MY LIFE IN CHINA AND AMERICA

BY

YUNG WING

Very truly yours
Yung Wing

TO

MY DEVOTED SONS

MORRISON BROWN

AND

BARTLETT GOLDEN YUNG

THESE REMINISCENCES

ARE AFFECTIONATELY DEDICATED

PREFACE

The first five chapters of this book give an account of my early education, previous to going to America, where it was continued, first at Monson Academy, in Monson, Massachusetts, and later, at Yale College.

The sixth chapter begins with my reëntrance into the Chinese world, after an absence of eight years. Would it not be strange, if an Occidental education, continually exemplified by an Occidental civilization, had not wrought upon an Oriental such a metamorphosis in his inward nature as to make him feel and act as though he were a being coming from a different world, when he confronted one so diametrically different? This was precisely my case, and yet neither my patriotism nor the love of my fellow-countrymen had been weakened. On the contrary, they had increased in strength from sympathy. Hence, the succeeding chapters of my book will be found to be devoted to the working out of my educational scheme, as an expression of my undying love for China, and as the most feasible method to my mind, of reformation and regeneration for her.iv

With the sudden ending of the Educational Commission, and the recall of the one hundred and twenty students who formed the vanguard of the pioneers of modern education in China, my educational work was brought to a close.

Of the survivors of these students of 1872, a few by dint of hard, persistent industry, have at last come forth to stand in the front ranks of the leading statesmen of China, and it is through them that the original Chinese Educational Commission has been revived, though in a modified form, so that now, Chinese students are seen flocking to America and Europe from even the distant shores of Sinim for a scientific education.

November, 1909,

CHAPTER I

BOYHOOD

I was born on the 17th of November, 1828, in the village of Nam Ping (South Screen) which is about four miles southwest of the Portuguese Colony of Macao, and is situated on Pedro Island lying west of Macao, from which it is separated by a channel of half a mile wide.

I was one of a family of four children. A brother was the eldest, a sister came next, I was the third, and another brother was the fourth and the youngest of the group. I am the only survivor of them all.

As early as 1834, an English lady, Mrs. Gutzlaff, wife of the Rev. Charles Gutzlaff, a missionary to China, came to Macao and, under the auspices of the Ladies' Association in London for the promotion of female education in India and the East, immediately took up the work of her mission by starting a girls' school for Chinese girls, which was soon followed by the opening of a school for boys also.

Mrs. Gutzlaff's comprador or factotum happened to come from the village I did and was, in fact, my father's friend and neighbor. It was through him that my parents heard about Mrs. Gutzlaff's school and it was doubtless through his influence and means that my father got me admitted into the school. It has always been a mystery to me why my parents should take it into their heads to put me into a foreign school, instead of a regular orthodox Confucian school, where my brother much older than myself was placed. Most assuredly such a step would have been more in play with Chinese public sentiment, taste, and the wants of the country at large, than to allow me to attend an English school; moreover, a Chinese cult is the only avenue in China that leads to political preferment, influence, power and wealth. I can only account for the departure thus taken on the theory that as foreign intercourse with China was just beginning to grow, my parents, anticipating that it might soon assume the proportions of a tidal wave, thought it worth while to take time by the forelock and put one of their sons to learning English that he

2

might become one of the advanced interpreters and have a more advantageous position from which to make his way into the business and diplomatic world. This I take to be the chief aim that influenced my parents to put me into Mrs. Gutzlaff's Mission School. As to what other results or sequences it has eventually brought about in my subsequent life, they were entirely left to Him who has control of all our devising and planning, as they are governed by a complete system of divine laws of antecedents and consequents, or of cause and effect.

In 1835, when I was barely seven years of age, my father took me to Macao. Upon reaching the school, I was brought before Mrs. Gutzlaff. She was the first English lady I had ever seen. On my untutored and unsophisticated mind she made a deep impression. If my memory serves me right, she was somewhat tall and well-built. She had prominent features which were strong and assertive; her eyes were of clear blue lustre, somewhat deep set. She had thin lips, supported by a square chin,—both indicative of firmness and authority. She had flaxen hair and eyebrows somewhat heavy. Her features taken collectively indicated great determination and will power.

As she came forward to welcome me in her long and full flowing white dress (the interview took place in the summer), surmounted by two large globe sleeves which were fashionable at the time and which lent her an exaggerated appearance, I remember most vividly I was no less puzzled than stunned. I actually trembled all over with fear at her imposing proportions—having never in my life seen such a peculiar and odd fashion. I clung to my father in fear. Her kindly expression and sympathetic smiles found little appreciative response at the outset, as I stood half dazed at her personality and my new environment. For really, a new world had dawned on me. After a time, when my homesickness was over and the novelty of my surroundings began gradually to wear away, she completely won me over through her kindness and sympathy. I began to look upon her more like a mother. She seemed to take a special interest in me; I suppose, because I was young and helpless, and away from my parents, besides being the youngest pupil in the school. She kept me among her girl pupils and did not allow me to mingle with what few boys there were at the time.

There is one escapade that I can never forget! It happened during the first year in the school, and was an attempt on my part to run away. I was shut up in the third story of the house, which had a wide open terrace on the top,—the only place where the girls and myself played and found recreation. We were not allowed to go out of doors to play in the streets. The boy pupils had their quarters on the ground floor and had full liberty to go out for exercise. I used to envy them their freedom and smuggled down stairs to mingle with them in their sports after school hours. I felt ill at ease to be shut up with the girls all alone way up in the third story. I wanted to see something of the outside world. I occasionally stole down stairs and ventured out to the wharves around which were clustered a number of small ferry boats which had a peculiar fascination to my young fancy. To gain my freedom, I planned to run away. The girls were all much older than I was, and a few sympathized with me in my wild scheme; doubtless, from the same restlessness of being too closely cooped up. I told them of my plan. Six of the older ones fell in with me in the idea. I was to slip out of the house alone, go down to the wharf and engage a covered boat to take us all in.

The next morning after our morning meal, and while Mrs. Gutzlaff was off taking her breakfast, we stole out unbeknown to any one and crowded into the boat and started off in hot haste for the opposite shore of Pedro Island. I was to take the whole party to my home and from there the girls were to disperse to their respective villages. We were half way across the channel when, to my great consternation, I saw a boat chasing us,

3

making fast time and gaining on us all the while. No promise of additional pay was of any avail, because our two oars against their four made it impossible for us to win out; so our boatmen gave up the race at the waving of handkerchiefs in the other boat and the whole party was captured. Then came the punishment. We were marched through the whole school and placed in a row, standing on a long narrow school table placed at one end of the school room facing all the pupils in front of us. I was placed in the center of the row, with a tall foolscap mounted on my head, having three girls on the right and three on the left. I had pinned on my breast a large square placard bearing the inscription, "Head of the Runaways;" there we stood for a whole hour till school was dismissed. I never felt so humiliated in my life as I did when I was undergoing that ordeal. I felt completely crestfallen. Some of the mischievous fellows would extract a little fun out of this display by taking furtive glances and making wry faces at us. Mrs. Gutzlaff, in order to aggravate our punishment, had ordered ginger snaps and oranges to be distributed among the other pupils right before us.

Mrs. Gutzlaff's school, started in September, 1835, was originally for girls only. Pending the organization and opening of the so-called "Morrison Education Society School," in the interval between 1835 and 1839, a department for boys was temporarily incorporated into her school, and part of the subscription fund belonging to the M. E. S. School was devoted to the maintenance of this one.

This accounts for my entrance into Mrs. Gutzlaff's School, as one of only two boys first admitted. Her school being thus enlarged and modified temporarily, Mrs. Gutzlaff's two nieces—the Misses Parkes, sisters to Mr. Harry Parkes who was afterwards knighted, by reason of the conspicuous part he played in the second Opium War, in 1864, of which he was in fact the originator—came out to China as assistants in the school. I was fortunately placed under their instruction for a short time.

Afterwards the boys' school under Mrs. Gutzlaff and her two nieces, the Misses Parkes, was broken up; that event parted our ways in life in divergent directions. Mrs. Gutzlaff went over to the United States with three blind girls,—Laura, Lucy and Jessie. The Misses Parkes were married to missionaries, one to Dr. William Lockhart, a medical missionary; the other to a Rev. Mr. MacClatchy, also a missionary. They labored long in China, under the auspices of the London Missionary Society. The three blind girls whom Mrs. Gutzlaff took with her were taught by me to read on raised letters till they could read from the Bible and Pilgrim's Progress.

On my return to my home village I resumed my Chinese studies.

In the fall of 1840, while the Opium War was still going on, my father died, leaving four children on my mother's hands without means of support.

Fortunately, three of us were old enough to lend a helping hand. My brother was engaged in fishing, my sister helped in housework, and I took to hawking candy through my own village and the neighboring one. I took hold of the business in good earnest, rising at three o'clock every morning, and I did not come home until six o'clock in the evening. My daily earnings netted twenty-five cents, which I turned over to my mother, and with the help given by my brother, who was the main stay of the family, we managed to keep the wolf away from our door. I was engaged in hawking candy for about five months, and when winter was over, when no candy was made, I changed my occupation and went into the rice fields to glean rice after the reapers. My sister usually accompanied me in such excursions. But unlike Ruth of old, I had no Boaz to help me out when I was short in my gleaning. But my knowledge of English came to my rescue. My sister told the head reaper that I could speak, read and write English. This awakened the curiosity of the reaper. He beckoned me to him and asked me whether I wouldn't talk some "Red Hair

4

Men" talk to him. He said he never heard of such talk in his life. I felt bashful and diffident at first, but my sister encouraged me and said "the reaper may give you a large bundle of rice sheaf to take home." This was said as a kind of prompter. The reaper was shrewd enough to take it up, and told me that if I would talk, he would give me a bundle heavier than I could carry. So I began and repeated the alphabet to him. All the reapers as well as the gleaners stood in vacant silence, with mouths wide open, grinning with evident delight. A few minutes after my maiden speech was delivered in the paddy field with water and mud almost knee deep, I was rewarded with several sheaves, and I had to hurry away in order to get two other boys to carry what my sister and I could not lug. Thus I came home loaded with joy and sheaves of golden rice to my mother, little dreaming that my smattering knowledge of English would serve me such a turn so early in my career. I was then about twelve years old. Even Ruth with her six measures of corn did not fare any better than I did.

Soon after the gleaning days, all too few, were over, a neighbor of mine who was a printer in the printing office of a Roman Catholic priest happened to be home from Macao on a vacation. He spoke to my mother about the priest wanting to hire a boy in his office who knew enough English to read the numerals correctly, so as to be able to fold and prepare the papers for the binders. My mother said I could do the work. So I was introduced to the priest and a bargain was struck. I returned home to report myself, and a few days later I was in Macao and entered upon my duty as a folder on a salary of $4.50 a month. My board and lodging came to $1.50—the balance of $3.00 was punctually sent to my mother every month. I did not get rich quickly in this employment, for I had been there but four months when a call for me to quit work came from a quarter I least expected. It had more the sound of heaven in it. It came from a Dr. Benjamin Hobson, a medical missionary in Macao whose hospital was not more than a mile from the printer's office. He sent word that he wanted to see me; that he had been hunting for me for months. I knew Dr. Hobson well, for I saw him a number of times at Mrs. Gutzlaff's. So I called on him. At the outset, I thought he was going to take me in to make a doctor of me, but no, he said he had a promise to fulfill. Mrs. Gutzlaff's last message to him, before she embarked for America with the three blind girls, was to be sure to find out where I was and to put me into the Morrison Education Society School as soon as it was opened for pupils.

"This is what I wanted to see you for," said Dr. Hobson. "Before you leave your employment and after you get the consent of your mother to let you go to the Morrison School, I would like to have you come to the hospital and stay with me for a short time so that I may become better acquainted with you, before I take you to the Morrison School, which is already opened for pupils, and introduce you to the teacher."

At the end of the interview, I went home to see my mother who, after some reluctance, gave her consent. I returned to Macao, bade farewell to the priest who, though reticent and reserved, not having said a word to me during all the four months I was in his employ, yet did not find fault with me in my work. I went over to the hospital. Dr. Hobson immediately set me to work with the mortar and pestle, preparing materials for ointments and pills. I used to carry a tray and accompany him in his rounds to visit the patients, in the benevolent work of alleviating their pains and sufferings. I was with him about a couple of months in the hospital work, at the end of which time he took me one day and introduced me to the Rev. Samuel Robins Brown, the teacher of the Morrison Education Society School.

CHAPTER II

The Morrison School was opened on the 1st of November, 1839, under the charge of the Rev. S. R. Brown who, with his wife, Mrs. Brown, landed at Macao on the 19th of February, 1839. Brown, who was afterwards made a D.D., was a graduate of Yale of the class of 1832. From his antecedents, he was eminently fitted to pioneer the first English school in China. I entered the school in 1841. I found that five other boys had entered ahead of me by one year. They were all studying primary arithmetic, geography, and reading. I had the start of them only in reading and pronouncing English well. We studied English in the forenoon, and Chinese in the afternoon. The names of the five boys were: 1. Wong Shing; 2. Li Kan; 3. Chow Wan; 4. Tong Chik; 5. Wong Foon. I made the sixth one and was the youngest of all. We formed the first class of the school, and became Brown's oldest pupils throughout, from first to last, till he left China in December, 1846, on account of poor health. Half of our original number accompanied him to this country, on his return.

The Morrison Education Society School came about in this way: Not long after the death of Dr. Robert Morrison, which occurred on the 1st of August, 1834, a circular was issued among the foreign residents on the 26th of January, 1835, calling for the formation of an Association to be named the "Morrison Education Society." Its object was to "improve and promote English education in China by schools and other means." It was called "Morrison" to commemorate the labors and works of that distinguished man who was sent out by the London Missionary Society as the first missionary to China in 1807. He crossed the Atlantic from London to New York where he embarked for China in the sailing vessel "Trident" on the 31st of January, 1807. He tried to land in Macao, but the jealousy of the Jesuits thwarted his purpose. He was obliged to go up to Canton. Finally, on account of the unsettled relations between the Chinese government and the foreign merchants there, he repaired to Malacca, and made that place the basis of his labors. He was the author of the first Anglo-Chinese dictionary, of three quarto volumes. He translated the Bible into Chinese; Leang Afah was his first Chinese convert and trained by him to preach. Leang afterwards became a powerful preacher. The importance and bearing of his dictionary and the translation of the Bible into Chinese, on subsequent missionary work in China, were fundamental and paramount. The preaching of his convert, Leang Afah, likewise contributed in no small degree towards opening up a new era in the religious life of China. His memory, therefore, is worthy of being kept alive by the establishment of a school named after him. Indeed, a university ought to have been permanently founded for that purpose instead of a school, whose existence was solely dependent upon the precarious and ephemeral subscriptions of transient foreign merchants in China.

At the close of the Opium War in 1840, and after the Island of Hong Kong had been ceded to the British government, the Morrison school was removed to Hong Kong in 1842. The site chosen for it was on the top of a hill about six hundred feet above the level of the sea. The hill is situated on the eastern end of Victoria Colony and was called "Morrison Hill" after the name of the school. It commands a fine view of the harbor, as that stretches from east to west. The harbor alone made Hong Kong the most coveted concession in Southern China. It is spacious and deep enough to hold the Navy of Great Britain, and it is that distinguishing feature and its strategic location that have made it what it is.

On the 12th of March, 1845, Mr. Wm. Allen Macy arrived in Hong Kong as an assistant teacher in the school. His arrival was timely, because the school, since its removal from Macao to Hong Kong, had been much enlarged. Three more classes of new pupils had been formed and the total number of pupils all told was more than forty. This was more than one man could manage. The assistant teacher was much needed. Brown continued his work in the school till the fall of 1846. Macy had a whole year in which to be broken into the work.

Between Brown and Macy there was a marked difference in temperament and character. Brown, on the one hand, showed evidences of a self-made man. He was cool in temperament, versatile in the adaptation of means to ends, gentlemanly and agreeable, and somewhat optimistic. He found no difficulty in endearing himself to his pupils, because he sympathized with them in their efforts to master their studies, and entered heart and soul into his work. He had an innate faculty of making things clear to the pupils and conveying to them his understanding of a subject without circumlocution, and with great directness and facility. This was owing in a great measure to his experience as a pedagogue, before coming out to China, and even before he entered college. He knew how to manage boys, because he knew boys' nature well, whether Chinese, Japanese or American. He impressed his pupils as being a fine teacher and one eminently fitted from inborn tact and temperament to be a successful school master, as he proved himself to be in his subsequent career in Auburn, N. Y., and in Japan.

Macy, the assistant teacher, was likewise a Yale man. He had never taught school before in his life, and had no occasion to do so. He possessed no previous experience to guide him in his new work of pedagogy in China. He was evidently well brought up and was a man of sensitive nature, and of fine moral sensibilities,—a soul full of earnestness and lofty ideals.

After the Morrison School was broken up in 1850, he returned to this country with his mother and took up theology in the Yale Theological Seminary. In 1854, he went back to China as a missionary under the American Board. I had graduated from Yale College then and was returning to China with him. We were the only passengers in that long, wearisome and most trying passage of 154 days from Sandy Hook to Hong Kong.

Brown left China in the winter of 1846. Four months before he left, he one day sprang a surprise upon the whole school. He told of his contemplated return to America on account of his health and the health of his family. Before closing his remarks by telling us of his deep interest in the school, he said he would like to take a few of his old pupils home with him to finish their education in the United States, and that those who wished to accompany him would signify it by rising. This announcement, together with his decision to return to America, cast a deep gloom over the whole school. A dead silence came over all of us. And then for several days afterwards the burden of our conversation was about Brown's leaving the school for good. The only cheerful ones among us were those who had decided to accompany him home. These were Wong Shing, Wong Foon and myself. When he requested those who wished to accompany him to the States to signify it by rising, I was the first one on my feet. Wong Foon was the second, followed by Wong Shing. But before regarding our cases as permanently settled, we were told to go home and ask the consent of our respective parents. My mother gave her consent with great reluctance, but after my earnest persuasion she yielded, though not without tears and sorrow. I consoled her with the fact that she had two more sons besides myself, and a daughter to look after her comfort. Besides, she was going to have a daughter-in-law to take care of her, as my elder brother was engaged to be married.

It may not be out of place to say that if it had depended on our own resources, we never could have come to America to finish our education, for we were all poor.

Doubtless Brown must have had the project well discussed among the trustees of the school months before he broached the subject to his pupils.

It was also through his influence that due provision was made for the support of our parents for at least two years, during our absence in America. Our patrons who bore all our expenses did not intend that we should stay in this country longer than two years. They treated us nobly. They did a great work for us. Among those who bore a conspicuous part in defraying our expenses while in America, besides providing for the support of our aged parents, I can recall the names of Andrew Shortrede, proprietor and editor of the "Hong Kong China Mail" (he was a Scotchman, an old bachelor, and a noble and handsome specimen of humanity), A. A. Ritchie, an American merchant, and A. A. Campbell, another Scotchman. There were others unknown to me. The Olyphant Sons, David, Talbot and Robert, three brothers, leading merchants of New York, gave us a free passage from Hong Kong to New York in their sailing vessel, the "Huntress," which brought a cargo of tea at the same time. Though late in the day for me to mention the names of these benefactors who from pure motives of Christian philanthropy aided me in my education, yet it may be a source of satisfaction to their descendants, if there are any living in different parts of the world, to know that their sires took a prominent part in the education of the three Chinese youths,—Wong Shing, Wong Foon and myself.

CHAPTER III

JOURNEY TO AMERICA AND FIRST EXPERIENCES THERE

Being thus generously provided for, we embarked at Whompoa on the 4th of January, 1847, in the good ship "Huntress" under Captain Gillespie. As stated above, she belonged to the Olyphant Brothers and was loaded with a full cargo of tea. We had the northeast trade wind in our favor, which blew strong and steady all the way from Whompoa to St. Helena. There was no accident of any kind, excepting a gale as we doubled the Cape of Good Hope. The tops of the masts and ends of the yards were tipped with balls of electricity. The strong wind was howling and whistling behind us like a host of invisible Furies. The night was pitch dark and the electric balls dancing on the tips of the yards and tops of the masts, back and forth and from side to side like so many infernal lanterns in the black night, presented a spectacle never to be forgotten by me. I realized no danger, although the ship pitched and groaned, but enjoyed the wild and weird scene hugely. After the Cape was doubled, our vessel ploughed through the comparatively smooth waters of the Atlantic until we reached the Island of St. Helena where we were obliged to stop for fresh water and provisions. Most sailing vessels that were bound from the East for the Atlantic board were accustomed to make St. Helena their stopping place. St. Helena, as viewed from the shipboard, presented an outward appearance of a barren volcanic rock, as though freshly emerged from the baptism of fire and brimstone. Not a blade of grass could be seen on its burnt and charred surface. We landed at Jamestown, which is a small village in the valley of the Island. In this valley there was rich and beautiful vegetation. We found among the sparse inhabitants a few Chinese who were brought there by the East India Company's ships. They were middle-aged people, and had their families there. While there, we went over to Longwood where was Napoleon's empty tomb. A large weeping willow hung and swept over it. We cut a few twigs, and kept them alive till we reached this country and they were brought to Auburn, N. Y., by Mr. Brown, who planted them near his residence when he was teaching in the Auburn Academy for several years before his departure for Japan. These willows proved to be fine, handsome trees when I visited Auburn in 1854.

From St. Helena we took a northwesterly course and struck the Gulf Stream, which, with the wind still fair and favorable, carried us to New York in a short time. We landed in New York on the 12th of April, 1847, after a passage of ninety-eight days of unprecedented fair weather. The New York of 1847 was altogether a different city from the New York of 1909. It was a city of only 250,000 or 300,000 inhabitants; now it is a metropolis rivaling London in population, wealth and commerce. The whole of Manhattan Island is turned into a city of skyscrapers, churches and palatial residences.

Little did I realize when in 1845 I wrote, while in the Morrison School, a composition on "An Imaginary Voyage to New York and up the Hudson," that I was to see New York in reality. This incident leads me to the reflection that sometimes our imagination foreshadows what lies uppermost in our minds and brings possibilities within the sphere of realities. The Chinese Education Scheme is another example of the realities that came out of my day dreams a year before I graduated. So was my marrying an American wife. Still there are other day dreams yet to be realized; whether or no they will ever come to pass the future will determine.

Our stay in New York was brief. The first friends we had the good fortune to make in the new world, were Prof. David E. Bartlett and his wife. He was a professor in the New York Asylum for the Deaf and Dumb, and was afterwards connected with a like institution in Hartford. The Professor died in 1879. His wife, Mrs. Fanny P. Bartlett, survived him for nearly thirty years and passed away in the spring of 1907. She was a woman highly respected and beloved for her high Christian character and unceasing activities for good in the community in which she lived. Her influence was even extended to China by the few students who happened to enjoy her care and instruction. I count her as one of my most valued friends in America.

From New York we proceeded by boat to New Haven where we had an opportunity to see Yale College and were introduced to President Day. I had not then the remotest idea of becoming graduate of one of the finest colleges of the country, as I did a few years afterwards. We went by rail from New Haven to Warehouse Point and from there to East Windsor, the home of Mrs. Elizabeth Brown, wife of Dr. Brown. Her parents were then living. Her father, the Rev. Shubael Bartlett, was the pastor of the East Windsor Congregational Church. I well remember the first Sabbath we attended his church. We three Chinese boys sat in the pastor's pew which was on the left of the pulpit, having a side view of the minister, but in full view of the whole congregation. We were the cynosure of the whole church. I doubt whether much attention was paid to the sermon that day.

The Rev. Shubael Bartlett was a genuine type of the old New England Puritan. He was exact and precise in all his manners and ways. He spoke in a deliberate and solemn tone, but full of sincerity and earnestness. He conducted himself as though he was treading on thin ice, cautiously and circumspectly. One would suppose from his appearance that he was austere and exacting, but he was gentle and thoughtful. He would have his family Bible and hymn book placed one on top of the other, squared and in straight lines, on the same spot on the table every morning for morning prayers. He always sat in the same spot for morning prayers. In other words, you always knew where to find him. His habits and daily life were as regular as clock work. I never heard him crack a joke or burst out in open laughter.

Mrs. Bartlett, Mrs. Brown's mother, was of a different makeup. She was always cheerful. A smile lighted up her features nearly all the time and for everyone she had a kind and cheerful word, while the sweet tone of her voice always carried with it cheerfulness and good will. Her genial temperament and her hospitality made the parsonage a favorite resort to all the friends and relatives of the family, who were quite numerous. It was always a puzzle to me how the old lady managed to make ends meet when her husband's salary was not over $400 a year. To be sure, the farm annually realized something, but Daniel, the youngest son, who was the staff of the old couple, had to work hard to keep up the prestige of the parsonage. It was in this parsonage that I found a temporary home while at school in Monson, and also in Yale.

CHAPTER IV

AT MONSON ACADEMY

We were in East Windsor for about a week; then we went up to Monson, Mass., to enter the Academy there. Monson Academy was, at one time, quite a noted preparatory school in New England, before high schools sprang into existence. Young men from all parts of the country were found here, undergoing preparation for colleges. It was its fortune, at different periods of its history, to have had men of character and experience for its principals. The Rev. Charles Hammond was one of them. He was in every sense a self-made man. He was a graduate of Yale; he was enthusiastically fond of the classics, and a great admirer of English literature. He was a man of liberal views and broad sympathies. He was well-known in New England as an educator and a champion of temperance and New England virtues. His high character gave the Academy a wide reputation and the school was never in a more prosperous condition than when he was principal. He took a special interest in us, the three Chinese students—Wong Shing, Wong Foon and myself—not so much from the novelty of having Chinese in the school as from his interest in China, and the possible good that might come out of our education.

In our first year in the Academy, we were placed in the English department. Greenleaf's Arithmetic, English Grammar, Physiology, and Upham's Mental Philosophy were our studies. In the last two studies we recited to the new preceptress, Miss Rebekah Brown, a graduate of Mt. Holyoke, the valedictorian of her class. She afterwards became the wife of Doctor A. S. McClean, of Springfield, Mass. She was a fine teacher and a woman of exceptional Christian virtues. She had an even and sweet temper, and was full of good will and good works. She and her husband, the good Doctor, took a genuine interest in me; they gave me a home during some of my college vacations, and helped me in various ways in my struggle through Yale. I kept up my correspondence with them after my return to China, and upon my coming back to this country, I was always cordially invited to their home in Springfield. It was on account of such a genuine friendship that I made Springfield my headquarters in 1872, when I brought the first installment of Government students to this country.

Brown placed us under the care of his mother, Mrs. Phoebe H. Brown. We boarded with her, but had a separate room assigned us in a dwelling right across the road, opposite to her cottage. Her widowed daughter with her three boys had taken up all the spare rooms in the cottage, which accounts for the want of accommodation for us.

In those primitive days, board and lodging in the country were very reasonable. Indigent students had a fair chance to work their way for an education. I remember we paid for board and lodging, including fuel, light and washing, only $1.25 a week for each, but we had to take care of our own rooms and, in the winter, saw and split our own wood, which we found to be capital exercise.

Our lodging was about half a mile from the academy. We had to walk three times a day to school and back, in the dead of winter when the snow was three feet deep; that gave us plenty of exercise, keen appetites and kept us in fine condition.

I look back upon my acquaintance with Mrs. Phoebe H. Brown with a mingled feeling of respect and admiration. She certainly was a remarkable New England woman— a woman of surpassing strength of moral and religious character. Those who have had the rare privilege of reading her stirring biography, will, I am sure, bear me out in this statement. She went through the crucible of unprecedented adversities and trials of life and came out one of the rare shining lights that beautify the New England sky. She is the authoress of the well-known hymn, "I love to steal awhile away from every cumbering care," etc., which breathes the calm spirit of contentment and resignation wherever sung.

The Rev. Charles Hammond, the principal of the academy when we joined it, was a graduate of Yale, as I stated before, and a man of a fine cultivated taste. He was an enthusiastic admirer of Shakespeare, who was his favorite poet; among orators he was partial to Daniel Webster. He had the faculty of inspiring his pupils with the love of the beautiful, both in ancient and modern literature. In our daily recitations, he laid a greater stress on pointing out the beauties of a sentence and its construction, than he did on grammatical rules, moods and tenses. He was a fine writer. His addresses and sermons were pointed and full of life. Like Dr. Arnold of Rugby, he aimed to build character in his pupils and not to convert them into walking encyclopedias, or intelligent parrots. It was through him that I was introduced to Addison, Goldsmith, Dickens, Sir Walter Scott, the Edinburgh Reviews, Macaulay and Shakespeare, which formed the bulk of my reading while in Monson.

During my first year in the Monson Academy, I had no idea of taking a collegiate course. It was well understood that I was to return to China at the end of 1849, and the appropriation was made to suit such a plan. In the fall of 1848, after Wong Shing—the eldest of the three of us—had returned to China on account of his poor health, Wong Foon and myself, who were left behind to continue our studies for another year, frequently met to talk over future plans for the end of the prescribed time. We both decided finally to stay in this country to continue our studies, but the question arose, who was going to back us financially after 1849? This was the Gordian Knot. We concluded to consult Mr. Hammond and Mr. Brown on the subject. They both decided to have the matter referred to our patrons in Hong Kong. Reply came that if we wished to prosecute our studies after 1849, they would be willing to continue their support through a professional course, if we were willing to go over to Scotland to go through the University of Edinburgh. This was a generous and noble-hearted proposal.

Wong Foon, on his part, after much deliberation, decided to accept the offer and go over to Scotland at the end of 1849, while, on my part, I preferred to remain in this country to continue my studies here with the view of going to Yale. Wong Foon's decision had relieved him of all financial anxieties, while the problem of how I was to pay my education bills after 1849, still remained to be solved. But I did not allow the perplexities of the future to disturb my peace of mind. I threw all my anxieties to the wind, trusting to a wise Providence to care for my future, as it had done for my past.

Wong Foon and I, having taken our decisive steps, dropped our English studies at the close of the school year of 1849, and in the fall of the same year we began the A B C's of our classical course. In the summer of 1850, we graduated from the academy. Wong Foon, by previous arrangements, went over to Scotland and entered the University of Edinburgh. I remained in this country and finally entered Yale. It was fully a decade since we had met for the first time in the Morrison School in Macao, in 1840, to become school-mates as well as class-mates. Now that link was broken.

Wong was in the University seven years. After completing his professional studies as a doctor, he returned to China in 1857. He was a fine scholar. He graduated the third man in his medical class. He also distinguished himself in his profession. His ability and skill secured for him an enviable reputation as one of the ablest surgeons east of the Cape of Good Hope at that time. He had a fine practice in Canton, where the foreign residents retained him as their physician in preference to European doctors. He was very successful and made quite a fortune before his death, which took place in 1879. Both the native and foreign communities felt his loss. He was highly respected and honored by Chinese and foreigners for his Christian character and the purity of his life.

CHAPTER V

MY COLLEGE DAYS

Before entering Yale, I had not solved the problem of how I was to be carried through the collegiate course without financial backing of a definite and well-assured character. It was an easy matter to talk about getting an education by working for it, and there is a kind of romance in it that captivates the imagination, but it is altogether a different thing to face it in a business and practical way. So it proved to me, after I had put my foot into it. I had no one except Brown, who had already done so much for me in bringing me to this country, and Hammond, who fitted me for college. To them I appealed for advice and counsel. I was advised to avail myself of the contingent fund provided for indigent students. It was in the hands of the trustees of the academy and so well guarded that it could not be appropriated without the recipient's signing a written pledge that he would study for the ministry and afterwards become a missionary. Such being the case, I made up my mind that it would be utterly useless for me to apply for the fund. However, a day was appointed for me to meet the trustees in the parsonage, to talk over the subject. They said they would be too glad to have me avail myself of the fund, provided I was willing to sign a pledge that after graduation I should go back to China as a missionary. I gave the trustees to understand that I would never give such a pledge for the following reasons: First, it would handicap and circumscribe my usefulness. I wanted the utmost freedom of action to avail myself of every opportunity to do the greatest good in China. If necessary, I might be obliged to create new conditions, if I found old ones were not favorable to any plan I might have for promoting her highest welfare.

In the second place, the calling of a missionary is not the only sphere in life where one can do the most good in China or elsewhere. In such a vast empire, there can be hardly any limit put upon one's ambition to do good, if one is possessed of the Christ-spirit; on the other hand, if one has not such a spirit, no pledge in the world could melt his ice-bound soul.

In the third place, a pledge of that character would prevent me from taking advantage of any circumstance or event that might arise in the life of a nation like China, to do her a great service.

"For these reasons," I said, "I must decline to give the pledge and at the same time decline to accept your kind offer to help me. I thank you, gentlemen, very much, for your good wishes."

Both Brown and Hammond afterwards agreed that I took the right view on the subject and sustained me in my position. To be sure, I was poor, but I would not allow my poverty to gain the upper hand and compel me to barter away my inward convictions of duty for a temporary mess of pottage.

During the summer of 1850, it seems that Brown who had been making a visit in the South to see his sister, while there had occasion to call on some of the members of "The Ladies' Association" in Savannah, Ga., to whom he mentioned my case. He returned home in the nick of time, just after I had the interview with the board of trustees of the academy. I told him of the outcome, when, as stated above, he approved of my position, and told me what he had done. He said that the members of the association agreed to help me in college. On the strength of that I gathered fresh courage, and went down to New Haven to pass my examination for entrance. How I got in, I do not know, as I had had only fifteen months of Latin and twelve months of Greek, and ten months of mathematics. My preparation had been interrupted because the academy had been broken up by the Palmer & New London R.R. that was being built close by. As compared with the college preparations of nine-tenths of my class-mates, I was far behind. However, I passed without condition. But I was convinced I was not sufficiently prepared, as my recitations in the class-room clearly proved. Between the struggle of how to make ends meet financially and how to keep up with the class in my studies, I had a pretty tough time of it. I used to sweat over my studies till twelve o'clock every night the whole Freshman year. I took little or no exercise and my health and strength began to fail and I was obliged to ask for a leave of absence of a week. I went to East Windsor to get rested and came back refreshed.

In the Sophomore year, from my utter aversion to mathematics, especially to differential and integral calculus, which I abhorred and detested, and which did me little or no good in the way of mental discipline, I used to fizzle and flunk so often that I really thought I was going to be dropped from the class, or dismissed from college. But for some unexplained reasons I was saved from such a catastrophe, and I squeezed through the second year in college with so low a mark that I was afraid to ask my division tutor, who happened to be Tutor Blodget, who had me in Greek, about it. The only redeeming feature that saved me as a student in the class of 1854, was the fortunate circumstance that I happened to be a successful competitor on two occasions in English composition in my division. I was awarded the first prize in the second term, and the first prize in the third term of the year. These prizes gave me quite an éclat in the college as well as in the outside world, but I was not at all elated over them on account of my poor scholarship which I felt keenly through the whole college course.

Before the close of my second year, I succeeded in securing the stewardship of a boarding club consisting of sophomores and juniors. There were altogether twenty members. I did all the marketing and served at the table. In this way, I earned my board through the latter half of my college course. In money matters, I was supplied with remittances from "The Ladies' Association" in Savannah, and also contributions from the Olyphant Brothers of New York. In addition to these sources of supply, I was paid for being an assistant librarian to the "Brothers in Unity," which was one of the two college debating societies that owned a library, and of which I was a member.

In my senior year I was again elected librarian to the same Society and got $30.00. These combined sums were large enough to meet all my cash bills, since my wants had to be finely trimmed to suit the cloth. If most of the country parsons of that period could get along with a salary of $200 or $300 a year (supplemented, of course, with an annual donation party, which sometimes carried away more than it donated), having as a general thing a large family to look after, I certainly ought to have been able to get through college with gifts of nearly a like amount, supplemented with donations of shirts and stockings from ladies who took an interest in my education.

The class of 1854, to which I had the honor and the good fortune to belong, graduated ninety-eight all told. Being the first Chinaman who had ever been known to go through a first-class American college, I naturally attracted considerable attention; and from the fact that I was librarian for one of the college debating societies (Linonia was the other) for two years, I was known by members of the three classes above, and members of the three classes below me. This fact had contributed toward familiarizing me with the college world at large, and my nationality, of course, added piquancy to my popularity.

As an undergraduate, I had already acquired a factitious reputation within the walls of Yale. But that was ephemeral and soon passed out of existence after graduation.

All through my college course, especially in the closing year, the lamentable condition of China was before my mind constantly and weighed on my spirits. In my despondency, I often wished I had never been educated, as education had unmistakably enlarged my mental and moral horizon, and revealed to me responsibilities which the sealed eye of ignorance can never see, and sufferings and wrongs of humanity to which an uncultivated and callous nature can never be made sensitive. The more one knows, the more he suffers and is consequently less happy; the less one knows, the less he suffers, and hence is more happy. But this is a low view of life, a cowardly feeling and unworthy of a being bearing the impress of divinity. I had started out to get an education. By dint of hard work and self-denial I had finally secured the coveted prize and although it might not be so complete and symmetrical a thing as could be desired, yet I had come right up to the conventional standard and idea of a liberal education. I could, therefore, call myself an educated man and, as such, it behooved me to ask, "What am I going to do with my education?" Before the close of my last year in college I had already sketched out what I should do. I was determined that the rising generation of China should enjoy the same educational advantages that I had enjoyed; that through western education China might be regenerated, become enlightened and powerful. To accomplish that object became the guiding star of my ambition. Towards such a goal, I directed all my mental resources and energy. Through thick and thin, and the vicissitudes of a checkered life from 1854 to 1872, I labored and waited for its consummation.

CHAPTER VI

RETURN TO CHINA

In entering upon my life's work which to me was so full of meaning and earnestness, the first episode was a voyage back to the old country, which I had not seen for nearly ten years, but which had never escaped my mind's eye nor my heart's yearning for her welfare. I wanted very much to stay a few years longer in order to take a scientific course. I had taken up surveying in the Sheffield Scientific School just as that department was starting into existence under Professor Norton. Had I had the means to prosecute a practical profession, that might have helped to shorten and facilitate the way to the goal I had in view; but as I was poor and my friends thought that a longer stay in this country might keep me here for good, and China would lose me altogether, I was for this and other reasons induced to return. The scientific course was accordingly abandoned. The persons who were most interested in my return to China were Pelatiah Perit of Messrs. Goodhue & Co., merchants in the China trade, and the Olyphant Brothers, who had taken such a lively interest eight years before in helping me to come over in their ship, the "Huntress." These gentlemen had no other motive in desiring me to return to China than

14

that of hoping to see me useful in Christianizing the Chinese, which was in harmony with their well-known broad and benevolent characters.

On the 13th of November, 1854, the Rev. William Allen Macy, who went out to Hong Kong to take the place of the Rev. Dr. Brown, as teacher in the Morrison Education Society School in 1845, went back to China as a missionary under the American Board, and we were fellow-passengers on board the sailing clipper ship "Eureka," under Captain Whipple, of Messrs. Chamber, Heisser & Co., of New York.

Winter is the worst season of the year to go on an eastern voyage in a sailing vessel, via the Cape of Good Hope. The northeast trade winds prevail then and one is sure to have head winds all the way. The "Eureka," in which Macy and myself were the only passengers, took that route to Hong Kong. We embarked on board of her as she rode in midstream of the East River. The day was bleak and bitingly cold. No handkerchiefs were fluttering in the air, waving a good voyage; no sound from the shore cheered u as the anchor was weighed, and as the tug towed us out as far as Sandy Hook. There we were left to our own resources. The sails were not furled to their full extent, but were reefed for tacking, as the wind was nearly dead ahead and quite strong. We found the "Eureka" to be empty of cargo, and empty even of ballast of any kind; for that reason she acted like a sailor who had just had his nip before he went out to sea. She tossed up and down and twisted from right to left, just as though she had a little too much to keep her balance. It was in such a fashion that she reeled her way from Sandy Hook to Hong Kong—a distance of nearly 13,000 nautical miles, which took her 154 days to accomplish. It was decidedly the most uninteresting and wearisome voyage I ever took in my life. The skipper was a Philadelphian. He had the unfortunate habit of stuttering badly, which tended to irritate a temper naturally quick and fiery. He was certainly a ludicrous object to look at. It was particularly in the morning that he might be seen pacing the quarter deck, scanning the sky. This, by the spectator, was deemed necessary for the skipper to work himself up to the right pitch, preliminary to his pantomimic performances in his battle with the head wind. All at once, he halted, stared at the quarter of the sky from whence the malicious head wind came. With a face all bloated and reddened by intense excitement, his eyes almost standing out of their sockets, and all ablaze with uncontrollable rage, with arms uplifted, he would clutch his hair as if plucking it out by the roots, gnash his teeth, and simultaneously he would jump up and down, stamping on the deck, and swear at the Almighty for sending him head winds. The air for the moment was split with his revolting imprecations and blasphemous oaths that were ejaculated through the laborious process of stammering and stuttering, which made him a most pitiable object to behold. In the early part of the voyage it was a painful sight to see him working himself up to that pitch of contortion and paroxysm of rage which made him appear more like an insane than a sane man, but as these exhibitions were of daily occurrence for the greater part of the voyage, we came to regard him as no longer deserving of sympathy and pity, but rather with contempt. After his passion had spent its force, and he subsided into his calmer and normal mood, he would drop limply into a cane chair, where he would sit for hours all by himself. For the sake of diversion, he would rub his hands together, and soliloquize quietly to himself, an occasional smile breaking over his face, which made him look like an innocent idiot. Before the voyage was half through, the skipper had made such a fool of himself through his silly and insane conduct about the wind, that he became the laughing stock of the whole crew, who, of course, did not dare to show any outward signs of insubordination. The sailing of the vessel was entirely in the hands of the first mate, who was literally a sea-tyrant. The crew was composed of Swedes and Norwegians. If it had been made up of Americans, the inhuman treatment by the officers might have driven them to desperate extremities, because the men were over-worked night and day in incessant tacking. The only time that they found a resting spell was when the ship was becalmed in the tropics when not a breath of wind was to be had for several days at a time. Referring to my diary kept in that memorable voyage,—it took us nearly two weeks to beat up the Macassar straits. This event tried our patience sorely. After it was passed, the skipper made the remark within the hearing of the Rev. Macy that the reason he had bad luck was because he had a Jonah on board. My friend Macy took the remark in a good-natured way and gave me a significant smile. We were just then discussing the feat of going through the Macassar straits and I remarked in a tone just loud enough to be heard by the old skipper that if I had charge of the vessel, I could take her through in less than ten days. This was meant as a direct reflection on the poor seamanship of the old fellow (for he really was a miserable sailor), as well as to serve as a retaliation for what he said a few minutes before, that there was a Jonah on board.

In the dead of winter, the passage to the East should have been taken around Cape Horn instead of the Cape of Good Hope, in which case we would no doubt have had strong and fair wind all the way from New York to Hong Kong, which would not only have shortened the voyage but also saved the captain a world of swearing and an incalculable amount of wear and tear on his nervous system. But as a passenger only, I had no idea of the financial motive back of the move to send the ship off perfectly empty and unballasted, right in the teeth of the northeast monsoon. I would have been glad to go around Cape Horn, as that would have added a new route to my journeying around the world, and furnished me with new incidents as well.

As we approached Hong Kong, a Chinese pilot boarded us. The captain wanted me to ask him whether there were any dangerous rocks and shoals nearby. I could not for the life of me recall my Chinese in order to interpret for him; the pilot himself understood English, and he was the first Chinese teacher to give me the terms in Chinese for dangerous rocks and shoals. So the skipper and Macy, and a few other persons who were present at the time, had the laugh on me, who, being a Chinese, yet was not able to speak the language.

My first thought upon landing was to walk up to the office of the "China Mail," to pay my respects to Andrew Shortrede, the proprietor and editor of the paper, and the friend who supported me for over a year, while I was in Monson Academy. After seeing him and accepting his hospitality by way of an invitation to take up my quarters in his house, I lost no time in hastening over to Macao to see my aged and beloved mother, who, I knew, yearned to see her long-absent boy. Our meeting was arranged a day beforehand. I was in citizen's dress and could not conveniently change the same for my Chinese costume. I had also allowed a pair of mustaches to grow, which, according to Chinese custom, was not becoming for an unmarried young man to do. We met with tears of joy, gratitude and thanksgiving. Our hearts were too full even to speak at first. We gave way to our emotions. As soon as we were fairly composed, she began to stroke me all over, as expressive of her maternal endearment which had been held in patient suspense for at least ten years. As we sat close to each other, I gave her a brief recital of my life in America, for I knew she would be deeply interested in the account. I told her that I had just finished a long and wearisome voyage of five months' duration, but had met with no danger of any kind; that during my eight years of sojourn in the United States, I was very kindly treated by the good people everywhere; that I had had good health and never been seriously sick, and that my chief object during the eight years was to study and prepare myself for my life work in China. I explained to her that I had to go through a preparatory school before entering college; that the college I entered was Yale—one of the leading colleges of the United States, and that the course was four years, which accounted for my long stay and delayed my return to China. I told her that at the end of four years I had graduated with the degree of A.B.,—analogous to the Chinese title of Siu Tsai, which is interpreted "Elegant Talent;" that it was inscribed on a parchment of sheep skin and that to graduate from Yale College was considered a great honor, even to a native American, and much more so to a Chinese. She asked me näively how much money it conferred. I said it did not confer any money at once, but it enabled one to make money quicker and easier than one can who has not been educated; that it gave one greater influence and power among men and if he built on his college education, he would be more likely to become the leader of men, especially if he had a well-established character. I told her my college education was worth more to me than money, and that I was confident of making plenty of money.

"Knowledge," I said, "is power, and power is greater than riches. I am the first Chinese to graduate from Yale College, and that being the case, you have the honor of being the first and only mother out of the countless millions of mothers in China at this time, who can claim the honor of having a son who is the first Chinese graduate of a first-class American college. Such an honor is a rare thing to possess." I also assured her that as long as I lived all her comforts and wants would be scrupulously and sedulously looked after, and that nothing would be neglected to make her contented and happy. This interview seemed to give her great comfort and satisfaction. She seemed very happy over it. After it was ended, she looked at me with a significant smile and said, "I see you have already raised your mustaches. You know you have a brother who is much older than you are; he hasn't grown his mustaches yet. You must have yours off." I promptly obeyed her mandate, and as I entered the room with a clean face, she smiled with intense satisfaction, evidently thinking that with all my foreign education, I had not lost my early training of being obedient to my mother. And if she could only have read my heart, she would have found how every throb palpitated with the most tender love for her. During the remaining years of her life, I had the rare privilege of seeing her often and ministered to her every comfort that it was in my power to bestow. She passed away in 1858, at the age of sixty-four, twenty-four years after the death of my father. I was in Shanghai at the time of her death. I returned to my native village in time to attend her funeral.

In the summer of 1855, I took up my residence in Canton, with the Rev. Mr. Vrooman, a missionary under the American Board. His headquarters were in Ham Ha Lan, in the vicinity of the government execution ground, which is in the south-western outskirts of the city, close to the bank of the Pearl River. While there, I began my Chinese studies and commenced to regain the dialect of Canton, which I had forgotten during my stay in the United States. In less than six months, the language came back to me readily, although I was still a little rusty in it. I was also making slow progress in recovering the written language, in which I was not well-grounded before leaving China, in 1346. I had studied it only four years, which was considered a short time in which to master the written language. There is a greater difference between the written and the spoken language of China than there is between the written and spoken English language. The Chinese written language is stilted and full of conventional forms. It is understood throughout the whole empire, but differently pronounced in different provinces and localities. The spoken language is cut up into endless dialects and in certain provinces like Fuhkien, Anhui and Kiangsu, the people are as foreigners to each other in the matter of dialects. Such are the peculiar characteristics of the ideographic and spoken languages of China.

During the six months of my residence in Canton, while trying to recover both the written and spoken languages, Kwang Tung province was thrown into a somewhat disorganized condition. The people of Canton attempted to raise a provincial insurrection or rebellion entirely distinct from the Taiping rebellion which was being carried on in the interior of China with marked success. To suppress and nip it in the bud, drastic measures were resorted to by Viceroy Yeh Ming Hsin, who, in the summer of 1855, decapitated seventy-five thousand people, most of whom, I was told, were innocent. My residence was within half a mile of the execution ground, as stated above, and one day, out of curiosity, I ventured to walk over to the place. But, oh! what a sight. The ground was perfectly drenched with human blood. On both sides of the driveway were to be seen headless human trunks, piled up in heaps, waiting to be taken away for burial. But no provision had been made to facilitate their removal.

The execution was carried on on a larger scale than had been expected, and no provision had been made to find a place large enough to bury all the bodies. There they were, left exposed to a burning sun. The temperature stood from morning to night in midsummer steadily at 90° Fahrenheit, and sometimes higher. The atmosphere within a radius of two thousand yards of the execution ground was heavily charged with the poisonous and pestilential vapor that was reeking from the ground already over-saturated with blood and from the heaps of corpses which had been left behind for at least two days, and which showed signs of rapid decomposition. It was a wonder to me that no virulent epidemic had sprung up from such an infectious spot to decimate the compact population of the city of Canton. It was a fortunate circumstance that at last a deep and extensive ravine, located in the far-off outskirts of the western part of the city, was found, which was at once converted into a sepulchral receptacle into which this vast human hecatomb was dumped. It was said that no earth was needed to be thrown over these corpses to cover them up; the work was accomplished by countless swarms of worms of a reddish hue and of an appearance that was perfectly hideous and revolting.

I was told that during the months of June, July and August, of 1855, seventy-five thousand people had been decapitated; that more than half of that number were declared to be innocent of the charge of rebellion, but that the accusation was made as a pretext to exact money from them. This wholesale slaughter, unparalleled in the annals of modern civilization, eclipsing even the enormities and blood-thirstiness of Caligula and Nero, or even the French Revolution, was perpetrated by Yeh Ming Hsin, who was appointed viceroy of Kwang Tung and Kwangsi in 1854.

Yeh Ming Hsin was a native of Han-Yang. Han-Yang is a part of the port of Hankau, and was destroyed with it when the Taiping rebels took possession of it. It was said that Yeh Ming Hsin had immense estates in Han-Yang, which were completely destroyed by fire. This circumstance embittered him towards the Taiping rebels and as the Taiping leaders hailed from Kwang Tung and Kwangsi, he naturally transferred his hatred to the people of those two provinces. It was in the lofty position of a viceroy that he found his opportunity to wreak his private and personal vengeance upon the Canton people. This accounts for his indiscriminate slaughter of them, and for the fact that he did not deign to give them even the semblance of a trial, but hurried them from life to death like packs of cattle to the shambles.

But this human monster did not dream that his day of reckoning was fast approaching. Several years after this appalling sacrifice of human life, in 1855, he got into trouble with the British government. He was captured by the British forces and banished to some obscure and remote corner in India where he led a most ignominious life, hated by the whole Chinese nation, and despised by the world at large.

18

On my return to headquarters, after my visit to the execution ground, I felt faint-hearted and depressed in spirit. I had no appetite for food, and when night came I was too nervous for sleep. The scene I had looked upon during the day had stirred me up. I thought then that the Taiping rebels had ample grounds to justify their attempt to overthrow the Manchu régime. My sympathies were thoroughly enlisted in their favor and I thought seriously of making preparations to join the Taiping rebels, but upon a calmer reflection, I fell back on the original plan of doing my best to recover the Chinese language as fast as I possibly could and of following the logical course of things, in order to accomplish the object I had at heart.

CHAPTER VII

EFFORT TO FIND A POSITION

Having at last succeeded in mastering the spoken language sufficiently to speak it quite fluently, I at once set to work to find a position in which I could not only support myself and mother, but also form a plan for working out my ideas of reform in China.

Doctor Peter Parker, who had been a medical missionary under the American Board for many years in Canton, was at that time made United States Commissioner as a temporary expedient, to take the place of an accredited minister plenipotentiary—a diplomatic appointment not yet come into existence, because the question of a foreign minister resident in Peking was still under negotiation, and had not been fully settled as a permanent diplomatic arrangement between the Peking government and the Treaty Powers. Dr. Parker was given the appointment of commissioner on account of his long residence in China and his ability to speak the Chinese language, but not on account of any special training as a diplomat, nor for legal knowledge. It was through Mr. M. N. Hitchcock, an American merchant of the firm of Messrs. King & Co., and a mutual friend of Dr. Parker and myself, that I became the Doctor's private secretary. I knew Dr. Parker while I was at Mrs. Gutzlaff's School, and he doubtless knew I had recently graduated from Yale, which was his Alma Mater also. His headquarters were in Canton, but he spent his summers in Macao. I was with him only three months. My salary was $15 a month (not large enough to spoil me at any rate). He had very little for me to do, but I thought that by being identified with him, I might possibly come in contact with Chinese officials. However, this was far from being the case. Seeing that I could neither learn anything from him, nor enlarge my acquaintance with the Chinese officials, I gave up my position as his secretary and went over to Hong Kong to try to study law. Through my old friend, Andrew Shortrede, who generously extended to me the hospitality of his house I succeeded in securing the position of the interpretership in the Hong Kong Supreme Court. The situation paid me $75 a month. Having this to fall back upon, I felt encouraged to go ahead in my effort to study law. Accordingly, I was advised to apprentice myself to an attorney or solicitor-at-law. In the English court of practice, it seems that there are two distinct classes of lawyers—attorneys or solicitors, and barristers. The first prepares in writing all evidences, facts, and proofs of a case, hands them to the barrister or counsel, who argues the case in court according to law.

I apprenticed myself to an attorney, who was recommended to me by my old patron and friend, Shortrede. I was not aware that by going into the British Colony in Hong Kong to become an attorney, I was stepping on the toes of the British legal fraternity, nor that by apprenticing myself to an attorney instead of to the new attorney-general of the Colony, who, without my knowledge, wanted me himself, I had committed another mistake, which eventually necessitated my leaving Hong Kong altogether.

First of all, all the attorneys banded themselves together against me, because, as they openly stated in all the local papers except the "China Mail," if I were allowed to practice my profession, they might as well pack up and go back to England, for as I had a complete knowledge of both English and Chinese I would eventually monopolize all the Chinese legal business. So they made it too hot for me to continue in my studies.

In the next place, I was not aware that the attorney-general wanted me to apprentice myself to him, for he did all he could in his capacity as attorney-general of the Colony to use his influence to open the way for me to become an attorney, by draughting a special colonial ordinance to admit Chinese to practice in the Hong Kong Colony as soon as I could pass my examinations. This ordinance was sent to the British government to be sanctioned by Parliament before it became valid and a colonial law. It was sanctioned and thus became a colonial ordinance.

In the meanwhile, Anstey, the attorney-general, found out that I had already apprenticed myself to Parson, the attorney. From that time forth I had no peace. I was between two fires—the batteries operated by the attorneys opened on me with redoubled energy, and the new battery, operated by the attorney-general, opened its fire. He found fault with my interpreting, which he had never done previously. Mr. Parson saw how things stood. He himself was also under a hot fire from both sides. So in order to save himself, he told me plainly and candidly that he had to give me up and made the article of apprenticeship between us null and void. I, on my part, had to give up my position as interpreter in the Supreme Court. Parson, himself, not long after I had abandoned my apprenticeship and my position as interpreter, for reasons satisfactory to himself, gave up his business in Hong Kong and returned to England. So master and pupil left their posts at pretty nearly the same time.

A retrospective view of my short experience in Hong Kong convinced me that it was after all the best thing that I did not succeed in becoming a lawyer in Hong Kong, as the theatre of action there would have been too restricted and circumscribed. I could not have come in touch with the leading minds of China, had I been bound up in that rocky and barren Colony. Doubtless I might have made a fortune if I had succeeded in my legal profession, but as circumstances forced me to leave the Colony, my mind was directed northward to Shanghai, and in August, 1856, I left Hong Kong in the tea clipper, "Florence," under Captain Dumaresque, of Boston. He was altogether a different type of man from the captain of the "Eureka" which brought me out in 1855. He was kind, intelligent and gentlemanly. When he found out who I was, he offered me a free passage from Hong Kong to Shanghai. He was, in fact, the sole owner of the vessel, which was named after his daughter, Florence. The passage was a short one—lasting only seven days—but before it was over, we became great friends.

Not long after my arrival in Shanghai, I found a situation in the Imperial Customs Translating Department, at a salary of Tls. 75 a month, equivalent to $100 Mexican. For want of a Chinese silver currency the Mexican dollar was adopted. This was one point better than the interpretership in the Hong Kong Supreme Court. The duties were not arduous and trying. In fact, they were too simple and easy to suit my taste and ambition. I had plenty of time to read. Before three months of trial in my new situation, I found that things were not as they should be, and if I wished to keep a clean and clear record and an untarnished character, I could not remain long in the service. Between the interpreters who had been in the service many years and the Chinese shippers there existed a regular system of graft. After learning this, and not wishing to be implicated with the others in the division of the spoils in any way or shape, I made up my mind to resign. So one day I called upon the Chief Commissioner of Customs, ostensibly to find out what my future

20

prospects were in connection with the Customs Service—whether or not there were any prospects of my being promoted to the position of a commissioner. I was told that no such prospects were held out to me or to any other Chinese interpreter. I, therefore, at once decided to throw up my position. So I sent in my resignation, which was at first not accepted. A few days after my first interview, Lay, the chief commissioner, strenuously tried to persuade me to change my mind, and offered as an inducement to raise my salary to Tls. 200 a month, evidently thinking that I was only bluffing in order to get higher wages. It did not occur to him that there was at least one Chinaman who valued a clean reputation and an honest character more than money; that being an educated man, I saw no reason why I should not be given the same chances to rise in the service of the Chinese government as an Englishman, nor why my individuality should not be recognized and respected in every walk of life. He little thought that I had aspirations even higher than his, and that I did not care to associate myself with a pack of Custom-house interpreters and inspectors, who were known to take bribes; that a man who expects others to respect him, must first respect himself. Such were my promptings. I did not state the real cause of my quitting the service, but at the end of four months' trial I left the service in order to try my fortune in new fields more congenial.

My friends at the time looked upon me as a crank in throwing up a position yielding me Tls. 200 a month for something uncertain and untried. This in their estimation was the height of folly. They little realized what I was driving at. I had a clean record and I meant to keep it clean. I was perfectly aware that in less than a year since my return to China, I had made three shifts. I myself began to think I was too mercurial to accomplish anything substantial, or that I was too dreamy to be practical or too proud to succeed in life. But in a strenuous life one needs to be a dreamer in order to accomplish possibilities. We are not called into being simply to drudge for an animal existence. I had had to work hard for my education, and I felt that I ought to make the most of what little I had, not so much to benefit myself individually as to make it a blessing common to my race. By these shifts and changes I was only trying to find my true bearing, and how I could make myself a blessing to China.

CHAPTER VIII

EXPERIENCES IN BUSINESS

The next turn I took, after leaving the Imperial Customs, was clerk in an English house—tea and silk merchants. During the few months that I was with them, I gained quite an insight into mercantile business, and the methods of conducting it, which proved to be profitable knowledge and experience to me later on. Six months after I had entered upon my new sphere as a make-shift, the firm dissolved partnership, which once more threw me out of a position, and I was again cast upon the sea of uncertainty. But during my connection with the firm, two little incidents occurred which I must not fail to relate.

One Thursday evening, as I was returning home from a prayer meeting held in the Union Chapel in Shanghai, I saw ahead of me on Szechuen Road in front of the Episcopal church, a string of men; each had a Chinese lantern swinging in the air over his head, and they were singing and shouting as they zigzagged along the road, evidently having a jolly, good time, while Chinese on both sides of the road were seen dodging and scampering about in great fright in all directions, and acting as though they were chased by the Old Nick himself. I was at a distance of about one hundred yards from the scene. I took in the situation at once. My servant, who held a lantern ahead of me, to light the way, was so frightened that he began to come back towards me. I told him not to be afraid, but walk right straight ahead. Pretty soon we confronted three or four of the fellows, half tipsy. One of them snatched the lantern from my servant and another, staggering about, tried to give me a kick. I walked along coolly and unconcerned till I reached the last batch of two or three fellows. I found these quite sober and in their senses and they were lingering behind evidently to enjoy the fun and watch the crowd in their hilarious antics. I stopped and parleyed with them, and told them who I was. I asked them for the names of the fellows who snatched my boy's lantern and of the fellow who tried to kick me. They declined at first, but finally with the promise that I would not give them any trouble, they gave me the name of one of the fellows, his position on the vessel, and the name of the vessel he belonged to. It turned out that the man was the first mate of the ship "Eureka," the very vessel that brought me out to China, in 1855, and which happened to be consigned to the firm I was working for. The next morning, I wrote a note to the captain, asking him to hand the note to his first officer. The captain, on receiving the note, was quite excited, and handed it to the first mate, who immediately came ashore and apologized. I made it very pleasant for him and told him that Americans in China were held in high esteem by the people, and every American landing in China should be jealous of the high estimation in which they were held and not do anything to compromise it. My motive in writing the note was merely to get him on shore and give him this advice. He was evidently pleased with my friendly attitude and extended his hand for a shake to thank me for the advice. He invited me to go on board with him to take a glass of wine and be good friends. I thanked him for his offer, but declined it, and we parted in an amicable way.

My second incident, which happened a couple of months after the first, did not have such a peaceful ending.

After the partnership of the firm, in whose employ I was, dissolved, an auction sale of the furniture of the firm took place. In the room where the auction was proceeding, I happened to be standing in a mixed crowd of Chinese and foreigners. A stalwart six-footer of a Scotchman happened to be standing behind me. He was not altogether a stranger to me, for I had met him in the streets several times. He began to tie a bunch of cotton balls to my queue, simply for a lark. But I caught him at it and in a pleasant way held it up and asked him to untie it. He folded up his arms and drew himself straight up with a look of the utmost disdain and scorn. I at once took in the situation, and as my countenance sobered, I reiterated my demand to have the appendage taken off. All of a sudden, he thrust his fist against my mouth, without drawing any blood, however. Although he stood head and shoulders above me in height, yet I was not at all abashed or intimidated by his burly and contemptuous appearance. My dander was up and oblivious to all thoughts of our comparative size and strength, I struck him back in the identical place where he punched me, but my blow was a stinger and it went with lightning rapidity to the spot, without giving him time to think. It drew blood in great profusion from lip and nose. He caught me by the wrist with both his hands. As he held my right wrist in his powerful grasp, for he was an athlete and a sportsman, I was just on the point of raising my right foot for a kick, which was aimed at a vital point, when the head partner of the firm, who happened to be near, suddenly stepped in between and separated us. I then stood off to one side, facing my antagonist, who was moving off into the crowd. As I moved away, I was asked by a voice from the crowd:

"Do you want to fight?"

I said, "No, I was only defending myself. Your friend insulted me and added injury to insult. I took him for a gentleman, but he has proved himself a blackguard."

22

With this stinging remark, which was heard all over the room, I retired from the scene into an adjoining room, leaving the crowd to comment on the incident. The British Consul, who happened to be present on the occasion, made a casual remark on the merits of the case and said, as I was told afterwards by a friend, that "The young man was a little too fiery; if he had not taken the law into his own hands, he could have brought suit for assault and battery in the consular court, but since he has already retaliated and his last remark before the crowd has inflicted a deeper cut to his antagonist than the blow itself, he has lost the advantage of a suit."

The Scotchman, after the incident, did not appear in public for a whole week. I was told he had shut himself up in his room to give his wound time to heal, but the reason he did not care to show himself was more on account of being whipped by a little Chinaman in a public manner; for the affair, unpleasant and unfortunate as it was, created quite a sensation in the settlement. It was the chief topic of conversation for a short time among foreigners, while among the Chinese I was looked upon with great respect, for since the foreign settlement on the extra-territorial basis was established close to the city of Shanghai, no Chinese within its jurisdiction had ever been known to have the courage and pluck to defend his rights, point blank, when they had been violated or trampled upon by a foreigner. Their meek and mild disposition had allowed personal insults and affronts to pass unresented and unchallenged, which naturally had the tendency to encourage arrogance and insolence on the part of ignorant foreigners. The time will soon come, however, when the people of China will be so educated and enlightened as to know what their rights are, public and private, and to have the moral courage to assert and defend them whenever they are invaded. The triumph of Japan over Russia in the recent war has opened the eyes of the Chinese world. It will never tolerate injustice in any way or shape, much less will it put up with foreign aggression and aggrandizement any longer. They see now in what plight their national ignorance, conceit and conservatism, in which they had been fossilized, had placed them. They were on the verge of being partitioned by the European Powers and were saved from that catastrophe only by the timely intervention of the United States government. What the future will bring forth, since the Emperor Kwangsu and Dowager Empress Chi Hsi have both passed away, no one can predict.

The breaking up of the firm by which I was employed, once more, as stated before, and for the fourth time, threw me out of a regular business. But I was not at all disconcerted or discouraged, for I had no idea of following a mercantile life as a permanent calling. Within the past two years, my knowledge of the Chinese language had decidedly improved. I was not in hot haste to seek for a new position. I immediately took to translating as a means of bridging over the breaks of a desultory life. This independent avocation, though not a lucrative one, nevertheless led the way to a wider acquaintance with the educated and mercantile classes of the Chinese; to widen my acquaintance was my chief concern. My translating business brought me in contact with the comprador of one of the leading houses in Shanghai. The senior partner of this house died in 1857. He was well-known and thought much of by both the Chinese and the foreign mercantile body. To attest their high regard for his memory, the prominent Chinese merchants drew up an elaborate and eulogistic epitaph on the occasion of his death. The surviving members of the firm selected two translators to translate the epitaph. One was the interpreter in the British Consulate General, a brother to the author of "The Chinese and their Rebellions," and the other was (through the influence of the comprador) myself. To my great surprise, my translation was given the preference and accepted by the manager of the firm. The Chinese committee were quite elated that one of their countrymen knew enough English to bring out the inner sense of their epitaph. It was adopted and engraved on the monument. My name began to be known among the Chinese, not as a fighter this time, but as a Chinese student educated in America.

Soon after this performance, another event unexpectedly came up in which I was again called upon to act; that was the inundation of the Yellow River, which had converted the northern part of Kiangsu province into a sea, and made homeless and destitute thousands of people of that locality. A large body of refugees had wandered to and flocked near Shanghai. A Chinese deputation, consisting of the leading merchants and gentry, who knew or had heard of me, called and asked me to draw up a circular appealing to the foreign community for aid and contributions to relieve the widespread suffering among the refugees. Several copies were immediately put into circulation and in less than a week, no less than $20,000 were subscribed and paid. The Chinese Committee were greatly elated over their success and their joy was unbounded. To give a finishing touch to this stroke of business, I wrote in the name of the committee a letter of acknowledgment and thanks to the foreign community for the prompt and generous contribution it had made. This was published in the Shanghai local papers—"The Shanghai Mail" and "Friend of China"—so that inside of three months after I had started my translating business, I had become widely known among the Chinese as the Chinese student educated in America. I was indebted to Tsang Kee Foo, the comprador, for being in this line of business, and for the fact that I was becoming known in Shanghai. He was a well-educated Chinese—a man highly respected and trusted for his probity and intelligence. His long connection with the firm and his literary taste had gathered around him some of the finest Chinese scholars from all parts of China, while his business transactions brought him in touch with the leading Chinese capitalists and business men in Shanghai and elsewhere. It was through him that both the epitaph and the circular mentioned above were written; and it was Tsang Kee Foo who introduced me to the celebrated Chinese mathematician, Li Jen Shu, who years afterwards brought me to the notice of Viceroy Tsang Kwoh Fan—the distinguished general and statesman, who, as will be seen hereafter, took up and promoted the Chinese Education Scheme. In the great web of human affairs, it is almost impossible to know who among our friends and acquaintances may prove to be the right clue to unravel the skein of our destiny. Tsang Kee Foo introduced me to Li Jen Shu, the latter introduced me to Tsang Kwoh Fan, who finally through the Chinese Education Scheme grafted Western education to the Oriental culture, a union destined to weld together the different races of the world into one brotherhood.

My friend Tsang Kee Foo afterwards introduced me to the head or manager of Messrs. Dent & Co., who kindly offered me a position in his firm as comprador in Nagasaki, Japan, soon after that country was opened to foreign trade. I declined the situation, frankly and plainly stating my reason, which was that the compradorship, though lucrative, is associated with all that is menial, and that as a graduate of Yale, one of the leading colleges in America, I could not think of bringing discredit to my Alma Mater, for which I entertained the most profound respect and reverence, and was jealous of her proud fame. What would the college and my class-mates think of me, if they should hear that I was a comprador—the head servant of servants in an English establishment? I said there were cases when a man from stress of circumstances may be compelled to play the part of a menial for a shift, but I was not yet reduced to that strait, though I was poor financially. I told him I would prefer to travel for the firm as its agent in the interior and correspond directly with the head of the firm. In that case, I would not sacrifice my manhood for the sake of making money in a position which is commonly held to be servile. I would much prefer to pack tea and buy silk as an agent—either on a salary or on commission. Such was my ground for declining. I, however, thanked him for the offer. This interview took place in the presence of my friend, Tsang Kee Foo, who without knowing the details of the conversation, knew enough of the English language to follow the general tenor of the talk. I then retired and left the manager and my friend to talk over the result. Tsang afterwards told me that Webb said, "Yung Wing is poor but proud. Poverty and pride usually go together, hand in hand." A few days afterwards Tsang informed me that Webb had decided to send me to the tea districts to see and learn the business of packing tea.

CHAPTER IX

MY FIRST TRIP TO THE TEA DISTRICTS

On the 11th of March, 1859, I found myself on board of a Woo-Sik-Kwei, a Chinese boat built in Woo-Sik, a city situated on the borders of the Grand Canal, within a short distance of the famous city of Suchau—a rival of the city of Hangchau, for wealth, population, silk manufacture, and luxury. The word "Kwei" means "fast." Therefore, Woo-Sik-Kwei means fast boats of Woo-Sik. These passenger boats which plied between the principal cities and marts situated near the waters of the canal and lake system in southern Kianksu, were usually built of various sizes and nicely fitted up for the comfort and convenience of the public. Those intended for officials, and the wealthy classes, were built on a larger scale and fitted up in a more pretentious style. They were all flat-bottom boats. They sailed fairly well before the wind, but against it, they were either tracked by lines from the mast to the trackers on shore, or by sculling, at which the Chinese are adepts. They can give a boat a great speed by a pair of sculls resting on steel pivots that are fastened at the stern, one on each side, about the middle of the scull, with four men on each scull; the blades are made to play in the water astern, right and left, which pushes and sends the boat forward at a surprisingly rapid rate. But in recent years, steam has made its way into China and steam launches have superseded these native craft which are fast disappearing from the smooth waters of Kiangsu province—very much as the fast sailing ships, known as Baltimore Clippers, that in the fifties and sixties were engaged in the East India and China trade, have been gradually swept from the ocean by steam.

At the end of three days, I was landed in the historic city of Hangchau, which is the capital of Chêhkiang. It is situated on a plain of uneven ground, with hills in the southwest and west, and northeast. It covers an area of about three or four square miles. It is of a rectangular shape. Its length is from north to south; its breadth, from east to west. On the west, lies the Si-Hoo or West Lake, a beautiful sheet of limpid water with a gravelly or sandy bottom, stretching from the foot of the city wall to the foot of the mountains which appear in the distance in the rear, rising into the clouds like lofty bulwarks guarding the city on the north.

The Tsientang River, about two miles distant, flanks the city on the east. It takes its rise from the high mountain range of Hwui Chow in the southeast and follows a somewhat irregular course to the bay of the same name, and rushes down the rocky declivities like a foaming steed and empties itself into the bay about forty miles east of the city. This is one of the rivers that have periodical bores in which the tidal waters in their entrance to the bay create a noise like thunder, and the waves rise to the height of eight or ten feet.

Hangchau, aside from her historic fame as having been the seat of the government of the Sung Dynasty of the 12th and 13th centuries, has always maintained a wide reputation for fine buildings, public and private, such as temples, pagodas, mosques and bridges, which go to lend enchantment to the magnificent natural scenery with which she is singularly endowed. But latterly, age and the degeneration of the times have done their work of mischief. Her past glory is fast sinking into obscurity; she will never recover her former prestige, unless a new power arises to make her once more the capital of a regenerated government.

On the 15th of March, I left Hangchau to ascend the Tsientang River, at a station called Kang Kow, or mouth of the river, about two miles east of the city, where boats were waiting for us. Several hundreds of these boats of a peculiar and unique type were riding near the estuary of the river. These boats are called Urh Woo, named after the district where they were built. They vary from fifty to one hundred feet in length, from stem to stern, and are ten or fifteen feet broad, and draw not more than two or three feet of water when fully loaded. They are all flat-bottom boats, built of the most limber and flexible material that can be found, as they are expected to meet strong currents and run against rocks, both in their ascent and descent, on account of the irregularity and rocky bottom of the river. These boats, when completely equipped and covered with bamboo matting, look like huge cylinders, and are shaped like cigars. The interior from stem to stern is divided into separate compartments, or rooms, in which bunks are built to accommodate passengers. These compartments and bunks are removed when room is needed for cargoes. These boats ply between Hangchau and Sheong Shan and do all the interior transportation by water between these entrepôts in Chêhkiang and Kiangsi. Sheong Shan is the important station of Chêhkiang, and Yuh-Shan is that of Kiangsi. The distance between the two entrepôts is about fifty lis, or about sixteen English miles, connected by one of the finest macadamized roads in China. The road is about thirty feet wide, paved with slabs of granite and flanked with greenish-colored cobbles. A fine stone arch which was erected as a land-mark of the boundary line separating Chêhkiang and Kiangsi provinces, spans the whole width of the road. On both sides of the key-stone of the arch are carved four fine Chinese characters, painted in bright blue, viz., Leang Hsing Tung Chu:

兩 省 通 衢

This is one of the most notable arch-ways through which the inter-provincial trade has been carried on for ages past. At the time when I crossed from Sheong Shan to Yuh-Shan, the river ports of Hankau, Kiukiang, Wuhu and Chinkiang were not opened to foreign trade and steam-boats had not come in to play their part in the carrying trade of the interior of China. This magnificent thoroughfare was crowded with thousands of porters bearing merchandise of all kinds to and fro—exports and imports for distribution. It certainly presented an interesting sight to the traveller, as well as a profound topic of contemplation to a Chinese patriot.

The opening of the Yangtze River, which is navigable as far as Kingchau, on the borders of Szechwan province, commanding the trade of at least six or seven provinces along its whole course of nearly three thousand miles to the ocean, presents a spectacle of unbounded possibilities for the amelioration of nearly a third of the human race, if only the grasping ambition of the West will let the territorial integrity and the independent sovereignty of China remain intact. Give the people of China a fair chance to work out the problems of their own salvation, as for instance the solution of the labor question, which has been so radically disorganized and broken up by steam, electricity and machinery. This has virtually taken the breath and bread away from nine-tenths of the people of China, and therefore this immovable mass of population should be given ample time to recover from its demoralization.

To go back to my starting point at Kang Kow, the entrance to the river, two miles east of Hangchau, we set sail, with a fair wind, at five o'clock in the morning of the 15th of March, and in the evening at ten o'clock we anchored at a place named the "Seven Dragons," after having made about one hundred miles during the day. The eastern shore in this part of the Tsientang River is evidently of red sandstone formation, for we could see part of the strata submerged in the water, and excavations of the stone may be seen strewn about on the shore. In fact, red sandstone buildings may be seen scattered about here and there. But the mountain about the Seven Dragons is picturesque and romantic.

Early the next day, we again started, but the rain poured down in torrents. We kept on till we reached the town of Lan Chi and came to anchor in the evening, after having made about forty miles. This is the favorite entrepôt where the Hupeh and Hunan congou teas were brought all the way from the tea districts of these provinces, to be housed and transhipped to Shanghai via Hangchau. Lan Chi is an entrepôt of only one street, but its entire length is six miles. It is famous for its nice hams, which are known all over China. On account of the incessant rain, we stopped half a day at Lan Chi. In the afternoon the sky began to clear and at twelve o'clock in the night we again started and reached the walled city of Ku Chow, which was besieged by the Taiping rebels in March, 1858, just a year before; after four months' duration the siege was raised and no great damage was done. We put up in an inn for the night. Ku Chow is a departmental city of Chêhkiang and is about thirty miles distant from Sheong Shan, already mentioned in connection with Yuh-Shan. We were delayed by the Custom House officials, as well as on account of the scarcity of porters and chair-bearers to take us over to Sheong Shan. We arrived at Yuh-Shan from Sheong Shan by chair in the evening. We put up in an inn for the night, having first engaged fishing boats to take us to the city of Kwangshun, thirty miles from Yuh-Shan, the next morning. After reaching Yuh-Shan, we were in Kiangsi territory, and our route now lay in a west by north direction, down stream towards the Po Yang Lake, whose southern margin we passed, and reached Nan Cheong, the capital of Kiangsi province. The city presented a fine outward appearance. We did not stop long enough to go through the city and see its actual condition since its evacuation by the rebels.

Our route from Nan Cheong was changed in a west by south direction, making the great entrepôt of Siang Tan our final goal. In this route, we passed quite a number of large cities that had nothing of special importance, either commercially or historically, to relate. We passed Cheong Sha, the capital of Hunan, in the night. We arrived at Siang Tan on the morning of the 15th of April. Siang Tan is one of the noted entrepôts in the interior of China and used to be the great distributing center of imports when foreign trade was confined to the single port of Canton. It was also the emporium where the tea and silk goods of China were centered and housed, to be carried down to Canton for exportation to foreign countries. The overland transport trade between Siang Tan and Canton was immense. It gave employment to at least one hundred thousand porters, carrying merchandise over the Nan Fung pass, between the two cities, and supported a large population along both sides of the thoroughfare. Steam, wars and treaties of very recent dates have not only broken up this system of labor and changed the complexion of the whole labor question throughout China, but will also alter the economical, industrial and political conditions of the Chinese Empire during the coming years of her history.

At Siang Tan, our whole party, composed of tea-men, was broken up and each batch began its journey to the district assigned it, to begin the work of purchasing raw tea and preparing it to be packed for shipment in Shanghai.

I stayed in Siang Tan about ten days and then made preparations for a trip up to the department of Kingchau in Hupeh province, to look into the yellow silk produced in a district called Ho-Yung.

We left Siang Tan on the 26th of April, and proceeded northward to our place of destination. Next morning at eight o'clock we reached Cheong Sha, the capital of Hunan province. As the day was wet and gloomy, we stopped and tried to make the best of it by going inside of the city to see whether there was anything worth seeing, but like all Chinese cities, it presented the same monotonous appearance of age and filth, the same unchangeable style of architecture and narrow streets. Early next morning, we resumed our boat journey, crossed the Tung Ting Lake and the great river Yangtze till we entered the mouth of the King Ho which carried us to Ho Yung. On this trip to hunt after the yellow silk—not the golden fleece—we were thirteen days from Siang Tan. The country on both banks of the King Ho seemed quiet and peaceful and people were engaged in agricultural pursuits. We saw many buffaloes and donkeys, and large patches of wheat, interspersed with beans. A novel sight presented itself which I have never met with elsewhere in China. A couple of country lassies were riding on a donkey, and were evidently in a happy mood, laughing and talking as they rode by. Arriving in Ho Yung, we had some difficulty in finding an inn, but finally succeeded in securing quarters in a silk hong. No sooner were we safely quartered, than a couple of native constables called to know who we were; our names and business were taken down. Our host, the proprietor of the hong, who knew the reason of our coming, explained things to the satisfaction of the men, who went away perfectly satisfied that we were honest traders and no rebel spies. We were left to transact our business unmolested. As soon as our object was known, numerous samples of yellow silk were brought for our inspection. We selected quite a number of samples, which altogether weighed about sixty-five pounds, and had them packed to be taken to Shanghai.

At the end of a fortnight, we concluded to take our journey back. Accordingly, on the 26th of May we bade Ho Yung farewell, and started for the tea district of Nih Kia Shi, in the department of Cheong Sha, via Hankau. We arrived at Hankau on the 5th of June, and put up in a native inn. The weather was hot and muggy, and our quarters were narrow and cut off from fresh air. Three days after our arrival, three deputies visited us to find out who we were. It did not take long to convince them that we were not rebel spies. We showed them the package of yellow silk, which bore marks of a war-tax which we had to pay on it, all along the route from Ho Yung to Hankau. We were left unmolested.

The port of Hankau had not been opened for foreign trade, though it was well understood that it was to be opened very soon. Before its capture by the Taiping rebels, or rather before the Taiping rebels had made their appearance on the stage of action, Hankau was the most important entrepôt in China. When the Taiping rebels captured Woochang in 1856, Hankau and Han Yang fell at the same time, and the port was destroyed by fire and was reduced to ashes. At the time of my visit, the whole place was rebuilt and trade began to revive. But the buildings were temporary shifts. Now the character of the place is completely changed and the foreign residences and warehouses along the water's edge have given it altogether a European aspect, so that the Hankau of today may be regarded as the Chicago or St. Louis of China, and in no distant day she is destined to surpass both in trade, population and wealth. I was in Hankau a few days before I crossed the Yangtze-Kiang to the black tea district of Nih Kia Shi.

We left Hankau on the 30th of June and went over to the tea packing houses in Nih Kia Shi and Yang Liu Tung on the 4th of July. I was in those two places over a month and gained a complete knowledge of the whole process of preparing the black tea for the foreign market. The process is very simple and can be easily learned. I do not know through what preparations the Indian and Assam teas have to go, where machinery is used, but they cannot be very elaborate. Undoubtedly, since the fifties, manual labor, the old standby in preparing teas for foreign consumption, has been much improved with a view of retaining a large percentage of the tea trade in China. The reason why a large percentage of the tea business has passed away from China to India is not because machinery is used in the one case and manual labor is retained in the other, but chiefly on account of the quality of the tea that is raised in the different soil of the two countries. The Indian or Assam tea is much stronger (in proportion to the same quantity) than the Chinese tea. The Indian tea is 2-1 to Chinese tea, in point of strength, whereas the Chinese tea is 2-1 to the Indian tea in point of delicacy and flavor. The Indian is rank and strong, but the Chinese tea is superior in the quality of its fine aroma. The higher class of tea-drinkers in America, Europe and Russia prefer China tea to Indian, whereas the laboring and common class in those countries take to Indian and Assam, from the fact that they are stronger and cheaper.

In the latter part of August I decided to return to Shanghai, not by way of Siang Tan, but via Hankau, down the Yangtze River to Kiu Kang and across the Poh Yang Lake. I arrived at Hankau again the second time on the 29th of August, having left there two months previous, in July. This time I came in a Hunan junk loaded with tea for Shanghai. At Ho Kow, the southern shore of the Poh Yang Lake, I had to follow the same route I took in March, and on the 21st of September I landed at Hangchau and from there I took a Woo-Sik-Kwei for Shanghai, where I arrived in the night of the 30th of September, the time consumed on this journey having been seven months—from March to October. It was my first journey into the interior of China, and it gave me a chance to gain an insight into the actual condition of the people, while a drastic rebellion was going on in their midst. The zone of the country through which I had passed had been visited by the rebels and the imperialists, but was, to all outward appearance, peaceful and quiet. To what extent the people had suffered both from rebel and imperialist devastations in those sections of the country, no one can tell. But there was one significant fact that struck me forcibly and that was the sparseness of population, which was at variance with my preconceived notions regarding the density of population in China which I had gathered from books and accounts of travelers. This was particularly noticeable through that section of Chêhkiang, Kiangsi, Hunan and Hupeh, which I visited. The time of the year, when crops of all kinds needed to be planted, should have brought out the peasantry into the open fields with oxen, mules, donkeys, buffaloes and horses, as indispensable accessories to farm life. But comparatively few farmers were met with.

Shortly after my arrival from the interior, in October, an English friend of mine requested me to go to Shau Hing to buy raw silk for him. Shau Hing is a city located in a silk district about twenty miles southwest of Hangchau, and noted for its fine quality of silk. I was about two months in this business, when I was taken down with fever and ague and was compelled to give it up. Shau Hing, like most Chinese cities, was filthy and unhealthy and the water that flowed through it was as black as ink. The city was built in the lowest depression of a valley, and the outlet of the river was so blocked that there was hardly any current to carry off the filth that had been accumulating for ages. Hence the city was literally located in a cesspool—a breeding place for fever and ague, and epidemics of all kinds. But I soon recovered from the attack of the fever and ague and as soon as I could stand on my legs again, I immediately left the malarial atmosphere, and was, in a short time, breathing fresher and purer air.

CHAPTER X

MY VISIT TO THE TAIPINGS

In the fall of 1859 a small party of two missionaries, accompanied by Tsang Laisun, planned a trip to visit the Taiping rebels in Nanking. I was asked to join them, and I decided to do so. My object in going was to find out for my own satisfaction the character of the Taipings; whether or not they were the men fitted to set up a new government in the place of the Manchu Dynasty. Accordingly, on the 6th of November, 1859, we left Shanghai in a Woo-Sik-Kwei boat, with a stiff northeast breeze in our favor, though we had to stem an ebb tide for an hour. The weather was fine and the whole party was in fine spirits. We happened to have an American flag on board, and on the spur of the moment, it was flung to the breeze, but on a sober second thought, we had it hauled down so as not to attract undue attention and have it become the means of thwarting the purpose of our journey. Instead of taking the Sung-Kiang route which was the highway to Suchau, we turned off into another one in order to avoid the possibility of being hauled up by the imperialists and sent back to Shanghai, as we were told that an imperial fleet of Chinese gun-boats was at anchor at Sung Kiang. We found the surrounding country within a radius of thirty miles of Shanghai to be very quiet and saw no signs of political disturbance. The farmers were busily engaged in gathering in their rice crops.

It might be well to mention here that during my sojourn in the interior, the Taiping rebels had captured the city of Suchau, and there was some apprehension on the part of foreigners in the settlement that they might swoop down to take possession of the city of Shanghai, as well as the foreign settlement. That was the reason the Sung Kiang River was picketed by Chinese gun-boats, and the foreign pickets were extended miles beyond the boundary line of the foreign concession.

We reached Suchau on the morning of the 9th of November without meeting with any difficulty or obstacles all the way, nor were we challenged either by the imperialists or rebels, which went to show how loosely and negligently even in time of war, things were conducted in China. On arriving at the Lau Gate of the city, we had to wait at the station where tickets were issued to those who went into the city and taken from those who left, for Suchau was then under martial law. As we wished to go into the city to see the commandant, in order to get letters of introduction from him to the chiefs of other cities along our route to Nanking, we had to send two of our party to headquarters to find out whether we were permitted to enter. At the station, close to the Lau Gate, we waited over an hour. Finally our party appeared accompanied by the same messenger who had been deputed by the head of the police to accompany them to the commandant's office. Permission was given us, and all four went in. The civil officer was absent, but we were introduced to the military commandant, Liu. He was a tall man, dressed in red. His affected hauteur at the start was too thin to disguise his want of a solid character. He became very inquisitive and asked the object of our journey to Nanking. He treated us very kindly, however, and gave us a letter of introduction to the commandant in Tan Yang, and furnished us with passports all the way through the cities of Woo Sik and Cheong Chow. In the audience hall of Commandant Liu, we were introduced to four foreigners—two Americans, one Englishman, and a French noble. One of the Americans said he was a doctor, the Englishman was supposed to be a military officer, and the

Frenchman, as stated above, claimed to be a nobleman. Doubtless they were all adventurers. Each had his own ax to grind. One of the Americans had a rifle and cartridges for sale. He asked quite an exorbitant price for them and they were summarily rejected. The Frenchman said he had lost a fortune and had come out to China to make it up. Our missionary companions were much pleased after being entertained by Lau in hearing him recite the doxology, which he did glibly. Towards evening, when we returned to our boat, he sent us a number of chickens and a goat to boot. We were thus amply provisioned to prosecute our journey to Tan Yang. We left Suchau on the morning of the 11th of November. On our arrival at Woo Sik, our passports were examined and we were very courteously treated by the rebels. We were invited to dinner by the chief in command. After that he sent us fruits and nuts, and came on board himself to see us off. We held quite a long conversation with him, which ended in his repeating the doxology.

November 12th we left Woo Sik and started for Cheong Chow. From Suchau onward we were on the Grand Canal. The road on the bank of the canal was in good condition. Most of the people we saw and met were rebels, traveling between Tan Yang and Suchau, and but few boats were seen passing each other. All the country surrounding the canal between those cities seemed to have been abandoned by the peasantry and the cultivated fields were covered with rank grass and weeds, instead of flourishing crops. A traveler, not knowing the circumstances, would naturally lay the blame wholly upon the Taiping rebels, but the imperialists in their conflicts with the rebels, were as culpable as their enemies. The rebels whom we met on the public road were generally very civil and tried in every way to protect the people in order to gain their confidence. Incendiarism, pillage, robbery and ill-treatment of the people by the rebels, were punished by death. We reached Cheong Chow in the night. We found nearly all the houses along the road between Woo Sik and Cheong Chow to be completely deserted and emptied of all their inmates. There were occasionally a few of the inhabitants to be seen standing on the bank with small baskets, peddling eggs, oranges and cakes, vegetables and pork. They were principally old people, with countenances showing their suffering and despair. On November 13, at six o'clock in the morning, we resumed our journey to Tan Yang. As we drew near Tan Yang, the people seemed to have regained their confidence and the fields seemed to be cultivated. The conduct of the rebels towards them was considerate and commendable. During the morning we saw a force of one thousand men marching towards Tan Yang. We did not quite reach Tan Yang and came to anchor for the night in plain sight of it.

Early next morning, we went into the city to see the Commandant Liu, to present to him the letter we received in Suchau, but he was absent from the city. The man next to Liu, a civilian, came out to meet us. He was very affable and treated us kindly and with great civility. One of our party referred to the religious character of the Taipings.

Chin then gave us his views of Christianity, as taught by Hung Siu Chune—the leader of the rebellion. He said:

"We worship God the Heavenly Father, with whom Jesus and the Holy Spirit constitute the true God; that Shang Ti is the True Spirit."

He then repeated the doxology. He said the rebels had two doxologies—the old and the new; they had discarded the new and adopted the old. He said, the Tien Wong—the Celestial Emperor—was taken up to Heaven and received orders from the Heavenly Father to come and exterminate all evil and rectify all wrong; to destroy idolatry and evil spirits, and finally to teach the people the knowledge of God. He did not know whether the Tien Wong was translated to Heaven bodily or in spirit, or both. He said the Tien Wong himself explained that he could not hold the same footing with God himself; that the homage paid to God was an act of religious worship, but that rendered to the Tien Wong was merely an act of court etiquette, which ministers and officers always paid to their sovereigns in every dynasty, and could not be construed as acts of worship. He also said that Tien Wong was a younger brother of Christ, but that it did not follow that he was born of the same mother. Tien Wong, he claimed, was a younger brother of Christ in the sense that he was especially appointed by God to instruct the people. Christ was also appointed by God to reform and redeem the world. With regard to the three cups of tea,—he said that they were intended as a thank-offering, and were not propitiatory in their character.

"Whenever we drink a cup of tea, we offer thanksgiving to the Heavenly Father. The three cups of tea have no reference to the Trinity whatever. One cup answers the same purpose. The number three was purposely chosen, because it is the favorite number with the Chinese,—it is even mentioned in the Chinese classics."

As for redemption, he said,—"No sacrificial offering can take away our sins; the power of redemption is in Christ; he redeems us and it is our duty to repent of our sins. Even the Tien Wong is very circumspect and is afraid to sin against God."

In the matter of the soldiery keeping aloof from the people in time of war, he said,—"It has been an immemorial custom, adopted by almost every dynasty, that the people should go to the country, and the soldiers be quartered in the city. When a city is captured or taken, it is easy to subjugate the surrounding country."

The places we saw in ruins, both at Suchau and all the way up the canal, were partly destroyed by Cheong Yuh Leang's troops in their retreat, partly by local predatory parties for the sake of plunder, and partly by the Taipings themselves. When Chung Wong was in Suchau, he did all he could to suppress incendiarism by offering rewards of both money and rank to those who took an active part in suppressing it. He issued three orders: 1. That soldiers were not allowed to kill or slaughter the inhabitants. 2. They were prohibited from slaughtering cattle. 3. They were prohibited from setting fire to houses. A violation of any of these orders was attended with capital punishment. When he came down to Woo Sik, he had a country elder decapitated for allowing local bandits to burn down the houses of the people. This was the information we gathered from our conversation with Chin. He also said that Ying Wong and Chung Wong were both talented men—not only in military but also in civil affairs.

He gave us a long account of the capture of different places by the rebels, and how they had been defeated before Nanking, when that city was laid siege to by the imperialists in the early part of 1860. He also showed us a letter by a chief at Hwui Chow regarding the utter defeat and rout of Tsang Kwoh Fan, who was hemmed in by an immense force of the rebels. Tsang was supposed to have been killed in the great battle. He said that Cheong Yuh Leang, the imperialist general, who laid siege to Nanking, after his defeat went to Hangchau for medical treatment for hemorrhage of the lungs; that all the country along the canal, north of the Yangtze, was in the hands of the rebels, and that Princes Chung and Ying were marching up the river to take possession of Hupeh, and that Shih Ta Kai, another chief, was assigned the conquest of Yun Nan, Kwai Chow and Sze Chune provinces. At that time Chin Kiang was being besieged by the rebels, and Chi Wong was in command of an army of observation in Kiang Nan. Such was the rambling statement given us by Chin regarding the disposition of the rebel forces under different chiefs or princes.

After dining with him in the evening, we repaired to our boat for the night. The next morning, November 15th, we again went into the city and called upon Liu, but, failing to see him, we again called upon Chin to arrange for the conveyance of our luggage and

32

ourselves from Tan Yang to Nanking. The aide told us to send all our things to Chin's office and that our boat, if left in Tan Yang until our return, would be well cared for and protected during our absence. So next morning, the 16th of November, we started on foot and walked fifteen miles from Tan Yang to a village called Po Ying, about six miles from the city of Ku Yung, where we halted to pass the night. We had some difficulty in securing a resting place. The people were poor and had no confidence in strangers. We, however, after some coaxing, were supplied with straws spread out on the ground, and the next morning we gave the old women a dollar. We had boiled rice gruel, cold chicken and crackers for our breakfast. When we reached Ku Yung about nine o'clock on the 17th of November, we found that every gate of the city was closed against us, as well as all others, because a rumor was afloat that the rebels before Chin Kiang were defeated, and that they were flocking towards Ku Yung for shelter. So we concluded to continue on our journey towards Nanking, though our missionary friends came near deciding to return to Tan Yang and wend our way back to Shanghai. We proceeded not far from Ku Yung, when we finally succeeded in getting chairs and mules to prosecute our journey.

On the 18th of November, after a trying and wearisome journey, we reached Nanking. I was the first one to reach the South Gate, waiting for the rest of the party to come up before entering. We were reported inside of the gate and messengers accompanied us to the headquarters of the Rev. Mr. Roberts, close by the headquarters of Hung Jin, styled Prince Kan.

After our preliminary introduction to the Rev. Mr. Roberts, I excused myself, and leaving the rest of the party to continue their conversation with him, retired to my quarters to clean up and get rested from the long and tedious journey. In fact, I had little or nothing to say while in Mr. Roberts' presence, nor did I attempt to make myself known to him. I had seen him often in Macao when in Mrs. Gutzlaff's school, twenty or more years before, and I had recognized him at once as soon as I set my eyes on him. He certainly appeared old to me, being dressed in his yellow satin robe of state and moving leisurely in his clumsy Chinese shoes. Exactly in what capacity he was acting in Nanking, I was at a loss to know; whether still as a religious adviser to Hung Siu Chune, or playing the part of secretary of state for the Taiping Dynasty, no one seemed able to tell.

The next day (the 19th of November) I was invited to call on Kan Wong. He was a nephew of Hung Siu Chune, the rebel chief who was styled Tien Wong or the Celestial Sovereign. Before Hung Jin came to Nanking, I had made his acquaintance, in 1856, at Hong Kong. He was then connected with the London Mission Association as a native preacher and was under Dr. James Legge, the distinguished translator of the Chinese classics. I saw considerable of him while in Hong Kong and even then he had expressed a wish that he might see me some day in Nanking. He was then called Hung Jin, but since he had joined his uncle in Nanking, he was raised to the position of a prince. Kan means "Protecting," and Kan Wong signifies "Protecting Prince." He greeted me very cordially and evidently was glad to see me. After the usual exchange of conventionalities, he wanted to know what I thought of the Taipings; whether I thought well enough of their cause to identify myself with it. In reply, I said I had no intention of casting my lot with them, but came simply to see him and pay my respects. At the same time, I wanted to find out for my own satisfaction the actual condition of things in Nanking. I said the journey from Suchau to Nanking had suggested several things to me, which I thought might be of interest to him. They were as follows:

1. To organize an army on scientific principles.
2. To establish a military school for the training of competent military officers.
3. To establish a naval school for a navy.

4. To organize a civil government with able and experienced men to act as advisers in the different departments of administration.

5. To establish a banking system, and to determine on a standard of weight and measure.

6. To establish an educational system of graded schools for the people, making the Bible one of the text books.

7. To organize a system of industrial schools.

These were the topics that suggested themselves to me during the journey. If the Taiping government would be willing, I said, to adopt these measures and set to work to make suitable appropriations for them, I would be perfectly willing to offer my services to help carry them out. It was in that capacity that I felt I could be of the most service to the Taiping cause. In any other, I would simply be an encumbrance and a hindrance to them.

Such was the outcome of my first interview. Two days later, I was again invited to call. In the second interview, we discussed the merits and the importance of the seven proposals stated in our first interview. Kan Wong, who had seen more of the outside world than the other princes or leaders, and even more than Hung Siu Chune himself, knew wherein lay the secret of the strength and power of the British government and other European powers, and fully appreciated the paramount importance and bearing of these proposals. But he was alone and had no one to back him in advocating them. The other princes, or leaders, were absent from the city, carrying on their campaign against the imperialists. He said he was well aware of the importance of these measures, but nothing could be done until they returned, as it required the consent of the majority to any measure before it could be carried out.

A few days after this a small parcel was presented to me as coming from Kan Wong. On opening it, I found to my great surprise a wooden seal about four inches long and an inch wide, having my name carved with the title of "E,"

which means "Righteousness," and designates the fourth official rank under that of a prince, which is the first. My title was written out on a piece of yellow satin stamped with the official seal of the Kan Wong. I was placed in a quandary and was at a loss to know its purport,—whether it was intended to detain me in Nanking for good or to commit me irretrievably to the Taiping cause, nolens volens. At all events, I had not been consulted in the matter and Kan Wong had evidently acted on his own responsibility and taken it for granted that by conferring on me such a high rank as the fourth in the official scale of the Taipings, I might be induced to accept and thus identify myself with the Taiping cause—of the final success of which I had strong doubts, judging from the conduct, character and policy of the leading men connected with it. I talked the matter over with my associates, and came to the decision that I must forthwith return the seal and decline the tempting bauble. I went in person to thank Kan Wong for this distinguished mark of his high consideration, and told him that at any time when the leaders of the Taipings decided to carry out either one or all of my suggestions, made in my first interview with him, I should be most happy to serve them, if my services were needed to help in the matter. I then asked him as a special favor for a passport that would guarantee me a safe conduct in traveling through the territory under the jurisdiction of the

Taipings, whether on business or pleasure. The passport was issued to me the next day, on the 24th of December, and we were furnished with proper conveyances and provisions to take us back to the city of Tan Yang, where our boat lay under the protection of Chin, second in command of the city, waiting our return from Nanking. We started on our return trip for Shanghai on the 27th of December by the same route as we came, and arrived safely in Tan Yang in the early part of January, 1861.

On my way back to Shanghai, I had ample time to form an estimate of the Taiping Rebellion—its origin, character and significance.

CHAPTER XI

REFLECTIONS ON THE TAIPING REBELLION

Rebellions and revolutions in China are not new and rare historic occurrences. There have been at least twenty-four dynasties and as many attendant rebellions or revolutions. But with the exception of the Feudatory period, revolutions in China (since the consolidation of the three Kingdoms into one Empire under the Emperor Chin) meant only a change of hands in the government, without a change either of its form, or principles. Hence the history of China for at least two thousand years, like her civilization, bears the national impress of a monotonous dead level—jejune in character, wanting in versatility of genius, and almost devoid of historic inspiration.

The Taiping Rebellion differs from its predecessors in that in its embryo stage it had taken onto itself the religious element, which became the vital force that carried it from the defiles and wilds of Kwangsi province in the southwest to the city of Nanking in the northeast, and made it for a period of fifteen years a constantly impending danger to the Manchu Dynasty, whose corruption, weakness and maladministration were the main causes that evoked the existence of this great rebellion.

The religious element that gave it life and character was a foreign product, introduced into China by the early Protestant missionaries, of whom Dr. Robert Morrison was the first English pioneer sent out by the London Mission, followed a decade later by the Rev. Icabod J. Roberts, an American missionary. These two missionaries may properly claim the credit, if there is any, of having contributed (each in his particular sphere) in imparting to Hung Siu Chune a knowledge of Christianity. Dr. Morrison, on his part, had translated the Bible into Chinese, and the Emperor Khang Hsi's dictionary into English; both these achievements gave the missionary work in China a basis to go upon in prosecuting the work of revising and of bringing the Bible to the Chinese standard of literary taste, so as to commend it to the literary classes, and in making further improvements in perfecting the Chinese-English dictionary, which was subsequently done by such men as Dr. Medhurst, Bishop Boone, Dr. Legge, E. C. Bridgeman, and S. Wells Williams.

Besides these works of translation, which undoubtedly called for further revision and improvement, Dr. Morrison also gave China a native convert—Leang Ahfah—who became afterwards a noted preacher and the author of some religious tracts.

Hung Siu Chune, in his quest after religious knowledge and truths, got hold of a copy of Dr. Morrison's Bible and the tracts of Leang Ahfah. He read and studied them, but he stood in need of a teacher to explain to him many points in the Bible, which appeared to him mysterious and obscure. He finally made the acquaintance of the Rev. Mr. Icabod J. Roberts, an American missionary from Missouri, who happened to make his headquarters in Canton. Hung Siu Chune called upon him often, till their acquaintance ripened into a close and lasting friendship, which was kept up till Hung Siu Chune succeeded in taking Nanking, when Mr. Roberts was invited to reside there in the double capacity of a religious teacher and a state adviser. This was undoubtedly done in recognition of Mr. Roberts' services as Hung's teacher and friend while in Canton. No one knew what had become of Mr. Roberts when Nanking fell and reverted to the imperialists in 1864.

It was about this time, when he was sedulously seeking Mr. Roberts' religious instructions at Canton, that Hung failed to pass his first competitive examination as a candidate to compete for official appointment, and he decided to devote himself exclusively to the work of preaching the Gospel to his own people, the Hakkas of Kwang Tung and Kwangsi. But as a colporter and native preacher, Hung had not reached the climax of his religious experience before taking up his stand as the leader of his people in open rebellion against the Manchu Dynasty.

We must go back to the time when, as a candidate for the literary competitive examinations, he was disappointed. This threw him into a fever, and when he was tossing about in delirium, he was supposed to have been translated to Heaven, where he was commanded by the Almighty to fill and execute the divine mission of his life, which was to destroy idolatry, to rectify all wrong, to teach the people a knowledge of the true God, and to preach redemption through Christ. In view of such a mission, and being called to the presence of God, he at once assumed himself to be the son of God, co-equal with Christ, whom he called his elder brother.

It was in such a state of mental hallucination that Hung Siu Chune appeared before his little congregation of Hakkas—migrating strangers—in the defiles and wilds of Kwangsi. Their novel and strange conduct as worshippers of Shangti—the Supreme Ruler—their daily religious exercises, their prayers, and their chanting of the doxology as taught and enjoined by him, had attracted a widespread attention throughout all the surrounding region of Kwangsi. Every day fresh accessions of new comers flocked to their fold and swelled their ranks, till their numerical force grew so that the local mandarins were baffled and at their wits' end to know what to do with these believers of Christianity. Such, in brief, was the origin, growth and character of the Christian element working among the simple and rustic mountaineers of Kwangsi and Kwang Tung.

It is true that their knowledge of Christianity, as sifted through the medium of the early missionaries from the West, and the native converts and colporters, was at best crude and elementary, but still they were truths of great power, potential enough to turn simple men and religiously-inclined women into heroes and heroines who faced dangers and death with the utmost indifference, as was seen subsequently, when the government had decided to take the bull by the horns and resorted to persecution as the final means to break up this religious, fanatical community. In their conflicts with the imperial forces, they had neither guns nor ammunition, but fought with broomsticks, flails and pitchforks. With these rustic and farming implements they drove the imperialist hordes before them as chaff and stubble before a hurricane. Such was their pent-up religious enthusiasm and burning ardor.

Now this religious persecution was the side issue that had changed the resistance of Hung Siu Chune and his followers, in their religious capacity, into the character of a political rebellion. It is difficult to say whether or not, if persecution had not been resorted to, Hung Siu Chune and his followers would have remained peaceably in the heart of China and developed a religious community. We are inclined to think, however, that even if there had been no persecution, a rebellion would have taken place, from the very nature of the political situation.

Neither Christianity nor religious persecution was the immediate and logical cause of the rebellion of 1850. They might be taken as incidents or occasions that brought it about, but they were not the real causes of its existence. These may be found deeply seated in the vitals of the political constitution of the government. Foremost among them was the corruption of the administrative government. The whole official organization, from head to foot, was honeycombed and tainted by a system of bribery, which passed under the polite and generic term of "presents," similar in character to what is now known as "graft." Next comes the exploitation of the people by the officials, who found an inexhaustible field to build up their fortunes. Finally comes the inevitable and logical corollary to official bribery and exploitation, namely, that the whole administrative government was founded on a gigantic system of fraud and falsehood.

This rebellion rose in the arena of China with an enigmatic character like that of the Sphinx, somewhat puzzling at the start. The Christian world throughout the whole West, on learning of its Christian tendencies, such as the worship of the true and living God; Christ the Savior of the world; the Holy Spirit, the purifier of the soul; the destruction of temples and idols that was found wherever their victorious arms carried them; the uncompromising prohibition of the opium habit; the observance of a Sabbath; the offering of prayers before and after meals; the invocation of divine aid before a battle—all these cardinal points of a Christian faith created a world-wide impression that China, through the instrumentality of the Taipings, was to be evangelized; that the Manchu Dynasty was to be swept out of existence, and a "Celestial Empire of Universal Peace," as it was named by Hung Siu Chune, was going to be established, and thus China, by this wonderful intervention of a wise Providence, would be brought within the pale of Christian nations. But Christendom was a little too credulous and impulsive in the belief. It did not stop to have the Christianity of the Taipings pass through the crucible of a searching analysis.

Their first victory over their persecutors undoubtedly gave Hung Siu Chune and his associates the first intimation of a possible overturning of the Manchu Dynasty and the establishment of a new one, which he named in his religious ecstasy "The Celestial Empire of Universal Peace." To the accomplishment of this great object, they bent the full force of their iconoclastic enthusiasm and religious zeal.

En route from Kwang Si, their starting point, to Nanking, victory had perched on their standard all the way. They had despatched a division of their army to Peking, and, on its way to the northern capitol, it had met with a repulse and defeat at Tientsin from whence they had turned back to Nanking. In their victorious march through Hunan, Hupeh, Kiang Si and part of An Hwui, their depleted forces were replenished and reinforced by fresh and new accessions gathered from the people of those provinces. They were the riffraff and scum of their populations. This rabble element added no new strength to their fighting force, but proved to be an encumbrance and caused decided weakness. They knew no discipline, and had no restraining religious power to keep them from pillage, plunder and indiscriminate destruction. It was through such new accessions that the Taiping cause lost its prestige, and was defeated before Tientsin and forced to retreat to Nanking. After their defeat in the North, they began to decline in their religious character and their bravery. Their degeneracy was accelerated by the capture of Yang Chow, Suchau, and Hangchau, cities noted in Chinese history for their great wealth as well as for their beautiful women. The capture of these centers of a materialistic civilization poured into their laps untold wealth and luxury which tended to hasten their downfall.

The Taiping Rebellion, after fifteen years of incessant and desultory fighting, collapsed and passed into oblivion, without leaving any traces of its career worthy of historical commemoration beyond the fact that it was the outburst of a religious fanaticism which held the Christian world in doubt and bewilderment, by reason of its Christian origin. It left no trace of its Christian element behind either in Nanking, where it sojourned for nearly ten years, or in Kwang Si, where it had its birth. In China, neither new political ideas nor political theories or principles were discovered which would have constituted the basal facts of a new form of government. So that neither in the religious nor yet in the political world was mankind in China or out of China benefited by that movement. The only good that resulted from the Taiping Rebellion was that God made use of it as a dynamic power to break up the stagnancy of a great nation and wake up its consciousness for a new national life, as subsequent events in 1894, 1895, 1898, 1900, 1901, and 1904-5 fully demonstrated.

CHAPTER XII

EXPEDITION TO THE TAIPING TEA DISTRICT

My Nanking visit was utterly barren of any substantial hope of promoting any scheme of educational or political reform for the general welfare of China or for the advancement of my personal interest. When I was thoroughly convinced that neither the reformation nor the regeneration of China was to come from the Taipings, I at once turned my thoughts to the idea of making a big fortune as my first duty, and as the first element in the successful carrying out of other plans for the future.

One day, while sauntering about in the tea garden inside the city of Shanghai, I came across a few tea-merchants regaling themselves with that beverage in a booth by themselves, evidently having a very social time. They beckoned to me to join their party. In the course of the conversation, we happened to touch on my late journey through the tea districts of Hunan, Hupeh and Kiang Si and also my trip to Nanking. Passing from one topic of conversation to another, we lighted upon the subject of the green tea district of Taiping in An Hwui province. It was stated that an immense quantity of green tea could be found there, all packed and boxed ready for shipment, and that the rebels were in possession of the goods, and that whoever had the hardihood and courage to risk his life to gain possession of it would become a millionaire. I listened to the account with deep and absorbing interest, taking in everything that was said on the subject. It was stated that there were over 1,000,000 chests of tea there. Finally the party broke up, and I wended my way to my quarters completely absorbed in deep thought. I reasoned with myself that this was a chance for me to make a fortune, but wondered who would be foolhardy enough to furnish the capital, thinking that no business man of practical experience would risk his money in such a wild goose adventure, surrounded as it was with more than ordinary dangers and difficulties, in a country where highway robbery, lawlessness and murder were of daily occurrence. But with the glamor of a big fortune confronting me, all privations, dangers and risks of life seemed small and faded into airy nothing.

My friend, Tsang Mew, who had been instrumental in having me sent traveling into the interior a year before, was a man of great business experience. He had a long head and a large circle of business acquaintances, besides being my warm friend, so I concluded to go to him and talk over the whole matter, as I knew he would not hesitate to give me his best advice. I laid the whole subject before him. He said he would consider the matter fully and in a few days let me know what he had decided to do about it. After a few days, he told me that he had had several consultations with the head of the firm, of which he was comprador, and between them the company had decided to take up my project.

The plan of operation as mapped out by me was as follows: I was to go to the district of Taiping by the shortest and safest route possible, to find out whether the quantity of tea did exist; whether it was safe to have treasure taken up there to pay the rebels for the tea; and whether it was possible to have the tea supply taken down by native boats to be transhipped by steamer to Shanghai. This might be called the preliminary expedition. Then, I was to determine which of the two routes would be the more feasible,—there being two, one by way of Wuhu, a treaty port, and another by way of Ta Tung, not a treaty port, a hundred miles above Wuhu. Wuhu and the whole country leading to Taiping, including the district itself, was under the jurisdiction of the rebels, whereas Ta Tung was still in possession of the imperialists. From Wuhu to Taiping by river the distance was about two hundred and fifty miles, whereas, by way of Ta Tung, the way, though shorter, was mostly overland, which made transportation more difficult and expensive, besides having to pay the imperialists a heavy war-tax at Ta Tung, while duty and war-tax were entirely free at Wuhu.

In this expedition of inspection, I chose Wuhu as the basis of my operation. I started with four Chinese tea-men, natives of Taiping who had fled to Shanghai as refugees when the whole district was changed into a theatre of bloody conflicts between the imperialist and rebel forces for two years. On the way up the Wuhu River, we passed three cities mostly deserted by their inhabitants, but occupied by rebels. Paddy fields on both sides of the river were mostly left uncultivated and deserted, overrun with rank weeds and tall grass. As we ascended towards Taiping, the whole region presented a heartrending and depressing scene of wild waste and devastation. Whole villages were depopulated and left in a dilapidated condition. Out of a population of 500,000 only a few dozen people were seen wandering about in a listless, hopeless condition, very much emaciated and looking like walking skeletons.

After a week's journey we reached the village of San Kow, where we were met and welcomed by three tea-men who had been in Shanghai about four years previous. It seemed that they had succeeded in weathering the storm which had swept away the bulk of the population and left them among the surviving few. They were mighty glad to see us, and our appearance in the village seemed to be a God-send. Among the houses that were left intact, I selected the best of them to be my headquarters for the transaction of the tea business. The old tea-men were brought in to co-operate in the business and they showed us where the tea was stored. I was told that in San Kow there were at least five hundred thousand boxes, but in the whole district of Taiping there were at least a million and a half boxes, about sixty pounds of tea to a box.

At the end of another week, I returned to Wuhu and reported all particulars. I had found that the way up from Wuhu by river to Taiping was perfectly safe and I did not anticipate any danger to life or treasure. I had seen a large quantity of the green tea myself and found out that all that was needed was to ship as much treasure as it was safe to have housed in Wuhu, and from there to have it transferred in country tea-boats, well escorted by men in case of any emergency. I also sent samples of the different kinds of green tea to Shanghai to be inspected and listed. These proved to be satisfactory, and the order came back to buy as much of the stock as could be bought.

I was appointed the head of all succeeding expeditions to escort treasure up the river to San Kow and cargoes of tea from there to Wuhu. In one of these expeditions, I had a staff of six Europeans and an equal number of Chinese tea-men. We had eight boxes of treasure containing altogether Tls. 40,000. A tael, in the sixties, according to the exchange of that period, was equal to $1.33, making the total amount in Mexican dollars to be a little over $53,000. We had a fleet of eight tea-boats, four large ones and four smaller ones. The treasure was divided into two equal parts and was placed in the two largest and staunchest boats. The men were also divided into two squads, three Europeans and three Chinese in one large boat and an equal number in the other. We were well provided with firearms, revolvers and cutlasses. Besides the six Europeans, we had about forty men including the boatmen, but neither the six tea-men nor the boatmen could be relied upon to show fight in case of emergency. The only reliable men I had to fall back upon, in case of emergency, were the Europeans; even in these I was not sure I could place implicit confidence, for they were principally runaway sailors of an adventurous character picked up in Shanghai by the company and sent up to Wuhu to escort the treasure up to the interior. Among them was an Englishman who professed to be a veterinary doctor. He was over six feet tall in his stocking feet, a man of fine personal appearance, but he did not prove himself to be of very stout heart, as may be seen presently. Thus prepared and equipped, we left Wuhu in fine spirits. We proceeded on our journey a little beyond the city of King Yuen, which is about half the way to San Kow. We could have gone a little beyond King Yuen, but thinking it might be safer to be near the city, where the rebel chief had seen my passport, obtained in Nanking, and knew that I had influential people in Nanking, we concluded to pass the night in a safe secluded little cove in the bend of the river just large enough for our little boats to moor close to each other, taking due precaution to place the two largest ones in the center, flanked by the other boats on the right and left of them; the smaller boats occupied the extreme ends of the line.

Before retiring, I had ordered all our firearms to be examined and loaded and properly distributed. Watchmen were stationed in each boat to keep watch all night, for which they were to be paid extra. The precautionary steps having thus been taken, we all retired for the night. An old tea-man and myself were the only ones who lay wide awake while the rest gave unmistakable signs of deep sleep. I felt somewhat nervous and could not sleep. The new moon had peeked in upon us occasionally with her cold smile, as heavy and dark clouds were scudding across her path. Soon she was shut in and disappeared, and all was shrouded in pitch darkness. The night was nearly half spent, when my ears caught the distant sound of whooping and yelling which seemed to increase in volume. I immediately started up to dress myself and quietly woke up the Europeans and Chinese in both boats. As the yelling and whooping drew nearer and nearer it seemed to come from a thousand throats, filling the midnight air with unearthly sounds. In another instant countless torch lights were seen dancing and whirling in the dismal darkness right on the opposite bank. Fortunately the river was between this marauding band and us, while pitch darkness concealed our boats from their sight. In view of such impending danger, we held a council of war. None of us were disposed to fight and endanger our lives in a conflict in which the odds were fearfully against us, there being about a thousand to one. But the English veterinary doctor was the foremost and most strenuous of the Europeans to advocate passive surrender. His countenance actually turned pale and he trembled all over, whether from fear or the chilly atmosphere of the night I could not tell. Having heard from each one what he had to say, I could do nothing but step forward and speak to them, which I did in this wise: "Well, boys, you have all decided not to fight in case we are attacked, but to surrender our treasure. The ground for taking such a step is that we are sure to be outnumbered by a rebel host. So that in such a dilemma discretion is the better part of valor, and Tls. 40,000 are not worth sacrificing our lives for. But by surrendering our trust without making an effort of some kind to save it, we would be branded as unmitigated cowards, and we could never expect to be trusted with any responsible commission again. Now, I will tell you what I propose to do. If the rebel horde should come over and attempt to seize our treasure, I will spring forward with my yellow silk passport, and demand to see their chief, while you fellows with your guns and arms must stand by the treasure. Do not fire and start the fight. By parleying with them, it will for the moment check their determination to plunder, and they will have a chance to find out who we are, and where I obtained the passport; and, even if they should carry off the treasure, I shall tell their chief that I will surely report the whole proceeding in Nanking and recover every cent of our loss."

These remarks seemed to revive the spirit and courage of the men, after which we all sat on the forward decks of our boats anxiously waiting for what the next moment would bring forth. While in this state of expectancy, our hearts palpitating in an audible fashion, our eyes were watching intently the opposite shore. All the shouting and yelling seemed to have died away, and nothing could be seen but torches moving about slowly and leisurely in regular detachments, each detachment stopping occasionally and then moving on again. This was kept up for over two hours, while they constantly receded from us. I asked an old boatman the meaning of such movements and was told that the marauding horde was embarking in boats along the whole line of the opposite shore and was moving down stream. It was three o'clock in the morning, and it began to rain. A few of the advance boats had passed us without discovering where we were. They were loaded with men and floated by us in silence. By four o'clock the last boats followed the rest and soon disappeared from sight. Evidently, from the stillness that characterized the long line of boats as they floated down stream, the buccaneering horde was completely used up by their looting expedition, and at once abandoned themselves to sound sleep when they got on board the boats. We thanked our stars for such a narrow escape from such an unlooked-for danger. We owed our safety to the darkness of the night, the rain and to the fact that we were on the opposite shore in a retired cove. By five o'clock all our anxieties and fears were laid aside and turned into joy and thankfulness. We resumed our journey with light hearts and reached San Kow two days later in peace and safety. In less than two weeks we sent down to Wuhu, escorted by Europeans and tea-men, the first installment, consisting of fifteen boatloads of tea to be transhipped by steamer to Shanghai. The next installment consisted of twelve boatloads. I escorted that down the river in person. The river, in some places, especially in the summer, was quite shallow and a way had to be dug to float the boats down. In one or two instances the boatmen were very reluctant to jump into the water to do the work of deepening the river, and on one occasion I had to jump in, with the water up to my waist, in order to set them an example. When they caught the idea and saw me in the water, every man followed my example and vied with each other in clearing a way for the boats, for they saw I meant business and there was no fooling about it either.

I was engaged in this Taiping tea business for about six months, and took away about sixty-five thousand boxes of tea, which was hardly a tenth part of the entire stock found in the district. Then I was taken down with the fever and ague of the worst type. As I could get no medical relief at Wuhu, I was obliged to return to Shanghai, where I was laid up sick for nearly two months. Those two months of sickness had knocked all ideas of making a big fortune out of my head. I gave up the Taiping tea enterprise, because it called for a greater sacrifice of health and wear upon my nervous system than I was able to stand. The King Yuen midnight incident, which came near proving a disastrous one for me, with the marauding horde of unscrupulous cut-throats, had been quite a shock on my nervous system at the time and may have been the primal cause of my two months' sickness; it served as a sufficient warning to me not to tax my nervous system by further

41

encounters and disputes with the rebel chiefs, whose price on the tea we bought of them was being increased every day. A dispassionate and calm view of the enterprise convinced me that I would have to preserve my life, strength and energy for a higher and worthier object than any fortune I might make out of this Taiping tea, which, after all, was plundered property. I am sure that no fortune in the world could be brought in the balance to weigh against my life, which is of inestimable value to me.

Although I had made nothing out of the Taiping teas, yet the fearless spirit, the determination to succeed, and the pluck to be able to do what few would undertake in face of exceptional difficulties and hazards, that I had exhibited in the enterprise, were in themselves assets worth more to me than a fortune. I was well-known, both among foreign merchants and native business men, so that as soon as it was known that I had given up the Taiping tea enterprise on account of health, I was offered a tea agency in the port of Kew Keang for packing teas for another foreign firm. I accepted it as a temporary shift, but gave it up in less than six months and started a commission business on my own account. I continued this business for nearly three years and was doing as well as I had expected to do. It was at this time while in Kew Keang that I caught the first ray of hope of materializing the educational scheme I had been weaving during the last year of my college life.

CHAPTER XIII

MY INTERVIEWS WITH TSANG KWOH FAN

In 1863, I was apparently prospering in my business, when, to my great surprise, an unexpected letter from the city of Ngan Khing, capital of An Whui province, was received. The writer was an old friend whose acquaintance I had made in Shanghai in 1857. He was a native of Ningpo, and was in charge of the first Chinese gunboat owned by the local Shanghai guild. He had apparently risen in official rank and had become one of Tsang Kwoh Fan's secretaries. His name was Chang Shi Kwei. In this letter, Chang said he was authorized by Viceroy Tsang Kwoh Fan to invite me to come down to Ngan Khing to call, as he (the Viceroy) had heard of me and wished very much to see me. On the receipt of the letter I was in a quandary and asked myself many questions: What could such a distinguished man want of me? Had he got wind of my late visit to Nanking and of my late enterprise to the district of Taiping for the green tea that was held there by the rebels? Tsang Kwoh Fan himself had been in the department of Hwui Chow fighting the rebels a year before and had been defeated, and he was reported to have been killed in battle. Could he have been told that I had been near the scene of his battle and had been in communication with the rebels, and did he want, under a polite invitation, to trap me and have my head off? But Chang, his secretary, was an old friend of many years' standing. I knew his character well; he wouldn't be likely to play the cat's paw to have me captured. Thus deliberating from one surmise to another, I concluded not to accept the invitation until I had learned more of the great man's purpose in sending for me.

In reply to the letter, I wrote and said I thanked His Excellency for his great condescension and considered it a great privilege and honor to be thus invited, but on account of the tea season having set in (which was in February), I was obliged to attend to the orders for packing tea that were fast coming in; but that as soon as they were off my hands, I would manage to go and pay my respects to His Excellency.

Two months after receiving the first letter, a second one came urging me to come to Ngan Khing as early as possible. This second letter enclosed a letter written by Li Sien Lan, the distinguished Chinese mathematician, whose acquaintance I had also made while in Shanghai. He was the man who assisted a Mr. Wiley, a missionary of the London Board of Missions, in the translation of several mathematical works into Chinese, among which was the Integral and Differential Calculus over which I well remember to have "flunked and fizzled" in my sophomore year in college; and, in this connection, I might as well frankly own that in my make-up mathematics was left out. Mr. Li Sien Lan was also an astronomer. In his letter, he said he had told Viceroy Tsang Kwoh Fan who I was and that I had had a foreign education; how I had raised a handsome subscription to help the famine refugees in 1857; that I had a strong desire to help China to become prosperous, powerful and strong. He said the viceroy had some important business for me to do, and that Chu and Wa, who were interested in machinery of all kinds, were also in Ngan Khing, having been invited there by the Viceroy. Mr. Li's letter completely dispelled all doubts and misgivings on my part as to the viceroy's design in wishing to see me, and gave me an insight as to his purpose for sending for me.

As an answer to these letters, I wrote saying that in a couple of months I should be more at liberty to take the journey. But my second reply did not seem to satisfy the strong desire on the part of Tsang Kwoh Fan to see me. So in July, 1863, I received a third letter from Chang and a second one from Li. In these letters the object of the viceroy was clearly and frankly stated. He wanted me to give up my mercantile business altogether and identify myself under him in the service of the state government, and asked whether or not I could come down to Ngan Khing at once. In view of this unexpected offer, which demanded prompt and explicit decision, I was not slow to see what possibility there was of carrying out my educational scheme, having such a powerful man as Tsang Kwoh Fan to back it. I immediately replied that upon learning the wishes of His Excellency, I had taken the whole situation into consideration, and had concluded to go to his headquarters at Ngan Khing, just as soon as I had wound up my business, which would take me a complete month, and that I would start by August at the latest. Thus ended the correspondence which was really the initiatory step of my official career.

Tsang Kwoh Fan was a most remarkable character in Chinese history. He was regarded by his contemporaries as a great scholar and a learned man. Soon after the Taiping Rebellion broke out and began to assume vast proportions, carrying before it province after province, Tsang began to drill an army of his own compatriots of Hunan who had always had the reputation of being brave and hardy fighters. In his work of raising a disciplined army, he secured the co-operation of other Hunan men, who afterwards took a prominent part in building up a flotilla of river gun-boats. This played a great and efficient part as an auxiliary force on the Yangtze River, and contributed in no small measure to check the rapid and ready concentration of the rebel forces, which had spread over a vast area on both banks of the great Yangtze River. In the space of a few years the lost provinces were gradually recovered, till the rebellion was narrowed down within the single province of Kiang Su, of which Nanking, the capital of the rebellion, was the only stronghold left. This finally succumbed to the forces of Tsang Kwoh Fan in 1864.

To crush and end a rebellion of such dimensions as that of the Taipings was no small task. Tsang Kwoh Fan was made the generalissimo of the imperialists. To enable him to cope successfully with the Taipings, Tsang was invested with almost regal power. The revenue of seven or eight provinces was laid at his feet for disposal, also official ranks and territorial appointments were at his command. So Tsang Kwoh Fan was literally and practically the supreme power of China at the time. But true to his innate greatness, he was never known to abuse the almost unlimited power that was placed in his hands, nor did he take advantage of the vast resources that were at his disposal to enrich himself or his family, relatives or friends. Unlike Li Hung Chang, his protégé and successor, who bequeathed Tls. 40,000,000 to his descendants after his death, Tsang died comparatively poor, and kept the escutcheon of his official career untarnished and left a name and character honored and revered for probity, patriotism and purity. He had great talents, but he was modest. He had a liberal mind, but he was conservative. He was a perfect gentleman and a nobleman of the highest type. It was such a man that I had the great fortune to come in contact with in the fall of 1863.

After winding up my business in New Keang, I took passage in a native boat and landed at Ngan Khing in September. There, in the military headquarters of Viceroy Tsang Kwoh Fan, I was met by my friends, Chang Si Kwei, Li Sien Lan, Wha Yuh Ting and Chu Siuh Chune, all old friends from Shanghai. They were glad to see me, and told me that the viceroy for the past six months, after hearing them tell that as a boy I had gone to America to get a Western education, had manifested the utmost curiosity and interest to see me, which accounted for the three letters which Chang and Li had written urging me to come. Now, since I had arrived, their efforts to get me there had not been fruitless, and they certainly claimed some credit for praising me up to the viceroy. I asked them if they knew what His Excellency wanted me for, aside from the curiosity of seeing a native of China made into a veritable Occidental. They all smiled significantly and told me that I would find out after one or two interviews. From this, I judged that they knew the object for which I was wanted by the Viceroy, and perhaps, they were at the bottom of the whole secret.

The next day I was to make my début, and called. My card was sent in, and without a moment's delay or waiting in the ante-room, I was ushered into the presence of the great man of China. After the usual ceremonies of greeting, I was pointed to a seat right in front of him. For a few minutes he sat in silence, smiling all the while as though he were much pleased to see me, but at the same time his keen eyes scanned me over from head to foot to see if he could discover anything strange in my outward appearance. Finally, he took a steady look into my eyes which seemed to attract his special attention. I must confess I felt quite uneasy all the while, though I was not abashed. Then came his first question.

"How long were you abroad?"

"I was absent from China eight years in pursuit of a Western education."

"Would you like to be a soldier in charge of a company?"

"I should be pleased to head one if I had been fitted for it. I have never studied military science."

"I should judge from your looks, you would make a fine soldier, for I can see from your eyes that you are brave and can command."

"I thank Your Excellency for the compliment. I may have the courage of a soldier, but I certainly lack military training and experience, and on that account I may not be able to meet Your Excellency's expectations."

When the question of being a soldier was suggested, I thought he really meant to have me enrolled as an officer in his army against the rebels; but in this I was mistaken, as my Shanghai friends told me afterwards. He simply put it forward to find out whether my mind was at all martially inclined. But when he found by my response that the bent of my thought was something else, he dropped the military subject and asked me my age and whether or not I was married. The last question closed my first introductory interview, which had lasted only about half an hour. He began to sip his tea and I did likewise, which according to Chinese official etiquette means that the interview is ended and the guest is at liberty to take his departure.

44

I returned to my room, and my Shanghai friends soon flocked around me to know what had passed between the viceroy and myself. I told them everything, and they were highly delighted.

Tsang Kwoh Fan, as he appeared in 1863, was over sixty years of age, in the very prime of life. He was five feet, eight or nine inches tall, strongly built and well-knitted together and in fine proportion. He had a broad chest and square shoulders surmounted by a large symmetrical head. He had a broad and high forehead; his eyes were set on a straight line under triangular-shaped eyelids, free from that obliquity so characteristic of the Mongolian type of countenance usually accompanied by high cheek bones, which is another feature peculiar to the Chinese physiognomy. His face was straight and somewhat hairy. He allowed his side whiskers their full growth; they hung down with his full beard which swept across a broad chest and added dignity to a commanding appearance. His eyes though not large were keen and penetrating. They were of a clear hazel color. His mouth was large but well compressed with thin lips which showed a strong will and a high purpose. Such was Tsang Kwoh Fan's external appearance, when I first met him at Ngan Khing.

Regarding his character, he was undoubtedly one of the most remarkable men of his age and time. As a military general, he might be called a self-made man; by dint of his indomitable persistence and perseverance, he rose from his high scholarship as a Hanlin (Chinese LL.D.) to be a generalissimo of all the imperial forces that were levied against the Taiping rebels, and in less than a decade after he headed his Hunan raw recruits, he succeeded in reducing the wide devastations of the rebellion that covered a territorial area of three of the richest provinces of China to the single one of Kiang Nan, till finally, by the constriction of his forces, he succeeded in crushing the life out of the rebellion by the fall and capture of Nanking. The Taiping Rebellion was of fifteen years' duration, from 1850 to 1865. It was no small task to bring it to its extinction. Its rise and progress had cost the Empire untold treasures, while 25,000,000 human lives were immolated in that political hecatomb. The close of the great rebellion gave the people a breathing respite. The Dowager Empress had special reasons to be grateful to the genius of Tsang Kwoh Fan, who was instrumental in restoring peace and order to the Manchu Dynasty. She was not slow, however, to recognize Tsang Kwoh Fan's merits and moral worth and created him a duke. But Tsang's greatness was not to be measured by any degree of conventional nobility; it did not consist in his victories over the rebels, much less in his re-capture of Nanking. It rose from his great virtues: his pure, unselfish patriotism, his deep and far-sighted statesmanship, and the purity of his official career. He is known in history as "the man of rectitude." This was his posthumous title conferred on him by imperial decree.

To resume the thread of my story, I was nearly two weeks in the viceroy's headquarters, occupying a suite of rooms in the same building assigned to my Shanghai friends—Li, Chang, Wha and Chu. There were living in his military headquarters at least two hundred officials, gathered there from all parts of the Empire, for various objects and purposes. Besides his secretaries, who numbered no less than a hundred, there were expectant officials, learned scholars, lawyers, mathematicians, astronomers and machinists; in short, the picked and noted men of China were all drawn there by the magnetic force of his character and great name. He always had a great admiration for men of distinguished learning and talents, and loved to associate and mingle with them. During the two weeks of my sojourn there, I had ample opportunity to call upon my Shanghai friends, and in that way incidentally found out what the object of the Viceroy was in urging me to be enrolled in the government service. It seemed that my friends had had frequent interviews with the Viceroy in regard to having a foreign machine shop established in China, but it had not been determined what kind of a machine shop should be established. One evening they gave me a dinner, at which time the subject of the machine shop was brought up and it became the chief topic. After each man had expressed his views on the subject excepting myself, they wanted to know what my views were, intimating that in all likelihood in my next interview with the Viceroy he would bring up the subject. I said that as I was not an expert in the matter, my opinions or suggestions might not be worth much, but nevertheless from my personal observation in the United States and from a common-sense point of view, I would say that a machine shop in the present state of China should be of a general and fundamental character and not one for specific purposes. In other words, I told them they ought to have a machine shop that would be able to create or reproduce other machine shops of the same character as itself; each and all of these should be able to turn out specific machinery for the manufacture of specific things. In plain words, they would have to have general and fundamental machinery in order to turn out specific machinery. A machine shop consisting of lathes of different kinds and sizes, planers and drills would be able to turn out machinery for making guns, engines, agricultural implements, clocks, etc. In a large country like China, I told them, they would need many primary or fundamental machine shops, but that after they had one (and a first-class one at that) they could make it the mother shop for reproducing others—perhaps better and more improved. If they had a number of them, it would enable them to have the shops co-operate with each other in case of need. It would be cheaper to have them reproduced and multiplied in China, I said, where labor and material were cheaper, than in Europe and America. Such was my crude idea of the subject. After I had finished, they were apparently much pleased and interested, and expressed the hope that I would state the same views to the Viceroy if he should ask me about the subject.

Several days after the dinner and conversation, the Viceroy did send for me. In this interview he asked me what in my opinion was the best thing to do for China at that time. The question came with such a force of meaning, that if I had not been forwarned by my friends a few evenings before, or if their hearts had not been set on the introduction of a machine shop, and they had not practically won the Viceroy over to their pet scheme, I might have been strongly tempted to launch forth upon my educational scheme as a reply to the question as to what was the best thing to do for China. But in such an event, being a stranger to the Viceroy, having been brought to his notice simply through the influence of my friends, I would have run a greater risk of jeopardizing my pet scheme of education than if I were left to act independently. My obligations to them were great, and I therefore decided that my constancy and fidelity to their friendship should be correspondingly great. So, instead of finding myself embarrassed in answering such a large and important question, I had a preconceived answer to give, which seemed to dove-tail into his views already crystallized into definite form, and which was ready to be carried out at once. So my educational scheme was put in the background, and the machine shop was allowed to take precedence. I repeated in substance what I had said to my friends previously in regard to establishing a mother machine shop, capable of reproducing other machine shops of like character, etc. I especially mentioned the manufacture of rifles, which, I said, required for the manufacture of their component parts separate machinery, but that the machine shop I would recommend was not one adapted for making the rifles, but adapted to turn out specific machinery for the making of rifles, cannons, cartridges, or anything else.

"Well," said he, "this is a subject quite beyond my knowledge. It would be well for you to discuss the matter with Wha and Chu, who are more familiar with it than I am and we will then decide what is best to be done."

This ended my interview with the Viceroy. After I left him, I met my friends, who were anxious to know the result of the interview. I told them of the outcome. They were highly elated over it. In our last conference it was decided that the matter of the character of the machine shop was to be left entirely to my discretion and judgment, after consulting a professional mechanical engineer. At the end of another two weeks, Wha was authorized to tell me that the Viceroy, after having seen all the four men, had decided to empower me to go abroad and make purchases of such machinery as in the opinion of a professional engineer would be the best and the right machinery for China to adopt. It was also left entirely to me to decide where the machinery should be purchased,—either in England, France or the United States of America.

The location of the machine shop was to be at a place called Kow Chang Meu, about four miles northwest of the city of Shanghai. The Kow Chang Meu machine shop was afterwards known as the Kiang Nan Arsenal, an establishment that covers several acres of ground and embraces under its roof all the leading branches of mechanical work. Millions have been invested in it since I brought the first machinery from Fitchburg, Mass., in order to make it one of the greatest arsenals east of the Cape of Good Hope. It may properly be regarded as a lasting monument to commemorate Tsang Kwoh Fan's broadmindedness as well as far-sightedness in establishing Western machinery in China.

CHAPTER XIV

MY MISSION TO AMERICA TO BUY MACHINERY

A week after my last interview with the Viceroy and after I had been told that I was to be entrusted with the execution of the order, my commission was made out and issued to me. In addition to the commission, the fifth official rank was conferred on me. It was a nominal civil rank, with the privilege of wearing the blue feather, as was customary only in war time and limited to those connected with the military service, but discarded in the civil service, where the peacock's feather is conferred only by imperial sanction. Two official despatches were also made out, directing me where to receive the Tls. 68,000, the entire amount for the purchase of the machinery. One-half of the amount was to be paid by the Taotai of Shanghai, and the other half by the Treasurer of Canton. After all the preliminary preparations had been completed, I bade farewell to the Viceroy and my Shanghai friends and started on my journey.

On my arrival in Shanghai in October, 1863, I had the good fortune to meet Mr. John Haskins, an American mechanical engineer, who came out to China with machinery for Messrs. Russell & Co. He had finished his business with that firm and was expecting soon to return to the States with his family—a wife and a little daughter. He was just the man I wanted. It did not take us long to get acquainted and as the time was short, we soon came to an understanding. We took the overland route from Hong Kong to London, via the Isthmus of Suez. Haskins and his family took passage on the French Messagerie Imperial line, while I engaged mine on board of one of the Peninsular & Oriental steamers. In my route to London, I touched at Singapore, crossed the Indian Ocean, and landed at Ceylon, where I changed steamers for Bengal up the Red Sea and landed at Cairo, where I had to cross the Isthmus by rail. The Suez Canal was not finished; the work of excavating was still going on. Arriving at Alexandria, I took passage from there to Marseilles, the southern port of France, while Haskins and his family took a steamer direct for Southampton. From Marseilles I went to Paris by rail. I was there about ten days, long enough to give me a general idea of the city, its public buildings, churches, gardens, and of Parisian gaiety. I crossed the English channel from Calais to Dover and went thence by rail to London—the first time in my life to touch English soil, and my first visit to the famous metropolis. While in London, I visited Whitworth's machine shop, and had the pleasure of renewing my acquaintance with Thomas Christy, whom I knew in China in the '50's. I was about a month in England, and then crossed the Atlantic in one of the Cunard steamers and landed in New York in the early spring of 1864, just ten years after my graduation from Yale and in ample time to be present at the decennial meeting of my class in July. Haskins and his family had preceded me in another steamer for New York, in order that he might get to work on the drawings and specifications of the shop and machinery and get them completed as soon as possble. In 1864, the last year of the great Civil War, nearly all the machine shops in the country, especially in New England, were preoccupied and busy in executing government orders, and it was very difficult to have my machinery taken up. Finally Haskins succeeded in getting the Putnam Machine Co., Fitchburg, Mass., to fill the order.

While Haskins was given sole charge of superintending the execution of the order, which required at least six months before the machinery could be completed for shipment to China, I took advantage of the interim to run down to New Haven and attend the decennial meeting of my class. It was to me a joyous event and I congratulated myself that I had the good luck to be present at our first re-union. Of course, the event that brought me back to the country was altogether unpretentious and had attracted little or no public attention at the time, because the whole country was completely engrossed in the last year of the great Civil War, yet I personally regarded my commission as an inevitable and preliminary step that would ultimately lead to the realization of my educational scheme, which had never for a moment escaped my mind. But at the meeting of my class, this subject of my life plan was not brought up. We had a most enjoyable time and parted with nearly the same fraternal feeling that characterized our parting at graduation. After the decennial meeting, I returned to Fitchburg and told Haskins that I was going down to Washington to offer my services to the government as a volunteer for the short period of six months, and that in case anything happened to me during the six months so that I could not come back to attend to the shipping of the machinery to Shanghai, he should attend to it. I left him all the papers—the cost and description of the machinery, the bills of lading, insurance, and freight, and directed him to send everything to the Viceroy's agent in Shanghai. This precautionary step having been taken, I slipped down to Washington.

Brigadier-General Barnes of Springfield, Mass., happened to be the general in charge of the Volunteer Department. His headquarters were at Willard's Hotel. I called on him and made known to him my object, that I felt as a naturalized citizen of the United States, it was my bounden duty to offer my services as a volunteer courier to carry despatches between Washington and the nearest Federal camp for at least six months, simply to show my loyalty and patriotism to my adopted country, and that I would furnish my own equipments. He said that he remembered me well, having met me in the Yale Library in New Haven, in 1853, on a visit to his son, William Barnes, who was in the college at the time I was, and who afterwards became a prominent lawyer in San Francisco. General Barnes asked what business I was engaged in. I told him that since my graduation in 1854 I had been in China and had recently returned with an order to purchase machinery for a machine shop ordered by Viceroy and Generalissimo Tsang Kwoh Fan. I told him the machinery was being made to order in Fitchburg, Mass., under the supervision of an

American mechanical engineer, and as it would take at least six months before the same could be completed, I was anxious to offer my services to the government in the meantime as an evidence of my loyalty and patriotism to my adopted country. He was quite interested and pleased with what I said.

"Well, my young friend," said he, "I thank you very much for your offer, but since you are charged with a responsible trust to execute for the Chinese government, you had better return to Fitchburg to attend to it. We have plenty of men to serve, both as couriers and as fighting men to go to the front." Against this peremptory decision, I could urge nothing further, but I felt that I had at least fulfilled my duty to my adopted country.

CHAPTER XV

MY SECOND RETURN TO CHINA

The machinery was not finished till the early spring of 1865. It was shipped direct from New York to Shanghai, China; while it was doubling the Cape of Good Hope on its way to the East, I took passage in another direction, back to China. I wanted to encircle the globe once in my life, and this was my opportunity. I could say after that, that I had circumnavigated the globe. So I planned to go back by way of San Francisco. In order to do that, I had to take into consideration the fact that the Union Pacific from Chicago to San Francisco via Omaha was not completed, nor was any steamship line subsidized by the United States government to cross the Pacific from San Francisco to any seaport, either in Japan or China at the time. On that account I was obliged to take a circuitous route, by taking a coast steamer from New York to Panama, cross the Isthmus, and from there take passage in another coast steamer up the Mexican coast to San Francisco, Cal.

At San Francisco, I was detained two weeks where I had to wait for a vessel to bridge me over the broad Pacific, either to Yokohama or Shanghai. At that time, as there was no other vessel advertised to sail for the East, I was compelled to take passage on board the "Ida de Rogers," a Nantucket bark. There were six passengers, including myself. We had to pay $500 each for passage from San Francisco to Yokohama. The crew consisted of the captain, who had with him his wife, and a little boy six years old, a mate, three sailors and a cook, a Chinese boy. The "Ida de Rogers" was owned by Captain Norton who hailed from Nantucket. She was about one hundred and fifty feet long—an old tub at that. She carried no cargo and little or no ballast, except bilge-water, which may have come from Nantucket, for aught I know. The skipper, true to the point of the country where they produce crops of seamen of microscopic ideas, was found to be not at all deficient in his close calculations of how to shave closely in every bargain and, in fact, in everything in life. In this instance, we had ample opportunity to find out under whom we were sailing. Before we were fairly out of the "Golden Gate," we were treated every day with salted mackerel, which I took to be the daily and fashionable dish of Nantucket. The cook we had made matters worse, as he did not seem to know his business and was no doubt picked up in San Francisco just to fill the vacancy. The mackerel was cooked and brought on the table without being freshened, and the Indian meal cakes that were served with it, were but half baked, so that day after day we practically all left the table disgusted and half starved. Not only was the food bad and unhealthy, but the skipper's family was of a very low type. The skipper himself was a most profane man, and although I never heard the wife swear, yet she seemed to enjoy her husband's oaths. Their little boy who was not more than six years old, seemed to have surpassed the father in profanity. It may be said that the young scamp had mastered his shorter and longer catechism of profanity completely, for he was not wanting in expressions of the most disgusting and repulsive kind, as taught him by his sire, yet his parents sat listening to him with evident satisfaction, glancing around at the passengers to catch their approval. One of the passengers, an Englishman, who stood near listening and smoking his pipe, only remarked ironically, "You have a smart boy there." At this the skipper nodded, while the mother seemed to gloat over her young hopeful. Such a scene was of daily occurrence, and one that we could not escape, since we were cooped up in such narrow quarters on account of the smallness of the vessel. There was not even a five-foot deck where one could stretch his legs. We were most of the time shut up in the dining room, as it was the coolest spot we could find. Before our voyage was half over, we had occasion to land at one of the most northerly islands of the Hawaiian group for fresh water and provisions. While the vessel was being victualed, all the passengers landed and went out to the country to take a stroll, which was a great relief. We were gone nearly all day. We all re-embarked early in the evening. It seemed that the captain had filled the forward hold with chickens and young turkeys. We congratulated ourselves that the skipper after all had swung round to show a generous streak, which had only needed an opportunity to show itself, and that for the rest of the voyage he was no doubt going to feed us on fresh chickens and turkeys to make up for the salted mackerel, which might have given us the scurvy had we continued on the same diet. For the first day or so, after we resumed our voyage, we had chicken and fish for our breakfast and dinners, but that was the last we saw of the fresh provisions. We saw no turkey on the table. On making inquiry, the cook told us that both the chickens and the turkeys were bought, not for our table, but for speculation, to be sold on arrival in Yokohama. Unfortunately for the skipper, the chickens and turkeys for want of proper food and fresh air, had died a few days before our arrival at the port.

Immediately upon reaching Yokohama, I took passage in a P. & O. steamer for Shanghai.

On my arrival there, I found the machinery had all arrived a month before; it had all been delivered in good condition and perfect working order. I had been absent from China a little over a year. During that time Viceroy Tsang Kwoh Fan, with the co-operation of his brother, Tsang Kwoh Chuen, succeeded in the capture of Nanking, which put an end to the great Taiping Rebellion of 1850.

On my arrival in Shanghai, I found that the Viceroy had gone up to Chu Chow, the most northerly department of Kiangsu province, close to the border line of Shan Tung, and situated on the canal. He made that his headquarters in superintending the subjugation of the Nienfi or Anwhui rebels, against whom Li Hung Chang had been appointed as his lieutenant in the field. I was requested to go up to Chu Chow to make a report in person regarding the purchase of the machinery.

On my journey to Chu Chow, I was accompanied by my old friend Wha Yuh Ting part of the way. We went by the Grand Canal from Sinu-Mew at the Yangtze up as far as Yang Chow, the great entrepôt for the Government Salt Monopoly. There we took mule carts overland to Chu Chow. We were three days on our journey. Chu Chow is a departmental city and here, as stated before, Viceroy Tsang made his quarters. I was there three days. The Viceroy complimented me highly for what I had done. He made my late commission to the States to purchase machinery the subject of a special memorial to the government. Such a special memorial on any political event invariably gives it political prominence and weight, and in order to lift me at once from a position of no importance to a territorial civil appointment of the bona fide fifth rank, was a step seldom asked for or conceded. He made out my case to be an exceptional one, and the following is the language he used in his memorial:

"Yung Wing is a foreign educated Chinese. He has mastered the English language. In his journey over thousands of miles of ocean to the extreme ends of the earth to fulfill the commission I entrusted to him, he was utterly oblivious to difficulties and dangers that lay in his way. In this respect even the missions of the Ancients present no parallel equal to his. Therefore, I would recommend that he be promoted to the expectancy of one of the Kiangsu subprefects, and he is entitled to fill the first vacancy presenting itself, in recognition of his valuable services."

His secretary, who drew up the memorial at his dictation, gave me a copy of the memorial before I left Chu Chow for Shanghai, and congratulated me on the great honor the Viceroy had conferred on me. I thanked the Viceroy before bidding him good-bye, and expressed the hope that my actions in the future would justify his high opinion of me.

In less than two months after leaving him, an official document from the Viceroy reached me in Shanghai, and in October, 1865, I was a full-fledged mandarin of the fifth rank. While waiting as an expectant subprefect, I was retained by the provincial authorities as a government interpreter and translator. My salary was $250 per month. No other expectant official of the province—not even an expectant Taotai (an official of the fourth rank)—could command such a salary.

Ting Yih Chang was at the time Taotai of Shanghai. He and I became great friends. He rose rapidly in official rank and became successively salt commissioner, provincial treasurer and Taotai or governor of Kiang Nan. Through him, I also rose in official rank and was decorated with the peacock's feather. While Ting Yih Chang was salt commissioner, I accompanied him to Yang Chow and was engaged in translating Colton's geography into Chinese, for about six months. I then returned to Shanghai to resume my position as government interpreter and translator. I had plenty of time on my hands. I took to translating "Parsons on Contracts," which I thought might be useful to the Chinese. In this work I was fortunate in securing the services of a Chinese scholar to help me. I found him well versed in mathematics and in all Chinese official business, besides being a fine Chinese scholar and writer. He finally persuaded me not to continue the translation, as there was some doubt as to whether such a work, even when finished, would be in demand, because the Chinese courts are seldom troubled with litigations on contracts, and in all cases of violation of contracts, the Chinese code is used.

In 1867, Viceroy Tsang Kwoh Fan, with Li Hung Chang's co-operation, succeeded in ending the Nienfi rebellion, and came to Nanking to fill his viceroyalty of the two Kiangs.

Before taking up his position as viceroy of the Kiangs permanently, he took a tour of inspection through his jurisdiction and one of the important places he visited was Shanghai and the Kiang Nan Arsenal—an establishment of his own creation. He went through the arsenal with undisguised interest. I pointed out to him the machinery which I bought for him in America. He stood and watched its automatic movement with unabated delight, for this was the first time he had seen machinery, and how it worked. It was during this visit that I succeeded in persuading him to have a mechanical school annexed to the arsenal, in which Chinese youths might be taught the theory as well as the practice of mechanical engineering, and thus enable China in time to dispense with the employment of foreign mechanical engineers and machinists, and to be perfectly independent. This at once appealed to the practical turn of the Chinese mind, and the school was finally added to the arsenal. They are doubtless turning out at the present time both mechanical engineers and machinists of all descriptions.

CHAPTER XVI

Having scored in a small way this educational victory, by inducing the Viceroy to establish a mechanical training school as a corollary to the arsenal, I felt quite worked up and encouraged concerning my educational scheme which had been lying dormant in my mind for the past fifteen years, awaiting an opportunity to be brought forward.

Besides Viceroy Tsang Kwoh Fan, whom I counted upon to back me in furthering the scheme, Ting Yih Chang, an old friend of mine, had become an important factor to be reckoned with in Chinese politics. He was a man of progressive tendencies and was alive to all practical measures of reform. He had been appointed governor of Kiangsu province, and after his accession to his new office, I had many interviews with him regarding my educational scheme, in which he was intensely interested. He told me that he was in correspondence with Wen Seang, the prime minister of China, who was a Manchu, and that if I were to put my scheme in writing, he would forward it to Peking, and ask Wen Seang to use his influence to memorialize the government for its adoption. Such an unexpected piece of information came like a clap of thunder and fairly lifted me off my feet. I immediately left Suchau for Shanghai. With the help of my Nanking friend, who had helped me in the work of translating "Parsons on Contracts," I drew up four proposals to be presented to Governor Ting, to be forwarded by him to Minister Wen Seang, at Peking. They were as follows:

FIRST PROPOSAL

The first proposal contemplated the organization of a Steamship Company on a joint stock basis. No foreigner was to be allowed to be a stockholder in the company. It was to be a purely Chinese company, managed and worked by Chinese exclusively.

To insure its stability and success, an annual government subsidy was to be made in the shape of a certain percentage of the tribute rice carried to Peking from Shanghai and Chinkiang, and elsewhere, where tribute rice is paid over to the government in lieu of taxes in money. This tribute rice heretofore had been taken to Peking by flat-bottom boats, via the Grand Canal. Thousands of these boats were built expressly for this rice transportation, which supported a large population all along the whole route of the Grand Canal.

On account of the great evils arising from this mode of transportation, such as the great length of time it took to take the rice to Peking, the great percentage of loss from theft, and from fermentation, which made the rice unfit for food, part of the tribute rice was carried by sea in Ningpo junks as far as Tiensin, and from thence transhipped again in flat-bottom boats to Peking. But even the Ningpo junk system was attended with great loss of time and much damage, almost as great as by flat-bottom scows. My proposition was to use steam to do the work, supplanting both the flat-bottomed scows and the Ningpo junk system, so that the millions who were dependent on rice for subsistence might find it possible to get good and sound rice. This is one of the great benefits and blessings which the China Merchant Steamship Co. has conferred upon China.

SECOND PROPOSAL

The second proposition was for the government to send picked Chinese youths abroad to be thoroughly educated for the public service. The scheme contemplated the education of one hundred and twenty students as an experiment. These one hundred and twenty students were to be divided into four installments of thirty students each, one installment to be sent out each year. They were to have fifteen years to finish their education. Their average age was to be from twelve to fourteen years. If the first and second installments proved to be a success, the scheme was to be continued indefinitely. Chinese teachers were to be provided to keep up their knowledge of Chinese while in the United States. Over the whole enterprise two commissioners were to be appointed, and the government was to appropriate a certain percentage of the Shanghai customs to maintain the mission.

THIRD PROPOSAL

The third proposition was to induce the government to open the mineral resources of the country and thus in an indirect way lead to the necessity of introducing railroads to transport the mineral products from the interior to the ports.

I did not expect this proposition to be adopted and carried out, because China at that time had no mining engineers who could be depended upon to develop the mines, nor were the people free from the Fung Shui superstition.[A] I had no faith whatever in the success of this proposition, but simply put it in writing to show how ambitious I was to have the government wake up to the possibilities of the development of its vast resources.

[A] The doctrine held by the Chinese in relation to the spirits or genii that rule over winds and waters, especially running streams and subterranean waters. This doctrine is universal and inveterate among the Chinese, and in a great measure prompts their hostility to railroads and telegraphs, since they believe that such structures anger the spirits of the air and waters and consequently cause floods and typhoons.—Standard Dictionary.

FOURTH PROPOSAL

The encroachment of foreign powers upon the independent sovereignty of China has always been watched by me with the most intense interest. No one who is at all acquainted with Roman Catholicism can fail to be impressed with the unwarranted pretensions and assumptions of the Romish church in China. She claims civil jurisdiction over her proselytes, and takes civil and criminal cases out of Chinese courts. In order to put a stop to such insidious and crafty workings to gain temporal power in China, I put forth this proposition: to prohibit missionaries of any religious sect or denomination from exercising any kind of jurisdiction over their converts, in either civil or criminal cases. These four propositions were carefully drawn up, and were presented to Governor Ting for transmission to Peking.

Of the four proposals, the first, third and fourth were put in to chaperone the second, in which my whole heart was enlisted, and which above all others was the one I wanted to be taken up; but not to give it too prominent a place, at the suggestion of my Chinese teacher, it was assigned a second place in the order of the arrangement. Governor Ting recognized this, and accordingly wrote to Prime Minister Wen Seang and forwarded the proposals to Peking. Two months later, a letter from Ting, at Suchau, his headquarters, gave me to understand that news from Peking had reached him that Wen Seang's mother had died, and he was obliged, according to Chinese laws and customs, to retire from office and go into mourning for a period of twenty-seven months, equivalent to three years, and to abstain altogether from public affairs of all kinds. This news threw a cold blanket over my educational scheme for the time being. No sooner had one misfortune happened than another took its place, worst than the first—Wen Seang himself, three months afterwards, was overtaken by death during his retirement. This announcement appeared in the Peking "Gazette," which I saw, besides being officially informed of it by Governor Ting. No one who had a pet scheme to promote or a hobby to ride could feel more blue than I did, when the cup of joy held so near to his lips was dashed from him. I was not entirely disheartened by such circumstances, but had an abiding faith that my educational scheme would in the end come out all right. There was an interval of at least three years of suspense and waiting between 1868 and 1870. I kept pegging at Governor Ting, urging him to keep the subject constantly before Viceroy Tsang's mind. But like the fate of all measures of reform, it had to abide its time and opportunity.

The time and the opportunity for my educational scheme to materialize finally came. Contrary to all human expectations, the opportunity appeared in the guise of the Tientsin Massacre. No more did Samson, when he slew the Timnath lion, expect to extract honey from its carcass than did I expect to extract from the slaughter of the French nuns and Sisters of Charity the educational scheme that was destined to make a new China of the old, and to work out an Oriental civilization on an Occidental basis.

The Tientsin Massacre took place early in 1870. It arose from the gross ignorance and superstition of the Tientsin populace regarding the work of the nuns and Sisters of Charity, part of whose religious duty it was to rescue foundlings and castaway orphans, who were gathered into hospitals, cared for and educated for the services of the Roman Catholic church. This beneficent work was misunderstood and misconstrued by the ignorant masses, who really believed in the rumors and stories that the infants and children thus gathered in were taken into the hospitals and churches to have their eyes gouged out for medical and religious purposes. Such diabolical reports soon spread like wild-fire till popular excitement was worked up to its highest pitch of frenzy, and the infuriated mob, regardless of death and fearless of law, plunged headlong into the Tientsin Massacre. In that massacre a Protestant church was burned and destroyed, as was also a Roman Catholic church and hospital; several nuns or Sisters of Charity were killed.

At the time of this occurrence, Chung Hou was viceroy of the Metropolitan province. He had been ambassador to Russia previously, but in this unfortunate affair, according to Chinese law, he was held responsible, was degraded from office and banished. The whole imbroglio was finally settled and patched up by the payment of an indemnity to the relatives and friends of the victims of the massacre and the rebuilding of the Roman Catholic and Protestant churches, another Catholic hospital, besides a suitable official apology made by the government for the incident. Had the French government not been handicapped by the impending German War which threatened her at the time, France would certainly have made the Tientsin Massacre a casus belli, and another slice of the Chinese Empire would have been annexed to the French possessions in Asia. As it was, Tonquin, a tributary state of China, was afterwards unscrupulously wrenched from her.

In the settlement of the massacre, the Imperial commissioners appointed were: Viceroy Tsang Kwoh Fan, Mow Chung Hsi, Liu * * * and Ting Yih Chang, Governor of Kiang Su. Li Hung Chang was still in the field finishing up the Nienfi rebellion, otherwise he, too, would have been appointed to take part in the proceedings of the settlement. I was telegraphed for by my friend, Ting Yih Chang, to be present to act as interpreter on the occasion, but the telegram did not reach me in time for me to accompany him to Tientsin; but I reached Tientsin in time to witness the last proceedings. The High Commissioners, after the settlement with the French, for some reason or other, did not disband, but remained in Tientsin for several days. They evidently had other matters of State connected with Chung Hou's degradation and banishment to consider.

CHAPTER XVII

Taking advantage of their presence, I seized the opportunity to press my educational scheme upon the attention of Ting Yih Chang and urged him to present the subject to the Board of Commissioners of which Tsang Kwoh Fan was president. I knew Ting sympathized with me in the scheme, and I knew, too, that Tsang Kwoh Fan had been well informed of it three years before through Governor Ting. Governor Ting took up the matter in dead earnest and held many private interviews with Tsang Kwoh Fan as well as with the other members of the Commission. One evening, returning to his headquarters very late, he came to my room and awakened me and told me that Viceroy Tsang and the other Commissioners had unanimously decided to sign their names conjointly in a memorial to the government to adopt my four propositions. This piece of news was too much to allow me to sleep any more that night; while lying on my bed, as wakeful as an owl, I felt as though I were treading on clouds and walking in air. Two days after this stirring piece of news, the memorial was jointly signed with Viceroy Tsang Kwoh Fan's name heading the list, and was on its way to Peking by pony express. Meanwhile, before the Board of Commissioners disbanded and Viceroy Tsang took his departure for Nanking, it was decided that Chin Lan Pin, a member of the Hanlin College, who had served twenty years as a clerk in the Board of Punishment, should be recommended by Ting to co-operate with me in charge of the Chinese Educational Commission. The ground upon which Chin Lan Pin was recommended as a co-commissioner was that he was a Han Lin and a regularly educated Chinese, and the enterprise would not be so likely to meet with the opposition it might have if I were to attempt to carry it out alone, because the scheme in principle and significance was against the Chinese theory of national education, and it would not have taken much to create a reaction to defeat the plan on account of the intense conservatism of the government. The wisdom and the shrewd policy of such a move appealed to me at once, and I accepted the suggestion with pleasure and alacrity. So Chin Lan Pin was written to and came to Tientsin. The next day, after a farewell dinner had been accorded to the Board of Commissioners before it broke up, Governor Ting introduced me to Chin Lan Pin, whom I had never met before and who was to be my associate in the educational scheme. He evidently was pleased to quit Peking, where he had been cooped up in the Board of Punishment for twenty years as a clerk. He had never filled a government position in any other capacity in his life, nor did he show any practical experience in the world of business and hard facts. In his habits he was very retiring, but very scholarly. In disposition he was kindly and pleasant, but very timid and afraid of responsibilities of even a feather's weight.

In the winter of 1870, Tsang Kwoh Fan, after having settled the Tientsin imbroglio, returned to Nanking, his headquarters as the viceroy of the two Kiangs. There he received the imperial rescript sanctioning his joint memorial on the four proposals submitted through Ting Yih Chang for adoption by the government. He notified me on the subject. It was a glorious piece of news, and the Chinese educational project thus became a veritable historical fact, marking a new era in the annals of China. Tsang invited me to repair to Nanking, and during that visit the most important points connected with the mission were settled, viz.: the establishment of a preparatory school; the number of students to be selected to be sent abroad; where the money was to come from to support the students while there; the number of years they were to be allowed to remain there for their education.

The educational commission was to consist of two commissioners, Chin Lan Pin and myself. Chin Lan Pin's duty was to see that the students should keep up their knowledge of Chinese while in America; my duty was to look after their foreign education and to find suitable homes for them. Chin Lan Pin and myself were to look after their expenses conjointly. Two Chinese teachers were provided to keep up their studies in Chinese, and an interpreter was provided for the Commission. Yeh Shu Tung and Yung Yune Foo were the Chinese teachers and Tsang Lai Sun was the interpreter. Such was the composition of the Chinese Educational Commission.

As to the character and selection of the students: the whole number to be sent abroad for education was one hundred and twenty; they were to be divided into four installments of thirty members each, one installment to be sent each year for four successive years at about the same time. The candidates to be selected were not to be younger than twelve or older than fifteen years of age. They were to show respectable parentage or responsible and respectable guardians. They were required to pass a medical examination, and an examination in their Chinese studies according to regulation— reading and writing in Chinese—also to pass an English examination if a candidate had been in an English school. All successful candidates were required to repair every day to the preparatory school, where teachers were provided to continue with their Chinese studies, and to begin the study of English or to continue with their English studies, for at least one year before they were to embark for the United States.

Parents and guardians were required to sign a paper which stated that without recourse, they were perfectly willing to let their sons or protégés go abroad to be educated for a period of fifteen years, from the time they began their studies in the United States until they had finished, and that during the fifteen years, the government was not to be responsible for death or for any accident that might happen to any student.

The government guaranteed to pay all their expenses while they were being educated. It was to provide every installment with a Chinese teacher to accompany it to the United States, and to give each installment of students a suitable outfit. Such were the requirements and the organization of the student corps.

Immediately upon my return to Shanghai from Nanking after my long interview with the Viceroy, my first step was to have a preparatory school established in Shanghai for the accommodation of at least thirty students, which was the full complement for the first installment. Liu Kai Sing, who was with the Viceroy for a number of years as his first secretary in the Department on Memorials, was appointed superintendent of the preparatory school in Shanghai. In him, I found an able coadjutor as well as a staunch friend who took a deep interest in the educational scheme. He it was who prepared all the four installments of students to come to this country.

Thus the China end of the scheme was set afloat in the summer of 1871. To make up the full complement of the first installment of students, I had to take a trip down to Hong Kong to visit the English government schools to select from them a few bright candidates who had had some instruction both in English and Chinese studies. As the people in the northern part of China did not know that such an educational scheme had been projected by the government, there being no Chinese newspapers published at that time to spread the news among the people, we had, at first, few applications for entrance into the preparatory school. All the applications came from the Canton people, especially from the district of Heang Shan. This accounts for the fact that nine-tenths of the one hundred and twenty government students were from the south.

In the winter of 1871, a few months after the preparatory school had begun operations, China suffered an irreparable loss by the death of Viceroy Tsang Kwoh Fan, who died in Nanking at the ripe age of seventy-one years. Had his life been spared even a year longer, he would have seen the first installment of thirty students started for the United States,—the first fruit of his own planting. But founders of all great and good works are not permitted by the nature and order of things to live beyond their ordained limitations to witness the successful developments of their own labor in this world; but the consequences of human action and human character, when once their die is cast, will reach to eternity. Sufficient for Tsang Kwoh Fan that he had completed his share in the educational line well. He did a great and glorious work for China and posterity, and those who were privileged to reap the benefit of his labor will find ample reason to bless him as China's great benefactor. Tsang, as a statesman, a patriot, and as a man, towered above his contemporaries even as Mount Everest rises above the surrounding heights of the Himalaya range, forever resting in undisturbed calmness and crowned with the purity of everlasting snow. Before he breathed his last, I was told that it was his wish that his successor and protégé, Li Hung Chang, be requested to take up his mantle and carry on the work of the Chinese Educational Commission.

Li Hung Chang was of an altogether different make-up from his distinguished predecessor and patron. He was of an excitable and nervous temperament, capricious and impulsive, susceptible to flattery and praise, or, as the Chinese laconically put it, he was fond of wearing tall hats. His outward manners were brusque, but he was inwardly kind-hearted. As a statesman he was far inferior to Tsang; as a patriot and politician, his character could not stand a moment before the searchlight of cold and impartial history. It was under such a man that the Chinese Educational Commission was launched forth.

In the latter part of the summer of 1872 the first installment of Chinese students, thirty in number, were ready to start on the passage across the Pacific to the United States. In order that they might have homes to go to on their arrival, it devolved upon me to precede them by one month, leaving Chin Lan Pin, the two Chinese teachers and their interpreter to come on a mail later. After reaching New York by the Baltimore and Ohio, via Washington, I went as far as New Haven on my way to Springfield, Mass., where I intended to meet the students and other members of the commission on their way to the East by the Boston and Albany Railroad. At New Haven, the first person I called upon to announce my mission was Prof. James Hadley. He was indeed glad to see me, and was delighted to know that I had come back with such a mission in my hands. After making my wants known to him, he immediately recommended me to call upon Mr. B. G. Northrop, which I did. Mr. Northrop was then Commissioner of Education for Connecticut. I told him my business and asked his advice. He strongly recommended me to distribute and locate the students in New England families, either by twos or fours to each family, where they could be cared for and at the same time instructed, till they were able to join classes in graded schools. This advice I followed at once. I went on to Springfield, Mass., which city I considered was the most central point from which to distribute the students in New England; for this reason I chose Springfield for my headquarters. This enabled me to be very near my friends, Dr. A. S. McClean and his worthy wife, both of whom had been my steadfast friends since 1854.

But through the advice of Dr. B. G. Northrop and other friends, I made my permanent headquarters in the city of Hartford, Conn., and for nearly two years our headquarters were located on Sumner Street. I did not abandon Springfield, but made it the center of distribution and location of the students as long as they continued to come over, which was for three successive years, ending in 1875.

In 1874, Li Hung Chang, at the recommendation of the commission, authorized me to put up a handsome, substantial building on Collins Street as the permanent headquarters of the Chinese Educational Commission in the United States. In January, 1875, we moved into our new headquarters, which was a large, double three-story house spacious enough to accommodate the Commissioners, teachers and seventy-five students at one time. It was provided with a school-room where Chinese was exclusively taught; a dining room, a double kitchen, dormitories and bath rooms. The motive which led me to build permanent headquarters of our own was to have the educational mission as deeply rooted in the United States as possible, so as not to give the Chinese government any chance of retrograding in this movement. Such was my proposal, but that was not God's disposal as subsequent events plainly proved.

CHAPTER XVIII

INVESTIGATION OF THE COOLIE TRAFFIC IN PERU

In the spring of 1873, I returned to China on a flying visit for the sole purpose of introducing the Gatling gun—a comparatively new weapon of warfare of a most destructive character. I had some difficulty in persuading the Gatling Company to give me the sole agency of the gun in China, because they did not know who I was, and were unacquainted with my practical business experience. In fact, they did not know how successfully I had carried on the Taiping Green Tea Expedition in 1860-1, in the face of dangers and privations which few men dared to face. However, I prevailed on the president of the company, Dr. Gatling himself, the inventor of the gun, to entrust me with the agency. Exactly a month after my arrival in Tientsin, I cabled the company an order for a battery of fifty guns, which amounted altogether to something over $100,000, a pretty big order for a man who it was thought could not do anything. This order was followed by subsequent orders. I was anxious that China should have the latest modern guns as well as the latest modern educated men. The Gatling Company was satisfied with my work and had a different opinion of me afterwards.

While I was in Tientsin, attending to the gun business, the Viceroy told me that the Peruvian commissioner was there waiting to make a treaty with China regarding the further importation of coolie labor into Peru. He wanted me to call on the commissioner and talk with him on the subject, which I did. In his conversation, he pictured to me in rosy colors how well the Chinese were treated in Peru; how they were prospering and doing well there, and said that the Chinese government ought to conclude a treaty with Peru to encourage the poorer class of Chinese to emigrate to that country, which offered a fine chance for them to better themselves. I told him that I knew something about the coolie traffic as it was carried on in Macao; how the country people were inveigled and kidnapped, put into barracoons and kept there by force till they were shipped on board, where they were made to sign labor contracts either for Cuba or Peru. On landing at their destination, they were then sold to the highest bidder, and made to sign another contract with their new masters, who took special care to have the contract renewed at the end of every term, practically making slaves of them for life. Then I told him something about the horrors of the middle passage between Macao and Cuba or Peru; how whole cargoes of them revolted in mid-ocean, and either committed wholesale suicide by jumping into the ocean, or else overpowered the captain and the crew, killed them and threw them overboard, and then took their chances in the drifting of the vessel.

Such were some of the facts and horrors of the coolie traffic I pictured to the Peruvian Commissioner. I told him plainly that he must not expect me to help him in this diabolical business. On the contrary, I told him I would dissuade the Viceroy from entering into a treaty with Peru to carry on such inhuman traffic. How the Peruvian's countenance changed when he heard me deliver my mind on the subject! Disappointment, displeasure and anger were visible in his countenance. I bade him good morning, for I was myself somewhat excited as I narrated what I had seen in Macao and what I had read in the papers about the coolie traffic. Indeed, one of the first scenes I had seen on my arrival in Macao in 1855 was a string of poor Chinese coolies tied to each other by their cues and led into one of the barracoons like abject slaves. Once, while in Canton, I had succeeded in having two or three kidnappers arrested, and had them put into wooden collars weighing forty pounds, which the culprits had to carry night and day for a couple of months as a punishment for their kidnapping.

Returning to the Viceroy, I told him I had made the call, and narrated my interview. The Viceroy, to make my visit short, then said, "You have come back just in time to save me from cabling you. I wish you to return to Hartford as quickly as possible and make preparations to proceed to Peru at once, to look into the condition of the Chinese coolies there."

On my return to Hartford, I found that Chin Lan Pin had also been instructed by the government to look after the condition of the Chinese coolies in Cuba. These collateral or side missions were ordered at Li Hung Chang's suggestion. I started on my mission before Chin Lan Pin did. My friend, the Rev. J. H. Twichell, and Dr. E. W. Kellogg, who afterwards became my brother-in-law, accompanied me on my trip. I finished my work inside of three months, and had my report completed before Chin started on his journey to Cuba. On his return, both of our reports were forwarded to Viceroy Li, who was in charge of all foreign diplomatic affairs.

My report was accompanied with two dozen photographs of Chinese coolies, showing how their backs had been lacerated and torn, scarred and disfigured by the lash. I had these photographs taken in the night, unknown to anyone except the victims themselves, who were, at my request, collected and assembled together for the purpose. I knew that these photographs would tell a tale of cruelty and inhumanity perpetrated by the owners of haciendas, which would be beyond cavil and dispute.

The Peruvian Commissioner, who was sent out to China to negotiate a treaty with Viceroy Li Hung Chang to continue the coolie traffic to Peru, was still in Tientsin waiting for the arrival of my report. A friend of mine wrote me that he had the hardihood to deny the statements in my report, and said that they could not be supported by facts. I had written to the Viceroy beforehand that he should hold the photographs in reserve, and keep them in the background till the Peruvian had exhausted all his arguments, and then produce them. My correspondent wrote me that the Viceroy followed my suggestion, and the photographs proved to be so incontrovertible and palpable that the Peruvian was taken by surprise and was dumbfounded. He retired completely crestfallen.

Since our reports on the actual conditions of Chinese coolies in Cuba and Peru were made, no more coolies have been allowed to leave China for those countries. The traffic had received its death blow.

CHAPTER XIX

END OF THE EDUCATIONAL MISSION

In the fall of 1875 the last installment of students arrived. They came in charge of a new commissioner, Ou Ngoh Liang, two new Chinese teachers and a new interpreter, Kwang Kee Cheu. These new men were appointed by Viceroy Li Hung Chang. I knew them in China, especially the new commissioner and the interpreter.

These changes were made at the request of Chin Lan Pin, who expected soon to return to China on a leave of absence. He was going to take with him the old Chinese teacher, Yeh Shu Tung, who had rendered him great and signal service in his trip to Cuba on the coolie question the year before. Tsang Lai Sun, the old interpreter, was also requested to resign and returned to China. These changes I had anticipated some time before and they did not surprise me.

Three months after Chin Lan Pin's arrival in Peking, word came from China that he and I were appointed joint Chinese ministers to Washington, and that Yeh Shu Tung, the old Chinese teacher, was appointed secretary to the Chinese Legation. This was great news to me to be sure, but I did not feel ecstatic over it; on the contrary, the more I reflected on it, the more I felt depressed. But my friends who congratulated me on the honor and promotion did not take in the whole situation as it loomed up before my mind in all its bearings. As far as I was concerned, I had every reason to feel grateful and honored, but how about my life work—the Chinese educational mission that I had in hand—and which needed in its present stage great watchfulness and care? If, as I reflected, I were to be removed to Washington, who was there left behind to look after the welfare of the students with the same interest that I had manifested? It would be like separating the father from his children. This would not do, so I sat down and wrote to the Viceroy a letter, the tenor of which ran somewhat as follows: I thanked him for the appointment which I considered to be a great honor for any man to receive from the government; and said that while I appreciated fully its significance, the obligations and responsibilities inseparably connected with the position filled me with anxious solicitude that my abilities and qualifications might not be equal to their satisfactory fulfilment. In view of such a state of mind, I much preferred, if I were allowed to have my preference in the matter, to remain in my present position as a commissioner of the Chinese mission in Hartford and to continue in it till the Chinese students should have finished their education and were ready to return to China to serve the State in their various capacities. In that event I should have discharged a duty to "Tsang the Upright," and at the same time fulfilled a great duty to China. As Chin Lan Pin had been appointed minister at the same time, he would doubtless be able alone to meet the expectations of the government in his diplomatic capacity.

The letter was written and engrossed by Yung Yune Foo, one of the old Chinese teachers who came over with the first installment of students at the same time Yeh Shu Tung came. In less than four months an answer was received which partially acceded to my request by making me an assistant or associate minister, at the same time allowing me to retain my position as Commissioner of Education, and in that capacity, to exercise a general supervision over the education of the students.

Ou Ngoh Liang, the new commissioner, was a much younger man than Chin. He was a fair Chinese scholar, but not a member of the Hanlin College. He was doubtless recommended by Chin Lan Pin. He brought his family with him, which consisted of his second wife and two children. He was a man of a quiet disposition and showed no inclination to meddle with settled conditions or to create trouble, but took rather a philosophical view of things; he had the good sense to let well enough alone. He was connected with the mission but a short time and resigned in 1876.

In 1876 Chin Lan Pin came as minister plenipotentiary and brought with him among his numerous retinue Woo Tsze Tung, a man whom I knew in Shanghai even in the '50's. He was a member of the Hanlin College, but for some reason or other, he was never assigned to any government department, nor was he ever known to hold any kind of government office. He showed a decided taste for chemistry, but never seemed to have made any progress in it, and was regarded by all his friends as a crank.

After Ou's resignation, Chin Lan Pin before proceeding to Washington to take up his official position as Chinese minister, strongly recommended Woo Tze Tung to succeed Ou as commissioner, to which Viceroy Li Hung Chang acceded without thinking of the consequences to follow. From this time forth the educational mission found an enemy who was determined to undermine the work of Tsang Kwoh Fan and Ting Yih Cheong, to both of whom Woo Tze Tung was more or less hostile. Woo was a member of the reactionary party, which looked upon the Chinese Educational Commission as a move subversive of the principles and theories of Chinese culture. This was told me by one of Chin's suite who held the appointment of chargé d'affaires for Peru. The making of Woo Tze Tung a commissioner plainly revealed the fact that Chin Lan Pin himself was at heart an uncompromising Confucian and practically represented the reactionary party with all its rigid and uncompromising conservatism that gnashes its teeth against all and every attempt put forth to reform the government or to improve the general condition of things in China. This accounts for the fact that in the early stages of the mission, I had many and bitter altercations with him on many things which had to be settled for good, once and for all. Such as the school and personal expenses of the students; their vacation expenses; their change of costume; their attendance at family worship; their attendance at Sunday School and church services; their outdoor exercises and athletic games. These and other questions of a social nature came up for settlement. I had to stand as a kind of buffer between Chin and the students, and defended them in all their reasonable claims. It was in this manner that I must have incurred Chin's displeasure if not his utter dislike. He had never been out of China in his life until he came to this country. The only standard by which he measured things and men (especially students) was purely Chinese. The gradual but marked transformation of the students in their behavior and conduct as they grew in knowledge and stature under New England influence, culture and environment produced a contrast to their behavior and conduct when they first set foot in New England that might well be strange and repugnant to the ideas and senses of a man like Chin Lan Pin, who all his life had been accustomed to see the springs of life, energy and independence, candor, ingenuity and open-heartedness all covered up and concealed, and in a great measure smothered and never allowed their full play. Now in New England the heavy weight of repression and suppression was lifted from the minds of these young students; they exulted in their freedom and leaped for joy. No wonder they took to athletic sports with alacrity and delight!

Doubtless Chin Lan Pin when he left Hartford for good to go to Washington carried away with him a very poor idea of the work to which he was singled out and called upon to perform. He must have felt that his own immaculate Chinese training had been contaminated by coming in contact with Occidental schooling, which he looked upon with evident repugnance. At the same time the very work which he seemed to look upon with disgust had certainly served him the best turn in his life. It served to lift him out of his obscurity as a head clerk in the office of the Board of Punishment for twenty years to become a commissioner of the Chinese Educational Commission, and from that post to be a minister plenipotentiary in Washington. It was the stepping stone by which he climbed to political prominence. He should not have kicked away the ladder under him after he had reached his dizzy elevation. He did all he could to break up the educational scheme by recommending Woo Tze Tung to be the Commissioner of Education, than whom he could not have had a more pliant and subservient tool for his purpose, as may be seen hereinafter.

Woo Tsze Tung was installed commissioner in the fall of 1876. No sooner was he in office than he began to find fault with everything that had been done. Instead of laying those complaints before me, he clandestinely started a stream of misrepresentation to Peking about the students; how they had been mismanaged; how they had been indulged and petted by Commissioner Yung; how they had been allowed to enjoy more privileges than was good for them; how they imitated American students in athletics; that they played more than they studied; that they formed themselves into secret societies, both religious and political; that they ignored their teachers and would not listen to the advice of the new commissioner; that if they were allowed to continue to have their own way, they would soon lose their love of their own country, and on their return to China, they would be good for nothing or worse than nothing; that most of them went to church, attended Sunday Schools and had become Christians; that the sooner this educational enterprise was broken up and all the students recalled, the better it would be for China, etc., etc.

Such malicious misrepresentations and other falsehoods which we knew nothing of, were kept up in a continuous stream from year to year by Woo Tsze Tung to his friends in Peking and to Viceroy Li Hung Chang. The Viceroy called my attention to Woo's accusations. I wrote back in reply that they were malicious fabrications of a man who was known to have been a crank all his life; that it was a grand mistake to put such a man in a responsible position who had done nothing for himself or for others in his life; that he was only attempting to destroy the work of Tsang Kwoh Fan who, by projecting and fathering the educational mission, had the highest interest of China at heart; whereas Woo should have been relegated to a cell in an insane asylum or to an institution for imbeciles. I said further that Chin Lan Pin, who had recommended Woo to His Excellency as commissioner of Chinese Education, was a timid man by nature and trembled at the sight of the smallest responsibilities. He and I had not agreed in our line of policy in our diplomatic correspondence with the State Department nor had we agreed as commissioners in regard to the treatment of the Chinese students. To illustrate his extreme dislike of responsibilities: He was requested by the Governor to go to Cuba to find out the condition of the coolies in that island in 1873. He waited three months before he started on his journey. He sent Yeh Shu Tung and one of the teachers of the Mission accompanied by a young American lawyer and an interpreter to Cuba, which party did the burden of the work and thus paved the way for Chin Lan Pin and made the work easy for him. All he had to do was to take a trip down to Cuba and return, fulfilling his mission in a perfunctory way. The heat of the day and the burden of the labor were all borne by Yeh Shu Tung, but Chin Lan Pin gathered in the laurel and was made a minister plenipotentiary, while Yeh was given the appointment of a secretary of the legation. I mention these things not from any invidious motive towards Chin, but simply to show that often in the official and political world one man gets more praise and glory than he really deserves, while another is not rewarded according to his intrinsic worth. His Excellency was well aware that I had no axe to grind in making the foregoing statement. I further added that I much preferred not to accept the appointment of a minister to Washington, but rather to remain as commissioner of education, for the sole purpose of carrying it through to its final success. And, one time in the heat of our altercation over a letter addressed to the State Department, I told Chin Lan Pin in plain language that I did not care a rap either for the appointment of an assistant minister, or for that matter, of a full minister, and that I was ready and would gladly resign at any moment, leaving him free and independent to do as he pleased.

This letter in answer to the Viceroy's note calling my attention to Woo's accusations gave the Viceroy an insight into Woo's antecedents, as well as into the impalpable character of Chin Lan Pin. Li was, of course, in the dark as to what the Viceroy had written to Chin Lan Pin, but things both in the legation and the Mission apparently moved on smoothly for a while, till some of the students were advanced enough in their studies for me to make application to the State Department for admittance to the Military Academy at West Point and the Naval Academy in Annapolis. The answer to my application was: "There is no room provided for Chinese students." It was curt and disdainful. It breathed the spirit of Kearnyism and Sandlotism with which the whole Pacific atmosphere was impregnated, and which had hypnotized all the departments of the government, especially Congress, in which Blaine figured most conspicuously as the champion against the Chinese on the floor of the Senate. He had the presidential bee buzzing in his bonnet at the time, and did his best to cater for the electoral votes of the Pacific coast. The race prejudice against the Chinese was so rampant and rank that not only my application for the students to gain entrance to Annapolis and West Point was treated with cold indifference and scornful hauteur, but the Burlingame Treaty of 1868 was, without the least provocation, and contrary to all diplomatic precedents and common decency, trampled under foot unceremoniously and wantonly, and set aside as though no such treaty had ever existed, in order to make way for those acts of congressional discrimination against Chinese immigration which were pressed for immediate enactment.

When I wrote to the Viceroy that I had met with a rebuff in my attempt to have some of the students admitted to West Point and Annapolis, his reply at once convinced me that the fate of the Mission was sealed. He too fell back on the Burlingame Treaty of 1868 to convince me that the United States government had violated the treaty by shutting out our students from West Point and Annapolis.

Having given a sketch of the progress of the Chinese Educational Mission from 1870 to 1877-8, my letter applying for their admittance into the Military and Naval Academies might be regarded as my last official act as a commissioner. My duties from 1878 onwards were chiefly confined to legation work.

When the news that my application for the students to enter the Military and Naval Academies of the government had proved a failure, and the displeasure and disappointment of the Viceroy at the rebuff were known, Commissioner Woo once more renewed his efforts to break up the Mission. This time he had the secret co-operation of Chin Lan Pin. Misrepresentations and falsehoods manufactured out of the whole cloth went forth to Peking in renewed budgets in every mail, till a censor from the ranks of the reactionary party came forward and took advantage of the strong anti-Chinese prejudices in America to memorialize the government to break up the Mission and have all the students recalled.

The government before acceding to the memorial put the question to Viceroy Li Hung Chang first, who, instead of standing up for the students, yielded to the opposition of the reactionary party and gave his assent to have the students recalled. Chin Lan Pin, who from his personal experience was supposed to know what ought to be done, was the next man asked to give his opinion. He decided that the students had been in the United States long enough, and that it was time for them to return to China. Woo Tsze Tung, the Commissioner, when asked for his opinion, came out point blank and said that they should be recalled without delay and should be strictly watched after their return. I was ruled out of the consultation altogether as being one utterly incompetent to give an impartial and reliable opinion on the subject. Thus the fate of the educational mission was sealed, and all students, about one hundred in all, returned to China in 1881.

The breaking up of the Chinese Educational Commission and the recall of the young students in 1881, was not brought about without a strenuous effort on the part of some thoughtful men who had watched steadfastly over the development of human progress in the East and the West, who came forward in their quiet and modest ways to enter a protest against the revocation of the Mission. Chief among them were my lifelong friend, the Rev. J. H. Twichell, and Rev. John W. Lane, through whose persistent efforts Presidents Porter and Seelye, Samuel Clemens, T. F. Frelinghuysen, John Russell Young and others were enlisted and brought forward to stay the work of retrogression of the part of the Chinese. The protest was couched in the most dignified, frank and manly language of President Porter of Yale and read as follows:

To The Tsung Li Yamun

or

Office for Foreign Affairs.

"The undersigned, who have been instructors, guardians and friends of the students who were sent to this country under the care of the Chinese Educational Commission, beg leave to represent:

"That they exceedingly regret that these young men have been withdrawn from the country, and that the Educational Commission has been dissolved.

"So far as we have had opportunity to observe, and can learn from the representations of others, the young men have generally made a faithful use of their opportunities, and have made good progress in the studies assigned to them, and in the knowledge of the language, ideas, arts and institutions of the people of this country.

"With scarcely a single exception, their morals have been good; their manners have been singularly polite and decorous, and their behavior has been such as to make friends for themselves and their country in the families, the schools, the cities and villages in which they have resided.

"In these ways they have proved themselves eminently worthy of the confidence which has been reposed in them to represent their families and the great Chinese Empire in a land of strangers. Though children and youths, they have seemed always to understand that the honor of their race and their nation was committed to their keeping. As the result of their good conduct, many of the prejudices of ignorant and wicked men towards the Chinese have been removed, and more favorable sentiments have taken their place.

"We deeply regret that the young men have been taken away just at the time when they were about to reap the most important advantages from their previous studies, and to gather in the rich harvest which their painful and laborious industry had been preparing for them to reap. The studies which most of them have pursued hitherto have been disciplinary and preparatory. The studies of which they have been deprived by their removal, would have been the bright flower and the ripened fruit of the roots and stems which have been slowly reared under patient watering and tillage. We have given to them the same knowledge and culture that we give to our own children and citizens.

"As instructors and guardians of these young men, we should have welcomed to our schools and colleges the Commissioners of Education or their representatives and have explained to them our system and methods of instruction. In some cases, they have been invited to visit us, but have failed to respond to their invitations in person or by their deputies.

"We would remind your honorable body that these students were originally received to our homes and our colleges by request of the Chinese government through the Secretary of State with the express desire that they might learn our language, our manners, our sciences and our arts. To remove them permanently and suddenly without formal notice or inquiry on the ground that as yet they had learned nothing useful to China when their education in Western institutions, arts and sciences is as yet incomplete, seems to us as unworthy of the great Empire for which we wish eminent prosperity and peace, as it is discourteous to the nation that extended to these young men its friendly hospitality.

"We cannot accept as true the representation that they have derived evil and not good from our institutions, our principles and our manners. If they have neglected or forgotten their native language, we never assumed the duty of instructing them in it, and cannot be held responsible for this neglect. The Chinese government thought it wise that some of its own youth should be trained after our methods. We have not finished the work which we were expected to perform. May we not reasonably be displeased that the results of our work should be judged unfavorably before it could possibly be finished?

"In view of these considerations, and especially in view of the injury and loss which have fallen upon the young men whom we have learned to respect and love, and the reproach which has implicitly been brought upon ourselves and the great nation to which we belong,—we would respectfully urge that the reasons for this sudden decision should be reconsidered, and the representations which have been made concerning the intellectual and moral character of our education should be properly substantiated. We would suggest that to this end, a committee may be appointed of eminent Chinese citizens whose duty it shall be to examine into the truth of the statements unfavorable to the young men or their teachers, which have led to the unexpected abandonment of the Educational Commission and to the withdrawal of the young men from the United States before their education could be finished."

CHAPTER XX

JOURNEY TO PEKING AND DEATH OF MY WIFE

The treatment which the students received at the hands of Chinese officials in the first years after their return to China as compared with the treatment they received in America while at school could not fail to make an impression upon their innermost convictions of the superiority of Occidental civilization over that of China—an impression which will always appeal to them as cogent and valid ground for radical reforms in China, however altered their conditions may be in their subsequent careers. Quite a number of the survivors of the one hundred students, I am happy to say, have risen to high official ranks and positions of great trust and responsibility. The eyes of the government have been opened to see the grand mistake it made in breaking up the Mission and having the students recalled. Within only a few years it had the candor and magnanimity to confess that it wished it had more of just such men as had been turned out by the Chinese Educational Mission in Hartford, Conn. This confession, though coming too late, may be taken as a sure sign that China is really awakening and is making the best use of what few partially educated men are available. And these few Occidentally educated men have, in their turn, encouraged and stimulated both the government and the people. Since the memorable events of the China and Japan war, and the war between Japan and Russia, several hundreds of Chinese students have come over to the United States to be educated. Thus the Chinese educational scheme which Tsang Kwoh Fan initiated in 1870 at Tientsin and established in Hartford, Conn., in 1872, though rolled back for a period of twenty-five years, has been practically revived.

Soon after the students' recall and return to China in 1881, I also took my departure and arrived in Tientsin in the fall of that year on my way to Peking to report myself to the government after my term of office as assistant minister had expired. This was the customary step for all diplomatic officers of the government to take at the close of their terms. Chin Lan Pin preceded me by nearly a year, having returned in 1880.

While paying my visit to Li Hung Chang in Tientsin, before going up to Peking, he brought up the subject of the recall of the students. To my great astonishment he asked me why I had allowed the students to return to China. Not knowing exactly the significance of the inquiry, I said that Chin Lan Pin, who was minister, had received an imperial decree to break up the Mission; that His Excellency was in favor of the decree, so was Chin Lan Pin and so was Woo Tsze Tung. If I had stood out alone against carrying out the imperial mandate, would not I have been regarded as a rebel, guilty of treason, and lose my head for it? But he said that at heart he was in favor of their being kept in the States to continue their studies, and that I ought to have detained them. In reply I asked how I could have been supposed to read his heart at a distance of 45,000 lis, especially when it was well known that His Excellency had said that they might just as well be recalled. If His Excellency had written to me beforehand not to break up the Mission under any circumstances, I would then have known what to do; as it was, I could not have done otherwise than to see the decree carried out. "Well," said he, in a somewhat angry and excited tone, "I know the author of this great mischief." Woo Tsze Tung happened to be in Tientsin at the time. He had just been to Peking and sent me word begging me to call and see him. Out of courtesy, I did call. He told me he had not been well received in Peking, and that Viceroy Li was bitter towards him when he had called and had refused to see him a second time. He looked careworn and cast down. He was never heard of after our last interview.

On my arrival in Peking, one of my first duties was to make my round of official calls on the leading dignitaries of the government—the Princes Kung and Ching and the presidents of the six boards. It took me nearly a month to finish these official calls. Peking may be said to be a city of great distances, and the high officials live quite far apart from each other. The only conveyances that were used to go about from place to place were the mule carts. These were heavy, clumsy vehicles with an axle-tree running right across under the body of a box, which was the carriage, and without springs to break the jolting, with two heavy wheels, one at each end of the axle. They were slow coaches, and with the Peking roads all cut up and seldom repaired, you can imagine what traveling in those days meant. The dust and smell of the roads were something fearful. The dust was nothing but pulverized manure almost as black as ink. It was ground so fine by the millions of mule carts that this black stuff would fill one's eyes and ears and penetrate deep into the pores of one's skin, making it impossible to cleanse oneself with one washing. The neck, head and hands had to have suitable coverings to keep off the dust. The water is brackish, making it difficult to take off the dirt, thereby adding to the discomforts of living in Peking.

I was in Peking about three months. While there, I found time to prepare a plan for the effectual suppression of the Indian opium trade in China and the extinction of the poppy cultivation in China and India. This plan was submitted to the Chinese government to be carried out, but I was told by Whang Wen Shiu, the president of the Tsung Li Yamun (Foreign Affairs), that for want of suitable men, the plan could not be entertained, and it was shelved for nearly a quarter of a century until recently when the subject became an international question.

I left Peking in 1882. After four months' residence in Shanghai, I returned to the United States on account of the health of my family.

I reached home in the spring of 1883, and found my wife in a very low condition. She had lost the use of her voice and greeted me in a hoarse low whisper. I was thankful that I found her still living though much emaciated. In less than a month after my return, she began to pick up and felt more like herself. Doubtless, her declining health and suffering were brought on partly on account of my absence and her inexpressible anxiety over the safety of my life. A missionary fresh from China happened to call on her a few days before my departure for China and told her that my going back to China was a hazardous step, as they would probably cut my head off on account of the Chinese Educational Mission. This piece of gratuitous information tended more to aggravate a mind already weighed down by poor health, and to have this gloomy foreboding added to her anxiety was more than she could bear. I was absent in China from my family this time nearly a year and a half, and I made up my mind that I would never leave it again under any conditions whatever. My return in 1883 seemed to act on my wife's health and spirit like magic, as she gradually recovered strength enough to go up to Norfolk for the summer. The air up in Norfolk was comparatively pure and more wholesome than in the Connecticut valley, and proved highly salubrious to her condition. At the close of the summer, she came back a different person from what she was when she went away, and I was much encouraged by her improved health. I followed up these changes of climate and air with the view of restoring her to her normal condition, taking her down to Atlanta, Georgia, one winter and to the Adirondacks another year. It seemed that these changes brought only temporary relief without any permanent recovery. In the winter of 1885, she began to show signs of a loss of appetite and expressed a desire for a change. Somerville, New Jersey, was recommended to her as a sanitarium. That was the last resort she went to for her health, for there she caught a cold which resulted in her death. She lingered there for nearly two months till she was brought home, and died of Bright's disease on the 28th of June, 1886. She was buried in Cedar Hill Cemetery in the home lot I secured for that purpose. Her death made a great void in my after-life, which was irreparable, but she did not leave me hopelessly deserted and alone; she left me two sons who are constant reminders of her beautiful life and character. They have proved to be my greatest comfort and solace in my declining years. They are most faithful, thoughtful and affectionate sons, and I am proud of their manly and earnest Christian characters. My gratitude to God for blessing me with two such sons will forever rise to heaven, an endless incense.

The two blows that fell upon me one after the other within the short span of five years from 1880 to 1886 were enough to crush my spirit. The one had scattered my life work to the four winds; the other had deprived me of a happy home which had lasted only ten years. The only gleam of light that broke through the dark clouds which hung over my head came from my two motherless sons whose tender years appealed to the very depths of my soul for care and sympathy. They were respectively seven and nine years old when deprived of their mother. I was both father and mother to them from 1886 till 1895. My whole soul was wrapped up in their education and well-being. My mother-in-law, Mrs. Mary B. Kellogg, assisted me in my work and stood by me in my most trying hours, keeping house for me for nearly two years.

CHAPTER XXI

MY RECALL TO CHINA

In 1894-5 war broke out between China and Japan on account of Korea. My sympathies were enlisted on the side of China, not because I am a Chinese, but because China had the right on her side, and Japan was simply trumping up a pretext to go to war with China, in order to show her military and naval prowess. Before the close of the war, it was impossible for me to be indifferent to the situation—I could not repress my love for China. I wrote to my former legation interpreter and secretary, two letters setting forth a plan by which China might prosecute the war for an indefinite time.

My first plan was to go over to London to negotiate a loan of $15,000,000, with which sum to purchase three or four ready built iron-clads, to raise a foreign force of 5,000 men to attack Japan in the rear from the Pacific coast—thus creating a diversion to draw the Japanese forces from Korea and give the Chinese government a breathing spell to recruit a fresh army and a new navy to cope with Japan. While this plan was being carried out, the government was to empower a commission to mortgage the Island of Formosa to some Western power for the sum of $400,000,000 for the purpose of organizing a national army and navy to carry on the war. These plans were embodied in two letters to Tsai Sik Yung, at that time secretary to Chang Tsze Tung, viceroy of Hunan and Hupeh. They were translated into Chinese for the Viceroy. That was in the winter of 1894. To my great surprise, Viceroy Chang approved of my first plan. I was authorized by cable to go over to London to negotiate the loan of $15,000,000. The Chinese minister in London, a Li Hung Chang man, was advised of my mission, which in itself was a sufficient credential for me to present myself to the minister. In less than a month after my arrival in London, I succeeded in negotiating the loan; but in order to furnish collaterals for it, I had to get the Chinese minister in London to cable the government for the hypothecation of the customs' revenue. I was told that Sir Robert Hart, inspector-general of customs, and Viceroy Li Hung Chang refused to have the customs' revenue hypothecated, on the ground that this revenue was hardly enough to cover as collateral the loan to meet the heavy indemnity demanded by Japan. The fact was: Viceroy Li Hung Chang and Chang Chi Tung were at loggerheads and opposed to each other in the conduct of the war. The latter was opposed to peace being negotiated by Li Hung Chang; but the former had the Dowager Empress on his side and was strenuous in his efforts for peace.

Hence Sir Robert Hart had to side with the Court party, and ignored Chang Chi Tung's request for the loan of $15,000,000; on that account the loan fell through, and came near involving me in a suit with the London Banking Syndicate.

I returned to New York and cabled for further instructions from Chang Chi Tung as to what my next step would be. In reply he cabled for me to come to China at once.

After thirteen years of absence from China, I thought that my connections with the Chinese government had been severed for good when I left there in 1883. But it did not appear to be so; another call to return awaited me, this time from a man whom I had never seen, of whose character, disposition and views I was altogether ignorant, except from what I knew from hearsay. But he seemed to know all about me, and in his memorial to the government inviting me to return, he could not have spoken of me in higher terms than he did. So I girded myself to go back once more to see what there was in store for me. By this recall, I became Chang Chi Tung's man as opposed to Li Hung Chang.

Before leaving for China this time, I took special pains to see my two sons well provided for in their education. Dr. E. W. Kellogg, my oldest brother-in-law, was appointed their guardian. Morrison Brown Yung, the older son, had just succeeded in entering Yale, Sheffield Scientific, and was able to look out for himself. Bartlett G. Yung, the younger one, was still in the Hartford High School preparing for college. I was anxious to secure a good home for him before leaving the country, as I did not wish to leave him to shift for himself at his critical age. The subject was mentioned to my friends, Mr. and Mrs. Twichell. They at once came forward and proposed to take Bartlett into their family as one of its members, till he was ready to enter college. This is only a single instance illustrative of the large-hearted and broad spirit which has endeared them to their people both in the Asylum Hill church and outside of it. I was deeply affected by this act of self-denial and magnanimity in my behalf as well as in the behalf of my son Bartlett, whom I felt perfectly assured was in first-class hands, adopted as a member of one of the best families in New England. Knowing that my sons would be well cared for, and leaving the development of their characters to an all-wise and ever-ruling Providence, as well as to their innate qualities, I embarked for China, this time without any definite and specific object in view beyond looking out for what opening there might be for me to serve her.

On my arrival in Shanghai, in the early part of the summer of 1895, I had to go to the expense of furnishing myself with a complete outfit of all my official dresses, which cost me quite a sum. Viceroy Chang Chi Tung, a short time previous to my arrival, had been transferred from the viceroyalty of the two Hoos to the viceroyalty of the two Kiangs temporarily. Instead of going up to Wu Chang, the capital of Hupeh, I went up to Nanking, where he was quartered.

In Viceroy Chang Chi Tung, I did not find that magnetic attraction which at once drew me towards Tsang Kwoh Fan when I first met him at Ngan Khing in 1863. There was a cold, supercilious air enveloping him, which at once put me on my guard. After stating in a summary way how the loan of $15,000,000 fell through, he did not state why the Peking government had declined to endorse his action in authorizing the loan, though I knew at the time that Sir Robert Hart, the inspector-general of the Chinese customs, put forward as an excuse that the custom dues were hardly enough to serve as collateral for the big loan that was about to be negotiated to satisfy the war indemnity demanded by the Japanese government. This was the diplomatic way of coating over a bitter pill for Chang Chi Tung to swallow, when the Peking government, through the influence of Li Hung Chang, was induced to ignore the loan. Chang and Li were not at the time on cordial terms, each having a divergent policy to follow in regard to the conduct of the war.

Dropping the subject of the loan as a dead issue, our next topic of conversation was the political state of the country in view of the humiliating defeat China had suffered through the incompetence and corruption of Li Hung Chang, whose defeat both on land and sea had stripped him of all official rank and title and came near costing him his life. I said that China, in order to recover her prestige and become a strong and powerful nation, would have to adopt a new policy. She would have to go to work and engage at least four foreigners to act as advisers in the Department for Foreign Affairs, in the Military and Naval Departments and in the Treasury Department. They might be engaged for a period of ten years, at the end of which time they might be re-engaged for another term. They would have to be men of practical experience, of unquestioned ability and character. While these men were thus engaged to give their best advice in their respective departments, it should be taken up and acted upon, and young and able Chinese students should be selected to work under them. In that way, the government would have been rebuilt upon Western methods, and on principles and ideas that look to the reformation of the administrative government of China.

Such was the sum and substance of my talk in the first and only interview with which Chang Chi Tung favored me. During the whole of it, he did not express his opinion at all on any of the topics touched upon. He was as reticent and absorbent as a dry sponge. The interview differed from that accorded me by Tsang Kwoh Fan in 1863, in that Tsang had already made up his mind what he wanted to do for China, and I was pointed out to him to execute it. But in the case of Chang Chi Tung, he had no plan formed for China at the time, and what I presented to him in the interview was entirely new and somewhat radical; but the close of the Japan War justified me in bringing forward such views, as it was on account of that war that I had been recalled. If he had been as broad a statesman as his predecessor, Tsang Kwoh Fan, he could have said something to encourage me to entertain even a glimpse of hope that he was going to do something to reform the political condition of the government of the country at the close of the war. Nothing, however, was said, or even hinted at. In fact, I had no other interview with him after the first one. Before he left Nanking for Wu Chang, he gave me the appointment of Secretary of Foreign Affairs for Kiang Nan.

On the arrival of Liu Kwan Yih, the permanent viceroy of the two Kiang provinces, Chang Chi Tung did not ask me to go up to Wu Chang with him. This I took to be a pretty broad hint that he did not need my services any longer, that I was not the man to suit his purposes; and as I had no axe to grind, I did not make any attempt to run after my grind-stone. On the contrary, after three months' stay in Nanking under Viceroy Liu Kwan Yih, out of regard for official etiquette, I resigned the secretaryship, which was practically a sinecure—paying about $150 a month. Such was my brief official experience with Viceroys Chang Chi Tung and Liu Kwan Yih.

I severed my official connection with the provincial government of Kiang Nan in 1896, and took up my headquarters in Shanghai—untrammeled and free to do as I pleased and go where I liked. It was then that I conceived the plan of inducing the central government to establish in Peking a government national bank. For this object I set to work translating into Chinese the National Banking Act and other laws relating to national banks from the Revised Statutes of the United States with Amendments and additional Acts of 1875. In prosecuting this work, I had the aid of a Chinese writer, likewise the co-operation of the late Wong Kai Keh, one of the Chinese students who was afterwards the assistant Chinese commissioner in the St. Louis Exposition, who gave me valuable help. With the translation, I went up to Peking with my Chinese writer, and, at the invitation of my old friend, Chang Yen Hwan, who had been Chinese Minister in Washington from 1884 to 1888, I took up my quarters in his residence and remained there several months. Chang Yen Hwan at that time held two offices: one as a senior member of the Tsung Li Yamun (Office for Foreign Affairs); the other, as the first secretary in the Treasury Department of which Ung Tung Hwo, tutor to the late Emperor Kwang Su, was the president. Chang Yen Hwan was greatly interested in the National Banking scheme. He examined the translation critically and suggested that I should leave out those articles that were inapplicable to the conditions of China, and retain only such as were important and practicable. After the translation and selection were completed, he showed it to Ung Tung Hwo, president of the Treasury. They were both highly pleased with it, and had all the Treasury officials look it over carefully and pass their judgment upon it. In a few weeks' time, the leading officials of the Treasury Department called upon me to congratulate me upon my work, and said it ought to be made a subject of a memorial to the government to have the banking scheme adopted and carried out. Chang Yen Hwan came forward to champion it, backed by Ung Tung Hwo, the president.

To have a basis upon which to start the National Bank of China, it was necessary to have the government advance the sum of Tls. 10,000,000; of this sum, upwards of Tls. 2,000,000 were to be spent on machinery for printing government bonds and bank-notes

70

of different denominations and machinery for a mint; Tls. 2,000,000 for the purchase of land and buildings; and Tls. 6,000,000 were to be held in reserve in the Treasury for the purchase of gold, silver and copper for minting coins of different denominations for general circulation. This Tls. 10,000,000 was to be taken as the initiatory sum to start the National Bank with, and was to be increased every year in proportion to the increase of the commerce of the Empire.

We had made such progress in our project as to warrant our appointing a committee to go around to select a site for the Bank, while I was appointed to come to the United States to consult with the Treasury Department on the plan and scope of the enterprise and to learn the best course to take in carrying out the plan of the National Bank. The Treasury Department, through its president, Ung Tung Hwo, was on the point of memorializing for an imperial decree to sanction setting aside the sum of Tls. 10,000,000 for the purpose indicated, when, to the astonishment of Chang Yen Hwan and other promoters of the enterprise, Ung Tung Hwo, the president, received a telegraphic message from Shing Sun Whei, head of the Chinese Telegraphic Co., and manager of the Shanghai, China Steamship Navigation Co., asking Ung to suspend his action for a couple of weeks, till his arrival in Peking, Ung and Shing being intimate friends, besides being compatriots, Ung acceded to Shing's request. Shing Taotai, as he was called, was well-known to be a multimillionaire, and no great enterprise or concession of any kind could pass through without his finger in the pie. So in this banking scheme, he was bound to have his say. He had emissaries all over Peking who kept him well posted about everything going on in the capital as well as outside of it. He had access to the most powerful and influential princes in Peking, his system of graft reaching even the Dowager Empress through her favorite eunuch, the notorious Li Ling Ying. So Shing was a well-known character in Chinese politics. It was through his system of graft that the banking enterprise was defeated. It was reported that he came up to Peking with Tls. 300,000 as presents to two or three princes and other high and influential dignitaries, and got away with the Tls. 10,000,000 of appropriation by setting up a bank to manipulate his own projects.

The defeat of the National Banking project owed its origin to the thoroughly corrupt condition of the administrative system of China. From the Dowager Empress down to the lowest and most petty underling in the Empire, the whole political fabric was honey-combed with what Americans characterize as graft—a species of political barnacles, if I may be allowed to call it that, which, when once allowed to fasten their hold upon the bottom of the ship of State were sure to work havoc and ruination; in other words, with money one could get anything done in China. Everything was for barter; the highest bid got the prize. The two wars—the one with Japan in 1894-5 and the other, the Japan and Russian War in 1904-5—have in some measure purified the Eastern atmosphere, and the Chinese have finally awakened to their senses and have come to some sane consciousness of their actual condition.

After the defeat of the national banking project at the hands of Shing Taotai, I went right to work to secure a railroad concession from the government. The railroad I had in mind was one between the two ports of Tientsin and Chinkiang; one in the north, the other in the south near the mouth of the Yangtze River. The distance between these ports in a bee line is about five hundred miles; by a circuitous route going around the province of Shan Tung and crossing the Yellow River into the province of Hunan through Anwhui, the distance would be about seven hundred miles. The German government objected to having this railroad cross Shan Tung province, as they claimed they had the monopoly of building railroads throughout the province, and would not allow another party to build a railroad across Shan Tung. This was a preposterous and absurd pretension and could not be supported either by the international laws or the sovereign laws of China. At that time, China was too feeble and weak to take up the question and assert her own sovereign rights in the matter, nor had she the men in the Foreign Office to show up the absurdity of the pretension. So, to avoid any international complications, the concession was issued to me with the distinct understanding that the road was to be built by the circuitous route above described. The road was to be built with Chinese, not with foreign capital. I was given six months' time to secure capital. At the end of six months, if I failed to show capital, I was to surrender the concession. I knew very well that it would be impossible to get Chinese capitalists to build any railroad at that time. I tried hard to get around the sticking point by getting foreign syndicates to take over the concession, but all my attempts proved abortive, and I was compelled to give up my railroad scheme also. This ended my last effort to help China.

I did not dream that in the midst of my work, Khang Yu Wei and his disciple, Leang Kai Chiu, whom I met often in Peking during the previous year, were engaged in the great work of reform which was soon to culminate in the momentous coup d'état of 1898.

CHAPTER XXII

THE COUP D'ETAT OF 1898

The coup d'état of September, 1898, was an event memorable in the annals of the Manchu Dynasty. In it, the late Emperor Kwang Su was arbitrarily deposed; treasonably made a prisoner of state; and had his prerogatives and rights as Emperor of the Chinese Empire wrested from him and usurped by the late Dowager Empress Chi Hsi.

Kwang Su, though crowned Emperor when he was five years of age, had all along held the sceptre only nominally. It was Chi Hsi who held the helm of the government all the time.

As soon as Kwang Su had attained his majority, and began to exercise his authority as emperor, the lynx eye of Chi Hsi was never lifted away from him. His acts and movements were watched with the closest scrutiny, and were looked upon in any light but the right one, because her own stand in the government had never been the legitimate and straight one since 1864, when her first regency over her own son, Tung Chi, woke in her an ambition to dominate and rule, which grew to be a passion too morbid and strong to be curbed.

In the assertion of his true manhood, and the exercise of his sovereign power, his determination to reform the government made him at once the cynosure of Peking, inside and outside of the Palace. In the eyes of the Dowager Empress Chi Hsi, whose retina was darkened by deeds perpetrated in the interest of usurpation and blinded by jealousy, Kwang Su appeared in no other light than as a dement, or to use a milder expression, an imbecile, fit only to be tagged round by an apron string, cared for and watched. But to the disinterested spectator and unprejudiced judge, Kwan Su was no imbecile, much less a dement. Impartial history and posterity will pronounce him not only a patriot emperor, but also a patriot reformer—as mentally sound and sane as any emperor who ever sat on the throne of China. He may be looked upon as a most remarkable historical character of the Manchu Dynasty from the fact that he was singled out by an all-wise Providence to be the pioneer of the great reform movement in China at the threshold of the twentieth century.

Just at this juncture of the political condition of China, the tide of reform had reached Peking. Emperor Kwang Su, under some mysterious influence, to the astonishment of the world, stood forth as the exponent of this reform movement. I determined to remain in the city to watch its progress. My headquarters became the rendez-vous of the leading reformers of 1898. It was in the fall of that memorable year that the coup d'état took place, in which the young Emperor Kwang Su was deposed by the Dowager Empress, and some of the leading reformers arrested and summarily decapitated.

Being implicated by harboring the reformers, and in deep sympathy with them, I had to flee for my own life and succeeded in escaping from Peking. I took up quarters in the foreign settlement of Shanghai. While there, I organized the "Deliberative Association of China," of which I was chosen the first president. The object of the association was to discuss the leading question of the day, especially those of reform.

In 1899, I was advised for my own personal safety, to change my residence. I went to Hong Kong and placed myself under the protection of the British government.

I was in Hong Kong from 1900 till 1902, when I returned to the United States to see my younger son, Bartlett G. Yung, graduate from Yale University.

In the spring of 1901, I visited the Island of Formosa, and in that visit I called upon Viscount Gentaro Kodama, governor of the island, who, in the Russo-Japan War of 1904-5 was the chief of staff to Marshal Oyama in Manchuria. In the interview our conversation had to be carried on through his interpreter, as he, Kodama, could not speak English nor could I speak Japanese.

He said he was glad to see me, as he had heard a great deal of me, but never had the pleasure of meeting me. Now that he had the opportunity, he said he might as well tell me that he had most unpleasant if not painful information to give me. Being somewhat surprised at such an announcement, I asked what the information was. He said he had received from the viceroy of Fuhkein and Chêhkiang an official despatch requesting him to have me arrested, if found in Formosa, and sent over to the mainland to be delivered over to the Chinese authorities. Kodama while giving this information showed neither perturbation of thought nor feeling, but his whole countenance was wreathed with a calm and even playful smile.

I was not disturbed by this unexpected news, nor was I at all excited. I met it calmly and squarely, and said in reply that I was entirely in his power, that he could deliver me over to my enemies whenever he wished; I was ready to die for China at any time, provided that the death was an honorable one.

"Well, Mr. Yung," said he, "I am not going to play the part of a constable for China, so you may rest at ease on this point. I shall not deliver you over to China. But I have another matter to call to your attention." I asked what it was. He immediately held up a Chinese newspaper before me, and asked who was the author of the proposition. Without the least hesitation. I told him I was the author of it. At the same time, to give emphasis to this open declaration, I put my opened right palm on my chest two or three times, which attracted the attention of everyone in the room, and caused a slight excitement among the Japanese officials present.

I then said, "With Your Excellency's permission, I must beg to make one correction in the amount stated; instead of $800,000,000, the sum stated in my proposition was only $400,000,000." At this frank and open declaration and the corrected sum, Kodama was evidently pleased and visibly showed his pleasure by smiling at me.

The Chinese newspaper Kodama showed me contained a proposition I drew up for Viceroy Chang Chi Tung to memorialize the Peking government for adoption in 1894-5, about six months before the signing of the Treaty of Shemonashiki by Viceroy Li Hung Chang. The proposal was to have the Island of Formosa mortgaged to a European Treaty power for a period of ninety-nine years for the sum of $400,000,000 in gold. With this sum China was to carry on the war with Japan by raising a new army and a new navy. This proposition was never carried through, but was made public in the Chinese newspapers, and a copy of it found its way to Kodama's office, where, strange to say, I was confronted with it, and I had the moral courage not only to avow its authorship but also a correction of the amount the island was to be mortgaged for.

To bring the interview to a climax, I said, should like circumstances ever arise, nothing would deter me from repeating the same proposition in order to fight Japan.

This interview with the Japanese governor of Formosa was one of the most memorable ones in my life. I thought at first that at the request of the Chinese viceroy I was going to be surrendered, and that my fate was sealed; but no sooner had the twinkling smile of Kodama lighted his countenance than my assurance of life and safety came back with redoubled strength, and I was emboldened to talk war on Japan with perfect impunity. The bold and open stand I took on that occasion won the admiration of the governor who then invited me to accompany him to Japan where he expected to go soon to be promoted. He said he would introduce me to the Japanese emperor and other leading men of the nation. I thanked him heartily for his kindness and invitation and said I would accept such a generous invitation and consider it a great honor to accompany him on his contemplated journey, but my health would not allow me to take advantage of it. I had the asthma badly at the time.

Then, before parting, he said that my life was in danger, and that while I was in Formosa under his jurisdiction he would see that I was well protected and said that he would furnish me with a bodyguard to prevent all possibilities of assassination. So the next day he sent me four Japanese guards to watch over me at night in my quarters; and in the daytime whenever I went out, two guards would go in advance of me and two behind my jinrickisha to see that I was safe. This protection was continued for the few days I spent in Formosa till I embarked for Hong Kong. I went in person to thank the governor and to express my great obligation and gratitude to him for the deep interest he had manifested towards me.

APPENDIX

An address by the Rev. Joseph H. Twichell, delivered before the Kent Club of the Yale Law School, April 10, 1878.

A visitor to the City of Hartford, at the present time, will be likely to meet on the streets groups of Chinese boys, in their native dress, though somewhat modified, and speaking their native tongue, yet seeming, withal, to be very much at home. He will also occasionally meet Chinese men who, by their bearing, will impress him as being gentlemen of their race.

These gentlemen are officers, and these boys are pupils of the Chinese Educational Mission, although one of the most remarkable and significant institutions of the age on the face of the whole earth. The object of the mission, now of nearly six years' standing, is the education in this country, through a term of fifteen years, of a corps of young men for the Chinese Government service; that Government paying the whole cost—an annual expense of about $100,000. The number of the officers is five, viz,—the two Imperial Commissioners in charge, a translator and interpreter and two teachers. The function of the teachers is to direct the Chinese education of the pupils, which proceeds pari passu with their Western education. The number of pupils was originally 120, but now 112, one having died and seven having, for various reasons, returned to China. A fine, large house recently erected by the Chinese Government in the western part of the City, at a cost of

74

fifty thousand dollars, is the headquarters of the Mission. There are the offices of the officers, and there is lodged the class that is present for examination and instruction in Chinese studies. For this purpose the pupils are divided into classes of about twenty, one coming as another goes, each staying at the Mission House two weeks at a time. A small part only of the whole number are permanently located in Hartford. Most of them are in other places, though not far away, generally two together attending school or receiving private instruction in families.

They come in yearly companies of thirty, beginning with 1872, and the last detachment is still chiefly engaged in learning our language.

The plan is to afford these boys the advantages of our best educational institutions—academies, colleges, and, to some extent, professional schools—to assign them, by and by, as they shall develop aptitude, to various special courses of study and training in the physical, mechanical and military sciences, in political history and economy, international law, the principles and practice of civil administration and in all departments and branches of knowledge, skill in which is useful for public government service in these modern times. And through the whole process of this education, it is to be impressed upon them that they belong and are to belong to their nation, for whose sake they are elected to enjoy these great and peculiar opportunities. The result will be, if all goes well and the plan is carried out,—and there is apparently nothing now to prevent it,—that in the year 1887 or thereabout there will go from this country to China a body of somewhere near a hundred men who have grown up under exceedingly favorable conditions from early youth to manhood here among us, destined to hold places of importance in the government and in the society of their native land, better equipped in all save experience to do for that land what most needs to be done, and inspired for their work with a more enlightened sense of patriotic duty and responsibility than any other hundred of her sons of their generation. And who can forecast or estimate the consequences that Divine Providence is thus preparing?

COMMISSIONER YUNG WING

Such in brief outline is the Chinese Educational Mission to the United States. The head and front of the whole marvellous enterprise, humanly speaking, is Commissioner Yung Wing. While others whose co-operation was indispensable, have, as will presently appear, contributed to it and still stand back of it, and justly share the credit of it with him, to him more than to any other man beside, probably more than to all other men beside, its existence is due. Its history, thus far, cannot be better told except in that connection, so intimately are the two histories related. But it becomes one who speaks of Yung Wing to observe the principle that we must be modest for a modest man, for so modest a man as he is is rare to find. He was born in 1828, of a worthy family in humble life, near the city of Macao in Southern China. In the year 1839 he became a pupil in a children's school, opened by Mrs. Gutzlaff, the wife of an English missionary, his parents consenting to it in the idea that it would be a profitable thing for him to learn the English language. Proving a bright scholar, he was in time promoted to the Morrison School, an institution founded by English merchants in Macao and named after Robert Morrison, the first English Protestant, but at this time under charge of the Rev. S. R. Brown, a teacher engaged by the Morrison Educational Society. When later this school was transferred to Hong Kong he went with it, and remained in it till he came to this country. He suffered, however, during this time serious interruption by the death of his father, which required him to go home and, a boy that he was, assist in the support of his family.

This he did by wages earned in the printing establishment of a Portuguese Roman Catholic mission in Macao.

In 1847, Mr. Brown, who had long noted his patient ardor in study, the marks of ability he showed and a certain original vigor of will and strength of character that were in him, brought him, at the age of sixteen, with two other native lads, also his pupils, of about the same age, to the United States; Andrew Shortrede, a large-hearted Scotchman, founder, proprietor and editor of The China Mail, published at Hong Kong, engaging to advance the means of their support for two years. The three boys were entered together at the academy in Monson, Mass., and were received into the family of Mr. Brown's mother, who lived at Monson, a royal woman whose name is memorable in the church of Christ as that of the author of the hymn, "I love to steal awhile away." It was while a member of her godly household that Yung Wing became a Christian believer.

It will not be out of place to state here, as a fact, the significance of which will be readily appreciated, that he caused the son who was born to him in 1876—his first-born—to be named in baptism Morrison Brown, an eloquent act of recognition and profession. Of Wing's two companions one, Wong Shing, was compelled, by want of health, to return to China the next year. There, in the office of The China Mail, he learned the art of printing. From 1852 or 1853 he was for several years connected with the press of the London Mission under Dr. Legge, now the eminent Professor of the Chinese Language and Literature in Oxford University. In 1873 he accompanied the second detachment of Chinese students to this country, and is at present under appointment as interpreter to the Chinese Legation soon to be established at Washington.

The other, Wong Fun, went to Scotland in 1850, and after two years general study entered the Medical Department of Edinburgh University, at which he graduated with very high honor. Returning to China in 1856, he began the practice of medicine in the city of Canton and is most highly esteemed on all that coast, both for his private character and for his professional talents, being held by many foreign residents the ablest physician in the whole region of the East beyond Calcutta. Wong Fun died Oct. 15th, 1878.

IN YALE COLLEGE

Yung Wing, after two years and a half spent at Monson, Mass., was, in 1850, though but poorly fitted for want of time, admitted to the Freshman Class in Yale College. His career in college was, in some respects, a remarkable one. Owing to his inadequate preparations, he did not, though he worked hard, take a high stand in general scholarship, yet he excelled in the departments of writing and metaphysics, and made a sensation that was felt beyond the college walls by bearing off repeated prizes for English composition. Throughout his entire course he contended with poverty, a circumstance the explanation of which deserves notice. When he became a Christian, at Monson, he heard and at once accepted his Divine call to devote his life to the Christian service of his nation. But the form of that service—what should it be? This question he had to answer, at least in part. The presumption was, and it was assumed by his friends and by the public so far as his case was known, that he would be a minister of the Gospel. But right then and there, after much careful and prayerful thinking, this boy of seventeen, though by no means doubting the value of Christian missions, fully recognizing the fact, indeed, that he himself was the direct fruit of Christian missions,—which, be it ever remembered, he was,—concluded, with an independence characteristic of him even at that age, that it was not best for him to be a missionary. He had a suspicion then, though indistinct, that he was wanted for something else. It was a costly conclusion and he was quite aware of it. It was against the views and hopes of the most of those who were around him, and by it, being without pecuniary means, he cut himself off from the resource of those charitable foundations that would have aided him as a student for the ministry. And so he was poor in college; he smiles now to remember how poor. Yet he received help from persons interested in him at New Haven and elsewhere, mainly through the medium of Professor Thatcher, whose care for him in that matter claims his liveliest gratitude to this day. And he got through. He came to college in his cue and Chinese tunic, but put off both in the course of his first year.

His nationality made him a good deal of a stranger, and this, together with his extreme natural reserve and his poverty, kept him from mingling much with the social life of college. He had not many intimates, yet he so carried himself from first to last as to merit and win the entire respect of all his class. It was in certain long walks and talks he had with his classmate, Carrol Cutler, now president of Western Reserve College, that he opened and discussed the project then forming in his mind of this Chinese Educational Mission. The idea was born, the dream was taking shape, but the way was long to its realization.

His graduation in 1854 was the event of the Commencement of that year. There were many, at least, who so regarded it, and some of them came to the Commencement principally for the sake of seeing the Chinese graduate. Among the latter was Dr. Bushnell of Hartford. He had heard of him and being strongly interested, according to the size of his great mind and heart, in the Chinese race, he desired to meet Yung Wing. An incident of their meeting on that occasion, which the writer has heard Dr. Bushnell tell, will bear repeating: When they were introduced, the Doctor gave it as one of his reasons for seeking the introduction that he desired to ascertain who had written certain newspaper articles on the Chinese question, as it then stood, which had attracted his attention as evincing marks of statesmanship. He thought Wing might know. Whereupon, as the Doctor said, Wing hung his head, and blushing like a girl, with much confusion of manner, confessed that he was their author. It is only fair to add that Mr. Wing says that he does not remember this incident. But it is equally fair to add again that in a case of this kind Dr. Bushnell's memory, or anybody else's, were more worthy to be trusted than Yung Wing's.

At the time of his graduation, Wing was as much tempted as it was possible for him to be, to change the plan of his life. He had been in this country long enough to become thoroughly naturalized here. He was, in fact, a citizen. All his tastes and feelings and affinities, intellectual and moral, made him at home here. Moreover, through the notice into which his graduation brought him, it came about that a very inviting opportunity was opened to him to remain and have his career here if he chose to. On the other hand, China was like a strange land to him. He had even almost entirely forgotten his native tongue. And there was nothing in China for him to go to. Except among his humble kindred, he had no friends there; nothing to give him any standing or consideration, no place, so to speak, to set his foot on. Not only so, but considering where he had been and what he had become, and the purpose he had in view, he could not fail to encounter, among his own people, prejudice, suspicion, hostility. A cheerless, forbidding prospect lay before him in that direction. The thought of going back was the thought of exile. He wanted immensely to stay. But there was one text of Holy Scripture that, all this while, he says, haunted him and followed him like the voice of God. It was this: "If any provide not for his own, and specially for those of his own house, he hath denied the faith, and is worse than an infidel." And by the words "his own" and "his own house," it meant to him the nation of which he was born. The text carried the day. The benefits which he had been, as it were, singled out from a whole people to receive, his sense of justice and gratitude alike would not let him appropriate to his own advantage. And so, though he knew not what should befall him, he set his face to return; and he went to do what he has done.

He sailed soon after his graduation for Hong Kong which, after a voyage of 151 days, he reached in the month of April, 1855. When the Chinese pilot came on board he found that he could, with some difficulty, understand what he said, though he could not make the pilot understand him, which shows the condition of his knowledge of Chinese on his arrival in the country. It took him all the time he was not otherwise employed for two years to acquire facility in the use of it.

TAKING FIRST STEPS IN LIFE

As for his grand scheme, he had settled it in his own mind that the first step to be taken toward carrying it out was to contrive a way of getting it before some influential public man or men—a thing itself of infinite difficulty. With this end in view, though, of course, to make his living also, he sought and obtained the position of private secretary to the Hon. Peter Parker, then Commissioner of the United States to China, hoping that it would be the means of affording him the access he desired. Becoming satisfied upon a sufficient trial that it was not likely to answer his expectations in this regard, he resigned the place after a few months. He now attempted another way of compassing the matter. There was at Hong Kong an English bar consisting of a dozen or so lawyers doing business for the foreign commercial houses of that City. Wing bethought him that the standing and acquaintance resulting from his becoming a member of that bar might not improbably bring him the opportunity he sought. Accordingly, he entered one of the offices as a student. But presently it got out among the lawyers who this young man was, what his education had been, and they saw that his competition with them for legal practice of a Chinese city was a thing not to be allowed if it could be prevented. And so his principal, pleading the commands of his legal brethren, informed him, with many courteous expressions of regret, that he must find another place to study law in. And as there was no other place, he had to give it up.

After this followed an interval of nearly two years, during which he occupied himself with Chinese and other studies, earning his bread by such commercial translation as he could find to do, and waited for the right thing to turn up. He then, in the same hope that led him to his previous experiments, took a place in the Customs Service at Shanghai. But neither did this, on trial, promise, in his judgment, a pou sto for his operations, and he soon abandoned it.

It was now 1860. Five years and nothing accomplished! To one only looking on the outside Yung Wing would appear to have thus far pursued an uncertain and rather thriftless course; but not if he penetrated his real policy and the purpose that lay ever nearest his heart; most assuredly not if he knew—what was the fact—that all this time that he was going from one thing to another and keeping himself poor, he was refusing offers of employment at rates of remuneration that to him, so long familiar with a straightened lot, seemed little short of princely. In 1860, however, overtures were made him by one of the leading silk and tea houses of Shanghai to enter its service as traveling inland agent, which, for the reason in part that it would send him touring through a wide extent of country and possess him, by observation, of a knowledge that he deemed would be useful to him, he determined to accept. This business he followed for a year, and then, seeing a good chance for it, set up in a business for himself which proved so profitable a venture that, had he continued in it, he would, to all appearances, have speedily become rich. As it was, he made a very considerable sum of money.

But in 1862 the door of the opportunity which he had been constantly feeling after from the day he landed in China, unexpectedly opened to him.

It was in this wise: While in the city of Shanghai, he made the acquaintance of a Chinese astronomer—a man of rank and of eminence in learning. Or rather, the astronomer, who had in some way gained intelligence of Wing's antecedents, sought his acquaintance for the sake of talking astronomy with him. In repeated interviews through which their acquaintance progressed to the degree of mutual friendly regard, Wing, who had carried away from college a better knowledge of astronomy than most graduates do, told him all he knew, which was a long advance upon his own previous acquisitions in that science. This astronomer was an officer of the great Tsang Kwoh Fan, viceroy of Kiang Su and Kiang Nan provinces, generalissimo of the Imperial forces and one of the very most prominent and leading men in the whole Empire. Through representations made to him by the astronomer, he soon sent a message to Yung Wing desiring to see him, and hinting a desire to take him into his service. Though returning a favorable reply to the message, under all the circumstances and for reasons that cannot be explained, Wing delayed responding to it in person for a considerable time. The situation was a delicate one, requiring extreme caution and circumspection on his part.

But at length he paid Tsang Koh Fan the promised visit. He felt the occasion to be a critical one, and when ushered into the great man's presence found it difficult to retain his composure. Tsang Koh Fan first bent upon him a long, intense, piercing gaze. As Wing says, he had never been looked at in his life as he was then. Then causing him to be seated, he required of him an account of his history, which he gave. He then questioned him as to his views respecting China,—her needs, her outlook, her public policy, and so on. A long conversation followed in which the Viceroy disclosed his views, to which Wing listened with amazement. For, behold, here was a man such as he had not supposed existed in that country—a man reared in China, and not a young man either—who had light in his head; who recognized the causes of many of the disadvantages China was contending with in taking her place among the family of nations; a man of marvellously liberal and progressive sentiments.

MADE A MANDARIN

The result of the interview was that Wing entered his service and was made a Mandarin of the fifth rank, there being nine degrees of that dignity in the Chinese official system. At this time the great Taiping rebellion was at its height and Tsang Koh Fan was in the field. In fact, the interview had taken place at his camp in Ngankin, on the Yang Tse River. The Viceroy first tendered Wing a military command which, on the score of lack of qualification, he asked leave to decline. He was then, shortly after, 1864, at his own suggestion, despatched abroad to purchase machinery for the manufacture of arms, for which purpose the expenditure of a large sum of money was intrusted to him. On this errand he visited France and England as well as the United States, but finally gave his orders here. On returning with his purchases to China in 1865, what he had done was so satisfactory to his chief that he was advanced to the next higher grade of official rank, viz,—the Fourth. The machinery he had bought was the foundation of the Kiang Nan Arsenal. It is curious to remark that the first work of a man whose supreme ambition it was, from Christian motives, to set his country forward in civilization, should have been the establishment of an arsenal. But it quite consisted with Yung Wing's ideas, which were intensely patriotic.

From 1865 to 1870 he was variously employed in different places, being under command now of one superior and now of another. Among the work that he did during this period, that of translation was prominent. He translated into Chinese Parson's Law of Contracts, and a book of English Law. He also translated large portions of Colton's Geography, deeming that geographical knowledge was as likely to prove beneficial to his countrymen as any.

But the thing that lay nearest his heart and that was continually before him, was the question of how to accomplish the plan he had so many years held in hope. He now had ample opportunity to expound and advocate it, and he did so with inexhaustible perseverance. The main argument he used was this: China, in her international relations, in her commercial and other intercourse with foreign peoples, suffers disadvantage and much detriment from want of men capable by education of acting as her representatives. She is forced to employ in many most important places, that ought to be occupied by her own citizens, foreigners by whom her interests are liable to be neglected or betrayed. Her forts, her ships of war, her military forces, her customs, are largely in charge of foreigners. How was it proper, he asked, that Anson Burlingame, an American, should be her chief agent in arranging a treaty with his own country and other western governments? This was his general line of reasoning.

The most to whom he brought the matter heard him with indifference, but there were three men upon whom he made an impression—all men of high rank and commanding influence. They were the Viceroy, Tsang Koh Fan, already named; Li Hung Chang, now Viceroy of the capital province of Chihli and the foremost Chinese statesman; and Ting Yi Tcheang, then Governor of the Province of Kiang Su. Yet these men, convinced as they were by Wing's reasons and avowedly favorable to his project, with all their eminence of position and their influence, were not ready to venture the attempt to carry it through with the Imperial Government. All the forces of conservatism would be opposed to it; the time for it had not come.

In 1867, however, the Governor Ting, who was the most willing of the three, had made representations to an Imperial Minister named Wan Cheang, on the strength of which he was advised to address a memorial on the subject to the Imperial Council at Peking, Wan Cheang undertaking to commend it to the attention of the Council. The situation was at this juncture moderately hopeful, but before the memorial reached the Council, the mother of Wan Cheang died, by which event he was, under the law of Chinese high official etiquette, retired from public life three entire years, and the whole business was set back to where it had been. These were years of great trial to Yung Wing. He was prospering, indeed, in one point of view, but the hope to which he was devoted was so long deferred that his heart was often sick. Understand that he was leading there in China an essentially solitary life. He had, soon after his return in 1855, in accordance with his views of what was due to his purpose, resumed his native dress and identified himself not only thus externally, but also in large measure in every other respect with his own people. Especially from the time he became a Chinese Government official, he had dwelt in Chinese society, and had disappeared almost wholly from other society. He had his books and kept up diligently with what was going on in the world of learning and letters outside—it was his only resource—but he was exceedingly alone and lonely notwithstanding. The discouragements to his endeavor that faced him were so numerous and so solid that he was sometimes half disposed to give it all up; but only half disposed.

One of the things that held him to it was not of a nature of an encouragement exactly, but it did excellently well as an antidote to the effect upon his spirits of his discouragements. It began to come to his ears now and than that his American and English friends in China were whispering it among themselves that he was a failure, that he had had a noble chance and had not known how to improve it; that he was impracticable; and that this scheme of his was utterly visionary and could never be successful. Whenever Wing heard of this, he set his teeth and took a new hold. But altogether his faith and manhood were put to an extreme test.

The end came though, as it always does in such cases, and came in a manner almost dramatic. In the month of June, 1870, occurred the woeful tragedy at Tientsin called the Tientsin Massacre, in which a considerable number of French Roman Catholic missionaries, male and female, were murdered by a Chinese mob. It followed that a commission appointed by the foreign powers, diplomatically represented in China, met that same year at Tientsin to investigate the outrage and determine the satisfaction that was to be required for it, together with a like commission appointed by the Chinese Government authorized to bring the affair to a settlement. The Chinese Commission consisted of five, and three of these five were the three men of whom mention has been made,—the viceroys Tsang Koh Fan and Li Hung Chang, and the Governor Ting Yi Tcheang.

AN OPPORTUNITY SEIZED

Yung Wing was at this time under official control of the last named, who, on being summoned to Tientsin, sent him word, for he was at a distance from him, to join the Commission at Tientsin as soon as possible, for his services would be needed there. Wing, though hastening, arrived late on the scene and found the business concluded. But on receiving an account of the difficulties that had attended its transaction, and observing that the commissioners were conscious of their disadvantage in it, he perceived an auspicious occasion for making a stroke in behalf of his scheme, and he made the most of it. He restated his arguments, enforcing them by the illustration of the case at hand, and insisted with the utmost earnestness that there ought to be no delay. And this time he prevailed. The three friends of his idea being together and countenancing one another, then and there agreed that they would at once take action to have the thing he proposed done, and would cast their united influence with the Government in its favor. They kept their agreement. They set their names to a memorial recommending the education of a corps of young men abroad for the Government service and at the Government expense. This memorial they forwarded to Pekin, where they backed it by all means in their power and to the effect that in the month of August, 1871, the measure recommended was adopted by the Imperial Government and a sum equal to $1,500,000 appropriated for its execution.

Mandarin Yung Wing was scarcely able to support the joy of his triumph. For two days, as he has told the writer, he could neither eat nor sleep. He walked on air, and he worshipped God. It was sixteen years after his return to China and twenty years after he set out for this goal that heaven had at last granted his prayer. To him the organization of the enterprise was principally committed. The feature of the long term of fifteen years resolved upon for the course of study and training to be pursued, is particularly due to him and reflects the size of the man, the type of his mind and character.

A school of candidates was at once opened at Shanghai from which the pupils were to be selected by competitive examination, and, as has been already stated, the first detachment of thirty arrived in the United States in 1872. The location of the Mission was also for him to determine. He might have procured its establishment in England, or France, or Germany; but as he himself had expressed it, the light that had enlightened him shone from America and from New England, and to America and New England he was resolved from the first this Mission should repair.

He was appointed Chief Commissioner of the Mission, receiving with the appointment his second promotion in rank, viz,—to the Third or Blue Button grade. With him was associated, as co-commissioner, a venerable scholar and dignitary,—Chin Lan Pin by name,—who, however, remained in this country less than two years, yielding his place to a younger man, Ngau Ngoh Liang, well-born, distinguished for learning, and a most agreeable gentleman.

The students of the Mission have thus far, with very few exceptions, exhibited excellent ability as scholars, and in many instances extraordinary ability, and with fewer exceptions still have been marked by their exemplary conduct. They have everywhere been most hospitably received. They are certainly worthy to be objects of the highest and most friendly interest to every Christian citizen of the United States.

Yung Wing was appointed, December 11, 1876, Associate Minister with his former colleague in the Educational Mission, Chin Lan Pin, to the United States, Peru and Spain. On this occasion he was again promoted in rank,—that is, to Second or Red Button grade, and invested with the title of Tao-tai (or Intendant) of the Province of Kiang Su.

He expects, on the now approaching arrival of Chin Lan Pin in the country, to take up his residence in Washington, yet not to relinquish the general superintendence of the institution which is so dear to him and has cost him so much, and in which are bound up his best patriotic hopes for his native land,—for he is a patriot from head to foot, in every fiber of his body. He loves the Chinese nation and believes in it, doubting not that there is before it a grand career worthy of its noble soil and of its august antiquity.

If it were the aim of the writer to magnify Yung Wing,—which it is not, but only to tell the story of the Chinese Educational Mission to the United States,—there are many things more that might be related of him, all going to show him to be of the stuff that heroes are made of, and one of the most significant characters in modern civilization. But because to relate them would be aside from the purpose in hand, and also because it would grievously offend Yung Wing to have them published, they are passed by. It must be said, for the last word, that even in attributing to him so much credit of the Educational Mission itself, the share he allows himself is very far exceeded. He is accustomed to assign the chief honor of it to those three men of China who helped it so potently with their influence. Tsang Koh Fan died in 1871. His portrait hangs on the wall of the Mission House in Hartford; and the portraits of the other two are there also. The boys are taught to reverence these men as their benefactors. And they are worthy of reverence. Their names deserve to be remembered, and will be, and not alone in China. Yet undoubtedly had there been no Yung Wing, that illustrious good deed of theirs had never been performed.

CPSIA information can be obtained
at www.ICGtesting.com
Printed in the USA
LVHW082340140719
624039LV00017BA/1133/P

9 781548 423551

GENERAL PSYCHOLOGY

With Spotlights on Diversity

Second Edition

Josh Gerow • Kenneth Bordens • Evelyn Blanch-Payne

Custom Publishing

New York   Boston   San Francisco
London   Toronto   Sydney   Tokyo   Singapore   Madrid
Mexico City   Munich   Paris   Cape Town   Hong Kong   Montreal

Pearson
Custom Publishing
is a division of

www.pearsonhighered.com

ISBN 10: 0-558-07800-1
ISBN 13: 978-0-558-07800-3

TABLE OF CONTENTS

CHAPTER NINE Personality

CHAPTER ELEVEN   Stress and Physical Health

CHAPTER TWELVE   The Psychological Disorders

CHAPTER THIRTEEN   Treatment and Therapy for the Psychological Disorders

CHAPTER FOURTEEN Social Psychology

PREFACE

The success of *General Psychology: With Spotlights on Diversity* has prompted this second edition revision. This is a new product developed from the authors' combined decades of expertise in psychology textbook writing, as well as input from teachers, students, and colleagues in the field. This exciting new text offers *Spotlight on Diversity* features, updated photos, colorful anatomical art, and a fresh approach with a new publisher, Pearson Custom Publishing. All of this combines to deliver a student-friendly, teacher-functional textbook that offers more features at a substantial savings. We are truly excited about the textbook you are now holding, and hope that excitement is evident in its pages.

Text Features and Benefits

What does this second edition of *General Psychology: With Spotlights on Diversity* offer?

- **A science-based approach to psychology, designed to enlighten and educate beginning students.** An introductory course may be our only chance to share with students the concepts, principles, methods, and challenges of psychology. Students who read this textbook will gain an appreciation of what psychology is and—equally important—what it is not. They will gain an understanding of what psychologists do and how they go about doing it. And they will become familiar with the vocabulary of psychology.

- **A text designed with applied theories of learning and memory to help students understand psychology.** The study of psychology should not be boring, or difficult. This text was written to make psychology accessible and practical for student learning. Pedagogical features include both a detailed outline and a "Preview" at the beginning of each chapter. Review and summary features, including "Before You Go On" and "A Point to Ponder or Discuss," reinforce key concepts, encourage critical thinking, and make psychology meaningful to real-world situations and students' everyday feelings and emotions.

- **A historical context to the science of psychology.** Students need to appreciate that everything of importance in psychology did not happen within the last six months—or six years. Everything "new" is not necessarily "improved." While this edition of *General Psychology* is as up-to-date as possible, the text discussion is enhanced with historical perspectives to provide added depth.

- **A focus on diversity of psychology in the twenty-first century.** The science of psychology now recognizes that matters of culture, ethnicity, gender, sexual orientation, and the like, are vital to a thorough understanding of psychology's content areas. Therefore, in addition to coverage of diversity issues within the body of the text, each chapter of *General Psychology* includes at least one *Spotlight on Diversity*, developed by author Evelyn Blanch-Payne, wherein *diversity* is discussed in its broadest sense. These *Spotlights* focus on such topics as minority and gender contributions to psychology; issues of intelligence and gender; cultural differences in perceptual organization; learning disabilities and the brain; sexual orientation. ethnic differences in drug and alcohol use and abuse; racial/ethnic disparities in healthcare, and the like.

- **A thorough, feature-filled, cost-controlled text.** Back in the 1970s and 80s, teachers seldom asked, "How much will this cost my students?" These days, instructors recognize it's important to keep education costs down. Indeed, a significant feature of *General Psychology* is its low cost to students. Pearson offers students the *General Psychology* text *and* the Student Study Guide at fraction of what most publishers charge for a text alone. You won't find a better introductory text at a lower price.

Student-Friendly Features

The pedagogical features of *General Psychology* are time-tested, proven effective, and designed to make learning interesting, meaningful, and as easy as possible. Students tell us that they *use* these features, because they *like* these features. They read the book, they learn from it, their test scores go up, and both students and instructors are pleased, as a result.

The text provides a variety of student-friendly features, designed to enhance learning and retention.

- **Chapter Outline and Preview**—Each chapter begins with a simple overview, rather than a distracting story or long lists of questions (which students tend to ignore). A *Preview* lists the issues to be addressed and provides a sense of direction and focus for what to expect in the chapter.
- **Before You Go On Questions**—This unique feature has been used by the text's authors for more than 20 years. The psychology behind this technique is straightforward: Interspersed questions foster distributed practice, indicating sensible "resting places" within each chapter to pause and reflect on what has just been read. As a review, these questions also help promote elaborative rehearsal. Students can self-test and reread a particular section if they need more time with a concept. Students have said they like these breaks and the opportunity to question themselves; they also find this feature especially helpful when reviewing and studying for exams.
- **Chapter Summary**—Each chapter ends with a *Chapter Summary,* in which answers are provided for the *Before You Go On* questions found throughout the text. This approach reinforces the value of the *Before You Go On* questions, and provides a nice, clear, focused summary for review and test preparation.
- **Glossary Terms**—For the beginning student, learning about psychology is, in large measure, a matter of vocabulary development. To assist in that process, key words and concepts are printed in the text in a **blue** boldface type and are defined immediately. Each term is then defined again in a running marginal glossary. All key terms are reassembled at the back of the text in an alphabetized glossary.
- **Points to Ponder or Discuss**—These questions are paired with the *Before You Go On* questions to provide an opportunity to pause, reflect, question, elaborate, and, indeed, ponder or discuss before rushing on to new material. This feature reflects our collective belief that a first course in psychology should promote critical thinking about psychological issues, not just rote memorization.
- **Examples and Applications**—Psychologists know that the more meaningful the material, the more effective the learning, and the better retention of that material. *General Psychology* provides everyday life examples and applications at every possible opportunity to demonstrate psychology's relevance to students' everyday lives.

- **An Extensive Student Study Guide**, available online *for free*, provides several additional learning aids for each chapter. Sections of the *Student Study Guide* can be downloaded and are easy to use. Major sections of the *Student Study Guide* include the following features:
  - a series of 15 short pieces, called *Study Tips*, intended to provide how-to-study information for beginning students;
  - a discussion of the usefulness of *flashcards* for mastering the basics of psychology, with examples provided for the first five chapters;
  - a set of *Practice Tests* of 40-50 multiple-choice and true-false test items, with answers provided in annotated form, indicating not only the correct answer, but also *why* that alternative is the best choice of those provided;
  - a list of all key words and concepts, with space for definitions;
  - a series of straightforward, simple projects, entitled *Experiencing Psychology*, that students can complete without instructor supervision
  - a series of active *Internet Links*, tied to each major A-level section of every chapter, that students can access to learn more about the content discussed in the text.

Teacher-Functional Features

General Psychology with Spotlights on Diversity 2/e works just as hard for the psychology instructor as it does for the student. Every effort has been made to make teaching as easy as possible. That commitment begins with a well-written, error-free, easy-to-read text.

- **An Instructor's Resource Kit** containing nearly *700 pages* of information, ideas, and teaching aids provides the most comprehensive instructor's guide available on the market. It is sure to offer innovative classroom ideas for both beginning and experienced teachers. In addition, instructors will be delighted with detailed chapter outlines, supplemental lecture topics, discussion ideas, classroom projects, demonstrations, updated timelines, critical-thinking exercises, and lists of suggested readings and media.
- **A Test Item File**, *written by the textbook authors*, includes well over 2000 multiple-choice items keyed to the text.
- **A Computerized Version of the Test Bank** is available, allowing an instructor to *easily* construct tests using items from the Test Item File and to *easily* add new items or revise existing ones.
- **Power Point Slides, WebCT, and a Website** are also available. An instructor's CD with Power Point presentations for each chapter make lectures easy to prepare. An instructor's website provides companion information and materials to round out lectures and projects.

What Is New in This Second Edition?

Anyone familiar with the first edition of *General Psychology with Spotlights on Diversity* will quickly realize that this is a not quick, simple, cosmetic revision. With the support of Pearson Custom, we have been able to reorganize several discussions, drop a few, and add several new pieces to the text. Here is an abridged list of some of the new topics or issues to be found in this new edition:

- A major new section on the differences between "Science" and "Pseudo-science"—and expansion of the issue of ethics in psychological research (Ch. 1)

- Expanded the discussion of neurogenesis and added a new section on epigenetics to the discussion of "Genetics and Psychological Traits" (Ch. 2)
- Added pieces on the danger of quiet "hybrid vehicles," a "new" basic taste: umani, the danger of cell-phone use while driving, and the role of the brain in the experience of illusions (Ch. 3)
- Added a piece on unconscious problem solving and decision making; expanded coverage of sleep apnea, and marijuana (Ch. 4)
- Expanded coverage of systematic desensitization and the role of classical conditioning in drug addiction (Ch. 5)
- Added new data on the role of schemas in memory and on overlearning; added new section on testing and practicing retrieval (Ch. 6)
- Added "conformation bias" to discussion of problem solving; updated section on age-, gender-, and ethnic- differences in IQ (Ch. 7)
- Added to sections on "infant memory," "gender identity," "social attachments," "puberty," "marriage and family in early adulthood," "transition to parenthood," "the elderly," and "death and dying" (Ch. 8)
- Added "The Biological Approach" to personality, with sections on physiological correlates of personality, and genetics and personality (Ch. 9)
- Made significant additions to "Eating Disorders"; Added new section on "Unconscious Emotional Reactions" (Ch. 10)
- Updated sections on "why people die," and "coping with HIV/AIDS" (Ch. 11)
- Updated sections on "insanity defense," "PTSD," "Alzheimer's dementia," "major depression," and "Schizophrenia"—added new section on, "A Disorder of Childhood: Autism" (Ch. 12)
- Updated sections on "ECT," "psychoactive drugs," and on "cognitive-behavioral therapy"—revised section on "Empirically Supported Therapies" (Ch. 13)
- Expanded coverage of "naïve realism," "implicit and explicit attitudes," and "attitude change"—made extensive additions to "prejudice and stereotypes"—updated sections on "interpersonal attraction," obedience," and "bystander intervention" (Ch. 14)

ABOUT THE AUTHORS

Josh R. Gerow began his college training at Rensselaer Polytechnic Institute, where he majored in chemistry. He earned his B.S. in psychology at the University of Buffalo, and his Ph.D. in experimental psychology at the University of Tennessee. His graduate area of specialization was developmental psycholinguistics. After teaching for two years at the University of Colorado, Denver Center, he joined the faculty of Indiana University–Purdue University at Fort Wayne (IPFW), where he still teaches. Dr. Gerow has conducted research and published articles in the field of instructional psychology, focusing on factors that affect performance in the introductory psychology course. His teaching background is extensive. During his more than 40 years as a college professor, he has taught courses in the psychology of learning, memory, the history of psychology, and his favorite course, General Psychology. He has brought college-level introductory psychology classes to high school students, and has made frequent presentations at regional and national conferences on the teaching of psychology. He has authored (or co-authored) sixteen editions of introductory psychology textbooks and the supplements that accompany those texts.

Kenneth S. Bordens received his Bachelor of Arts degree in psychology from Farleigh Dickinson University (Teaneck, New Jersey campus) in 1975. He earned a Master of Arts and Doctor of Philosophy degrees in Social Psychology from the University of Toledo in 1979. After receiving his Ph.D., he accepted a position at Indiana University–Purdue University at Fort Wayne (IPFW), where he has taught for the past 30 years. Dr. Borden's main research interest is in psychology and the law. Specifically, he has published several studies on juror and jury decision making. His most recent research is on the impact on jurors of consolidating multiple plaintiffs in complex trials. He has co-authored several editions of three textbooks (*Research Design and Methods: A Process Approach; Psychology and the Law: Integrations and Applications;* and *Social Psychology*), in addition to three editions of *Psychology: An Introduction*, with Dr. Gerow. He currently is writing a text on statistics. Dr. Bordens teaches classes in social psychology, child development, research methods, the history of psychology, and introductory psychology.

Evelyn Blanch-Payne is currently teaching psychology at Georgia State University. She received her doctoral degree in Educational Psychology from Kent State University. Her areas of research interest and her publication history include Ethnicity and Breast Cancer Awareness, Faculty Teaching Styles, Learning Styles of College Students, Cognitive-Behavioral Changes of Mental Health Consumers, and End-of-life Care Preferences. She was a contributor to *The Handbook for Enhancing Undergraduate Education in Psychology* for the American Psychological Association, and has been a presenter at many professional conferences. She has served as Principle Investigator for a Title III research grant, and as a Faculty Fellow at the John F. Kennedy Space Center, NASA. She has been the recipient of numerous teaching awards, including Outstanding Teacher, Most Distinguished Faculty Member, Student Choice Award, and Who's Who Among American Teachers Award in 2000, 2002, and 2005. Blanch-Payne holds professional memberships in several organizations and associations of psychology.

1

The Science of Psychology and Its Research Methods

PREVIEW

Psychology may well be the best class you will take in your college career. After all, it is about you, your family, and your friends. It is about why people think and feel and behave as they do. It is about how all of us find out about the world in which we live and how we learn and remember things. This class will cover all sorts of issues you have wondered about for a long time. It may not answer all of your questions, and it may even raise a few new ones, but it will set you off on a new path of discovery.

This first chapter is necessarily quite general. It just seems logical to start off with at least a general discussion about what psychology is, where modern psychology has come from, and how psychologists go about their work. In many ways you can think of this first chapter as an outline, with details to be filled in as we go along. We will begin with an examination of a rather standard, "textbook," definition of psychology, looking at what it is that psychologists study and why we may call their endeavors scientific. Then we will take a brief glance at psychology's past. To understand the discipline as it exists today requires that we appreciate something of its origins and early efforts. Having traced the work of past psychologists, we add a thumbnail sketch of contemporary approaches to psychology.

If psychology is a science, it is so because psychologists use scientific methods in their efforts to understand affects (emotions), behaviors, and cognitions. As part of our introductory discussion, we need to consider those scientific methods in more detail. We will cover the methods used by psychologist-practitioners later, mostly in Chapter 13, which looks at treatment and therapy for psychological disorders. In this chapter, we focus on the methods used to increase our basic knowledge and understanding of psychological functions.

There is some technical terminology to deal with in this discussion of methodology, but please don't lose sight of the basic procedures. In essence, they are really very simple. And they all start with observations. As much as anything else, to be a good scientist, one must be observant.

We then consider what can be done with careful observations about affect, behavior, or cognitions so that they can be used to predict yet other behaviors. The process involved is called correlation, and we will encounter many correlational studies in the chapters that follow. Most of what is known in psychology today has been learned by doing experiments. As we will see, doing an experiment is fairly simple, but doing a good, carefully controlled experiment is a different matter.

As you study this chapter, keep in mind all of the other science classes you have taken. You soon will discover that the only real difference between psychology and all the other sciences is in their subject matter—not in their methodology.

TOWARD A DEFINITION

We will continue to expand on it throughout the rest of this text, but here is a definition of psychology that we can work with for now: **Psychology** is the science that studies behavior and mental processes. This rather simple definition may not tell you a whole lot just yet, but it does raise a couple of points worthy of your time.

The definition claims for psychology the status of "science." We will explore that claim in some detail later in this chapter. It also claims that the subject matter of this science is behavior and mental processes. Mostly, psychologists focus their study on the behaviors and/or the mental processes of their fellow humans. Although unstated in our definition, psychologists often study non-human animals as well. We will see many examples of psychological research that uses animals in an effort to help us

psychology the science that studies behavior and mental processes

understand human behaviors or mental processes. At the same time, some psychologists study the behavior and mental activity of animals simply because they find them interesting and worthy of study in their own right.

Before we get into what it means to say that psychology is a science, let's take a closer look at just what it is that psychologists study.

The Subject Matter of Psychology

Psychologists study behavior. **Behavior** is what organisms do—their actions and reactions. The behaviors of organisms are observable and measurable. If we wonder whether a rat will press a lever in some situation, we can put a rat in that situation and watch. If we are interested in your ability to draw a circle, we can ask her to draw one and observe her efforts. Observable, measurable behaviors offer an advantage as objects of study. They are *publicly verifiable.* That is, several observers (the public) can observe the same behavior and confirm its existence and nature. Several observers, for example, can determine whether a rat pressed a lever and even measure the extent, speed, and force with which it did so. We can agree that you correctly drew a circle and not a triangle or an oval. If you were interested in the extent to which violent movies might contribute to physical aggression, you would most likely focus on overt, observable, aggressive behaviors, rather than on how such movies make a viewer feel or think.

Psychologists study mental processes. As we shall soon see, psychology was actually defined as the science of mental processes (or "consciousness") when it first emerged as a separate discipline late in the nineteenth century.

There are two kinds of mental processes: cognitive and affective. **Cognitions** are mental events, such as perceptions, beliefs, thoughts, ideas, and memories. Cognitive processes include activities such as perceiving, thinking,

Courtesy of Fancy/Veer/Corbis.

knowing, deciding, and remembering. **Affect** is a term that refers to our feelings, emotions, or moods.

Here we have a scheme we will encounter repeatedly: the **ABC**s that make up the subject matter of psychology. Psychology is the science that studies **a**ffect, **b**ehavior, and **c**ognition. To say that we understand a person at any given time, we must understand what that person is feeling (A*ffect*), doing (B*ehavior*), and thinking (C*ognition*).

At this point you might be wondering why we are making a distinction between affect, behavior and cognition since they all seem to be so closely related. One reason is that behaviors are directly observable; affects and cognitions are not. We must infer your affects or from the observation of your behaviors. For example, we may infer that you are sad (an affective state) if we see you sitting slumped and crying. We may infer that jurors used certain pieces of evidence in coming to their decision (a cognitive process) on the basis of what they tell us in post-trial interviews.

Psychologists find it useful, and occasionally necessary, to define the subject matter of their investigation by using operational definitions. An **operational definition** defines concepts in terms of the procedures used to measure or

behavior what organisms do—their actions and reactions

affect one's feelings, moods, or emotions

cognitions mental events; such as perception, beliefs, thoughts, ideas, and memories

operational definition a definition of concepts in terms of the procedures used to measure or create those concepts

create them. A few examples will help. Suppose you wanted to examine the relationship between exposure to television and performance in school. Before you got very far, you would have to define just what you meant by "exposure to television," and you would have to specify how you would go about measuring "performance in school." That is, you would have to generate operational definitions for the issues you were going to study. You might, for example, define "exposure to television" in terms of the average number of hours spent watching television each week, measured for a 3-month period. "Performance in school" might simply be the grades earned in certain classes.

Even a condition as common as "hunger" needs an operational definition when we refer to it in science. For example, what if we wanted to compare the maze learning of hungry rats with rats that had plenty to eat? What do we mean by a "hungry rat"? We might provide an operational definition, specifying that—at least for our study—a hungry rat is one that you have deprived of food for 24 hours (thus defining a concept in terms of the procedures used to create it). Alternatively, we might have operationally defined a hungry rat as one that had lost 20 percent of its normal body weight.

As important as operational definitions are when considering behavior, they become even more important when we start considering mental processes (affects and cognitions). For example, how could you define "anxiety" in a study comparing the exam performance of students who experience either high or low levels of anxiety when they take tests? How might you define intelligence in a study designed to compare the intelligence of students who have had exposure to a preschool program with students who have not had such exposure? A person's intelligence and/or level of anxiety are internal, non-observable, mental events. Your only recourse is to use operational definitions and specify how we intend to measure these concepts. For example, you might operationally define anxiety in terms of observable, measurable changes in physiological reactions such as heart rate, blood pressure, and/or sweat gland activity. You might operationally define intelligence as a score on a certain psychological test.

Operational definitions have their limitations. They may oversimplify truly complex concepts (surely, there is more to "intelligence" than a test score). They also may allow for ambiguity (changes in some physiological reactions may reflect mental states other than just "anxiety"). Nonetheless, such definitions allow us to specify exactly how we are to measure those processes we are studying and, thus, help us to communicate clearly with others. We shall see many examples of operational definitions throughout this text.

BEFORE YOU GO ON

1. What is the definition of psychology?
2. What are the ABCs of psychology's subject matter?
3. What is an operational definition and why is it important in science?

Points to Ponder or Discuss
How would you operationally define "creativity"?
If you want to know how people really feel or what they think about some issue, what are some of the problems that might arise from simply asking them how they feel or what they think?

Psychology: Science and Practice

We have underscored the point that psychology takes a scientific approach to leaning about affect, behavior, and cognition. However, as you probably already know there are there are many ways to find out about our world and our selves. As you go through life, you encounter a wide range of experiences and form beliefs corresponding to these experiences. You use a number of strategies to help you understand and make sense of what you experience. Your beliefs about your world come from many sources. Some are formed as a matter of faith (for example, there is a God—or there isn't). Some beliefs come through tradition, passed on from generation to generation, accepted simply because "they say it is so." Sometimes we credit our beliefs about the human condition to common sense (for example, "absence makes the heart grow fonder." But then that same common sense tells us "out of sight, out of mind."). Some of our beliefs derive from art, literature, poetry, and drama (for example, some of our ideas about romantic love may have roots in Shakespeare's *Romeo and Juliet* or in the latest song from today's hottest recording star). All of these ways of learning about behaviors and mental processes have some value in certain contexts, but each has its pitfalls. What you believe about the existence of God, for example, might be very different from what someone else believes. Traditions from different cultural groups may lead to very different behaviors on the same issue (e.g., sanctioning suicide bombing or not).

Because of the pitfalls inherent in many of the everyday strategies we use to make sense of the world, psychologists prefer to rely on a different way of finding out about mental processes and behavior. Psychologists (as well as other scientists) maintain that there is a better way to understand the world around you: The application of the values and methods of science. As we shall see later,

Courtesy of Steve Cole/amanaimages/Corbis.

it is only through the application of scientific methods and principles can we arrive at scientific laws to help describe and explain mental processes and behavior.

Memories of previous biology or chemistry classes notwithstanding, the goal of science is make the world easier to understand (Mitchell & Jolley, 2001, p. 3). Scientists do this by generating scientific laws about their subject matter. Simply put, *scientific laws* are statements about one's subject matter can be verified—not on the basis of faith, tradition, or common sense, but through logical reasoning and observation (Herganhahn, 2001, p. 7). Generally, there are two criteria used to determine whether a particular discipline (like psychology) is a true **science**: 1) The discipline has an organized body of knowledge (a set of scientific laws), and 2) The discipline uses scientific methods to acquire that knowledge. So, how does psychology rate on these two criteria?

Over the years, psychologists have accumulated a great deal of information about the behaviors and mental processes of organisms, both human and non-human. Still, many intriguing questions remain unanswered. Some answers that psychology currently offers to very important, relevant questions are

Some of the beliefs that we acquire about the world "such as "If you get your head wet, you'll catch a cold!" come from tradition, passed on from one generation to another.

science a discipline that demonstrates 1) an organized body of knowledge (a set of scientific laws), and 2) the use of scientific methods

incomplete and tentative. For example, psychologists can tell us many of the "risk factors" that increase the chances of developing certain psychological disorders, but cannot say with assurance what really causes those disorders. And, although there has been considerable progress on the question, psychologists are not at all sure exactly how children go about acquiring their language skills. Not having all the answers can be frustrating, but that is part of the excitement of psychology today—there are still so many things to discover! The truth is, however, that psychologists have learned a lot, and what they know is reasonably well organized. In fact, you have in your hands one version of the organized body of knowledge that is psychology: your textbook.

It is important that you keep in mind that in a science an organized body of knowledge is always a work in progress. Like a living organism, the body of knowledge undergoes change when new information is discovered and old theories are discarded in favor of newer ones more consistent with new knowledge. For example, early in the history of psychology there was something called the "variability hypothesis" which suggested that male behavior was more highly variable than female behavior. Assumed cognitive and emotional differences between men and women were believed to relate to this difference in behavioral variability. Careful and incisive research by Leta Stetter Holingworth (1914), an early female pioneer in psychology, went a long way calling into question both the assumed variability discrepancy between men and women as well as the social significance of any variability that did exist. Holingworth's work (as well as the work of others in the field) led to a change in the body of knowledge on the subject.

Psychology meets the second requirement of a science because what is known in psychology has been learned through the application of **scientific methods**—methods of acquiring knowledge that involve observing a phenomenon, for-

mulating hypotheses about it, making additional observations, refining and re-testing hypotheses (Bordens & Abbott, 2008). Scientific methods reflect an attitude or an approach to discovery and problem-solving. It is "a process of inquiry, a particular way of thinking," rather than a prescribed set of procedures that must be followed rigorously (Graziano & Raulin, 1993, p. 2). Science involves an attitude of being both skeptical and open-minded about one's work (Mitchell & Jolley, 2001).

Although the actual techniques used by psychologists and other scientists may differ, there is a general set of principles that guide scientific research in all sciences, leading to a common process to uncover scientific knowledge. The process goes something like this: The scientist (e.g., the psychologist) makes some observations about his or her subject matter. For example, you might notice that children seem to be more physically violent after playing a violent role-playing video game. On the basis of your initial observation you develop a hypothesis. A **hypothesis** is a tentative explanation of some phenomenon that can be tested to establish its validity (Bordens & Abbott, 2008). Essentially, a hypothesis is an educated guess about one's subject matter. In psychology, hypotheses are stated in such a way as to link together two things: factors believed to control behavior and the behavior itself. In our example, you might develop the following hypothesis: "Playing violent video games leads to aggressive behavior."

No matter how sound or valid this hypothesis may sound to the scientist—or to others—it cannot be accepted as an explanation. The hypothesis must be tested under carefully controlled conditions. First, you must operationally define what "playing violent video games" is and what constitutes "aggressive behavior." New observations need to be made under controlled conditions to determine if the hypothesized relationship exists. If after such controlled observations it turns out that children

scientific methods techniques of acquiring knowledge that involve observing phenomena, formulating hypotheses about them, making additional observations, and refining and re-testing hypotheses

hypothesis a tentative explanation of a phenomenon that can be tested and either supported or rejected

who play violent video games *are* more aggressive than children who do not, the hypothesis has received support.

Playing violent video games => more aggressive behavior

One reality about scientific research is that once a hypothesis is confirmed, the research process does not stop. In our example, for instance, does playing *all* types of violent video games increase aggression and is this relationship true for children of *all* ages? Maybe only those video games that are highly realistic and encourage identification with characters increase aggressive behavior. It may be that only younger children are affected by playing violent video games. The point here is that finding support for your initial hypothesis often raises more questions than are answered.

Here is an important point to remember about science, the scientific method, and hypotheses. A scientific hypothesis may be rejected because there is no data to support it. Based on evidence, a hypothesis may be supported, but it cannot be "proven" as true. No matter how much evidence one finds to support a hypothesis, scientists—always open-minded—realize that new hypotheses may come along that do a better job of explaining what has been observed. Thus, psychologists avoid statements or claims that their research "proves" something. Rather, we couch our interpretations of results in terms of a hypothesis being supported or rejected. As an example, evidence once indicated that stress alone caused stomach ulcers. We now understand that biological infection causes many types of ulcers and stress has nothing to do with such ulcers.

The Science of Psychology and Pseudoscience

We have taken great pains to point out that psychology is a science because it adheres to the rules and methods employed by a science to acquire knowledge. Does this mean that everything you encounter relating to psychology

and its phenomena is based on careful scientific scrutiny? Unfortunately, the answer to this question is "no." There is a great deal of dross out there (dross means, "worthless, commonplace, or trivial" matters), especially in the popular media that is not based on careful scientific research. For example, is it really possible that you will experience greater physical and psychological well-being if you tape a patch to the bottom of your foot at night to draw out toxins from the body? Will you actually get more and higher quality sleep if you take that pill with a special blend of herbs and enzymes before you go to bed? And, can autistic children learn to communicate effectively through a "facilitator"? Many of the claims made in commercials and by seemingly legitimate psychologists are simply false because they are based on pseudoscientific claims and not on carefully conducted scientific studies.

The term **pseudoscience** literally means "false science." According to Robert Carroll (2006), "pseudoscience is [a] set of ideas based on theories put forth as scientific when they are not scientific." Some notorious examples of pseudoscience include phrenology (determining personality by reading the bumps on one's head), eye movement desensitization and reprocessing therapy (EMDR) (moving ones eyes back and forth rapidly while thinking about a problem), and astrology (using the position of the stars and planets to explain behavior and predict the future), and facilitated communication (using a trained communication facilitator to help an autistic person communicate with others).

Scott Lillenfeld (2005) lists several qualities that define a pseudoscience:

1. Using *ad hoc* hypotheses to explain away falsification of a pseudoscientific idea or claim. These hypotheses provide ways to escape criticism.
2. No mechanisms for self-correction and consequent stagnation of ideas or claims. This means that disconfirmed ideas are not corrected based on new information.

pseudoscience a set of ideas based on theories put forth as scientific when they are not

3. Reliance on a confirmational strategy rather than a disconfirmational one to test ideas or claims. Testimonials are often provided to confirm the worth of the product of procedure. Generally, this is not the best way to test the effectiveness of a claim.

4. Shifting the burden of proof to skeptics and critics away from the proponent of an idea or a claim. Proponents of a product often challenge skeptics to prove the claims wrong, when it is the job of the person making he claim to provide supporting evidence for claims made.

5. Over-reliance on anecdotal evidence and testimonials to support an idea or claim. Little or no empirical research is offered to support claims. Instead, personal anecdotal experience and glowing testimonials are used as evidence for a claim.

6. Avoidance of the peer review process that would scientifically scrutinize ideas and claims. Real scientists subject their evidence to review by experts in the field to assess its reliability. Pseudoscientific claims are usually not subject to such scrutiny.

7. A failure to build on an existing base of scientific knowledge with new information.

8. Excessive use of impressive sounding jargon that lends false credibility to ideas and claims. Such jargon may sound impressive, but it does little to support the claims,

9. Failure to specify conditions under which ideas or claims would not hold true.

Lillenfeld points out that no one of the above is sufficient to identify an idea or claim as pseudoscientific. However, the greater the number of the above qualities an idea or claim has, the more confident you can be that the idea or claim is based on pseudoscience and not legitimate science.

You should hone your skills on distinguishing between pseudoscientific claims and those backed up by actual science. This will put you in a better position to separate the gold from the dross in the popular media and make you a better more critical consumer of information in our culture. Besides, maybe you won't be so inclined to plop down your $19.95 (plus shipping and handling) for those Japanese foot pads that supposedly make you feel better; even if they do double your order if you call within the first 20 minutes of the offer! Caveat Emptor!!!

The Science of Psychology Applied

The goal of many psychologists is to use scientific methods to learn about their subject matter. But, while all psychologists are scientists, most are scientist-practitioners. Sometimes these psychologists are called "service providers." This means that they are not so much involved in discovering new laws about behavior and mental processes as they are in *applying* what is already known. Of those psychologists who are practitioners, most are clinical or counseling psychologists. Their goal is to apply what is known to help people deal with problems that affect their ability to adjust to the demands of their environments, including other people.

Psychological practitioners can be found in many places, not just clinical settings where therapy and treatment are conducted. Even before the dust settled after the World Trade Center bombings of September 2001, psychologists (and other mental health professionals) rushed to New York City to try to offer some relief from the pain and suffering of that horrendous trauma (Martin, 2002; Murray, 2002, pp. 30–33). Just four years later, mental health professionals became an integral part of the "recovery teams" assigned to the Southeast Gulf coast in response to Hurricane Katrina.

Other scientist-practitioners apply psychological principles to issues that arise in the workplace. These practitioners are industrial-organizational, or I/O psychologists. Sport psychologists use what they know about affect, behavior, and cognition to improve the performance of athletes. Other practitioners advise attorneys on how best to present arguments in the courtroom. Some intervene to reduce ethnic prejudices and to teach others how differing cultural values affect behaviors. Some establish programs to reduce roadside litter or increase the use of automobile safety belts, while still others help people train their pets. Educational and school psychologists work to apply what they know about learning, memory, and other cognitive processes to make teacher-student interactions as effective as possible. In short, psychology as a discipline is often about helping people, and it is about helping people in many ways—not just through counseling and therapy.

The science of psychology and the practice of psychology are not mutually exclusive endeavors. Many practitioners in clinical, industrial, or other applied settings are also active scientific researchers. And much of the research conducted in psychology originates as a response to the real-world problems of practitioners.

The Goals of Psychology

One of the lessons that psychologists learned long ago is that it is dangerous to generalize. Any statement that begins, "All psychologists . . ." is likely to be in error; there will be exceptions. Still, in the spirit of this first chapter, it may be useful to consider the goals of psychology as the science of behavior and mental processes. These are goals held by nearly all scientists.

1. *Observe and describe.* Science begins with the careful observation and description of its subject matter. Before we can explain what happened, we need a reliable (consistent) description of what happened. Before we can solve a problem, we need a complete description of the essential aspects of the problem. Before we can act

to minimize the prejudice shown to members of a minority group in a work setting, we need an objective description of the extent of current prejudice. Before we can work to improve the pattern of communication within a family, we need a complete description of what that communication pattern is now.

2. *Understand and explain.* Once psychologists agree on an adequate description of a behavior, affect, or cognition, their goal is to understand it. In most cases that means coming to know its likely causes. Scientists aim to know the reasons why an event occurs. Questions asking "why" something happens are difficult to answer. "Why do people become terrorists?" A minor reformation of that question might be, "Under what circumstances do people turn to terrorism?" As we said earlier, as evidence accumulates, we may come to support some hypotheses (for example, economic and social conditions, being the recipient of violence as precursors for terrorism) and eliminate others (for example, mental illness).

3. *Predict.* With the understanding of a phenomenon should come the ability to predict it. Prediction is a powerful goal for a science. "In these conditions, the terrorism is likely to continue, but under different circumstances, we may expect the terrorism to diminish." If we can *describe* what tasks we want an employee to do and *understand* what it takes to do those tasks well, we should be able to *predict* which applicants for the job are most likely to succeed at it.

4. *Influence and control.* If scientists can predict events, it seems logical that they can then influence or control them. Clearly, this is not always the case. For example, astronomers may describe, understand, and predict the movement of the planets, but it is not likely

(at least for now) that they can control them. Meteorologists may be able to predict (some) weather patterns, but they are not able to control the weather (to any significant degree). Influence or control is a particularly important goal for scientist-practitioners. If a therapist can explain why someone is feeling depressed, that therapist then would like to arrange circumstances that will alleviate that depression. If a child psychologist understands why a toddler is acting badly, then he or she can take appropriate actions to influence that toddler's behaviors. Your instructor would like to do everything possible to influence you to do your best in this class. Clearly, the ability to influence or control behaviors carries with it some serious risks and responsibilities. For this reason, psychologists adhere to strict standards of ethical behaviors—an issue we will address soon.

BEFORE YOU GO ON

4. Why can we make the claim that psychology is a science?
5. What is pseudoscience and why should you learn to distinguish it from real science?
6. What are "scientist-practitioners" in psychology?
7. What are the major goals of the science of psychology?

Points to Ponder or Discuss
In what ways have you seen the science of psychology applied to problems or issues in your own life? Find and example in the news media or in an advertisement of a claim made based on pseudoscience. Track down the basis for the claims made and see if you can find some real science on the issue or claim.

APPROACHES TO PSYCHOLOGY, PAST AND PRESENT

No two psychologists approach their subject matter in exactly the same way. Each brings unique experiences, expertise, values, and—yes—prejudices to the science of behavior and mental processes. This is true today and has always been the case. In this section, we add to our definition of psychology by considering some of the major perspectives, or approaches, that have emerged throughout psychology's history.

Psychology's Roots in Philosophy and Science

Psychology did not suddenly appear as the productive scientific enterprise we know today. The roots of psychology are found in philosophy and in science.

We credit philosophers for suggesting that it is reasonable to seek explanations of human behaviors at a human level. Early explanations tended to refer to God—or the gods. If someone suffered from fits of terrible depression, for example, it was believed that person had offended the gods. A few philosophers successfully argued that they might be able to explain why people behave, feel, and think as they do without constant reference to God's intentions in the matter. Ancient philosophers, such as Aristotle (384 BCE–322 BCE), began to think and write about many of the issues that interest modern psychologists: Perception, learning, memory, development, and psychopathology. These ancient philosophers laid the groundwork for the subject matter of modern psychology.

The French philosopher René Descartes (1596–1650) is a good example of another philosopher who had a profound effect on modern psychology. Descartes liked to think about thinking. As he "lay abed of a morning thinking" (which his schoolmaster allowed because he was so good at it), he pondered how the human body and mind produced the very process he was engaged in—thinking. Descartes saw the human body as a piece of machinery: intricate and complicated to be sure, but machinery nonetheless. If the body consisted essentially of tubes, gears, valves, and fluids, its operation must be subject to natural physical laws, and those laws could be discovered. This is the philosophical position known as **mechanism**.

Descartes went further. According to the doctrine of **dualism**, humans possess more than just a body: They have minds. It is likely, thought Descartes, that the mind similarly functions through the actions of knowable laws, but getting at these laws would be more difficult. Here's where Descartes had a truly important insight: We can learn about the mind because the mind and the body *interact* with each other. That interaction takes place in the brain. In these matters, Descartes' position is called **interactive dualism**: dualism because the mind and the body are separate entities and interactive because mind and body influence each other. Thus, René Descartes introduced the real possibility of understanding the human mind and how it works. It is worth mentioning here that we shall see (first in Chapter 2) examples of this process of mind and body interacting when consider how neuroscientists can now *see* physical changes occurring the brains of people engaged in mental, cognitive processes, thanks to new techniques of imaging the brain at work.

Nearly a hundred years later, a group of British thinkers brought that part of philosophy concerned with the workings of the mind very close to what was soon to become psychology. This group got its start from the work of John Locke (1632–1704). Locke was sitting with friends after dinner one evening discussing philosophical issues when it became clear that no one in the group really understood how the human mind understands anything, much less how it grasps complex philosophical issues. Locke announced that within a week he could provide the group with a short explanation of the nature of human understanding. What was to have been a simple exercise took Locke many years to finish, but it gave philosophers a new set of ideas to ponder.

One of Locke's major concerns was how we come to represent the world "out there" in the internal world of the mind. Others (including Descartes) had asked this question, and many assumed that we are born with many basic ideas about the world, ourselves, and, of course, God. Locke thought otherwise. He believed that we are born into the world with our minds quite empty, like blank slates. (The mind as a blank slate, or *tabula rasa*, was not new with Locke; Aristotle had introduced the notion in the third century BCE) So how does the mind come to be filled with all of its ideas and memories? Locke's one word answer was: experience. Locke and his followers came to be known as British **empiricists**, those who credit experience and observation as the source of mental life. Their philosophical doctrine is known as empiricism. Generally speaking, the major contribution of the early philosophers to the emergence of psychology as a science was to make psychology empirical.

Philosophers had gone nearly to the brink of defining a new science. They had raised intriguing questions about the mind, how it worked, where its contents (ideas) came from, how ideas could be manipulated, and how the mind and body might influence each other. Could the methods of science provide answers to any of the philosophers' questions? A few natural scientists and physiologists believed that they could.

mechanism associated with Descartes, the notion that if the body consists essentially of tubes, gears, valves, and fluids, its operation must be subject to physical laws, and those laws can be discovered

dualism associated with Descartes, the position that humans posses more than just a body; they have a mind

interactive dualism Descartes' position that the mind and body are separate entities and interact or influence each other; knowing the body provides knowledge of the mind

empiricists those who credit experience and observation as the source of mental life

During the nineteenth century, natural science was progressing on every front. Charles Darwin (1809–1882) was a naturalist/biologist. In 1859, just back from a lengthy sea voyage that took him to the Galapagos Islands, Darwin published *On the Origin of Species*, which laid out his ideas on evolution. Few non-psychologists were ever to have as much influence on psychology. Darwin confirmed that the human species was a part of the natural world of animal life. His work paved the way for the methods of science to be applied to understanding this creature of nature called the human being.

Darwin made it clear that all species of this planet are related to one another in a nearly infinite number of ways. After Darwin, scientists believed that what science discovered about the sloth, the ground squirrel, or the rhesus monkey might enlighten them about the human race. Another Darwinian concept that fit well into psychology was *adaptation*. Species will survive and thrive only to the extent that they can, over the years, adapt to their environments. Psychologists were quick to realize that adaptation to one's environment was often a mental as well as a physical process.

A year after the publication of *On the Origin of Species*, a German physicist, Gustav Fechner (1801–1887), published a volume that was unique as a physics text. Fechner applied his training in the methods of physics to the psychological processes involved in sensation. How are psychological judgments made about events in the environment? What, Fechner wondered, was the relationship between the physical characteristics of a stimulus and the psychological experience of that stimulus? For example, if the intensity of a light were doubled, would an observer see that light as twice as bright? Fechner found that the answer was no. Using the scientific procedures we would expect from a physicist, Fechner went on to determine the precise relationship between the physical aspects of stimuli and a person's psychological experience of those stimuli (Link, 1995). Fechner succeeded in applying the methods of science to a psychological question about the mind and experience.

The mid-1800s also found physiologists reaching a much better understanding of how the human body functions. By then it was known that nerves carried electrical messages to and from various parts of the body, that nerves serving vision are different from those serving hearing and the other senses, and that they also are different from those that activate the muscles and glands. Of all the biologists and physiologists of the nineteenth century, the one whose work is most relevant to psychology is Hermann von Helmholtz (1821–1894). In the physiology laboratory, Helmholtz performed experiments and developed theories on how long it takes the nervous system to react to stimuli, how we process information through our senses, and how we experience color. These are psychological issues, but in the mid-1800s there was no independent, recognized science of psychology.

BEFORE YOU GO ON

8. How did the philosophies of Descartes and Locke prepare the way for psychology?
9. What contributions did Darwin and early physiologists make to the emergence of psychology?

A Point to Ponder or Discuss
If John Locke had not "invented" empiricism or if Charles Darwin had not "invented" evolution, would they have been invented by someone else, sooner or later?

The Early Years: Structuralism and Functionalism

It is often claimed that the science of psychology began in 1879, when Wilhelm Wundt (1832–1920) opened his laboratory at the University of Leipzig. Wundt had been trained to practice medicine, had studied physiology, and had served as a laboratory assistant to the great Helmholtz. Wundt also held an academic position in philosophy. Here was a scientist-philosopher with an interest in such psychological processes as sensation, perception, attention, word-associations, and emotions.

Although we could credit others with getting psychology started (e.g., Fechner or Helmholtz), Wundt was the first researcher who clearly saw his work as the start of a new, separate scientific endeavor. He wrote in the preface of the first edition of his *Principles of Physiological Psychology* (1874), "The work I here present is an attempt to mark out a new domain of science."

For Wundt, the new domain of psychology was to be the scientific study of the mind. Wundt and his students wanted to systematically describe the elements of mental life, the bits and pieces of conscious experience. Beyond that, Wundt wanted to see how the elements of thought were related to one another and to events in the physical environment—the latter notion picked up from the work of Fechner. Under carefully controlled laboratory conditions, Wundt's hypotheses were tested and then re-tested. Because the scientists in Wundt's laboratory were mostly interested in describing the structure of the mind and its operations, Wundt's approach to psychology became known as **structuralism** (although Wundt himself did not call his psychology "structuralism").

As Wundt's new laboratory was flourishing in Germany, an American philosopher at Harvard University, William James (1842–1910), was making known his opposition to the type of psychology being studied in Leipzig.

James agreed that psychology should study consciousness and use scientific methods. He defined psychology as "the science of mental life," a definition very similar to Wundt's. However, he thought the German-trained psychologists were off-base trying to discover the contents and structures of the human mind. James argued that consciousness could not be broken down into elements. He believed consciousness to be dynamic, a stream of events, personal, changing, and continuous. According to James, psychology should be concerned not with the structure of the mind, but with its function. Taking Darwin's lead, James thought the focus of psychology should be on the practical uses of mental life, because the survival of species requires that a species adapt to its environment. James and his followers wondered how the mind functions to help organisms adapt and survive in the world.

James's practical approach to psychology found favor in North America, and a new type of psychology emerged, largely at the University of Chicago. Psychologists there continued to focus on the mind, but emphasized its adaptive functions. This approach became known as **functionalism**. Functionalists still relied on experimental methods and introduced the study of animals to psychology, again reflecting Darwin's influence. Indeed, one of the most popular textbooks of this era was *The Animal Mind* (1908) by Margaret Floy Washburn (1871–1939), the first woman to be awarded a Ph.D. in psychology—from Cornell University in 1894. She addressed questions of animal consciousness and intelligence. Functionalism was open to a wide range of topics—as long as they related in some way to mental life, adaptation, and practical application. Child, abnormal, educational, social, and industrial psychology all can be traced back to functionalism.

In the early days of American psychology, earning a graduate-level education or any academic appointment was

Courtesy of Hulton Archive/Stringer/Getty Images.

Wilhelm Wundt (1832–1920)

structuralism Wundt's approach to psychology, committed to describing the structures of the mind and their operation

functionalism the approach to psychology that focuses on the mind, but emphasizes its adaptive functions

very difficult for women, no matter how capable (Furumoto & Scarborough, 1986; Scarborough & Furumoto, 1987). Still, one woman, Mary Calkins (1863–1930), so impressed William James that he allowed her into his classes, although Harvard would not allow her to enroll formally, nor would Harvard award her a Ph.D., for which she had met all requirements. Calkins was offered her degree from Radcliffe College, essentially the women's equivalent of Harvard. Calkins respectfully declined the degree because she felt she should have received the degree from Harvard where she did her graduate work. Calkins was awarded honorary degrees from both Columbia University, in 1909, and Smith College, in 1910. Mary Calkins went on to do significant experimental work on human learning and memory and, in 1905, was the first woman elected president of the American Psychological Association. Christine

Ladd-Franklin (1847–1930) received her Ph.D., but not until 40 years after it was earned and Johns Hopkins University lifted its ban on awarding advanced degrees to women (in 1926). In the interim, she authored an influential theory on how humans perceive color.

In the latter part of the nineteenth century and early twentieth century bright young students were drawn to the science of psychology. During this time, new academic departments and laboratories began to prosper throughout the United States and Canada. Psychology was well under way as the scientific study of the mind, its structures, or its functions. However, the young science of psychology was about to be revolutionized by the new thinking of John Watson early in the twentieth century. John Watson turned psychology's attention from the study of the mind to the study of behavior.

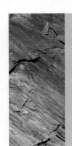

BEFORE YOU GO ON

10. Compare and contrast the structuralism of Wundt with the functionalism of James.

A Point to Ponder or Discuss
Can you think of any reasons why structuralism happened to flourish in Germany, while functionalism was so much more popular in the United States?

Behaviorism

When John B. Watson (1878–1958) was growing up, his devoutly religious mother pushed him toward becoming a minister. While Watson was a student at Furman University his mother died, removing one of the main pressures he felt to enter the ministry. Instead, Watson enrolled instead as a graduate student in psychology at the University of Chicago. As an undergraduate, he had read about the new science of psychology, and he thought Chicago, where many leading functionalists were, would be the best place to study. He was soon

disappointed, however. It turned out he had little sympathy or talent for attempts to study mental processes with scientific methods. Even so, he stayed on at the university as a psychology major, studying the behavior of animals, eventually earning his Ph.D. in psychology.

With his new Ph.D. in hand, Watson went to Johns Hopkins University. Shortly after his arrival, he changed both the focus and definition of psychology almost single-handedly. In 1913, Watson published the article *Psychology as the behaviorist views it,* which is also known as the "behaviorist manifesto." In this article, Watson defined psychology in the following way: "Psychology as the behaviorist views it is a purely objective experimental branch of natural science" (Watson, 1913, p. 158). Watson argued further that if psychology was to become a mature, productive science, it had to give up the preoccupation with consciousness and mental life and concentrate instead on events that could be observed and measured directly. He felt that psychology should give up the study of the mind (which could not be observed directly) and study behavior (which could be observed directly). His new approach became known as **behaviorism.**

Watson and the behaviorists never denied that people think or have ideas or feelings. They said only that such processes were not the proper subjects of scientific investigation. After all, no one can share the thoughts or feelings of someone else. Watson argued that the study of psychology should leave private, mental events to the philosophers and theologians and instead make psychology as rigorously scientific as possible. Watson once referred to behaviorism as "common sense grown articulate. Behaviorism is a study of what people do" (Watson, 1926, p. 724).

Throughout the first half of the twentieth century behaviorism became the dominant force in psychology. No one epitomized the behaviorist approach to psychology more than B.F. Skinner (1904–1990). Skinner took Watson's ideas and spent a long and productive career in psychology trying to demonstrate that we can predict and control the behaviors of organisms by studying the relationships between their observable responses and the circumstances under which those responses occur (Lattal, 1992). What mattered most for Skinner was how changes in the environment caused changes in observable behavior.

Behaviorists did not address the question of why a rat turns left in a maze by talking about what the rat wanted or what the rat was thinking at the time.

Rather, they tried to specify the environmental conditions (the presence of food, perhaps) under which a rat is likely to turn left. For more than 50 years, Skinner consistently held to the argument that psychology should be defined as "the science of behavior" (Skinner, 1987; 1990).

Wundt's structuralism, the functionalism of the early American psychologists, and the behaviorism of Watson were academic approaches to psychology. Ever since the late 1800s, other approaches to the science of behavior and mental processes have had a significant impact. Some were influential in the past and continue to influence the way we think about psychology today. We will briefly consider three.

Psychoanalytic Psychology

Early in the twentieth century, Sigmund Freud (1856–1939), a practicing physician in Vienna, became intrigued with what were then called "nervous disorders." He was struck by how little was known about those disorders. As a result, he chose to specialize in the identification and treatment of "nervous disorders," a discipline now called *psychiatry.*

Freud was not a laboratory scientist. Most of his insights about the mind came from his careful observations of his patients and himself. Freud's works were particularly perplexing to the behaviorists. Just as they were arguing against a psychology that concerned itself with consciousness, here came Freud declaring that we are often subject to forces of which we are not aware. Our feelings, actions, and thoughts (A, B, and C again) are often under the influence of the unconscious mind, wrote Freud, and many of our behaviors are expressions of instinctive strivings. Freud's views were completely at odds with Watson's. We call the approach that traces its origin to Sigmund Freud and that emphasizes innate strivings and the unconscious mind **psychoanalytic psychology.** Psychoanalytic psychology can be viewed as the beginning of modern

behaviorism the approach to psychology, first associated with Watson, that claims psychology should give up the study of the mind and focus on observable behaviors

psychoanalytic psychology associated with Freud, the approach to psychology that emphasizes innate strivings and the unconscious mind

Courtesy of Roger Ressmeyer/Corbis.

Carl Rogers (1902–1987)

humanistic psychology the approach to psychology that takes the position that the individual, or self, should be of central concern

gestalt psychology the approach to psychology that focuses on perception, concerned with how we select and organize information from the outside world

clinical psychology. As you might imagine, we shall have much to say about Freud and psychoanalysis later.

Humanistic Psychology

In many respects, humanistic psychology arose as a reaction against behaviorism and psychoanalysis (Clay, 2002). The leaders of this approach were Carl Rogers (1902–1987) and Abraham Maslow (1908–1970). **Humanistic psychology** takes the position that the individual, or the self, should be the central concern of psychology. In other words, if psychologists concern themselves only with stimuli in the environment and observable responses to those stimuli, they dehumanize psychology by leaving out the person. Humanists critiqued the behaviorists by noting that caring, intention, concern, will, love, and hate are real phenomena and worthy of scientific investigation whether they can be directly observed or not. Humanists believed attempts to understand people without considering such processes were doomed. To the humanistic psychologists, the Freudian reliance on instincts was too controlling. Our biology notwithstanding, we are—or can be—in control of our destinies. Rogers, Maslow, and their intellectual heirs emphasized the possibility of personal growth and achievement. This approach led Rogers to develop a system of psychotherapy and Maslow to develop a theory of human motivation.

Gestalt Psychology

In the first quarter of the twentieth century, a group of German scientists took an approach to psychology that was decidedly different from that of Wundt, James, Watson, or Rogers. Under the leadership of Max Wertheimer (1880–1943), this approach became known as Gestalt psychology. **Gestalt psychology** focuses on perception, concerned in particular with how we select and organize information from the outside world. "Gestalt" is a German word difficult to translate literally into English. It means roughly "configuration," "whole," or "totality." In general terms, if you can see the big picture—if you can focus on the forest rather than the trees—you have formed a gestalt. Gestalt psychologists argued that to analyze perception or consciousness into discrete, separate entities would destroy the very essence of what was being studied. "The whole is more than the sum of its parts," they said. When we look at a drawing of a cube, we do not see the individual lines, angles, and surfaces, but naturally combine these elements to form a whole, a gestalt, which we experience as a cube. The Gestalt school of psychology was important in that it focused attention away from breaking consciousness into component parts or studying only observable behavior. It led psychology to view psychological events such as perception in a more holistic way.

See Table 1.1 for a brief summary of this discussion.

BEFORE YOU GO ON

11. What are some of the assumptions or basic ideas that typify behaviorism, psychoanalysis, humanistic psychology, and Gestalt psychology?

A Point to Ponder or Discuss
Suppose that Sigmund Freud, John Watson, Carl Rogers, and Max Wertheimer met by chance on a train. What do you think they might have talked about? On what would they have agreed and on what would they have disagreed?

TABLE 1.1

INTERACTIVE DUALISM	René Descartes	the body is mechanical; the mind can be known	*Psychology's history—a brief summary.*
EMPIRICISM	John Locke	experience fills the mind with ideas	
EVOLUTION	Charles Darwin	all organisms are related and adapt to the environment	
PHYSICS	Gustav Fechner	finds lawful relation between stimuli and experience	
PHYSIOLOGY	von Helmholtz	science addresses psychological questions	
STRUCTURALISM	Wilhelm Wundt	establishes science of mind— structure and operations	
FUNCTIONALISM	William James	how the mind functions to help us adapt	
BEHAVIORISM	John B. Watson	psychology is the science of behavior	
PSYCHOANALYSIS	Sigmund Freud	innate drives and levels of consciousness	
HUMANISTIC PSYCH.	Carl Rogers	the self, or person, is what really matters	
GESTALT PSYCHOLOGY	Max Wertheimer	focus on perception, selection, and organization	

SPOTLIGHT
ON DIVERSITY

Minority Pioneers

The early history of psychology usually reads as if only white males were involved in the enterprise. The contributions of women or minorities (and there were many) often went unacknowledged (Minton, 2000). Within the last 25 years, historians of psychology have identified several psychologists whose lives and efforts enriched the discipline. Here, we will briefly list just a few.

Francis Cecil Sumner (1895–1954)

The first African American to receive a Ph.D. in psychology was Francis Sumner (Sawyer, 2000). He was the last graduate student of the well-known and respected functional psychologist, G. Stanley Hall, at Clark University in Massachusetts. Sumner's doctoral dissertation was on the "Psychoanalysis of Freud and Jung." He received his degree in 1920 (Guthrie, 1998; Houston, 1990). Sumner was proficient in five foreign languages, was interested in the psychology of religion, and was a pioneer in expanding opportunities for African Americans in education. He published two articles on strategies for getting more young black students to pursue graduate education. (And a major thrust of his argument was for better, segregated opportunities for graduate education.) After a teaching stint at the West Virginia Collegiate Institute, he became Chair of the Department of Psychology at Howard University in Washington, D.C. Howard soon became a leading institution for the training of black psychologists.

Kenneth Clark (1914–2005) and Mamie Clark (1917–1983)

Kenneth Clark was born in the Panama Canal Zone, but when he was five years old, he moved with his mother and younger sister to Harlem in New York City. Clark attended Howard University, where he was a student of Francis Sumner. At Howard, Clark led demonstrations against segregation and met Mamie Phipps, who was to become his wife and collaborator. In 1940, Kenneth Clark became the first African American to receive a Ph.D. in psychology from Columbia University, and in 1943, Mamie Clark was the second. Kenneth took an academic position at City College of New York, where he remained until he retired in 1975. In 1970, he became the first black person to become president of the American Psychological Association. Mamie never secured an academic appointment. About her search for employment, she said the following: "It soon became apparent to me that a black female with a Ph.D. in psychology was an unwanted anomaly in New York City in the early 1940s" (O'Connell & Russo, 2001, p. 271).

A major focus of the Clarks' research was the development of self-esteem and self-perceptions of young children. In a series of studies (Clark & Clark, 1939, 1947), they demonstrated that black children showed a preference for white dolls over dolls of color, even as early as the age of three. Most of the black children said that the white dolls looked "nice" and that the black dolls looked "bad." The Clarks concluded that these preferences were due to racial segregation. These oft-cited works were significant factors in the landmark 1954 Supreme Court case of *Brown v. Board of Education* (Tomes, 2004). Kenneth Clark died on May 5, 2005. Ronald Levant, President of the American Psychological Association, was invited to speak at the funeral. Noting that Clark was APA's first non-Caucasian president, Levant described Kenneth Clark as the psychologist who ". . . had the most profound, dramatic and lasting impact on the twentieth century" (Levant, 2005, p. 5).

Joseph L. White (1932–)

Joseph White (a 2003 Helms Award recipient) earned his Ph.D. in 1961 from Michigan State in clinical psychology. He was a pioneer in the field of Black psychology and is often referred to as the "Godfather of Black psychology." In 1970, he published an article in *Ebony* magazine entitled "Toward a Black Psychology," which challenged traditional psychological theories and truly initiated the era of African American and ethnic psychology. Dr. White met with the executive council of APA to remove or reform the all-too-common conclusion in psychology texts that blacks were an inferior race. He demanded that more blacks be admitted to doctoral programs. Dr. White is the author of several papers and three books: *The Psychology of Blacks: An African-American Perspective* (1990; 1984); *The Troubled Adolescent* (1989); *Black Man Emerging: Facing the Past and Seizing a Future in America* (1998). Joseph White has enjoyed a distinguished career in the field of psychology and mental health as a teacher, administrator, mentor, clinical supervisor, writer, consultant, and practicing psychologist. He sought to encourage African Americans and Hispanics to obtain a college education. He is currently Professor Emeritus of Psychology and Psychiatry at the University of California.

Courtesy of Robert Maass/Corbis.

Kenneth Clark (1914–2005)

Robert V. Guthrie (1932–2005)

Just a few weeks after he was born in Chicago, Robert Guthrie moved with his family to Richmond, and then to Lexington, Kentucky. Growing up in the segregated South had a profound influence on Guthrie, who, at the time, thought his career options were severely limited (O'Conner, 2001). He attended Florida A&M University, spent a stint in the military, and after returning from the conflict in Korea, resumed his education at Florida A&M. Following another seven years in the military, he moved his family to San Diego, California, where he earned his Ph.D. in 1970 from the United States International University. After serving as an assistant professor at the University of Pittsburgh for three years and as research psychologist studying multicultural issues at the National Institute of Education in Washington, D.C., Guthrie returned to San Diego to work at the Navy Personnel Research and Development Center in 1976. In was in that year that his book, *Even the Rat Was White: A Historical View of Psychology*, first appeared (Guthrie, 1976/2004). It was a remarkable text. African-American psychologists and students told Guthrie that his book was "heaven-sent," although mainstream psychology rather ignored it. "They thought that I was being somewhat revolutionary and divisive, driving a wedge between black and white psychologists," Guthrie explained (Cross, 1998). That attitude has changed, and *Even the Rat Was White* is now hailed as an "excellent piece of histiography that offers a good, hard look at racism in the development of psychology" (Cross, 1998). Among other things, Guthrie's book tells about the lives and work of African-American psychologists who otherwise might have been forgotten.

George Isidore Sanchez (1906–1972)

Born in Albuquerque, George Sanchez worked as a teacher, principal, and administrator in Bernalillo County, New Mexico, from 1923 until 1930, when he began graduate school at the University of Texas. He was the first Hispanic male to receive an Ed.D. degree from the University of California at Berkeley, in 1934. Sanchez ("the founder of Chicano psychology") expanded on work he had begun while working on his master's degree on the use of standardized tests for Spanish-speaking children (Tevis, 2001). His major work on this topic was a critical review of group differences and Spanish-speaking children (Guthrie, 1976/2004). He was a major force in the American Southwest, working for equalization of school funding for all children. At the University of Texas, he served as Chairman of the Department of History and Philosophy of Education and as Director of the Center for International Affairs. He directed a Carnegie Foundation survey of Taos County, which later resulted in his book *Forgotten People: A Study of New Mexicans.*

Psychologists have come to celebrate the contributions of women and minority groups to the field of psychology. Interest in these groups and in their contributions has grown steadily since the mid-1980s. Psychology in the late twentieth century is no longer Eurocentric, but more importantly, psychology increasingly emphasizes gender, race, culture, ethnicity, and class. Today, psychologists are working to replace the old image in the field of psychology with a new one that is more culturally inclusive.

Contemporary Approaches to the Science of Psychology

Psychology has come a long way since those few students gathered around Wilhelm Wundt in his laboratory back in the late 1800s. At the end of the twentieth century, there were over 500,000 psychologists at work in the world, approximately 166,000 employed in the United States in 2006 (Bureau of Labor Statistics, 2008). Organized in 1892, the American Psychological Association (APA) is the oldest professional organization of psychologists. The APA claims about 150,000 members and lists 55 divisions (including divisions of General Psychology, Teaching of Psychology, Military Psychology, Psychotherapy, Health Psychology, International Psychology, Aesthetics and the Arts, and the like) to which its members may belong (American Psychological Association, 2008). The Association for Psychological Science (APS), formed in 1988 and currently has approximately 18,000 members dedicated to the advancement of scientific psychology (Association for Psychological Science, 2008).

Each psychologist brings a unique set of personal experiences, training, and values to the science and practice of psychology. What unites them all, of course, is the search for a better understanding of affects, behaviors, and cognitions. Additionally, there are a few major, general approaches or perspectives that psychologists take to their research. Here we review some of the more common approaches that guide psychologists in their work. Some have a history dating to psychology's earliest days, while others are more contemporary. Approaches used by the scientist-practitioners of psychology (such as those engaged in treatment and therapy for psychological disorders, industrial/organizational psychology, environmental psychology, and sport psychology) will be covered in later chapters.

The biological approach. Underlying all of our thoughts, feelings, and behaviors is a living biological organism, filled with tissue, fibers, nerves, and chemicals. Psychologists who take a biological perspective seek to explain psychological functioning in terms of genetics and the operation of the nervous system, the brain in particular. The argument is that, ultimately, every single thing you do, from the simplest blink of an eye to the deepest, most profound thought you've ever had, can be explained by biochemistry. To be sure, experience may modify or alter one's biological structure (Newcombe, 2002). For example, what are the changes that take place in our brains as memories are formed? Psychologists who subscribe to a biological point of view might look at cases of violence in our schools as a reflection of an inherited predisposition, some sort of hormonal imbalance, and/or a problem with the activity of an area deep in the center of the brain known to be involved in raw, primitive emotions, such as fear and rage.

The evolutionary approach. Yes, psychologists with this point of view are closely allied with those who have a biological perspective. However, they take a broader, long-range view of human and animal behaviors. Although this tradition can trace its roots to Darwin, it is one of the newer perspectives in psychology (Buss, 1999; de Waal, 1999; 2002). Here, the argument is that we should try to explain behaviors and mental processes in terms of how they promote the species' survival and how they help members of the species adapt to their environments. It is something of an oversimplification, but the point is that we do what we do in order to pass our genes along to those who will survive us. We are altruistic (we voluntarily help others) on the chance that they will help us later or that they will assist our offspring (McAndrew, 2002; Penner, et al., 2005).

An evolutionary approach may suggest that members of the human race are becoming more aggressive (even violent), because in the long run, aggressive behaviors are adaptive.

The cognitive approach. We have seen that cognitions include such mental contents as ideas, beliefs, knowledge, and understanding. Psychologists who favor a cognitive approach argue that the focus of our attention should be on how an organism processes information about itself and the world in which it lives. Just what *do* we believe? Why do we seem to remember some things, yet forget others? How do we make decisions or solve problems? How do humans acquire their language? What is intelligence? Now that's quite a list of questions, but it only scratches the surface of the issues that cognitive psychologists pursue. As a subfield of psychology, cognitive psychology is one of the fastest growing (Anderson, 2000).

The developmental approach. Developmental psychologists look at the organism as it grows and develops throughout its lifespan. Some focus their study on children, some are interested in the challenges of adolescence, while others look for patterns and individual differences throughout adulthood. As the number of older persons in the population increases, more psychologists are shifting their concern to older adults, their strengths as well as their weaknesses. Psychologists who favor this approach combine the perspectives and methods of many other types of psychologists. This is, they may be interested in several different psychological processes, such as learning and memory, solving problems, making social adjustments, sensing and perceiving the world, reacting to stress, and so on. What unites the scientists who follow this approach is the focus on describing and understanding the factors that influence how these processes change through the lifespan of the individual.

The cross-cultural approach. If psychologists understood all there was to know about the affects, behaviors, and cognitions of young, white, middle-class American males, they would know a lot—surely, more than they know now. But, would we not still have to ask, "What about females? What about older adults? What about the poor? What about Mexicans or Australians or Germans?" Is there any reason to believe that what is true of young, middle-class American males is also true of elderly, poor, Jordanian women? Of course not. Recognizing the importance of such differences is the thrust of the cross-cultural approach to psychology (Hall, 1997; Lehman, Chiu, & Schaller, 2004; Shweder, 1999; Triandis & Suh, 2002). Even very basic psychological issues, such as what an individual finds reinforcing or what motivates an individual to action, vary enormously from culture to culture. How East Asians and Americans perceive and account for cause-and-effect relationships may be significantly different (Norenzayan & Nisbett, 2000). How people of different cultures define mental illness and the treatment or therapy options that are available differ significantly from one culture to another (Lopez, 2000; Triandis, 1996).

Recognizing the people live in a variety of cultural and ethnic environments, one of the goals of cross-cultural psychology is to examine cultural sources of psychological diversity.

Courtesy of Phillipe Lissac/Godong/Corbis.

Positive psychology. Two psychologists, Martin Seligman and Mihaly Csikszentmihalyi, recently introduced an approach to psychology that is qualitatively different from those mentioned so far. They, and a growing group of colleagues, call this new perspective "positive psychology" (Aspinwall & Staudinger, 2003; Buss, 2000, Myers, 2000; Seligman & Csikszentmihalyi, 2000). On the surface, the approach seems simple. For too long, psychologists followed the medical perspective of looking to diagnose, understand, and "fix" that which is "wrong." This new approach says that instead of a focus on mental illness, we should focus on mental health. Instead of trying to understand depression, we should seek to understand happiness. What leads to a sense of well-being, to enjoyment, to individuals and communities that thrive? Positive psychology asks about the kinds of families that produce children who flourish, the kinds of work situations that lead to productivity and worker satisfaction. Seligman says that there are three pillars to positive psychology, "First, the study of subjective well-being—life satisfaction and contentment when about the past; happiness, joy, and exuberance when about the present; and optimism, faith and hope when about the future . . . The second pillar is the study of positive individual traits—intimacy, integrity, leadership, altruism, vocation and wisdom, for example. Third,

the study of positive institutions" (Quoted in Volz, 2000).

Here is an example of research consistent with the goals of positive psychology. Psychologists conducted a study designed to determine which variables were most associated with being very happy as an undergraduate (Diener & Seligman, 2002). The study concluded that very happy people had stronger romantic and other social relationships and were a bit more extroverted and agreeable. They did not exercise any more than average, nor did they participate in religious activities any more often than others. Although the happiest undergraduates occasionally experienced a negative mood, they experienced positive feelings most of the time. The study found the very happiest college students sampled were highly social, spending less time alone than those in the other groups.

This is quite enough for now. You get the point: There are many ways to approach the scientific study of behavior and mental processes. No one way is best. And few psychologists adhere to only one perspective. Most understand the benefits of these approaches. You often will encounter these approaches as you continue your study of psychology. Now let's look at those methods used by psychologists that help to qualify psychology as a science.

BEFORE YOU GO ON

12.   Briefly describe the thrust of the approaches to psychology identified as biological, evolutionary, cognitive, developmental, cross-cultural, and positive.

A Point to Ponder or Discuss
Which of the approaches discussed in this section would you adopt if you were a psychologist?

SPOTLIGHT
ON DIVERSITY

Women in Psychology

During the first 50 years of psychology's existence as a science, prominent women in the field were few. Those who survived in the discipline did so largely on the fringes. This is certainly not the case of the role of women in psychology now. Acknowledging that the danger of making such lists (it being so very easy to overlook someone), we here present an alphabetical list of some of the women who guided and built the science of psychology over the past half-century. Many of these women are still very active in the field, and their contributions to psychology are mentioned elsewhere in this text.

Mary D. S. Ainsworth

Mary D. Salter Ainsworth was born in Ohio, but grew up in Toronto, where her family moved in 1918. She became interested in psychology upon reading William McDougall's *Character and the Conduct of Life* in high school. She earned her Ph.D. in developmental psychology from the University of Toronto in 1939. She married Leonard Ainsworth in 1950 and moved to England. She worked with John Bowlby on the devastating effects of parent-child separations, which had become so common in England during World War II. In 1955, she joined the faculty of Johns Hopkins University and moved to the University of Virginia in 1974, from which she retired in 1984. Her best-known work is on the attachments—and the sense of security—that develop between infants and those who care for them. She developed a laboratory for observing infants and parent/caregiver attachment. Her research revealed four patterns of attachment: secure, avoidant, ambivalent and disorganized.

Anne Anastasi

Often referred to as the "guru of psychological testing," Anne Anastasi was born in New York City and entered college as a math major. Her interests in individual differences prompted a switch to psychology. She combined her background in mathematics with her interests in psychology and earned a Ph.D. from Columbia University in two years, graduating in 1930. She became most interested in how culture and experience affect a person's intellectual development. She provided guidance to generations of psychologists about the use and misuse of psychological tests, intelligence tests in particular. First published in 1954, her textbook *Psychological Testing* is a classic. The book was revised for a seventh edition in 1996 and has become a classic in psychological testing. Dr. Anastasi has contributed a great deal to test construction, evaluation and test interpretation.

Linda Bartoshuk

Linda Bartoshuk is Professor of Surgery and Psychology at the Yale University School of Medicine. She did her undergraduate work at Carleton College and received her Ph.D. from Brown University in 1966. She is one of the world's foremost experts on the sense of taste. She is particularly interested in genetic variations in the ability to taste, and she has identified a range of abilities from non-tasters to super-tasters, and has studied the relationship between the senses of taste and pain. She has also done considerable research on the various pathologies of taste and how taste receptors in the mouth are related to the brain's processing of taste. Most recently, her research has focused on super-tasters' taste buds and heightened taste sensations that affect food preferences. Dr. Bartoshuk has conducted research on oral pain and oral analgesia in cancer patients with oral lesions.

Sandra Lipsitz Bem

Sandra Bem was born in Pittsburgh and received her bachelor's degree in psychology from Carnegie Mellon University. She went to the University of Michigan for her graduate The Science of Psychology and Its Research Methods 19 studies and was awarded her Ph.D. in developmental psychology at the age of 23. After a return to Carnegie Mellon with her husband Daryl, they moved to Stanford University from 1971 to 1978. Next they headed for Ithaca, New York, where—among other things—Sandra Bem became the Director of Women's Studies at Cornell University. She is best known for her work on gender identity and the development of gender roles. She wrote the *Bem Sex Role Inventory (BSRI)*, which assesses both masculine and feminine characteristics. Bem noted that most people have *both* characteristics to some degree. She coined the term "androgynous" for those individuals who have a balance, or near-balance, of masculine and feminine traits. She has written extensively on gender, but she published one of her most acclaimed works in 1993, *The Lenses of Gender: Transforming the Debate on Sexual Inequality.*

Eleanor Gibson

Eleanor Gibson spent her academic career at Cornell University, often working in collaboration with her husband James. She received her Ph.D. in experimental psychology from Yale University in 1966. She had always been intrigued by the writings of the Gestalt psychologists and committed to the study of perception from the very start of her career. She focused on the development of perception—a process of making the whole into a collection of distinct and separate parts. Her most famous contribution was the creation of the "visual cliff" (in collaboration with Richard Walk). The "visual cliff" is a solid glass tabletop below which half of the surface appeared to drop off to the floor. Gibson and Walk discovered that children as young as six months old would refuse to cross over the half of the surface that appeared to drop off—no matter how much they were encouraged or enticed. The researchers concluded that these children could perceive the apparent depth, and that depth perception is not a learned skill.

Carol Gilligan

Born in New York City, Carol Gilligan majored in literature at Swarthmore College, but she switched to psychology at Radcliffe University where she earned a master's degree in clinical psychology. She was awarded a Ph.D. in social psychology from Harvard University in 1964. While at Harvard, Gilligan studied with Lawrence Kohlberg, who was working on his stage theory of moral development. Her research led Gilligan to believe that men and women approach moral dilemmas in a different way. According to Gilligan, one gender is not necessarily any more "moral" than the other, but there are differences in the way the genders perceive what is right or wrong, proper or improper. Her most cited writing is *In a Different Voice: Psycho-*

logical Theory and Women's Development. This work has been hotly debated ever since it was published in 1982. Gilligan remains at Harvard, still very active in the Gender Studies program. Her book *Meeting at the Crossroads: Women's Psychology and Girls' Development* was written in 1992.

Elizabeth F. Loftus

One of the most recognized names in contemporary psychology is Elizabeth Loftus, Distinguished Professor of Psychology and Social Behavior at the University of California at Irvine. Born in Los Angeles, Loftus received her B.A. in math and psychology in 1966. She became intrigued by human memory as a graduate student at Stanford University, which awarded her a Ph.D. in 1970. Loftus's major contributions to psychology have been on eyewitness testimony, the fallibility of long-term memories, and the notion of "repressed memories." Her expertise in these socially important areas has often thrust her into the limelight. She has testified on the fallibility of memory in more than 200 trials. She has also published 19 books and nearly 200 articles on the subject of the unreliability of personal memory retrieval.

Eleanor Maccoby

Any discussion among psychologists about sex roles and gender development will soon, and often, include the name Eleanor Maccoby. Maccoby received her undergraduate degree from the University of Washington in Seattle. Her master's degree and Ph.D. (in experimental psychology) were both from the University of Michigan. From the start, the focus of Maccoby's research—first at Harvard University, then at Stanford University—was the socialization of children. Maccoby studied the factors and forces that mold a child's socialization (including some early studies on the effects of television) and concluded that the role of parents in the process is often overestimated. Her most-cited writing (with C. N. Jacklin) is *The Psychology of Sex Differences,* a review and analysis of more than 1600 studies, which was published in 1974. As her career progressed, Eleanor Maccoby shifted the focus of her research from preschool children to those in middle childhood and then, finally, to adolescents.

Janet Taylor Spence

Born in Ohio, Janet Spence began her college career at Oberlin College, where she received a degree in 1945. She went to graduate school at Yale University, met her husband-to-be, Kenneth Spence (a very prominent psychologist as well), and transferred after just one year to the University of Iowa, where she earned her Ph.D. in 1949. Janet Taylor Spence's first academic achievements were in the area of anxiety and behavior. She was particularly interested in chronic, non-situational anxiety and how it might influence the course of learning. One of the first things she discovered was that psychologists had no instrument to measure anxiety. She developed the Taylor Manifest Anxiety Scale, a test that is in common use today. After four years at the University of Iowa, Janet and Kenneth Spence moved to the University of Texas. There, Janet Spence's interests shifted to women's studies and gender differences. She focused on competency and what it means for women to be competent in their own right, and she developed another test, the Attitudes Toward Women Scale. Janet Taylor Spence served a four-year term as Chair of the Department of Psychology and became the sixth woman to be elected president of the American Psychological Association in 1984.

Past Presidents of the American Psychological Association
The American Psychological Association (APA) was founded in 1892, and G. Stanley Hall served as its first president. Many famous psychologists have served as president of the APA, including ten women:

1905— Mary Whiton Calkins
1921— Margaret Floy Washburn (note the gap in time here)
1972— Anne Anastasi
1973— Leona E. Tyler
1980— Florence L. Denmark
1984— Janet T. Spence
1987— Bonnie R. Strickland
1996— Dorothy W. Cantor
2001— Norine G. Johnson
2004— Diane F. Halpern
2007— Sharon Stephans Brehm

In the beginning, women struggled to get a foothold in psychology, just as they did within all academic arenas. Few professions can count as many women within their ranks as psychology. Not only are women well represented, but they are some of psychology's brightest stars, doing work of enduring value. Indeed, over half of the graduate students enrolled in psychology programs in the United States are women.

RESEARCH METHODS: MAKING OBSERVATIONS

Our discussion of research in psychology begins with observational methods because observation is at the heart of any research in psychology. Remember the goals of psychology. Before we can explain what people do (much less why they do it), we first must make valid observations of what people do. There are several ways psychologists make observations, and there are steps psychologists take to ensure that their observations are valid and reliable.

Naturalistic Observations

Naturalistic observation involves carefully and systematically watching behaviors as they occur naturally, with a minimum of involvement by the observer. There is a logical appeal to the notion that if you are trying to understand what organisms do, you should simply watch them in action, noting their behaviors and the conditions under which those behaviors occur.

Although it may seem straightforward and appealing, naturalistic observation does present a few difficulties. If we want to observe people (or any other organisms) acting naturally, we must make sure they do not realize that we are watching them. In other words, we try to make *unobtrusive observations* of behavior. So, for example, a scientist observing chimpanzees in the wild might observe from a specially constructed "blind" which hides her from the chimpanzees. This is important because as you know from your own experience, people may act very differently if they believe that they are being watched. You may do all sorts of things—naturally— in the privacy of your own home that you would never do if you thought someone was observing you.

naturalistic observation the method of systematically watching behaviors as they occur naturally, with a minimum involvement of the observer

A second potential difficulty is **observer bias**, which occurs when the observer's own motives, expectations, and previous experiences interfere with the objectivity of the observations being made. Observer bias is largely a matter of recording what observers expect or want to see happen rather than noting what actually occurred (Mitchell & Jolley, 2001, p. 76). It may be difficult for a researcher to be truly objective in her observations of children in a preschool setting if she knows that the hypothesis under investigation is that boys are more verbally aggressive than girls. One remedy is to have observers note behaviors without knowing the hypothesis under investigation. Another protection against observer bias is to use several observers and to rely only on those observations that are verified by a number of observers. Two other steps can help reduce observer bias: 1) provide the clearest possible operational definitions for the variables or interest, and 2) provide the best possible training for the observers before they go into the field.

A third potential difficulty of naturalistic observation is that the behaviors you want to observe may not be there when you are. Say that you are interested in conformity and wish to observe people conforming to group pressure in the real world. Where would you go? Where are you likely to observe conformity happening naturally? Yes, some environments might be more likely to produce conformity than others, but there are no guarantees. And if you start manipulating events so that conformity will be more likely, you clearly are no longer engaged in naturalistic observation. To use this method, one often has to be lucky—and almost certainly patient.

Difficulties notwithstanding, naturalistic observation can be the most suitable method available. For example, studying chimpanzees in zoos and laboratories will tell us little about how chimpanzees behave in their natural habitat. Psychologists also have been frustrated in their attempts to study the language

Courtesy of Bloomimage/Corbis.

development of young children. By the time they are three years old, children demonstrate many interesting language behaviors. However, these children may be too young to appreciate and follow the instructions that experiments require. Nor are they likely to respond sensibly to questions about their own language use. Perhaps all we can do is to carefully watch and listen to young children as they use language, trying to determine what is going on by observing them behaving naturally as they interact with their environments, including the people within them.

Surveys

When it is important to make observations about a large number of people, we may use a survey method. Doing a **survey** involves systematically asking a large number of persons the same question or set of questions on a particular topic. You may ask a person questions face-to-face, in a telephone interview, on a written questionnaire, or via an Internet questionnaire.

If we wanted to know, for example, whether there is a relationship between one's income level and the type of television programs one watches regularly, we could ask about these issues in a survey of a large number of people. A survey can

Although there are potential pitfalls, many researchers argue that the best way to study behavior is to observe how it occurs naturally.

observer bias a problem that arises when an observer's own motives, expectations, and previous experiences interfere with the objectivity of the observations being made

survey a data collection method of systematically asking a large number of persons the same question or set of questions

case history a method in which one person—or a small group of persons—is studied in depth, often over a long period of time

sample a subset, or portion, of a larger group (population) that has been chosen for study

tell us what a given segment of the population thinks or feels about some issue and can provide insights about preferences for products, services, or political candidates. If the cafeteria staff on your campus really wanted to know what students preferred to eat, they could survey a sample of the student population.

For survey results to be valid, the sample surveyed must be sufficiently large and representative of the population from which it was drawn. A **sample** is a subset, or portion, of a larger group (population) that has been chosen for study. The point is that we would like to be able to generalize, or extend, our observations beyond just those in our survey sample. Cafeteria managers who survey only students attending morning classes on Tuesdays and Thursdays may make observations that do not generalize to the larger population of students on campus.

As you can imagine, there are other potential problems with survey data beyond the lack of adequate sampling. For one thing, people do not always respond truthfully. "Oh, I only watch news programs or the PBS channel if I watch TV at all" may be the truth, but it may not be. Question formulation is also very important. Just think of all the ways in which you could ask about cafeteria food. "Do you prefer pizza or vegetable soup?" "What is your favorite food?" "Is there anything you wouldn't eat?"

Case Histories

The case history method provides another type of observational informa-

tion. In a **case history** approach, one person—or a small group of persons—is studied in depth, often over a long period of time. Use of this method usually involves a detailed examination of a wide range of issues. The method is *retrospective*, which means that one starts with a given state of affairs (a situation that currently exists) and go back in time to see if there might be a relationship between this state of affairs and previous experiences or events.

As an example, let's say you were interested in the choices college students make when they decide on a major course of study. Why do some students major in psychology, while others choose chemistry or art history as a major? Perhaps the case history method could be helpful. How would you proceed? You would choose a sample of students, perhaps seniors, from each major and ask them a series of penetrating (one hopes) questions about such matters as previous educational experiences, what their parents do/did as a career, which teachers they liked the best in high school, their favorite hobbies and on and on. You would look for are answers that are reasonably consistent within each group of majors but different from those students of other majors.

As we shall see, Freud based most of his theory of personality on his intensive examination of the case histories of his patients (and of himself). An advantage of the case history method is that it can provide a wealth of information about a few individuals. The disadvantage is that we have to be particularly careful when we try to generalize beyond those individuals we have studied.

BEFORE YOU GO ON

13. Compare and contrast the use of naturalistic observation, surveys, and the case history method in psychology.

A Point to Ponder or Discuss
You have a hypothesis: People who like sports have more friends than people who do not like sports. How would you conduct three different studies, each using one of the methods described above to test your hypothesis? What would be the strengths and weaknesses of each method?

RESEARCH METHODS: LOOKING FOR RELATIONSHIPS

Although the range of specific research techniques available to psychologists is vast, they generally fall into two categories: correlational or experimental. In **correlational research**, variables are observed and measured but are not manipulated. A *variable* is something that can take on different values—as opposed to a constant, which has but one value. For example, intelligence is a variable because when we measure it a range of different sores can result. Manipulating a variable simply means changing its value. Correlational research depends on measuring the values of variables and looking for relationships between or among them. For example, if you were interested in the play patterns of boys and girls in a daycare center, you could observe play times and categorize play behaviors (e.g., being aggressive or helping, playing with others or alone) while noting the child's gender. Correlational methods could then tell you if there were relationships between the variables you noted while making no attempt to influence any of those variables.

In **experimental research**, investigators actually manipulate a variable (or more than one) and then look for a relationship between those manipulations and changes in the value of some other variable. Say, for example, a researcher was interested in factors that influence children's willingness to donate candy to needy children. The researcher has one group of children watch a pro-social television program in which the central character behaves generously. At the same time, a second group watches a "neutral" show, in which the central character does not behave generously. Afterward, all the children are asked to play a game in which part of their winnings may be donated to needy children. In this case, the researcher manipulates one variable (behavior of the character in the show) and measures another (generosity—operationally defined as the number of pieces of candy donated in a game) to see if there is a relationship between the two.

Correlational Research

As we have noted, correlational research involves measuring variables and looking for a relationship among them. This sort of study can be useful in several situations. If it is not possible (or proper) to manipulate a variable of interest, then correlational research is the available option. For instance, in a study of the relationship between birth defects and alcohol consumption, you surely would not want to encourage pregnant women to drink alcohol, particularly if it were your hypothesis that doing so would have negative consequences! But you might be able to locate women who did drink to varying degrees during their pregnancies and use that information to see if the drinking is related to birth defects. Correlational research is often used in the early stages of an investigation just to determine if relationships between selected variables do exist. For example, based on correlational data on alcohol consumption and birth defects, subsequent experimental research (using animal participants) might further explore the biological link between the two variables. Research that involves the age of the participants is correlational by necessity; after all, you cannot manipulate a person's age.

Because of the prevalence and importance of correlational research, let's work through an example in some detail. Imagine that we are interested in discovering whether a relationship (a correlation) exists between reading ability and performance in a class in introductory psychology. First, we need to generate operational definitions of the variables of interest. How are we to measure "reading ability" and "performance in introductory psychology"? The latter variable is easy: Performance in class shall be the total number of points earned on classroom exams. Measuring reading ability is more of a

correlational research a scientific method seeking associations between variables that are observed and measured, but not manipulated

experimental research a scientific method in which investigators manipulate a variable (or more than one) and look for a relationship between those manipulations and changes in the value of some other variable

challenge. We could design our own test of those behaviors we believe reflect degrees of reading ability, but we're in luck. Several established tests of reading ability already are available. We decide on an old standard: The Nelson Denny Reading Test, or the NDRT (Brown, 1973).

Now we are ready to collect some data (make some observations). We give a large group of students the reading test (the NDRT). Once those tests are scored, we have one set of numbers. At the end of the semester we add up points earned by those same students in their introductory psychology class, and we have our second set of numbers. For each student, then, we have a pair of numbers—one for reading ability, the other for performance in class. Our goal is to see if these numbers are correlated.

The Correlation Coefficient

Once identified variables have been measured, the correlational method is really more statistical than psychological. Our pairs of numbers are entered into a calculator or computer. A series of arithmetic procedures is applied, following prescribed formulas. The result (denoted by a lower-case r) is the **correlation coefficient**, a number with a value between −1.00 and +1.00 that tells us about the nature and the extent of the relationship between the variables we have measured. What does this number

mean? How can just one small number tell us about a relationship between responses? In truth, it takes some experience to be truly comfortable with the interpretations of correlation coefficients. What we can say is that there are two aspects of the coefficient that deserve our attention: its sign and its magnitude.

The sign of a correlation coefficient will be either positive (+) or negative (−). A **positive correlation coefficient**, say r = +0.80, tells us that as values of one variable increase, the values of the other variable increase as well. As the values of one variable decrease, the values of the other variable also go down. In other words, changes in the values of each variable are in the same direction. In our example, a positive correlation means that high scores on the reading test are associated with high point totals in the psychology class. It also means that students with low reading scores tend to be the ones who do poorly in the class. As it happens, there are data that tells us that the correlation between these two variables is positive (Gerow & Murphy, 1980). Figure 1.1(A) depicts a positive correlation coefficient and shows what a graph of scores in our example might look like. Here we see a major use of correlation: If we determine that two responses are correlated, we can use one (say a reading test score) to predict the other (a grade in a psychology class).

positive correlation coefficient a value between 0.00 and +1.00 that tells us that as values of one variable increase, the values of the other variable increase as well

correlation coefficient a number with a value between +1.00 and −1.00 that tells us about the nature and the extent of a relationship between the variables that have been measured

---

FIGURE 1.1

Graphical representations of (A) positive, (B) negative, and (C) zero correlations, using examples cited in the text.

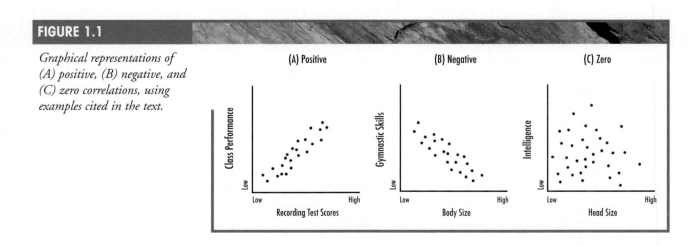

What if our calculations yield a correlation coefficient that is a negative number? A negative sign indicates a negative, or inverse, relationship between our variables. A **negative correlation coefficient** means that as the value of one variable increases, the value of the other variable decreases. The direction of change is different for each variable. For example, if you were to measure body size to see if it was related to gymnastic ability, it is likely that you would find a negative correlation. Large body sizes (high scores) are typically associated with (predict) poor gymnastic ability (low scores), and small body sizes are associated with good gymnastic ability. Although these two sets of scores are negatively correlated, we still can use body size to predict gymnastic ability. Figure 1.1(B) shows data depicting a possible negative correlation between gymnastic skills and body size. Negative correlations are not as common as positive ones, but if you think about it, you can come up with examples. As automobiles get larger (scores go up) their gas mileage decreases (scores go down). As you get older you will come to appreciate that many skills are negatively correlated with age. As we get older (scores go up) we become less and less able to do things that we were once able to do (scores go down).

What does the numerical value of a correlation coefficient indicate? Again, it takes practice to get used to working with numbers with values such as −0.46, +0.55, or +0.003, but the basics are fairly straightforward. The closer the value of our calculated correlation coefficient gets to either extreme, +1.00 or −1.00, the stronger the relationship between the variables we have measured. That is, as r gets close to +1.00 or −1.00 (say, +0.84 or −0.93) the more confidence we have in our ability to predict one variable by knowing the other. The closer our coefficient gets to zero (say, +0.04 or −0.003) the less confidence we have in making predictions. In the example with which we are working,

reading test scores tend, in fact, to be correlated with psychology grades with a coefficient of about +0.55. That means that, in general, students who read well do well in the class and that students who read poorly do poorly in the class, but there are many exceptions to this rule of thumb. If our correlation turned out to be +0.95, then we would have much more confidence in predicting a class grade on the basis of a reading test score. With r = +0.95, there will be very few exceptions in the association between reading test scores and introductory psychology exam point totals. Another reality is that the larger the sample (the more observations made), the greater the confidence we can put in our correlation coefficient, no matter its value. In other words, a correlation coefficient of +0.95 based on a study of 100 students is not as valuable as it would be if it had been based on a study of 1,000 students.

What if our correlation coefficient turns out to be zero, or nearly so (say r = −0.003)? In this case we would conclude that the two sets of observations we have made are simply not related to each other in any consistent, useful way. Imagine that we worked from the faulty logic that, for college students,

negative correlation coefficient a value between 0.00 and −1.00 that tells us that as values of one variable increase, the values of the other variable decrease

Clearly, there is a correlation between gymnastic ability and overall body size—and a negative correlation it is—but that correlation alone does not help us draw any conclusions about cause and effect.

Courtesy of Kevin Dodge/Corbis.

intelligence is a function of brain size and that head size is a good measure of brain size (actually, neither assertion is true). If we measured both the head sizes and grade-point averages of many students, we would find that the correlation between these two measures would be very close to zero. (Note that our "problem" here is not our hypothesis that intelligence and grade point averages are related. The problem is that we have used a very poor operational definition of intelligence.) As correlation coefficients approach zero, predictability decreases. Figure 1.1(C) shows what a graph of data from two unrelated variables would look like.

As you read through this text, you will encounter many studies that use a correlational analysis of measured observations. As you do, there are two important points to keep in mind. First, just because a correlation between two variables exists, we have no evidence that changes in one variable *cause* changes in the other. It is simply inappropriate to infer that a cause-and-effect relationship exists between two variables based solely on correlational research. This is the case even if the two variables are highly correlated with each other and even if logic tells us that one could cause the other.

It does make sense, doesn't it, that an inability to read well would cause some students to perform poorly in an introductory psychology class, where reading is so important? If all we know is that reading ability and class performance are correlated, we can make no statement about cause and effect.

The second important thing to keep in mind about correlations is that even when the value of a correlation coefficient is very high, we cannot make specific predictions for individual cases. Reading ability and course grades in psychology are positively correlated. By and large, in general, students who read well will do well in the course and those who read poorly are likely to get lower grades. But, there will be exceptions. A few poor readers may get very high scores in their psychology class, perhaps motivated to achieve as never before. A few good readers may do poorly, perhaps slacking off and not studying enough. Even if we know a student's reading test score, we can offer only general probabilities about what that student's final class grade might be. Like most of our scientific observations in psychology, statements of correlation hold true only by and large, in the long run, or more often than not.

BEFORE YOU GO ON

14. For what reasons do psychologists do correlational research?
15. What does a correlation coefficient tell us?

A Point to Ponder or Discuss
We have provided a few examples of possible correlations. Can you generate pairs of observations that are likely to be characterized by a positive, negative, or near-zero correlation coefficient?

RESEARCH METHODS: DOING EXPERIMENTS

A major goal of any science—and psychology is no exception—is to establish

clear causal connections among variables of interest. Although it is useful to know that a relationship exists between variables based on correlational research, what we often really want to know is whether those variables are related in a cause-and-effect manner. For example, as a researcher, you may want to know if alcohol consumption during pregnancy *causes* birth defects. Does exposure to second-hand smoke *cause* lung cancer? Does being reared in an impoverished environment *cause* lower intelligence? As useful as correlations are, the only way to establish causal relationships is to conduct well-designed experiments. An **experiment** is a series of operations used to investigate whether changes in the values of one variable cause measurable changes in another variable while all other variables are controlled or eliminated. That's quite a mouthful, but the actual procedures are not difficult to understand.

When researchers perform an experiment, they are no longer content to discover that two measured observations are simply related; they want to be able to claim that, at least to some degree, one causes the other. To see if such a claim can be made, researchers manipulate the values of one variable to see if those manipulations cause a measurable change in the values of another variable. An **independent variable** is the variable that the experimenter manipulates. The experimenter determines its value, and nothing the participant in the experiment does will affect its value. For example, if you were interested in the effects of alcohol on birth defects, you could give three groups of pregnant mice different amounts of alcohol in their diets (0.0 oz. per day, 0.5 oz. per day, or 1.0 oz. per day). As the experimenter, you determine which groups get which dosage, i.e., the alcohol is your independent variable. On the other hand, a **dependent variable** (or a "dependent measure") provides a measure of the participants' behavior. An experimental hypothesis, then, is that values of the dependent variable will, indeed, depend upon the independent variable manipulation the participants received. In our example, some measure of the number and/or extent of birth defects would be our dependent variable, or measure.

In its simplest form, an experiment will have two groups of participants. Those in the **experimental group** are exposed to some value of the independent variable. For example, in an experiment on the effects of alcohol on the driving ability of college students, ten students in the experimental group could be given an amount of alcohol equivalent to three mixed drinks. Then, we ask these students to "drive" a course on a driving simulator—very much like an arcade video game. We discover that these students average four accidents in a 15-minute testing session. Is there any way we can claim that the alcohol they drank before driving had anything at all to do with those accidents? No, not really. Why not? There are lots of reasons. For one thing, these 10 students might be among the worst drivers ever and be prone to accidents whether they have a drink or not. In order to show that it was the alcohol causing the poor performance, we would need a second group of students—students of comparable driving skills—who receive a nonalcoholic beverage that tastes exactly like the alcoholic one. Participants in this group comprise the control group. In general terms, a **control group** receives a zero level of the independent variable. The control group is the baseline against which the performance of the experimental group is

Courtesy of moodboard/Corbis.

experiment a series of operations used to investigate whether changes in one variable cause measurable changes in another variable, while all other variables are controlled or eliminated

independent variable the variable in an experiment that the experimenter manipulates

dependent variable (or "dependent measure") a measure of the behavior of the participants in an experiment

experimental group participants in an experiment exposed to some value of the independent variable

control group participants in an experiment who receive a zero level of the independent variable

A well-controlled experiment can support or refute the hypothesis that a "study skills class" can improve classroom performance.

judged. Thus, even in the simplest of experiments, one must have at least two levels of the independent variable, where one will be zero.

Before we work through another example in some detail, there is one other term to introduce. A **placebo** is something given to participants that has no identifiable effect on the dependent variable. In our example, the placebo was the nonalcoholic beverage given to members of the control group. When the effectiveness of new drugs is tested, one group receives the real medication, while another (control) group gets a pill, injection, or capsule that is in every way similar to the new medication, but which, in fact, has no active ingredients. That is, they receive a placebo—and no one in the experiment knows until afterward if he or she is receiving a medication or a placebo.

Now let's work through another example, just to be sure we have our terminology well in mind. While checking out "study skills" on the Internet, you read an article claiming that students can do better on classroom tests simply by learning how to take tests. (Remember, all good science begins with observation.) You decide to test this notion experimentally. Your hypothesis: Taking a class on test-taking skills will have a positive influence on classroom exams.

You get some volunteers from your introductory psychology class and divide them into two groups. One group (A) agrees to take a 3-hour class on test-taking strategies, while the other group (B) takes a 3-hour class on making and sticking to a budget while in college. At the end of the semester—with the students' permission—you will compare the exam scores of the two groups.

Now for some terminology. Your *hypothesis* is that training on test-taking strategies will improve performance in an introductory psychology class. You have manipulated whether the participants in our study get that training, so getting the training is your *independent variable* (which in this example has only two values, either training or no train-

ing). You believe that such training will improve performance. What will you measure to see if this is so; that is, what will be your *dependent variable?* You observe the scores the students in your study earned on classroom exams throughout the term. You discover that Group A (those who had training) scored, on the average, nearly a whole letter-grade better than did the students in the control group who did not have the training (Group B). It looks as though you have confirmed your hypothesis.

Before we get too carried away, there is yet one more type of variable we need to consider. **Extraneous variables** are those factors, other than the independent variables, that can influence the dependent variable of an experiment. To conclude that changes in one's dependent variable are caused by the manipulations of the independent variable, these extraneous variables need to be controlled or eliminated. These factors should be considered and dealt with before an experiment begins. In our example, what extraneous variables might be involved? Other than just taking a test-taking class, what factors might have produced the effect we demonstrated? For one thing, we had better be able to show that the students in both our groups were of essentially the same academic ability before we began. We would have a serious problem if we discovered that the students in Group A were honor students, while those in Group B were struggling to get by in all their classes. When we are done with an experiment and find measurable differences in our dependent variable, we want to be able to claim that these differences were caused by our manipulation of the independent variable and nothing else. Indeed, the quality of an experiment is determined by the extent to which extraneous variables are anticipated and eliminated. This matter of control is so important that we will have more to say about it in the next section. Figure 1.2 reviews the steps in our example experiment.

---

placebo something given to participants that has no identifiable effect on the dependent variable

extraneous variables those factors, other than the independent variable, that can influence the dependent variable of an experiment and need to be controlled or eliminated

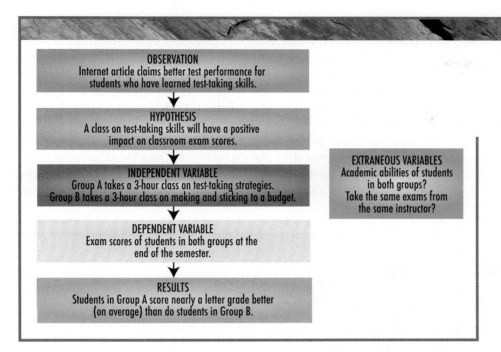

FIGURE 1.2

Some of the steps, or stages, in doing a simple experiment. In this example, which group (A or B) is the "control group" and which is the "experimental group"?

Doing Experiments: Exercising Control

The essence of doing an experiment is to look for changes in the value of a dependent variable that are caused by changes in the value of an independent variable. To claim that observed changes are due solely to the manipulation of the independent variable, we have to show that extraneous variables have been controlled, or eliminated. (Indeed, the word extraneous means "not essential.")

Think back to our example experiment on the effects of alcohol on students' driving performance in a simulator. We would like to say that it was our manipulation of the amount of alcohol that produced the differences in driving measures between our control group (no alcohol) and the experimental group (three alcoholic beverages). To do this, we needed to have eliminated from consideration anything else that might have affected the students' driving abilities. For example, we would use the same driving test for all of the participants, run the experiment in the same room with the same equipment, read instructions to the participants in the same manner, and score their driv-

ing performance using the same criteria. And, as we mentioned earlier, we would have taken every step to ensure that the driving abilities of the two groups were equal, or as nearly so as reasonable, before we began.

To make sure that members of your control group and experimental group begin the experiment on an equal footing, you might try a number of things. You might try to match the participants on the measure of interest. A more common technique is to use **random assignment**, which means that each participant in the research has an equal chance of being assigned to any one of the groups in the experiment. In our driving example, if we used random assignment, good, bad, and average drivers would have been equally likely to be in either the experimental group or the control group. When using random assignment, individual differences will, in the long run, equalize across groups.

Another way to control for differing past experiences of participants in an experiment is called a **baseline design**. Although there are several such designs, each amounts to arranging conditions so that each participant serves in both the experimental and in the control group

random assignment a procedure by which each participant in a research program has an equal chance of being assigned to any of the groups in an experiment

baseline designs techniques of arranging conditions so that each participant serves in both the experimental and in the control group conditions

conditions. For instance, if you wanted to see if a given drug caused an increase in running speed of white rats in an activity wheel using a baseline design. First you would measure the running speeds of some rats without giving them the drug (a control, or baseline, measure), and then you would check their running speed after they were given the drug. At the same time, another group of rats would run in the activity wheel first under the influence (if any) of the drug and then later without the drug. Changes in running behavior (the dependent variable) could then be attributed to the drug (the independent variable). There are some scientists who argue that this experiment could be done with just one rat. Over the course of weeks, you would have the rat run in the activity wheel many times under the influence of the drug and many times without the drug.

BEFORE YOU GO ON

16. What are the basic elements involved in doing an experiment?

A Point to Ponder or Discuss
A TV ad tells you, "Four out of five doctors surveyed preferred Brand X for the treatment of back pain." Is Brand X necessarily the best for back pain? Why or why not? What uncontrolled variables might be reflected in this result?

generalization (in experiments) the ability to apply results beyond the restrictive conditions of an experimental setting

field experiments those done not in a laboratory, but in the "real world"

The Generality of Psychological Research

We have made a strong case for identifying and exercising tight control over extraneous variables when conducting experimental research. This control is necessary if research is to produce unambiguous results free of confounding variables. However, there is a cost to be paid for the tight control found in many psychological experiments. As it happens, experiments that tightly control extraneous variables often are not very realistic. Yes, in an experiment to determine the effect of alcohol on driving ability, it is wise to control for all other factors that could affect driving skills other than the amount of alcohol consumed. But, in the real world, people drive vastly dissimilar cars in a wide variety of weather, road, and traffic conditions. With extraneous variables controlled, one often must still wonder if one's results really apply to life in the real world. The ability to apply results beyond the restrictive conditions of an experiment is known as **generalization**. There is often a negative correlation between the extent of experimental control and generalization. In other words, the tighter the control, the less likely the results can be generalized.

Not all psychological research is conducted under tightly controlled laboratory conditions. Some experiments, known as **field experiments**, are done in the "real world." Instead of bringing participants into the laboratory, the researcher essentially brings the laboratory to the participants. One imaginative example is a study conducted by Middlemist, Knowles, and Matter back in 1976. The researchers were interested in how people might react to invasions of their personal space—an invisible "bubble" that extends up to four feet from an individual. One person typically enters another person's personal space by invitation only. The researchers knew that an uninvited invasion of a person's personal space was psychologically arousing. They wondered if it might be physiologically arousing as well.

They did their experiment in a public men's room (i.e., in a lavatory, not a laboratory). In one condition (close), the third of three urinals was closed off, leaving only a center urinal and an adjacent urinal available. In the other condition (far), the center urinal was closed off. As a participant took a position at one urinal, a confederate (someone in on the project) positioned himself at the remaining urinal. A third confederate hidden in a toilet stall timed how long it took the participant to begin urination and how long urination lasted. This may sound extraordinarily strange, but these are two well-accepted measures of physiological arousal and stress. Indeed, in the close condition, onset was delayed and duration of urination was much shorter than in the far condition.

Conducting an experiment in a natural environment can give one greater assurance that results will generalize beyond the confines of the experiment. However, don't forget the trade-off. There is likely to be some loss of control of extraneous variables. In this example experiment, it was not possible to control the amount of commotion in the hallway outside the lavatory, the possibility of interruption by others, or just how badly the participants needed to be in that lavatory in the first place.

Which should be of greater concern, tight control or generality? This question has no simple answer beyond the obvious one that a researcher should try to strike a balance. Still, another broad rule of thumb applies: If the research is primarily designed to test some theory or model, then the experimenter should be more concerned with tight control and less concerned with generality. On the other hand, if the intent is to apply the results of one's research to a real-world problem, then the experimenter should be more concerned with generality than with tight control.

Using a Meta-analysis

Before we leave this section, there is one additional research technique that

Courtesy of moodboard/Corbis.

deserves mention. Some experiments or correlational studies are impossible (or prohibitively expensive) to do on a large scale, with many participants.

For example, ethics (and common sense) prohibit us from purposely rearing children in isolation, deprived of environmental stimulation. However, researchers might be able to locate a few adolescents who had relatively isolated, deprived childhoods and compare them on some relevant measures with teenagers who had apparently normal childhoods and with a third group who seemed to have extraordinarily stimulating childhood experiences. Whatever the findings, based on only a few adolescents, and with many variables left uncontrolled, results would be tentative at best. But what if, over the years, many similar studies had been conducted by different researchers in different parts of the world? Although no single study would be convincing by itself, what if there were some way to combine the results of all (or most) of these studies? Such is precisely the intent of a **meta-analysis**, a statistical procedure of combining the results of many studies to see more clearly the relationship, if any, between or among variables. A meta-analysis has the advantage of minimizing the errors that can plague smaller studies (Schmidt, 1992). As Rosenthal and DiMatteo put it, "Meta-analysis

In order to determine how people might react to crowded conditions, it might be worthwhile to go out into the real world, find people in crowded conditions, and observe how people are responding.

meta-analysis a statistical procedure of combining the results of many studies to see more clearly the relationship(s), if any, between or among variables allows researchers to arrive at conclusions that are more accurate and more credible than can be presented in any one primary study or in a non-quantitative, narrative review" (2001, p. 61).

Just as one example of a meta-analytic study, consider the now classic work of Janet Hyde and her associates (Hyde et al., 1990), which examined gender differences in mathematics performance. These researchers examined 100 studies that involved the testing of a combined total of 3,175,188 participants! (It is difficult to imagine one single research project on any issue involving over three million people.) The researchers found very few differences between males and females in mathematical performance. Females show a slight edge in computational skills in elementary school and middle school, while males tend to do a little better in mathematical problem-solving in high school and college—particularly on tests of advanced mathematics. But the differences that were found were small and, in most comparisons, there were no differences at all. These are the sorts of conclusions that any one study, no matter how well conceived, is unlikely to provide.

BEFORE YOU GO ON

17. In doing experiments, what is the relation between generalization and control?
18. What is the essence of a meta-analysis?

A Point to Ponder or Discuss
What, in general, is the relation between the size of an experiment (i.e., the number of participants involved) and the usefulness of that experiment? Is a large experiment necessarily better than a smaller one?

ETHICS IN PSYCHOLOGICAL RESEARCH

Imagine that you find yourself in the following situation: You sign up for an experiment as part of your psychology course requirements. You think the study simply involves taking some kind of test. When you arrive for the study you are, in fact, given a test to take. A few minutes later the experimenter returns and says that you did better on the test than almost anyone else and that he suspects that you cheated. He explains that this is a serious infraction and will have to report you and take disciplinary action against you. You are incredulous because you did not cheat, and you find yourself getting more and more worried about what might happen. However, no amount of explaining dissuades the experimenter from reporting you. Then, the experimenter says that if you admit to cheating on the exam he will simply withhold credit for participating in the experiment. You reluctantly admit to cheating, even though you were innocent. At this point, the experimenter tells you that the accusation was a ruse and that the real purpose of the study was to see if you would accept a "plea bargain," involving a lesser punishment.

The scenario we just described is very similar to the method used by Gregory, Mowen, and Linder (1978) to study plea-bargaining. How do you think you would feel had you been a participant in this experiment? Would you be upset that you had been lied to? Or, would you be relieved to find out that you were not in trouble with the experimenter? Should researchers be allowed to deceive research participants in order to study something like plea-bargaining? Are the interests of science worth the anxiety such a study causes in participants? All of these questions are relevant to the issue of ethics in psychological research; an issue that has been important to psychologists for more than 50 years.

More often than not, the goals of science are noble goals: finding a cure for cancer, developing programs to help disadvantaged children in school, discovering the causes of Alzheimer's dementia, or learning about plea-bargaining. But does having a noble goal justify *any and all* research practices? Are there ethical boundaries that should not be crossed in the quest for scientific knowledge and practical applications of that knowledge? Not every research practice is justified, no matter how noble the goals of researchers. Researchers must never cross some ethical boundaries. Researchers in psychology must adhere to a strict code of ethics developed by the American Psychological Association (APA) when conducting research. The purpose of the APA's ethical code is to protect research participants from potentially harmful experiments and to ensure their well-being.

As a discipline, psychology has a unique problem with regard to ethics. To be sure, ethical standards are important in the application of psychological knowledge, be it in diagnosis, therapy, counseling, or training. But in psychology, concerns about ethics also are crucial in the gathering of information. After all, the objects of psychological research are living organisms. Their physical and psychological welfare must be protected as their behaviors and mental processes are investigated.

Psychologists have long been concerned with the ethical implications of their work. Since 1953, the American

Psychological Association has regularly revised the "Ethical Principles of Psychologists and Code of Conduct" for practitioners and researchers. The most recent revision was published in December of 2002 (APA, 2002).

Ethics and Research with Human Participants

How are the current ethical guidelines applied to psychological research? In planning research, psychologists assess potential risks to participants. What potential dangers, physical or psychological, might accompany participation? Even if potential risks are deemed slight, they need to be considered. Researcher Gregory Kimble put it this way: "Is it worth it? Do the potential benefits to science and eventually to animal and human lives justify the costs to be extracted here and now?" (Kimble, 1989, p. 499). Seldom will any one psychologist be required to make the ultimate decision about the potential benefits or risks of research. An institutional review board typically reviews research proposals to ensure that all research meets the requirements of ethical research practice.

Here are some other ethical issues related to research in psychology:

1. Participants' *confidentiality* must be guaranteed. Most studies designate participants using identification numbers, not names. No matter what participants are asked to do or say, they should be confident that no one except the researchers will have access to their responses.

2. Participation in research should be *voluntary*. No one should feel coerced or compelled to participate in psychological research. For example, college students cannot be offered extra credit for participating in psychological research unless other options are available for earning the same amount of extra

credit. Volunteers should be allowed the option of dropping out of any research project, even after it has begun.

3. Persons should be in research projects only after they have given *informed consent*. Participants must know the risks of participation, why a project is being done, and what is expected of them. In some cases, it is not possible to fully disclose the true nature and purpose of a study to participants. Some small amount of deception may be required. In these cases, the amount of deception needs to be balanced against the potential benefits of the research and justified to the relevant institutional review board.

4. Participants should be *debriefed* after the research has been completed, especially in cases where the nature of the research required incomplete disclosure to the participants. That means that the project and its basic intent should be fully explained to all those who participated in it. Participants should also be provided with a copy of the results of the project when they are available.

Think back to the Middlemist et al. (1976) field experiment on the physiological effects of invasions of personal space. What are some ethical questions raised by that experiment? Were the participants informed in advance of their participation? Did the participants have an opportunity for informed consent? Is it ethical to engage in clandestine observation of a private behavior? These and perhaps other questions must be considered when evaluating any research project, especially one done in the field. Special care must be exercised and additional guidelines must be followed when children or persons from specialized populations (for example, mentally-retarded persons) participate in experiments.

Ethics and the Use of Animals in Research

Ethical guidelines published by the APA for the use of animals in research are quite stringent. In certain cases, the guidelines for animals are more stringent than those for humans. Current APA guidelines include the following points:

1. Obtaining, caring for, using, and disposing of animals used in research must comply with all federal, state, and local laws and be consistent with professional standards.

2. A psychologist trained in the care and use of animals must supervise any procedures involving animals and is ultimately responsible for the comfort, health, and humane treatment of the animals.

3. The psychologist must ensure that all assistants are trained in research methods and the care, maintenance, and handling of the animal species being used.

4. Roles assigned to assistants must be consistent with their training.

5. Efforts must be made to minimize any discomfort, infection, illness, or pain of animal subjects.

6. Procedures that subject animals to pain, stress, or privation should be used only when no alternatives are available.

7. When an animal's life is to be terminated, it must be done rapidly with an effort to minimize pain.

8. Proper anesthesia must be used for all surgical procedures.

In addition to these APA guidelines government regulations must be followed. These government regulations specify how animal research subjects are to be treated, housed, and cared for. Just like research using humans, research using animals must be reviewed to make sure it is ethical before it can start.

BEFORE YOU GO ON

19. What are the major ethical guidelines for research using human participants and for research using animal participants?

A Point to Ponder or Discuss

Think about the research scenario that opened this section on research ethics and consider it in the light of the APA's ethical code. What, if any, ethical violations were committed? Can you think of a way to do the study and get the same results while adhering more closely to the APA ethical code?

SOME KEY PRINCIPLES TO GUIDE US

Over the years, a few over-arching, principles have emerged that seem to touch upon nearly every area of psychological investigation. If you get these points firmly in mind now, at the start, you will see them again and again as you read on.

1. ***Explanations in psychology often involve INTERACTIONS.*** This is another way of saying that nothing is simple. In case after case, we find that a psychological explanation involves the interaction of powerful underlying forces. How much of our identity (our affects, behaviors, and cognitions) is the result of inheritance, or our biological *nature?* How much of our identity reflects the influences of the environment and our experiences with it, or our *nurture?* Is intelligence inherited (nature) or the result of experience with the environment (nurture)? Is aggressiveness inborn (part of one's nature), or is it learned (an aspect of one's nurture)? Does alcoholism reflect a person's innate nature, or is it a learned reaction to events in the environment? Why do some people react to stress by becoming depressed, while others develop physical symptoms, and yet others seem not to be bothered?

   The position that psychologists take is that most behaviors and mental processes result from the interaction of both inherited predispositions and environmental influences. That is, a psychological characteristic is not the result of either heredity or experience, but reflects the interaction of both. "For all psychological characteristics, inheritance sets limits on, or sets a range of potentials for, development. Environment determines how near the individual comes to developing those potentials" (Kimble, 1989, p. 493). General acceptance of the notion that genetics are an important contributors to individual differences is a relatively recent phenomenon in psychology, dating back only to the 1980s (Plomin, 1990).

Courtesy of Ilona Habben/zefa/Corbis.

Psychologists believe that musical talent (for example) reflects the interaction between genetic or inherited predispositions and nurturing environmental opportunities. Either without the other would not be likely to produce high levels of performance.

Another case of interaction that we'll encounter later is that between a person's internal dispositions, or personality, and the situation in which that person finds himself or herself. Which determines what a person will do, the situation, or personality? Both. They interact. For example, Bob may be a very outgoing, extroverted, sociable sort of person. It's just the way he is. But it's easy to imagine situations (surrounded by "important," powerful employers, perhaps) in which Bob may act far more reserved and less social, isn't it?

There is no observation in psychology more universally accepted than that "there are individual differences." Each of these students has reached the same milestone of graduation, but each reached that goal by a uniquely individual collection of affects, behaviors, and cognitions.

Courtesy of Brand X/Corbis.

2. ***There are individual differences.*** No two people are exactly alike. This is psychology's most common and well-documented observation. Given the diversity of genetic make-ups and environments— which include social and cultural pressures—it is not surprising that people can be so different from one another. Not only is each organism unique, but also no organism is exactly the same from one point in time to another. You are not the same person today that you were yesterday. Learning and experience have changed you, probably not in any great, significant way. But, what may have been true of you yesterday may not be true of you today. Do you see the complication this causes for the science of psychology? Because of the variability that exists among people, virtually all psychological laws are statements made "in general, in the long run, more often than not." Our example of reading abilities predicting grades in psychology classes made this point. Although we know that there is an association (a correlation) between reading ability and grades (in general) we really cannot make a specific prediction for one individual based on one reading test score.

3. ***Our experience of the world often matters more than what it in the world.*** What we perceive and what we remember are surely dependent

upon events as they occurred. But, as we shall see (in Chapters 3 and 6), they are also influenced by many previous experiences as well. The main idea here is that, as active agents in the world, we each select, attend to, interpret and remember different aspects of the same world of events. That is, our view of the world comprises two forms of reality: objective and subjective. Objective reality is what is actually there. For example, when a crime occurs, certain events take place: There is a perpetrator, some incident occurs in a specific way (e.g., a robbery), and there are consequences of that action (e.g., stolen money, personal injury, and the like). Your *experience* of these objective events comprise *subjective reality*. Point of view, personal expectations and prejudices, stress levels, and other factors determine what aspects of the objective event are processed and stored in your memory. This is why eyewitness accounts of a crime so often differ, sometimes drastically. Witnesses construct their own versions of subjective reality that becomes, for them, "what happened." More often than not, it is one's subjective reality that determines one's reactions and behaviors.

BEFORE YOU GO ON

20. Describe three major principles that will appear repeatedly throughout this text.

A Point to Ponder or Discuss
Granted that scientific laws in psychology are made "in general, in the long run," how would you proceed if you really wanted to understand one individual and make predictions about that person's behaviors in a given situation?

CHAPTER SUMMARY

1. **What is the definition of psychology?**

   Psychology is simply defined as the scientific study of behavior and mental processes.

2. **What are the ABCs of psychology's subject matter?**

   Psychologists study the behaviors ("B" of our ABCs) and mental processes of organisms. Mental processes are of two types: Affective processes ("A") (involving feelings, emotions, or moods) and cognitive processes ("C") (involving knowledge, beliefs, perceptions, memories, and the like). When psychologists study the behaviors of organisms, they study their observable actions and reactions.

3. **What is an operational definition and why is it important in science?**

   Operational definitions do not state what a concept *is*, rather they specify the techniques or procedures used to measure or create the concept of concern. Operational definitions have the advantage of making it very clear exactly what a scientist means when using terminology. For example, rather than entering a philosophical discussion of the nature of intelligence, a scientist will use an operational definition, specifying exactly how (in the research under consideration) "intelligence" is to be measured, perhaps with a particular intelligence test.

4. **Why can we make the claim that psychology is a science?**

   Two requirements must be met for a discipline to qualify as a science. It must demonstrate an organized body of knowledge of its subject matter, and it must confine itself to the use of scientific methods. Although there remain many intriguing unanswered questions about behavior and mental processes, psychologists have learned a great deal and have done so using the methods of science.

5. **What is pseudoscience and why should you learn to distinguish it from real science?**

   Pseudoscience (literally "false science") is a set of ideas based on theories that are presented as being scientific when they are not. Pseudoscientific claims are often made by people who represent themselves as scientists, but are provided with no evidence to substantiate them. There often is reliance upon anecdotal evidence and personal tes-timony to back pseudoscientific claims. If nothing else, developing the ability to distinguish between real science and pseudoscience will make one a better consumer of information.

6. **What are "scientist-practitioners" in psychology?**

   Scientist-practitioners are those psychologists who are not so much interested in discovering new scientific laws about affect, behavior, and cognition as they are in applying what is already known to real-world issues. Most scientist-practitioners are clinical or counseling psychologists who work to help people deal with psychological problems, or disorders.

7. **What are the major goals of the science of psychology?**

   In common with all the sciences, psychology aims to accurately observe and describe, understand or explain, predict, and (whenever possible) control or influence its subject matter.

8. **How did the philosophies of Descartes and Locke prepare the way for psychology?**

   Several philosophical doctrines set the stage for the emergence of psychology as a science. Descartes' doctrines of mechanism (the body is essentially a machine) and interactive dualism (the mind and body are separate but interacting systems) helped move philosophical thinking about explanations for human nature away from theology. The British philosopher, John Locke, added the doctrine of empiricism (knowledge is acquired through one's experience). These notions seemed to call out for scientific answers as well as philosophical conjecture.

9. **What contributions did Darwin and early physiologists make to the emergence of psychology?**

   Early natural scientists, such as Darwin, showed that the methods of science could be used to help understand animal behaviors. Scientists like Fechner applied the methods of physics to the study sensation and perception. Physiologists such as Helmholtz were busy in the nineteenth century looking for the physical mechanisms that were related to the human experiences of hearing and seeing. Some early physiologists claimed that the origins of mental processes were in the brain.

Overall, the efforts of natural scientists and physiologists in the 1800s helped to make psychology a scientific endeavor.

10. **Compare and contrast the structuralism of Wundt with the functionalism of James.**

Wundt and the structuralists used rigorous scientific methods in an attempt to discover the elements of mental life, both affect and cognitions. Their basic question was, "What are the elemental units of the mind and how do they interact?" James and his students agreed that rigorous scientific methods should be used to study the nature of mental life. However, they did not believe that consciousness could be analyzed into component parts because, among other things, consciousness was constantly changing. The basic question for James was, "How do the mind and consciousness function to help the organism adapt to its environment?"

11. **What are some of the assumptions or basic ideas that typify psychoanalysis, behaviorism, humanistic psychology, and Gestalt psychology?**

Behaviorism, begun by John Watson, focused only on those overt behaviors of organisms that could be directly measured. Mental life and consciousness were not to be part of psychology's subject matter. The psychoanalytic approach, associated with Sigmund Freud, emphasized mental activities that formed and motivated behaviors. The approach claims that most behaviors reflect both the unconscious mind and instinctive forces. Humanistic psychologists, following the lead of Abraham Maslow and Carl Rogers, believe that psychology's central concern should be the self, one's perception of one's self, free will, and personal growth. Focusing on external forces—be they environmental or instinctive—is dehumanizing. Gestalt psychology, begun in Germany with the work of Max Wertheimer, stressed the laws of perception and how individuals select and organize information from the outside world. Mental life cannot be broken into parts without destroying the whole.

12. **Briefly describe the thrust of the approaches to psychology identified as biological, evolutionary, cognitive, developmental, cross-cultural, and positive.**

Psychologists who take a biological approach to the study of behavior and mental processes suggest that these processes have an underlying biological or genetic basis that needs to be understood. The evolutionary approach takes the long-range view that psychological functioning can best be understood in terms of how a species comes to adapt to its environment. The psychodynamic (or psychoanalytic) approach seeks to understand the impact of innate, largely unconscious processes and the influence of early childhood experiences. The cognitive approach concentrates on how organisms process information about themselves and the world in which they live, dealing with matters such as perception, learning, memory, problem-solving, or decision-making. Developmental psychologists may be concerned with behaviors, emotions, or cognitions, but tend to focus on factors that impact on how these characteristics develop over an organism's life span. A cross-cultural approach acknowledges that one's cultural context has a major influence on one's psychological functioning and argues that psychology should take into account matters of gender, race, and ethnicity. Positive psychology is the name of a subfield that focuses on what is good and right about behavior and mental processes rather than focusing on problems and illness. It seeks to understand the subjective well being of individuals and institutions. Please remember that these approaches are not mutually exclusive and that this list is not exhaustive.

13. **Compare and contrast the use of naturalistic observation, surveys, and the case history method in psychology.**

Science begins with the careful observation of one's subject matter. With naturalistic observation, one watches and notes the behaviors of persons or animals as they behave in their natural environments. Care must be taken that the subject of study is unaware that he or she is being observed and that the observer's values and prejudices do not influence the observations. Surveys can be used to obtain small amounts of information from a large number of persons, while using the case history method can uncover detailed observations of a small number of individuals.

14. **For what reasons do psychologists do correlational research?**

Correlational research is useful when one cannot manipulate the variables of interest but still wants to know about possible relationships between measured observations. If two variables are correlated, knowing the value of one can help predict the value of the other.

15. **What does a correlation coefficient tell us?**

How, and the extent to which, variables are lawfully related is indicated by the correlation coefficient, symbolized by the letter r. If r is a positive number, then increases in the value of one variable are associated with (or predict) increasing values of the other variable. If the correlation coefficient is a negative number, then as the values of one variable increase, the values of the other variable decrease (i.e., the variables are related, but inversely). Correlation coefficients that approach zero (either + or −) tell us that the measured variables are simply not related in any lawful, predictable way.

16. **What are the basic elements involved in doing an experiment?**

Unlike correlational studies, experiments are designed to demonstrate a cause-and-effect relationship between variables. An experimenter manipulates the values of an independent variable, which is hypothesized to have a predicted effect on some other, dependent variable. To see if this is the case, the dependent variable (whose value should "depend" upon the independent variable) is measured. In order to claim that manipulations of an independent variable caused the measured changes in the dependent variable, one must also demonstrate that anything else that could have produced the measured effects (called extraneous variables) has been controlled or eliminated.

17. **In doing experiments, what is the relation between generalization and control?**

Generality refers to the extent to which results can be applied beyond the conditions of an experiment, often to real-world situations. There is often a trade-off of giving up some experimental control (as in field experiments) in order to produce results of high generality.

18. **What is the essence of a meta-analysis?**

Meta-analysis is a research technique that allows one to combine and compare the results of many similar studies of the same issue or of the same variables. By relying on the results of studies using many participants, and from different times and places, patterns of results may appear that would not be noticed in single, smaller studies.

19. **What are the major ethical guidelines for research using human participants and for research using animal participants?**

The ethical guidelines furnished by the American Psychological Association include mention of such issues as maintaining the confidentiality of participants; ensuring that participation is voluntary and that one may voluntarily withdraw at any time; disclosing the purposes, methods, and risks of participation at the beginning of the research; and debriefing participants fully at the end of the research. Psychologists also follow guidelines for the care and handling of animals in research. Animals must be housed according to strict standards, a trained psychologist must supervise any procedures involving animals, and every effort must be made to minimize pain, illness, infection, and discomfort.

20. **Describe three major principles that will appear repeatedly throughout this text.**

Some findings in psychology are so common, so over-arching, that they may be referred to as key principles. Three such generalizations are that 1) One's nature (biological inheritance) and one's nurture (one's experience in the environment) *interact* to produce a person's psychological characteristics, 2) Making specific predictions for individuals is difficult because in so many ways, no people are exactly alike, nor is one person exactly the same over two points in time, and 3) Objective reality (what really happened in the world) is often much less important in predicting one's responses to events than subjective reality (one's experience of what happened, flavored by beliefs and values already stored in memory).

The Biological Bases of Psychological Functioning

PREVIEW

At first glance, as you skim this chapter, it may look a lot more like biology than what you expected in a psychology text. Perhaps it is. But, here is the point: All of your behaviors, from the simple blink of an eye to rapid sequences of complex motions; every emotion you have ever experienced, from mild annoyance to extreme fear; your every thought, from the trivial to the profound—all of these can be reduced to molecules of chemicals racing in and out of the tiny cells that comprise your nervous system.

Every day, huge array of sights, sounds, smells, tastes, and tactile stimuli bombard you. Some go unnoticed; some are ignored; some elicit a response on your part. Most of the time, we take these reactions for granted. Now, they are the focus of this chapter. The processes of getting information to and from the brain (and other parts of your body) involve a beautifully complex set of actions on a cellular level.

We will take a building-block approach to this discussion of the physiological/biological underpinnings of psychological functioning. We will begin by considering the structures and functions of the individual nerve cell. As remarkable as these microscopically tiny cells are, they would have little impact without their ability to pass information from one part of the body to another in nerve fibers. We will see that nerve cells communicate with one another through a remarkable set of chemical actions. Before we go on, we will survey how scientists organize their discussion of nervous systems, and we will briefly examine a system of glands and hormones that can significantly affect psychological functioning—the endocrine system. We will take a brief look at the genetic basis of one's psychological traits—a discussion foreshadowed in Chapter 1, and an issue that will reappear over and over again.

Then, we can put together what we have been discussing into the truly complex structures of the central nervous system, or the CNS. The CNS is composed of the spinal cord and the brain. In our discussion of the spinal cord we see the first indication of how stimuli from the environment produce behaviors—simple reflexive reactions.

Then, there is the brain. No more complex structure exists in nature than the human brain. It is in the brain that conscious, voluntary actions begin, emotions are experienced, and cognitions are formed, manipulated, and stored. Before we get to specific structures and their actions, it is sensible to consider how **neuroscientists**—scientists concerned with the development, structure, function, chemistry, pharmacology and pathology of the nervous system—have learned what is known about the brain.

Because of the brain's complexity, it is necessary to study its structures and their functions one at a time. Although we will examine the parts of the brain one at a time, we must keep in mind that all these structures are part of an integrated, unified system in which all the parts work together and influence one another in complex ways.

NEURONS: THE BUILDING BLOCKS OF THE NERVOUS SYSTEM

Our exploration of the nervous system begins with the nerve cell, or **neuron**. This microscopic cell transmits information—in the form of neural impulses—from one part of the body to another. Neurons were not even recognized as separate structures until around the end of the 19th century. To underscore how small neurons are, consider that there are approximately 125 million light-sensitive neurons that line the back of each human eye, an estimated 1 billion neurons in the spinal cord, and about 100 billion neurons in the brain (Zillmer & Spiers, 2001). Add to these staggering numbers that a single neuron may, on average, establish 10,000 connections with other neurons (Beatty, 1995).

neuroscientists scientists concerned with the development, structure, function, chemistry, pharmacology, and pathology of the nervous system

neuron the microscopically small cell that transmits information in the form of nerve impulses from one part of the body to another

The Structure of Neurons

Even though, much like snowflakes, no two neurons are exactly alike, there are some commonalities among neurons. Figure 2.1 illustrates these shared features.

All neurons have a **cell body**, the largest concentration of mass in the neuron. The cell body contains the nucleus of the cell, which holds the genetic information that keeps the cell functioning. A neuron's cell body is gray in color; thus, large numbers of cell bodies packed together (as in the brain) are referred to as "gray matter." Protruding from a neuron's cell body are several tentacle-like structures, called dendrites, and one particularly long structure called the axon. Typically, **dendrites** reach out to receive messages, or neural impulses, from nearby neurons. These neural impulses are sent to the cell body and down the **axon** to other neurons, muscles, or glands. Some axons are quite long—as long as two to three feet in the spinal cord. Within a neuron, impulses go *from dendrite to cell body to axon,* and most of the distance traveled is along the axon.

The neuron in Figure 2.1 has a feature not found on all neurons. This axon has a cover, or sheath, made of myelin. **Myelin** is a white substance composed of fat and protein, and myelin is found on about half the axons in an adult's nervous system. Myelin is not an outgrowth of the axon itself, but is produced by other cells throughout the nervous systems. Myelin covers an axon in lumpy segments, separated by gaps, or "nodes," rather than in one continuous coating. It is largely the presence of myelin that allows us to distinguish between the gray matter (cell bodies, dendrites, and bare, unmyelinated axons) and white matter (myelinated axons) of nervous-system tissue. We tend to find myelin on axons that carry impulses relatively long distances. For

cell body the largest concentration of mass in the neuron, containing the nucleus of the cell

dendrites protuberances that reach out to receive messages, or neural impulses, from other nearby neurons

axon a long protuberance extending from the neuron's cell body that carries neural impulses to other neurons, muscles, or glands

myelin a white substance composed of fat and protein that covers, insulates, and protects about half of the axons in an adult's nervous system

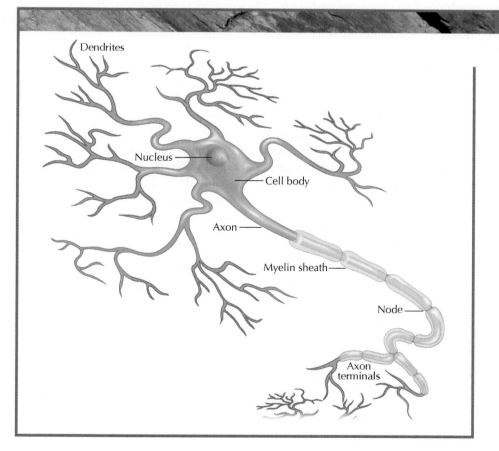

FIGURE 2.1

A typical neuron with its major structures.

Dendrites

Nucleus

Cell body

Axon

Myelin sheath

Node

Axon terminals

instance, most neurons that carry messages up and down the spinal cord have myelin on their axons, whereas most of those that carry impulses back and forth across the spinal cord do not.

Myelin serves several functions. It protects the long and delicate axon. It also acts as an insulator, separating the activity of one neuron from those nearby. Myelin speeds impulses along the length of the axon. Myelinated neurons carry impulses nearly ten times faster than unmyelinated ones—up to 150 yards per second, or well over 300 miles an hour!

The loss of protective, impulse-speeding myelin can have devastating effects. It is the loss of myelin that produces a number of disorders, the most common of which is *multiple sclerosis (MS)*, in which myelin is destroyed and replaced by scars of hardened tissue. (A medical term for scar or scab is "sclera," and with this disease many such sclera are formed—hence, the term "multiple sclerosis.") This neurological illness affects nearly 10 of every 10,000 young adults, a rate that is 50% higher than it was 25 years ago (National Multiple Sclerosis Society, 2007). Symptoms of MS are usually first noticed in the early 20s. Although not considered a fatal disease, multiple sclerosis can cause blurred vision, poor balance and coordination, slurred speech, numbness, paralysis, or blindness—largely depending upon where in the body the myelin is lost. Symptoms may be permanent, or they may come and go. There is no known cure, but there are medications that modify the course of the disease, slow its progression, and improve functioning (National Multiple Sclerosis Society, 2008).

Whether covered with myelin or not, axons end in a branching series of bare end points called **axon terminals** (or "terminal buttons"). At the axon terminal, each neuron communicates with other neurons. So to review: Within a neuron, impulses travel from the dendrites to the cell body, to the axon (which may be myelinated), and then to axon terminals.

Although neurons continue to develop after birth, it is safe to say that we are born with the most neurons we will ever have. In fact, we are born with about twice as many neurons as we'll ever use. What happens to the unused neurons? Those that are not strengthened by experience eventually die off. For example, an infant (6 to 10 months old) has neural circuitry that allows him or her to distinguish among most human speech sounds. Experience with parents or caregivers speaking their native language around the infant strengthens those neurons important to that native language. Neurons which are not important to the native language die off. The "use it or lose it" nature of neurons means that infants actually become less able to discriminate among speech sounds as they develop to a certain point because of the neurons they have lost. The result is that an infant who at 6 to 10 months of age could discriminate among many speech sounds can no longer do so at 10 to 12 months of age (Werker, 1989). In a sense then, we are born with a "generic brain" and our experience determines which neurons die off. While unnecessary neurons die off, bear in mind also the interconnections between neurons become more numerous and complex as the brain develops.

The fact that dead neurons are not (normally) replaced with new ones makes neurons unique among cells. We constantly make new blood cells to replace lost ones; if we did not, we could never donate a pint of blood. Lost skin cells are rapidly replaced by new ones. You rinse away skin cells by the hundreds each time you wash your hands. Neurons are different: Once they're gone, they're gone forever. We are in luck, however, because the functions of lost neurons can often be taken over by surviving neurons.

There also is recent evidence that new neurons *can* be generated in the primate brain even in adulthood (Gage, 2003; Shors et al., 2001; Wise, 2003). **Neurogenesis** is the term used to describe the production of functioning

axon terminal a branching series of bare end points where an axon ends

neurogenesis the term used to describe the production of functioning neurons after birth

neurons after birth. Reports of successful neurogenesis began to appear in the late 1990s. At first, the research involved neurons in the brains of rats, mice, and shrews (Gross, 2000; Kempermann & Gage, 1999). Early on, it still seemed unlikely that neurogenesis could be demonstrated in the human brain. We now know better. At first, neurogenesis was demonstrated in a lower brain center (the hippocampus) and, more recently, even in higher areas of the brain, the cerebral cortex (Brandner, Vantini, & Schneck, 2000; Eriksson et al., 1998; Kempermann, 2002; Mezey, 2003). These results suggest that the brain may have the capacity to regenerate lost neurons, but certainly not at the rate that new neurons grow before birth and in very early childhood. There is also evidence emerging that neurogenesis may be disrupted by diabetes (Beauquis et al., 2008). In one experiment, reduced neurogenesis was found in parts of the brain associated with depression and in the hippocampus (associated with memory) (Beauquis et al., 2008). For obvious reasons, the issue of neurogenesis is one of the most active areas of research in all of science.

Have you noticed that discussing the structure of the neuron is nearly impossible without referring to its function: the transmission of neural impulses? We have seen that neural impulses are typically received by dendrites, passed on to cell bodies, then to axons, and ultimately to axon terminals. We know that myelin insulates some axons and speeds neural impulses along, but what exactly is a neural impulse? We will explore the neural impulse in the next section.

BEFORE YOU GO ON

1. What are the major parts of a neuron?
2. What is myelin, and what functions does it serve?
3. What is neurogenesis, and why is it important?

A Point to Ponder or Discuss
If we have fewer neurons in our brains now than we did when we were born, what are the implications for a) the rapidity of neural development before birth and b) the importance of adequate stimulation of the brain soon after birth?

The Function of Neurons

The function of a neuron is to transmit neural impulses from one place in the nervous system to another. Let's start with a definition. A **neural impulse** is a rapid, reversible change in the electrical charges within and outside a neuron. When a neuron transmits an impulse (when a neuron "fires"), this change in electrical charge travels from the dendrites to the axon terminal. Now let's take a closer look at how a neuron transmits an impulse.

Neurons exist in a complex biological environment. As living cells, they are filled with and surrounded by fluids. Only a very thin membrane (like a skin) separates the fluids inside a neuron from those outside. These fluids contain chemical particles called ions. **Chemical ions** are particles that carry a small, measurable electrical charge that is either positive (+) or negative (−). Electrically charged ions float around in all the fluids of the body, but they are heavily concentrated in the fluids in and near the nervous system. If you examine the distribution of ions inside and outside the axon of a neuron, you will find that the inside of the axon has more negative charge than the outside. (See Figure 2.2A.) All that means is that there are more negative ions than positive ions inside the axon. Conversely, there are

chemical ions chemical particles that carry a small electrical charge, either positive (+) or negative (−)

neural impulse a rapid, reversible change in the electrical charge within and outside a neuron

FIGURE 2.2

When a neuron is "at rest," the electrical charge inside that neuron has a significantly more negative charge (–70 mV) than is found outside the neuron (A). When the neuron fires, an "action potential" occurs and travels rapidly down the neuron (B). At this point, polarity reverses, and the inside actually becomes positively charged compared to the outside (+40 mV).

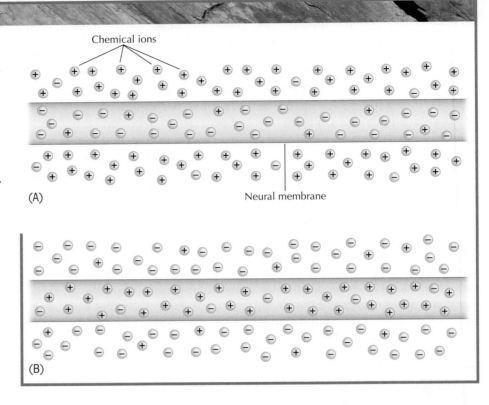

Chemical ions

(A)

Neural membrane

(B)

resting potential the tension that results from the positive and negative ions' attraction to each other (about –70 mV)

action potential the electrical charge that results when the ions within the neuron become more positive than the ions within the neuron (about +40 mV)

more positive ions than negative ions outside the neuron's axon. When a neuron is not transmitting an impulse, or not firing, that neuron is said to be "at rest." When it is at rest, the physiology of the neuron keeps the inside of the axon negatively charged compared to the outside. A tension develops between the electrical charge of ions that have been trapped inside the neuron (those predominantly negative ions) and the electrical charge of ions that have been trapped outside the neuron (predominantly positive ions). Positive and negative ions are attracted to each other; however, they cannot come into contact because the neuron's membrane separates them.

The tension that results from the positive and negative ions' attraction to each other is called a **resting potential**. The resting potential of a neuron is about –70 millivolts (mV), which makes a neuron somewhat like a tiny battery. A D-cell battery (the sort used in a flashlight) has two aspects (or poles): one positive and the other negative. The

electrical charge possible with one of these batteries (the resting potential) is 1500 mV, much greater than that of a neuron. The resting potential of a neuron is negative 70 mV because we measure the *inside* of a neuron relative to the *outside*, and the negative ions are concentrated inside. At rest, the neuron is in a polarized state.

When a neuron is stimulated to fire, or produce an impulse, the electrical tension of the resting potential is released. Very quickly, the polarity of the neuron changes—a process called *depolarization*. Depolarization occurs when the axon membrane suddenly allows positively charged ions to flood into the interior of the axon, drastically changing the electrical potential of the axon. Then the membrane allows positively charged ions to exit the axon. For an instant (about one one-thousandth of a second), the electrical charge within the neuron becomes more positive than the area outside the neuron. This new charge is the **action potential**, which is about +40 mV (Figure 2.2B). The pos-

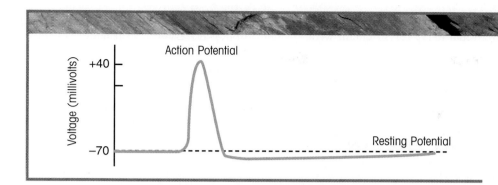

FIGURE 2.3

Changes in electrical potential that occur during the firing of a neuron. Note that the voltage is negative (–70 mV) when the neuron is "at rest," and positive (+40 mV) during the firing of the impulse. Note, too, that the entire process lasts but a few milliseconds.

itive sign here indicates that the inside of the neuron is now more positive than the outside (there are more positive ions inside than outside). In a fraction of a second, the neuron returns to its original state with the tension redeveloped and, after a few thousandths of a second, it is ready to fire again.

Before the neuron returns to its normal resting state, it becomes hyperpolarized. That is, its negative charge is more negative than the normal –70mV. This hyperpolarization occurs because the neuron's membrane allows too many negative ions back through the membrane, making the inside of the cell too negative. For a few thousandths of a second, there is a **refractory period** during which the neuron cannot fire. Eventually, the membrane returns to normal as the distribution of ions across the cell membrane restores itself.

To repeat, when a neuron is at rest, there is a difference between the electrical charges inside and outside the neuron (the inside is more negative). When the neuron is stimulated to fire, the difference reverses, so that the inside becomes slightly positive. The tension of the resting potential then returns (see Figure 2.3). Note: As an impulse "travels down a neuron," *nothing physically travels from one end of the neuron to the other.* The only movement is the movement of the electrically charged ions into and out of the neuron through its membrane.

Neurons don't fire every time they are stimulated. That is to say, they don't always transmit a neural impulse when they are stimulated. A neuron either fires or it doesn't, a fact called the **all-or-none**

principle. There is no such thing as a weak or strong neural impulse; the impulse is there or it isn't. The depolarization of the neuron during the action potential is an all-or-none proposition. This raises an interesting psychological question: How does the nervous system react to differences in stimulus intensity? How do neurons react to the difference between a bright light and a dim one, a soft sound and a loud one, or a tap on the shoulder and a slap on the back? Remember, neurons do not fire partially, so we cannot say that a neuron fires partially for a dim light and fires to a greater degree for the brighter light. Part of the answer involves neural thresholds.

As we just said, neurons do not generate impulses every time they are stimulated. Each neuron has a level of stimulation that must be reached to produce an impulse. The minimum level of stimulation required to fire a neuron is the **neural threshold**. This concept, coupled with the all-or-none principle, is the key to understanding how we process stimuli of varying intensities. High-intensity stimuli (bright lights, loud sounds, etc.) do not cause neurons to fire more vigorously; they stimulate *more* neurons to fire. And, as it happens, those neurons will fire more frequently as well. High-intensity stimuli are above the neural threshold of a greater number of neurons than are low-intensity stimuli. The difference in our experience of a flashbulb going off near our faces and how we see a candle at a distance reflects the number of neurons involved and the rate at which they fire, not the degree or extent to which they fire.

refractory period the brief time during which a neuron, having just fired, cannot fire again

neural threshold the minimum level of stimulation required to get a neuron to fire

all-or-none principle the observation that a neuron either fires or it doesn't

Now that we have examined the individual nerve cell in detail, we are ready to learn how neurons communicate with each other—how impulses are transmitted from one cell to another. How impulses travel between neurons is just as remarkable, but quite different from how impulses travel within neurons.

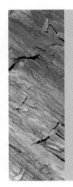

BEFORE YOU GO ON

4. What is the nature of a neural impulse?
5. What is the all-or-none principle, and what are neural thresholds?

A Point to Ponder or Discuss

Neural impulses begin when stimuli activate one's sense receptors. In what other ways might neural impulses begin? Once neurons begin to fire and send impulses on to other neurons, what do you suppose stops the process, i.e., when does neural transmission stop?

FROM ONE NEURON TO ANOTHER: THE SYNAPSE

The location at which a neural impulse is relayed from one neuron to another is called the **synapse**. At these synapses, neurons do not touch each other. Instead, there is a microscopic gap between the axon terminal of one neuron and the dendrites (or cell body) of another neuron. This gap is called the **synaptic cleft**. What happens at the synapse is shown in Figure 2.4.

Synaptic Transmission

At the end of an axon, there are many branches which themselves end at axon terminals. Throughout any neuron, but concentrated in its axon terminals, are incredibly small containers called **vesicles**, which hold complex chemicals called neurotransmitters. After crossing the synaptic cleft, complex chemical molecules called neurotransmitters act to excite or inhibit the transmission of a neural impulse in the next neuron.

When an impulse reaches the axon terminal, the vesicles burst open and release the neurotransmitters they have been holding. The released neurotransmitters flood out into the synaptic cleft.

Once in the synaptic cleft, some neurotransmitter molecules move to the membrane of a nearby neuron where they may fit into **receptor sites**: special places on a neuron where neurotransmitters can be received. Think of the neurotransmitter as being a key that fits into a particular lock on the receptor site. If the key fits into the lock, the neurotransmitter attaches to the receptor site in the membrane of the next neuron (Figure 2.4).

Then what happens? Actually, any number of things can happen. Let's look at a few. The most logical scenario for synaptic activity is that the neurotransmitters float across the synaptic cleft, enter into (or "bind to") receptor sites in the next neuron in a chain of nerve cells, excite that neuron to release the tension of its resting potential, and fire a new impulse down to its axon terminals. There, new neurotransmitter chemicals are released from vesicles, which cross the synaptic cleft and stimulate the next neurons in the sequence. For obvious reasons, the process is called **excitatory**.

As it happens, there are many places throughout our nervous systems where the opposite effect occurs. In this case, when they are released, the

---

receptor sites special places on a neuron where neurotransmitters can be received

synapse the location at which a neural impulse is relayed from one neuron to another

synaptic cleft a microscopically small gap between the axon terminal and the dendrites (or cell body) of another neuron

vesicles incredibly small containers that hold complex chemicals called neurotransmitters

excitatory the name of the process in which neurotransmitter chemicals are released from the vesicles, cross the synaptic cleft, and stimulate the next neuron to fire

FIGURE 2.4

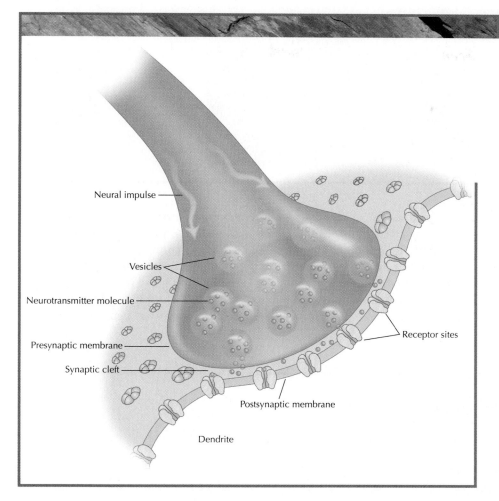

A synapse, in which transmission is from upper left to lower right. As an impulse enters the axon terminal, vesicles release neurotransmitter chemicals into the synaptic space, or cleft. The neurotransmitter then either excites or inhibits an impulse in the next neuron.

Neural impulse

Vesicles

Neurotransmitter molecule

Presynaptic membrane

Synaptic cleft

Receptor sites

Postsynaptic membrane

Dendrite

neurotransmitters flood across the synaptic cleft, bind to receptor sites, and prevent that next neuron from firing. This synaptic process is referred to as being **inhibitory**. Sometimes neurotransmitters are released at a synapse and simply do not find a receptor site to bind to, and thus have no excitatory or inhibitory effect.

A small complication: Neurotransmitters themselves are not properly classified as being either excitatory or inhibitory. Excitation or inhibition is not a function of the chemicals themselves. Rather, what happens at the synapse is a function of the *interaction* of the neurotransmitter and the receptor site to which it binds. In other words, at some synapses a neurotransmitter may inhibit impulse transmission, but in a different location, at a

different synapse, that same neurotransmitter may excite impulse transmission.

The final step in synaptic transmission is the elimination of the neurotransmitter from the synaptic cleft. This is done in one of two ways: destruction by an enzyme or reuptake. Some neurotransmitters are broken down by special enzymes secreted into the synaptic cleft, and eventually leave the body as waste. Other neurotransmitters are reabsorbed by the membrane of the neuron from which they came through a process called **reuptake**.

Many drugs used to treat psychological disorders mimic the action of neurotransmitters and either over-stimulate neural impulse transmission or overly inhibit synaptic activity. Some drugs (the antidepressant Prozac is an example) affect the breakdown or reuptake of

inhibitory the name of the process in which neurotransmitters flood across the synaptic cleft, bind to receptor sites, and prevent the next neuron from firing

reuptake the process by which neurotransmitters are reabsorbed by the membrane of the neuron from which they came

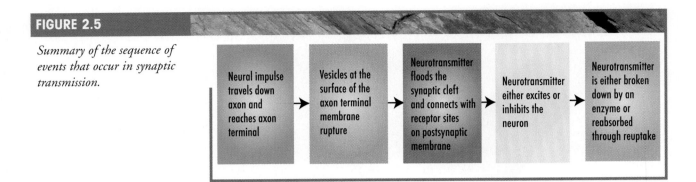

FIGURE 2.5

Summary of the sequence of events that occur in synaptic transmission.

| Neural impulse travels down axon and reaches axon terminal | Vesicles at the surface of the axon terminal membrane rupture | Neurotransmitter floods the synaptic cleft and connects with receptor sites on postsynaptic membrane | Neurotransmitter either excites or inhibits the neuron | Neurotransmitter is either broken down by an enzyme or reabsorbed through reuptake |

neurotransmitters. The sequence of events in synaptic transmission is summarized in Figure 2.5. Please note that synaptic transmission also occurs at the synapse of neurons and other kinds of cells. When a neuron forms a synapse with a muscle cell, for instance, the release of a neurotransmitter from the neuron's axon terminals may excite that muscle to contract momentarily. Similarly, neurons that form synapses with the cells of a gland may cause that gland to secrete a hormone when stimulated by the appropriate neurotransmitter.

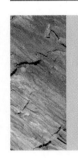

BEFORE YOU GO ON

6. Describe the synapse and, in general terms, what happens there.

A Point to Ponder or Discuss
How do you suppose researchers discovered neurotransmitters and the mechanisms by which they produce excitatory and inhibitory reactions at the synapse?

Neurotransmitters

To understand how neurotransmitters work, we must examine both the key and the lock: the neurotransmitter and its receptor site. Not long ago, scientists believed that neurons produced and released only two different neurotransmitters: one that excited neural impulse transmission and another that inhibited neural impulse transmission. Now we realize that this view is much too simplistic. Researchers have since identified more than 100 neurotransmitters, and it is virtually certain that there are many others yet to be discovered (Greengard, 2001). With respect to receptor sites, the once-held view that each neurotransmitter had one-and-only-one type of recep-

tor site is no longer valid. One neurotransmitter may have more than one type of receptor site (Cooper, Bloom, & Roth, 1996). Thus, there are subtypes of receptor sites for each of the various brain chemicals. The search for these receptor sites has become one of the hottest areas of brain research.

The discovery of more neurotransmitters and receptor-site subtypes teaches us more about the biochemistry of the brain and how it works. The belief that there were only a couple of types of neurotransmitters placed a limitation on the nature and complexity of synaptic communication. More neurotransmitters, receptor sites, and specialized sites indicate a potential for clearer and more complex communication within the nervous system. For example, imagine that a part of the brain that processes emotion receives separate signals indicating two different emotions (fear and surprise). Were there only one neurotransmitter and receptor site involved, the different emotions could not be recognized. More neurotransmitters and receptor sites allow the independent signals to be separated, sorted, and more clearly recognized (Wilson, 1998).

Despite the complex biochemistry of the nervous system, it is useful to describe the activity of some of the neurotransmitters that have been discovered. We will encounter these neurotransmitters again when we discuss the actions of many drugs; when we consider how memories are formed; and when we explore possible causes of, and treatment for, some psychological disorders. For now, let's briefly note five better-known neurotransmitters.

Acetylcholine (pronounced "uh-see-til-koh´-leen"), or ACh, is found throughout the nervous system, where it acts as either an excitatory or inhibitory neurotransmitter, depending on where it is found. It is a common neurotransmitter and was the first to be discovered (in the 1920s). Although some acetylcholine can be found in the brain, most is found outside the brain in the peripheral nervous system. Most commonly, when acetylcholine is released, it binds with receptor sites on muscle cells, stimulating a contraction. But ACh works to inhibit activity in heart-muscle cells—an excellent example of one neurotransmitter having both excitatory and inhibitory effects.

One form of food poisoning, *botulism*, blocks the release of acetylcholine at neuron/muscle-cell synapses, which can cause paralysis of the respiratory system and death unless an antidote is given. The poisonous drug *curare* works in much the same fashion. Some other poisons (e.g., the venom of the black widow spider) have just the opposite effect, causing excess amounts of ACh to be released, resulting in muscle contractions or spasms so severe as to be deadly. Nicotine is a chemical that in small amounts tends to increase the normal functioning of ACh, but in large doses acts to override the normal action of acetylcholine—a reaction that can lead to muscle paralysis and even death. Acetylcholine has been associated with memory formation and the maintenance of levels of overall arousal. Low levels of acetylcholine have been tied to the loss of cognitive functioning in patients with Alzheimer's disease.

Norepinephrine is a common and important neurotransmitter that is involved in maintaining levels of vigilance and activation. It is associated with high levels of emotional arousal, such as increased heart rate, blood pressure, and perspiration. When there is an abundance of norepinephrine in a person's brain or spinal cord, feelings of arousal, agitation, even anxiety may result. (Cocaine increases the release of norepinephrine, leading to a state of agitation and a "high" mood state.) Too little norepinephrine in the central nervous system is associated with feelings of depression.

Dopamine, a neurotransmitter that also helps to regulate mood, is one that intrigues psychologists. Dopamine is involved in a wide range of reactions. Either too much or too little dopamine within the nervous system seems to produce a number of effects, depending primarily on which system of nerve fibers in the brain is involved. Among other things, dopamine seems to act to tell us which of our activities are rewarding or pleasurable. When hungry rats eat or thirsty rats drink, for example, levels of dopamine increase in their brains. Dopamine has been associated with the thought and mood disturbances of some psychological disorders, such as schizophrenia (Walker et al., 2004). As we shall see shortly, dopamine is also associated with the loss of movement. Dopamine acts mostly as an inhibitor. With too little dopamine, we find a loss of voluntary movement; too much dopamine and we find involuntary tremors.

Serotonin is produced in a small area low in the brain, very near the spinal cord, but it is found throughout the brain. Its action in the nervous system is quite complex and not yet completely understood. We do know, however, that serotonin is involved in the sleep/waking cycle. An increase in levels of serotonin in parts of the brain is related to sleep onset (Rosenzweig, Leiman, & Breedlove, 1996). Serotonin also plays a role in depression. Depleted levels of serotonin are related to depressive symptoms. Certain drugs that increase serotonin levels (often by blocking reuptake) reduce depressive symptoms. Low levels of serotonin have been associated with aggressive behavior (Coccaro, Kavoussi, & McNamee, 2000).

Endorphins (plural because there are several) are natural pain suppressors. The pain threshold—the ability to tolerate different levels of pain—is, in part, a function of endorphin production

(Watkins & Mayer, 1982). With excess levels of endorphins, we experience little pain; a deficit results in an increased experience of pain. When we are under extreme physical stress, endorphin levels rise. Long-distance runners, for instance, often report a euphoric "high" after they run great distances, as though endorphins have kicked in to protect them against the pain of physical exhaustion. For some individuals, risky behaviors like skydiving or surfing enormous waves seem to cause pleasure because of the production of endorphins.

We easily could continue this list, but we turn now to what neurotransmitters do: They are the agents that bind to receptor sites and then either excite or inhibit the transmission of neural impulses throughout the nervous system. That excitation or inhibition has an enormous effect on our thoughts, feelings, and behavior. Table 2.1 summarizes these important neurotransmitters.

TABLE 2.1	
A summary of some major neurotransmitters.	**Acetylcholine** found throughout the nervous system; stimulates muscle contractions; associated with memory formation and overall levels of arousal
	Norepinephrine maintains vigilance and activation; associated with high levels of emotional arousal
	Dopamine involved in regulating mood and in determining reward and pleasurable stimuli; associated with mood and thought disturbances and the impairment of movement
	Serotonin complex interactions involving sleep/wake cycles; plays a role in depression and in aggression
	Endorphins act as natural pain suppressors; may cause pleasure in some engaged in risky behaviors

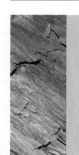

BEFORE YOU GO ON

7. Name and briefly describe the actions of four neurotransmitters.

A Point to Ponder or Discuss
Let us say that Drug X raises one's awareness, increases activation and energy levels, and improves cognitive functioning. Drug Y, on the other hand, has just the opposite effects. On the basis of what you know about neural impulse transmission so far, how might you account for the differences between these two drugs?

THE HUMAN NERVOUS SYSTEMS: THE BIG PICTURE

Now that we know how neurons work individually and in combination, let's consider the context in which they function. Behaviors and mental activities require large numbers of integrated neurons working together in complex, organized systems. Figure 2.6 depicts these systems.

The major division of the nervous systems is determined wholly on the basis of anatomy. The **central nervous system (CNS)** includes all neurons and supporting cells found in the spinal cord and brain. This system of nerves is the most complex and most intimately involved in the control of behavior and mental processes. The **peripheral nervous system (PNS)** consists of all neurons in our body not in the CNS—the nerve fibers in our arms, face, fingers, intestines, and so on. Neurons in the peripheral nervous system carry impulses from the central nervous system to the muscles and glands or to the CNS from receptor cells.

The peripheral nervous system is divided into two parts, based largely on the part of the body being served. The **somatic nervous system** includes those neurons that are outside the CNS and serve the skeletal muscles and pick up impulses from our sense receptors such as the eyes and ears. The other component of the PNS is the autonomic nervous system (ANS). "Autonomic" essentially means "automatic." This name implies that the activity of the ANS is largely (but not totally) independent of central nervous system control. The nerve fibers of the **autonomic nervous system** are involved in activating the

central nervous system (CNS) all neurons and supporting cells found in the spinal cord and brain

peripheral nervous system (PNS) all neurons not in the CNS; the nerve fibers in our arms, legs, face, torso, intestines, and so on

somatic nervous system those neurons that are outside the CNS, serve the skeletal muscles and pick up impulses from our sense receptors

autonomic nervous system (ANS) the system involved in activating the smooth muscles, such as those of the stomach, intestines, and glands

FIGURE 2.6

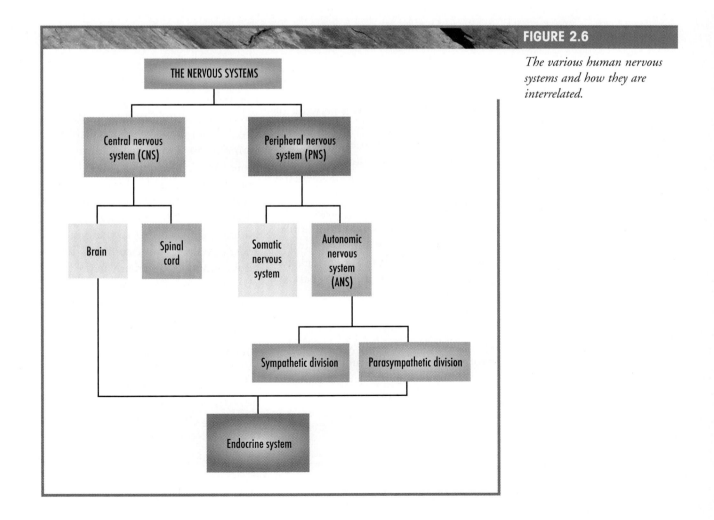

The various human nervous systems and how they are interrelated.

smooth muscles, such as those of the stomach and intestines, and the glands. The ANS provides feedback to the CNS about this internal activity.

The ANS also consists of two parts: the sympathetic division and the parasympathetic division. These two components commonly work in opposition to each other. The **sympathetic division** is active when we are emotionally aroused or excited, as we might be when riding up that first incline of a roller coaster. The **parasympathetic division** is active when we are relaxed and quiet, as we might be after a long day at the amusement park, half asleep

in the back seat on the drive home. Both divisions of the ANS act on the same organs, but they do so in opposite ways.

There is good reason to categorize the various organizations of neurons: It makes a very complex system easier to understand, and it reminds us that not all neurons in our body are doing the same thing for the same reason at the same time. Note that the outline of Figure 2.6 is very simplified to this extent: The nerve fibers in each of the systems have profound influences on one another. They are not at all as independent as our diagram might imply.

| sympathetic division (of the ANS) is active when we are emotionally aroused or excited

| parasympathetic division (of the ANS) is active when we are relaxed and quiet

BEFORE YOU GO ON

8.   Name the major divisions of the human nervous systems, and briefly describe what they do.

A Point to Ponder or Discuss
Imagine you are walking barefoot in the dark and step on a tack. Which of your various nervous systems might be involved, and how?

The Endocrine System

The **endocrine system** is a network of glands that affect behaviors by secreting chemicals called hormones. All hormones travel through the bloodstream and can affect organs far from where the hormones are produced. Many hormones produced by the glands of the endocrine system are chemically similar to neurotransmitters and have similar effects. The endocrine system's glands and hormones are controlled by parts of the brain and by the autonomic nervous system. Although not composed of neurons and synapses, the endocrine system is relevant to our discussion for two reasons. First, its function is like that of the nervous system: to transmit information from one part of the body to another. Second, hormones exert a direct influence on behavior.

| endocrine system a network of glands that affects behavior by secreting chemicals called hormones

Consider the so-called sex hormones, testosterone and estrogen. These hormones are found in both males and females, but testosterone is much more common in males, while estrogen is more common in females. High levels of testosterone in males have long been associated with increased aggression (Booth et al., 2003; Dabbs et al., 1995); but the relationship between testosterone and aggression is quite complex. Testosterone functions differently in the brains of males before birth (prenatal) and at puberty. During prenatal development, the male genetic code produces high levels of testosterone in the male brain, which causes the male brain to be wired for aggression—known as the *organization function* of testosterone. Then, at puberty, testosterone serves an *activation* function for aggression. Generally, research on animal subjects has confirmed the organization and activation functions of testosterone level. The connection between testosterone and aggression is complicated by findings that aggression (particularly the activation of aggressive behaviors) is influenced not just by the "male" testosterone, but also by the "female" estrogen. Recent research indicates that what seems to matter most is the relative levels or balance of the two hormones.

Let us consider three more endocrine glands—the pituitary, the thyroid, and the adrenal glands. (Glands in our bodies that are not part of the endocrine system because their secretions do not enter the bloodstream are called *exocrine glands*. Tear glands and sweat glands are two examples.)

Perhaps the most important endocrine gland is the **pituitary gland**. It is often referred to as the master gland, reflecting its direct control over the activity of many other glands in the system. The pituitary is nestled under the brain and secretes many different hormones. One hormone released by the pituitary is *growth hormone*, which regulates the growth of the body during its fastest physical development. Extremes of overproduction or underproduction cause the development of giants or dwarfs. The so-called "growth spurt" associated with early adolescence is due to the activity of the pituitary gland. It is the pituitary gland that stimulates the release of hormones that regulate the amount of water held within the body. It is the pituitary that directs the mammary glands in the breasts to release milk after childbirth. In its role as master over other glands, the pituitary regulates the output of the thyroid and the adrenal glands, as well as the sex glands.

The **thyroid gland** is located in the neck and produces a hormone called thyroxin. Thyroxin regulates the pace of the body's functioning—the rate at which oxygen is used and the rate of body function and growth. When a person is easily excited, edgy, having trouble sleeping, and has lost weight, a person may have too much thyroxin in his or her system, a condition called *hyperthyroidism*. Too little thyroxin leads to a lack of energy, fatigue, and an inability to do much, a condition called *hypothyroidism*.

The **adrenal glands**, located on the kidneys, secrete a variety of hormones into the bloodstream. The hormone adrenaline (more often referred to as epinephrine) is very useful in times of stress, danger, or threat. Adrenaline quickens breathing, causes the heart to beat faster, directs the flow of blood away from the stomach and intestines to the limbs, dilates the pupils of the eyes, and increases perspiration. When our adrenal glands flood epinephrine into our system during a perceived emergency, we usually feel the resulting reactions; but, typical of endocrine-system activity, these reactions may be delayed.

For example, as you drive down a busy street, you see a child dart out from behind a parked car and race to the other side of the street. You slam on the brakes, twist the steering wheel, and swerve to avoid the child. As the child scampers away, oblivious to the danger, you proceed down the street. Then, about a block later, your body reacts to the near miss: your heart pounds, a lump forms in your throat, your mouth dries, and your palms sweat. Why does your reaction come when the incident is over and you are out of danger? The delay in your body's reaction is because your reaction is largely hormonal. Your body's adrenal glands secrete epinephrine, and it takes time for this substance to travel through the bloodstream to the heart, pupils of the eyes, and the brainstem. You begin to feel effects once the epinephrine reaches these places.

adrenal glands secrete a variety of hormones into the bloodstream that are very useful in terms of stress, danger or threat

pituitary gland the master gland, reflecting its direct control over the activity of many other glands in the endocrine system

thyroid gland regulates the pace of the body's functioning—the rate at which oxygen is used and the rate of body function and growth

BEFORE YOU GO ON

9. What is the function of the endocrine system in general, and the pituitary gland, thyroid gland, and adrenal glands in particular?

A Point to Ponder or Discuss
Can nervous systems or endocrine systems similar to those in humans be found in so-called "lower species," such as dogs and cats? Why, or why not?

Genetics and Psychological Traits

At conception, a new cell is formed, one that contains a set of chromosomes, molecules of DNA, and genes from both the mother's ovum and the father's sperm. With conception, inheritance is over, but its effects most certainly are not.

What we inherit are chromosomes, DNA, and genes, which, in turn, produce certain chemicals—largely enzymes and proteins. The DNA, chromosomes and genes are what we commonly refer to as *genetics.* Your genetic makeup influences you throughout your life in ways of great interest to psychologists. To be sure, we do not inherit our mother's talent for music, our father's aggressiveness, or Aunt Tillie's mental illness. We do not inherit behaviors. We inherit chemicals. But, such assertions may be overly literal. There is considerable evidence that many of our behaviors, cognitive skills, and emotional reactions are influenced greatly by genetic factors. The term **behavior genetics** (or, "behavioral genetics") is the name given to the discipline that studies the effects of genetics on psychological functioning.

Perhaps we should ask where all this considerable evidence about the role of genetics in our affect, cognitions, and behavior comes from. In truth, most of the evidence is indirect—there is no one piece of research to point to. Instead, we have the accumulated weight of data from a number of different types of studies. Three types of research have proven to be particularly useful in illustrating the role of genetics in behavior.

1. ***Inbreeding studies:*** A typical inbreeding study involves mating organisms with a certain trait, while also breeding organisms that do not display that trait. If environmental conditions are held nearly constant over several generations, we may conclude that observed differences in the two strains of organisms are due to the genes they inherited through the inbreeding. We are all familiar with the practical results of such studies. Consider the breeding of horses for speed, cattle for muscle tissue, or dogs for their retrieval skills. Clearly, these studies are not done with humans, so researchers are then faced with the task of arguing that whatever results they do find for rats, monkeys, horses or dogs apply for humans as well.

2. ***Family history studies:*** This approach to determining the influence of heredity is the oldest of the three, first employed systematically by Sir Francis Galton in the 1800s, when he concluded that "genius" tended to "run in families" and thus had a genetic basis (Galton, 1879).

The logic is that when a trait tends to show up more consistently within groups that are genetically related than it does otherwise, we may assume some genetic basis for

behavior genetics the discipline that studies the effects of genes on psychological functioning

that trait. For example, the psychological disorder schizophrenia occurs in the general population at a rate of about one person in 100. But, if you have a brother or sister (sibling) with the disorder, your odds of having schizophrenia are about one in ten. If that sibling happens to be an identical twin (which means both of you have exactly the same set of genes), then your odds are one in two (Gottesman, 2001). Studying twins and comparing the traits of identical twins and fraternal twins (conceived and born at about the same time, but genetically no more similar than any brother and sister) have produced other intriguing insights. Genetics may account for some part in such diverse traits as aggression, depression, shyness, extroversion, and personal mannerisms (Ely, Lichenstein & Stevenson, 1999; Loehlin, 1992). Later we will see that there is similar evidence of a genetic basis for general intelligence (Chapter 7) and Alzheimer's Disease (Chapter 12).

Please keep in mind that there are all sorts of problems with studies of family histories and twins. Obviously, persons from the same family share more than a set of genes. They are reared in very similar environments, and, most of the time, the more closely related two people are, the more similar their environments. Family history research cannot tell us that environmental factors are irrelevant, but it can show us that genetic transmission is influential. Even with studies of twins separated at (or near) birth, difficulties remain: a) there simply are not many such cases, and b) if twins are reared in different homes, how can we begin to quantify *how* different the two environments really are—particularly when adoption agencies usually look to place adopted children in homes as similar to their original ones as possible.

3. **Searching for the direct influence of specific genes:** The Human Genome Project was established in 1990 as an international effort of research scientists to determine the location of *all* human genes and to read the entire set of genetic instructions encoded in human DNA. This mission was completed in April 2003 with the publication of the full and complete sequence of the human genome (NHGRI, 2002). The effort and the results are mind-boggling—and often misinterpreted. What a wonderful thing to be able to map and identify individual human genes! The potential is enormous, but, at the moment, it is little more than a promise, a beginning with an unclear path ahead.

Researchers have identified genes on specific chromosomes that are associated with a range of outcomes, including Alzheimer's disease, general intelligence, schizophrenia, alcoholism, and muscular dystrophy (Hillier et al., 2005; McGuffin, Riley, & Plomin, 2001; Plomin et al., 2002). The media may be excused perhaps for a bit of over-exuberance, but many reports in the press have been misleading. *"Scientists Find Smart Gene!"* and *"Cause of Alzheimer's Disease Linked to Gene!"* are the sorts of headlines that have appeared from time to time. Think back to Chapter 1, and remember our discussion of correlation in which we made the point that discovering an association between two events (the location of a gene and the symptoms of a disease, for example) does not imply a known cause-and-effect relation. Then remember our discussion of *interactionism.* The environment produces powerful influences on behavior, the choices one makes, and on the course of a disease—

even if there is a known genetic association with that disease (Moffitt, Caspi, & Rutter, 2005). And thirdly, remember that in psychology, little is as simple as it first appears. As one group of researchers put it,

> Frequent news reports claim that researchers have discovered the 'gene for' such traits as aggression, intelligence, criminality, homosexuality, feminine intuition, and even bad luck. Such reports tend to suggest, usually incorrectly, that there is a direct correspondence between carrying a mutation in the gene and manifesting the trait or disorder. Rarely is it mentioned that traits involving behavior are likely to have a more complex genetic basis. (McGuffin, Riley, & Plomin, 2001, p. 1232).

These authors go on to say that "ultimately, the human genome sequence will revolutionize psychology and psychiatry," but there are many steps to be taken and many problems to be solved along the way. If nothing else, the social and ethical issues involved in this line of research are nearly overwhelming.

Before we leave the topic of genetic influences, we must explore another level of genetic influence. For many years, scientists believed that when the human genome sequence was cracked it would open up our understanding of genetic influence and perhaps lead to cures for many diseases. However, genetic scientists now tell us that such an understanding will not come from disentangling the genome sequence alone (Weidman, Dolinoy, Murphy, & Jirtle, 2007). A true understanding of the relationship between genetics and complex systems like behavior and diseases will also require understanding *epigenetics*. **Epigenetics** refers to a complex biochemical system that exists above the basic level of one's DNA code (genetics) that can affect the overt expression of genetically influenced traits. Epigenetics influence the expression of genetic codes by switching genes on or off and can affect the expression of genetic predispositions across many generations (Pennisi, 2001). You can think of epigenetics as a mechanism that instructs genes how to function. To complicate matters further, the epigenetic code can be modified by environmental factors such as maternal health or nutrition, which, in turn, can increase susceptibility to a range of diseases and conditions (Weidman et al., 2007).

Let's take a quick look at how this works. In one experiment genetically identical female mice were fed one of two diets (Dolinoy, Weidman, Waterland, & Jirtle, 2006). One group of mice received a diet high in soy (equivalent to a human consuming a diet high in soy products), whereas a second group was on an identical diet except that the soy was eliminated (corn was substituted). The mice were impregnated and eventually the offspring were observed for coat color and changes in their epigenetic structure. Dolinoy, et al. found that the offspring of mice exposed to the high soy diet displayed a mottled yellow-brown coat and the offspring of mice exposed to the non-soy diet showed the more common solid yellow coat. More significantly, the researchers found that the epigenetic structure of the two sets of offspring differed, resulting in not only the modified coat color but also to a resistance to obesity later in life. Thus, what the offsprings' mothers ate affected the coat color and susceptibility to obesity in genetically (in terms of the underlying DNA structure) identical mice. Researchers believe that with further research it might be possible to change susceptibility to a range of diseases (e.g., cancer, diabetes, Alzheimer's) by manipulating epigenetic structure.

epigenetics a complex biochemical system, above the level of one's DNA code that can affect the expression of genetically influenced traits

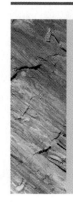

THE SPINAL CORD

The central nervous system consists of the brain and the spinal cord. In this section, we consider the structure and function of the spinal cord, reserving our discussion of the brain for the next section.

The Structure of the Spinal Cord

The spinal cord is a mass of interconnected neurons within the spinal column that looks rather like a section of rope or thick twine. It is surrounded and protected by the hard bone and cartilage of the vertebrae. A cross-sectional view of the spinal column and the spinal cord is illustrated in Figure 2.7. A few structural details need to be mentioned. Note that the spinal cord is located in the middle of the spinal column, which extends from the lower back to high in the neck just below the brain. Note also that nerve fibers enter and leave the spinal cord from the side. Neurons or nerve fibers that carry impulses toward the brain or spinal cord are called **sensory neurons** or sensory fibers. Neurons and nerve fibers that carry impulses away from the spinal cord and brain to muscles and glands are called **motor neurons** or motor fibers. Neurons within the central nervous system are called **interneurons**.

Notice also that the center area of the spinal cord consists of gray matter, while the outside area is light white matter. This color difference means that the center portion is filled with cell bodies, dendrites, and unmyelinated axons, while the outer section is filled with myelinated axons. These observations about the structure of the spinal cord are the key to understanding its functions.

The Functions of the Spinal Cord

The spinal cord has two major functions. One, the *communication* function, involves transmitting impulses rapidly to and from the brain. When sensory impulses originate in sense receptors below the neck and make their way to the brain, they do so through the spinal cord. When the brain transmits motor impulses to move or activate parts of the body below the neck, those impulses first travel down the spinal cord. For example, if you stub your toe, pain messages travel up the spinal cord and register in the brain. When you decide to reach for that cup of coffee and bring it toward your mouth, impulses originating in your brain move to the muscles in your back, arm, and hand by traveling first down the spinal cord.

Impulses to and from various parts of the body leave and enter the spinal

sensory neurons those that carry impulses toward the brain or spinal cord

motor neurons those that carry impulses away from the spinal cord and brain to muscles and glands

interneurons those within the central nervous system

FIGURE 2.7

A cross-sectional view of the spinal column. Only the white matter and gray matter in the center represent actual spinal cord tissue. Note that spinal nerves enter and leave the spinal cord at its sides.

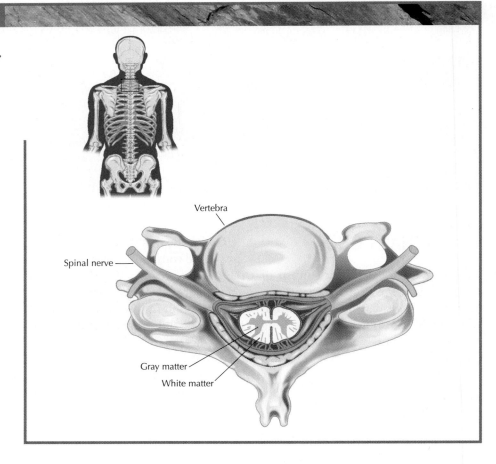

Vertebra

Spinal nerve

Gray matter

White matter

Courtesy of Reuters/Corbis.

Christopher Reeve

cord at different points. Impulses to and from the legs, for example, enter and leave at the very base of the spinal cord (see Figure 2.8). If the spinal cord is damaged, the communication function may be disrupted. The consequences of such an injury are disastrous, resulting in a loss of feeling and a loss of voluntary movement (that is, paralysis) of the muscles in those parts of the body served by the spinal cord below the injury. The higher in the spinal cord that damage takes place, the greater is the resulting loss.

In May 1995, the late actor Christopher Reeve was attempting to jump his thoroughbred, Eastern Express, over what is called a "rail jump." The horse balked, throwing Reeve headfirst to the ground. At impact, the uppermost vertebrae of his spinal column were crushed, and his spinal cord was severed. Reeve, perhaps best known for his movie portrayal of Superman, was instantly paralyzed. In Reeve's case, his injury led to *quadriplegia,* or the loss of function of all four limbs, because his injury was so high on the spinal cord. Had his injury been lower, he might have had *paraplegia,* loss of function in the parts of the body below the injury. In addition, impulses from the brain that normally stimulate the muscles of the diaphragm to contract were cut off. For nearly eight years, a mechanical ventilator filled Reeve's lungs with air. In March of 2003, a small device was surgically implanted in his diaphragm muscles to regularly stimulate contractions, not unlike a pacemaker does for the heart muscle. Two weeks later, he was able to breathe on his own for nearly two hours before resuming the use of a ventilator. Patients who undergo this procedure typically learn to breathe on their own for longer and longer periods

FIGURE 2.8

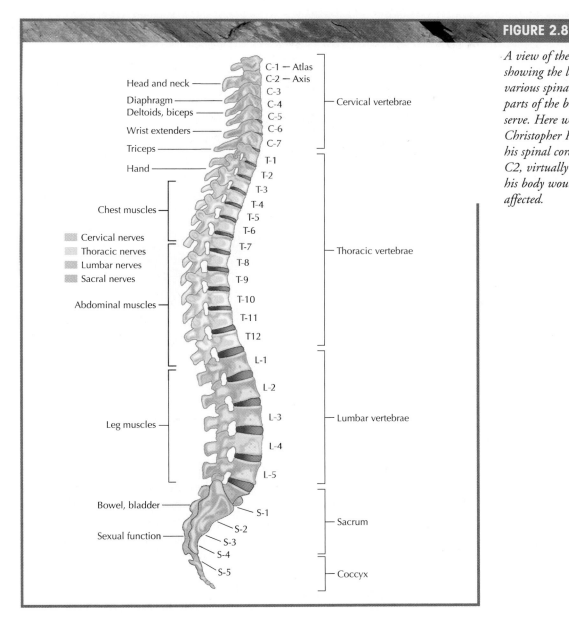

A view of the spinal column, showing the location of the various spinal nerves and the parts of the body that they serve. Here we can see that if Christopher Reeve had severed his spinal cord at or near level C2, virtually every muscle in his body would have been affected.

Head and neck
Diaphragm
Deltoids, biceps
Wrist extenders
Triceps
Hand
Chest muscles

Cervical nerves
Thoracic nerves
Lumbar nerves
Sacral nerves

Abdominal muscles

Leg muscles

Bowel, bladder
Sexual function

C-1 — Atlas
C-2 — Axis
C-3
C-4
C-5
C-6
C-7

Cervical vertebrae

T-1
T-2
T-3
T-4
T-5
T-6
T-7
T-8
T-9
T-10
T-11
T12

Thoracic vertebrae

L-1
L-2
L-3
L-4
L-5

Lumbar vertebrae

S-1
S-2
S-3
S-4
S-5

Sacrum

Coccyx

as their atrophied diaphragm muscles regain strength. Reeve became a spokesman and role model for the nearly 200,000 Americans who have spinal cord injuries. He died on October 10, 2004, at the age of 52. (To learn more about Reeve and the foundation he began, visit www.christopherreeve.org)

Since Reeve's injury there have been advancements in the treatment of spinal cord injuries. One example is spinal hypothermia treatment, which, if applied soon after an injury, may improve a patient's prognosis. In this treatment an ice-cold saline solution is injected into the patient's bloodstream, which chills the entire body. The treatment prevents swelling and hemorrhaging around the injury. An example of the effectiveness of this treatment is Kevin Everett, a tight end who played for the NFL team the Buffalo Bills. On September 9, 2007, Everett suffered a severe spinal cord injury resulting from a headfirst collision with another player. Very soon after his injury he received the hypothermia treatment. After undergoing surgery, Everett showed significant improvement in voluntary movement of his arms and legs. His recent reports say

FIGURE 2.9

A spinal reflex. Stimulation of receptor cells in the skin, in turn, stimulate sensory neurons, interneurons, and motor neurons. Although a response is made without the involvement of the brain, impulses also travel up fibers in the spinal cord's white matter to the brain.

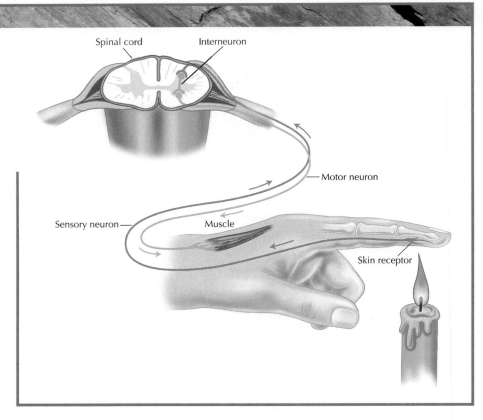

that he is walking on his own and that his prognosis is positive.

The second major function of the spinal cord is its *integrative function* and involves mediating spinal reflexes. **Spinal reflexes** are simple, automatic behaviors that occur without conscious voluntary action of the brain. To understand how these reflexes work, see Figure 2.9. In this drawing of the spinal cord, we have added receptor cells in the skin, sensory neurons, motor neurons to muscles in the hand, and have labeled the neurons within the spinal cord as interneurons.

Let's trace your reaction to holding the tip of your finger over a burning candle. Receptor cells in your fingertip respond to the heat of the flame, sending neural impulses racing along sensory neurons, up your arm and shoulder, and into the spinal cord. Then two things happen at almost the same time. Impulses rush up the ascending pathways of the spinal cord's white matter to your brain (very quickly you learn how

silly putting a finger near a flame was). Impulses also travel on interneurons and leave the spinal cord on motor neurons to your arm and hand, where muscles are stimulated to contract, and your hand jerks back.

This is a simple spinal reflex. Impulses travel *in* on sensory neurons, *within* on interneurons, and *out* on motor neurons. Here we have an environmental stimulus (a flame), activity in the central nervous system (neurons in the spinal cord), and an observable response (withdrawal of the hand). Notice that, for this sequence of events of the spinal reflex, the involvement of the brain is not at all necessary.

There are a few observations we must make about the reflex of the type shown in Figure 2.9. First, the fact that impulses enter the spinal cord and immediately race to the brain is not indicated in the drawing. In a situation such as the candle example, you may jerk your hand back "without thinking about it," but very soon thereafter you are aware of what has happened. Awareness occurs in the brain, not in the spinal cord. It is also true that some reflexes are simpler than the one in Figure 2.9. The reflex in this drawing shows three types of neurons—sensory, motor, and interneurons. Some spinal reflexes involve only sensory neurons and motor neurons, which directly interact within the spinal cord. The common knee-jerk reflex is an example—sensory neurons and motor neurons synapse directly with no interneurons involved.

THE "LOWER" BRAIN CENTERS

Perched atop your spinal cord, encased in bone, is a wonderful, mysterious organ: your brain. Your brain is a mass of neurons, supporting cells, blood vessels, and ventricles (interconnected cavities containing fluid). Your brain accounts for a small fraction of your body weight, but due to its importance, it receives almost 20 percent of the blood in your body. Your brain contains a storehouse of memories and is the seat of your emotions and motivation. It regulates your breathing and the beating of your heart.

For convenience, we will divide the brain into two major categories of structures. We first discuss the role of some of the "lower" brain centers, which are involved in several important aspects of behavior. Then we will examine the role of the cerebral cortex, the outer layers or covering of the brain that, generally speaking, controls higher mental functions.

The "lower" centers of the brain contain vital structures involved in regulating crucial, involuntary functions like respiration and the heartbeat. Although we may call these structures "lower," they are by no means unimportant. Lower brain centers are "lower" in two ways.

First, they are physically located beneath the cerebral cortex. Second, these brain structures develop first—both in an evolutionary sense and within the developing human brain. These lower brain structures are the structures we most clearly share with other animals and upon which our very survival depends. Use Figure 2.10 to locate the lower brain structures as we discuss them.

The Brainstem

As you look at the spinal cord and brain, you cannot tell where one ends and the other begins. There is no abrupt division of these two aspects of the central nervous system. Just above the spinal cord there is a slight widening of the cord that suggests the transition to brain tissue. At this point of widening, two structures form the brainstem: the medulla and the pons.

The lowest structure in the brain is the medulla. In many ways, the medulla acts like the spinal cord in that its major functions involve involuntary reflexes. There are several small structures called nuclei (collections of neural cell bodies) in the **medulla** that control such functions as coughing, sneezing, tongue movements, and reflexive eye movements. You do not think about blinking

medulla the lower brain center that controls such functions as coughing, sneezing, respiration, heart function, and reflexive eye movements

FIGURE 2.10

Some of the major structures of the human brain, of which the cerebral cortex is clearly the largest.

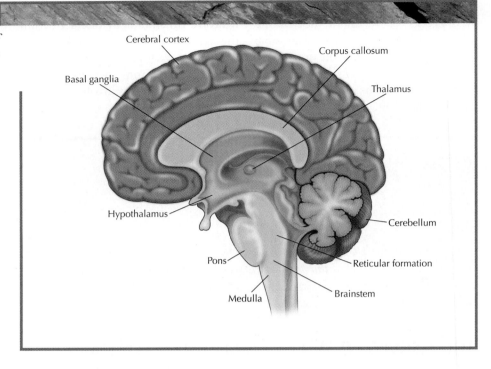

cross laterality the process of nerve fibers crossing from one side of the body to the opposite side of the brain

pons a relay station, or bridge, relaying sensory messages from the spinal cord and the face to higher brain centers, and relaying motor impulses from higher centers in the brain down to the rest of the body

your eye as something rushes toward it, for example; your medulla produces that eye blink reflexively.

The medulla contains nuclei that control breathing reflexes, mediate blood pressure levels, and regulate the muscles of the heart to keep it beating rhythmically. We can control the nuclei of the medulla, but only within limits. For example, the medulla controls our respiration (breathing), but we can override the medulla and hold our breath. We cannot, however, hold our breath until we die, as some children occasionally may threaten. We can hold our breath until we lose consciousness, which is to say until we give up voluntary control; then the medulla takes over and breathing resumes.

At the level of the medulla, most nerve fibers to and from the brain cross from right to left and vice versa. That is, motor neurons from the left side of the brain cross over to control the right side of the body. Motor neurons from the right side of the brain cross to control the left side of the body. Similarly, sensory nerve fibers from each side of the body cross over to carry information to the opposite side of the brain. This crossover explains why electrically stimulating the correct area in the left side of the brain produces a movement in the right arm. It also explains why a cerebral stroke in the left side of the brain causes loss of movement in the right side of the body. The arrangement of nerve fibers crossing from one side of the body to the opposite side of the brain is called **cross laterality**, and the crossing takes place in the brainstem.

Just above the medulla is a structure called the pons. (The pons is one structure; there is no such thing as a "pon.") The **pons** serves as a relay station or bridge, sorting out and relaying sensory messages from the spinal cord and the face up to higher brain centers and similarly relaying motor impulses from higher centers of the brain down to the rest of the body. The cross laterality that begins in the medulla continues in the pons. Nuclei in the pons are also partially responsible for the rapid eye movement that occurs when we dream. Other centers in the pons are involved in determining when we sleep and when we awaken.

BEFORE YOU GO ON

14. Where are the medulla and the pons, and what do they do?
15. What is meant by cross-laterality?

A Point to Ponder or Discuss

One way to study how the various structures in the central nervous system work is to contemplate what would happen if those structures were damaged or destroyed. For example, what would be the result of an accident that damaged the medulla? What if the pons were destroyed?

The Cerebellum

The cerebellum sits behind your pons, tucked up under the base of your skull. Your cerebellum (literally, "small brain") is about the size of your closed fist and is the second-largest part of your brain. Its outer region (its cortex) is convoluted, that is, the tissue is folded in upon itself, creating many deep crevices and lumps.

The major role of the **cerebellum** is to smooth and coordinate rapid body movements. Most intentional voluntary movements originate in higher brain centers (the motor area of the cerebral cortex) and are coordinated by the cerebellum. Because of the close relationship between body movement and vision, many eye movements originate in the cerebellum. Curiously, the cerebellum, as small as it is, contains nearly half of all the neurons in the human brain (Zillmer & Spiers, 2001, p. 93).

Our ability to stoop, pick a dime off the floor, and slip it into our pocket involves a complex series of movements smoothed and coordinated by our cerebellum. When athletes practice or rehearse a movement, such as a golf swing or a gymnastic routine, we may say that they are trying to "get into a groove," so that their trained movements can be made simply and smoothly. In a way, the athletes are training their cerebellums, which play an important role in coordinating "automatic" movements. Examples would be catching a fast line drive hit right to you, playing a well-practiced piano piece, or quickly reaching out to save a priceless vase you just knocked off a table with your elbow. It appears that such movements are not reflexive, but rather the cerebellum learns to make them—a process that is the focus of research by neuroscientists interested in how one's learning experiences are represented in the brain.

Few behaviors are as well coordinated or as well learned as the rapid movements needed to speak. The next time you're talking to someone, focus on how quickly and effortlessly your lips, mouth, and tongue are moving, thanks to the cerebellum. Damage to the cerebellum slurs speech. In fact, damage to the cerebellum disrupts all coordinated movements. Someone with cerebellum damage may shake and stagger when he or she walks. To the casual observer such a person may appear to be drunk. (On what region of the brain do you suppose alcohol has a direct effect? The cerebellum.)

Damage to the cerebellum can disrupt motor activity in other ways. If the outer region (or "cortex") of the cerebellum is damaged, involuntary trembling occurs when the person tries to move (called "intention tremors"). Damage to inner, deeper areas of the cerebellum leads to "tremors at rest," and the limbs or head may shake or twitch rhythmically even when the person tries to remain still.

cerebellum the lower brain center that smoothes and coordinates rapid bodily movements

Courtesy of Randy Faris/Corbis.

The ability of an athlete—beginner or professional—to perform a complex, coordinated series of movements, smoothly and in the same fashion with each repetition, requires the involvement of the cerebellum.

| **reticular formation** an ill-defined collection of nerve fibers involved in one's level of activation or arousal

| **basal ganglia** lower brain centers that are involved in the planning, initiating, and coordinating of large, slow movements

| **Parkinson's disease** a disorder involving the basal ganglia in which the most noticeable symptoms are impairment of movement and involuntary tremors

The Reticular Formation

The reticular formation is hardly a brain structure at all. It is a complex network of nerve fibers that begins in the brainstem and works its way up through and around other structures to the top portions of the brain.

What the **reticular formation** does, and how it does so, remain something of a mystery; but, we do know that it is involved in determining our level of activation or arousal. It influences whether we are awake, asleep, or somewhere in between. Electrical stimulation of the reticular formation can produce electroencephalographic patterns of brain activity associated with alertness. Classic research has shown that lesions of the reticular formation cause a state of constant sleep in laboratory animals (Lindsley, et al., 1949; Moruzzi & Magoun, 1949). In a way, the reticular formation acts like a valve that either allows sensory messages to pass from lower centers up to the cerebral cortex or shuts them off, partially or totally. We don't know what stimulates the reticular formation to produce these effects.

The Basal Ganglia

A curious set of tissues is the basal ganglia. The basal ganglia are a collection of small, loosely connected structures deep within the center of the brain. Like the cerebellum, the basal ganglia primarily control motor responses. Unlike the cerebellum, the **basal ganglia** are involved in the planning, initiation, and coordination of large, slow movements. Although the basal ganglia are clearly related to the movements of some of our body's larger muscles, there are no direct pathways from the ganglia down the spinal cord and to those larger muscles.

Researchers have come to better understand the functions of the basal ganglia as they have come to better understand **Parkinson's disease**, a disorder involving the basal ganglia in which the most noticeable symptoms are impairment of movement and involun-

tary tremors. At first patients with Parkinson's may have tightness or stiffness in the fingers or limbs. As the disease progresses, patients lose their ability to move themselves, or they are able to move but only with great effort. Walking, once begun, involves a set of stiff, shuffling movements. In advanced cases, voluntary movement of the arms is nearly impossible. Parkinson's is more common with increasing age, afflicting approximately 1 percent of the population. It has been diagnosed in actor Michael J. Fox, attorney Janet Reno, and boxer Muhammed Ali. On April 5, 2005, Pope Paul II died of complications resulting from Parkinson's disease.

The neurotransmitter dopamine is usually found in great quantity in the basal ganglia. Indeed, the basal ganglia are the source of much of the brain's dopamine. In Parkinson's disease, the cells that produce dopamine die off and as they do, levels of the neurotransmitter decline. As dopamine levels in the basal ganglia become insufficient to meet the body's needs, symptoms of the disease appear with all their behavioral consequences. Treatment, you might think, would be to inject dopamine back into the basal ganglia. Unfortunately, that is just not possible because there is simply no way to get the chemical in there so that it will stay. But another drug, L-dopa (in pill form), has the same effect: L-dopa increases dopamine availability in the basal ganglia and slows the course of the disease as a result.

One treatment for Parkinson's disease that has received considerable attention of late is the transplantation of stem cells from embryos directly into the brain of someone suffering from the disease. Stem cells are found in embryonic tissue and are, in a sense, "pre-cells" in that they have not yet developed to become the kind of cell they ultimately will be. When in the proper environments, stem cells develop into blood cells, skin cells, bone cells—or brain cells. After many studies demonstrated that cells from the fetuses of rats would grow in the brains of adult rats and increase the amount of dopamine there, the procedure was tried with humans. The results have been promising. Studies have shown that transplanting stem cells taken from ("harvested" from) aborted human embryos, into the brains of persons with Parkinson's disease *can* slow or even reverse the course of the disease (Cohen et al., 2001; Juengst & Fossel, 2000; Langston, 2005; Takagi, 2005; Vastag, 2003). As you are well aware, the process of gathering cells from aborted embryos has become a political issue in the United States.

Work on stem cell transplantation continues, but the picture has become more complicated. There are several sources of stem cells including embryonic, adult, and neural. Each of these types of stem cells may hold promise for relief from Parkinson's symptoms. Early successes with embryonic stem cells was tem-pered by variable outcomes (Trzaska & Rameshwar, 2007). In some patients, there was improvement in the months after the procedure, but over time the benefits of the stem cells diminished and were accompanied by negative side effects. A bit more success has been found with adult stem cells. With adult stem cells patients experienced relief from Parkinson's symptoms but experienced fewer negative side effects (Cell Medicine, 2008). Even more promising is a procedure in which a patient receives his or her own neural stem cells. One patient treated with this experimental procedure showed marked improvement in Parkinson's symptoms (Cell Medicine, 2008). Although promising, this therapy is still considered to be experimental and the procedures used need to be refined before further clinical trials are attempted (Goya, Tyers, & Barker, 2008).

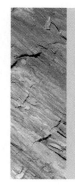

BEFORE YOU GO ON

16. What are the major functions of the cerebellum and the reticular formation?
17. What are the basal ganglia, and what is their relation to Parkinson's disease?

A Point to Ponder or Discuss
The ethical, moral, legal, and political issues involved in harvesting cells of any sort for any purpose from aborted embryos are very complex. Have you formed any opinions on these issues, and would you be willing to share those opinions with others?

The Limbic System

The **limbic system** is more a collection of small structures than a single unit. It is particularly important in controlling the behaviors of animals, which do not have as well-developed cerebral cortexes as humans. In humans, the limbic system controls many of the complex behavioral patterns that are often considered to be instinctive. The limbic system is located in the middle of the brain. Figure 2.11 shows the limbic system's major parts: amygdala, septum, hippocampus, and hypothalamus.

Within the human brain, parts of the limbic system are intimately involved in the display of emotional reactions. One structure in the limbic system, the *amygdala*, produces reactions of rage or aggression when stimulated, while another area, the *septum*, has the opposite effect, reducing the intensity of emotional responses when it is stimulated. The influence of the amygdala and the septum on emotional responding is immediate and direct in nonhumans. In humans, its role is more subtle, reflecting the influence of other brain centers. There is little doubt that

limbic system a collection of small structures in the center of the brain involved in emotionality and memory formation

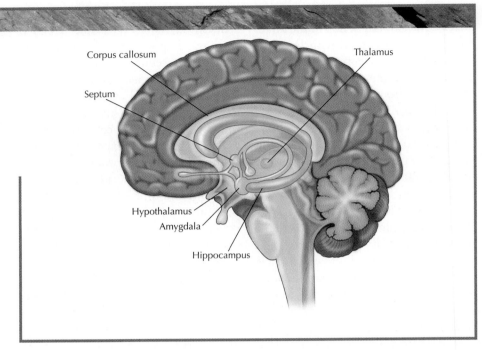

FIGURE 2.11

A view of the brain showing structures deep within it. Among these, the septum, amygdala, and hippocampus constitute the limbic system. Given its proximity, it is easy to see why many scientists include the hypothalamus as part of the limbic system as well.

Corpus callosum

Thalamus

Septum

Hypothalamus

Amygdala

Hippocampus

the amygdala is involved in most cases of depression, but exactly how is not yet clear (Davidson et al., 2002).

The amygdala also plays an important role in other emotions as well. For example, the amygdale is important when deciding whether or not a stimulus is dangerous (Ekman, 1992; LeDoux, 1995). The amygdala also appears to be involved in positive emotions such as sympathy and empathy. The results of one experiment, for example, found that arousal of empathy was associated with activation of a neural circuit in the brain that included the amygdala (Völlm et al., 2006). Interestingly, playing a violent video game is associated with a reduction in activity of structures in this circuit, including the amygdala (Weber, Ritterfeld, & Mathiak, 2006).

Another structure in the limbic system, called the *hippocampus*, is less directly involved in emotion and more involved with the formation of memories. (Vargha-Khadem et al., 1997). People with a damaged hippocampus are often unable to "transfer" experiences (e.g., a birthday party) into permanent memory storage (Wheeler & McMillan,

2001). They may remember events for short periods and may be able to remember events from the distant past, but only if these events occurred before the hippocampus was damaged. Interestingly, damage to the hippocampus does not interfere significantly with verbal aspects of memory—learning and remembering a list of words, for example (Vargha-Khadem et al., 1997).

The *hypothalamus* is a structure that plays a complex role in motivational and emotional reactions. Among other things, it influences many of the functions of the endocrine system, which, as we have seen, is involved in emotional responding. Actually, the hypothalamus is not unitary; instead, it is a collection of smaller structures known as nuclei. Each nucleus plays a different role in the regulation of motivation and emotion. And, we should note, there are those who do not list the hypothalamus as a part of the limbic system *per se*, but see it as a quite separate organ.

The major responsibility of the hypothalamus is to monitor critical internal bodily functions. One subsection, for example, mediates feeding behaviors. Destruction of this nucleus in a rat results in a condition (called hyperphagia) that causes the animal to lose its ability to regulate food intake and become obese. (As you can imagine, researchers who study the various eating disorders have been very interested in the hypothalamus (e.g., Polivy & Herman, 2002). In a similar way, the anterior hypothalamus is involved in the detection of thirst and regulation of fluid intake.

The hypothalamus also plays a role in aggression. Stimulation of the lateral nucleus in a cat produces aggression that looks much like predatory behavior. The cat is highly selective in what it attacks and stalks its prey before pouncing. Stimulation of the medial nucleus results in an anger-based aggression. The cat shows the characteristic signs of anger (arched back, ears flattened, hissing and spitting) and will attack anything in its way. Interestingly, the role of the hypothalamus in hunger and aggression is not as simple as it may seem. For example, if you apply mild stimulation to the lateral nucleus, a cat will show signs of hunger (but not aggression). Increase the strength of the stimulation to the same site, and a cat will display aggression.

The hypothalamus also acts something like a thermostat, triggering a number of automatic reactions should we become too warm or too cold. This small structure is also involved in aggressive and sexual behaviors. It acts as a regulator for many hormones. The hypothalamus has been implicated in the development of sexual orientations, an implication we'll discuss in later chapters when we study needs, motives, and emotions.

The Thalamus

The thalamus sits below the cerebral cortex and is intimately involved in its functioning. Like the pons, the **thalamus** is a relay station for impulses traveling to and from the cerebral cortex. Many impulses traveling from the cerebral cortex to lower brain structures, the spinal cord, and the peripheral nervous system pass through the thalamus. Overcoming the normal function of the medulla (for example, by holding your breath) involves messages that pass through the thalamus. The major role of the thalamus, however, involves the processing of information from the senses.

In handling incoming sensory impulses, the thalamus collects, organizes, and then directs sensory messages to the appropriate areas of the cerebral cortex. Sensory messages from the lower body, eyes, and ears, (but not the nose) pass through the thalamus. For example, at the thalamus, nerve fibers from the eyes are spread out and projected onto the back of the cerebral cortex. It is believed by many neuroscientists that the thalamus "decides" what information will be sent to the cortex, and thus, what will enter consciousness, but empirical data to support this hypothesis has proven difficult to obtain.

thalamus a relay station for impulses to and from the cerebral cortex

---

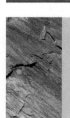

BEFORE YOU GO ON

18. What are the major structures of the limbic system, and what are their functions?
19. Describe the placement and functions of the thalamus.

A Point to Ponder or Discuss
Given the importance of the limbic system in regulating sexual impulses, eating, drinking, body temperature and memory, why do you suppose that there is, as yet, no surgical procedure for humans that can directly influence the structures of this system?

THE CEREBRAL CORTEX

The human brain is a homely organ. There is nothing pretty about it. If anything, its consistency resembles that of warm desert gelatin. When we look at a human brain, the first thing we are likely to notice is the large, soft, lumpy, creviced outer covering of the cerebral cortex (cortex means "outer bark," or covering). The cerebral cortex of the human brain is significantly larger than any other brain structure. It is the complex and delicate **cerebral cortex** that makes us uniquely human by giving us our ability to think, reason, and use language.

How Neuroscientists Study the Brain

The complexity of the billions of neurons that make up the spinal cord and the brain is truly awesome. That we know as much as we do about their tiny and delicate structures is a credit to the neuroscientists who have taken up the challenge of trying to understand this most important system of nerve fibers (Friston, 2005; Saxe, Carey, & Kanwisher, 2004). In this section, we pause and very briefly review a few approaches that neuroscientists have used to gain insights into how the brain works.

Accident and injury—One way to find out how parts of the central nervous system function is to work backward, asking what happens to an organism's behaviors or mental processes if a part of its brain is damaged by accident or injury. If, for example, a person were found to be blind after suffering a traumatic injury to the back of the brain, we might hypothesize that vision is normally coded there. Neurologist Pierre-Paul Broca (1824–1880) used this method to discover that speech production is processed in a small area toward the front, and usually on the left side, of the brain. Broca's conclusions were based on his observations of human brains during autopsies. Boca noticed that autopsies for those who had

similar speech disorders revealed noticeable damage in this very same area of the brain. Logic led Broca to suspect that normal speech functions are controlled by this portion of the brain, now called *Broca's Area.*

Surgical intervention—No one can control the precise location or the extent of damage that occurs as the result of accident or disease. What can be done is to surgically cut (*lesion*) or remove (*ablate*) some particular portion of brain matter to see what the effects might be. Obviously, no one cuts into human brains motivated solely by the curiosity of what might happen as a result. The procedure is used sparingly, only for a justified medical purpose, or with animal subjects. The logic here is the same as for naturally occurring damage to the brain. A small lesion is made in a rat's brain. That rat then refuses to eat, even when previously attractive food is made readily available. The procedure is repeated with other rats, and the results are the same. It then can be reasonably concluded that the lesioned part of the brain plays a role in the feeding behaviors of rats.

Electrical stimulation—An *electrode* is a fine wire that can be eased into a specific area of the brain. Once in position the electrode delivers a tiny electric current, stimulating that portion of the brain. This technique was first used with success in the early 1870s (Sheer, 1961). About a hundred years later, Wilder Penfield of McGill University used a stimulating electrode to map out many of the functions of the brain (Penfield, 1975; Penfield & Rasmussen, 1950).

Most of the time, when an electrode stimulates a part of the brain, there is simply no discernable reaction. Sometimes, however, the results are striking. A mild electric current is delivered to the tissues near the surface of the very back of the brain. The patient (whose brain has been exposed for a justified medical reason) reports having a visual experience—a flash of lights not unlike fireworks. Here is some evidence supporting the notion that visual informa-

cerebral cortex the large, convoluted outer portion of the brain that makes us uniquely human, giving us our abilities to think, reason, and use language

tion is processed at the back of the brain. A stimulus from an electrode high in the left side of the brain produces a muscle twitch in the patient's right arm, although the patient claims not to have moved. Perhaps this area of the left side of the brain controls muscles in the right arm.

Electrical recording—Neural impulses, you will recall, are largely changes in electrical charges that sweep down nerve fibers. Some recording electrodes are so small and so sensitive that they can be used to detect electrical changes in individual neurons. Most recordings of single cell activity are made in nonhumans, particularly those animals that have large neurons, such as the squid. Single-cell recordings allowed David Hubel and Thorton Wiesel to locate individual cells in the brains of cats and monkeys that respond only to very specific types of visual stimulation. The work of these researchers (which earned them a Nobel Prize) suggests that the entire visual field (what we see) is represented in the brain, although in somewhat distorted form. Their work also confirms that visual processing occurs at the back of the brain.

In 1929, Hans Berger, a German psychiatrist who had been using the technique for nearly twenty years, reported that electrodes attached to a person's scalp could pick up and record the general electrical activity of the human brain. Recordings of the electrical activity of the brain are called **electroencephalograms**, or **EEGs**, for short. Electroencephalograms do not provide much in the way of detailed information about the specific activity of small areas of the brain, but they do provide a wealth of information about overall activity, and they are the most common indicator of levels, or stages of sleep. A variant of the EEG is the *MEG*, or *magnetoencephalogram*, a recording of the finer, smaller magnetic fields produced by the electrical changes that take place when neurons fire. The process is very expensive and still experimental, but it can produce a three-dimensional image

of where activity is taking place within the brain as, for example, a person views a variety of stimuli. So far, the most promising uses of MEG technology are in making accurate diagnoses for epilepsy (Knowlton, 2003; Knowlton & Shih, 2004; Parra, Kalitzin, & Silva, 2004).

Imaging the brain—One way to study areas of the intact, functioning brain is to look at them. Several techniques and instruments have been developed to do just that—with a precision and accuracy never imagined in the early days of X-ray technology. A major step was taken when computer technology joined with X-ray procedures to produce a **CT scan** (sometimes called a CAT scan) of the brain. *CT* stands for **computed tomography**. The procedure takes a series of thousands of X-ray pictures of the brain from many angles. The images are fed into a computer that enhances their quality and combines them into a set of pictures of "slices" of the brain. The technique is totally noninvasive, meaning no blood is shed and the patients experience is no more traumatic than a long session of X-rays. CAT scans may tell us about the structures of the brain, the **PET scan** (that's **positron emission tomography**), and its more recent derivatives, give insights about the function of the intact brain. A small amount of a harmless, short-lived, radioactive substance, called a "tracer," is attached to glucose and injected into the bloodstream. In areas of heightened activity in the brain, the glucose is metabolized ("burned up" or used) quickly. This increased rate of activity is recorded on the scan. It is a bit crude, but different areas of the brain are highlighted by activity reflected in the tracer when a subject is asked to engage in different cognitive tasks, such as remembering and focusing on an event from the day before, or imagining a view from the bedroom window (Cabeza & Nyberg, 2000).

What is probably the best, most commonly used noninvasive device for imaging the brain is *magnetic resonance*

CT scan (computed tomography) the procedure for taking a series of thousands of X-ray pictures of the brain from many angles

PET scan (positron emission tomography) a scanning technique that provides insights about the functions of the intact brain

electroencephalograms (EEGs) recordings of the electrical activity of the brain

functional magnetic resonance imaging (fMRI) a technique that allows for the measurement of molecules of blood in the brain, taken as an indicator of neural activity

imaging (the *MRI*), and the newer **functional magnetic resonance imaging**, or **fMRI**. This technique allows for the measurement of the movement of molecules of blood, taken as an indicator of neural activity. One advantage of the MRI and fMRI over the PET scan is obvious: no radioactive materials of any sort. The other advantage is that the fMRI images are more precise and faster. Even short bursts of neural activity can be noticed. Research looking at how the brain functions while a person is engaged in some task (usually cognitive) seems limited only by the imagination of the neuroscientists involved (D'Esposito, Zorahn, & Acguirre, 1999; Dogil, et al., 2002). Studies have contrasted the processing of information by people with severe psychological disorders and people with no signs of disorder (Wright et al., 2000). The fMRI has also been used to investigate the brain responses associated with maternal responsiveness (Squire, & Stein, 2003).

BEFORE YOU GO ON

20. Briefly outline some of the techniques that have been used to study the functions of structures in the brain.

A Point to Ponder or Discuss
If you had access to a fMRI—and the staff to operate it—what sorts of questions about imaging brain functions would you like to investigate?

Lobes and Localization

Figure 2.12 presents two views of the cerebral cortex: a top view and a side view. You can see that the deep folds of tissue provide us with markers for dividing the cerebrum into major areas. The most noticeable division of the cortex can be seen in the top view: the deep crevice that runs down the middle of the cerebral cortex from front to back, dividing it into the left and right cerebral hemispheres.

A side view of a hemisphere (Figure 2.12 shows us the left one) allows us to see the four major divisions of each hemisphere, called "lobes." The *frontal lobes* (plural because there are a left and a right) are the largest and are defined by two large crevices called the central fissure and the lateral fissure. The *temporal lobes* are located at the temples below the lateral fissure, with one on each side of the brain. The *occipital lobes*, at the back of the brain, are defined somewhat arbitrarily, with no large fissures setting them off, and the *parietal lobes* are wedged behind the frontal lobes and above the occipital and temporal lobes.

Using the methods outlined in the previous section, researchers have learned much about what normally happens in the various regions of the cerebral cortex, but many of the details of cerebral function are yet to be understood. Neuroscientists have mapped three major areas of the cortex: *sensory areas*, where impulses from sense receptors are sent; *motor areas*, where most voluntary movements originate; and *association* areas, where sensory and motor functions are integrated and where higher mental processes are thought to occur. We now review each of these in turn, referring to Figure 2.13 as we go along.

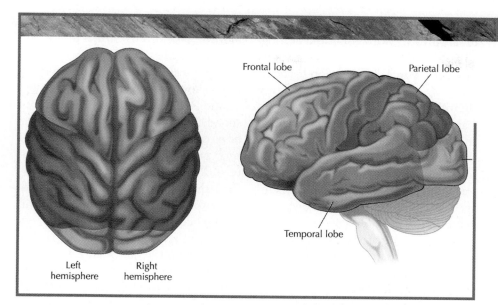

FIGURE 2.12

Frontal lobe

Parietal lobe

Temporal lobe

Left hemisphere

Right hemisphere

The human cerebral cortex is divided into left and right hemispheres, which, in turn, are divided into frontal, temporal, occipital, and parietal lobes.

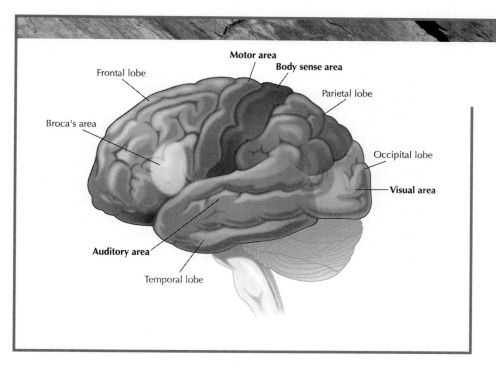

FIGURE 2.13

Motor area

Body sense area

Frontal lobe

Parietal lobe

Broca's area

Occipital lobe

Visual area

Auditory area

Temporal lobe

A side view of the left cerebral hemisphere, showing the four lobes of the cerebral cortex and areas of localization of function.

Sensory Areas

Let's review for a minute. Receptor cells (specialized neurons) in our sense organs respond to stimulus energy from the environment. These cells then pass neural impulses along sensory nerve fibers, eventually to the cerebral cortex. Senses in our body below our neck first send impulses to the spinal cord. Then it's up the spinal cord, through the brainstem, where they cross from left to right and from right to left, on up to the thalamus, and beyond to the cerebrum. After impulses from our senses leave the thalamus, they go to a **sensory area**, an area of the cerebral cortex that receives impulses from the senses. The sensory area involved depends on which sense was activated.

sensory areas those parts of the cerebral cortex that receive impulses from the senses

Large areas of the human cerebral cortex are involved with vision and hearing. Virtually the entire occipital lobe processes visual information (labeled "visual area" in Figure 2.13). Auditory (hearing) impulses go to large centers ("auditory areas") in the temporal lobes. In addition to being involved in hearing, the undersides of the temporal lobes have a curious function. If certain parts of the underside of the temporal lobes are damaged, a condition called *prosopagnosia* exists. In this disorder, a person loses the ability to recognize faces (but not voices).

Bodily senses (touch, pressure, pain, etc.) send impulses to a strip at the very front of the parietal lobe (labeled "body sense area" in Figure 2.13). In this area of the parietal lobe, researchers have mapped out specific regions that correspond to the various parts of the body. Looking at such a "map," we find that some body parts—the face, lips, and fingertips, for example—are overrepresented in the body sense area of the cerebral cortex, reflecting their high sensitivity.

Finally, let's remind ourselves of cross laterality, the crossing over of information from senses on the left side of the body to the right side of the brain, and vice versa, that occurs in the brain stem. When someone touches your right arm, that information ends up in your left parietal lobe. A tickle to your left foot is processed by the right side of your cerebral cortex.

Motor Areas

We have seen that some of our actions, at least very simple and reflexive ones, originate below the cerebral cortex. Although lower brain centers, such as the basal ganglia, may be involved, most voluntary activity is initiated in the **motor areas** of the cerebral cortex in strips at the very back of the frontal lobes. These areas (again, there are two of them, left and right) are directly across the central fissure from the body sense areas in the parietal lobe (see Figure 2.13). We need to make the dis-

claimer that the actual decision to move probably occurs farther forward in the frontal lobes.

Electrical stimulation techniques have allowed neuroscientists to map locations in the motor areas that correspond to, or control, specific muscles or muscle groups. As is the case for sensory processing, some muscle groups (e.g., those that control movements of the hands and mouth) are represented by disproportionally larger areas of cerebral cortex.

As you know, cross laterality is also at work with the motor area. It is your right hemisphere's motor area that controls movements of the left side of your body, and the left hemisphere's motor area that controls the right side. Someone who has suffered a cerebral stroke (a disruption of blood flow in the brain that results in the loss of neural tissue) in the left side of the brain will have impaired movement in the right side of his or her body.

Association Areas

Once we have located the areas of the cerebral cortex that process sensory information and initiate motor responses, there is a lot of cortex left over. The remaining areas of the cerebral cortex are called **association areas**, which are areas of the cerebrum where sensory input is integrated with motor responses and where cognitive functions such as problem-solving, memory, and thinking occur. There is an association area in each of the two frontal, parietal, and temporal lobes. The occipital lobes are so "filled" with visual processing that there is no room left for occipital association areas.

There is considerable support for the idea that the "higher mental processes" occur in the association areas. Frontal association areas are involved in many such processes (Schall, 2004). Remember Pierre-Paul Broca's discovery that normal speech functions are controlled by this portion of the brain, now called Broca's area (see Figure 2.13). Broca's

association areas regions of the cerebral cortex where sensory input is integrated with motor responses and where cognitive functions, such as memory, problem solving and thinking occur

motor areas those parts of the cerebral cortex in which most voluntary movement is initiated

area controls the production of speech. That is, it coordinates the actual functions needed to express an idea. A person with damage to Broca's area shows an interesting pattern of speech defects. If asked a question, like "Where is your car?" a person with Broca's area damage might be able to tell you, but only in broken, forced language. For example, the person might say, "Car . . . lot . . . parked by . . . supermarket."

Another part of the brain involved in language and speech processing is Wernicke's area, located in the left temporal lobe. This area is involved in speech comprehension and with organizing ideas. A bundle of nerve fibers connects Wernicke's and Broca's areas so that the language comprehended and organized in Wernicke's area is transmitted to Broca's area, which then coordinates the speech output. If Wernicke's area is damaged (or if the neural fibers connecting it to Broca's area are damaged), a different speech problem is manifested. If a person with Wernicke's area damage is asked where the car is parked, the answer that comes out will be in grammatically correct language. The catch is that it will make no sense whatsoever.

For example, the person might say, "The seashore beautiful this time of year."

Damage to the very front of the right frontal lobe or to an area where the parietal and temporal lobes come together often interrupts or destroys the ability to plan ahead, to think quickly, reason, or think things through (Greene & Haidt, 2002). Interestingly, these association areas of the brain involved in forethought and planning nearly cease to function when one is feeling particularly happy (e.g., George et al., 1995). It is this area of the brain that is surgically disconnected from other brain centers in a "prefrontal lobotomy," a procedure commonly used in the 1950s and 1960s as a treatment for some extreme cases of mental disorders.

We should not get carried away with cerebral localization of function. Please do not fall into the trap of believing that separate parts of the cerebral cortex operate independently or that they have the sole responsibility for any one function. Avoiding these traps will be particularly important to keep in mind as we look at the division of the cerebral cortex into right and left hemispheres.

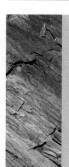

BEFORE YOU GO ON

21. Describe the location of each of the four lobes of the cerebral cortex.
22. Briefly describe the functions of the sensory areas, the motor areas, and the association areas of the cortex.

A Point to Ponder or Discuss
Infants who are born with only one cerebral hemisphere, or who have one hemisphere surgically removed, seem to develop with the full range of cognitive functions. How might this be possible?

The Two Cerebral Hemispheres: Splitting the Brain

The ancient Greeks knew that the cerebral cortex was divided into two major sections, or hemispheres. That the cerebral cortex is divided in half seems quite natural. After all, we have two eyes, arms, legs, lungs, and so forth. Why not two divisions of the brain? In the last 40 years, interest in this division into hemispheres has heightened as scientists have accumulated evidence that suggests that each half of the cerebral cortex may have primary responsibility for its own set of mental functions.

In most humans, the left hemisphere is the larger of the two halves, contains a higher proportion of gray matter, and is considered the *dominant hemisphere* (active to a greater degree in more tasks). We have already noted that the major language centers are housed in the left cerebral hemisphere. At least this is true for nearly all right-handed people. For some left-handers, language may be processed primarily by the right hemisphere. Because humans are so language-oriented, little attention was given to the right hemisphere until a remarkable surgical procedure performed in the 1960s gave us new insights about the cerebral hemispheres (Sperry, 1968, 1982; Springer & Deutsch, 1981).

Normally, the two hemispheres of the cerebral cortex are richly interconnected by a network of hundreds of thousands of fibers collectively called the **corpus callosum** (see Figure 2.10). Through the corpus callosum, one side of our cortex remains in constant and immediate contact with the other. Separating the functions of the two hemispheres is possible, however, through a surgical technique called a *callosotomy* or more simply a **split-brain procedure**, which is neither as complicated nor as dangerous as it sounds. The procedure was first performed on a human in 1961 by Joseph Brogan to lessen the severity of the symptoms of epilepsy. As an irreversible treatment of last resort, the split-brain procedure has been very successful. Although the procedure destroys the corpus callosum's connections between the two hemispheres, it leaves in tact other connections between the two hemispheres (for example, the superior colliculus). These other connections allow for the transfer of some information between the two hemispheres. For example, in patients with a callosotomy some sensorimotor information is transferred between hemispheres by the superior colliculus (Savazzi et al., 2007).

Most of what we know about the activities of the cerebral hemispheres has been learned from split-brain subjects, both human and animal. One of the things that make this procedure remarkable is that, under normal circumstances, split-brain patients behave normally. Only in the laboratory, using specially designed tasks, can we see the results of independently functioning hemispheres of the cerebral cortex (Corballis, Funnell, & Gazzaniga, 2002; Foerch, 2005; Gazzaniga, Ivry, & Mangun, 2002; Metcalfe et al., 1995).

Experiments with split-brain patients confirm that speech production is a left-hemisphere function in most people. Imagine you have your hands behind your back. I place a house key in your left hand and ask you to tell me what it is. Your left hand feels the key. Impulses travel up your left arm, up your spinal cord, and cross over to your right cerebral hemisphere (remember cross laterality). You tell me that the object in your left hand is a key because your brain is intact. Your right hemisphere quickly passes the information about the key to your left hemisphere, and your left hemisphere directs you to say, "It's a key."

Now suppose that you are a split-brain patient. You cannot answer my question even though you understand it perfectly. Why not? Your right brain knows that the object in your left hand is a key, but without an intact corpus callosum, it cannot inform the left hemisphere where speech production is located. Under the direction of the right cerebral hemisphere, you would be able to point with your left hand to the key placed among other objects before you. Upon seeing your own behavior, your eyes would communicate that information to your left hemisphere.

A major task for the left hemisphere is the production of speech and the processing of language. But we must remain cautious about making too much of the specialization of function. When the results of the first research efforts on split-brain patients were made public, many people, less skeptical than the researchers themselves, jumped to faulty, overly simplistic conclusions. (Remember our discussion of pseudoscience in Chapter 1?) We now know that virtually no behavior or mental process is the

corpus callosum the structure that richly interconnects the two hemispheres of the cerebral cortex

split-brain procedure a surgical technique that destroys the corpus callosum's connections between the two hemispheres of the cerebral cortex

product of one hemisphere alone. For example, Gazzaniga (1998) reports of one split-brain patient who learned to speak from the right hemisphere 13 years after surgery severed the corpus callosum.

Still, what about the right hemisphere? The clearest evidence is that the right hemisphere dominates the processing of visually presented information (Bradshaw & Nettleton, 1983; Kosslyn, 1987). Putting together a jigsaw puzzle, for instance, uses the right hemisphere more than the left. Skill in the visual arts (e.g., painting, drawing, and sculpting) is associated with the right hemisphere. It is involved in the interpretation of emotional stimuli and in the expression of emotions. While the left hemisphere is analytical and sequential, the right hemisphere is considered better able to grasp the big picture—the overall view of things—and tends to be somewhat creative. It may be that some illnesses, such as depression, are associated more with one hemisphere than the other. Activating the brain's healthier "other half" produces overall improvement (Schiffer, Stinchfield, & Pascual-Leone, 2002).

These possibilities are intriguing. While it seems that there are differences in the way the two sides of the cerebral cortex normally process information, these differences are slight, and many are controversial. In fact, the more we learn about hemispheric differences, the more we discover similarities. And let us not lose sight of the enormous ability of the human brain to repair itself. In 2003, the Associated Press published a "human interest" story about Christina Santhouse, a 16-year-old high-school student. When she was 9 years old, the entire right cere-bral hemisphere of her brain was surgically removed. The treatment was for an advanced case of Rasmussen's encephalitis, a neurological disease that gradually eats away brain tissue. The surgery was done at Johns Hopkins Hospital, where over 100 such "hemispherectomies" have been performed. Yes, Christina suffers from side effects of the procedure (e.g., partial paralysis in her left arm and leg and the loss of peripheral vision in one eye), but in most ways, the fully functioning left hemisphere has managed to take over the functions of the missing right hemisphere and to serve the teenager very well.

We should be careful about overgeneralizing, but the left hemisphere of the cerebral cortex is involved in processing language and words, as when working a crossword puzzle. A major task of the right hemisphere of the cerebral cortex is organizing the visual patterns, as is required for the visual arts.

Courtesy of Macduff Everton/ Getty Images.

Courtesy of John Lund/Drew Kelly/Getty Images.

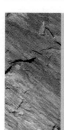

BEFORE YOU GO ON

23. What is the split-brain procedure, and what has been learned from it?

A Point to Ponder or Discuss
Might it be possible to train or educate one hemisphere of the brain while ignoring the other? Imagine that you wanted to strengthen the abilities of your right cerebral hemisphere. How might you proceed?

SPOTLIGHT
ON DIVERSITY

Learning Disabilities and the Brain

Since the earliest attempts at formal education, it has been realized that some children seem significantly less able than others to learn. Such children have been called "slow," "feebleminded," and/or "retarded." It was only about 50 years ago when an effort began in earnest to separate from those children who were challenged at all levels of intellectual functioning, those children "who have disorders in development of language, speech, reading, and associated communication skills." This proposal, by Samuel Kirk, a professor of special education at the University of Illinois was made in April 1963. Parents who heard Dr. Kirk soon thereafter established The Association for Children with *Learning Disabilities*—a term not used before (Armstrong, 1987, pp. 6–7). As discussed earlier in this chapter, the human brain has approximately 100 billion neurons and about one trillion supportive cells. We know that the brain reproduces and creates as many as 250,000 cells per minute in the early stages of development. Are there some connections between learning disabilities and brain development in children? Decreases in brain connection and brain cells are linked to lower IQ scores, developmental problems, and lower achievement test scores (Fiedorowicz et al., 2001).

Today, a learning disability is defined as "a disorder in one or more of the basic psychological processes involved in understanding or in using language, spoken or written, that may manifest itself in an imperfect ability to listen, think, speak, read, write, spell, or do mathematical calculations. Learning disabilities adversely affect the ability of the child to communicate and meet the challenges of education" (Culbertson, 2001, p. 261). Estimates suggest that approximately 8–15 percent of the public school population includes children with learning disabilities. The most common learning disabilities are *dyslexia* (an impairment of reading skills), *dyscalculia* (an impairment of arithmetic skills), and *dysgraphia* (an impairment of writing skills) (Culbertson & Edmonds, 1996).

From the beginning, it has been assumed that learning disabilities reflect some specific brain dysfunction that interferes with normal learning processes, and that there may be many different sources for structural damage to the brain that causes such disabilities. Only recently has significant progress been made in locating these abnormalities in the brain (McCardle, Scarborough, & Catts, 2001). Most successes have been in the area of understanding the causes of dyslexia, but there also has been some fruitful research on dyscalculia. We will here highlight a few such studies.

Dyslexia affects millions of Americans and neuroimaging has shown that the brain of the dyslexic individual develops more slowly than that of an unaffected person. This research suggests that the delayed brain development is a major factor in contributing to learning problems. Neuroimaging studies of children with dyslexia have focused on problems in the left, rear ("posterior") portions of the cerebral cortex, toward the back of the temporal lobes, near the parietal and the occipital lobes (Pugh et al., 2001). Disabled children tend to rely on frontal and right hemisphere areas, rather than left posterior areas when reading (Pugh et al., 2001). Additionally, there seems to be a disruption of the normal connections between brain regions normally involved in reading—the left side of the visual association areas and nearby areas in the left temporal and parietal lobes (Simos et al., 2000). Research by Beverly Wright and Steven Zecker of Northwestern University (2004) finds that many of the brain abnormalities associated with learning problems, including dyslexia, can be accounted for by the hypothesis "that the brains of affected individuals develop more slowly than those of their unaffected counterparts. In addition, it seems that brain changes occurring at ≈ [about] 10 years of age, presumably associated with puberty, may prematurely halt this slower-than-normal development when improvements would normally continue into adolescence" (Wright & Zecker, 2004, p. 9942). On a positive note, it seems that behavioral remediation programs (focusing on auditory processing and oral language production) not only improve language use and reading skills, but also produce increased activity in the very areas of the left side of the brain usually seen as disrupted in dyslexic individuals (Temple et al., 2003).

There is simply much less data available on the nature, course, and causes of dyscalculia than dyslexia, perhaps because it is less common (Fuchs & Fuchs, 2002). The brain region most commonly cited as being involved in dyscalculia (often called "mathematics disabilities," or "MD") is very close to those associated with dyslexia—areas in the left posterior parietal lobe. In part, this may be due to the overlap between the underlying mechanisms for processing numbers and words (Cohen & Dehaene, 2000). An argument for at least the partial involvement of areas near the visual cortex reflects the observation that many individuals with dyscalculia simply cannot form visual images of quantities represented by numbers (Bell, 1991; Paivio, 1981). That is to say, people with this disability struggle to form a visual image of what "5" *looks like*. As soon as you read that last sentence, you probably formed several such images, perhaps things like five fingers or toes, a basketball team, or even five hash marks (/////) on a piece of paper. If nothing else, it is clear that much more research needs to be done on the neurological underpinnings of learning disabilities.

Children with learning disabilities often have behavioral problems, which may involve mental conditions such as attention deficit hyperactivity disorder (ADHD) (Kessler, Chiu, & Walters (2005). Children with ADHD—approximately 20–30 percent of the population—also have a specific learning disability (Wender, 2000). The characteristics of ADHD are inattention, hyperactivity, and impulsivity. ADHD is a condition that generally becomes apparent during the preschool and early school years. It is difficult for children with ADHD to control their behaviors and/or pay attention. Professionals have identified three subtypes of attention deficit hyperactivity disorder: **predominantly hyperactive/impulsive type** (that does not show significant inattention); **predominantly inattentive type** (that does not show significant hyperactive-impulsive behavior) sometimes called ADD; and the **combined type** (that displays both inattentive and hyperactive-impulsive symptoms) (Wender, 2000).

Wender (2000) identified the following signs and symptoms:

- Fails to give close attention to details or makes careless mistakes
- May have poorly formed letters or words or messy writing
- Has difficulty sustaining attention in tasks or play activities
- Does not follow through on instructions and fails to finish schoolwork or chores
- Avoids or strongly dislikes tasks (such as schoolwork) that require sustained mental effort

- Forgetful in daily activities
- Has difficulty organizing tasks and activities
- Loses things necessary for tasks or activities (pencils, assignments, tools)
- Shows difficulty engaging in leisure activities quietly
- Acts as if "driven by a motor" and cannot remain still
- Blurts out answers to questions before the questions have been completed, often interrupts others

The hope is, as techniques for imaging the intact, functioning brain continue to evolve, so will our understanding of these disabilities. And, as you can see, when we speak of "diversity," we mean more than differences based on gender or ethnicity.

The Two Sexes: Male and Female Brains

The anatomical differences between women and men are obvious. When we discuss the function of the brain, however, we may fairly ask if there are any differences between the brains of men and women. Remember, we are asking about general differences; no two human beings' brains are precisely the same. If there are differences in the anatomy of male and female brains, we then must ask if these differences are significant. Do they have a measurable impact on psychological functioning?

It turns out that what appears to be a loaded question can be resolved fairly easily. Except for those differences in the brains of males and females that are directly related to reproductive function (which *are* significant), there are very few differences of real consequence (e.g., Unger & Crawford, 1992). (We shall see in Chapter 10 that it is the hypothalamus of the brains of men and women that are most involved in sexuality and are most different.)

Here's an example of research in this area. One intriguing possibility is that the hemispheres of the cerebral cortex are more separate and distinct (more lateralized) in males than in females. At least one part of the corpus callosum in the brains of females is consistently larger than it is in the brains of males. There is also evidence that women are more likely to recover from strokes than are men, perhaps because functions lost as a result of damage in one hemisphere can be taken over more easily by the other, undamaged hemisphere (McGlone, 1977, 1978, 1980). Another implication—usually unspoken—is that intellectual functioning in women is more "balanced" than in men, whereas men are more likely to excel in the functioning of one hemisphere or the other. Further research failed to find any differences in lateralization (Bleier et al., 1987). Nor is there evidence that differences in lateralization are associated with any differences in cognitive abilities between men and women (e.g., Unger & Crawford, 1992). There is a difference in the lateralization of the brains of left-handed persons and right-handed persons (brains of left-handed persons are less lateralized), but there are no significant differences in the cognitive abilities of left- and right-handed persons (Kocel, 1977). Just to complicate this complex issue a bit more, it also seems to be the case that in some memory tasks, men use both sides of their brains or right-side dominance, while women show activity predominantly in the left hemisphere (Speck et al, 2000). And, one recent meta-analysis demonstrated that women have a significantly worse outcome following a traumatic brain injury than to do men (Farace & Alves, 2000), while another report of two studies—on post-traumatic recovery in mice—found no gender differences in one, and a better recovery rate for females in the other (Hall, Gibson, & Pavel, 2005).

Just as some scientists were prepared to give up researching gender-based differences in lateralization, researchers at Yale University, Drs. Sally and Bennett

Shaywitz (she's a psychologist; he's a neurologist) published their work (Shaywitz et al., 1995). The Shaywitzes watched the functioning intact brains of men and women as they read nonsense words and tried to determine if the words rhymed. The Shaywitzes used functional magnetic resonance imaging (fMRI) because it shows glimpses of areas of the brain that are active during even a very brief task. The Shaywitzes found that when men attempted to sound out nonsense words, they used a small portion of their left cerebral cortex near Broca's area. Women used the same area, but they also involved a similar area on the right side of their brains. Interestingly, the men and women performed the task equally well; the differences were only in how their brains approached the task. Sounds like progress, right? Well, no. A few years later, Frost et al. (1999) published their research, arguing that there are no substantive differences in the organization of language in males and females (see also Gernsbacher & Kaschak, 2003).

Still, every once in a while, a tidbit of research comes along that suggests that it is too early to drop this line of investigation. For example, it seems that women do recall or recognize emotional information better than men do. A study by researchers of the State University of New York at Stony Brook and Stanford University (Canli, 2002), reports that women's recollections of emotionally stimulating photographs were 10 to 15 percent more accurate than men's recollections of similar photographs. Note first that this difference is not a large one. But also note that the study also looked at the brain activity of the participants while they watched the photographs and while they tried to recall them. The conclusion: Women's neural response to emotional scenes was significantly more active than that of men.

Another interesting experiment looked at the possibility that the greater preference of males for playing video games relates to differences in brain functioning (Hoeft, Watson, Kesler, Bettinger, & Reiss, 2008). Using functional magnetic resonance imaging, these researchers investigated brain activity in males and females while they played a video game. They found greater activity in parts of the limbic system associated with reward and addiction in males, compared to females. The authors believe this may help explain why males are more likely than females to become "hooked" on video games.

Another line of research with potentially useful results has to do with gender differences in brain aging and brain disease. Brain cells die off ("atrophy") at different rates and in different places (subregions) for males and females. Perhaps most importantly, there is simply more brain atrophy with aging in males than in females (Xu et al., 2000). Additionally, females show a higher incidence of Alzheimer's disease (a degenerative brain disease) than males. Interestingly, the incidence of Alzheimer's disease is lower in women on hormone replacement therapy for other conditions. This suggests that the gender difference in Alzheimer's disease is related in some way to the level of sex hormones present in the brain (Compton, van Amelsvoort, & Murphy, 2001). Further, normal brain aging gender differences also relate to differing levels of sex hormones.

BEFORE YOU GO ON

24. What are the differences between the brains of males and the brains of females?

A Point to Ponder or Discuss
Assume that researchers discover a significant difference in some small region of the adult brains of men and women. How could one determine how much of the difference is due to genetics and biology and how much of the difference is due to environment and culture?

CHAPTER SUMMARY

1. **What are the major parts of a neuron?**

   A neuron is the basic cell of the nervous system. Every neuron has three parts: the cell body, dendrites, and axon. The cell body contains the structures needed to sustain the life of the neuron. Dendrites extend from the cell body and receive messages from other neurons, while the axon extends from the cell body and carries the neural message away from the cell body. At their ends, axons branch out to form several axon terminals.

2. **What is myelin, and what functions does it serve?**

   Myelin is a white fatty substance that coats the axons of some neurons of the nervous system. The myelin sheath covers the axon in segments, rather than in one continuous covering. The myelin sheath has several functions. First, it protects the delicate axon from damage. Second, it insulates the axon against signals from other neurons. Third, it speeds the rate of the neural impulse as it travels down the axon.

3. **What is neurogenesis, and why is it important?**

   Once neurons die—and they so regularly—they are not normally replaced with new ones. Their functions may be taken over by other nearby nerve cells. Recently, research evidence has documented *neurogenesis* in humans as well as in animal species. Under the right conditions, new neurons can be generated in the adult brain. So far, there are severe limits on how many new neurons can be produced, but the promise for the future is great.

4. **What is the nature of a neural impulse?**

   A neural impulse is the electrical signal, or activity, that travels down the axon after a neuron has been stimulated. The resting potential of a neuron is its electrical charge while it is at rest, −70mV. This indicates that the inside of the axon is negatively charged relative to the outside. The lining up of negative ions on the inside and positive ions on the outside creates tension along the axon. The action potential is the change in the electrical charge in an axon after the neuron is stimulated, which is +40mV.

5. **What are the all-or-none principle and neural thresholds?**

   The all-or-none principle is the name for the observation that if a neuron fires, the neural impulse occurs at full force, or not at all. Thus, there is no such thing as a strong or weak neural impulse; it is either present or not. Neural thresholds describe the minimal level of stimulation necessary to get a neuron to transmit an impulse of its own. Some neurons have very low thresholds (and, thus, are very sensitive), while some have high thresholds (and require considerable stimulation before they fire).

6. **Describe the synapse and, in general terms, what happens there.**

   A synapse is the location where two neurons communicate with each other. The neurons do not physically touch; there is a small gap called the *synaptic cleft* separating the axon of one neuron from the dendrite or cell body of the next. Communication between neurons across the synaptic cleft is accomplished chemically. When the neural impulse reaches the axon terminal, a neurotransmitter is released into the synaptic cleft. It is through this chemical that the neural impulse is communicated across the synapse.

7. **Name and briefly describe the actions of four neurotransmitters.**

   Neurotransmitters are chemicals that flood the synaptic cleft, often transmitting a neural impulse from one neuron to another. Neurotransmitters may have an excitatory function when they reach certain receptor sites, causing the next neuron to fire. Others have an inhibitory function, which makes it more difficult for the next neuron to fire. Approximately 100 neurotransmitters have been identified. *Acetylcholine* is a neurotransmitter that can have an excitatory or inhibitory function, depending on where it is found. It commonly works in synapses between neurons and muscles and may also play a role in memory. *Norepinephrine* is involved in mood regulation and physiological reactions associated with levels of arousal. *Dopamine* is a neurotransmitter that has been associated with psychological disorders of thought and mood, as well as voluntary movements. *Endorphins* are natural pain suppressors.

8. **Name the human nervous systems and briefly describe what they do.**

The *central nervous system (CNS)* includes all of the neurons and supporting cells found in the brain and spinal cord. It is a complex system involved in the control of behavior and mental processes. The *peripheral nervous system (PNS)* consists of all of the neurons in our body that are not in the central nervous system. It includes the nerve fibers in our arms, face, fingers, intestines, etc. Neurons in the peripheral nervous system carry impulses either from the central nervous system to the muscles and glands or to the central nervous system from receptor cells. The somatic and autonomic nervous systems are subdivisions of the peripheral nervous system. The *somatic nervous system* includes the neurons that serve the skeletal muscles and pick up impulses from our sense receptors. The *autonomic nervous system (ANS)* is composed of the nerve fibers that activate the smooth muscles, such as those of the stomach, intestines, and glands. The autonomic nervous system has two subsystems. *The sympathetic system* is activated under conditions of excitement or arousal, and the *parasympathetic system* is activated when a person is relaxed and calm.

9. **What is the function of the endocrine system in general, and the pituitary gland, thyroid gland, and adrenal glands in particular?**

The endocrine system is a network of glands that influence behaviors through the secretion of chemicals called *hormones*. The hormones, which circulate through the blood system, can have an effect on behavior. The *pituitary gland* is often called the "master gland" because it controls many other glands in the endocrine system. It is located under the brain and secretes a variety of hormones. Pituitary hormones affect growth, lactation, regulation of the amount of water held in the body, and the regulation of other glands. The *thyroid gland*, located in the neck, produces a hormone, thyroxin, which regulates the body's "pace" (e.g., the rate at which oxygen is used). Hyperthyroidism occurs when too much thyroxin in the blood results in excitability, edginess, insomnia, and weight loss. Too little thyroxin leads to hypothyroidism, associated with fatigue and lack of energy. The *adrenal glands*, located on the kidneys, secrete a variety of hormones into the blood. One such hormone, adrenaline, is released during times of danger. It increases respiration and heart and perspiration rates, directs the flow of blood away from the digestive system toward the limbs, and causes pupils to dilate.

10. **How have researchers studied the effects of genes on psychological functioning?**

Psychologists have long been interested in the influence that one's genes have on psychological functioning. Although it is true that a single gene may not produce any discernable effect on its own, there is ample evidence that the DNA and genes inherited from one's parents are important in molding a person's affects, behaviors, and cognitions. *Inbreeding studies* demonstrate that many characteristics can be bred into generations of animals. *Family history and twin studies* demonstrate a correspondence between observed traits and genetic similarity. The *Human Genome Project* has recently mapped all human genes and the set of genetic "instructions" encoded in human DNA. Scientists hope to find the genes (or more likely sets of genes) that are associated with certain measured human traits. Although the task is complex and behavior will always have an environmental component, the project has amazing possibilities to advance our understanding of how genetics contributes to behavior.

11. **What role do epigenetics play in the expression of one's underlying genetic code?**

By definition, *epigenetics* refers to a complex set of biochemical systems that exist above the basic level of one's DNA (genetic code) that can affect the over expression of genetically influenced traits. In simplified form, this means that having a particular gene for a given characteristic does not mean that that characteristic will be expressed. The person's epigenetics influence whether a given gene (or genes) will be switched on or off. Additionally, recent research suggests that how one's epigenetics actually influence the underlying DNA can be influenced by environmental factors, such as health, nutrition, and exposure to toxins. In practical terms, this means, for example, having a set of genes that could predispose a person to a particular disease does not at all mean that the person will actually contract that disease.

12. **What are sensory neurons, motor neurons, and interneurons?**

Sensory neurons carry information (in the form of neural impulses) from the body to the central nervous system. *Motor neurons* carry information from the central nervous system to muscles and glands in the body. *Interneurons* are those neurons located and functioning within the central nervous system.

13. **What is the basic structure of the spinal cord, and what are its two functions?**

The spinal cord, which is encased in the spinal column, is a mass of interconnected neurons resembling a piece of rope that extends from the lower back to just below the brain. It has nerve fibers that carry messages to and from the brain and to and from the body. The spinal cord also is involved in reflex actions. When a receptor is stimulated (e.g., your hand touches a hot surface) sensory neurons transmit the information to the spinal cord. There, interneurons form synapses with motor neurons that then send impulses to muscles in your arm and hand to withdraw your hand. At the same time, however, information is transmitted up the spinal cord, and you consciously experience the pain. Note that some reflexes do not involve interneurons to mediate sensory experience and motor response, and instead work through direct synaptic connections between sensory and motor neurons. These synapses are located within the spinal cord.

14. **Where are the medulla and the pons, and what do they do?**

Like the spinal cord, the medulla's major functions involve involuntary reflexes. There are several small structures, called nuclei (collections of neural cell bodies), in the medulla that control functions such as coughing, sneezing, tongue movements, and reflexive eye movements. The medulla also sends out impulses that keep your heart beating and your respiratory system breathing. The pons serves as a relay station, sorting and relaying sensory messages from the spinal cord and the face to higher brain centers, and reversing the relay for motor impulses coming down from higher centers. The pons is also responsible, at least in part, for the sleep/waking cycle and the rapid movement of our eyes that occurs when we dream.

15. **What is meant by cross laterality?**

Cross laterality means that the right side of your brain controls the left side of your body, while the left side of your brain controls the right side of your body. In the same fashion, sensory impulses from the right side of your body cross to be received by the left side of your brain, and sensory impulses from the left side of your body are registered in the right side of your brain.

16. **What are the major functions of the cerebellum and the reticular formation?**

The cerebellum is located under the base of the skull. Its cortex (outer layer) is convoluted. The major function of the cerebellum is to smooth out and coordinate rapid body movements. Most voluntary movements originate in the higher brain centers and are coordinated by the cerebellum. Damage to the cerebellum can lead to a variety of motor problems including loss of coordination, tremors, and speech problems. The reticular formation is more a network of nerve fibers than a true brain structure. Most of the functions of the reticular formation remain a mystery. However, we know it is involved in alertness and the sleep/waking cycle.

17. **What are the basal ganglia, and what is their relation to Parkinson's disease?**

The basal ganglia are a collection of small, loosely connected structures deep in the middle of the brain. The basal ganglia primarily control the initiation and the coordination of large, slow movements. In Parkinson's disease, the cells in the basal ganglia that produce the neurotransmitter dopamine die, and the levels of dopamine in the basal ganglia drop. This loss of dopamine is thought to produce the characteristic motor problems associated with the disease.

18. **What are the major structures of the limbic system, and what are their functions?**

The limbic system is a collection of structures rather than a single one. The limbic system is composed of the amygdala, hippocampus, septum, and hypothalamus. The limbic system controls many of the behaviors that we consider instinctive. When stimulated, the amygdala evokes reactions of rage or aggression. It also helps you to decide whether or not a stimulus is dangerous. The septum reduces the intensity of emotional responses when it is stimulated. The influence of the amygdala and the septum on emotional responding is immediate and direct in non-humans. In humans, it is more subtle, which reflects the influence of other brain centers.

The hippocampus is involved with forming memories. Persons with damage to the hippocampus have difficulty transferring memories from temporary memory storage to permanent storage. The hypothalamus is a part of the limbic system involved in the mediation of motivation. It is not a unitary structure, but rather a collection of smaller structures called nuclei. Each nucleus plays a different role. The major function of the hypothalamus is to monitor and control internal body functions such as hunger, thirst, and body temperature, as well as to regulate many hormones.

19. Describe the placement and functions of the thalamus.

The thalamus is a lower brain structure located just below the cerebral cortex. It relays impulses traveling to and from the cortex. The primary function of the thalamus is to relay sensory information to the cerebral cortex, and perhaps to regulate access to consciousness.

20. Briefly outline some of the techniques that have been used to study the functions of structures in the brain.

Over the years, neuroscientists have used a variety of techniques for learning about the human brain. When accident or injury damages a part of the brain and then has an effect on behavior, assumptions might be made about that structure's usual function. Surgically lesioning or ablating small parts of the brain can also indicate what their normal functions might be. Stimulating small areas of the brain with an electrode has allowed scientists to "map out" some of the functions that occur in the stimulated areas, and tiny recording electrodes can indicate which areas of the brain are active when an organism is stimulated. The electroencephalogram (EEG) is a recording of the overall electrical activity of the brain and has been most useful in determining levels of arousal or wakefulness.

More recently, imaging techniques have been found to be very efficient in showing the structure and the function of the human brain in a noninvasive way. CAT-scans produce thousands of X-ray images of the brain that are then assembled by a computer to give a three-dimensional view of the brain. PET-scans show areas of the brain that become active by recording the amount of radio-active "tracer" elements released during a task. The MRI and fMRI use magnetism to detect tiny movements of blood molecules, and they can give detailed images of even short bursts of neural activity in the brain.

21. Describe the location of each of the four lobes of the cerebral cortex.

The cerebral cortex, also known as the cerebrum, is associated with those higher mental processes that make us human. The lobes of the cerebral cortex are divisions of each of the two cerebral hemispheres. The *frontal lobes* are defined by two large crevices called the central and lateral fissures, and are located at the front of the brain. The *temporal lobes* are located at the temples, below the lateral fissure on each side of the brain. The *occipital lobes* are located at the very back of the brain, and the *parietal lobes* are sandwiched between the frontal, occipital, and temporal lobes.

22. Briefly describe the functions of the sensory areas, the motor areas, and the association areas of the cortex.

The sensory areas of the brain are portions of the brain specialized for receiving neural impulses from the senses. Nearly all of the occipital lobe is dedicated to receiving information from visual stimuli. Impulses relating to hearing are directed to the temporal lobes. Information from the body senses go to the body sense areas located in the parietal lobe. The motor areas of the cerebral cortex initiate and control most voluntary motor movements. The motor areas of the cortex are located at the back of the frontal lobes. The association areas of the cortex are the parts of the cortex not directly involved in the mediation of sensory and motor activities. The association areas make up a large portion of the cortex and are involved in the integration of sensory input, motor responses, and higher cognitive functions (e.g., problem-solving and memory).

23. What is the split-brain procedure, and what has been learned from it?

The split-brain procedure is a surgical technique performed to relieve the symptoms of severe epilepsy. The procedure involves removing the corpus callosum. The result is that the two hemispheres become disconnected and can be studied independently. In most people, the left hemisphere of the cerebrum is larger and is referred to as the "dominant hemisphere" because it is active in so many tasks and because it is the seat of language in most people. The differences in function of the two hemispheres of the cortex are quite minimal, but the right hemisphere seems to be specialized for visual and spatial information. Artistic skills like painting and sculpting are also associated with the right hemisphere, as is the interpretation of emotional stimuli.

24. **What are the differences between the brains of males and the brains of females?**

The cerebral hemispheres of the brain may be slightly more lateralized in the male brain than in the female brain. In females, the corpus callosum is larger, which implies greater cooperation between the hemispheres. The brains of females also seem slightly more active in processing and recollecting emotional stimuli. Despite these minor differences, there are many more similarities. Those differences that are significant tend to be in mid-brain structures, such as the hypothalamus, and are related to sexuality and sexual functioning.

Sensation and Perception

3

PREVIEW

This chapter on sensation and perception forms a nice "bridge" between the discussion of matters biological and matters psychological. Although we will begin talking about special neurons (receptor cells) and neural pathways to the brain, in actuality we are beginning our discussion of consciousness, learning, and memory. Before you can learn about or remember some event in the world you must perceive that event. You must select, organize, and interpret the event. And before you can do that, you must first sense the event. That is, you must gather information about the event and put it in a form your brain can appreciate. Your senses take energy from the world around you (in the form of light, sound, tastes, smells, physical pressures, etc.) and change that energy into the only energy there is in your brain: neural impulses.

Over the next several chapters we will be refining this simplistic summary statement: We cannot remember what we have not learned, we cannot learn that of which we are not conscious, we cannot be conscious of that which we have not perceived, and we cannot perceive that which we have not sensed.

Processing information begins with sensation. After discussing a few ideas relevant to all the human senses, we will take a look at each of the senses in turn. For each sense, the most basic issues are a) what is the nature of the stimulus for this sense, and b) what is the receptor system for this sense? We devote more space to vision because vision *is* a vital sense for humans and because more is known about it than the other senses.

The scientific study of the human senses—and your experience—should convince you just how incredibly sensitive sense receptors are. In fact, our senses are so good that they present us with much more information than we can possibly process. Perception allows us to sort from the myriad incoming signals only a very few to which we pay attention and react, only a select few

that we make meaningful, organize, interpret, recognize, and remember.

Much of the discussion on perception originates with the Gestalt psychologists, who began their study of perception at the start of the twentieth century. It was they who first recognized a difference between what we sense and what we perceive. Perception is largely a matter of selection and organization. To select some aspects of sensory input while ignoring others, we must first be paying attention to the world around us. What we attend to (and thus perceive) is partly determined by the characteristics of the stimulus events in our environment and partly determined by our internal characteristics. Once we have attended to and selected information for processing, we attempt to organize it in sensible, meaningful ways. The factors that guide that process of organization are the subject of the remainder of Chapter 3.

A PRELIMINARY DISTINCTION

This chapter begins our discussion of **information processing**—how we find out about the world, make judgments about it, learn from it, and remember what we have learned. Although sensation and perception cannot be separated in our personal experience, we will separate them here, in our discussion. The initial stages of information processing involve sensation and perception.

Sensation is the action of detecting external stimuli and converting those stimuli into nervous-system activity. Sensation yields our immediate experience of the stimuli in our environment. The psychology of sensation deals with how our various senses do what they do. **Sense receptors** are the specialized neural cells in the sense organs that change physical energy into neural impulses. In other words, each of our sense receptors is a **transducer**—a mechanism that converts energy from one form to another. A light bulb is a transducer. It converts

---

information processing the means by which we find out about the world, make judgments about it, learn from it, and remember what we have learned

sensation the action of detecting external stimuli and converting those stimuli into nervous system activity

sense receptors the specialized neural cells in the sense organs that change physical energy into neural impulses

transducer a mechanism that converts energy from one form into another

electrical energy into light energy (and a little heat energy). Your eye is a sense organ that contains sense receptors that transduce light energy into neural energy (neural impulses). Your ears are sense organs that contain receptors that transduce the mechanical energy of sound waves into neural energy.

Compared to sensation, perception is a more active, complex, even creative, process and acts on the stimulation received and recorded by the senses. **Perception** is a process that involves the selection, organization, and interpretation of stimuli. Perception is a more cognitive and central process than sensation. We may say that our senses *present* us with information about the world, and our perception *represents* (re-presents) that information, often flavored by our motivations, our expectations, and our past experiences. In other words, ". . . we sense the presence of a stimulus, but we perceive what it is" (Levine & Shefner, 1991, p. 1).

CONCEPTS RELATED TO ALL SENSORY PROCESSES

Before we get into how each sense organ transduces physical energy from the environment into neural energy, we need to consider a few concepts common to all of our senses.

Think about a solar battery powered calculator. In the dark, it will not work. In dim light, it might show some signs of life. In normal light, the calculator's display is bright and easy to read, and all of the calculator's features work properly. The calculator's solar power cell requires a minimum amount of light to work. This minimum is the threshold level of stimulation for that device. Light intensities below the threshold will not allow the calculator to work. Light intensities at or above the threshold allow the calculator to operate properly.

Your sense organs operate in a manner similar to the solar cell in the calculator. A minimum intensity of a stimulus must be present for the receptor cells within the sense organ to transduce the physical stimulus from the environment (for example, light, sound, pressure on your skin) into a neural impulse that your nervous system can interpret. This minimum intensity is known as the **sensory threshold,** or the minimum intensity of stimulus energy needed to operate your sense organs.

Physiologists and psychologists have studied sensory thresholds for over a century. It was research on sensory thresholds that contributed to psychology's emergence as a unique science. **Psychophysics** is the study of relationships between the physical attributes of stimuli and the psychological experiences they produce. It is one of the older fields of psychological research. Many methods of psychophysics were developed even before Wundt opened his psychology laboratory in Leipzig in 1879.

There are two ways to think about psychophysics. First, at an applied level, the techniques of psychophysics are designed to assess the sensitivity of our senses, providing answers to such questions as, "Just how good *is* your hearing after years of playing in a rock band?" Second, at a theoretical level, psychophysics provides a systematic means of relating the physical world to the psychological world. Now we might ask, "How much of a change in the physical intensity of this sound will it take for you to experience a difference in loudness?" Psychophysical methods are designed to measure sensory thresholds, indicative of the sensitivity of our sense receptors. There are two types of sensory thresholds: absolute thresholds and difference thresholds.

Absolute Thresholds

Imagine sitting in a dimly lit room staring at a small box. The side of the box facing you is covered by a sheet of cloudy plastic. Behind the plastic is a light bulb. The light bulb's intensity can be decreased to the point where you

sensory threshold the minimum intensity of stimulus energy needed to operate sense organs

perception the process that involves the selection, organization, and interpretation of stimuli

psychophysics the study of relationships between the physical attributes of stimuli and the psychological experiences they produce

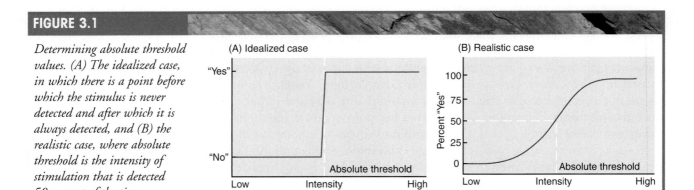

FIGURE 3.1

Determining absolute threshold values. (A) The idealized case, in which there is a point before which the stimulus is never detected and after which it is always detected, and (B) the realistic case, where absolute threshold is the intensity of stimulation that is detected 50 percent of the time.

absolute threshold the physical intensity of a stimulus that a person reports detecting 50 percent of the time

cannot see it at all or increased so that you can see it very clearly. There are many intensity settings between these extremes. At what intensity will the light first become visible to you? Common sense suggests that there should be an intensity level below which you cannot see the light and above which you can. That level is called your absolute threshold. In other words, *sensory thresholds are inversely related to sensitivity*: as threshold values decrease, sensitivity increases. The lower the threshold of a sense receptor, the more sensitive it is.

Let us return to our imaginary experiment. A light's intensity is repeatedly varied, and you are asked to respond, "Yes, I see the light," or "No, I don't see it." (In this study, you are not allowed to say you do not know or are not sure.) When this experiment is done, it shows something strange. The intensity of the light can be reduced so low that you never report seeing it and raised so high that you always report seeing it. However, in between there are light intensities to which you sometimes respond "yes" and other times respond "no." In other words, at an identical intensity, sometimes you see the light and other times you don't. Figure 3.1 shows the difference between an idealized set of results from an experiment to determine absolute thresholds and a more realistic set of results.

In reality then, absolute thresholds are not absolute. They change from moment to moment, reflecting subtle changes in the sensitivity of our senses. Absolute thresholds also reflect such factors as momentary shifts in our ability to pay attention to the task at hand. Because they have no truly absolute measures of sensory sensitivity, psychologists use the following operational definition: **absolute threshold** is the physical intensity of a stimulus that a person reports detecting 50 percent of the time. In other words, intensities below threshold are detected less than 50 percent of the time, and intensities above threshold are detected more than 50 percent of the time. Absolute thresholds apply to all of our senses, not just vision.

What good is the concept of absolute threshold? Determining absolute thresholds is not just academic. Audiologists use absolute threshold to test hearing. Sound system design engineers need to know about absolute thresholds; stereo speakers that do not reproduce sounds above threshold levels are not of much use. Engineers who design warning lights must be certain they are well above absolute threshold. You make regular use of absolute thresholds in daily living. How much perfume do you need to use for it to be noticed? How low must you whisper so as not to be overheard in a classroom? Do you really smell natural gas in the house, or is it your imagination? Can one basil leaf in the tomato sauce be detected, or will two be required? As it happens, our sense receptors are remarkably sensitive, as the examples in Figure 3.2 show.

FIGURE 3.2

Vision	A candle flame seen from a distance of 30 miles on a clear, dark night
Hearing	The ticking of a watch under quiet conditions from a distance of 20 feet
Taste	One teaspoon of sugar dissolved in two gallons of water
Smell	One drop of perfume in a three-room apartment
Touch	The wing of a bee dropped on your cheek from a height of 1 centimeter

Examples of absolute threshold values for the five senses (i.e., these stimuli will be detected 50 percent of the time).

Signal Detection

When we are asked to determine whether a stimulus has been presented, we are being asked to judge if we can detect a signal against a background of other stimuli and randomly changing neural activity called "noise." When we consider thresholds this way, we are using signal detection theory. **Signal detection theory** states that stimulus detection is a decision-making process of determining if a signal exists against a background of noise (Green & Swets, 1966).

According to signal detection theory, one's absolute threshold is influenced by many factors in addition to the actual sensitivity of one's senses. Random nervous system activity has to be accounted for, as do the person's expectations, attention, and biases. For example, in experiments to determine absolute threshold, people are more likely to respond positively when asked if they can detect a stimulus. In other words, when in doubt, people tend to say "yes" (Block, 1965).

Remember the study that launched this discussion of psychophysics? The intensity of a light in a box changes and you are asked if you can detect that light. Your absolute threshold is taken to be the intensity of light to which you respond, "yes" 50 percent of the time. Signal detection theory considers all the factors that might have prompted you to say "yes" at any exposure to the light. What might some of these factors be?

One might be the overall amount of light in the room. Wouldn't you be more likely to detect the signal of the light in a room that was totally dark? What if you were offered a $5 reward each time you detected the light? Wouldn't you tend to say, "yes" more often, whether you were really sure of yourself or not? By the same token, if we were to fine you $1 for each time you said "yes" when the light was not really on, might you be more conservative, saying "yes" only when you were sure of yourself? Might we expect a difference in your pattern of saying "yes" or "no" depending on whether you were tested midmorning or late in the day? Recall the earlier example of absolute threshold in which we asked whether one basil leaf could be detected in a sauce, or if two would be required? Might not many variables influence your decision, including what else you had to eat or drink just before tasting the sauce?

Difference Thresholds

Imagine a friend makes an incredible claim. She claims she can taste the differences among different colored M&M candies. Of course, you are skeptical and decide to design an experiment to test her amazing taste abilities. You blindfold her and feed her pairs of M&Ms, one at a time, giving her a small drink of water between each M&M. Sometimes you give her different colored pairs of M&Ms, and other times you give her matching

signal detection theory the position that stimulus detection is a decision-making process of determining if a signal exists against a background of noise

pairs. You keep track of the number of times she correctly discriminates between the pairs of M&Ms. To your amazement, your friend can detect the difference among the differently colored M&Ms!

This example may be silly, but actually, we are often called upon to detect differences between or among stimuli that are above our absolute thresholds. The issue is not whether the stimuli can be detected, but whether they are in some way different from each other. So, a difference threshold is the smallest difference between stimulus attributes that can be detected. As you may have anticipated, we find the same complication that we encounter when we try to measure absolute thresholds. A person's difference threshold for any stimulus attribute varies slightly from moment to moment. Again, to be above the **difference threshold**, the differences between stimuli must be detected more than 50 percent of the time.

Here's an example: You are presented with two tones. You hear them both clearly (they are above your absolute threshold) and report that they are equally loud. If the intensity of one of the tones is gradually increased, it will eventually reach a point at which you can just barely detect that it has become louder. This **just noticeable difference**, or **jnd**, is the amount of change in a stimulus that makes a stimulus just detectably different from what it was.

The concept of just noticeable difference, or difference threshold, is relevant in many contexts. A parent tells a teenager to "turn down that music!" The teenager reduces the volume, but is the difference enough for the parent to notice? Do the shoes and dress match closely enough? Will anyone notice if we use dried herbs and spices instead of the more expensive fresh ones a recipe calls for? While painting a room, you run out of paint. Does the new paint (from a different batch) match the old paint closely enough to be below the difference threshold?

Sensory Adaptation

Sensory adaptation occurs when our sensory experience decreases with continued exposure to a stimulus. There are many examples of sensory adaptation. When we jump into a pool or lake, the water feels very cold. After a few minutes we adapt and are urging

sensory adaptation what occurs when our sensory experience decreases with continued exposure to a stimulus

difference threshold the minimum difference between stimuli that is detected 50 percent of the time

just noticeable difference (jnd) the amount of change in a stimulus that makes it just detectably different from what it was

Courtesy of Chris Windsor/Getty Images.

With time spent in the dark, the ability to see low illumination light increases. In a few minutes, this girl will be able to see much more than she did when she first entered the cave. Of course, the process is dark adaptation.

Studying absolute thresholds is not just an academic exercise. There are many practical applications. Why put an expensive herb or spice in a sauce if no one can taste it? Just how much of a spice do you need to add so that it can be detected? These are questions of psychophysics.

Courtesy of Andersen Ross/Getty Images.

our friends reassuringly, "Come on in; the water's fine." When cabbage is cooking, the odor is nearly overwhelming, but we adapt and soon do not notice it. When the refrigerator turns on, the compressor's motor makes a noise that quickly blends in with other kitchen noises. We really do not notice the noise again until it stops.

These common examples of sensory adaptation imply our ability to detect a stimulus depends largely on the extent to which our sense receptors are being newly stimulated or have adapted. In fact, our sense receptors respond best to changes in stimulation (Rensink, 2002, Rensink, O'Regan, & Clark, 1997). The constant stimulation of a receptor leads to adaptation and a lower chance that the stimulation will be detected.

Psychologists also use *adaption* in a different sense. What happens when you move from a brightly to a dimly lit area? You enter a darkened movie theater on a sunny afternoon. At first you can barely see, but in a few minutes, you see reasonably well. What happened? We say that your eyes have "adapted to the dark." **Dark adaptation** refers to the process in which the visual receptors become *more* sensitive with time spent in the dark. Light adaptation occurs when you move from a darkened area to an illuminated one. For example, imagine you need to use the bathroom in the middle of the night. You stumble out of bed. Without thinking, you reach for the light switch and are nearly blinded by the light, which, as you know, can even be painful. After a very short period of time, you adapt to the light and are no longer bothered by it. While you are asleep, your eyes are maximally dark-adapted (that is, they are very sensitive to light). When you turn on the light, the visual sense receptors in your eyes fire nearly all at once, flooding your brain with visual stimulation. It takes a much less time for your eyes to light-adapt than to dark-adapt.

dark adaptation the process in which the visual receptors become more sensitive with time spent in the dark

---

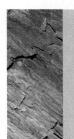

BEFORE YOU GO ON

1. How do the processes of sensation and perception differ?
2. Briefly describe absolute thresholds, difference thresholds, and signal detection theory.
3. What is sensory adaptation?

A Point to Ponder or Discuss
You are trying to explain sensory thresholds to someone who has never taken a psychology class. What examples can you generate to illustrate that sensory thresholds are relevant to everyday life?

VISION

If you could have only one of your senses, which one would you choose? Each of our senses helps us process different information about the environment. Many of us enjoy eating and might choose the sense of taste. Others delight in listening to music and might choose the sense of hearing. None of us would wish to give up the sense of touch during intimate moments. Perhaps the strongest case would be for the sense of sight. An entire lobe of the brain (the occipital) is given over to the processing of visual information, and we equate visual experience with truth or reality, as in the expression, "Seeing is believing."

The Stimulus for Vision: Light

The stimulus for vision is a form of electromagnetic energy we call light. Understanding the nature of light can help us understand how vision works. Light

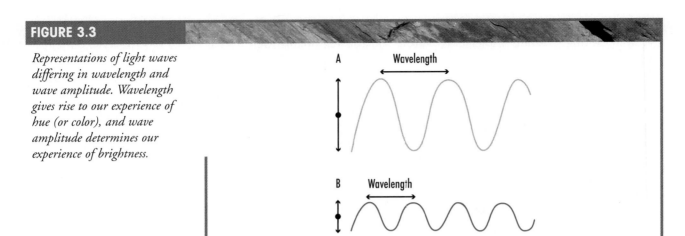

FIGURE 3.3

Representations of light waves differing in wavelength and wave amplitude. Wavelength gives rise to our experience of hue (or color), and wave amplitude determines our experience of brightness.

radiates from its source in waves. Light waves have three important physical characteristics, each related to psychological experience: wave amplitude, wavelength, and wave purity.

Light energy varies in its intensity. Differences in intensity correspond to physical differences in the *wave amplitude* of light. Refer to Figure 3.3, and assume that the two waves represent two different light waves. One of the physical differences between light A and light B is their amplitude. Our psychological experience of wave amplitude, or intensity, is brightness. The difference between a bright and a dim light is due to the difference in wave amplitude.

Wavelength is the distance between any point in a wave and the corresponding point on the next wave, or cycle. In Figure 3.3 wave A has a longer wavelength than does B. It is difficult to imagine distances so small, but the length of a light wave can actually be measured. The unit of measurement is the *nanometer (nm)*, which is equal to one one-billionth of a meter.

Wavelength determines the hue, or color, of the light we perceive. The human eye responds only to radiant energy with a wavelength between roughly 380 nm and 760 nm. This is the range of energy that constitutes the *visible spectrum* (see Figure 3.4). As light waves increase from the short 380 nm wavelengths to the long 760 nm wavelengths, we experience these changes as gradually moving from violet, to blue, to

green, yellow-green, yellow, orange, and to red—the color spectrum. Waveforms of energy with wavelengths shorter than 380 nm (e.g., X-rays and ultraviolet rays) are too short to stimulate the receptors in our eyes and go unnoticed. Waveforms of electromagnetic energy with wavelengths longer than 760 nm (e.g., radar and microwaves) are too long to stimulate the receptor cells in our eyes.

Here is an apparently easy problem: We have two lights, one red (700 nm) and the other yellow-green (550 nm). We adjust the physical intensities of these two lights so that they are equal. Will the lights appear equally bright? Actually, they won't. Even with their amplitudes equal, and even though amplitude does determine brightness, the yellow-green light appears much brighter than a red one. It also appears brighter than a blue light of the same amplitude. Wavelength and wave amplitude interact to produce apparent brightness. Wavelengths in the middle of the spectrum (such as yellow-green) appear brighter than do wavelengths of light from either extreme if their amplitudes are equal. We *can* get a red light to appear as bright as a yellow-green one, but to do so we will have to increase its amplitude, which requires more energy and is thus more expensive. Perhaps the lights on emergency vehicles should be yellow-green, not red. With everything else being equal, yellow-green lights appear brighter than red ones.

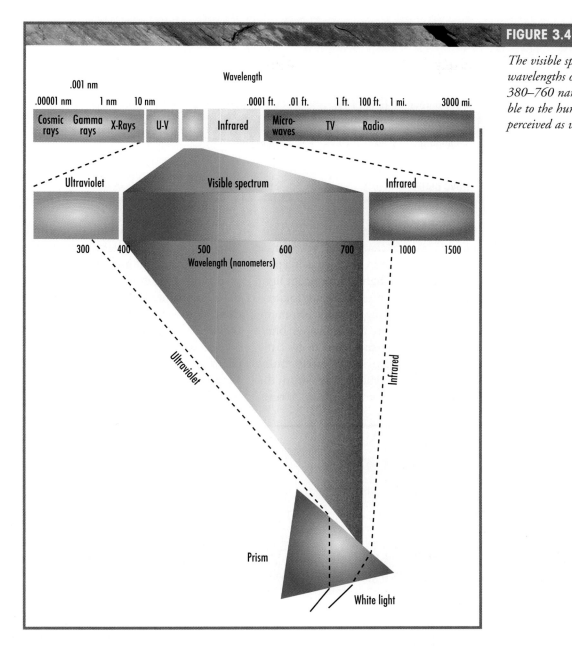

FIGURE 3.4

The visible spectrum, in which wavelengths of approximately 380–760 nanometers are visible to the human eye and are perceived as various hues.

Now consider a third characteristic of light waves: their *saturation*—the degree of purity of a light. Imagine a light of medium amplitude with all of its wavelengths exactly 700 nm long. Because the wavelengths are all 700 nm, it would appear red. Moreover, it would appear as a pure, rich red. We call such a light *monochromatic* because it consists of light waves of one (mono) length or hue (chroma). Monochromatic light is said to be highly saturated. We seldom see such lights outside the laboratory because producing a pure, monochromatic, light is expensive. The reddest of red lights we see

in our everyday experience have other wavelengths of light mixed with the predominant 700 nm red. (If the 700 nm wave did not predominate, the light would not look red.) Even the red light on top of a police car has some violet, green, and yellow light in it.

As different wavelengths are mixed into a light, it lowers in saturation and looks pale and washed out. Light of the lowest possible saturation, a light consisting of a random mixture of wavelengths, is **white light**. It is something of a curiosity that white light is in fact as *impure* a light as possible. A pure light

white light a light of the lowest possible saturation, consisting of a random mixture of wavelengths

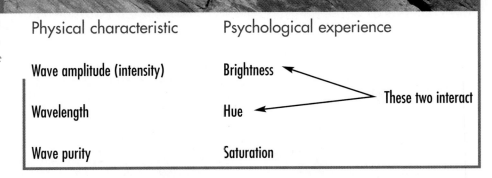

FIGURE 3.5

Relationships between physical characteristics of light and our psychological experience of that light.

Physical characteristic	Psychological experience
Wave amplitude (intensity)	Brightness
Wavelength	Hue
Wave purity	Saturation

These two interact

has one wavelength; a white light contains many wavelengths. A true white light is as difficult to produce as is a pure monochromatic light. Fluorescent light bulbs generate a reasonable approximation, but their light contains too many wavelengths from the short or blue-violet end of the spectrum to be truly white. Light from incandescent bulbs contains too many light waves from the orange and red end of the spectrum, even if we paint the inside of the bulb with white paint. A prism can break a beam of white light into its various parts to produce a rainbow of hues. Where did all those hues come from? They were there all along, mixed together to form the white light.

We have seen that three physical characteristics of light influence our visual experience. These relationships are summarized in Figure 3.5.

BEFORE YOU GO ON

4. What are the three major characteristics of light and what psychological experience does each produce?

A Point to Ponder or Discuss
The stimulus for vision is light, not paint. Why, then, do we see a red barn as red? What would we see if we were to cover the barn with green paint? For that matter, what is the difference between red and green paint?

The Receptor for Vision: The Eye

Vision involves transducing light-wave energy into the neural energy of the nervous system, i.e., causing neurons to transmit impulses to the brain. The sense receptor for vision is the eye, a complex organ composed of several structures. Most of them are involved in focusing light on the back of the eye where the actual transduction of light energy into neural energy takes place.

Figure 3.6 illustrates the structures of the human eye. The **cornea** is the tough,

round, virtually transparent outer shell of the eye. The cornea has two functions: to protect the delicate structures at the front of the eye and to bend light rays so that they can be focused at the back of the eye. In fact, the cornea does about three-fourths of the bending of light waves.

The **pupil** is an opening through which light enters the eye. The **iris** (the colored part of your eye) can expand or contract depending on the intensity of light striking the eye. In bright light, the iris contracts and lets only small amounts of light into the eye. Conversely, in dim light the iris expands and allows more light to enter. The iris of the eye also

pupil the opening through which light enters the eye

iris the colored part of the eye that can expand or contract depending upon the intensity of light striking the eye

cornea the tough, round, virtually transparent outer shell of the eye that begins focusing light waves

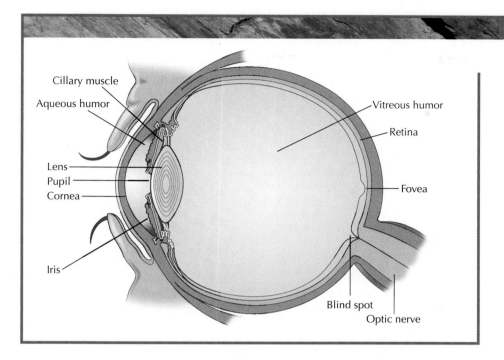

FIGURE 3.6

The major structures of the human eye.

enlarges when people view images of attractive members of the opposite sex (Tombs & Silverman, 2004). The **lens** is a flexible structure whose shape is controlled by powerful **ciliary muscles** that expand or contract to reflexively change the shape of the lens that brings an image into focus. The lens becomes flatter when we try to focus on an object at a distance and rounder when we try to view something up close. The changing of the shape of the lens is called **accommodation.** Often an image does not focus on the back of the eye as it should because of the shape of the lens or because of a failure of accommodation. Sometimes, even a healthy lens and ciliary muscles can't focus on an image because of the shape of the eyeball. The result is either nearsightedness or farsightedness. With age, lenses harden and ciliary muscles weaken, making it difficult to focus.

As you can see in Figure 3.6, the eye is filled with two fluids. The **aqueous humor** (humor means fluid) provides nourishment to the cornea and the other structures at the front of the eye. The aqueous humor is constantly produced and supplied to the space behind the cornea, filtering out blood to keep the fluid clean. If the fluid cannot easily pass out of this space, pressure builds

within the eye, causing distortions in vision or, in extreme cases, blindness. This disorder is known as *glaucoma.* The interior of the eye (behind the lens) is filled with a thicker fluid called **vitreous humor.** Its major function is to keep the eyeball spherical.

At the back of the eye is the **retina,** where vision begins to take place. Light energy is transduced into neural energy here. The retina is really a series of layers of specialized nerve cells at the back surface of the eye. The location of the retina and its major landmarks is shown in Figure 3.6. Figure 3.7 shows the retina in more detail.

To describe the retina, let's move from the back of the retina toward the front. The layer of cells *at the very back* of the retina contains the receptor cells for vision, the transducers or "photoreceptors" of the eye. It is here that light wave energy is changed into neural energy. Photoreceptor cells come in two types: **rods** and **cones.** They are so named because they look like tiny rods and cones. Their tips respond to lightwave energy and begin neural impulses. The impulses travel down the rods and cones and pass on to—form a synapse with—other cells arranged in layers. Within these layers there is considerable

lens a flexible structure that changes its shape in order to focus images on the back of the eye

ciliary muscles powerful muscles that expand or contract to reflexively change the shape of the lens to focus an image on the retina

vitreous humor the thick fluid in the center of the eye (behind the lens) with the major function of keeping the eyeball spherical

retina the place where vision begins to take place; where light wave energy is transduced into neural energy

accommodation the process of changing the shape of the lens

aqueous humor the material that provides nourishment to the cornea and other structures at the front of the eye

rods/cones the photo-receptor cells (transducers) found in the retina

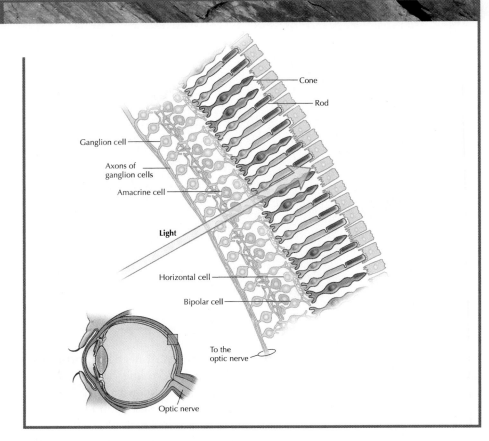

FIGURE 3.7

The major features of the human retina.

Cone

Rod

Ganglion cell

Axons of ganglion cells

Amacrine cell

Light

Horizontal cell

Bipolar cell

To the optic nerve

Optic nerve

---

optic nerve the collection of neurons that leaves the eye and starts back toward other parts of the brain

fovea the place in the retina where visual acuity is best in daylight or in reasonably high levels of illumination

blind spot the place at which nerve impulses from the rods and cones, having passed through many layers of cells, leave the eye

---

combination and integration of neural impulses. No rod or cone has a single direct pathway to the cerebral cortex of the brain. Impulses from many rods and cones are combined within the eye by bipolar cells and ganglion cells among others. Fibers from ganglion cells form the **optic nerve**, the collection of neurons that leaves the eye and starts back toward other parts of the brain.

The fovea and the blind spot are two main features of the retina (Figure 3.6). The fovea is a small area of the retina where there are few layers of cells between the entering light and the cone cells that fill the area. The fovea contains no rods but many tightly packed cones. It is at the **fovea** our visual acuity—or ability to discern detail—is best, at least in daylight or in reasonably high levels of illumination. When you thread a needle, you focus the image of the needle and thread on the fovea.

The **blind spot** is the place at which the nerve impulses from the rods and cones, having passed through many layers of cells, exit the eye. There are no

rods or cones at the blind spot—nothing is there except the optic nerve threading its way back into the brain. Because there are no rods or cones, there is no vision there. Figure 3.8 shows you how to locate your blind spot.

More on Rods and Cones and What They Do

Let's continue our discussion about rods and cones—the two types of receptor cells in our retinas. The fact that the retina of the eye contains two different types of cells was first observed by Max Schultze in 1865 (Goldstein, 1999). Although they are both nerve cells, rods and cones are very different. In each eye, there are about 120 million rods but only 6 million cones. Rods and cones are distributed unevenly throughout the retina. Cones are concentrated in the center of the retina in the fovea, and rods are concentrated on the periphery in a band or ring around the fovea.

Cones function best in medium to high levels of light (as in daylight, for

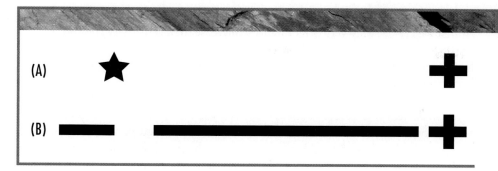

FIGURE 3.8

This figure provides two ways to locate your blind spot.
(A) Close your right eye and stare at the cross (+). Hold the page about a foot from your left eye and slowly move the page around until the star falls on your blind spot and disappears.
(B) Close your right eye and stare at the cross (+). Hold the page about a foot from your left eye and slowly move the page around until the break in the line falls on your blind spot. The line will then appear to be unbroken.

example) and are primarily responsible for our experience of color. On the other hand, rods operate best under conditions of reduced light (as in twilight). Rods are more sensitive to low-intensity light, but do not discriminate among wavelengths of light, which means that rods do not contribute to our appreciation of color.

To a degree, you can verify these claims about cones and rods with your own experiences. Do you find it difficult to distinguish among colors at night or in the dark? The next time you are at the movies eating pieces of different-colored candy, see if you can tell them apart without holding them up to the light of the projector. You probably will not be able to tell a green piece from a red one because they all will appear black. You cannot distinguish colors very well in a dark theater because you are seeing them primarily with your rods, which are very good at seeing in the reduced illumination but unable to distinguish among wavelengths of light.

If you are looking for something small outside on a moonlit night, you proba-

bly won't see it if you look directly at it. Imagine changing a tire at night and losing a lug nut in the gravel. If you look directly at it, the image of the lug nut falls on your fovea. Remember, your fovea consists almost entirely of cones and cones do not operate well in relative darkness, so you won't see the nut. To increase your chance of finding it, you have to get the image of the nut to fall on the periphery of your eye, where rods are concentrated.

One of the reasons nocturnal animals (e.g., many varieties of owls) function so well at night is because their retinas are packed with rods, which enable them to see well in the dark. Usually, such animals have little or no fovea, far fewer cones, and are color-blind.

Consider another piece of evidence for the idea that our rods and cones provide two distinct types of visual experience. As we have seen, dark adaptation is the process of our becoming more sensitive (our thresholds lowering) as we spend time in the dark. Figure 3.9 shows the dark-adaptation process. It illustrates that time spent in the dark increases our

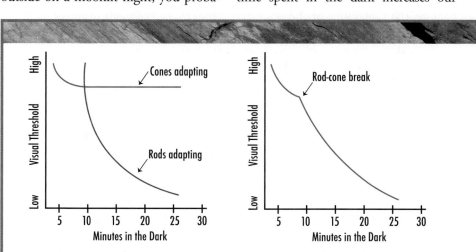

FIGURE 3.9

The dark adaptation curve. In the graph on the left, we see that the cones begin adapting immediately, but then begin "dropping out" at about the 10-minute mark. Rods then begin adapting and continue until about 30 minutes have been spent in the dark. When these two curves are combined to give us a view of what happens in general with time spent in the dark, we have the curve at the right, which shows the "rod-cone break."

sensitivity or lowers our threshold levels. At first we can see only very bright lights (the light reflected from the movie screen, for example). Later we can see dimmer lights (reflected from people in the theater), and soon we can see still-dimmer lights (reflected from pieces of candy) as our threshold drops. The entire dark adaption process takes about 20 to 30 minutes.

But something strange is going on. The dark-adaptation curve (Figure 3.9) is not smooth and regular. After eight to ten minutes, the shape of the curve changes. This break in the smoothness of the curve is called the *rod-cone break*.

For eight or nine minutes, the cones increase their sensitivity (represented by the first part of the curve). But cones are basically daylight receptors and not designed for seeing in the dark. After a few minutes, they have become as sensitive as they can get; therefore, they drop out of the curve. At about the same time, the rods lower their threshold and become even more sensitive (represented by the part of the curve after the "break"). This explanation of the different actions of rods and cones in dark adaption has remained unchallenged for over 70 years.

BEFORE YOU GO ON

5. Describe the structures of the eye that are involved in focusing images onto the back of the eye (the retina).
6. Describe the structures of the retina, noting the different functions of the rods and the cones.

A Point to Ponder or Discuss
Think about the structures of the eye mentioned in this section. As you consider each in turn, describe the effect on vision if that structure were damaged or destroyed.

The Visual Pathway after the Retina

Considerable visual processing takes place within the layers of the retina; there are, after all, many more rods and cones in the retina than there are ganglion cell fibers leaving it. Visual information continues to change as it races back to the visual area of the occipital lobe of the cerebral cortex.

To trace the pathway of nerve fibers between the eyes and the cortex, we need to introduce the concept of left and right visual fields. When you view the world, everything to your left is in your left visual field, whereas everything to your right is in your right visual field. In Figure 3.10 the left visual field is red and the right visual field is purple. Stimuli in our left visual field end up being represented in our right occipital lobe, and

stimuli in our right visual field in our left occipital lobe—a sort of cross laterality.

Where and how fibers in the optic nerve get directed to the occipital lobe occurs largely in the **optic chiasma**. Notice in Figure 3.10 that, in fact, each eye receives light energy from both visual fields. Light that enters your left eye from the left initiates neural impulses that cross to the right side of the brain at the optic chiasma, whereas light that enters our left eye from the right visual field initiates neural impulses that go straight back to the left hemisphere. Now see if you can describe what happens to light that enters the right eye.

From the optic chiasma, nerve fibers pass through other centers in the brain including a cluster of cells on each side of the brain called the *superior colliculus*. This cluster controls the movement of our eyes as we scan a patterned stim-

optic chiasma where fibers in the optic nerve get directed to the occipital lobe

FIGURE 3.10

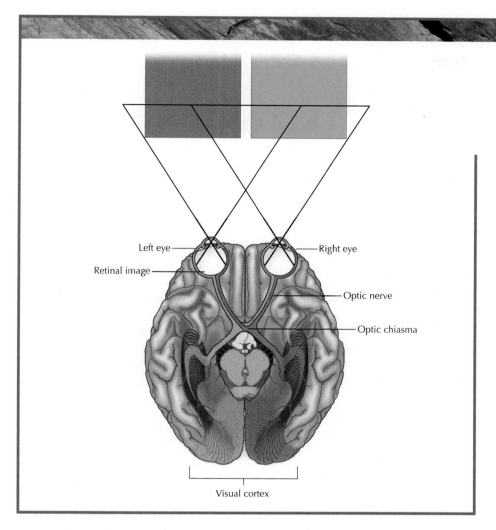

Left eye

Right eye

Retinal image

Optic nerve

Optic chiasma

Visual cortex

In keeping with the principle of cross laterality, stimuli from the left visual field are sent to the right occipital lobe for further processing, whereas stimuli from the right visual field are sent to the left occipital lobe.

ulus, perhaps fixing our gaze on some aspect of the pattern. Curiously, people who are totally blind because of damage to the occipital lobes of their cerebral cortex can often locate visual stimuli in space. That is, they can point to a light they cannot "see"—probably an example of the superior colliculus at work. Beyond the superior colliculus, nerve cells form synapses with neurons in the thalamus, and the thalamus projects neural impulses to the layers of cells in the visual cortex of the occipital lobe.

Vision doesn't really "happen" in our eyes. The eye contains the transducers, but seeing occurs in the brain. The brain reassembles a myriad of neural impulses into one image in our awareness—a single, complete visual field, not one divided into left and right. It is the cerebral cor-

tex that detects and interprets patterns of light, shade, color, and motion.

Color Vision and Color Blindness

How the eye responds to various intensities of light is fairly simple. High-intensity lights cause a greater number of neurons to fire more rapidly. Low intensity lights cause fewer neurons to fire less frequently. How the eye responds to differing wavelengths of light to produce differing experiences of hue or color, however, is far more complex. Two theories of color vision, both proposed many years ago, have received research support. As is often the case with competing theories, both are likely to be partially correct.

FIGURE 3.11

The relative sensitivities of three types of cones to lights of differing wavelengths. Although there is considerable overlap, each type is maximally sensitive to wavelengths corresponding to the primary hues of light: blue, green, and red.

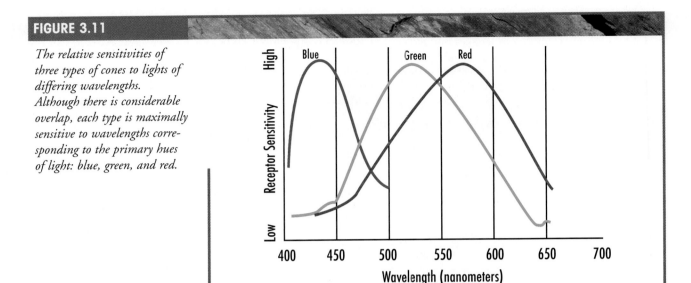

trichromatic theory a theory of color vision proposing that the eye contains three (tri) distinct receptors for color (chroma)

opponent-process theory a theory of color vision proposing that color vision works by means of three pairs of mechanisms that respond to different wavelengths of light: a blue-yellow processor, a red-green processor, and a black-white processor

The older of the two, the trichromatic theory, was first proposed by Thomas Young early in the nineteenth century and was revised by noted physiologist Hermann von Helmholtz roughly 50 years later. As its name suggests, the **trichromatic theory** proposes that the eye contains three (tri-) distinct receptors for color (chroma). Although there is some overlap, each receptor responds best to one of three primary hues of light: *red, green, or blue.* These hues are primary because the careful combination of the three produces all other colors. Many of us see this principle in action everyday because the picture on a television set is produced using patterns of very small red, green, or blue dots of light. From these three wavelengths, all other colors are constructed or integrated. (Don't confuse the three primary hues of light with the three primary colors of pigment, which are red, blue, and yellow. The primary colors of paint, dye, pastel, crayon, etc., can be mixed together to form all other pigment colors. Our eyes respond to light, however, not pigment, and the three primary hues of light are red, green, and blue.)

Because the sensitivity of the three types of receptors overlaps, when our eyes are stimulated by a non-primary color—for example, orange—the orange-hued light stimulates each receptor to varying degrees to produce the experience of orange. What gives this theory credibility is that there are three types of cones in the retina and each plays a role in color vision (Figure 3.11).

Dissatisfied with the Young-Helmholtz theory, Ewald Hering proposed the **opponent-process theory** in 1870. Hering proposed color vision works by means of three pairs of mechanisms that respond to different wavelengths of light: a blue-yellow processor, a red-green processor, and a black-white processor.

Each mechanism is capable of responding to either of the two hues that give it its name, but not to both. That is, the blue-yellow processor can respond to blue or to yellow, but not both simultaneously. The second mechanism responds to red or to green, but not both. The third codes brightness. Thus, the members of each pair work in opposition, hence the theory's name. If blue is excited, yellow is inhibited. If red is excited, green is inhibited. A light may appear to be a mixture of red and yellow, but it cannot be seen as a mixture of red and green because red and green cannot be excited at the same time. (It is difficult to imagine what a "reddish green" or "bluish yellow" would look like. Can you picture a light that is bright and dim at the same time?)

There are some signs that Hering was on the right track. Researchers have found excitatory-inhibitory mechanisms such as he proposed for red-green, blue-yellow, and black-white. They are not at the level of rods and cones in the retina as Hering thought, but at the layer of the ganglion cells (see Figure 3.7) and in a small area of the thalamus.

Support for Hering's theory also comes from experience with negative afterimages. If you stare at a bright green figure for a few minutes and then shift your gaze to a white surface, you will notice an image of a red figure. Where did *that* come from? While you stared at the green figure, the green component of the red-green process fatigued because of the stimulation it received. When you stared at the white surface, red and green components were equally stimulated; but because the green component was fatigued, the red predominated and produced the image of a red figure.

Evidence supporting both theories of normal color vision comes from studies of persons with color-vision defects. Defective color vision of some sort occurs in about 8 percent of males and slightly less than 0.5 percent of females. Most cases are genetic. It makes sense that if cones are our receptor cells for the discrimination of color, people with a deficiency in color vision would have some problem with their cones. This would be consistent with the Young-Helmholtz theory. In fact,

there is a noticeable lack of one type of cone in the most common of the color-vision deficiencies (dichromatism); which type depends on the color that is "lost." Those people who are red-green colorblind, for instance, have trouble distinguishing between red and green. People with this type of problem also have trouble distinguishing yellow from either red or green. The deficiency is not in actually seeing reds or greens. It is in distinguishing reds and greens from other colors. Put another way, someone who is red-green colorblind can clearly see a bright red apple; the problem is that it looks no different than a bright green apple.

Some color-vision defects can be traced to cones in the retina, but damage to cells higher in the visual pathway is implicated in some rare cases of color-vision problems. When such problems do occur, there are losses for both red and green or both yellow and blue as predicted by the opponent-process theory (Schiffman, 1990).

Because cone cells that respond differently to red, blue, and green light have been found in the retina, we cannot dismiss the trichromatic theory. However, there also are cells that operate the way the opponent-process theory predicts, so we cannot dismiss that theory either. Which one is right? Probably both. Our experience of color likely depends on the interaction of cone cells and opponent-process cells within our visual pathway—a marvelous system indeed.

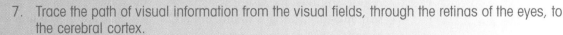

BEFORE YOU GO ON

7. Trace the path of visual information from the visual fields, through the retinas of the eyes, to the cerebral cortex.
8. Briefly discuss how we experience the hue or color of light.

A Point to Ponder or Discuss
How might we test the color vision of animals? That is, how do you know if a dog, or a cat, or a pigeon sees the world in the same fully colorful way you do?

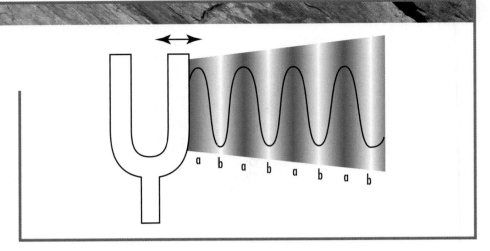

Sound waves are manifested as changes in air pressure produced as the tines of the tuning fork vibrate back and forth.

AUDITION: THE SENSE OF HEARING

Vision is an important sense. Try this experiment on your own: Blindfold yourself and spend part of your day without your sense of sight. Try to do your normal everyday activities without your eyes. You will realize almost immediately just how heavily you rely on vision. But consider for a moment the quantity and quality of information you *do* receive from your other four senses. You may gain a new appreciation of how well they inform you of the wonder of your environment: the aroma and taste of well-prepared barbecue, the sounds of birds and music, the touch and feel of textures and surfaces, the sense of where your body is and what it is doing, the feedback from your muscles as you move. We now turn to these "lesser" senses, beginning with hearing, or audition.

The Stimulus for Hearing: Sound

As the stimulus for vision is light, the stimulus for hearing is sound. Sound is a series of air pressures (or other medium, such as water) beating against the ear. These pressures constitute sound waves. As a source of sound vibrates, it pushes air against our ears in waves (see Figure 3.12). Like light waves, sound waves have three major physical charac-

teristics: amplitude, frequency (the inverse of wavelength), and purity. And, as is the case for light, each is related to a different psychological experience.

The amplitude of a sound wave depicts its intensity—the force with which air strikes the ear. The physical intensity of a sound determines the psychological experience of loudness—the higher its amplitude, the louder the sound. Quiet, soft sounds have low amplitudes.

The physical intensity of sound is measured in units of force per unit area (or pressure). Loudness, however, is a psychological characteristic, measured by people's experiences, not by instruments. The **decibel scale** of sound intensity measures perceived loudness. Its zero point is the absolute threshold, or the lowest intensity of sound that can be detected. Our ears are very sensitive receptors and respond to very low levels of sound intensity. If our ears were any more sensitive, we would hear molecules of air bouncing against our eardrums. Individual receptor cells for sound, deep in our ears, need only to be displaced by the diameter of a hydrogen atom to produce the experience of sound (Hudspeth, 1997). Figure 3.13 lists a few examples of common sounds in decibel units.

If sound intensities are high enough, we literally can "feel" sound. Sounds in the 90–120 decibel range (such as those produced by jet aircraft engines or fast-moving trains) are often felt as much as heard. Because sounds this

decibel scale a scale of sound intensity measuring perceived loudness

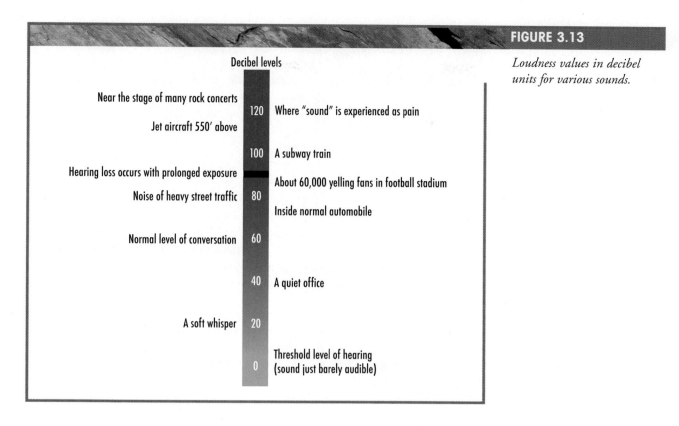

FIGURE 3.13

Loudness values in decibel units for various sounds.

loud are common in dance clubs and at concerts, the shift from hearing a sound to feeling it has been named "the rock and roll threshold" (Dibble, 1995; McAngus-Todd & Cody, 2000). Prolonged exposure to very loud, high intensity sounds can cause deafness. When then-President Bill Clinton turned 51, he was fitted with hearing aids. His hearing loss was attributed— at least in part—to his playing a saxophone in a jazz band. Hearing loss among rock musicians is a real and serious concern. There is even a web page (www.hearnet.com) posting advice and treatment options under the title page, "Hearing Education and Awareness for Rockers." On the other hand, the San (or "Bushmen") of the Kalahari Desert in Africa have significantly better hearing at an older age than do natives of the United States. There may be several reasons for this, but the relative quiet of their desert environment seems to be a significant factor (Berry, et al., 1992). Granting that long-term exposure to very loud sounds can cause hearing problems, a recent concern has focused on a problem that some people have

with *quiet*. It is generally a good idea to get out of the path of a moving car or truck. We can see cars and trucks coming at us, and when they approach from behind, we can hear them. The problem: Today's hybrid cars are so quiet that they often operate with virtually no sound being produced by the vehicle. This is a danger for all of us, but particularly for those of us who are visually impaired and rely heavily on their sense of hearing (Rosenblum, 2008). A piece of legislation, called the "Pedestrian Safety Enhancement Act of 2008" (H.R. 5734) was introduced into the 110th Congress on April 9. The bill requires a federally funded study of how to make vehicles noisier than they normally are (at slow speeds). The added sound is likely to be something like a running car engine or the sound of tires on pavement.

The second physical characteristic of sound is wave frequency, or the number of times a wave repeats itself within a given time period. For sound, frequency is measured in terms of how many waves of pressure are exerted every second. The unit of sound frequency is

TABLE 3.1

A summary of the ways in which the physical characteristics of light and sound waves affect our psychological experiences of vision and hearing.

Physical characteristic	Psychological experience for vision	Psychological experience for hearing
Wave amplitude	Brightness	Loudness
Wavelength or frequency	Hue	Pitch
Wave purity or mixture	Saturation	Timbre

timbre the psychological quality or character of sound that reflects its degree of purity

the hertz, which is abbreviated Hz. If a sound wave repeats itself 50 times in one second, it is a 50-Hz sound; 500 repetitions is a 500-Hz sound.

The psychological experience produced by sound-wave frequency is *pitch*. Pitch is our experience of how high or low a tone is. The musical scale represents differences in pitch. Low frequencies correspond to bass tones, such as those made by foghorns or tubas. High frequencies correspond to high-pitched sounds, such as the musical tones produced by flutes or the squeals of smoke detectors.

Just as the human eye cannot see all possible wavelengths of radiant energy, the human ear cannot hear all possible sound-wave frequencies. A healthy human ear responds to sound-wave frequencies between 20 Hz and 20,000 Hz. If air strikes our ears at a rate less than 20 times per second, we do not hear a sound. Nor can we hear sound vibrations faster than 20,000 Hz. Many animals can hear sounds with frequencies above 20,000 Hz, such as those produced by dog whistles.

A third characteristic of sound waves is wave purity or complexity. Just as we seldom experience monochromatic lights, we seldom experience pure sounds. A pure sound would be one in which all waves from the sound source vibrate at exactly the same frequency. Pure sounds can be produced electronically and approximated by tuning forks, but most real-world sounds are complex mixtures of many different sound-wave frequencies. A tone of middle C on the piano is a tone of 256 Hz. (The piano wire vibrates 256 times per second.) A pure 256-Hz tone consists of sound

waves (vibrations) of only that frequency. As it happens, the piano's middle C has many other wave frequencies mixed in with the predominant 256-Hz wave frequency. (If the 256-Hz wave did not predominate, the tone wouldn't sound like C.)

The psychological quality or character of a sound that reflects its degree of purity is called **timbre**. For example, each musical instrument produces a unique variety or mixture of overtones, so each type of musical instrument sounds a little different from others. If a trumpet, a violin, and a piano play the same note, equally loudly, we can still tell the instruments apart because of our experience of timbre.

We learned that the opposite of a pure light is white light—a light made up of all wavelengths of the visible spectrum. Again we see the parallel between vision and audition. If a sound source produces all the possible sound-wave frequencies, it sounds similar to the buzzing noise one hears when a radio is tuned to a position between stations. This soft, buzzing sound, containing a range of many audible sound frequencies, is useful in masking or covering other unwanted sounds. We call a random mixture of sound frequencies white noise, just as we refer to a random mixture of wavelengths of light as white light.

The analogy between light and sound and vision and hearing is striking. Both types of stimulus energy can be represented as waves. In both cases, each of the physical characteristics of the waves (amplitude, length or frequency, and purity or complexity) is correlated with a psychological experience (Table 3.1).

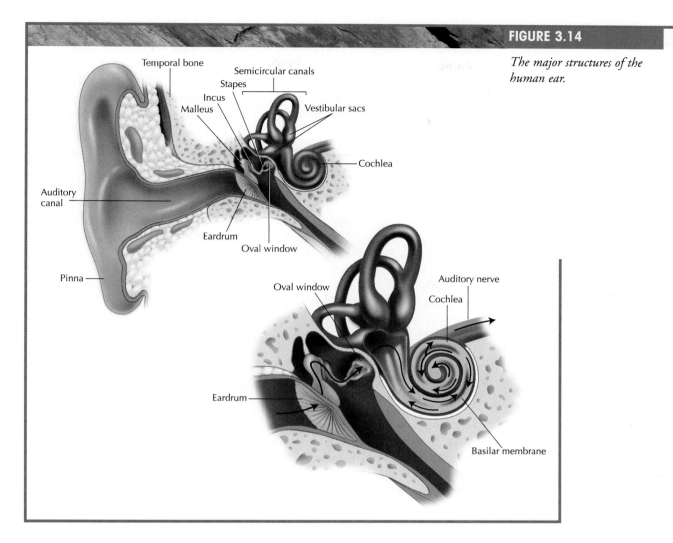

FIGURE 3.14

The major structures of the human ear.

The Receptor for Hearing: The Ear

The energy of sound wave pressures is transduced into neural impulses deep inside the ear. As is the case with the eye's, most of ear's structures simply transfer energy from without to within. The major structures of the ear are depicted in Figure 3.14 and we will refer to it as we trace the path of sound waves from the environment to the receptor cells.

The outer ear is called the **pinna**. Its function is to collect sound waves from the air around it and funnel them through the auditory canal toward the eardrum. Airwaves push against the eardrum (technically, the *tympanic membrane*) setting it in motion so that it vibrates at the same rate as the sound source. The eardrum then passes vibra-

tions to three very small bones (collectively called *ossicles*) in the middle ear. They are, in order, from the eardrum inward, the *malleus, incus,* and *stapes* (pronounced *stape-eez*). These bones then amplify and pass the vibrations to the oval window membrane, which is like the eardrum only smaller.

When sound waves pass beyond the oval window, the vibrations are in the inner ear. The major structure of the inner ear is the snail-like **cochlea**, which contains the actual receptor cells for hearing. As the stapes vibrates against the oval window, a fluid inside the cochlea is set in motion at the same rate. When the fluid within the cochlea moves, the *basilar membrane* is bent up and down. The basilar membrane is a small structure that runs about the full length of the cochlea. Hearing takes place when tiny

pinna the outer ear

cochlea the snail-like structure of the inner ear that contains the receptor cells for hearing mechanical receptors called *hair cells* are stimulated by the vibrations of the basilar membrane. Through a process not yet fully understood, the mechanical pressure of the basilar membrane causes the hair cells to bend. The neural impulses leave the ears, traveling on the auditory nerves toward the temporal lobes. Thus, most of the structures of the ear are responsible for amplifying and directing waves of pressure to the hair cells in the cochlea where the neural impulse begins.

BEFORE YOU GO ON

9. What are the three main physical characteristics of sound, and what psychological experience is produced by each?
10. Describe the major structures of the human ear and note their role in hearing.

A Point to Ponder or Discuss
Loss of hearing often can be characterized as "conduction deafness" or "nerve deafness." What do you suppose the difference is, and which is more likely to be treatable with hearing aids?

THE CHEMICAL SENSES

Taste and smell are referred to as the "chemical senses" because the stimuli for both are molecules of chemical compounds. For taste, the chemicals are dissolved in liquid (usually, the saliva in our mouths). For smell, they are dissolved in the air that reaches the smell receptors high inside our noses. The technical term for taste is **gustation**; for smell, it is **olfaction**.

If you have ever eaten while suffering from a serious head cold, you appreciate the extent to which our experiences of taste and smell are inter-related. Most foods seem to lose their taste when we cannot smell them. This is why we differentiate between the *flavor* of foods (which includes qualities such as odor and texture) and the *taste* of foods. A simple test demonstrates this point. While blindfolded, eat a small piece of peeled apple and a small piece of peeled potato. See if you can tell the difference between the two. You shouldn't have any trouble. Now hold your nose very tightly and try again. Without your sense of smell, you will likely find telling the difference much more challenging.

| **gustation** the technical term for the sense of taste |

| **olfaction** the technical term for the sense of smell |

Taste (Gustation)

Our experience of the flavors of foods depends so heavily on our sense of smell, texture, and temperature that we sometimes have to wonder if there is truly a sense of taste. Well, there is. Even with odor and texture held constant, tastes can vary.

Scientists have long claimed that taste has four basic psychological qualities (and many combinations of these four): sweet, salty, sour, and bitter. Most foods derive their special taste from a unique combination of these four basic taste sensations. You can easily generate a list of foods that produce each of these sensations. It is more difficult to think sour and bitter-tasting foods because we do not like bitter and sour tastes and have learned to avoid them. Beyond that, specific taste preferences are culturally conditioned—a reality you may have experienced the first time you visited a restaurant that serves food from another culture. Even newborns can discriminate among the four basic taste qualities. A newborn will, for example, make a face, wrinkle his nose, and turn away when a sour liquid such

FIGURE 3.15

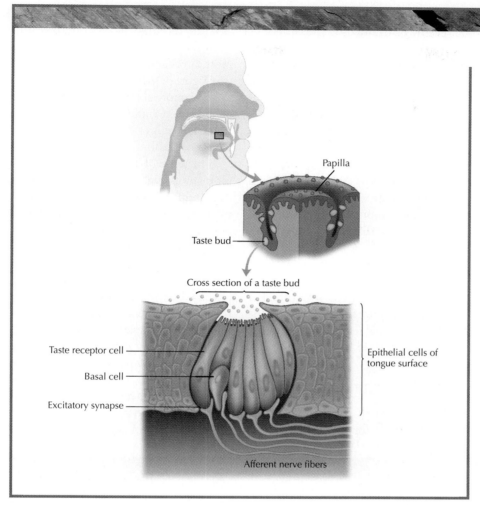

Enlarged view of a taste bud, the receptor for gustation.

Papilla

Taste bud

Cross section of a taste bud

Taste receptor cell

Basal cell

Excitatory synapse

Epithelial cells of tongue surface

Afferent nerve fibers

as grapefruit juice is placed in his or her mouth. As people age, they often develop new preferences for certain foods, but such changes have more to do with learning and experience than with our gustatory receptors. With old age, however, as taste buds begin to fail, people often use more sugar, salt, pepper, and other seasonings.

Over the past decade, neuroscientists have added a fifth taste quality to the list of basic tastes: *umami* (Chandrashekar et al., 2006; Soldo, Blank, & Hofmann, 2003; Palmer, 2007). The name "umami" comes from the Japanese word "umai," which means "delicious." The taste is difficult to describe, but is most often referred to as "savory-ness" or "meatiness." The experience of umami is created by a specific amino acid, glutamate (the main ingredient in the flavor-enhancing com-

pound monosodium glutamate (MSG) commonly found in so much oriental cooking). The recognition of umami as a basic taste became widespread with word of the discovery of a separate, independent receptor cell for glutamate in the taste buds (Chaudhari, Landin, & Roper, 2000; Nelson et al., 2002).

The receptor cells for taste are located in the tongue and are called **taste buds**. We have about 10,000 taste buds, and each one consists of several parts (Figure 3.15). When parts of taste buds die (or are killed by foods that are too hot, for example), they regenerate. This capacity to regenerate makes taste a unique sense because taste buds are nerve cells and most nerve cells do not regenerate when they die.

Taste buds respond primarily to chemicals that produce one of the five

taste buds the receptor cells for taste, located in the tongue

basic taste qualities. These receptors are not evenly distributed on the surface of the tongue; receptors for sweet tastes are concentrated at the tip of the tongue, for example. Nonetheless, all five qualities of taste can be detected at all locations of the tongue. You may have seen drawings of the tongue that indicate the locations where the basic tastes are processed. We now know that such simplified drawings are simply incorrect. In addition to responding to the various chemicals that we put in our mouths—our taste buds also respond to different temperatures (Cruz & Green, 2000). In fact, as many as half of the neurons in mammalian taste pathways—from the taste buds to the brain—respond to temperature. For example, warming the very tip of the tongue from a cold temperature gives rise to the experience of sweetness.

Smell (Olfaction)

The sense of smell is not well understood. Receptors for smell are hair cells located high in the nasal cavity, very close to the brain itself. The pathway from these receptors to the brain is the most direct and shortest of all the senses (see Figure 3.16). Researchers would like to know more about how molecules suspended in air and gases stimulate the small hair cells of the olfactory receptors to fire neural impulses.

The sense of smell is very important for many animals. Many animals, including humans, emit chemicals called **pheromones** that produce distinctive odors. Pheromones are sometimes released in urine, or by cells in the skin, or from special glands (in some deer, this gland is located near the rear hoof). One purpose of pheromones is to mark territory, to let others of the same species know of your presence. If you take a dog for a walk and he urinates on almost every signpost, he is leaving a pheromone message that says, "I have been here; this is my odor; this is my turf." As you might suspect, dog's have a significantly more sensitive sense of smell than humans

pheromones chemicals that produce distinctive odors that may be related to attracting members of the opposite sex

FIGURE 3.16

The olfactory system, showing its proximity to the brain and transducers for smell—the hair cells.

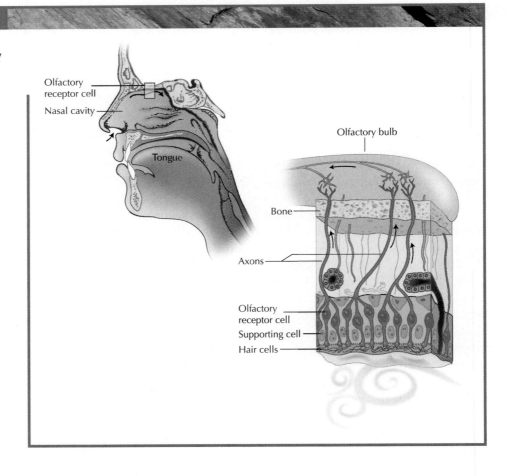

(from 300 to 10,000 *times* more [Goldstein, 2002, p. 475]), and the canine nose is more sensitive to pheromones than nearly anything else (Leinders-Zufall, et al., 2000).

Although recent evidence suggests that pheromone detection does occur through the same pathways as are other odors the primary organ involved in the detection of pheromones is the **vomeronasal organ (VNO)** (Wang et al., 2006). The VNO in most animals appears to be involved in detecting pheromones that regulate behaviors like mating, territoriality, and aggressiveness (Beekman, 2002; Firestein, 2001; Luo, Fee, & Katz, 2003). Indeed, when structures for the detection of pheromones are destroyed in mice, those mice fail to engage in sexual or aggressive behaviors (Mandiyan Coats, & Shah, 2005). In humans, the VNO may also be involved in sexual attraction (Benson, 2002; Jacob et al., 2002). Human pheromones may influence men's and women's brains (the hypothalamus) differently (Savic et al., 2001). In fact, enterprising companies have manufactured perfumes for men and women that supposedly stimulate the VNO. Even though it makes sense that the VNO would be involved in human sexuality (as it is in animal sexuality), the data are not overwhelming, and human sexuality certainly includes other signals beyond pheromones (Benson, 2002; Cutler, Friedmann, & McCoy, 1998).

THE SKIN, OR CUTANEOUS, SENSES

Most of us don't often think about our skin. We scratch it, scrape it, cut it, and wash it, but we surely don't pay much attention to it. Figure 3.17 shows some of the structures found in a hair-covered area of human skin. Each square inch of our multi-layered skin contains nearly 20 million cells, and among these cells are many special sense receptors. Skin receptor cells may be divided into those with *free nerve endings* and those with some sort of covering—called *encapsulated nerve endings*, of which there are many types. The special sense receptors in our skin somehow give rise to our psychological experience of touch or pressure and of warm and cold.

vomeronasal organ (VNO) the primary organ involved in the detection of pheromones

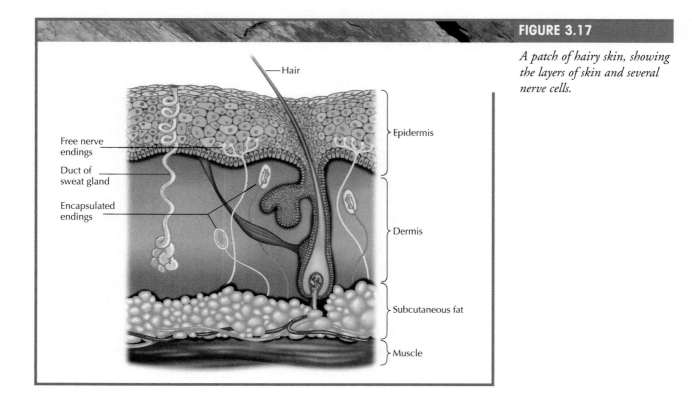

FIGURE 3.17

A patch of hairy skin, showing the layers of skin and several nerve cells.

FIGURE 3.18

A demonstration that our sense of what is hot can be constructed from sensations of what is warm and cold. Even if you know that the coiled tubes contain only warm and cold water, when you grasp the tubes they will feel very hot.

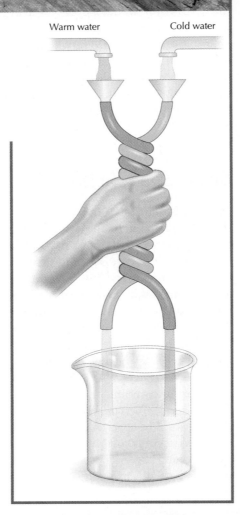

Warm water   Cold water

tiny hairs on their posteriors that detect even the minutest changes in air flow. This sense (which few other organisms have) allows a cockroach to "surmise the direction of an attack and scurry away to avoid being eaten" (or squished) (Rinberg & Davidowitz, 2000, p. 756).

By carefully stimulating very small areas of the skin, scientists can locate areas that are sensitive to temperature. It seems that warm and cold temperatures each stimulate specific locations on the skin. Even so, no consistent pattern of receptor cells is found at these locations, called temperature spots. That is, no one has yet located specific receptor cells for cold or hot. Most researchers believe the experience of hot comes from the simultaneous stimulation of warm and cold temperature spots. Researchers devised a rather ingenious experiment to test their hypothesis. They ran cold water through one metal tube, and warm water through another. They coiled the tubes together (Figure 3.18). Persons touching the coiled tubes reported both tubes felt hot.

THE POSITION SENSES

We take for granted our ability to know how and where our bodies are positioned in space. Without thinking, we seem to know how our bodies are positioned in regard to the pull of gravity. Our senses also let us know where parts of our body are in relation to one another. We can tell if we are moving or standing still. And, unless we have a special reason to pay attention to them (for example, being on a roller coaster), we usually adapt quickly to these sensory messages and virtually ignore them.

Our sense of sight gives us most of the information about where we are in space. If we need to know, we simply look around. However, even with our eyes closed, we have two systems to help us sense our position in space. One, the **vestibular sense**, tells us about balance, about where we are in relation to gravity, and about acceleration or deceleration.

We can easily discriminate between a light touch and a strong jab in the arm and between vibrations, tickles, and itches. An appealing hypothesis is that different receptors in the skin are responsible for each kind of sensation, but the facts do not support this hypothesis. Although some types of receptor cells are more sensitive to some types of stimuli, current thinking is that our ability to discriminate among types of cutaneous sensation is due to the unique combination of responses the many receptor cells have to various types of stimulation.

As good as our cutaneous senses are, those of the common cockroach are—in some ways—even better. Cockroaches are incredibly good at avoiding a swat from a newspaper or a stomp from the heel of a shoe because of the

vestibular sense the sense that tells us about balance, where we are in relation to gravity, and about acceleration or deceleration

The receptors for the vestibular sense are on either side of the head near the inner ears. Five chambers are located there: three semicircular canals and two vestibular sacs (Figure 3.14 on page 113). Each of these chambers is filled with fluid. When your head moves in any direction, the fluid in your semicircular canals moves, drawn by gravity or the force of the head accelerating in space. The vestibular sacs contain fluid with very small solid particles floating in it. When you move, these particles are forced against one side of a sac, and they stimulate hair cells that start neural impulses. These neural impulses have been traced to the temporal and parietal lobes of the cerebral cortex and to the hippocampus in the midbrain (Kahane et al., 2003). When the receptor cells in the vestibular sacs or semicircular canals are over-stimulated, the result may be motion sickness. Because of the space program, body position awareness and the discomfort of motion sickness have become hot research topics in psychology in the last decade. As a result of the international space station, researchers are getting their first chance to see the effects of long-term "weightless" as humans spend months at a time living in space (Lackner & DiZio, 2005).

Receptors for the **kinesthetic sense** are concentrated in the joints, but they are also found in muscles and tendons. Kinesthetic sense receptors sense the position and movements of parts of the body and send impulses to the brain through pathways in the spinal cord. The way the kinesthetic receptors operate is an excellent example of reflex action. Consider something as simple as bending your elbow. At the same time that muscles in the front of your upper arm (biceps) contract, the corresponding muscles in the back of your arm (triceps) automatically relax. Our kinesthetic receptors, operating reflexively through the spinal cord, take care of the details without our having to think about them. In fact, about the only time you notice your kinesthetic system is when it stops working well, such as when your leg "falls asleep" and you have trouble walking.

kinesthetic sense the sense that informs us about body position with receptors in joints, muscles, and tendons

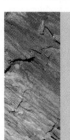

BEFORE YOU GO ON

11. What are the stimuli and the receptors for the senses of gustation and olfaction?
12. Briefly describe the cutaneous senses and the position senses.

A Point to Ponder or Discuss
Is cutaneous sensation the same all over your body, or are some areas more sensitive to touch and pressure than others? How might sensitivity to touch over different body areas be tested?

PAIN: A SPECIAL SENSE

The sense of pain is a curious and troublesome one for scientists interested in sensory processes. Pain, or the fear of it, can be a strong motivator; people will do all sorts of things to avoid pain. Pain is surely unpleasant, but it is also very useful. Pain alerts us when a problem occurs somewhere in our bodies and prompts us to take steps to remove the source of the pain. More than 80 percent of all visits to the doctor are

Courtesy of Mike Powell/Corbis.

Bungee chord jumping can put a real strain on one's kinesthetic and vestibular senses. Bouncing at the end of what amounts to a huge rubber band challenges a person's ability to orient in space—or determine just which way is "up."

prompted by pain (Turk, 1994). A World Health organization study found that nearly one-quarter of primary-care patients at 15 centers around the world reported persistent pain (Gureje et al., 1998). Yet, feelings of pain are private sensations and are sometimes difficult to share or describe.

What is pain? What causes the experience of pain? What are its receptors? We have only partial answers to these questions. Many stimuli cause pain. Intense stimulation of any sense receptor may produce pain. Too much light, intense pressure on the skin, excessive temperature, very loud sounds, and "hot" spices can all cause pain. In certain circumstances, even a light pinprick can be painful. Our skin's surface has many receptors for pain, but they can also be found deep inside our bodies—consider stomachaches, headaches, and lower back pain. Researchers have long suspected that the brain plays a crucial role in the experience of pain, but only recently have they been able to find areas (in the thalamus and the parietal lobe of the cerebral cortex that are intimately involved in the sensation of pain is the only "sense" for which they cannot find a specific center in the cerebral cortex (Loyd & Murphy, 2006; Mohr et al., 2005; Seghier et al., 2005; Smith, 2007; Tracey, 2005).

One theory about our experience of pain that has gained considerable favor claims that a "gate control mechanism" (high in the spinal cord) opens to let pain messages race to the brain or closes so that messages never reach the brain (Melzack, 1973; 1999; Melzack & Wall, 1965). This "mechanism" is not purported to be a physical, physiological structure, but more the influence of a combination of factors, such as a person's attitudes, mood, expectations, and behaviors (Turk, 1994). Here again we see the *interaction* of biological and psychological factors producing what appears to be single experience (Keefe, Abernathy, & Campbell, 2005; Keefe & Francis, 1999).

Regardless of the theories used to explain it, pain is a significant issue for many Americans. As many as 50 million

Americans experience chronic and debilitating pain, usually from conditions such as arthritis, migraines, or back problems (Clay, 2002; Lozada & Altman, 2001). Fortunately, even without a full understanding of how pain is sensed, health professionals have techniques that they can use to reduce, or manage, the experience of pain. If pain really is experienced in the brain, what can be done to keep pain messages from reaching those brain centers?

Drug therapy is one choice for pain management. When administered systematically, opiates such as morphine seem to inhibit pain messages both at the spinal cord level and at the specific site of the pain. Unfortunately, drug treatments for pain—particularly pain associated with a disease or illness—often have very unpleasant side effects (Keefe, Abernathy, & Campbell, 2005, pp. 605–607).

Hypnosis and cognitive self-control (trying hard to convince yourself that your pain is not bad and will soon go away) have both been effective in lessening the experience of pain. That psychological processes can inhibit pain is reinforced by data on placebo effects. A placebo is a substance (perhaps a pill) that a person *believes* will be useful in treating some symptom, such as pain. When a person takes a placebo that he or she believes will alleviate pain, endorphins are released in the brain, effectively blocking pain-carrying impulses from triggering the experience of pain (Zubieta et al., 2005).

Counter irritation is another technique used to treat pain from or near the surface of the skin. The technique involves forcefully (but not painfully, of course) stimulating an area of the body near the location of the pain. Dentists have learned that rubbing the patient's gum near the spot where Novocain is to be injected significantly reduces the patient's experience of pain during the injection.

Acupuncture also is effective in the treatment of pain (Ulett, 2003). No one yet knows why this ancient Chinese practice works as well as it does. In some cases, acupuncture doesn't work at all. These cases usually involve patients who are skeptical of the treatment's value, which suggests that acupuncture has a placebo effect for some patients. As many as 12 million acupuncture therapies for pain management are performed in the United States each year, even though acupuncture may be less effective than pain-killing drugs (Taub, 1998).

Each person's response to pain is unique. Many factors influence how each of us responds to pain including prior experiences, memories of those experiences, and attitudes about pain. In addition, each person's tolerance of pain may be partly genetic. Researchers have isolated a gene that produces an enzyme called COMT. Each person has two copies of this gene, one from each parent. Further, it seems that there are two versions of the gene. One is particularly good at producing and regulating the body's natural painkillers, the endor-

phins. A person who has inherited two such forms of the COMT gene appears very stoic and resistant to pain. The second version is not as good at regulating and producing endorphins; consequently, a person who has inherited two of the second version seems to have a particularly low threshold for pain. About half of the population has one gene of each type and tolerates pain at levels between the two extremes (Zubieta et al., 2003).

Gender and cultural differences can influence the expression or display of pain. In Japan, for instance, individuals are socialized not to show pain or any intense feeling. In Western cultures, men are often socialized not to show pain and to "take it like a man." Mental health professionals sometimes find it more difficult to diagnose and treat men who have been socialized to hide their pain because information about pain can be vital to an accurate diagnosis or successful treatment.

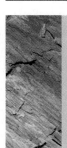

BEFORE YOU GO ON

13.   What produces the sensation of pain, and what actions can control the experience of pain?

A Point to Ponder or Discuss
At first, it might appear desirable to be completely pain free. Upon reflection, what are some of the drawbacks of being unable to experience pain?

PAYING ATTENTION: PERCEPTUAL SELECTIVITY

In a grand old lecture hall at the University of Tennessee, nearly 600 students settled down to listen to the day's lecture on perception. Suddenly a student burst through the closed doors at the rear of the hall. This student stomped down the center aisle of the classroom, screaming and yelling obscenities at the professor: "You failed me for the last time, you so-and-so!" The class was stunned. No one moved as the student leaped over the

lectern to grab the professor. The two struggled briefly, then—in full view of everyone—a gun, a chrome-plated revolver, appeared. Down behind the lectern they fell. Kaboom! The students sat frozen in their seats as the professor lay moaning on the floor and the student ran from the room through the same side door that the professor had entered earlier. Six hundred students just sat there, silent, unmoving. At just the proper dramatic moment, the professor slowly drew himself up to the lectern. And in a calm, soft voice said, "Now I want everyone to write down exactly what you saw."

salient detail an aspect or detail of the environment that captures our attention

peripheral detail aspects of the environment that do not draw our attention and make up our perceptual background

The preceding story was a clever classroom demonstration witnessed by one of your textbook's authors (Gerow) when he was in graduate school. The irate student was the professor's graduate assistant, and the point of the demonstration was to test students' ability to perceive events.

You can guess what happened. The "irate student" was described as being from 5'4" to 6'3" tall, weighing between 155 and 230 pounds, and wearing either a blue blazer or a gray sweatshirt. But the most remarkable misperception had to do with the revolver. When the professor first reached the lectern, he reached into his suit-coat pocket, removed the gun, and placed it on top of his notes. When the student crashed into the room, the first thing the professor did was to reach for the gun and point it toward the student. In fact, the student never had the revolver. It was the professor who fired the shot that startled the class, sliding the gun to the floor as he fell. Fewer than 20 of the 600 students in class that day reported the events as they really occurred. The overwhelming majority of witnesses claimed that a crazy student had burst into the classroom with a gun in his hand.

Try to imagine how you might have reacted if you had been in class that morning. You sit in class listening to your professor lecture, and from time to time, your mind wanders (we hope not too frequently). You think that wearing your new shoes was not a good idea. Your feet hurt. To your left, a student rips open a bag of chips. You turn your head, annoyed. You smell someone's perfume and think what a pleasant fragrance it is. You can feel the pen in your hand as you write. Your senses are being bombarded simultaneously by all sorts of information, sights, sounds, tastes, odors, even pain. Suddenly, someone enters the room and begins arguing with your professor. A scuffle breaks out. You see a gun and hear a shot. Your heart is pounding, you are breathing heavily, and you don't know what to do next.

What determines which stimuli attract our attention and which get ignored? One thing is for sure: You cannot attend to every stimulus at once. Typically, we select a few details to which we attend. A detail that captures our attention is called a **salient detail**. Salient details not only catch our attention, but we remember them more often and more vividly than we recall peripheral details. **Peripheral details** do not draw our attention; they make up our perceptual background. The competition among stimuli to be selected in (salient) or ignored (peripheral) is not just academic. For example, this same issue applies to the debate over the use of cell-phones while driving. Nearly 120 million Americans use cell-phones, and 85 percent of them report using their phones while driving. One series of studies concluded that cell-phone use disrupts driving behaviors by diverting attention from salient details (road conditions, traffic, etc.) to other cognitive tasks (what is being said on the cell-phone) (Strayer & Johnston, 2001). A report of the National Highway Safety Administration has reported some intriguing, and grim, data: An analysis of vehicle crashes and "near crashes," showed that three-quarters of the cases involved some form of driver inattention within three seconds before the event. The two most common distracters were drowsiness and cell-phone use (Klauer et al., 2006). It turns out that "hands free" cell-phone use is as distracting—and dangerous—as hand-held cell-phone use (Strayer & Drews, 2007). Yet another study indicated that drivers who talk on their cell-phones may be just as impaired as those who drink and drive (Strayer, Drews, & Couch, 2006).

In this section, we will discuss some of the variables that influence what we attend to and what we ignore. These variables are of two general types: stimulus factors and personal factors. By *stimulus factors* we mean those characteristics that make some stimuli more compelling than others no matter who perceives them. By *personal factors* we mean those characteristics of the perceiver that influence which stimuli get attended to or perceived. Personal factors may be transient, such as the emotional arousal that accompanies witnessing an accident, or more stable, such as poor vision or personal prejudices.

Stimulus Factors in Perceptual Selectivity

The most important stimulus factor in perceptual selection is *contrast*, the extent to which a stimulus is different from stimuli around it. One stimulus can contrast with other stimuli in a variety of ways. We are more likely to attend to a stimulus if its *intensity* is different from the intensities of other stimuli. Generally, the more intense a stimulus, the more likely we are to select it for further processing. We are more likely to attend to an irate student in a classroom if he is shouting rather than whispering. A bright light is usually more attention grabbing than a dim one; an extreme temperature is more likely to be noticed

Courtesy of Martin Ruegner/Getty Images.

If ever there were a situation in which we would want a stimulus to stand out as a figure against a background, it would be for a railroad-crossing signal as a train approaches. Those lights had better be bright and flashing.

than a moderate one. Yet, context can make a difference. A shout is more compelling than a whisper, unless everyone is shouting; then it may be the soft, quiet, reasoned tone that gets our attention. If we are faced with a barrage of bright lights, a dim one may be the one we process more fully.

The same argument holds for *size*. In most cases, the bigger the stimulus, the more likely we are to attend to it. There is little point in building a small billboard to advertise your motel or restaurant. You want to construct the biggest billboard you can in hopes of attracting attention. Still, faced with many large stimuli, we may attend to the one that is smaller. The easiest player to spot on a football field is often the place-kicker, who tends not to be as large and not to wear as much protective padding as the other players.

A third dimension for which contrast is relevant is *motion*. Motion is a powerful factor in determining visual attention. Walking through the woods, you may nearly step on a chipmunk before you notice it, as long as it stays still— an adaptive camouflage that chipmunks do well. If it suddenly moves to escape, you easily notice it as it scurries across the leaves.

Although intensity, size, and motion are three characteristics of stimuli that readily come to mind, there are others. Indeed, any way in which two stimuli are different (i.e., contrast) can provide a dimension that determines which stimulus we attend to. (Even a small grease spot attracts attention if it is in the middle of a solid yellow tie.) Because contrast guides attention, important terms are printed in **boldface type** throughout this book—so you will notice them, attend to them, and recognize them as important stimuli. No doubt that every student in that Tennessee classroom the morning the "crazed" student rushed the lectern attended to several salient details of the situation because the demonstration contrasted vividly with what every student usually sees and hears in a lecture class.

Another stimulus characteristic that determines attention is *repetition*. With all else being equal, the more often a stimulus is presented, the more likely it will be attended to. Note that we have to say, "all else being equal" or we develop contradictions. If stimuli are repeated too often, they lose their novelty and we adapt to them. Even so, there are many examples of the value of repetition in getting someone's attention. Instructors seldom mention key concepts just once. In this book, we repeat the definitions of important terms in the text, in the margins, and again in the glossary at the end of the book. Television advertisers invest heavily in repeating their commercials—often to the point that we cannot ignore them.

There are many ways in which stimuli differ. The larger the contrast between any stimulus and those around it, the more likely that stimulus will capture our attention. All else being equal, the more a stimulus is presented, the more likely that it will be perceived and selected for further processing.

Personal Factors in Perceptual Selectivity

Sometimes the stimuli are less important than the perceiver. In other words, sometimes what is there to be seen matters less than who is doing the seeing. Imagine two students watching a football game on television. Both are pre-

Courtesy of Ashley Cooper/Corbis.

sented with identical images from the same screen. One asks, "Wow, did you see that tackle?" The other responds, "No, I was watching the cheerleaders." Their difference in perception cannot be attributed to the nature of the stimuli because both students received the same information from the same TV. The difference must have arisen from the characteristics of the perceivers, or personal factors, which we categorize as motivation, expectation, or past experience.

After a multiple-choice exam, an instructor collects answer sheets and then goes over each of the test questions. Students have marked their answers on the exams, and thus can get immediate feedback. One student is particularly worried about item #12. It was a difficult item for which he chose alternative *d*. The instructor gets to item #12 and clearly says, "The answer to number twelve is *b*." The student responds, "Yes! I knew I got that one right!" But wait a minute! The instructor said "*b*." True, but the student wanted to hear her say "*d*" so badly, that is what he perceived. He selected (attended to) a stimulus that was not even there.

We often perceive what we want to perceive, and we often perceive what we expect to perceive. We may not notice stimuli when they are present simply because we did not know that they were coming—we did not expect them. When we are psychologically ready, or predisposed to perceive something, we have formed a **mental set**.

Here is an example from the research of Mack and Rock (1998). Participants in this study gaze at a screen upon which a simple cross pattern is flashed very quickly. The stimulus is rather like a large plus (+) sign. They are to report which arm of the cross is longer, the horizontal line or the vertical line. After a few presentations, and without warning, a small figure (a square, a circle, a triangle, or a slanted line) is added to the stimulus of the cross pattern. Participants are asked to identify the small figure that was added. Even though they looked right at it, none could recognize

mental set the cognitive process of being psychologically ready or predisposed to perceive something

Personal factors, such as past experience, motivation, and mental set can influence which stimuli are selected for processing. A trained and experienced bird-watcher is likely to notice more birds than will a naive beginner.

FIGURE 3.19

How we perceive the world is determined at least in part by our mental set, or our expectations about the world. How many THEs did you see when you first glanced at this figure? Why?

the figure at a rate any better than guessing, because they simply were not expecting such a stimulus to appear.

Take a second to glance quickly at the message in Figure 3.19. What does the message say? (If you have seen this before, you will have to try it with someone who hasn't.) Many people say the message is "Paris in the spring." In fact, *the* appears twice in the triangle: "Paris in the the spring." Most people familiar with the English language (and with this phrase) do not expect to see two adjacent *the's*. Following their mental set, they report seeing only one. Others may develop a different mental set. Their reasoning may go something like this: "This is a psychology text, so there is probably a trick here, and I'm going to find it." In this instance, such skepticism is rewarded. There is a trick, and if their mental set is to find one, they do. The inability to change a set way of perceiving a problem may interfere with finding a solution to that problem. What we call "creative" problem-solving is often a matter of perceiving aspects of a problem in new or unexpected ways. Thus, even as complex a cognitive process as problem-solving often hinges on basic perceptual processes.

When we say that what we attend to is a result of motivation and expectation, we are claiming that what we perceive is often influenced by our past experiences. Much of our motivation and many of our expectations develop from past experiences. We are likely to perceive, or expect to perceive, what we have perceived in the past. Perhaps a personal

example will make this clear. I (Gerow) took a course in comparative psychology and part of the course work was to examine the behaviors of birds, because one of the teachers was an ornithologist (a scientist who studies birds). All students were required to go bird-watching very early one morning. I still remember that outing vividly: cold, tired, wet, clutching the thermos of coffee, slopping through the marshland looking for birds as the sun was just rising. After 20 minutes of this unpleasantness, the instructor had identified 10 or 11 different birds, but I could only report that, "I don't know what sort of duck it was, but I thought I saw a duck." The differences in perception between my instructor and me that cold, wet morning can be explained in terms of motivation (he did care more than I) but also in terms of his past experiences (he knew where to look and what to look for).

Our perception of stimuli in the world is usually accomplished without conscious effort, and the process can be influenced by several factors, some of which depend on the stimuli themselves. What we perceive is determined to some extent by the bits and pieces of information we receive from our senses, called **bottom-up processing**. We may attend to a particular stimulus because it is significantly larger, smaller, more colorful, louder, or slower than the other stimuli around it. We then try to organize, identify, and store that stimulus in our memory. On the other hand, whether or how stim-

bottom-up processing a process that occurs when what we perceive is determined in large extent by the bits and pieces of information we receive from our senses

top-down processing a process that occurs when what one selects and perceives depends largely on what the perceiver already knows

uli are perceived also can be influenced by the motivation, expectations, and experiences of the perceiver. In this case, selection of stimuli is a matter of applying concepts and information

already processed. When what one selects and perceives depends on what the perceiver already knows, this is **top-down processing**.

BEFORE YOU GO ON

14. What stimulus and personal factors influence which stimuli we select for processing (salient) and which ones we ignore (peripheral)?

A Point to Ponder or Discuss
The American judicial system relies on testimony of eyewitnesses in prosecuting crimes. Given what you have learned about perception, do you think the courts should rely on eyewitness testimony?

ORGANIZING OUR PERCEPTUAL WORLD

One of our basic perceptual reactions to the environment is to select certain stimuli from among all those that activate our receptors so they may be processed further. A related perceptual process is to organize and interpret those bits and pieces of experience into meaningful, organized wholes. We do not hear individual sounds of speech; we perceive words, phrases, and sentences (Feng & Ratnam, 2000). Our visual experience is not one of bits of color and light and dark, but of identifiable objects and events. We don't perceive a warm pat on the back as responses from hundreds of individual receptors in our skin. Although the visual world is projected onto a two-dimensional retinal surface, our experience is in three dimensions.

Perceptual organization was of considerable interest to the Gestalt psychologists. Perhaps you recall that *gestalt* is a German word that means "configuration" or "whole." You form a gestalt when you see the "big picture." When you perceive the whole as being more than the sum of its parts, you have formed a gestalt.

A very basic principle of Gestalt psychology is the **figure-ground relation-**

ship. Those stimuli that are attended to and grouped together are figures, whereas all the rest are the ground. As you focus your attention on the words on this page, they form figures against the ground (or background, if you'd prefer) provided by the rest of the page and everything else within your field of vision. When you hear your instructor's voice during a lecture, it is the figure against the ground of all other sounds in the room. The irate student who barged into the classroom to confront a professor became a perceptual figure rather quickly. Do you see the relationship between these classic, Gestalt terms (figure and ground) and the more modern, technical terms (salient and peripheral details) we discussed in the last section? What the Gestalt psychologists called a *figure*, we also can call a *salient detail* of our sensory world. Those stimuli that make up our perceptual *ground* are the *peripheral details*. Figure 3.20 provides a few visual examples of the figure-ground relationship.

Gestalt psychologists were intrigued by how we group and organize individual sensory stimuli to form meaningful, perceptual gestalts. As with perceptual selection, many factors influence how we organize our perceptual world. Again, it will be useful to consider both stimulus factors, or bottom-up processing, and personal factors, or top-down processing.

figure-ground relationship the name for the process in which those stimuli that are attended to and grouped together are figures, and all the rest is ground

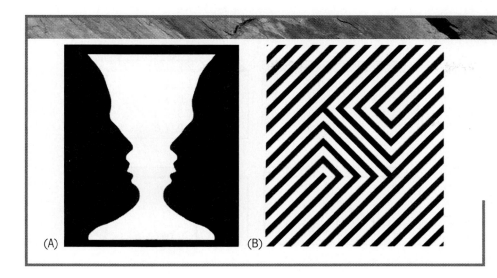

FIGURE 3.20

(A) A classic reversible figure-ground pattern. What do you see here? A white vase, or two black profiles facing each other? Can you see both figures clearly at the same time? (B) After a few moments' inspection, a small square should emerge as a figure against a ground of diagonal lines.

Grouping Stimuli with Bottom-Up Processing

Bottom-up processing occurs when we select stimuli as they enter our senses and process them "higher" into our cognitive systems by organizing them, interpreting them, making them meaningful, and storing them in memory. When we talk about bottom-up processing in this context, we are talking about forming gestalts, putting salient details of stimuli together based solely on the characteristics of the stimuli themselves. We also call these *stimulus factors* and will consider five of the most influential: proximity, similarity, continuity, common fate, and closure.

1. ***Proximity.*** Glance quickly at Figure 3.21(A). Without giving it much thought, what did you see? A bunch of Xs, yes; but more than that, there were two identifiable groups of Xs, weren't there? The group of Xs on the left seems somehow separate from the group on the right, whereas the Xs within each group seem to go together. This illustrates what the Gestalt psychologists called **proximity**, or **contiguity**—events occurring close together in space or time are perceived as belonging together and being part of the same figure.

Proximity operates on more than just visual stimuli. Sounds that occur together (are contiguous) in speech are perceived together to form words or phrases. In written language there are physical spaces between words on the printed page (in speech, there usually are short pauses between words and between one sentence and the next). Thunder and lightning usually occur together, thunder following shortly after the lightning. As a result, it is difficult to think about one without also thinking about the other.

2. ***Similarity.*** Now glance at Figure 3.21(B) and describe what you see. A collection of Xs and Os are clearly organized into a simple pattern—as two columns of Xs and two of Os. Perceiving rows of alternating Xs and Os is possible, but difficult, demonstrating the Gestalt principle of **similarity**. Stimuli that are alike or share properties tend to group together in our perception—a "birds of a feather are perceived together" sort of thing. Most of us perceive Australian koalas as bears because they look so much like bears, when, in fact, they are related to kangaroos and wallabies.

3. ***Continuity.*** The Gestalt principle of **continuity** (or **good continuation**) is

proximity the observation that events occurring close together in space or time are perceived as belonging together and being part of the same figure

similarity the observation that stimuli that are alike or share properties tend to be grouped together in our perceptions

continuity (or good continuation) a process that operates when we see things as ending up consistent with the way they began

FIGURE 3.21

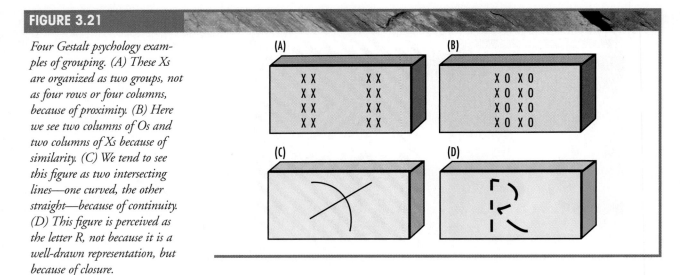

Four Gestalt psychology examples of grouping. (A) These Xs are organized as two groups, not as four rows or four columns, because of proximity. (B) Here we see two columns of Os and two columns of Xs because of similarity. (C) We tend to see this figure as two intersecting lines—one curved, the other straight—because of continuity. (D) This figure is perceived as the letter R, not because it is a well-drawn representation, but because of closure.

closure the process by which we tend to fill in gaps or spaces in our perceptual world

common fate the tendency to group together in the same figure those elements of a scene that appear to move together in the same direction and at the same speed

operating when we see things as ending up consistent with the way they started. Figure 3.21(C) illustrates this point with a simple line drawing. The clearest, simplest, easiest way to organize this drawing is as two separate but intersecting lines, one straight, the other curved. It is difficult to imagine seeing this figure any other way.

Continuity may account for how we organize some of our perceptions of people. Aren't we surprised when a hardworking, award-winning high school honor student does poorly in college and flunks out? That is not the way we like to view the world. We would not be as surprised to find that a student who barely made it through high school fails to pass at college. We want things to continue as they began, as in "as the twig is bent, so grows the tree."

4. **Common fate.** Common fate is the tendency to group together in the same figure those elements of a scene that appear to move together in the same direction and at the same speed. Common fate is like continuity, but it applies to moving stimuli. Remember our example of a chipmunk sitting motionless on the leaves in the woods? As long as both the chipmunk and the leaves remain still, the chipmunk is not noticed. When it does move, all the parts of the chipmunk move together, sharing a common fate, and we see a chipmunk (not disconnected legs and ears and a torso) scurrying away.

5. **Closure.** One of the most commonly encountered Gestalt principles of organization, or grouping, is **closure.** We tend to fill in spaces or gaps in our perceptual world. Closure provides an excellent example of perception as an active process. It underscores the notion that we constantly seek to make sense out of our environment, whether that environment presents us with sensible stimuli or not. This concept is illustrated by Figure 3.21(D). At a glance, we see this figure as the letter R, but, of course, it is not. That is not the way to make an R. However, because of closure, it may well be the way we perceive an R.

As an example of closure, make an audiotape of a casual conversation with a friend, and write down exactly what you both say (which is not easily done). A truly faithful transcription will reveal that many words and sounds were left out. Although they were not actually there as stimuli, they were not missed by the listener, because he or she filled in the gaps (closure) and understood what was being said.

FIGURE 3.22

An example of subjective contour.

A phenomenon that many psychologists believe is a special case of closure is the perception of **subjective contours**, in which arrangements of lines and patterns enable us to see figures that are not actually there. If that sounds a bit strange, look at Figure 3.22, in which we have an example of subjective contour. In this figure, you can "see" a solid triangle that is so clear it nearly jumps off the page. There is no accepted explanation for subjective contours (Rock, 1986; Sobel & Blake, 2003), but it seems to be another example of our perceptual processes filling in gaps in our perceptual world in order to provide us with sensible information. And, that "filling in gaps" seems most likely to occur in the cerebral cortex, not in the eye or the optic nerve pathways (Lee & Nguyen, 2001; Maertens et al., 2008).

Grouping Stimuli with Top-Down Processing

Remember that when we refer to top-down processing, the implication is that we take advantage of motivations, expectations, and previously stored experiences in order to deal with incoming stimuli. In terms of perceptual organization, this means that we often perceive stimuli as going together, as part of the same gestalt or figure, because we want to, because we expect to, or because we have perceived them together in the past.

We can think of no better example in our own experience than the one used at the beginning of our discussion of perception. Nearly 600 students claimed to see something that did not happen. The problem was not one of perceptual selection. After all, everybody saw the gun. The problem was one of organization—with whom did they associate the gun? No student was *mentally set* for the professor to bring a gun to class. No one *wanted* to see the professor with a gun. And no one had *experienced* a professor with a gun in class before. (Seeing crazed students in classes with guns is not a common experience either, but with television and movies and similar events showing up in the daily news, it is certainly a more probable one.)

Here is another simple example of top-down processing influencing our perception of reality. Examine the short sentence presented in Figure 3.23. Even at a glance, you have little difficulty discerning the meaning of this short phrase. The cat sat by the door. Now note that the "H" in both instances of the word "THE" and the "A" in the words "CAT" and "SAT" are identical. Your senses could not discriminate between these two figures, except that they occurred in a meaningful context. Without past experience with the English language, and a passing knowledge of cats, doors, and sitting, the stimuli of Figure 3.23 would make little sense.

subjective contours a perceptual phenomenon in which arrangements of lines and patterns enable us to "see" figures that are not actually there

FIGURE 3.23

THE CAT SAT
BY THE DOOR.

An example of top-down processing.

BEFORE YOU GO ON

15. What characteristics of stimuli (salient characteristics) guide bottom-up organization of the information presented by one's senses?
16. How does top-down processing influence how incoming sensory messages are organized or grouped together?

A Point to Ponder or Discuss
In which professions might we find persons using the Gestalt principles of organization?

PERCEIVING DEPTH AND DISTANCE

One way we organize visual stimuli is to note *where* they are. We perceive the world as three-dimensional. As long as we pay attention (surely a required perceptual process), we won't fall off cliffs or run into buildings. We know with considerable accuracy just how far we are from objects. What is remarkable about this ability is that light reflected from objects and events in our environment falls on two-dimensional retinas. The depth and distance in our world is not something we directly sense; it is something we perceive.

The ability to judge depth and distance accurately is a vital, adaptive skill. Our ability to make such judgments reflects the fact that we are responding to a large number of cues to depth and distance. Some cues are built into our visual systems and are referred to as *ocular cues*. Other cues are part of our environment and they are called physical, or pictorial cues.

Ocular Cues

Some of the cues we get about distance and depth reflect the way our eyes

retinal disparity a binocular cue to depth caused by the fact that when we look at a nearby 3-dimensional object, each eye gets a somewhat different view of it

convergence a cue to 3-dimensionality that occurs when our eyes turn toward each other when we view something close

work. Cues that involve both eyes are called *binocular cues* (*bi* means "two"). When we look at a nearby three-dimensional object, each eye gets a somewhat different view of it, a phenomenon called **retinal disparity**. Hold a pen with a clip on it a few feet in front of your eyes. Rotate the pen until the clip can be viewed by the left eye, but not by the right. (You check that by first closing one eye, then the other, as you rotate the pen.) Now each eye (retina) gets a different (disparate) view of the same object. It is a cue that what we are looking at must be solid or three-dimensional. Otherwise, each eye would see the same image, not two different ones (Figure 3.24).

Another binocular cue to depth and distance is **convergence**—our eyes turning toward each other when we view something up close. As we gaze off into the distance, our eyes aim outward in almost parallel fashion. As we focus on objects close to us, our eyes come together, or converge, and we interpret that convergence as an indication that what we are looking at is close to us. Convergence is also illustrated in Figure 3.24. If you consider convergence and retinal disparity together, you get some hint about the depth-perception abilities of certain animals. Those with their two eyes located at the front of their heads (dogs, cats, frogs, and primates, for example) have significantly better depth perception than do those animals with one eye located on each side of their heads (such as horses, rabbits, birds, and fish).

The remaining depth-perception cues are *monocular*, implying that they require only one eye to have their influence. (Even the physical cues that follow are monocular cues because they can be appreciated with only one eye.) A unique monocular cue, at least for relatively short distances, is **accommodation**—the changing of the shape of the lens by the ciliary muscles to focus images on the retina. When we focus on distant objects, accommodation flattens our lens, and when we focus on nearby objects, our lens gets rounder or fatter. Although the process is reflexive and occurs automatically, our brains react to the activity of our ciliary muscles in terms of the distance of an object from our eyes. Accommodation doesn't function well as a cue for distances beyond arm's length because the changes in the activity of the ciliary muscles are too slight to be noticed. But it is within arm's length that decisions about distance are often critical.

Physical Cues

The physical cues to distance and depth are those we get from the structure of our environment. These are sometimes called "pictorial cues" because artists use them to create the impression of three-dimensionality on a two-dimensional canvas or paper. Here are six of the more important physical cues to distance and depth.

1. *Linear perspective*: This cue can best be illustrated with a familiar example. If we were to stand in the middle of the road and look off into the distance, the sides of the road would appear to come together in the distance. Using this pictorial cue in drawing takes some time and experience to develop.

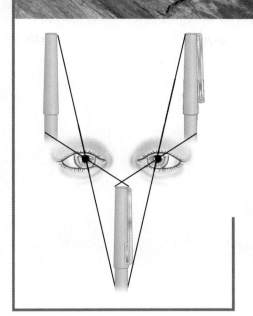

FIGURE 3.24

When looking at a three-dimensional object, such as a pen, the right eye sees a slightly different image than does the left eye—a phenomenon called retinal disparity. This disparity gives us a cue that the object we are viewing is three-dimensional. Here we also note convergence—our eyes turn toward each other when we view an object that is close to us.

accommodation the process of the changing of the shape of the lens by the ciliary muscles to focus images on the retina

2. *Interposition*: This cue to distance reflects our appreciation that objects in the foreground tend to partially obscure objects in the distance. One of the reasons a professor knows that people sitting in the back of a classroom are farther away than people sitting in the front row is the information that he or she gets from interposition. People (and other objects) in the front partially block the professor's view of the people sitting behind them.

3. *Relative size*: This commonly used cue is based on the assumption that few things change size but many things move nearer or farther away. Objects that are nearer to us cast a larger image on our retinas than objects that are farther away. So, all else being equal, we tend to judge the object that produces the larger retinal image as being closer to us.

4. *Texture gradient*: This commonly used cue can be illustrated with an example. If we were to stand on a gravel road and look down, the texture of the roadway would be visible. We could see individual pieces of gravel. As we look farther down the road, the texture gradually changes, and details give

(A) Courtesy of Rudy Sulgan/Corbis.

(B) Courtesy of Richard T. Nowitz/Corbis.

(C) Courtesy of Craig Aurness/Corbis.

A) Linear perspective is a common and clear cue to distance. B) With interposition, objects in the foreground (closer to us) partially obscure our view of objects farther away. C) We all know that hot air balloons are about the same size, and thus judge those that appear larger as being closer to us—relative size. D) Texture gradient refers to the notion that when up close and nearby, we can discern the bits and pieces of small objects that gradually seem to become indistinguishable as they are farther away from us. E) Motion parallax refers to the fact that when we move past a stable view (as when a passenger in a train) objects that are close or nearby seem to whiz by us quickly, while objects that are farther away remain in our sight line for a longer period of time.

(D) Courtesy of Ron Chapple/Corbis.

(E) Courtesy of Hill Street Studios/Blend Images/Corbis.

way. Finally, at a sufficient distance, the road appears to be without texture. We interpret this gradual change (gradient) in texture as a change in distance. Here is a related observation, known well by golfers: People tend to overestimate the distance of an object (e.g., a flag in the center of a green) when it is observed across a gap, such as a steep ravine, or valley. The same distance can be judged much more accurately if viewed over flat or rolling terrain, where the ground is continuously in view—allowing for texture gradient effects to operate (Sinai, Ooi, & He, 1998).

5. ***Patterns of shading.*** This cue is a favorite of sketch artists. Drawings without shading look flat and two-dimensional. Artists striving for life-like realism use shading of tree trunks and apples and show them casting shadows. After all, shadows distinguish three dimensional from two-dimensional objects, and tell us a great deal about the shape and solidity of the object casting them.

6. ***Motion parallax:*** This cue has an unfamiliar name, but it is something we are all familiar with. When we are riding in a car at a modest speed, we perceive nearby utility poles and fence posts as racing by, objects farther away from the car as moving more slowly, and mountains or trees way off in the distance as hardly moving at all. This difference in apparent motion is known as motion parallax. Max Wertheimer's observation of this phenomenon during a train ride in 1910 is what first got him interested in perception and eventually led him to create Gestalt psychology.

BEFORE YOU GO ON

17. List and describe those cues that allow us to perceive depth and distance.

A Point to Ponder or Discuss
What would it be like to see the world with only one eye?

THE CONSTANCY OF VISUAL PERCEPTION

Perceptual constancies help us organize and interpret the stimulus input we get from our senses. Because of the constancy of perception, we recognize a familiar object as being the same regardless of how far away it is, the angle from which we view it, or the color or intensity of the light reflected from it. You can recognize your textbook whether you view it from a distance or close up, straight on or from an angle, in a dimly or brightly lighted room, or in blue, red, or white light; it is still your textbook, and you will perceive it as such regardless of how your senses detect it. Were it not for perceptual constancy, each sensation might be perceived as a new experience, and little would appear familiar to you.

Size constancy is the tendency to see objects as unchanging in size regardless of the size of the retinal image they produce. A friend standing close to you may fill your visual field. At a distance, the image of the same person may take up only a fraction of your visual field. The size of the image on your retina may be significantly different, but you know very well that your friend has not shrunk but has simply moved farther away. Our ability to discern that objects remain the same size depends on many factors, but two of the more important are the quality of the depth-perception cues available to us, and our familiarity with the stimulus object.

Shape constancy refers to our perception that objects maintain their shape even though the retinal image they cast may change. Shape constancy may be demonstrated with any familiar object, such as a door. As you look at a door from various angles, the shape of the image of the door on your retina changes radically. Straight on, it appears to be a rectangle; partially open, a trapezoid; from the edge or fully open, a straight line. But despite the retinal image, shape constancy ensures you still see a door (Figure 3.25).

Brightness constancy causes familiar objects to be perceived with their usual brightness regardless of the actual amount or type of light under which they are viewed. The white shirt or blouse you put on this morning may be sensed as light gray when you pass through a shadow, or as even a darker gray when night falls, but it is still perceived as a white shirt and in no way darker than it was in the morning. Picture a brick wall on a sunny day. Upon it fall the shadows of nearby trees and shrubs. Although the brightness of the light presented to your eyes from the

shape constancy the perception that objects maintain their shape, even though the retinal image they cast may change

brightness constancy the process that causes familiar objects to be perceived with their usual brightness, regardless of the actual amount or type of light under which they are viewed

size constancy the tendency to see objects as unchanging in size, regardless of the size of the retinal image that they produce

FIGURE 3.25

At the level of the retina, we experience different images; yet we know we are looking at the same door because of shape constancy.

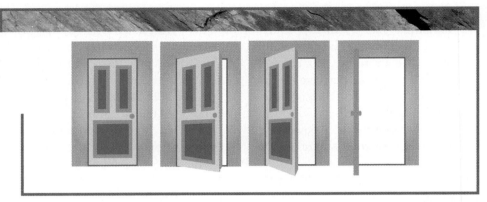

FIGURE 3.26

A few classic geometrical illusions. In each case, you know the answer, but the relevant questions are: (A) Are the vertical and horizontal lines the same length? (B) Is the brim of the hat as wide as the hat is tall? (C) Are the two horizontal lines the same length? (D) Are the two horizontal lines the same length? (E) Are the two diagonals part of the same line? (F) Are the long diagonal lines parallel? (G) Are the two center circles the same size?

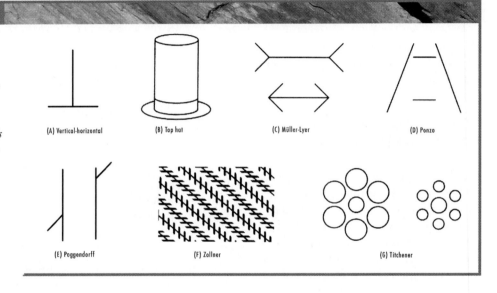

(A) Vertical-horizontal   (B) Top hat   (C) Müller-Lyer   (D) Ponzo

(E) Poggendorff   (F) Zollner   (G) Titchener

color constancy the process that allows one to perceive the color of a familiar object as constant, despite changing lighting conditions

illusions experiences in which our perceptions are at odds with reality

shaded part of the wall is considerably less than from the unshaded part, you still perceive the wall as all of the same brightness. The same principle holds for color perception.

Color constancy allows you to perceive the color of a familiar object as constant, despite changing lighting conditions. For example, if you know you put on a white shirt this morning, you would still perceive it as white even if we were to illuminate it with a red light. Under a red light, the shirt might appear red to someone else, but not to you because of color constancy.

When Constancy Fails: Geometric Illusions and Impossible Figures

By now you appreciate that the relationship between the "real world" and your perceptual world is not as straightforward as you might have thought. What is perceived is often flavored by factors beyond the physical reality that stimulates our sense receptors. Illusions and impossible figures illustrate the complex interaction between physical reality and our psychological experience. **Illusions** are experiences in which our perceptions are at odds with reality.

Several simple and compelling geometrical illusions are presented in Figure 3.26. Figure 3.26(A) depicts the vertical-horizontal illusion. Figure 3.26(B) is the same illusion in slightly more meaningful terms. Are the lines in Figure 3.26(A) the same length? Yes, you know they are. But do they *appear* to be the same length? No, they do not. The vertical line seems much longer than the horizontal one. The hat in Figure 3.26(B) seems to be considerably taller than it is wide.

Impossible figures—examples of conflicting visual information.

Notice that the vertical-horizontal illusion works even after you measure the two lines because of the first of three fundamental facts about illusions: They do not depend on our ignorance of the situation.

The second fact about illusions is that they do not occur at the retina. Figure 3.26(C) is the well-known Müller-Lyer illusion named for the man who first drew it. The top line would still appear longer than the bottom one even if the two (equal) lines were presented to one eye and the arrow-like vanes were presented to the other. The third fact about illusions is that their effects do not depend on eye movements. Illusions appear vividly even when they are flashed before the eyes too quickly for the eyes to scan. Some recent research has shed some light on this notion that illusions are more a function of the brain at work than a function of how our eyes work. Apparently, our brains have an amazing, and adaptive, ability to see into the very near future, noting not only what is there, but what is likely to occur in the next fraction of a second. Think of this phenomenon in terms of being able to catch or hit a ball. To do so accurately, our brains need to note where that ball is right now, *and* where it is likely to be in the next split second. That is, our brains seek to make sense of visual stimuli, to provide a sensible perception of events that may not be, in fact, as sensible as our eyes might tell us that they are (Changizi et al., 2008; Changizi & Widders, 2002; Nijhawan, 2002).

Illusions of the sort presented in Figure 3.26 are not new. Scientists have been investigating illusions for well over a hundred years. How do geometrical illusions give rise to visual experiences at odds with the physical reality detected by the eyes? Frankly, psychologists do not know. Several factors seem to work together to create illusions. Illusions are evidence that our perceptual constancies can be over-applied. Illusions depend largely on how we perceive and interpret clues to the size of objects in a three-dimensional world and on the inferences we make about the world from experience (Bach & Poloschek, 2006; Fermüller & Malm, 2004; Goldstein, 2002; Gregory, 1977; Plug & Ross, 1994).

Illusions remind us that perception involves more than simple sensation. Perception involves the organization and interpretation of the information we get from our senses; consequently, the world is not always exactly as our senses make it appear. This final point is made even more dramatically with what are known as impossible figures (Figure 3.27).

BEFORE YOU GO ON

18.   List and describe the perceptual constancies as represented in vision.

A Point to Ponder or Discuss
Can you think of perceptual constancies that occur in sensory dimensions other than vision? Can you think of any perceptual illusions that involve motion, not just static figures?

SPOTLIGHT
ON DIVERSITY

Cultural Differences in Perceptual Organization

Sensation is a matter of physics and physiology. Energy levels above threshold initiate neural impulses in sense receptors. There is every reason to believe that everyone's sense receptors work in pretty much the same way. Perception, however, is a different matter altogether. As we have seen, which stimuli are selected for further processing *and* how those stimuli are organized and interpreted often depends on the person doing the perceiving. We called these personal factors and referred to the *top-down processing* of information. How we interpret the perceptual world depends on our motivation, our expectations, and our personal experiences. Cultural experiences, in particular, significantly influence perceptions.

Cues to Depth and Distance in the Real World
Even something as "natural" as perceiving depth and distance is susceptible to cultural constraints. Here is a classic example. Colin Turnbull (1961) reported that the Bambuti people of the African Congo live much of their lives in the dense Ituri Forest, where they seldom can see much farther than 100 feet. When Turnbull first took his Bambuti guide out of the forest onto the open, grassy plains, the guide, Kenge, was disoriented with regard to cues for distance. Kenge thought that buffalo grazing a few miles away were tiny insects because he responded more to retinal size than relative size as a cue to distance. When Turnbull told Kenge that "the insects were buffalo, he roared with laughter and told me not to tell such stupid lies" (Turnbull, 1963). As it happens, with just a little training in how the real, physical world can be represented, most cultural differences in the perception of depth disappear (Mshelia & Lapidus, 1990).

Pictorial Representations of Depth and Distance
Consider the drawing in Figure 3.28. In your opinion, if the man with the spear were trying to kill an animal, which would it be, an antelope or an elephant? Because you respond to such pictorial cues to depth and distance as relative size and interposition, the answer is obvious: the antelope. The elephant is too far away in the background. When pictures such as this one were shown to people who live in remote areas of Africa, many failed to respond to the "standard" pictorial cues, and responded that the man was trying to kill the elephant (Deregowski, 1972, 1973; Hudson, 1960). In this study, the problem was not one of judging depth or distance in the real, three-dimensional world, but of interpreting physical cues as represented in a picture or a drawing (Serpell & Deregowski, 1980). Once again, with just a little training in how the real, physical world can be represented in pictures or drawings, most cultural differences in the perception of depth disappear (Mshelia & Lapidus, 1990).

A Simple Illusion and "The Carpentered World" Hypothesis
A reasonable explanation of the Müller-Lyer illusion (Figure 3.26(C)) is that the vanes of the arrows can be taken to represent corners, as in a room. Figure 3.29(A) gives you an idea of this concept. Whether corners are near to us or far away, we are presented with perspective cues to their distance. Hence, we see the arrows in the illusion as representing corners and edges. This view is known as the "carpentered world

FIGURE 3.28

Which animal—the antelope or the elephant—is the hunter about to spear? One's response to this question depends on the interpretation of pictorial or physical cues to depth and distance. Such interpretations vary across cultures.

hypothesis" (Davidoff, 1975; Gregory, 1977). In fact, the effects of the Müller-Lyer illusion are hard to find in cultures such as that of the Zulu in Africa who have lived in circular houses with arched doorways and domed roofs throughout most of history (Segall, Campbell, & Herskovits, 1966). The carpentered world hypothesis sounds pretty good, doesn't it? As is often the case, it may be too simple an explanation. Look at Figure 3.29(B). There are no angles or edges here, but even we who live in a highly carpentered world tend to see circles B and C as being closer together than circles A and B—even though they are not.

Psychologists know cultural experiences play a role in many of our affects, behaviors, and cognitions. Early on, we see that cultural experiences even influence as fundamental a psychological process as perception.

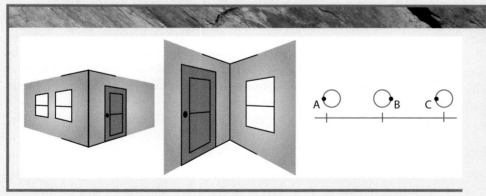

FIGURE 3.29

(A) One attempt to "explain" the Müller-Lyer illusion as the representation of edges and corners, and a variant of the Müller-Lyer illusion. (B) The distance between circles A and B is equal to the distance between circles B and C. An explanation in terms of edges and corners no longer seems reasonable.

CHAPTER SUMMARY

1. **How do the processes of sensation and perception differ?**

   Sensation is the process of receiving information from the environment and changing it into nervous-system activity. The process of changing external stimuli into a form that the nervous system can interpret is called *transduction*. *Perception* is the process of selecting, organizing, and interpreting stimuli. Sensation and perception differ in that perception is a more active, cognitive, and central process.

2. **Briefly describe absolute thresholds, difference thresholds, and signal detection theory.**

   Conceptually, an absolute threshold is the minimum amount of stimulus necessary to trigger a reaction from a sense organ. However, because sensory sensitivity is not constant or stable, an *absolute threshold* is defined as the physical intensity of a stimulus that a person reports detecting 50 percent of the time. On the other hand, a *difference threshold* refers to the minimum difference between stimuli that can be detected 50 percent of the time. A *just noticeable difference* (or *jnd*) is the amount of change in a stimulus that makes it just noticeably different from another stimulus. According to *signal detection theory*, stimulus detection is a decision-making process. The decision is whether a stimulus is present against a background of noise. Stimulus detection depends on many factors, such as the sensitivity of one's sense organs, attention, expectations, motivations, and biases.

3. **What is sensory adaptation?**

   Sensory adaptation occurs when one's sensory experience decreases as a result of continued exposure to a stimulus. For example, when you first walk down a city street, you may think the noise of the traffic is very loud. As you continue to stroll, even though the noise level is unchanged, you tend not to notice the traffic sounds because of adaptation. Indeed, sense organs are better able to detect changes in stimulation, not continuous stimulation.

4. **What are the three major characteristics of light and what psychological experience does each produce?**

   Light is a form of electromagnetic energy that radiates from its source in waves. Light has three properties: *wave amplitude* (the height of the wave),

wavelength (the distance between peaks of the wave, measured in nanometers), and *wave purity* (the number of different types of waves making up the stimulus). Differences in wave amplitude determine the brightness of light—the higher the wave, the brighter the light. Wavelength determines the hue or color of the light. The visual spectrum for the human eye ranges from 380 to 760 nanometers. The experience of hue gradually shifts from violet, to blue, to green, to yellow, and to red as wavelengths increase from 380 nm to 760 nm. Finally, wave purity refers to its saturation. The more saturated a light wave the more pure its hue. The purest light is monochromatic and is made up of light waves of energy that are all of the same length. A random mixture of wavelengths produces the lowest saturation, or white light.

5. **Describe the structures of the eye that are involved in focusing images onto the back of the eye (the retina).**

   The *cornea* is a tough, virtually transparent structure, and is the first to bend light to focus an image onto the back of the eye. The *pupil* (the opening through which light passes) and the *iris* (the colored part of the eye) work to expand or contract, letting in more or less light respectively. In dim light the pupil will be larger, and in bright light it will be smaller. The *lens* is a flexible structure whose shape is controlled by the *ciliary muscles*. The ciliary muscles change the shape of the lens to focus light as it enters the eye. The lens becomes flatter when we try to focus on a distant object and more round when we try to focus on a nearby object. This changing of the shape of the lens is called *accommodation*.

6. **Describe the structures of the retina of the eye, noting the different functions of the rods and the cones.**

   The retina is a series of photosensitive layers located at the back of the eye. The layer of cells at the very back of the retina contains the *photoreceptors*, which actually transduce light energy into neural impulses. There are two types of photoreceptors: rods and cones. *Rods* are responsible for low-light vision and do not provide any information about color or hue. *Cones* are responsible for daylight vision and the experience of color. Signals from the rods and cones are processed through the *bipolar cells* and *ganglion cells* that begin to combine and integrate neural impulses. Fibers from the ganglion cells form the *optic nerve.* Cones are concentrated in the *fovea* (near the center of the retina) where there are few layers of cells between the light entering the eye and the cones. In the fovea the cones are densely packed and there are no rods. The rods are found outside the fovea, in the retina's periphery. Visual acuity is highest at the fovea. The point where the optic nerve connects to the eye is called the *blind spot.* There are no rods or cones at this spot; consequently, there is no vision there.

There are about 120 million rods, but only 6 million cones. Rods and cones differ not only in location and number, but also in function. The cones work most efficiently in medium to high levels of light and are responsible for the experience of color. Conversely, the rods work most effectively in low light. As a consequence, they are responsible for twilight and night vision. Rods do not discriminate among different wavelengths of light; therefore the rods are not involved in color vision.

7. **Trace the path of visual information from the visual fields, through the retinas of the eyes, to the cerebral cortex.**

The *left visual field* contains all the visible stimuli to the observer's left side, while the *right visual field* contains all those stimuli off to the observer's right side. Images from the left visual field are processed in the right side of the brain, and images from the right visual field are processed in the left side of the brain. Once nerve fibers leave the eye at the blind spot, they travel to the *optic chiasma,* where some are sent straight back and others cross to the opposite side of the brain. From the optic chiasma, impulses travel to the occipital lobes of the cerebral cortex where visual experiences are processed.

8. **Briefly discuss how we experience the hue or color of light.**

The two theories of color vision are the *Young-Helmholtz trichromatic theory* and *Hering's opponent-process theory.* Both theories attempt to explain how the visual system codes wavelengths of light to produce the experience of color. According to the trichromatic theory, there are three types of cones, each maximally sensitive to one of the three primary hues: red, green, and blue. According to Hering's opponent-process theory, there are three pairs of mechanisms involved in our experience of color: a blue-yellow processor, a red-green processor, and a black-white processor. Processors respond to either of the characteristics for which they are named, but not to both at the same time. There is evidence to support both theories, some of which comes from our understanding of why some people have defects in color vision.

9. **What are the three main physical characteristics of sound, and what psychological experience is produced by each?**

Like light, sound may be represented as a waveform of energy with three major physical characteristics: wave amplitude, frequency, and purity. Wave amplitude provides our experience of the loudness of a sound. Frequency determines pitch, and purity determines timbre.

10. **Describe the major structures of the human ear and note their role in hearing.**

Most of the structures of the ear (pinna, auditory canal, eardrum, malleus, incus, stapes, and oval window) intensify and transmit the pressure of sound waves to the fluid in the cochlea, which then vibrates the basilar membrane. The basilar membrane stimulates tiny hair cells to transmit neural impulses along the auditory nerve to the temporal lobes of the cerebral cortex.

11. **What are the stimuli and the receptors for the senses of gustation and olfaction?**

The chemical senses are gustation (taste) and olfaction (smell). For both, the stimuli are chemical particles dissolved either in a liquid (for taste) or the air (for smell). The receptors for taste are cells in the taste buds located on the tongue. Taste appears to have five primary qualities: sweet, salty, sour, bitter, and umami. For smell, the sense receptors are hair cells that line the upper regions of the nasal cavity.

12. **Briefly describe the cutaneous senses and the position senses.**

The cutaneous senses are the senses of touch, pressure, warmth, and cold. Specific receptor cells for each of these so-called skin senses have not yet been identified, although they no doubt include free nerve endings and encapsulated nerve endings, which most likely work together. One of our position senses is the vestibular sense, which responds to the movement of small particles suspended in a fluid within our vestibular sacs and semicircular canals and informs us about orientation with regard to gravity or accelerated motion. The other position sense is the kinesthetic sense, which uses receptors in our tendons, muscles, and joints to inform us about the orientation of various parts of our bodies.

13. **What produces the sensation of pain, and what actions can control the experience of pain?**

A wide variety of stimuli can give rise to our experience of pain, from high levels of stimulus intensity to light pinpricks, and to internal stimuli of the sort that produce headaches. The central nervous system is involved in the experience of pain, perhaps as a gate-control mechanism in the spinal cord that either blocks or sends impulses carrying information about pain to the brain. Any mechanism that can effectively block the passage of pain impulses can control our experience of pain. This is directly accomplished by the action of endorphins and counter-irritation. The experience of pain can be controlled by medications, hypnosis, placebo effects, self-persuasion, and/or acupuncture.

14. **What stimulus and personal factors influence which stimuli we select for processing (salient) and which ones we ignore (peripheral)?**

A *salient detail* is some aspect of the environment that captures our attention and, thus, is perceived. *Peripheral details* are those stimuli that are not attended to and, thus, remain in the background. Stimulus characteristics can determine which will be attended to. We are more likely to attend to a stimulus if it *contrasts* with others around it in terms of intensity, size, motion, novelty, or any other physical characteristic. The *repetition* of a stimulus also increases the likelihood that we will attend to it. The selection of stimuli is partly based on characteristics of the perceiver. Such factors as *motivation, expectation (or mental set),* and *past experience* often determine which stimuli become salient rather than peripheral. When characteristics of the perceiver are influential, we say that information is processed from the top down, rather than from the bottom up.

15. **What characteristics of stimuli (salient characteristics) guide bottom-up organization of the information presented by one's senses?**

How we organize or group objects and events in our experience depends in part on the characteristics of the available stimuli, such as proximity (occurring together in space or time), similarity (the extent to which stimuli share physical characteristics), continuity (the extent to which stimuli appear to end as they began), common fate (seeing together elements of a scene that move together), and closure (filling in gaps in our perceptual world in a sensible way). When these factors influence organization, we have bottom-up processing again.

16. **How does top-down processing influence how incoming sensory messages are organized or grouped together?**

These factors originate in our cognitive systems and are referred to as personal factors. The personal factors that affect perceptual organization are the same as those that influence attention: motivation, mental set, and past experience. Simply put, we perceive stimuli as belonging together because we want to perceive them together, we expect them to be together, or we have experienced them being grouped together in the past.

17. **List and describe those cues that allow us to perceive depth and distance.**

We are able to perceive three-dimensionality and distance, even though we sense the environment on two-dimensional retinas because of the many cues with which we are provided. Some have to do with the visual system and are called ocular cues. Retinal disparity involves each eye getting a slightly different view of three-dimensional objects. Convergence occurs when we look at something near our eyes and they move in toward each other. Retinal disparity and convergence are called binocular cues because they require both eyes. Accommodation, a monocular cue requiring only one eye, occurs when our lenses change shape to focus images as objects move toward or away from us.

Cues for depth and distance also come from the environment, including many physical cues such as linear perspective (parallel lines seem to come together in the distance), relative size (everything else being equal, the smaller the stimulus, the farther away we judge it to be), interposition (near objects partially obscure our view of more distant objects), texture gradients (details of texture that we can see clearly up close are difficult to determine at a distance), patterns of shading, and motion parallax (as we move toward stationary objects, those close to us seem to move past us more rapidly than do objects in the distance).

18. **List and describe the perceptual constancies as represented in vision.**

Perceptual constancies are mechanisms that help us organize and interpret the stimulus input we receive from our senses. The perceptual constancies allow us to recognize a familiar object for what it is, regardless of the image it forms on our retinas. Size constancy is the tendency to see objects as being of constant size regardless of the size of the retinal image. Shape constancy refers to our perception that objects maintain their shape even though the retinal image they cast may change (as when they are viewed from different angles). Brightness constancy means that the apparent brightness of familiar objects is perceived as being the same regardless of the actual amount or type of light under which they are viewed. Finally, color constancy allows us to see the color of objects as stable despite being illuminated with different-colored lights.

Varieties of Consciousness

4

PREVIEW

Many of the early psychologists (Wilhelm Wundt and William James, for example) *defined* psychology as the science of consciousness. Dealing with consciousness scientifically proved to be a very tricky business. Indeed, after years of struggling with a science of consciousness, psychologists abandoned it altogether and turned their attention to observable behaviors, as John B. Watson (and behaviorism) claimed they should. But consciousness would not go away, and within the last 40 years, the study of consciousness has re-emerged, resuming its place in mainstream psychology.

The chapter begins with a focus on "normal waking consciousness"—and that distortion of consciousness called sleep. We still can rely on William James' characterization of consciousness as a point of departure for our discussion. We will rely on another famous person from psychology's early days, Sigmund Freud, to begin our consideration of the levels of consciousness. A related and significant question is the extent to which we may be able to process information without awareness—without being fully conscious of doing so.

Sleep is an alteration of consciousness that happens to everyone. We will see how scientists describe sleep and look at the phenomenon of rapid-eye-movement sleep, during which dreams occur. As necessary as sleep is to all of us, there are millions of Americans who are chronically deprived of adequate amounts of sleep or who suffer from one of several disorders of sleep. These are the issues that conclude this discussion.

Consciousness normally changes throughout the day when we are awake and varies throughout the night as we sleep. These changes in consciousness are quite natural, automatic, and involuntary. We do not really decide when we will go to sleep, when we will dream, or when we will spontaneously awaken. These alterations in consciousness just "happen." For roughly the second half of this chapter, we direct our attention to those altered states of consciousness that require some effort to attain. Throughout human history in nearly every culture, people have sought ways to influence their state of consciousness.

We consider three processes that alter consciousness: hypnosis, meditation, and the use of psychoactive drugs. The use of hypnosis has become a standard practice in clinical and counseling psychology. There are situations in which altering consciousness through hypnosis can be useful. However, there are limits on just what hypnosis can accomplish. We will try to separate fact from fiction. Meditation is an ancient practice for which exaggerated claims are often made. While there can be benefits derived from meditative practices, again, there are limits. The most popular means of altering personal consciousness, at least in Western cultures, is through the use of drugs. We will discuss stimulants, depressants, hallucinogens, and two drugs that do not fall clearly into these categories, marijuana and ecstasy.

TOWARD A DEFINITION

"Consciousness" is a commonly used term. It is one of those wonderful concepts that everyone appears to understand and no one seems able to define precisely. Consciousness seems to be something that people have and rocks do not. Dogs and cats may have some sort of consciousness, but the issue gets terribly muddy if one considers plants. Consciousness does seem to take on different meanings, forms, or types (Anthony, 2002; Crick & Koch, 1998; 2003; Baars, 2003). Philosophers say things such as, "The notion of consciousness is notoriously obscure" (Armstrong, 1981, p. 55), while neuroscientists look for ways in which "some active neuronal processes in your head correlate with consciousness, while others do not" (Crick & Koch, 1998, p. 97), or "ways in which physical processes in the brain give rise to subjective experience" (Chalmers, 1995, p. 63).

Francis Crick of the Salk Institute and Christof Koch of the California Institute of Technology say, "Everyone has a rough idea of what is meant by being conscious. For now, it is better to avoid a precise definition of consciousness because of the dangers of premature definition." (1998, p. 98). Still, there is something comforting about even an imprecise definition. Here is a common approach: **Consciousness** is the subjective awareness of the environment and of one's own mental processes. Normal consciousness, then, shows two aspects: a) a perceptual consciousness or an awareness of the world around us, and b) an introspective consciousness or awareness of those thoughts, feelings, and perceptions that are active in our own minds—a sort of awareness of one's self (Armstrong, 1999, p. 119; Blakemore, 2001). With this as a working definition, we might ask how best to characterize consciousness.

NORMAL WAKING CONSCIOUSNESS

We probably have no better description of consciousness than that provided by William James over a hundred years ago (1890, 1892, 1904). According to James, there are four aspects of normal, waking consciousness. Keep these four factors in mind—in your own consciousness—as we work through this chapter.

1. *Consciousness is always changing.* Consciousness does not hold still. It cannot be held before the mind for study. "No state once gone can recur and be identical with what was before," James wrote (1892, p. 152).

2. *Consciousness is a very personal experience.* Consciousness does not exist without someone to have it. My consciousness and yours are separate and different. The only consciousness that I can experience with certainty is mine. You may try to tell me about yours, but I will never be able to fully appreciate the state of mind that is your consciousness.

3. *Consciousness is continuous.* Our awareness of our environment and of our own mental processes cannot be broken into pieces. There are no gaps in our awareness. We cannot tell where one thought begins and another leaves off. James wrote, "Consciousness, then, does not appear to itself chopped up in bits. Such words as 'chain' or 'train' do not describe it fitly as it presents itself in the first instance. It is nothing jointed; it flows. A 'river' or 'stream' is most naturally described. In talking of it hereafter, let us call it the stream of thought, of consciousness (1890, p. 243). Since 1890, reference to the term "stream of consciousness" can be found in many settings, most notably in English literature.

4. *Consciousness is selective.* Awareness is often a matter of making choices, of selectively attending to some aspect of experience while ignoring others. "We find it [consciousness] always doing one thing, choosing one out of several of the materials so presented to its notice, emphasizing and accentuating that and suppressing as far as possible all the rest" (James, 1890, p. 139).

consciousness the subjective awareness of the environment and of one's own mental processes

Courtesy of Bettmann/Corbis.

William James, Harvard philosopher and pioneer in psychology, had much to say about consciousness that is still accepted as reasonable.

Here we clearly see the interdependence of the processes of perception and consciousness.

You can appreciate why studying human consciousness scientifically, or experimentally, has been a challenge. An even more slippery notion is that consciousness is not an either/or proposition; it functions to different degrees, or levels.

BEFORE YOU GO ON

1. Although it may be imprecise, present a characterization of normal, waking consciousness.

A Point to Ponder or Discuss
In what ways might we compare the consciousness of a human with that of an ape, a dog, a bat, a spider, a dandelion, or a rock?

LEVELS OF CONSCIOUSNESS

The observation that levels, or the extent, of one's consciousness may vary throughout the day seems intuitively obvious. At times we are wide-awake, paying full attention to nearly everything around us, processing all sorts of information. At other times our minds "wander" and we find ourselves without focus—not paying attention, or processing much information of any sort from anywhere. And, of course, when we are asleep, there are long periods when we are seemingly unaware of anything that is happening either in the environment or in our own minds.

It also seems intuitively obvious that the higher the level of our consciousness, the better able we are to process (i.e., interpret, understand, recall, or react to) information. Is it not more likely that you will remember something said in class if your consciousness is focused—if you are truly attentive, wide-awake, and straining your attention to understand what is being said? Are you not more likely to trip over something on the sidewalk if you are daydreaming about your weekend plans rather than remaining fully conscious of the environment around you?

Now we come to an interesting question: Is it even possible to process information without being aware of it at all? Can we process information unconsciously? The idea of an unconscious aspect of mind has a long history in philosophy and psychology (Blakemore, 2001; Crick & Koch, 2000; Dijksterhuis & Nordgren, 2006; Fazio & Olson, 2003; Merikle & Daneman, 1998). In this section, we focus first on a classic view of the unconscious—as proposed by Sigmund Freud—and then consider some contemporary research.

The Freudian View of Levels of Consciousness

Sigmund Freud was trained in medicine and can rightfully be called the Father of **psychiatry**, that field of medicine that studies, diagnoses, and treats mental disorders. Early in his career, Freud became intrigued by what were then called "nervous disorders." He was struck by how little was known about disorders wherein a person's psychological experiences and mental life seemed to produce pain and suffering for which there was no medical explanation. Freud proposed an elaborate theory of personality and put his ideas about human nature into practice by developing new techniques

psychiatry the field of medicine that studies, diagnoses, and treats mental disorders

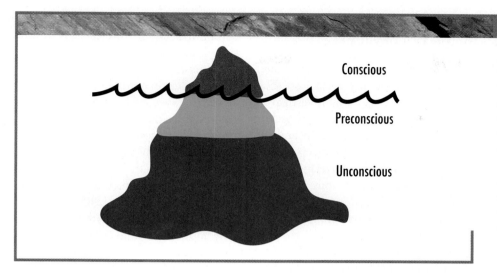

FIGURE 4.1

In the theories of Sigmund Freud, the mind is likened to an iceberg, where only a small potion of one's mental life is available in normal waking consciousness; more is available, with some effort of retrieval, at a preconscious level; and most is stored away at an unconscious level from which intentional retrieval occurs only with great effort.

for treating mental disorders. A central aspect of both his theory and his therapy was Freud's view of consciousness.

Freud's vision of consciousness is often depicted as an iceberg nearly totally submerged in the sea (Figure 4.1). This iceberg analogy is one that Freud used himself. What does it imply? Freud wrote that only a very small portion of a person's mental life was readily available to awareness at any given time. Ideas, memories, feelings, or motives of which we are actively aware are said to be **conscious**. At the moment, we hope you are conscious of the words you are reading, what they mean, and how you can relate them to your own experience. Aspects of our experience of which we are not conscious at any moment, but that can easily be brought to awareness, are stored at a **preconscious** level. Right now you may not be thinking about what you had for dinner last night or what you might have for dinner tonight, but with just a little effort these matters— now in your preconscious—can be brought into your conscious awareness.

Cognitions, feelings, or motives that are not available at the conscious or the preconscious level are said to be in the **unconscious**. At this level are ideas, desires, and memories of which we are not aware and cannot easily become aware. This is a strange notion: There are thoughts and feelings stored in our minds of which we are completely

unaware. Freud theorized that the unconscious level of mind can and does influence us. Much of the content of our unconscious mind is there, Freud reasoned, because thinking about or dwelling on these issues would cause anxiety and distress. A husband, for instance, who constantly forgets his wedding anniversary and occasionally cannot even remember his wife's name when he tries to introduce her, may be having some unconscious conflict or doubts about being married in the first place. (There are, of course, other explanations!) Unconscious mental content passing (we might say "erupting," "slipping," or "bursting") through the preconscious can show itself in dreams, humor, and slips of the tongue. It could be significant that following a lively discussion of some issue, Dan says to Heather, "That's one of the breast discussions I've had about that," when he meant to say, "That's one of the best discussions . . ." As we will see, many Freudian techniques of psychotherapy are aimed at helping the patient learn about and deal with the contents of his or her unconscious mind.

Demonstrating levels of consciousness as Freud proposed them has proven difficult in controlled laboratory research. Nonetheless, Freud's ideas about levels of consciousness have gained wide acceptance in psychology, particularly among clinical psychologists.

conscious the level of consciousness containing ideas, memories, feelings, or motives of which we are actively aware

preconscious the level of consciousness containing aspects of our experience of which we are not conscious at the moment, but that easily can be brought into awareness

unconscious the level of consciousness containing cognitions, feelings, or motives that are not available at the conscious or preconscious level

Contemporary Investigations of the Unconscious

Interest in the unconscious is not limited to Freud and other psychoanalysts. Currently, researchers are investigating whether (and how) the unconscious mind can process information and can influence behavior. There are several ways in which psychologists have approached the study of the unconscious.

Subliminal perception is the process of perceiving and responding to stimuli presented at intensity levels that are below one's absolute threshold of conscious processing. In many contexts, this is called implicit processing.

The German word *limen* means threshold. A stimulus presented at a level below your threshold to detect it would be a sub-threshold stimulus. [But, curiously, we retain the German in this instance and refer instead to a "subliminal stimulus."] On the face of it, then, "subliminal perception" is a contradiction in terms. How can one possibly perceive a stimulus that is below threshold level?

Can a subliminal message implanted in an advertisement induce you to buy a product? Can you improve your memory (or your self-confidence or your sex life, etc.) by listening to tapes with subliminal messages embedded within other material? Although a belief in this sort of subliminal perception is widespread, the answer to these questions is clearly no. For example, in one experiment, motivated participants listened to audiotapes that were supposed to improve their memory, while others listened to tapes designed to enhance self-esteem through subliminal suggestion (Greenwald et al., 1991). The participants were not aware that the labels of some of the tapes had been switched so that some who believed they were using the memory tape were actually using the self-esteem tape (and vice versa). The results showed little evidence for the power of subliminal messages. Although there was some improvement in memory and self-esteem for everyone,

neither effect could be attributed to the subliminal tapes. Interestingly, more than one-third of the participants had the illusion of improvement. It seems that if a person genuinely believes that self-help tapes will work and invests money and time in them, he or she can become convinced that the tapes work and may actually show some improvement (Greenwald, Klinger, & Schuh, 1995; Strahan, Spencer, & Zanna, 2005; Vokey & Read, 1985).

Does the failure of subliminal self-help tapes mean that it is not possible to process any information subliminally? The answer here is also no. Subliminal messages that are complex and meaningful (like those on subliminal tapes, either audio or video) cannot be processed unconsciously. However, more simple stimuli can. In one experiment, for example, a person sits in front of a small screen. A word is flashed on the screen so dimly and so quickly that the person does not report seeing the word. Let's say the word is STARS. Now, two words that the subject can see clearly are flashed on the screen. The task is to choose the word that is related in some way to the word that was not seen. Let us say the words used in this example are STRIPES and PENCILS. Even when subjects claim they are only guessing, they choose STRIPES significantly more frequently than chance would predict. If the "unconscious prompt" had been ERASERS, not STARS, they would more likely choose PENCILS. It is as if the initially presented word influenced their choice (Abrams & Greenwald, 2000; Bar & Biederman, 1998; Kouider & Dupoux, 2005; Labroo, Dhar, & Schwarz, 2008; Mitchell, 2006). For that matter, simply having read a list of words increases the ability of subjects to recognize those words later when they are flashed very briefly on a computer screen, even if the subjects do not recognize that the words have been read before (Jacoby & Dallas, 1981).

Blindsight is a phenomenon that occurs in individuals with damage to the primary visual areas of the cerebral

subliminal perception the process of perceiving and responding to stimuli presented at levels that are below one's absolute threshold of conscious processing

Courtesy of image100/Corbis.

For several decades, people have been concerned about mindcontrol through subliminal advertising. The notion is that a message (say, "Buy Popcorn") would be flashed on a movie screen so rapidly that the audience would not be conscious of its appearance, but the message would subliminally enter their minds. Everyone would then rise and head to the concession stand for popcorn. The technique never did work. A message as complicated as "Buy Popcorn" requires a long exposure in order to be processed—a long enough exposure to be very distracting to moviegoers.

cortex. Despite the fact that these individuals are blind in the area of the visual field associated with the damage, some visual capacity remains–even though there is no awareness of this capacity. In normal vision, visual pathways extend from the retina through the lateral geniculate body and then on to the primary visual cortex, back in the occipital lobes. If something happens to damage this pathway, a person will be rendered blind in that part of the visual field served by the damaged area. However, the damage may not eliminate vision altogether. The phenomenon of blindsight, a rare occurrence, was first reported by Lawrence Weiskrantz (1986). In the course of research with patients having damage to the visual cortex, Weiskrantz noted that a person who reported that he or she could not "see" a stimulus presented in the damaged area of the visual field, could, when encouraged to guess, correctly identify the presence of a stimulus above chance levels. For example if a dot of light were moved across the blind area of a person's visual field, that person would claim to have seen nothing. But when pressured to guess the direction of the dot's movement, they could correctly report the direction at a level significantly above chance (Blakemore, 2001; Scharli & Haiman, 1999;

Wessinger & Fendrich, 1997; Kentridge & Heywood, 1997).

This phenomenon has been demonstrated in other aspects of vision. In one case, a patient with brain damage could not identify even the simplest of shapes. However, when she was asked to place a letter in a mail slot, she successfully adjusted the position of the envelope to fit the slot. Thus, ". . . the loss of certain kinds of activity in certain crucial areas of the visual cortex impairs or extinguishes visual awareness, without necessarily abolishing visually guided behavior" (Zeman, 1998, p. 1696). An analogous phenomenon can be found with hearing (called "deaf hearing"). In one experiment, a deaf patient was found to react reflexively to sounds and later identified auditory stimuli above chance levels when asked to guess whether a stimulus was presented (Garde & Cowey, 2000).

Why does blindsight occur? The answer to this question is not clear. It may be that subcortical visual pathways that remain intact after a lesion or surgery are responsible for blindsight (Kentridge & Heywood, 1999). There also is evidence that fibers and tissue that were spared damage within the primary visual pathways may account for blindsight (Scharli & Harman, 1999; Scharli, Harman, & Hogben, 1999). Currently, there is no single accepted explanation of blindsight. Researchers in the area do accept that "blindsight is unlike normal, near-threshold vision and that information about the stimulus is processed by blindsighted persons in an unusual way" (Azzopardi & Cowey, 1997).

A team of researchers under the direction of Ap Dijksterhuis, of the University of Amsterdam in The Netherlands, has been collecting data in support of the theory that many complex cognitive tasks—such as problem solving and decision making—occur at an unconscious level (Dijksterhuis & Nordgren, 2006; Dijksterhuis et al., 2006; Dijksterhuis & Meurs, 2006; Ruys, Dijksterhuis, & Corneille, 2008)). Indeed, these researchers believe that not only do we often use unconscious processes to make decisions and solve problems, but also that unconscious processing is often superior to effortful, conscious processing.

For example, in one experiment (Dijksterhuis, 2004), people were asked to choose the best of four apartments to rent. Everyone was given the same information about each apartment, a list of 12 features. Some descriptions of these hypothetical apartments were positive (this apartment is rather sizeable) or negative (this apartment has an unfriendly landlord). One apartment was described in largely positive terms, making it quite desirable. A second apartment was described by a majority of negative features, while the other two were described in neutral terms. So, in

a brief period of time, each person was given 48 tidbits of information about the apartments to be considered.

Then came the experimental manipulation. One group of participants had to decide which apartment they would chose to rent immediately after reading the long list of descriptions. A second group was told to consciously think about each of the apartments for three minutes before making a decision. Right after reading the descriptions, the third group was distracted by a meaningless task that prevented conscious thought. "Ironically, the unconscious thinkers [those in the third group] performed significantly better than the conscious thinkers and the immediate choosers. In fact, for participants who had to choose immediately or who engaged in conscious thought, the task was too difficult in the sense that they did not, on average, indicate greater liking of the desirable apartment than the undesirable apartment. Only the unconscious thinkers reported the appropriate preference for the desirable apartment" (p. 96).

What do you make of these results? One interpretation is that when one is faced with a difficult decision, involving several choices and a good bit of information (e.g., Which classes should I take next semester? or, How will I start my term paper?) *not* consciously thinking about one's options may be the best course of action. That is, sometimes the advice to "sleep on it," may be the best option.

BEFORE YOU GO ON

2. What is meant by "levels of consciousness," and how did Freud characterize such levels?
3. What does research on phenomena such as subliminal perception and blindsight tell us about the unconscious processing of information?
4. Is there any evidence that the unconscious can be helpful in anything other than very simple tasks?

A Point to Ponder or Discuss
Personal experience may lead one to report that his or her level or degree of consciousness shifts and changes throughout the day, but self-reports of mental states tend to be unreliable. How might we operationally define "levels of consciousness" in someone else without taking his or her word for it?

SLEEP

Sleep reduces our alertness, awareness, and perception of events occurring around us. Sleep is more an altered state of awareness than a total loss of consciousness. After all, we remain aware enough of the extent of the bed not to fall off (very often). Parents who are able to "sleep through anything" awaken quickly at the muffled cry of their child in a room down the hall.

We seldom are aware or conscious of our own sleeping, even though we may spend more than 200,000 hours of our lifetime asleep. Just as the level or degree of our awareness varies, so does our sleep vary in its level or quality throughout the night, and from night to night.

The Stages of a "Good Night's Sleep"

How do we know when someone is asleep? Self-reports are notoriously unreliable. A person who claims that he or she "didn't sleep a wink last night" may have slept soundly for many hours (Dement, 1974; Espie, 2002). Our best indicators of sleep are measurements of brain activity and muscle tone. The **electroencephalograph (EEG)** is an instrument that measures and records the electrical activity of the brain. It does so by means of small electrodes pasted onto the scalp. Each electrode is measuring the summation of the action potentials of hundreds of the neurons that lie below it. The process is slightly messy, but it is in no way painful. The **electromyogram** (EMG) similarly produces a record of a muscle's activity, tone, or state of relaxation.

When you are awake and alert, your EEG pattern shows fast, small, irregular patterns called *gamma waves* and *beta waves*. Gamma waves occur more than 30 times per second, while beta waves occur between 12 and 30 times per second. You have fast eye movements as you look around at objects and events in your environment, and your breathing may be fast and shallow or slow and deep, depending on your level of physical activity.

When you are in a calm, relaxed state with your eyes closed but not yet asleep, your EEG pattern shows a rhythmic cycle of brain-wave activity called *alpha waves*. In this pre-sleep stage, your brain produces smooth EEG waves cycling eight to twelve times per second. If, as you lie still, you start worrying about an event of the day or trying to solve a problem, the alpha waves become disrupted and are replaced by an apparently random pattern of heightened electrical activity typical of that found in wakefulness.

As you enter sleep, your brain waves change as alpha waves give way to the brain waves that occur during the stages of sleep. The transition between the waking state and the sleep state is not sudden or abrupt. The onset of sleep is more like someone gradually turning down the brightness of a light than shutting off a switch. Once asleep, EEG tracings of the activity of the brains of sleeping subjects reveal that sleep can be divided into five stages. As we review these stages, refer the EEGs for each stage of sleep shown in Figure 4.2.

Stage 1 Sleep: This is a very light sleep. Sometimes it is referred to as *descending stage 1 sleep* because it represents a descent from wakefulness into sleep. The smooth cyclical alpha pattern disappears and is replaced by the slower theta waves (4–7 cycles per second). The amplitude (magnitude) of the electrical activity becomes more regular. Breathing becomes more regular, heart rate slows, and blood pressure decreases. Some slow, rolling eye movements may occur, or the eyes may be still. If aroused from sleep, individuals report being in a light sleep or just "drifting off" to sleep. This stage does not last long—generally less than ten minutes. Then one starts to slide into stage 2 sleep.

Stage 2 Sleep: In this stage, the EEG pattern is similar to Stage 1—low amplitude, with no noticeable wavelike pattern. The difference is that now there are *sleep spindles* in the EEG record—brief bursts of electrical activity (12–14 cycles per second) that occur with regularity

electroencephalograph (EEG) an instrument that measures and records the electrical activity of the brain

electromyogram (EMG) a record of a muscle's activity, tone, or state of relaxation

FIGURE 4.2

EEG records showing the general electrical activity of the brain for a person at various stages of sleep and wakefulness.

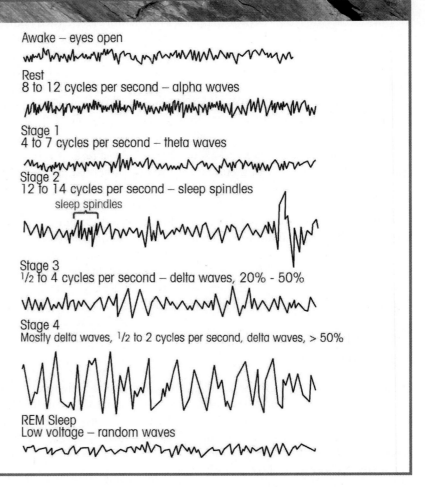

Awake – eyes open

Rest
8 to 12 cycles per second – alpha waves

Stage 1
4 to 7 cycles per second – theta waves

Stage 2
12 to 14 cycles per second – sleep spindles

sleep spindles

Stage 3
¹/2 to 4 cycles per second – delta waves, 20% - 50%

Stage 4
Mostly delta waves, ¹/2 to 2 cycles per second, delta waves, > 50%

REM Sleep
Low voltage – random waves

(every 15 seconds or so). In addition to sleep spindles, we also see *K-complexes* in the EEG record. A K-complex is indicated by a large, sharp waveform made up of a single positive wave followed by a single negative wave. Both sleep spindles and K-complex patterns may be signs of the brain's efforts to turn off incoming sensory messages from the environment (Zillmer & Spears, 2001, pp. 410–413).

Stage 3 Sleep: With this stage, one is getting into deep sleep. There is an overall reduction in the brain's electrical activity. *Delta wave* activity now becomes obvious in the EEG. Delta waves are high, slow waves (from 0.5 to 4 cycles per second). In this stage, delta waves constitute between 20 percent and 50 percent of the EEG pattern. Internal functions (heart rate, breathing,

temperature) become slower and lower. It is going to be difficult to wake the sleeper now.

Stage 4 Sleep: Now the person is in deep sleep. The EEG record is nearly filled with slow, recurring delta waves (as opposed to Stage 3 sleep, where delta waves made up only a portion of brain-wave activity). Readings from an electromyogram indicate that muscles have become almost totally relaxed. About 15 percent of a night's sleep will be spent in this stage. It is during this period of sleep that the pituitary gland releases growth hormone and the immune system is most active. Infants spend a great deal of time in this "restorative stage" of sleep—and adults will increase their Stage 4 sleep time after periods of unusual exertion and physical activity.

REM and NREM Sleep

In the early 1950s, Nathaniel Kleitman and Eugene Aserinsky made a remarkable observation. They discovered that sometimes during sleep a person's eyes move rapidly under his or her closed eyelids. These eye movements are called **rapid eye movements** and are said to occur during REM sleep. Perhaps the most remarkable thing about REM sleep is that, persons awakened tend to report clear, vivid dreams. Sometimes rapid eye movements are totally absent—periods called non-REM, or NREM sleep (Aserinsky & Kleitman, 1953; Kleitman, 1963b). A person awakened during a period of NREM sleep who can report anything tends to report, not vivid dreams, but fragmented thoughts.

The last segment of Figure 4.2 is a typical REM sleep EEG tracing. Note how similar this part of the figure is to the EEG for wakefulness. Indeed, there are areas of the visual cortex (in the occipital lobe) and elsewhere in the brain where neural activity is greater during REM sleep than at any time during the waking day. Paradoxically, REM sleep produces a muscular immobility, called **atonia**, caused by the total relaxation of the muscles. Atonia seems to be the body's way of preventing the dreamer from reacting to the action of the dreams. For most persons, atonia is occasionally interrupted by slight muscle twitches, but some people thrash about wildly during REM sleep, a condition reasonably called REM sleep disorder.

During REM sleep there is often an excitement of the sex organs, males having a penile erection, females having a discharge of vaginal fluids (although this latter finding is not as common). Breathing usually becomes shallow and rapid. Blood pressure levels may skyrocket and the heart rate increases, all while the person lies "peacefully" asleep. Scientists have long suspected that the marked increase in physiological activity during REM sleep is related to heart attacks, strokes, and other cardiovascu-lar problems that can develop during sleep (King et al., 1973; Kirby & Verrier, 1989; Somers et al., 1993).

If awakened during REM sleep, a person reports a vivid, story-like dream about 85 percent of the time. At first, scientists believed that the rapid eye movements during REM sleep were being made as the dreamer literally viewed, or scanned, images produced by the dream. As a result of this belief and the speed of the eye movements, scientists concluded that dreams lasted only a few seconds. We now know that dreams last far longer and that a dreamer's rapid eye movements are unrelated to the content of dreams.

Periods of REM sleep occur throughout the night and normally last from a few minutes to half an hour, and account for about 25 percent of the sleep of adult humans. About 90 to 120 minutes each night are spent in REM sleep. A person's first REM episode (first dream) will typically occur about 90 minutes after entering Stage 1 sleep, followed by another episode about an hour later. As the person reaches the fifth, sixth, and seventh hours of sleep the number of REM periods increases dramatically. As a person goes through a night's sleep, that person tends to have longer REM episodes and more vivid dreams. Remember, of course, that these are averages and "typical" patterns, and not necessarily those followed by every sleeper every night.

Dreaming

If, indeed, every person dreams every night, as research indicates, is it not reasonable to ask what function dreams have? Why do we dream every night? Why do we dream what we dream? The meaning of dreams has interested people at least as far back as the time of the ancient Greek philosophers. For example, Aristotle believed that dreams were simply the contents of sensory experiences that manifested themselves during sleep. Aristotle did not attach much significance to dreams because he viewed

rapid eye movements (REM) times when a sleeping person's eyes move quickly under his or her closed eyelids; associated with dreaming

atonia a period of muscular immobility

Everyone dreams, every night. Rapid eye movements (REM) are fairly reliable indicators of someone in a dream state.

manifest content the content of a dream of which the dreamer is aware

latent content the "true" underlying meaning of a dream that resides in a person's unconscious mind

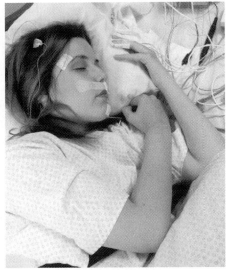

Courtesy of Yoav Levy/Getty Images.

activation-synthesis theory the proposal that dreams are activated by brainstem mechanisms, sending impulses up to the cerebral cortex, where they are synthesized and made meaningful

them as leftovers from the day's sensory experiences. In other words, for Aristotle, dreams were simply a re-experiencing of the events of the day.

One of the more influential views of the nature of dreams was that of Sigmund Freud (1900a) in his book *Interpretation of Dreams*. Recall that Freud emphasized the role of the unconscious in our everyday lives. Freud saw dreams as a way to uncover the mischief going on in the unconscious. In fact, in a lecture at Clark University in 1910, Freud said, "interpretation of dreams is in fact the *via regia* [royal road] to the interpretation of the unconscious."

Freud's theory of dreams focused on the importance of the meaning of dreams. He suggested that many dreams serve a wish-fulfillment purpose. That is, the content of a dream is related to something you need or want. So, if you are thirsty when you go to bed and you dream of drinking water, your wish for water has been fulfilled in the dream. (This particular notion was tested by sleep researcher William Dement many years ago. He kept people from drinking any liquids before going to sleep, awakened them when they began a REM stage of sleep, and discovered that many were, indeed, dreaming about drinking, or wanting to and being unable to do so [Dement, 1976].)

Freud also suggested that all dreams are related to (but not simply a replay of) events in the few days preceding the dream.

In his theory of dreams, Freud made a distinction between two types of dream content. **Manifest content** was the content of which the dreamer was aware. For example, if you were to awake and remember a dream of being chased by a motorcycle-riding bear in a clown suit, that is the manifest content. Of course, the manifest content was important but only as a pathway to the latent content. The **latent content** is the "true," underlying meaning of the dream that resides in a person's unconscious mind. Arriving at the (largely symbolic) latent content was quite an art, because latent content shows itself in a highly disguised form. So the bear riding the motorcycle could be a dramatization of some unconscious thought (e.g., a desire to get away from your parents). Unlocking latent content was made even more difficult because, as Freud noted, something vivid in the manifest content may relate to something insignificant in the latent content and vice versa. That is, maybe a bear and a motorcycle chase are unimportant, compared to the clown suit which, perhaps, signals the embarrassment that you feel about the way your mother dresses in public.

Although Freud's theory on dreams was comprehensive and well articulated, not everyone agreed with it. For example, Carl Jung (a fellow psychoanalytic theorist) believed that dreams were more transparent and their symbols more closely related to universal human concerns (Hobson, 1988). Despite these differences, the psychoanalytic theory dominated most of the thinking on dreams in the twentieth century.

Alan Hobson and his colleagues proposed another quite different theory of dreams (Hobson, 1995; Hobson & McCarley, 1977; McCarley & Hobson, 1981). Their theory is known as the **activation-synthesis theory**. According to it, dreams are activated by physiological mechanisms in the brainstem, probably in the pons. Dream activation produces and sends impulses up through higher levels of the brain. These impulses do not come from the outside environment; instead, they are produced in the brainstem. Once these impulses reach the cerebral cortex, they are synthesized by being related to existing memories, interpreted, and made meaningful. Although the exact nature of synthesis is mysterious, it appears as if the brain is trying to make sense of what are likely to be random patterns of neural activity. The involvement of memories (mostly recent ones) in the synthesis process provides the "plot" or "story" for the dream. Hobson (1988) maintains that dreams are "neither obscure nor bowdlerized, but rather transparent and unedited" (p. 214). Hobson's position is in sharp contrast to Freud's view of dreams as being highly disguised and distorted.

Which position is "correct" is still open to debate. Some psychologists and psychiatrists adhere to Freud's theory of dreams, claiming that they find it useful in understanding a patient's problems or needs. However, like almost all of Freud's theoretical concepts, his theory of

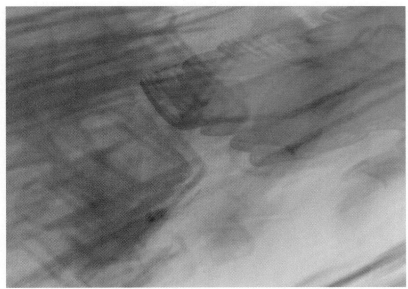

Courtesy of John Foxx/Getty Images.

dreams has little empirical support. Conversely, the activation-synthesis theory is based on years of research on both animals and humans. What is most important, however, is that both approaches say that our dreams have meaning and the content of our dreams is important to us. The major difference lies in the characterization of a dream as being highly distorted (psychoanalysis) or transparent (activation-synthesis).

Why we dream what we dream is a question that continues to intrigue researchers, as it intrigued Sigmund Freud so many years ago. Imagine that you awaken and remember a dream of raindrops falling into a vividly colorful pool. What could that mean? Need it mean anything?

BEFORE YOU GO ON

5. Briefly describe the different stages of sleep and how they are measured.
6. What is the difference between REM and NREM sleep?
7. How do Freud and Hobson characterize the content of dreams?

A Point to Ponder or Discuss
Everyone sleeps and everyone dreams (at least everyone experiences REM sleep). What ideas can you generate to explain why everyone seems to have a need to sleep and dream?

SLEEP DISORDERS

A good night's sleep is wonderful. Indeed, some people have no difficulty sleeping and likely take a good night's sleep for granted. Others experience problems, either in falling sleep or during sleep. Still others fall asleep when they do not intend to. Collectively these problems are called sleep disorders and are the focus of this section.

Insomnia

At some time, each of us has suffered from **insomnia**—the inability to fall asleep or stay asleep when we want to. Insomnia may last a few days, or it may go on for weeks or months. Insomnia is a very common complaint in the family doctor's office, and once established, it may last for years (Shocat, et al, 1999). Insomnia can be brought on by many things, such as excitement over upcoming events, life stress, psychological disorders, and a host of illnesses (Espie, 2002; Perlis, Smith, & Pigeon, 2005; Rothenberg, 1997; Silber, 2005). Insomnia may occur if we over-stimulate our autonomic nervous systems with drugs such as caffeine. Chronic, debilitating insomnia affects nearly 30 million Americans, women more commonly than men, and the elderly about one and one-half times as often as younger adults (Espie, 2002). Estimates of Americans who suffer less chronic, but still debilitating bouts of insomnia approach 16 million (Pawaskar et al., 2008).

An interesting finding from the sleep laboratory is that many people who believe they are not getting enough sleep are, in fact, sleeping much more than they think. The phenomenon is called *pseudoinsomnia*, and one hypothesis is that such people spend several dream episodes each night dreaming that they are awake and trying to get to sleep. Then, in the morning, they remember their dreams and come to believe that they haven't slept at all (e.g., Dement, 1974).

In the quest for that elusive good night's sleep, many persons with insomnia resort to medications to help them fall or stay asleep. Prescribing sleeping pills (common in nursing homes) and using over-the-counter medications to treat insomnia can cause more problems than they solve. The medications (usually sedatives or depressants) may have a positive effect for a while, but eventually dosages have to be increased as tolerance builds. When the drugs are discontinued, a rebound effect occurs that often makes it more difficult to get to sleep than it had been before. For these reasons, sleep experts recommend that drugs be used only for transient, short-term insomnia, limited to four weeks or less.

Many cases of insomnia have roots in learning and the development of poor sleep habits. For example, after a poor night's sleep or two, a person might begin to dwell on not being able to sleep, which may lead to anxiety at bedtime. In such circumstances people learn to associate the bedroom with anxiety and negative feelings, which are incompatible with the relaxation that is needed to fall asleep. A study by Libman and his associates (1997), found that good and poor sleepers differ on several behavioral dimensions. When good sleepers do wake up in the middle of the night, they are able to fall back to sleep quickly. On the other hand, poor sleepers tend to engage in counterproductive activities such as tossing and turning, looking at the clock, or worrying about personal problems.

Because so many cases of insomnia relate to cognitive, affective, and behavioral problems, a person suffering from insomnia may find success with techniques that target unproductive sleep-related thoughts and behaviors. Table 4.1 summarizes several behavioral techniques that can be used to fall asleep (Pawlicki & Heitkemper, 1985).

According to the National Commission on Sleep Disorders Research (NCSDR), we are a nation of people badly in need of a good night's sleep. For many of us, a few nights of less sleep than needed is of little consequence. For others, like interstate truck drivers—who regularly get fewer than five hours of sleep a night—the consequences can be deadly.

Courtesy of Momatiuk—Eastcott/Corbis.

TABLE 4.1

1. Avoid drinking alcohol or caffeine within 4-6 hours of bedtime.

2. Avoid the use of nicotine before bedtime—or at any time during the night, should you get up.

3. Engage in exercise during the day, but not just before bedtime.

4. Work at establishing a regular bedtime and a regular time for getting up each morning.

5. Avoid sleeping pills. As helpful as they may be at first, they can make matters worse in the long run.

6. Do your best to minimize light, noise, and extreme temperatures where you sleep.

7. Eat a light snack before bedtime, but avoid anything approaching a large meal.

8. Don't use your bed for studying, reading, or watching television. At bedtime, turn off the radio.

9. If you feel that you have to nap during the day, do so sparingly. One good nap now and then is all right. A series of several short naps is ultimately disruptive.

10. Should you awaken during the night and find that you are unable to get back to sleep, get out of bed. Go to another room. Your bed is for sleeping, not for worrying. Similarly, don't let yourself fall asleep someplace else. Return to your bed when—and only when—you are sleepy.

Techniques recommended for getting a good night's sleep.

Cognitive-behavioral techniques can be helpful in treating insomnia. In one study, for example, several behavioral techniques were assessed including stimulus control instructions (use one's bedroom only for sleep, get up and leave bed if one doesn't fall asleep in a reasonable time, wake at a regular time, do not take naps), relaxation training, biofeedback, and cognitive therapy (Bootzin & Rider, 1997). Stimulus-control techniques had the strongest effect in treating insomnia and have been found to be effective in helping persons with insomnia fall asleep after they had quit using sleep aiding medications (Riedel et al., 1998). Indeed, mental health professions generally agree that cognitive-behavioral therapy (discussed in Chapter 13) is an effective way to treat insomnia (Espie, 2002; Espie et al., 2001; Siversten et al., 2006).

Narcolepsy

Narcolepsy involves going to sleep, even during the day, without any intention to do so. Periods of narcoleptic sleep can overcome a person, regardless of the number of hours of sleep obtained the night before. Several other symptoms can accompany narcolepsy: a sudden decrease in muscle tone even while awake, a paralysis upon falling asleep, or a series of dream-like images at the point of going to sleep or waking up.

Narcolepsy is associated with a loss of specific types of neurons in the hypothalamus (Thannickal et al., 2000). Hypocretins are manufactured within these specialized neurons in the hypothalamus and sent throughout the brain. These hypocretins are complex chemicals (called peptides) that act very much like neurotransmitters. Hypocretin levels are normally greatest during periods of wakeful activity—and during REM sleep. Levels are lowest during the quiet, still, periods of NREM sleep. Narcolepsy may be brought on by a sudden drop in hypocretin levels (Siegel, 2004). A reduction in the hypothalamus of those neurons that normally produce hypocretins is strongly associated with narcolepsy.

The big problem with narcolepsy (in addition to the embarrassment it may

narcolepsy the sleep disorder that involves going to sleep, even during the day, without any intention of doing so

cause) is the total loss of muscle tone that happens when the person is awake. This loss can occur without warning but it is usually triggered by an emotional event, either happy or sad. A person with narcolepsy can have an attack before giving a speech or after hearing a funny joke. The danger in suddenly going to sleep or losing muscle control during daily activities (such as driving a car) is obvious.

Sleep Apnea

Apnea (literally "without breath") means a sudden stoppage in breathing. If we were to stop breathing when awake and conscious, we could do something about it. When awake, we exercise conscious, voluntary control over our breathing. We cannot do so, however, when we are asleep. **Sleep apnea** involves patterns of sleep during which breathing stops entirely. Sleep apnea is widespread, affecting as many as 12 million Americans. Although anyone can suffer from sleep apnea, it is most common among men who are overweight (American Sleep Apnea Association, 2001). A recent epidemiological study of sleep apnea reported that the prevalence of the disorder (associated with daytime sleepiness) was between 3% and 7% for adult men and between 2% and 5% of adult women in the general population. Additionally, prevalence increases significantly with age, found in only 3.2% of males between the ages of 20 to 44 years, in 11.3% of males between the ages of 45 to 64 years, and 18.1% of males between the ages of 65 to 100 years (Punjabi, 2008).

Episodes of sleep apnea are usually short. When apnea episodes are longer—say, a minute or two—carbon dioxide in the lungs builds to such a level that the sleeper is awakened, draws a few gasps of air, and returns to sleep, probably oblivious to what just happened. Potential consequences of sleep apnea include hypertension, coronary heart disease, stroke, psychiatric problems, impotence, and memory loss (Golbin, Somers, & Caples, 2008; Lopez-Jimenez, Sert, & Somers, 2008; Yaggi et al., 2008). Not surprisingly, perhaps, there is a strong correlation between sleep apnea and insomnia (Lavie, 2007).

Sleep apnea is also suspected as a cause of Sudden Infant Death Syndrome, or SIDS. In SIDS, apparently healthy infants (without major illness, but sometimes with a slight infection or cold) suddenly die in their sleep. Roughly two infants per thousand fall victim to SIDS.

sleep apnea patterns of sleep during which breathing stops entirely

---

BEFORE YOU GO ON

8. Describe the sleep disorders insomnia, narcolepsy, and sleep apnea.

A Point to Ponder or Discuss
Do you get enough sleep? Have you experienced insomnia (or any of the other sleep disorders)? How would you deal with insomnia if you were to develop it?

---

hypnosis an altered state of consciousness characterized by a) a marked increase in suggestibility, b) a focusing of attention, c) an exaggerated use of imagination, d) an unwillingness or inability to act on one's own, and e) an unquestioning acceptance of distortions of reality

HYPNOSIS

Hypnosis is a state of consciousness that typically requires the voluntary cooperation of the person being hypnotized. **Hypnosis** is characterized by a) a marked increase in suggestibility, b) a focusing of attention, c) an exaggerated use of imagination, d) an unwillingness or inability to act on one's own, and e) an unquestioning acceptance of distortions of reality (Hilgard & Hilgard, 1975). Being hypnotized is not like going to sleep. Few of the characteristics of sleep are to be found in the hypnotized subject. EEG patterns, for example, are significantly different.

Hypnosis has been used for various purposes and with varying degrees of success. As you know, it has been used as entertainment, as a routine in which members of an audience are hypnotized—usually to do silly things. It has been used to access memories of events not in immediate awareness. It has been touted as a treatment for a wide range of physical and psychological disorders. In this section, we will examine hypnosis and the research concerning its effectiveness for various purposes.

Can everyone be hypnotized? No, probably not. Susceptibility to hypnosis varies: "Some people respond to almost all suggestions; others respond to none; most show moderate levels of response." (Kirsch & Braffman, 2001, p. 58). Contrary to popular belief, a person cannot be hypnotized against his or her will. Some hypnotists claim that they can hypnotize anyone under the right conditions, which is why we hedged and said "probably" not (Lynn et al., 1990).

Although not everyone can be easily hypnotized, some people are excellent subjects, can readily be put into deep hypnotic states, and can learn to hypnotize themselves (Hilgard, 1975, 1978). A few traits are correlated with one's ability to be hypnotized. The most important factor seems to be the ability to engage easily in daydreaming and fantasy, to be able to "set ordinary reality aside for awhile" (Wilkes, 1986, p.25), and become totally "engaged" or absorbed in a particular task (Barnier & McConkey, 2004; Council & Green, 2004). In fact, it turns out that being susceptible to hypnosis is not extraordinary. Some people simply are more open to imaginative suggestibility (Kirsch & Braffman, 2001). Other factors that may identify a good subject for hypnosis include a degree of passivity or willingness to cooperate (at least during the

Courtesy of Bruce T. Brown/Getty Images.

All sorts of claims have been made for hypnosis. Indeed, under hypnosis, people will do some pretty silly things—but they are not likely to do anything that they would not do otherwise. Hypnosis has many serious and beneficial applications.

hypnotic session), and a proneness to fantasy (Barber, 2000; Braffman & Kirsch, 1999).

Can I be made to do things under hypnosis that I would not ordinarily do? Next to being unknowingly hypnotized, the greatest fear associated with hypnosis is that it will somehow force a person to do things that he or she would not ordinarily do. Can a hypnotist make you do something dangerous or embarrassing? The bottom line is this: Under the influence of a skilled hypnotist, you may do some pretty silly things and do them publicly. But, under the right circumstances, you might do those same things without being hypnotized. It is unlikely you would do under hypnosis anything that you would not do otherwise. However, under certain (unusual) circumstances, people can do outrageous—and dangerous—things, which is why hypnosis should be used with great caution.

Does hypnosis really represent a truly altered state of consciousness? The issue is in dispute. Some believe that hypnosis is really no more than a heightened level of suggestibility (Barber, 1972; 2000; Spanos & Barber, 1974; Kirsch, 2000), whereas others believe it to be a special state, separate from the compliance of a willing subject. When hypnotized people are left alone, they usually maintain the condition induced by their hypnosis. Those who are not hypnotized, but simply complying with a hypnotist, revert quickly to normal behaviors when left alone (Hilgard, 1975). The EEG recordings of the brain activity of hypnotized individuals reveal few, if any, alterations from normal consciousness (Barber, Spanos, & Chaves, 1974).

A person in a hypnotic state seems to be aware of what he or she is doing, but in a strange way. Within the hypnotized subject is what Hilgard calls a "hidden observer" who may be aware of what is going on. In one study (Hilgard & Hilgard, 1975), a person was hypnotized and told that he would feel no pain as his hand was held in a container of ice water (usually very painful). When asked, the person reported feeling little pain, just as expected. The hypnotic suggestion was working. The Hilgards then asked the person if "some part of him" was feeling any pain and directed him to indicate the presence of such pain by using his free hand to press a lever (or to write out a description of what he was feeling). Although he continued to say he had no feeling of pain, the free hand (on behalf of the "hidden observer") indicated that it "knew" there was pain in the immersed hand.

Can hypnosis be used to alleviate physical pain?
Yes. It will not (it cannot) cure the underlying cause, but it can be used to control the feeling of pain (Keefe, Abernethy, & Campbell, 2004). Hypnosis can be used to create hallucinations (perceptual experiences that occur without sensory input) in the hypnotized subject. Hallucinations are said to be positive when a person perceives something that is not there and negative when a person fails to perceive something that is there. Pain reduction uses negative hallucinations. If a person is a good candidate for it, hypnosis has a significant chance of blocking a portion of perceived pain from conscious awareness (Alden & Heap, 1998; Hilgard & Hilgard, 1975; Liossi & Hatira, 2003; Montgomery et al, 2000; 2002).

Hypnosis has recently received attention as a means of controlling pain in older adults. Pain in older adults is a common phenomenon, often related to chronic illnesses, depression, social isolation, and sleep problems (Chodosh, et al., 2001). Hypnosis holds allure as a pain management tool because of its noninvasive nature and the possibility of treating pain without the side effects of medications. Using hypnosis to manage pain in older adults has met with considerable success and is becoming more and more common (Ashton et al., 1997; Cuellar, 2005; Gay, Philippot, & Luminet, 2002).

Is it true that one can remember things under hypnosis that could not otherwise be remembered?
Probably not. This question may be the most hotly contested issue related to hypnosis. In the sense of, "Can you hypnotize me to remember psychology material better for the test next Friday?" the answer is almost certainly no. Someone might be able to convince you under hypnosis (that is, successfully suggest to you) that you had better remember your psychology and thus motivate you to remember. But there is no evidence that hypnotic suggestion can directly improve your ability to learn and remember new material. In the more restrictive sense of, "I don't remember all the details of the accident and the trauma that followed. Can hypnosis help me recall those events more clearly?" the answer is less certain. Distortions of memory can easily occur in normal states. In hypnotic states a person is by definition in a suggestive state and susceptible to distortions in recall furnished or prompted by the hypnotist (even assuming that the hypnotist has no reason to cause such distortions). To the extent that hypnosis can reduce feelings of anxiety and tension, it may help in the recollection of anxiety-producing memories. The evidence on this issue is neither clear nor convincing in either direction.

What of the related questions, "Can hypnosis take me back in time (regression) and make me remember what it was like when I was only three or four years old?" or "Can hypnosis help me recall experiences from past lives?" Here, we do have a clear-cut answer, and the answer is no. So-called age-regression hypnotic sessions have simply not proven to be valid (e.g., Nash, 1987; Spanos et al., 1991). Often there is no way to verify the validity of memories "recovered" during age or past-life regression.

The use of hypnosis to refresh the memory of a witness in a legal proceeding presents a particular concern: the potential for hypnosis to lead to the creation of *pseudomemories*, or false memories. Under hypnosis, a person is in a highly suggestible state and may be susceptible to having facts or events that never occurred implanted. The research on pseudomemories is inconclusive. Some studies show that hypnosis does not lead to high levels of pseudomemory-creation (Sheehan & Statham, 1989; Weekes, Lynn, Green, & Brentar, 1992); whereas, other studies do show an increase in pseudomemories, especially among those who are highly susceptible to hypnosis (Sheehan, Statham, & Jamison, 1991; Sheehan, Green, & Truesdale, 1992).

BEFORE YOU GO ON

9. What is hypnosis, who can be hypnotized, and for what purposes is hypnosis of value?

A Point to Ponder or Discuss
Why would anyone want to alter his or her normal state of consciousness? Are some reasons for doing so more valid than others?

MEDITATION

Meditation is a self-induced state of consciousness characterized by a focusing of attention and relaxation. It is often associated with Eastern cultures, where it has been practiced for centuries. Meditation became popular in North America in the 1960s and psychologists began to study it seriously during this time. In this section we will examine meditation and the benefits some of its practitioners claim to derive from it.

Among the more popular forms of meditation are those that require mental focusing or concentration, such as *transcendental meditation (TM)*. In TM, a meditator begins by assuming a comfortable position and becoming calm and relaxed. The meditator then focuses his or her attention to one particular stimulus. This focus could be on some bodily function, such as breathing, or on some softly spoken or chanted word or phrase, or *mantra*, such as "ooom," "one," or "calm." The meditator blocks other external or internal stimuli from consciousness. The meditator's challenge is to stay relaxed, peaceful and calm. Meditation's practitioners claim that a state of meditation cannot be forced, but reaching an altered state of awareness through meditation is not difficult.

Once a person is in a meditative state, measurable physiological changes do take place that allow psychologists to claim meditation to be an altered state of consciousness. The most noticeable is a predominance of alpha waves in the EEG record. Such waves characterize a relaxed state of the sort experienced just before one enters into sleep. Breathing slows and becomes deeper, oxygen intake is reduced, and the heart rate and blood pressure may decrease (Cahn & Polich, 2006; Schneider et al., 2005).

Without a doubt people enter meditative states of consciousness. What is

meditation a self-induced state of altered consciousness characterized by a focusing of attention and relaxation

Courtesy of Milena Boniek/PhotoAlto/Corbis.

Techniques of meditation are relatively easy to learn. Meditation is surely a relaxing process. What benefits, if any, it provides beyond relaxation are very much in doubt.

far less certain is if these people derive any benefits from the practice. One of the major claims for meditation is that it is a simple, very effective, even superior way to enter into a state of relaxation. The reduction of somatic (bodily) arousal is taken to be one of the main advantages of meditation. The claim is that by meditating, one can slow bodily processes and enter into a state of physical as well as psychological calm. Researcher David Holmes (1984, 1985, 1987) has reviewed the evidence for somatic relaxation through meditation. On several measures of arousal/relaxation, including heart rate, respiration rate, muscle tension, and oxygen use, Holmes concluded that there are no differences between meditating persons and people who are "simply" resting or relaxing.

Another claim made for meditation is that those who practice it are better able to cope with stress, pressure, or threatening situations. Once again, Holmes reports that he could find no evidence to support this claim. In fact, in four of the studies he reviewed, Holmes found that under mild threat, meditating subjects showed greater arousal than did non-meditating subjects. We must add two important notes here: First, some psychologists have taken issue with Holmes' methods and conclusions and argue that meditation *does* offer advantages over simply resting, suggesting also that "resting" is a difficult concept to define (Shapiro, 1985; Suler, 1985; West, 1985). Second, Holmes does not argue that meditation is useless. He simply says that with regard to somatic arousal there is no evidence that it is any better than resting.

Some advocates of meditation claim its benefits reach far beyond relaxation and somatic arousal reduction. Many psychologists are skeptical of the claims that meditation can raise one's consciousness to transcendental heights of new awareness and thus make one a better person because these claims are not able to be verified in the laboratory. The official U. S. website for transcendental meditation (www.tm.org) provides an astounding list of meditation's benefits: increased IQ, enhanced creativity, higher productivity, improved perception, better health, smoother relations at work, and better quality of life. In addition, the website claims meditation has the twin powers to reduce crime and reverse aging.

A recent large-scale study prepared for the U. S. Department of Health and Human Services reviewed the results of more than 800 research studies of the benefits of meditation (Ospina et al, 2007). One noteworthy result of this project was that most of the studies that were found in the research literature were of poor quality. The bottom-line conclusion of the authors was that "Many uncertainties surround the practice of meditation. Scientific research on meditation practices does not appear to have a common theoretical perspective and is characterized by poor methodological quality. Firm conclusions on the effects of meditation practices in healthcare cannot be drawn based on available evidence" (p. v).

BEFORE YOU GO ON

10.   What is meditation and what are its benefits?

A Point to Ponder or Discuss
Assume that you agree with the argument that total mental and somatic relaxation is a good thing.
How might you attain such a state?

ALTERING CONSCIOUSNESS WITH DRUGS

In this final section, we will discuss some of the chemicals that alter consciousness by inducing changes in perception, mood, or behavior. Because they can alter psychological processes, these chemicals are referred to as **psychoactive drugs**.

Drugs have been used for centuries to alter consciousness. At least initially, psychoactive drugs are taken to achieve a state of consciousness the user considers to be positive, pleasant, or even euphoric. No reasonable person would take a drug because he or she expected to have an unpleasant or bad experience. Nonetheless, the use of drugs that alter mood, perception, and behaviors has seriously negative outcomes in many cases, and a few definitions are required to advance our discussion of these outcomes:

1. ***Dependence:*** a state in which a) the use of a drug is required to maintain bodily functioning (called physical dependence), or b) continued use of a drug is believed to be necessary to maintain psychological functioning at some level (called psychological dependence). "I just can't face the day without my three cups of coffee."

2. ***Tolerance:*** a condition in which the use of a drug leads to a state in which more and more of it is needed to produce the same effect. "I used to get high with just one of these; now I need three."

3. ***Withdrawal:*** a powerfully negative response, either physical or psychological (including reactions such as headaches, vomiting, and cramps), that results when one stops taking a drug. "When I take these, I may not feel great, but it sure hurts when I stop."

4. ***Addiction:*** an extreme dependency, physical or psychological, in which signs of tolerance and painful withdrawal are usually found (American Psychiatric Association, 2000). Addiction also implies seeking a short-term gain (for example, a pleasurable feeling) at the expense of long-term negative consequences (Miller, 1992). "No way I'm gonna give it up; no matter what. It feels too good."

Another important distinction we should make is between drug use and drug abuse. We are dealing with *abuse* when we find a) a lack of control, as evidenced by daily impairment and continued use, even knowing that one's condition will deteriorate; b) a disruption of interpersonal relationships or difficulties at work that can be traced to drug usage; and c) indications that maladaptive drug use has continued for at least one month (American Psychiatric Association, 2000). In this distinction is the reality that, although drug use may not have negative consequences, drug abuse will. The United States Department of Health and Human Services (HHS) claims that drug and alcohol abuse contributes to the deaths of more than 120,000 Americans each year and costs taxpayers more than $294 billion

psychoactive drugs those chemicals that alter psychological processes

TABLE 4.2

A few examples of common psychoactive drugs.

DRUG TYPE	EXAMPLE	COMMENTS
STIMULANTS	CAFFEINE	found in coffee, tea, colas, and chocolate, increases CNS activity and metabolism, disrupts sleep
	NICOTINE	activates excitatory synapses, leads to tolerance and addiction
	COCAINE	produces short-lived "high"; raises blood pressure and heart rate; masks fatigue; blocks reuptake, highly addictive
	AMPHETAMINES	release excess neurotransmitters; slower than cocaine; mask fatigue
DEPRESSANTS	ALCOHOL	decreases nervous system activity; impairs decision-making; reduces inhibitions; leads to dependency and addiction
	OPIATES	analgesics; produce feelings of calm and ease; lead to addiction
	HEROIN	produces "rush" of euphoria; reduces pain; highly addictive
	BARBITURATES	slow nervous system activity; move from calm to sleep to coma to death; cause addiction
HALLUCINOGENS	LSD	produces hallucinations, usually visual; increases serotonin levels; raises levels of emotionality
OTHERS	MARIJUANA	alters mood; slight depressant; in high doses, causes cognitive deficits and chromosomal abnormalities; when taken at early age, leads to other drug use/abuse
	ECSTASY	produces euphoria and lessening of inhibitions; can have hallucinogenic properties; may cause confusion, depression, anxiety, and paranoia

stimulants psychoactive drugs that stimulate or activate an organism, producing a heightened state of arousal and elevation of mood

annually (HHS, 2001). In truth, no clear line divides drug use and drug abuse. For that matter, no clear lines divide drug use, drug dependency, and drug addiction (Byrne, Jones, & Williams, 2004; Gilvarry, 2000). Instead, a continuum runs from total abstinence through heavy social use to addiction (Robinson & Berridge, 2003).

There are many psychoactive drugs. We will focus on the more common ones (Table 4.2).

Stimulants

Chemical **stimulants** do just that—they stimulate or activate an organism, producing a heightened sense of arousal and an elevation of mood. Most of the time, these drugs also activate neural reactions, but at this level we have to maintain a healthy respect for the complexity of the brain and the various ways stimulants interact with its parts. For example, one stimulant administered directly to one part of a cat's reticular formation can awaken and arouse a sleeping cat, but if that same stimulant is administered to a different area of a cat's reticular formation, the cat will go to sleep.

Caffeine is one of the most widely used stimulants. It is found in many foods and drinks (soft drinks, coffee, tea, and chocolate), as well as in several varieties of painkillers. In moderate amounts, it seems to have no serious or life-threatening effects. At some point, a mild dependence may develop. Caffeine temporarily increases cellular metabolism (the process of converting food into energy), which then results in a burst of newfound energy. It also blocks the effects of some inhibitory neurotransmitters in the brain. Caffeine disrupts sleep, making it more difficult to fall and to stay asleep.

Giving up caffeine after long or excessive use may result in withdrawal pains. If you drink a lot of coffee and cola during the week, but stop on the weekend, you may get caffeine withdrawal headaches. By the same token, if you drink coffee to help stay awake during an all-night study session, you may find yourself fatigued a few hours after your last cup. If you are especially unlucky, this fatigue will arrive just as your exam does!

Nicotine is a popular stimulant found in cigarettes. Nicotine is absorbed into the lungs and reaches the brain very quickly—in a matter of seconds. Nicotine stimulates central nervous system activity, but it also relaxes muscle tone slightly, which may explain why smokers claim a cigarette relaxes them. Nicotine produces its effects by activating excitatory synapses in both the central and peripheral nervous systems. Most smokers (but not all) develop a tolerance to nicotine, requiring more and more to reach a desired state of stimulation. Nicotine is addictive, despite earlier claims to the contrary (Maxhom, 2000).

Smokeless tobacco has become a popular alternative to smoking in the last two decades. In fact, 20.4 percent of boys between the ages of nine and twelve report having used smokeless tobacco (Centers for Disease Control, 1999), as do nearly nine percent of college students (Rigotti, Lee, & Wechsler, 2000). Even without the smoke, the nicotine in smokeless tobacco is absorbed into the blood and gets to the brain almost as quickly as nicotine from cigarettes and is just as addictive. (We will have much more to say about the effects of nicotine addiction on health in Chapter 11.)

Cocaine is a stimulant derived from leaves of the coca shrub (native to the Andes region of South America). The allure of cocaine is the rush of pleasure and energy it produces when it first enters the bloodstream. Cocaine enters the bloodstream various ways depending upon how the user chooses to ingest it. If it is snorted in powder form, cocaine enters through the nose's mucous membranes. If it is smoked in its base form, cocaine enters through the lungs. Cocaine can also be injected directly into the bloodstream in liquid form. The length of a cocaine high varies depending on the method of ingestion, but 15–20 minutes is an average.

Cocaine use elevates the blood pressure, increases the heart rate, and blocks the reuptake of two important neurotransmitters: norepinephrine and dopamine. As a result, for a time, excess amounts of these two neurotransmitters are available in the nervous system. Norepinephrine acts in the central and the peripheral nervous systems to provide arousal and the sense of extra energy. Dopamine acts in the brain to produce feelings of pleasure and euphoria.

Some of the effects of cocaine use are permanent and others are long lasting, even though the high lasts only a few minutes. Not only is the rush produced by cocaine short-lived, but a letdown approaching depression follows. As users well know, one way to combat letdown and depression is to take more of the drug, a vicious cycle that leads to dependency and addiction. Cocaine is such a powerfully addictive drug that many can become psychologically and physically dependent on it after using it only once or twice. Because cocaine is illegal, determining the number of cocaine users or addicts is difficult; however, according to the National Institute on Drug Abuse (1999a), an estimated 1.7 million people in the United States over the age of 12 are current users. Cocaine addiction tends to run in families and current research is exploring a genetic basis for it.

Amphetamines are synthetically manufactured stimulants that usually come in the form of capsules or pills, and are known by many street names: bennies, wake-ups, uppers, dexies, or jellie babies. In addition to blocking reuptake, amphetamines release excess dopamine and norepinephrine into the nervous system. The action of amphetamines is considerably slower and less widespread than that of cocaine. Once an amphetamine takes effect, it gives users a feeling of being alert, awake, aroused, filled with energy, and ready to go. These results are relatively short-lived. The drug does not create alertness so much as it masks fatigue, which ultimately overcomes the user when the drug wears off. These are not the only effects of amphetamine use; it has a direct effect on the heart and circulatory system, causing, for example, irregular heartbeat and increased blood pressure.

Methamphetamine (or "meth," "chalk," or "ice," among other street names) is chemically related to amphetamine, but its effects on the central nervous system are faster and greater. Methamphetamine is easy to make, requiring no sophisticated apparatus, and is usually manufactured in small illegal "labs." The powdery substance can be taken orally, snorted, injected intravenously, or smoked. The latter two methods create an intense sensation called a "rush" or a "flash" that lasts only a few minutes, but is described as extremely pleasurable. Users usually become addicted very quickly. Methamphetamine releases high levels of dopamine, which enhance mood and body movement. At the same time, "meth" damages or destroys cells that produce dopamine (and serotonin), causing symptoms like those of Parkin-

son's disease (National Institute on Drug Abuse, 2005). In 2004, an estimated 1.4 million Americans aged 12 or older reported using methamphetamine within the previous year, and 12.3 million had used it in their lifetimes (Substance Abuse and Mental Health Services Administration, 2005).

Depressants

Depressants reduce awareness of external stimuli, slow bodily functioning, and decrease levels of overt behavior. Predictably, a person's reaction to depressants depends largely on how much is taken. In small doses, they may produce relaxation, a sense of freedom from anxiety, and a loss of stifling inhibitions. In greater amounts, they can result in sedation, sleep, coma, or death.

Alcohol is the most common of all depressants and its use started many thousands of years ago—perhaps as long ago as 8000 B.C. (Monastersky, 2003; Ray & Ksir, 1987). Over 100,000 deaths a year in the United States are attributed to alcohol. Alcohol use has been associated with myriad problems with newborns. Interestingly, just over 50 percent of alcohol consumption in the United States ($22.5 billion worth) is by 12- to 20-year-old illegal underage drinkers and by adult excessive drinkers (more than two drinks a day) (Foster, Vaughan, Foster, & Califano, 2003).

Perhaps the first thing to keep in mind about alcohol is that it *is* a depressant. Some folks may feel that alcohol stimulates them to be more entertaining, but alcohol actually slows their nervous system activity. Alcohol increases urination, leading to an overall loss of fluids. It raises visual thresholds, making it more difficult to detect dim lights. Alcohol affects mood, leading to friendly elation as levels rise and to depression, anger, and fatigue as alcohol levels drop.

The specific effects of alcohol reflect several interacting factors. Primary among them (again) is amount. What matters most is the amount of alcohol that gets into a person's bloodstream.

depressants psychoactive drugs that reduce awareness of external stimuli, slow bodily functioning, and decrease levels of overt behavior

Blood alcohol level (BAL) is affected by how much one drinks and by how fast the alcohol can get into the bloodstream. How fast the alcohol reaches the bloodstream is affected by what else is in the stomach and the sex of the drinker (females absorb alcohol faster than males). Because the alcohol will be more quickly absorbed, Drinking on an empty stomach is more dangerous than drinking while eating or soon after. One-tenth of one percent of alcohol in the bloodstream is enough to declare a person legally drunk in most states. At this level, brain activity is so depressed that decision-making is distorted and motor coordination is impaired (and both are required to drive safely). Drinking more than one mixed drink, one glass of wine, or one can of beer per hour is enough to raise blood alcohol levels.

Opiates, such as morphine and codeine, are called *analgesics* because they can be used to reduce or eliminate pain. In fact, opiates were first used for this purpose. In small doses, they create feelings of well-being, ease, relaxation, and a trance-like state. Unlike alcohol, opiates seem to have little effect on motor behavior. However, they produce dependence and addiction, and withdrawal causes extreme pain and depression.

Heroin is an opiate, originally (in the 1890s) derived from morphine but considered less addictive—a notion soon proven wrong. Strong dependency and addiction occur rapidly. An estimated 500,000 persons in the United States are addicted to heroin, and nearly half of them live in New York City. As with other drugs, heroin may owe its addictive nature to its rapid entry into the brain. Methadone, a drug used in some heroin treatment programs for long-term users, shares many of heroin's chemical properties and effects but is slower to reach the brain, tends not to produce heroin's "rush," and is somewhat less addictive.

The psychological effects of heroin (beyond whatever painkilling use it may have) are mostly related to one's emotional state and mood. Unlike alcohol or other opiates, heroin use does not

Courtesy of KG-Photography/zefa/Corbis.

Psychoactive drugs are chemicals that alter psychological processes. The use and abuse of such chemicals can have profound personal, social, and economic consequences.

normally produce hallucinations or thought disturbances. But regular heroin users quickly build a tolerance for the drug and require more of the drug to get high. Larger doses can cause breathing to stop, often for periods long enough to result in death.

Barbiturates are synthetically produced sedatives of which there are over 2,500 varieties (Doweiko, 1993). All barbiturates slow nervous system activity—in small amounts producing a sense of calm and tranquility, in higher doses producing sleep or coma. This tranquilizing effect is achieved by either blocking receptor sites of excitatory synapses or enhancing the effects of inhibitory neurotransmitters. Barbiturates also depress the cells and organs outside the central nervous system, slowing muscular responses and reducing respiration and heart rates. All barbiturates produce dependency if used regularly. Some are addictive, producing strong withdrawal symptoms when discontinued. As always, once addiction develops, getting off these drugs is very difficult.

Hallucinogens

Hallucinogens have unpredictable effects on consciousness. One obvious reaction to these drugs is the formation of hallucinations. That is, users often report seeing things when there is nothing there, or seeing things that are there

hallucinogens psychoactive drugs with unpredictable effects on consciousness, including the formation of hallucinations

Courtesy of Tom & Dee Ann McCarthy/Corbis.

All psychoactive drugs are not illegal narcotics. The nicotine in cigarettes and alcohol both influence psychological functioning. However, in most places, they are illegal if used by minors.

in ways others do not. Contrary to popular belief, hallucinations are not only visual. Nonetheless, hallucinations of hearing, smell, taste, and touch are much less common. There are nearly a hundred different types of hallucinogens, and many have been used for centuries. In many cultures, these drugs are used in religious practices to induce trance-like states intended to help the user communicate with the supernatural. In such settings, the drug may be given to young people by their elders, and "unauthorized" use, or abuse of the drug, is nearly unheard of (Chagnon, 1983; Grob & Dohkin de Rois, 1992).

LSD (lysergic acid diethylamide), a potent and popular hallucinogen, was introduced in the United States in the 1940s. LSD raises levels of emotionality and can produce profound changes in perception—usually vivid, visual hallucinations. Finding that levels of the neurotransmitter serotonin increased when LSD was given to animals was an early step to uncovering how the drug works (Jacobs, 1987). This finding was not surprising, because LSD and similar hallucinogens (e.g., mescaline) have chemical compositions similar to serotonin. Serotonin has its effects, both excitatory and inhibitory, on many areas of the brain. LSD acts on serotonin receptor sites, much like a neurotransmitter. Small doses of either can produce major behavioral effects.

LSD usually does not alter mood as much as it exaggerates a user's present mood. From the start, LSD's mood magnifying capability has been recognized as what makes the drug so dangerous. The person drawn to experiment with LSD is likely seeking escape from an unpleasant situation. He or she may be depressed or feeling hopeless. LSD will most likely worsen this user's mood by exaggerating already unpleasant feelings. The result will not be relief and escape, but instead a "bad trip."

Marijuana

Marijuana is a difficult drug to categorize. It can act as a depressant. In small doses, its effects are similar to those of alcohol: decreased nervous system activity and depressed thought and action. In larger doses, marijuana often acts as a hallucinogen, producing hallucinations and/or alterations in mood.

Marijuana is produced from the cannabis, or hemp plant, the source of most of the rope manufactured for sailing ships in the eighteenth century. Grown by George Washington and other prominent colonists, hemp was an important cash crop in the American colonies. During World War II, the plants were grown in great numbers throughout the Midwest. The cannabis plant is hardy, and many of the remnants of those early farms still grow in Illinois and Indiana, where every summer, adventurers come in search of a profitable—albeit illegal—harvest. More marijuana is grown in the United States than anywhere else in the world. Use of the drug is widespread. Indeed, marijuana is the most commonly used illicit drug in the United States. More than 83 million Americans age 12 and older have tried marijuana at least once, according to the National Household Survey on Drug Abuse (NHSDA, 2002). Thirty-nine percent of males (and 26 percent of females) arrested in 1999 tested positive for marijuana use (National Institute on Drug Abuse, 2003; Department of Justice, 2000).

The active ingredient in marijuana is the *tetrahydrocannabinol*, or *THC*. THC is also the active ingredient in **hashish**, a similar but more potent drug, also made from the cannabis plant. Although marijuana, in large doses, has been found to increase overall levels of some neurotransmitters, researchers do not know exactly how it produces this effect. However it works, marijuana has become more potent than in times past. Levels of THC found in marijuana increased dramatically between 1980 and 1997 (ElSohly et al., 2000).

Our society finds it difficult to deal with marijuana. In the United States, it is illegal to sell, possess, or use the drug. There is some evidence that users of marijuana may rapidly develop a tolerance for it, but there is little evidence that it is addictive. Is marijuana dangerous? One would think certainly, if for no other reason than that it is usually smoked, and smoking is a danger to one's health. And, smoking marijuana is more dangerous than cigarette smoking in terms of causing many respiratory problems. Strangely enough, there is evidence that smokers of marijuana–even heavy, long-term smokers–do *not* have an increased risk of developing lung cancer (Tashkin et al., 2006). In fact, the researchers reported that smokers of marijuana had a slightly *smaller* risk of developing lung cancer than did non-smokers in the control group!

Marijuana is dangerous in the sense that alcohol is dangerous. Excessive use leads to impaired judgment, impaired reflexes, unrealistic moods, poor physical coordination, and hallucinations. Excessive use is also related to deficits in tasks requiring sustained attention and cognitive flexibility. Heavy users of marijuana also show lower verbal intelligence quotients than light users as well as all sorts of cognitive deficits, including impaired memory skills (Pope et al., 2001; Pope & Yurgelun-Todd, 1996; Solowij et al., 2002). There is evidence that (even with genetic and environmental factors controlled) use of marijuana before the age of 17 is a significant risk factor for other drug use and drug-related problems (Lynskey et al., 2003). Additionally, a team of British scientists concluded that marijuana smoking increases the risk of developing serious symptoms of psychological disorders, such as schizophrenia or depression (Moore et al., 2007).

The use of marijuana may have genetic implications (it can produce chromosomal abnormalities in non-humans). It can adversely affect the body's immune system and white blood cells. It is partially responsible for lowering the sperm count in male users. It can impair memory function, affecting memories of recent events in particular. It has predictably negative effects when taken during pregnancy, resulting in smaller babies, increased numbers of miscarriages, and so on (Doweiko, 1993).

Ecstasy

Ecstasy (a common name for MDMA) is a drug that is classified as a *psychedelic amphetamine*. Because of its euphoric effects, ecstasy has become a very popular drug over the past 20 years, especially among young people. One survey conducted in Boston found that 14 percent of boys and 7 percent of girls in high school were using ecstasy (Erowid, 2001). According to the National Institute on Drug Abuse (NIDA) more than 11 million persons aged 12 or older have used ecstasy at least once in their lifetimes (NIDA, 2006).

Ecstasy produces feelings of emotional openness and euphoria, fewer critical thoughts, and fewer inhibitions. It has also been associated with greater trust and fewer barriers between people (NIDA, 2001; 2006). Because of these effects, ecstasy is popular with young adults and adolescents attending concerts or raves (all night dance parties). A person can feel the effects of ecstasy in as little as 30 minutes, and the euphoria can last as long as three to four hours. Regular users may develop a tolerance for the drug, requiring higher and higher doses to obtain the desired effects.

As is the case with most drugs, ecstasy has a downside. On the physical side, ecstasy use has been associated with symptoms such as teeth clenching, nausea, blurred vision, rapid eye movement, faintness, and chills or sweating (NIDA, 2006). It can cause a dangerous increase in body temperature that can lead to kidney failure. On the psychological side, ecstasy use can produce confusion, sleep problems, depression, severe anxiety, and paranoia. These adverse reactions may be immediate or may occur weeks after taking the drug. Ecstasy may damage parts of the brain associated with thought and memory—probably from damage to the serotonin systems in the brain (Parrott et al., 1998; Reneman et al., 2001; Schilt et al., 2007). The seriousness of side effects is tied to the dose taken. As tolerance develops and higher doses are taken, ecstasy users have more pronounced negative side effects. Finally, ecstasy can interact with other drugs. For example—and not surprisingly—ecstasy interacts negatively with alcohol and antidepressant medications (NIDA, 2001, 2006).

BEFORE YOU GO ON

11. Describe and note the effects on consciousness of these psychoactive drugs: caffeine, nicotine, cocaine, amphetamines, methamphetamine, alcohol, opiates, barbiturates, LSD, marijuana, and ecstasy.

A Point to Ponder or Discuss
Given the obvious and inherent danger of psychoactive drugs, why do millions of people use these drugs, sometimes regularly, and sometimes to the point of addiction?

SPOTLIGHT
ON DIVERSITY

Ethnic and Gender Differences in Drug and Alcohol Use and Abuse

In our discussion of psychoactive drugs, we differentiated between drug use and drug abuse, and between addiction and dependence. Another relevant distinction is that between legal and illicit drugs. *Illicit drugs* are those whose use, possession or sale is illegal. Note that the term illicit also applies to legally available drugs that are used without a prescription. Also note that drugs that are quite legally used and sold by adults—alcohol is the best example—become illicit when used by persons younger than 21.

After rising slowly but surely for nearly two decades, illicit drug use among adolescents in the United States began to drop slightly in the late 1990s. Now, as then, there are significant differences in drug use as a function of race or ethnicity and gender (Kann et al., 2000; Marsiglia et al., 2004). The National Survey on Drug Use and Health (NSDUH) revealed several differences in illicit drug use among the major racial/ethnic groups they surveyed in 2002 and 2003 (SAMHSA, 2003). Figure S-1 shows the percentage of persons in each group who reported using illicit drugs in the month preceding the survey. A rate decrease between the two years reported here was

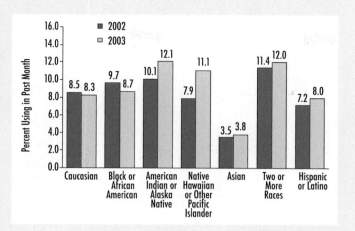

Figure S-1. *Past-month illicit drug use among persons aged 12 or older by race/ethnicity: 2002 and 2003 (with permission, from SAMSHA, 2003).*

significant only for Black/African Americans (from 9.7 percent to 8.7 percent). Comparable data for 2004 was recently released (SAMHSA, 2005). These data show few changes of significance from those of 2003. The percentage of Hispanic or Latino respondents to the survey who reported having used illicit drugs in the previous month dropped (from 8.0% to 7.2%), and the data for those of two or more races rose from 12.0 percent to 13.3 percent.

Data from the 2005 National Survey on Drug Use and Health reveal gender differences with regard to illegal drug use. Using the same question of illicit drug use within the previous month, a higher percentage of men (9.8) than women (6.1) agreed that they had used such drugs (SAMHSA, 2005). These data were consistent with those reported the previous two years. Males are almost twice as likely as females to use marijuana (8.0 to 4.3 percent). Women are much more likely than men to use antidepressant drugs, or sedatives prescribed for depression, anxiety, or sleep disorders, but there are no gender differences in the non-medical (illicit) use of prescription drugs (Simoni-Wastila, 1998). As it happens, once they begin using drugs, women are as likely as men to become addicted, but it appears that men are more likely to begin illicit drug use. Adolescent girls are more likely to have their first experience with illicit drugs in private or with a friend or two; whereas, boys are more likely to have their first encounter in larger social settings in the company of their peers (Van Etten & Anthony, 1999).

An interesting insight on gender differences and drug use is the relationship between "sex-linked" personality characteristics and substance use patterns. For example, (Kulis, Marsiglia, & Hecht, 2002) have shown that interpersonal dominance typically associated with masculinity predicted more substance use for adolescents of both genders; whereas, nurturing qualities that are often associated with femininity predicted refusals to offers to use illicit drugs. One feminist and gender socialization perspective suggests that young females' use of drugs may be related to self-image, weight loss, and depression, different causative factors from those for adolescent males (Slater, Guthrie, & Boyd, 2001).

Caucasians are significantly more likely than any other ethnic group to use alcohol (SAMHSA, 2005). Figure S-2 depicting alcohol use data for 2003 shows us that 54.4 percent of White Americans reported the use of alcohol, compared to 42.0 percent of American Indians or Alaska Natives, 41.5 percent of Hispanics, 39.8 percent of Asians, and 37.9 percent of African Americans during the month prior to the survey. Comparable data are reported for binge drinking (five or more drinks on at least one occasion in the 30 days prior to the survey) and heavy drinking (binge

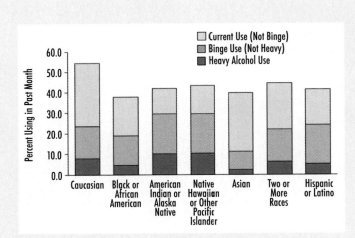

Figure S-2. *Current, binge, and heavy alcohol use among persons aged 12 or older, by race/ethnicity: 2003 (with permission, from SAMSHA, 2003).*

drinking on five or more days in the past month). These percentages were virtually unchanged in the 2004 data recently released. Data not reflected in Figure S-2 tell us that the rate of underage (and hence illicit) drinking remained relatively constant from 2002 through 2004, with about 10.8 million persons aged 12 to 20 reporting drinking alcohol in the month prior to the survey interview—and of these, 7.4 million were binge drinkers and 2.4 million met the criterion for "heavy drinking" (SAMHSA, 2005).

With regard to gender, males are more likely than females to consume alcohol. The 2003 National Survey on Drug Use and Health showed that 57.3 percent of males aged 12 or older were current drinkers compared with 43.2 percent of females in the same age group (SAMHSA, 2003). There may be gender-role expectations surrounding the use of alcohol and drugs. For example, personality variables such as behavioral aggression are associated with male use of alcohol, while emotional warmth and concern for others was inversely associated with alcohol use for females (Huselid & Cooper, 1992; Thomas, 1996).

CHAPTER SUMMARY

1. **Although it may be imprecise, present a characterization of normal, waking consciousness.**

   Consciousness is the awareness or perception of the world around us and of our own mental processes. William James described the four aspects of normal waking consciousness: 1) It is always changing (it cannot be held in mind to be studied). 2) Consciousness is a personal experience (each person's consciousness is different from every other person's). 3) Consciousness is continuous (it cannot be broken down into separate pieces). 4) Consciousness is selective (allowing one to selectively attend to some things while ignoring others).

2. **What is meant by "levels of consciousness," and how did Freud characterize such levels?**

   Levels of consciousness refer to the notion that we experience different degrees of awareness of self and the environment (e.g., wide-awake and attentive, wandering, sleepy). We perform at optimal levels when we are at the highest level of consciousness. At the unconscious level, we may be able to process information without being aware of the fact we have done so. Sometimes bits and pieces of experience enter our consciousness, without our paying attention to them.

   Freud believed that consciousness occurred on three levels: *conscious*, *preconscious*, and *unconscious*. He also argued that consciousness was much like an iceberg, with only a small portion (the conscious mind) above the surface. The conscious mind was said to represent the ideas, memories, feelings, and motives of which we are actively aware. Just below the waterline is the preconscious. In the preconscious are mental processes of which we are not immediately aware but which we can access quite easily (e.g., what we did yesterday). Deep under the water is the unconscious, containing ideas, desires, and memories and the like, of which we are not aware and cannot easily become aware

3. **What does research on phenomena such as subliminal perception and blindsight tell us about the unconscious processing of information?**

   Research suggests that unconscious processing of information is possible. In *subliminal perception*, a stimulus is flashed at a rate or intensity below one's threshold of detection. That is, the person is not consciously aware of it (reports no knowledge of the stimulus). Generally, subliminal processing of complex messages is not likely. However, we are sensitive to some stimuli presented below the level of awareness. The subliminal presentation of one word, for example, may influence one's perception of subsequently presented words. *Blindsight* also provides some evidence for unconscious processing. Blindsight may occur in a person who is blind due to damage to the primary visual area of the cerebral cortex. Even with such blindness, a person may, for example, correctly report the direction in which a dot of light is moving, while at the same time claiming not to "see" the light.

4. **Is there any evidence that the unconscious can be helpful in anything other than very simple tasks?**

   Recent evidence suggests that the unconscious processing of complex information is often used to help make decisions and solve problems. In fact, the unconscious processing of information actually may lead to improved decision-making and problem solving.

5. **Briefly describe the different stages of sleep and how they are measured.**

   The stages of sleep are measured using an EEG, or electroencephalogram, a device that measures electrical activity in the brain. In the period preceding sleep, while you are calm and relaxed, your brain produces alpha waves (8 to 12 cycles per second). Sleep has four stages, each with a distinct EEG pattern. In Stage 1 sleep, theta waves (4–7 cycles per second) replace alpha waves, heart rate slows, breathing becomes more regular, and blood pressure decreases. The eyes move slowly or remain still. A person awakened during Stage 1 sleep reports being in a light sleep or drifting off to sleep. During Stage 2 sleep, the EEG shows sleep spindles. Sleep spindles are brief, high amplitude bursts of electrical activity (12–14 cycles per second) that appear about every 15 seconds. During Stage 2, a person enters deeper sleep, but he or she still can be easily awakened. During Stage 3 sleep, high and slow delta waves (.5 to 4 cycles per second) comprise between 20 and 50 percent of the EEG pattern. A person's normal bodily functions slow during Stage 3 sleep, and it is difficult to wake a person at this stage. In Stage 4 sleep, the EEG shows a pattern comprised almost entirely of delta waves. Stage 4 sleep accounts for about 15 percent of a night's sleep.

6. **What is the difference between REM and NREM sleep?**

REM sleep refers to periods during which the sleeping person's eyes can be seen moving rapidly under his or her eyelids. Rapid Eye Movement (REM) sleep is the period during which vivid, story-like dreams occur. The eye movements are not associated with "watching" a dream, but are a by-product of brain activation. *NREM sleep (or non-REM sleep)* describes periods of sleep without these rapid eye movements. Persons awakened during NREM sleep report fewer and more fragmented dreams. Periods of REM sleep occur throughout the night and usually last between a few minutes and half an hour. The length of REM periods and the vividness of dreams increase as sleep progresses. REM sleep accounts for about 20 to 25 percent of the sleep of adults. Every person experiences REM sleep and dreams, but not everyone can remember dreams in the morning. Yet, during a normal night's sleep, each of us has several dreams. Unless we make a conscious effort to remember a dream, we are unlikely to do so. During REM sleep, muscles are totally relaxed (a condition called atonia), sex organs are aroused, blood pressure increases markedly, and breathing becomes shallow and irregular.

7. **How do Freud and Hobson characterize the content of dreams?**

Freud developed an elaborate system for explaining dreams. According to Freud, dreams originate in the unconscious and provide some keys to the unresolved conflicts that explain behaviors. Freud called the elements the dreamer was aware of and could recall *manifest content*. Using psychoanalysis, Freud and his disciples could decode dreams to reveal their hidden symbolic meanings. Freud called these hidden meanings *latent content*. More recently, Hobson developed the activation-synthesis theory. He did not attach any special hidden meanings to dreams. Instead, he suggested that dreams were caused by incidental activation of the visual system by lower brain centers and attempts of higher brain centers to synthesize (give meaning to) this near random neuronal activity.

8. **Describe the sleep disorders insomnia, narcolepsy, and sleep apnea.**

Insomnia is the inability to fall asleep or stay asleep. It may occur in brief episodes or become chronic, lasting for weeks or months. Insomnia may be brought on by anticipation of an important event, stress, illness, or drug use. Chronic insomnia affects about 30 million Americans. Women report more insomnia than men do. Older adults report more insomnia than younger adults. Interestingly, many people who report insomnia actually get more sleep than they think they do, a condition called pseudoinsomnia. Although many people take medications to sleep better, they may not get the relief they expect. Persons with insomnia can build tolerances for initially effective medications. When the insomnia sufferers stop taking these medications, they can rebound and find sleep even more elusive than before the medications started. Some medications also disrupt Stage 3 and Stage 4 sleep. For all these reasons, most sleep experts advise against long term use of sleep aids. Some cases of insomnia result from learning and perpetuating poor sleep habits. After sleeping poorly for a night or two, a person may begin to worry about not sleeping and the worry may become self fulfilling. Eventually, this person may develop negative thoughts, emotions, and behaviors related to sleep. Individuals experiencing this form of insomnia may benefit from cognitive and behavioral treatments.

Narcolepsy involves unintentionally falling asleep, even during the day. The symptoms of narcolepsy are excessive sleepiness, and muscle weakness or paralysis. Narcoleptics may experience paralysis or dreamlike hallucinations upon falling asleep or upon waking up. Although only 50,000 cases have been diagnosed, narcolepsy may affect as many as 350,000 Americans.

Sleep apnea involves periods of sleep during which the sleeper stops breathing entirely. Apnea appears mostly in obese, middle-aged males, but a form of apnea may be responsible for sudden infant death syndrome. Short episodes of sleep apnea are not dangerous, but long ones are obviously life threatening.

9. **What is hypnosis, who can be hypnotized, and for what purposes is hypnosis of value?**

Hypnosis is an induced state of consciousness under which a person is susceptible to suggestion. Only the willing can be hypnotized, and susceptibility to hypnosis varies from person to person. A person may be a better subject for hypnosis if he or she possesses a vivid imagination; a passive nature; a willingness to cooperate; a penchant for reading, running, or acting.

Hypnosis has been successfully used to help people manage pain. Although hypnosis is not a cure, it can help control pain. Hypnosis cannot improve memory for learned information (for example, for a test), nor can it make people recall long-forgotten childhood memories or past lives. However, hypnosis has been used to ease the anxiety surrounding the recall of emotionally traumatic events.

10. **What is meditation and what are its benefits?**

Meditation is a self-induced state of consciousness characterized by an extreme focusing of attention and relaxation. There are several types of meditation. The practice of transcendental meditation generally includes assuming a comfortable position, relaxing, and directing attention to a particular stimulus (like breathing) or to a softly spoken word called a mantra. When meditating, a person breathes more slowly and produces alpha waves on an EEG, indicating a relaxed state. Proponents of meditation claim that it is an easy way to relax. They also claim it can help a person cope better with stress, pressure, and threatening situations. Although meditation can be relaxing, it has not been scientifically proven to be better than other ways of relaxing.

11. **Describe and note the effect(s) on consciousness of these psychoactive drugs: caffeine, nicotine, cocaine, amphetamines, methamphetamine, alcohol, opiates, barbiturates, LSD, marijuana, and ecstasy.**

Psychoactive drugs are substances that influence psychological functioning. *Caffeine*, found in coffee, tea, colas, and chocolate, is characterized as a stimulant drug. It produces a heightened sense of arousal and an elevation of mood. Withdrawal effects are common after lengthy use of caffeine. *Nicotine* is a stimulant, commonly found in tobacco products. Even the tobacco companies admit that nicotine is an addictive drug. *Cocaine* is a highly addictive stimulant that produces a short-lived euphoria, or "high." The *amphetamines* (plural because there are several varieties) are synthetically produced stimulants once thought to mimic, but to be safer than, cocaine. They act on the body more slowly than cocaine does, but they still produce a sense of alertness and arousal that is relatively short-lived. Amphetamines seem to mask fatigue more than they create additional energy. *Methamphetamine* is a synthetic drug related to amphetamine but with greater potency and likelihood of inducing addiction.

Alcohol is a depressant. It reduces awareness and slows bodily functions. The most popular of the depressants, alcohol contributes to over 100,000 deaths each year in the United States. Whether a person becomes dependent upon alcohol seems to depend on both genetic and socio-cultural factors. *Opiates* (such as codeine and morphine) are called analgesics because of their pain-killing capabilities. They are addictive. *Heroin* is a very addictive opiate to which users quickly develop tolerance. Heroin users need ever increasing amounts of the drug to maintain the same level of pleasure and withdrawal symptoms are extreme. *Barbiturates* are synthetic sedatives of which there are many varieties. In small doses, barbiturates create a sense of calm and relaxation by slowing nervous system activity. In higher doses, they produce sleep and in sufficient doses they can even be fatal.

Hallucinogens (such as *LSD*) are drugs that alter mood and perceptions. They get their name from their ability to induce hallucinations (perceptual experiences without the benefit of sensory input). In short, users of hallucinogens have experiences unrelated to what is going on in their environment. Hallucinogens may intensify already unpleasant moods. The active ingredient in *marijuana* is the chemical compound THC. Smoking marijuana may be more dangerous to the respiratory system than is the smoking of regular cigarettes, but research also tells us that it does not increase the risk of developing lung cancer. Long-term marijuana use has been associated with impaired judgment, unrealistic mood, impaired coordination, and hallucinations. Early marijuana use has been associated with later use and abuse of other psychoactive drugs. Marijuana may also impair the immune system and have negative consequences when taken a short time before pregnancy or during pregnancy. *Ecstasy* is a drug with the qualities of amphetamines and hallucinogens that produces feelings of emotional openness, reduces critical thoughts, and decreases inhibitions. Ecstasy creates feelings of euphoria and makes users more open and trusting of others. The drug has short- and long-term negative physical side effects (e.g., nausea, blurred vision, rapid eye movement, faintness, and chills or sweating) and negative psychological side effects (e.g., confusion, sleep problems, depression, and severe anxiety).

5

Learning

PREVIEW

Directly or indirectly, learning influences every aspect of our being. Learning affects how we perceive the world, how we interact with it as we grow and develop, how we form social relationships, and how we change during psychotherapy. As we said in Chapter 1, who we are reflects the interaction of our biological/genetic constitution and our learning experiences. Indeed, the human organism is poorly suited to survive without learning. If we are to survive, much less prosper, we must profit from our experiences.

In this chapter we begin by considering how psychologists define learning. Learning surely produces changes in an organism's psychological functions (affect, behavior, and/or cognition), but we will see that some such changes can be attributed to processes other than learning. We begin our discussion with a simple form of learning, called classical conditioning. (Although *learning* and *conditioning* are technically not synonymous, they can be used interchangeably. We follow common usage here by referring to the most basic and fundamental type of learning as *conditioning*.) Most of our descriptions will be based on the work of pioneering psychologist Ivan Pavlov. In fact, many psychologists refer to classical conditioning as "Pavlovian conditioning" in his honor. The essential processes of classical conditioning are straightforward, and we will illustrate them by talking about dogs learning to salivate when bells ring. Don't worry. Before we are through, we will show how important Pavlov's salivating dogs are to our everyday human experiences.

We then turn our attention to operant conditioning and observational learning. In operant conditioning, what matters most are the consequences of an organism's behaviors. The premise of operant conditioning is that behaviors are shaped by the consequences that they have produced in the past. Learning becomes a matter of increasing the rate of those responses that produce positive consequences and decreasing the occurrence of those behaviors that produce negative consequences. We shall see that much of human behavior can be explained in terms of operant conditioning.

We begin by defining some basic terms. What is operant conditioning and how might it be demonstrated? As we did with classical conditioning, we will take a close look at a laboratory demonstration of operant conditioning, and, because the concept of reinforcement is so central in operant conditioning, we will spend a good deal of time examining some of the principles of reinforcement—and punishment.

Chapter 5 closes with a brief discussion of some cognitive approaches to learning. Classical conditioning and operant conditioning focus entirely on observable changes in behavior. By definition, cognitive approaches consider relatively permanent changes in the thinking of an organism that may or may not be observable in that organism's behavior. We focus on the cognitive and social aspects of Bandura's Theory of Observational Learning.

WHAT IS LEARNING?

Undoubtedly, learning is a critical psychological process. Psychologists say that **learning** is demonstrated by a relatively permanent change in behavior that occurs as the result of practice or experience. This standard definition raises some points worth exploring.

First, when we say that learning is *demonstrated by* a change in behavior, we mean that learning (like many psychological processes) cannot be observed directly. Literally, no one can directly observe, or measure, what you have learned. Thus, we distinguish between "learning," which is an internal process

| **learning** a process demonstrated by a relatively permanent change in behavior that occurs as the result of practice or experience

that is not observable and "perform-ance," which is overt, observable behav-ior. All we can measure directly is your performance, or behavior. To determine if you have learned, we ask you to per-form, to do something, and then make inferences about your learning based upon your performance. Unfortunately, performance does not always adequately reflect learning. For example, you may learn a great deal while studying for a test. However, you may test poorly because you are ill, anxious, or distracted. This example works both ways. Occa-sionally a non-studying student may do reasonably well on a multiple-choice test by making a few lucky guesses.

Learned changes in behavior are *rel-atively permanent*. That is, they are not fleeting, short-lived, or cyclical changes, such as those due to fatigue or brief shifts in motivation. For example, a typ-ical typist increases keyboarding effi-ciency between 8 AM and 10 AM. The improvement should not be attributed to learning, but to *warm-up*. That same typist might not function as well at the end of the day—a change in behavior

better attributed to fatigue than to for-getting. These are measurable changes in behavior, but they are not due to learn-ing because learned changes are rela-tively permanent.

Learned changes in behavior result from *practice* or *experience*. Yet, some other behavioral changes may be due to maturation. The fact that birds fly, sala-manders swim, or humans walk has more to do with genes and physical develop-ment than with learning. Indeed, some changes in our behaviors are due to auto-matic physiological reactions and are not learned. For example, we do not learn to see in the dark when we enter a dark the-atre. A series of automatic physiological changes causes our eyes to adapt.

As students, we are in the habit of seeing all learning as good. Yet, this is not always the case. We can learn mal-adaptive, ineffective habits just as read-ily as we learn good, adaptive ones. No one really enjoyed the first cigarette that he or she smoked. Yet many people have learned the very maladaptive habit. Learning is simply reflected in a change in behavior, be it for better or worse.

Courtesy of Larry Bray/Getty Images.

We tend to think of learning as a good thing–and usually it is. However, it also is true that people learn all sorts of behav-iors or habits that are ineffec-tive or downright maladaptive. Hardly anyone can clam to truly have enjoyed their first cigarette, but (sadly) many peo-ple have learned the habit and, having done so, find it difficult to quit.

BEFORE YOU GO ON

1. How do psychologists define learning?

A Point to Ponder or Discuss
How could you demonstrate whether an observed behavior—say a chick's pecking at pieces of grain—
was learned or inherited?

THE BASICS OF CLASSICAL CONDITIONING

classical conditioning a learning process in which a neutral stimulus is paired with a stimulus that reliably elicits an unconditioned response

When we think about learning, we typically think of such things as memorizing the Bill of Rights, studying for an exam, or learning to drive a car. However, our study of learning begins in a less common setting: over a hundred years ago in the laboratory of a Russian physiologist who taught dogs to salivate in response to tones. How salivating dogs illuminate the way humans learn is difficult to imagine, but please be patient.

Late in the nineteenth century, Ivan Pavlov was studying digestion—work for which he would be awarded a Nobel Prize in 1904. Pavlov focused on the salivation reflex in dogs. He knew that he could get his dogs to salivate by forcing food powder into their mouths. He measured the number of drops of saliva that were produced each time food powder was introduced. Salivation is a reflex—an unlearned, automatic response that occurs in the presence of a specific stimulus. Every time Pavlov presented the food powder, his dogs salivated.

Pavlov then made one of the more important discoveries in psychology. He noticed that his dogs sometimes began salivating *before* he put food in their mouths. They would salivate at the sight of the food or at the sight of the laboratory assistant who usually delivered the food. In fact, it was not Pavlov, but one of his laboratory assistants, S. G. Vul'fson, who first made this observation (Domjan, 2005; Toades,

1997). Understanding and explaining his lab assistant's observation and its implications for behavior became Pavlov's lifelong goals (1927, 1928). The phenomenon he studied is now called **classical conditioning,** (or Pavlovian conditioning), a learning process in which a neutral stimulus (for example, Vul'fson) is paired with a stimulus (for example, the food) that elicits an unconditioned response (for example, salivation). After conditioning, the neutral stimulus (Vul'fson) alone elicits a new, conditioned response (salivation), much like the original unconditioned response. In the abstract that may not make much sense, but as we go through the process step by step, you will come to realize that classical conditioning is simple and straightforward.

To demonstrate classical conditioning, we first need a stimulus that consistently produces a predictable response. The relationship between this stimulus and the response it elicits is usually an unlearned, reflexive one. Given this stimulus, the same response always follows. Here is where the food powder comes in. If we present the food powder to a dog, the salivation reliably follows. We call the stimulus an unconditioned stimulus (UCS) and the response to it an unconditioned response (UCR). A UCS (food powder) produces a UCR (salivation) with no prior learning. That is, a dog does not need to learn to salivate at food. It happens naturally. Thus, anytime you see the term "unconditioned" you will know that there is no learning involved.

Russian physiologist Ivan P. Pavlov (center), surrounded by some of his students and associates, observes a dog in a testing apparatus.

Courtesy of Bettmann/Corbis.

Now we need a neutral stimulus that, when presented, produces a minimal response, or a response of no particular interest. For this neutral stimulus, Pavlov chose a tone. At first, when you sound a tone, a dog will respond. It will perk up its ears and orient itself toward the sound. We call this response an **orienting reflex**, a simple, unlearned response of attending to a new or unusual stimulus. Imagine students sitting in class while repairs are going on in the hallway. Occasionally, a hammering sound occasionally attracts the attention of students, and they reflexively orient toward the noise.

Pavlov found that after hearing the tone for a while, the dog would get used to the tone and ignore it. This process is called **habituation**, a simple form of learning in which an organism comes to disregard a stimulus of little or no consequence. Essentially, the dog learns not to orient toward the tone. (Just as students habituate to the hammering and no longer orient toward it.) We are ready to go. We have two stimuli: a tone that produces a minimal response and food powder (UCS) that reliably produces salivation (UCR).

Neutral Stimulus (NS)⟶No Response
    (a tone)   (no salivation)

UCS ⟶ UCR
(food powder)   (salivation)

Once we get our stimuli and responses straight, the rest is easy. Next, you pair the two stimuli. That is, they are presented at about the same time—the tone first, then the food. The salivation then occurs automatically in response to the food. We have a neutral stimulus, then a UCS, followed by the UCR (or tone-food-salivation).

Neutral
Stimulus (NS) + UCS ⟶ UCR
  (a tone)   (food powder) (salivation)

Each pairing of the two stimuli is a conditioning trial. Over several trials conditioning, or learning, takes place and a relatively permanent change in behavior results. After a number of trials, the tone by itself makes the dog salivate. Now the dog salivates to both the food powder and the tone. The tone is no longer "neutral" because it produces a response, so we call the tone a conditioned stimulus (CS). To keep the salivation response the tone elicits separate from the salivation response the food powder produces, we call salivating to the tone a conditioned response (CR), indicating that it has been conditioned, or learned. Thus, the term "conditioned" deals with the learned part of classical conditioning.

CS ⟶ CR
(a tone)   (salivation)

orienting reflex a simple, unlearned response of attending to a new or unusual stimulus

habituation a simple form of learning in which an organism comes to disregard a stimulus of little or no consequence

Let's review:

1. We start with two stimuli: the neutral stimulus (soon to be the CS), which elicits no UCR, and the UCS, which elicits the UCR.
2. We repeatedly present the CS and UCS together.
3. As a result, when we present the CS alone, it now elicits a CR.

The same type of stimulus—a tone, for example—can be either a neutral stimulus (before learning occurs) or a conditioned stimulus (when it elicits a learned response). Similarly, the same type of response (salivation, for example) can be either an unconditioned response (if it is elicited without learning) or a conditioned response (if it is elicited as the result of learning).

If you have a pet, you have no doubt seen classical conditioning. You may have observed your pet exhibit a range of excited, anticipatory behaviors every time it hears you open the cabinet where its food is kept. The open door (CS) was paired with the food inside (UCS), which produces the same sort of reaction (CR) that was originally reserved for the food (UCR).

Classical conditioning occurs not only in dogs and cats, but in humans also. You demonstrate a classically conditioned response when pictures or aromas of your favorite foods cause you to salivate. If you become worried when you see your instructor enter the classroom carrying exam papers, you are displaying a classically conditioned response.

There are two technical points we need to make. The CR and UCR are not identical. The CR is usually weaker than the UCR no matter how many times the CS and the UCS are paired. For example, a dog will not produce as much saliva in response to the tone (as a CR) as it once did in response to the food powder (as a UCR). Second, how you pair the conditioned stimulus and the unconditioned stimulus matters. You can present two stimuli at about the same time in many different ways: simultaneously, UCS then CS, CS then UCS, and with varying time intervals in between. Of all the alternatives, the method that consistently works best is CS followed within a second or so by the UCS, or, again, tone-food-salivation. (You may think of it this way: Classical conditioning is a matter of "ding—food—slobber.")

BEFORE YOU GO ON

2. Describe how dogs can be classically conditioned to salivate at the sound of a tone.

A Point to Ponder or Discuss
Unconditioned responses are those that reliably and naturally occur in the presence of stimuli without any previous learning. How many unconditioned responses in humans can you list?

PROCESSES AND PHENOMENA OF CLASSICAL CONDITIONING

Now that we have covered the basics of classical conditioning, we can examine a classical conditioning experiment.

Acquisition

Acquisition is the stage of classical conditioning during which the CS and UCS are paired and the strength of the CR increases (for example, a dog acquires the response of salivating to a tone). When conditioning begins, the

acquisition the stage of classical conditioning during which the CS and the UCS are paired and the strength of the CR increases

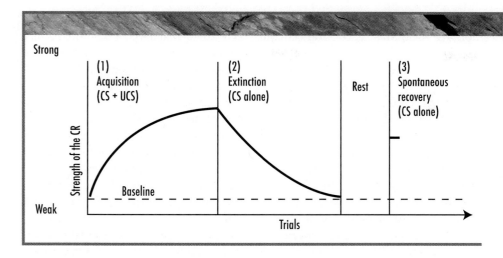

FIGURE 5.1

*The stages of conditioning
(1) Acquisition is produced by
the repeated pairing of a CS
and a UCS. The strength of
the CR increases, rapidly at
first, then slows, and eventually levels off. (2) Extinction is
produced by presenting the CS
without pairing it with the
UCS. The strength of the CR
then decreases. (3) After a rest
interval; (and following
extinction), spontaneous recovery is demonstrated by a partial return of the CR.*

extinction the stage of classical conditioning in which the
strength of the CR decreases
with repeated presentations of
the CS alone

conditioned stimulus (CS) does not produce a conditioned response (CR),
which is why we refer to it as a neutral
stimulus at this point. After a few pairings of the CS and UCS (conditioning
trials), we can demonstrate the presence
of a CR. To do that, of course, we will
have to present the conditioned stimulus (CS) by itself. We now discover that
there is some saliva produced in
response to the tone presented alone.
The more trials of the CS and UCS
together, the more the dog salivates in
response to the tone presented alone.
Over repeated trials, the strength of the
CR (the amount of saliva produced in
response to the tone) increases rapidly
at first, then slows, and eventually levels off (Figure 5.1).

Extinction and Spontaneous Recovery

Assume we have a well-conditioned dog
producing a strong CR. Continuing to
present the CS-UCS pair adds little to
the amount of saliva we get when we
present the CS alone. Now we go
through a series of trials during which
the CS (the tone) is presented but is *not*
paired with the UCS (food powder). The
result is that the CR will weaken. As we
continue to present the tone without following it with food powder, the CR
becomes progressively weaker; the dog
salivates less and less and eventually will

stop salivating to the tone. This is called
extinction—the process in which the
strength of a CR decreases with repeated
presentations of the CS alone (that is, the
tone without the food powder).

It would appear that we are right
back where we started. Because we have
extinguished the CR, our dog no longer
salivates when we present the tone. Let's
return our dog to the kennel for a rest.
Later, when the dog comes back to the
laboratory and we sound the tone, the
dog salivates again! Not a lot, perhaps,
but the salivation returns, or recovers. It
recovers automatically, or spontaneously,
so we call this phenomenon spontaneous recovery. Figure 5.1 illustrates
extinction and spontaneous recovery.

Spontaneous recovery is the return
of the extinguished CR after a rest interval. Spontaneous recovery has two
important implications. First, one series
of extinction trials may not be sufficient
to eliminate a conditioned response.
Because of the possibility of spontaneous recovery, we may need several
series of extinction trials to overcome the
conditioned response. Second, what
happens during extinction is not "forgetting"—at least not in the usual
sense. The conditioned response is not
forgotten; it is *suppressed*. That is, the
learned salivation response (CR) is still
there, but it is not showing up in performance during extinction, which is
why it can (and does) return later in

spontaneous recovery the
stage of classical conditioning
that occurs after extinction and
following a rest interval in
which the extinguished CR
automatically reappears in
response to the CS

stimulus generalization a process in classical conditioning in which a conditioned response is elicited by stimuli similar to the original CS

spontaneous recovery. Another indication that the learned association between the CS (e.g., the tone) and the UCS (e.g., the food powder) is not lost during extinction is that relearning is always faster (takes fewer trials) than the initial learning. That is, if we again pair the CS with the UCS, relearning of the CR takes fewer trials than the original acquisition—even though there was no indication of a CR at the end of extinction. On the contrary, if we continue to present the CS alone (without the UCS) after spontaneous recovery, the strength of the CR diminishes as it did during extinction.

Generalization and Discrimination

During the course of conditioning, assume we consistently use a tone of a given pitch as the conditioned stimulus. After repeated pairings of this tone with food powder, a dog salivates when the tone is presented alone. What will happen if we present a tone that the dog has not heard before? Typically, the dog will salivate in response to the new tone also. This response will probably not be as strong as the original CR (there may not be as much saliva). How strong it will

be depends on how similar the new tone is to the original CS. The more similar the new tone is to the original, the more saliva will be produced. This is **stimulus generalization**—a process by which a conditioned response is elicited by stimuli similar to the original CS.

An unconditioned stimulus need not be paired with all possible conditioned stimuli. If you choose a mid-range tone as a CS, a conditioned response automatically generalizes to other, similar tones. If a dog is conditioned to salivate to a tone of middle pitch, it will also salivate to higher and lower tones through generalization (Figure 5.2). Notice that the CR gets weaker and weaker as the new CS differs more and more from the original CS tone. This phenomenon is called the *generalization gradient.*

Discrimination learning, on the other hand, occurs when the dog learns to discriminate between different stimuli, emitting the CR in the presence of some stimuli and not others. In a sense, generalizing a response from one stimulus to others is the opposite of coming to discriminate among them. To produce discrimination learning, we would present a dog with many tones, but would pair the UCS food powder with only one of them—the CS to which we

discrimination learning a process in classical conditioning in which an organism learns to discriminate between different stimuli, emitting a CR in response to some stimuli, but not to others

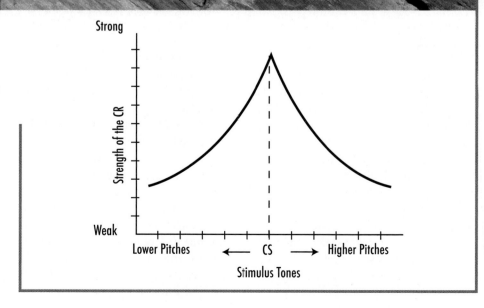

FIGURE 5.2

The generalization gradient. Presenting stimuli other than the CS may produce a CR. How much conditioned response is produced depends on the similarity between the new stimulus and the original CS.

want the dog to salivate. For example, we might pair food powder with a tone of middle C. A lower tone, say, A, would also be presented to the dog but would not be followed by food powder. At first the dog would salivate some in response to the lower tone (stimulus generalization), but eventually our dog would learn to discriminate and stop salivating to the A.

BEFORE YOU GO ON

3. What are acquisition, extinction, spontaneous recovery, generalization and discrimination, and how are they demonstrated in classical conditioning?

A Point to Ponder or Discuss
Are there examples of stimulus generalization and discrimination in your everyday life? Can you identify a voice on the telephone? Can you tell one brand of spaghetti sauce from another? How might these be examples of classical conditioning?

THE SIGNIFICANCE OF CLASSICAL CONDITIONING

It is time to leave our discussion of dogs, tones, salivation, and Pavlov's laboratory and turn our attention to the practical application of classical conditioning. Examples of classically conditioned human behaviors are everywhere. Many of our physiological reactions have been classically conditioned to certain stimuli in our environments. As we have noted, the sights or aromas of certain foods may produce a CR of salivation or of hunger pangs. The sight, sound, or mention of some (food-related) stimuli may produce a rumbling nausea in the pit of the stomach. Certain stimuli can make us sleepy. In addition, in each case the response is not naturally occurring, but has been learned, or classically conditioned.

One of the more significant aspects of classical conditioning is its role in the development of emotional responses to stimuli in our environment. Few stimuli naturally, or instinctively, produce an emotional response. Yet think of all the things that do directly influence how we feel. For example, very young children seldom seem afraid of spiders, snakes, or airplane rides. (Some children actually seem to enjoy them.) How many adults do you know who have learned to be afraid of these things? There are many stimuli in our environments that evoke fear. There are stimuli that produce feelings of pleasure, calm, and relaxation. What scares you? What makes you feel relaxed? Why? Might you feel upset in a certain store because of an unpleasant experience you once had there? Might you happily anticipate a trip to the beach because of a very enjoyable vacation you had there as a child? Do you shudder at the sight of a police car or smile at the thought of a payroll envelope? In each case, your response may have been classically conditioned. (Of course, not all our learned emotional reactions are classically conditioned.)

Classical conditioning is relevant to our everyday lives. It also continues to intrigue psychologists searching to understand its underlying processes (Domjan, 2005; Pearce & Bouton, 2001). Psychologists also are interested in finding new ways to apply conditioning in the real world. In this section, we briefly explore a few examples of classic and contemporary work in classical conditioning.

A Classic Example: The Case of "Little Albert"

In 1920, John B. Watson (yes, the founder of behaviorism) and his student assistant, Rosalie Rayner, published a summary research article about their attempts to classically condition a child nicknamed "Little Albert." Although Watson and Rayner's summary oversimplified matters (Samuelson, 1980), the Little Albert project involved the classical conditioning of an emotional response—fear.

Watson and Rayner gave eleven-month-old Albert many toys to play with. Among other things, he was allowed to play with a live white rat. Albert showed no apparent sign of fearing it. At this point, the rat was a neutral stimulus (NS) with respect to fear. Then conditioning began. One day as Albert reached for the rat, Rayner made a sudden, loud noise by striking a metal bar with a hammer. The loud noise frightened Albert. Two months earlier Watson and Rayner had established that a sudden loud noise would frighten Albert. At least he behaved in a way that Watson and Rayner felt indicated fear.

After repeated pairings of the rat and the loud noise, Albert's reaction to the rat underwent a relatively permanent change. At first, Albert would start to reach toward the rat, but then he would recoil and cry, often trying to bury his head in his blanket. He was making emotional responses to a previously neutral stimulus (NS) that did not elicit those responses before it was paired with a sudden loud noise. This pairing sounds like classical conditioning: The rat is the CS and the sudden loud noise is the UCS that elicits the UCR of an emotional fear response. After repeated pairings of the rat and the noise (CS and UCS), the rat elicits the same sort of fear response (or CR). The procedures used to condition Little Albert are depicted in Figure 5.3.

Watson and Rayner then demonstrated that Albert's fear of the white rat generalized to all sorts of stimuli: a dog (in fact, a brown, spotted dog, not a white one), a ball of cotton, even a Santa Claus mask with a white beard and mustache. In some cases, however, Watson and Rayner did not test for generalization as they should have. They occasionally paired the loud noise (UCS) with new stimuli before testing to see what Little Albert's reaction might have been (Harris, 1979).

Several issues have been raised concerning Watson and Rayner's demonstration of learned fear—not the least of

FIGURE 5.3

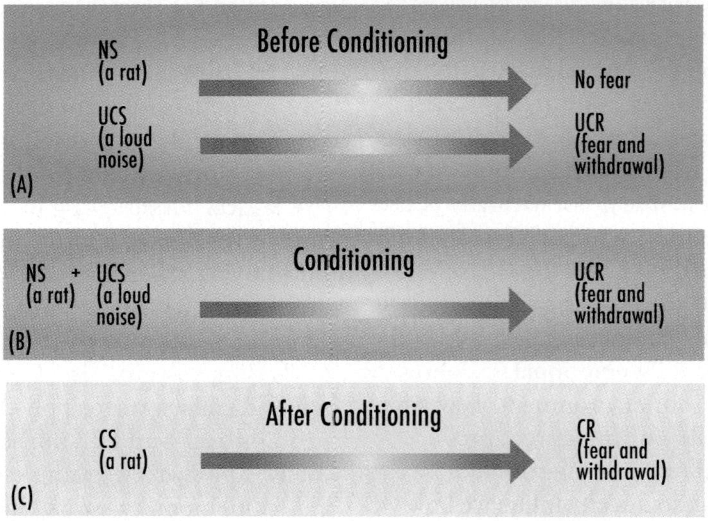

Conditioning Little Albert to fear a neutral stimulus (NS) by pairing it with a fear-producing stimulus (UCS). The NS becomes a CS when it has been associated with the UCS and will come to elicit a learned fear response (CR).

which is the unethical treatment of Albert. It is unlikely that anyone would attempt such a project today. Watson had previously argued (1919) that emotional experiences of early childhood could affect an individual for a lifetime, yet he purposely frightened a young child (and without the advised consent of the boy's mother). Albert's mother took him home before Watson and Rayner had a chance to undo the conditioning. They were convinced that they could reverse Little Albert's fear, but as fate would have it, they never got the chance. A number of researchers who tried to replicate Watson and Rayner's experiment, despite the ethical considerations, were not very successful (Harris, 1979).

Even with these disclaimers, it is easy to see how the Little Albert demonstration can be used as a model for how fear or any other emotional response can develop. When the project began, Albert didn't respond fearfully to a rat, a cotton ball, or a Santa Claus mask. After a few trials of pairing a neutral stimulus (the rat) with an emotion-producing stimulus (the loud noise), Albert appeared to be afraid of all sorts of white, fuzzy objects.

BEFORE YOU GO ON

4. Briefly describe Watson and Rayner's "Little Albert" demonstration.

A Point to Ponder or Discuss
Consider those stimuli that frighten you. Is your fear an unlearned, natural reaction or conditioned? Can you recollect the circumstances in which any of your fear responses were conditioned to the stimuli that elicit them?

An Application: Treating Fear

Many things in this world are life threatening and downright frightening. Being afraid of some stimuli is an adaptive, rational, and wise reaction. Occasionally, however, some people experience distressing fears of stimuli that are not threatening in any real or rational sense. Some people are intensely afraid of heights, spiders, the dark, riding on elevators, or flying. Psychologists say that these people are suffering from a **phobic disorder**—an intense, irrational fear of an object or event that leads a person to avoid contact with it. There are many possible explanations for how phobic disorders occur, but one likely explanation is classical conditioning. This accounting for phobias suggests that a previously neutral stimulus (a spider, for example) is associated with a fear-inducing event (perhaps a painful spider bite). Through a process of association, the previously neutral stimulus (the CS) comes to elicit a fear response that, through generalization, all sorts of spiders and bugs may also elicit the fear response.

Classical conditioning is an effective way to treat fears and phobias. Mary Cover Jones (1924) made one of the earliest attempts to apply classical conditioning to the elimination of a fear. Jones worked with a young boy with a fear of rabbits. Jones began pairing a pleasing food with the presence of the rabbit. By itself, the food did not elicit fear, but rather feelings of pleasure. By pairing the food with the rabbit, Jones conditioned the boy to substitute pleasure for fear in the presence of the rabbit. Over 30 years later, Joseph Wolpe described in detail how classical conditioning could be used to treat fears (1958, 1969, 1981, 1997). Wolpe's technique is called **systematic desensitization**. Its goal is to gradually teach a patient to associate positive feelings with a previously feared stimulus.

phobic disorder an intense, irrational fear of an object or event that leads a person to avoid contact with it

systematic desensitization a process for treating phobias in which the goal is to gradually teach (through classical conditioning) a patient to associative positive feelings and relaxation with a previously feared stimulus

There are three stages of systematic desensitization. First, the therapist instructs or trains the client to relax. Relaxing can be difficult, but most clients can learn to enter a relaxed state quickly with minimal training. The second stage is to construct an "anxiety hierarchy"—a list of stimuli that gradually decrease in their ability to elicit anxiety. For example, a hierarchy for a person attempting to overcome a fear of speaking in public might include the following: giving a formal speech to a large group, being called on in class, talking to a small group of strangers, being introduced to two people, talking with friends, talking to a friend on the phone. The third stage involves conditioning.

The client relaxes completely and thinks about the stimulus that is lowest on the anxiety hierarchy. The client is then to think about the next higher stimulus, and the next, and so on, all the while remaining as relaxed as possible. As they move up the list, the therapist monitors the client's level of tension. If anxiety seems to be overcoming relaxation, the client is told to stop and move back down the hierarchy to a less anxiety-provoking item.

Systematic desensitization is more than the simple extinction of a previously conditioned fear response. A new response (relaxation) is acquired to replace the old one (fear). This process is called *counter-conditioning* and works on the premise that a person cannot be both relaxed and anxious at the same time. If a stimulus is repeatedly paired with being relaxed, classical conditioning will produce calm. For many people, systematic desensitization can be effective. It works best for fears or anxieties associated with specific, easily identifiable stimuli; it is less successful for a diffuse, generalized fear, for which hierarchies are difficult to generate. Because it is simple, straightforward, and, after all, a relaxing procedure, systematic desensitization works particularly well for older patients with phobias (Pagoto et al., 2006). It has even proven effective as a means of training (classically conditioning) autistic children to remain calm and relaxed in the presence of loud noises, often a very aversive stimulus for such children (Koegel, Openden, & Koegel, 2007).

Classical Conditioning's Role in Drug Addiction

In Chapter 4, we defined drug addiction as the joint occurrence of tolerance and withdrawal symptoms. Tolerance is said to occur when more and more of a substance (say, a drug such as caffeine or heroin) is needed to arrive at a set, desired reaction. Withdrawal symptoms include all sorts of negative reactions (such as depression, cramps, or agitation) that occur when a person stops using a drug.

Some tolerance to a drug's use can be biological. The body may increase its ability to break down and rid itself of a drug. Increased use of a drug also may produce changes in synaptic activity. Indeed, a significant part of drug tolerance may be psychological and based upon classical conditioning (Carroll, 2003; Crombag & Robinson, 2004; Robinson & Berridge, 2003; Woods & Ramsey, 2000).

Shepard Siegel and his colleagues have done much of the work connecting addiction and classical conditioning

Classical conditioning can play a part in drug addiction. If the same location is repeatedly associated with the use of a drug, more and more of that drug will be needed to reach a desired "effect"—a conditioned tolerance. If the user then tries that same amount of drug in a totally new environment, the dosage may be deadly.

Courtesy of Katy Winn/Corbis.

(Siegel et al., 2000; Siegel & Ramos, 2002; Siegel, 2005). When drug addicts take their drugs in the same environment (a common phenomenon), aspects of that environment can become stimuli that produce a classically conditioned response that leads to tolerance. In that same environment (a complex CS), a larger and larger dose is needed to produce the full effect desired by the user. The stimuli in that familiar environment produce an anticipatory reaction opposite to the drug's reaction (as if to prepare the user's body for what is about to occur). Indeed, under normal conditions, the body's attempts to anticipate and adapt are useful survival skills (Domjan, 2005).

If the drug user chooses to use in a new environment, however, he or she will be without the stimuli for the conditioned tolerance and without the learned compensatory reaction. As a result, in this new environment, the same (usual) amount of drug can cause a potentially fatal overdose. In one study of ten former heroin addicts who had nearly died of drug overdoses, Siegel (1984) found that seven of the ten had changed something about the circumstances in which they used the heroin—and those changes were nearly fatal because the environmental cues were not present to produce the usual classically conditioned tolerance reactions.

Given the role of conditioning in drug tolerance, it would behoove drug addiction therapists to consider conditioning when treating drug addiction. In fact, some researchers suggest that drug addiction therapists should extinguish the association between environmental stimuli present when an addict uses a drug and the physical reaction to the drug as part of addiction therapy (Conklin, 2006; Milekie et al., 2006; Siegel, 2005).

A Question: Can Any Stimulus Serve as a CS?

Pavlov and generations of psychologists after him believed that any stimulus paired with an unconditioned stimulus could serve as an effective conditioned stimulus. It is easy to see how they came to this conclusion because a wide variety of stimuli *can* be paired with food powder and, as a result, come to elicit salivation.

Yet we now know that pairings must be made with care if classical conditioning is to result. Not every stimulus pairs with an unconditioned stimulus to produce classical conditioning. For example, a rat can be conditioned to fear the sound of a tone by presenting that tone and following it with an electric shock. It does not take many pairings of the tone and the shock for the conditioned response (fear of tone) to develop—a straightforward example of classical conditioning. Assume we take a second rat and present it with a tone followed by a shock. However, from time to time, we give the rat the shock without the preceding tone. Yet, we see to it that both rats get an equal number of tone-shock pairings. Will this second rat demonstrate a conditioned response to the tone presented alone? No, it won't. Although this second rat experienced the same number of tone-shock pairings, it will not be conditioned (Rescorla, 1968, 1987; 1988; 2000).

As our example illustrates, the capacity of a stimulus to act as a CS depends upon the extent to which that stimulus predicts another stimulus (Rescorla & Wagner, 1972). In the original Pavlovian demonstration, the tone was highly informative. Every time the tone was presented, food powder followed. As a result, the tone was an effective CS. Rescorla's experiments show that if a tone does not reliably predict a shock (some shocks occur without the preceding tone), that tone will not be an effective CS no matter how many times it is paired with the UCS.

If dogs and rats can learn which stimuli predict other stimuli, isn't it reasonable to think humans also capable of being similarly conditioned? We may experience a pleasant feeling when we see a picture of a mountain stream because the stream is associated with a favorite vacation. The fact that we left for that vacation on a Tuesday is not relevant. Mountain streams predict fun and good times; Tuesdays do not. We have not been conditioned to associate a fireplace mantle with the pain of being burned, even though we may have received our first burn from a fire in fireplace. Little Albert's fear of a rat generalized to many stimuli, but he did not develop a fear of blankets, even though he was sitting on one every time Rayner created the loud noise that Albert came to associate with the rat.

Think back to the early discussion in Chapter One of the *functional psychologists*. One of their premises was that psychologists should study those processes (mostly mental) that functioned to help an organism survive and thrive in its environment. It is in this spirit that several researchers have come to focus on classical conditioning's usefulness for survival—what they call a "functional perspective" on Pavlovian conditioning (Domjan, 2005; Hollis, 1997). From a functional point of view it makes perfect sense that the most effective conditioned stimuli would be those that already occur naturally in the environment, already paired with (perhaps minimally so) unconditioned stimuli. The rattling sound of a rattlesnake is an obvious example of a potential CS. With training and practice, other cues, like the shape of the snake's head or the pattern of the multi-colored scales on its back could also come to act as conditioned stimuli. The short of it is this: Some stimuli—naturally—make better conditioned stimuli than others.

Must the CS–UCS Interval Be Brief?

Pavlov thought that the time between CS and UCS was a critical variable in classical conditioning. For nearly 50 years researchers assumed the most appropriate interval between the CS and UCS was a very brief one—a few seconds at most. Learning textbooks taught that the shorter the interval between the

CS and UCS, the faster conditioning would be. Yet, newer research on how taste aversions (strong dislikes) are formed has uncovered an example of classical conditioning that challenges the assumption that the CS–UCS interval must be brief.

Many experiments have confirmed that rats and people (and other animals) can be classically conditioned to avoid particular foods (Garcia et al., 1966; Gemberling & Domjan, 1982; Revulsky & Garcia, 1970). For example, rats eat a food with a distinctive taste and are subsequently given a poison or treated with X-rays so that they develop nausea. However, the nausea does not occur until hours after the food has been eaten. (In a few days, the rats are perfectly normal and healthy again.) Even though there has been a long delay between the flavored food (CS) and the feelings of nausea (UCS), the rats learn to avoid the food, often in just one trial. Patients taking chemotherapy may experience nausea as side effect and can develop a strong taste aversion for the particular food they ate hours before treatment—even if that food was something pleasant, such as ice cream (Bernstein, 1978).

Courtesy of Jon Feingersh/zefa/Corbis.

Someone eats a huge meal and a few hours later develops severe stomach cramps. The classical conditioning of taste aversion tells us that the person is much more likely to associate the discomfort and illness with what was eaten rather than with any of the other stimuli that were present during the meal.

The time between CS and UCS in taste aversion studies contradicts the assumption that the CS and UCS need to be presented together to be effective. A related issue is why the taste of previously eaten food should so commonly serve as the CS for nausea that occurs hours later. That is, why is the nausea associated with the taste of food instead of some other stimulus event? Imagine this scenario: You order a piece of pumpkin pie at a restaurant. Hours later, you suffer severe stomach cramps and nausea. Why are you likely to associate your illness with the food you ate but not the chair you sat on or the music you heard during dinner? At least part of the answer is that we may have a biological predisposition, a bias, for making some associations easily (for example, taste and nausea), and others with difficulty or not at all (for example, music and nausea). As we pointed out in the previous section, associations with a functional basis may be among those that are easily formed (Domjan, 2005; Shettleworth, 2001). Food followed by nausea is an association made easily because it is biologically adaptive to learn quickly not to eat certain things.

BEFORE YOU GO ON

5. How can classical conditioning be used in the treatment of phobias?
6. What role might classical conditioning play in drug addiction?
7. What makes a stimulus a good candidate to be a conditioned stimulus?
8. Does the interval between the CS and UCS always have to be brief?

A Point to Ponder or Discuss
The Department of Homeland Security's warning system for terrorist threats uses colors from green (for safety) to red (for very high alert). Some argue people may learn to ignore the warnings if repeated red alerts are raised and resolved without incident. If this concern is valid, what role might classical conditioning play?

THE BASICS OF OPERANT CONDITIONING

Although he did not "discover" it, Harvard psychologist B. F. Skinner did most of the early research on operant conditioning. In fact, the techniques of operant conditioning had been in use for hundreds of years before Skinner was born. What Skinner did was bring that earlier work and those techniques into the laboratory. There he studied operant conditioning with a unique vigor that helped us realize its significance.

Defining Operant Conditioning

Skinner used the term **operant** to refer to a behavior or behaviors an organism uses to operate on its environment to produce certain effects. Operant behaviors are controlled by their consequences. Operant behaviors maintain or increase their rate if they are reinforced and decrease their rate if they are not reinforced or are punished (Skinner, 1983; Staddon & Ceruti, 2003). Thus, **operant conditioning** changes the rate, or probability, of responses on the basis of the consequences that result from those responses. Skinner was careful not to claim that the future governs what happens in the present, but rather that past experiences can influence present ones. Skinner put it this way: ". . . behavior is shaped by its consequences, but only by consequences that lie in the past. We do what we do because of what

operant conditioning a form of learning that changes the rate or probability of responses on the basis of the consequences that result from those responses

operant a behavior or behaviors an organism uses to interact with its environment in order to produce certain effects

FIGURE 5.4

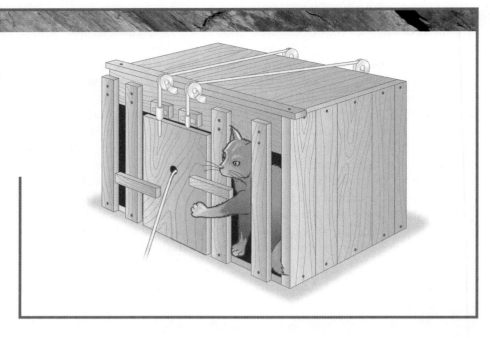

After noting that cats became more and more proficient at escaping from his "puzzle box," E. L. Thorndike came to believe that they were demonstrating lawful behaviors. Those behaviors could be explained, Thorndike argued, in terms of his law of effect.

law of effect responses are acquired when followed by a "satisfying state of affairs, and if responses are not followed by a satisfying state of affairs, or lead to "discomfort," an organism will tend not make that response again

has happened, not what will happen" (Skinner, 1989).

Actually, we find the first clear statement of operant conditioning in the work of Columbia University psychologist Edward L. Thorndike, who was trying to uncover the laws of learning. In one experiment, he placed a cat inside a wooden "puzzle box." The door of the box was latched with a wooden peg. If manipulated correctly, the peg could be moved and the latch opened. Once the cat opened the latch, it could dine on a piece of fish that Thorndike had placed outside the box (Figure 5.4). When first placed in the box, the cat engaged in a wide range of behaviors: clawing, licking, biting, scratching, hissing, and stretching. However, eventually—and, at first, by chance—the cat unlatched the door and ate the food. The next time the cat was in Thorndike's "puzzle box," it exhibited many of the same behaviors, but it unlatched the door and escaped a bit sooner. Over a series of trials, Thorndike's cat reduced its irrelevant behaviors and unlatched the door more and more quickly. After some experience, a cat placed in the box would go immediately to the latch, move the peg,

open the door, and eat the fish. Thorndike had discovered a law of learning—the law of effect.

The **law of effect** embodies the basics of operant conditioning, claiming that responses are learned ("stamped in," Thorndike said) when followed by a "satisfying state of affairs" (Thorndike, 1911). On the other hand, if a response is not followed by a satisfying state of affairs, or if a response leads to "discomfort," an organism will tend not to make that response again. Thorndike seemed to be saying, "We tend to do, and continue to do, those things that make us feel good." This seemingly simple observation is profound because it is true. Behaviors are shaped by their consequences.

Examples of operant conditioning are all around us. Imagine a father at the supermarket with his toddler seated in a shopping cart. The youngster is screaming at the top of his lungs, "I want a candy bar! Candy bar!" Father is doing a good (and an appropriate) job of ignoring this unruly behavior until he spies a neighbor coming down the next aisle. The neighbor has her three children with her, all of whom are acting like angels. What is a parent to do? He races by the checkout lanes, grabs a chocolate bar, and gives it to his child. He has reinforced the child's tantrum by giving the child the candy (he has cre-ated a satisfying state of affairs). What is likely to happen on the next visit to the store? Screaming worked this time, so it will be tried again. Reinforced behaviors tend to recur.

BEFORE YOU GO ON

9.   What is Thorndike's law of effect, and how is it related to operant conditioning?

A Point to Ponder or Discuss
Which of your behaviors today are behaviors for which you have been reinforced before? That is, how many of your behaviors have been operantly conditioned?

Demonstrating Operant Conditioning

To demonstrate operant conditioning in the laboratory, Skinner built a special apparatus, which he called an *operant chamber* (Figure 5.5). Although Skinner never used the term, and said he did not like it (1984), some psychologists con-tinue to call this device a "Skinner box." The chamber pictured here is designed for rats. Its two distinguishing features are a small lever that protrudes from one wall and a small cup that holds rat food. When the lever is pressed all the way down, the apparatus automatically dis-penses food pellets one at a time into the food cup.

FIGURE 5.5

A drawing of a typical operant chamber.

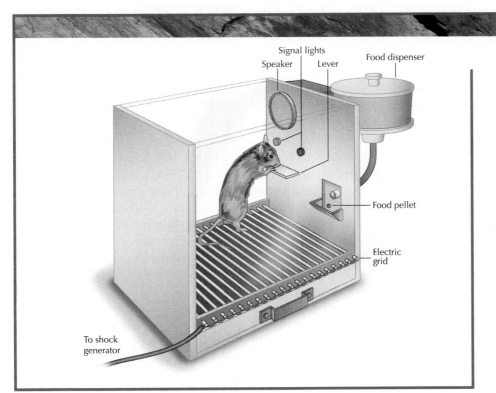

Now that we have our chamber, we need a learner. If we put a hungry rat into the chamber and do nothing else, the rat will occasionally press the lever. There is, after all, little else for the rat to do. A rat naturally explores the environment and tends to manipulate objects in it. The rate at which the rat freely presses the lever is called its *base rate* of responding. Typically, a rat will press the lever eight to ten times an hour.

After a period of observing the rat, we activate the food dispenser so that a food pellet is delivered every time the lever is pressed. As predicted by the law of effect, the rate of the lever-pressing response increases. The rat may eventually press the lever 500 to 600 times an hour. Learning has taken place because there has been a relatively permanent change in behavior as a result of experience.

Here is a little subtlety: Has the rat learned to press the lever? In any sense can we say that we have taught the rat a lever-pressing response? No. The rat "knew" how to press the lever and did so long before we introduced the food pellets as a reward for its behavior. The change that occurred here was in the rate of the response, not in its nature.

The Course of Operant Conditioning

One of the givens of operant conditioning is that before a response can be reinforced, that response must occur. If your rat never presses the lever, it will never get a pellet. What if you place your rat in an operant chamber and discover that, after grooming itself, it stops, stares off into space, and settles down, facing away from the lever and the food cup? Your operant chamber is prepared to deliver a food pellet as soon as your rat presses the lever, but you may have a long wait.

In such circumstances, you could use a procedure called **shaping**—reinforcing successive approximations of the response, you ultimately want to condition. You have a button that delivers a pellet to the food cup of the operant

chamber even though the lever is not pressed. When your rat turns to face the lever, you deliver a pellet, reinforcing that behavior. This is not exactly the response you want, but at least the rat is facing in the correct direction. You do not give your rat another pellet until it moves toward the lever. It gets another pellet for moving even closer to the lever. The next pellet doesn't come until the rat touches the lever. Eventually the rat will press the lever to deliver a pellet by itself. Shaping is over, and the rat is on its own. Shaping seldom goes quite as smoothly as just described. One alternative to shaping that is sometimes used to train large animals is called putting through (Frieman, 2002, p. 143). The animal is guided through a behavioral routine and then rewarded when that routine has been completed. Using language, humans can coax or guide one another to engage in new behaviors ("Come on now, put your hands over your head and lean forward. Lean a little more, a little more. There; now just fall into the pool headfirst. You can do it. You can dive!")

Once an organism emits the responses you wish to reinforce, the procedures of operant conditioning are simple. Immediately following the response, a reinforcer is provided. As responses produce reinforcers, those responses become more and more likely to occur. The increase in response rate that follows reinforcement will generally be slow at first, become more rapid, and eventually level off. This stage in which response rates increase is acquisition. Figure 5.6 is a curve showing the stages of operant conditioning. Note that the vertical axis is a measure of rate of response, not response strength. What increases in acquisition for operant conditioning is the rate of a response.

Once an organism is responding at a high rate, what will happen if reinforcers are withheld? Let us say that because we have reinforced its lever pressing, a rat is pressing a lever at a rate of 550 times an hour. From now on, however, it will receive no more food

shaping the process of reinforcing successive approximations of a response one ultimately wants to operantly condition

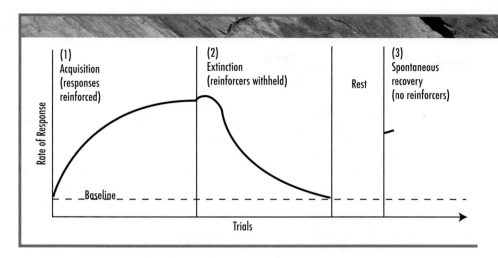

FIGURE 5.6

The stages of operant conditioning. (1) During acquisition, response rates increase as responses are reinforced. (2) In extinction, reinforcers are withheld, and response rates return to their original baseline rates. In spontaneous recovery, an increase in response rate is noted following a rest interval after extinction. Note that the vertical axis indicates a measure of the rate of a response, not its strength.

pellets for its efforts—no more reinforcement. Although we expect the rat to stop pressing the lever, it does not. Quite the opposite happens for the first few non-reinforced behaviors. In fact, both the rate of responding and the force of each response increase. The rat hits the lever more and harder than it did before. Eventually, however, the rate of lever pressing gradually decreases to the base rate (not to zero, because it didn't start at zero), and extinction has occurred. In operant conditioning, **extinction** is the decrease in the rate of a response as reinforcers are withheld.

Now assume that extinction has occurred and that the rat has been removed from the operant chamber and returned to its home cage for a few days. When we again deprive it of food and return it to the chamber, what will it do? The rat will go to the lever and begin to press it again. Although the lever pressing has undergone extinction, lever pressing will resume once the rat is given a rest interval. This return of an extinguished response following a rest interval is called **spontaneous recovery**. Figure 5.6 shows extinction and spontaneous recovery.

What happens to the spontaneously recovered response depends on what you do next. If you withhold reinforcement, the behavior again undergoes extinction. That is, the rate of responding falls. If you reinforce the operant response, the behavior is reacquired and regains its heightened rate.

Generalization and Discrimination

In classical conditioning, we saw that a response conditioned to one stimulus could be elicited by other, similar stimuli. We have a comparable process in operant conditioning, and again we call it **generalization**—a process in which responses that are conditioned in the presence of a specific stimulus appear in the presence of other, similar stimuli. For example, little Leslie receives a reinforcer for saying "doggie" as a neighbor's poodle wanders across the front yard. "Yes, Leslie, good girl. That's a good doggie." Having learned that calling the poodle "doggie" earns her parental approval, Leslie tries the response again with a German shepherd. Leslie's operantly conditioned response of saying "doggie" in the presence of a poodle has generalized to the German shepherd. Her parents no doubt reinforce her again. The problem, of course, is that Leslie may over-generalize "doggie" to virtually any furry, four-legged animal and start calling cats and raccoons "doggie" also. When a child turns to a male stranger and utters "DaDa," generalization can be blamed for the embarrassing mislabeling.

The process of generalization can be countered by discrimination training. **Discrimination training** is basically a matter of differential reinforcement. In other words, responses made to appropriate

generalization in operant conditioning, a process in which responses conditioned in the presence of specific stimuli also appear in the presence of other, similar stimuli

extinction in operant conditioning, the decrease in the rate of a response that occurs as reinforcers are withheld

spontaneous recovery in operant conditioning, the automatic return of an extinguished response following a rest interval

discrimination training in operant conditioning, a matter of differential reinforcement—responses made to appropriate stimuli are reinforced, while responses made to inappropriate stimuli are not reinforced

Many learned behaviors–bicycle riding, for example–are often acquired through a series of small steps. Get up. Get your balance. Pedal. Steer. Keep that balance. The process is much like shaping, acquiring successive approximations of the ultimate complex pattern of required behaviors.

Courtesy of Fancy/Veer/Corbis.

stimuli will be reinforced, while responses made to inappropriate stimuli will be ignored or extinguished (by withholding reinforcers, not by punishing the response). To demonstrate how discrimination training works, consider a strange question: Are pigeons color-blind? Disregarding why anyone would care, how might you go about testing the color vision of a pigeon? The standard tests we use for people certainly will not work.

In an operant chamber, a pigeon can be readily trained to peck at a single lighted disk to earn a food reward. Soon the pigeon pecks the disk at a high rate. Now the pigeon is presented with two lighted disks, one red, and the other green. Otherwise, they are identical: the same shape, brightness, and size. Can the pigeon tell the difference? We make the green disk the discriminative (positive) stimulus because pecking at it earns a reinforcer. Pecks at the red disk are not reinforced. The position of the colored disks is randomly altered so that we do not just demonstrate that the pigeon can tell left from right.

At first, the pigeon responds to the red and green disks at about the same rate. But in short order, the pigeon is ignoring the red disk and pecking only at the green one, for which it receives its reinforcer (Figure 5.7). In order to maintain such behavior, the pigeon must be able to discriminate between the two colored disks. We still do not know what red or green looks like to a pigeon, but we may conclude that pigeons can tell the difference between the two. This result makes sense because pigeons have cones in their retinas and, as you will recall, cones are the receptors for color vision. Some varieties of owl are virtually without cone receptor cells and thus are color-blind. When tested, these owls cannot discrim-

FIGURE 5.7

Discrimination training. Response rates for a pigeon presented with a green disk and a red disk. Pecks at the green disk are reinforced; those at the red disk are not.

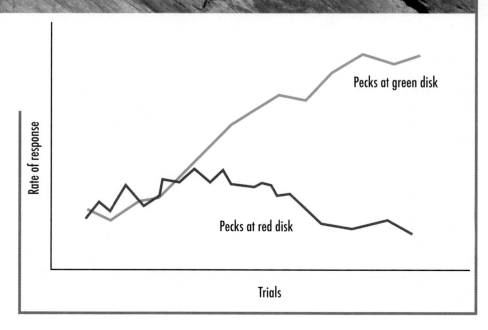

inate between red and green and appear frustrated, squawking and flapping their wings.

Please do not think that generalization and discrimination learning apply only to young children, rats, and pigeons. A great deal of our own learning involves learning when behaviors are appropriate and likely to be reinforced and when they are inappropriate and likely to be ignored or punished. You have learned that many of the behaviors reinforced at a party are inappropriate responses to make in the classroom. You may have learned that it is okay to put your feet up on the coffee table at home but not when you are at your employer's house or at Grandma's. Learning to interact with people from different cultures is also a matter of discrimination learning. In Saudi Arabia, for example, if two people approach a door at the same time, the person on the right always enters first. Being courteous by holding the door open for someone to the left of you and insisting that they enter is a generalized response that is simply not proper in all situations.

BEFORE YOU GO ON

10. Describe the steps involved in demonstrating operant conditioning.
11. Describe generalization and discrimination in operant conditioning, providing examples of each.

A Point to Ponder or Discuss
What are the similarities and the differences between classical and operant conditioning?

REINFORCEMENT

Clearly, reinforcement is a crucial concept in operant conditioning. At this point, it is useful to make a distinction between reinforcement and a reinforcer. **Reinforcement** refers to the *process* of strengthening a response. Reinforcement is a procedure for increasing the probability of a behavior. A **reinforcer** refers to the actual stimulus used in the process of reinforcement. A reinforcer is the stimulus (for example, the food pellets) used in the process of reinforcement.

Skinner and his students have long argued that we should define reinforcers only in terms of their effect on behavior. Reinforcers are stimuli. If a stimulus presented after a response increases the rate or likelihood of that response, then that stimulus is a reinforcer regardless of its nature. Imagine the following scenario: A parent spanks his four-year-old child each time the child pulls the cat's tail. The parent then notices that instead of pulling the tail less, the child is actually pulling the tail more often. If the operant behavior we are trying to influence is pulling of the cat's tail, then the spanking is serving as a reinforcer because the frequency of the operant behavior has increased. Although the parent originally saw the spanking as punishment for the tail-pulling behavior, the child is being reinforced by the attention from the parent! In short, predicting ahead of time which stimuli will act as reinforcers may be difficult. We need to observe the effect of a stimulus on the level of a behavior before we know if that stimulus is really a reinforcer.

Culture influences what will or will not be reinforcing. In many cultures (mostly Eastern, Asian, and African), the group is valued above the individual. In such cultures, reinforcing an individual's achievements will have less effect than in those cultures (mostly Western) in which individual effort and achievement are valued (Brislin, 1993). In Chinese culture, a student learns for the purpose of becoming a more virtuous person.

reinforcement the process of increasing the rate or probability of a response

reinforcer the actual stimulus used in the process of reinforcement that increases the rate or probability of a response

primary reinforcers those that do not require previous experience to be effective; they are related to an organism's survival and usually are physiological or biological in nature

secondary reinforcers a conditioned, acquired, or learned reinforcer

Attempts to reinforce such a student's learning using reinforcers for self-improvement will be misguided (Li, 2003; 2004). In traditional Hawaiian culture, the sense of family is strong, and personal independence is not a valued goal. Thus, the Hawaiian child may not be motivated by individual rewards (gold stars, grades) to the extent that his or her Caucasian counterpart may be. The point is that we cannot predict whether a stimulus will be reinforcing until we try it. Keep in mind that a stimulus is reinforcing only if it increases the rate or the likelihood of the response it follows.

Primary and Secondary Reinforcers

As we have seen, reinforcers are defined in terms of their effects on behavior—events that increase the rates or probabilities of behaviors that they follow are said to be reinforcing. When we distinguish between primary and secondary reinforcers, the issue is the extent to which those reinforcers are natural and unlearned or acquire their reinforcing capability through learning or experience.

A **primary reinforcer** does not require previous experience to be effective. In some way, a primary reinforcer is related to the organism's survival and are usually physiological or biological in nature. Food for a hungry organism or water for a thirsty one are primary reinforcers. Providing a warm place by the fire to a cold, wet dog involves primary reinforcement. A **secondary reinforcer** is a conditioned, acquired, or learned reinforcer. Nothing about secondary reinforcers makes them inherently reinforcing in any biological sense, yet they strengthen responses. Most of the reinforcers we all work for are of this sort. Money, praise, high grades, and promotions are good examples. Money, in itself, is not worth much. But previous experience has convinced most of us of the reinforcing nature of money because it can be traded for things we need (such as food) or value (such as a new car). Thus, money can serve to increase the rate of a variety of responses. Let us remind ourselves again of the extent to which culture influences which stimuli are likely to be seen as reinforcing. In non-Western cultures, money for individual achievement may not be a very effective secondary reinforcer at all. In many Asian or South American cultures, money allocated to a group is more likely to become an acquired reinforcer (Brislin, 1993; Li, 2004).

Positive and Negative Reinforcers

Now that we have distinguished primary from secondary, we can make one more distinction. A **positive reinforcer** is a stimulus that increases or maintains the response the rate of a response that it follows. This sounds familiar and even redundant: If something is positive, it ought to be reinforcing. Examples include such stimuli as food for hungry organisms, water for thirsty ones, high grades for well-motivated students, and money, praise, and attention for most of us. Remember, the intention of the person doing the reinforcing does not matter at all.

positive reinforcer a stimulus given to an organism after a response is made that increases (or maintains) the rate of that response

Courtesy of David Arky/Corbis.

Many people will engage in all sorts of behaviors, and work very hard, in order to earn blue ribbons. For such people, these ribbons have become secondary (learned or acquired) reinforcers.

A **negative reinforcer** is a stimulus that increases (or maintains) the rate of a response that precedes its *removal.* To increase the rate of a response with negative reinforcement, one presents an aversive stimulus before the behavior to be learned is emitted. For example, you administer an electric shock to a rat in an operant chamber. Any behavior that immediately precedes the removal of the negative reinforcer will increase in rate. So, if we want the rat to learn to press a lever, we make termination of the negative reinforcer contingent upon the lever press. When the rat presses the lever, the shock is terminated. It is the removal of an aversive event that is reinforcing.

Negative reinforcer is a strange term, isn't it? If a stimulus is negative, how can it be a reinforcer? Remember that the key word here is *reinforcer,* and reinforcers increase the rate of responses. In terms of Thorndike's law of effect, negative reinforcement must produce some satisfying state of affairs. It does. The reinforcement comes not from the delivery or presentation of negative reinforcers, but from their removal. You should be careful not to confuse negative reinforcement (which increases the strength of a behavior) and punishment (which decreases the strength of behav-

ior). They are two different processes with opposite effects on behavior.

So negative reinforcers are stimuli that increase the probability of a response when they are removed. They may include such stimuli as shocks, enforced isolation, or ridicule—exactly the sorts of things a person would work to avoid or escape. It may sound strange, but negative reinforcement is desirable. If you are offered negative reinforcement, take it. Figure 5.8 illustrates how positive and negative reinforcers work.

One clear demonstration of negative reinforcement can be found in **escape conditioning**. In this procedure, an organism learns to get away from (escape) a painful, noxious, aversive situation once in it. If an appropriate response is made and the escape is successful, the organism is reinforced and will tend to make the same response again (and probably more quickly). The organism has escaped from a negative reinforcer and has received negative reinforcement. A rat in an operant chamber is given a constant shock through the metal floor of the chamber. As soon as the rat presses a lever, the shock stops. The lever press has been reinforced. Because an unpleasant, painful stimulus was terminated, negative

negative reinforcer a stimulus that increases (or maintains) the rate of a response that precedes it removal

escape conditioning a process in which an organism learns to get away from (escape) a painful, noxious, aversive situation once in it

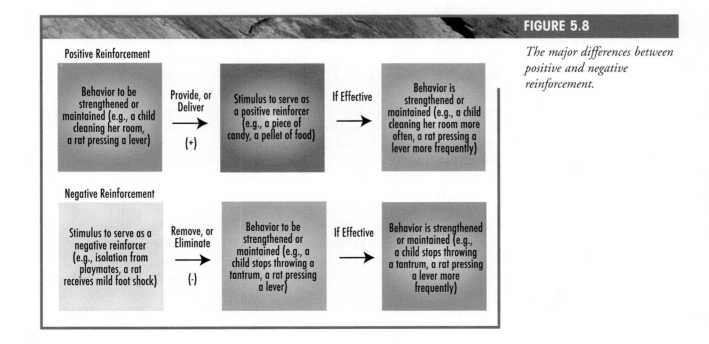

FIGURE 5.8

The major differences between positive and negative reinforcement.

reinforcement occurred. The negative reinforcer was the shock, and the learning was escape conditioning. You take an aspirin when you have a headache and are reinforced because the pain stops. You are likely to take aspirin the next time you have a headache. When a prisoner is released early for "good behavior," the good behavior is being reinforced. The process is negative reinforcement because the negative stimulus of imprisonment has been removed. A child who learns to clean up his or her room to prevent parental nagging has engaged in escape conditioning.

In **avoidance conditioning**, an organism learns to get away from (avoid) an unpleasant, painful, aversive situation before it occurs. A dog is placed in a long box divided into a left and right compartment by a chest-high barrier in the middle. Now in the left compartment, a light (signal) turns on. Five seconds later a strong, painful shock is delivered to the floor of the box. The dog hops around, squeals, barks, and eventually jumps into the right compartment where there is no shock. Thus the dog has been negatively reinforced for jumping. Now a light comes on in the right compartment, followed five seconds later by a shock to the floor. Yelping, barking, and scratching occur, but the dog rather quickly jumps back to the left compartment. One more trial: light, five-second delay, shock, jump. Now the dog is once again in the right compartment of the box. The next time the light comes on, the dog jumps into the left side of the box within five seconds, thus *avoiding* the shock. On each subsequent trial, the dog jumps the barrier when the light comes on. It has learned to avoid the shock.

This example is impressive in a couple of ways. Here, the removal of a painful stimulus is used to bring about a relatively permanent change in behavior. In just three trials we have trained a dog to jump over a hurdle when a light comes on. One of the most noteworthy aspects of avoidance conditioning is that responses acquired this way are highly resistant to extinction. After all, once the jump is made to the signal light, the shock is no longer required. Our dog will continue to jump for a long time. Keep in mind, however, that we are here using a shock as a negative reinforcer, not as punishment. We are not shocking the dog for doing anything in particular. Indeed, when the appropriate response is made, the shock is avoided. It is also important to realize that a response for avoiding the shock is readily available. There is something that the dog can do to avoid the shock. All it has to do is jump to the other side. When dogs, for example, are shocked at random intervals in a situation from which there is no escape or way to avoid the shock, an unusual thing happens. The dogs eventually reach a state where they appear to give up. They just lie down and passively take the administered shock. This behavior pattern is called **learned helplessness**. Once acquired, learned helplessness is very difficult to overcome. That is, if dogs are then given an opportunity to escape the shock, they have great difficulty learning to do so, and some dogs are never able to learn it at all (Seligman, 1975; 1991).

Are there examples of avoidance conditioning in human behaviors? Of course there are. As you drive down the road on a day when there is good visibility and little traffic, do you see if you can go just as fast as your car will take you? One would hope not. You probably keep your speed fairly close to the posted limit, trying to avoid the consequences of being stopped and given a ticket. This response is most likely if you have ever received a speeding ticket (or tickets) in the past. When Wayne says "uncle" to get Ken to stop twisting his arm, Ken stops, thereby reinforcing Wayne's saying "uncle." If this negative reinforcement is effective, in order to avoid the pain of arm-twisting, Wayne will be more likely to say "uncle" in the future when Ken asks him to. (Note that Ken could have used a positive reinforcer to get Wayne to say "uncle," perhaps by offering him five dollars to do so.)

avoidance conditioning a process in which an organism learns to get away from (avoid) a painful, noxious, aversive situation before it occurs

learned helplessness a phenomenon of learning that there is no escape from a punishing situation or stimulus and passively giving in to it without resistance

Here's one more hint for you. Do not think of positive and negative reinforcement in terms of good and bad, but in terms of plus (+) and minus (–). When using positive reinforcement, one adds (+) a stimulus, and in negative reinforcement one takes away, or subtracts (–), a stimulus. And remember, any time you see the term reinforcement or reinforcer, you know that we are talking about attempts to increase the rate of a behavior.

BEFORE YOU GO ON

12. Define the concepts of reinforcer and reinforcement, distinguishing between primary and secondary reinforcers as well as between positive and negative reinforcers.

A Point to Ponder or Discuss
Despite the apparent effectiveness of avoidance conditioning in training dogs to do things like jump over hurdles, psychologists usually recommend using shaping and positive reinforcement. How would you train a dog to jump over a hurdle or barrier?

Schedules of Reinforcement

In all of our discussions and examples so far, we have implied that operant conditioning requires that a reinforcer be provided after every desired response. It is true that it may be best at the start to reinforce each response as it occurs. But as response rates begin to increase, there is good reason for reinforcing responses intermittently.

The procedure in which each and every response is reinforced after it occurs is called a **continuous-reinforcement (CRF) schedule**. One problem with CRF schedules is that earning a reinforcer after each response soon may reduce the effectiveness of that reinforcer. For example, once a rat has eaten its fill, it will no longer find food pellets a worthwhile reinforcer for its behavior, and the rat will have to be removed from the operant chamber until it becomes hungry again (Skinner, 1956). In addition, responses acquired under a CRF schedule tend to go through the extinction process very quickly. Once reinforcement is withheld, response rates decrease drastically.

Alternatives to reinforcing every response are *partial (or intermittent) reinforcement schedules*. As the names imply, these are strategies for reinforcing a response less frequently than every time it occurs (Staddon & Cerutti, 2003). There are several kinds of partial reinforcement schedules, but we will review only four: the fixed-ratio, fixed-interval, variable-ratio, and variable-interval schedules.

With a **fixed-ratio schedule (FR)**, one establishes (fixes) a ratio of reinforcers to responses. In an FR 1:5 (or 1/5) schedule, for example, a reinforcer is delivered after every five responses. A 1:10 fixed-ratio schedule for a rat in an operant chamber means that the rat receives a pellet only after every tenth lever press. Fixed ratio schedules are favorites of employers and educators: "I'll pay you 25 cents for every 12 gizmos you assemble," or "You'll earn ten points of credit for every three book reports you hand in." Understandably, there is a high and steady rate of responding under a fixed-ratio schedule. After all, the more one responds, the more reinforcement occurs. Most organisms pause briefly immediately following reinforcement. Psychologists refer to this interlude as the post-reinforcement pause. Responses acquired under an FR schedule are more resistant to extinction than those acquired under a CRF schedule. (Technically, a continu-

fixed ratio (FR) schedule a procedure in which one establishes (fixes) a ratio of reinforcers to responses

continuous reinforcement (CRF) schedule a procedure in which each and every desired response is reinforced after it occurs

One of the best examples of variable ratio schedules of reinforcement are the rates at which gambling devices, such a slot machines, pay off or "reinforce" the user. Think about the consequences of that reinforcement schedule for those who use such devices.

Courtesy of George B. Diebold/Corbis.

fixed interval (FI) schedule a procedure in which time is divided into set (fixed) intervals, and after each interval, a reinforcer is delivered when the next appropriate response occurs

variable ratio (VR) schedule a schedule in which one varies (changes) the ratio of reinforcers to responses

variable interval (VI) schedule a schedule in which one randomly varies the time interval between reinforcers

ous reinforcement schedule is a fixed-ratio schedule with a 1:1 ratio.)

With a **fixed-interval schedule (FI)**, time is divided into set (fixed) intervals. After each interval, a reinforcer is delivered when the next response occurs. An FI 30-second schedule calls for the delivery of a food pellet for the first lever press a rat makes after each 30-second interval passes. With such a schedule, you know from the start that you won't be dispensing more than two pellets every minute. Note that the rat does not get a pellet just because 30 seconds has elapsed; it gets a pellet for the first response it makes *after* the fixed interval. Employers who provide payroll checks every Friday, or at some other set interval, are reinforcing using a fixed-interval schedule. Under an FI schedule, response rates decrease immediately after a reinforcer, and then increase as the time for the next reinforcer approaches. FI schedules also produce responses that are resistant to extinction.

There are two variable schedules of reinforcement: a **variable-ratio schedule (VR)** and a **variable-interval schedule (VI)**. From the learner's point of view, these schedules are very much alike. They differ from the perspective of the

dispenser of reinforcers. With a VR schedule, one varies the ratio of reinforcers to responses. With a VR 1:5 schedule, the experimenter provides one reinforcer for every five responses *on average*, but always in a different ratio. The first reinforcer may come after five responses, the next after six, the next after nine, the next after one, and so on. On the average, the ratio of reinforcers to responses is 1:5, but the actual ratios vary. From the learner's point of view, this is a random schedule. Slot machines are one commonly cited example of a VR schedule. They pay off (reinforce) on a variable-ratio schedule where the ratios are usually quite large. The variable-ratio schedule produces a high rate of responding with no post-reinforcement pauses. Behavior maintained on a VR schedule is very resistant to extinction.

Variable-interval (VI) schedules follow the same logic as variable-ratio schedules. The difference is that for VI schedules, time intervals are established randomly. For a rat on a VI 30-second schedule, a food pellet comes following the first lever press response after a 30-second interval; the next follows the first response after a 50-second interval; then after a ten-second interval, and so on. For a VI 30-second schedule, the varied intervals average 30 seconds in length. An instructor who wants to keep a class studying regularly and attending class consistently may give quizzes on a variable-interval schedule. The students will learn that quizzes are coming, but they will never know exactly when. VI schedules generally produce a slower but very steady pattern of performance. If you know when your exams are coming, you may slack off until just before test time. If they occur randomly throughout the semester, you are more likely to keep up your studying so that you will be prepared when the professor gives a test.

This terminology is standard, but it is somewhat technical. The main point to remember is that operant conditioning does not require that each response be reinforced. The scheduling of rein-

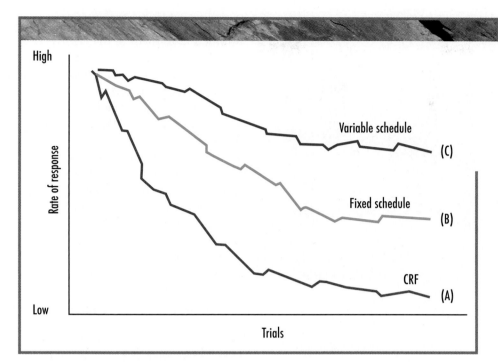

FIGURE 5.9

The effects of a schedule of reinforcement on extinction. These are three hypothetical extinction curves following operant conditioning on (A) continuous reinforcement (CRF), (B), a fixed schedule (FR or FI), and (C), a variable schedule (VR or VI).

forcers influences the pattern of the learned responses. Maintaining behavior on a partial schedule of reinforcement also affects a behavior's resistance to extinction. A behavior maintained on a partial schedule of reinforcement is more resistant to extinction than one maintained on CRF (see Figure 5.9).

Another point should be made regarding the scheduling of reinforcers. No matter whether one is using a continuous, fixed or variable reinforcement schedule, reinforcers should come immediately after the desired response. Delayed reinforcement is likely to be ineffective. We are not saying that delaying reinforcement destroys the possibility of learning, but in most cases, the more immediate

the reinforcer, the better the learning. In one classic study, for example, rats were reinforced for entering a black box instead of a white one. The task was learned readily when reinforcers were delivered immediately. If the delivery of reinforcers was delayed only a second or two, very little learning took place; with a ten-second delay, there was no learning at all (Grice, 1948). Say parents buy tickets to Saturday's circus to reward their son's good behavior with the babysitter on Tuesday night. The length of time between good behavior and reward may create problems. By Saturday afternoon, the trip may reinforce the inappropriate behaviors of Saturday morning, not the good behaviors of last Tuesday.

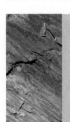

BEFORE YOU GO ON

13. Describe the ways reinforcers can be scheduled.

A Point to Ponder or Discuss
Parents of two combative young children are about to embark on a 1200-mile driving vacation. What techniques of operant conditioning might these parents use to minimize fighting on the trip?

Courtesy of David P. Hall/Corbis.

"Negative punishment" is a strange sounding term. It amounts to punishing behavior by taking away, or removing something of value, as in, "No, you cannot go out and play with your friends this afternoon, after what you did at lunch today."

PUNISHMENT

punishment in operant conditioning, a process that occurs when a stimulus delivered to an organism decreases the rate of probability of the response that preceded it

We have talked about the varieties and the scheduling of reinforcers. Now let us consider punishment. **Punishment** occurs when a stimulus delivered to an organism *decreases* the rate or probability of the response that preceded it. Punishment is usually unpleasant, noxious, or painful physically (e.g., a spanking) or psychologically (e.g., ridicule). The purpose of punishment is to decrease the rate of a behavior that preceded it.

It is worth noting again the difference between punishment and negative reinforcement, two concepts that are often confused. Punishment, as we just defined, involves the delivery of a noxious stimulus *after* a behavior, that is intended to decrease the strength of the response. Negative reinforcement, which we defined earlier in this chapter, involves presenting a noxious stimulus *before* a behavior occurs. Any behavior that removes the noxious stimulus will be reinforced and strengthened. So, even though a punish*er* and a negative reinforc*er* may be the same stimulus (for example, an electric shock), the processes of punish*ment* and negative reinforce*ment* employing that stimulus have opposite effects on behavior.

Predicting which stimuli will be punishing is as difficult to do as predicting which stimuli will be reinforcing. Once again, the intentions of the person doing the punishing are irrelevant. The only way to know that something is a punisher is to observe its effect on behavior. We may think that we are punishing Jon for his temper tantrum by sending him to his room, but what if Jon enjoys being in his room? We may have inadvertently reinforced Jon's temper tantrums by rewarding them. The only way to know for certain is to see how Jon behaves after the trip to his room. If Jon throws fewer tantrums, sending him may have been a punishment.

We can think of punishers as being positive and negative in the same way reinforcers are. Positive punishment means delivering (adding, +) a painful, unpleasant stimulus (e.g., a slap on the hand) following an inappropriate response. Negative punishment means removing (subtracting, −) a valued, pleasant stimulus (e.g., "No TV for a week!") following an inappropriate response. Another example is the use of "time out" sessions. Time outs work particularly well with children in groups. If one child begins acting inappropriately (say, by yelling or bullying others), that child is taken aside and placed away from the other children in a quiet setting for a period of time. Punishment takes the form of removing the valuable opportunity for social interaction and play.

Is punishment an effective way of controlling behavior? Yes, it can be. Punishment can be an impressive modifier of behavior. A rat has learned to press a lever to get food. Now you want the rat to stop pressing the lever, and you are unwilling to simply let extinction run its course. You pass an electric current through the lever so that the rat gets a strong shock each time it touches the lever. What will happen? Actually, several things may happen, but—if your shock is strong enough—there is one thing of which we can be sure: The rat will stop pressing the lever. If punishment is effective, why do psychologists argue against using it, particularly on misbehaving children?

Even used correctly, punishment has many potential drawbacks. And often it is not used correctly. We will examine punishment in general and spanking in particular.

1. To be effective, punishment should be delivered immediately after the infraction. The logic is the same as for the immediacy of reinforcement. Priscilla is caught in mid-afternoon throwing flour all over the kitchen. Father says, "Just wait until your mother gets home." For the next three hours, Priscilla's behavior is angelic. When mother gets home, what is punished—Pricilla's flour tossing or the appropriate behaviors that followed?

2. To be effective, punishment needs to be administered consistently. If one chooses to punish a certain behavior, it should be punished whenever it occurs, and that is often difficult to do. Threatening punishment ("If you do that one more time . . ." "I'm warning you . . ." "You'd better stop right now, mister.") but not delivering on the threat simply reinforces a child to ignore the caregiver.

3. Punishment may decrease (suppress) overall behavior levels. Although an effectively punished response may end, so may other responses. For example, the rat that has been shocked for pressing the bar will stop, but it may only cower motionless in the corner of the operant chamber.

4. When responses are punished, alternatives should be introduced. Think about your rat for a minute. The poor thing knows to press the lever when it is hungry. Indeed, you reinforced the rat for making that response, but now it gets a shock instead of a food pellet. With no alternative response to get food, the rat is in an irresolvable conflict. The rat may become fearful, anxiety-ridden, and even aggressive. That is, punishment does not convey information about *what to do*; it only communicates *what not to do*. Rub-

bing your puppy's nose in a mess on the carpet doesn't teach the puppy what to do when it needs to relieve itself, but taking it outside might.

Now let us consider the use of the physical punishment of children—spanking—as a separate case. Few child-rearing issues get people more emotional than whether hitting or spanking a child is always, never, or occasionally warranted (Kazdin & Benjet, 2003). Spanking is an issue that involves religious beliefs ("spare the rod and spoil the child" [Proverbs 13:48]), political actions (Spanking has been outlawed in several countries, including Sweden, Israel, Austria, and Germany [Gershoff, 2002]), and family traditions ("My folks spanked me, and look at me; I turned out okay."). If nothing else, corporal punishment is a common phenomenon in the United States, where 74 percent of parents of children younger than 17 years of age and 94 percent of parents of three- and four-year olds use spanking as a discipline technique (Benjet & Kazdin, 2003; Gallop, 1995; Straus & Stewart, 1999; Straus, Sugarman, & Giles-Sims, 1997).

Before we go any further, let us define **spanking** as punishment that is "a) physically non-injurious; b) intended to modify behavior; and c) administered with an opened hand to the extremities or buttocks" (Friedman & Schonberg, 1996, p. 853). Clearly, no one can be in favor of child abuse: Striking a child with a fist or an object so as to cause bleeding, bruising, scarring, broken bones, and the like. What about spanking? Does it work? As you might imagine, we have to be very careful here, but yes, spanking does work in the sense that it can be an effective means to get a child to stop engaging in a given behavior (Gershoff, 2002; Kazdin & Benjet, 2003; Baumrind, Larzelere, & Cowan, 2002). Are there negative consequences of using spanking as a disciplinary measure? Yes, there are several. Spanking diminishes the quality of parent-child relationships, may result (in the long term) in diminished mental health, and may lead to an increase in criminal and

spanking a form of punishment that is physically non-injurious, intended to modify behavior, and administered with an opened hand to the extremities or buttocks

antisocial behaviors (Gershoff, 2002; Straus, Sugarman, & Giles-Sims, 1997). Spanking may also convey the message that hitting is an acceptable outlet for frustration and may lead to bullying—particularly the bullying of smaller children (Strassberg et al., 1994).

Almost all the research on the effects of spanking is correlational. Researchers look for differences in parental spanking behaviors and then correlate those differences with targeted outcome behaviors. The problem, of course, is that correlational data tell us about relationships, but not about cause and effect. Just because spanking correlates with certain outcomes, does not mean that spanking caused those outcomes.

So, what is a parent to do? A reasonable strategy would be to search for other—non-physical—means of disciplining. Responsible parents know that sometimes children do things that deserve punishment. At issue is not should there be punishment, but how it can be best accomplished. If, from time to time, a parent loses control and spanks a child, well, so be it; it happened. There seems to be little reason to agonize over such an action—so long as it is isolated. Problems with physical forms of discipline are most closely associated with the habitual, continual use of spanking to control behavior. Effective parents provide both rewards and reinforcement for good behavior and swift and consistent discipline with positive alternatives for inappropriate behavior.

BEFORE YOU GO ON

14. What is punishment and when is it likely to be an effective means of controlling behavior?
15. What is the difference between punishment and negative reinforcement and how does each affect behavior?

A Point to Ponder or Discuss
Imagine you have chosen not to spank or hit your child. What other ways could you punish inappropriate or dangerous behaviors?

COGNITIVE APPROACHES TO SIMPLE LEARNING

Cognitive approaches to learning accent changes in an organism's system of cognitions—its mental representations of itself and its world. Cognitive learning involves the acquisition of knowledge or understanding, which may or may not be reflected in behavior. Recall that when we defined learning we said that learning is demonstrated by changes in behavior. The implication is that there may be less than a perfect correspondence between what one has learned and how one performs. We anticipated this issue with our coverage of the work of Rescorla on classical conditioning. There we noted that a stimulus acts as an effective conditional stimulus only when it informs the organism about something happening in its world as in, "When this tone sounds, food will follow." Extracting useful information from one's experience in the world is largely a cognitive task. In this section, we will review the work of two cognitive theorists: Edward Tolman and Albert Bandura.

Latent Learning and Cognitive Maps

The brain of a rat is not very large, and its cerebral cortex is small indeed. Can a rat use that brain to "think"—to form and manipulate cognitions? Can rats figure things out? They can form simple associations. They can learn to associate a light with a shock and a lever-press response with a reinforcer, and they can modify their behaviors on the basis of these associations. Can they do more?

Consider a classic experiment performed over 75 years ago by E. C. Tolman and C. H. Honzik (1930). At the time of this experiment, it was well established that a rat could learn to run through a complicated maze to get to a goal box containing a food reward. Tolman and Honzik, however, wanted to investigate just what the rats were learning when they negotiated a maze.

They constructed a maze and divided the rats into three groups. One group of hungry rats was given a series of exposures (trials) to the maze. Each time the rats ran from the starting point to the goal box, they received a food reward. Over the course of 16 days, the rats in this group improved steadily in maze-running. Their error rate dropped from about nine per trial to just two. A second group of rats also explored the maze for 16 days. However, these rats were not given a food reward for making it to the end of the maze. Instead, they were removed from the maze. The average number of errors made by these rats also dropped from about nine errors per trial to about six. That this second group improved suggests that simply being removed from the maze was some reinforcement. Even so, after 16 days, the group receiving the food reinforcer still outperformed the other group in maze-running.

A third group of rats was allowed to explore the maze on their own for ten days. These rats were not given a food reward for reaching the goal box; instead, they were removed from the maze. Beginning on day 11, the rats received a food reinforcer for reaching the goal box. The rats received food reinforcers for the remainder of the 16-day experiment. Introducing the food reward significantly altered the behaviors of the rats. Before the food was introduced the rats had made only slight improvements in maze running. After the food was introduced, the rats demonstrated far

Courtesy of Jon Riley/Getty Images.

If it were not for our ability to form cognitive maps, we soon would be disoriented in complex, busy environments, such as a shopping mall. We need to "know" where we parked our car and where the store we want to visit is located.

better maze running abilities. In fact, on days 13 through 16, they made fewer errors than did the rats that received food all along! The performance of all three groups is shown in Figure 5.10.

What do you make of this experiment? Why did that third group of rats do so much better after the food reward was introduced? Did they learn something about the maze before they received reinforcement for getting to the goal box? Did they "figure out" the maze early on but decline to rush to the goal box until there was a good reason to do so? Tolman thought so. He argued that the food rewarded a change in performance when the actual learning had taken place earlier. This sort of undisplayed learning is called **latent learning** because it does not appear in behavior until it is reinforced.

During their first ten days in the maze, the rats of group three developed what Tolman called a *cognitive map*. A **cognitive map** is a mental picture of the environment, including significant landmarks. The rats knew about the maze, but they had no reason to rush to the goal box until day 11. Tolman (1932) called his approach "purposive behaviorism." Tolman's experiments illuminated the difference between performance and

latent learning a "hidden" learning that is not shown in behavior until it is reinforced (until there is a reason for doing so)

cognitive map a mental picture or representation of the physical environment, noting specific landmarks when possible

FIGURE 5.10

The performance of rats in a complicated maze were (A) never rewarded for reaching the end of the maze, (B) rewarded every time they reached the end of the maze, and (C) rewarded for reaching the end of the maze only on days 11–16 (Tolman & Honzik, 1930).

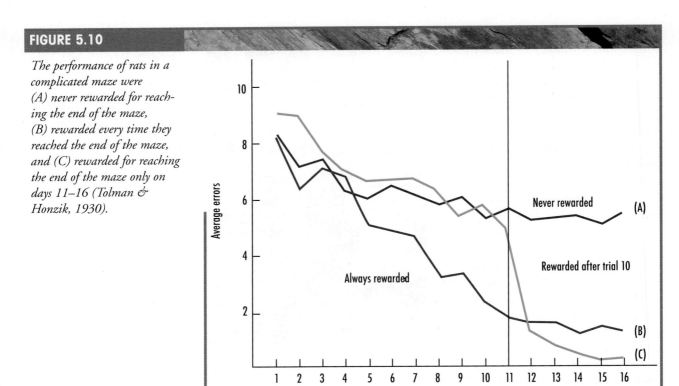

| social learning theory associated with Bandura, the position that learning often takes place through the observation and imitation of models

learning and focused attention on the cognitive aspects of learning. The ability of Tolman and Honzik's rats as cognitive map makers is impressive. Yet species of small birds use cognitive maps to locate seeds they have hidden. Researchers estimate that these birds can map at least 2,500 hiding places (Vander Wall, 1982).

You also use latent learning and cognitive maps. You may take the same route home from campus every day. If an accident blocks your usual route, won't you be able to use your knowledge of other routes (a cognitive map) to get home? When you park in a large lot, what do you do as you walk away from your car? Do you look around, trying to develop a mental image, a cognitive representation, of the parking lot? You are meeting a friend in a new building on campus. You arrive early, so you stroll around for a few minutes. Isn't it likely that this apparently aimless behavior will be useful if you have to locate a classroom in that building next semester? If you know that The GAP is on the mall's ground floor, just before the food court, aren't you using a cognitive map?

Social Learning Theory

Albert Bandura emphasizes learning as a social activity. For this reason, his theory is called the **social learning theory** (Bandura, 1974, 1982, 2001a, 2001b). His theory recognizes that learning often takes place through the observation and imitation of models.

According to social learning theory, there are three possible outcomes associated with learning from the behavior of others. First, a person can learn a new behavior from a model. Second, a person can diminish or stop (Bandara's term is inhibit) a behavior in his or her repertoire if the person sees the model punished for the behavior. Finally, a person can resume (disinhibit) a behavior already in the person's repertoire after watching a model perform or be rewarded for the behavior.

The classic study of observational learning was reported by Bandura, Ross, and Ross (1963). Ninety-six preschoolers were randomly assigned to one of four experimental conditions. One group of children observed an adult model act aggressively toward a large inflated plastic "Bobo" doll. The adult model vigorously attacked the doll. Children in the second group watched a movie featuring the same aggressive behaviors directed toward the doll. The third group watched a cartoon featuring a cat aggressively attacking Bobo. Children in the fourth group were the control group and did not observe interactions of any kind with Bobo.

Then the children were tested individually. Each child was allowed to play briefly with new and interesting toys. Next each child was led to a room with fewer, older, and less-interesting toys, including a small Bobo doll. Each child was left alone in the room while researchers, hidden from view, watched the child's behavior.

The children who had seen Bobo attacked by the models were much more aggressive in their play than were the children in the control group. Indeed, most of the children in the first three groups even attacked the Bobo doll the exact manner the models had.

According to social learning theory, the children had learned simply by observing. As with latent learning, the learning was separated from performance. The children had no opportunity to imitate (to perform) what they had learned until they had a Bobo doll of their own. The learning that took place during observation was internal, or cognitive.

Reinforcement and punishment can play a major role in observational learning. For example, a follow up study added a twist to the experiment just described: The adult models were either rewarded or punished for attacking Bobo. Children who observed the model being punished for attacking the doll engaged in very little aggressive behavior toward their own dolls. Those who saw the model receive reinforcement imitated the model's behaviors in considerable detail (Bandura, 1965).

Learning about the consequences of behavior by observing what happens to someone else is vicarious reinforcement or vicarious punishment. **Vicarious reinforcement** leads to acquisition of new behaviors or disinhibition of behavior; whereas **vicarious punishment** leads to inhibition of behavior.

The application of this sort of data can be very straightforward. For example, Bandura's research suggests that children can learn many potential behaviors by watching TV. Subsequent research confirms that children can learn aggressive behavior from watching violent television programs (Anderson & Bushman, 2002; Bushman & Anderson, 2001; Carnagey, Anderson, & Bartholow, 2007; Donnerstein, 2005; Landhuis et al., 2007). There is a consistent relationship between the amount of violent television a child watches and the level of aggressive behavior displayed. Indeed, six professional associations, including the American Psychological Association and the American Medical Association, released a joint statement saying, "at this time, well over 1,000 studies . . . point overwhelmingly to a causal connection between media violence and aggressive behavior in some children" (Joint Statement, 2000, p. 1). Supporters of social learning theory are especially concerned about television programs depicting situations in which inappropriate behaviors go unpunished (Donnerstein, 2005). Social learning theory suggests that it would be most unfortunate for one of a child's TV heroes to be rewarded for inappropriate behavior. As it happens, reinforced behaviors of valued models are more likely to be imitated than punished behaviors of less-valued models (Bandura, 1965).

Violent video games also can transmit aggression via observational learning. Much of the early research on this issue did not show any significant relationship between playing violent video games and aggression. More recent research does. For example, Anderson and Dill (2000) found a correlation between self-reported violent video game play and aggressive delinquent

vicarious reinforcement/ vicarious punishment learning about the consequences of one's own behaviors by observing what happens to someone else who engages in those behaviors

Bandura's social learning theory tells us that people often learn new behaviors by watching and "modeling" their own behaviors after those they observe.

Courtesy of Sigrid Olsson/Getty Images.

behavior among college students. Participants who frequently played video games were most likely to show delinquent aggressive behavior. However, the relationship was not as simple as it first appears. Anderson and Dill found that individuals with an aggressive personality were most likely to show high levels of aggression after exposure to video game violence. This relationship was stronger for males than females. In a follow-up laboratory experiment, participants played either a violent or non-violent video game, and then played a competitive game against what the participant believed was an opponent (actually, the opponent's responses were controlled by a computer). The participant was told that whoever pressed a button first after seeing a stimulus could punish the other player with a burst of noise. Anderson and Dill found that playing a violent video game led to higher levels of aggression than playing a non-violent video game. Other research shows that when individuals (male or female) play a video game competitively, they display a more aggressive style of play than individuals playing cooperatively (Anderson & Morrow, 1995).

Learning through observation and imitation is common. Your television on any Saturday provides many examples, particularly if you watch a PBS station. All day long there are people (role models) trying to teach us how to paint landscapes, build desks and cabinets, do aerobic exercises, improve our golf games, remodel the basement, repair a faucet, or prepare a low-calorie meal. The basic message is "Watch me and see how I do it and then try it yourself."

BEFORE YOU GO ON

16.   Describe latent learning and social learning theory and provide examples of both.

A Point to Ponder or Discuss
Some behaviors may be harder to learn through imitation. Which behaviors might be hard to learn from exposure to models?

SPOTLIGHT
ON DIVERSITY

Ethnic Differences in Learning Styles

When we hear "diversity in the classroom," we usually think of diversity of students—in terms of age, gender, ethnicity, socioeconomic background or disability. In this SPOTLIGHT, we discuss a different aspect of diversity—the diversity of learning styles. By *learning styles* we mean those unique learning preferences for perceiving, conceptualizing, and problem solving that students bring to the classroom (Willis 1992).

We must begin this discussion with something of a *caveat*. Although belief in the notion of learning styles is widespread, there is very little hard evidence that student learners have some sort of fixed way of interacting with information that is consistently superior to other ways of learning. The notion of learning styles is intuitive; it makes sense. Some people learn in ways that are different from the ways in which others people learn. The problem is that—like lots of good, sensible ideas—there is little research evidence to support such a notion (Krätzig & Arbuthnott, 2006; Stahl, 1999). In truth, when researchers look closely at learning styles, they are often hard pressed to find truly reliable, valid instruments (tests) to measure learning styles (Harrison, Andrews & Saklofske, 2003). Most of the instruments used to assess learning styles are self-report inventories (Delahoussaye, 2002; Loo, 2002). Having it said that, it remains true that many students (and teachers) strongly believe that they have a strong *preference* for how to-be-learn materials are presented. So here, we are using "learning style" more in the sense of a preferred format for processing information than some sort of built-in pre-wired cognitive mechanism.

Psychologists and educators have developed several ways to analyze learning styles. One popular such system measures learning styles along three dimensions: *perceptual modality, information processing,* and *personality patterns.*

Perceptual modalities are measurements of the ways learners encode information through the senses—or believe they encode information through the senses. The goal for a teacher, then, is to understand which of the senses a student uses most efficiently and teach accordingly. The argument goes that visual learners must see to believe. Aural learners prefer listening in class. Verbal learners are likely to absorb reading materials and lectures more easily than other students, and tactile/kinesthetic learners prefer a "hands on" approach. Two cautions: most students learn using all perceptual modalities, and the vast majority fall in the middle along these dimensions. **Information processing** measures how learners think, solve problems, and remember information. Learners have preferred ways of organizing, interpreting, and retaining information. **Personality patterns** involve measuring beliefs, feelings, and values—those different aspects of self and identity that students bring to class.

Cultural background may influence learning styles (Felder & Brent, 2005). For example, one cross-cultural study looked at the learning styles of accounting students from Australia, Taiwan, and Hong Kong (Auyeung & Sands, 1997). Students from Taiwan and Hong Kong were generally found to have more abstract (thinking) and reflective (watching) learning styles, while the Australian students possessed more concrete (feeling) and active (doing) learning styles. An earlier study of adult managers from India, East Africa, and the United Kingdom found significant differences in learning styles and attributed those differences to the prevailing attitudes and norms of the different cultures in which the managers worked (Hayes & Allinson, 1988).

Several studies have explored cultural differences in the learning styles of ethnic groups within the United States. Ramirez and Castaneda (1974), for example, found that Caucasian American students of European ancestry tend to be the most *field-independent learners*, while Hispanic American, American Indian, and African American students tend to be *field-dependent*. Field-independent persons develop structure themselves, can pull out cues embedded in a context, prefer to work alone, are object- and task-oriented, and are analytical thinkers. Field-independent students are also more likely to seek individual recognition and prefer classroom activities that involve abstract concepts and work unrelated to their personal experiences (Kinsella, 1995). On the other hand, field dependent students tend to need cues from the environment, prefer external structure provided by others, are people-oriented, intuitive thinkers, and often remember material in a social context. The field-dependent style (associated with Hispanic, Asian, American Indian, and African American students) is usually more holistic, passive, and socially-motivated. Field dependent students are group-oriented and cooperative, often wanting to listen to the views of others before making decisions (Nuby, Ehle, & Thrower, 2001). They tend to be highly visual/spatial, contextual, and intuitive in their approach to learning.

Hispanic Americans—Moll & Diaz (1987) described traditional Hispanic culture as tightly organized and noted that it places high expectations of social conformity upon members. They argued that the traditional culture of Hispanics partially accounts for the fact that many Hispanic students are strongly field-dependent, group-oriented, cooperative learners. Although field dependency decreased as Hispanic students moved away from traditional values, Hispanic learners seldom become as field independent as Caucasian and Asian males. Hispanic students are often kinesthetic learners; whereas, Caucasians and African-American students are significantly more auditory and visual in their processing of information (Dunn, Griggs, & Price, 1993; Yong & Ewing, 1992).

According to Sanchez (2000), Hispanic students exhibit a high need for feedback, prefer concrete—as opposed to abstract—learning experiences, prefer group activities, and learn better from "hands-on" activities. Cooperative learning is more highly favored among Hispanic children than among African-American children (Vasquez, 1990). Indeed, the Hispanic culture's emphasis on cooperation can make some Hispanic students uncomfortable with conventional classroom competition.

African Americans—African-American students generally prefer visually presented materials. African American students are more holistic—looking for the "big picture"—in their approach to learning, while Caucasian students tend to be more systematic, more self-regulated, and less open-minded (Willis, 1992). African American students are more field dependent, and Caucasians are more field independent. In addition, African-American students prefer experimentation, improvisation, and harmonious interaction with others and the environment (Franklin, Hale, & Bailey, 2001; Shade, 1992). Cooperative learning groups are particularly effective for African-American students (Kagan, 1986).

Boykin (1983) has identified nine dimensions of the African American culture that influence learning: spirituality, harmony, movement, verve, affect, communalism, expressive individualism, orality, and social time perspective. Boykin sees in these nine dimensions ways in which African Americans perceive the world. When teachers design instruction taking these nine dimensions into account, African-American students perform better than with traditional techniques.

Asian Americans—Although less research has been done on Asian-American students, it appears that they tend to use logical, sequential reasoning (Doktor, 1982). They are more likely to use abstract concepts, be field-independent, and employ reflective learning styles (Pang & Cheng, 1998). As we noted in this chapter, students from Eastern cultures may come to the classroom with a different view of the purpose of learning. In Western cultures, the goal of learning is to develop and use the mind to understand the world. In Eastern cultures, the goal of learning is to the help the learner to become a more virtuous person (Li, 2002; 2005).

Asian American secondary school students prefer kinesthetic learning to auditory or visual learning. They do not prefer cooperative learning (Park & Chi, 1999). Asian students are—in general, of course —more overtly thinking-oriented than feeling-oriented in their learning, basing their decisions on logic and analysis rather than on the feelings of others or emotion (Nelson, 1995). Compared with American students of European ancestry, Asian American learners place greater value on reflection and self-examination (Condon, 1984). They show a concern for precision and for not taking risks in conversation.

Native Americans—Prior to the 1980s, little research had been done on Native American learning styles (Swisher, 1990). Even today some researchers doubt whether a distinctly Native American learning style exists. Learning styles vary among tribes and among Native Americans in the same tribe (MacIvor, 1999). However, some studies indicate that Native American students tend to be field-dependent and use global holistic learning styles (Chrisjohn & Peters, 1989; Das, Kirby, & Jarman, 1992; Nuby & Oxford, 1997; Pewewardy, 1999). In general, Native Americans are visual learners and are accustomed to learning from examples and by demonstration because Native American tribal elders and parents prefer to teach using these methods (Swisher & Pavel, 1994).

Native American students are reflective and thoughtful in their learning styles rather than impulsive (Nuby & Oxford, 1997). Reflective learners are apt to carefully consider options before responding. In the classroom, Native American students spend much more time watching and listening and less time talking than do Caucasian students (Gilliland, 1999). Hilliard (2001) proposes that the reluctance of some Native American students to attempt problems in class may be due to the fear of being shamed if they are not successful. To their less culturally attuned teachers, their reluctance may appear to be passivity or a lack of motivation. The Native American student places great value on membership in the family and tribe and on the leadership of elders. These values may be in conflict with the emphasis on individual achievement found in the traditional American classroom (Cleary & Peacock, 1999).

Conclusion

Every student brings to the learning situation certain preferences in perceiving, processing, and remembering information. To use the common term, every student has a unique learning style; however, there appear to be some consistent differences among learning styles based upon culture, ethnicity, and race.

CHAPTER SUMMARY

1. **How do psychologists define learning?**

   Learning is demonstrated by a relatively permanent change in behavior that occurs as the result of practice or experience. We can use the same definition for "conditioning" in that it is a simple, basic, form of learning.

2. **Describe how dogs can be classically conditioned to salivate at the sound of a tone.**

   In classical, or Pavlovian, conditioning, a neutral stimulus (a tone) that originally does not elicit a response (salivating) is paired with another stimulus (food powder) that reliably elicits the response. As a result, the once-neutral stimulus acquires the ability to elicit a response similar to the one that the stimulus produces reflexively (the dog learns to salivate at the tone). The unconditioned stimulus, or UCS, is the stimulus that reliably elicits a reflexive response. In the case of Pavlov's dogs the UCS was food powder. The unconditioned response, or UCR, is the reflexive response elicited by the UCS. In the case of Pavlov's dogs, the UCR is salivating. In classical conditioning, the relationship between the UCS and UCR is unlearned. The conditioned stimulus, or CS, is the previously neutral stimulus, which, after being paired with the UCS, comes to elicit a learned response that resembles the UCR. In this case, the CS is the tone. The learned response is called the conditioned response (CR). The CR is not identical to the UCR, but instead is typically weaker.

3. **What are acquisition, extinction, spontaneous recovery, generalization and discrimination, and how are they demonstrated in classical conditioning?**

   In classical conditioning, *acquisition* refers to the process of learning an association between the CS and the UCS. Acquisition is represented by an increase in the strength of the CR as the CS and the UCS continue to be presented together. If the CS is repeatedly presented without the UCS, the strength of the CR decreases. This gradual decrease is the process of *extinction. Spontaneous recovery* occurs if an organism is given a rest period following extinction of a CR. After the rest period and presentation of the CS, the CR is once again observed. If the CS and UCS are paired again, reacquisition of the CR occurs. If the CS is again presented alone, the CR again extinguishes.

   In *generalization*, a response (CR) conditioned to a specific stimulus (CS) will also be elicited by other, similar stimuli. The more similar the new stimuli are to the original CS, the greater the resultant CR. As the new stimulus becomes more and more dissimilar to the original CS, the CR becomes progressively weaker. In many ways, *discrimination* is the opposite of generalization. Discrimination is learning to make a CR in response to a specific CS (paired with the UCS) while learning not to make the CR in response to other stimuli, which are not paired with the UCS.

4. **Briefly describe Watson and Rayner's "Little Albert" demonstration.**

   Classical conditioning has its most noticeable effect on emotion or mood. Most of the stimuli to which we respond emotionally have probably been classically conditioned to elicit those responses. In the Watson and Rayner 1920 "Little Albert" demonstration, a sudden loud noise (the UCS) was paired with the presentation of the neutral stimulus, a white rat. As a result of such pairings, 11-month-old Albert came to display a learned fear response (a CR) to the originally neutral rat (now the CS). The conditioned fear generalized to other similar stimuli. The "Little Albert" demonstration has been used to explain learned emotional reactions to events in our environments.

5. **How can classical conditioning be used in the treatment of phobias?**

   Phobic disorders (phobias) are those in which a person experiences an irrational and intense fear of something that is not truly dangerous. Wolpe and others have found that the disorder can be treated using systematic desensitization. Systematic desensitization involves training a person to relax and stay relaxed while thinking about a hierarchy of stimuli that are more and more likely to elicit anxiety or fear. If relaxation can be conditioned to thoughts of anxiety-producing stimuli, the sense of calm and relaxation will come to replace the competing response of anxiety.

6. **What role might classical conditioning play in drug addiction?**

Drug addiction involves both the painful symptoms of withdrawal and the development of tolerance to the effects of a drug. When a drug is taken repeatedly in the same environment, the reaction to the drug can become conditioned to stimuli in that environment. This conditioning to the environment blunts or reduces the reaction to the drug itself and more and more drug is required to achieve the desired effect. In a novel environment—one without the conditioned stimuli—tolerance effects are reduced. Consequently, a dose that would have been "safe" in the old setting can result in an overdose in the new setting.

7. **What makes a stimulus a good candidate to be a conditioned stimulus?**

For many years, psychologists assumed that any stimulus paired with a UCS could serve as a conditioned stimulus, but newer research has demonstrated that some stimuli are not readily associated in classical conditioning. Classical conditioning is largely a process of learning about relationships between events in the world. Biology may limit the forms of conditioning that are likely to occur easily. The key factor in determining if a stimulus will become an effective CS is whether it reliably predicts the occurrence of another stimulus. Regardless of the number of times the stimuli are paired, a stimulus will not be an effective CS if it does not predict another stimulus.

8. **Does the interval between the CU and UCS always have to be brief?**

In the early days of classical conditioning, researchers thought the CS—UCS interval had to be brief for conditioning to occur. We now know that some stimuli can be associated even after a long delay. Learned taste aversion is one example. A taste can be associated with feelings of illness after a delay of several hours. Taste aversion may allow for conditioning with a long delay because of a biological predisposition to develop taste aversion for things eaten just prior to illness. Such a delay is adaptive for organisms because it may stop an organism from eating a harmful food a second time.

9. **What is Thorndike's law of effect, and how is it related to operant conditioning?**

E.L. Thorndike first demonstrated of what we now call operant conditioning. He placed a cat in a "puzzle box" and noticed that, at first, the cat's behaviors were random. Eventually the cat hit upon a wooden peg that opened the box and gave the cat access to food. On successive trials the cat became more efficient until it went to the peg right away. The *law of effect* states that learning occurs when a response is followed by a "satisfying state of affairs." The law of effect is very similar to B. F. Skinner's short description of operant conditioning: Behaviors are controlled by their consequences. Operant conditioning occurs when the probability, or rate, of a response is changed as a result of the consequences that follow that response. Reinforced responses increase in rate and unreinforced responses decrease in rate.

10. **Describe the steps involved in demonstrating operant conditioning.**

Skinner constructed a special apparatus he called an *operant chamber*. The chamber allowed Skinner to control an organism's environment during learning. A typical chamber for a rat had a bar or lever and a food cup. A hungry rat was placed in the chamber and was reinforced (with a pellet of food) for the appropriate operant behavior (depressing the bar or lever). Acquisition occurs as an organism learns to associate a behavior with its consequence. In operant conditioning, acquisition is produced by reinforcing a response so that its rate increases.

Shaping is used initially to establish a response, that is, to get an organism to make a desired response. Shaping occurs by reinforcing successive approximations of a behavior to the desired one. At each stage of the shaping process, approximations of the desired behavior are reinforced. *Extinction* occurs when one withholds reinforcement from a previously reinforced behavior. For a rat in an operant chamber, the rate of responding and the force exerted on the lever will both increase over the first few trials after reinforcement is withheld. Eventually, extinction decreases the response to its original baseline rate. After a rest interval, a previously extinguished response will return at a rate above baseline; that is, in the same situation, it will *spontaneously recover*.

11. **Describe generalization and discrimination in operant conditioning, providing examples of each.**

Generalization has occurred when a response reinforced in the presence of one stimulus also occurs in the presence of other, similar stimuli. A pigeon reinforced for pecking at a red disk demonstrates generalization when it also pecks at a pink disk. A reinforced verbal response of "doggie" in the presence of a cocker spaniel may generalize to other dogs (and cats). *Discrimination* involves differential reinforcement—reinforcing responses to some stimuli while extinguishing responses to other (inappropriate) stimuli. A pigeon can learn to discriminate between a red disk and a green one by being reinforced to peck at one but not the other. You (probably) have learned to discriminate cans that contain soft drinks from cans that contain beer.

12. **Define the concepts of reinforcer and reinforcement, distinguishing between primary and secondary reinforcers as well as between positive and negative reinforcers.**

Reinforcement refers to the process of strengthening a response. A *reinforcer* is the actual stimulus used in the process of reinforcement. A reinforcer is any stimulus that increases or maintains the rate of a response, regardless of the nature of the stimulus. A *primary reinforcer* is a stimulus that is in some way biologically important or related to an organism's survival, such as food for a hungry organism or warm shelter for a cold one. No learning is required for a primary reinforcer to strengthen or maintain behavior. On the other hand, a *secondary reinforcer* strengthens or maintains response rates only because of an earlier learning experience. Secondary reinforcers have no direct biological significance for an organism. Instead, they take on reinforcing qualities by being associated with something else. Secondary reinforcers include praise, money, and letter grades.

A *positive reinforcer* is a stimulus that increases or maintains the rate of the response it follows. Food for hungry animals, water for thirsty animals, and high grades for well-motivated students are examples of positive reinforcers. A *negative reinforcer* is an aversive stimulus presented before an operant behavior occurs. When the behavior is emitted, the aversive stimulus is removed. Any behavior that comes immediately before the removal of the negative reinforcer will be strength-ened or maintained. Thus, the removal of an aversive stimulus is negatively reinforcing. Both escape and avoidance conditioning are examples of negative reinforcement.

13. **Describe the ways reinforcers can be scheduled?**

On a *continuous reinforcement schedule (CRF)*, an organism is reinforced for each and every response made. Behaviors maintained on a continuous schedule extinguish quickly. On a partial reinforcement schedule an organism is not reinforced for every response made. The *FR (fixed-ratio) schedule* calls for delivering one reinforcer after a set number of responses (e.g., one reinforcer after every five responses). The *FI (fixed-interval) schedule* calls for a reinforcer at the first response following a specified, or fixed, interval. A *VR (variable-ratio) schedule* randomly changes the ratio of reinforcers to responses, but maintains a given ratio as an average. A *VI (variable-interval) schedule* calls for a reinforcer for the first response after a time interval whose length is randomly varied. In general, responses reinforced with partial reinforcement schedules are more resistant to extinction than are responses reinforced each time they occur. Responses acquired under variable schedules tend to be most resistant to extinction.

14. **What is punishment and when is it likely to be an effective means of controlling behavior?**

Punishment is the process of decreasing the strength of a behavior by delivering a painful, unpleasant, or aversive stimulus after a behavior. Punishment is intended to eliminate or to reduce the rate of a behavior. Punishment can involve either administering a punisher or withdrawing a stimulus that an organism desires. For example, a child can be spanked or lose television privileges. Punishment can be effective in suppressing a response when it is strong enough and is delivered immediately after the response. Punishment must also be used consistently to be effective. Inconsistent punishment reduces effectiveness of present punishment and desensitizes the organism to the effects of future punishment. The punishment of one response should be paired with the reinforcement of another, more appropriate response. Spanking children has several drawbacks: it leads only to temporary suppression of behavior, it provides children with aggressive role models, and it teaches children that aggression is the way to deal with frustration and anger.

15. **What is the difference between punishment and negative reinforcement, and how does each affect behavior?**

Although both negative reinforcement and punishment involve the use of unpleasant, noxious, even painful stimuli, there effects on behavior are essentially opposite. When a given behavior is followed by an unpleasant or painful stimulus (i.e., is punished), the rate of that behavior will decrease. When an unpleasant or painful stimulus is removed when a given behavior occurs (i.e., negatively reinforced), the rate of that behavior will increase.

16. **Describe latent learning and social learning theory and provide examples of both.**

According to E. L. Tolman, latent learning is the acquisition of information (an internal, mental, cognitive process) that may or may not be demonstrated in performance. *Latent learning* is learning that has not yet been revealed by performance. Implicit in the concept is a distinction between learning and performance. Rats can learn their way around a maze but not demonstrate what they know until they are reinforced with food. Billy may not be willing to show us he can play our song on the piano until we drop a few dollars in his tip jar. *Cognitive maps* are mental pictures of the environment including key landmarks. In searching for a classroom in an unfamiliar building, we create a cognitive map for possible later use—another example of latent learning.

Albert Bandura's *social learning theory* emphasizes observation and imitation in the acquisition of behaviors. We learn by imitating models. An individual can acquire a totally new behavior by imitation. An individual can learn by imitation to inhibit (decrease or stop) a behavior that he or she was performing. Or, a person can learn to disinhibit (resume) a behavior in his or her repertoire from watching the behavior of models. A commonly cited example of social learning is children's learning of aggressive behaviors from violent television programs. Vicarious reinforcement occurs when a person sees a model reinforced for some behavior, and it increases the likelihood that the person will imitate the model. Vicarious punishment occurs when a person sees a model punished for a behavior, and it makes it less likely that the person will imitate the model.

Memory

6

PREVIEW

It is nearly impossible to imagine life without memory. As students of psychology, we care about memory in an academic, study-learn-test sense, but memory's value goes well beyond exams. All of those things that define us as individuals—our feelings, beliefs, attitudes, and experiences—are stored in our memories.

We will begin this chapter by defining memory. This is not an easy task, as human memory is complex, multifaceted, creative, and elusive. We will consider how information and experiences get into memory and how they are stored there. We will explore the possibility that memory is of several types and examine what the varieties of memory might be. We will also investigate the physiological changes that occur when new memories are formed.

Basics in hand, we will turn to why we forget things. Because forgetting is a matter of retrieval failure, we will focus on factors that affect the retrieval of information from memory. A well-learned habit, a textbook definition, a personal experience, or a briefly stored telephone number: All are useless if we cannot retrieve them when we need them.

What factors influence whether information can be retrieved on demand? What can be done to make successful retrieval more likely? Answering these questions requires examining four related factors: a) how memory is measured, b) how encoding strategies influence retrieval, c) how encoding is scheduled, and d) how interference can influence retrieval. Throughout this discussion, we will assume that the information to be remembered is stored in memory. That is, we will focus on retrieval, not retention. Occasionally, we may feel that we have "forgotten" something when it was never stored in memory in the first place.

MEMORY AS INFORMATION PROCESSING

A popular approach to human memory regards it as the final step in a series of psychological activities that process information. The processing of information begins when sense receptors are stimulated above threshold levels. The process of perception then selects and organizes the information provided by the senses. Memory makes and stores a record of perception.

Although we commonly give a single label to memory, it is not a single structure or process. Instead, **memory** is a set of systems involved in the acqui-

memory a set of systems involved in the acquisition, storage, and retrieval of information

There are few topics in all of psychology as relevant to college students as the study of human memory—particularly at exam time.

Courtesy of Tetra Images/Corbis.

sition, storage, and retrieval of information. Memory consists of systems that can hold information for periods ranging from a fraction of a second to a lifetime. These systems have storage capacities that range from very limited, like a few simple sounds, to vast—complex events, the details of an entire human life (Baddeley, 1998).

Using memory involves three interrelated activities. The first is **encoding**, the process of putting information into memory, or forming cognitive representations of information. Encoding is an active process involving a decision (perhaps unconscious) as to which details of an experience to place into memory. Once representations of experience are encoded in memory, they must be kept there. Not surprisingly, this process is called **storage**. In order to use information stored in memory, it must be gotten out again—a process called **retrieval**. So if memory involves the interrelated processes of encoding, storing, and retrieving information, how shall we describe

those "systems" in which these processes operate?

Some psychologists argue that memory is made up of separate storehouses, each with its own characteristics and mechanisms for processing information. These psychologists support *multistore models of memory* (Cowan, 1993; Tulving, 1985). Of these, the most widely known is Atkinson and Shiffrin's **Modal Memory Model** (1968). In this model, information is processed through three distinct memory storage systems: sensory memory, short-term memory (STM), and long-term memory (LTM). Although newer research (Bradley 1998) has raised questions about it, the modal memory model is still popular and worth exploring. We will look at sensory memory, short-term memory, and long term-memory and ask the same questions for each. What is its *capacity*. How much information can it handle? What is its *duration*. For how long can information be held without further processing? How is information *encoded*. In what form is it stored?

encoding the process of putting information into memory, or forming cognitive representations of experiences

Modal Memory Model a way of looking at memory, i.e., that information is processed through three distinct memory storage systems: sensory memory, short-term memory (STM), and long-term memory (LTM)

storage the process of holding encoded information in memory

retrieval the process of finding and moving information out of memory for use

---

BEFORE YOU GO ON

1. How can memory be characterized as a stage of information processing?

A Point to Ponder or Discuss
Sometimes we can remember events or experiences vividly and nearly without effort. At other times (as on exams), we cannot remember what we want to when we want to even with great effort. What might account for these differences?

SENSORY MEMORY

Sensory memory stores large amounts of information for very short periods (a few seconds, or less). There may be sensory memory systems for each of your senses, but psychologists usually consider only vision and hearing. Visual sensory memory, or *iconic memory*, is the sensory store associated with vision. Think of information in iconic memory as similar to a photocopy that lasts for only about a half second (Sperling, 1960, 1963). The storage system for hearing is called *echoic*

memory, which, as its name implies, is something like a brief echo—one that can last for five to ten seconds. Being able to detect unusual, and potentially dangerous stimuli quickly "is a fundamental ability that helps ensure the survival of biological organisms" (Tiitinen et al., 2002, p. 90). This ability does not seem to involve paying attention to incoming stimuli, and thus is seen as a function of sensory memory. The rapid (nearly instantaneous) recognition of an auditory stimulus as being new, different, or novel apparently takes place in

sensory memory a variety of memory that stores large amounts of information for brief periods (a few seconds or less)

the auditory cortex of the brain on the side opposite the ear that is stimulated (Alain, Woods, & Knight, 1998).

The concept of such very brief memory systems is a strange one (we usually do not think about remembering something for only a few seconds), but it has a place in information-processing models. Information stored in our memories must first have entered through our senses. Before you can recall what a lecturer had to say, you must first hear it. To remember a drawing from this book, you must see it. To remember the aroma of fried onions, you must have smelled them. A sensory memory does not pass through our sensory systems immediately; instead, it is held there for a brief time. Even after a stimulus is gone, its imprint forms a sensory memory.

Sensory memory seems very large. Not long ago, psychologists believed that sensory memory could hold as much as a person's sense receptors could respond to at any one time. In other words, they believed everything above sensory thresholds—everything to which the senses reacted—was stored in sensory memory. Such claims may have overstated the capacity of sensory memory. Although sensory memory can hold much more information than we can adequately attend to, it has limits.

Sensory memory is typically viewed as being a rather mechanical or physical type of storage. In other words, information is not encoded in sensory memory; instead, it is taken in the form the receptors deliver it. It is as if stimuli from the environment make an impression on our sensory systems, reverberate momentarily, and then rapidly fade or are replaced by new stimuli.

Here are two demonstrations of sensory memory. In a reasonably dark area, stand about 20 feet away from a friend who is pointing a flashlight at you. Have your friend swing the flashlight in a small circle, making about one revolution per second. What do you see? You *experience* a circle of light. At any one instant, however, you are seeing only where the light is, and you are experiencing from your sensory memory where the light has just been. If your friend moves the light more slowly, you will see the light and a "tail" of light following it, but you will no longer see a full circle because the image of the light's position will have decayed from sensory memory. (A similar situation occurs with a streak of lightning. In fact, the lightning is only in the sky for about two-tenths of a second. It is the impression of lightning in sensory memory that we experience.)

Have you ever had someone ask you a simple question, to which you reply "Huh? What'd you say?" Then, before the person repeats the question, you answer it (which may, in turn, provoke the response: "Why didn't you answer me in the first place?"). Perhaps you did not hear the full question initially, but while it was still reverberating, or echoing, in your sensory memory, you listened to it again and formed your answer.

Many students find strange the idea of sensory memory as a very brief storage space for large amounts of minimally processed information, but it is a real phenomenon, at least for vision and audition. Perhaps that fraction of a second or two of storage in sensory memory gives us the extra time we need to attend to information so that we can move it along in our memory.

BEFORE YOU GO ON

2. What is the nature of sensory memory?

A Point to Ponder or Discuss
Perhaps sensory memory is pertinent only to the psychology laboratory. Can you think of any other examples of it from your own experience?

SHORT-TERM MEMORY (STM)

Information easily enters sensory memory; but once there, where does it go? Most of it fades rapidly or is quickly replaced with new stimuli. But with a little effort, we can process material from our sensory memories more fully by moving it to short-term memory. **Short-term memory (STM)** is a level, or store, in human memory with a limited capacity and, without the benefit of rehearsal, a brief duration.

Short-term memory is referred to as *working memory* by researcher Alan D. Baddeley (1982, 1992, 1998, 2001). Baddeley sees working memory as a workbench or desktop where we assemble and use information to which we pay attention. In his view, STM has subcomponents called buffers or processors.

These subcomponents include a processor of visual and spatial information (what do things look like, and where are they in space), a buffer for sounds (used when we read or "talk" to ourselves in our heads), and an executive processor (for moving information from one kind of memory to another on our mental desktop). Thus, short-term memory holds information in our consciousness ever so briefly while we "work" with it (Jonides, Lacey, & Nee, 2005).

Figure 6.1 depicts the model of memory we are building. At the top the diagram shows stimuli from the environment activating our senses and moving directly to sensory memory. In the middle is short-term memory. We can move information into short-term memory from sensory memory or from long-term memory *by attending to it.*

short-term memory (STM) a level, or store in memory with a limited capacity and, without the benefit of rehearsal, a brief duration

FIGURE 6.1

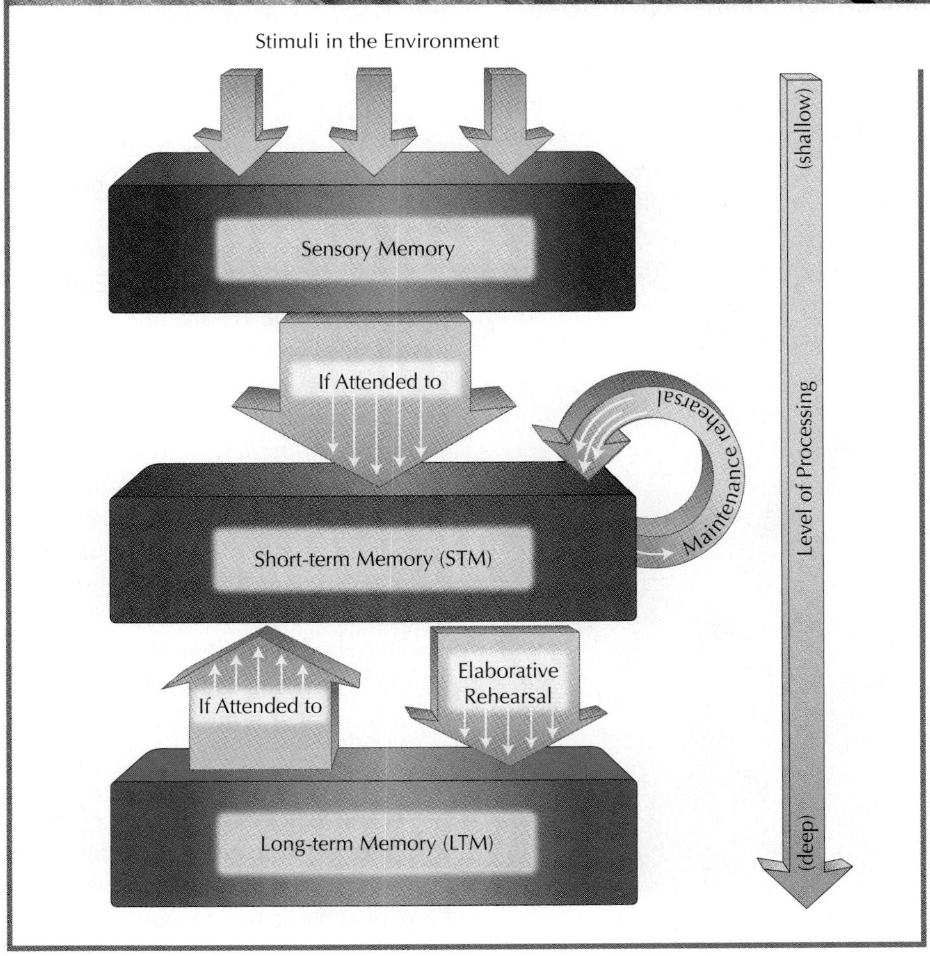

A simplified model of human memory.

The Duration of STM

Interest in short-term memory can be traced to two experiments reported independently in the late 1950s (Brown, 1958; Peterson & Peterson, 1959). In the 1959 experiment, researchers showed students three consonants for three seconds. Presenting the letters for three seconds ensured that the students had time to attend to and encoded them into STM. The students were then asked to recall the three letters after retention intervals ranging from zero to 18 seconds. This task does not sound difficult. Anyone can remember a few letters for 18 seconds. In this study, however, students were kept from rehearsing the letters during the retention interval. Instead, they were given a "distraction" task to perform right after they saw the letters. They were to count backward, by threes, from a three-digit number.

If you were a participant, researchers would have shown you three consonants (KRW, for example) and then immediately asked you to start counting backward from a three digit number like 397 by threes—397, 394, 391, 388, and so on. The experiment required you to count aloud as rapidly as possible. The researchers intended the counting to distract you from rehearsing. Under these conditions, your correct recall of the letters will depend on the length of the retention interval. If you are asked after just a few seconds of counting, you will do pretty well. If you have to count for 15 to 20 seconds, your recall will drop to almost zero. Distracted by counting, you cannot rehearse the letters and soon will not be able to recall them.

This laboratory example is not entirely abstract as the following scenario shows. Having studied for hours, you decide to reward yourself with a pizza. Never having called Pizza City before, you turn to the yellow pages to find the number: 555-5897. Repeating the number to yourself, you close the phone book and dial. Darn, the line is busy! Well, you'll call back in a minute.

Just as you hang up, the doorbell rings. It is the paper carrier and you owe $13.60. Discovering that you do not have enough cash to pay for the paper and a pizza, you write a check. Your thought process goes something like this: "Let's see, what is today's date? Oh yeah, September 9th. How much did you say I owed you? Oh yes, $13.60, and a dollar and a half for a tip, comes to $15.10. This is check number 1079; I had better write that down. There you go. Thanks a lot."

The paper carrier leaves, and you resume studying. Then you recall the pizza. Now five or six minutes have passed since you got a busy signal from Pizza City. As you go to redial, you cannot remember the number. Assuming you have no redial feature on your phone, you go back to the phone book. Once you attended to it, Pizza City's telephone number was active in your short-term memory only long enough to dial. Because of your not being able to rehearse the number and the other numbers entering as interfering information, you found that you were unable to access the original phone number.

We can increase the duration of short-term memory by rehearsing the information stored there. The rehearsal we use to keep material active in our short-term

Most of the time when we look up a telephone number, we only need to (or want to) remember that number long enough to get it dialed successfully. That is, all we want to do is attend to it in order to get it into short-term memory.

Courtesy of Steve Prezant/Corbis.

memory is **maintenance rehearsal** (or rote rehearsal); it amounts to little more than the simple repetition of the information already in our STM. To get material into STM (encoding), we have to attend to it. Each time we repeat the material, we are re-attending to it.

The 15 to 20 second duration of STM is long enough for us to use it in many everyday activities. Usually all we want to do with a telephone number is remember it long enough to dial it. We also use STM to do math, particularly math "in our heads." Multiply 28 by 6 without paper and pencil. "Let's see. Six times 8 is 48. Now I have to keep the 8 and carry the 4." Stop right there. Where do you "keep the 8" and store the 4 until they are needed? Right, in STM. For that matter, where did the notion that 6×8 equals 48 come from? Where did what *multiply* means come from? Right again. This information entered STM, not through our senses and sensory memory, but from long-term storage (see Figure 6.1). The executive processor of working memory led you to the information needed to solve this simple problem.

Language processing is another example of STM in action. Reading a long sentence like this one, you need a place to store the beginning until you get to the end—so that you can comprehend the sentence before deciding whether it's worth remembering.

Having discussed short-term memory's duration, we will now deal with its capacity. Just how much information can we hold in STM for that 15- to 20-second duration?

The Capacity of STM

In 1956 George Miller wrote a paper about "the magical number seven, plus or minus two." In his paper, he argued that the capacity of short-term memory is very small—limited to just five to nine (or 7 ± 2) bits, or "chunks," of information. Remember, to encode information into short-term memory, one must attend to that information. Limits on attention span also provide limits on how much we can process into STM.

Subsequent research indicates Miller may have overestimated short-term memory's capacity. In the context of STM, a *chunk* is a technical, but imprecise term (Anderson, 1980). A **chunk** is the representation in memory of a meaningful unit of information. Thus, Miller claims that we can store 7 ± 2 meaningful pieces of information in STM. Some studies have shown that short-term memory may hold only four or five "chunks" or, perhaps, even fewer (Cowan, 2001, 2005; McElree, 2001). Interestingly, there now is evidence (using both hearing speakers and deaf American Sign Language users) that the capacity of STM for spoken items is close to 7 ± 2, but for the same information presented visually, the capacity drops to 5 ± 1 (Boutla et al., 2004).

We can easily attend to, encode, and store five or six letters in short-term memory. Holding the letters YRDWIAADEFDNSYE in short-term storage, however, would be a challenge. Fifteen randomly presented letters exceed the capacity of STM for most of us. But what if we were asked to remember the words Friday and Wednesday? Keeping these two simple words in STM is easy, even though they contain the same 15 letters. Here we are storing two chunks of meaningful information, not 15. In fact, we can easily store 50 letters in short-term memory if we recode them into the one meaningful chunk: days of the week.

We can readily store a telephone number in short-term memory. Adding an area code makes the task somewhat more difficult because the ten digits now come fairly close to the upper limit of our STM capacity. Notice how we tend to cluster the digits of a telephone number into a pattern. The digit series 2 1 9 5 5 5 3 6 6 1 is more difficult to deal with as a simple string than when it is seen and encoded as a telephone number: (219) 555-3661 (Bower & Springston, 1970). Grouping the digits

maintenance rehearsal the simple repetition of the information already in STM in an effort to keep it there

chunk the representation in memory of a meaningful unit of information

into chunks lets us see them in a new, more meaningful way.

At best, short-term memory works rather like a leaky bucket. From the vast storehouse available in sensory memory, we scoop up some information (and not much, at that) by paying attention to it and holding it for a while until we use it, hang onto it with maintenance rehearsal, move it along to long-term storage, or lose it.

BEFORE YOU GO ON

3. Describe short-term, or working, memory.

A Point to Ponder or Discuss
When would more effective chunking of information improve your memory?

LONG-TERM MEMORY (LTM)

Long-term memory (LTM) holds large amounts of information for long periods. Experience tells us that the capacity of long-term memory is huge—virtually limitless. Playing along with television trivia game shows, we may impress ourselves with the vastness of what we have stashed in LTM. How much can be stored in human memory may never be measured, but we can never learn so much that there will not be room for more.

How Long Do Long-Term Memories Last?

From experience, we know that we remember some things for a long time. Assuming you remain disease and injury free, you are not likely ever to forget some information, such as your name or the words to the song "Happy Birthday."

It is difficult to imagine an experiment that could measure how long information or experiences remain in LTM. Yet, certainly, we cannot remember some things we once knew. Why do we forget some things? Do we forget them because the information is no longer in our long-term memories—it just isn't there anymore? Or do we for-

get them because we are unable to get the information out of LTM—it is still there but somehow not accessible?

As an adult, you have a large number of memories, some pleasant, some unpleasant. You may remember proms and football games from high school. Perhaps you have some fond memories of a teacher or a friend from grade school. How about memories for pre-school events? Is there an age before which lasting memories are not possible, or, as some argue, do we all carry memories of our own births and even in utero experiences? Recent evidence suggests, "The earliest scientifically documented childhood memories recalled by adults happened to them when they were around 2 years of age." (Howe, 2000, 2003, p. 63). Even though infants—even newborns—can *form* memories, they do not *retain* these early memories into adulthood.

How Does Information Get into Long-Term Memory?

Simple repetition (maintenance rehearsal) is used to keep material active in short-term memory. This type of rehearsal is one way to move information from STM to LTM. Within limits, the more a bit of information is repeated, the more likely it will be remembered beyond the limits of short-

---

long-term memory (LTM)
that level or store of memory that holds large amounts of information for long periods of time

term memory. However, simple repetition is seldom sufficient to process information into long-term storage. Simply attending to information—the essence of repetition—is not an efficient means of encoding it into long-term memory.

To move information into long-term memory, we need to think about it, organize it, form images of it, and make it meaningful—relate it to something already in our long-term memories. In other words, to get information into LTM, we need to use **elaborative rehearsal**. A term proposed by Craik and Lockhart (1972), elaborative rehearsal is not an either/or process. Instead, information can be elaborated to greater or lesser degrees. When we do no more than attend to an item, as in maintenance rehearsal, our processing is fairly minimal, or shallow, and that item is likely to remain in memory for a relatively short time. The more we rehearse an item elaboratively, the deeper into memory it is processed. The more we elaborate on it, the easier it becomes to remember.

Consider a hypothetical experiment in which students are asked to respond to a list of words in different ways. In one instance, they are asked to count the number of letters in each word on the list. In another, they are asked to generate a word that rhymes with each one they read. In a third, they are asked to use each word in a sentence. The words are processed at progressively deeper levels as students focus on a) the simple physical structure of the words, b) the sounds of the words as they are said aloud, and c) the meaning of the words and their roles in sentence structure. In such experiments, as processing (elaboration) increases, recall of the words being processed increases also (Cermak & Craik, 1979; Craik & Tulving, 1975).

Are There Different Types of Long-Term Memories?

From experience, we know that we can retrieve what we have stored in LTM in various forms. We can remember the definitions of words. We can visualize people and events from the past. We can recall the melodies of songs. We can recollect how our bodies moved when we first tried to roller-skate.

Are there different long-term memory storage systems that encode and store information differently? Apparently there are. Psychologists generally accept that long-term memory is divided into two subsystems: declarative memory and nondeclarative memory (Gabrieli, 1998; Squire, 1992; Thompson, 2005). **Declarative memory** (sometimes explicit memory) includes memory systems from which information can be intentionally recalled. Declarative memory includes subsystems for verbally oriented, factual information (semantic memory) and memory for events (episodic memory). **Nondeclarative memory** (sometimes implicit or procedural memory) involves the acquisition, retention, and retrieval of performance skills such as tying one's shoelaces, swinging a golf club, or riding a bicycle. Retrieval from implicit memory occurs without conscious awareness; it just seems to happen automatically.

Declarative memory is divided into semantic memory and episodic memory (Tulving, 1972, 1983, 2002). In **semantic memory**, we store all our vocabulary, simple concepts, and rules (including those for using language). Within semantic memory, we store our knowledge of the world. Our semantic memories are filled with facts, both important and trivial. Can you answer these questions?

Who opened the first psychology laboratory in Leipzig in 1879?

How many stripes are there on the American flag?

Is "Colorless green ideas sleep furiously" a well-formed grammatically correct sentence?

What do dogs eat?

If you can, you found the answers in your long-term semantic memory.

Information in semantic memory is stored in an organized fashion. Psychologists are not yet sure how to

elaborative rehearsal the process of moving information into long-term memory by thinking about it, organizing it, forming images of it, and making it meaningful—relating it to something already in LTM

declarative memory (explicit memory) memory systems from which information can be readily retrieved

nondeclarative memory (procedural memory) the type of LTM in which well-learned chains of responses are stored

semantic memory the type of long-term memory in which vocabulary, simple concepts, and rules are stored

characterize the complex structure of semantic memory, but they have put forth several ideas. At the very least, concepts elicit each other as associations. If we ask you to say the first thing that comes to mind when you hear the word "hot," aren't you likely to say "cold"? When people are asked to recall a list of randomly presented words from various categories (e.g., pieces of furniture, fruits, sports, and colors), they do so by category, recalling first furniture, then names, then fruits, and so on. Psychologists call this process *category clustering* (Bousfield, 1953).

Even when we are without an obvious way to cluster a list of words, we organize them anyway. Psychologists call the phenomenon *subjective organization* because individuals create and impose their own personal (subjective) organization on the list (Tulving, 1966).

Over the past 20 years, scientists have proposed several hierarchical network models to describe the structure of semantic LTM. Each is somewhat different, but all propose that concepts (e.g., animal, bird, canary, yellow) or propositions (e.g., birds are animals, birds can fly, canaries are birds, canaries are yellow) in semantic memory interrelate in highly structured, predictable ways.

Semantic long-term memory is also abstract. For example, although we know how many stripes are on the American flag and what dogs usually eat, we have difficulty remembering how, why, or when we acquired that information. Information in semantic memory is not tied in any way to our memories of our own life experiences.

In **episodic memory** we store the memories of our life events and experiences. Episodic memory is time-related and stores experiences in chronological order (Eichenbaum & Fortin, 2003; Tulving, 2002). Episodic memory registers, or catalogues, all of our life's events. That is, episodic memories are of specific, not abstract, events. An eyewitness account of a crime is drawn from episodic memory. The answers to these questions draw upon episodic memory:

What did you have for lunch yesterday?

Did you sleep well last night?

How did you spend last summer's vacation?

What did your dog eat yesterday?

What was your fifth birthday like?

Some researchers claim that there is a separate category of episodic memory called *autobiographical memory* (e.g., Baddeley, 1990; Berseheid, 1994). Auto-

episodic memory the type of LTM in which memories of life events and experiences are stored

Psychologists believe that there are several varieties of long-term memory. In procedural *memory are stored all our well-learned habits of how to do things, like tie our shoes, ride a bicycle, or sign our name. In* episodic *memory we have stored memories of the events of lives, with truly important events, like the death of a loved one in* autobiographical *memory. In* semantic *memory are stored all the facts, ideas, vocabulary and meanings we have learned—such as those that are put into LTM when we study.*

Courtesy of Bloomimage/Corbis.

Courtesy of Russell Underwood/Corbis.

Courtesy of JGI/Jamie Grill/Getty Images.

biographical memory contains memories of significant life events. A memory of what you ate for lunch last Monday may be in your episodic memory, but your memory of your first day in college is probably in autobiographical memory, as well. Children develop autobiographical memory between three and three and a half years of age, at around the time they begin to talk to themselves and others about the events of their lives (Howe, 2003; Nelson, 1993).

An altogether different type of long-term memory is nondeclarative (or procedural) memory. In this memory, we store responses and chains of responses that we have learned well, such as how to ride a bicycle, type, shave, or apply makeup. Simply stated, procedural memory stores the basic procedures of our lives. What we have stored here is retrieved and put into use with little or no effort. At one time in your life, handwriting was quite difficult, as you strained to form letters and words correctly. But by now, your writing skills, or procedures, are so ingrained that you can retrieve the processes involved almost without thinking. In fact, if you try to explicitly remember and describe each aspect of a procedural memory, you will find the task difficult. Doubt that? Try to explain step-by-step how to tie a shoe. John Anderson (1987) calls the information in this subsystem procedural knowledge, or "knowing how." The other types of LTM hold what Anderson calls declarative knowledge, or "knowing that."

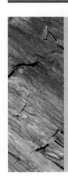

BEFORE YOU GO ON

4. What are the capacity and duration of long-term memory?
5. What are possible varieties of long-term memory?

A Point to Ponder or Discuss
If elaborative rehearsal is required to process information into long-term memory, why do we seem to remember so many things for which we have no recollection that we elaborated on them at all?

On the Accuracy of Long-Term Memories

When we try to remember a fact that we learned in school many years ago, it is easy to determine the accuracy of our recall: either we know it or we don't.

Testing the accuracy of declarative, semantic memory is easy compared to testing the accuracy of episodic or autobiographical memories. Determining the accuracy of our memories for past experiences is difficult at best and sometimes simply impossible. Do we *really* remember all the details of the family vacation we took when we were six years old, or are we recalling bits and pieces of what actually happened along with fragments of what we have been told happened, and adding in other details to reconstruct a likely story? Most times, recalling experiences accurately from the distant past is not terribly crucial. Yet, at other times, accuracy can be critical. We consider two such situations: repressed memory and eyewitness memory. First, let us take a look at the constructive nature of memory in general.

A popular misconception is that human memory works much like a camcorder (or DVD burner). That is,

reconstructive memory the notion that we store only features of what has been experienced and then retrieve those features and construct a meaningful story about what was encoded and stored

when an experience is placed into memory, the record button is pressed (encoding), and the experience is captured perfectly on tape (storage). Information is gathered from storage by pressing the rewind button, followed by the play button (retrieval). Although this view of memory is simple, it is not accurate. In reality, we store only features of what has been experienced, and then, we retrieve those features and construct what was encoded and stored in memory using a process called **reconstructive memory** (Bartlett, 1932).

Retrieval from memory involves reconstruction, so memories may be inaccurate because information is left out or added (Lindsay et al, 2004; Loftus, 2002, 2003; Schacter, Norman, & Koutstaal, 1998). Newer research suggests that the construction process involves—as Frederick Bartlett suggested over 70 years ago—storing patterns of features in which each feature represents a different aspect of what is experienced. Furthermore, the features are stored in different parts of the brain. Consequently, no single part of the brain houses a complete memory. Retrieval of a memory is much like putting together a jigsaw puzzle. Features stored in various parts of the brain are reactivated, and they, in turn, reactivate other features. This reactivation process continues until a memory is reconstructed (Schacter et al., 1998; Thompson, 2005).

As Bartlett first noted, sometimes the reconstruction process results in inaccurate reports of what is in memory. Recall of information from memory may not be accurate for several reasons. At the time of encoding, inadequate separation of similar episodes may cause a person to forget a feature as specific to a given episode. Weak connections among the features associated with an event stored in memory can cause one to reconstruct the memory inaccurately. Finally, retrieval cues may match more than one set of features representing more than one event. As a result, the mind may not

repressed memory a stored memory that so disturbs a person that he or she pushes it deep into the unconscious and can no longer retrieve it readily

be able to find and retrieve the event sought. In short, memories are not always fixed or accurate representations of what has been experienced.

Can people be fooled into believing they remember things that never happened? One researcher draws this conclusion: "There is ample evidence that people can be led to believe that they experienced things that never happened. In some instances, these beliefs are wrapped in a fair amount of sensory detail and give the impression of being genuine recollections" (Loftus, 2004, p. 147). In one study, Elizabeth Loftus and her colleagues had people evaluate advertisements. One advertisement for Disneyland showed Bugs Bunny in the Magic Kingdom. The ad's text referred to meeting Bugs Bunny as being the perfect ending to a perfect day. The participants were then asked about their childhood experiences at Disneyland (Braun, Ellis, & Loftus, 2002). Initially, about 16 percent of those who saw the Bugs Bunny advertisement claimed to have met him at Disneyland. The more often people saw the Bugs Bunny advertisement, the greater the percentage that remembered him at Disneyland. The details of people's recollections were often very rich, even though these were "constructed" memories. After all, Bugs Bunny is a Warner Brothers character and has never appeared at any Disney theme park.

The possibility of repressed memories also illustrate the importance of accuracy in retrieval from long-term storage. A **repressed memory** is one that so disturbs a person that the person pushes it deep into the unconscious and can no longer readily retrieve it.

Psychologists generally accept that people repress painful memories (Baddeley, 1990; Brown, Scheflin, & Hammond, 1998; Gold et al., 1994; Loftus, 1994). Repressed memories have been associated with several psychological symptoms, including eating disorders, depression, and anxiety. One controversial theory is that sexual abuse during childhood is at the root of these and other disorders and the memories of abuse have been repressed. Proponents of this theory believe treatment requires recovering and dealing with the repressed memories of abuse.

For Sigmund Freud, repression was a central theoretical concept. Yet, he recognized the possibility for error in reports of childhood sexual abuse that he heard from patients. Of these reports, Freud (1943) wrote the following: "Sexual experiences in childhood reconstructed and recollected in analysis are on some occasions undeniably false, while others are just as certainly quite true, and that in most cases truth and falsehood are mixed up" (p. 321). Freud recognized memories recovered in therapy could be true, false, or a blend of the two.

Elizabeth Loftus (1993, 1997, 2003) has challenged the authenticity of the repressed memories of some adults who claim they were abused as children. Loftus has never argued that child abuse does not occur. Nor does she argue that therapists regularly prompt or encourage false memories. She does argue that not every repressed memory of child abuse is accurate. Some people come to believe that they were abused as children to help explain the difficulties they are encountering as adults (Goodman et al., 2003; McNally, 2003a, 2003b, 2003c; Powell & Boer, 1994). Most people who were sexually abused when they were children do remember quite well the sorts of things that happened to them, often wishing that they could forget—or repress—them (Alexander et al., 2005).

The accuracy of long-term memory is also critical in eyewitness testimony. If, in fact, memories are often inaccurate, we may need to reconsider the weight our legal system gives to eyewitness testimony (Kassin et al., 2001; Ross et al., 1993; Wells & Olson, 2002, 2003). Many wrongful convictions are the result of errors in the recollections of eyewitnesses. Over 100 persons convicted

Courtesy of PhotoLink/Getty Images.

There may be no more critical an application of psychological research on memory than that on the validity of memories presented during eyewitness testimony.

before DNA was used for identification have now been exonerated. Of those, more than 75 percent were victims of mistaken eyewitness identification (Loftus, 2004; Scheck, Neufeld, & Dwyer, 2000; Wells & Olson, 2003; Wells, Memon, & Penrod, 2006).

The challenges posed to eyewitnesses occur at each phase of the memory process: encoding, storage, and retrieval. When you encode information, you select information to be placed into memory. For any event, it is likely that not all details of an event are equally attended to and encoded. Only details that are salient to the individual are encoded. For example, if you saw a person with a gun holding up a bank, you might encode information about the gun, the robber's clothing, his height, and his weight—particularly if he were very heavy or very thin. Other information (e.g., the color of the robber's shoes) may not be encoded.

Once information is encoded, it must be stored for later use. As we have seen, human memory is a dynamic, constructive process. Information placed into storage can be influenced by information already there and/or information that enters at a later time.

Imagine that you witnessed a robbery. At first, you believe the robber drove away in a green car. However, the next day you read in the newspaper that another witness described the getaway car as blue. Through a process of compromise memory (Loftus, 1979) you may blend green and blue and come to believe the car was a bluish-green.

Saul Kassin of Williams College and his colleagues surveyed experts on eyewitness testimony and found that the experts agreed on many of the issues related to such testimony (2001). Survey results are summarized in Table 6.1.

TABLE 6.1

Statements and observations about eyewitness testimony on which experts in the field agree (from Kassin et al., 2001).

1. An eyewitness' testimony about an event can be affected by how the questions put to that witness are worded.

2. Police instructions can affect an eyewitness's; willingness to make an identification.

3. Eyewitness testimony about an event often reflects not only what the witness actually saw, but information he or she obtained later.

4. An eyewitness's; perception and memory for an event may be affected by his or her attitudes and expectations.

5. Hypnosis increases suggestibility to leading and misleading questions.

6. An eyewitness's confidence is not a good predictor of his or her identification accuracy.

7. The presence of a weapon impairs the eyewitness's ability to accurately identify the perpetrator's face.

8. The rate of memory loss for an event is greatest right after the event and then levels off over time.

9. The less time an eyewitness has to observe an event, the less accurately he or she will remember it.

10. Eyewitnesses sometimes identify as a culprit someone they have seen in another situation or context.

BEFORE YOU GO ON

6.   What does the research on repressed memories of childhood trauma and on eyewitness testimony contribute to the discussion of the accuracy of long-term memory?

A Point to Ponder or Discuss
In our discussion on perception we noted that we often perceive what we expect to, or want to, or have perceived in the past. How might selective perception limit the accuracy of long-term memory?

SPOTLIGHT
ON DIVERSITY

Does Gender Affect Memory?

Are there gender differences in memory? Back in 1974, Maccoby & Jacklin failed to find significant gender differences on a wide range of ordinary memory tasks. This classic study—credited with igniting interest in the long-running search for stable sex differences in cognitive processing—looked at memory tasks that involved declarative long-term memory. For example, given a list of words to memorize today, would there be a difference in the recall of that list by males and females three weeks later? In this and similar tasks, the answer is "No." But what about for other varieties of memory?

There are significant and stable sex differences in both encoding and retrieval for episodic and/or autobiographical memory (Agnieszka, 2003; Herlitz, Nilsson, & Backman, 1997; Herlitz & Yonker, 2002). This finding has appeared in dozens of studies using a variety of techniques. In a test of recall of one's life events, for example, women generate recollections of more events, both positive and negative in their emotional flavor (Seidlitz & Diener, 1998). Fujita, Diener, & Sandvik (1991) tell us that women recall more emotional autobiographical events than men in timed tests, produce memories more quickly or with greater emotional intensity in response to provided cues, and report more vivid memories than their spouses for events related to their first date, last vacation, and a recent argument. Women's recall of gender-related memories from early childhood is faster and more complete than men's (Friedman & Pines, 1991). Sex differences also have been reported for the episodic memories of children, with greater length and detail in the reports of girls (Davis, 1999). When older adults are tested, for example by asking for oral life histories in semi-structured interviews, again researchers find that "women's memory styles were markedly more specific or episodic than were men's styles," suggesting that perhaps "women place a greater value on purposeful reminiscence than do men" (Pillemer et al., 2003, p. 525). Several studies suggest that men and women focus on different aspects of their autobiographical memories, with emotional loading being an important component for women, but not so for men. Men *do* have autobiographical memories of life experiences, but women have memories that are richer and more commonly associated with social context—memories of others, family, friends, and associates (Cowan & Davidson, 1984; Schwartz, 1984; Thorne, 1995).

In a related research study, Lindholm & Christianson (1998) found women outperformed men in eyewitness memory for a violent murder. The investigators claim that women's memories of such events may be better because women have more elaborate categories for encoding information about people. The study's authors speculate that such differences may be due to socialization: Males and females may be socialized and attend to—and hence remember—different sorts of information. For example, women seem to be better able to process information about people because women have learned to attend to more detail about people than have men.

Recent advances in neuroimaging have allowed researchers to see evidence of a neural basis for sex differences in processing episodic memories. These differences appear in images of the amygdala, a small structure of the limbic system that is associated with emotionality (Hamann, 2005). In one study (Canli et al, 2002), an fMRI recorded the brain activation of 12 men and 12 women while they rated their emotional arousal in response to neutral or emotionally negative pictures. Three weeks later, they all took a recognition test. All participants remembered the emotionally negative pictures better than the neutral ones, but women remembered the negative pictures significantly better than the men did. The fMRI showed that during the encoding of the pictures and at later testing the *right hemisphere* (side) of the amygdala was the more active in men, but the *left hemisphere* was the more active in women during these same periods. These results confirmed those of a similar study reported two years earlier (Canli et al., 2000) and have been reconfirmed by researchers at the University of California's Irvine campus (Cahill et al., 2004).

Conclusion

There may very well be no gender differences at all in the sorts of memory processing commonly done by college students: studying and remembering information for exams. However, men and women do differ significantly in the extent to which episodic or autobiographical memories are formed and recalled. Brain imaging studies reveal that the sexes use different sides of the amygdala in encoding and recalling emotionally charged memories.

WHERE AND HOW ARE MEMORIES FORMED IN THE BRAIN?

No one should be shocked to learn that memories reside in our brains. This much we know. But researchers still would like to know where memories are stored and how they are formed. New brain imaging techniques offer exciting possibilities for better answers to these two very old questions.

Where Are Memories Formed?

Karl Lashley (1890–1958), a student of John B. Watson, spent over 30 years trying to find the particular part of the brain where memories were stored. Lashley taught rats, cats, and monkeys to negotiate complex mazes. He then systematically removed or lesioned (cut) portions of the cerebral cortexes of these animals. Once he destroyed a part of the brain, Lashley tested the animal to see if it could still negotiate the maze. Lashley was hoping to discover where memories resided. Instead, he discovered that specific memories do not have specific locations in the brain.

Researchers now recognize a few limitations of Lashley's studies. For one thing, his studies were almost exclusively limited to maze running. Lashley may have been correct that memories for mazes are not stored in a single location in the brain. Nevertheless, other types of memories seem to have predictable locations. Individual experiences of sight, sound, or touch are usually stored in, or near, the relevant sensory area of the cerebral cortex. Memories of faces and of animals may have storage places of their own (Squire, 1992; Thompson & Krupa, 1994).

One brain imaging study examined which areas of the cortex were activated when participants were exposed to and asked to remember pictures or sounds.

The imagings showed that "the regions activated during the recall test comprised a subset of those activated during the separate perception task in which subjects actually viewed pictures and heard sounds" (Wheeler, Petersen, & Buckner, 2000, p. 11125; Gabrieli et al., 1998). Researchers at the University of Michigan also report that short-term memory storage locations are the same ones that were active in the *perception* of the information being stored. Even information brought to STM from LTM activates an area of the brain (mostly in the parietal and temporal lobes) that was activated when the information was initially processed (Jonides, Lacey, & Nee, 2005; Jonides et al., 2008).

Another limitation of Lashley's work is that it focused only on the cerebral cortex. Some evidence suggests that many lower brain centers are intimately involved in encoding and storing information (Deadwyler & Hampson, 2004; Gluck & Myers, 1995; Mishkin & Appenzeller, 1987). For example, we know that rabbits can be classically conditioned to close the protective tissue (*nictitating membrane*) that covers their eyes, in response to the sound of a tone. Once this response has been learned, the only way to destroy the association is to make small lesions in areas of the cerebellum. For rabbits, then, we know that "the essential memory trace was formed and stored in the cerebellum" (Thompson, 2005, p.5).

Most human memories are stored in the cerebral cortex, but lower brain structures also likely play roles in memory. For instance, the hippocampus appears vital to memory consolidation—taking experiences in short-term or working memory and moving them into long-term storage. Much of what we know about the role of the hippocampus we have learned from observing people who have lost at least one aspect of memory to illness or disease (Baddeley, 1990; Milner et al., 1968; Squire, 1992).

One patient known only as H.M. suffered from severe epilepsy. For nearly 11 years, he experienced an average of one major convulsive attack and several partial seizures every day. Having not found relief using conventional treatments, the patient chose radical surgery. Surgeons severed parts of the temporal lobe and removed the hippocampus from both sides of H.M.'s brain. The surgery was successful and greatly diminished H.M.'s epileptic seizures but left his sensory, perceptual, and intellectual functions mostly intact.

However, the surgery had disastrous effects on H.M.'s memory. He could not form new long-term memories. Failure to recall events before his surgery would have meant a diagnosis of **retrograde** (backward-acting) **amnesia**—the loss of memory of events that occurred before the onset of the amnesia. However, this was not the problem. H.M. could remember all that had happened to him before his surgery. He could not form memories of events that happened after the surgery. H.M. had **anterograde** (forward-acting) **amnesia**. If asked what year it was, H.M. would say, "1953"—the year the surgery was performed. If you were to interact with H.M. and then leave for a few minutes, he would not recognize you when you returned.

Consider the fate of Clive Wearing, a bright musician who suffered brain damage as the result of contracting encephalitis. He, too, was left after treatment with an inability to form new, lasting memories. Researchers recorded one recurring effect of Mr. Wearing's memory loss: "If his wife left the room for a few minutes, when she returned he would greet her with great joy, declaring that he had not seen her for months and asking how long he had been unconscious. Experienced once, such an event could be intriguing and touching, but when it happens repeatedly day in, day out, it rapidly loses its charm" (Baddeley, 1990, p. 5). Unlike H.M., Mr. Wearing also had signs of retrograde amnesia. His recollections of events before his illness were spotty and seldom included detail. Yet, his memory for making beautiful music remained.

From these and other similar cases, researchers reason that if only the

retrograde (backward-acting) amnesia the loss of memories of events that occurred before the onset of the amnesia

anterograde (forward-acting) amnesia the inability to form memories of events that happen after the onset of the amnesia

hippocampus is damaged and the rest of the brain is unscathed, the degree of amnesia (retrograde or anterograde) is considerably less than that of H.M. or Mr. Wearing, each of whom also had damage to his temporal lobes.

How Are Memories Formed?

When human memories are formed, changes occur in the cerebral cortex that are influenced by the action of the hippocampus. That may sound simple enough, but what sorts of changes? Exactly what is changed and in what ways? Answers are not yet available, and the hints suggest the processes involved are incredibly complex (Nee et al., 2008). If the nervous system is in some way altered as memories are formed, that alteration must be at the level of the neuron or the synapse.

Even by the late 1970s, researchers could see some evidence that memory formation produces changes at the synapse (Bartus et al., 1982; Lavond et al., 1993; Olson et al., 2006). One change that occurs is that, with experience, the synapse becomes more efficient. More specifically, when a synapse stimulates another neuron several times, future synaptic transmission at that site becomes easier (Kalat, 2001; Lang et al., 2004). *Glutamate*, the most abundant neurotransmitter in the brain, is also involved in learning and memory. Repeated stimulation at a glutamate receptor site causes a change in the ion balance on the postsynaptic membrane. This changed ion balance allows glutamate to stimulate a neuron at the synapse more easily.

If memories form because repetition, experience, or practice allow neurotransmitters to work more effectively at the synapse, what would happen if the action of those neurotransmitters were disrupted or blocked? Most of us would predict that memories formed at the synapses that used those neurotransmitters would be disrupted. Using neurotransmitters serotonin and acetylcholine, researchers have done such studies and they support the predicted outcome.

Other researchers claim that experience does not increase (or alter in any way) the neurotransmitter released at synapses. Instead, these researchers point to changes in the postsynaptic membrane as the source of the increase in synaptic efficiency. The most common changes are thought to be increases in the number of effective or useful receptor sites (Lynch & Baudry, 1984). As synapses are used repeatedly, the number of receptor sites increases. The increase in receptor sites makes synapse use more efficient.

In brief, the formation of memories involves both the formation of new synapses, and making some synaptic transmissions easier than they once were. What remains to be seen is whether the increased efficiency at the synapse is because more neurotransmitters are present or because physical changes in the membranes of neurons allow the same amount of neurotransmitters to work more effectively.

BEFORE YOU GO ON

7.   Where are memories formed and stored in the brain, and what sorts of physiological changes occur there?

A Point to Ponder or Discuss
Damage to different parts of the brain can cause retrograde or anterograde amnesia. How would you determine if a patient had anterograde or retrograde amnesia (or both), and what would this information tell you concerning where the patient's brain might be damaged?

RETRIEVAL AND HOW WE MEASURE IT

We now turn our attention to some practical matters, particularly for college students. *What factors affect our ability to retrieve information from long-term memory storage?* For now, matters of physiological underpinnings are of no concern. We have encoded some information in memory. Someone asks us for that information. What will determine whether we can respond successfully? In part, our ability to successfully retrieve the information depends how that information is asked for.

There are several ways we can retrieve information from memory. In some cases, we may be asked directly. For example, when you are taking an exam, you are consciously and actively trying to retrieve information from memory. In other instances, retrieval of information is not so direct or conscious. For example, you may have learned to play golf many years ago. When you try the game now, you find your skills are rusty. However, with just a bit of practice, you can return to your old form quickly. Because you retained some of your previous learning, you were able to relearn golf more easily.

Direct, Explicit Measures of Memory

Measures of retrieval are called direct, or explicit, when someone is asked to consciously or purposefully retrieve specified information from memory (as on a classroom exam).

One direct measure of memory is recall. **Recall** occurs when someone produces information to which he or she has been previously exposed. There are different types of recall tasks. In *free recall*, the learner is allowed to recall information in any order. For example, a teacher gives a student a list of 15 words to learn and then tests the student's recall by asking her to write the words *in any order.*

Free recall provides the fewest retrieval cues to aid the retrieval process. We merely specify the information wanted and say, "Go into your long-term memory, locate that information, get it out, and write it down." Another type of recall is *serial recall,* in which a person is required to recall information in the order in which it was presented. For example, a child learning the alphabet will be required to recall letters in the order learned. In another form of recall, called *cued recall,* some retrieval cues are provided. For example, if we asked you to learn a list of word pairs (cat–dog, car–boat, etc.), we might use the first word in each pair as a cue. You would be given the first word and asked to answer with the second.

Another explicit measure of memory is recognition. For **recognition**, we ask someone to identify material previously experienced. An eyewitness picking a suspect out of a lineup is a good example of a recognition task. The witness was exposed to a perpetrator at the scene of the crime. An image of the perpetrator's face was encoded into memory. During a lineup, the witness is asked if he or she recognizes the perpetrator. Recognition memory is a two-step process. First, the individual must retrieve information stored in memory (the memory of the perpetrator's face, for example). Second, the individual must compare that memory to the people in the lineup to determine whether the perpetrator is present.

Recognition memory is a more sensitive measure of memory than recall. In other words, we can often recognize things that we cannot recall. For example, have you ever recognized an acquaintance walking toward you but been unable to recall the person's name? In virtually every case, retrieval by recognition is superior to retrieval by recall (Bahrick, 1984; Schacter, 1987). Figure 6.2 depicts some clear-cut (and classic) data on this point. Over a two-day period, tests of retrieval by recognition are superior to tests of retrieval by recall.

recognition the process in which someone is asked to identify material previously experienced

recall the process that occurs when someone produces information to which he or she has been previously exposed

FIGURE 6.2

Differences in retrieval scores for the memory of nonsense syllables over a two-day period. In one case, retrieval is measured with a test for recall, whereas in the other case, retrieval is measured with a test for recognition (Luh, 1922).

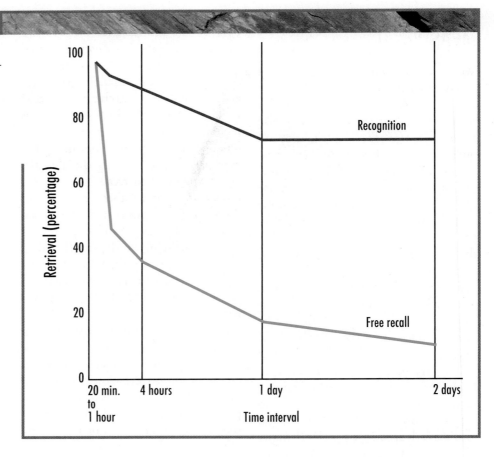

Most students would rather take a multiple-choice exam, in which they only have to recognize the correct response from among a few alternatives, than a fill-in-the-blank test (or a short-answer or essay test), which requires recall. Consider these two questions, each of which is after the same information. (1) The physiologist best associated with the discovery of classical conditioning was _____, and (2) The physiologist best associated with the discovery of classical conditioning was a) Thorndike b) Helmholtz c) Pavlov d) Skinner. For the first question, recall is required; for the second question, recognizing Pavlov's name is all that is needed.

Despite the differences between recall and recognition, the two forms of retrieval have common elements. Both involve the retrieval of material stored in declarative memory, either semantic or episodic (Hayman & Tulving, 1989; Tulving, 1983, 2003).

Indirect, Implicit Measures of Memory

Indirect or implicit measures of memory are more subtle than either recall or recognition. With indirect measures, a person demonstrates that information is stored in memory when he or she takes advantage of previous experiences without consciously trying to do so.

For example, suppose a student in a memory experiment returns to the laboratory two weeks after memorizing a list of 15 words and cannot recall or recognize any of the list words. We might be a bit surprised, but we would be wrong to assume that nothing had been retained from the earlier learning experience. What if we ask this student to relearn the list? Two weeks ago, it took ten presentations of the list before the student learned the words. Now, relearning the same list takes only seven trials. Relearning being easier than initial learning is a common finding in memory research.

Relearning is the change in performance that occurs when a person is required to learn material for a second time. Relearning almost always takes fewer trials, or less time, than did the original learning. The difference is attributed to the benefit provided by the person's memory of the original learning. Because relearning does not require the direct, conscious retrieval of information from memory, it qualifies as an indirect, or implicit, test of memory retention.

Among other things, research on implicit tests of memory supports the hypothesis that information is stored in various types of long-term memory. Although we may think of the relearning of verbal materials, such as words, as a typical example of an indirect measure of memory, many implicit tests of retention focus on procedural memories, or procedural knowledge. You will recall from our previous discussion that procedural memories include the storage of knowing how to go about doing things, such as speaking, typing, tying a shoelace, speaking, or riding a bicycle. Remembering how to do such things is virtually automatic or unconscious. When we specifically try to recall how to do them—when we really pause and think about what we're doing—our performance often deteriorates. Of procedural memories, one researcher writes the following: "In some sense, these performances reflect prior learning, but seem to resist conscious remembering" (Roediger, 1990, p. 1043).

Consider the story of a man with amnesia. He stumbles out of the woods

Courtesy of moodboard/Corbis.

Some memories—such as how to move one's fingers rapidly while playing a saxophone—are recalled implicitly, nearly defying conscious efforts to recall the sequence of such memories.

three days after going hunting. He approaches a farmhouse and knocks on the door. He remembers nothing—not his name, nor where he is from, nor whether he is married—nothing. However, when invited in, he sits at the table and eats a bowl of soup with perfect table manners, all the while telling those around him in perfectly good English that he cannot remember a thing. As extensive as his amnesia may be, his implicit recall—largely from procedural memory—is flawless.

> **relearning** the change in performance that occurs when a person is required to learn material for a second time

---

BEFORE YOU GO ON

8.   In what ways does how one is asked influence retrieval from long-term memory?

A Point to Ponder or Discuss
Well-practiced skills are often said to be "second nature," or almost automatic. Why are attempts to consciously recall such chains of behavior—as they are being performed—so disruptive?

FIGURE 6.3

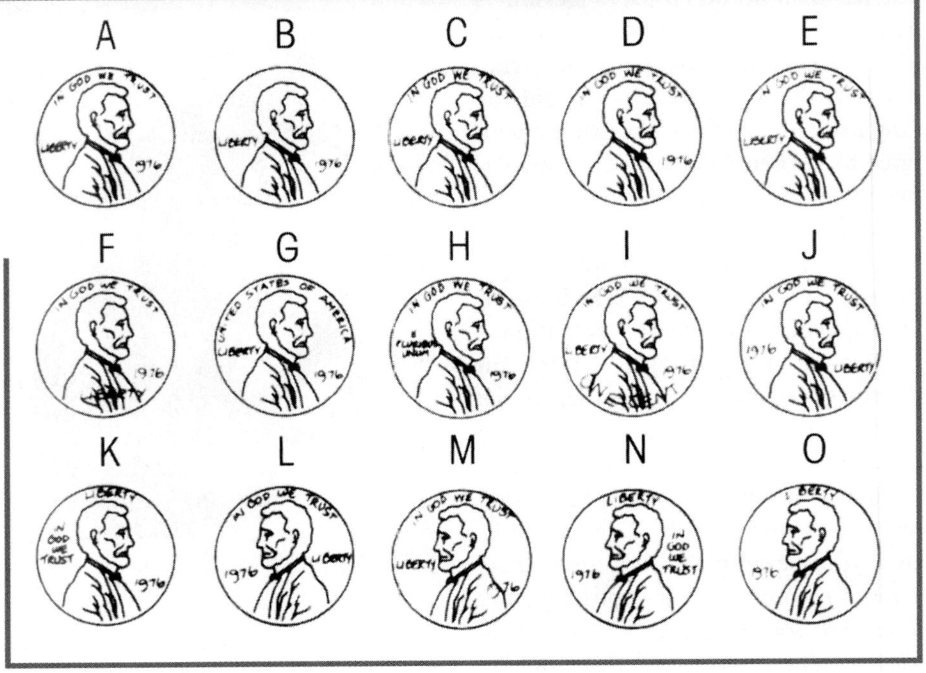

Fifteen drawings of the head of a penny. The fact that we cannot easily identify the correct rendition emphasizes that simple exposure to a stimulus does not guarantee it will be adequately encoded in long-term memory (Nickerson & Adams, 1979).

RETRIEVAL AND HOW WE ENCODE MEMORIES

Encoding, storage, and retrieval are interrelated memory processes. The issue in this section is simple: If you do not encode information properly, you will have difficulty retrieving it. You have had countless encounters with pennies. Can you draw a picture of a penny, locating all its features (recall)? Can you recognize an accurate drawing of a penny (See Figure 6.3)? In fact, few of us can, and even fewer can recall all of the essential features of a penny. Nearly 90 percent fail to note that the word *Liberty* appears behind Lincoln's shoulder (Nickerson & Adams, 1979; Rubin & Kontis, 1983). Such retrieval failures do not result from a lack of experience but from a lack of proper encoding. Few of us have ever sat down to study (encode) exactly what a penny looks like. We will cover four encoding issues: context effects, meaningfulness, mnemonic devices, and schemas.

encoding specificity principle the assertion that how one retrieves information depends upon how it was encoded in the first place

The Power of Context

Retrieval is more successful when it occurs in a situation as near to the one present at encoding as possible. When cues present at encoding are also present at retrieval, retrieval is better. The **encoding specificity principle** asserts that how we retrieve information depends on how it was encoded in the first place (Newby, 1987; Tulving & Thompson, 1973). We not only encode and store particular items of information, but also note and store the context in which those items occur. Indeed, there is even evidence for a cortical basis for the hypothesis, in that areas of the brain that are active during the encoding of visually-presented stimuli are precisely the same as those that are active upon the retrieval of those stimuli (Vaidya et al., 2002). The encoding specificity principle is as valid for animals as for humans. Of the ability of animals to recall, one researcher writes, "Ease of retrieval . . . is quite strongly influenced by the context in which the animal is asked to retrieve it. The closer the test context is to training conditions and the more unique the context is for specific memories, the better the retrieval" (Spear et al., 1990, pp. 190–191).

Here is a hypothetical experiment that demonstrates encoding specificity (based on Tulving & Thompson, 1973). Students are asked to learn a list of 24 common words. Half the students are given cue words to help them remember each item on the list. For the stimulus word *wood*, the cue word is *tree;* for *cheese*, the cue is *green,* and so on for each of the 24 words. The other students receive no such cues during their memorization (i.e., while encoding). Later, students are asked to recall as many words from the list as they can. Presenting the cue at recall improves performance for those students who were presented with it when they first learned the words. On the other hand, presenting the cue at recall to the other group actually lowers their recall. A fair conclusion for our experiment: If learning takes place without a cue, recall will be better without it.

Books about how to study in college often recommend that you choose one place for studying. Your kitchen table is not likely to be a good choice because it is associated with eating experiences (and many others). That is, the context of a kitchen is not a good one for encoding information unless you expect to be tested for retrieval in that same context—which seems very unlikely. This advice was reaffirmed by a series of experiments by Steven Smith (1979). He had students learn some material in one room and then tested their recall for that material in either the same room or a different one. When a new room—a different context with different cues—was used, retrieval scores dropped substantially. Simply instructing students to try to remember and think about the room in which learning took place helped recall considerably.

These context effects may be related to *state-dependent memory.* The idea here is that, to a degree, retrieval depends on the extent to which a person's state of mind at retrieval matches the person's state of mind at encoding (Leahy & Harris, 1989, p. 146). If learning takes place while a person is under the influence of a drug, for example, being under the influence of that drug at retrieval often has beneficial effects (Eich et al., 1975). For example, in one study, college students drank a sweetened beverage containing either caffeine or a placebo before they studied 40 pairs of words. The next day, they were tested for their memory of the words, again drinking a beverage with caffeine or a placebo. Those who drank the same beverage on both days recalled more words than did those who drank different beverages (Creeley & Keleman, 2003).

Now classic research by Gordon Bower (Bower, 1981; Bower & Mayer, 1989) suggests that mood can predict retrieval. Using moods (sad or happy) induced by posthypnotic suggestion, Bower found that retrieval was best when mood at retrieval matched mood at learning. Unfortunately, this "mood-dependent memory" effect has proven to be unreliable. Neither the circumstances under which it occurs nor the mechanisms that produce it are well understood (Eich, 1995; Eich et al., 1994). Still, there is evidence that a given mood or frame of mind tends to evoke memories that are consistent with that mood (e.g., Blaney, 1986). Simply put: When you are in a good mood, you tend to remember pleasant things, and when you are in a bad or depressed mood, you tend to remember unpleasant, depressing things.

For sure, emotionally arousing experiences are easier to recall than are emotionally neutral events (Levine & Bluck, 2004). Emotional arousal may help to explain what Brown and Kulik (1977) call flashbulb memories—memories that are unusually clear and vivid. You may have flashbulb memories of your first kiss, your high school graduation, or a traffic accident. Although flashbulb memories are particularly clear and

meaningfulness the extent to which to-be-remembered items elicit existing associations in memory

vivid, they are not necessarily any more complete or accurate than other memories. Although we seem to recall these events in vivid detail, much of that detail may be wrong or may never have happened (McCloskey et al., 1988; Neisser, 1982, 1991; Wright, Gaskill, & O'Muircheartaigh, 1998). A recent confirmation of the inconsistency found in flashbulb-type memories comes from a study by Jennifer Talarico and David Rubin of Duke University. The day after the horrific attack on the World Trade Center on September 11, 2001, students recorded their memories of first hearing about the disaster. They also recorded their recollections of everyday events. One, six, or 32 weeks later, the students recalled the traumatic and everyday events with equal accuracy. However, the students rated their memories of the traumatic events as more vivid and accurate than their memories of everyday events (2003).

The Usefulness of Meaningfulness

A psychology professor has a hypothesis. She believes she can determine the learning ability of students by noting where they sit in a classroom. The best, brightest students choose seats farthest from the door. Poorer students sit by the door, apparently interested in getting easily in and out of the room. (There may be some truth to this, but we are not serious.) To make her point, she does an experiment. Students seated away from the door are asked to learn a list of words. They are read the list only once. A second list of words is needed for the students seated by the door because they have already heard the first list. The list the "smart students" hear contains words such as *university, registrar, automobile, environmental,* and *psychology.* As predicted, they have little problem recalling this list even after just one presentation. The students huddled by the door get the second list: *insidious, tachistoscope, sophistry, flotsam,* and *episcotister,* and

the like. The professor's hypothesis will be confirmed.

This obviously is not a fair experiment. Those students sitting by the door will yell foul. The second list is far more difficult to learn and recall than the first. The words on the first list are more familiar and easier to pronounce. The major difference between these lists is the **meaningfulness** of the items—the extent to which they elicit existing associations in memory. The university, registrar, automobile list is easy to remember because each word is meaningful. Each word makes us think of many other things or produces many associations. These items are easy to elaborate. Words like episcotister are more difficult because they evoke few if any associations.

An important observation: Meaningfulness is not a characteristic or feature built into materials to be learned. Meaningfulness resides in the learner. *Episcotister* may be a meaningless collection of letters for many, but for others it is a word rich in meaning, a word with which they can readily form associations. What is or is not meaningful is a function of individual experiences. (An episcotister, by the way, is an apparatus used in psychology—usually in experiments on visual perception. To make this word truly meaningful, you might want to research episcotisters.)

It follows, then, that one of your tasks as a learner is to do whatever you can to make the material you are learning as meaningful as possible. You need to seek out and form associations between what you are learning and what you already know. You need to rehearse elaboratively what you are encoding so that you can retrieve it later. You need to ask questions about what you are studying. What does this mean? What does it make me think of? Does this remind me of something I already know? How can I make this more meaningful? Perhaps you now see the reason for including "Before You Go On" questions within each chapter.

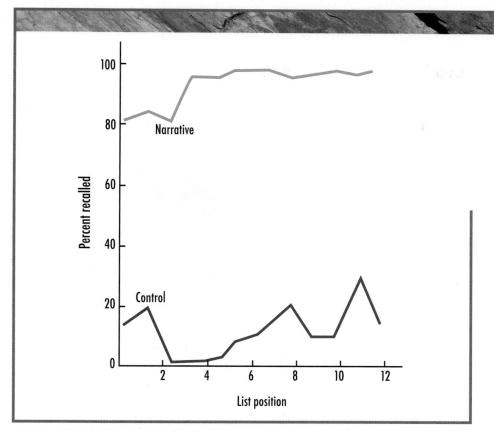

FIGURE 6.4

Percent correct recall for words from 12 lists learned under two study conditions. In the narrative condition, students made up short stories to relate the words meaningfully, whereas in the control condition, simple memorization without any mention of a specific mnemonic device was used (after Bower & Clark, 1969).

The Value of Mnemonic Devices

Retrieval is enhanced when we elaborate on the material we are learning—when we organize it and make it meaningful during the encoding process. Now we will look at a few specific encoding techniques, or **mnemonic devices**, that can aid our retrieval by helping us to organize and add meaningfulness to new material. The use of mnemonic techniques has been around, and the focus of psychological inquiry for many years.

Research by Bower and Clark (1969), for example, shows us that we can improve retrieval of otherwise unorganized material if we weave that material into a meaningful story—a technique called **narrative chaining**. A group of college students learned a list of ten simple nouns in a specific order. This is not a terribly difficult task, and the students had little trouble with it. Then they were given another list of ten nouns to learn, and then another, and

another until they had learned 12 lists. These students were given no instructions other than to remember each list of words in order.

A second group of students learned the same 12 lists, but they were asked to make up stories that used each of the words on each list in order. After each list was presented, both groups were asked to recall the list of words they had just heard. At this point, there was no difference in the recall scores for the two groups. Then came a surprise. After all 12 lists had been recalled, the students were tested again on their recall for each of the lists. Students were given a word from one of the 12 lists and were asked to recall the other nine words from that list. Now the difference in recall between the two groups of students was striking (see Figure 6.4). Students who used a narrative-chaining technique recalled 93 percent of the words (on average), but those who did not organize the words recalled only 13 percent. The message is clear and consistent with

mnemonic devices techniques that aid retrieval by helping one to organize and add meaningfulness to new material

narrative chaining the process that aids retrieval by the weaving of unorganized materials into a meaningful story

FIGURE 6.5

An illustration of how the key word method can be used to help foreign language retrieval. The Spanish word for "duck" is pato, pronounced "pot-oh."

what we have learned so far: Organizing unrelated words into sensible stories helps us remember them.

Forming *mental images* can also improve memory. Using imagery at encoding to improve retrieval has proven to be very helpful in many different circumstances. Canadian psychologist Allan Paivio contends that visual images provide a unique way of encoding meaningful information; thus, we are at an advantage when we can encode not only what a stimulus means, but also what it looks like (Paivio, 1971, 1986). Imagery helps us retrieve words such as horse, rainbow, and computer more readily than words such as treason, session, and effort.

Assume that you want to learn the meanings of a large number of Spanish words. You could use simple rote repetition, but this technique is tedious and inefficient. Richard Atkinson (1975) suggests imagining a connection that visually ties the word to a key word. He called this the key word method of study. The Spanish word for "horse," for example, is *caballo*, which is pronounced *cab-eye-yo*. To remember this association, you might choose eye as the key word and picture a horse kicking someone in the eye. If that is too gruesome, you might imagine a horse with a very large

eye. The Spanish word for "duck" is *pato*. Here your key word might be pot, and you could picture a duck wearing a pot on its head (Figure 6.5) or sitting in a large pot on the stove. Atkinson's learning method may sound strange, but research suggests that it works (Pressley et al., 1982).

The same basic technique works whenever you need to remember any paired items. Gordon Bower (1972), for example, asked students to learn lists of pairs of English words. Some students were instructed to form mental images that showed an interaction between the two words. One pair, for instance, was piano-cigar. Students who formed images of the word pairs were much better at recalling them.

Is it true that the more strange and bizarre the image, the better you will be able to recall it? The research is divided. Some suggests that common, interactive images work better (Bower, 1970; Wollen et al., 1972), but other research shows bizarre images work better to promote recall (Worthen & Marshall, 1996). For example, Worthen (1997) found that recall was better when a strange image was used (for example a cat with a bowl hovering over its tail) than when a more common image (a cat drinking from a bowl) was used. Strange

Courtesy of Corbis.

Having a complete, complex schema *for playing chess makes it easier to recall the placement of pieces on a chessboard—so long as those placements reflect a true game situation. If pieces are placed randomly on the board, a chess-playing schema will be of little value, and may even interfere with attempts to remember the placement of the chess pieces.*

images were better regardless of whether subjects generated their own or researchers provided them. If Worthen is right, it may be easier to learn a piano-cigar word pair by picturing a piano smoking a cigar than by picturing a cigar in an ashtray on a piano.

The last imagery-related mnemonic device may be the oldest. It is attributed to the ancient Greek poet Simonides and is called the **method of loci** (Yates, 1966). The learner imagines a familiar location (loci are locations)—such as her house or apartment and places the material she is trying to recall in various places throughout her house in a sensible order. When the time comes for her to recall the material, she walks through her chosen locations mentally, recalling the information stored at each.

Mnemonic devices do not have to be formal techniques with special names. You used a mnemonic device to remember how many days are in each month when you learned the ditty, "Thirty days

hath September, April, June, and November. All the rest have. . . ." Some students originally learned the colors of the rainbow in order (we called it the visible spectrum in Chapter 3) by remembering the name "ROY G. BIV," which is not terribly meaningful, but it does help us remember "red, orange, yellow, green, blue, indigo, and violet." You have likely used mnemonic devices to organize and make meaningful all sorts of study material. In each case, your retrieval was improved when you found a method to organize otherwise unrelated material in a meaningful way.

The Role of Schemas

The encoding specificity principle tells us that how we retrieve information is affected by how it was encoded. One process that influences how we encode and retrieve information is our use of schemas. A **schema** is an internal, organized, general knowledge system stored in long-term memory. Schemas come in a variety of forms. A *person schema* helps us organize information about the characteristics of people (for example, attractiveness, weight, and height) and store them in memory. A *role schema* includes information and expectations about how individuals in certain roles should behave. For example, when a person is in the role of "professor," that person is expected to come to class, lecture, give exams, and assign final grades. *Event schemas* (sometimes called "scripts") include our ideas about how events are to occur. For example, we know what should happen at a basketball game or a ballet performance.

Schemas help us organize information about our world. They help us remember things by allowing us to organize related information and activate that information when needed. For example, the single most important factor in a reader's comprehension turns out to be the reader's prior knowledge of the subject, or existing schema (Mayer, 2004). Generally, we remember information we have a schema for better than information we must

schema an internal, organized knowledge system stored in long-term memory

method of loci the mnemonic technique in which the learner imagines a familiar location and "places" the material to be retrieved in various places throughout that location in a sensible order

create a new schema for. Moreover, schemas direct our search for new information. We pay more attention to information that is consistent with an existing schema than to information that is not. One demonstration of the power of schemas used computer graphics simulations displayed on a head-mounted display utilizing stereo imaging and head tracking. Participants in this experiment were shown several "environments" (such as an academic's office), some which were constructed to match common schemas, while some contained information inconsistent with the scene(s) being viewed. Graphic displays that approximated common schemas were recognized and remembered to a much better degree than those that contained inconsistent details (Mania, Robinson, & Brandt, 2005).

Another clever demonstration of the action of schemas in action presented people with an image of a standard clock with the numbers represented as Roman numerals. When asked to draw the clock from memory, almost all participants mistakenly represented the "four" as "IV" rather than "IIII," which is commonly used on clock faces, including the one used in the experiment (French & Richards, 1993). A recent study showed that stimuli consistent with previously formed schemas were processed much more quickly than those for which previously formed schemas were not available (Tse et al., 2007).

Think in terms of your memory. If you were asked to recall all the details of your last trip to the dentist, wouldn't you rely on your knowledge of what it is like to go to the dentist in general—your schema? Wouldn't you supplement the actual recall of your last specific visit by adding details consistent with your schema?

BEFORE YOU GO ON

9. In what ways does encoding information influence the later retrieval of that information?

A Point to Ponder or Discuss
How can you use meaningfulness, mnemonics, schemas, and encoding specificity to learn and remember the material in this chapter?

RETRIEVAL AND HOW WE SCHEDULE PRACTICE

Retrieval depends on how information is encoded, rehearsed, or practiced. Retrieval also depends upon how much and how often we practice. Some students do not do well on exams because they simply do not have (or make) enough time to study. Other students underachieve because they do not schedule wisely the time they have.

Overlearning

Once we decide to learn something, we read, practice, and study the material until we know it. We study until we are satisfied that we have encoded and stored the information in our memories, and then—usually—we quit. That is, we do not engage in **overlearning**, the process of practicing or rehearsing material over and above what is needed to learn it.

Consider this example and how it might apply to your study habits. A student comes to the laboratory to learn a list of syllables such as *DAX, WUJ, PIB, LEP,* and *ZUW.* There are 15 such items on the list, and they have to be presented repeatedly before the student can recall all of them correctly. Having correctly recalled the items once, the student is asked to return in two weeks for a test of his recall. Not surprisingly, he doesn't do very well on the recall test.

overlearning the process of practicing or rehearsing information over and above what is necessary to learn it

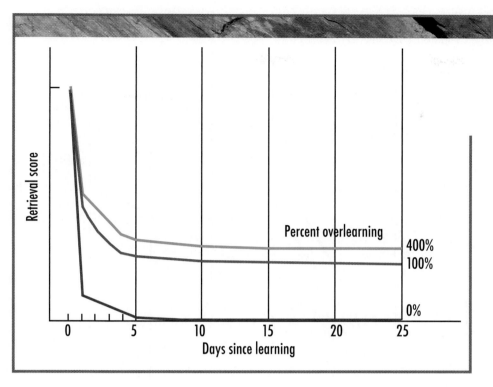

FIGURE 6.6

Idealized data showing the short-term and long-term advantages of overlearning. Note the "diminished returns" with additional overlearning (Krueger, 1929).

What do you think would have happened if we had continued to present the list of syllables at the time of learning, well beyond the point at which it was first learned? Let us say the list was learned in 12 trials. We ask the student to practice the list for six additional presentations (50 percent overlearning—practice that is 50 percent above that required for learning). What if we required an additional 12 trials (100 percent overlearning), or an additional 48 trials (400 percent overlearning)? The effects of overlearning are well documented and predictable. The recall data for this imaginary experiment might look like those in Figure 6.6. Note three things about these data:

1. Learners forget much of what they learn and do so quickly. (Researchers have reconfirmed this finding many times since Hermann Ebbinghaus first reported it in 1885.)

2. Overlearning improves retrieval and has its greatest effects the longer the time between learning and retrieval.

3. Overlearning produces diminishing returns; i.e., 50 percent overlearning is much more useful than no overlearning; 100 percent overlearning is somewhat better than 50 percent; and 400 percent overlearning is only slightly better than 100 percent.

Lest we rush to judgment, there also is some data that suggests that as logical as it may be to herald the benefits of overlearning, those benefits may be short-lived. Studying until mastery is achieved and then continuing with additional study immediately following may not be such an efficient use of a student's time (Rohrer et al., 2005; Rohrer & Pashler, 2007). It may be that investing overlearning spread out over time would be the best course of action. That is where we turn next.

Scheduling, or Spacing, Practice

Some of the oldest data in psychology tell us that retrieval will be improved if practice (encoding) is spread out over time, interspersed with intervals of rest.

FIGURE 6.7

Improvement in performance as a function of the distribution of practice time. The task involved was printing the letters of the alphabet upside-down and backward with 20 one-minute trials separated by rest intervals of various lengths (Kientzle, 1946).

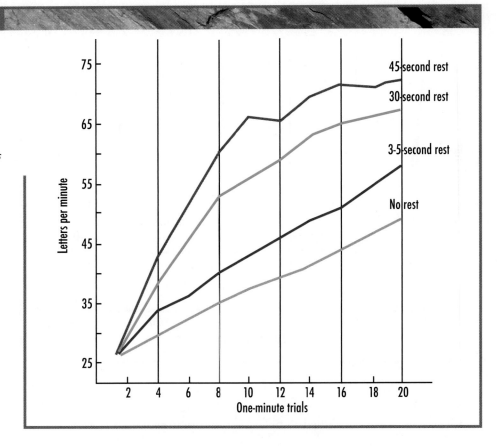

The data in Figure 6.7 are standard. This experiment, first performed in 1946, provides such reliable results that it is commonly used as a student project in psychology laboratory classes. The task is to write the letters of the alphabet, upside down and from right to left.

Researchers divide participants into four groups and give each group the opportunity to practice the task under different conditions. The massed-practice group works with no break between trials. The three distributed-practice groups receive the same amount of practice, but get to rest between each one-minute trial. One group gets a three-to five-second rest between trials, a second group receives a 30-second rest, and a third group gets a 45-second rest.

Participants in all four groups begin at about the same (poor) level of performance (see Figure 6.7). After 20 minutes of practice, all groups show improvement. However, the data show a distinct pattern. The massed practice (no rest) group does the worst, and the 45-second rest group does the best.

The conclusion from years of research: Distributed practice is superior to massed practice in nearly every case (Cepeda et al., 2006; Rohrer & Pashler, 2007). Of course, there are exceptions. Some tasks are disrupted by rigidly scheduled breaks and have their own built-in places breaks should be taken. A student working advanced calculus problems may find a break in the middle of a problem counterproductive. Several short periods with rest periods between are more efficient than a single marathon cram session. Cramming is better than not studying at all, but still far from the best way to study. (Here we have another justification for placing our "Before You Go On" questions throughout each chapter. They mark places to pause, review, and reinforce—before plunging into new material.)

BEFORE YOU GO ON

10. How do overlearning and the scheduling of practice affect retrieval?

A Point to Ponder or Discuss
Starting now, what can you change in the way that you study that will be consistent with the points raised in this section?

RETRIEVAL AND HOW WE OVERCOME INTERFERENCE

Think back to third grade. Can you remember the name of the student who sat behind you? Most of us can't. You may be able to guess (remember memory has a constructive nature), but there seems to be no way you can directly access and retrieve that name from long-term memory with certainty. Maybe the name is simply no longer there. It may be lost forever. Perhaps you never encoded that name in a way that would allow you to retrieve it effectively. Perhaps the name of that student is in your memory, but you cannot access it because you have been in so many classes since third grade. So much has happened and entered your memory that the name is "covered up" and being interfered with by information that entered later.

What is the name of the student who sat behind you in your most recent class? That may be a little easier, but remembering with confidence is probably still not easy. Again, our basic retrieval problem may be one of interference. Assuming that what we are searching for is still there, we may not be able to retrieve it because so many previous experiences are getting in the way, interfering with retrieval.

Retroactive Interference

That interference can disrupt retrieval is an old idea in psychology. For example, experiments in the 1920s demonstrated that students who were active for a period after learning had more difficulty remembering what they had learned than did students who slept for the same period (Jenkins & Dallenbach, 1924). Researchers have validated this principle using a large and surprising range of experimental subjects. Figure 6.8 depicts

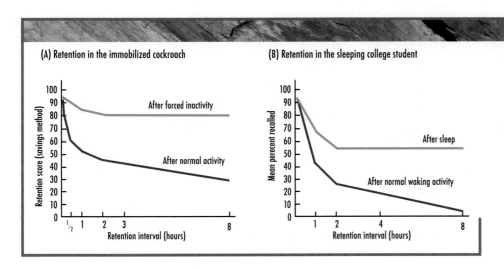

FIGURE 6.8

These groups illustrate how activity following learning can interface with the retrieval of the learned behavior or materials. In both cases, normal waking activity caused more interference than did forced inactivity (for cockroaches) or sleeping (for college students) (Minami & Dallenbach, 1946).

TABLE 6.2

Designs of experiments to demonstrate retroactive interference and proactive interference.

(A) Retroactive interference

	Learn	Learn	Test
Experimental group	Task A	Task B	Retrieval of Task A
Control group	Task A	Nothing	Retrieval of Task A

(B) Proactive interference

	Learn	Learn	Test
Experimental group	Task A	Task B	Retrieval of Task B
Control group	Nothing	Task B	Retrieval of Task B

Note: If interference is operating, the control group will demonstrate better retrieval than will the experimental group.

retroactive interference the process of inhibiting the retrieval of learned material by the acquisition of information learned after the to-be-remembered information

data from two experiments, one with college students who learned a list of nonsense syllables, and the other with cockroaches that learned to avoid a part of their cage. Student or roach, subjects who engaged in normal waking activity performed worse on tests of retrieval than their resting counterparts for all retention intervals.

Interference that *follows* the learning to be remembered or retrieved is called

Courtesy of Richard Klune/Corbis.

Growing up and learning to drive in North America means that we have learned to drive down the right side of a road. If one then travels to England and drives a car rented there one first finds that the steering wheel is on the "wrong side" of the car and that people drive down the "wrong side of the road." Here we have proactive interference—all those previous experiences are going to interfere with what now needs to be done.

retroactive interference. Let us look at a hypothetical learning experiment to illustrate the concept. Students are randomly assigned to an experimental group or a control group. Both groups are required to learn a list of nonsense syllables. Once they learn the list, students in the experimental group are asked to learn a second similar list. At the same time, control group students are told to rest quietly.

Both groups are asked to remember the first list of nonsense syllables. The control group will do better than the experimental group. For the experimental group, the second list interferes with the retrieval of the first (Table 6.2(A))

Retroactive interference is common. A student who studied French in high school takes a few Spanish courses in college and now cannot remember much French. The Spanish keeps getting in the way. Two students are scheduled to take a psychology test tomorrow at 9 AM. Both are equally able and motivated. One is taking only the psychology class. She studies for two hours, watches TV for two hours, and goes to bed. She comes in the next morning to take the test. The second student also studies psychology for two hours, but then she reads a chapter and a half from her sociology textbook. After reading sociology, she goes to bed, comes to psychology class, and takes the test. Everything else being equal, this second student will be at a disadvantage. The sociology she studied will retroactively interfere with her retrieval of the psychology she learned.

Proactive Interference

Proactive interference occurs when *previously* learned material interferes with the retrieval of more recently learned material. Let us return to hypothetical experiment with two groups of students. This time the experimental group learns a list of syllables and the control group rests quietly. Both groups then learn a second list of syllables. This time we test for the retrieval of the second list. Again, the control group students have an advantage because the first list is not in their memories to interfere with retrieval of the second. However, their advantage

is not as great as it was last time because proactive interference disrupts retrieval less than retroactive interference. How can students use this principle to study more effectively? Students should study their most important assignment last.

Many factors influence the extent of both retroactive and proactive interference. For example, meaningful, well-organized material is less susceptible to interference than is less meaningful material, such as nonsense syllables. As a rule, the more similar the interfering material is to the material being retrieved, the greater will be the interference (McGeoch & McDonald, 1931). The student who had to study for a psychology test and read a sociology text will experience more interference (retroactive or proactive) than will a student who has to study for the psychology test and work on calculus problems.

proactive interference the process that occurs when previously learned material inhibits the retrieval of more recently learned material

---

BEFORE YOU GO ON

11. What are retroactive and proactive interference, and how do they affect retrieval?

A Point to Ponder or Discuss
Imagine you have three exams on Monday. How will you schedule your studying to minimize the effects of interference?

A FINAL NOTE ON PRACTICING RETRIEVAL

In these last few sections, we have reviewed quite a bit of data and have summarized a number of laboratory experiments dealing with factors that affect our ability to retrieve information from memory. That ability often depends on how retrieval is measured and the quality of cue that are available to us at the time of retrieval. We have seen that the quality and the quantity of one's learning, or encoding, influence memory retrieval. We need to spend time with the material we are learning.

We need to try to encode that material in a meaningful and well-organized way, whenever possible matching cues available at retrieval with those present at encoding. We have to do what we can to avoid interference effects.

Now we need to add one more point: *The retrieval of information from long-term memory is enhanced when one practices retrieval.* In other words, retrieval is a practicable skill. This observation turns out to be true for the retrieval of all sorts of information by all sorts of organisms, but it is particularly relevant in the context of retrieving information in the classroom (Leeming, 2002; Roediger & Karpicke, 2006(a), 2006(b)).

Here is one way to think about this: What do classroom quizzes, tests, and exams really measure? Teachers often claim that they are measuring what you—as a student—have learned about a given body of knowledge. In fact, what a classroom test measures is not what you have learned as much as what you can remember (retrieve) at the time of the test! Now, of course, what you can retrieve on a test is surely a function of what you have learned, or studied, and we already have seen that there are several steps you can take to enhance your learning of classroom materials.

The point being made here is that it is powerfully advantageous to practice your retrieval of material. How do you that? Testing. Test yourself before your instructor gives you a test that will impact your grade. Once you have understood a section of your test, pause and try to imagine how you might be tested on that information. If your instructor goes on and on in class about some particular point, you might guess that the point will show up on the next test. How will your instructor ask you about that material? (If you have not yet figured it out, that is precisely why we include Practice Tests in the student study guide materials that accompany this textbook.) Two leading researchers in this area, Henry Roediger and Jeffrey Karpicke put it this way, "A powerful way of improving one's memory for material is to be tested on that material. Tests enhance later retention more than additional study of the material [over-learning], even when tests are given without feedback" (2006a, p. 181).

BEFORE YOU GO ON

12. What does it mean to say that retrieval is a practicable skill?

A Point to Ponder or Discuss
Many students find it useful to study with other students. There are many reasons why this might be a good idea (many of them social, of course). How may the discussion of this last section be used to guide the behaviors of students in a study group?

CHAPTER SUMMARY

1. **How can memory be characterized as a stage of information processing?**

   Memory is a set of systems involved in the *encoding, storage,* and *retrieval* of information. Memory is composed of systems that can hold information for periods ranging from fractions of a second to a lifetime. The storage capacities of memory systems range from very limited to vast. The information processing view of memory sees it as the end product of sensation, perception, and learning. In this view, encoding refers to the active process of deciding what should be placed into memory and forming cognitive representations for encoded information. Storage refers to the process of keeping information in memory after cognitive representations have been formed. Retrieval is the process of getting information out of memory. The *multistore model of memory* holds that there are a number of separate memory storage systems, each with its own ways of processing information. This model of memory divides memory into sensory memory, short-term memory, and long-term memory.

2. **What is the nature of sensory memory?**

   Sensory memory is a memory storage system that holds large amounts of information for very short periods of time. *Iconic memory* is the sensory storage system associated with vision, and it can hold information for about a half second. *Echoic memory* is the sensory store associated with hearing, and it can hold auditory information for five to ten seconds.

3. **Describe short-term, or working, memory.**

   Short-term memory (STM) is a storage system in which information can be held for several seconds (occasionally up to one minute) before it fades or is replaced. Encoding information into this memory requires that we attend to it. Information may enter short-term storage from sensory memory or be retrieved from long-term memory. We keep material in STM by re-attending to it, a process called maintenance rehearsal. The capacity of short-term memory is approximately 7 ± 2 "chunks" of information, where a *chunk* is an imprecise measure of a unit of meaningful material. Finding creative ways to chunk information can allow STM to hold more information.

4. **What are the capacity and duration of long-term memory?**

   Long-term memory is a storage system that houses large amounts of information for long, virtually limitless, periods. Barring illness or injury, a person can reasonably expect long-term memory to hold memories for a lifetime. Researchers have not yet devised a means to measure the capacity of long-term memory, but it appears to be nearly limitless.

5. **What are possible varieties of long-term memory?**

   Declarative memory is a storage system with subsystems for verbally oriented, factual information (semantic memory) and for events (episodic memory). *Nondeclarative* memory (procedural memory) involves memory for the acquisition, retention, and retrieval of performance skills. Semantic memory is the subsystem of declarative memory where we store our vocabulary, simple concepts, and rules for language use. Information is stored in semantic memory in an organized fashion. Information is best encoded into semantic long-term memory by elaborative rehearsal. *Episodic memories* record life events and experiences. They are tied to specific times and places. There is a separate category of episodic memory known as autobiographical memory, which stores important events from one's life. Procedural memory is part of the nondeclarative memory system. In this storage system we keep recollections of learned responses or chains of responses. Procedural memories involve knowing how to perform a skill (for example, riding a bike or hitting a golf ball).

6. **What does the research on repressed memories of childhood trauma and on eyewitness testimony contribute to the discussion of the accuracy of long-term memory?**

   Despite the popular conception of memory as working like a camcorder, recording information exactly for later playback, memory is a *constructive process.* Only features of an experience or event are stored, and recall involves a reconstruction of those features. According to this view, stored features are scattered in different areas of the brain. When we want to remember something, a feature is activated that sets off a chain reaction in other related features. Ultimate recall, then, can be influenced by several events other than the to-be-recalled event itself.

Repressed memories are events presumed to be in one's long-term memory, but very difficult to recall, or bring into consciousness, because they produce anxiety. Some psychologists have challenged the accuracy of repressed memories. The debate is not just academic. Courts of law have accepted testimony from adults concerning repressed memories of sexual abuse during childhood. The accuracy of repressed memories of child sexual abuse remains a very controversial topic.

Many factors, other than the actual event itself, can influence the recollections of eyewitnesses. Overall, the research on eyewitness memory suggests that information held in long-term memory is not permanent or unchangeable. It can be susceptible to many outside influences.

7. **Where are memories formed and stored in the brain, and what sorts of physiological changes occur there?**

In ways yet unknown, human memories are probably stored throughout the cerebral cortex. The hippocampus is surely involved in the consolidation of long-term memories, as studies of patients with amnesia have shown. Memories for events are probably stored at, or very near, those cortical locations that originally processed the event. At the neural level, synaptic pathways that are used repeatedly become more and more efficient in their ability to transmit neural impulses. Neurotransmitters are better able to function at the synapse. Improved neurotransmitter function is more likely a result of changes in the receptor sites of post-synaptic neurons than it is of any change in the neurotransmitters themselves. Discovering the precise physiological changes that occur as memories are formed, stored, and retrieved is one of the most active areas of research in neuroscience today.

8. **In what ways does how one is asked influence retrieval from long-term memory?**

The ability to retrieve information stored in long-term memory (LTM) is partially determined by how one is asked to do so. An explicit measure of memory asks that a person consciously or purposefully retrieve information from memory. Recall and recognition both qualify as explicit measures. *Recall* involves asking a person to produce information to which he or she has been pre-viously exposed. Recall is a process that involves going into memory and pulling out as much identified information as possible. *Recognition* is a direct measure of memory in which the information to be retrieved is presented and a person is asked if it can be identified as familiar. Recognition is a two-step process involving retrieving information and then comparing it to what is to be recognized. A decision must be made as to whether the information has been experienced before. Retrieval measured by recognition is generally superior to retrieval measured by recall.

Implicit tests of memory assess the extent to which previously experienced material is helpful in subsequent tasks. Implicit tests of memory do not require conscious efforts to recall information. For example, *relearning* shows us that, even when information can be neither recalled nor recognized, it will be easier to relearn than it was to learn in the first place. Relearning is the change in performance when a person is required to learn material for a second time. Relearning almost always requires fewer trials than the original learning did because some material learned previously remains in memory.

9. **In what ways does encoding information influence the later retrieval of that information?**

Retrieval depends heavily on encoding. For example, the greater the extent to which the cues or context available at retrieval match the cues or context available at encoding, the better retrieval will be. Even matching a person's state of mind at encoding and retrieval may improve retrieval. The *encoding specificity principle* suggests that we not only encode what we are trying to learn, but also encode aspects about the place where the learning occurred. Recall for information will be easier if memory is tested in the same place that learning occurred.

Meaningfulness reflects the extent to which material is associated with, or related to, information already stored in memory. In general, the more meaningful the material, the easier it will be to retrieve. Meaningfulness resides in the individual and not in the material to be learned. *Mnemonics* are specific encoding techniques that can help us retrieve information. They help us organize and add meaningfulness to new information at encoding by taking advantage of existing memories. For example, narrative chaining involves making up a story that meaningfully weaves together otherwise unorganized words or information. Forming mental images of information to be remembered is also helpful. The *method of loci* is an imagery method in which one "places" pieces of information at various locations (loci) in a familiar setting and then retrieves those pieces of information by mentally traveling through the setting. Schemas are organized, general knowledge systems stored in LTM. Based on past experiences, schemas summarize essential features of common events or situations. They are used to guide the organization of and give meaning to new information. The more relevant one's available schemas for to-be-remembered information, the better encoding and retrieval will be.

10. **How do overlearning and the scheduling of practice affect retrieval?**

Overlearning is the rehearsal or practice of material beyond what is necessary for immediate recall. Within limits, the more one engages in overlearning, the greater the likelihood of accurate retrieval. Retrieval also is affected by how one schedules study (or encoding) sessions. In massed practice, study or rehearsal occurs in a single uninterrupted session. Distributed practice occurs in segments with rest between them. In almost all cases, distributed practice produces better retrieval than massed practice.

11. **What are retroactive and proactive interference, and how do they affect retrieval?**

Retroactive interference occurs when material or information cannot be retrieved because it is blocked by material or information learned later. *Proactive interference* occurs when information cannot be retrieved because it is blocked by material or information learned earlier. Typically, retroactive interference lowers retrieval more than proactive interference does.

12. **What does it mean to say that retrieval is a practicable skill?**

Learning cannot be measured directly. All one can do is measure performance (retrieval) and, on that basis, make determinations about the extent to which learning was successful. Retrieval is a practicable skill. The more one engages in testing for stored information, the better will be the retrieval of that information.

"Higher" Cognitive Processes

7

PREVIEW

As this chapter's title implies, cognitive mental processes can be divided into lower and higher. Because these categories overlap and interrelate, the difference is not always clear. Nevertheless, here it is: The lower cognitive processes are tied to the immediate environment. They involve selecting stimuli for our attention, organizing and interpreting those stimuli (perception), encoding them for storage (memory), and making relatively permanent changes in our behaviors and/or mental processes as a result (learning). On the other hand, higher cognitive processes are built upon lower ones. They are not tied to direct experience. Instead, they use and manipulate cognitions that have already been processed.

We begin by discussing thinking, a term that includes forming concepts, reasoning and making decisions. Then, we examine two higher cognitive processes: solving problems and using language. We focus on problem solving because it requires that we have the right set of concepts to consider, that we can reason logically, and that we make sound decisions. It is in the context of problem solving that we review what psychologists mean by "creativity."

Then we consider language. Arguably, the use of language sets humans apart. Other species may have complex means of communicating, but only humans have language—at least as we shall define it.

The second half of this chapter deals with intelligence. Defining intelligence is difficult. Most likely intelligence is not a singular, unitary talent, or process: People can be intelligent or act intelligently in many ways. When doing research on intelligence, psychologists operationally define it—recall that an operational definition specifies how a concept is measured. Therefore, we will look at some popular measurements of intelligence. Psychologists call these measurements intelligence tests. We will define psychological tests generally,

and see what makes some tests better than others. We will examine group differences in measured intelligence. Finally, we will consider individual differences in measured intelligence, looking at giftedness and retardation.

SOME THOUGHTS ABOUT THINKING

Thinking is a term that refers to cognitive processes that build on existing cognitions—perceptions, ideas, experiences, and memories. Thinking uses concepts: The answer to "Find the reciprocal of 25?" requires thinking about what a reciprocal is. Thinking involves reasoning: "I don't really like chemistry and I am earning Cs and Ds in it. I like psychology and haven't earned anything but As in my psychology classes. Maybe I ought to switch majors." Thinking involves problem solving: "I missed class on Wednesday; how can I get the notes?" Thinking can be creative: "How can I do this differently and better?" Thinking is largely a matter of the ability of the human system of cognitions to go beyond and manipulate information that is readily available in the environment (Markman & Genter, 2001).

In Chapter 1, we introduced you to John Locke. Locke suggested that our minds contain *ideas* and that those ideas come from our experience (a notion psychologists agree with). In today's terminology, however, Locke's *ideas* are called concepts. **Concepts** are mental categories or classes into which we place the events and objects we experience. Concepts are what we use when we think. Concepts are crucial to the survival of thinking beings: "Is the plant edible or poisonous? Is that person friend or foe? Was the sound made by a predator or by the wind?" All organisms assign objects and events in the environment to separate classes or categories. This allows them to respond differently, for example, to nutrients and poisons, and to predators and prey. Any species lacking this ability would quickly

---

thinking a term referring to cognitive processes that build on existing cognitions—perceptions, ideas, experiences, and memories

concepts mental categories or classes into which we place the events and objects that we experience

become extinct" (Ashby & Maddox, 2005, p. 150).

Think about chairs. Really. Take a moment and think about them. As you do, pay attention to what you are doing. Images come to mind. You may imagine armchairs, dining-room chairs, rocking chairs, high chairs, chairs in the classroom, easy chairs, overstuffed chairs, broken chairs, and so on. As you thought about chairs, did one chair—some standard, definitional chair—come to mind? Are there defining characteristics of chairs? Most have four legs, although beanbag chairs have none. Most chairs are used for sitting, although people also stand on chairs to reach high places. Most chairs have backs, but if the back gets too low, you have a stool, not a chair. Most chairs are made for one person; if they get too wide they become benches, love seats or sofas.

In fact, most concepts in our memories are "fuzzy" (Labov, 1973). What is the difference between a river and a stream? Somehow we know, but because these concepts are not exact, they are difficult to distinguish. Fuzzy concepts are precisely why we say things such as, "Technically speaking, a tomato is a fruit, not a vegetable." Or, "Actually, a spider really is not an insect." One way to deal with this complication is to follow the lead of Eleanor Rosch (1978). She argued that we think about concepts in terms of **prototypes**—members of a category that typify or represent the category to which they belong.

Rosch suggests that, within our concept of chair, are certain examples that are more typical—more "chair-ish"—than others. The same principle applies to birds. A robin may be a prototypic bird. Crows are less prototypic. Vultures are even less so, and that penguins even *are* birds may be difficult to remember because they seem so different from the prototype. Concepts, then, are the mental representations of our experience. They are what we talk about when we communicate. They are what we manipulate when we think and when we solve problems.

Reasoning is the process of reaching conclusions that are based on either a set of general (cognitive) principles or an assortment of acquired facts and observations. There are two major categories of reasoning, *inductive* and *deductive*, but some instances of reasoning do not fall neatly into either category.

When fictional detectives or real-life crime scene investigators pull together many pieces of evidence to determine who committed a crime—and when and how it was committed—they are reasoning inductively. **Inductive reasoning** leads to a likely general conclusion based on separate, specific facts and observations. Indeed, reasoning inductively is not easy. Errors can enter the process in many ways: Are the facts and observations accurate in the first place? Are they relevant? Do these facts also support a different, but just as logical, conclusion? We will treat reasoning as a subset of problem-solving in the next section.

Many of the same barriers to effective inductive reasoning also apply to deductive reasoning. **Deductive reasoning** leads to specific conclusions about events based on a small number of general principles (concepts again). In a way, deductive reasoning is inductive reasoning in reverse. You have a few general concepts that cover life on campus. Eighteen to 28 year olds who walk around

prototypes members of a category that typify or best represent the category to which they belong

reasoning the process of reaching conclusions that are based either on a set of general (cognitive) principles, or on an assortment of acquired facts and observations

inductive reasoning mental processes that lead to a likely general conclusion based upon separate, specific facts and observations

deductive reasoning mental processes that lead to specific conclusions based on a small number of general principles

We might think of a robin as a prototypic member of the general concept of "birds." Penguins are less prototypical, and sometimes it is easy to forget that penguins really are birds.

Courtesy of Momatiuk - Eastcott/Corbis.

camps, sit in classrooms and carry textbooks are likely to be students. Indeed, these general principles of college life have grown from personal experience as well as from reading and hearing about college students. So when you see 24-year-old Bob walking across campus and into a psychology class, with textbooks under his arm, you deduce that

Bob is a college student. And well he may be. Can you imagine possibilities for this scenario in which Bob is *not* a college student? Again, we will treat deductive reasoning as a special case of problem-solving, where the problem takes the form, "Given what you know about the world, how can you explain this particular event or observation?"

BEFORE YOU GO ON

1. What is "thinking," and to what extent does it involve concepts, reasoning, and problem solving?

A Point to Ponder or Discuss
Do non-humans think? How would we know for sure whether they did or did not? What might they think about?

PROBLEM SOLVING

In their 1954 text, *Experimental Psychology*, Woodworth and Schlosberg began their chapter on problem solving with this observation: "If the experimentalist could show us how to think clearly, and how to solve our problems successfully and expeditiously, his social contribution would be very great" (p. 814). Their hope has yet to be fulfilled. Our daily lives are filled with problems of various sorts. Some are simple, straightforward, and even trivial; others are complex and crucial. Here we focus on cognitive, or intellectual, problems—those that require the manipulation of cognitions for their solution. The first thing to do is define what a problem is, and then we can consider how to go about solving one.

Sometimes our goals are obvious, our situation is clear, and the way from where we are to where we want to be is also obvious. In such cases, we do not have a problem, do we? Suppose you're hungry for breakfast and you have eggs, bacon, bread, and butter. You also have a stove, pans, a spatula and the know how to cook. Further assume you like

to eat eggs, bacon, and buttered toast. With little hesitation, you will engage in the appropriate behaviors and reach your goal. More plainly, you will cook and eat.

A **problem** exists when there is a discrepancy between one's present state and one's perceived goal state and no readily apparent way to get from one to the other. When the path to attaining your goal is not clear, a problem exists, and you need to engage in problem-solving behaviors—as might be the case if halfway through making breakfast you were to discover you had no butter or margarine.

A problem, then, has three major components: a) an *initial state*—the situation as it exists, or is perceived to exist, at the moment; b) a *goal state*—the situation as the problem solver would like it to be; and c) possible routes or *strategies* for getting from initial state to goal state.

Psychologists also distinguish between well-defined and ill-defined problems. *Well-defined* problems are those in which both the initial state and the goal state are clear. We know what the current situation is and what the

problem a situation that exists when there is a discrepancy between one's present state and one's perceived goal state and no readily apparent way to get from one to the other

goal is, and we may even know some of the possible ways to go about getting from one to the other. "What English word can be made from the letters *teralbay*?" We see that this question presents a problem. We understand what the question is asking, have some ideas about how we might go about answering it, and will surely know when we have succeeded. "How do you get home from campus if you discover that your car won't start?" Again, we know our initial state (on campus with a car that won't start), and we will know when we have reached our goal (we're at home), but we have to find a different way to get there.

Most problems we face are *ill-defined*. In such cases, we have neither a clear idea of what we are starting with, nor a clearly identified solution. "What should my college major be?" Many high school seniors (and a few college seniors) do not even know what their options are. They have few ideas about how to investigate college majors. And once they have selected a major, they are not at all sure that their choice was the best one—which may explain why so many college students change their majors so often. Ill-defined problems usually involve several variables that are difficult to define (much less control), so psychologists usually study problems that are reasonably well-defined.

BEFORE YOU GO ON

2. What is a problem, and how do a well-defined and an ill-defined problem differ?

A Point to Ponder or Discuss
List five or six problems you faced yesterday and determine whether each is well-defined or ill-defined.

Problem Representation

Once we realize we are facing a problem, the first thing we should do is put it in some form that allows us to think about it in familiar terms. We need to represent the problem in our minds, interpreting the problem so that the initial state and the goal state are as clear as we can make them. We also need to note any restrictions on how we can go about seeking solutions. In short, we need to understand the nature of the problem and make it as meaningful as possible by relating it to information in our memories.

By examining a few problems of the sort that have been used in the psychology laboratory, we can see that how we represent a problem can be critical. Consider the following classic example (from Duncker, 1945):

> One morning, exactly at sunrise, a Buddhist monk began to climb a tall mountain. A narrow path, only a foot or two wide, spiraled around the mountain to a glittering temple at the summit. The monk ascended at varying rates of speed, stopping many times along the way to rest and eat dried fruit, which he carried with him. He reached the temple shortly before sunset. After days of fasting and meditation, he began his journey back down along the same path, starting at sunrise again and walking at variable speeds, with many pauses along the way. His average speed going down was, of course, greater than his average climbing speed. Show that there is a spot along the path that the monk occupied on both trips at precisely the same time of day.

Many of the problems we face in daily living are "ill-defined." "It's getting to be dinner time. I'd like to prepare something nice for my friends who just stopped by. What do I have on hand, and what can I do with what I have?"

Courtesy of Cultura/Corbis.

Thinking about this problem as it is presented here can be maddening. As is often the case with real-life problems, this statement contains a lot of irrelevant information. Problem representation often requires sorting out what matters from and what does not. The fact that the man is a monk is not relevant, nor is that the destination is a temple, nor that dried fruit is eaten, nor that the path is narrow, nor that the trip was made on two different days.

You might represent this problem in terms of just one climber making the trip in one day. Or, better still, imagine two climbers: one starting from the top and the other starting from the bottom. Because they both take the same path, they will meet at some point during the day. Representing the problem this way, makes the truth that the monks will meet easy to see. Representing this mountain-climbing problem by sketching ascending and descending pathways also makes it easier to solve.

Drawing is not always the best way to represent a problem. Representing the following problem visually would not be wise:

Imagine that you have a very large sheet of paper, 1/100 of an inch thick. Imagine folding

it over on itself so that now you have two layers of paper. Fold it again so that there are four layers. It is impossible to actually fold a sheet of paper 50 times, but imagine that you could. About how thick would the paper be if it were folded over on itself 50 times? (From Adams, 1974)

It sounds simple. Unfortunately, estimating the thickness of a piece of paper folded 50 times is difficult. Some people guess a few inches. Others guess a few feet. Many more have no idea at all. Representing this problem visually does not help. The person who represents the problem using exponents is more likely to arrive at an accurate answer. Actually, 50 folds would increase the paper's thickness by a factor of 2^{50}. That comes to about 1,100,000,000,000,000 inches, roughly the distance from the earth to the sun!

Very often, representing a problem well is the key to solving it. Once you recognize a problem, your first step in solving it should be to find ways to represent it in a variety of ways. A successful representation helps to eliminate nonessential information and connects the problem to those you have solved before. Even when they are well represented, some problems defy easy solution. (Much of what we call "creativity" is little more than the ability to represent problems in novel or unique ways.) We now turn to how to generate solutions.

Problem-Solving Strategies

Once you have an adequate representation of the initial state of a problem and have a clear idea of what an acceptable goal state might be, you still have to figure out how to get to that goal. Not surprisingly, problem solvers use strategies. In this context, a **problem-solving strategy** is a systematic plan for generating possible solutions that can be tested to see if they are correct. Cognitive strategies permit the problem solver to exercise some control over the task at hand.

problem-solving strategy a systematic plan for generating possible solutions to a problem that can be tested to see if they are correct

They allow solvers to choose the skills and knowledge they bring to bear on any particular problem at any time. We will consider two problem-solving strategies: algorithms and heuristics.

An **algorithm** is a strategy that, if correctly applied, guarantees a solution to the problem eventually. An algorithm explores and evaluates all possible solutions in a systematic way until the correct one is found. For this reason, algorithm is sometimes called a *generate-test strategy*. (Hypotheses are generated and then tested one at a time.) Given their computation speed, computers are frequently programmed to solve problems using algorithms.

Simple anagram problems (letters of a word shown in a scrambled fashion) can be solved using an algorithmic strategy. "What English word has been scrambled to make uleb?" With sufficient patience, you can systematically rearrange these four letters until you hit on a correct solution: leub, lueb, elub, uleb, buel, beul, blue. There it is, blue. With only four letters to deal with, finding a solution generally doesn't take very long; there are only 24 possible arrangements of four letters ($4 \times 3 \times 2 \times 1 = 24$).

On the other hand, consider the eight-letter anagram teralbay. In fact, there are 40,320 possible combinations of these eight letters: $8 \times 7 \times 6 \times 5 \times 4 \times 3 \times 2 \times 1 = 40{,}320$ (Reynolds & Flagg, 1983). Unless you happen to start in a good place, you may waste time trying bad combinations. If we were attempting a ten-letter anagram, we would have 3,628,800 combinations to check!

Imagine that you go to the supermarket to buy a jar of horseradish. You're sure the store has horseradish, but you do not know where it is. You could go up and down every aisle, checking first the top shelf, then the second, then the third, until you spied the horseradish. This algorithmic strategy would work if the store carried horseradish and if you searched carefully enough. Shopping this way would be inefficient. We don't use algorithms to grocery shop; instead, we use heuristics.

Courtesy of Steve Prezant/Corbis.

A **heuristic** is an informal, rule-of-thumb strategy of generating and testing problem solutions. For solving problems, heuristics are generally more efficient than algorithms, but they do not offer a guarantee of eventual success. In many cases, heuristics save time by searching for solutions in the places they are most likely to be found. A heuristic strategy for finding horseradish might take you to various sections in the store in the order you believed to be most reasonable. You would not waste time searching the cereal aisle or the frozen food section—required if you were using an algorithmic strategy. Another, even more reasonable, heuristic would be to ask an employee.

If you tried the teralbay anagram problem, it is likely you used a heuristic strategy. To do so, you rely on your experience with the English language. (You take advantage of pre-existing cognitions.) You seriously consider only those letter combinations you know occur frequently. You generate and test the most common combinations first. You don't worry much about the possibility that the solution may contain a combination such as *brty*. Nor do you search for a word with an *aae* string in

You are in the supermarket, and a problem arises. You have horseradish on your list and don't know where to find it. An algorithmic strategy would be to go up and down every aisle, looking on every shelf. It might take you a long time, but you would find the horseradish. A heuristic strategy would be to begin your search in those areas where you thought the horseradish might be. Better yet would be the strategy of asking a store employee where the horseradish is displayed.

algorithm a strategy that, if correctly applied, guarantees a solution to a problem eventually

heuristic an informal, rule-of-thumb strategy of generating and testing problem solutions

it. You explore words that end in *able* because you know these to be fairly common. But that doesn't work. What about *br* words? No, that doesn't work. How about words with *tray* in them? *Traybeal*? No. *Baletray*? No. "Oh! Now I see it: *betrayal*." This heuristic strategy is a means-ends analysis, a strategy in which one always keeps the final goal in mind, but first works toward reaching

subgoals. In the teralbay example, subgoals are letter combinations that make sense or are commonly found. Once subgoals are reached, they are manipulated in an attempt to reach the final goal. The horseradish search also involved a means-ends analysis: First find the right section of the store, and then search for the specific product.

BEFORE YOU GO ON

3. Beginning with problem representation, describe the steps in effective problem solving.

A Point to Ponder or Discuss
Generate your own examples of problems that could be solved with either algorithmic or heuristic strategies. For each, which strategy is likely to be more effective?

Barriers to Effective Problem Solving

It is difficult, often impossible, to solve problems without relying heavily on one's memory. If you could not remember the recipe for something you wanted for dinner, you would have difficulty buying the ingredients. If couldn't remember the layout of the streets around campus, you would have a struggle getting home if your usual route was blocked by construction. Regardless of the type of problem or the strategy employed to solve it, solving problems effectively requires that we use our memories. There are times, however, when previous experiences (and memories of them) create difficulties in problem solving. We will look at three such cases: mental sets, functional fixedness, and biased heuristics.

Perceptions can be influenced by expectations or by an individual's mental set. We often perceive what we are set to perceive. The concept of mental set is also very relevant in problem solving. A **mental set** is a tendency to perceive or respond to something in a given, or set, way. It is, in essence, a cog-

nitive predisposition. We may have expectations that interfere with effective problem solving.

A classic example of how an inappropriate mental set can interfere with problem solving is shown in Figure 7.1. When presented with this problem, most people assume (form a mental set) that their lines must stay within the square formed by the nine dots. Only when people set aside this assumption can they solved the problem. Figure 7.5 on page 294 provides one solution to the nine-dot problem.

Mental sets do not *necessarily* interfere with problem-solving. The appropriate mental set can be helpful. For example, if we had told you to look beyond the confines of any imagined square when attempting the nine-dot problem, that mental set—which seems strange out of context—could have made the problem easier to solve.

Mental sets may lead to less-than-efficient problem-solving strategies. Consider the following incident. Moe and Larry were helping Curley move to a new apartment. Moe rented a truck with swinging back doors, which rested against the truck's sides once opened.

mental set a tendency to perceive or respond to something in a given, or set, way

After a full day of moving, it was time to close the truck. When Moe, Larry, and Curley tried to swing the back doors shut, they found a car in the way. With their mental set squarely fixed on the car being in the way, and failing to locate the owner of the car, they struck upon what to them was the only logical solution: Pick up and move the car. Moe, Larry and Curley picked up the front of the car, bouncing it along, and moved it enough that they could close the doors. It was only after they were in the truck, driving away that it dawned on them that they could have closed the doors easily by driving the truck forward a few feet!

Functional fixedness is a type of mental set defined as the inability to discover an appropriate new use for an object because of experience using the object for some other purpose (and was first described by Duncker in 1945). The problem-solver fails to see a solution to a problem because he or she has "fixed" some "function" to an object that makes it difficult to see how it could help with the problem at hand.

Maier (1931) provided a good—and classic—example of functional fixedness. Two strings are hung from the ceiling, but they are so far apart a person cannot reach them both at the same time. The goal is to hold on to both strings at once. There are other objects in the room, including a pair of pliers. One solution is to tie the pliers to one string and start them swinging like a pendulum. As the person holds the other string, the string with the pliers attached can be grasped as it swings over close to the person. Because many people do not see pliers as useful (functioning) for anything but tightening and loosening things, they are unable to visualize the pliers as a potential pendulum weight. They have "fixed" the "function" of the pliers in their mind. You have broken the barrier of functional fixedness when, unable to locate a screwdriver, you retrieve a knife from the silverware drawer or a dime from your pocket and tighten a screw with it.

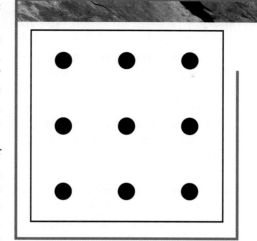

FIGURE 7.1

Without lifting your pen or pencil from the page, connect these nine dots with four straight lines.

Some real life problems require a choosing a "best" alternative from many possibilities. Looked at this way, decision-making tasks are like the problems in this chapter. Problem solving requires using past experience to devise strategies for reaching goal states. Occasionally our heuristic strategies—those rules of thumb used to guide problem solving—are biased because of misperceptions of past experience. Such biases create barriers to effective problem solving.

Some decision-making strategies require us to estimate the probability of events, and many of these strategies are notoriously poor (Hastie & Park, 1986; Payne et al., 1992). Most of the research on judging probabilities and frequencies has been reported by Daniel Kahneman and Amos Tversky (1973, 1974, 1979, 1984; Tversky & Kahneman, 1974).

The **availability heuristic** is the assumption that things that readily come to mind are more common (or occur more frequently) than things that do not come as readily to mind. For example, I show you a list of names that includes 19 famous women and 20 less-famous men. Later, you will almost certainly overestimate the number of women on the list because the famous names were more available to you. The media (newspapers, TV, radio) often draw our attention to events (make them available) in such a way that we tend to overestimate how often they

functional fixedness a type of mental set; the inability to discover an appropriate new use for an object because of experience using the object for some other purpose

availability heuristic the assumption that things that readily come to mind are more common than are things that do not come to mind so readily

happen. When reports of terrorist bombings at a foreign airport make the news, many Americans cancel their travel plans, overestimating the risk. Most people overestimate the number of people killed in plane crashes compared to those killed in car crashes because airplane crashes get more media attention. As a result, airplane crashes are more available in our memories.

The **representativeness heuristic** is the assumption that judgments about the most prototypic member of a category will hold for all members of the category. For example, you know that a particular group of men consists of 70 percent lawyers and 30 percent engineers. You are told that one of the men, chosen at random, has hobbies that include carpentry, sailing, and mathematical puzzles. Is this man an engineer or a lawyer? If you believe these hobbies are representative of engineers, not lawyers, you may say that the man is an engineer; even though it is more than twice as likely he is a lawyer.

Which group includes more tobacco chewers: professional baseball players or college students? The answer is college students (because there are so many of them, even though a smaller percentage of them use chewing tobacco). If you flip a coin and it turns up heads five times in a row, what is the chance of getting tails on the next flip? The probability is no better than it has been all along—50/50. (The fact that heads have appeared the previous five times is of absolutely no consequence to the coin.)

There are other heuristics that can bias our decision-making. Multiple-choice test items require you to decide which of a number of alternatives best answers a question. A problem-solving heuristic that may cause trouble making such decisions is called the **positive test strategy**—the strategy that claims that if something works, don't drop it to try something else (Klayman & Ha, 1987). This is the heuristic that suggests "If it isn't broken, don't fix it." This approach is often a sensible, but there *are* instances when even better solutions—more useful decisions—could be found if only one kept looking. Have you fallen into the trap of saying that alternative A was the correct answer to a multiple-choice test item, only to discover later that alternatives B and C were also correct, making alternative D, "all of the above," the best answer?

And finally, consider what is called the **confirmation bias**—the notion that we tend to select from among several options the one that best fits with what we have suspected to be true for some time. In other words, when we have to decide if a new piece of information is true or false, the information that confirms what we have believed all along is likely to be accepted as true, but if it goes against previously developed beliefs, it will be discounted as false. In short, we tend to seek and accept information that is consistent with what we already believe—even if that information is patently false (Aronson, Wilson, & Akert, 2005; Reich, 2004).

Successful problem solving requires that we break out of the restraints imposed by improper mental sets, functional fixedness, and some heuristic strategies.

---

representativeness heuristic the assumption that judgments about the most prototypic member of a category will hold for all members of that category

positive test strategy the procedure that claims that if something works, one should not drop it to try something else that might work better

confirmation bias the notion that we tend to select from among several options the one that best fits with what we have suspected to be true for some time

Although one is much more likely to be hurt or killed in an automobile accident on the ride to the airport, a newscast of a terrorist threat or a plane crash may keep people from flying because they significantly overestimate the risks involved. This is an example of the availability heuristic.

Courtesy of Ashley Cooper/Corbis.

CREATIVITY

"Creativity refers to the potential to produce novel ideas that are task-appropriate and high in quality" (Sternberg, 2001c, p. 360). So, "creative" means more than unusual, rare, or different (Runco, 2004). Creative solutions should be put to the same test as more ordinary solutions: Do they solve the problem at hand?

Creative solutions generally involve a reorganization of problem elements. Creativity is often a matter of learning—not how to do something—but how to do something in a different way. It also requires being flexible and resisting the pressure to go back to "the old way" (Stokes, 2001). As we mentioned, creativity is often noticeable in the problem representation stage of problem solving where seeing a problem in a new light or combining elements in a new way can lead to creative solutions.

What is the relationship between creativity and intelligence? Researchers disagree. Many researchers view creativity as separate from intelligence (Runco, 2004, p. 679). However, some creative solutions are so breathtakingly brilliant that many feel that some relationship between intelligence and creativity must exist (Simonton, 1984; Sternberg, 2001c). At the very least, creative problem solving requires some knowledge of the field (e.g., art, chemistry, music, writing, astronomy) that the creative person works in (Nakamra & Csikszentmihalyi, 2001). People who generate creative solutions tend to be highly motivated and generally optimistic (Hennessey & Amabile, 1988; Isen, 1999). And although most people (many psychologists included) assume that creativity is an innate talent, ". . . there is considerable evidence that hard work and intrinsic motivation—which can be supported or undermined by the social environment—also play central roles" (Amabile, 2001). The same idea is expressed in an old saying about golf: "It seems the more I practice, the luckier I get."

Solving problems creatively may involve **divergent thinking**—starting with one idea and generating from it a number of new ones. On the other hand, **convergent thinking** takes many ideas or bits of information and attempts to reduce them to a single possible solution (Figure 7.2). All problem solving uses convergent thinking, but creative problem-solving uses divergent thinking to explore possibilities.

Businesses search for "creative problem solvers"—innovators who will create the next generation of wireless telephones or discover new uses for the Internet (Fontenot, 1993). Employers solicit for employees willing to "think outside the box." Yet the data suggest that most creative discoveries are not *that* different from ordinary problem solving (Weisberg, 1993). Creative

divergent thinking the process of starting with one idea and generating from it a number of new ones

convergent thinking the process of taking many ideas or bits of information and attempting to reduce them to a simple solution

FIGURE 7.2

A schematic representation of convergent and divergent thinking in the context of problem solving.

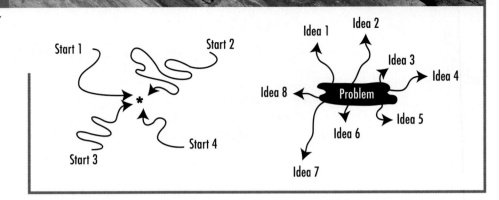

problem solvers are usually motivated experts in their fields (Sternberg & Lubart, 1996). Businesses have found that efforts to reinforce creativity at work are effective (Runco, 2004; Simonton, 1997). Creativity boosting measures include such things as allowing time for reflective thought, promoting collaboration among workers from different parts of the business, forbidding negative assessments of new ideas during brainstorming sessions, and permitting periods of play and exploration. Because businesses sell products in competitive markets, they are concerned with both utility (does it work?) and uniqueness (is it different?).

BEFORE YOU GO ON

5. What do psychologists mean when they speak of creativity, particularly in the realm of problem solving?

A Point to Ponder or Discuss
Are there any areas of your life in which you feel you have the potential for creativity? What steps could you take to express that potential?

LANGUAGE

Language sets humans apart. The philosopher Suzanne Langer put it this way:

> Language is, without a doubt, the most momentous and at the same time most mysterious product of the human mind. Between the most clear animal call of love or warning or anger, and a man's least, trivial word, there lies a whole day of Creation or in a modern phrase, a whole chapter of evolution. (1951, p. 94)

Let's Talk: What Is Language?

How shall we characterize this mysterious product of the human mind called language? Here is a classic definition: **Language** is a large collection of arbitrary symbols that have a common, shared significance for a language-using community and that follow certain rules of combination (Morris, 1946).

Before we examine this definition, we need to make a distinction between *communication* and *language*. Communication is the act of transferring information from one point to another.

language a large collection of arbitrary symbols that have a common shared significance for a language—using community, and that follow certain rules of combination

Language, on the other hand, is a specific means of communication. You may find yourself arguing with someone who insists that animals (e.g., chimpanzees, dolphins, bees) use language. They do not. They do have elaborate communication systems. For example, chimpanzees use vocalizations and gestures to communicate messages. However, this and other animal communication systems do not qualify as a language. You will see why as we discuss the definition of language further and examine language's properties in greater detail.

Language consists of a large number of *symbols* that can be combined in an infinite number of ways to produce an infinite number of utterances. The symbols that constitute language are commonly referred to as words—labels we have assigned to concepts, or our mental representations. When we use the word *chair* as a symbol, we don't use it to label just one specific instance of a chair. We use the word as a symbol to represent our concept of chairs. As symbols, words need not stand for real things in the real world. We have words to describe objects or events that cannot be perceived, such as *ghost* or, for that matter, *mind*. With language we can communicate about owls and pussycats in teacups and a four-dimensional, time-warped hyperspace. Words stand for cognitions, or concepts, and we have a great number of them.

Language use is a social process, a means of communicating our understanding of events to others. One property of all true languages is **arbitrary symbolic reference**, which means that there need be no resemblance between a word and its referent. In other words, there is no requirement for using the particular symbol for a given object. You call what you are reading a *book* (or a *textbook*, to use a more specific symbol). As speakers of English, we agreed to use the symbol book to describe what you are reading. But we didn't have to. We could have agreed to call it a *relm*, or a *poge*. The symbols of a language are arbitrary, but—once established by com-

Courtesy of Frans Lanting/Corbis.

mon use or tradition—they become part of the language and must be learned and applied consistently by each new user of the language.

Notice also that the arbitrary reference for symbols in one's language can change over time. Think how the symbols "gay" or "cool" or "web" have changed in terms of what they reference today compared to just 50 years ago. Consider the new symbols that have entered the language because of new technologies, such as *blog* or *ipod*, or *podcast*. Or consider how the meanings of symbols can change. A symbol that once referred to a canned meat product now refers to unsolicited junk email (*spam*), and savvy folks talk about *burning* digital music to a *CD*.

To be part of a language, at least in a practical sense, language symbols need to have shared significance for a language-using community. That is, people have to agree on both the symbols and their meanings. *Semanticity* refers to the meaning that words take on in language and gives language its power. You and I might decide to call what you are now reading a *relm*, but we would be in a tiny language-using community.

There has been a long-standing debate among psycholinguists about whether primates (chimpanzees and great apes in particular) possess language skills. They certainly have elegant systems of communication, and they surely can be taught to communicate with humans (and other primates) in ways that appear to use language.

arbitrary symbolic reference refers to the fact that there is no necessary relationship between a word and what it symbolizes; the relationship is arbitrary

The final part of our definition tells us that the symbols of a language must follow certain *rules of combination*. What this means is that language is structured and rule-governed. What makes language use a special form of communication is the fact that it is governed by rules of combination. For one thing, rules dictate how we can and cannot string symbols together in language. In English we say, "The small boy slept late." We do not say, "Slept boy late small the." Well, we could say it, but it would not communicate anything.

Using language is a remarkably creative, generative process. The ability of language users to express an infinite number of ideas with a finite number of symbols is called *productivity*. Almost every time we use language, we use it in ways that are different from how we have used it before. Still, as native speakers, we are able to apply the underlying rules of language to these new situations without much difficulty. Yet another characteristic of language is *displacement*, the ability to communicate about the "not here" and the "not now." We can

use language to talk about yesterday's lunch and tomorrow's class schedule. We can talk about things that are not here, never were, and never will be. Language is the only form of communication that allows us to do so.

Finally, language and speech are not synonymous terms. Speech is one way in which language is expressed as behavior. There are others, including writing, coding (as in Morse code), or signing (as in American Sign Language).

These properties of language set it apart from animal communication systems. No known animal communication system has the properties of language we have just described. For example, chimpanzee vocalizations and gestures have specific meaning (not arbitrary symbolic reference). They also cannot be combined to express an infinite number of ideas (they lack productivity), and they refer only to the here and now (there is no capacity for displacement). Although animals communicate with one another, they do not have true language.

BEFORE YOU GO ON

6.   What are the defining characteristics of language?

A Point to Ponder or Discuss
Other than language as we use it every day, can you think of any other system of unitary symbols with a common shared significance for some user community that follow rules of combination? Would mathematics qualify? How about music? What are the similarities and differences?

Describing the Structure in Language

Psycholinguistics is a hybrid discipline of psychology and linguistics. When psycholinguists analyze a language, they usually do so at three levels. The first level involves the sounds that are used when we express language as speech. The second level deals with the meaning of words and sentences, and the third level

involves the rules used for combining words and phrases to generate sentences. At each of these three levels, we can see structure and rules at work.

The individual speech sounds of a language are called **phonemes**. They are the sounds we make when we talk to one another. Phonemes by themselves have no meaning, but when we put them together in the proper order, they result in a meaningful utterance. For

| **phonemes** the individual speech sounds of a language

example, the word *cat* consists of three phonemes: an initial consonant sound (a "k" sound here), the vowel sound of "a," and the consonant sound, "t." *Phonological rules* govern how phonemes are combined to form words and phrases. If we were to interchange the consonant sounds in *cat*, for example, we would have an altogether different utterance, *tack*, with an altogether different meaning. Language usage, therefore, requires knowing which speech sounds are part of that language and understanding how they may be combined to form larger language units. There are approximately 45 phonemes in English. (And because those 45 sounds are represented by only 26 letters in our alphabet, it is little wonder that many of us have trouble spelling.) As noted above, language is productive; thus, we can express an infinite number of ideas with a limited set of speech sounds.

Describing a language's phonemes—noting which sounds are relevant and which combinations are possible–is only a small part of a language's complete description. Meaning must also be examined in the analysis of a language. The study of meaning is called **semantics**. Researchers who study semantics examine the morpheme in detail. **Morphemes** are the smallest units of meaning in a spoken language—a collection of phonemes that means something. In many cases, a morpheme is a word. For example, *write* is a morpheme and a word; it has meaning, and it is not divisible into smaller, meaningful units. Such a morpheme is called a *free morpheme* because it can stand alone. Other morphemes, known as *bound morphemes*, are not words and cannot stand alone. Prefixes (for example, *re-* and *un-*) and suffixes (for example, *-ing* and *-ed*) are bound morphemes because they must be attached to another morpheme to be used properly. Many words are a combination of free and bound morphemes. *Rewrite*, for example, consists of two morphemes, *write* (a free morpheme) and *re* (a bound morpheme),

which in this context means roughly, "do it again." *Tablecloth* is another word composed of two morphemes, *table* and *cloth* (both free morphemes).

The use of morphemes is governed by morphological rules. For example, we cannot go around making nouns plural in any way we please. The plural of *ox* is *oxen*, not *oxes*. The plural of *mouse* is *mice*, not *mouses*, *mousen*, or *meese*. If you want to write something over again, you have to *rewrite* it, not *write-re* it. Note (again) how morphemes are verbal labels for concepts (mental representations). Asking you to rewrite something would make no sense if we did not share the concepts of "writing" and "doing things over again."

There is one aspect of our language that obviously uses rules: the generation of sentences—stringing words (or morphemes) together to create meaningful utterances. **Syntax** describes the rules that govern how sentences are formed or structured in a language. The formal expression of the syntax of a language is **grammar**.

Understanding the syntax, or syntactic rules, of one's language involves a peculiar sort of knowledge, or higher cognitive process. We all know the rules of English in the sense that we can—and do—use them. But few of us could explain those rules to someone else. We say that people have a *competence*, a

semantics the study of meaning

morphemes the smallest units of meaning in a spoken language—a collection of phonemes that mean something

syntax the rules that govern how sentences are formed or structured in a language

grammar the formal expression of the syntax of a language

Our awareness of proper syntax tells us immediately that the utterance, "The puppies are playing in the yard" is acceptable, but that "Yard the playing in puppies are" is not acceptable. Notice that we know that the second utterance is unacceptable even if we are not able to specify why it is wrong, or which grammatical rules have been violated.

Courtesy of DLILLC/Corbis.

cognitive skill that governs language use. That skill allows us to judge the extent to which an utterance is a meaningful, well-formed sentence. We know that "The dog looks terrifying" fits the rules of English and that "The dog looks barking" does not. And, somehow, we recognize that "The dog looks watermelon" is downright absurd. At the same time, we recognize that "Colorless green ideas sleep furiously" does fit the rules of English, even though it does not make sense (Chomsky, 1957). It may be a silly thing to say, but we realize that it is a grammatically correct thing to say.

We also know that these two utterances communicate the same message, even though they look (and sound) quite different from one another:

> *The student read the textbook.*
> *The textbook was read by the student.*

In either case, we know who is doing what. Another linguistic intuition that demonstrates our competence with the rules of language lies in our ability to detect ambiguity. Look at these two sentences:

> *They are cooking apples.*
> *They are cooking apples.*

There is no doubt that the two sentences above appear identical. But upon reflection, we realize that they may be communicating different (ambiguous) ideas. In one case, we may be talking about what some people are cooking (apples, as opposed to spaghetti). In another interpretation, we may be identifying a variety of apple (those best-suited for cooking, as opposed to those best-suited for eating raw). In yet another case, we may be describing what is being done to the apples (cooking them, as opposed to eating them). You may be able to think of other interpretations. This is not an isolated example of ambiguity in language. There are many. Consider the ambiguity of the following statements: "The shooting of the marines was terrible," or "Flying airplanes can be dangerous."

Language Use as a Social Process

The main purpose of language is communication. Language helps us share our thoughts, feelings, intentions, and experiences with others. In that sense, using language is a social behavior. **Pragmatics** is the study of how language is related to the social context in which it occurs. Our understanding of sarcasm (as in, "Well, this certainly is a beautiful day!" when in fact it is rainy, cold, and miserable), or simile (as in, "Life is like a sewer . . ."), or metaphor (as in, "His slam dunk to start the second half was the knockout blow"), or cliché (as in, "It rained cats and dogs") depends on many things, including an appreciation of the context of the utterance and the intention of the speaker. The rules of conversation (turn-taking) are also part of the pragmatics of speech. That is, we have learned that it is most efficient to listen while others speak, and to speak while they listen. When someone violates this rule, it is difficult to have a conversation.

Pragmatics involves making language decisions based on the social situation at hand. Think about how you modify your language usage when you talk to your best friend, a preschool

pragmatics the study of how language is related to the social context in which it occurs

It is our knowledge of a language's pragmatics that informs us that the statement, "It's raining cats and dogs" is not to be taken literally.

Courtesy of Anthony Redpath/Corbis.

child, a college professor, or a driver who cuts you off at an intersection. Contemporary concerns about "political correctness" seem relevant here, don't they? In most contexts, words such as *pig, Uncle Tom, boy,* and *girl* are reasonable and proper; in other contexts, they can evoke angry responses. Cultural differences also play a role in pragmatics. For example, in some American Indian cultures, periods of silence—even lengthy periods of silence—during conversation are common and acceptable. Someone unfamiliar with this pragmatic reality, however, might become anxious or upset when long pauses disrupt the flow of their conversation (Brislin, 1993, pp. 217–221). As you can imagine, translations from one language and culture to another can cause huge changes in meaning. Two favorite examples (from Berkowitz, 1994) involve the translation of American advertising slogans into Asian languages. "Finger Lickin' Good" in Chinese means "Eat Your Fingers Off" and "Come alive with the Pepsi Generation" in Taiwanese means "Pepsi will bring your ancestors back from the dead."

BEFORE YOU GO ON

7. How are the rules and structures of language reflected in the use of phonemes, morphemes, and syntax?
8. What is the study of pragmatics, and what does it tell us about language use?

A Point to Ponder or Discuss
In what ways do specific languages (e.g., English, French, Swahili, etc.) differ from each other?

JUST WHAT IS INTELLIGENCE?

Intelligence is a troublesome concept in psychology. We all know what we mean when we use the word, but we have a terrible time trying to define intelligence concisely. Consider the varying concept of intelligence in the following statements.

- Is John's failure in school due to his lack of intelligence or to some other factor—his motivation, perhaps?
- Locking your keys in the car was not a very intelligent thing to do.
- A student with any intelligence can see the difference between positive and negative reinforcement.

In this section, we will develop a working definition of intelligence and review some of the ways in which psychologists have described the concept of intelligence.

To guide our study throughout this discussion, we will accept two definitions of intelligence: one academic and theoretical, the other practical and operational. For our theoretical definition of **intelligence**, we will use a definition offered by David Wechsler (1975, p. 139): "The capacity of an individual to understand the world about him [or her] and his [or her] resourcefulness to cope with its challenges." This definition, and others like it, sounds sensible at first, but it does present some ambiguities. Just what does "capacity" mean in this context? What is meant by "understand the world"? What if the world never really challenges one's "resourcefulness"? Would such people be considered less intelligent? Although there are difficulties with Wechsler's definition, most psychologists today take a similar approach to intelligence, emphasizing adaptation, problem solving, and finding ways to meet one's goals.

intelligence the capacity of an individual to understand the world and his or her resourcefulness to cope with its challenges

g-factor according to Spearman, one's general, overall intelligence

s-factors according to Spearman, a collection of a person's specific cognitive skills

Defining a concept operationally can help us understand an abstract concept. In other words, as E. G. Boring put it in 1923, "Intelligence is what the intelligence tests measure" (Hunt, 1995, p. 356). Before we get to a discussion of intelligence tests, it will be helpful to spend a bit of time reviewing some of the ways in which psychologists have thought about and described intelligence.

Classic Models of Intelligence

Most theoretical models of intelligence are attempts to categorize or organize cognitive or intellectual abilities into groupings that make sense. British psychologist Charles Spearman was one of the pioneers of mental testing and the inventor of many statistical procedures used to analyze test scores. Spearman's characterization of intelligence came from his analysis of scores earned by people on a wide range of psychological tests designed to measure cognitive skills. What impressed Spearman was that, no matter what cognitive ability a specific test was designed to measure, some people always seemed to do bet-

ter than others. People who scored high on some tests tended to score high on most of the tests. It seemed as if there was an intellectual power that facilitated performance in general. Spearman (1904) concluded that intelligence consists of two things: a general intelligence, called a **g-factor**, and a collection of specific cognitive skills, or **s-factors**. Spearman believed that "g" was somehow independent of knowledge and content —it went beyond knowing facts. The g-factor involved the ability to understand and apply relationships in all sorts of content areas. In this view, everyone has some degree of general intelligence (which Spearman thought was inherited), and everyone has specific skills that are useful in some tasks, but not in others.

When L. L. Thurstone examined correlations among the various tests of cognitive abilities he administered, he arrived at a different conclusion than Spearman's. Thurstone (1938) saw little evidence to support the notion of a general g-factor of intellectual ability. Instead, he claimed that abilities fall into seven categories, which he called *primary mental abilities*. These abilities

Contemporary views of intelligence see it expressed in many forms beyond the academic sense with which we usually associate the term. Intelligence and giftedness can be expressed in many ways—including artistic endeavors.

Courtesy of The Irish Image Collection/Corbis.

Courtesy of Plush Studios/Blend Images/Corbis.

included such things as the ability to understand ideas, concepts, and words; the ability to use numbers; the ability to remember lists of things; and the ability to visualize and mentally manipulate complex forms and designs. Thurstone argued that each factor in his model is independent, and that to know a person's intelligence requires that you know how he or she fares on all seven factors.

J. P. Guilford (1967) proposed a model that was even more complicated than either Spearman's or Thurstone's theories. Guilford claimed that intelligence can be analyzed as three intersecting *dimensions*. Guilford claimed that any intellectual task could be described in terms of the *mental operations* used in the task, the *content* of the material involved, and the *product* or outcome of the task. Each of these three dimensions has a number of possible values. There are five operations, four contents, and six possible products, yielding 120 possible combinations. (In 1988, Guilford increased the possible number of combinations to 150 by adding two more operations to his theory.)

Philip Vernon (1960, 1979) suggested we think of intelligence as a collection of skills and abilities arranged in a hierarchy. At the top is a general cognitive ability similar to Spearman's "g." Under it are two factors. One is a verbal, academic sort of intelligence; the other is a mechanical, practical sort. Either of these, in turn, is thought of as consisting of more-specific intellectual skills. The verbal-academic skill, for example, consists of numerical and verbal abilities, among others. Each of these can be broken down further (verbal skills include word usage and vocabulary, for instance), and then further still, because vocabulary includes knowing synonyms and antonyms. Seeing intelligence as including a general factor and a structured set of specific factors provided a model that combined some of the thinking of Spearman, Thurstone, and Guilford.

More Contemporary Models of Intelligence

During the past 25 years, theories about the nature of intelligence have taken a different approach than those reviewed above. First, recent theories assume that intelligence is a multidimensional concept; i.e., rather than talking about a singular intelligence, we should be talking about *intelligences*. Second, newer theories view intelligence as an active processing of information, rather than a trait that one either has or doesn't have to some degree.

The contemporary model that best characterizes the concept of "multiple intelligences" belongs to Howard Gardner of Harvard University's Graduate School of Education (1983, 1993, 2003a, 2003b). Gardner suggests that people can display intelligence in any one of several different ways. "I was claiming that all human beings possess not just a single intelligence (often called 'g' for general intelligence). Rather, as a species we human beings are better described as having a set of relatively autonomous intelligences" (Gardner, 2003a, p. 4).

Just how many "intelligences" might we possess, and what might they be? First, Gardner acknowledges a scholastic/academic intelligence, made up of *mathematical/logical* and *verbal/linguistic abilities*. He characterizes the combination of these two intelligences as formulating the concept of "intelligence" used by both scholars and laypeople. Gardner maintains that scholastic/academic abilities are the strengths of a law professor. And if one is a law professor, these abilities are wonderful, useful strengths to have. There are, however, other ways to be intelligent. *Spatial intelligence* is demonstrated by the ability to know where you are, where you've been, and how to get to where you want to be. People with strong spatial intelligence are good at visualizing things, like how furniture will look in a room—without physically moving it around. This is an intelligence characteristic of successful architects, designers, surgeons—and those who blaze trails through the jungle. *Musical intelligence* is rather self-evident. It is the ability needed not only to produce, but also to appreciate pitch, rhythm, tone, and the subtleties of music. We often speak of musicians as having a "gift" or great "talent." Isn't that exactly what law professors have—a talent or a gift—but for more academic pursuits? *Body-kinesthetic intelligence* is reflected in the ability to control one's body and to handle objects, as found in skilled athletes, dancers, and craftspeople. *Interpersonal intelligence* is exemplified by the ability to get along with others, and to "read other people" (Rosnow et al., 1995). You would expect successful teachers, therapists, politicians, and salespeople to display this sort of intelligence. *Intrapersonal intelligence* amounts to a keen self-awareness, and is required for people to understand themselves, to realize their strengths and weaknesses, and to look their best.

Gardner anticipated that, over time, he would add to his list of the seven intelligences. In fact, in 1995 he added *naturalistic intelligence* to his list. People with this intellectual strength are particularly in tune with their natural environment and the patterns that it presents. This would be a handy intelligence for anyone who lived off the land, or for someone who was a naturalist or biologist. Gardner is toying with adding a ninth intelligence, which he calls *existential intelligence*, reflecting the ability to deal easily with matters mystical, or even religious. He calls this "the intelligence of big questions," but he is not yet comfortable with it as a freestanding variety of intelligence, leaving his list at "eight and a half" (Gardner, 2003a, p. 7).

Obviously, a person can find success in life with any one (or more) of these multiple intelligences, but which intelligences are most-highly valued depends on the demands of one's culture. Highly technological societies, such as ours, value the first two types of intelligence. In cultures where one must climb tall trees or hunt wild game for food, body/kinesthetic skills are valued—as they are in the American subculture we call "professional athletics." Interpersonal skills are valuable in cultures that emphasize family and group activities over individual accomplishment. Again, as in so many areas, context matters.

Robert Sternberg is a Yale University cognitive psychologist who also views intelligence as multifaceted (1997, 1999, 2004; Sternberg, Grogorenko, & Kidd, 2005). He focuses on how one *uses* intellectual abilities, rather than trying to describe a particular set of skills or talents. Where Gardner emphasizes the autonomy, or separateness, of his varieties of intelligence, Sternberg sees intelligent behavior as a reflection of three different processes, or components, working together. What matters most for Sternberg is how people achieve success in their lives, given the socio-cultural context in which they live. It is largely a matter of how people set about to solve the problems that arise in their lives.

Sternberg's *Triarchic Theory of Intelligence* has three components:

1. ***Analytic:*** This involves analyzing, comparing, judging, processing information, evaluating ideas, and the like. College students need this sort of intelligence when they are asked to do such things as compare and contrast Helmholtz's and Hering's theories of color vision. "What is the problem here?" "How shall I get started?" "What will I need to see this through?" "How will I know when I have succeeded?"

2. ***Practical:*** This involves the sort of thinking required to solve real problems in the real world. You are at the library late at night and discover that your car won't start. What will you do? You will rely on those skills that Sternberg would say exemplify practical intelligence—knowing which friend is most likely to come to your aid, or having the phone number of a "road-side assistance" service readily available, for instance.

3. ***Creative:*** This component of intelligence comes into use when we face new problems or challenges; when old solutions no longer work, and a creative one is needed. "How can I generate a mnemonic device to help me remember all these different approaches to intelligence?"

Sternberg is quick to point out that his first component of intelligence is much easier to measure with standard psychological tests than are the other two. From this theoretical perspective, people are intelligent to the extent to which they understand their strengths and weaknesses, work to apply their strengths whenever they can, and continue to try to improve their weaknesses.

Finally, let us examine the work of John Mayer and Peter Salovey. They introduced the term "emotional intelligence" into psychology's vocabulary (Mayer & Salovey, 1994, 1995, 1997; Mayer & Geher, 1996). The concept was an immediate hit with the general public. It was discussed on television talk shows and in popular news magazines. Daniel Goleman's 1995 book on the topic, *Emotional Intelligence*, became a nonfiction bestseller. Emotional intelligence is characterized by the ability to accurately 1) *perceive* emotions, 2) *generate* emotion so as to assist thought, 3) *understand* emotions, and 4) *regulate* emotions so as to promote better emotion and thought.

Some people are successful in life, particularly in social situations, not because they are so "smart" in a cognitive, academic sense, but because they are good at controlling their own feelings and are sensitive to the feelings of others (Salovey & Grewal, 2005). Consider your response to the following situation. As you drive down a four-lane highway, you notice a construction sign indicating that the left lane is closed ahead. You move to the right lane. Whizzing by you and the other drivers who have responded to the warning sign is a driver in a red car who zips down the left lane until the very last minute, jogging back to the right just before hitting the barricades. Is this driver rude, aggressive, obnoxious, and worthy of scorn and rage? Or did he or she simply not attend to the warning sign? Perhaps the driver was responding to an emergency. Being able to weigh such alternatives and monitor one's own response accordingly is a sign of emotional intelligence. Here's another example. As a manager, you need to discipline an employee. Doing so in a constructive way, without causing embarrassment, resentment, or anger would demonstrate emotional intelligence. Do you see a bit of Sternberg (applying intelligence to solve problems) and a bit of Gardner (interpersonal and intrapersonal intelligence) here? The concept of emotional intelligence (EQ, as opposed to IQ) seems sensible. Can EQ be measured? Is it a scientifically useful term for assessing and predicting behavior? These questions are now actively under research review (Brackett, Mayer, & Warner, 2004; Ciarrochi, Chan, & Caputi, 2000; Grewald & Salovey, 2005; Salovey & Grewald, 2005).

BEFORE YOU GO ON

9. Offer both a theoretical and an operational definition of intelligence.
10. Briefly describe the models of intelligence offered by Spearman, Thurstone, Guilford, Vernon, Gardner, and Sternberg.

A Point to Ponder or Discuss
From your own personal perspective, what do you see as the strengths and the weaknesses of the characterizations of intelligence presented in this section?

PSYCHOLOGICAL TESTS OF INTELLIGENCE

Just as there are several ways to define intelligence, there several ways to measure it. Most involve psychological tests. Although the focus of our discussion here is intelligence, we must recognize that psychological tests have been devised to measure the full range of human traits and abilities. For that reason, we start with a few words about tests in general.

The Characteristics of Psychological Tests

A **psychological test** is an objective, standardized measure of a sample of behavior, used as an aid in the understanding and prediction of behavior (Anastasi, 1988; Kaplan & Saccuzzo, 2001). A psychological test measures behavior, because that is all we can measure. We cannot directly measure feelings, aptitudes, abilities, or intelligence. We can make inferences about such things on the basis of our measures of behavior, but we cannot measure them directly.

Psychological tests can measure only a sample of a one's behaviors. If we want to know about your tendency to be aggressive, for example, we cannot very well ask you everything that relates to aggression in your life. However, we can sample (i.e., identify a portion of) the behaviors of interest. Based on those results, we can then assume that your responses to a sample of items will predict, or be similar to, responses to unasked questions. Sampling is used in many testing situations. One example is a classroom final exam that asks you about only a sample of the material you have learned.

A psychological test should also be objective, meaning it should fairly and consistently evaluate the behaviors being measured. In other words, if several examiners (at least those with the same level of expertise) give the test, their evaluations and interpretations of the responses should be about the same. If the same responses to a psychological test lead one psychologist to say that a person is perfectly normal, a second to consider the person a mass of inner conflict, and a third to wonder why this person is not in a psychiatric institution, we have a problem—and it is probably with the objectivity of the test.

The quality of a psychological test depends on the extent to which it has three characteristics: *reliability*, *validity*, and *adequate norms*. A test's **reliability** refers to its ability to produce the same or highly similar results across similar testing situations. Suppose someone gives you a test and, on the basis of your responses, claims that you have an IQ slightly below average—94, let's say. Three weeks later, you retake the same test and are told that your IQ is now 127, nearly in the top 3 percent of the population. We have not yet discussed IQ scores, but we can agree that a person's IQ as a measure of intelligence should not change by 33 points in a matter of three weeks.

When people worry about the usefulness of a test, their concern is usually with validity. Measures of **validity** tell us the extent to which a test actually measures what it claims to be measuring. In other words, validity is the extent to which there is agreement between a test score and the quality or trait that the test is believed to measure (Kaplan & Saccuzzo, 2001). There are different forms of validity. *Face validity* is the lowest level of validity. If the items on a test cover a wide range of topics related to the behavior being evaluated, the test is said to have face validity. In other words, the test looks—at face value—as though it is measuring what it claims to be measuring. *Predictive validity* occurs when the results of a test predict a behavior known to be related to what is being tested. For example, intelligence test scores should reliably predict (be correlated with) school performance. *Concurrent validity* is established by demonstrating that a test produces

---

reliability the extent to which a test produces the same or highly similar results across similar testing situations

psychological test an objective, standardized, measure of a sample of behavior

validity the extent to which a test actually measures what it claims to be measuring

scores that correlate well with another established test in the area. Finally, *construct validity* involves the results of a test relating to a construct predicted by a theory. For example, if a theory of intelligence predicts that "intelligent" people are successful in life, then test scores should correlate highly with success. In general, although it may be acceptable to demonstrate validity in one way, the more dimensions along which a test is valid, the better.

There is one more issue that we must address: the adequacy of test norms. Suppose that you have filled out a long questionnaire designed to measure the extent to which you are outgoing. You know that the test is a reliable and valid instrument. You are told that you scored a 50 on the test. So what? What does *that* mean? It does not mean that you answered 50 percent of the items correctly—on this test there are no correct or incorrect answers. The point is this: If you do not have a basis of comparison, one test score by itself is meaningless. You have to be able to compare your score with the scores of other people like you who have also taken the test. Results of a test taken by a large group of people whose scores are used to make comparisons are called **test norms**. By using test norms in our example above, you may discover that a score of 50 is average—or that it reflects a very high or very low level of extroversion.

As we review some psychological tests used to measure intelligence, keep in mind the many ways in which psychologists have described or defined intelligence. Given the difficulty that psychologists have coming to any agreement on the nature of intelligence, you should not be surprised to learn that not all psychologists are pleased with the intelligence tests that are currently available.

test norms results of a test taken by a large group of people whose scores are used to make comparisons

---

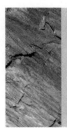

BEFORE YOU GO ON

11. What is a psychological test, and by what criteria is the quality or value of a test judged?

A Point to Ponder or Discuss
How could your instructor assess the quality of your next classroom exam?

The Stanford-Binet Intelligence Scales and the Concept of IQ

Alfred Binet (1857–1911) may not have authored the first test of intelligence (that distinction goes to Sir Francis Galton [1822–1911]), but Binet's was the first effort to stand the test of time. The fifth-edition revision of his test was published in the spring of 2003 (Roid, 2003). Binet was the leading psychologist in France early in the twentieth century. Of great concern in those days were children in the Paris school system who seemed unable to profit from the educational experiences they were being given. Binet and his collaborator,

Theodore Simon, wanted to identify students who should be placed in special (remedial) classes, where their education could proceed more efficiently than it had in the standard classroom.

Binet theorized that *mental age* (how well children performed on academic tasks) was more important than *chronological age* (how old the children were) as a means for evaluating students' classroom success. He reasoned that no matter how long it had been since a child's birth, if that child could answer questions and perform as well as an average 8-year-old, then that child had a mental age of 8 years. If the child performed as an average 10-year-old, that child had a mental age of 10 years.

In 1912, William Stern furthered Binet's theory by introducing the concept of the intelligence quotient, or IQ. Stern recognized that having the intellectual abilities of an 8-year-old is unremarkable for a child of 8, but for a child of 6 it is quite remarkable, indeed. In addition, there might be cause for concern if a 10-year-old child has the mental age of an 8-year-old. Stern used a simple formula to evaluate a child's intelligence based on his or her age. As you know, a quotient is the result derived when you divide one number by another. In dividing 8 by 6, the quotient is 1.33. **IQ** was determined by dividing the person's mental age (MA) by his or her actual, chronological age (CA). This quotient was then multiplied by 100. For example, if an 8-year-old girl had a mental age of 8, she would be average, and her IQ would equal 100:

$$IQ = \frac{MA}{CA} \times 100 = \frac{8}{8} \times 100 = 1 \times 100 = 100$$

If the 8-year-old were above average, with the intellectual abilities of an average 10-year-old, her IQ would be 125 (10/8 × 100, or 1.25 × 100). If she

were below average, say with the mental abilities of an average 6-year-old, her computed IQ would be 75.

It did not take long for psychologists to find fault with the traditional IQ. It was argued that mental age itself was an ambiguous measure of mental ability (Cohen et al., 1988). Two individuals with the same IQ could have very different levels of intelligence. For example, a 6-year-old with an MA of 7 has an IQ of 116.7. A 12-year-old with an MA of 14 has the same IQ, despite the fact that the 12-year-old is two mental years above his or her chronological age and the 6-year-old is only one year above. As a result of this type of discrepancy, psychologists developed the deviation IQ that is now used. The **deviation IQ** uses established group norms and allows for comparing intelligence scores across age groups. Because it is a term ingrained in our vocabulary, we will continue to use the term "IQ" for a measure of general intelligence—even though psychologists norm groups, and no longer calculate MAs or compute quotients. Figure 7.3 presents the idealized distri-

FIGURE 7.3

An idealized curve that shows the distribution of scores on the Stanford-Binet Intelligence Scale taken by a very large sample of the general population. The numbers at the top of the curve indicate the percentages of the population expected to score within the range of scores indicated; that is 68 percent earn scores between 85 and 115, 95 percent score between 70 and 130, and 99 percent earn scores between 55 and 145.

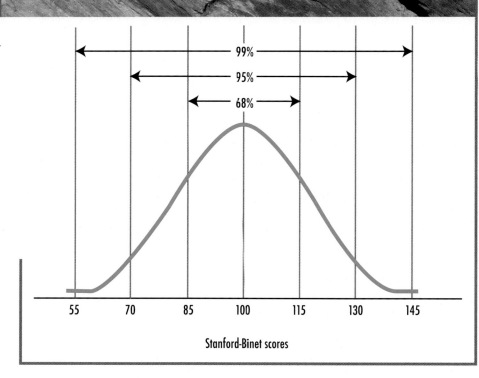

bution of scores on the Stanford-Binet test, reflecting scores of a huge sample of the population. Note that the average IQ score is 100 *by definition*. Also note that about two-thirds of the population has an IQ score between 85 and 115, and that scores above 130 or below 70 are quite rare.

Binet's first test appeared in 1905 and was an immediate success. It caught the attention of Lewis M. Terman at Stanford University, who supervised a translation and revision of the test in 1916. Since then, the test has been called the Stanford-Binet Intelligence Scales and has undergone subsequent revisions.

The test is individually administered—one examiner, one examinee—and takes about an hour. Items are arranged by age level. An 8-year-old child who appears to be of average intelligence might be started on the set of items that most 7-year-olds can answer. If a child seems "slow," an examiner might start with items from the 6-year-old level. The test then proceeds up the age range until the child fails a prescribed number of items. The items themselves vary. There are vocabulary items: "What does 'breakfast' mean?" "What is an anvil?" There are numerical questions: "If I had 12 pencils and gave you 5 of them, how many would I have left?" "What is 28 divided by 7?" There are tests of working memory: "Listen to this sentence, and then repeat it to me. . . ." Some items test spatial relations: "Here is a puzzle that should be a duck. Can you put these five pieces together so that they look like a duck?" Some questions are on general information: "Who lives in a castle?" "What is wrong with this picture?" (This is asked as the child is shown a picture of a wagon with three wheels.) There are other types of items, but you get the idea. The test publishers claim that the Stanford-Binet Intelligence Scales can be used for people between the ages "2 to 90+ years,"

although it is, in fact, used primarily for children aged 16 and under.

As did Binet's original test, the current edition yields an overall test score that reflects "g," or general intellectual ability, described as "what an individual uses when faced with a problem that he or she has not been taught to solve" (Thorndike et al., 1986, p.3).

Underlying "g" are three factors: crystallized abilities, fluid-analytic abilities, and short-term memory. *Crystallized abilities* represent those skills needed for acquiring and using information about verbal and quantitative concepts. These abilities are influenced by schooling and could be called an academic ability factor. *Fluid-analytic abilities* are those needed to solve problems that involve figural or non-verbal types of information. They involve the ability to see things in new and different ways, and are less tied to formal schooling. The third factor at this level is short-term memory. Items that test one's ability to hold information in memory for short periods can be found on Binet's original test.

The next level of abilities provides more specific, content-oriented definitions of the factors from the previous level. For example, at this level, crystallized abilities are divided into verbal and quantitative reasoning, fluid-analytic abilities are seen as abstract/visual reasoning, and there is no ability at this level under short-term memory. At the base of the hierarchy are the 15 subtests that constitute the actual Stanford-Binet test.

What all of this means is that the 2003 revision of the Stanford-Binet test acknowledges that a person's measured intelligence should be reflected in more than just one test score. Not only can one determine an overall g score (the only score available from earlier editions), but scores for each factor at each level can be calculated, as well. There are also scores for the 15 subtests by themselves.

BEFORE YOU GO ON

12.   How was IQ calculated when it was first introduced, and how is it calculated today?
13.   Briefly describe the Stanford-Binet Intelligence Scales.

A Point to Ponder or Discuss
What do you think of the idea of skipping a child ahead a grade, or holding a child back a grade, in school, based simply on scores of a test like the Stanford-Binet?

The Wechsler Tests of Intelligence

David Wechsler published his first intelligence test in 1939. Unlike the Stanford-Binet test that existed at the time, it was designed for use with adult populations, and it attempted to reduce the heavy reliance on verbal skills that characterized Binet's tests. With a major revision in 1955, the test became known as the *Wechsler Adult Intelligence Scale (WAIS)*. It was revised in 1981 and again in 1997, and is known as the *WAIS-III*. The WAIS-III is appropriate for persons between 16 and 74 years of age, and is one of the most commonly used of all psychological tests.

A natural extension of the WAIS was the *Wechsler Intelligence Scale for Children (WISC)*, originally published 11 years after the WAIS. With updated norms and several new items (among other things, it is designed to minimize bias against any ethnic group or gender), the *WISC-IV* appeared in 2003. It is appropriate for children ages 6 to 16 (there is some overlap with the WAIS-III). A third test in the series is for younger children, between the ages of 4 and 6. It is called the *Wechsler Preschool and Primary Scale of Intelligence,* or *WPPSI*. It was published in 1967, was revised in 1989, and again in 2002, as the *WPPSI-III*. There are subtle differences among the three Wechsler tests, but each is based on the same logic. Therefore, we will consider only one, the WAIS-III, in detail.

The WAIS-III consists of 14 subtests organized in two categories, a *verbal scale*, and a *performance scale*. Table 7.1 lists the subtests of the WAIS-III and describes some of the items found on each.

Items on each subtest are scored (some of the performance items have time limits that affect scoring). As is now the case with the Stanford-Binet, each subtest score is compared to a score provided by the test's norms. How an individual's score compares to the scores of people in the norm group (others of the same sex and age who have already taken the test) determines the standard score for each Wechsler subtest. In addition to one overall score (essentially, the IQ score), the Wechsler tests provide separate verbal and performance scores, which can tell us something about a person's particular strengths and weaknesses.

BEFORE YOU GO ON

14.   Briefly describe the Wechsler Adult Intelligence Scale.

A Point to Ponder or Discuss
What reasons or justifications can you generate for administering an IQ test to a 25-year-old adult? That is, what purpose(s) might be served by such testing?

TABLE 7.1

The subtests of the Wechsler Adult Intelligence Scale, Third Edition, WAIS-III.

VERBAL SUBTESTS	
Vocabulary	person must provide an acceptable definition for a series of words
Similarities	person must indicate the way(s) in which two things are alike; for example, "In what way are a horse and a cow alike?"
Arithmetic	simple math problems must be answered without paper and pencil; for example, "How far will a bird travel in 90 minutes at the rate of 10 miles per hour?"
Digit span	person is to repeat a series of digits, given at the rate of one per second, both forward and backward
Information	person must answer questions about a variety of topics dealing with one's culture; for example, "Who wrote Huckleberry Finn?" or "How many members are there in the U.S. Congress?"
Comprehension	test of judgment, common sense, and practical knowledge; for example, "Why do we bury the dead?" or "Why do we have prisons?"
Letter-number	letters and numbers in scrambled order, person is to re-order them correctly; for sequencing example, "Given Z, 3, B, 1, 2, A," the correct response would be, "1, 2, 3, A, B, Z."
PERFORMANCE SUBTESTS	
Picture completion	person must identify or name the missing part or object in a drawing; for example, a truck with only three wheels
Digit symbol coding	each nine-digit "key" is paired with a simple symbol; given a random series of digits, the person must provide the paired symbol within a time limit.
Block design	using blocks whose sides are all red, all white, or diagonally red and white, person must copy a pattern provided on a card
Matrix reasoning	person is presented with non-verbal, figural stimuli and is to describe a pattern or relationship between the stimuli
Picture arrangement	series of cartoon-like pictures must be arranged in order to tell a story
Object assembly	free-form jigsaw puzzles must be put together to form familiar objects
Symbol search	person is given a geometric figure and must locate that figure from among five figures in a search group of figures as quickly as possible

GROUP DIFFERENCES IN MEASURED INTELLIGENCE

For the remainder of this chapter, we will be focusing on IQ scores. Please keep in mind that IQ is simply a convenient abbreviation for intelligence as it is measured by psychological tests. We should not equate IQ with one's intelligence. IQ scores reflect only one particular measure of intelligence.

Recognizing that there are individual differences in intelligence, can we make any general statements about differences in IQ? For example, as a group, who are smarter, women or men? Do we become

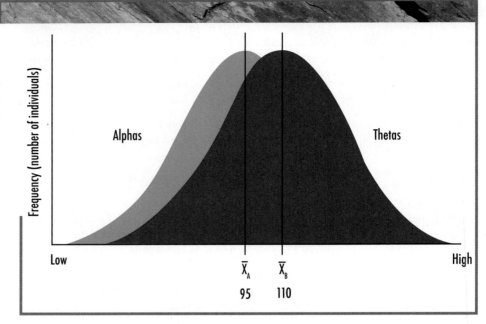

FIGURE 7.4

Hypothetical distributions of IQ scores for two groups (Alphas and Thetas). The average IQ for Thetas is higher than that for Alphas, but there is considerable overlap between the two distributions. That is, some Alphas have IQs higher than the average for Thetas (110), and some Thetas have IQs lower than the average for Alphas (95).

more or less intelligent with age? Are there differences in intelligence among ethnic groups? Simple answers to such questions are often misleading and, if interpreted incorrectly, can be harmful to some groups of people.

Reported average differences in IQ test scores are often misleading. Let us imagine that two large groups of people are tested: 1,000 *Alphas* and 1,000 *Thetas*. On average, the IQ score for Alphas is 95, and for Thetas, it is 110. An appropriate statistical analysis tells us that the difference of 15 points is too large to attribute to chance. Are Thetas smarter than Alphas? Yes, on average, they are—that is exactly what has been discovered.

Now look at Figure 7.4. Here are two curves that represent the IQ scores from the study. We can see the difference in the averages of the two groups. However, there are several Thetas whose IQs are below that of the average Alpha. And there are several Alphas with IQs above that of the average Theta. We may draw conclusions about average IQs, but making definitive statements about individual Thetas and Alphas is just not possible.

In addition, being able to demonstrate a significant difference between the average IQs of two groups in itself tells us nothing about *why* those differences exist. Are Thetas genetically superior to Alphas? Maybe, maybe not. Have Alphas had equal access to the sorts of experiences that IQ tests ask about? Maybe, maybe not. Are the tests biased to provide Thetas with an advantage? Maybe, maybe not. Learning that two groups of people have different average IQ scores usually raises more questions than it answers.

Gender Differences in IQ

Here is a question to which we have a reasonably definitive answer: Is there a difference between the IQs of males and females? The answer is no. Very few studies report any differences between men and women on tests of general intelligence, or IQ. With a few notable exceptions, what differences have been found seem to be getting smaller (Halpern, 1997; Halpern et al., 2007; Hyde, 2005; Jackson & Rushton, 2006). As researcher Diane Halpern wrote, commenting on sex differences in cognitive abilities, "Experimental results are based on group averages, and no one is average" (2004, p. 139).

Note that there may be no measured differences between the IQs of men and women because IQ tests are, in fact, constructed to minimize or eliminate any such differences (Brody, 1992). Usually, if an item on an intelligence test discriminates between males and females, it is dropped from the test.

When we look beyond global measures of IQ, there are some signs of gender differences on specific intellectual skills (which offset each other on general IQ tests). For example, males score significantly higher than females on tests of spatial relations—particularly on tests that require one to visualize how a three-dimensional object would look when rotated in space (Eagly, 1995; Halpern et al., 2007). What is curious about this rather specialized ability is that males perform better than females on such tasks from an early age, widening the gap through the school years, even though this particular ability is only marginally related to academic course work—which suggests that these sex differences cannot be attributed to differences in educational opportunity. The advantage that males have in mentally manipulating objects in space may partially explain why boys consistently outscore girls on 3-D video games (Cutmore et al., 2000).

Educational experiences may explain some of the differences found on tests of mathematical ability. Scores on tests of mathematics skills are well correlated with the number and type of math classes taken while a student is in high school. For many reasons, males enroll in more advanced math (and science) courses than do females. It is not surprising, then, that by the time they leave high school, there are differences between men and women on tests of mathematical ability (particularly for those that assess mathematical reasoning and problem-solving). There are no differences in overall mathematical abilities between boys and girls through elementary school, and, in fact, early on, when math involves learning facts and calculations, girls actually show an advantage

over boys (Halpern, 2004). Further, there is evidence that overall average differences between males and females on tests of mathematical reasoning have declined steadily over the past 25 years (Hyde, 2005). In fact, a recent study (Hyde et al., 2008) has demonstrated that differences in math scores for males and females have vanished completely—attributable mostly (the authors assert) because now girls are taking as many advanced classes in mathematics as are boys!

A somewhat different argument is that although average differences may be small, significant differences remain in the respective proportions of males and females who score at the very top or the very bottom of ability tests (Benbow et al., 2000; Feingold, 1995). For example, an analysis by Larry V. Hedges and Amy Nowell of the University of Chicago examined the performances of male and female teenagers on tests of mental ability over 30 years (1995). In every case, average differences were small. However, on some tests, there were disproportionately larger numbers of boys at the top or the bottom of the distributions of scores. Seven times as many boys as girls scored in the top 5 percent on science tests, and twice as many boys as girls scored in the top 5 percent on math tests. On the other hand, boys were much more likely than

Some psychologists argue that by the time they are in high school, boys generally outscore girls on tests of mathematics and science because of the different courses they are encouraged to take. As more girls are drawn to classes in math and science, the argument goes, gender differences in test scores will continue to decline.

Courtesy of Tom Stewart/Corbis.

girls to score near the bottom of the distribution on tests of perceptual speed and reading comprehension. Boys showed a very large disadvantage on tests of writing skills. One intriguing aspect of this study was that differences in the scores of males and females showed remarkably little change between 1960 and 1992, the dates of the testing sessions used in the research.

Girls tend to earn higher scores on tests of verbal abilities, such as writing and language use—particularly when the tests involve topics or content with which females tend to be familiar. In fact the average scores of boys and girls on tests of reading literacy show an advantage for girls regardless of the country in which testing is done (Halpern et al., 2007; Ogle et al., 2003).

BEFORE YOU GO ON

15. What differences in intelligence, if any, are there between males and females?

A Point to Ponder or Discuss
As it happens, a substantial majority of college students (and college graduates) these days are women. Why do you suppose that is the case?

Age Differences in IQ

You know a great deal more now than you did when you were 12. You knew more when you were 12 than you did when you were 10. Many 12-year-olds think they know more than their parents do. What we know about changes with age, even how much we know changes with age, but neither provides a measure of intelligence. IQ scores are computed so that, by definition, they remain consistent with age. The IQ of the average 12-year-old is 100, the same as the IQ of the average 30-year-old and the average 60-year-old, regardless of which test is used. But what happens to the IQ of an individual as he or she ages? If Kim's IQ is 112 at age 4, will it still be 112 at age 14, or 40?

Infant and preschool IQ tests have proven to be poor predictors of IQ at older age. IQ scores of children younger than 7 simply do not correlate well with IQs measured later. This does not mean that testing young children is without purpose. Having even a rough idea of the intellectual abilities of young children is often useful, particularly if there

is concern about mental retardation or belief that the child might be exceptional. The resulting scores may not predict adult intelligence well, but they might help in assessing the development of the child compared to other children.

What about intellectual changes throughout our lives? You may have guessed the correct answer: yes, no, and it depends. Most of the data on age differences in IQ have been gathered using a cross-sectional method, in which tests are given at about the same time to many people of varied ages. The results of these tests indicate that overall IQ peaks in the early 20s, remains stable for about 20 years, and then declines sharply. A different approach is to test the same individuals repeatedly, over a period of time. This is the longitudinal method. With this method, things do not look quite the same, showing people's IQ scores steadily rising until their late 30s or early 40s. Scores then stabilize for about 20 years, and begin falling steadily after people reach their late 60s (Schaie, 1996).

Studies of cognitive abilities demonstrate that it might be better to ask about specific intellectual skills, rather than to measure general intelligence. For example, vocabulary test scores usually increase as a person ages (Blum et al., 1970; Salthouse, 2003), whereas verbal fluency test scores often steeply decline beginning at age 30 (Schaie, 1996). One longitudinal study of more than 300 bright, well-educated adults showed a slight increase in general intellectual performance throughout adulthood (ages 18 to 54) on the *Wechsler Adult Intelligence Scale* (Sands et al., 1989). A closer look at scores for people between the ages of 40 and 61 showed improvement on the Information, Comprehension, and Vocabulary subtests, but a decline in scores on Digit Symbol and Block Design (see Table 7.1 on page 283 to review these subtests).

With age, the ability to acquire new information or solve new and different types of problems may decline, but there is no reason to expect a decline in those intellectual abilities already acquired. Research supporting this idea comes from the National Institute on Aging (Grady et al., 1995). Older volunteers (average age 69) had greater difficulty than younger volunteers (average age 25) recognizing pictures of faces they had been shown 15 minutes earlier. Using PET scan imaging techniques, which show the brain centers that are active during a given task, the researchers noted that fewer areas of the brain were active when the older subjects tried to memorize the faces. They could not remember the faces because they had not encoded them effectively.

Researcher Timothy Salthouse of the University of Virginia and his colleagues have compiled some very compelling data on cognitive skills and aging. Across many studies, four tests were used: a) a *vocabulary test* (select best synonym), b) a *speed test* (classify pairs of patterns as same or different as rapidly as possible), c) a *reasoning test* (identify the geometric pattern that best fits in the larger pattern from which a piece is missing), and d) a *memory test* (recall

Courtesy of Tom Grill/Corbis.

a list of words after each of three auditory presentations). Summarizing the results of several studies is rather easily done. Scores on the *vocabulary test* were high with increased age, until about the mid-50s; after that, they declined slightly or remained stable. For the other three tests, there were large, consistent, and steady declines in the scores from age 20 until age 80. These age-related effects are clearly apparent before the age of 50. Remarkably, within age groups, variability in the test scores was not that great. The steep declines in speed, reasoning, and memory test scores were not a reflection of some people doing very badly, while most did okay, and a few did well; declines were across the board (Salthouse, 2004; Salthouse & Ferrer-Caja, 2003).

If testing shows dramatic declines in three out of four cognitive skills as we age, why isn't this decline more noticeable? Why aren't there greater negative consequences of the age-related cognitive declines? Salthouse offers four explanations (2005).

1. Cognitive ability of any sort is just one factor contributing to successful functioning in most activities of daily living.

From childhood to early adulthood to late adulthood, a person's measured IQ is not likely to change very much. What may very well change as we age is the nature of our intelligence—what we know, not how much we know.

2. Unlike psychological tests that ask you to "do your best," few real-life situations require people to perform at their maximum levels.

3. People adapt to age-related changes (physical and cognitive) by modifying their environments and daily routines to minimize cognitive challenges.

4. "The greater experience and knowledge associated with increased age probably reduces the need for the type of novel problem solving that declines with age" (p. 142).

BEFORE YOU GO ON

16. What intellectual changes, if any, take place as a result of aging?

A Point to Ponder or Discuss
On many tests of cognitive skills, scores tend to peak as people reach their mid-20s. What, if anything, could someone do to maintain those skills with increasing age?

SPOTLIGHT
ON DIVERSITY

Racial and Ethnic Differences in IQ

That there are significant differences between the IQ test scores of African Americans and Caucasian Americans is not a new discovery. It was one of the conclusions drawn from the testing of Army recruits during World War I. Since then, many studies have reconfirmed the fact that—on average—Caucasians score about 15 points higher on general intelligence (IQ) tests than do African Americans (Hunt & Carlson, 2007; Lynn, 2006). African Americans also earn lower scores on performance tests and on tests designed to minimize the influence of one's cultural background (so-called "culture-fair tests") The nagging question, of course, is why? Why do these differences appear?

The proposed answers have been controversial, and point to several possibilities: a) The tests are biased and unfair. Current IQ tests may reflect mainstream life and the experiences of Caucasian Americans to a greater extent than they reflect the experiences of most African Americans or Hispanics. b) Differences in IQ scores can be attributed to environmental factors, such as available economic or educational opportunities, or the extent to which one is exposed to a wide range of stimuli. c) There are genetic factors that place some groups at a disadvantage. d) There are cultural differences in motivation and attitude about test performance. In most Western cultures, poor performance on an academic test is typically attributed to factors other than one's effort, "The test was bad, my teachers were lousy, and I had the flu." In most Asian cultures, failure is more likely to be attributed to lack of effort, "I didn't work hard enough to prepare, and will try harder next time."

Test bias may account for some of the differences in IQ scores, but assume for the moment that available techniques for assessing IQ (general intelligence) are as valid as they can be. First, let us remind ourselves that even the best and fairest of tests measures only one or a few of the various possible dimensions of intelligence. What then? Some (e.g., Suzuki & Valencia, 1997) find intelligence tests to be racially biased and unfairly favorable to middle- and upper-class test-takers. Others (e.g., Gregory, 1999) argue that current intelligence tests do a very good job of establishing standards of intellectual competence and potential.

In the 1950s and 1960s, social scientists were confident that most, if not all, of the differences between the average IQ scores of Caucasians and African Americans could be accounted for in terms of environmental, socio-cultural, and motivational factors. There may not have been a lot of research to support this position, but the logic was compelling and consistent with prevailing attitudes. African Americans were at a disadvantage on standard IQ tests because they were often denied access to enriching educational opportunities. Their generally lower socioeconomic status deprived them of many of the experiences that could raise their IQ scores. Still, there remain those who argue that at least some of the differences in IQ scores earned by Caucasians and by African-Americans is due to heredity, or to genetic factors (Rowe, 2005; Rushton & Jenkins, 2005).

To understand why the issue of the inheritance of IQ has not yet been resolved requires that we keep in mind three points:

a) Any evidence that genetic factors may affect differences in intelligence *within* races does not imply that genetic factors influence differences in intelligence *between* races;

b) A failure to identify specific environmental causes of racial differences in IQ is insufficient reason to drop the environmental factors argument; and

c) Just because researchers have not identified the specific environmental factors that can cause racial differences in IQ does not mean we must accept any genetic explanations.

One intriguing hypothesis about why African Americans might not score as well on standard IQ tests comes from an experiment conducted by Steele and Aronson (1995). According to Steele and Aronson, when a person is asked to perform a task for which there is a negative stereotype attached to their group, that person will perform poorly because the task is threatening. They call this a *stereotype threat*. To test the hypothesis that members of a group will perform more poorly on tasks related to prevailing negative stereotypes, African American and Caucasian participants took a test composed of items from the verbal section of the *Graduate Record Exam*. One-third of the participants were told that the test was a diagnostic tool for measuring their intellectual ability (diagnostic condition). One-third was told that the test was a laboratory tool for studying their problem-solving ability (nondiagnostic condition). The final one-third was told that the test was being used to measure their problem-solving ability, and would present a challenge to them (nondiagnostic/challenge condition).

The results of this experiment showed that when the test was said to be diagnostic of their intellectual abilities, African American and Caucasian participants differed significantly, with African Americans performing more poorly than Caucasians. However, when the test was presented as nondiagnostic, African American and Caucasian participants did equally well. Overall, across the three conditions, African Americans performed most poorly in the diagnostic condition. Steele and Aronson point out that this is a pattern consistent with impairments caused by test anxiety, evaluation apprehension, and competitive pressure. Stereotype threat has been demonstrated in several different settings (Aronson, Quinn, & Spencer, 1998). In one study, white males were selected to participate because of their high ability in math and their strong self-confidence in math. When they appeared for the experiment, some participants were told that the research was part of a study "concerned with understanding why Asians appear to outperform other students in tests of math ability" (Aronson et al., 1999, p. 33). They were then exposed to materials supporting that contention. Students in the stereotype-induced condition performed much worse than did other students who received no such messages about Asians' math ability. It seems likely that the negative influence of a stereotype threat results in a reduction of working memory that, in turn, interferes with the cognitive processing of test items (Schmader & Johns, 2003).

What does this tell us about the performance of African Americans and Caucasians on intelligence tests? The argument favoring the theory of stereotype threat suggests that when African Americans are faced with tests that are diagnostic of intellectual ability, they will not perform well, because they believe they are not supposed to perform well on such tests. Further, the argument, (never proposed by Steele and Aronson, but widely publicized by others) is that eliminating the stereotype threat would eliminate any African American-Caucasian difference in IQ test performance. This argument sounds reasonable, but it is flawed. While it may be true that making test-takers aware of their lower ability to complete a test successfully may produce lower test scores than they would have earned minus the stereotype awareness (that is, what Steele and Aronson reported when they first coined the term "stereotype threat"), it is a leap beyond the data to use the "Steele and Aronson experiment as evidence that stereotype threat is the primary *cause* of African American-Caucasian differences in test performance" (Sackett, Hardison, & Cullen, 2004, p. 7, emphasis added). But, on the other hand, when students are told about the possibility of a "stereotype threat" before begin their test-taking, any possible effects of the phenomenon disappear (Johns, Schmader, & Martens, 2005).

So where do we stand on the issue of racial-ethnic differences in IQ? We stand in a position of considerable uncertainty. For one thing, even the very concept of race is being challenged as a meaningful descriptor of people. We would do well to keep in mind the following: "Whether intelligence is largely genetically or largely environmentally determined is actually irrelevant in the context of group differences. The real issue is whether intelligence can be changed, an issue that does not go hand in hand with the issue of heritability" (Angoff, 1988, p. 713). And the argument over the causes for racial differences may someday become moot. Among other things, the gap between African Americans and Caucasians on intelligence tests has been closing (Dickens & Flynn, 2001; Williams & Ceci, 1997). The narrowing of the gap is related more to gains by African Americans than to declines by Caucasians.

BEFORE YOU GO ON

17.   Comment on differences in IQ scores earned by African Americans and Caucasians.

A Point to Ponder or Discuss
Imagine that you wanted to create an "IQ test" that was significantly biased so as to favor African American women between the ages of 50 and 65. What sorts of questions would put this group at an advantage over Caucasian males between the ages of 15 and 30?

EXTREMES OF INTELLIGENCE

When we look at the IQ scores earned by large, random samples of people, we find that they are distributed in a predictable pattern. The most frequently occurring score is the average score, 100. Most other earned scores are close to this average. In fact, about 95 percent of all IQ scores fall between 70 and 130 (see Figure 7.3). We end this chapter by considering those people who score at the extremes. People in these two "tails" of the IQ distribution are, by definition, at opposite ends of a spectrum, but they do share certain attributes, including a certain sense of "differentness." Children and adolescents who are either intellectually gifted or mentally retarded "have in common a desire, reinforced by well-meaning adults and peers, to 'be like everyone else,' that is, to be more like the norm" (Robinson, Zigler, & Gallagher, 2000).

The Mentally Gifted

There are several ways in which a person can be gifted. As we have seen, many contemporary theories of intelligence speak of intelligences. In all cases, however, there is the expectation that a gifted individual can do something better, with more precision, more impact than can most of us. People can be gifted (we often say "talented") in as many human endeavors as one can imagine. There are gifted musicians, athletes, glassblowers, ballet dancers, public speakers, nurturers, and racecar drivers. Such people are said to be "gifted" because they excel at their task, whatever it might be. They do something better than nearly everybody else. But here we are talking about intelligence, and in particular, intelligence of an academic sort—the sort measured by IQ tests. The intellectually gifted are people of exceptionally high IQ, with scores of 130 or above. Some reserve the label "gifted" for those with IQs above 135. In either case, we are dealing with

a very small portion of the population: fewer than 3 percent.

How can we describe intellectually gifted individuals? Actually, there have been few large-scale attempts to understand mental giftedness or the cognitive processing of people at the very upper end of the IQ distribution (Robinson, Zigler, & Gallagher, 2000; Winner, 2000). A lot of what we do know about the mentally gifted comes from a classic study begun by Lewis M. Terman in the early 1920s (yes, this is the same Terman who revised Binet's IQ test in 1916). Terman supervised the testing of more than 250,000 children throughout California. His research group at Stanford University focused on those children who earned the highest scores, 1,528 in all, each with an IQ above 135. Lewis Terman died in 1956, but the study of those mentally gifted individuals who were between the ages of 8 and 12 in 1922 continues. Ever since their inclusion in the study, and at regular intervals, they continue to be retested, surveyed, interviewed, and polled by psychologists and others (Friedman et al., 1995; Goleman, 1980).

The Terman study has its drawbacks: choosing a narrow definition of gifted in terms of IQ alone is one; failing to account for the educational or socioeconomic level of each child's parents is another. The researchers also may have excluded from the sample those children who showed any signs of psychological disorders or problems, whether their IQ scores were high enough or not. Nonetheless, the study is an impressive one simply because it continued for so long. What can this longitudinal analysis tell us about people with very high IQs?

Most of Terman's results fly in the face of the classic stereotype of the bright child as a skinny, anxious, clumsy, sickly kid who wears thick glasses (Sears & Barbee, 1977). In fact, if there is any overall conclusion to be drawn from the Terman-Stanford study it is that, in general, gifted children experience advantages in virtually everything. They are taller, faster, better coordinated, have better eyesight, fewer emotional problems, and tend to stay married longer than average. These findings have been confirmed by other researchers, studying different samples of subjects (Deary et al., 2007; Gottfredson, 2004; Gottfredson & Deary, 2004; Winner, 1996; 2000). Many obvious things are also true: The mentally gifted received more education; found better, higher-paying jobs; and had brighter children than did people of average intelligence. However, if we have learned anything by now, it is that we shouldn't over generalize. Not all of Terman's children (occasionally referred to as *Termites*) grew up to be rich and famous or live happily ever after. Many did, but not all.

The Mentally Retarded

Our understanding of mental retardation has changed markedly over the past 25 years. We have seen changes in treatment and care and great strides in prevention. There have also been significant changes in how psychology defines mental retardation.

Intelligence, as measured by IQ tests, is often used to confirm suspected cases of mental retardation. However, psychologists believe that there is more to retardation than IQ alone. The American Association of Mental Retardation (AAMR) defines **mental retardation** as: "a disability characterized by significant limitations both in intellectual functioning and in adaptive behavior as expressed in conceptual, social, and practical adaptive skills" (AAMR, 2002).

The IQ cutoff for mental retardation is usually taken to be 70, with IQs between 70 and 85 considered "borderline" or "slow." Standard IQ cutoff scores for the four major degrees of retardation are listed below:

- IQ 50–69: mildly mentally retarded (approximately 80 percent of all cases of retardation)
- IQ 35–49: moderately mentally retarded (approximately 12 percent of all cases of retardation)
- IQ 20–34: severely mentally retarded (approximately 8 percent of all cases of retardation)
- IQ less than 19: profoundly mentally retarded (less than 1 percent of all cases of retardation) (American Psychiatric Association, 2002)

As you review this list, keep two things in mind. First, these scores are suggested limits. Given what we know about IQ tests, it is ridiculous to claim after one administration of a test that a person with an IQ of 69 is mentally retarded, while someone with an IQ of 71 is not. Second, a diagnosis of mental retardation is not (or should not be) made on the basis of IQ score alone. Of late, there has been much controversy over where to place the upper limit of mental retardation, with some (e.g., the American Association of Mental Retardation) arguing that it should be at 75 rather than 70. To fit the AAMR definition of mental retardation, the symptoms of the below-average intellectual functioning must show up before age 18.

In many circles, the term "developmentally delayed" is beginning to replace the narrower term "mentally retarded," and it is suggested that a more appropriate term is "an individual with mental retardation," rather than a "mentally retarded individual" (Robinson, Zigler, & Gallagher, 2000). Diagnosis may come after the administration of an IQ test, but initial suspicions generally come from perceived delays in developmental patterns of behavior.

By making "limitations in adaptive behavior" a part of the definition, the AAMD is acknowledging that there is more to getting along in this world than possessing the intellectual and academic skills that IQ tests emphasize. Being mentally retarded does not mean being helpless, particularly for those at borderline or mild levels of retardation. Of major consideration is the ability to adapt to one's environment. In this regard, skills such as the ability to dress oneself, follow directions, make change, or find one's way home from a distance become relevant (Coulter & Morrow, 1978).

mental retardation a disability characterized by significant limitations both in intellectual functioning and in adaptive behavior as expressed in conceptual, social, and practical adaptive skills

No matter the definition of retardation, the population of citizens with mental retardation or developmental delay is large. Approximately 3 percent of the population at any one time falls within the IQ range for retardation. Two other relevant estimates are that nearly 900,000 children and young adults between the ages of 3 and 21 with mental retardation are being served in public schools, and that nearly 200,000 persons with mental retardation are found in community residential facilities: state and county mental hospitals and nursing homes. Let us now turn to a brief discussion of the causes, treatment, and prevention of mental retardation.

The Causes, Treatment, and Prevention of Mental Retardation

About one-fourth of mental retardation reflects a problem that developed before, during, or just after birth. Between 15 and 20 percent of those persons referred to as mentally retarded were born prematurely—at least three weeks before the due date, or at a weight below 5 pounds, 8 ounces.

We all appreciate that the health of the mother during pregnancy and the health of the father at conception can affect the health of the child. Several prenatal conditions can cause developmental delays. These include rubella, hypertension, exposure to X-rays, low oxygen intake, maternal syphilis, and the mother's use of drugs—from powerful narcotics to the frequent use of aspirin, alcohol, or nicotine. To greater and lesser degrees, all of these can be linked to mental retardation. In addition, some cases stem from difficulties or injuries during the birth process itself.

As we have seen, the extent to which normal levels of intelligence are inherited is open to debate. Some types of mental retardation, however, are clearly genetic in origin (Plomin & McGuffin, 2003, pp. 218–219). One of the clearest examples is the intellectual retardation accompanying *Down syndrome*, first noted in 1866. No one knows exactly why it happens, but occasionally a fetus develops with 47 chromosomes, instead of the usual 46 that combine to create 23 pairs. It is known that Down syndrome is more likely to occur as the age of either parent increases. The physical signs are well known: small, round skull; flattened face; large tongue; short, broad nose; broad hands; and short, stubby fingers. Children born with Down syndrome experience delayed behavioral development in childhood. A Down syndrome child may fall into any level of retardation. Many are educable and lead lives of considerable independence, although, even as adults, many will require supervision to some extent.

Fragile X syndrome is a variety of mental retardation with a genetic basis that was discovered more recently—in the late 1960s (Bregman et al., 1987; Kaufman & Reiss, 1999). Although it can occur in females, it is found primarily in males. Males with Fragile X syndrome usually have long faces, big ears, and, as adults, large testes. Individuals with this form of retardation have difficulty processing sequences of events or events in a series, which means that they have problems with language skills. One curiosity is that, whereas males with Down's syndrome show a gradual but steady decrease in IQ scores with age, males with Fragile X syndrome show their most noticeable declines during puberty.

Most cases of mental retardation do not have obvious causes. About one-half to three-quarters of mental retardation cases do not have known biological or genetic causes.

Dealing effectively with mental retardation has been difficult. Special education programs have helped, but not all have been successful. Preparing teachers and mental health professionals to be sensitive to the wide range of behaviors and feelings of which mentally retarded persons are capable has also helped. Working with some mildly retarded and moderately retarded children to raise their IQs has also resulted in impressive changes. For severely and profoundly retarded persons, however, the outlook is not as bright—at least in terms of raising IQ points. But we always need to remind ourselves that quality of life is not necessarily a function of IQ. The emphasis in recent years has been less on overall intellectual growth and more on those specific skills and abilities that can be improved.

As strange—and as frustrating—as it may be, there are still many more questions about how best to accommodate exceptional children with intellectual deficits than there are answers. For example, mainstreaming—placing mildly retarded and borderline children in regular classroom settings—has been a common practice for several years. Is it a beneficial practice? Is it any better than segregating exceptional children in special schools or special classrooms? As yet, there is simply no clear-cut evidence one way or the other (Detterman & Thompson, 1997).

There is greater hope in the area of prevention. As we all continue to appreciate the influences of the prenatal environment on the development of cognitive abilities, mothers and fathers can be better educated about how their behaviors affect the development of their unborn children. An excellent example of how mental retardation can be prevented concerns a disorder called *phenylketonuria*, or *PKU*. This disorder is genetic in origin, and more than 50 years ago, it was found to be a cause of mental retardation. PKU results when a child inherits genes that fail to produce an enzyme that normally breaks down chemicals found in many foods. Although a newborn with PKU usually appears normal, a simple blood test can detect the disorder soon after birth. Once PKU has been detected, a prescribed diet (which must be maintained for about four years) can reduce or eliminate any of the retardation effects of the disorder.

BEFORE YOU GO ON

18. What does it mean to be "intellectually gifted" or an "individual with mental retardation," and what are some of the causes of the latter?

A Point to Ponder or Discuss
Imagine that you were a teacher of a sixth-grade class. How do you think you would deal with having two students with IQ scores of 140 or higher? How would you deal with having two students with IQ scores of, say, 60?

FIGURE 7.5

A possible solution to the nine-dot problem. Note that one has to break the "mental set" that the four lines must remain inside the rectangle defined by the dots.

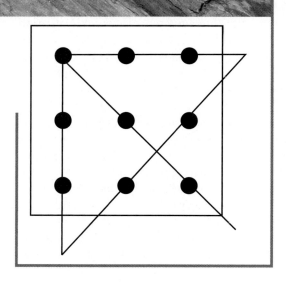

CHAPTER SUMMARY

1. **What is meant by "thinking," and to what extent does it involve concepts, reasoning, and problem solving?**

   Thinking is a general term that refers to the use of perceptions, ideas, and memories—cognitive processes not tied to direct experience. Thinking also involves the manipulation of *concepts*—the mental representations of categories or classes of events and of objects of our experience. Thinking is often taken to be synonymous with problem-solving and reasoning. *Reasoning* is a matter of coming to conclusions that are based either on a set of general principles (deductive reasoning) or on a set of specific acquired facts and observations (inductive reasoning).

2. **What defines "a problem," and what is the difference between a well-defined and an ill-defined problem?**

   A problem has three components: a) an *initial state*—the situation as it exists, b) a *goal state*—the situation as the problem-solver would like it to be, and c) *routes or strategies* for getting from the initial state to the goal state. Whether a problem is well-defined or ill-defined is a matter of the extent to which the elements of the initial state and goal state are well-delineated and clearly understood by the problem solver. An example of a well-defined problem might be that which you face when a familiar route home from campus is blocked. An example of an ill-defined problem might be that which you face when you have to write a term paper on the topic of your choice.

3. **Beginning with problem representation, describe the steps that can be taken to solve problems effectively.**

   Problem representation involves the mental activity of thinking about a problem and putting it into familiar terms. A proper representation of a problem will make it easier to solve. Algorithms and heuristics are types of strategies, or systematic plans, used to solve problems. *Algorithms* involve a systematic search of all possible solutions until the goal is reached; with algorithms, a solution is guaranteed. A *heuristic* strategy—of which there are many—is an informal, rule-of-thumb approach that involves generating and testing hypotheses that may (or may not) lead to a solution in a sensible, organized way.

4. **Describe how a mental set, functional fixedness, and the use of inappropriate heuristic strategies may become barriers to effective problem solving.**

   A *mental set* is a predisposition to perceive or respond in a particular way. Mental sets develop from past experience and involve the continued use of strategies that have been successful in the past. Because past ways of perceiving or solving a problem may not be appropriate for the problem at hand, mental sets can hinder effective problem solving. *Functional fixedness* is a type of mental set in which an object is seen as serving only a few fixed functions. We tend to judge as more likely or more probable those events readily available to us in memory—the *availability heuristic*. We also tend to overgeneralize about events that are prototypic representatives of a category or concept—the *representativeness heuristic*. Additionally, the *positive test strategy* may have us accept a successful solution that is still not the best solution to a problem.

5. **What do psychologists mean when they speak of "creativity," particularly in the realm of problem-solving?**

   Creativity is seen as the potential to produce novel ideas that are task-appropriate (solve the problem at hand, for example) and are high in quality. An individual usually has a sound knowledge base in the domain in which creativity is demonstrated. Creativity often involves divergent thinking, in which a large number of alternative possibilities are generated for testing; it is seen as a useful technique in problem solving. Convergent thinking, on the other hand, involves taking a large number of ideas or possibilities and reducing them to one or a few.

6. **What are the defining characteristics of language?**

   Language is a complex and creative cognitive skill used for communication. A language consists of a large number of arbitrary symbols (usually words) that are combined in accordance with certain rules to stand for, or label, our conceptualization of objects and events that have meaning for users of that language. The use of language is a generative process that, among other things, allows us to communicate about the "not here" and the "not now."

7. **How are the rules and structures of language reflected in the use of phonemes, morphemes, and syntax?**

A *phoneme* is the smallest unit of sound in the spoken form of a language (i.e., a speech sound). How phonemes can be combined in a language follows strict rules. *Morphemes* are the smallest units of meaning in a language, including words, prefixes, and suffixes. How morphemes are ordered, or structured, in language affects their meaning. *Syntax* refers to the rules that govern the way morphemes are ordered, or structured, to produce sentences. Language speakers are competent in the use of these rules, even though they may not be able to state them explicitly. We can determine intuitively (without being able to explain why) when utterances are syntactically correct and when they are not. We can tell when two sentences that take different forms are communicating the same idea or message. We can identify ambiguous sentences and can often remove that ambiguity, but only when we are aware of a larger context in which the utterance occurred.

8. **What is the study of pragmatics, and what does it tell us about language use?**

Pragmatics is the study of how the social situation, or context, in which language is used influences the meaning of what is being said. An appreciation of that context allows us to recognize the use of sarcasm, simile, metaphor, and the like.

9. **Offer both a theoretical and an operational definition of intelligence.**

Theoretically, intelligence is said to be the capacity of an individual to understand the world and use resourcefulness to cope with its challenges. Operationally, intelligence can be defined as that which intelligence tests measure.

10. **Briefly describe the models of intelligence offered by Spearman, Thurstone, Guilford, Vernon, Gardner, and Sternberg.**

Based on his analysis of a wide range of psychological tests to measure cognitive skills, Spearman viewed intelligence as consisting of a general factor ("g") and a number of specific abilities ("s"). Thurstone saw intelligence as a combination of seven unique and primary mental abilities. Guilford argued that there are as many as 150 cognitive skills that comprise one's intelligence. Vernon suggested that intellectual skills or cognitive abilities could be arranged in a hierarchy, from general at the top to specific at the bottom. Gardner proposes a theory of multiple intelligences—different, autonomous ways in which a person may be intelligent. His list includes: mathematical/logical, verbal/linguistic, spatial, musical, body-kinesthetic, interpersonal, intrapersonal, and naturalistic abilities. Sternberg focuses on how one uses intelligence, and argues for an organized set of three cognitive processes, working together, and present in individuals to varying degrees. His three components are a) analytic—involving analyzing, comparing, judging, and evaluating ideas; b) practical—involving what it takes to solve real problems in the real world; and c) creative—involving the discovery of new or different solutions to problems.

11. **What is a psychological test, and by what criteria is the quality or value of a test judged?**

A psychological test is an objective, standardized measure of a sample of behavior. To be a "good," quality test, an instrument must demonstrate a) *reliability*—that it measures something consistently, b) *validity*—that it measures what it says it's measuring, and c) adequate *norms* that can be used to assign meaning to an individual score.

12. **How was IQ calculated when it was first introduced, and how is it calculated today?**

The IQ, or intelligence quotient, was originally determined by dividing an individual's mental age (MA), as determined by testing, by that individual's chronological age (CA), and multiplying the result by 100. The formula is $IQ = MA/CA \times 100$. IQ scores are now determined by comparing the test score of an individual with the scores earned by large norm groups of other people of the same age. By definition, if a person earns the same test score as the average of the norm group, his or her IQ is 100.

13. **Briefly describe the *Stanford-Binet Intelligence Scales*.**

First published in 1905, the Stanford-Binet is the oldest test of general intelligence. Its most recent revision (2003) yields an overall score ("g"), as well as scores for a number of abilities assumed to underlie general intelligence. The test is individually administered, and it consists of 15 subtests, each assessing a specific cognitive task. Scores on the test compare the performance of an individual to that of others of the same age level.

14. **Briefly describe the *Wechsler Adult Intelligence Scale*.**

The three Wechsler scales are individually administered tests of general intelligence, each appropriate for a specific age group. The *Wechsler Adult Intelligence Scale (WAIS)* is a commonly used test for persons between 16 and 74 years of age. The WAIS consists of verbal and performance subtests of varied content. Hence, three scores can be determined: an overall score, a score on the verbal subtests, and a score on the performance subtests. Scores on the Wechsler tests are standard scores, comparing one's abilities to those of others of the same age.

15. **What differences in intelligence, if any, are there between males and females?**

When comparing test scores of any two groups of individuals, it is important to remember that, even if there are differences on average, the score of any individual in one group can be above or below the average for the other group. There are no significant differences between men and women on virtually any test that yields a general IQ score. There are such differences on tests of spatial relations skills and advanced math skills (males score higher—but recent studies show that this difference is no longer evident), and verbal fluency and writing skills (females score higher).

16. **What intellectual changes, if any, take place as a result of aging?**

Overall intelligence does tend to rise steadily until people reach their late 30s or early 40s. Then it remains stable for about 20 years, and steadily declines after people reach their late 60s. Various skills and abilities are differentially affected by age. Although vocabulary skills continuously increase until the age of 50, they become stable or slightly diminished after that age. The cognitive skills involved in forming new memories, reasoning, and problem-solving quickly peak in one's early 20s. After that, they show a steady, continuous fall throughout life. With age, most people are able to compensate for these losses so that they are hardly noticeable.

17. **Comment on differences in IQ scores earned by African Americans and Caucasians.**

There are reliable differences between the IQs of African Americans and Caucasians, with most studies putting the average difference at about 15 points in favor of Caucasians. Asian American students, on average, perform better on tests of academic achievement—mathematics in particular. The data on racial differences tell us nothing, however, about their source. Arguments have been made favoring genetic and environmental causes, including the emphases each culture puts on testing and performance.

18. **What does it mean to be "intellectually gifted" or an "individual with mental retardation," and what are some of the causes of the latter?**

Giftedness can mean several things, in addition to overall intellectual ability as measured by IQ tests (usually an IQ over 130 or 135). Other abilities in which individuals may be gifted include psychomotor skills, the visual and performing arts, leadership, creativity, and abilities in specific academic areas. The Terman-Stanford research tells us that people who are mentally gifted experience other physical, educational, social, and economic advantages.

Mental retardation is indicated by below-average intellectual functioning (IQ scores of less than 70), originating before the age of 18, and associated with impairment in adaptive behavior (as well as academic behaviors). In addition to genetic causes (as in Down's syndrome and Fragile X syndrome), most of the known causes of mental retardation involve the health of the parents at conception, and the care of the mother and fetus during pregnancy and delivery. Drug use, lack of oxygen, and poor nutrition have been implicated in mental retardation. In other words, many causes of mental retardation appear to be preventable.

Development through the Lifespan 8

PREVIEW

From conception to death, human beings are united by shared developmental events. On the other hand, each of us is unique. Developmental psychologists study both the common patterns of development and the ways we differ as we grow and develop throughout our lives. We tend to think that a person's development begins at birth. In fact, growth and development begin earlier, at conception and with the first division of one cell into two, so that is where we will start.

The focus of the first half of this chapter is children. We will begin with the basics of sensory and perceptual development—asking how does the child experience its world? The centerpiece of any discussion of the psychology of children is usually their cognitive development. Because it is such a classic and has inspired so many, the approach of Jean Piaget is a reasonable place to begin. We will then look at "information-processing approaches" of describing and accounting for the cognitive development of children. We then will consider several areas of concern to developmental psychologists that are really quite social in nature. One is moral reasoning. How do children come to appreciate what is right and what is wrong? Another area of interest is Erik Erikson's psychosocial approach to development (which, in fact, covers the lifespan). A third socially-oriented focus of child psychology is the development of gender identity—how children come to appreciate that boys are different from girls. And finally, we introduce what has become a significant concern, not only for psychologists, but also for makers of public policy: social attachments, their possible benefits, and how secure attachments can be fostered by society's institutions.

Throughout this chapter, we will use growth and development to mean different things. *Growth* refers to simple enlargement—getting bigger. *Development* refers to a differentiation of structure or function. Something develops when it appears for the first time and remains. Thus we say that the nervous system develops between week two and week eight after conception.

A timeline of the development of an individual tells us that the most rapid development and most dramatic changes occur between conception and around 11 years of age. So much happens during this time span—physical growth, the development of memory, language, and social relationships—that it is easy to lose sight of the fact that development is a lifelong process. Although the changes we see in development after childhood are not as rapid or dramatic as those seen during childhood, development progresses until the day we die. Hence, we continue the story of human development past childhood, through adolescence, and into early, middle, and late adulthood.

For over 100 years, psychologists have struggled to determine how best to characterize adolescence. Interestingly, most of the research on adolescent development has focused on their troubles, conflicts, and problems. Indeed, little has been written about the "normal" development of teenagers. Research has focused on how teenagers adjust or fail to adjust to the stresses of adolescence and how to help them adjust better. We will follow the lead of the researchers, addressing the issues of physical maturation and individual identity formation.

We divide adulthood (somewhat artificially) into three sub-stages: early, middle, and late. Although there are no sharp dividing lines, each sub-stage reflects a different set of challenges and adjustments, involving family, career, retirement and—ultimately—one's own mortality. Having begun this chapter with a section of prenatal development and birth, we end it with a section on death and dying.

PRENATAL DEVELOPMENT

Human development begins at conception, when the father's sperm cell unites with the mother's ovum. At that time, all of the genes on the 23 chromosomes from each parent pair off within a single cell. That one action transmits all inherited characteristics. Within the next 30 hours, the one cell will divide and become two cells. In three days, there may be about ten to 15 cells; after five days, there will be slightly more than 100. No one knows exactly how many cells the human organism has at birth, but "about 200 billion" is a common guesstimate (Shaffer & Kipp, 2007).

The time from conception to birth, the **prenatal period**, is divided into three stages: germinal, embryonic, and fetal. Each stage has its own landmarks of growth and development. Many events that can have lifelong consequences occur during the sensitive prenatal period.

Once the sperm fertilizes the egg, the first new cell, called the **zygote**, is formed. During the germinal stage of prenatal development, the zygote begins to move down the fallopian tube toward the uterus. As it travels to the uterus, the zygote undergoes rapid cell growth, eventually forming into a hollow ball called the blastocyst. The **germinal stage** lasts from the time of fertilization until the blastocyst implants itself into the uterus—about two weeks.

The blastocyst is interesting. Its outer layer of cells is genetically programmed to develop into the placenta (this forms the interface between the blood systems of the mother and unborn child—the two blood systems do not intermix directly), the amniotic sac (the sac the fetus will grow in), and the umbilical cord (which connects the fetus to the placenta). The inner layer of cells is programmed to become the fetus itself. The blastocyst includes hundreds of cells, and for the first time it is clear that not all of the cells are exact repli-

Courtesy of John-Francis Bourke/zefa/Corbis.

cas of one another. That is, there is now some differentiation among cells.

The **embryonic stage** lasts about six weeks. During this period, the embryo (as the developing organism is now called) develops at a rapid rate, and all of the organ systems of the body are laid in place. At the beginning of this stage, only three types of cells can be identified: a) those that will become the nervous system, the sense organs, and the skin; b) those that will become the internal organs; and c) those that will become the muscles, blood vessels, and the skeleton. By the end of the embryonic stage, we can identify the face, eyes, ears, fingers, and toes.

During the embryonic stage, the unborn child is most sensitive to environmental influences. Most prenatal problems occur during this stage. For example, if the heart, eyes, and hands do not differentiate and develop during this embryonic period, there will be no way to compensate later. The central nervous system is at risk throughout all of the prenatal period, but particularly in weeks three through six. The reason for this heightened sensitivity is simple: organs are most vulnerable when they are growing rapidly. Two months after

Child psychologists study the ways in which children grow and develop. They look for common patterns that apply to all children, and also look for ways in which children can differ from one another.

prenatal period the time from conception to birth

zygote the first new cell resulting from conception

germinal stage the period of development that lasts from the time of fertilization until the blastocyst implants itself into the uterus—about 2 weeks

embryonic stage the period of development during which the embryo develops at a rapid rate, and all of the organ systems of the body are laid in place—lasts about 6 weeks

fetal stage the period of development during which the organs of the body continue to increase in complexity and size, and also begin to function–includes months 3 through 9

point of viability that time at which the fetus could survive if it were born

conception, the embryonic stage draws to a close. The one-inch-long embryo now has a primitive nervous system able to respond to a light touch with a simple reflex movement.

The final stage of prenatal development is the longest, the **fetal stage**. It includes months three through nine. Not only do the organs of the body continue to increase in complexity and size, but they also begin to function. The arms and legs move spontaneously by the end of the third month. In two more months, these movements will be substantial enough for the mother to feel them. At the end of the fifth month, the fetus can be ten inches long. Internal organs have developed, but not to the point of sustaining life outside the uterus. The brain has developed, but neurons within it have not formed many synapses.

Development and growth continue through the last few months of pregnancy. The most noticeable change, at least to the mother, is the significant increase in weight and movement of the fetus. Sometime during the seventh month, most fetuses have reached the **point of viability**—the point at which the fetus could survive if it were born. Although the fetus may be able to survive outside the mother, it will almost certainly require medical intervention and care to do so. Even so, birth in the seventh month often leads to difficulties later on. Normally, during its last few weeks in the uterus, the fetus grows more slowly. Its movements may be more powerful, but its overall activity is slowed because of the cramped quarters. After nearly 270 days, the fetus is ready to enter the world.

BEFORE YOU GO ON

1. Briefly describe the three stages of the prenatal period.

A Point to Ponder or Discuss
Is there any indication to the expectant mother of the shifts from the germinal to the embryonic to the fetal stages of prenatal development?

Environmental Influences on Prenatal Development

In the vast majority of cases, the growth and development of the human organism from zygote to fetus progresses according to the blueprint laid down in the genes. However, in the prenatal stage, things outside the mother can affect the human organism. Most external influences on prenatal development have negative consequences.

The old expression, "You are what you eat" has some truth. In the same way, before we are born, we are what our mothers eat. Malnourished mothers

have more miscarriages, stillbirths, and premature births. Newborns with low birth weight (four pounds or less) who survive have a much greater risk of cognitive deficits, even as they approach adolescence (Taylor et al., 2000). At a minimum, the newborn of a malnourished mother will also be malnourished.

Deficiencies in specific vitamins and minerals influence the prenatal organism. A mother's calcium deficiencies affect the development of bones and teeth in the fetus, for instance. As is the case for many nutrients, it may very well be the mother who suffers more. If there is not enough calcium in the mother's system, "the fetal need for calcium will be met at the expense of the mother" (Hughes & Noppe, 1985, p. 140). Expectant mothers should increase their intake of folic acid (found in foods such as fruits, green vegetables, tuna, and beans). Using supplements that provide up to 0.5 mg a day is also recommended. Folic acid can help prevent birth defects—spina bifida and cleft palate, in particular (Botto et al., 2002; Itika et al., 2001; Torpy, 2005). However, taking vitamins can be overdone. Overdosing some vitamins (especially vitamins A and D, and folic acid, too, for that matter) can have negative effects for both mother and unborn child. Expectant mothers should eat a balanced, sensible diet.

There is ample evidence that smoking cigarettes has harmful effects on the unborn child. Smoking during pregnancy is associated with low birth weight, premature birth, and stillbirths (Pollack, Lantz, & Frohna, 2000; Torpy, 2005). Infants born to smokers require more stimulation to arouse from sleep (Franco et al., 1999) and have a higher risk of hearing defects. Children whose mothers smoked a pack of cigarettes a day during pregnancy have a 75 percent increase in the risk for mental retardation, even when other risk factors (e.g., maternal age, education, and alcohol use) were controlled (Drews & Murphy, 1996). As they get older, the children of mothers who smoked during pregnancy have more behavioral problems such as aggression and hyperactivity (Mick et al., 2002; Orlebeke, Knol, & Verhulst, 1999) and they perform worse on visual perceptual tasks (Fried & Watkinson, 2000), compared to children of nonsmokers. Recently, researchers in Spain discovered that smoking in pregnancy causes genetic damage to the unborn fetus. One common type of chromosome damage linked to maternal smoking increases the risk of blood cancers (like leukemia) (de la Chica et al., 2005).

So, the bad news is that smoking during pregnancy relates to a wide range

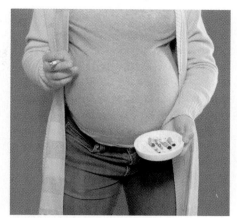

Courtesy of E. Dygas/Getty Images.

Protecting the unborn is often just a matter of common sense and maintaining a healthy lifestyle. One unhealthy behavior known to have negative consequences during prenatal development is smoking. There is no "safe level" of smoking for pregnant women.

of problems. And yet many expectant mothers continue to smoke. In 2000 (the most recent data available), over 400,000 mothers smoked during pregnancy (NCHS, 2003). There is some good news, however. First, the percentage of pregnant mothers who smoke declined from 38% in 1990 to 11.4% in 2003 (Center for Disease Control and Prevention, 2004). Second, if a mother stops smoking early in pregnancy, she can avoid some of the negative effects of smoking. For example, if a pregnant woman stops smoking between her first visit to the doctor and the 32nd week of pregnancy, she reduces the risk her child will have low birth weight, small head size, and abnormal brain size (Lindley et al., 2000).

Alcohol is a drug that can seriously damage unborn children. Alcohol quickly and directly passes through the placenta from the mother to the fetus. Alcohol then collects in organs that have high water content, most ominously in the gray matter of the brain. To make things worse, the fetus eliminates alcohol at half the rate of the mother. The bottom line is that alcohol gets into the fetus easily and stays in for a long time.

Heavy drinking (three drinks or more per day) or binge drinking during vulnerable periods of organ development significantly increases the chance of having smaller babies with retarded

fetal alcohol syndrome (FAS)
a problem in which smaller
babies with retarded growth,
poor coordination, poor muscle
tone, and intellectual retardation result when the mother
consumes alcohol during
pregnancy

growth, poor coordination, poor muscle tone, intellectual retardation, and other problems, collectively referred to as **fetal alcohol syndrome** (FAS) (Jones et al., 1973). Lower alcohol consumption during critical periods of pregnancy can produce a condition that is less severe than full-blown fetal alcohol syndrome known as *fetal alcohol effects*. Alcohol also can have subtle effects on development at low to moderate doses. For example, light alcohol consumption (as little as one drink per day) during early or mid-pregnancy is related to deficits in fine motor skills (Barr et al., 1990). The more alcohol the mother drinks, the greater the impairment in fine motor skills. Children whose mothers drank even small amounts of alcohol during pregnancy are at an increased risk for behavior problems later in life (Sood et al., 2001). Among other things, such children are much more likely to be diagnosed with attention-deficit hyperactivity disorder (Mick et al., 2002) and are much more likely to have alcohol-related problems of their own, even at the age of 21 (Baer et al., 2003; Streissguth et al., 2004).

Mothers who use or abuse psychoactive drugs such as heroin or cocaine during pregnancy may seriously harm their unborn children. For example, 70 percent of newborns of mothers who used heroin during pregnancy showed symptoms of drug withdrawal (e.g., tremor, irritability, hyperactivity and respiratory problems) after birth (Weintraub et al., 1998). Deficits related to cocaine use during pregnancy can be found in preschool children (largely a slowing of language development) and early grade school (largely behavior problems in school) (Delaney-Black et al., 2004; Estelles et al., 2005; Lewis et al., 2004).

Here is yet another concern for pregnant women: "Developmental, learning, and behavioral disabilities are a significant public health problem. Environmental chemicals can interfere with brain development during critical periods, thereby impacting sensory, motor, and cognitive function" (Koger, Schettler, & Weiss, 2005, p. 243). Over and above what a pregnant woman eats, drinks, and smokes during pregnancy, there are throughout the environment toxins and pollutants that can adversely affect her unborn child. Environmental factors cause many developmental defects. Researchers estimate that at least three percent, perhaps as many as 25 percent of developmental defects result directly from neurotoxic environmental exposures (Costa et al., 2004). Many developmental defects might be prevented if people knew that—in addition to alcohol, drugs, and cigarette smoke— exposure to pesticides and other toxic substances has adverse effects during prenatal development (Koger, Schettler, & Weiss, 2005).

Having said all of this, we need to caution against over-reactions. Yes, ingesting a potentially harmful substance such as alcohol does increase the likelihood of birth defects and mental retardation. But there are a few things to bear in mind. Some mothers and fetuses are simply more resilient than others. Second, the physical health of the mother is important. Harmful substances are less harmful when the mother is healthy. Third, exposure to multiple harmful substances is more damaging than exposure to one. In short, exposure to a harmful substance does not mean birth defects or retardation will certainly result. On the other hand, a pregnant woman should be prudent about harmful substances. Pregnant women should avoid as many harmful substances as possible, get good prenatal care, eat a healthy diet, and follow a doctor's advice.

What About Dad?

As you were reading through the last section on nourishment, drugs, and environmental toxins did it sound at all sexist to you? Everything we have covered puts the focus on mothers—what mothers should and should not do. Eat a balanced diet. Don't drink. Don't do drugs. Don't smoke. There has been little concern expressed about the father's role in the process. A review of the literature looked at factors that influence the pathological development of children and adolescents and found that only one percent of the 577 studies cited focused on the role of fathers (Phares & Compas, 1993). A more recent review (Phares et al., 2005) looked at the same issues and questions. They looked at 514 research studies—dealing mostly with mental illness and clinical child issues (or, developmental psychopathology)—and found that "there continues to be a dearth of research on fathers and developmental psychopathology" (p. 736). However fathers have not been totally ignored. Researchers are examining the role of fathers in the physical problems of their children (Lamb, 2004). For example, consider research into the causes of Down syndrome, a collection of birth defects associated with mental retardation. Down syndrome is the result of a child being born with 47 chromosomes per cell instead of the standard 23 pairs. It was assumed that a problem with the mother's ovum caused this syndrome since the likelihood of having a child with Down syndrome increases as the mother's age increases.

Psychologists now recognize that the age of the father is related to some cases of Down syndrome. As many as one-third of all Down syndrome cases reflect difficulties with the father's sperm, and the syndrome is more likely in children whose fathers have jobs that subject them to toxic chemicals. Recent research confirms that a father's age is a risk factor for schizophrenia in children. The study examined the medical records of over 50 thousand members of the Swedish army. It found that advancing paternal age is associated with an increased risk of developing schizophrenia. Indeed, the odds of developing this

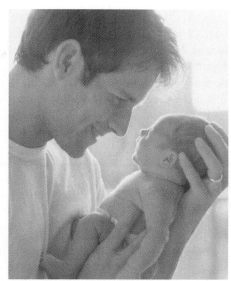

Courtesy of LWA-Dann Tardif/Corbis.

Over the last two decades, psychologists have become more interested in the role of fathers in the growth and development of prenatal and newborn children.

devastating mental disorder increase by 30 percent for each 10-year increase in the father's age. The researchers see these results as strong evidence that schizophrenia is caused by mutation of the father's DNA rather than by inherited personality traits (Zammit et al., 2003). Alcohol use by fathers has also been implicated as a probable cause of prenatal and birth abnormalities, but nearly all of this research has been on rats and mice (Hood, 1990). There is increasing support for counseling fathers about their role in the development of fetal alcohol syndrome (Gearing, McNeill, & Lozier, 2005). Research also supports the hypothesis that advanced *paternal age* is a significant risk factor for the development of autism (Reichenberg et al., 2006).

There is no getting around the father's role in sexually transmitted diseases (STDs). Syphilis and genital herpes can cause miscarriage, low birth weight, and impaired cognitive functioning. Acquired immune deficiency syndrome (AIDS) can be passed from mother to child during pregnancy, during the birth process or after birth, but—fortunately—less than one-fourth of those children born to mothers who are HIV-infected will themselves be infected. Rates of HIV-infected new-borns are in decline: There were an estimated 1,760 such cases in 1991, but fewer than 400 in the year 2000. This decline reflects the fact that fewer HIV-infected women are becoming pregnant and the fact that the drug *zidovidine* (ZDV) is at least somewhat effective in combating the virus. For those infants who become infected, the outlook is not good. Although some survive to adolescence, nearly all will die of AIDS and will have to adjust to a world in which their mothers died of AIDS.

BEFORE YOU GO ON

2. Summarize those factors that can negatively affect prenatal development.

A Point to Ponder or Discuss
Movies in the 1930s and 1940s glamorized smoking and many people smoked heavily. At that time, the harmful effects of smoking had not been proven. How did so many children survive so many smoking parents? (Or did they?)

SENSORY AND PERCEPTUAL DEVELOPMENT

neonate the name given to a newborn

A newborn, or **neonate**, comes into the world capable of responding to a wide range of stimuli. At birth, a newborn's senses are not fully developed, but some (for example, smell and taste) are more advanced than others (for example, vision) (Shaffer, 2002).

The neonate's ability to sense even subtle changes is remarkable. However, there are limitations. The ability of the eyes to focus on an object, for example, does not fully develop until the child is about 4 months old. The neonate can focus well on objects held one to two feet away, but everything nearer or farther appears out of focus. This means that even newborns can focus on the facial features of the persons cradling or feeding them. Visual acuity—the ability to discern detail—shows a threefold to fourfold improvement in the first year. Newborns can detect differences in brightness, and they soon develop the

ability to detect surfaces, edges, and borders. The neonate sees the world in color but cannot make clear distinctions among some hues (blue, green, and yellow seem most troublesome). By the age of 3 months an infant displays full color vision (Adams & Courage, 1998).

When does the perception of depth and distance develop? Neonates show some reactions to distance. They will, for example, close their eyes and squirm away if you rush an object toward their face. In the late 1950s, Cornell University psychologists Eleanor Gibson and Richard Walk built an apparatus designed to test the depth perception of young children (Gibson & Walk, 1960). The *visual cliff*, as it is called, is a deep box covered by a sheet of thick, clear Plexiglas. The box is divided into two sides, one shallow, the other deep, separated by a centerboard. Gibson and Walk found that 6-month-old children would not leave the centerboard to venture out over the deep side of the box, even to get to their mothers. By crawling age, then, the child seems to perceive depth and respond to it appropriately.

It seems likely that the perception of depth develops before the age of 6 months. When neonates (who obviously cannot crawl!) are placed on the Plexiglas over the deep side of the visual cliff box, their heart rates *decrease*, indicating that they at least notice the change in visual stimulation (Campos et al., 1978). When 7-month-old infants are placed over the deep side of the visual cliff, their heart rates *increase*. The increase in heart rate is taken as indicating fear—a response that develops after the ability to discriminate depth (Bertenthal & Campos, 1989). There is also ample evidence that retinal disparity (the discrepancy in images received by the retinas of the two eyes) does not develop until the fourth month after birth. So, in rudimentary form, neonates sense depth, but reacting appropriately to depth cues requires experiences and learning that come later.

Form and pattern perception also develop rapidly during the first year of life. Infants prefer patterned stimuli over unpatterned stimuli (Bednar & Miikkulainen, 2002; Fantz, 1961) and prefer moving over stationary stimuli (Slater et al., 1985). When given a choice of looking at a face-like stimulus and another patterned stimulus, infants prefer to look at the face-like stimulus. A newborn just a few hours old recognizes a picture of its mother's face and prefers to look at it over any other face paired with it (Walton et al., 1992; Walton & Bower, 1993). Infants also can discriminate among facial expressions of emotions and spend more time looking at facial expressions of joy than of anger (Malatesta & Izard, 1984).

The senses other than vision are more highly developed at birth. Neonates can hear nearly as well as adults. There is evidence that even the fetus can discriminate among certain sounds, and certainly a 3-day-old newborn is able to discriminate the sound of its mother's voice from other sounds (DeCasper et al., 1994; Kolata, 1987).

Courtesy of altrendo images RR/Getty Images.

The newborn comes into the world with many of its senses functioning very well indeed. Vision takes some time to develop. The ability to discriminate among a range of colors develops by the age of 3 months. Clear focus on nearby objects, such as toys, is apparent at the age of 4 months. Visual acuity increases three-fold during a child's first year.

Newborns respond to differences in taste and smell. They discriminate among the four basic taste qualities of salty, sweet, bitter, and sour. Neonates show a preference for sweet tastes, and show displeasure to bitter and sour tastes (Shaffer & Kipp, 2007). Although they are unable to use it then, the sense of smell is established before birth. Immediately after birth, neonates respond predictably, drawing away and wrinkling their noses in reaction to a variety of strong odors (Bartoshuk & Beauchamp, 1994). A one- or two-week-old neonate can distinguish its mother's smell from the smell of an unfamiliar woman (Cernoch & Porter, 1985). Neonates also can detect touch and temperature differences and can definitely feel pain.

In summary, newborns appear to have a wide range of sensory and perceptual abilities. For certain, the neonate may need time to learn what to do with the sensory information it acquires, but many of its senses are gathering information. How the newborn processes information received from its senses depends on the development of its mental, or cognitive, abilities. This next step is the subject we turn to now.

BEFORE YOU GO ON

3. Summarize the sensory-perceptual abilities of the neonate.

A Point to Ponder or Discuss
If a 3-day-old infant can recognize the face or the voice (or both) of its mother, what does that tell us about the newborn's memory?

COGNITIVE DEVELOPMENT

Cognitive development is the age-related changes in learning, memory, perception, attention, thinking, and problem solving. From the moment a person is born, changes take place in the basic psychological processes underlying cognition. Developmental psychologists look at cognitive development from two perspectives. First, there is the structural-functional approach developed by Jean Piaget. According to this approach, there are age-related changes in the structures involved in cognition, but the functions remain fixed. In Piaget's theory, at each stage of development, a child uses a qualitatively different form of intelligence. Second, there is the information-processing approach, which is not a unified theory like Piaget's. Instead, those advocating this approach focus on quantitative changes in basic information-processing systems like memory, attention, and learning. From the information-processing approach, cognitive development means that a child becomes a faster, more efficient processor of information. The information-processing systems we are born with grow and develop; they are not replaced by qualitatively different systems as suggested by Piaget.

Piaget's Stages of Development

Jean Piaget proposed a comprehensive theory that describes the course of cognitive development from birth through adolescence. Like Freud, Piaget was not trained as a psychologist. In 1919, Piaget left Switzerland and went to France to work with Alfred Binet to help develop the first IQ test. Piaget became fascinated with the incorrect answers children gave to items on the test. He noticed that children of about the same age gave very similar incorrect answers. Piaget eventually concluded that cognitive development involved qualitative changes in the ways that children think. He dedicated the rest of his life to studying how children develop.

According to Piaget, intelligence has two aspects: structures and functions. Piaget argued that the structures of

In Piaget's sensorimotor stage of development, children learn about their world by sensing and doing—by actively engaging in their world and attending to consequences.

Courtesy of James Woodson/Getty Images.

knowledge (intelligence) are integrated mental representations that children construct to make sense of the world. He called these structures **schemas** (Piaget, 1952). Functions are the mechanisms that help children understand and adapt to the environment. Functions are the processes the child uses to discover the objects and events of his or her world and to create new or different schemas. Unlike the structures, which change with age, functions do not change.

A major cognitive function for Piaget is that of **adaptation**—developing the appropriate schemas to meet the demands of the environment. How does a child get along in the world? By using the appropriate schemas. Where do these schemas come from? Adaptation. Adaptation is composed of two complementary processes: assimilation and accommodation. **Assimilation** occurs when a child incorporates new information into an existing schema. Having grown up in a family that includes two small dogs, Cynthia encounters the neighbor's large collie. The simplest adaptive function is to assimilate this new object into her existing schema of "dog." When Cynthia comes to experience her first cat, she attempts to apply the same schema to this new object. Now Cynthia's assimilation is not correct in this instance, but she has made errors of assimilation before—as when she learned that, although bite-sized, thumbtacks are not edible. The process of **accommodation** allows a child to modify his or her schemas to account for objects and experiences (or to create wholly new schemas if need be). Indeed, it is by adaptation that an infant organizes its schemas into "things edible" and "things not edible." It is by accommodation that a child learns the difference between petting the dog's tail and pulling the dog's tail.

Piaget theorizes that a child passes through four qualitatively different stages of cognitive development. These four stages are as follows: sensorimotor stage (birth to two years), preoperational stage (2 to 7 years), concrete operations stage (7 to 11 years), and formal operations stage (12 years and up). Movement through these stages was unidirectional (in this order with no turning back) and universal (the same for all cultures). Piaget believed the order of the stages never changed, but children moved through the stages at widely differing speeds.

In the **sensorimotor stage** (birth to two years), children discover by sensing (sensori-) and by doing (motor). A child may come to appreciate, for example, that a quick pull on a dog's tail (a motor activity) reliably produces a loud yelp (a sensory experience), perhaps followed, in turn, by parental attention. One of the most useful schemas to develop in the sensorimotor stage is that of *causality*. Infants gradually come to realize that events may have knowable causes and that some behaviors cause predictable reactions. Pushing a bowl of oatmeal off the high chair causes a mess *and* gets Mommy's attention: if A, then B—a very practical insight.

Another important discovery during this stage is that objects exist even when they are not in view. Early in this stage, an object that is out of sight is more than out of mind. The object ceases to exist. By the end of the sensorimotor period, children have learned that objects still exist even if they cannot be seen and that their reappearance can be anticipated. This awareness is called **object permanence**. Yet another useful skill learned during the sensorimotor period is *imitation*. As long as it is within its range of abilities, a baby will imitate almost any behavior it sees. The baby has developed a cognitive strategy that will be used for a lifetime: imitating a model.

Throughout most of the **preoperational stage** (2 to 7 years), a child's thinking is self-centered, or egocentric. According to Piaget, the child has difficulty understanding life from someone else's perspective. In this usage, egocentrism does not imply a selfish, emotional sort of reaction. It simply refers

---

schemas according to Piaget, integrated mental representations that children construct to make sense of the world

adaptation according to Piaget, the process of developing the appropriate schemas to meet the demands of the environment

assimilation according to Piaget, a process that occurs when a child incorporates new information into an existing schema

accommodation according to Piaget, the process that allows a child to modify his or her schemas in order to account for new objects or experiences (or to create new schemas)

sensorimotor stage Piaget's stage of cognitive development (birth to 2 years) in which children discover by sensing (sensori-) and by doing (motor)

object permanence the awareness that objects still exist even if they cannot be seen and that their reappearance is anticipated

preoperational stage Piaget's stage of cognitive development (2 to 7 years) in which a child's thinking is self-centered, or egocentric

to a limitation on children's thinking when they are in the early years of preoperational thought. Imagine two 4-year-olds seated at a table with a large paper maché mountain on it. One child sees several small plastic sheep "grazing" on his side of the mountain. At the other end of the table sits another child looking at the same mountain, but on her side there are no sheep. This situation (a variant of one actually constructed by Piaget) creates great difficulties for these two children because each assumes that the other has exactly the same view, either with or without sheep.

In the preoperational stage, children begin to develop symbols, usually in the form of words, to represent concepts. At this stage, children do not know how to manipulate symbols in a consistent, rule-governed way. It's not until the end of this period that they can play word games or understand why riddles about rabbits throwing clocks out of windows in order to "see time fly" are funny. Children at this stage also have great difficulty with "abstract" concepts, such as those involved with religious beliefs. On the other hand, they are quite capable of playing "make believe," pretending to be mommies and daddies, for instance.

Children in the **concrete operations stage** (7 to 11 years) begin to develop many new concepts and show that they can manipulate those concepts. For example, they can organize objects into categories: balls over here, blocks over there, plastic soldiers in a pile by the door, and so on. Each of these items is recognized as a toy, ultimately to be put away in the toy box and not in the closet, which is where clothes go. It is in this period that rule-governed behavior begins. At this stage, the child learns to use rules to classify, rank, order, or categorize the concrete, observable objects of the world.

A sign of the beginning of the concrete operations stage is the ability to solve conservation problems. **Conservation** is the awareness that changing the form or the appearance of something

does not change what it really is. Piaget concluded that conservation marked the end of the preoperational stage based upon many observations. We can show size conservation by giving two equal-size balls of clay to a 4-year-old. One ball is then rolled into a long cigar shape, and the child will now assert that it has more clay in it than the ball does. A 7-year-old will seldom hesitate to tell you that each form contains the same amount of clay. The 7-year-old has moved on to the next stage of cognitive development.

As its name suggests, in the concrete operations stage children begin to use and manipulate (operate on) concepts and ideas. However, their manipulations are still very concrete—tied to real objects in the here and now. An 8-year-old can be expected to find her way to and from school, even if she takes a side trip along the way. What she will have difficulty doing is telling you exactly how she got from one place to another. Drawing a sensible map is difficult for her. If she stands on the corner of Maple Street and Sixth Avenue, she knows where to go next to get home. Dealing with the concrete reality, here and now, is easy. Dealing with such knowledge in abstract terms is harder.

The logical manipulation of abstract, symbolic concepts characterizes the last of Piaget's stages: **formal operations** (12 and older). At this stage children use abstract, symbolic reasoning. By the age of 12, most children can develop and mentally test hypotheses—they can solve problems mentally.

In the stage of formal operations, youngsters can reason through hypothetical problems: "What if you were the only person in the world who liked rock music?" "If nobody had to go to school, what would happen?" Similarly, children are now able to deal with questions that are contrary to fact: "What if John F. Kennedy or Ronald Reagan were still president of the United States?" The stages of Piaget's theory and the cognitive milestones associated with each are summarized in Table 8.1.

concrete operations stage
Piaget's stage of cognitive development (7 to 11 years) in which children begin to develop many new concepts and show that they can manipulate those concepts

formal operations stage
Piaget's stage of cognitive development (12 and older) characterized by the logical manipulation of abstract, symbolic concepts

conservation the awareness that changing the form or appearance of something does not change what it really is

TABLE 8.1

1. Sensorimotor stage (ages birth to 2 years)
   "Knows" through active interaction with environment
   Becomes aware of cause-effect relationships
   Learns that objects exist even when not in view
   Crudely imitates the actions of others

2. Preoperational stage (ages 2 to 6 years)
   Begins by being very egocentric
   Language and mental representations develop
   Objects are classified on just one characteristic at a time

3. Concrete operations stage (ages 7 to 12 years)
   Develops conservation of volume, length, mass, etc.
   Organizes objects into ordered categories
   Understands relational terms (e.g., bigger than, above)
   Begins using simple logic

4. Formal operations stage (ages over 12)
   Thinking becomes abstract and symbolic
   Reasoning skills develop
   A sense of hypothetical concepts develops

Piaget's stages of cognitive development.

Reactions to Piaget

There is no doubting Piaget's significant influence. He dedicated his career to the study of children. Later research has validated many of his insights and contributions. Finding evidence of Piaget's stages is one of the success stories of cross-cultural research. The stages just reviewed have been identified in children around the world (Brislin, 1993; Segall et al., 1990). There are still individual differences, of course. Remember the example of conservation that involved estimating the amount of clay when it is rolled into different shapes? Sons and daughters of potters understand the conservation of sizes of clay with great ease (Price-Williams et al., 1969). In other words, a child's experience does matter.

Piaget's theory has been criticized on two counts: First, the borders between stages are not as clear-cut as his theory suggests, and second, Piaget underestimated the cognitive abilities of preschool children (Bjorklund, 2000; Flavell, 1982, 1985; Wellman & Gelman, 1992).

For example, the egocentrism said to characterize the child in the preoperational stage may not be as flagrant as Piaget believed. In one study (Lempers et al., 1977), children were shown a picture pasted inside a box. They were asked to show the picture to someone else. In showing the picture, they turned it so that it would be right-side up to the viewer. Every child over two years old showed some appreciation for giving the viewer the proper perspective. In addition, young children (18 months old) readily ascribe goals and intentions to the action of others. That is, preschoolers can observe someone else doing something and appreciate why they are doing it (Meltzoff, 1995). According to Piaget, they should not have this ability until quite a bit later.

Some of Piaget's observations and assumptions have come under attack. This is to be expected in science, particularly for so grand a theory. Nonetheless, Piaget made important contributions. He focused attention on the social and emotional development of children and had considerable influence on the American educational system.

He showed that children are not just passive receptacles during development, but rather are active participants in their own cognitive development. Jean Piaget contributed a theory of cognitive development in children that was so detailed, so thought-provoking, so well grounded in observation that it will continue to challenge researchers for years to come.

BEFORE YOU GO ON

4. What is the general nature of Piaget's approach to cognitive development in children?
5. Briefly describe each of the four stages of Piaget's theory.
6. What are some of the criticisms of Piaget's theory? Do these criticisms mean that his theory is "wrong?"

A Point to Ponder or Discuss
Can you relate any of the themes and/or characters of PBS's Sesame Street *to the stages of cognitive development proposed by Piaget?*

The Information-Processing Approach

Piaget's theory served as a catalyst for developmental psychologists to explore cognitive development. The information-processing approach grew out of research that developmental psychologists conducted on infant learning, memory, and attention. Let's briefly review research in these areas.

Newborns are able to perform simple learning tasks. A neonate (only two hours old) is stroked on the forehead and seems not to respond. This stroking stimulus is then paired with a sugar solution delivered to the infant's lips. The unconditioned stimulus of the sugar solution elicits the unconditioned response of turning the head and making sucking movements. After several trials of pairing the stroking of the forehead and the sugar solution, the baby turns its head and makes sucking movements simply when its forehead is touched (Blass et al., 1984). This sequence is an example of classical conditioning. Head-turning and sucking movements of neonates can also be brought under the control of operant conditioning. These responses occur at higher rates when they are followed by reinforcers such as sugar solutions, the sound of the mother's voice, or the recorded sound of the mother's heartbeat (Moon & Fifer, 1990). It seems that newborns learn very quickly to make attachments with primary caregivers based largely on their sense of smell—a sort of accelerated learning that virtually disappears about ten days after birth (Moriceau & Sullivan, 2004).

Imitation is the ability to reproduce a behavior that is observed. There is evidence that infants as young as one week old can imitate simple facial expressions (Meltzoff & Moore, 1983). Infants can learn to recognize individual faces soon after birth, and learning to appreciate the full range of facial features and expressions continues through months, even years, of experience with faces (Bednar & Miikkulainen, 2002). True imitation of complex behaviors is not reliably evident until the child is eight to 12 months old. Once developed, imitation plays an important role in the transmission of a wide range of behaviors, including prosocial behaviors (e.g., helping) and antisocial behaviors (e.g., acting aggressively).

To benefit from learning, one must be able to store and retrieve information. Memory is the cognitive system that performs these tasks. Memory can be demonstrated in very young infants. For example, many years ago, Friedman (1972) reported a demonstration of memory in neonates only one to four days old. Babies were shown a picture of a simple figure—a checkerboard pattern, for example—for 60 seconds. Experimenters recorded how long the baby looked at the stimulus. After the same pattern was shown repeatedly, the baby appeared bored and gave it less attention. When a new stimulus pattern was presented, the baby stared at it for the full 60 seconds of its exposure. So what does this have to do with memory? The argument is that, for the neonate to stare at the new stimulus, it must have formed some memory of the old one. How else would it recognize the new pattern as being new or different? If the new stimulus pattern were very similar to the old one, the baby would not give it as much attention as it would if it were totally different.

By the time the infant is 2 to 3 months old, it can remember an interesting event for several days (Shaffer, 2002). In one classic experiment, Rovee-Collier (1984) tied one end of a string to the foot of an infant and the other end to a mobile. Each time the infant kicked its foot, the mobile moved. When tested days later, infants 2 to 3 months old remembered the relationship and they got upset if they kicked their feet and the mobile did not move. Memory for the event was also evident after three weeks if the experimenters provided the infant with a retrieval cue (moved the mobile). In another experiment (Schrores, Prigot, & Fagan, 2007), 3-month old infants learned to move a mobile with their foot in the presence of an odor (coconut or cherry). Infant memory was tested one or five days later either in the presence of the odor that accompanied original learning (i.e., coconut used during learning and recall), in the presence of

the unused odor (i.e., coconut used during learning and cherry during recall), or no odor. The results showed that infants memory of the relationship between the odor and memory over both retention intervals.

Over the course of infancy, recall memory shows improvement. However, an infant's memory is constrained because areas of the brain's frontal lobe associated with memory retention and retrieval do not really begin to mature until shortly before the child is 2 years old. Indeed, retrieval of events from four months earlier is almost impossible for 13-month-old children, but children who are 21 months old or 28 months old easily recall events from four months earlier (Liston & Kagan, 2002).

By the time children are 2 to 3 years of age, their memories have improved noticeably. By far, however, the most impressive gains in childhood memory take place between 3 and 12 years of age. Children make huge strides in both short-term and long-term memory.

Children's memories improve as they become better at using memory strategies such as rehearsal, organization, using retrieval cues, and elaboration.

Imitation is a powerful tool for the processing of information—even for young children.

Courtesy of Daniel Bosler/Getty Images.

The use of spontaneous verbal rehearsal to learn material gets progressively better with age. Flavell (1977) found that only 10 percent of kindergartners used verbal rehearsal without being told to do so, but 60 percent of second-graders and 85 percent of fifth-graders used rehearsal spontaneously. Interestingly, younger children have the ability to rehearse (which helps memory) if they are told to do so. Additionally, children use more efficient rehearsal strategies as they get older. Young children (5 to 8 years old) rehearse one item at a time, whereas older children (12 years old) rehearse items in related clusters (Guttentag, Ornstein, & Siemans, 1987). Elaboration, you may recall from our discussion in Chapter 6, is a sophisticated memory strategy that involves working to make material meaningful, perhaps by forming mental images of material to be learned. Generally, elaboration is a memory strategy discovered later in childhood and rarely used before adolescence. While a younger child can improve memory using rote rehearsal, the same child will not improve memory much if they are told to use elaboration.

BEFORE YOU GO ON

7. Briefly describe what psychologists know about the abilities of young children to learn and remember.

A Point to Ponder or Discuss
We noted (in Chapter 6) that encoding information into semantic memory requires paying attention to that information. How much of a very young child's inability to remember very much is due to the child's inability to pay attention? How would you demonstrate such a relationship?

MORAL DEVELOPMENT

How children learn to reason and judge right and wrong is an aspect of cognitive development that has received considerable attention. Piaget included the study of moral development in his theory, arguing that morality is related to cognitive awareness and that children are unable to make moral judgments until they are at least three or four years old (Piaget, 1932, 1948).

Lawrence Kohlberg has offered a theory that focuses on moral development (1963, 1969, 1981, 1985). Like Piaget's approach, Kohlberg's is a theory of stages—of moving from one stage to another in an orderly fashion. Kohlberg's data came from young boys who responded to questions about stories that involve moral dilemmas. A commonly cited example concerns whether a man should steal a drug in order to save his wife's life after the pharmacist who invented the drug refuses to sell it to him. Should the man steal the drug? Why or why not?

On the basis of the children's responses to such dilemmas, Kohlberg proposed three levels of moral development, with two stages (or "orientations") at each level. His theory includes the six stages summarized in Table 8.2. For example, a child at the level of **preconventional morality** would reason that the man should not steal the drug because "he'll get caught and be put in jail" or that he should steal the drug because "the drug didn't cost all that much." A person at the first level of moral reasoning is mostly concerned about the rewards and punishments that come from breaking a rule. A child who

preconventional morality
Kohlberg's stage of moral development in which moral reasoning is mostly concerned about the rewards and punishments that come from breaking a rule

TABLE 8.2

Level 1	Preconventional morality	*Kohlberg's stages of moral development.*
1. Obedience and punishment orientation	Rules are obeyed simply to avoid punishment: "If I take the cookies, I'll get spanked."	
2. Naive egotism and instrumental orientation	Rules are obeyed simply to earn rewards: "If I wash my hands, will you let me have two desserts?"	
Level 2	**Conventional (conforming) morality**	
3. Good boy/girl orientation	Rules are conformed in order to avoid disapproval and gain approval: "I'm a good boy 'cause I cleaned my room, aren't I?"	
4. Authority-maintaining orientation	Social conventions blindly accepted to avoid criticism from those in authority: "You shouldn't steal because it's against the law, and you'll go to jail if the police catch you."	
Level 3	**Postconventional morality**	
5. Contractual-legalistic orientation	Morality is based on agreement with others to serve the common good and protect the rights of individuals: "I don't like stopping at stop signs, but if we didn't all obey traffic signals, it would be difficult to get anywhere."	
6. Universal ethical principle orientation	Morality is a reflection of internalized standards: "I don't care what anybody says—what's right is right."	

says the man should steal the drug because "it will make his wife happy, and most people would do it anyway," or that he shouldn't steal the drug because "you always have to follow rules, even if the situation is serious" is reflecting a type of reasoning at the second level, **conventional morality**. At this level, judgments are based on an accepted social convention—social approval and disapproval matter as much as or more than anything else. The argument that he should steal the drug because "human life is more important than a law," or that "he shouldn't steal the drug for a basically selfish reason, which in the long run would promote more stealing in the society in general" is an example of moral reasoning at the third level of **postconventional morality**. Moral reasoning at this highest level

Courtesy of altrendo images/Getty Images.

conventional morality
Kohlberg's stage of moral development in which moral judgments are based on an accepted social convention

postconventional morality
Kohberg's stage of moral development in which moral reasoning at this highest level reflects complex, internalized standards

"No one is watching. I easily can slip this into my purse and get out of here without anyone noticing. But should I? What if I get caught?" Such dilemmas were the subject of Lawrence Kohlberg's research on moral development.

reflects complex, internalized standards. Notice that in this approach, what matters are not the choices a child makes, but the reasoning behind those choices.

The evidence suggests that the basic thrust of Kohlberg's theory has merit. It also has cross-cultural application. To varying degrees, Kohlberg's descriptions have been tested in several nations in samples drawn from several cultures. Those nations include Israel, India Turkey, and Nigeria (Nisan & Kohlberg, 1982; Snarey, 1987; Snarey et al., 1985). Remember: It is not the choice, but how the choice is made that matters. For example, conventional morality depends on accepted social norms, and cultures differ concerning what is "accepted as social convention." Regardless of what the culture accepts, the important thing is how the subject reasons.

Problems with the Kohlberg's theory also exist. For one thing, there may be a "disconnect" between how people reason, how they feel about a given circumstance, and how they actually behave. Just because someone "knows what's right" and "feels what's right," does not mean that person will actually do what is right. Among other things, the nature of the situation (and in particular the social pressures of that situation) may overpower internal moral cognitions (Thoma & Rest, 1999). And, "although people occasionally make moral judgments in their everyday lives to reveal solutions to moral dilemmas, as Kohlberg's model assumes, they more often make moral decisions that advance their adaptive interests" (Krebs, 2000, p. 132).

It also turns out that few people (including adults) function at the higher stages of moral reasoning described by the theory. This is particularly true in cultures that emphasize group or communal membership, such as the Israeli kibbutz or tribal groups in New Guinea, more than individuality (Snarey, 1987).

This observation brings us to a key concept in cross-cultural psychology: the dimension of *individualism-collectivism* (Bhawuk & Brislin, 1992; Erez & Early, 1993; Triandis, 1990, 1993). People in some cultures are socialized from early childhood to take others (the family, the tribe, the neighborhood, the society) into account when setting goals or making decisions. Such a tendency toward collectivism is found more commonly in Asia and South America. People in other cultures are socialized to think mostly about themselves and their own behaviors, a sort of "pull yourself up by your own boot straps; make it on your own; you'll get what you deserve" mentality. This tendency toward individualism is common in North America and Western Europe. What we are talking about is a dimension of comparison here; even within the same culture, individualism and collectivism vary. This discussion relates to Kohlberg's theory because most measures of moral reasoning put a high value on the sort of thinking found in individualistic (largely Western) cultures and devalue the sorts of thinking typical of collective cultures. This does not mean that Kohlberg was wrong, of course. It just means that what is true for one culture may not be true for another, and neither is necessarily any "better" or more moral.

A similar argument has been raised about Kohlberg's theory as it applies to females (Ford & Lowery, 1986). Remember: All of Kohlberg's original data came from the responses of young boys. Later, when girls were tested, some studies suggested that the girls showed less advanced moral development than did boys. Carol Gilligan argues that the moral reasoning of females is simply different from the moral reasoning of males. Males (at least in Western cultures) are concerned with rules, justice, and an individual's rights. As a result, they approach moral dilemmas differently than do females, who characteristically are more concerned with caring, personal responsibility, and interpersonal relationships (Gilligan, 1982).

Researchers are not trying to determine if men are more or less moral in their thinking than women. Instead, they want to know if men and woman develop different styles of moral reasoning. So far, research has shown that gender differences sometimes do not emerge (Knox, Fagley, & Miller, 2004) or that any differences between men and women in resolving moral conflicts are small (Darley & Schultz, 1990; Donneberg & Hoffman, 1988; Gilligan, 1993), and that both males and females consider justice and concern for others when reasoning about moral issues (Smetana, Kilen, & Turiel, 1991). Additionally, the gender of the main character in a moral dilemma used in research interacts with participant gender. If the main character and participant making a moral judgment are the same gender, higher levels of moral reasoning are used than if the main character and participant are of opposite sexes (McGillicuddy-DeLisi, Sullivan, & Hughes, 2003).

BEFORE YOU GO ON

8. Summarize Kohlberg's approach to moral reasoning and discuss its strengths and weaknesses.
9. Summarize what is known about gender differences in moral reasoning.

A Point to Ponder or Discuss
What is the likelihood that a 5-year-old understands a dilemma about getting prescriptions for a dying wife, or for that matter, that an adult could relate to a dilemma about children sharing toys? That is, how much are moral dilemmas themselves age-related?

ERIKSON'S PSYCHOSOCIAL THEORY OF DEVELOPMENT

Psychologist Erik Erikson (1902–1994), like Piaget, proposed a stage theory of human development (Erikson, 1963, 1965, 1968). Unlike Piaget, Erikson focused on more than cognitive development. Erikson's theory is based on his observations of a wide range of people of various ages. As we will see, his theory extends from childhood through adolescence into adulthood and has a cross-cultural basis. Erikson was born in Germany, studied with Anna Freud (Sigmund Freud's daughter) in Vienna, and then came to the United States to do his research. Erikson's views were influenced more by Freud than by Piaget. Unlike Freud, however, Erikson focused on the social environment, which is why his theory is called *psychosocial.*

Erikson lists eight stages of development through which a person passes. These stages are not so much time periods as they are a series of conflicts (or social crises) that need to be resolved. Erikson uses a pair of terms to describe the conflict in each of his eight stages. Erikson implies that we all resolve the conflicts in order and face them at about the same age. Table 8.3 summarizes Erikson's eight stages of development.

Only the first four stages apply to children. In fact, a strength of Erikson's view of development is that it covers the entire life span. For now, we will stick to the part of Erikson's theory that applies to children, the first four crises. However, we will return to consider the other stages throughout the chapter.

During the first year of life, a child's greatest struggle centers on the establishment of a sense of *trust or mistrust.* There is not much a newborn can accomplish on its own. If its needs are met, the child develops a sense of safety and security, optimistic that the world is a predictable place. If a child's needs are not met, the child develops mistrust—feelings of frustration and insecurity.

TABLE 8.3

Erikson's theory of development.

Approximate age	Crisis	Adequate resolution	Inadequate resolution
0–1½	Trust vs. mistrust	Basic sense of safety	Insecurity, anxiety
1½–3	Autonomy vs. self-doubt	Perception of self as agent capable of controlling own body and making things happen	Feelings of inadequacy to control events
3–6	Initiative vs. guilt	Confidence in oneself as initiator, creator	Feeling a lack of self-worth
6–puberty	Competence vs. inferiority	Adequacy in basic social and intellectual skills	Lack of self-confidence, feelings of failure
Adolescent	Identity vs. role confusion	Comfortable sense of self as a person	Sense of self as fragmented; shifting, unclear sense of self
Early adult	Intimacy vs. isolation	Capacity for closeness and commitment to another	Feeling of aloneness, separation; denial of need for closeness
Middle adult	Generativity vs. stagnation	Focus on concern beyond oneself to family, society, future generations	Self-indulgent concerns; lack of future orientation
Later adult	Ego-integrity vs. despair	Sense of wholeness, basic satisfaction with life	Feelings of futility, disappointment

During the period of *autonomy versus self-doubt*, from ages one and one-half to three years, the child develops a sense of self-esteem. The child begins to act independently, to dress and feed himself or herself, for example. Physically more able, the child strikes off on his or her own, exploring ways of assuming personal responsibility. Frustration at this level of development leads the child to feel inadequate and doubt self-worth.

Erikson calls the period from ages three to six *initiative versus guilt*. Now the child struggles to develop as a contributing member of social groups, particularly the family. If the child is encouraged, he or she should develop initiative—a certain joy of trying new things. Asking a 5-year-old what the family should do this evening can help the child learn to develop initiative to think and plan. Without such encouragement, a child is likely to feel guilty and resentful.

The final childhood period, *competence versus inferiority*, lasts from about age six to puberty. During this period, the child is challenged to move beyond the safety and comfort of the family. Development happens "out there" in the neighborhood and at school. The child begins to learn those skills needed to become a fully functioning adult in society. If the child's efforts are constantly belittled or ignored, the child may develop a sense of inadequacy and inferiority and remain dependent on others as an adult.

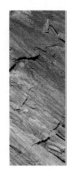

BEFORE YOU GO ON

10. Describe the first four stages of Erikson's theory of development.

A Point to Ponder or Discuss
In terms of psychosocial development, what is to become of the (theoretical) child who is so protected, so sheltered, that he or she never really experiences the social realities of choices and conflicts, much less crises?

DEVELOPING GENDER IDENTITY

The theories of Piaget, Kohlberg, and Erikson deal with how (and when) children develop concepts or cognitions about themselves and the world in which they live. In this section we'll focus on the concept of **gender**—one's sense of maleness or femaleness, as opposed to one's sex, which is a biological term. Gender has been defined as "the socially ascribed characteristics of females and males, their roles and appropriate behaviors" (Amaro, 1995, p. 437), and "the meanings that societies and individuals ascribe to female and male categories" (Eagly, 1995, p. 145).

One of the first proclamations made upon the birth of a baby is "It's a girl!" or "It's a boy!" Parents wrap little girls in pink, boys in blue, and dress an infant or small child in clothes that proclaim the child is a boy or a girl. And, these labels matter! In one study (Condry & Condry, 1976), for example, male and female adults watched a videotape of an infant (which could not be identified as male or female on the tape) being presented with four different stimuli (e.g., a teddy bear). Half of the participants were told that the infant they were observing was male and the other half were told that the infant was a female. Participants rated the infant's behavior on a number of rating scales. The results

gender one's sense of maleness or femaleness

Courtesy of Peter Cade/Getty Images.

Courtesy of Solus-Veer/Corbis.

Children develop a sense of gender identity by the time they are 2 or 3 years old. Parents often encourage gender development—if unwittingly, perhaps—when they provide toy cars and trucks for boys and dolls for girls.

showed that when the participants believed that the infant was a male, the infant's behavior was more likely to be described as "active" and "potent" than if participants believed that the infant was a female. Interestingly, children as young as 3 years old showed the same gender bias (Haugh, Hoffman, & Cowen, 1980).

As infants, boys develop a bit more slowly, have a little more muscle tissue, and are somewhat more active, but even these differences are slight (e.g., Eaton & Enns, 1986). During the first year of life there are virtually no differences in temperament or "difficulty" between boys and girls (Thomas & Chess, 1977). Many adults believe that there ought to be differences between little boys and little girls (Paludi & Gullo, 1986), and they choose toys, clothing, and playmates based on what they believe is acceptable (Schau et al., 1980). However, when averaged over many studies, there are few areas in which parents consistently treat their sons and daughters differently (Lytton & Romney, 1991).

The only area in which North American parents show significant differentiation is in the encouragement of different sex-typed activities for girls and boys. For example, in one study (Snow et al., 1983), fathers were more likely to give dolls to 1-year-old girls than to boys of the same age. However, even at this age, children prefer certain toys; when offered dolls, boys are less likely to play with them. In the first few years of school, girls and boys place different values on activities and see themselves as good at different things. Girls tend to value (and see themselves as competent in) reading and instrumental music, but boys tend to value math and sports (Eccles et al., 1993).

Children's peer groups are significant for both girls and boys (Maccoby, 1988, 1990). By the age of three or four,

girls and boys gravitate toward playmates of the same sex, a pattern that is shown cross-culturally. Boys tend to dominate in mixed-sex interactions. In fact, by school age, boys prefer to play in groups, while girls prefer to either play alone to interact with only one other girl (Benenson & Heath, 2006). Boys tend to use direct commands to influence others, whereas girls tend to use polite suggestions, which work with other girls but not with boys (Serbin et al., 1984). Girls develop more intense friendships and are more distressed when those friendships end. Interactive styles that develop in same-sex groups in childhood are the foundation for differences in social relationships of adult men and women, with more supportive, intimate relationships among women and more direct, hierarchical relationships among men (Maccoby, 1990).

At what age do boys and girls begin to see each other as "different"? When do children develop gender identity, that sense or self-awareness of maleness or femaleness? Even 5-month-old infants are able to distinguish gender in faces shown to them in pictures (Fagan & Singer, 1979; Walker-Andrews et al., 1991). Most children develop a sense of gender identity by two or three years old (Paludi & Gullo, 1986). By the age of four, most children demonstrate gender stereotypes, showing that they believe that certain occupations, activities, or toys go better with males and some go better with females. By the time they start school, most children associate various personality traits with men and with women. This pattern crosses cultural lines (Williams & Best, 1990). Once gender identity is established, it remains invulnerable to change. By late childhood and early adolescence, peer pressure intensifies gender differences (McHale et al., 2001).

Cognitive psychologists believe that, once children can discriminate between the sexes, they develop schemas for gender-related information. A schema, you will recall, is an organized system of general information, stored in memory, which guides the processing of new information. For example, children remember toys better if they are gender-consistent than if they are gender-inconsistent. That is, male children remember male-oriented toys better than female-oriented toys, and the reverse is true for female children (Cherney & Ryalls, 1999). This effect extends to children being asked to remember situations depicting gender-consistent versus gender-inconsistent information (Signorella, Bigler, & Liben, 1997). In one experiment, male and female children (kindergarten to third grade) were asked to recall a series of pictures depicting men and women in either traditional or nontraditional roles. The results showed that male children remembered more pictures showing a male in a traditional male role (e.g., firefighter) than a male in a nontraditional role (e.g., school teacher). Female children remembered more pictures showing a female in a traditional role than in a nontraditional role (Liben & Signorella, 1993). The study's authors believe this gender difference is most likely due to distorting or forgetting material inconsistent with the child's gender schemas.

All of this might leave you with the impression that gender schemas and sex-typed behaviors (e.g., gender-related preferences for different types of toys) result from social forces operating on the child (e.g., parents, the media) to produce differences between males and females. This is undoubtedly true, as decades of research shows. However, remember from Chapter 1 that there is also a biological perspective in psychology. Can some of the differences in gender identity and behavior differences between males and females be related to biological factors? The answer to this question is yes. One interesting fact supports the role of biology in gender-related differences in behavior: Monkeys show the same sex-typed toy preferences as to human children (Alexander & Hines, 2002; Hassett, Siebert, & Wallen, 2004)!

In one experiment, Alexander and Hines allowed male and female vervet monkeys to interact with a number of toys, two of which were "male toys" (a car and a ball) and two "female toys" (a doll and a cooking pot). Alexander and Hines found that the male monkeys spent more time interacting with the car and ball; whereas the female monkeys spent more time interacting with the doll and pot. Alexander (2003) believes that findings such as these suggest that exposure to male hormones during prenatal development contributes to differential brain development for males and females (the fancy term for this is *sex-dimorphic development* of the brain). There is evidence supporting this idea (Berenbaum & Hines, 1992, for example). Specifically, Alexander suggests that evolutionary pressures have resulted in differences in how males and females process visual information, with males paying more attention to object movement and location and females to form and color. Further, this biological difference may lead to "preparedness" for a male or female gender role that is reinforced by gender socialization (Alexander, 2003).

This leads us to an age-old question in psychology: Where do gender differences come from? Are they primarily a product of social forces, or are they more closely related to biological differences? In many respects, this question oversimplifies the origins of gender (or any) behavior differences. Gender-related behavior and preferences are undoubtedly the result of a complex interaction between biological, cognitive, and social factors (Iervolino, Hines, Golombok, Rust, & Plomin, 2005).

DEVELOPING SOCIAL ATTACHMENTS

We adapt and thrive in this world to the extent that we can profit from our relationships with other people. The roots of social development can be found in early infancy—in the formation of attachment. **Attachment** is a strong and reciprocal emotional relationship between a child and mother or primary caregiver (Bowlby, 1982). Attachment has survival value, "increasing the chances of an infant being protected by those to whom he or she keeps proximity" (Ainsworth, 1989, p. 709). A well-formed attachment provides a child with freedom to explore the environment, become curious, solve problems, and learn to get along with peers (Collins & Gunnar, 1990).

Forming an attachment between infant and parent is not automatic; it requires regular interaction and give-and-take. Strong attachments are most likely if the parent is sensitive and responsive to the child. *Sensitivity* refers to the parent's ability to correctly read the signals coming from an infant (for example, identifying when the infant is hungry—as opposed to sleepy—by the infant's crying pattern). *Responsiveness* refers to how the parent responds to the child's signals—for example, picking up the infant when he or she cries, changing the diaper as soon as it is soiled, feeding the infant regularly, and so on. One study found that mothers who did not respond appropriately to their in-

fants were more likely to show an insecure attachment (Harel & Scher, 2003).

Simply spending time with an infant is usually not enough to produce successful attachment. Spontaneous hugging, smiling, eye contact, and vocalizing all help attachment. Attachment is fostered by qualities such as warmth and gentleness. When the process is successful, we say that the child is "securely attached." Forming an attachment is a two-way street. Parents become more easily attached when a baby reciprocates by smiling, cooing, and clinging when attended to (Pederson et al., 1990). About 65 percent of American children become securely attached by the age of one year—a percentage close to that found in seven other countries (van Ijzendoorn & Kroonenberg, 1988).

Are there long-term benefits of becoming securely attached? Yes. Secure attachment is related to: a) sociability (less fear of strangers, better relationships with peers, more popularity, and more friends), b) higher self-esteem, c) better relationships with siblings, d) fewer tantrums (or less aggression), e) less concern by teachers over controlling behaviors in the classroom, f) more empathy and concern for the feelings of others, g) fewer behavioral problems at later ages, and h) better attention spans (from Bee, 1992). Securely attached children also show greater persistence at problem-solving and are less likely to seek help from adults when injured or disappointed (Goldsmith & Harman,

attachment a strong and reciprocal emotional bond or relationship between a child and his or her primary caregiver

1994). It is also likely that attachment patterns set in early childhood retain their influences indefinitely (Fraley, 2002).

Infants can and do form attachments with persons other than their mothers. Father-child attachments are common and beneficial for the long-term development of the child (Grych & Clark, 1999; Lamb, 1977, 1979). One researcher found that she could predict how much a baby showed signs of attachment to its father simply by knowing how often Dad changed the baby's diaper. There is no evidence that fathers are less sensitive to the needs of their children than are mothers, but they may be a little more physical and a little less verbal in their interactions (Parke & Tinsley, 1987).

Finally, we need to consider how those children who spend time—sometimes a lot of time—in daycare facilities form attachments. In the United States, more than half the mothers of children younger than three work, and their children are cared for, at least in part, by others. Studies suggest children placed in high-quality daycare benefit cognitively and socially (Burchinal et al., 2000; Lamb, 1998; NICHD, 2002). But, how do these children fare with respect to attachment? It depends largely on the quality of the care the children get—no matter where they get it. Children who receive warm, supportive, attentive care; adequate stimulation; and opportunities for exploration demonstrate secure attachment (Erel, Oberman, & Yirmiya, 2000; NICHD, 2002; Phillips et al., 1987). The influence of daycare on attachment depends on the likelihood that the child would have received good, warm, supportive, loving care at home (Scarr & Eisenberg, 1993). Additionally, the quality of daycare and quality of maternal care combine to affect attachment security. Children who experience both low-quality daycare and insensitive/unresponsive parenting show the poorest attachment security (NICUD Early Child Care Research Network, 1997).

The benefit or harm of non-parental childcare also depends on the age of the

Courtesy of Yellow Dog Productions/Getty Images.

child. "There is little dispute about the conclusion that children who enter daycare at 18 months, 2 years, or later show no consistent loss of security of attachment to their parents" (Bee, 1992, p. 510). The debate centers on children younger than one year old, and some evidence suggests that secure attachment is less likely among children not cared for at home during their first year (Belsky, 1990; Belsky & Rovine, 1988; Hennessy & Melhuish, 1991; Lamb & Sternberg, 1990). Two other studies suggest that early infant daycare has little effect on a child's later social and emotional development. One study in France found no difference in aggression and other behavior problems between 3- to 4-year-old children who had attended daycare during the first three years of life and those who had not (Balleyguier & Meihuish, 1996). Early daycare has also been found to affect neither mother-infant interactions or cognitive outcomes for the child (Caruso, 1996). A recent study looked at the formation of secure attachment with primary professional caregivers. One variable in the study was the extent to which the children were more or less temperamentally irritable

Although parents may be concerned—and occasionally feel guilty—about putting their children in a daycare facility, the research tells us that children can do well, even thrive, in such settings. The critical factor—which takes some investigation on the part of parents—is the quality of the care offered at daycare and preschool facilities.

before the study began. Attachment depended only on the extent of the children's individual experience of positive caregiver interactions in the day care center—regardless of the rated irritability of the children (De Schipper, Tavecchio, & Van Ijzendoorn, 2008). So, what we know is that forming positive attachments with caregivers is a beneficial process in childhood, and who the caregiver is (mother, father, professional daycare worker) matters much less than the quality of the interactions between that primary caregiver and the child.

BEFORE YOU GO ON

13. What is the significance of social attachments formed in infancy and early childhood?

A Point to Ponder or Discuss
You have been hired as a consultant by a chain of daycare facilities. What sorts of things should they do to ensure proper attachment between caregiver and child?

SPOTLIGHT
ON DIVERSITY

Parenting Styles

Psychologists have long been interested in how *parenting styles* influence the development of children. In this context, "parenting styles" are the over-arching, general, strategies that parents use to influence the affects, behaviors, and cognitions of their children (Barber, 1996, 1998; Eisenberg et al., 2005).

The first "model of parenting styles" was proposed by Diana Baumrind of the University of California's Institute of Human Development (1971, 1989, 1991). Baumrind's approach is based on the degree of "demandingness" or control, and the degree of responsiveness or warmth, parents react to their children with (Maccoby & Martin, 1983). Baumrind identified three parenting styles: *indulgent, authoritarian,* and *authoritative.*

The *indulgent parenting style* (often referred to as *"permissive"*) was quite popular in the 1950s and 1960s. Parents stressed acceptance, love and relationship building and were less likely to set limits. Permissive parents are highly attuned to their children's developmental and emotional needs but place few demands on them, and permit them to make their own decisions. Permissive-indulgent parents exercise little parental control and tend to work to meet their child's needs (Radziszewska et al., 1996). A subset of the indulgent parenting style is the "permissive-neglectful" parent (Maccoby & Martin, 1983). The permissive-neglectful parent exercises no control and does not respond to the child's needs. They are indifferent to their children and have low levels of responsiveness and demandingness. Sometimes referred to as "uninvolved," such parents allow their children freedom, expect little responsibility, and are distant in their relationship. Children raised by parents who used the *indulgent parenting style* tend to be creative and original, but they have difficulty getting along with others. They also tend to be aggressive when they do not get their way.

The *authoritarian parenting style* imposes rules (usually without explaining them), expects strict obedience, and often uses physical/verbal punishment as a means of control. Parents who use this style seldom take into account the child's feelings and/or opinions. The child's needs may be considered, but authoritarian parents are not usually warm in their social interactions with their children (Darling & Steinberg, 1993). Children reared with the authoritarian parenting style are generally withdrawn and have low self-esteem. Interestingly, this parenting style was dominant throughout most of Western history. In the distant past, society changed very slowly, and society's norms (rules) also evolved slowly. Thus, the authoritarian style was an easy and efficient way to teach the "right" course of action to children in the clearest possible way.

Parents who use an *authoritative parenting style* set clear rules, and enforce them consistently, but they are flexible in explaining rules based upon the needs of the child. Authoritative parents involve their children in decision-making and have high expectations (Darling & Steinberg, 1993; Eisenberg, 2005). Such parents allow more autonomy during adolescence and show warmth in parenting their children. Baumrind, (1971, 1991) reports that an authoritative parenting style produces children who have the highest levels of academic achievement, self-esteem, self-reliance, and social skills. The authoritative parenting style tends to nurture psychosocially adapted children (Steinberg, Darling, & Fletcher, 1995; Steinberg, Dornbusch, & Brown, 1992).

In the United States, most parents (at least among members of the middle-class of European decent) use the authoritative parenting style. Steinberg, Darling & Fletcher (1995) argue that authoritative parenting predicts positive psychosocial behaviors and fewer problem behaviors during adolescence for all ethnic groups. Higher academic achievement is typically associated with lower parental authoritarianism and higher parental authoritativeness (Steinberg, Elmen, & Mounts, 1989). The outcomes of the authoritative parenting style are similar across ethnic groups—at least for socialization and general adjustment. However, there are ethnic differences associated with academic performance and authoritative parenting style (Steinberg, Dornbusch & Brown, 1992).

Are parenting styles similar across ethnicity? Some research indicates they are. Parenting styles are very similar across ethnic groups, and family influences largely transcend ethnicity (Lamborn et al., 1991; Steinberg, 2001; Steinberg et al., 1991; Steinberg et al., 1994). However, there may be some differences in how different ethnic groups rate different parenting styles. For instance, Sonnek (1999) claims that the major characteristics of the authoritarian style of parenting are rated as a negative trait by Caucasian Americans, but they are rated as a positive trait by Hispanic Americans.

African Americans are more likely than whites to rear their children using the authoritative parenting style (Radziszewska et al., 1996). They are more likely to be strict, use physical discipline, and have defined behavioral standards for their children. Even so, African American parents balance this strictness with love, affection, and support. The authoritative style works best for African American children by helping them learn to be self-assertive and independent. Strong bonding with extended family is typical of the way African Americans parent their children. Grandparents and older siblings take part in teaching and disciplining younger children. As a result, roles overlap in many African American families.

The typical "nuclear" American family includes a father, mother, and child—or children. This vision of the family is regularly reinforced on television and in magazines. However, in many cases it is just wrong. For example, about 41 percent of African American children, 30 percent of Hispanic American children, 15 percent of Caucasian American children live in single parent homes with the mother as head of the household. The reality within many ethnic groups is extended families rear children and the model family may not be the nuclear family portrayed in the media. That is, for many families, children are raised not just by Mom and Dad, but by grandparents, uncles, aunts, and cousins (Levitt, Guacci-France, & Levitt, 1993).

Socioeconomic status appears to influence parenting styles within the African American family. According to Hoffman (2003), the authoritative parenting style is generally practiced among poorer families while middle class African American families are more authoritarian.

Asian Americans tend to practice authoritarian parenting styles (Dornbusch et al., 1987). The authoritarian parenting style is typically associated with lower academic grades. However, Asian American children generally excel academically (Sue & Okazaki, 1990). Chao and Sue suggest that the controlling behavior of Asian American parents does not have the same effect on their children because Asian American parents typically are not hostile or coercive and their emphasis on obedience promotes educational excellence.

Asian American parents generally seek a strong attachment between parent and child (Suzuki, 1980). Asian American children are taught to obey, to respect, and to honor their elders (Chao, 1994). Family ties are close and group success is favored over individual success. High value is placed on interdependence and the family unit over individuality (Yee et al., 1998).

Psychologist Judith Rich Harris takes a different view of the role of parents in socializing children. She developed a "group socialization theory" that claims that parents—no matter what their style—play only a small role in the social and intellectual development of their children. In her 1998 book, *The Nurture Assumption*, Harris argues children learn what behaviors and values are appropriate in different environments *from those environments*. Children learn from parents, but they also learn from peers, from classmates, and from teachers. Children don't assume that what works in one place will work somewhere else. Harris concedes the differences in a child's behaviors between home and school may be subtle and minimal—if the child is from a "typical" home. However she notes that differences are ". . . most noticeable in the one [child] whose parents belong to a different culture from the others in the neighborhood—the child of immigrant or deaf parents, for instance." (Harris, 1999, p. 8).

Conclusion

There are three parenting styles: authoritative, authoritarian, and indulgent. Parenting styles can influence attitudes, values, emotional growth, and social interactions of children. Parenting styles can predict psychosocial competence, academic performance, and social development. The effects of parenting styles may vary within and across ethnic groups. For example, Caucasian Americans' authoritarian parenting style generally produces children with relatively strong school performance, low behavioral problems, but problematic self-development. For African Americans, authoritarian parenting does not seem to create self development issues for children.

ADOLESCENT DEVELOPMENT

Adolescence is a period of transition from the dependence of childhood to the independence of adulthood. It begins at puberty (sexual maturity) and lasts through the teen years—the second decade of life.

We can view adolescence from different perspectives. In biological terms, adolescence begins with **puberty**—sexual maturity and an ability to reproduce—and concludes with the end of physical growth in the late teen years. In psychological terms, adolescence has its own set of cognitions, feelings, and behaviors. Psychologists emphasize the development of problem-solving skills and an increased reliance on the use of symbols, logic, and abstract thinking. In adolescence, teens struggle to form their own identities and learn to appreciate themselves and their self-worth. In social terms, adolescents occupy a place in their societies "in between"—not yet an adult, but no longer a child. In this context, adolescence usually lasts from the early teen years through graduation from the highest education level, when a person is thought to enter the adult world.

Whether we accept a biological, psychological, or social perspective, we are usually talking about people who, in our culture, are between 12 and 20. Psychologists still struggle with how to characterize adolescence: Is it a time of personal growth, independence, and positive change? Or is it a period of rebellion, turmoil, and negativism?

The pessimistic view of adolescence is the older of the two, attributed to G. Stanley Hall (who wrote the first textbook on adolescence in 1904) and to Anna Freud (who applied psychoanalytic theory to adolescents). They claim that adolescence normally involves difficulty and adjustment: "To be normal during the adolescent period is by itself abnormal" (Freud, 1958, p. 275). In this view, "Adolescents may be expected to be extremely moody and depressed one day and excitedly 'high' the next. Explosive conflict with family, friends, and authorities is thought of as commonplace" (Powers et al., 1989, p. 200). The teen years present conflicts and pressures that require difficult choices, and some teenagers react to these pressures in maladaptive ways (Larson & Ham, 1993; Quadrel et al., 1993; Takanishi, 1993).

Adolescence requires changes and adjustments, but those adjustments and changes are usually made in psychologically healthy ways (Jessor, 1993; Millstein et al., 1993; Steinberg & Morris, 2001). As adolescents struggle for independence and for self-expression, some behave recklessly. Such behaviors often reflect the socialization process of the teenagers' culture (Arueff, 1995; Compas et al., 1995). Still, most teenagers meet the challenges of the period without developing significant social, emotional, or behavioral difficulties (Steinberg, 1999). However, there is a "wide variability that characterizes psychological development during the second decade of life" (Compas et al., 1995, p. 271). Some struggle more than others. Those that struggle may be at a disadvantage. For example, one study found that high levels of parent-adolescent conflict are associated with poor academic achievement (Dotterer, Hoffman, Crouter, & McHale, 2008).

For certain, adolescence presents a series of challenges. In the next two sections, we will examine two of the challenges faced by an adolescent: puberty and identity formation.

adolescence a developmental period of transition from the dependence of childhood to the independence of adulthood, beginning at puberty and lasting through the teen years—the second decade of life

puberty the onset of sexual maturity and the ability to reproduce

The Challenges of Puberty

Two biological changes mark the onset of adolescence. First, there is a marked increase in height and weight, known as a *growth spurt*, and second, there is sexual maturation. The growth spurt usually occurs in girls before it does in boys. Girls begin their growth spurt as early as age nine or ten and then slow down at about age 15. Boys generally show increased rates of growth between the ages of 12 and 17. Males usually do not reach adult height until their early twenties; females generally attain maximum height by their late teens (Tanner, 1981).

Some of the challenge of early adolescence is a direct result of the growth spurt. Increases in height and weight often occur so rapidly that they are accompanied by real, physical "growing pains," particularly in the arms and legs. The growth spurt seldom affects all parts of the body uniformly, especially in boys. Boys of 13 and 14 often appear clumsy and awkward as they try to coordinate their large hands and feet with the rest of their body. Boys also experience changes in their vocal chords. As the vocal cords lengthen, the pitch of the voice lowers. This transition is seldom smooth, and a teenage boy may suffer weeks of squeaking and cracking as the pitch of his voice descends.

Puberty occurs when one becomes physically capable of sexual reproduction. With puberty, comes an increase in levels of sex hormones—androgens in males and estrogens in females. (We all have androgens *and* estrogens in our bodies. Males simply have more androgens; females have more estrogens.) Boys seldom know when their own puberty begins. For some time they have erections and nocturnal emissions of seminal fluid. Male puberty begins when live sperm appear in the semen. Most boys have no idea when that happens; such determinations require a laboratory test. In females, the onset of puberty is recognizable. It is indicated by the first menstrual period, called **menarche**.

With puberty, adolescents are biologically ready to reproduce. Psychological maturity, however, does not come automatically with sexual maturity. Some boys and girls reach puberty before their peers and are called early bloomers; other boys and girls reach puberty later and are

menarche the first menstrual period, indicative of the beginning of puberty in females

Adolescence begins at puberty, a period during which there are many physical changes for both girls and boys. For boys, the pitch of the voice is likely to change and facial hair begins to grow.

Courtesy of Stockbyte/Getty Images.

called late bloomers. Reaching puberty well before or well after others of the same age may have some psychological effects, although few are long lasting.

Let us first get an idea of what early and late puberty means. Puberty is expected to occur between 10 and 15 years of age for girls and between 11 and 16 for boys. In fact, this age range is quite large and subject to change. For example, in the United States 150 years ago, the average age of menarche was 16; now it is close to 12, although this trend is leveling off (Euling et al., 2008).

What are the advantages and disadvantages of early maturation? A girl who enters puberty early will probably be taller, stronger, faster, and more athletic than other girls (and many boys) in her class at school. She is more likely to be approached for dates, have earlier sexual encounters, and marry at a younger age than will her peers. She may have self-image and self-esteem problems, and be more susceptible to emotional problems, particularly if she puts on weight and shows marked breast development (Ge, Conger, & Elder, 1996). An early age of menarche is a risk factor for the development of breast cancer (Golub et al., 2008). Early maturing girls (compared to a normal control group) show more behavior problems and more difficulty relating to their parents and peers (Tremblay & Frigon, 2005).

Because of the premium put on physical activity in boys, the early-maturing boy is at a greater advantage than the early-maturing girl. He will have more dating and sexual experiences than his peers, which will raise his status. He will have a better body image and higher self-esteem. Also, physically mature adolescents are expected by parents, teachers, and friends to show higher levels of emotional and social maturity (Jaffe, 1998). This presents the physically mature adolescent with quite a challenge because physical development is usually faster than both social and emotional development. Indeed, early-maturing boys (often influenced by older peers) are at greater risk for all sorts of problems,

including delinquency, drug and alcohol use (Dick et al., 2000; Patton et al., 2004; Williams & Dunlap, 1999), and depression (Kaltiala-Heino, Kosunen, & Rimpela, 2003). The early-maturing boy will experience more sexual arousal earlier, will become sexually active sooner than age-mates who reach puberty later (Ostovich & Sabini, 2005), and is at higher risk for the development of testicular cancer (Golub et al., 2008). Alfred Kinsey and his associates first put forth these very hypotheses in 1948 (Kinsey, Pomeroy, & Martin, 1948, pp. 297–326).

Late-maturing boys may carry a sense of inadequacy and poor self-esteem into adulthood. They also tend to be more psychologically immature and experience more anxiety over their sexuality than those who mature more "normally" (Lindfors et al., 2007). Late maturity for girls has virtually no long-term negative consequences. In retrospect, some women feel blooming late was an advantage because they had the extra time to pursue broadening interests, rather than becoming "boy-crazy" like their peers in early adolescence (Tobin-Richards et al., 1984).

The consequences of early- and late-occurring puberty are reasonably well known. What is less certain is why some teens (and even pre-teens) experience puberty when they do, but recent studies have pointed to increased obesity and weight gain as a risk factor for early puberty in girls. No such relationship was found for boys (Kaplowitz, 2008). In one large study, a higher body mass index score (a measure of obesity) in girls as young as 36 months of age, and a higher rate of change in body mass index between age 36 months and first grade were found to be associated with an earlier onset of puberty across various measures (Lee et al., 2006).

There also is accumulating evidence that earlier and faster maturation is related to the quality of family relationships—at least for girls. Families characterized by stress, conflict, and a lack of closeness tend to see their children reaching puberty at younger ages (Belsky, Steinberg, & Draper, 1991; Kim & Smith, 1998). Of particular importance for the timing of menarche is the role played by the father. In homes with a supportive and affectionate father, menarche tends to occur later (Ellis et al., 1999). The absence of the biological father is strongly associated with early menarche (Kanazawa, 2001; Maestripieri et al., 2004). Two other predictors of early onset of puberty for girls are a history of mood disorders (i.e., depression) in the mother and the presence of a stepfather in the home (Ellis & Garber, 2000).

BEFORE YOU GO ON

15. What is puberty, and what are the consequences of reaching puberty earlier or later than age-mates?

A Point to Ponder or Discuss
The timing of puberty seems to have a greater effect on boys than on girls. Why do you suppose this is so?

The Challenges of Identity Formation

Adolescents around the world give the impression of being great experimenters. They experiment with hairstyles, music, religions, drugs, sexual outlets, fad diets, part-time jobs, part-time relationships, and part-time philosophies of life. To adults, it often appears that most of a teenager's commitments are part-time. Teens are busy trying things out, doing things their own way, and grandly searching for Truth.

identity crisis the struggle to define and integrate the sense of who one is, what one is to do in life, and what one's attitudes, beliefs, and values should be

Courtesy of Beth Dixson/Solus-Veer/Corbis.

Teens are great experimenters. They are trying to fashion some sense of identity, some sense of who they are as individuals in the world.

Adolescents are experimenters because one of the major tasks of adolescence is the resolution of an **identity crisis**—the struggle to define and integrate the sense of who one is, what one is to do in life, and what one's attitudes, beliefs, and values should be. The concept of identity formation is associated with Erik Erikson (1963), in whose view the search for identity is the fifth stage of psychosocial development and occurs during the adolescent years. During adolescence we come to grips with questions like "Who am I?" "What am I going to do with my life?" "What is the point of it all?" (Habermas & Bluck, 2000).

For many young people, resolving their identity crisis is simple. In such cases, the adolescent experiences little confusion and little conflict in attitudes, beliefs, or values. Many teenagers slide easily into the values and sense of self they began to develop in childhood. For other teenagers, however, the conflict of identity formation is quite real. They have a sense of giving up the values of parents and teachers in favor of new ones—their own. Physical growth, physiological changes, increased sexuality, and the perception of societal pressures to decide what they want to be when they "grow up" may lead to what Erikson calls role confusion. Role confusion occurs when the teenager's desire to be independent, to be true to his or her values, does not fit the values of the past, of childhood. As a result, the teenager experiments with various roles, trying them on to see which ones work, often to the dissatisfaction of bewildered parents.

It seems that most of the process of forging a new and independent sense of self takes place rather late in adolescence. Most of the conflicts between parents and teenagers over independence occur early in adolescence and then gradually decline (Smetna & Gaines, 1999). Further, it seems that black adolescents are more likely to develop a sense of self-esteem and identity than are white adolescents and that developing a sense of ethnic identity is one of the contributing factors to this observation (Gray-Little & Hafdahl, 2000; Phinney, Cantu, & Kurtz, 1997).

Another perspective on identity formation comes from the work of James Marcia (1980). According to Marcia, identity development begins in infancy but becomes a dominant theme in adolescence. In adolescence the teenager develops a plan for movement into adulthood. Marcia has identified four ways teenagers can resolve identity issues: identity achievement, foreclosure, identity diffusion, and moratorium. *Identity achievers* have chosen and accepted a career and ideological path for themselves. A person in *identity foreclosure* is also set on a career and ideological path. However, that path was chosen by someone else—most likely the parents. *Identity diffusers* are individuals who have not yet set a career or ideological path, even if they have gone through a decision-making process. Finally, those in *moratorium* are in a state of struggle over their futures. Individuals in moratorium are in a "crisis."

Alan Waterman (1985) looked at identity status across eight cross-cultural studies of individuals of varying ages. Waterman found that identity achievement is most frequently found for college juniors and seniors. Foreclosure and identity diffusion are most common for younger children (sixth to tenth grade). Moratorium was less common for most age groups, except for students in their first two years of college where around 30 percent were in moratorium. Finally, once an identity has been formed it may not be stable. Individuals typically fluctuate among identity statuses (for example, between moratorium and identity achievement) (Lerner, 1988).

BEFORE YOU GO ON

16. What is meant by "identity formation" in adolescence, and what factors influence its development?

A Point to Ponder or Discuss
Have you reached Marcia's stage of identity achievement? What factors have influenced your development of a sense of self and self-esteem?

DEVELOPMENT DURING EARLY ADULTHOOD

Generally, adulthood brings changes that are not as dramatic as those of our childhood and adolescence. As adults, we try to accommodate physical changes and psychological pressures without drawing attention to ourselves. Adulthood means the possibility that health may become a concern for the first time. Finally, as adults, we may have to adjust to marriage, parenthood, career, the death of friends and family, retirement, and, ultimately, our own mortality.

Following the lead of Erikson (1968) and Levinson (1978, 1986), we will consider adulthood in terms of three overlapping periods, or seasons: early adulthood (roughly ages 18 to 45), middle adulthood (ages 45 to 65), and late adulthood (over age 65). Before we proceed, a few cautions are in order. Although there is support for developmental stages in adulthood, these stages may be better defined by the individual adult than by the developmental psychologist. Some psychologists find little evidence of orderly transitions in adulthood, while others find that there are gender differences in what determines the stage of adult life.

Nothing so clearly marks the transition from adolescence to adulthood as the capacity to make choices and commitments independently. The sense of identity fashioned in adolescence is now put into action. In fact, the achievement of a sense of self by early adulthood is a good predictor of the success of intimate relationships later in adulthood (Kahn et al., 1985). With adulthood, there are new and often difficult choices to be made. Advice may be sought from elders, parents, teachers, or friends, but adults make their own choices. Should I get married? Which job should I pursue? Do I need more education? What sort? Where? Should we have children? How many? Adolescents may dream about these things, but adults must decide them.

One conceptualization of adulthood casts the developmental stage in terms of *the maturity principle*: "People become more dominant, agreeable, conscientious, and emotionally stable over the course of their lives. These changes point to increasing psychological maturity over development, from adolescence to middle age" (Costa, Roberts, & Shiner, 2005, p. 468). There are two—quite different—views of what adult maturity means (Hogan & Roberts, 2004). The humanistic view holds that maturity is measured by how much a person is achieving personal growth and higher levels of self-actualization, and is becoming more creative and open to feelings. Actually, the data do not support this view. People do not grow increasingly open to experience. If anything, they become *less* open to new ideas and experiences (Small et al., 2003). The second view of maturity equates maturity with the capacity to be a productive member of society. In this view, maturity includes becoming more deliberate and decisive, but also requires becoming more considerate and charitable (Caspi, Roberts, & Shiner, 2005). The data support this second view.

Levinson (1986, p. 5) calls early adulthood the "era of greatest energy and abundance and of greatest contradiction and stress." In terms of our physical development, we peak during our twenties and thirties, and we are apparently willing to work hard to maintain that physical condition. On the one hand, young adulthood is a season for finding our niche, for working through aspirations of our youth, and for raising a family. On the other hand, it is a period of stress, finding the "right" job, taking on parenthood, and keeping a balance among self, family, job, and society. Let us take a look at two important decision-making processes of young adulthood: the choice of mate and family, and the choice of job or career.

Marriage and Family

Erikson (1963) claims that early adulthood revolves around the choice of *intimacy versus isolation*. Failure to establish close, loving, intimate relationships may result in loneliness and long periods of social isolation. Marriage is not the only source of interpersonal intimacy, but it is the first choice of most Americans. Increasing numbers of young adults are delaying marriage, but 85 percent of us marry (at least once).

Young adults may value marriage, but the choice of whom to marry is of no small consequence. Social scientists have learned that mate selection is a complex process. At least three factors influence the choice of a marriage partner (Newman & Newman, 1984). The first is *availability.* Before we can develop an intimate relationship with someone, we need the opportunity to establish the relationship. The second factor is *eligibility.* Here, matters of age, religion, race, politics, and background come into play. Once we find a partner who is available and eligible, a third factor enters the picture: *attractiveness.* In this context, attractiveness means physical attractiveness, but judgments of physical beauty depend on who is doing the judging. In most cases, a potential partner's attractiveness also involves psychological characteristics, such as understanding, emotional supportiveness, and shared values and goals.

Do opposites attract? When psychologist David Buss reviewed the evidence on mate selection, he concluded that, in marriage, they do not. He found that "we are likely to marry someone who is similar to us in almost every variable" (Buss, 1985, p. 47). Mates are most likely to be similar in age, education, race, religion, and ethnic background, followed by attitudes and opinions, mental abilities, socioeconomic status, height, weight, and even eye color. Buss and his colleagues found that men and women are in nearly total agreement on the characteristics they seek in a mate (Buss & Barnes, 1986). Table 8.4 presents 13 such characteristics ranked by men and women. Men and women differ significantly in ranking only two: good earning potential and physical attractiveness. More recent studies also find considerable agreement between males and females for desired traits, but males do rely more heavily on physical attractiveness as a significant factor than to females (Todosijević, Ljubinković, & Araničić, 2003).

Let's pause here and remind ourselves of two points that have come up before. First, the conclusions of the studies just cited are true only in general, on the average. There may be happy couples that have few of the traits listed in Table 8.4 in common. Second, these conclusions hold only in Western, largely Anglo, North American cultures. Buss and

Courtesy of Maria Teijeiro/Getty Images.

A major marker of early adulthood is gaining independence from one's parents. At the same time, early adulthood is marked by interdependence—often in the form of marriage and the beginning of a new family.

many others are studying global preferences in selecting mates. In one report of their efforts (Buss et al., 1990), people from 33 countries on six continents were studied. There were some similarities among all of the cultures studied, but cultures tended to rank traits differently. The trait that varied most across cultures was *chastity.* Respondents from China, India, Indonesia, Iran, Taiwan, and Arab Palestine placed great importance on chastity in a potential mate. Samples from Ireland and Japan placed moderate importance on chastity. In contrast, samples from Sweden, Finland, Norway, the Netherlands, and West Germany generally judged chastity to be irrelevant or unimportant. You will note that chastity is nowhere to be found on the list of characteristics in Table 8.4.

Choosing a marriage partner is not always a matter of making sound, rational decisions, regardless of one's culture. Several factors, including romantic love and the realities of economic hardship, sometimes affect such choices. Research also indicates that what people state as their preferences for traits of a mate do not necessarily match the traits of their actual choices for marriage (Todd et al., 2007). As sound and sensible as a choice of partner may seem, approximately 50 percent of all first marriages end in divorce, and 75 percent of

TABLE 8.4

Characteristics sought in mates.

Rank (most important)	Male choices	Female choices
1	Kindness and understanding	Kindness and understanding
2	Intelligence	Intelligence
3	Physical attractiveness	Exciting personality
4	Exciting personality	Good health
5	Good health	Adaptability
6	Adaptability	Physical attractiveness
7	Creativity	Creativity
8	Desire for children	Good earning capacity
9	College graduate	College graduate
10	Good heredity	Desire for children
11	Good earning capacity	Good heredity
12	Good housekeeper	Good housekeeper

second marriages suffer the same fate (Gottman, 1994). In the United States, first marriages last an average of ten years.

Just as men and women tend to agree on what matters in choosing a mate, so do they agree on what matters in maintaining a marriage. Both sexes list such things as liking one's spouse as a friend, agreeing on goals, having similar attitudes and interests, and a shared commitment to making the marriage work (Karney & Bradbury, 1995). One of the best predictors of a successful marriage is how successfully marriage partners were able to maintain close relationships (such as with parents) *before* marriage.

The Transition to Parenthood

Beyond establishing an intimate relationship, becoming a parent is often taken as a sure sign of adulthood—that "psychological maturity" to which we referred earlier. For many couples, parenthood is more a matter of choice than ever before because of more available means of contraception and new treatments for infertility. Having a family fosters **generativity**, which Erikson claims, reflects a concern for family and for a person's impact on future generations. Although such con-

cerns may not become central until a person is over age 40, parenthood usually begins much sooner.

A baby changes established routines. Few couples have a realistic vision of what having children will do to their lives. The freedom for spontaneous trips, intimate outings, and privacy is exchanged for the joys of parenthood. As parents, men and women take on the responsibilities of new social roles—of father and mother. These new adult roles add to the already established roles of being male or female, son or daughter, husband or wife. It seems that choosing to have children (or at least choosing to have a large number of children) is becoming less popular.

What changes occur in a relationship when a child is born? Marital satisfaction tends to drop when a child is born (Lawrence, Rothman, Cobb, Rothman, & Bradbury, 2008). This is true even among couples who were satisfied with their marriages before a child is born. Additionally, Lawrence et al. found that an unplanned child results in greater marital dissatisfaction than does a planned child. Interestingly, the higher the level of marital satisfaction *before* a child is born, the steeper the decline

generativity a concern for family and for a person's impact on future generations

in marital satisfaction *after* a child is born (Lawrence et al., 2008). The good news is that marital satisfaction increases once the children leave the nest. Glenn (1990), after reviewing the literature in this area, concluded that the U-shaped curve representing marital satisfaction before, during, and after the child-rearing years is one of the more reliable findings in the social sciences.

Why does marital dissatisfaction increase after the birth of a child? The most likely explanation is that the birth of a child increases role conflict (playing more than one role at a time, such as wife and mother) and role strain (a role's demands exceed a person's abilities) (Bee, 1996).

Career Choice

By the time a person has become a young adult, he or she generally has chosen a vocation. In today's marketplace, however, most people change careers several times in their work lives. Nevertheless, choosing wisely and finding satisfaction in the work chosen go a long way toward determining self-esteem and identity. For women in early adulthood, being employed outside the home is a major determinant of self-worth. Dual-career families, in which both the woman and the man pursue lifelong careers, are common (Barnett, & Hyde, 2001). In 2006, women made up 46 percent of the workforce in the United States (U. S. Department of Labor, 2006).

Selection of a career is driven by many factors, such as family influences and the desire to earn money. Choosing a career path involves seven stages (Turner & Helms, 1987).

1. ***Exploration***: The person knows something needs to be done, but he or she has not defined the alternatives or developed plans for making a choice.

2. ***Crystallization***: The person is considering some real alternatives. Advantages and disadvantages of some potential careers are examined. The person eliminates some

Courtesy of Sven Hagolani/zefa/Corbis.

career options, but he or she has not made a choice.

3. ***Choice***: For better or worse, the person reaches a decision and feels relief and optimism that it will all work out.

4. ***Career clarification***: The person begins to invest themselves in their career decision. The person fine tunes the choice: "I know I want to be a teacher; but what do I want to teach and to whom?"

5. ***Induction***: The person acts on the career decision and faces a series of potentially frightening challenges to the person's values and goals: "Is this really what I want to do?"

6. ***Reformation***: The person discovers that changes need to be made if he or she is to fit in with fellow workers and do the job as expected: "This isn't going to be as simple as I thought. I'd better take a few more classes."

7. ***Integration***: The job and the work become part of the person and vice versa. In this final period, a person feels considerable satisfaction.

Occasionally a person makes a poor career decision. Fortunately, as soon as the person realizes it, he or she can repeat the steps in hopes of reaching the self-satisfaction that comes in the final stage.

Another indicator of adult status is one's choice of career or vocation. Yes, one may change jobs throughout one's life span, but career choice is another indicator of individual commitment.

BEFORE YOU GO ON

17. What characterizes early adulthood?
18. What are some of the factors involved in getting married, having children, and choosing a career?

A Point to Ponder or Discuss
What characteristics do you look for in a potential mate? How do you feel about becoming a parent, and how do you see parenthood affecting your life? What factors matter to you in choosing a career?

DEVELOPMENT DURING MIDDLE ADULTHOOD

As the middle years of adulthood approach, many aspects of life have become settled. By the time most people reach the age of 40, their place in the framework of society is fairly set. They have chosen their lifestyle and have grown accustomed to it. They have a family (or have decided not to). They have chosen their life work and advanced in their professions: "Most of us during our forties and fifties become 'senior members' in our own particular worlds, however grand or modest they may be" (Levinson, 1986, p. 6). In reality, the notion of a mid-life crisis is mostly a myth (Costa & McCrae, 1980; McCrae & Costa, 1990).

There are several tasks that a person must face in the middle years, beginning with adjusting to physiological changes. Middle-aged persons can surely engage in many physical activities, but they must know their limits. Heading out to the backyard for pickup basketball with the neighborhood teenagers is something a 45-year-old may have to think twice about.

While career choices have been made, in middle age one comes to expect satisfaction with work. If career satisfaction is not attained, a mid-career job change is possible. Of course, there are also situations in which changing jobs in middle age is more a matter of necessity than choice. In either case, the potential exists for crisis and conflict or for growth and development.

A major set of challenges that middle-aged persons face is dealing with family members. At this stage in life, parents are often in the throes of helping their teenagers adjust to adolescence and prepare to "leave the nest," while at the same time caring for their own parents. Adults in this situation have been referred to as "the sandwich generation" (Neugarten & Neugarten, 1989). In fact, family members provide nearly 80 percent of all day-to-day health care for the elderly. The stress and strain of dealing with the care of both one's own children or teenagers and one's parent(s) can be enormous (Chishol, 1999; Spillman & Pezzin, 2000).

By middle adulthood, most people have chosen their career paths and have developed lifestyles that allow for leisure time. At the very least, this scenario is often presented as an integral part of "the American dream."

Courtesy of Kevin Dodge/Corbis.

One task of middle adulthood is similar to Erikson's crisis of generativity versus stagnation. People shift from thinking about all they have done with their life to thinking about what they will do with what time is left, and how they can leave a mark on future generations.

Although all the "tasks" we have noted so far are interdependent, this is particularly true of these last two: relating to a spouse as a person and developing leisure-time activities. As children leave home and financial concerns diminish, there may be more time for a person's spouse and for leisure. In the eyes of adults, these tasks can amount to enjoying each other, enjoying status, enjoying retirement, vacations, and travel. In truth, taking advantage of these opportunities in meaningful ways provides a challenge for some adults whose lives have previously been devoted to children and career.

BEFORE YOU GO ON

19. Describe middle adulthood.

A Point to Ponder or Discuss
If there is no such thing as a "mid-life crisis," why do so many people use the concept to explain their behaviors and the behaviors of others?

DEVELOPMENT DURING LATE ADULTHOOD

The transition to late adulthood generally occurs in our early to mid-sixties. Persons over the age of 65 constitute a sizable and growing proportion of the population. By the year 2030, nearly 20 percent of Americans will be over 65—about 66 million persons (Armas, 2003; Torres-Gil & Bikson, 2001). According to a Census Bureau report, by the year 2050, the number of persons over age 65 will be 78.9 million—and these persons will have an average life span of 82.1 years. The data also tell us that aging is largely a women's issue. The vast majority of those over age 80 are women, and the number of older ethnic minority adults is increasing more rapidly than for the population in general.

What It Means to Be Old

Ageism is the name given to discrimination and/or prejudice against a group on the basis of age. Ageism is particularly acute in our attitudes about the elderly. One misconception about the aged is that they live in misery. We cannot ignore some of the difficulties that come with aging, but matters may not be as bad as commonly believed. The elderly do generally lose some of their sight and hearing, but these problems do not always mean a loss of quality of life. But as Skinner (1983) suggested, "If

ageism discrimination and/or prejudice against a group or an individual solely on the basis of age

There is little doubt that late adulthood can bring health problems as well as sensory and cognitive loss, but for most older persons this is also a stage of life for retirement, reflection, and relaxation.

Courtesy of Andersen Ross/Getty Images.

you cannot read, listen to book recordings. If you do not hear well, turn up the volume of your phonograph (and wear headphones to protect your neighbors)."

Some cognitive abilities decline with age, but others develop to compensate for most losses (Grady et al., 1995). About 5.4 million people (22.2%) in the United States age 71 years or older demonstrate some cognitive impairment without dementia (e.g., Alzheimer's Disease) (Plassman et al., 2008). Despite efforts to improve the cognitive skills of the elderly, there has been little change in this number in recent years (Rodgers, Ofstedal, & Herzog, 2003). More years of education predict higher cognitive test scores, and a slower decline in those test scores over time (Alley, Suthers, & Crimmins, 2007). Some apparent memory loss may reflect more of a choice of what one wants to remember than an actual loss. Mental speed is reduced, but the accumulated experience of living longer often compensates for lost speed.

Children have long since left the nest, but they are still in touch, and now there are grandchildren to spoil. Further, the children of the elderly have reached adulthood themselves and are more able and likely to provide support for aging parents. Most elderly adults live in family settings. In fact, only about 13 percent of Americans over the age of 65 live in nursing homes (AAHSA, 2003). However, the number of elderly living in nursing homes increases with age, reaching about 25 percent for individuals aged 85 and older. In 1995, a majority of individuals over the age of 65 (67 percent) lived with their families (American Association of Retired Persons, 1997). A health risk of concern is the dramatic increase in overweight and obesity among older adults. Between the period 1976–1980 and 1999–2002, the percentage of persons who were overweight rose from 57 percent to 73 percent and the percentage judged obese doubled, from 18 percent to 36 percent (Administration on Aging, 2004).

Emerging research evidence suggests that those older adults who do experience chronic illness (diabetes, arthritis, cardiovascular disease, and cancer, for example) can take significant strides in fighting off declining health by becoming actively engaged in their own care. Active control strategies (referred to as "health-engagement control strategies," or HECS), such as investing time and energy in addressing one's health concerns, seeking help when it is needed, and making commitments to overcome threats to physical health can have remarkably helpful effects, not only on physical health but also for improving the simple activities of daily living (Wrosch & Schults, 2008; Wrosch et al., 2007; Wrosch et al., 2006). Obviously, there are limits to getting elderly people with serious health problems engaged in their own care. One rule of thumb seems obvious: The sooner the better. A time will come when health issues become so severe that successfully engaging in HECS is not likely.

Some individuals dread retirement, but most welcome it as a chance to do things they have planned on for years (Kim & Moen, 2001). Many people over the age of 65 become *more* physically active after retiring, perhaps from a desk job. Three factors contribute to one's sense of well being once retired: a) the extent of available economic resources, b) social relationships with a spouse, family and friends, and c) personal resources, such as physical health, education, and self-esteem (Kim & Moen, 1999; Moen, Kim, & Hofmeister, 2001).

Until recently, almost all research on the effects of retirement focused on males. As more women enter the workforce and retire from it, so is the study of retirement changing. More women age 55–69 than ever are in the American work force (Administration on Aging, 2004). Two conclusions seem warranted: First, women appear to have more negative attitudes toward retirement, and, second, having an employed spouse extends the working life of both members of the couple (Han & Moen, 1999; Quick & Moen, 1998; Reitzes, Multran, & Fernandez, 1998).

We often assume that old age necessarily brings with it poor health. However, in 1994 only 28 percent of elderly individuals reported their health to be fair or poor. That compares to a 10 percent rate for non-elderly individuals. Finally, only 5 percent of individuals between the ages of 65 and 69 reported needing assistance for important daily activities (American Association of Retired Persons, 1997). That is not to say that older people do not have health problems; of course they do. But what seems to matter most—as is true for all of us—is the extent to which those problems can be managed successfully (Brod et al., 1999). Acute short-lived illnesses occur less frequently among older Americans (but when they do occur, they tend to be more severe). Elderly Americans have more chronic illness, such as arthritis, rheumatism, osteoporosis, arteriosclerosis, and hypertension (Cavenaugh & Blanchard-Fields, 2002). Another medical issue of greater concern to the elderly is over-medication and drug interactions. The average 85-year-old takes eight to ten prescription medications (Giron et al., 2001). Not only is this costly, but it can produce what are known as "adverse drug events" (ADEs). ADEs usually are the result of an accumulation and inter-action of several drugs rather than any one medication (Tune, 2001).

Developmental psychologists find it useful to think about persons over 65 as divided into two groups: the *young-old* and the *old-old*. This distinction is not made on the basis of actual age, but on the basis of psychological, social, and health characteristics (Neugarten & Neugarten, 1986). This distinction reinforces the notion that aging is not some sort of disease. The young-old group is the large majority of those over 65 years of age (80 to 85 percent). They are "vigorous and competent men and women who have reduced their time investments in work or home-making, are relatively comfortable financially and relatively well-educated, and are well-integrated members of their families and communities" (Neugarten & Neugarten, 1989). By comparison, the old-old are those who are struggling, whose health is deteriorating and whose financial affairs and social support systems are lacking. And there are those who *do* make the distinction between young-old and old-old solely on the basis of age, with the differentiation usually made at age 75.

The concept of successful aging was, until recently, mostly ignored. Most research on the elderly has focused on average age-related losses. John Rowe and Robert Kahn (1987) argue that "the role of aging per se in these losses has often been overstated and that a major component of many age-associated declines can be explained in terms of lifestyle, habits, diet, and an array of psychosocial factors extrinsic to the aging process" (p. 143). The argument is that the declines, deficits, and losses of the elderly are not the result of advanced age but of factors over which we all can exercise some degree of control. The major contributors to decline in old age include such things as poor nutrition, smoking, alcohol use, inadequate calcium intake, failure to maintain a sense of autonomy or control over life circumstances, and lack of social support (as long as the support does not erode self-control). Attention to these factors may not lengthen the life span, but they should extend what Rowe and Kahn call the "health span, the maintenance of full function as nearly as possible to the end of life" (1987, p. 149). Close family relationships and involvement in effective exercise programs predict successful aging (Bieman-Copland, Ryan, & Cassano, 1998; Valliant & Valliant, 1990). If it comes from the initiative of the individual, a growing dependency on others can be a positive, adaptive strategy for successful aging (Baltes, 1995).

Death and Dying

Of the two sure things in life, death and taxes, death is the surer. There are no loopholes. About 55 million people die each year, worldwide, nearly 2.4 million in the United States (Gillick, 2000). Dealing with the reality of our own death is the last major crisis we face in life. A century ago, most people died in their homes, and death was an event witnessed by everyone, even children. Now, a majority of Americans die in hospitals and nursing homes (Leming & Dickinson, 2002, p. 3). Many people never have to deal with their own death in psychological terms. These are the people who die young or suddenly. Still, most people do have time to contemplate their own death, and they usually do so in late adulthood.

Much attention was focused on the confrontation with death in the popular book, *On Death and Dying* by Elisabeth Kübler-Ross (1969, 1981). Her description of the stages one goes through when facing death come from hundreds of interviews she did with terminally ill patients. Kübler-Ross suggests the process has five stages:

1. ***Denial***—a firm, simple avoidance of the evidence; a sort of "No, this can't be happening to me" reaction;

2. ***Anger***—often accompanied by resentment and envy of others, along with a realization of what is truly happening; a sort of "Why me? Why not someone else?" reaction;

3. ***Bargaining***—a matter of dealing, or bartering, usually with God; a search for more time; a sort of "If you'll just grant me a few more weeks, or months, I'll go to church every week—no, every day" reaction;

4. ***Depression***—a sense of hopelessness that bargaining won't work, that a great loss is imminent; a period of grief and sorrow over both past mistakes and what will be missed in the future; and

5. ***Acceptance***—a rather quiet facing of the reality of death, with no great joy or sadness, simply a realization that the time has come.

Kübler-Ross' description may be idealized. Many dying patients do not fit this pattern at all (Butler & Lewis, 1981). Some may show behaviors consistent with one or two of the stages, but seldom all five. Although she never meant her stages to be taken as a prescription, there is some concern that this pattern of approaching death may be viewed as the "best" or the "right" way to go about it. The concern is that caretakers may try to force dying people into and through these stages, instead of letting each face the inevitability of death in his or her own way (Bowling, 2000; Kalish, 1976, 1985).

Although elderly people have to deal with dying and death, they are less morbid about it than are adolescents (Lanetto, 1980). Older people may fear the process of dying, but they have much less concern about the event of death (Leming & Dickinson, 2002). Most older Americans are

One inevitable outcome of living is dying. In fact, older persons are less morbid about death than are adolescents, and express less fear of dying than do younger adults.

Courtesy of altrendo images/Getty Images.

comfortable talking about death and dying, but most restrict such conversations to family member. Only 17 percent report that they have talked with their physicians about their end of life wishes. Most are concerned that they not become burdens to their families (AARP, 2005). One study found that adults over age 60 do think about and talk about death more frequently than do the younger adults surveyed. However, of all of the adults in the study, the oldest group expressed the least fear of death, some even saying that they were eager for it (Fortner & Neimeyer, 1999).

BEFORE YOU GO ON

20. Summarize the major aspects of late adulthood.

A Point to Ponder or Discuss
Have you ever—seriously—contemplated your own death? Do you think your attitudes and feelings about death will change as you get older?

CHAPTER SUMMARY

1. **Briefly describe the three stages of the prenatal period.**

   The prenatal period of development begins at *conception* when the egg is fertilized by a sperm and ends with birth. The first new cell created at fertilization is the *zygote*. The zygote begins to divide as it moves down the fallopian tube toward the uterus. A hollow ball of cells forms, called the *blastocyst*. The *germinal period* lasts for about two weeks and ends when the blastocyst implants itself in the uterine wall. During the *embryonic stage*, which lasts about six weeks, all of the organ systems of the body are put into place. The embryo is most susceptible to prenatal problems that could lead to defects. By the end of this stage, the embryo is one inch long, has a functioning nervous system, and is capable of simple reflexive movements. The *fetal stage* is the longest, spanning the last six months of pregnancy. The organs laid down during the embryonic stage increase in complexity and size and begin to function. The arms and legs develop, and the brain develops rapidly. The age of viability, or the age at which the fetus could survive if born prematurely, is reached in the seventh month.

2. **Summarize those factors that can negatively affect prenatal development.**

   A mother's diet can affect prenatal development. Malnutrition in the mother or deficiencies of specific vitamins or minerals are usually shared by the embryo or the fetus. Cigarette smoking can cause retarded prenatal growth and increased risk of hearing defects, miscarriages, stillbirths, and neonatal death. Alcohol is a drug that reaches the fetus easily. It stays in the fetus longer than it stays in the mother and collects in organs with a high water content (like the gray matter of the brain). Exposure to high levels of alcohol throughout pregnancy or binge drinking during a vulnerable period of organ development can lead to fetal alcohol syndrome. *Fetal alcohol syndrome* includes retarded physical growth, poor coordination, poor muscle tone, intellectual retardation, and other problems. Even light alcohol consumption can lead to deficits in motor skills. Mothers who use or abuse psychoactive drugs put their infants at risk for low birth weights, difficulty regulating the sleep-waking cycle, and drug addiction, as well as a host of other problems.

3. **Summarize the sensory-perceptual abilities of the neonate.**

   Most of the neonate's senses function reasonably well from birth. The eyes can focus at arm's length, although they will require a few months to focus on objects over a range of distances. Depth perception may be present at—or soon after—birth, but responding to it reasonably takes time, up to about 6 months. The newborn sees the world in color, but color vision will not fully develop until the age of 3 months. Hearing and auditory discrimination are quite good, as are the senses of taste, smell, and touch.

4. **What is the general nature of Piaget's approach to cognitive development in children?**

   Cognitive development refers to the age-related changes in learning, memory, perception, attention, thinking, and problem solving. Piaget's is a stage theory that says there are qualitative, age-related changes in the structures and functions that underlie intelligence. Piaget proposed that there are cognitive structures called *schemas* that help a child deal with information. During development these structures undergo significant change. The functions involved in cognitive development do not change with age. A major function is *adaptation*. Adaptation consists of two sub-processes: assimilation (incorporating new information into existing schemas) and accommodation (adjusting existing schemas, or adding new schemas, to account for new information).

5. **Briefly describe each of the four stages of Piaget's theory.**

   During the *sensorimotor stage* (birth–2) a baby develops schemas (assimilating new information and accommodating old concepts) through an interaction with the environment by sensing and doing. The baby begins to appreciate cause-and-effect relationships, imitates the actions of others, and by the end of the period, develops a sense of object permanence. Egocentrism is found in the *preoperational stage* (2–7). The child appears unable to appreciate the world from anyone else's perspective. In addition, children begin to develop and use symbols in the form of words to represent concepts. In the *concrete operations* stage (7–11), a child organizes concepts into categories, begins to use simple logic and understand relational terms.

The beginning of this stage is marked by conservation—coming to understand that changing something's form does not change its nature or quantity. The essence of the *formal operations* stage (12–older) is the ability to think, reason, and solve problems symbolically or in an abstract rather than a concrete, tangible form.

6. **What are some of the criticisms of Piaget's theory? Do these criticisms mean that his theory is "wrong?"**

Piaget's theory of cognitive development has been very influential and has received support from cross-cultural studies, but it has not escaped criticism. The theory has been criticized on two grounds: First, there is little evidence that cognitive abilities develop in a series of well-defined stages (that is, the borders between stages are poorly defined), and second, Piaget may have underestimated the cognitive abilities of preschool children. These criticisms do not mean that Piaget's theory is wrong; it just means that some few aspects of it might have been misguided.

7. **Briefly describe what psychologists know about the abilities of young children to learn and remember.**

Newborns just a few hours old give evidence of learning through both classical and operant conditioning. They also show the ability to imitate simple facial expressions. Imitation of complex behaviors is not reliably shown until the child is between eight and 12 months old. Imitation becomes an important channel of learning as the child gets older, contributing to the development of prosocial and antisocial behaviors. Neonates (in one study, only one to four days old) can demonstrate memory. They will attend to a new visual pattern after ignoring a familiar one, showing an appreciation of the difference between familiar and new. By the time infants are 2 to 3 months of age, they can remember an interesting event for up to three weeks. Children as young as 3 years can form coherent representations of events, but the most impressive changes in memory occur between the ages of 3 and 12 years. As children get older they are better able to use the memory strategies of rehearsal, organization, using retrieval cues, and elaboration (which is discovered later than the other strategies).

8. **Summarize Kohlberg's approach to moral reasoning and discuss its strengths and weaknesses.**

Kohlberg claims that moral reasoning develops through three levels of two stages each. First, a person decides between right and wrong on the basis of avoiding punishment and gaining rewards (*preconventional morality*), then on the basis of conforming to authority or accepting social convention (*conventional morality*), and finally on the basis of one's understanding of the common good, individual rights, and internalized standards (*postconventional morality*). Although much of the theory has been supported, there is evidence that many individuals never reach the higher levels of moral reasoning.

9. **Summarize what is known about gender differences in moral reasoning.**

There may be deficiencies in applying Kohlberg's theory equally to both genders or to all cultures, wherein what is "moral" or "right" may vary. It also seems to be the case that how a child or adult reasons about moral issues need not be reflected in actual behaviors. As Carol Gilligan first pointed out, there also may be differences in *how* males and females think through moral dilemmas, although these differences are likely to be small. No one has argued that males have "better" or "worse" moral reasoning skills than do females; it just may be that they are slightly different.

10. **Describe the first four stages of Erikson's theory of development.**

Of Erikson's eight stages of development, four occur during childhood. These stages are described in terms of crises or conflicts that need resolution and include the following: a) trust versus mistrust (whether the child develops a sense of security or anxiety), b) autonomy versus self-doubt (whether the child develops a sense of competence or doubt), c) initiative versus guilt (whether the child gains confidence in his or her own ability or becomes guilty and resentful), and d) competence versus inferiority (whether the child develops confidence in intellectual and social skills or develops a sense of failure and lack of confidence.) Because each of the stages in Erikson's theory involves the individual (here, the child) interacting with others, it is called a theory of psychosocial development.

11. **What is gender identity and when does it develop?**

Gender identity is the sense or self-awareness of one's maleness or femaleness and the roles that males and females traditionally play in one's culture. Most children have a sense of their own gender by the age of 2 to 3 years, with gender identity most strongly reinforced by peer groups and play activities. A child's cognitive sense of gender stereotypes may flavor how new information is accommodated.

12. **What factors appear to contribute to gender-related differences in behavior?**

Typical of many such questions, this one has no specific answer. There seems to be a biological/hormonal/genetic basis to some gender differences, but many also clearly seem to be the product of learning and socialization processes. Once again we see a complex interaction among biological, cognitive, and social influences.

13. **What is the significance of social attachments formed in infancy and early childhood?**

Attachment is a strong emotional relationship formed early in childhood between the child and primary caregiver(s). It has survival value in an evolutionary sense, keeping the child in proximity to those who can best care for him or her. Secure attachment in childhood has been associated with improved cognitive performance and self-esteem later in life. A secure attachment is most likely to occur if the parents (or other caregivers) are optimally sensitive and responsive to the infant and develop a reciprocal pattern of behavior with the infant. Fathers, as well as mothers, demonstrate appropriate attachment-related behaviors. To date, most evidence is that daycare for children (particularly for those older than two) does not have negative consequences (depending mostly on the quality of care). The extent to which a child will become securely attached has more to do with the quality of caregiver/child interactions than who does the interacting.

14. **What two conflicting views of adolescence have been put forward in psychology?**

Physically, adolescence begins with puberty (attainment of sexual maturity) and lasts until the end of physical growth. Historically, the period has been seen as one of stress, distress, and abnormality. More contemporary views see adolescence as a period of challenges, but a period that most teenagers survive with no lasting negative consequences.

15. **What is puberty, and what are the consequences of reaching puberty earlier or later than age-mates?**

Two significant physical developments mark adolescence: a *spurt of growth*, seen at an earlier age in girls than in boys, and the beginning of sexual maturity, a period called *puberty*. As adolescents, individuals are for the first time physically prepared for sexual reproduction and begin to develop secondary sex characteristics. The consequences of reaching puberty early are more positive for males than females. Being a late bloomer has a more negative effect on teens of both sexes, although the long-term consequences for both are few and slight.

16. **What is meant by "identity formation" in adolescence, and what factors influence its development?**

The challenge of identity formation is to establish a personal identity that is separate from the parents. Thus, one major task of adolescence, to use Erikson's terms, is the resolution of an identity crisis, which is the struggle to define and integrate the sense of who one is, what one is to do in life, and what one's attitudes, beliefs, and values should be. Another point of view is that of James Marcia. Marcia's four dimensions of identity formation are identity achievement, foreclosure, identity diffusion, and moratorium. Resolution through identity achievement means that a person has gone through a period of decision making and has settled on a self-chosen career and ideological path. An individual in foreclosure has had an ideological and career path chosen by someone else, most likely the parents. Individuals who have not yet chosen an ideological or career path, but may have gone through a decision-making phase, are said to be identity diffusers. Those in moratorium are in "crisis" and are in a state of struggle over the future. Identity achievement is most common among college juniors and seniors. Foreclosure and identity diffusion are most often seen in younger children in sixth to tenth grades.

17. **What characterizes early adulthood?**

Early adulthood (ages 18 to 45) is characterized by both psychological maturity and choices and commitments made independently. The young adult assumes new responsibilities and is faced with decisions about career, marriage, and family. For Erikson, the period is marked by the conflict between intimacy and social relationships on the one hand, and social isolation on the other.

18. **What are some of the factors involved in getting married, having children, and choosing a career?**

Mate selection and marriage are two issues that young adults face. Individuals tend to "match" on a variety of characteristics (e.g., age, education, or race). Many marriages fail, but most young adults list a good marriage as a major source of happiness in their lives. Many factors determine the selection of a mate. There is little support for the notion that opposites attract. Characteristics of desired mates vary among cultures. Before the birth of the first child, marital satisfaction is high. During the child-rearing years, marital satisfaction declines, but it recovers again after the children leave the home. The birth of a child adds stress to a marriage through role conflict and role strain. Choosing a career or occupation is a decision of early adulthood. Choosing the right career contributes in positive ways to self-esteem and identity. It is a process that goes through several stages: exploration, crystallization, choice, career clarification, induction, reformation, and integration. Occasionally, a person makes a poor career choice and may have to begin the process all over again.

19. **Describe middle adulthood.**

Middle adulthood (ages 45 to 65) may be troublesome for some, but most find middle age a period of great satisfaction and opportunity. Toward the end of the period, the individual begins to accept his or her own mortality in several ways. Tasks of middle age involve adapting to one's changing physiology, occupation, aging parents and growing children, social and civic responsibilities, and the use of leisure time.

20. **Summarize the major aspects of late adulthood.**

The number of elderly is growing rapidly—reaching nearly 66 million by the year 2030. Although there may be sensory, physical, and cognitive limits forced by old age, fewer than 30 percent of elderly people rate health problems as a major concern. Although some elderly are isolated and lonely, fewer than 13 percent live in nursing homes. Older people may be concerned about death, but they are neither consumed by it nor morbid about it. With good nutrition, the development of a healthy lifestyle, proper social support, and the maintenance of some degree of autonomy and control over one's life, "successful aging" can become even more common than it is today. This is another way of saying that we can increase the already large percentage (80 to 85 percent) of those over the age of 65 who have been characterized as young-old, as opposed to old-old.

Worldwide, over 55 million people die each year. Elisabeth Kübler-Ross described five stages of the dying process. The first stage is denial—involving avoidance of evidence of impending death. The second stage is anger, which is often accompanied by resentment and envy of others who are not dying. Bargaining is the third stage, in which the dying person tries to make a deal with God for more time. The fourth stage is depression, or a sense of hopelessness that bargaining won't work, sorrow over past mistakes, and what will be missed in the future. The final stage is acceptance, in which the dying person finally accepts the reality of death with no great joy or sadness. As Kübler-Ross acknowledged, not all dying patients progress through the five stages of death she outlined. There is also the danger that caretakers might force people to go through the stages. Elderly people have to deal with death (their own and that of others) more than individuals of other ages. They tend to be less morbid about it than adolescents, but they think about it more than younger adults. However, elderly people express less fear of death than younger individuals, which is not to say that they are not anxious about dying. In fact, some even express eagerness for death.

Personality

9

PREVIEW

Personality is a word that we use regularly without giving much thought to exactly what it means. Personality seems to exist in greater or lesser degrees, as in, "She is so bubbly! She's just Miss Personality." Apparently, personality also can have degrees of goodness. It can be evaluated as being great or awful or somewhere in between, as in, "True, he doesn't look like much, but he sure has a great personality." We like to think that we are reasonably accurate in our assessments of the personalities of others—and, the truth is, we probably are.

A major task of this chapter is to describe some of the approaches to and theories of personality. We will define both "theory" and "personality." Then, we will discuss five approaches to the study of personality.

Because it is the oldest and arguably the most elegant of the theories of personality, Sigmund Freud's psychoanalytic theory of personality is our point of beginning. One reflection of the value of Freud's theory is that it has attracted the attention and the interest of so many other psychologists. After covering the psychoanalytic approach, we consider the personality theories of behavioral psychologists and learning theorists. The contrast with Freud's approach is immediately clear. As opposed to accepting the focus of either psychoanalytic or behavioral approaches to personality, some psychologists have claimed that our first focus should be cognitive. We will take a brief look at a couple of personality theories proposed by cognitive psychologists.

Of the six approaches discussed in this chapter, the humanistic theories of Rogers and Maslow often appeal most to students—partly because they allow for the possibility that people can take charge of their own lives, that they are not ruled by inner drives or rewards from the environment. We shall also discuss the trait theories of personality. Whereas most theories of personality try to explain why people think, act, and feel as they do, trait theories have no such interest. Their goal is to describe human personality, and theirs will be the last approach to personality we consider. Finally, we discuss the biological approach to personality. This approach, as you shall see, differs markedly from the "grand" theories of personality we cover in this chapter.

Most psychologists who claim personality as one of their areas of interest are not trying to devise a new grand theory to describe or explain human nature. Most are instead involved in research that focuses on one or a few aspects of the complex concept we call personality.

For example, we'll explore the extent to which personality explains a person's behavior. Psychologists first raised this question nearly forty years ago: Is a person's behavior determined by the situation (external factors) or the person's traits and personality (internal factors). Debate once raged, but that question has been largely resolved, and we will explore the answers research has uncovered.

We'll investigate gender differences in personality, where the major research question is clear: Are there any reliable differences—in general, of course—between the personalities of men and those of women? Finally, we will address some of the ways psychologists measure or assess personality.

INTRODUCING PERSONALITY THEORIES

A theory is a series of assumptions or beliefs; in our particular case, these assumptions are about people and their personalities. Theories are designed both to describe and to explain. The beliefs that constitute a theory are based on observations and are logically related to one another. A theory should lead—through reason—to specific, testable hypotheses. In short, a **theory** is an organized collection of testable ideas used to describe and explain a particular subject matter.

theory an organized collection of testable ideas used to describe and explain a particular subject matter

What then is personality? Few terms have been as difficult to define. Actually, each personality theory we will study has its own definition. But just to get us started, we will say that **personality** includes those affects, behaviors, and cognitions of people that characterize them in a number of situations over time. (Here again is our ABC mnemonic.) In addition, personality includes those dimensions we can use to discern non-physical differences among people. With personality theories, we are looking for ways to do two things: to describe how people remain the same over time and in different circumstances and to describe differences that we know exist among people (Baumeister, 1987; Mischel, 2004). Note that personality originates from within and is something a person brings to his or her interactions with the environment (Burger, 2000), but personality also reflects the influences of one's culture or social context (McAdams & Pals, 2006).

Personality psychologists have three interrelated goals or missions (Funder, 2001a). The theoretical mission of psychologists who specialize in understanding personality is "to account for individuals' characteristic patterns of thought, emotion, and behavior together with the psychological mechanisms—hidden or not—behind those patterns" (Funder, 2001b, p. 198). The empirical mission of personality psychologists is to gather and analyze observations on how personalities, environmental situations, and behaviors are inter-related. What Funder (2001a) calls "perhaps the most important mission" of personality psychology is "institutional"—to bring together the contributions of many of psychology's sub-fields so as to better understand the whole person.

> **personality** those affects, behaviors, and cognitions of individuals that characterize them in a number of situations over time

---

BEFORE YOU GO ON

1. What is meant by "theories of personality"?

A Point to Ponder or Discuss
In what ways do psychologists view personality differently from the way the term is used in everyday speech?

THE PSYCHOANALYTIC APPROACH

We begin our discussion of personality with Freud's psychoanalytic theory because he was the first to present a unified theory of personality.

Freud's theory of personality has been one of the more influential and controversial in all of science. There are many facets to his theory, but two basic premises characterize Freud's approach: he relied on innate drives to explain much of human behavior, and he believed in the power of unconscious forces to mold and shape behavior.

Freud's ideas about personality arose from his reading of the great philosophers, observations of his patients, and intense examination of himself. His private practice—focusing on mental disorders—provided Freud with the opportunity to develop techniques to treat his patients and a general theory of personality to explain his observations. We will review Freud's ideas about psychotherapy in Chapter 13. Here we consider his theory of the structure and dynamics of human personality.

conscious the level of consciousness containing ideas, memories, feelings, or motives of which we are actively aware

preconscious the level of consciousness containing aspects of our experience of which we are not aware at the moment, but that can easily be brought into awareness

life instincts (eros) impulses for survival, including those that motivate sex, hunger, and thirst

libido the driving force of the id; the sexual/sensual energy by which the id operates

death instincts (thanatos) opposed to life instincts, inborn impulses that are largely directed at destruction and aggression

unconscious the level of consciousness containing cognitions, feelings, or motives that are not available at the conscious or preconscious level

Basic Instincts and Levels of Consciousness

According to Freudian theory, our behaviors, thoughts, and feelings are largely governed by innate biological drives, which he refers to as instincts. These instincts are inborn impulses or forces that rule our personalities. In Freudian theory, all of our many drives or instincts can be grouped into two categories.

In the first category are the **life instincts (eros)**, or impulses for survival, including those that motivate sex, hunger, and thirst. Each instinct has its own energy that compels us into action (drives us). Freud called the psychic energy through which the sexual instincts operate **libido**. The second category includes all the instincts opposed to life instincts. These instincts are **death instincts (thanatos)** and are largely impulses of destruction. Directed inward, they give rise to feelings of depression or suicide; directed outward, they result in aggression. The death instincts also propel us toward behaviors that endanger our own lives or well-being, such as smoking or dangerous sports. Life itself, according to Freud, is an attempt to resolve conflicts between these two natural but opposed sets of instincts.

Freudian personality theory holds that information, feelings, wants, drives, desires, and the like are found at various levels of awareness or consciousness. Mental events of which we are actively aware at the moment are **conscious**. Aspects of our mental life of which we are not conscious at any moment but that can be easily brought to awareness are stored at a **preconscious** level. For example, if you think about your plans for the evening and find your mind already has a conception, Freud would say you had plans in your preconscious mind even though you were not aware of them until you focused on them and thereby moved them to the conscious mind. (If this all sounds a bit familiar, good. It should. We first introduced Freud's ideas on consciousness in Chapter 4.)

Cognitions, feelings, and motives that are not conscious or preconscious are said to be in the **unconscious**. In the unconscious we keep ideas, memories, and desires of which we are not aware and cannot easily become aware. Remember the significance of the unconscious level of the mind in Freudian theory: Even though we are unaware of the thoughts and feelings stored there, we are still deeply influenced by them. Freud believed the contents of a person's unconscious, passing through the preconscious, might show in slips of the tongue, humor, anxiety-based symptoms, or dreams. He also believed that most of our mental life takes place on the unconscious level and that unconscious forces could explain behaviors that otherwise seemed irrational and beyond understanding.

The Structure of Personality

Freud believed that the mind operates on three interacting levels of awareness: conscious, preconscious, and unconscious. He also proposed that personality consists of three separate, though interacting, structures or subsystems: the id, ego, and superego. Each of these structures has its own job to do and its own principles to follow.

Sigmund Freud was the first to present a unified theory of personality. He relied on innate drives to explain much of human behavior, and he believed in the power of unconscious processes to mold and shape personality.

Courtesy of Bettmann/Corbis.

The **id** is the totally inborn portion of personality. It resides in the unconscious level of the mind, and it is through the id that basic instincts are expressed. The driving force of the id is libido, or sexual energy; although it may be more fair to say "sensual" rather than "sexual" so as not to imply that Freud was always talking about adult sexual intercourse. The id operates on the **pleasure principle**, indicating that the major function of the id is to find satisfaction for basic pleasurable impulses. Although the other divisions of personality develop later, our id remains with us always and is the basic energy source in our lives. The id manifests itself in our everyday lives when we act impulsively. For example, if you go ahead and buy that new iPhone even though you will have trouble paying your rent that month you are acting on irrational impulses from the id. But, at least temporarily, it feels good to buy the iPhone, satisfying the id's quest for pleasure.

The **ego** is the part of the personality that develops through one's experience with reality. In many ways, it is our "self"—at least the self of which we are consciously aware at any time. It is the rational, reasoning part of our personality. The ego operates on the **reality principle**. One of the ego's main jobs is to find satisfaction for the id, but in ways that are reasonable and rational. The ego may delay gratification of some libidinal impulse or find a socially acceptable outlet for some need. Freud said that "the ego stands for reason and good sense while the id stands for untamed passions" (Freud, 1933). So, if you decide not to buy that iPhone (even though you really want it) so you can pay your rent, you are responding to the realistic demands of the ego.

The last of the three structures of personality to develop is the **superego**, which we can liken to one's sense of morality or conscience. It reflects our internalization of society's rules. The superego operates on the **idealistic principle**. One problem with the superego is that it, like the id, has no contact with

Courtesy of Inti St. Clair/Getty Images.

reality and, therefore, often places unrealistic demands on the individual. For example, a person's superego may have that person believe that he or she should always be kind and generous and never harbor unpleasant or negative thoughts about someone else. The superego demands that a person do what it deems right and proper, no matter what the circumstances. Failure to do so may lead the person to feel guilt and shame. Using our iPhone example, if you bought the phone, even though you did not really have the money, the superego would make you feel guilty and ashamed of yourself.

It falls to the ego to try to maintain a realistic balance between the conscience of the superego and the libido of the id.

Although the dynamic processes underlying personality in Freud's theory may appear complicated, the concepts are not as complicated as they sound. A simple illustration may help explain how these three structures of personality interact in a person facing a moral dilemma. Suppose a bank teller discovers an extra $50 in his cash drawer at the end of the day. He certainly could use an extra $50. "Go ahead. Nobody will miss it. The bank can afford a few dollars here and there. Think of the fun you can have with an extra $50," is the basic

Carla goes to her local ATM to pick up $60 in cash—something she has done many times before. But this time, the ATM gives her $80! What will she do with the extra $20? Her id may tell her to keep it. "After all, it wasn't your mistake!" Her superego may argue otherwise. "Now Carla, you know that's not your money and that you should go inside and return it." Her ego may have to resolve this conflict in as rational a way as possible.

id the totally inborn portion of personality, residing in the unconscious; it is through the id that basic instincts are expressed

pleasure principle the basis of operation of the id—to find satisfaction for basic pleasurable impulses

ego the part of the personality that develops through one's experiences with reality; the rational, reasoning part of our personalities

reality principle the basis of operation of the ego—to find satisfaction for the id, but in ways that are reasonable and rational

superego one's sense of morality or conscience, reflecting one's internalization of society's rules

idealistic principle the basis of operation of the superego—to promote what is good or right, regardless of pressure from the id

repression the most basic defense mechanism—referred to as motivated forgetting

defense mechanisms unconsciously applied techniques that protect the conscious self (ego) against strong feelings of anxiety

sublimation a defense mechanism involving the repression of unacceptable sexual or aggressive impulses and allowing them to surface in socially acceptable behaviors that are not openly sexual or aggressive

denial a defense mechanism in which a person refuses to acknowledge the realities of an anxiety-producing situation

rationalization making up excuses for one's behaviors, rather than facing their (anxiety-producing) causes or consequences

Fantasy is a defense mechanism often used by college students. Particularly when experiencing a good deal of stress and anxiety, there is something quite helpful in letting your mind wander to think about peace and quiet and far away places.

message from the id. "The odds are that I'll get caught if I take this money. Although I sure could use that money, I know that stealing is wrong," reasons the ego. "You shouldn't even think about taking that money. Shame on you! It's not yours. It belongs to someone else and should be reported," the superego protests. The interaction of the three components of personality isn't always this simple and straightforward, but this example illustrates the general idea.

The Defense Mechanisms

If the ego cannot find acceptable ways to satisfy the drives of the id, or if it cannot deal with the demands of the superego, conflict and anxiety result. Then ways must be found to combat the resulting anxiety. Freud observed that we use **defense mechanisms**, *unconsciously* applied techniques that protect the conscious self (the ego) against strong feelings of anxiety. We will look next at some of the more common ego defense mechanisms Freud identified.

Courtesy of Stephanie Rausser/Getty Images.

Repression is the most basic defense mechanism. It is sometimes referred to as motivated forgetting, which gives you a good idea of what is involved. Repression is a matter of forgetting about some anxiety-producing event or desire. For example, Paul had a teacher with whom he did not get along. After spending an entire semester trying to do his best, Paul failed the course. The following summer, while Paul was walking with his girlfriend, the teacher approached, and Paul could not remember the instructor's name. He had repressed it. Forgetting about everything and everyone who ever caused you anxiety is not an adaptive response. Still, repressing anxiety-producing memories into the unconscious can protect us from dwelling on unpleasantness.

Sublimation is a defense mechanism involving the repression of unacceptable sexual or aggressive impulses and allowing them to surface in socially acceptable behaviors that are not sexual or aggressive. For example, if a young man has sexual urges for his sister, he can repress these urges and channel them into an acceptable behavior. He may channel the sexual energy into art and become an accomplished artist. An individual without artistic talent might channel sexual energy into a hobby or excelling at a job.

Denial is an anxiety defense mechanism in which a person refuses to acknowledge the realities of an anxiety-producing situation. When a patient first hears that he or she has a terminal illness from a physician, the patient may refuse to believe the doctor. Rather than face a frightening possibility, the patient just goes into denial; the patient refuses to believe or accept that the diagnosis is accurate.

Rationalization amounts to making up excuses for one's behaviors rather than facing the (anxiety-producing) real causes and unpleasant consequences of one's behaviors. For example, Kevin failed his psychology midterm because he didn't study for it and didn't attend several of the lectures. However, Kevin hates to admit, even to himself, that his failure is due to his own decisions and his own stupidity. Instead, he rationalizes, "It really wasn't my fault. I had a terrible instructor. The test was grossly unfair. We used a lousy book. And I've been fighting the flu all semester."

Fantasy provides an escape from anxiety through imagination or daydreaming. It is a defense mechanism commonly used by college students. After a week of exams and term paper deadlines, isn't it pleasant to sit back in a comfortable chair and fantasize about graduating from college with honors? An occasional fantasy is a normal and acceptable reaction to stress and anxiety. Yet, there are potential dangers. One needs to be able to keep the real separate from the fantasy. In addition, having a fantasy by itself will not solve the problem or relieve the anxiety. Daydreaming about academic success may improve one's mood, but it is not likely to improve one's grades.

Projection is a matter of seeing one's own unacceptable, anxiety-producing thoughts, motives, or traits in others. For example, under enormous pressure to do well on an exam, Kirsten decides to cheat. But at exam time, her conscience (superego) won't let her. Because of projection, Kirsten may think that she sees cheating going on all around her. Projection is a mechanism often used by people who feel aggression or hostility toward others. When people feel hostile, they often project their aggressiveness onto others, coming to believe that others are "out to get them."

Regression involves a return to earlier, more primitive, even childish levels of behavior that were once effective in securing the desired outcome. We see regression most often in children. Imag-

ine a 4-year-old who, until recently, was an only child; his mother has just returned from the hospital with his new baby sister. The 4-year-old is no longer the center of attention. To try to gain back some of the attention he has lost, he reverts to earlier behaviors and starts wetting the bed, screaming for a bottle, and crawling on all fours.

The defense mechanism of **displacement** is most often used by those seeking to cope with aggression. The defense involves redirecting aggression at a substitute person or object rather than expressing it directly, which would cause anxiety. For example, Dorothy expects to get promoted at work, but she is passed over. She's angry at her boss but feels, perhaps correctly, that blowing her top at her boss will be harmful, so she displaces her hostility toward her husband, her children, or the family cat.

This list of defense mechanisms is not an exhaustive one, but it has the more common ones and should give you an idea of what Freud had in mind. There are two additional points that deserve special mention. First, using defense mechanisms is natural. You should not be alarmed if some of these mechanisms sound like reactions you have used. In moderation, defense mechanisms help us to cope with everyday life. Second, although they are normal, these mechanisms can become a detriment to mental health. If we successfully use a defense mechanism to ease the pain of anxiety, we may no longer feel a need to search for the true causes of our anxiety. Thus, we will not resolve the conflicts that produced the anxiety in the first place. After all, if these mechanisms do nothing else, they distort reality, at least to some degree. We'll have more to say about this point when we discuss effective and ineffective strategies for dealing with stress and anxiety.

fantasy the defense mechanism that provides escape from anxiety through imagination or daydreaming

displacement the defense mechanism that involves redirecting aggression at a substitute person or object rather than expressing it directly

projection seeing one's own unacceptable, anxiety-producing thoughts, motives, or traits in others

regression a return to earlier, more primitive, childish levels of behavior that were once effective in securing desired outcomes

The Psychosexual Development of Personality

Psychoanalytic theories of personality development have been around for many years. In general, psychoanalytic theories propose the following four things: a) Behavior is guided by both conscious and unconscious forces. b) The basic structure of personality develops over time. c) Personality develops through a series of stages. d) An individual's personality develops according to how well an individual moves through the stages of development.

In Freud's oral stage of psychosexual development (ages birth to 1 year) pleasure and satisfaction come from oral activities: eating, sucking, biting, making noises and the like.

Courtesy of Norbert Schaefer/Corbis.

Freud put a lot of stock in the biological bases of personality, relying on concepts such as drive and instinct. His biological orientation also flavored his view of personality development. According to Freud, personality develops naturally, in a biologically based series of overlapping stages. One of Freud's most controversial assumptions about human behavior was that even infants and young children were under the influence of the sexual strivings of the id and its libidinal energy. The outlet for the sexual impulses (again, "sensual" may be closer to Freud's meaning) of young children is not the reproductive sex act. But Freud thought that much of the pleasure derived by children is essentially sexual; hence, we refer to Freud's developmental stages as *psychosexual.* Freud claimed that there are four such stages and one "period" during which no significant developmental challenges arise.

1. ***Oral Stage*** (birth to 1 year). Pleasure and satisfaction come from oral activities: feeding, sucking, and making noises.
2. ***Anal Stage*** (age 1 to 3 years). Sometime in their second year, children develop the ability to control their bladder and bowel habits. At this time, the anus becomes the focus of pleasure. Satisfaction is gained through bowel control. Children in this stage can display aggression (the id again) particularly against parents by having bowel movements at inappropriate

times or by refusing "to go" when placed on the potty chair. Here we see the thoughtful, reasoning ego emerging and exercising some control. After all, the parents can't *make* the child do what they want him or her to do. The child is in control and that control can give the child feelings of great satisfaction.

3. ***Phallic Stage*** (age 3 to 5 years). In this stage children become aware of their sexuality. The genitals become more important than the mouth and the anus as the source of pleasure. Masturbation or fondling of the genitals may become a common practice.

Freud admitted that he did not understand women or the psychology of women very well (Fadiman & Fragen 1994, p. 8). Often, he offended the feminists of his day. (Yes, there were feminists at that time, and Freud was well aware of their criticisms.) One of the things that got him in trouble was suggesting that, in the phallic stage, girls come to realize that they do not have a penis and feel inferior, "lacking," and jealous as a result (Freud, 1933, p. 126). Freud said that such *penis envy* led mature women to desire children—a male child in particular, who will bring the "longed-for penis" with him. This theory hardly endeared Freud to feminists in his day, nor is it particularly popular with feminists of today.

During this stage of development, children tend to form close (sexually based) attachments to the parent of the opposite sex, and feelings of jealousy or fear of the same-sex parent may arise. Freud named this pattern of reaction the *Oedipus complex* in boys and the *Electra complex* in girls. It is in the phallic stage that the superego begins to develop. The Oedipus/Electra complex is the central crisis of the phallic stage. The resolution of the Oedipus/Electra complex results in the formation of gender-role identity, sexual orientation, and emotions relating to intimacy.

4. ***Latency Period*** (age 6 years until puberty). During this period, sexual development stops. However, the ego develops rapidly during this stage. Children are focused on learning about the world and how it operates. Sexual development can wait. Sexuality is repressed. At this stage, children tend to choose friends of the same sex. You have no doubt heard the protestations of a 9-year-old boy, "Oh, yuck; kiss a girl? No way! Yuck!" And you counsel, "Just wait; soon girls won't seem so yucky."

5. ***Genital Stage*** (after puberty). With puberty comes a renewal of sexual impulses, a reawakening of desire, and an interest in matters sexual, erotic, and sensual. During this stage the person must deal with new relationships with members of the opposite sex. Relating to the opposite sex is the greatest challenge of this stage. Unresolved conflicts from earlier stages come to the forefront during this stage. Unless a person has learned to identify his or her unconscious impulses and conflicts on a conscious and rational level, the person will experience some degree of difficulty dealing with these challenges (Hill, 1998).

Events in these psychosexual stages of development can produce profound effects on later development. At each stage of development—except for the latency period—there is a "crisis" that must be resolved. If it is not resolved, then there will be an over-investment of psychic energy at that stage, and a person is said to have a *fixation* in that stage. Please be clear on this point: A fixation does not mean that a person is stuck in a particular stage, failing to move on to the next stage. Instead, a fixation means that the failure to resolve a crisis will leave an indelible mark on the personality that becomes visible in that person's adult personality. For example, the crisis in the oral stage of development is weaning. If weaning is accompanied by stress and anxiety, the crisis may not be fully resolved. In adults this unresolved crisis may show up as an excessive need for oral stimulation and gratification. That is, the mouth will continue to be a source of pleasure, as demonstrated in overeating, fingernail biting, talkativeness, or smoking. A person who smokes several packs of cigarettes per day could be said to have an oral fixation. But then again, maybe not. Freud (an avid cigar smoker himself) really did say that, "Sometimes a cigar is just a cigar." As we have seen, the crisis that must be dealt with in the anal stage is toilet training. Toilet training accompanied by high levels of stress and anxiety can lead to an anal fixation. Adult manifestations of such an anal fixation are people who are overly neat and orderly (known as an *anal-retentive personality*) or extremely disorganized and messy (an *anal-expulsive personality*).

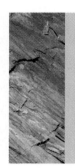

BEFORE YOU GO ON

3. What are the essential elements of Freud's psychosexual stages of development?

A Point to Ponder or Discuss
If you wanted to find evidence—for or against—the notions of Oedipus or Electra Complexes during the phallic stage of development, how might you proceed? What data would be relevant to this question?

The Psychoanalytic Approach after Freud

Sigmund Freud was a prolific writer and a persuasive communicator. His ideas were challenging, and they attracted many followers. Freud founded a psychoanalytic society in Vienna with an inner circle of colleagues and friends who shared his ideas. However, some colleagues did not agree with all aspects of his theory. Among other things, many of them were bothered by the very strong emphasis on biological instincts and libido and what they perceived as a lack of concern for social influences. Some of these analysts proposed theories of their own. These analysts became known as *neo-Freudians*. Because they had their own ideas, they had to part from Freud; he would not tolerate disagreement with any aspect of his theory from those within his inner circle.

The theories proposed by the neo-Freudians are complex and comprehensive. Each consists of logically interrelated assumptions, and it is not possible to do justice to any theory of personality in a short paragraph or two. However, we can sketch the basic idea(s) behind the theories of a few neo-Freudians.

Alfred Adler (1870–1937). As the psychoanalytic movement began to take shape, Adler was one of Freud's closest friends. However, Adler left Freud's inner circle and, in 1911, founded his own psychoanalytic approach to personality. Two things seemed most to offend Adler: 1) the negativity of Freud's views (for example, the death instinct) and 2) the idea of sexual libido as the prime impulse in life.

Adler argued that we are a product of the social influences on our personality. We are motivated not so much by drives and instincts as we are by goals and incentives. For Adler, the future and one's hope for what it held were often more important than one's past. In Adler's theory, the goal in life is the achievement of success or superiority. This goal is fashioned in childhood when, because we are then weak and vulnerable, we develop an **inferiority complex**—the feeling that we are less able than others to solve life's problems and get along in the world. Although we may seem inferior as children, with the help of social support and our own creativity, we can overcome and succeed. Simply striving for superiority, to be the best, was viewed by Adler as a healthy reaction to early feelings of inferiority only when it was balanced with a sort of "social interest" or "community feeling," or a genuine desire to help and serve others.

Carl Jung (1875–1961). Carl Jung left Freud's inner circle in 1913. Freud had chosen Jung to be his successor, but shortly thereafter the two men disagreed about the role of sexuality and the nature of the unconscious—two central themes in psychoanalysis. Jung was more mystical in his approach to personality and, like Adler, was more positive about a person's ability to control his or her own destiny. He believed the major goal in life is to unify all of the aspects of our personality, conscious and unconscious, introverted (inwardly directed) and extroverted (outwardly directed). Libido was energy for Jung, but not sexual energy. It was energy for personal growth and development.

Jung readily accepted the idea of an unconscious mind and expanded on it, arguing for two types of unconscious: the *personal unconscious*, which is very much like Freud's notion, and the *collective unconscious*, which contains those very basic ideas that go beyond an individual's own personal experiences. Jung believed that the collective unconscious contained concepts common to all of humanity and inherited from all past generations. The contents of our collec-

tive unconscious include what Jung called *archetypes*—universal forms and patterns of thought. These are basic "ideas" that transcend all of history. Jung's archetypes include themes that recur in myths: motherhood, opposites, good, evil, masculinity, femininity, and the circle as a symbol of journeys that come full circle, returning to their point of origin, or of the complete, whole self.

Karen Horney (1885–1952). Trained as a psychoanalyst in Germany, Karen Horney (pronounced "horn-eye") came to the United States in 1934. She accepted a few Freudian concepts but significantly changed most of them. Horney believed that the idea of levels of consciousness made sense, as did anxiety and repression, but she theorized that the prime impulses that drive or motivate behavior are not biological and inborn, nor are they sexual and aggressive. A major concept for Horney was *basic anxiety*, which grows out of childhood when the child feels alone and isolated in a hostile world. If parents properly nurture their children, children overcome basic anxiety. If parents are overly punishing, inconsistent, or indifferent, however, children may develop *basic hostility* and

inferiority complex (according to Adler) the feeling that we are less able than others to solve life's problems and get along in the world

Courtesy of Bettmann/Corbis.

Karen Horney held onto many principles of psychoanalysis, but is called a "neo-Freudian" because she parted ways with Freud on several critical issues.

may feel hostile and aggressive toward their parents. However, young children cannot express hostility toward their parents openly, so the hostility gets repressed (to the unconscious), building even more anxiety.

Horney did emphasize early childhood experiences, but from a perspective of social interaction and personal growth. Horney claimed that there are three distinct ways in which people interact with each other. In some cases, people *move away from others*, seeking self-sufficiency and independence. The idea here is, "If I am on my own and uninvolved, you won't be able to hurt me." On the other hand, some *move toward others* and are compliant and dependent. This style of interaction shields against anxiety in the sense: "If I always do what you want me to do, you won't be upset with me." Horney's third interpersonal style involves *moving against others*. In this third case, the effort is to be in control, gain power, and dominate: "If I am in control, you'll have to do what I want you to." Horney's ideal state is a balance among these three styles, but she argued that many people have one style that predominates in their dealings with others.

Horney also disagreed with Freud regarding the biological basis of differences between men and women. Freud's theories have been challenged many times for their male bias (Fisher & Greenberg, 1977; Jordan et al., 1991). Karen Horney was one of the first to do so.

Evaluating the Psychoanalytic Approach

Now that we have reviewed a few major ideas from a very complex approach to personality, can we make any judgments about its worth or contributions? You may already know the answer. There are critics and supporters of each of the theoretical approaches in this chapter. However, each approach can tell us something about ourselves and about human personality in general.

The psychoanalytic approach, particularly as modified by the neo-Freudians, is the most comprehensive and complex of the theories we will review. Psychologists have debated the relative merits of Freud's works for decades, and the debate continues, with efforts to generate more empirical research (Funder, 2001). On the positive side, Freud and psychoanalytic theorists focused our attention on the importance of the childhood years and suggested that some (even biologically determined) impulses may affect our behaviors even though we are unaware of them. Although Freud may have overstated the matter, he contributed significantly by drawing our attention to sexuality and sexual impulses as influences on personality and human behavior. Freud's concept of defense mechanisms as reactions to anxiety has generated a great deal of research and has been generally accepted (Baumeister, Dale, & Sommers, 1998; Feshbach et al., 1996), as has his notion that the unconscious may influence our pattern of responding to the world (Westen, 1998).

On the other hand, many psychologists have been critical of psychoanalytic theory. We have seen how the neo-Freudians tended to downplay innate biological drives and take a more social approach to personality development than did Freud. A major criticism of the psychoanalytic approach is that so many of its insights cannot be tested. Freud thought of himself as a scientist, but he tested none of his ideas about human nature experimentally. Some seem beyond testing. Just what is *libidinal energy*? How can it be measured? How would we recognize it if we saw it? Concepts such as id, ego, and superego may sound sensible enough, but how can we prove or (more importantly) disprove their existence? Such a heavy reliance on instincts, especially with sexual and aggressive overtones, as explanatory concepts goes beyond where most psychologists are willing to venture.

BEFORE YOU GO ON

4. Summarize the contributions of the neo-Freudians, and provide a general statement evaluating the psychoanalytic approach to personality.

A Point to Ponder or Discuss
How might a psychoanalytically oriented psychologist account for the success or failure of students in a Psychology 101 class?

THE BEHAVIORAL-LEARNING APPROACH

Many early-20th century American psychologists scoffed at the psychoanalytic approach, regardless of who happened to propose it. From the beginning, American psychology favored the observable and the measurable. As a result, the approach to personality in America was oriented toward the laboratory and theories of learning. Explaining personality in terms of learning and observable behaviors seemed a reasonable course of action. In this section we briefly review some of the behavioral approaches to personality.

John B. Watson (1878–1958) and his followers in behaviorism argued that psychology should turn away from the study of consciousness and the mind because the contents of mental life were unverifiable and ultimately unscientific. They argued that the science of psychology should instead study observable behavior. Yet here were Freud and other psychoanalysts arguing that *unconscious* and *preconscious* forces were determiners of behavior. "Nonsense," the behaviorists would say. "We don't even know what we mean by consciousness, and here you want to talk about levels of unconscious influence!"

Watson emphasized the role of the environment in shaping behaviors. Behaviorists did not accept the Freudian notion of inborn traits or impulses, whether they were called drives, id, libido, or anything else. Learning was

Courtesy of Jim Zuckerman/Corbis.

what mattered most. A personality theory was not needed. A theory of learning would include all the details about personality that one would ever need.

Who we are is determined by what we have learned and early learning experiences count heavily—on this point Watson and Freud would have agreed. Even our fears are conditioned (remember Watson's "Little Albert" study?). So convinced was Watson that instincts and innate impulses had little to do with the development of behavior that he could write, albeit somewhat tongue in cheek, "Give me a dozen healthy infants, well-formed, and my own specified world to bring them up in, and I'll guarantee to take any one at random and train him to become any type of specialist I might

Theorists who take a behavioral-learning approach to personality argue that who we are in this world is a reflection of our learning and our experiences. While many women in our society acquire what is often referred to as "gender-appropriate" careers, others acquire a different set of expectations.

select—doctor, lawyer, artist, merchant, chief, and yes, even beggarman and thief, regardless of his talents, penchants, tendencies, abilities, vocations, and race of his ancestors" (Watson, 1925).

B.F Skinner (1904–1990) avoided any reference to internal variables to explain behavior, which is the essence of what we normally think of as personality. Skinner believed that psychology should focus on observable stimuli, observable responses, and the relationships among them. He argued that one should not go meddling about in the mind of an organism. Behavior is shaped by its consequences. Some behaviors result in reinforcement and thus tend to be repeated. Other behaviors are not reinforced and, thus, tend not to be repeated. Consistency in behavior simply reflects the consistency of the organism's reinforcement history. A pivotal question, from Skinner's point of view, is how can external conditions be manipulated to reinforce the behaviors we want?

John Dollard (1900–1980) and **Neal Miller** (1909–2002) tried to use learning theory to explain personality and how it developed. What matters for a person's personality, they argued, was the system of habits developed in response to cues in the environment. Behaviors are motivated by biological primary drives (upon whose satisfaction survival depended) and learned drives, which developed through experience. Motivated by drives, habits that get reinforced are repeated and become part of the stable collection of habits that constitute personality. For example, repression into the unconscious is simply learned forgetfulness; forgetting about some anxiety-producing experience is reinforcing and, consequently, tends to be repeated. It was Miller (1944) who proposed that conflict could be explained in terms of tendencies (habits) to approach or avoid goals and has little to do with the id, ego, and superego or with unconscious impulses of any sort.

Albert Bandura (b. 1925) is a behaviorist willing to consider the internal cognitive processes of the learner. He claims that many aspects of personality are learned, but often through observation and social influence (Bandura, 1999; 2001a). For Bandura, learning is more than forming connections between stimuli and responses or between responses and reinforcers; it involves a cognitive rearrangement and representation of the world. His approach argues that you learn to behave honestly by observing others, for example. If you see your parents being honest and see their behaviors being rewarded, you may learn to behave honestly.

Evaluating the Behavioral-Learning Approach

Many critics of the behavioral-learning approach to personality argue that Watson, Skinner, and others dehumanize personality and that even the social learning theory of Bandura is too deterministic. The essence of their criticism is captured in this question: If everything a person does, thinks, or feels is in some way determined by his or her environment or learning history, what then does the person—or the person's personality—contribute? In the behaviorist world, the critics say there is nothing—or very little—for the *person*, for personality, to contribute. As a result of the limited importance of the concept of personality to behavioral theorists, Behavioral-learning approaches to personality often are not theories at all, at least not very comprehensive theories. To their credit, learning theorists demand that theoretical terms be carefully defined and that hypotheses be verified experimentally. Many of the ideas reflected in this approach to personality theory have been successfully applied in behavior therapy.

BEFORE YOU GO ON

5. What is the essence of the behavioral-learning approach to personality, and what are some of its strengths and weaknesses?

A Point to Ponder or Discuss
Which aspects of your personality do you think reflect your learning experiences?

THE COGNITIVE APPROACH

Cognitive theorists believe that basic cognitive processes (for example, memory and accessing information) intersect with patterns of thought and perception normally thought to be involved in personality and that theorists should focus on such cognitions (Funder, 1997).

George Kelly (1955) proposed an early cognitive theory of personality. According to Kelly, every person has a set of *personal constructs* that direct his or her thoughts and perceptions. These personal constructs are a part of one's long-term memory and direct to a degree how information is stored and processed in other memory stores. Unfortunately, Kelly developed his theory just as the "cognitive revolution" in psychology was beginning, and he never really connected his notion of personal constructs and the then-developing ideas about human cognitive functioning (Funder, 1997, 2001a).

Walter Mischel, a student of Kelly, made the connection between Kelly's personal constructs and human cognition. Mischel (1973, 1999, 2004) has proposed a cognitive model of personality with four "person variables":

1. ***Cognitive and behavioral construction competencies:*** This set of competencies includes personal abilities such as intelligence, social skills, and creativity. These compe-

tencies are part of one's procedural memory, or memory involving how to do things.

2. ***Encoding strategies and personal constructs:*** The conceptual categories a person uses to make sense out of the world fall into this division. They include beliefs about one's self (for example, "I am a friendly person") and make up part of one's declarative memory.

3. ***Subjective stimulus values:*** Here a person houses his or her expectations about achieving goals, as well as the weight placed on possible outcomes for goal achievement (for example, rewards).

4. ***Self-regulatory systems and plans:*** This dimension includes strategies for self-reinforcement and how those strategies control cognitions. Items within this dimension would also be part of a person's procedural memory.

Cantor and Kihlstrom (1987) propose another cognitive approach. Their approach focuses on an individual's *social intelligence*, which includes all those skills, abilities, and knowledge that a person brings to social situations (McAdams, 1990). People use their social intelligence to solve immediately pressing *life tasks*. A life task, for example, could be attending college or deciding on a career. According to this view, individuals face a range of different life tasks over time. An individual must use his or her social intelligence and problem-solving strategies to deal with these tasks. Individuals facing life tasks must make use of information that they have stored in declarative and procedural memory (McAdams, 1990).

Cantor and Langston (1989) report results from a study that tracked first year college students. Researchers identified two major packages of strategies used by the students to deal with life tasks. The first group of students used *defensive pessimism*, which involves approaching life tasks with a "worst case scenario" in mind. Generally, these students set low expectations for themselves and felt anxious about facing life tasks. The second group of students used a more optimistic package of strategies. As a result, the second package identified *optimists* who approach life tasks with positive expectations, experience less anxiety, and generally have more positive attitudes toward academic tasks. This study found that pessimists and optimists did not differ in their first-semester college performance. Although in this study optimists performed no better academically than their more pessimistic peers, there is ample evidence that optimists reap other benefits, including better physical health (Myers, 2000; Scheier & Carver, 1992).

Evaluating the Cognitive Approach

The cognitive approach to personality still does a good job explaining our observations about personality and what we know about human cognition. In short, Kelly's and Mischel's cognitive approach to personality has withstood the test of time. In fact, during the 30 years since Mischel first proposed his theory, it has undergone only one change: the addition of a fifth, affective factor. Other cognitive systems have also been proposed that incorporate the time-honored cognitive concepts of schemes and scripts. More recently, a rich new area of research has arisen from the blending of cognitive and trait the-

ories of personality (Funder, 1997). More information on the trait approach comes later in this section.

THE HUMANISTIC-PHENOMENOLOGICAL APPROACH

To some degree, the humanistic-phenomenological approach to personality contrasts with both the psychoanalytic and behavioral approaches. It claims that people can shape their own destinies and chart their own courses of action despite biological, instinctive, or environmental influences. The humanistic view may be thought of as more optimistic than either the Freudian approach (with its death instincts and innate impulses) or the learning approach (with its emphasis on control exerted by forces of the environment). It tends to focus more on the "here and now" and less on early childhood experiences as important molders of personality. The humanistic-phenomenological view emphasizes the wholeness or completeness of personality, rather than its structural parts. What matters most is how people perceive themselves and others, which is essentially what phenomenological means.

Carl Rogers' (1902–1986) approach to personality is referred to as a person-centered or "self" theory. Like Freud, Rogers developed his views of human nature through the observation of clients in a clinical setting. (Rogers preferred the term *client* to *patient* and the term *person-centered* to *client-centered* to describe his approach.) Rogers believed that the most powerful human drive is the one to become fully functioning.

To be *fully functioning* implies that the person is striving to become all that he or she can be. To be fully functioning is to experience "optimal psychological adjustment, optimal psychological maturity, complete congruence, complete openness to experience . . ." (Rogers,

1959, p. 235). Fully functioning people live in the present, get the most from each experience, don't mope over opportunities lost or anticipate events to come. Fully functioning people do not act only to please others. Instead, they are open to their own feelings and desires, aware of their inner selves, and regard themselves positively.

Helping children function fully requires that we offer children what Rogers calls *unconditional positive regard.* For children, some behaviors bring reward, and others do not. How children behave often influences how they are regarded by those they care about. If children behave well, then others regard them positively. Conversely, if children behave badly, then others regard them negatively. Thus, children tend to receive only conditional positive regard. If they do what is expected or desired, then they get rewarded. As a result, children try to get rewards and avoid punishment; they try to act in ways that please others. For children, feelings of self-worth depend on others who may reward them, not reward them, or punish them. Rogers also argued that we should separate the child's behaviors from the child's self. That means that we may punish a child for doing a bad thing, but never for being a bad child (for example, "I love you very much, but what you have done is dangerous, and I told you not to, and therefore you will be punished"). Helping people achieve positive self-regard is one of the major goals of Carl Rogers' person-centered therapy.

Note that what matters here is not so much what *is*, but what is *felt* or *perceived*. Your true self (whatever it may be) is less important than your image of yourself. How you experience the world is what matters, clearly a phenomenological point of view. You may be an excellent piano player but if you feel you play poorly that perception or self-regard is what matters most.

Abraham Maslow's (1908–1970) basic criticism of psychology was that it

Courtesy of Troy Aossey/Getty Images.

Carl Rogers, a humanistic personality theorist, argued that children profit from receiving "unconditional positive regard," being hugged or rewarded, not for doing something in particular (conditional: if–then) but simply for doing nothing.

was altogether too pessimistic and negative. People's behaviors were dictated by a hostile environment or depraved instincts, many of which propelled people on a course of self-destruction.

Maslow took a more optimistic view of human nature and the motives for human behavior. He saw humans as motivated by the necessity to meet their needs. He regarded the meeting of needs as a positive, or at the worst, a neutral part of living (Maslow, 1954).

Because Maslow's goal was to help people realize their fullest potential (to "self-actualize"), he focused his study upon the very highest achieving people in society and sought to understand the characteristics which produced achievement (see Table 9.1). Compare this point of view with that of Freud, who drew many of his ideas about personality from interactions with his patients, people who hardly could be categorized as self-actualizers. Maslow did not limit himself to achievers alive in his day: Most of his self-actualizers were historical figures, such as Thomas Jefferson and Eleanor Roosevelt.

TABLE 9.1

Some of the characteristics or attributes of self-actualizers.

1. They tend to be realistic in their orientation.

2. They accept themselves, others, and the world for what they are, not for what they should be.

3. They have a great deal of spontaneity.

4. They tend to be problem-centered, rather than self-centered.

5. They have a need for privacy and a sense of detachment.

6. They are autonomous, independent, and self-sufficient.

7. Their appreciation of others (and of things of the world) is fresh, free, and not stereotyped.

8. Many have spiritual or mystical (although not necessarily religious) experiences.

9. They can identify with mankind as a whole, and share a concern for humanity.

10. They have a number of interpersonal relationships, some of them very deep and profound.

11. They tend to have democratic views in the sense that all are created equal and should be treated equally.

12. They have a sense of humor that tends more to the philosophical than the hostile.

13. They tend to be creative in their approaches.

14. They are hard-working.

15. They resist pressures to conform to society.

Evaluating the Humanistic-Phenomenological Approach

The humanistic-phenomenological approach has a number of strengths. For one, it reminds us of the wholeness of personality and of the danger in analyzing something as complex as personality in artificial bits and pieces. Additionally, the humanistic approach is more positive and optimistic, stressing personal growth and development. This view contrasts with Freud's darker, more pessimistic approach. As we will see in our discussion of psychotherapy, the humanistic-phenomenological approach has had a significant impact on many therapists and counselors.

Humanistic theories also have some drawbacks. A major problem with this approach is much like the basic problem with Freud's theory: It seems to make sense, but how do we go about testing any of the observations and statements made by proponents of the approach? Many of the key terms are defined in general, fuzzy ways. What is self-image? How do we really know when someone is growing? How can we document the advantages of unconditional positive regard? In many ways, what we have is a blueprint for living, a vision for the nature of personality, not a scientific theory. In addition, some critics claim that the notions of striving to become fully functioning or self-actualized are both naïve and far from universal.

BEFORE YOU GO ON

6. What is the basic thrust of approaches to personality that are classified as cognitive or humanistic-phenomenological?

A Point to Ponder or Discuss
Of our ABCs—affect, behavior, and cognition—which is the most important? That is, granting that who you are in the world is a reflection of your feelings, your actions, and your stored knowledge, which one of these three plays the largest role in your personality?

THE TRAIT APPROACH

Trait theories of personality have a markedly different flavor than any of the approaches we have looked at thus far. Trait theories have two important aspects. First, the trait approach is an empirical one, relying on research using carefully constructed tests. Second, the trait approach focuses on individual differences in personality and not on measuring which traits are dominant in a given individual (Funder, 1997). Personality psychologist Arnold Buss put it this way: "Trait psychologists typically seek to reveal the psychological dimensions along which people differ and ways in which traits cluster within individuals" (1989, p. 1379). We may define a **trait** as "any distinguishable, relatively enduring way in which one individual differs from others" (Guilford, 1959a, p. 5).

Traits are descriptive dimensions. That is, any trait (friendliness, for example) is not a simple either/or proposition. Friendliness falls on a continuum, ranging from extremely unfriendly to extremely friendly, with many possibilities in between. To be useful, traits need to be measurable so we can assess the extent to which people may differ on those traits (Ozer & Reise, 1994; Wiggins & Pincus, 1992). We will briefly summarize two classic trait theories and then look at a contemporary trait theory.

Three Classic Examples

For **Gordon Allport** (1897–1967), personality traits exist within a person and help explain the consistency in that person's behavior. The argument is that in various situations, a personality trait of friendliness might produce a range of specific responses, but those responses would be, in their essence, very much alike.

Allport proposed two types of personality traits: *common traits* and *personal traits* (personal dispositions) (Allport, 1961). By common traits Allport means those aspects of personality shared by almost everyone, even if to greater or lesser degrees. Aggressiveness is an example of a common trait, as is intelligence. These are traits we can use to make comparisons among people. Personal traits or dispositions, on the other hand, are unique to just some persons. How one displays a sense of humor (sharp wit, cutting sarcasm, philosophical puns, dirty jokes, and so on) is usually thought of as being a unique disposition.

Allport then went on to claim that personal traits have three subtypes: cardinal, central, and secondary. A *cardinal trait* is so overwhelming that it influences virtually everything a person does. The personalities of few of us are ruled by cardinal traits. Allport could imagine only a few examples (Don Quixote, the Marquis de Sade, Mohandas Gandhi, and Don Juan among them). No, people's

trait (personality) any distinguishable, relatively enduring way in which one individual differs from others

behaviors are not likely to be influenced by cardinal traits, but central traits. These can usually be described in just one word. They are the five to ten traits that best characterize someone (for example, honesty, friendliness, neatness, outgoingness, fairness, and kindness). Finally, each of us is occasionally influenced by secondary traits. These traits seldom govern many of our reactions but may be found in specific circumstances. For example, people who are basically very calm and easygoing, even when threatened (reflecting their central traits), may become very aggressive and excited when threatened in their own homes by intruders.

Another classic trait theory is that of **Raymond Cattell** (1905–1998). Cattell's is an empirical approach, relying on psychological tests, surveys, and questionnaires. Talking about personality traits without talking about how they are measured made little sense to Cattell. Cattell used a technique called factor analysis—a correlational procedure

that identifies groups of highly related variables that are assumed to measure the same underlying factor (here, a personality trait). The logic is that, if you know that some people are outgoing, you do not need to test them to see if they are sociable or extroverted; because these traits are all highly inter-related, such information would be redundant.

Cattell argued for two major types of personality traits (1973, 1979). *Surface traits* are clusters of behaviors that go together, like those that make up curiosity, trustworthiness, or kindliness. These traits are easily observed and can be found in many settings. More important than surface traits are the few underlying traits from which surface traits develop. These underlying traits are called *source traits*. One's pattern of source traits determines which surface traits get expressed in behavior. Source traits are harder to measure than surface traits because they are not directly observable. Cattell's source traits are listed in Table 9.2.

TABLE 9.2

Sixteen source traits are identified by Cattell. (Each trait is a dimension.)

Reserved (detached, aloof)	◄─► **Outgoing** (participating)	**Trusting** (accepting)	◄─► **Suspicious** (circumspect)
Less intelligent (dull)	◄─► **More intelligent** (bright)	**Practical** (down-to-earth)	◄─► **Imaginative** (absentminded)
Affected by feelings (easily upset)	◄─► **Emotionally stable** (calm)	**Forthright** (unpretentious)	◄─► **Shrewd** (astute, worldly)
Submissive (obedient, easily led)	◄─► **Dominant** (assertive)	**Self-assured** (secure, complacent)	◄─► **Apprehensive** (insecure, troubled)
Serious (sober, taciturn)	◄─► **Happy-go-lucky** (enthusiastic)	**Conservative** (disinclined to change)	◄─► **Experimenting** (experimenting)
Expedient (disregards rules)	◄─► **Conscientious** (moralistic, staid)	**Group-dependent** (a joiner)	◄─► **Self-sufficient** (resourceful)
Timid (shy, restrained)	◄─► **Venturesome** (socially bold)	**Uncontrolled** (follows own urges)	◄─► **Controlled** (shows willpower)
Tough-minded (rejects illusions)	◄─► **Sensitive** (tender-minded)	**Relaxed** (tranquil, composed)	◄─► **Tense** (frustrated, driven)

A third classic trait theory approach to personality is that of **Hans Eysenck** (1916–1997). Eysenck's model is a hierarchy, with three "supertraits" at the top. Below these are the more common sorts of personality traits, and still farther down are clusters of habitual patterns of behavior. At the lowest level are specific behaviors or responses (1967, 1982, 1990). The first of Eysenck's supertraits is the dimension of *extraversion—introversion*. An extravert would likely be sociable, lively, active, excitable, carefree, and the like. An introvert would tend to be quiet, passive, sober, reflective, and the like. Eysenck never thought of extraversion-introversion as "either-or," but as a dimension, from one extreme to the other, with most people falling in between. People toward the extraversion end would be expected to engage in certain behaviors, such as choosing to study with others, joining clubs, and seeking new experiences. People toward the introversion end would be expected to study alone, avoid joining clubs, and mostly engage in familiar activities.

The second supertrait proposed by Eysenck was called *neuroticism*, which is a dimension with emotional stability at one end and emotional instability at the other. Emotional stability predicts a person who tends to remain calm, reasonable, even-tempered, and in control. Emotional instability predicts a person who tends to be more restless, anxious, moody, or excitable. Combining both dimensions, Eysenck created a system with four basic personality types: extraverted-stable, extraverted-unstable, introverted-stable, and introverted-unstable.

Late in his career, Eysenck added a third supertrait dimension to his model called *psychoticism*. People rated high on psychoticism tend to be aggressive, impulsive, self-centered, antisocial, and even hostile. Those rated low tend to be warm, caring, empathic, and involved.

A Contemporary Perspective: The Big Five

We've looked at just two theories that have tried to identify relatively enduring personality traits, and we've generated quite a list. Allport focused on common traits and personal dispositions, and Cattell found many surface traits and a smaller number of source traits. Which scheme is right? Which set is more reasonable? Is there any set of personality traits that researchers agree upon?

It may surprise you to learn that personality psychologists are coming to a consensus concerning which traits have the most research support as descriptors of personality. This consensus approach is referred to as the *Five-Factor Model* (Caspu, Roberts, & Shiner, 2005; De Raad, 1998; John & Srivasta, 1999; Ozer & Reise, 1994; McCrae & Costa, 1986, 1997, 1999). What dimensions of personality are referred to as the "Big Five"?

Although many researchers agree five major dimensions (the "Big Five") suffice to characterize human personality, some researchers still disagree on exactly how to describe these five. A few researchers (John & Srivastava, 1999) support a "Big Three" approach. The following is a compilation from several sources (listed above). Please note that there is no particular ranking involved in this list. That is, Dimension I is not to be taken as any more important or more common than Dimension IV.

1. ***Dimension I — Extraversion/ Introversion*** embodies such things as assurance, talkativeness, openness, self-confidence, and assertiveness, on the one hand, with silence and passivity on the other. The extravert seeks stimulation, particularly from social situations, and is a generally happy person (Lucas & Fujita, 2000).

2. ***Dimension II — Agreeableness*** (sometimes *Friendliness*) has altruism, trust, caring, and providing

emotional support at one end, and hostility, indifference, selfishness, and distrust on the other.

3. ***Dimension III—Conscientiousness*** is a "will to achieve." It includes self-control, dependability, planning, thoroughness, and persistence, paired with carelessness, impulsivity, negligence, and unreliability. As you might imagine, this dimension correlates well with educational achievement.

4. ***Dimension IV—Neuroticism*** is an emotionality dimension. In many ways, this is the extent to which one is emotionally stable and able to handle most of the stress that one encounters or, at the other extreme, is anxious, depressed, or in some way psychologically disordered. It includes such things as nervousness and moodiness.

5. ***Dimension V—Openness to Experience and Culture.*** (In this context, "culture" refers to aspects of experience such as art, dance, literature, music, and the like.) This factor includes such characteristics as curiosity, imagination, and creativity. Persons rated low on this dimension are quite focused, with narrow interests and little desire to try different things, such as travel.

The recurrent finding that all personality traits can be reduced to just five (with these names or names like these) is remarkable. Each of these five traits represents a dimension of possible habits and individual responses that a person may bring to bear in any given situation.

These five traits have emerged from over 50 years of research in many cultures (McCrae & Costa, 1999; Stumpf, 1993; Wiggins & Pincus, 1992). They have emerged regardless of the individuals being assessed, and "the Big Five have appeared now in at least five languages, leading one to suspect that something quite fundamental is involved here" (Digman, 1990, p. 433). On the other hand, Revelle (1987) noted that "the agreement among these descriptive dimensions is impressive, [but] there is a lack of theoretical explanation for the how and the why of these dimensions" (p. 437).

Evaluating the Trait Approach

As we have already mentioned, trait approaches to personality are different from the others, even in their basic intent. Trait theories have a few obvious advantages. First, they provide us not only with descriptive terms, but also with the means of measuring the important dimensions of personality. Second, they give us an idea of how measured traits are related to one another. On the other hand, debate continues concerning the number of traits that are important in personality and predicting behavior. Even with the so-called Big Five traits, which is the most widely accepted trait theory today, there continues to be disagreement concerning whether the five traits are completely independent and whether personality can be reduced down to five traits (Paunonen & Jackson, 2000).

The basic relevance or value of personality traits also varies from one culture to another (Segall, Lonner, & Berry, 1998). The notion of individual personality traits seems to be more relevant and sensible in individualistic societies, such as ours and most other Western cultures. In these cultures, people are viewed as individuals, and knowing about the characteristics of those individuals is viewed as helpful. If people are viewed in terms of their membership in a group or a collective (as in collectivistic cultures, such as are found in Asia and South America), then their individual traits will be of less interest than their roles, duties, group loyalties, and responsibilities, for example (Kitayama et al., 1997; Shwedler & Sullivan, 1993).

So, as we might have predicted, when we try to evaluate the various approaches to—or theories of—personality, there are no real winners or losers. Each approach has its shortcomings, but each also adds something to our appreciation of the complex concept of human personality.

THE BIOLOGICAL APPROACH

Now that we have reviewed the classic "psychological" approaches to personality, we turn our attention to another approach to personality: The biological approach. The **biological approach** to personality focuses on biological, physiological, and genetic mechanisms to describe and explain personality. Generally, we can categorize the biological approach into two subcategories: Physiological explanations (focusing on the role of brain anatomy and physiology) and genetic/evolutionary explanations (Funder, 2007). You may recall that in Chapter 2 we briefly discussed the role of biological forces in cognition and behavior. In the sections that follow we expand that discussion and focus on how various biological factors relate to personality.

Physiological Correlates of Personality

As noted above, this approach focuses on the role of brain anatomy and physiology to account for personality characteristics. Researchers attempt to localize parts of the brain that are linked to various personality traits. Generally, research in this area shows a relationship between brain anatomy and physiology and certain aspects of personality.

One early example of attempting to connect brain activity with personality was Han Eysenck's (1967) arousal the-ory. According to this theory, differential activity in the *ascending reticular activating system* (ARAS) related to individual differences in the introversion-extraversion personality dimension, with introverts showing higher levels of activity in the ARAS than extraverts. Presumably, the higher level of ARAS activity in introverts causes them to seek out social situations that result in low levels of additional arousal (Bullock & Gilliland, 1993). Eysenck (1967) provided some evidence for his arousal theory, but subsequent research led to mixed results (Bullock & Gilliland, 1993). However, Bullock and Gilliland did provide some support for the arousal theory of introversion-extraversion. They found higher levels of activity in the ARAS among introverts than extraverts. Other research shows that activity in the lateral orbital and medial prefrontal cortex of the brain is associated with "persistence" (Gusnard et al., 2003).

Another line of research has investigated the relationship between neurotransmitters and personality. In one study (Gera et al., 1999) a positive correlation was found between levels of norepinephrine and the personality trait that is generally called "sensation seeking" (the tendency to seek out novel, stimulating situations). Higher levels of norepinephrine were correlated with greater sensation seeking. Similarly, research shows a relationship between serotonin and the personality traits of endurance and neuroticism (Dragan & Oniszczenko, 2006).

biological approach (to personality) focuses on biological, physiological, and genetic mechanisms to describe and explain personality

Genetics and Personality

Research and theory concerning the relationship between genetics and personality have a long and controversial history in psychology. One of the earliest attempts to link heredity and personality was made by Sir Francis Galton (1865). Galton stated clearly that "I find that talent is transmitted by inheritance in a very remarkable degree" (p. 157). Clearly, Galton believed that talent (as well as other traits) was inherited from one's parents. Statements like these sowed the seeds of controversy because scientists like Galton also believed that one could improve the human race through selective breeding, an idea that was eventually misapplied in the eugenics movement. More controversy emerged when philosophers and scientists began to question whether heredity or environment was responsible for personality and behavior. Because of these controversies, talking about the relationship between genetics and personality fell out of favor. It was not until fairly recently that scientists began to consider this relationship once again. A "new" discipline emerged known as *behavior genetics*, which looks at how personality (and other traits) might be related to heredity.

What does the field of behavior genetics tell us about the relationship between genetics and personality? Generally, research shows a moderately strong link between genetics and various personality traits. For example,

Plomin (1990) reports that there is an "average" relationship between genetics and the personality traits of extraversion and neuroticism. Similarly, Plomin reports moderate relationships between genetics and characteristics such as achievement, intimacy, aggression, harm avoidance and traditionalism. Other research by Jang, Livesley and Vernon (1996) shows similar moderate relationships between genetics and traits making up the big five personality profile (neuroticism, openness, agreeableness, extraversion, and conscientiousness). Similarly, "subjective well-being" (a tendency to be satisfied with one's life situation) also appears to have a significant genetic component (Weiss, Bates, & Luciano, 2008).

In the preceding discussion you may have noticed that most of the relationships between genetics and personality traits are moderate. This suggests that personality traits cannot be fully accounted for by genetics. In fact, studies in behavior genetics show that the environment also contributes substantially to personality characteristics. Generally, research shows that aspects of the non-shared environment (those aspects of the environment that differ among children in a family) contribute in a significant way to personality along with genetics. So, the bottom line appears to be that both genetics and the environment relate to, and contribute to the formation of one's personality characteristics.

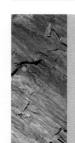

BEFORE YOU GO ON

9. How do brain anatomy and physiology relate to personality?
10. What role does heredity (genetics) play in personality?

A Point to Ponder or Discuss
How might heredity and environment combine to influence the development of various personality traits?

SPOTLIGHT
ON DIVERSITY

Gender and Ethnic Differences in Self-Esteem and Locus of Control

Personality traits allow us to describe people and to express differences among them. We can note Kathy's assertiveness and Juan's sociability. We can say that Chuck is friendlier than Steve or that Melissa is more impulsive than Jesse. Personality psychologists have been intrigued by the extent to which personality traits can characterize *groups* of people. The two groups studied most closely in this regard are men and women. We know that intelligence, or cognitive ability, is a major component of a person's personality. We learned (in Chapter 7) that there are few specific differences between men and women in intellectual abilities, and none at all in intelligence overall. This remains true even though "American women have received more college degrees than men every year since 1982, and the gap is widening every year" (Halpern, 2004, p. 135). What about other personality traits?

Let us review some of the data for two traits, self-esteem and locus of control. In this context, *self-esteem* reflects the judgments or attitudes about themselves that people make, and usually maintain, which reflect approval or disapproval. It is one's self-evaluation, or feeling of value. The first major, meta-analytic study of gender differences in personality was done by Eleanor Maccoby and Carol Jacklin and published in 1974. It turned up very little evidence for gender differences in self-esteem. However, Maccoby and Jacklin's research stimulated many others to look again at personality and gender.

The data on differences between *adult* males and females remain rather equivocal. In fact, there have been *so many* studies of gender differences in self-esteem (literally, thousands) that some psychologists claim this line of research should be stopped (Scheff & Fearon, 2004). Differences in self-esteem that appear in adolescence tend to be small, but at least there is a consistency in this research: Most studies find males have higher levels of self-esteem (Chubb, Fertman, & Ross, 1997; Kling et al., 1999; Robins & Trzesniewski, 2005; Thomas & Daubman, 2001). Those differences seem to peak at about the ninth-grade level and be most pronounced in students from predominantly white high schools. Researchers are now examining the factors that lead to gender differences in self-esteem, such as same- and different-gender friendships, athleticism, and parenting style.

When psychologists speak of *locus of control*, they mean the source of an individual's reinforcement and satisfaction. People with an *internal locus of control* believe that their destinies are in their own hands, under the control of their own abilities, motivation, and effort. *External locus of control* implies that forces outside the individual are what matters—luck, fate, chance, the actions of others, and the like (Chubb, Fertman, & Ross, 1997: Rotter, 1954, 1956). Internal locus of control has been correlated with several positive outcomes, from staying in high school, to reducing anxiety, to being generally well adjusted.

Does research show gender differences in locus of control? Researchers do not yet know for certain—particularly for adolescents. One of the few consistent findings is that as adolescents grow older, they tend to become more *internal* in their locus. One large study (Cairns et al., 1990) reported significant gender differences, with females being more *external* in their locus of control than were males. However, at about the same time, two studies found no gender differences at all (Adame, Johnson, & Cole, 1989; Dellas & Jernigan, 1987). A major review study (Archer & Waterman, 1988) confirmed the reality: Of 22 studies reviewed, six showed that girls used more *external* control, one had girls using more *internal* control, and the rest reported no differences based on gender.

Psychologists looking for group differences have also looked at racial and ethnic differences. Researchers have considered the connections between the self-esteem of members of a racial/ethnic group and the value placed upon those members by the culturally dominant group. Members of a group—usually on the basis of race or ethnicity—who come to feel that the larger society devalues them in some way, may be said to be *stigmatized* (Crocker, Major, & Steele, 1998). The standard assumption has been that stigmatized individuals internalize the negative view of the society. Thus, levels of self-esteem in stigmatized groups should parallel the degree to which they are devalued by the culturally dominant group (Twenge & Crocker, 2002).

"Members of non-stigmatized groups should have higher self-esteem than members of stigmatized groups, and among stigmatized groups, those who are more valued (e.g., Asian Americans) should have higher self-esteem than those who are less valued (e.g., blacks and Latinos in the United States)" (Major & O'Brien, 2005, pp. 406-407). Sound sensible? Maybe, but that's not what the data say. Indeed, in a meta-analysis, African Americans had higher self-esteem than did white Americans, who had higher self-esteem than did Latino Americans who had higher self-esteem than did Asian Americans and Native Americans (Twenge & Crocker, 2002). And, if you were to compute a combined measure of self-esteem for African, Latino, and Asian Americans, that combined measure would be higher than the same measure for white Americans (Crocker et al., 1994). The task now for personality psychologists and social psychologists is to explain these—largely unexpected—group differences in self-esteem.

Another intriguing line of research on self-esteem asks what is the real worth of a high, positive sense of self? Today we hear a great deal about efforts to boost or bolster self-esteem—particularly that of children and adolescents. Those engaged in this effort assume that a positive self-evaluation is a good thing and that those who can develop self-esteem will succeed in school and at work and achieve happiness. By now, we hope, you question assumptions like these. That is exactly what psychologist Roy Baumeister and his colleagues did; they questioned the value of having a high level of self-esteem. They published their work under the title *Exploding the Self-Esteem Myth*, which ought to give you an idea of their findings (Baumeister et al., 2003, 2005). Indeed they found no real connection between high self-esteem and genuine achievement, ability, or successfulness. The only characteristic correlated strongly with high self-esteem was the ability to make friends easily.

Finally, what can we say about *locus of control* and ethnicity? When Janet Helms (1990) looked at locus of control and race, she discovered an interesting relationship. African Americans with a positive racial identity tended to have an internal locus of control, a sort of, "I am who I am, and I can get this done" attitude. African Americans who tended to view the world—and their place in it—from a European/white perspective had more of an external locus of control, believing that others mostly controlled their fate.

Asian Americans present a complex picture with regard to locus of control. Their heritage emphasizes the group and interdependency. In many cases, Asian Americans allow decisions to be made by others, even if those others are not members of a close group (such as family members). European Americans generally place high value on personal autonomy and decisions made by one's self (i.e., an internal locus). In contrast, Asian Americans tend to value group autonomy and group decisions (i.e., an external locus) (Chiu & Hong, 2005; Hong et al., 2001; Menon et al., 1999).

What can we conclude about personality differences in groups, based on gender or ethnicity? The study of gender differences is the older of the two arenas of study. Research has generally concluded that, if there are gender differences in personality traits, they are few and small. However, what matters is how people perceive personality differences in the real world. Looking for racial, cultural, ethnic differences in personality is a newer enterprise. There may be some differences, determined by the context of culture, but their importance in day-to-day living has yet to be established. For nearly every descriptor we can imagine, there are more differences *within* identifiable groups than there are *between* them.

A DEBATE RESOLVED: IS THERE A PERSONALITY?

Each approach to personality has its own perspective. There is one theme, however, that they all have in common: They all address the *consistency* of personality. Someone with an "overdeveloped superego" should be consistently conscientious and feel guilty whenever established standards are not met. Someone who has learned to behave aggressively should behave aggressively in a range of settings. Someone trying to "grow personally and self-actualize" should be consistently open to a wide variety of new opinions and ideas. Someone with a trait of extraversion should appear outgoing and extraverted most of the time.

Nearly 40 years ago, this very basic assumption about personality was challenged by Walter Mischel (1968). One problem with arguing for the consistency of personality is that personality just may not be consistent at all (Council, 1993; Epstein, 1979; Mischel, 1968, 1979; Mischel & Peake, 1982). Think carefully about your own behavior and your own personality. Assume for the moment you think of yourself as easygoing. Are you always easygoing, easy to get along with? Are there some situations in which you would be easygoing, but others in which you might fight to have your way? Are there some situations in which you tend to be social and outgoing, yet different situations in which you prefer to be alone and not mix in? Such was the thrust of Mischel's challenge: Personality characteristics appear to be consistent only when they are viewed in similar or consistent situations.

We may observe consistency in the personality of others for two reasons: First, it is convenient. We like to think that we can quickly and accurately categorize people. If we see someone do something dishonest—say, pick up change left as a tip for a waiter—we find it convenient to label that person as basically dishonest. It is easy to assume that the aggressive, mean football player will probably be mean and aggressive off the field as well. Such assumptions may not be true, but they do make it easy to form judgments about others. Second, we tend to see others only in a restricted range of situations, where their behaviors and attitudes may very well be consistent. The real test would be to see those people in varied situations on many occasions (Kendrick & Funder, 1991; Mischel, Shoda, & Mendoza-Denton, 2002).

As you might suspect, arguments challenging the very definition of personality created quite a stir. Since Mischel raised the challenge, there has been much research and debate on this issue. We now see that things may not be as unstable and situation-bound as Mischel first suggested. One analysis, using methodology borrowed from the field of behavior genetics, argues that most of the variability we see in behaviors reflects individual differences, even more than the pressures of the situation (Vansteelandt & Van Mechelen, 1998; McCrae & Costa, 1994; Wiggins & Pincus, 1993).

In fact, most personality theorists today agree that the debate about personality traits versus the situation as determinants of behavior "can at last be declared about 98% over" (Funder, 2001, p. 199). Depending on how you look at it, neither side won, or both sides won. Research supports that some personality-related characteristics are stable over time and in many different situations. Indeed, even Mischel acknowledges that *on the average*—averaged over many situations, or in the aggregate—people show "stable overall individual difference: on the whole, some people are more sociable than others, some are more open-minded, some are more punctual, and so on" (Mischel, 2004, p. 3; Mischel & Shoda, 1998; Michel, Shoda, & Smith, 2004). The research also supports the notion that it is folly not to take into account the situation in which behaviors occur.

One outcome of the debate over the relative importance of personality and situational variables is known as *interactionism*, or the transactional approach. This approach says that how an individual behaves is a function of an interaction of personality characteristics and the individual's perception of the situation. Neither personality characteristics (inside the person) nor the situation (external environment) can fully explain an individual's reaction. For one thing, personality traits may not be consistent; no one claims that they cannot change and adjust over time. On the other hand, a person's internal dispositions may very well determine in part the sorts of situations a person gets himself or herself into. Again, Mischel puts it this way:

> . . . if different situations acquire different meanings for the same individual, as surely they do, the kinds of appraisals, expectations and beliefs, affects, goals, and behavioral scripts that are likely to become activated in relation to particular situations will vary. Therefore, there is no theoretical reason to expect the individual to display similar behaviors in relation to different psychological situations unless they are functionally equivalent in meaning. (2004, p. 5)

Predicting what will happen in any situation depends largely on the interaction of an individual's internal dispositions ("personality" and the dynamics of the situation. A friendly pick-up game of basketball easily can turn highly competitive—even hostile—if the score gets close and a group of friends gathers to act as a cheerleading audience.

Courtesy of Kevin Dodge/Corbis.

Let's say that Robin agrees to a friendly racquetball game, just for the exercise. At first all goes well, and Robin, a superior player, takes it easy on her opponent. After all, they are just playing for the exercise. In the second game, Robin's opponent makes a few good shots and moves ahead in the score. Then Robin notices a small group of spectators watching them play. As the situation changes, so does Robin's perception of it: "This is no longer fun and games," Robin thinks to herself as she starts smashing low line drives off the front wall. Within just a few minutes,

Robin's behavior is now considerably different. The situation has been altered (that is, the situation is no longer functionally the same in meaning), and her behavior becomes aggressive and forceful. A perceived challenge to her ability brought out competitive reactions. Robin's personality also brought about a change in the situation; to some degree, her competitiveness turned a friendly game into an athletic contest. With interactionism we have an approach that acknowledges the impact of the environment but also allows for the influence of stable, internal personality traits.

BEFORE YOU GO ON

11. How would you characterize the person-situation debate, and how has it been resolved?

A Point to Ponder or Discuss
Think about your own personality traits or dispositions. Are there some that are more stable, more consistent across more situations? What accounts for the difference(s) between those traits that appear more stable across situations and those that seem more bound to the situation at hand?

PERSONALITY MEASUREMENT OR ASSESSMENT

As we know, personality is a difficult concept to define. Most definitions include the idea that there are characteristics of an individual that remain fairly consistent over time and over many (if not all) situations. Psychologists are especially keen to measure those characteristics in ways which are reliable (produce consistent results) and valid (actually measure what they are supposed to).

Why do psychologists engage in personality assessment? There are three main reasons for the measurement of personality. The first reason is related to mental illness and psychological disorders. One question that a psychologist may ask in a clinical setting is, "What is

wrong with this person?" In fact, the first question is often, "Is there anything wrong with this person?" (Burisch, 1984). If there were an adequate measure of some personality trait, say, shyness, and if enough people were measured on that trait, a person's score could then be compared to scores of the norm group. In this way, a psychologist could assess whether a client's score on shyness was "normal,"—at or near the average, or norm—or "abnormal"— significantly different from the average or norm. Thus, aiding psychologists in adequate and proper diagnosis of patients is one aim of personality measurement.

A second purpose for personality assessment is theory building, where there are a number of inter-related questions. Which personality traits can be measured? How can traits be organized within the person? Which traits are the most important for describing personality? Is this trait bound to some particular cultural setting (Ozer & Reise, 1994)? For trait theorists, finding answers to these questions is obviously the major purpose for constructing personality measurement devices.

The third purpose involves the extent to which knowledge of personality traits can be used to predict some target behavior or behaviors. This is a practical concern, particularly in vocational placement. For example, if we know that Joe is dominant and extroverted, what does that knowledge tell us about his leadership potential? Or about the likelihood that he will succeed as a sales manager? For that matter, what personality traits best describe a successful astronaut, police officer, or secretary?

In brief, personality assessment has three goals: diagnosis, theory building, and behavior prediction. These goals often interact. A clinical diagnosis made in the context of some theoretical approach is often used to predict possible outcomes, such as which therapy is most appropriate for a given patient.

Now let's consider a few of the assessment techniques that are used to discover the nature of someone's personality.

Behavioral Observations

As you and I develop our impressions of the personalities of friends and acquaintances, we usually do so by relying on **behavioral observation**, which, as its name suggests, involves drawing conclusions about someone's personality on the basis of observations of his or her behaviors. We judge Maria to be bright because she was the only one who knew the answer to a question in class. We feel that Dan is submissive because he always seems to do whatever his wife demands.

As helpful as our observations may be, there might be problems with the casual, unstructured observations you and I normally make. Because we have observed only a few behaviors in a few settings, we may be over-generalizing when we assume that those same behaviors will show up in new or different situations. Maria may never again know the answer to a question in class. Dan could have given in to his wife only because we were there. That is, the behaviors that we observe may not be typical at all.

Nonetheless, behavioral observation can be an excellent source of information, particularly when the observations being made are purposeful, careful, and structured and when steps are taken to make the observations reliable and valid and to ensure our sample is representative (Funder, 1995). Among other things, the accuracy of one's observations is related to the degree of acquaintance between the observer and the person being observed (Paulus & Bruce, 1992). Behavioral observations are commonly a part of a clinical assessment. The clinical psychologist may note several behaviors of a client as potentially significant—the style of dress, manner of speaking, gestures, postures, and so on.

Consider an example. A child is reportedly having trouble at school, behaving aggressively, and being generally disruptive. A psychologist may visit the school and observe the child's behaviors in the natural setting of the classroom. It could be that the child behaves aggressively and engages in fighting behavior, but only when the teacher is in the room. Otherwise, the child is pleasant and passive. Perhaps, the child's aggressive behaviors are a ploy to get the teacher's attention.

To add to his or her observations, a psychologist may role-play as a means to collect information. Role-playing is acting out a given life situation. "Let's say that I'm a student and you're the teacher, and that it's recess time," the psychologist says to a child. "Let's pretend that somebody takes a toy away from me, and I hit him on the arm. What will you do?" What is of interest here is the child's

behavioral observation a method of drawing conclusions about someone's personality on the basis of observations of his or her behaviors

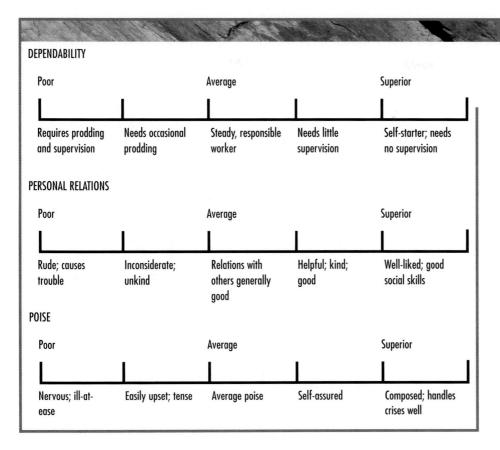

FIGURE 9.1

A graphic rating scale such as this might be used by an employer evaluating current or potential employees.

DEPENDABILITY

Poor — Average — Superior

Requires prodding and supervision | Needs occasional prodding | Steady, responsible worker | Needs little supervision | Self-starter; needs no supervision

PERSONAL RELATIONS

Poor — Average — Superior

Rude; causes trouble | Inconsiderate; unkind | Relations with others generally good | Helpful; kind; good | Well-liked; good social skills

POISE

Poor — Average — Superior

Nervous; ill-at-ease | Easily upset; tense | Average poise | Self-assured | Composed; handles crises well

response in a role-reversal situation. Can the child mentally "step back" from the situation and be realistic about what the teacher should do?

Observational techniques can be supplemented with a rating scale (such as the one in Figure 9.1). Rating scales provide many advantages over casual observation. For one thing, they focus the attention of the observer on a set of specified behaviors to be observed. Rating scales also yield a more objective measure of behavior. With rating scales, behaviors can be observed by several raters. If you use several raters to observe the same behaviors (say, children at play in a nursery school), you can check on the reliability of their observations. If all five of your observers agree that Timothy engaged in hitting behavior on the average of six times per hour, the consistency of that assessment adds to its usefulness.

BEFORE YOU GO ON

12. What are three potential goals of personality assessment, and to what extent is behavioral observation a useful technique?

A Point to Ponder or Discuss
Consider your best friend. Which four or five personality traits best describe your friend's personality? Which traits might your friend think are most important for describing your personality?

Minnesota Multiphasic Personality Inventory (MMPI) a paper-and-pencil personality test that measures several personality dimensions with the same set of (567) items

interview a method that yields data of what people say about themselves, rather than what they do

Interviews

We can learn some things about people just by watching them. We can also learn about some aspects of personality by simply asking people about themselves. In fact, the interview is "one of the oldest and most widely used, although not always the most accurate, of the methods of personality assessment" (Aiken, 1984, p. 296). Interviews are popular largely because they are simple and flexible.

The data of the interview are what people say about themselves, rather than what they do. Interview results are usually impressionistic and not easily quantifiable (although some interview techniques are more structured and objective than others). The interview is more a technique of discovering generalities than uncovering specifics.

A major advantage of the interview is its flexibility. The interviewer may decide to drop a certain line of questioning if it produces no useful information and pursue some other area of interest (Whetzel & McDaniel, 1997). Over 20 years ago, studies demonstrated very clearly that most interviews had very little reliability and even less validity (Tenopyr, 1981). Interviews were nearly abandoned as a means of assessing personality. However, the low marks that interviewing received held only for free-form, rambling, unstructured interviews. *Structured interviews*, on the other hand, are characterized by a specific set of questions to be asked in a prescribed order. This structured interview, then, becomes more like a psychological test to the extent that it is objective and standardized and asks about a particular sample of behavior. Studies of structured interviews show that their reliability and validity can be very high (Campion, Palmer, & Campion, 1997, 1998; Landy et al., 1994).

Paper-and-Pencil Tests

Observational and interview techniques barely qualify as psychological tests. Remember our definition of a psychological test: an objective, standardized measure of a sample of behavior. (You might find it useful to review our discussion of tests and the qualities of a good, useful test in Chapter 7.) Here, we'll focus on one of the most often-used paper-and-pencil personality tests, the **Minnesota Multiphasic Personality Inventory**, or **MMPI** for short. The test is called multiphasic because it measures several personality dimensions with the same set of items.

The MMPI was designed to aid in the diagnosis of mental disorders and, hence, is not designed to identify personality traits. The MMPI is the most researched test in psychology and remains one of the most commonly used (Lubin et al., 1984). The test remains popular largely because it has been shown repeatedly to be a reliable and valid measure of a set of personality characteristics (Lilienfeld, Wood, & Garb, 2000; Wood et al., 2002). In 1990, a revision of the MMPI (the MMPI-2) became available. The revision made two major changes and several lesser ones. Antiquated items (sensible in 1940, but no longer relevant 50 years later) and offensive items (having to do with religion or sexual practices) were replaced. The norm group for the MMPI-2 was much larger (2,600 people) than for the MMPI (about 700 people) and is supposed to be more representative in regard to cultural background, ethnicity, and the like (Ben-Porath & Butcher, 1989). Indeed, the evidence suggests that the MMPI-2 scores of American blacks and Hispanics, as well as selected international samples, are very similar to the general U.S. norm group (Butcher, Lim, & Nezami, 1998; Greene, 2000). The authors of the MMPI-2 intended to update and improve the test but not change the basic design or meaning of test scores.

The MMPI-2 consists of 567 true/false questions about feelings, attitudes, physical symptoms, and past experiences. It is a *criterion-referenced* test, which means that items on the test are referenced to one of the criterion groups—either normal persons or patients with a diagnosis of a particular mental disorder. Some of the items appear sensible. "I feel like people are plotting against me" seems like the sort of item someone with paranoia would call "true," whereas normal persons would tend to respond "false." Many items, however, are not as obvious. "I like to visit zoos" is not an MMPI-2 item, but it might have been if individuals of one diagnostic group responded to the item differently from other people. What the item appears to be measuring is irrelevant. What matters is whether people of different groups respond differently to the item. Psychologists do not make even a tentative diagnosis of a psychological disorder on the basis of a person's response to just a few items. Instead a diagnosis is based upon the interpretations of sets of scores by a trained, experienced psychologist.

The MMPI-2's *validity scales* consist of items from among the 567 that assess the extent to which the test-taker is attending to the task at hand or is trying to present herself or himself in a favorable light instead of responding truthfully to the items. For example, responding "true" to several statements such as "I always smile at everyone I meet" would lead an examiner to doubt the validity of the test-taker's responses.

Although the MMPI-2 is commonly used, it is not the only paper-and-pencil test of personality. The *California Personality Inventory*, or CPI, was written using only people who were not diagnosed as having a psychological problem or disorder. It assesses 18 personality traits, including dominance, self-acceptance, responsibility, and sociability. Because it is designed to measure several traits, it can also be referred to as a multiphasic test.

Some multiphasic tests were designed in conjunction with a particular personality theory. For example, Cattell's trait theory approach investigated a number of potential personality traits. Cattell's *16 PF Questionnaire* (in which PF stands for personality factors) measures these traits. Analysis of responses on this test results in a personality profile that can be compared to one gathered from a large norm group.

Finally, many personality questionnaires or inventories are designed to measure just one trait and, thus, are not multiphasic. One example is the *Taylor Manifest Anxiety Scale*. Taylor began with a large pool of items, many of them from the MMPI, and then asked psychologists to choose those items they thought would best measure anxiety. The 50 items most commonly chosen by psychologists constitute this widely accepted test. A more recent test, the *Endler Multidimensional Anxiety Scale*, not only assesses anxiety, but its designer also claims it can distinguish between anxiety and depression (Endler et al., 1992).

Projective Techniques

A **projective technique** asks a person to respond to ambiguous stimuli. The stimuli can be any number of things, and there are no clearly right or wrong answers. Projective procedures are unstructured and open-ended. Because there is so little content in the stimulus being presented, the idea is that the person will project some of himself or herself into the response. In many ways, projective techniques are more like aids to interviewing than psychological tests (Korchin & Scheldberg, 1981).

Some projective techniques are very simple. The word association technique, introduced by Galton in 1879, is a projective procedure. "I will say a word, and I want you to say the first thing that pops into your head. Do not think about your response; just say the first thing that comes to mind." There are no right answers. Psychologists hope this technique yields some insight into the problems of a patient.

A similar technique is the unfinished sentences, or sentence-completion, test. For example, a sentence is begun "My greatest fear is . . ." The person is asked to complete the sentence. Although published tests are available (e.g., the *Rotter Incomplete Sentences Blank*), many psychologists prefer to make up their own. Again, there are no right or wrong responses, and interpreting responses is subjective, but a skilled examiner can gain new insights about a person's personality.

projective technique an assessment device that asks a person to respond to ambiguous stimuli

FIGURE 9.2

A sample Rorschach-like inkblot. The subject is asked what the inkblot represents, and what he or she sees in it. Because the stimulus is so ambiguous, the notion is that the subject will "project" some of his or her self into any response.

Courtesy of Glyn Jones/Corbis.

Of the projective techniques, none is as well known as the *Rorschach inkblot test.* This technique was introduced in 1921 by Hermann Rorschach (see Figure 9.2). There are ten cards in the Rorschach test: Five are black on white, two are red and gray, and three are multicolored. People are asked to tell what they see in the cards or what the inkblot represents.

Scoring Rorschach tests has been controversial. Standard scoring procedures require attending to many factors: what the person says (content), where the person focuses attention (location), mention of detail versus global features, reaction

to color or open spaces, and how many distinct responses a person gives. Many psychologists question the use of the Rorschach as a diagnostic instrument. Much of what it tells an examiner may be gained directly. For example, Rorschach responses referring to sadness, death, and dying may indicate a depressed person. Are the inkblots really needed to discover such depression? As a psychological test, the Rorschach seems neither reliable nor valid (Hamel, Gallagher, & Soares, 2001; Lilienfeld, 1999; Lilienfeld, Wood, & Garb, 2000; Wood et al., 2002). Many psychologists appear to agree because the use of Rorschach is on the decline in clinical practice (Piotrowski, Belter, & Keller, 1998). Now it is used primarily as an aid to assessment.

The Thematic Apperception Test, or TAT, was devised by Henry Murray in 1938. This test is a series of ambiguous pictures about which a person is asked to tell a story. The person is asked to examine the pictures and describe what is going on, what led up to the situation, and what the outcome is likely to be. The theory behind the design is that a person's hidden needs, desires, and emotions will be projected into his or her stories. The test is called a *thematic* test because scoring depends largely on the interpretation of the themes of the stories. Scoring manuals are available, but scoring and interpretation are usually subjective and impressionistic. It is likely the TAT is popular for the same reasons that the Rorschach was: Psychologists are used to it, comfortable with the insights it provides, and willing to tolerate a little subjectivity so long as it serves the larger purpose of a reasonable diagnosis.

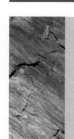

BEFORE YOU GO ON

13. How might interviews be helpful in determining a person's personality?
14. Describe the MMPI-2 and the projective techniques, the Rorschach and the TAT in particular.

A Point to Ponder or Discuss
What might you conclude about a person who looked at all of the inkblots of the Rorschach test and said, "I'm sorry, but these just look like inkblots to me."?

CHAPTER SUMMARY

1. **What is meant by "theories of personality"?**

   A *theory* is an organized collection of testable ideas used to explain a particular subject matter, such as personality. *Personality* includes the affects, behaviors, and cognitions that characterize an individual in a number of situations over time. Personality also includes those dimensions that we can use to judge people to be different from one another. Personality resides within an individual and includes characteristics that he or she brings to interactions with the environment.

2. **Briefly summarize the major features of Freud's psychoanalytic approach to personality, commenting on his reference to basic instincts, levels of consciousness, the structure of personality, and defense mechanisms.**

   Freud's theory of personality was and is both influential and controversial. There are two basic premises to Freud's theory: a reliance on innate drives to explain human behavior and an acceptance of the role of the unconscious in motivating behavior. Freud proposed that at any given time, we are aware, or conscious, of only a few things. With a little effort, some ideas or memories can be accessed from our *preconscious*. Others—those in our unconscious mind—can be accessed only with great difficulty. Freud believed that *unconscious* motives could explain behaviors that seem irrational and that most of our mental lives take place on the level of the unconscious. Freud believed that human behavior was guided by innate biological drives called *instincts*. He divided instincts into two broad categories: The *life instincts*, or eros, are related to survival and include motives for hunger, thirst, and sex. The *death instincts*, thanatos, are related to destruction, such as depression and aggression. The *libido* is the psychic energy through which the instincts operate.

   The three structures of personality, according to Freud, are the *instinctive id*, operating on the *pleasure principle* and seeking immediate gratification; the *ego*, or sense of self that operates on the *reality principle*, mediating needs in the context of the real world; and the *superego*, or sense of morality, which operates on the *idealistic principle*, attempting to direct one to do what is right and proper. *Defense mechanisms* are unconscious devices employed to defend the ego against feel-

   ings of anxiety. They include *repression*, or motivated forgetting, in which anxiety-producing ideas or experiences are forced into the unconscious; *denial*, in which one refuses to acknowledge the reality of anxiety-producing situations; *rationalization*, in which one generates excuses for anxiety-producing behaviors rather than facing the real reasons for those behaviors; *fantasy*, in which a person uses daydreaming to escape the anxieties of daily living; *projection*, in which one sees in others those traits or desires that make one anxious when seen in oneself; *regression*, in which one retreats to earlier, primitive levels of behavior that were once effective as a means of dealing with anxiety; and *displacement*, in which one's anxiety-producing motives or behaviors are directed at some "safe" object or person rather than at the person for whom they are intended.

3. **What are the essential elements of Freud's psychosexual stages of development?**

   Psychoanalytic theories of personality are based on four assumptions: a) Behavior is influenced by both conscious and unconscious forces; b) the structure of personality develops over time; c) personality develops in stages; and d) an individual's personality develops according to how well an individual moves through the stages of development.

   Freud believed that personality developed in stages, each related to some expression of sexuality, or sensuality. At each of Freud's psychosexual stages, there is a "crisis'" to be resolved. If there were an overinvestment of psychic energy at any stage, a fixation could take place. The first stage of development is the oral stage, in which pleasure and satisfaction derive from oral activities such as sucking, feeding, and noise-making. The second stage is the anal stage, in which the control of bladder and bowel movements becomes a source of satisfaction and pleasure. The third stage is the phallic stage, in which one becomes aware of one's sexuality and forms a close attachment with the opposite-sex parent. During the latency period (which is not a true stage because there is no crisis), sexuality is "put on hold." The final stage is the genital stage, which follows puberty, and wherein there is a reawakening of sexual, sensual desires.

4. **Summarize the contributions of the neo-Freudians, and provide a general statement evaluating the psychoanalytic approach to personality.**

Adler, Jung, and Horney each parted with Freud on theoretical grounds, while remaining basically psychoanalytic in their respective approaches to personality. For Adler, social influences and inferiority complexes mattered much more than did innate drives. Jung was less biological and more positive; he expanded on Freud's view of the unconscious mind, adding the notion of the collective unconscious. Horney rejected the notion of instinctual impulses and discussed instead the concept of basic anxiety and how one reacts to it as the sculptor of one's personality.

The strengths of the psychoanalytic approach include the fact that Freud and other psychoanalytic theorists focused attention on the importance of the childhood years and the role of the unconscious and biological factors in motivating behavior. The greatest weakness of the approach is that many of its central concepts cannot be empirically tested.

5. **What is the essence of the behavioral-learning approach to personality, and what are some of its strengths and weaknesses?**

Many psychologists have argued that personality can be explained using learning principles and observable behavior. Watson emphasized behavior and argued that psychology should abandon mental concepts. Skinner emphasized the notion of conditioning and how one's behaviors are shaped by their consequences. Dollard and Miller tried to explain personality development in terms of learning and habit formation. Bandura stressed the role of observation and social learning in the formation of personality. The behavioral-learning approach has been criticized for dehumanizing personality and being too deterministic. The various learning approaches to personality are not really comprehensive theories. However, on the positive side, the approach demands that terms be carefully defined and verified experimentally.

6. **What is the basic thrust of approaches to personality that are classified as cognitive or humanistic-phenomenological?**

According to the cognitive approach, basic information-processing strategies such as memory and attention intersect with patterns of thought and perception normally thought to be involved in

personality. An early cognitive theory proposed by Kelly suggested that personal constructs, which are a part of long-term memory, direct an individual's thoughts and perceptions. Mischel's approach to personality more clearly linked personality constructs with cognitive psychology. According to Mischel, there are four "person variables" that make up personality. These are: cognitive and behavioral competencies, encoding strategies and personal constructs, subjective stimulus values, and self-regulatory systems and plans. Cantor and Kihlstrom proposed that social intelligence is at the heart of personality. Social intelligence includes all the skills, abilities, and knowledge that a person brings to social situations, and it is used to deal with a wide range of life tasks. Two major life task "packages" are optimism and pessimism, which are characteristic ways that a person deals with life tasks. Although the two approaches are very different, they appear equally successful in dealing with some life tasks.

The humanistic-phenomenological theories of Rogers and Maslow are alike in several ways, emphasizing the integrity of the self and the power of personal development. Both theorists challenge the negativity and biological bias of psychoanalytic theory, as well as the environmental determinism of behaviorism. On the positive side, this approach reminds us of the wholeness of personality and the inherent dangers in trying to break down a complex concept like personality into artificial segments. Another strength of the approach is its focus on personal growth and striving. The approach has been used successfully in psychotherapy. On the negative side, the central concepts of the approach are difficult to test.

7. **What are trait theories of personality?**

A personality trait is a characteristic and distinctive way in which an individual may differ from others. Trait theories are attempts to discover and organize that set of traits which could be used to describe the characteristics of an individual and also to characterize ways in which any individual may differ from others.

8. **Briefly describe the classic approaches to trait theories of Allport, Cattell, and Eysenck, and the more contemporary approach, known as "The Big Five."**

According to the classic trait theory of Allport, there are two varieties of traits: common traits and personal dispositions. The first variety is found in virtually everyone, and the second variety is unique to some individuals. Cattell also divides the world into two varieties of traits: surface traits, which are readily observable, and source traits, from which surface traits develop. Eysenck's model of personality is hierarchical, with three major "supertraits," or dimensions: extraversion-introversion, neuroticism, and psychoticism. Where people fall within these dimensions predicts more common personality traits and behaviors.

More recent research in personality trait theory suggests that, from all of those traits that have been proposed, five emerge most regularly, although there is still no agreement on what to call these dimensions. One version calls them: a) Extraversion-Introversion, b) Agreeableness or Friendliness, c) Conscientiousness or Will, d) Neuroticism, or Stability-Instability, and e) Openness to Experience and Culture. The trait approach has provided a powerful way of describing and measuring personality dimensions. Modern trait theories have made great strides in showing how traits predict behavior. On the other hand, there is still debate over the number of traits that are involved in personality and whether the so-called "Big Five" traits are independent of one another and can adequately represent personality.

9. **How do brain anatomy and physiology relate to personality?**

One biological approach to the study of personality tries to find correlates of personality variables with activity in some prescribed region of the brain. For example, there is reason to believe that where one falls on the dimension or trait of introversion-extraversion is related to the activity of one's ascending reticular activating system. Another approach seeks relationships between consistent personality patterns and particular neurotransmitters. For example, high levels of "sensation-seeking" are correlated with high levels of norepinephrine.

10. **What role does heredity (genetics) play in personality?**

Scientists have long sought to determine the extent to which one's personality is determined by genetic factors (one's "nature") or by the forces and influences of the environment (one's "nurture"). That search continues even now. Indeed, moderate relationships have been found between some genetic make-up and some personality traits, including extraversion, neuroticism, subjective well-being, and each of the so-called "Big Five" traits. Although some aspects of personality may very well be grounded in one's genes, it is inappropriate to say that any aspect of personality "is inherited."

11. **How would you characterize the person-situation debate, and how has it been resolved?**

An issue of interest among psychologists who study personality is the extent to which we can claim that there are internal, individual traits that are consistent over time and situations. An individual's personal characteristics should be discernible at least within a range of situations. The debate over the stability or consistency of personality variables that began in the late 1960s is essentially over. A point of view called *interactionism* has emerged that says that predicting how a person will respond in a certain situation is determined by the interaction of (relatively) stable personality characteristics and that person's perception of the situation.

12. **What are three potential goals of personality assessment, and to what extent is behavioral observation a useful technique?**

Psychologists would like to be able to reliably and validly measure or assess an individual's personality so that they may a) identify and make a proper diagnosis of any psychological disorder, b) construct reasonable theories of personality, or c) use such measurements or assessments to predict future behaviors for that person. Behavioral observation involves drawing inferences about an individual's personality based on observations of his or her overt behaviors. Behavioral observation can be an important tool for assessing personality, particularly when the observations are made in a purposeful, careful, and structured way; if steps are taken to ensure reliability and validity of observations; and if the sample of individuals observed is representative.

13. **How might interviews be helpful in determining a person's personality?**

Interviews simply ask people about their own behaviors and personality traits. The major advantages of the interview are ease and flexibility. An interviewer may expand productive lines of questioning and abandon lines of questioning that are not informative. Unfortunately, unstructured interviews lack validity. On the other hand, structured interviews (which give up flexibility) are as reliable and valid as any psychological test.

13. **Describe the MMPI-2 and the projective techniques, the Rorschach and the TAT in particular.**

Multiphasic instruments attempt to measure several characteristics or traits with the same set of items. The *Minnesota Multiphasic Personality Inventory*, or MMPI, was designed (in the early 1940s and revised as the MMPI-2 in 1990) as an aid to diagnosis. The test includes 567 true/false items that discriminate among persons of differing diagnostic categories and that assess the extent to which the subject is doing a thorough and honest job of answering the questions. There are other multiphasic paper-and-pencil tests, such as the California Personality Inventory or Cattell's *16 PF Questionnaire*, and many tests of individual personality traits.

With a projective technique, the assumption is that, in responding to an ambiguous stimulus, a person will project aspects of his or her personality into test responses. Projective techniques include word association tests, sentence completion tests, the Rorschach test, and the TAT. The *Rorschach inkblot test* is a projective technique that was introduced in 1921 by Hermann Rorschach. The test includes ten cards showing inkblot patterns. An individual is asked what the inkblot represents. Scoring the test involves attending to what the person says, where the person focuses attention, mentions of detail, and how many direct responses are made. The *TAT* is a projective technique introduced by Henry Murray in 1938. The test consists of a series of ambiguous pictures. The individual taking the test is required to tell a story to go with each picture, describing what is going on in the picture and the likely outcome. Scoring is based upon the themes of the stories told by the person being examined. Although the projective techniques continue to be used in clinical practice, there is scant evidence that any of them have any useful degree of reliability or validity.

Motivation and Emotion

10

PREVIEW

In this chapter, our focus will be on questions that begin with *why*. "Why did she do that (as opposed to her doing nothing)?" "Why did she do that (as opposed to her doing something else)?" "Why does she keep doing that (as opposed to her stopping)?" As you can see, the study of motivation gets us involved with attempts to explain the causes of certain behaviors.

We will define motivation and then explore several different theories of motivation. As is often the case, no one approach tells us all we would like to know about motivation, but each adds something to our appreciation of motivated behavior. We look at instincts, needs and drives, incentives, homeostasis, arousal, and cognitive dissonance as concepts that can explain why we do what we do and why we keep on doing it.

Some human drives have a basis in physiology. We will consider temperature regulation and thirst drives. We'll examine eating behaviors, addressing not only why we eat, but also the related issues of overweight, obesity, and the eating disorders. Human sexual motivation is complex, involving forces and pressures beyond the simply biological. We will look at sexual orientation and sexual dysfunctions. Next we will examine motives that have no clear biological basis, called psychologically based motives. These psychologically based motives include achievement, power, and affiliation.

Since becoming a discipline in the late 1900s, psychology has included the study of emotions. Psychologists have learned a great deal about emotions, but they still have some basic questions: What are emotions and where do they come from? How can we increase the frequency and intensity of pleasant emotions and decrease unpleasant ones?

Even though some emotions are unpleasant—fear, shame, jealousy, and rage—most of us would not give up our ability to experience emotions. Such a bargain would mean that we would also give up the capacity to feel love, joy, satisfaction, and ecstasy. Life without these emotions would be flat, cold, and drab.

We begin this discussion of emotions by asking the question: How would you define emotion? We will next look at how scientists have attempted to organize or classify the emotions. We will briefly discuss whether it is possible to experience emotions unconsciously. We then turn to the physiological bases of emotions. Emotions require the central nervous system, to be sure, but it is the autonomic nervous system that is most intimately involved. Ever since William James at the end of the nineteenth century, psychologists have tried to provide a systematic and comprehensive "theory" of emotion. We will briefly review four such attempts. We will discuss the outward display of emotion and how internal emotional states are communicated from one organism to another. Finally, we will briefly discuss frustration and anger and the behavioral consequences of both.

WHAT MOTIVATES US?

Here we are using "motivation" to describe a force that initiates behaviors—that gets an organism going—energized to do something and to keep doing it. Motivation involves two sub-processes. The first is arousal—an organism's level of activation or excitement. The second sub-process provides direction, or focus, to the organism's behaviors. More than being simply aroused and active, a motivated organism must behave with a purpose or goal. Thus, **motivation** is the process that arouses, directs, and maintains behavior.

From the very beginning of psychology, psychologists have tried to develop a theory to summarize motivated behaviors. In short, psychologists have attempted to find one general theory to explain why organisms tend to do what they do. We will review some of the theories psychologists have put forth.

| **motivation** the process that arouses, directs, and maintains behaviors

Courtesy of Randy Wells/Corbis.

Courtesy of James Hager/Getty Images.

Why do salmon swim upstream—against horrific odds? Why do birds build nests as they do? In both cases we may "explain" these behaviors in terms of inborn, innate instincts to do so. However, the concept of instinct has not proven to be useful for explaining human behaviors.

Instincts

During the 1880s, psychologists often explained behaviors in terms of **instincts**—unlearned, complex patterns of behavior that occur in the presence of certain stimuli. Why do birds build nests? A nest-building instinct. When conditions are right, birds build nests. It's what birds do. Why do salmon swim upstream to mate? Instinct. Swimming upstream at mating season is part of a salmon's nature. These behaviors can be modified by the animal's experiences, but the force behind them is unlearned or instinctive. It is simply part of their nature to engage in these behaviors.

Instincts may explain the behaviors of birds and salmon, but what about humans? William James (1890) reasoned that because they are more complex, humans had to have more instincts than do "lower" animals. William McDougall championed the instinctual explanation of human behaviors (McDougall, 1908). He said that 11 basic instincts motivate human behaviors: repulsion, curiosity, flight, reproduction, gregariousness, acquisitiveness, parenting, construction, self-assertion, self-abasement, and pug-

nacity. McDougall discovered not all human behaviors fit into his categories, so he added seven more instincts. Each time a behavior pattern did not fit the categories, psychologists created a new instinct to explain it.

As lists of human instincts got longer and longer, the problem with this approach became obvious—explaining behavior patterns by alluding solely to instinct re-labels the behaviors and explains nothing. Even so, the psychologists who argued for instincts contributed two important ideas to psychology: We engage in some behaviors for reasons that are basically biological, or physiological, and these behaviors are more inherited than learned.

Needs and Drives

Another approach explains the whys of behavior in terms of needs and drives. We will look at two needs and drives theories.

Clark Hull's ideas about motivation were dominant in the 1940s and 1950s (Hull, 1943). In Hull's system, a **need** is defined as a lack or shortage of some biological essential required for survival.

instincts unlearned, complex patterns of behavior that occur in the presence of certain stimuli

need a lack or shortage of some biological essential required for survival

drive a state of tension, arousal, or activation—aimed at satisfying a need

secondary drives those drives that are derived from learning experiences

It is difficult to argue that one would jump out of a plane— even with an experienced co-jumper—in order to satisfy a need to reduce tension. It may be that such folks are seeking a heightened state of arousal.

Courtesy of Darryl Leniuk/Getty Images.

Deprivation gives rise to needs. When an organism is deprived of food, it develops a need for food. Needs give rise to drives. A **drive** is a state of tension, arousal, or activation. If an organism is in a drive state, it is aroused and directed to engage in some behavior to satisfy the drive by reducing the underlying need. Needs produce tensions (drives) that the organism seeks to reduce; hence, this approach explains behaviors in terms of drive reduction.

Whereas instincts are tied to specific patterns of behavior, needs and drives are not. Drives can explain why we do what we do and still allow for the influence of experience and the environment. Going without food may give rise to a need, which in turn gives rise to a drive, but how the organism behaves as a result depends upon that organism's experiences and learning history.

One problem with Hull's drive-reduction approach centers on the biological nature of needs. To claim that needs result only from biological deprivations seems overly restrictive. Perhaps not all of the drives that activate a person's behavior are based on biological needs. Humans often engage in behaviors to satisfy learned drives. These **secondary drives** are a product of learning experiences, as opposed to *primary drives*, which are based on unlearned, physiological needs. In fact, most of the drives that arouse and direct our behaviors have little to do with biology. You may feel you need a new car. Your brother may convince himself that he needs a new set of golf clubs, and you will both work very hard to save the money to buy what you need. You may say you are "driven," but it is difficult to imagine how your new car or your brother's golf clubs could be satisfying some sort of biological need. A lot of advertising is directed at trying to convince people that certain products and services are needed, even though, in fact, they have little to do with survival.

A second problem with Hull's approach is that organisms often continue behaving a certain way even after their biological needs are met. Drives are states of arousal or tension. Hull claims that we behave as we do to reduce tension or arousal. Yet we know that sky divers jump out of airplanes, rock climbers risk life and limb to scale sheer cliffs, monkeys play with mechanical puzzles even when solving those puzzles leads to no other reward, and children explore the pots and pans in kitchen cabinets even when repeatedly told not to. These behaviors do not appear to be reducing tension, do they? We might suggest, as some psychologists have, that these organisms are trying to satisfy an exploration drive, a manipulation drive, or a curiosity drive. But then we risk explaining why people behave as they do by generating longer and longer lists of drives—the same problem we had when we tried to explain behavior in terms of more and more instincts.

So what do these complications to Hull's theory mean? It seems that people often do behave in ways that reduce drives and thereby satisfy needs. How drives are satisfied, or needs are reduced, may reflect each organism's learning history. The concept of drive reduction is a useful one and is still very much with us in psychology, but it is not a complete explanation for motivated behaviors.

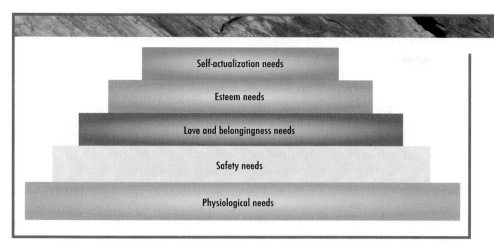

FIGURE 10.1

Maslow's hierarchy of needs.

We associate Abraham Maslow with the humanistic movement in psychology. Humanistic psychologists emphasize the person and his or her psychological growth. Maslow combined his concern for the person with Hull's drive reduction theory and proposed that human behavior does, in fact, respond to needs. Not all of those needs are physiological. Maslow believed that the needs that motivate human action are few and are arranged hierarchically (Maslow, 1943; 1970). Figure 10.1 summarizes Maslow's hierarchy of needs.

Maslow's approach is a stage theory. He proposes that we are motivated first by *physiological needs*—the basic needs related to survival—food, water, and shelter. Until these needs are met, we will not be concerned with anything else. Once physiological needs are under control, we are still motivated, but now by *safety needs*—the need to feel secure, protected from potential dangers. We are now motivated to see to it that the cupboard has food for later, the heating bill is paid, and enough money is saved to protect against sudden calamity. The hierarchical nature of this theory is already clear. We are not going to worry about what we'll be eating tomorrow if there's not enough to eat today, but if today's needs are taken care of, we can then focus on the future.

Once we meet our safety needs, we become concerned about *love and belongingness needs*—needs for someone else to care about us, to love us. If these needs are satisfied, we become concerned with meeting our *needs for esteem*. We want to be recognized for our achievements and efforts. These needs are not physiological, but social. Now our behaviors are motivated by our awareness of others and a concern for their approval. We move on to higher stages in the hierarchy only if needs at lower stages are met.

Ultimately, we may reach the highest stage in Maslow's hierarchy: the *need for self-actualization*. We self-actualize when we become the best we can be, taking the fullest advantage of our potential. We are self-actualizing when we strive to be as creative or productive as possible. Pervin (2001) describes self-actualization as "the tendency of an

A homeless person who spends the better part of his day on the sidewalk begging food is likely to be focusing on needs low on Maslow's hierarchy. Only when these needs are met might we expect any concern at all for matters of belongingness, self-esteem, or self-actualization.

Courtesy of Viviane Moos/Corbis.

organism to grow from a simple entity to a complex one, to move from dependence toward independence, from fixity and rigidity to a process of change and freedom of expression" (p. 177).

Maslow's arrangement of needs in a hierarchy reflects the values of Western culture, particularly the values of individualism and achievement. The theory, after all, is about how individuals working hard can overcome obstacles, achieve goals, and satisfy needs. People achieve at different levels and reach different levels on Maslow's hierarchy. Some never get beyond basic survival needs. Few persons ever fully achieve self-actualization. Most Americans meet their basic needs but never fully satisfy their social needs.

As a comprehensive theory of human motivation, Maslow's hierarchy has some difficulties. Perhaps the biggest stumbling block is that the world will not cooperate with the theory. Maslow's neat ordering of needs does not always fit how people really behave. Individuals will freely give up satisfying basic survival needs for the sake of "higher" principles (as in hunger strikes). For the sake of love, people may abandon their own needs for safety and security. Little empirical research supports Maslow's approach to ranking needs in a hierarchy, but the theory still has intuitive appeal. As a result, Maslow's theory of human motivation still has admirers both inside and outside of psychology.

BEFORE YOU GO ON

1. How do psychologists define *motivation,* and how have they used the concepts of instincts, needs, and drives to account for motivated behaviors?

A Point to Ponder or Discuss
When they are hungry, chickens—even very young chickens—peck at the ground as if searching for bits of grain. How could you determine whether this behavior pattern is instinctive or learned?

Incentives

Another alternative to a drive reduction approach to motivation focuses on the end state, or goal, of behavior, not needs or drives within the organism. In this view, organisms are motivated by external stimuli, or **incentives**. Incentives are external events that are said to pull our behavior from without. Drives are internal events that push our behavior from within. We are pushed by internal drives, but pulled by external incentives.

When a mountain climber says she climbs a mountain "because it is there," she is indicating that she is motivated by an incentive. After enjoying a large meal, we may order a piece of cherry cheesecake, not because we need it in any physiological sense, but because it is there on the dessert cart and looks so good (and because previous experience tells us that it is likely to taste good as well).

Some parents want to know how to motivate their child to clean up his or her room. We can interpret this case in terms of establishing goals or incentives. What the parents want is a clean room, and they would like to have the child clean it. What those parents really want to know is how they can get their child to value, work for, and be reinforced by a clean room. If they want the child to be motivated to clean the room, the child needs to learn the value or incentive of having a clean room. How to teach a child that a clean room is a thing to be valued is another story, involving other incentives the child values. For now, let us acknowledge that establish-

incentives the end states, or goals, of behaviors that organisms are motivated to attain ing a clean room as a valued goal is the major task at hand, and having a clean room is not an innate, inborn need.

If you think this sounds like our discussion of operant conditioning, you are right. Remember, the basic tenet of operant conditioning is that behaviors are controlled by their consequences. We tend to do (are motivated to do) what leads to reinforcement (positive incentives), and we tend not to do what leads to punishment or failure of reinforcement (negative incentives).

Balance or Equilibrium

A concept that has proven useful in understanding motivation is balance or equilibrium. The idea is that we are motivated to reach and maintain a state of balance. But what are we motivated to balance? Sometimes balance involves physiological processes that need to be kept at some level or within a restricted range of activity. Sometimes equilibrium is required among our thoughts or cognitions. We will review three approaches to motivation that emphasize maintaining a state of equilibrium, or functioning at an optimum level: homeostasis, arousal, and cognitive dissonance.

Walter Canon was among the first to refer to a need for equilibrium (1932). Cannon was concerned with our internal physiological reactions, and his term for a state of balance within those reactions was **homeostasis**. The idea is that each of our physiological processes has a balanced set point of operation. An organism's set point is a level of activity that is normal or most suitable. When anything upsets this balance, we become motivated, driven to do whatever we can to return to our set point, that optimal homeostatic level of activity. If we drift only slightly from our set point, we are returned to homeostasis by our physiological mechanisms without our even being aware of the change. If automatic processes do not return us to homeostasis, we may have to take action, motivated by the drive to return to our set point and regain homeostasis.

Everyone has normal set levels for body temperature, blood pressure, heart rate, basal metabolism (the rate at which energy is used by bodily functions), and so on. If any of these processes deviates from its set point, or homeostatic level, we become motivated to do something that will return us to our state of balance. Cannon's concept of homeostasis was devised to explain physiological processes, but the ideas of balance and optimal level of operation have been applied to psychological processes as well.

Arousal refers to one's overall level of activation or excitement. A person's level of arousal may change from day to day and within the same day. After a good night's sleep and a brisk morning shower, you may have a high arousal level. (Your arousal may also be high as your instructor moves through class handing out exams.) Late at night, after a busy day at school, you may have a low level of arousal. Your arousal level is at its lowest when you are in the deepest stages of sleep.

Arousal theories of motivation (Berlyne, 1960, 1971; Duffy, 1962; Hebb, 1955) claim that there is an optimal level of arousal (an "arousal set point") that organisms are motivated to maintain. Remember, drive reduction theories argue that we are motivated to reduce tension or arousal by satisfying the needs that give rise to drives. Arousal theories argue that sometimes we seek ways to increase arousal to maintain our optimal arousal level. If you are bored and in a rut, you may think going to an action-adventure movie is a good idea. On the other hand, if you've had a busy, hectic day, you may want to just stay home and do nothing.

This approach is like Cannon's idea of homeostasis but in terms that are more general. It suggests that for any situation there is a "best," or most efficient, level of arousal. To do well on an exam, for example, requires that a student have a certain level of arousal. If a student is tired, bored, or just doesn't care, the student will probably perform poorly. If, on the other hand, a student is so worried,

arousal one's overall level of activation or excitement

homeostasis a state of balance or equilibrium among internal physiological processes

FIGURE 10.2

For each task we attempt, there is an optimal level of arousal. What that level is depends on several factors, including the difficulty of the task. In other words, it is possible to be too aroused (motivated), just as it is possible to be underaroused (Hebb, 1955).

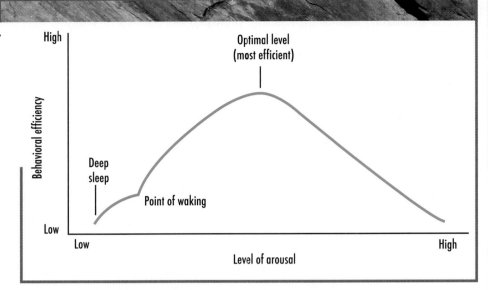

uptight, and anxious that he or she can barely function, the student will also probably perform poorly. The relation between arousal and performance efficiency is depicted in Figure 10.2.

Arousal theory also takes into account the difficulty or complexity of the activity. For simple tasks, a high level of arousal may be optimal, but that same level of arousal would be disastrous for difficult, complex tasks (Brehm & Sell, 1989). For example, students who are judged to be poorly, moderately, or highly motivated tried a series of difficult anagrams (identifying a word whose letters have been scrambled). Highly motivated students did significantly worse than did the moderately motivated students (Ford et al., 1985). For very simple tasks—such as pounding on a large rod every time it pops into view—the higher the arousal the better. The idea that optimal levels of arousal vary with the difficulty of a task can be traced to a 1908 article by Yerkes and Dodson—even though the concept of "arousal" did not reappear in the research literature until many decades later (Winton, 1987).

For some reason, optimal levels of arousal vary widely from person to person. Some people seem to need and seek particularly high levels of arousal and excitement in their lives. Such people are referred to as "sensation seekers" (Zuckerman et al., 1978, 1980). They enjoy skydiving or mountain climbing and look forward to the challenge of driving in heavy city traffic. In fact, some evidence suggests a genetic basis for individual differences in sensation seeking, or risk-taking (Ebstein et al., 1996).

How deep does the human need for equilibrium go? Many psychologists recognize our desire to maintain a state of balance among our ideas or beliefs (our cognitions), as well as among our physiological processes and levels of arousal. That is, we are motivated to maintain what Leon Festinger (1957) calls a state of consonance among our cognitions.

For example, you believe yourself to be a good student. You study hard for an exam in biology and think that you are prepared. You judge the exam to be a fairly easy one. But you fail the test! That's hard to accept. You believe you studied adequately and that the test wasn't difficult. But now you also know you failed the test. These cognitions do not fit together. They are not consonant; they are not balanced. You are experiencing **cognitive dissonance**—a state of tension or discomfort that exists when we hold and are aware of inconsistent cognitions. Festinger argues, we are motivated to bring about a change in

cognitive dissonance a motivating state of tension or discomfort that exists when we hold or are aware of inconsistent ideas, beliefs, or cognitions

our system of cognitions when we experience cognitive dissonance. You may come to believe you are not such a good student after all. You may come to believe that your paper was unfairly graded. Or you may come to believe you are a poor judge of an exam's difficulty. This theory does not predict what will happen, but it does predict that cognitive dissonance produces motivation to return to a balanced state of cognitive consonance.

These days, almost all smokers experience cognitive dissonance. They know smoking is dangerous, yet they continue to smoke. Some reduce their dissonance by convincing themselves that, although smoking is bad for a person's health in general, it really isn't that bad for them in particular, at least not when compared to perceived "benefits." Another possible dissonance reducer is convincing one's self that if they stopped smoking, they would gain weight (which is seldom true) (White, McKee, & O'Malley, 2007).

Summing Up: Applying Motivational Concepts

You and your friends have spent a relaxing spring day backpacking in the mountains. After a full day in the fresh mountain air, everyone has eaten large servings of beef stew and baked beans. You have even found room for dessert: toasted marshmallows and a piece of chocolate squeezed between two graham crackers.

As your friends settle around the campfire and darkness begins to overtake the campsite, you excuse yourself. You need to walk off some of that dinner, so you decide to take a stroll down a narrow trail. As you meander down the trail, you feel totally relaxed, at peace with the world. When you are about 200 yards from the campsite, you think you hear a strange noise in the woods off to your left. Looking back down the trail, you can barely see the campfire's glow through the trees and underbrush. Well, maybe you'd better not venture

Courtesy of Don Mason/Blend Images/Corbis.

much farther, perhaps just over that ridge, and then—suddenly—a large growling black bear emerges from behind a dense thicket! It takes one look at you, bares its teeth, and lets out a mighty roar!

In this situation, and in many similar but less dramatic ones, we can be sure of one thing: Your reaction will involve both emotional and motivational states. You will certainly become emotional. Encountering a bear in the woods is not something that one does with reason and intellect alone. You will be motivated to do something; getting away from that bear seems reasonable. We will return to this meeting-a-bear-in-the-woods story soon, when we discuss emotion.

For now, let us apply the theoretical approaches we have been discussing to explain your behavior. Let's say that, upon seeing the bear, you throw your arms straight up in the air, scream at the top of your lungs, and sprint back to camp. Your friends, still sitting around the campfire, can see and hear you coming. How might they explain your behaviors?

1. "Clearly, it's a matter of instinct. Humans have a powerful and useful instinct for avoiding large animals in the wild. In this instance, running away is just an unlearned,

Have you ever bought a car, thinking that you just made the best deal possible, only to discover later that the car had dozens of problems, including a few major—and expensive— ones? If so, you probably experienced cognitive dissonance, wondering how anyone as bright as you are could have made such an error in judgment.

natural, instinctive reaction to a specific stimulus."

2. "No, I think that the fear that arose upon seeing the bear created a tension—a drive—that needed to be relieved. There were several options available, but in your need to reduce your fear, you chose to run away."

3. "Why do you folks keep relying on all this internal instinct-need-drive nonsense? Previous learning experience, even if it was secondhand, or vicarious, taught you that bears in the wild are incentives to be avoided. They are negative goals. You ran back here simply to reach the goal of safety with us, your friends."

4. "I see your reaction as an attempt to maintain a state of equilibrium or balance. Seeing that bear was certainly an emotional experience that increased many physiological functions. Your running away was just one way to try to return those physiological functions to their normal, homeostatic levels."

5. "Why get so complicated with physiological functions? Why not just say that your overall arousal level was much higher than normal—higher than you wanted it to be—so you ran away from the bear simply to lower your level of arousal?"

6. "The same argument can be made for your cognitions—and cognitive dissonance reduction. You know that you like being safe and free of pain. You believe that bears in the woods can be a significant source of pain. These two ideas are in conflict. You needed to do something to resolve the dissonance. In this case, you chose to run away."

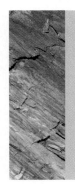

BEFORE YOU GO ON

2. How can incentives, homeostasis, arousal, and cognitive dissonance be useful in explaining motivated behaviors?

A Point to Ponder or Discuss
You hear a teacher moan, "Teaching would be so much easier if my students were motivated." What do you suppose that teacher is moaning about? How would you advise this teacher to motivate his or her students?

TEMPERATURE REGULATION

Now that we have reviewed a few theoretical approaches to motivation, we can turn to a few specific examples. As we go through this discussion, we will follow convention and use the term *drive* when talking about activators of behavior that have a known biological or physiological basis (for example, a hunger drive) and will use the term *motive* for those that do not (for example, a power motive).

You probably don't give your body temperature much thought beyond the fuzzy notion that 98.6 degrees Fahrenheit is "normal." Indeed, you probably do not consider regulating body temperature a motivated behavior. However, it is in the sense that you are motivated to maintain homeostasis when your body's automatic responses fail to. Whenever anything happens to raise or lower your body temperature above or below its homeostatic set point range, you become motivated. You become driven to return your body temperature to its normal, balanced 98.6 degrees. In passing, body

Courtesy of image100/Corbis.

Courtesy of image100/Corbis.

We are driven to maintain our body temperatures within rather strict limits. When our autonomic nervous systems cannot adequately deal with temperature extremes, we will be motivated to do something to raise or lower our body temperatures in order to return to some homeostatic level.

temperature fluctuates throughout the day, and 98.2 degrees is a better estimate of normal, average body temperature (Mackowiak et al., 1992).

Imagine that you are outside on a bitterly cold day and are improperly dressed for the low temperature and high wind. Your body temperature starts to drop. Automatically your body responds to elevate your temperature back to its normal level: Blood vessels in the hands and feet constrict, forcing blood back to the center of the body to conserve heat (as a result, your lips turn blue); you shiver (those involuntary muscle movements create small amounts of heat energy); and you get "goose bumps" as the skin thickens to insulate against the cold. These are the sorts of automatic physiological reactions Cannon had in mind when he wrote about homeostasis.

Now imagine that you are fully dressed and walking across a desert at noon on a hot day in August. Your temperature rises. Automatically, blood is diverted to the surface of your body, and your face becomes flushed. You perspire, and as moisture on the surface of the skin evaporates, the skin is cooled, as is the blood now near the surface—all in an attempt to return your body's temperature to its homeostatic level.

Two centers deep within your brain act as a thermostat and initiate the temperature regulation process. They are located in the hypothalamus, a midbrain structure near the limbic system that is involved in several physiological drives (see Figure 10.3). One center is particularly sensitive to elevated body temperatures, and the other to lowered temperatures. Together they act to mobilize the body when normal balance is upset. If your body's temperature does not return to normal, you may be driven to take some voluntary action. You may have to get inside, out of the cold or heat. You may need to put on or take off clothing. You may need to turn on the furnace or the air conditioner. Over and above what your brain may do automatically, you may have to engage in learned behaviors in order to maintain homeostasis.

FIGURE 10.3

A section of the human brain, showing the location of the hypothalamus.

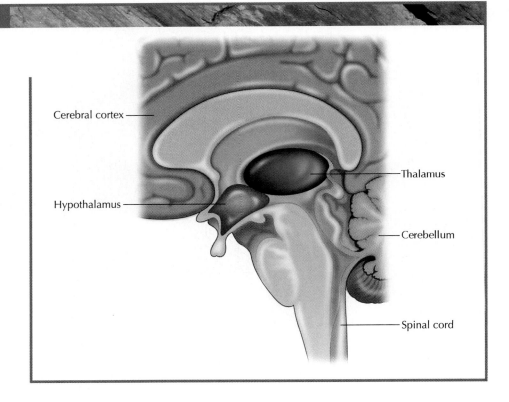

Cerebral cortex

Hypothalamus

Thalamus

Cerebellum

Spinal cord

THE THIRST DRIVE AND DRINKING BEHAVIORS

We need water for survival. If we don't drink, we die. As the need for water increases, it gives rise to a thirst drive. The intriguing issue is not so much that we need to drink, but how we know we are thirsty. What actually causes us to seek liquid and drink it?

Internal Physiological Cues

For a long time, psychologists thought that we drank to relieve discomfort caused by the dryness of our mouths and throats. The unpleasantness of a dry mouth and throat can cause a person to drink, but there must be more to drinking behavior than this. Animals with their salivary glands removed, whose mouths and throats are constantly dry, drink no more than normal animals (they drink smaller amounts more frequently). Normal bodily processes (such as urination, exhaling, and perspiration) cause us to lose about

two liters of water a day (Levinthal, 1983). That water needs to be replaced, but what motivates us to do so?

About two-thirds of the fluid in our bodies is within our cells (cellular); the remaining one-third is in the spaces between our cells (free water). The body has two mechanisms sensitive to losses of fluid (Adrogué & Madius, 2000). The hypothalamus monitors fluid loss within cells. One small center turns on the thirst drive when fluid levels are low, and another turns off the thirst drive when the body has enough fluid. When the body has a shortage of water between cells, the brain stimulates a thirst drive through a complex chain of events involving the kidneys. The kidneys stimulate the production of a hormone that leads to a thirst drive (Stephanides, Wilson, & Sinert, 2001).

External Psychological Cues

Sometimes we drink because we have a physiological need for water. At other times, however, we drink because of external factors or incentives. The aroma of freshly brewed coffee could stimulate us to order a second (unneeded) cup. A frosty glass of iced tea may look too good to refuse. We might drink a cold beer or a soda simply because it tastes good, whether we need the fluid it contains or not.

Here's an interesting example of the interaction of physiological needs and learned behaviors. Anyone who exercises should know to replenish the water lost to perspiration. Particularly when it's hot, athletes are reminded to drink lots of fluids. Actually, athletes used to get far different advice. Up until the late 1960s, they were advised not to drink during exercise because it was believed that ingesting fluids diminished athletic performance (Noakes, 2003). In 1969, an article appeared with the title, "The Danger of an Inadequate Water Intake during Marathon Running" (Wyndham & Strydom, 1969). Many people misinterpret the sensible advice. They drink significantly more fluids (water or "sports drinks") than they have lost during their exercise. The results can be tragic. Indeed, the *over-consumption* of a sports drink before and during the 2002 Boston Marathon was cited as the cause of one runner's death during the race (Hew et al., 2003; Noakes, 2003). The issue is largely one of homeostasis: A person should replace lost fluids but not go beyond the homeostatic, set point level.

Courtesy of tetra images/Getty Images.

We do *need water, and sometimes we drink because we are thirsty. But, in many cases, we drink because a beverage looks tasty, or because others around us are drinking, or because past experience tells us that this beverage tastes good.*

Psychological and environmental factors are still important in satisfying even a drive with obvious physiological roots like thirst. *What* we drink will be influenced by previous learning experiences. Maybe we have seen a commercial for a sports drink and been influenced to try it. Finally, the environment also plays a key role in what we drink because we can only drink what we have. We may want a particular brand of sports drink, but we will probably settle for whatever is in the vending machine at the gym.

BEFORE YOU GO ON

3. How is temperature regulation a physiological drive?
4. What factors motivate us to drink?

A Point to Ponder or Discuss

A marathon runner knows the importance of replenishing bodily fluids during practice and during a race, but also knows not to overdo it. How can that runner discover exactly how much water or fluid to drink?

THE HUNGER DRIVE AND EATING BEHAVIORS

Our need for food is as obvious as our need for water. If we don't eat, we die. Again, the more interesting questions center upon the sources of human motivation. What gives rise to the hunger drive? What motivates us to eat? As it happens, many factors motivate a person to eat. Some are physiological. Some are psychological and reflect learning experiences. Some involve social pressures. In this section we will review these factors and also take a look at two food-related problems: obesity and eating disorders.

Internal Physiological and Genetic Factors

How do we know that we are hungry? When we skip a meal, we feel a rumble in our stomach. Are these rumblings a reliable cue for hunger? Walter Cannon designed an ingenious experiment to find out. He had subjects swallow an uninflated balloon. The balloon was inflated so that it pressed against the stomach wall. Researchers attached one end of a small tube to the balloon and the other end to an instrument that recorded each time the subject's stomach contracted. A telegraph key also was attached to the recording device. The subject was to press the key each time he felt a hunger pang. Cannon found that subjects' feelings of hunger correlated closely with stomach contractions, leading him to conclude that stomach contractions were the motivators for eating.

However, the role of stomach contractions in hunger is not quite so simple. People and animals with no stomachs and people and animals with intact stomachs eat the same amounts of food. In short, cues from our stomachs don't seem to be important in producing our hunger drive. Researchers have identified two structures that seem to be involved in the hunger drive: the hypothalamus (again) and the liver.

Theories of hunger that focus on the hypothalamus are *dual-center theories* because two regions in the hypothalamus are involved in food intake. The ventromedial hypothalamus is a "no-eat" center that lets us know when we've had enough, and the lateral hypothalamus is an "eat" center that gives rise to feelings of hunger (van den Pol, 1999). Removing or lesioning the eat center (leaving the no-eat center intact) in rats leads to starvation, but lesioning the no-eat center (leaving the eat center intact) leads to extreme overeating. Electrical stimulation of the no-eat center causes even a food-deprived rat to stop eating (Friedman & Stricker, 1976).

Although these animal studies indicate the hypothalamus is involved in hunger, they do not explain why normal organisms eat. What activates the brain's hunger-regulating centers in a normal organism? Scientists do not know for certain, but several hypotheses have been suggested. Some scientists propose that the body responds to levels of blood sugar (glucose), that can converted into energy (metabolized) for the body's use. When we haven't eaten for a while and our levels of glucose are low, we are stimulated to eat. When our glucose levels are adequate, we stop eating. Glucose levels may be monitored for us by our liver.

Another view holds that we respond, through a complex chain of events, to levels of fat stored in our bodies. When fat stores are adequately filled, we feel no hunger. If fat supplies are depleted, we begin to feel hunger. Once again, the liver is involved in monitoring levels of stored fat.

A third hypothesis emphasizes internal, physiological cues and relies heavily on the concept of set point, or homeostasis. Proponents of this position claim that a person's overall body weight—like blood pressure, heart rate, or body temperature—is physiologically regulated (Nisbett, 1972). If this theory is correct, the body makes many adjustments to maintain the set point: "Being so regulated, weight normally is maintained at a particular level or set point, not only by the control of food intake, as is often assumed, but also by complementary adjustments in energy utilization and expenditure" (Keesey & Powley, 1986). If this theory is accurate, it may explain why dieting and exercise programs often fail. If weight is governed by set points and homeostasis, weight loss should trigger an effort to return to the set point level. The result may be to abandon the diet, cut down on exercise, or both. Conversely, if a person eats too much—more than is necessary to keep a homeostatic level of energy consumption and storage—he or she will be motivated to expend energy to return to set point levels. Scientists still do not know what mechanisms determine a person's set point body weight and energy utilization levels to begin with. Evidence suggests these set points are influenced by genetics and feeding patterns during infancy.

Powerful genetic forces may determine a person's body size and the distribution of fat within the body (Stunkard, 1988; Stunkard et al., 1986). One experiment looked at the effects of overeating on 12 pairs of adult (ages 19 to 27) male identical twins (Bouchard et al., 1990). After eating normally for two weeks, the men were required to consume 1,000 excess calories six days a week over a 100-day period. By the end of the study, some twin pairs had gained considerably more weight than other twin pairs. Yet, there were virtually no differences in weight gain within each pair of twins. In addition, where the excess weight was stored (for example, the waist or hips) also varied among pairs, but not within twin pairs. The researchers concluded that "the most likely explanation for the intrapair similarity . . . is that genetic factors are involved" (p. 1477). A related study looked at the body weights of twins reared together or apart and found that regardless of where or how the twins were reared, there was a significant relationship between genetic similarity and body mass (Stunkard et al., 1990). Even early childhood environments had little or no effect. Such data tell us that genetic factors are important in both the ultimate determination of body weight and size and the distribution of fat within the body. But these data do not tell us that the only factors in the determination of body size are genetic (Brownell & Rodin, 1994; Sobal & Stunkard, 1989).

There is one other series of studies to consider before we leave this discussion. In 1994 researchers at the Howard Hughes Medical Institute of Rockefeller University announced that they had isolated a specific gene related to eating and obesity. They called it the obese gene, or *the ob gene* (Barinaga, 1995). This gene controls the amount of a hormone named *leptin* (after the Greek word for thin) in the bloodstream. This hormone tells the brain how much fat is stored in the body. When something goes wrong with the gene, insufficient amounts of ob protein are available, and the organism continues to eat, "unaware" that it already has adequate (or more than adequate) fat stored away. The result is an overweight organism (Batterham et al., 2003; Friedman, 2000).

External Psychological Factors

We know from our own experiences that eating behaviors are influenced by factors beyond our physiology. We often respond to external cues. The stimulus properties of foods—aroma, taste, or appearance—may be enough to get us to eat. We may not want any dessert after a large meal until the waitress shows us a piece of chocolate cake. Eating that cake has nothing to do with internal physiological conditions (reminding us of the incentive approach to motivation described earlier).

Sometimes people eat more from habit than from need. We may fall into habits of eating at certain times, tied more to the clock than to internal cues from our bodies. "It's 12 o'clock. It's lunch time; so let's eat." Some people seem unable to watch TV without poking food into their mouths, a behavioral pattern motivated more by learning than by physiology.

Occasionally we eat simply because others around us are eating. This "socially facilitated" eating has been observed for many years and in several species (Harlow, 1932; Tolman, 1969). If a caged chicken is allowed to eat its fill of grain, it eventually stops eating. When other hungry chickens are placed in the cage and begin to eat, the full chicken starts right in eating again. Its behaviors are not noticeably different from those of the chickens just added to the cage.

Overweight people may be less sensitive to internal hunger cues and more sensitive to external eating cues from the environment (Schachter, 1971), although there is evidence that this is not always true (Rodin, 1981). We do know that many people who are overweight tend to underestimate the amount of food (calories) they eat each day, even when they are in a controlled weight-loss program. They fail to lose weight because they really are not dieting, even though they believe they are. They also tend to overestimate their level of exercise and physical activity (Lightman et al., 1992).

An intriguing phenomenon related to environmental pressures for eating is the so-called *French paradox*: the observation that the mortality rate from heart disease is substantially lower among the French than among Americans. This is true in spite of the fact that the French have higher blood cholesterol levels and eat a highly palatable diet containing much more fat, including saturated fat (Rozin et al., 1999). The French also are significantly leaner than Americans. Several hypotheses have been advanced to explain this paradox. One of the more popular—although not necessarily more important—is that the French drink significantly more red wine than do Americans, and, in moderation, red wine can be beneficial for cardiovascular health (Renaud & Logeril, 1992). A recent study suggests that, although the French take much longer to eat, they eat significantly smaller portions (Rozin et al., 2003). Even portions of foods available in supermarkets are smaller in France than in the U.S. The authors suggest that researchers focus more on the cultural and social factors that surround the eating experience. Another hypothesis is that the lower rate of obesity among the French is due to a statistical artifact (Law & Wald, 1999). Over the past decades, the French have been consuming foods with greater levels of animal fats. It takes several years for the effects of higher fat consumption to show up in health statistics. Thus, in a few years the French (as well other Europeans whose diets have similarly changed) may show obesity rates comparable to those in the United States (Baarschers, 2005).

BEFORE YOU GO ON

5. List some internal and external factors that motivate eating behaviors.

A Point to Ponder or Discuss
What accounts for the gradual, but measurable changes in the diets of Europeans over the last few decades?

Obesity

We don't see the gradual increase in size of the people on our planet as an epidemic, but we should. Americans have become more obese: "The average weight of Americans increased consistently over the last half of the twentieth century" (Harnack, Jeffery, & Boutelle, 2000, p. 1479). The health consequences of obesity are global: "Obesity claims an increasing number of lives worldwide" (Kelner & Helmuth, 2003, p. 845). Overweight and obesity have technical definitions, expressed in terms of the *body mass index*, or *BMI*. The body mass index is the quotient of a person's weight (in kilograms) divided by the square of the person's height (in meters), or BMI = kg/m^2. A body mass index score between 19.9 and 25 indicates overweight, and a BMI score of 30 or more indicates obesity.

According to the Centers for Disease Control (2005a), an estimated 65 percent of American adults 20 years and older can be classified as overweight or obese (a BMI of at least 25). Additionally, the CDC (2008a) estimates that 35 percent of American adult men are obese (a BMI of 30 or more).

Data for overweight children (6–11 years old) are sobering as well. According to the CDC (2008b), compared to the years spanning 1976–1980 where 6.5 percent of 6–11 year-old children were classified as overweight, there were more overweight children between 2003–2004 (18.8%). Similar increases were shown for children aged 2–5 years (an increase from 5% to 13.9%) and aged 12–19 (an increase from 5% to 17.4%). The news is equally bad for male and female children aged 12–19 years who are white, non-Hispanic black, and Mexican American. For all three groups there were substantial increases of overweight children from 1988–1994 to 2003–2004 (CDC, 2008c). However, the greatest increase in this age range was for non-Hispanic black females who showed an increase

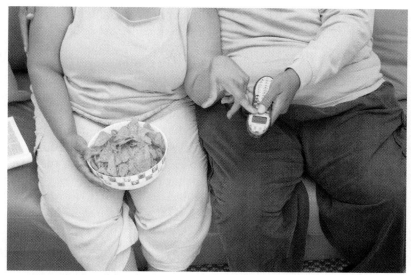

Courtesy of moodboard/Corbis.

Obesity is reaching epidemic proportions, and the best long-term response is making significant lifestyle changes in terms of caloric intake and exercise.

from 13.2 percent (1988–1994) to 25.4 percent (2003–2004). The data are also dismal for black and Hispanic youngsters (ages 4 to 12), for whom the percentage of those who are obese more than doubled between 1986 and 1998 (Strauss & Pollack, 2001). Severe or morbid obesity is indicated by a BMI of at least 40, or more than 100 pounds overweight. A typical male with a BMI of 40 would be 5-foot-10 and weigh 300 pounds. Think about this: In the 14 years between 1986 and 2000, the prevalence of severe obesity quadrupled from about 1 in 200 Americans to 1 in 50. That's over 4 million persons (Sturm, 2003). A recent study of 27,000 people from 52 countries confirmed that obesity is a significant risk factor for heart attacks. Interestingly, the standard body-mass index was only slightly related to heart attacks. What mattered more—in this worldwide sample—was waist and hip circumferences, particularly the ratio of waist size to hip size (Yusuf et al., 2005). The implication is that simply weighing too much is less important than is carrying the bulk of that weight around one's waist.

So what causes obesity and what can be done about it? Part of the answer is genetic. Some people are born with a genetic predisposition to become over-weight. Remember, simply inheriting such a predisposition does not make a person fat; it may be easier for such people to gain weight and more difficult for them to lose it, however. Scientists are trying to find specific genes (or sets of genes) that are more common in persons who are obese and have difficulty controlling their appetites or their eating behaviors (Couce et al., 1997; Farooqi et al., 2003; Guttmacher & Collins, 2003; Branson et al., 2003). As with so many other phenomena, obesity is related to a complex interaction of several genetic factors and the environment (Centers for Disease Control and Prevention, 2005b).

The causes of obesity are partly at the level of biochemistry and hormones. We learned the protein *leptin* plays a major role in regulating eating behaviors by providing feedback of a sense of being hungry or of being full. As it happens, people who become obese seem relatively insensitive to the messages provided by this protein, but other related hormones (peptide YY3–36, for instance) do seem to be effective both for persons of normal weight and for those who are obese or overweight (Batterham et al., 2003; Bloom, 2003).

The bad news for overweight persons looking for a quick fix from the pharmaceutical industry is that those chemicals that appear to influence appetite and eating carry serious side effects (Sinton, Fitch, & Gershenfeld, 1999). And, as one researcher put it, "the body's weight-control systems have apparently been designed to protect more against weight loss than weight gain" (Marx, 2003, p. 846). The good news is that environmental, cultural, and behavioral factors (over which one might have some control) also contribute in a significant way to weight gain (CDC, 2008d). Remember our earlier discussion of the French paradox as one example. The so-called obesity epidemic is at least in part induced by an environment that promotes eating large quantities of food (Brownell, 2002; Hill & Peters, 1998).

Even the experts disagree on whether dieting can be effective in the long run (Brownell, 1993, 2002). The long term results of dieters are not encouraging: "Fully 95 percent of those starting a weight-loss program will return to their original weight within five years" (Martin et al., 1991, p. 528). Surely, you have heard the message before: Consistent, long-term weight loss requires a shift in lifestyle. Eat a little less; exercise a little more. The only problem for this regimen—particularly in a society that is geared to near-instant gratification—is that results will be slow in coming. One team of researchers estimates that small changes in behavior, such as 15 minutes per day of walking or eating one or two fewer bites at each meal could prevent weight gain for most of the population (Hill et al., 2003).

Eating Disorders

Few of us eat properly all the time. Some of us simply eat too much—too many saturated fats in particular—sometimes resulting in overweight or obesity. In contrast, other people eat too little. When a person refuses to maintain a normal weight, he or she is probably suffering from an eating disorder. The two most common eating disorders are anorexia nervosa and bulimia nervosa. They are separate disorders, but a person can show symptoms of both at the same time. Indeed, some researchers suggest that there is but one eating disorder with different manifestations (VanderHam et al., 1997). Approximately 11 million Americans suffer from eating disorders, over 90 percent of them women (National Eating Disorders Association, 2008).

Anorexia nervosa is characterized by an inability (or refusal) to maintain one's body weight. It is essentially a condition of self-starvation, accompanied by a fear of becoming fat and a feeling of being overweight in spite of being considerably underweight (more than 15 percent below normal) (APA, 2000). The anorexic person stays abnormally

anorexia nervosa an eating disorder characterized by an inability (or refusal) to maintain one's body weight thin by eating far less, or being more physically active, or both. Eating disorders have a mortality rate of nearly 20 percent. The mortality rate from these disorders is greater than for any other psychological disorder, including depression (Sullivan, 1995; Vitiello & Lederhendler, 2000). Among females ages 15–24 in the general population, eating disorders have a mortality rate about 12 times higher than the death rate due to all other causes combined (Spearing, 2001).

Bulimia nervosa (or simply, bulimia) is characterized by episodes of binge eating followed by purging—usually self-induced vomiting or the use of laxatives to rapidly rid the body of just-eaten food (APA, 2000). Binge eating episodes are often well planned, anticipated with a great deal of pleasure, and involve rapidly eating large amounts of high-calorie, sweet-tasting food. Like the anorexic patient, the person with bulimia is very likely to be female, upper class, and concerned about weight (Mulholland & Mintz, 2001). Unlike a person with anorexia nervosa, a bulimic patient need not be well below normal body weight. Another difference involves denial: "The anorexic denies to others and herself that any problem or abnormal eating behavior exists, whereas the bulimic usually denies the existence of a problem to others, but clearly recognizes that her eating is abnormal" (Sherman & Thompson, 1990, p. 4). Additionally, bulimia nervosa (but not anorexia) is strongly associated with impulsivity, which shows itself in sexual promiscuity, suicide attempts, drug abuse, and stealing or shoplifting (Matsunaga et al., 2000; Polivy & Herman, 2002).

What causes eating disorders, and what can be done to treat them effectively? Eating disorders have several interacting causes. The value that Western cultures place on thinness is certainly one factor. We are constantly being bombarded with messages that communicate the same theme: "To be thin is good; to be fat is bad." Many young girls idolize super-thin fashion models, dancers, and

Courtesy of Peter Dazeley/Getty Images.

Some people are simply thin, but some who are significantly under normal body weight may be suffering from an eating disorder, such as bulimia—which involves eating and then purging.

bulimia nervosa an eating disorder characterized by episodes of binge eating followed by purging—usually self-induced vomiting or the use of laxatives to rapidly rid the body of just-eaten food

entertainers. The average American woman is 5'4" and 140 pounds, yet the average American fashion model is 5'11" and 117 pounds. Over 40 percent of girls in the first, second, and third grades want to be thinner. More than 75 percent of girls desire to weigh less by adolescence. The cultural emphasis on feminine thinness is likely to contribute to the greater dissatisfaction among women with their weight and body shape (Rolls et al., 1991). University of Toronto Researchers Janet Polivy and C. Peter Herman call media messages a "background cause." As they put it, ". . . idealized media images are at best a background cause of Eds [eating disorders]. Exposure to the media is so widespread that if such exposure were *the* cause of Eds, then it would be difficult to explain why anyone would *not* be eating disordered" (2002, p. 192). Other research has examined the degree to which people accept (or internalize) the ideals of attractiveness the media portrays. Researchers have named this concept "thin-ideal internalization" (Thompson et al., 1999; Thompson & Stice, 2001). Everyone is exposed (even over-exposed) to images and arguments that physical attractiveness and being thin are ideals to be highly valued, but not everyone "buys into" that message. Some do. Some internalize attitudes and messages from family, friends, and media and fully accept that being thin is a good thing (Cusumano & Thompson, 2001; Hohlstein, Smith, & Atlas, 1998). Finally, there is evidence that individuals with anorexia process images of themselves differently from images of others (Sachdev, Mondraty, Wen, & Guilford, 2008). Sachde et al. found that anorexics showed less activation in certain brain areas than control subjects when viewing images of themselves. Sachdev et al. suggest that these differential activation patterns in anorexics (compared to controls) may underlie distortions in body image.

Psychologists have had some success finding specific behavioral or personality traits that might contribute to the development of an eating disorder. Adolescent girls with eating disorders tend to have strong needs for achievement and approval. There is also a relationship between "self-oriented perfectionism" and anorexia (Castro-Fornieles et al., 2007). In another study, high levels of perfectionism was associated with longer duration of anorexia (Nilsson, Sundbom, & Hägglöf, 2008). Patients with eating disorders are often depressed, but the depression may be a response to an eating disorder rather than a cause (Garner et al., 1990). Parenting and family style may contribute to the development of eating disorders. Anorexia nervosa patients do tend to come from very rigid, rule-governed, overprotective families. In one study, symptoms of anorexia were related to high levels of maternal control (Canetti, Kanyas, Lerer, Latzer, & Bachar, 2008). Bulimic patients often experienced inordinate blame and rejection in childhood (Bruch, 1980; Yates, 1990). Also, lack of proper attachment in early childhood has been noted as a potential contributor to eating disorders (Ward et al., 2000). These findings are useful guidelines in understanding eating disorders, but they will not apply in every case.

Researchers have considered physiological causes of eating disorders. The National Institute of Mental Health claims "Eating disorders are not due to a failure of will or behavior; rather, they are real, treatable medical illnesses in which certain maladaptive patterns of eating take on a life of their own" (Spearing, 2001). There is some evidence that abnormalities in brain serotonin levels may relate to anorexia and bulimia (Kaye, 2008). There is a small but significant genetic component to the eating disorders; relatives of patients with eating disorders are four to five times more likely to develop the disorder than are people in the general population (Klump, McGue, & Iacono, 2000; Strober et al., 2000). Also, a brain protein called brain-derived neurotrophic factor (BDNF) which is associated with eating behavior appears to be associated with eating disorders. Genetically regulated levels of BDNF in the brain have been found to play a role in anorexia and bulimia (Mercader et al., 2008).

Bulimic patients do not feel full after they eat, even after they binge (Walsh et al., 1989) possibly because bulimic patients are deficient in the hormone cholecystokinin (CCK). CCK, normally produced in the small intestine, signals that a person is full and need eat no more. When drug treatment elevates CCK levels in bulimic patients, they often show fewer symptoms of the disorder.

The prognosis, or prediction of the course of a disorder, for anorexia nervosa is particularly poor. Nearly 50 percent of those released from treatment relapse within one year (Yates, 1990). Treatment is usually medical, aimed at restoring body weight and nutrition. Hospitalization may be required. Interestingly, no effective drug treatments have been found for anorexia nervosa (Barlow & Durand, 2002). Nearly all forms of psychotherapy have been tried, but with little consistent success, and no one form of therapy is significantly more effective than any other. Psychotherapy focuses on the patient's distorted body image and low self-esteem. Psychotherapy is far more likely to be successful when the patient's family is involved. If all members of the family participate in therapy, prognosis is much better than if the patient is left on her (or his) own.

The outlook for bulimia nervosa is usually much better, but even so, about a third of patients still have the disorder five years after initial treatment (Fairburn et al., 2000). At least bulimic patients are seldom malnourished and, thus, do not require hospitalization. For persons with bulimia, the prognosis is better with family-oriented therapy than with individual therapy (Fairburn et al., 1993). With bulimic patients there has been some short-lived success with antidepressant medications (Geracioti & Liddle, 1988; Walsh et al., 1997), but when one looks at long-term success, the data are not as encouraging (Fairburn et al., 2000; Walsh, 1995; Walsh et al., 1991).

BEFORE YOU GO ON

6. What is "obesity," and what are some of the probable causes of the so-called "obesity epidemic"?
7. Describe anorexia nervosa and bulimia nervosa and comment on possible causes and treatments for them.

A Point to Ponder or Discuss
If you knew someone with an eating disorder (and likely you do), how would you persuade this person to seek treatment?

SEXUAL MOTIVATION AND HUMAN SEXUAL BEHAVIORS

Sex can be a powerful motivator. Sexual motivation varies considerably, not only among individuals, but also among species. Sexuality involves a complex interplay of physiological, cognitive, and affective processes. We begin with a discussion of the physiological basis for sexual motivation. We next explore the cognitive and affective aspects of sexual motivation and finally we consider sexual orientation in this chapter's Spotlight on Diversity.

On the physiological level, the sex drive is unique in many ways. For one thing, survival does not depend on its satisfaction. If we do not drink, we die; if we do not regulate our body temperatures, we die; if we do not eat, we die. If we do not have sex—well, we don't die. The survival of a species requires an adequate number of its members to respond successfully to a sex drive, but an individual member can get along without doing so. Second, most physiologically based drives, including thirst and hunger, provide mechanisms that ultimately replenish or maintain the body's energy. When it is satisfied, the sex drive depletes the body's energy. Third, the sex drive is not present—in the usual sense—at birth, but appears only after puberty. The other physiological drives are present and even most critical early in life.

A fourth unique quality of the sex drive is the extent to which internal and external forces have differing degrees of influence on sexual behaviors, depending on the species involved. Internal, physiological states are much more important in "lower" species than in humans. For example, sex for rats is simple and straightforward. If adequate testosterone (the male sex hormone) is present, and if the opportunity presents

For most animals—bears included—sexual behaviors are biologically and hormonally driven. Such is clearly not the case for humans, for whom learning, experience, and reacting to family, peer, and societal pressures are also relevant.

Courtesy of Xinhua/Corbis.

itself, a male rat will engage in sexual behaviors. If adequate levels of estrogen (a female sex hormone) are present, and if the opportunity arises, the female rat will engage in sexual behaviors. For rats, learning or experience has little to do with sexual behaviors—they are tied closely to physiology, to hormone level. There is virtually no difference between the mating behaviors of sexually experienced rats and virgin rats. Furthermore, if the sex glands of rats are removed, sexual behaviors cease. Removal of the sex glands from experienced male cats and dogs ("higher" species than rats) produces a gradual reduction in sexual behaviors. However, an experienced male primate ("higher" still) may persist in sexual behaviors for the rest of his life, even after the sex glands have been surgically removed. (The same seems true for most human males, but the data are sketchy.)

Yet biology alone cannot adequately account for human sexual behaviors. Hormones may provide humans with an arousing force toward sexual behaviors, but hormones may be neither necessary nor sufficient to account for them. It is obvious, for example, that physiological mechanisms cannot account for what a person does when sexually aroused or with whom he or she does it. Sexual behaviors are shaped by society, religion, family, and personal experience. Particularly in societies such as ours, where sexual behaviors are so influenced by learning experiences, one easily could come to believe that sexual drives are acquired through learning and practice alone. (Satisfying the sex drive also may involve considerable unlearning many of the prohibitions acquired in childhood and adolescence.) Sex manuals of the "how-to" variety sell well, and sex therapy has become a standard practice for many clinical psychologists helping people to cope with the pressures that external factors put on their "natural" sexual motivation.

With regard to sexuality, men and women differ in a few important ways. Having reviewed the research data, UCLA psychologist Letitia Peplau lists four male-female differences regarding human sexuality (2003).

1. ***Sexual Desire***—Compared with women, men are more interested in sex, fantasize more about sex, and want sex more often (Baumeister, 2000; Baumeister, Catanese, & Vohs, 2001). Men are significantly more likely to buy X-rated videos than women are. Men masturbate more frequently than women. Peplau takes these measures as indicative of men's greater sexual desire.

2. ***Sexuality and Relationships***—Women are more likely than men to require commitment and a relationship before engaging in sexual behaviors. Men are more likely to see sexuality simply in terms of intercourse and physical pleasure (Regan & Berscheid, 1999). Women's sexual fantasies usually involve a familiar partner, affection, and commitment, but men's sexual fantasies involve strangers and multiple partners.

3. ***Sexuality and Aggression***—We noted in Chapter 9 a significant gen-

der difference in aggression, particularly overt, physical aggression: Men are more physically aggressive. For example, men are commonly more assertive, even coercive, and more prone to be the ones who initiate physical sexual contact (Felson, 2002; Impett & Peplau, 2003). As Peplau put it, "Although women use many strategies to persuade men to have sex, physical force and violence are seldom part of their repertoire" (2003, p. 38).

4. *Sexual Plasticity*—Women's beliefs and attitudes about sexual issues can be changed by societal and environmental influences to a greater degree than can men's (Baumeister, 2000). The sexual activities of women are significantly more variable than are those of men, being more frequent when in an intimate relationship, dropping to near zero following a break-up.

Courtesy of Randy Faris/Corbis.

Research tells us that males are more interested in sex for the sake of sex, while females are more interested in commitment and intimacy.

In her review, Peplau repeatedly makes the point that the male-female differences listed above apply to both homosexuals and heterosexuals. It is to that difference—homosexual and heterosexual orientation—that we turn next.

BEFORE YOU GO ON

8. What factors motivate or influence sexual behaviors in humans?

A Point to Ponder or Discuss
Have you examined your own attitudes about homosexuality? For example, do you believe that homosexuality is a biologically based orientation and not a choice?

SPOTLIGHT
ON DIVERSITY

Sexual Orientation

The complexities of human sexuality are no more apparent than when we consider **homosexuality**—sexual attraction and arousal to members of the same sex. (Heterosexuality involves attraction and sexual arousal to members of the opposite sex.) Psychologists argue that homosexuality should be referred to as an *orientation*, not as a sexual preference. It is certainly not to be considered a sexual disorder. Like handedness or language, sexual orientation is not chosen voluntarily (Committee

homosexuality sexual arousal and attraction to members of the same sex

on Lesbian and Gay Concerns, 1991; Money, 1987). Some even recommend that the descriptor "homosexual" not be used to refer to persons of a same-sex orientation because of the negative stereotypes associated with the term. The term homosexuality focuses only on the sexual nature of a relationship, while ignoring the affective preferences and identity issues (Kelly, 1995). According to Kelly, someone can have an emotional (i.e., affective) orientation toward members of the same sex yet never express it in sexual behavior because of social pressures. The term *gay*, used to refer to males with a same-sex orientation, and *lesbian*, the term for women with a same-sex orientation, are preferred terms of reference. For the sake of simplicity, we will use the terms homosexuality and heterosexuality, but acknowledge that these terms do not fully reflect the complexity of human sexual orientations.

Homosexuality and heterosexuality are not mutually exclusive categories, but are endpoints of a dimension of sexual orientations. Alfred Kinsey and his colleagues (1948, 1953) first brought the prevalence of homosexuality to the attention of the general public. Kinsey devised a seven-point scale of sexual orientation, with those who are exclusively heterosexual at one end and persons who are exclusively homosexual at the other. Kinsey found that about half the males who responded to his surveys fell somewhere between the endpoints. Kinsey's methods were rather crude, and psychologists are now more conscious of the fact that answers given to sensitive questions often depend on how those questions are asked.

Even though homosexuality is now more openly discussed than it was in the 1940s and 1950s, it is still difficult to get accurate estimates of the number of persons who are exclusively or predominantly homosexual. Estimates suggest that about 1–2 percent of North American males are exclusively homosexual and that 8 to 10 percent have had more than an occasional homosexual encounter (Billy et al., 1993). When asked if they are sexually attracted to persons of the same gender, 6.2 percent of men and 4.4 percent of women responded affirmatively. When asked if they have had a sexual encounter with someone of the same gender within the *past year*, 2.7 percent of the men and 1.3 percent of the women responded "yes." When this question was rephrased to *since puberty*, comparable figures were 7.1 percent and 3.8 percent, respectively (Laumann et al., 1994). Finally, note that trends in same gender sexual behavior differ for females and males: Between 1990 and 2002, females reported a significant increase in same gender sex, but males reported no significant change for the same period (Turner et al., 2005).

There are few differences between persons with homosexual and heterosexual orientations in the pattern of their sexual responsiveness. Most homosexuals have experienced heterosexual sex. They simply find same-sex relationships more satisfying. Compared to married heterosexual partners, lesbian couples report more intimacy, more autonomy, and more equality in their relationships (Kurdek, 1998). Generally, homosexual couples are more at ease and more comfortable with their sexual relationship than most heterosexual couples, and when therapy is needed, the issues are much the same, focusing on developing clear communication, exploring personal values, expectations within the relationship, and matters related to developing as individuals as well as partners (Glick, & Berman, 2000). Comparative studies have produced some insights: "Relative to partners from married heterosexual couples, partners from gay and lesbian couples tend to assign household labor more fairly, resolve conflict more constructively, experience similar levels of satisfaction, and perceive less support from family members but more support from friends" (Kurdek, 2005, p. 251).

Psychologists have no generally accepted theory about why a person displays a particular sexual orientation. Still, it is safe to assume that a homosexual orientation results from an interaction of genetic, hormonal, and environmental factors. There is ample evidence that homosexuality has something of a genetic basis, and tends to "run in families" (Bailey & Pillard, 1991; Pool, 1993; Whitam et al., 1993). There also is evidence that the relationship between biological factors and sexual orientation is stronger for males than it is for females (Hershberger, 2001).

There are no differences in sex hormone levels of adult heterosexuals and adult homosexuals (Gladue, 1994; Tuiten et al., 2000). Providing gay males and lesbians with extra sex hormones may increase overall sex drive, but it has virtually no effect on sexual orientation. One hypothesis is that *prenatal* hormonal imbalances may affect sexual orientation in adulthood. This hypothesis claims that embryos (genetically male or female) exposed to above-average concentrations of female hormones will develop into adults attracted to persons having masculine characteristics (Ellis & Ames, 1987; Gladue et al., 1984; Money, 1987).

In 1991, Simon LeVay of the Salk Institute in San Diego published an article on his research that became headline news. LeVay performed a postmortem examination of the brains of 19 gay men, 16 heterosexual men, and six heterosexual women. He found an area in the hypothalamus that was significantly smaller in the gay men. In gay men, this area was precisely the same size as that found in the hypothalamus of women. LeVay did not claim that he had located the cause of homosexual orientation. His research led only to an association from which a cause-and-effect conclusion is not warranted. But LeVay's work does suggest why male homosexuality is present in most human populations, despite cultural constraints. His work suggests homosexuality is a biological phenomenon (Barinaga, 1991; Byne et al., 2000).

So where does research on the relationship between brain structure and sexual orientation leave us? Although there is some evidence to support the hypothesis that the brains of homosexuals and heterosexuals differ, it is by no means conclusive. Research in this area is plagued by methodological problems, reliance on postmortem studies, and failure to replicate results (Gallo, & Robinson, 2000). As the biological evidence accumulates, psychologists remain unwilling to totally abandon hypotheses that emphasize environmental influences. One thing, however, is clear: Sexual orientation cannot be attributed to any one early childhood experience. Still, intriguing tidbits do surface from time to time. One study (Bearman & Bruckner, 2001) focused on general socialization experiences of childhood by looking at the same gender romantic attraction of fraternal twins. The investigators found that a male adolescent with a female fraternal twin was (16.8%) more likely to show same gender attraction than a male adolescent with a male fraternal twin. Bearman and Bruckner suggest that socialization experiences account for the difference. A male with a female twin may not be subjected to as many socialization experiences that punish feminine behaviors as those with a male twin.

What might we conclude today about the how a person comes to be heterosexual or homosexual? Consistent with so many other complex behavior patterns, the ultimate explanation may be biopsychosocial. As one researcher put it: "With a larger data base . . . we may be able to construct a biosocial model in which different events—genetic, hormonal, and environmental—occurring at critical times are weighted for their impact on the development of sexual orientation. Associated with this model would be the idea that not all men and women arrive at their sexual orientation following the same path" (Gladue, 1994).

PSYCHOLOGICALLY BASED MOTIVES

Many of your behaviors can be analyzed in terms of physiologically based needs and drives. That you had breakfast this morning soon after you got up may have been your response to a hunger drive. That you got dressed may have been your attempt to control your body temperature, which also may have influenced your choice of clothes. Some sexual motivation may also have affected what you chose to wear today.

On the other hand, many of our behaviors are aroused and directed (which is to say, motivated) by nonbiological forces. In this section we will review three learned or social motivators: achievement, power, and affiliation and intimacy motivation.

Achievement Motivation

Henry Murray introduced the hypothesis that people are motivated to varying degrees by a need to achieve to psychology in 1938. The **need to achieve (nAch)** is the acquired need to meet or exceed some standard of excellence in one's behaviors. David McClelland and his associates have devoted themselves to finding ways to measure nAch and determining its implications (McClelland, 1985; McClelland et al., 1953; Smith, 1992).

Although there are short paper-and-pencil tests for the purpose, nAch is usu-

ally assessed by means of the *Thematic Apperception Test (TAT)*. This is a projective test in which people are asked to tell short stories about a series of ambiguous pictures depicting people in various settings (we first introduced the TAT in the previous chapter). Psychologists interpret and score the stories using a series of objective criteria that note references to attempting difficult tasks, succeeding, being rewarded for one's efforts, setting short- and long-term goals, and so on. There are no right or wrong responses. Instead, psychologists make judgments about the references to achievement a person projects into the pictures.

One of the first things McClelland and his colleagues found was that there are consistent differences in measured levels of the need to achieve. A reliable finding about people with high need for achievement is that, when given a choice, they attempt tasks in which success is not guaranteed (otherwise, there is no challenge) but in which there still is a reasonable chance of success. Both young children (McClelland, 1958) and college students (Atkinson & Litwin, 1960) who were high in nAch were observed playing a ring-toss game in which the object was to score points by tossing a small ring over a peg from a distance. The farther away from the peg one stood, the more points one could earn for each successful toss. In both studies, students with high nAch scores stood at a moderate distance from the peg. They did not stand so close as to guarantee success, but they did not stand so far away that they would almost certainly fail. People with low achievement motivation scores tended to go to either extreme—very close, earning few points for their successes or so far away that they rarely succeeded.

People with high achievement needs are not always interested in their own success or achievement at the expense of others. Particularly in collectivist societies, people may work very hard to achieve goals that are available only to

need to achieve (nAch) the acquired need to meet or exceed some standard of excellence in one's behaviors

Courtesy of moodboard/Corbis.

Someone motivated by a need to achieve (nAch) has an acquired need to meet or exceed some standard of excellence.

the group of which they are a part (Brislin, 1993).

McClelland would argue that you are reading this text at this moment because you are motivated by a need to achieve. You want to do well on your next exam. You want to get a good grade in this course, and you have decided that to do so you need to study the assigned text material. Some students, however, may read assignments not because they are motivated by a need to achieve, but because they are motivated by a fear of failure (Atkinson & Feather, 1966). In such cases, the incentive is negative (avoid an F) rather than positive (earn an A). Individuals motivated by a fear of failure tend to take few risks. They choose either simple tasks or impossible ones. If the task is simple, they are bound to do well. If the task is impossible, they cannot be made responsible for failure.

It seems that the need to achieve is learned, usually in childhood. Children who show high levels of achievement motivation are those who have been encouraged in a positive way to excel ("Leslie, that grade of B is very good. You must feel proud!" versus "What! Only a B?"). Children with a high need to achieve are generally encouraged to work things out on their own, perhaps with parental support and encouragement ("Here, Leslie, see if you can do this" as opposed to "Here, dummy, let me do it; you'll never get it right!"). McClelland believes almost everyone can learn achievement motivation and has developed training programs for that purpose (McClelland & Winter, 1969).

Power Motivation

Some people are motivated to be in control, to be in charge of both the situation and of others. In such cases, we speak of a **need for power** (McClelland, 1982; Winter & Stewart, 1978). Psychologists also measure the need for power by interpreting stories generated using the Thematic Apperception Test.

A high need for power is, in itself, neither good nor bad. Instead, psychologists evaluate the purposes for which power is used in the stories.

People with high power needs like to be admired. They prefer to control the fate of others, usually by manipulating access to information. They strive to put themselves in a position to say, "If you want to get this job done, you'll have to come to me to find out how to do it." People with low power needs tend to avoid situations in which others have to depend on them and tend to be submissive in interpersonal relationships. Although the situation is changing slowly in Western cultures, men are more commonly found in positions of power than are women (Darley & Fazio, 1980; Fiske & Glick, 1995; Mulac et al., 1985). However, there are no reliable differences between men and women in measured needs for power (Winter, 1988).

The Needs for Affiliation and Intimacy

Another psychologically based motivator is the **need for affiliation**—a need to be with others, to work with others toward some end, and to form friendships and associations. Individuals with a high need for affiliation express a stronger desire to be with friends than those with a low need for affiliation. For example, college men with a high need for affiliation tend to pick living arrangements that enhance the likelihood of meeting others. As a result, men with a high need for affiliation had more housemates and were more willing to share a room than those with a low need for affiliation (Switzer & Taylor, 1983). Additionally, there are some gender differences in the need for affiliation. For example, teenage girls express a greater desire to spend time with friends of the same sex than teenage boys do (Wong & Csikzentmihalyi, 1991).

A high need for affiliation is often at odds with a need for power. If a person

need for affiliation the need to be with others, to work with others toward the same ends, and to form friendships and associations

need for power the need to be in control, to be in charge of both the situation and of others

Courtesy of Bob Krist/Corbis.

Students who join a fraternity may be responding to a need for affiliation—the need to be with others and work with others toward the same end, whatever it might be.

need for intimacy the need to form and maintain close affectionate relationships

loneliness a subjective psychological state in which there is a discrepancy between relationships we would like to have and those that we actually have

is simultaneously motivated to be in control and to be with others in a truly supportive way, that person may feel conflicted. For the same reason, it is harder to exercise power over people whose friendship you value than over people whose friendship is of little concern. Some people can balance these conflicts. Many politicians are people who have both high power and high affiliation needs and they enjoy the exercise of power but also value being public figures and being surrounded by aides and advisors (Winter, 1987). Of course, affiliation and achievement motives need not always go together. Success can be earned either with others (high affiliation) or on one's own (low affiliation).

Although psychologists are quite confident that achievement and power motives are learned and culturally determined, they are less confident about the sources of affiliation motivation. Some

scientists argue that the need to affiliate and be with others is partly biological. On the one hand, we are social animals for whom social isolation is difficult, especially when we are young. On the other hand, some of the degree to which we value affiliation must have been learned.

Merely affiliating with others does not always satisfy our social needs. Individuals also may have a **need for intimacy**, or a need to form and maintain close affectionate relationships (McAdams, 1982). Intimacy in a relationship involves sharing and disclosing personal information. Individuals with a high need for intimacy tend to be warm and affectionate and to express concern for others. Women are more likely to show a higher need for intimacy than men do (McAdams, 1989).

What happens when our needs for affiliation and intimacy are not met? In this situation, we feel loneliness. **Loneliness** is a subjective, psychological state that arises when there is a discrepancy between relationships we would like to have and those we actually have (Peplau & Perlman, 1982). Being alone does not constitute loneliness. Some people prefer to be alone and probably have low need for affiliation and intimacy. Some people are only temporarily lonely, but others are chronically lonely. These persons have few, if any, close relationships. In many cases, these individuals lack social skills. Lonely persons also tend to have negative expectations for social interactions. That is, they enter social settings (for example, a party) apprehensive and expecting to fail. They then act in ways that fulfill this expectation.

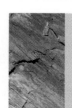

BEFORE YOU GO ON

9.   Describe the needs for achievement, power, affiliation, and intimacy.

A Point to Ponder or Discuss
What motivated you to take this class? How do you feel about it now?

Courtesy of Cultura/Corbis.

Courtesy of Cal Crary/Getty Images.

Emotions give flavor and coloring to our lives, whether those emotions are sadness, joy, or anger.

Courtesy of Corbis.

DEFINING AND CLASSIFYING EMOTIONS

Try to recall the last time you experienced an emotion of some significance—perhaps the fear of going to the dentist, the joy of receiving an A on an exam, the sadness at the death of a friend, or the anger at being unable to register for a class you wanted to take. You may be able to identify four components to your emotional reaction:

1. You experience a subjective feeling, or affect, which you may label fear, joy, sadness, anger, or the like.
2. You have a cognitive reaction; you recognize, or "know," what has happened.
3. You have an internal, physiological reaction, involving glands, hormones, and internal organs.
4. You engage in an overt behavioral reaction. You tremble as you approach the dentist's office. You run down the hallway, a broad smile on your face, waving your exam over your head. You cry at the news of your friend's death. You shake your fist and yell at the registrar when you find you can't get in the class you wanted.

When a behavior we can observe arises from an emotion, we begin to see how emotions and motivation are related. Emotions are motivators (Greenberg & Safran, 1989; Lang, 1985; Lazarus, 1991a, 1991b, 1993). To be motivated is to be aroused to action. Emotional experiences also arouse behaviors.

There has been considerable debate in psychology (and beyond) concerning how to define emotion (Soloman, 2003). As one researcher puts it, ". . . there is no consensus on a definition of the term emotion, and theorists and researchers use it in ways that imply different processes, meanings, and functions" (Izard, 2007, p. 260). For now, we will define an **emotion** as an experience that includes a subjective feeling, a cognitive interpretation, a physiological reaction, and a behavioral expression.

How are emotions classified? Psychologists have developed several ways. In psychology's first laboratory, Wilhelm Wundt was concerned with emotional reactions. He described emotions using three intersecting dimensions: pleasantness-unpleasantness, relaxation-tension, and calm-excitement.

More recently, Carroll Izard (1972, 1977, 1993) proposed a classification scheme with nine primary emotions.

emotion an experience that includes a subjective feeling, a cognitive interpretation, a physiological reaction, and a behavioral expression

TABLE 10.1

Plutchik's eight primary emotions and how they relate to adaptive behavior.

Emotion or feeling	Common stimulus	Typical behavior
1. Anger	Blocking of goal-directed behavior	Destruction of obstacle
2. Fear	A threat or danger	Protection
3. Sadness	Loss of something valued	Search for help and comfort
4. Disgust	Something gruesome or loathsome	Rejection; pushing away
5. Surprise	A sudden, novel stimulus	Orientation; turning toward
6. Curiosity	A new place or environment	Explore and search
7. Acceptance	A member of own group; something	Sharing; taking in; incorporating of value
8. Joy	Potential mate	Reproduction; courting; mating

From these basic nine, all other emotions can be constructed. Izard's nine primary emotions are fear, anger, shame, contempt, disgust, distress, interest, surprise, and joy. In Izard's theory, these nine emotions are primary emotions because they cannot be dissected into simpler, more basic emotions and each has its own underlying physiological basis. All other emotions are some combination of two or more of these nine.

Robert Plutchik (1980a, b) argued for eight primary emotions. For Plutchik, these eight emotions are primary because each is directly tied to some adaptive pattern of behavior; they are emotions related to survival. Table 10.1 lists each of Plutchik's eight primary emotions and its adaptive significance. For Plutchik, all other emotions are variants of the primary ones. For example, while rage may be an extreme emotion, it is essentially the same as anger. Anger in a weaker form is annoyance (Plutchik, 1980b).

Richard Lazarus (1991a, b; 1993) has proposed a theory of emotion that stresses the motivational role of emotions. He claims that emotions are the result of specific relationships or interactions between a person and his or her environment. Some relations are perceived as (potentially) harmful to a person's sense of well-being and yield negative emotions, such as anger, anxiety, fear, shame, or guilt. These are emotions a person is motivated to avoid. Some relations are (potentially) beneficial, give rise to positive emotions, such as joy, pride, gratitude, and love, and are emotions a person is motivated to seek or approach. Lazarus's list of basic emotions and their relational themes is presented in Table 10.2.

None of the approaches to classifying emotions listed so far has proven to be completely satisfactory. Psychologists continue to propose theories to account for the nature of an emotional reaction (Berkowitz, 1990; Buck, 1985; Ekman, 1993; Mathews & MacLeod, 1994; Ortony et al., 1988; Russell, 2003).

Theorists do not agree on the exact number of primary emotions or how they combine to form other emotions. Ortony and Turner (1990) listed more than a dozen different theories each with its own set of basic, or primary, emotions. A similar review by Plutchik (1994) lists 16, and none is in complete agreement with any other. Theorists agree on one thing: emotions represent a *valenced state*, meaning that emotions can be classified as being either positive (relief or happiness, and the like) or negative (fear, anger,

Emotion	Relational theme
Anger	A demeaning offense against me and mine
Anxiety	Facing an uncertain, existential threat
Fright	An immediate, concrete, and overwhelming physical danger
Guilt	Having transgressed a moral imperative
Shame	Failing to live up to an ego ideal
Sadness	Having experienced an irrevocable loss
Envy	Wanting what someone else has
Jealousy	Resenting a third party for the loss of, or a threat to, another's affection or favor
Disgust	Taking in or being too close to an indigestible (metaphorically speaking) object or idea
Happiness	Making reasonable progress toward the realization of a goal
Pride	Enhancement of one's ego-identity by taking credit for a valued object or achievement, either one's own or that of some group with which one identifies
Relief	A distressing goal-incongruent condition that has changed for the better or gone away
Hope	Fearing the worst, but wanting better
Love	Desiring or participating in affection, usually—but not necessarily—reciprocated
Compassion	Being moved by another's suffering and wanting to help

or shame, and the like) (Russell, Bachorowski, & Fernández-Dols, 2003). Unfortunately, theorists are still arguing over how best to distinguish between positive and negative emotions. For example, should fear be classified as a negative or positive emotion? Intuitively, fear seems negative, but fear can guide a person's behavior in positive or adaptive ways. After all, to be without fear in the real world would be very dangerous.

So where does this leave us? As sensible as it may sound to try to construct a system of basic, primary, emotions—particularly if such a system had a physiological or evolutionary foundation—such an attempt will prove difficult at best. One problem is that there is less than total agreement on just what *basic* or *primary* means when we are talking about emotions. "Thus, the question 'Which are the basic emotions?' is not only one that probably cannot be answered, it is a misdirected question, as though we asked, 'Which are the basic people?' and hoped to get a reply that would explain human diversity" (Ortony & Turner, 1990, p. 329).

All theorists agree that being emotional is partly a physiological, visceral response. To put it plainly, being emotional is a gut-level reaction. Being emotional involves more than our thinking, reasoning cerebral cortex. We turn next to the physiological aspects of emotion.

BEFORE YOU GO ON

10. What do psychologists mean when they talk about emotion?
11. What has become of attempts to identify and classify basic, or primary, emotions?

A Point to Ponder or Discuss
If you were to list primary emotions, which ones would be on your list, and how would you include some and exclude others?

PHYSIOLOGICAL ASPECTS OF EMOTION

Imagine yourself in the following situation. After backpacking in the mountains and enjoying a large meal, you find yourself eye to eye with a growling bear. What will you do now? Undoubtedly, you will have an emotional reaction to the growling bear. You will experience affect (call it fear, if not panic). You will have a cognitive reaction (realizing you've just encountered a bear and that you'd rather you hadn't). You will engage in some overt behavior (either freezing in your tracks or racing back to the camp). A significant part of your reaction in this situation (or one like it) will be internal, physiological, and "gut-level." Responding to a bear in the wild is not something people do purely intellectually. When we are emotional, we respond viscerally.

Our biological reaction to emotional situations takes place at several levels. Both the Autonomic Nervous System (ANS) and the brain play key roles in our biological reactions to emotional situations.

The Role of the Autonomic Nervous System

The autonomic nervous system (ANS) consists of two parts that serve the same organs but have nearly the opposite effect on those organs. The **parasympathetic division** is actively involved in maintaining a relaxed, calm, and unemotional state. As you strolled down

the path into the woods, the parasympathetic division of your ANS automatically directed your digestion. Your body diverted blood from the extremities to the stomach and the intestines. Your body's salivary glands produced extra saliva to aid digestion. With your stomach full, and with blood diverted to it, you felt somewhat drowsy as your brain responded to the lower blood supply. Your breathing and heart rate were slow and steady. Again, the parasympathetic division of your ANS controlled all of these activities.

Suddenly, there's that bear! As with any emotional response, the **sympathetic division** of your ANS now takes over. Automatically, many physiological changes take place—changes that are usually quite adaptive.

1. Your pupils dilate, letting in as much available light as possible. As a result, your visual sensitivity is increased.
2. Your heart rate and blood pressure increase (your body needs energy as quickly as possible).
3. Your digestion stops and blood is redirected from the digestive tract to the limbs and brain. You have a bear to deal with, so digestion can wait. Blood goes to the arms and legs where it can be used in what is called a fight-or-flight response.
4. Your respiration increases, becoming deeper and more rapid; you'll need all the oxygen you can get.
5. Your body perspires. As moisture is brought to the surface of the skin and evaporates, it cools your body and helps conserve energy.

sympathetic division the component of the ANS that is actively involved in states of emotionality

parasympathetic division the component of the ANS that is actively involved in maintaining a relaxed, calm, and unemotional state

6. Your blood sugar increases, making more energy readily available.

7. Your blood will clot more readily than normal—a valuable adaptation for obvious reasons.

Some of these changes made by the sympathetic division of the ANS are made directly (for example, stopping salivation and stimulating the cardiac muscle). Others are made indirectly through the release of hormones into the bloodstream (mostly epinephrine and norepinephrine from the adrenal glands). Because part of the physiological aspect of emotion is hormonal, it takes a few seconds. If you were confronted by a bear, you probably would not notice, but the sweaty palms, gasping breaths, and "butterflies in your stomach" take a few seconds to develop.

Is the autonomic and endocrine system reaction the same for every emotion? That question is difficult to answer. It remains a source of controversy among researchers in psychology. At best, differences in physiological reactions for various emotions are very slight. There appears to be a small difference in the hormones produced during rage and those produced during fear. There may be differences in the biological bases of emotions that prepare us for confrontation or for retreat—fight or flight (Blanchard & Blanchard, 1988). This issue has been controversial in psychology for many years and is likely to remain so (Blanchard & Blanchard, 1988; Plutchik, 1994; Selye, 1976).

The Role of the Brain

When we become emotional, our sympathetic nervous system does not just spring into action on its own. Autonomic nervous system activity is matched with central nervous system activity.

Two brain structures intimately involved in emotionality are the limbic system and the hypothalamus—that small structure in the middle of the brain so centrally involved with physiological drives. The limbic system consists of several small structures (the *amygdala* may be the most important for emotionality) and is a lower brain structure. These structures are "lower" in the sense of being well below the cerebral cortex and in the sense of being present (and important) in the brains of "lower" animals, such as rats and cats.

The limbic system is most involved in emotional responses to threatening situations—those that call for confrontation or retreat. Electrical stimulation or destruction of portions of the limbic system reliably produces a variety of changes in emotional reaction. The amygdala's primary role appears to be in determining the emotional significance of a stimulus. Different parts of the amygdala become active depending upon the emotion involved. For example, positive emotions (winning an important game) are associated with activity in the *left side* of the amygdala, but unpleasant emotions (losing that important game) are associated with activity in the *right side* of the amygdala (Zalla et al., 2000). In another study, researchers found sadness activated the amygdala (Wang et al., 2005). Stimuli associated with fear and anger also activate different regions of the amygdala (Whalen et al., 2001). It is as if this small structure in the limbic system somehow helps us discriminate among different emotions. In a similar vein, stimulating certain areas of the hypothalamus (considered by some to be a key part of the limbic system) produces strong emotional reactions—including those that lead cats to attack and kill any nearby prey (Flynn et al., 1970). Psychologists do not fully understand how the limbic system operates in emotionality, but findings like these suggest it is a complex neural circuit deep in the brain and that it works to mediate emotional states.

The cerebral cortex's role in emotionality seems to be largely to interpret and inhibit neural impulses from lower brain centers. That is, the limbic system and hypothalamus appear to be the sources for raw, extreme—and undirected—emotional reactions. The cortex interprets impulses from these lower centers along with other information available to it and then modifies and directs the emotional reaction accordingly. In short, the cerebral cortex provides the cognitive aspect of an emotion. The cerebral cortex plays a vital role in the interpretation and memory of emotional events. When you get back to camp, you will use your cortex to describe the emotional details of encountering the growling bear. Emotional reactions tend to be processed in the right hemisphere of the brain; the left hemisphere is usually unemotional (Boraod, 1992; Damasio et al., 2000; LeDoux, 1995). Beyond that, current research indicates that no specific, particular parts of the cerebral cortex are associated with any specific emotional reaction (Barrett & Wager, 2006).

BEFORE YOU GO ON

12. Describe the role of the autonomic nervous system and the brain in emotion.

A Point to Ponder or Discuss
Describe the physiological bases of an emotional reaction that is more likely and less dramatic than meeting a bear in the woods. For example, what are the physiological bases of discovering you aced an exam you had been worried about?

THEORIES OF EMOTION

We have just examined how the body reacts physiologically to an emotion-producing stimulus. Yet, the role these physiological reactions play in our experience of emotions is unclear. Are they a by-product of our emotions? Or, are they the central component of what we experience as emotions? We shall explore these questions next as we look at several theories of emotion put forth by psychologists. Simply put, theories of emotion are systematic attempts to explain how we become emotional and how the various components of an emotion interact.

The James–Lange Theory of Emotion

Pioneering psychologist William James proposed a theory of emotion that put the body's physiological response at the center of emotions (1884). At around the same time Danish researcher Carl Lange developed similar ideas about emotions, so their theory is now called the *James–Lange theory* of emotion.

James wrote, ". . . the bodily changes follow directly the PERCEPTION of the exciting fact, and that our feeling of the same changes as they occur IS the emotion" (James, 1884, pp. 189–190). So, according to James, the bodily changes that accompany exposure to an emotion-producing stimulus comprise our emotions. Without the physiological changes, there would be no emotion. James regarded the fact that we do not ordinarily experience emotion without the physiological response of the body as proof of his theory.

For example, imagine you are on an airplane and another passenger suddenly jumps up and screams that he is hijacking the plane. Almost immediately your heart pounds, you sweat, and your breathing accelerates. In James' view, you are not afraid because of the hijacker. Rather, you are afraid because your body is telling you to be afraid. James rejected the idea that one mental state (perceiving the hijacker) could cause another (the emotion of fear). Finally, if in response to the hijacker your body were not to undergo physical/physiological changes, you would not experience emotion. This fact, for James, was evidence that his theory was correct.

James knew his theory was inconsistent with the accepted, common sense view of how emotions worked. Common sense says we cry because we are sad, or we laugh because we are happy. James believed the opposite: We are sad because we cry, we are happy because we laugh, and we are afraid because we tremble. As you might expect, James' anti-intuitive view created quite a stir and provoked a good bit of criticism. As simple schematics, the common-sense approach and the James–Lange approach might look like this:

Common Sense Approach

Stimulus→Experience of Emotion→ Appropriate Response

James–Lange Approach

Stimulus→Appropriate (internal) Response→Experience of Emotion

The Cannon-Bard Theory of Emotion

A former student of William James, Walter Cannon (1927), sharply criticized his teacher's theory of emotion and called for it to be abandoned for several reasons. Chiefly, Cannon was skeptical that people could actually differentiate among the subtle physiological changes that accompany most emotional states and thus identify the emotions they were experiencing. Cannon argued that most people could tell the difference between crying and trembling, but that most physiological/visceral reactions in emotional situations were far more subtle.

Cannon, along with his colleague Philip Bard (1934) proposed a different theory of emotion. According to the *Cannon–Bard theory* of emotion, the brain plays a central role in the experi-

ence of emotion. According to Cannon, ". . . the neural arrangements for emotional expression reside in sub-cortical centers, and that these centers are ready for instant and vigorous discharge when they are released from cortical restraint and are properly stimulated" (Cannon, 1927, pp. 119–120). According to Cannon, the *thalamus* was the part of the brain most intimately involved in emotional experience: ". . . the peculiar quality of the emotion is added to simple sensation when the thalamic processes are roused (Cannon, 1927, p. 120). Cannon maintained that the bodily changes discussed by James took place almost simultaneously with the activation of the thalamus. A schematic of this approach might look like this:

Cannon–Bard Approach

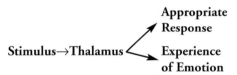

Stimulus→Thalamus Appropriate Response / Experience of Emotion

The issues raised by James and Cannon decades ago are still relevant in the debate over the nature of emotions. Psychologists are still trying to uncover the exact relationship between physiological arousal and emotional experience. Some recent research suggests that James and

A common-sense approach to emotion would argue that these young ladies are crying because they are sad. The James–Lange approach to emotion would argue quite the opposite—that because they are crying, they feel sad.

Courtesy of Corbis.

Lange may have had it right all along. For example, some research suggests different emotions might produce different patterns of physiological activity that then activate different pathways in the brain (Davidson et al., 1994). Additionally, if a person is asked to produce a certain facial expression (e.g., a smile), he or she experiences the correct corresponding emotion (e.g., joy) (Ekman, Levenson, & Friesen, 1983). Finally, improved imaging techniques reveal that certain areas of the brain become active when people try to monitor their own internal processes (Critchley et al., 2004). Quite possibly, James and Lange were at least partially correct when they proposed that emotional experience follows physiological responses.

The Two-Factor Theory of Emotion

In the first half of the twentieth century, psychology was dominated by behaviorism—the school of thought that advocated studying observable stimuli and responses. The behaviorists' strong empirical leanings caused them to avoid studying the internal aspects of emotions. Consequently, interest in the study of emotions waned. Starting in the 1950s, something of a "cognitive revolution" took psychology by storm. Tired of the rigid adherence to behaviorism, psychologists began to study internal psychological processes again. The study of emotions was once again at the forefront of American psychology.

During the cognitive revolution, the *two-factor theory* of emotion emerged (Schachter & Singer, 1962). According to Schachter and Singer, two factors are essential to emotional experience: physiological arousal and situation-appropriate cognition (Cornelius, 1996). According to this theory (diagrammed below), an emotion-producing stimulus causes a physiological response (much like the one suggested by William James). However, for that arousal to be interpreted as an emotion it must be accompanied by certain cognitions (thoughts) that label the emotional experience. Let's return to our hijacking example. Your body becomes physiologically aroused when you perceive the hijacker shouting. Cognitively, you immediately tie the arousal to the presence of the hijacker. The cognitively mediated emotion you experience is fear.

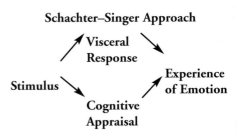

Schachter and Singer (1962) conducted an imaginative experiment to test their theory. Participants were told that they were taking part in an experiment testing the effects of a vitamin supplement on vision. One group was given an injection of epinephrine (which causes diffuse physiological arousal much like the arousal that accompanies emotion). The second group was given an injection of saline solution (a placebo that produces no physiological reactions). Within each group, participants were given one of three types of information about the effects of the injection. In the "epinephrine-informed group" participants were given accurate information on what to expect from the injection (pounding heart, shaking hands, flushed face). In the "epinephrine-misinformed group," participants were misinformed about the effects of the injection (itchiness, headache, numbness). Finally, in the "epinephrine-ignorant group," participants were told that there would be no side effects.

In the second phase of the experiment, participants were taken to a room to wait for the drug to take effect. In the waiting room there was another person working for the experimenters (the "stooge"). For half of the participants the "stooge" behaved euphorically (balling up paper and shooting baskets, playing around with a hoola hoop). For the other half, the "stooge" behaved angrily (complaining about a required questionnaire, ripping up the questionnaire).

Schachter and Singer measured participants' emotions using direct observation, participant pulse rates, and a mood questionnaire. Participants who were misinformed or uninformed about the effect of the injection showed the most euphoric emotion. Those who were correctly informed experienced less euphoric emotion. Schachter and Singer theorized that misinformed and uninformed participants used the behavior of the stooge as a way to label (cognitively) their unexplained arousal. Participants who were correctly informed about the injection could correctly attribute their arousal to the drug and had no need to use the stooge's behavior to help label the arousal. Unfortunately, the data from the angry stooge condition did not support Schachter and Singer's theory.

Schachter and Singer's theory and research reignited interest in studying emotions. Unfortunately, other researchers not only failed to replicate Schachter and Singer's results but produced results that contradicted Schachter and Singer (Cornelius, 1996; Marshall & Zimbardo, 1979; Maslach, 1979). For these reasons, some researchers are skeptical about the theory. Regardless, Schachter and Singer's theory was immensely important because it refocused attention on emotions and served as a catalyst for further research and additional theories (Cornelius, 1996).

The Cognitive Appraisal Theory of Emotion

At around the same time that Schachter and Singer proposed their theory of emotion, other cognitive psychologists were working on their own versions of a cognitively based theory of emotion. The *cognitive appraisal theory* of emotion, for example, argues that how one appraises (evaluates) a situation determines both emotion and behavior. In this context, *appraisal* is defined as the "process by which we judge the personal relevance of our situation, for good or ill" (Cornelius, 1996, p. 114). Imagine two people in an airplane going skydiv-

ing for the first time. On the one hand, Skydiver 1 looks at the 5,000-foot drop to earth and appraises the situation as "dangerous"—and *as a consequence* experiences fear. On the other hand, Skydiver 2 looks out the door and appraises the situation as "challenging" and *as a consequence* experiences exhilaration. According to the cognitive appraisal theory of emotion, these two skydivers experienced different emotions because they appraised the same situation very differently. These appraisals go beyond our mere knowledge of stimuli and events. Rather, they are *judgments* about stimuli and events (Cornelius, 1996). Emotion simply cannot occur without cognitive appraisal, but not all stimuli are equally likely to arouse emotion (Arnold, 1960). For a stimulus to arouse emotion, it must be relevant to us or relevant to someone important to us. So, our hypothetical skydiver feels fear because jumping is personally relevant to her. That is, jumping will have personal consequences for her.

More contemporary cognitive models of emotion focus on emotion as a process rather than a static experience (Scherer, 1999; Planalp, 1999). The *process model of emotion* generally includes five parts: a precipitating event, a cognitive appraisal, physiological changes, behavior tendencies/behaviors, and regulation (Planalp, 1999). In this model, emotions are ongoing experiences that can change over time as situations change.

Let's return to our hypothetical skydivers. The skydiver approaches the open airplane door and looks down (precipitating event) and appraises her situation as dangerous (cognitive appraisal). As a result, she feels butterflies in her stomach and breaks a sweat (physiological change) and withdraws from the door (behavior). She sits back down in the plane and calms herself (regulation). Intending to jump, she again approaches the door. The precipitating event is the same, but now it seems less dangerous. The physiological reactions diminish, and she successfully jumps.

Notice this example focuses on how the *process* of emotion works. The skydiver experiences fear, but the fear is not an end point, as it is in static models of emotion. Our skydiver regulates her emotions and eventually jumps out of the plane. Many real-world emotional situations require a process of appraisal and regulation. For example, Folkman and Lazarus (1985) found that students used different emotional regulation strategies to cope with taking a midterm exam. Before the exam, students used "informational support." Before the exam, students used coping mechanisms to improve their probable results (e.g., studying with other students). After the exam, students relied more on "emotional support" to help them cope with the potential consequence. Folkman and Lazaraus pointed out that an essential component in coping was the *process* that changed over time and as the situation changed.

Cognitive appraisal theories of emotion emphasize the appraisal process in understanding emotions. Klaus Scherer (1984; 1986; 1999) has described the appraisal process in considerable detail in his *component process model* of emotion. According to Scherer (1999), appraisal involves a series of *stimulus evaluation checks* (SECs) in a fixed order: novelty (Is this a new or familiar situation?), pleasantness (Is the stimulus pleasant or unpleasant?), goal/need significance (Will this behavior help me reach a goal?), coping potential (How well will I be able to cope with this situation?), and norm compatibility (Does the behavior called for violate a norm, or some "rule" of appropriateness with which I am familiar?) (1986).

Scherer sees emotion and appraisal as constantly operating to gather and check information in changing situations. So, let's go back to our skydiver once again. The first level of appraisal is whether the skydiver has done this before. Higher levels of fear are natural for a person facing a new experience (first time skydiving). In the second level appraisal, the skydiver determines if the situation is pleasant or unpleasant. If she sees the situation as unpleasant, she will likely experience a negative emotion. At the third level, the skydiver might conclude that no important goal is served by jumping out of the plane. Fourth, she determines how to cope with the situation (e.g., withdrawing from the door). Finally, she compares her behavior with that of her fellow skydivers. If everyone else has jumped, she may jump as well.

Unconscious Emotions

Each of the theories we just covered makes a key assumption about the experience of an emotion: that emotions are a conscious experience. That is, when you are confronted by that pesky bear in the woods you are aware consciously of your fear. There is ample evidence, acquired from decades of research, that we are consciously aware of our emotional states. However, is it possible that you could also have emotional reactions that are unconscious and below your level of awareness? Some researchers think so.

For example, Winkielman and Berridge (2004) suggest that is possible to have unconscious emotions. They argue that is not much of a conceptual leap to move from the existence of implicit attitudes and other cognitive functions, which operate unconsciously, to unconscious emotions. The results of a recent experiment by Ruys and Stapel (2008a) provide evidence for unconscious emotions. Ruys and Stapel presented participants with emotion-producing pictures (e. g., a growling dog, a dirty, unflushed toilet) or a nonemotional picture so rapidly that they were below their level of awareness. Ruys and Stapel measured emotional reactions by having participants rate the extent to which they felt a number of emotions (fear and disgust among them) and by completing a word completion task. Ruys and Stapel found that the participants completed words in the direction of the emotion-producing picture they saw. That is, if a participant saw a fearful picture (the growling dog) they were more likely to complete words indicating fear. Similarly, ratings of one's mood and emotion was in the direction of the picture presented. Participants who saw the disgusting picture were more likely to report feelings of disgust than those exposed to the fearful or neutral pictures. In another similar study Ruys and Stapel (2008b) found that unconscious exposure to emotional facial expressions elicits an emotional response consistent with that expression. So, participants unconsciously exposed to an angry face were likely to report feeling angry.

Results like these have some interesting implications for our emotional lives. Ruys and Stapel (2008a) suggest that unconscious emotions might explain situations in which you feel an emotion, but can't put your finger on why. For example, you may get up one morning and after a while feel angry or depressed, seemingly with no reason. Perhaps you are having an unconscious emotional response to a dream you had but cannot remember or maybe to an angry person you saw on the television news that morning.

BEFORE YOU GO ON

13. What do the James–Lange and the Cannon–Bard theories say about the roots of emotion?
14. What are the two-factor and cognitive appraisal theories of emotion?
15. What are unconscious emotions and how might they affect your daily emotional experiences?

A Point to Ponder or Discuss
Take the four major components of emotion: subjective feeling (affect), physiological reaction, cognitive appraisal, and overt behavior. Under what circumstances can any of these exist independent of the other three?

OUTWARD EXPRESSIONS OF EMOTION

Psychologists have long been intrigued by how animals communicate their inner emotional states to one another. Charles Darwin was one of the first to popularize the idea animals use facial expressions. More than a hundred years later, psychologists are still refining Darwin's original hypothesis. For example, it is not likely that facial expressions conveying emotion are "broadcast" for the benefit of all who see them. At least some facial expressions are directed only at specific observers. Nor is it likely that receivers of facial expressions conveying emotion can interpret ("decode") such messages simply and reflexively (Russell, Bachorowski, & Fernández-Dols, 2003, p. 343).

In the wild, it is often useful for one animal to recognize emotional state of another animal: Is it angry? Is it a threat? Is it just curious, or is it looking for dinner? Is it sad, looking for comfort, or is it sexually aroused, looking for a mate? An animal's inability to correctly read outward expressions of emotion could result in the animal becoming food. Survival requires that animals correctly perceive the emotional state of other animals.

Animals have many instinctive and ritualistic patterns of behavior they can use to communicate aggressiveness, sexual attraction, submission, and other emotional states. To a degree far beyond most other members of the animal kingdom, humans can use language to describe their emotions to one another. The spoken word adds layers of complexity to interpreting emotions from observations alone. Indeed, research tells us that emotional states can be reflected in *how* we speak, even if our message is not related to emotion at all (Bachorowski & Owren, 1995; Scherer, 1986).

Humans, like animals, use body language to communicate their emotional condition (Birdwhistell, 1952; Fast, 1970). For example, if we were to observe someone sitting quietly, slumped slightly forward with head down, we would likely conclude the person was feeling sad. Even if we only were to observe from a distance, we could reach the same conclusion. Humans similarly interpret postural cues and gestures as being associated with fear, anger, happiness, and so on. These associations appear to be learned and subject to cultural influences.

Darwin recognized facial expression as a cue to emotion in animals, especially mammals. Might the same principle apply in humans, too? Do all humans use substantially the same facial expressions to communicate their emotions? A growing body of evidence supports the hypothesis that facial expressions of emotional states are innate responses, only slightly sensitive to cultural influence—but the relation between facial expression and underlying emotion is far from simple (Adelmann & Zajonc, 1989; Oatley & Jenkins, 1992; Russell, Bachorowski, & Fernández-Dols, 2003).

Paul Ekman and his colleagues have conducted several studies trying to find a reliable relationship between emotional state and facial expression across cultures (Ekman, 1972, 1992, 1993; Ekman et al., 1987). In one study, college students were shown several series of six pictures. Each series showed one person's face expressing six emotions: happiness, disgust, surprise, fear, sadness, or anger (Ekman, 1973). When students from the United States, Argentina, Japan, Brazil, and Chile were asked to identify the emotion being experienced by the faces in the photographs, their answers agreed to a remarkable degree. While this study is interesting, its critics noted that the participants were all college students and most likely shared many experiences despite their cultural differences. Even though Ekman's participants came from different countries, their agreement could be explained by their common experiences rather than by an innate tendency to express the same emotions through similar facial expression. Despite the criticism, it is very likely that some facial expressions—for happiness, for example—can be readily identified across cultures, but others—such as disgust—are difficult to interpret cross-culturally (Elfenbein & Ambady, 2002).

Another study of facial expression (Ekman et al., 1983) has shown that making a face associated with an emotion can cause distinctive physiological changes that mimic the emotion (see also Adelmann & Zajonc, 1989; Laird, 1984; Matsumoto, 1987; Schiff & Lamon, 1989). Strange as it sounds, if you raise your eyebrows, open your eyes widely, and raise the corners of your mouth, you will produce an internal physiological change similar to what occurs when you are happy. You may find yourself genuinely smiling as a result.

As one lion approaches another, each needs to have a pretty good idea of the emotional state of the other.

Courtesy of O. Alamany & E. Vicens/Corbis.

BEFORE YOU GO ON

16.   What factors are involved in the communication of emotion from one organism to another?

A Point to Ponder or Discuss
Actors communicate feelings or emotions their characters are experiencing. What methods do actors use to accomplish this task?

BEHAVIORAL MANIFESTATIONS OF EMOTION: THE FRUSTRATION-AGGRESSION HYPOTHESIS

Facial expression and posture are not the only ways people express emotions. Emotions often directly motivate or influence behavior. For example, imagine you accidentally cut off another motorist on your way home from school. You think nothing of it because it was accidental. In your rearview mirror, you see the other driver inches from your rear bumper. He pulls next to you, screams something unkind, and gestures rudely at you. Next, he tries to run you off the road. You decide to pull over and let this "maniac" pass you.

In this example, the other motorist was obviously emotional. His emotional episode escalated into aggression. Social psychologists define **aggression** as any behavior intended to inflict physical and/or psychological harm on another organism (for example, you) or the symbol of that organism (for example, your car). The frustration-aggression hypothesis is the classic explanation for aggression in situations such as the one just described. The original **frustration-aggression hypothesis** stated that ". . . aggression is always a consequence of frustration . . . the occurrence of

aggressive behavior always presupposes the existence of frustration and, contrariwise . . . the existence of frustration leads to some form of aggression" (Dollard et al., 1939, p. 1). In other words, we behave aggressively when we are frustrated.

Frustration can vary in strength, depending on three factors. The first factor is the intensity of the original drive or motivation. If you are very thirsty and receive nothing to drink, your frustration will be greater than if you are only slightly thirsty and receive nothing. The second factor is the degree to which the goal-directed behavior is blocked or thwarted. If a water fountain dribbled just enough water for you to drink a little bit, you would be less frustrated than if it did not work at all. The third factor is the number of frustrating events that have preceded your present frustration. If your thwarted attempt to get a drink from a water fountain occurred immediately after another frustrating event (the soda machine taking your money without dispensing a soda), you would experience more frustration than if it had not. Thus, frustrating experiences are cumulative. The motorist you cut off may have reacted aggressively because he had experienced several frustrating events. Perhaps he didn't get a raise, he had to work late, he hit rush hour traffic, and then you cut him off.

The original frustration-aggression hypothesis stated that frustration *always* leads to aggression. In fact, frustrated

aggression any behavior intended to inflict physical and/or psychological harm to another organism or the symbol of that organism

frustration-aggression hypothesis the position that aggression is always a consequence of frustration

Courtesy of Somos Images/Corbis.

Becoming angry when frustrated—perhaps by other drivers—is seldom very useful, but anger and aggression are common reactions to frustration.

people restrain themselves from aggression regularly. In some cases the possibility of punishment deters frustrated people from aggression. In our example, if a police car was right behind the frustrated driver, he might not have acted aggressively out of fear of being arrested.

The frustration-aggression hypothesis stirred controversy nearly from the moment it was proposed. Some theorists questioned whether frustration inevitably led to aggression (Miller, 1941). Others suggested that frustration leads to aggression only under very specific circumstances, such as when the blocked response is important to the individual (Blanchard & Blanchard, 1984).

Criticism and additional research produced refinements in the original frustration-aggression hypothesis. For example, Berkowitz (1989; 1993) proposed that frustration and aggression were connected by negative affect, such as anger. Berkowitz believed that aggression only occurred when the frustration of goal-directed behavior led to anger. If no anger was aroused, no aggression could result.

What factors, then, lead to the arousal of anger? There are several situational factors that can turn frustration into aggression (Berkowitz & Harmon-Jones, 2004;

Anderson & Bushman, 2002). One factor is how we judge the *intent* of a person who is the source of our frustration. If we believe the person deliberately frustrated or harmed us, we will be angrier than if we believe the person did so accidentally. When people decide to become aggressive, they often consider the intentions of those who have wronged them to be more important than the actual behaviors (Ohbuchi & Kambara, 1985). Of course, this does not mean that people do not get angry when someone inadvertently frustrates them (Herrald & Tomaka, 2002). For example, have you ever gotten frustrated—and angry—sitting in traffic, even though all the drivers around you bear no responsibility for your frustration? Indeed, aggression is sometimes directed against those who have no connection to the source of the initial frustration (Pederson, Gonzales, & Miller, 2002).

Another factor that can contribute to anger, and ultimately to aggression, is the perception that we have been treated unjustly (Baron, 1999). For example, fans at sporting events have been known to pelt officials with projectiles following a call against their team. In these cases, the fans are (usually) reacting to what they perceive as an injustice. As it happens, even frustration that is fully justified can lead to aggressive behaviors (Dill & Anderson, 1995).

Those who perceive they have been wronged see their aggression as a way of restoring justice and equity. The motorist you cut off on the highway may have been just trying to "even the score" with you. Anger is more likely to be aroused by perceived inequity and injustice than by the frustration of the event itself (Sulthana, 1987). People who feel they are powerless may be more likely to resort to aggression (Richardson, Vandenberg, & Humphries, 1986). As world events remind us daily, riots and terrorism are often the weapons of choice among those with little power, low status, and a sense of being unjustly treated.

As a final note about anger, it appears anger can be aroused simply by those bodily changes that normally accompany anger (Berkowitz & Harmon-Jones, 2002). In one experiment, some participants clinched their fists (a behavior that often accompanies anger) while they described an experience from their lives. Other participants did the same thing without clinching their fists. The clinched fist group displayed anger more intensely in their descriptions (Jo, 1994). The studies show a straight-forward relationship: the more bodily manifestations for anger, the more intensely anger is felt. In another study, participants who made an angry facial expression and struck an angry body posture reported feeling more anger than participants who did only one or the other (Flack, Laird, & Cavallaro, 1999).

BEFORE YOU GO ON

17. What is the frustration-aggression hypothesis, and what factors influence the progression from becoming frustrated to becoming aggressive?

A Point to Ponder or Discuss
Frustration can lead to anger, which can lead to aggression. What other causes of human aggression can you think of that have little to do with frustration as we have defined it?

CHAPTER SUMMARY

1. **How do psychologists define *motivation*, and how have they used the concepts of instincts, needs, and drives to account for motivated behaviors?**

   Motivation is the process that arouses, directs, and maintains an organism's behaviors. *Instincts* are complex patterns of unlearned behavior that occur in the presence of certain stimuli. Instinct approaches to explaining why humans do what they do have not proven to be satisfactory. *Needs* are shortages of some biological necessity. Deprivation leads to a need, which gives rise to a *drive*, which arouses and directs an organism's behavior. Many drives are more learned than biologically based. Maslow devised a system that places needs in a hierarchy, from physiological survival needs to a need to self-actualize.

2. **How can incentives, homeostasis, arousal, and cognitive dissonance be useful in explaining motivated behaviors?**

   Focusing on *incentives* explains behaviors in terms of goals and outcomes rather than internal driving forces. Incentives may be thought of as goals—external stimuli that attract (positive goals) or repel (negative goals). The basic idea of balance or equilibrium theories is that organisms are motivated to reach and maintain a state of balance—a set point level of activity. *Homeostasis*, for example, is a drive to maintain a state of equilibrium among internal physiological conditions, such as blood pressure, metabolism, and heart rate. Other theorists argue for a general drive to maintain a balanced state of *arousal*, with an optimal level of arousal being best suited for any given task or situation. Leon Festinger claims that we are motivated to maintain consonance, or balance, among cognitive states, thereby reducing, if not eliminating, *cognitive dissonance*.

3. **How is temperature regulation a physiological drive?**

   Temperature regulation can be viewed as a physiological drive because we have a need (are driven) to maintain our body temperatures within certain strict (homeostatic) levels. Doing so involves voluntary as well as involuntary responses.

4. **What factors motivate us to drink?**

   We are motivated to drink for several reasons, including a need to relieve dryness in our mouths and throats and to maintain a homeostatic level of fluid within our bodies (which is monitored by the hypothalamus). We also engage in drinking behavior in response to external cues (incentives), such as taste, aroma, or appearance. In addition, drinking behavior can be driven by our previous learning experiences.

5. **List some internal and external factors that motivate eating behaviors.**

   Several factors affect eating behaviors. Internal factors include cues mediated by the hypothalamus, which may be responding to stored fat levels, blood sugar levels, or other indicators that our normal homeostatic balance has been disrupted. Associated with this view is the position that body weight is maintained at a set point by both food intake and exercise levels. Awareness of being full may be stimulated by a hormone (leptin) produced under the control of an obesity gene. There is evidence that body size may be significantly determined by genetic factors. The stimulus properties of foods may motivate eating, as may habit patterns and social pressures.

6. **What is "obesity," and what are some of the probable causes of the so-called "obesity epidemic"?**

   Obesity is expressed in terms of a body mass index (BMI) of a person's weight in kilograms divided by height in meters. A BMI of 30 indicates obesity; a BMI of 35 indicates severe, or morbid, obesity. Rates of obesity have risen dramatically in the past 50 years, and rates of morbid obesity quadrupled between 1986 and 2000. Healthcare officials speak in terms of an epidemic. Part of the problem may be genetic. Part of the problem may be a relative insensitivity to the hormone *leptin*. There are few easy remedies for excessive weight. Still, cultural, environmental, and behavioral factors do contribute to overweight and can contribute to weight loss. Simply eating less and exercising more really can help.

7. **Describe anorexia nervosa and bulimia nervosa and comment on possible causes and treatments for them.**

The eating disorders *anorexia nervosa* and *bulimia* are most commonly found in females. These disorders afflict nearly 8 million Americans. The anorexic patient is essentially engaged in self-starvation, significantly reducing body weight (to levels more than 15 percent below normal). Bulimia involves recurrent binging and purging of large amounts of (usually) sweet, high-calorie foods. We do not know what causes eating disorders, but cultural, family, genetic, and hormonal influences have been implicated. A risk factor for both disorders is thin-ideal internalization—"buying into" the notion that thin is good and fat is bad. The prognosis for anorexia is poor. Initially, patients with anorexia usually receive medical treatment designed to restore body weight. Neither drug treatment nor psychotherapy has been particularly successful in treating anorexia. In the short term, antidepressant medications—especially when paired with psychotherapy—can be effective in treating bulimia. However, research suggests family-oriented therapy and cognitive therapies are most effective for treating bulimia.

8. **What factors motivate or influence sexual behaviors in humans?**

The sex drive is an unusual physiological drive because: a) individual survival does not depend on its satisfaction; b) unlike thirst and hunger, which replenish the body's energy, the sex drive depletes bodily energy when satisfied; c) it is not fully present at birth, but appears later; and d) the extent to which it is influenced by learned or external influences varies among species. The sex drive in humans may have a hormonal basis, but the pressures of culture, family, and peers have a strong influence on its expression. Surely what a person does, or with whom he or she does it, is influenced more by learning and experience than by biology. When compared to women, men have a greater interest in sex, a greater sexual desire, are less likely to require any sort of commitment from a sex partner, are more likely to use aggression or coercion in sex, and are less likely to change their sexual attitudes or behaviors.

9. **Describe the needs for achievement, power, affiliation, and intimacy.**

Achievement motivation, based on the *need to achieve (nAch),* is a need to attempt and succeed at tasks so as to meet or exceed a standard of excellence. Achievement needs are usually assessed by interpreting short stories generated in response to the *Thematic Apperception Test,* or TAT, in which one looks for themes of striving and achievement. The *need for power* is the need to be in charge, to be in control of a situation. *Affiliation needs* involve being motivated to be with others, to form friendships and interpersonal relationships. The *need for intimacy* is the need for close affectionate relationships. Individuals with a high need for intimacy tend to be warm, affectionate, and concerned for others. Although psychologists believe that achievement and power needs are learned and socially influenced, they are not as certain about the origins of affiliation and intimacy needs. These latter two needs may have a biological basis.

10. **What do psychologists mean when they talk about emotion?**

Psychologists claim that an emotional reaction has four components: a) the experience of a subjective feeling, or affective component; b) a cognitive appraisal or interpretation; c) an internal, visceral, physiological reaction; and d) an overt behavioral response.

11. **What has become of attempts to identify and classify basic, or primary, emotions?**

Dating back to Wundt in the 1800s, psychologists have attempted to categorize emotional reactions. Wundt believed that emotions had three intersecting dimensions: pleasantness-unpleasantness, relaxation-tension, and calm-excitement. Izard identified nine primary emotions: fear, anger, shame, contempt, disgust, distress, interest, surprise, and joy. Izard believed each of the nine had a unique physiological basis. Further, he believed that all other emotions were combinations of the primary emotions. Plutchik proposed eight basic emotions with many combinations and degrees. Other theorists have proposed as many as dozens or as few as two primary emotions. Richard Lazarus' theory of emotion highlighted the motivational aspects of emotion. He believed that we learn to seek out certain emotions (joy, pride, and love, for example) and to avoid others (fear, anger, guilt, for example). For the most part, psychologists agree that emotions represent valenced states—that they are either positive or negative. Psychologists have yet to reach agreement concerning just what positive and negative means in regard to emotion. The inconsistency among theories of emotion is proof that the task of finding basic emotions is extremely difficult. As a result of the inconsistency, some psychologists regard the whole effort as misguided.

12. **Describe the role of the autonomic nervous system and the brain in emotion.**

Some of our reactions when we become emotional are produced by the sympathetic division of the autonomic nervous system. These reactions occur to varying degrees and depend on the situation, but they generally include dilation of the pupils, increased heart rate and blood pressure, cessation of digestive processes, deeper and more rapid breathing, increased perspiration, and elevated blood sugar levels. Other reactions are indirectly caused by the release of the hormones epinephrine and norepinephrine into the blood. These reactions require a few seconds to take effect. Two brain structures closely involved in emotional reactions are the hypothalamus and the limbic system. The limbic system is most involved in confrontation or retreat responses. The hypothalamus also produces strong emotional reactions. The role of the cerebral cortex in emotional responding is not well understood. However, the cortex appears to play mainly an inhibitory role in emotionality. The cerebral cortex interprets impulses from the hypothalamus and limbic system and then modifies and directs the emotional reaction. Thus, the most prominent role of the cortex in emotional responding is cognitive in nature, giving meaning to emotional experiences.

13. **What do the James–Lange and the Cannon–Bard theories say about the roots of emotion?**

The *James–Lange theory* of emotion says that an emotion-producing stimulus causes physiological changes in the body (e.g., in the autonomic nervous system) and that the perception of these changes *is* the emotion. This view was challenged by the *Cannon–Bard theory*, which says that an emotion-producing stimulus produces activity in the subcortical areas of the brain, most notably the thalamus. The activity of the thalamus is what separates an emotion from a simple reaction to a non-emotional stimulus. Modern research has lent some support to the James–Lange explanation. Research shows that different emotions can produce different patterns of physiological activity and that self-induced bodily changes can elicit an emotional experience. There is also support for

Cannon's idea that the thalamus is important in the experience of emotions.

14. **What are the two-factor and cognitive appraisal theories of emotion?**

According to the *two-factor theory of emotion*, there are two important processes in the experience of emotion. The first process is physiological arousal. In response to an emotion-producing stimulus, the body produces a physiological response. The second process is a cognitive and involves attaching an appropriate label to the physiological arousal. Although some early research supported this theory, it has been called into question by recent findings. Despite its shortcomings, the two-factor theory rekindled interest in studying emotions.

The *cognitive appraisal theory of emotion* is a newer theory. It says that our thoughts and judgments about a stimulus or situation are central to the emotion that we experience. A cognitive theory of emotion proposed by Magda Arnold suggests that every emotion involves physiological arousal, an appraisal of the emotion-stimulus (e.g., pleasant versus unpleasant), and an assessment of the personal relevance of the stimulus. The process model of emotion suggests that emotions are ongoing experiences, rather than static events. In this model emotions have five components: precipitating event, cognitive appraisal, physiological changes, behavior tendencies/behaviors, and regulation. Klaus Scherer proposed a process theory of emotion called the content process model. According to this model, appraisal involves a series of *stimulus evaluation checks* (SECs). These checks occur in a fixed order: novelty (Is this a new or familiar situation?), pleasantness (Is the stimulus pleasant or unpleasant?), goal/need significance (Will this behavior help me reach a goal?), coping potential (How well will I be able to cope with this situation?), and norm compatibility (Does the behavior called for violate a norm?).

15. **What are unconscious emotions and how might they affect your daily emotional experiences?**

Unconscious emotions are emotions that are experienced below your normal level of awareness. Most traditional theories of emotion suggest that emotions are experienced consciously. Although this is true, research also shows that emotions are also experienced unconsciously. Unconscious emotions may relate to emotional states we experience that we cannot easily explain.

16. **What factors are involved in the communication of emotion from one organism to another?**

Charles Darwin was among those who popularized the theory that facial expressions provide information about internal states. In the years since Darwin, scientists have sought to better understand the role of facial expressions in the communication of emotions. For certain, communicating emotions via facial expressions has survival value. Recent research has revealed new complexities in how facial expressions convey emotions. Some facial expressions with emotional content are messages intended for a specific receiver. Paul Ekman and his colleagues claim to have identified facial expressions that appear to be universal. These include happiness, disgust, surprise, sadness, anger, and fear. Subjects from five countries were able to accurately identify these six emotions in photographs of faces. Again, further research indicates that some emotional states (happiness, for example) are easier to interpret than others (such as fear and disgust). In addition to facial expressions, humans use postural cues and language to communicate how they feel.

17. **What is the frustration-aggression hypothesis, and what factors influence the progression from becoming frustrated to becoming aggressive?**

Social psychologists define aggression as any behavior that is intended to inflict physical and/ or psychological harm on another organism or the symbol of that organism. The frustration-aggression hypothesis is one explanation of aggression. In its original form (Dollard and colleagues, 1939) it stated that aggression is always the result of frustration and that frustration always leads to aggression. Frustration occurs when a goal-directed behavior is blocked. The extent of frustration is influenced by three factors. The first factor is the strength of the drive. The stronger the original drive to perform a behavior, the more frustration results if that behavior is blocked. The second factor is the degree or extent to which a goal-directed behavior is blocked. The more complete the impediment, the more frustration results. A totally blocked behavior is more frustrating than a partially blocked behavior. The third factor is the accumulated number of frustrating experiences. The greater the number, the more frustration will result. In fact, frustration does not always lead to aggression and aggression often occurs without frustration. In light of these facts, scientists have updated the hypothesis: Frustration will lead to aggression only if it arouses a negative emotion such as anger. Research has produced some insights into the conditions under which we become angry. Anger can be aroused if we perceive that a person intended to harm us, if we feel we have been treated unjustly, or if we feel powerless.

Stress and Physical Health

11

PREVIEW

Stress is a consequence of living. No college student (or faculty member) is unfamiliar with stress. This chapter covers what psychologists have learned about stress, its causes, and our reactions to it. Our study of stress is divided into two main sections. First we will see—at least in general terms—what psychologists mean when they talk about stress and where stress comes from. What are the common sources of stress in our lives? The full answer is complex, but we will focus on three major categories of events that produce stress: frustration, conflict, and life events. Second, we will examine how people respond to stress. We shall see that some reactions to stress are positive and healthy, while others are maladaptive.

Health Psychology became the 38th professional division within the American Psychological Association in 1978. It now has more than 3,000 members—a fairly constant number over the past five years, but an increase of 200 percent over 1980 membership (Keeton, 2003). As its name suggests, health psychology is the study of psychological or behavioral factors that affect physical health and illness. Stress is surely one of those factors. As researchers, health psychologists seek to understand the relationships between psychological functioning and physical health. As applied psychologists, or practitioners, health psychologists help patients cope with physical diseases and illnesses, and they help people try to prevent health problems before they occur.

The involvement of psychologists in the medical realm of physical health is based on four assumptions:

1. Certain behaviors increase the risk of certain chronic diseases.
2. Changes in behaviors can reduce the risk of certain diseases.
3. Changing behaviors is often easier and safer than treating many diseases.
4. Behavioral interventions are comparatively cost-effective (based on Kaplan, 1984).

Thinking about physical health and illness in this way reflects the biopsychosocial model. As its name implies, this approach emphasizes the *interaction* of biological factors (such as a person's genetic predispositions), psychological factors (such as a person's reactions to stress or awareness of the risk of certain behaviors), and social factors (such as the influence of a person's cultural and family values or social support). You may remember our citing this sort of *interactionism* at the end of Chapter 1 as one of the key principles in psychology today.

Here, we examine two major thrusts of health psychology: research and practice. We'll look at the relationships between psychological variables and physical health, where researchers still ask the basic questions: What is it about psychological functioning that influences a person's physical health? Is it stress? Are there personality traits that predict illness, disease, and bad health? Then we'll consider how psychologists are joining the fight against illness and disease. In this regard, we'll focus on two important health problems: smoking and sexually transmitted diseases. Throughout these discussions, please keep in mind that we have foreshadowed many relevant issues in the coverage of drug and alcohol use and abuse (Chapter 4), and overweight and obesity (Chapter 10)—both of these are physical health problems strongly influenced by psychological factors.

STRESS: A FEW EXAMPLES TO WORK WITH

Stress is so common that it is, arguably, unavoidable. Being "stressed out" seems to be a universal condition—particularly among college students. In that spirit, a list of potentially stressful events could be endless. In this introductory section, we list a few (fictitious) examples that we will refer to throughout this chapter.

- It's Friday, and you have a chance to get away for the weekend. Unfortunately, you have two big exams Monday and need the weekend to study.
- Lindsay is almost done typing a term paper when suddenly the power goes out. Having failed to save her work, she'll have to redo it all.
- Cindy and Jerry have known each other since grade school. They dated throughout high school and college. Next week, family and friends will celebrate their marriage.
- Doug wants to make the basketball team, but the coach tells him that he is just too short to play.
- Marian is excited about going to Germany in a student-exchange program, but she's also very nervous about getting along in a new country.
- After 11 years on the road as a salesperson, Wayne is being promoted to district sales manager—an office job with a substantial raise in pay.
- Jake cut his smoking back to one pack a day and was considering starting an exercise program. Having just suffered a heart attack, he is in intensive care.
- Three-year-old Trudy keeps asking her mother for a cookie. Mother steadfastly refuses because it's almost dinner time. Trudy returns to her room and promptly pulls an arm off her favorite doll.
- You are late for class and driving rapidly down a two-lane road. A driver pulls out in front of you and drives ten miles per hour below the speed limit.
- Shirley wants to be a concert pianist, but her music teacher tells her she does not have the talent or discipline.

Life is filled with stress, frustration, and conflict. These are the types of stressful events people encounter every day. We will refer to these examples throughout this chapter.

Courtesy of Purestock/Getty Images.

Even if the choices that one has to make involve pleasant, positive alternatives (e.g., "Which dessert(s) should I choose?"), the very process of having to make such choices can create stress.

STRESSORS: THE CAUSES OF STRESS

Although each of us knows stress and how it feels, psychologists have struggled with how to characterize stress for nearly 60 years. **Stress** may be defined as a complex set of reactions made by an individual under pressure to adapt. In other words, stress is a response that people make to their "appraisal that important goals have been harmed, lost, or threatened" (Folkman & Moskowitz, 2004, p. 747). Stress happens inside people. Stress includes physiological reactions and unpleasant feelings (for example, increased heart rate and experienced anxiety). Stress can be so unpleasant that it motivates us. If nothing else, when we feel stress, we want to take action to reduce it or to eliminate it altogether.

Stress can be produced by many circumstances or events. These sources of stress are called **stressors**. We will consider three types of stressors: frustration, conflict, and life events. Then, once we see where stress comes from, we will consider techniques people use to cope with it.

stress a complex set of reactions made by an individual under pressure to adapt

stressor the source of stress

Frustration-Induced Stress

Motivated behaviors are *goal-directed.* Whether by internal processes (drives) or external stimuli (incentives), we are pushed or pulled toward our positive goals and away from our negative goals. However, people do not always reach all of their positive goals. Have you gotten everything you've ever wanted? Nor are people able to avoid their negative goals perfectly. Have you always been able to avoid unpleasantness, pain, or sorrow? Do you know anyone who has?

Sometimes we never reach a particular goal. At other times, we progress more slowly or with greater difficulty than we would like. In either case, we become frustrated. **Frustration** is the blocking or thwarting of goal-directed behavior—blocking that may be total and permanent or partial and temporary (see Figure 11.1).

Stress resulting from frustration is a normal, commonplace reaction. Frustration is a stressor, and the stress it produces is part of life. In no way does experiencing stress as a result of frustration imply weakness, illness, or pathology. Remember: How individuals react to the stressors in their lives is what matters most.

Someone who is frustrated and stressed may not be thinking clearly enough to wonder about the source of the stress. However, in order to respond adaptively, it helps to recognize the source of the blocking—the particular stressor—keeping us from our goals. There are two basic types of frustration: environmental and personal.

Environmental frustration implies that the blocking of one's goal-directed behavior is caused by something or somebody in the environment. (Note that psychologists identify sources of frustration, but they do not assign blame.) Remember our example of Lindsay, who lost her term paper when the power went out? Her frustration is environmental. Lindsay wanted to get her term paper done. Her goal-directed behavior led her to use her computer. Something in her environment—a momentary power outage—kept her from reaching her goal. And remember Trudy? She wanted a cookie, but her mother said, "No, it's dinner time." Trudy was also frustrated by her environment, but in a slightly different way. She wanted a cookie, and her mother blocked that motivated behavior. Environmental frustration, in which the source of the blocking is another person, is sometimes called *social frustration.*

Occasionally we are frustrated because of an internal or personal reason. This is called *personal frustration.* Doug fails to make the basketball team because he is too short. Shirley, who wants to be a concert pianist, may be frustrated because she does not have sufficient talent. Some of us have learned that getting older can be stressful. When we have difficulty doing things that used to be easy, we may feel stress. In this case, the stress is frustration-induced and an example of personal frustration.

Conflict-Induced Stress

Sometimes we cannot satisfy a particular drive or motive because it is in conflict with other motives that are influencing us at the same time. That is, stress may result from conflicting motives. *Motivational conflicts* imply a choice has to be made. When the choice is relatively easy, the stress will be slight; when the choice is harder, the resulting stress will be greater. When discussing conflicts, we talk about positive goals

 frustration the blocking or thwarting of goal-directed behavior

FIGURE 11.1

A depiction of frustration, the blocking or thwarting of goal-directed behavior.

and negative goals. Positive goals are those that one wishes to approach, and negative goals are those that one wishes to avoid. There are four major types of stress-inducing motivational conflicts.

Conflicts are necessarily unpleasant, stress-producing situations, even when the goals involved are positive. In an **approach-approach conflict**, an organism is caught between two (or more) alternatives, and each of them is positive, or potentially reinforcing (Figure 11.2). If alternative A is chosen, a desired goal will be reached. If B is chosen, a different desirable goal will be attained. Conflict arises because only one alternative may be chosen.

Resolving an approach-approach conflict yields something positive, no matter which alternative is chosen. If Carla enters an ice cream shop with only enough money to buy one scoop of ice cream, she may experience a conflict when faced with all the flavors that are available that day. Typical of conflict, she will sway back and forth among alternatives. However, when she decides, she will walk out of the store with an ice cream cone of some flavor she likes. Her life might have been easier (less stressful) if the store had just one flavor and she didn't have to make a choice.

Sometimes the choices we have to make are much more serious. What will be your college major? On the one hand, you would like to go to medical school and be a surgeon (that's a positive incentive or goal). On the other hand, you would like to study composition and conducting at a school of music (also a clearly positive goal). At the moment, you cannot do both. Premed students take different courses than music majors do. Both are constructive, desirable alternatives, but at registration you have to make a choice, one that will have long-lasting repercussions. The long-lasting consequences of such a conflict qualify it as a stressor.

Perhaps the most stress-inducing of all motivational conflicts are the **avoidance-avoidance conflicts** (Figure 11.3). In this type of conflict, a person is faced with several alternatives, and each of them is negative or in some way punishing.

Avoidance-avoidance conflict is common in the workplace. Imagine that you are a supervisor of a large department. Your department has been doing well and is making a profit, but management directs you to cut your operating budget 20 percent by next month. There are ways you can reduce expenses—limit travel, cut down on supplies, reduce pay, eliminate expense accounts—but each involves an action you would rather not take. If you do nothing at all, you may lose your job. The result may be stress, and the stressor is an avoidance-avoidance conflict.

With **approach-avoidance conflicts**, a person is in the position of considering only one goal (Figure 11.4). What makes this situation a conflict is that the

FIGURE 11.2

A diagram of an approach-approach conflict. In such a conflict, a person is faced with two (or more) attractive, positive goals and must choose between or among them.

FIGURE 11.3

A diagram of an avoidance-avoidance conflict. In such a conflict, a person is faced with two (or more) unattractive, negative goals, and must choose between or among them. This is sometimes referred to as a "no-win" situation.

FIGURE 11.4

A diagram of an approach-avoidance conflict. Here, a person is faced with only one goal. What makes this a conflict is that the goal has both positive and negative aspects or features.

approach-approach conflict a situation in which an organism is caught between two or more alternatives and each of them is positive, or potentially reinforcing

avoidance-avoidance conflict a situation in which a person is faced with several alternatives, each of them negative or in some way punishing

approach-avoidance conflict a situation in which a person is faced with only one goal and would like to reach that goal, but at the same time would like not to

person would very much like to reach that goal, but at the same time would very much like not to. It is a matter of "Yes, I'd love to . . . Well, I'd rather not . . . Maybe I would . . . No, I wouldn't . . . yes . . . no." Consider starting a relationship with someone special. On the one hand, such a relationship might be wonderful. On the other hand, asking for a date puts you in a position to be rejected.

People in approach-avoidance conflicts vacillate between alternatives—motivated to approach and, at the same time, motivated to avoid. Marian in our opening examples is in an approach-avoidance conflict. She wants to go to Germany and be an exchange student, but she fears leaving the country she knows.

Multiple approach-avoidance conflicts may be the most common of the conflicts experienced by adults (see Figure 11.5). This type of conflict arises when an individual is faced with a number of alternatives, each one of which is in some way both positive and negative.

Perhaps you and some friends are shopping on a Saturday morning. You realize that it is getting late, and you all are hungry. Where will you go to lunch? You have a multiple approach-avoidance conflict here. "We could go to Bob's Diner, where the food is cheap and the service is fast, but the food really isn't very good. We could go to Cafe Olé, where the food is better, but service is a little slower, and the food is more expensive. Or we could go to The Grille, where the service is elegant and the food is superb, but the price is very high." Granted this is not an earth-shaking dilemma, but each alternative has pluses and minuses to be considered. The more difficult the choice is, the greater the stress that can result.

Think of your decision to go to college. First, there was the multiple approach-avoidance conflict of whether to go at all: "I could forget about it, just stay here; get a good job; lay back and be happy, but all my friends are going, and college graduates do make more money than high school graduates." Now that you have decided to go, the conflict becomes a choice among colleges. All of the pluses and minuses of each college need to be considered: Stay at home and go to school nearby? Stay in state for lower tuition, but move away from home? Get away and go some place you have always wanted to live?

Life is filled with such conflicts, and some of them can cause extreme stress. Possible conflicts include "What will I do with the rest of my life?" "Should I stay at home with the children (+ and –), or should I have a career (+ and –)?" "Should I get married or stay single, or is there another way (+ and – in each case)?" "Should I work for company A (+ and –), or should I work for company B (+ and –)?" Clearly, such lists could go on and on. Reflect on the conflicts you have faced during the past few weeks. Can you categorize each of them into one of the four types listed here?

Life-Induced Stress

Frustration and conflict and the stress that goes with them are unavoidable parts of life. There are other sources of stress that do not fit neatly into our descriptions of conflict or frustration. Psychologists have looked at events and changes that occur in life as potential sources of stress.

multiple approach-avoidance conflict a situation in which an individual is faced with a number of alternatives, each one of which is at the same time and in some way both positive and negative

FIGURE 11.5

A diagram of multiple approach-avoidance conflict. In such a conflict, a person is faced with two (or more) alternatives, each of which has both positive and negative aspects or features, and a choice must be made between or among the alternatives.

In 1967, Thomas Holmes and Richard Rahe published the first version of their *Social Readjustment Rating Scale*, or *SRRS* (Holmes & Holmes, 1970). The basic idea behind this scale is that stress results whenever life situations change. The scale provides a list of potentially stressful life events. The original list of such events was drawn from the reports of patients suffering from moderate to high levels of stress in their lives. Marriage was arbitrarily assigned a value of 50 stress points, or life-change units. With "marriage = 50" as their guide, the patients rated a number of other life changes by how stressful they were in comparison. The death of a spouse got the highest rating (100 units), followed by divorce (73 units), pregnancy (40 units), trouble with the boss (23 units), changing to a new school (20 units), and minor violations of the law (11 units). In a rather direct way, the SRRS gives us a way to measure the stress in our lives.

There is a positive correlation between scores on the *SRRS* and the incidence of physical illness and disease. People with *SRRS* scores between 200 and 299 have a 50-50 chance of developing symptoms of physical illness within the next two years, whereas 80 percent of those with scores above 300 develop symptoms within the same time period. Several studies that have looked at *SRRS* scores and health problems have found positive correlations (Adler et al., 1994; Brett et al., 1990). The logic is that stress predisposes one to physical illness (Krantz & McCeney, 2002). But correlations do not tell us about cause and effect. Some of the *SRRS* items mention physical illness or are health-related. So it is no surprise to find that scores are related to levels of physical illness.

Socioeconomic status, or SES, is a measure that reflects income, educational level, and occupation. Sensibly, there is a negative correlation between socioeconomic level and experienced stress (Adler et al., 1999; Bradley & Corwyn, 2002; Sapolsky, 2005). SES is

Courtesy of Ariel Skelley/Getty Images.

Moving into a new home is an exciting and surely positive life event, But no matter how positive it may be, the process is bound to be stressful.

related to stress in at least two ways: a) Persons of higher socioeconomic status are less likely to encounter negative life events, such as unemployment, poor housing, frequent household moves, and less access to quality health care (McLeod & Kessler, 1990; Sapolsky, 2005), and b) Persons of low SES have fewer resources to deal with stressful life events when they occur.

It does not take a lot of imagination to think of life situations likely to produce stress. For example, being a working mother is a stressor. Indeed, working mothers experience stress to a much greater extent than working fathers do (Chandola, Brunner, & Marmot, 2006; Light, 1997; Matthews et al., 1997). Isn't it logical that being a single parent or being a college student with children can be stressful? Certainly, being diagnosed with a serious, life-threatening disease is a stress-producing life event (Anderson, 1997).

Richard Lazarus (1981, 1991c, 1993, 2000) has long argued that psychologists should focus on smaller and less dramatic life changes as sources of accumulating stress. For Lazarus it is not the major life changes, but the little hassles that cause the most stress. What often

socioeconomic status (SES) a measure that reflects income, educational level, and occupation

matters most are life's little *hassles*—the traffic that goes too slowly, the toothpaste tube that splits, ants at a picnic, the cost of a pizza compared to what it was just a few years ago. Major life-change events are too large to affect us directly. What causes us stress is the way big events produce little, irritating changes and hassles in our lives. Being retired may mean no friendly conversation at coffee-break time. A spouse who returns to work may make life more difficult; the other spouse may have to cook dinner for the first time. Thus, stress is not so much a reaction to an event itself but to the hassles it creates. Also, large traumatic events are rare (one hopes), and "thus their cumulative effect on health and well-being may not be as great as that of minor yet frequent stressors, such as work deadlines and family arguments" (Almeda, 2005, p. 64).

Lazarus and his colleagues created a scale to assess how hassled people are (Kanner et al, 1981). Respondents to the Hassles Scale, as it is called, indicate which hassles they have experienced and rate the severity of the resulting stress. The ten most-commonly cited daily hassles for college students and for middle-aged adults are listed in Table 11.1. *The Hassles Scale* turns out to predict physical health problems and anxiety and depression better than the *Social Readjustment Rating Scale* (DeLongis et al., 1988).

The events in our lives that we view as stressors do not have to be negative or unpleasant. Many events we look forward to bring with them hassles and stress (Folkinan & Moskowitz, 2000; Somerfield & McCrae, 2000). For example, everybody is happy about Cindy and Jerry getting married—a pleasant, positive life event. At the same time—as any married person will attest—weddings and the preparations for them are stressors. New conflicts arise. If Aunt Sarah is invited, does that mean that Aunt Louise must be invited as well? Cindy and Jerry are planning an outdoor reception. What if it rains? And there's Wayne the experienced salesman, now a sales manager. Wayne may have become used to being on the road and setting his own hours. Now that he has a promotion ("good news"), his daily routine may be drastically altered by his being confined to an office. These changes could stress Wayne.

TABLE 11.1

Ten common stressors in the lives of middle-aged adults and college students.

For Middle-aged Adults:	For College Students:
1. Concerns about weight	1. Troubling thoughts about the future
2. Health of a family member	2. Not getting enough sleep
3. Rising prices of common goods	3. Wasting time
4. Home maintenance (interior)	4. Inconsiderate smokers
5. Too many things to do	5. Physical appearance
6. Misplacing or losing things	6. Too many things to do
7. Yard work or outside home maintenance	7. Misplacing or losing things
8. Property, investments, or taxes	8. Not enough time to do the things you need to do
9. Crime	9. Concerns about meeting high standards
10. Physical appearance	10. Being lonely

BEFORE YOU GO ON

1. Define the terms *stress* and *stressor*.
2. Describe the stressors characterized as frustration, conflict, and life events.

A Point to Ponder or Discuss
What stressors (large and small) did you experience last week? Sort these stressors into the three categories discussed in this section.

INDIVIDUAL DIFFERENCES IN RESPONDING TO STRESSORS

Different people respond to stressors in different ways. What constitutes a stressor and what someone may do when he or she experiences stress can vary considerably from person to person. Some fall apart at weddings; others find them only mildly stressful. For some people, simple choices are difficult to make; for others, choices are not enough, and they seek challenges. Stress even affects the same person differently at different times. For example, being caught in slow-moving traffic might drive you up the wall. In the same situation a few days later, you are not bothered at all. So remember that reactions to stressors vary from time to time and from person to person.

Some researchers argue that the amount of stress experienced and the means of coping with stress are not different for men and women (Baum & Grunberg, 1991; Lazarus, 1993). Others, however, argue that there are significant differences between how males and females deal with stress (Taylor et al., 2000). Whereas males are more likely to display a "fight-or-flight" response to stress, females (and not just human females at that) are more likely to respond with what Taylor and her colleagues call a "tend-and-befriend" response. A father at home alone with a sick and crying child is likely to scurry around to find someone to look after the baby. A mother in the same situation is more likely to call her older sister or mother, seeking advice.

Some people seem so generally resistant to the negative aspects of stress they are said to have *hardy personalities* (Ford-Gilboe & Cohen, 2000; Kobasa, 1979, 1982, 1987). Hardiness in this context is related to three things: a) *challenge*—being able to see difficulties as opportunity for change and growth, not as a threat to status; b) *control*—being in charge of what is happening and believing that a person is the master of his or her fate; and c) *commitment*—being engaged or involved with life, its circumstances and consequences, not just watching life go by from the sidelines.

Some responses to stress are more effective or adaptive than others. Stress often follows as a natural consequence of being alive and motivated in the real world. Unfortunately, people occasionally develop ineffective or maladaptive strategies for dealing with stressors, meaning that, in the long run, they will not be successful in reducing stress. Before we consider strategies for dealing with stress, let's look more closely at the physiological reactions to stressors.

SELYE'S GENERAL ADAPTATION SYNDROME

Stressors produce a series of physiological reactions within us no matter how we ultimately cope with stress. In this way, stress is much like our other reactions to emotion-producing stimuli in

Final exams are just one week away. Sarah learns that her father has suffered a severe heart attack. She sits in the hospital waiting room uncertain of his prognosis and worried about what she should do. The longer such a scenario continues, the greater the accumulated stress. In such an example we can see all three stages of Hans Selye's General Adaptation Syndrome.

Courtesy of ColorBlind Images/Blend Images/Corbis.

General Adaptation Syndrome the most widely accepted description of the physiological reactions to chronic stressors, including alarm, resistance, and exhaustion stages

our environments. When we experience stress, demands are made on the physiological systems of our bodies. Hans Selye's **General Adaptation Syndrome,** or GAS, is the most widely accepted description of the physiological reactions to chronic (long-lasting) stressors. According to Selye (1956, 1974), the reaction to stressors occurs in three stages: alarm, resistance, and exhaustion.

The first response to the perception of a stressor is *alarm.* Any perceived threat produces rapid and noticeable changes in the sympathetic division of the autonomic nervous system: Blood pressure and heart rate increase, pupils dilate, digestion stops, and blood rushes to the extremities of the body. The adrenal glands enlarge and secrete norepinephrine into the bloodstream, mobilizing the body's resources and increasing blood

sugar. This strong, often dramatic, reaction cannot last long. It usually lasts no more than several minutes, a few hours at the most.

Imagine Pat, a college student. Pat is strongly motivated to do well in his courses. It is just past midterm, and he gets word from home that his father has had a massive heart attack. Near panic, he drives 16 hours straight home and rushes to the hospital. His father has never been seriously ill before, but now he's in coronary intensive care. The shock and disbelief nearly overwhelm Pat in his initial alarm stage. (You can follow this example of the General Adaptation Syndrome in Figure 11.6.)

In *resistance,* the second stage of the GAS, the cause of stress remains present. Pat's body continues to fight off the challenge of the stressor. His father begins to show signs of recovery, but he will remain in coronary intensive care for three more days and will be hospitalized longer still. Pat is powerless to help his father, but he feels that he can't go back to school right now. Every day he stays, he gets further behind in school.

Pat's body mobilized resources in the alarm stage of the GAS. Without a way to escape the source of his stress, he stays aroused and his body's resources continue to drain. If new stressors appear, Pat will be less able to deal effectively with them. More than that, he will be even more sensitive to new stressors that

FIGURE 11.6

Selye's General Adaptation Syndrome calls for three levels of largely physiological reactions to stressors. In the alarm reaction, resources are quickly mobilized as the sympathetic division of the ANS springs into action. If the stressor remains, the organism enters a defensive resistance stage. Following prolonged exposure to a stressor, the energy necessary for adaptive resistance may become depleted in a stage of exhaustion.

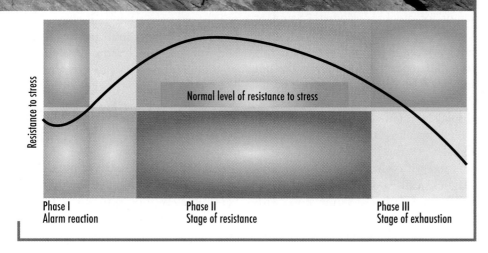

Resistance to stress

Normal level of resistance to stress

Phase I
Alarm reaction

Phase II
Stage of resistance

Phase III
Stage of exhaustion

he might have otherwise ignored. He will become more vulnerable to physical illness and infection. He may develop high blood pressure, ulcers, skin rashes, or respiratory difficulties. Pat may appear in control, but his father's condition and his looming exams eat away at him, intruding into his awareness.

If Pat cannot cope with the stress, he will reach exhaustion. In this stage, his bodily resources are nearly depleted. He is running out of energy and time. Pat may break down—physically, psychologically, or both. Pat may become depressed. Although the resistance stage may last for several months, resources run out. In extreme cases (e.g., if stressors remain or even worsen over months), the exhaustion stage may result in death.

Some of the particulars of Selye's syndrome have been challenged, but ample evidence supports its basic tenets. Indeed, many studies document stress as a risk factor for infectious disease and even premature death (Antoni & Lutgendorf, 2007; Krantz & McCeney, 2002; Matthews & Gump, 2002; Robles, Glaser, & Kiecolt-Glaser, 2005). One study actually found a mechanism that linked stress to aging and premature death: Individual cells age faster in people with a lot of chronic stress. The study compared the length of a structure in white blood cells (*telomere*—known to be related to aging) in mothers of chronically ill children and mothers of healthy children. The mothers with high stress levels had telomere lengths indicating an equivalent aging of ten years (Epel et al., 2004).

For Selye, stress is a three-stage mobilization of the body's resources to combat real or perceived threats to our well-being. In that sense, the process *is* adaptive—at least through the stage of resistance. Unfortunately, we have a limited supply of adaptive resources, and repeated exposure to stressors has a cumulative effect. So dire consequences can result when someone faces several stressful situations simultaneously or nearly simultaneously. Selye's model focuses on how a person responds to stressors physiologically. It does not take into account how a person may respond to stressors in more cognitive and behavioral ways. In short, it does not consider how people think about stress and what strategies are effective in overcoming stress. In the next section, we will look at what works and what doesn't in the battle against stress.

BEFORE YOU GO ON

3. Comment on individual differences in how people respond to stressors.
4. Describe the stages of Selye's General Adaptation Syndrome.

A Point to Ponder or Discuss
Do you have a "hardy personality"? Do you know anyone who does? To what extent do you think that "hardiness" in this context can be learned or developed?

EFFECTIVE STRATEGIES FOR COPING WITH STRESS

In the long run, the most effective way to deal with stress is to learn from it. Learning is defined as a relatively permanent change in behavior that occurs as the result of practice or experience. Responding to a stressor with learning makes particularly good sense for frustration-induced stress. In a frustrating situation, the pathway to our goal is being blocked. An adaptive way to handle such a stressor is to learn a new way

FIGURE 11.7

Reacting to frustration with learning is the most effective long-term reaction to stressors. That is, when one's goal-directed behaviors are continually blocked or thwarted, one should consider bringing about a relatively permanent change in those behaviors, or consider changing one's goals altogether.

to reach our goal or to learn to modify our goal (see Figure 11.7).

In fact, much of our everyday learning is motivated by frustration-induced stress. You have learned many new responses to cope with frustration. Having been frustrated once (or twice) by locking yourself out of your house or car, you learn to hide a spare set of keys where you can easily find them. Having been caught in a blizzard (or a tropical storm) with no cookies in the house, you have learned to bake them. You may have learned as a child to get what you wanted from your parents by smiling sweetly and asking politely. In each of these cases, what motivated the learning was the stress resulting from frustration.

Learning motivated by stress may also teach the value of escape and avoidance. You now know how to avoid getting into many motivational conflicts. You may have learned that a sensible thing to do once you are in a conflict is to escape from the situation altogether or to make major changes in what is motivating you. In some ways, stress can be seen as a positive force in our lives because it produces the stimuli that motivate learning. If we were never challenged, never set difficult goals, never faced stressful situations, we would miss out on many opportunities for personal growth. The stress we experience is unpleasant at the time, but it can produce many positive consequences (Carver & Scheier, 1999; Folkman & Moskowitz, 2000, 2004; Tedeschi, Park, & Calhoun, 1998).

emotion-focused strategies techniques that deal with how one feels and how to change the way one feels when dealing with stress and stressors

problem-focused strategies techniques that deal with finding the underlying situation that is causing one's stress and taking steps to deal with it

To say that we should respond to stressful situations by learning new, effective behaviors is sensible enough, but are there specific measures that we can take to help alleviate stress? Indeed, there are. Here are eight such strategies.

Identify the Stressor

Remember that stress is a reaction to any one of several types of stressors. If you experience stress in your life, the first thing to ask is, "Where is this stress coming from?" Are you having difficulty resolving a motivational conflict? What positive or negative goals are involved? Is your goal-directed behavior being blocked? If so, what is the source of your frustration? What recent changes or events in your life are upsetting or problematic? Any successful strategy for coping with stress will require change and effort on your part. The first thing to do is to make sure your efforts are directed at the real source of your stress.

Efforts for dealing with stress can be categorized as being emotion-focused or problem-focused (Folkman & Moskowitz, 2004; Lazarus & Folkman, 1984). The difference is self-evident. Strategies that are **emotion-focused** deal with how you feel and with finding ways to change the way you feel. This strategy is often the first reaction to stressors: "I feel stressed out and miserable; how can I feel better?" Real progress, however, usually requires looking beyond how you feel at the moment to find the underlying situation causing your present feelings—a **problem-focused strategy**: "Where did this stress come from, and how can I make it go away?"

Remove or Negate the Stressor

Once a stressor has been identified, the next logical question is, "Can anything be done about it?" Do I have to stay in this situation, or can I bring about a change? If an interpersonal relationship has become a nagging source of stress, might this be the time to think about breaking it off? If the stress at work has become overwhelming, might this be a good time to consider a different job? The issue is one of taking control, of trying to turn a challenge into an opportunity. Granted, this process sounds cut and dried, even easy. What makes the process difficult is that there usually is affect involved—often very strong emotional reactions. What we are describing here is largely a cognitive, "problem-solving" approach. If it is going to be at all successful, negative emotions have to be set aside, at least for the time being. Recall that people with "hardy personalities" are likely to take control of stressful situations. These are the people who know how to avoid many of the negative consequences of stress. Further evidence of the value of being proactive comes from studies of the terminally ill. People with terminal illnesses fare much better if they take control, find out everything there is to know about their illness, seek second and third opinions, and make the most of what time they have left (Antoni & Lutgendorf, 2007; van der Pompe, Antoni, & Heijnen, 1998).

Reappraise the Situation

We should assess whether the stressors in our lives are real or (even partially) imagined threats to our well-being. Making this determination is part of what is called a *cognitive reappraisal* of one's situation (Folkman & Moskowitz, 2000; Schultz & Decker, 1985). In the context of stress management, cognitive reappraisal means rethinking a situation to put it in the best possible light.

Is that co-worker really trying to do you out of a promotion? Do you really care if you are invited to the party? Must you earn an A on the next test to pass the course? Are things really as bad as they seem? Lazarus (1993, p. 9) sees cognitive reappraisal as realizing that "people should try to change the noxious things that can be changed, accept those that cannot, and have the wisdom to know the difference"—a paraphrase of an ancient Hebrew prayer.

Courtesy of Amana Productions Inc./Getty Images.

Meichenbaum (1977) has argued that we can deal with a lot of stress simply by talking to ourselves, replacing negative statements (such as, "Oh boy, I'm really in trouble now. I'm sure to be called on, and I'll embarrass myself in front of the whole class") with coping statements (such as, "I'll just do the best I can. I am as prepared as anybody in here, and this will all be over soon"). This cognitive approach takes practice, but it can be very effective.

Inoculate Against Future Stressors

Among other things, this strategy involves accepting and internalizing much of what we have been saying about stress and stressors being a part of everyone's experience. Inoculation is largely a matter of convincing yourself that stress has occurred before, will occur again, and that this, too, will pass. It is a matter of anticipation and preparation—truly coming to accept the reality that "worrying about this won't make it any better," or "no matter how bad things look, I'll be able to figure out some plan to deal with it." Surgery patients recover faster and with fewer post-surgical complications if they are fully informed before their surgery of what they can expect, how

One positive way of dealing with stress is cognitive reappraisal— what Meichenbaum calls "talking to ourselves, trying to convince ourselves that things are not really as bad as they may seem. A good strategy is to replace negative thoughts, such as, "Oh boy, I'm in trouble now. I'm going to be next to give my speech in class, and I'm bound to just sound stupid!" with more positive thoughts, such as "Hey, I'm as prepared as I possibly can be. No one, not even the professor expect me to be a pro. I surely can do this as well as anybody else in here. I'll just do my best, and in a few minutes this all will be over!"

they are likely to feel, and what they can do to aid in their own recovery.

Aspinwall and Taylor (1997) refer to this sort of response to stressors as "proactive coping." It is a matter of: a) building a reserve of resources (including time, finances, and social support), b) anticipating future stressors, c) making early appraisals of those future stressors, d) engaging in coping strategies early on, and e) contemplating and using feedback about strategies that have worked in the past (Aspinwall, 2003; Folkman & Moskowitz, 2004, p. 757). People in high-stress occupations (emergency-room personnel, for example) can be trained to anticipate stressors and deal with these stressors even before they occur. This stress-exposure training or SET, as it is called, can reduce the experience of stress and increase performance on the job (Driskell & Johnston, 1998; Salas & Cannon-Bowers, 2001).

Inoculating yourself against future stressors often amounts to developing a sense of optimism that generally good things, as opposed to bad things, will happen to you. Optimistic people "routinely maintain higher levels of subjective well-being during times of stress than do people who are less optimistic" (Scheier & Carver, 1993, p. 27). Optimism also predicts better adjustment in one's first year away at college, less depression among mothers following childbirth, better rates of recovery from heart surgery, and better overall physical health (Aspinwall & Taylor, 1992; Cohen & Pressman, 2006; Pressman & Cohen, 2005; Scheier & Carver, 1992, 1993).

Take Your Time with Important Decisions

Stress often accompanies the process of making tough decisions. You are frustrated. A goal-directed behavior is being blocked. You have to decide if you will pursue a different course of action. Which course of action? Would it be wiser to change your goal? Do you want

to do this (+ and –) or do you want to do that (+ and –)? We may make matters worse by rushing a decision "just to have it over with," even granting that occasionally we are faced with deadlines. We may add to an already-stressful situation by racing to conclusions before we have all the facts and before we have explored all the costs and benefits associated with the alternatives (Hogan, 1989). For example, if you can't make up your mind about buying a new car, don't make a quick purchase. Instead, why not rent the same model for a few days to be sure you will be happy with it?

The strategies listed above are suggestions for coping with a stressor. As problem-focused strategies, these are the only effective, long-term ways to deal with stressors. In the short-term, however, there are some things that can combat the unpleasant feelings or affects that accompany stress. We'll look at three emotion-focused strategies.

Learn Techniques of Relaxation

Learning to relax may not easy to accomplish, but the logic behind the strategy is simple to understand: Feeling stressed and being relaxed are not compatible responses. If you can relax, the experience (feelings) of stress will be diminished. Hypnosis, meditation, and relaxation training have all been used to help patients relax.

A variety of operant conditioning called biofeedback can provide relief from the tension associated with stress (Kamiya et al., 1977; Shirley et al., 1992). **Biofeedback** is "the process of providing information to an individual about his [or her] bodily processes in some form which he [or she] might be able to use to modify those processes" (Hill, 1985, p. 201). For example, a person's heart rate is constantly monitored, and the rate is fed back to the person in the form of an audible tone. As heart rate increases, the tone becomes higher.

biofeedback the technique of providing information about internal bodily processes in such a form that the person might be able to modify those processes

When heart rate decreases, the tone gets lower. Once the person learns (through the feedback) what his or her heart rate is doing, the person may gain some control over that response. Positive change (a lower heart rate) is reinforced by the lower tone the person hears and the knowledge that the person has succeeded. As a result of being reinforced, the stress-fighting responses increase in their frequency (Kaplan, 1991; Linden & Moseley, 2006; Nakao et al., 2003).

Engage in Physical Exercise

Exercise can be part of a program to prevent stress in the first place. Creating such a program requires common sense. Deciding tomorrow you will run five miles a day, rain or shine, may create more stress than it eliminates. Exercise should be enjoyable, not overly strenuous, and help you feel better about yourself. Even when you become stressed, you can benefit from exercise. There is a good deal of evidence that physical exercise (aerobic exercise in particular) helps combat stress (Anshel, 1996; Hays, 1995). Physical exercise helps once stress is experienced, but it is difficult to say if exercise combats stress directly or does so indirectly by improving overall physical health, stamina, self-esteem, and self-confidence.

Seek Social Support

Finally, social support helps persons experiencing stress. Perhaps no one

Courtesy of Lori Adamski Peek/Getty Images.

A reasonable program of physical exercise can help to fight off the feelings of stress. It is important that one's exercise program is reasonable enough that it does not become a stressor in its own right.

knows precisely how you feel or has experienced exactly the same situation, but all of us have known stress, and we all know the types of situations that give rise to it. Social support from friends and relatives or from others, such as physicians, clergy, therapists, or counselors can be very helpful (Adler & Matthews, 1994; Berghuis & Stanton, 2002; Coyne & Downey, 1991). If at all possible, one should not face stress alone.

Now that we have reviewed some steps to help alleviate stress, let's consider some reactions to stress that are not as adaptive.

BEFORE YOU GO ON

5. Briefly summarize both problem-focused and emotion-focused strategies that can help cope with stress.

A Point to Ponder or Discuss
No doubt you have used several of the strategies in this section when you have experienced stress. Are there any you have not tried? Have you learned anything that might help you combat stress?

INEFFECTIVE STRATEGIES FOR COPING WITH STRESSORS

Coping effectively with stress generally requires change. If you do not change, you fixate and accept the same stress from the same stressor. Fixation is seldom an adequate reaction to stress. The adage, "If at first you don't succeed, try, try again" is sound advice. But there is also a point where sensible people recognize that a particular course of action is not likely to work. At some point, we must give up and try something else.

In a way, *procrastination* is a form of fixation, isn't it? Your term paper is due in two weeks, but you can't seem to get started, deciding to put it off until this weekend. The weekend brings the usual diversions, and the stress of dealing with the paper is momentarily postponed. The catch is that you are going to pay a price. Eventually, you will have to do the paper. Then, just before the deadline, you will probably experience more stress than ever before. A long-term study of procrastination in college students found that procrastinators experienced less stress and fewer illnesses

early in the semester, but as the semester progressed, they reported greater stress, more illness, and more serious illnesses. And procrastinators earned significantly lower grades. As the authors of this study put it, "Procrastination thus appears to be a self-defeating behavior pattern marked by short-term benefits and long-term costs" (Tice & Baumeister, 1997). In addition to failing to adjust one's behavior or goals or attempting to ignore the problem, there are two other maladaptive reactions to stressors: aggression and anxiety.

There are many causes of aggression, but one source of aggressive behaviors is stress—in particular, the stress from frustration. A student expecting an A on a paper gets a C-, returns to her room, and throws her hairbrush at the mirror, shattering it. Judging it to be moving too slowly, a driver in a hurry rams the bumper of the car ahead. Remember Trudy, who was frustrated because she couldn't have a cookie and then tore the arm off her doll? At one time, psychologists proposed that frustration was the only cause of aggression, the so-called **frustration-aggression hypothesis** (Dollard et al., 1939). Supporters of this hypothesis claimed that frustration could produce several different reactions, including aggression, but that aggression was always caused by frustration.

Psychologists now recognize other possible sources of aggression (some view it as innate or instinctive, but others see it as a response learned through reinforcement or modeling that need not be stimulated by frustration). However, frustration remains a prime candidate as the cause of aggression. Although not much good in the long run, a flash of aggressive behavior often follows stress (Berkowitz, 1978, 1982, 1989, 1990).

You are in the parking lot trying to get home from class, and your car won't start. Over and over you crank the ignition. Continuing to turn the key without success is a good example of fixation—it is not doing you any good, but you keep at it, perhaps until you run

frustration-aggression hypothesis the claim (now discredited) that frustration can produce several different reactions, including aggression, but that aggression was always caused by frustration

Aggression often follows frustration and stress. But aggression in itself does nothing to remove or alleviate the stressor. And there are causes of aggression other than frustration.

Courtesy of Andreas Kuehn/Getty Images.

down the battery. Still frustrated, you swing open the door, get out, kick the front left fender, throw up the hood, and glower at the engine. You're mad! Having released a bit of tension, you might feel better for a few seconds, but being angry and kicking at the car or yelling at someone who offers to assist will not help you solve your problem.

Another negative consequence of stress is **anxiety**—a general feeling of tension, apprehension, and dread that involves predictable physiological changes. Anxiety is difficult to define precisely, but everyone seems to know what you are talking about when you refer to it. Like stress, it is a reaction we all have experienced. Often anxiety accompanies stress. Anxiety is an unpleasant emotional component of the stress response. As much as for any other reason, we want to rid ourselves of stress to reduce our anxiety.

Sometimes the stress and anxiety in a person's life become more than he or she can cope with effectively. The person's anxiety starts to interfere with normal adaptations to the environment and to other people. The anxiety becomes all-consuming. More anxiety follows, and then more distress, and more discomfort, and more pain. For many people—tens of millions of people in the United States and Canada—the anxiety that accompanies stress is so discomforting and so maladaptive that it leads to a psychological disorder.

> **anxiety** a general feeling of tension, apprehension and dread that involves predictable physiological changes

BEFORE YOU GO ON

6. Describe three ineffective, inappropriate reactions to stress.

A Point to Ponder or Discuss
At some time or another, most of us have reacted to stress by fixating, becoming aggressive, or feeling anxious. When you have any of these reactions, how do you respond? That is, how can you make these ineffective strategies effective?

PSYCHOLOGICAL FACTORS THAT INFLUENCE PHYSICAL HEALTH

Is there a relationship between a person's personality and that person's physical health? Can individual psychological evaluations predict physical as well as psychological disorders? Is there a disease-prone personality? Are some lifestyles unhealthy? "Why do some people get sick and some stay well?" (Adler & Matthews, 1994, p. 229; Schneiderman, 2004). The tentative answer to each of these questions is yes. There is a positive correlation between some personality variables and physical health.

The Type A Personality

Although researchers had been exploring the link between psychology and physical health for years, they first caught the attention of the public with a series of studies examining the association between coronary heart disease (CHD) and the **Type A behavior pattern** (TABP). As originally defined, a Type A person is a competitive, achievement-oriented, impatient individual who typically works at many tasks at the same time, is easily aroused, and is often hostile or angry (Friedman & Rosenman, 1959). The symptoms of coronary heart disease include chest pains and heart attacks, and it is caused by a buildup of substances (cholesterol, for example) blocking the

> **type A behavior pattern (TABP)** characterizes a person who is competitive, achievement-oriented, impatient, who typically works at many tasks at the same time, is easily aroused, and prone to hostility and anger

supply of blood to the heart. People who show none of the characteristics of the TABP and who are relaxed and easygoing are said to have a *Type B behavior pattern*.

From the early 1960s to the early 1980s, several studies reported a positive relationship between CHD and behaviors typical of the Type A personality (Jenkins, 1976; Rosenman et al., 1975; Wood, 1986). The National Institutes of Health declared the Type A behavior pattern an independent risk factor for heart disease (National Institutes of Health, 1981). The Type A personality pattern was implicated in hypertension (chronic high blood pressure) even when no other signs of coronary heart disease were present (Irvine et al., 1991). It all seemed clear. Find people with the Type A behavior pattern, intervene to change their behaviors, and watch the incidence of coronary heart disease decline. But, as we have said repeatedly, complex problems seldom have simple solutions.

Data began to surface that did not show a clear relationship between TABP and coronary heart disease (Fishman, 1987; Hollis et al., 1990; Matthews, 1982, 1988; Wright, 1988). Perhaps Type A people were not more at risk for heart disease than anyone else. Perhaps studies that failed to find a relation between TABP and CHD were flawed.

As it happens, both of these hypotheses appear to be valid. For one thing, the Type A behavioral pattern is complex and difficult to assess. It is likely that simple paper-and-pencil inventories—which had been used in many studies—fail to identify a large number of people with the TABP.

It also may be that the TABP as originally defined is too global a pattern of behaviors (Adler & Matthews, 1994). Perhaps there is a set of behaviors within the general definition of Type A behaviors that does predict coronary heart disease. The best bet seems to be that the "active ingredients" of TABP that are most predictive of CHD are *anger*, impatience, and *hostility*. Of particular interest is something called "cynical hostility"—being suspicious, moody, distrusting, and quick to get upset and criticize others (Bunde & Suls, 2006; Hemmingway & Marmot, 1999; Krantz & McCeney, 2002; Williams & Schneiderman, 2002). A large-scale study by the Committee on Health and Behavior of the National Institute of Medicine (2001) concluded that "Strong links have been identified between the trait of hostility and the incidence of and mortality from heart disease" (p. 5), a finding consistent with a nine-year study that found that men high in hostility had more than twice the risk of dying of a cardiovascular incident than did men low in hostility (Everson et al., 1997).

This line of inquiry shows how research science works. Researchers refine and test hypotheses, working toward a closer approximation of truth. The original research showing a link between certain behavior patterns and CHP is tested and refined. Part of the excitement of research in psychology is that there is so much work to be done to understand the connections between disease and the mind. In this case, more work still needs to be done. Better techniques of diagnosing Type A behavior patterns are needed, as is research on the mechanisms that underlie whatever relationships there may be between

Feeling under pressure to get things done on time, becoming hostile when all does not go well, and trying to do too many things at once may be some of the "ingredients" of the Type A Behavior Pattern.

Courtesy of Mark Scott/Getty Images.

TABP and coronary heart disease. As an example, consider a study of 2,394 men aged 50 to 64 who were assessed for CHD. They also were assessed on three measures of Type A personality, as well as other CHD risk factors. After nine years, there was no increased risk of coronary heart disease associated with *any* of the measures of TABP. The researchers did conclude that: a) If a man is likely to have a heart attack, he will have it sooner rather than later if he has a Type A personality, and b) Being Type A increases exposure to potential triggers of heart problems (such as alcohol and/or cigarette smoke) rather than directly producing cardiovascular problems (Gallacher et al., 2003). Then, just one month later, a report of a major study was issued that clearly did associate hostility and impatience with hypertension—a major risk factor for CHD (Yan et al., 2003). More research is also needed on which changes in Type A persons would be likely to reduce their chances of heart disease (Winett, 1995). After all, most of the traits of the TABP are the same ones many Americans value and imitate in their quest to "get ahead."

BEFORE YOU GO ON

7.   What is the relationship, if any, between the Type A behavior pattern and physical health?

A Point to Ponder or Discuss
Do you have a Type A or a Type B personality?

Why People Die: The Unhealthy Lifestyle

Death is unavoidable, and people die for many reasons. On the other hand, many deaths are premature and preventable. Let us review a few statistics.

In 2005, in the United States, 2,448,07 deaths occurred (CDC, 2008a, p. 3). In order, the ten leading causes of those deaths were heart disease, cancer, stroke, chronic respiratory disease, accidents, diabetes, Alzheimer's disease, influenza, kidney disease, and suicide. Continuing a trend of several years, heart disease and cancers accounted for a little more than half (53.3 percent) of all deaths, and the ten causes listed here accounted for nearly 80 percent (Arias et al., 2003; Minino & Smith, 2001).

Remember the model of disease and health called the biopsychosocial model? Many health psychologists wonder how many of our nation's deaths (just over two million annually) can be traced to psychological or behavioral factors. We are already aware of a few potentially unhealthy behaviors from the research on the Type A behavior pattern: hostility, anger, and time-urgency as risk factors for cardiovascular disease (which, includes both heart disease and stroke).

The Director of the Centers for Disease Control, Dr. Julie Gerberding, spoke at a National Health Council meeting in October 2003. Her focus was on obesity in America. Commenting on rising rates of obesity, she said, "Unfortunately, poor diet and lack of exercise have almost caught up with tobacco as being the leading cause of death in the United States." What other risk factors contribute to an "unhealthy lifestyle"?

Risk factors for coronary heart disease include cigarette smoking, obesity, a sedentary lifestyle, family history, and such psychosocial factors as depression, anxiety, lack of social support, and work-related stress (Frasure-Smith &

A major premise of health psychology is that many health problems have more to do with behaviors and choices than with bacteria and viruses. Cigarette smoking and overeating are behaviors that lead directly to negative health consequences. Engaging in risky behaviors with motorcycle stunts and tricks on the street can lead to all sorts of problems (and doing so without a helmet or protective clothing is even worse).

Courtesy of Leah Warkentin/Design Pics/Corbis.

Lespérance, 2005; Grundy, 1999; Hemingway & Marmot, 1999; Rozanski, Blumenthal, & Kaplan, 1999). Obviously, many of these factors interact and make matters worse. For example, cigarette smoking, alcohol consumption, and depression work together to interrupt normal sleep patterns, and together they pose a much greater risk of coronary heart disease than any single factor by itself (Kiecolt-Glaser et al., 2002). Persons who live an unhealthy lifestyle also increase their risk of cancer. Poor diet, stress, lack of exercise, excessive exposure to ultraviolet rays, lack of social support, and tobacco use are risk factors for cancer (Glanz, 1997; Glanz et al., 1999; Lerman, Rimer, & Glynn, 1997; McKenna et al., 1999). In the case of cancer, positive behaviors that can reduce one's risk include taking steps to ensure early diagnosis (getting PAP smears for cervical cancer, mammograms for breast cancer, PSA blood tests for prostate cancer, and the like) (Schneiderman et al., 2001). One's educational level also matters. "Despite increased attention and substantial dollars directed to groups with low socioeconomic status, within race and gender groups, *the educational gap in life expectancy is rising* (Meara, Richards, & Cutler, 2008 [emphasis added])

Globally, 35 million people will die in 2005 from heart disease, stroke, cancer, and other chronic diseases—and 80 percent of those deaths will occur in low-income and middle-income countries. By focusing on just two lifestyle changes—reducing smoking and obesity—the hope is to cut this death rate by two percent a year, thus averting 36 million deaths by 2015 (Strong et al., 2005).

An unhealthy lifestyle may involve behaviors that are fatal—failing to wear safety belts or recklessness at work or at play, for instance. By their nature, accidents are haphazard, unpredictable, and unforeseen, but, caution, safety training, and awareness can reduce accidents. Health psychologists promote such things as smoke-free spaces, safe work places, exercise programs at work, and air bags in cars. At the same time, many health psychologists work with individuals who want to change behaviors and develop a healthier lifestyle.

Remember that many causes of death—even death at a young age—are largely determined by biology (infections, for example) and not directly susceptible to significant changes in lifestyle. A woman with high cholesterol can change her diet and exercise rigorously and still, after six months, not change her cholesterol level. On the other hand, you may know a 93-year-old who eats saturated fats daily—butter, fried foods, sausage, and ice cream are the bulk of his diet. Yet he has no cholesterol build-up and the blood pressure of a healthy teenager. Sometimes, it is just in the genes.

For the remainder of this chapter, we will examine two areas where psychologists have been particularly active: helping people stop smoking and helping people prevent or cope with sexually transmitted diseases.

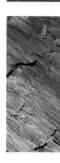

BEFORE YOU GO ON

8. What are some of the components of an unhealthy lifestyle?

A Point to Ponder or Discuss

Everyone knows that smoking, eating too much, and not exercising are strongly associated with health problems. Why do people behave in ways they know to be unhealthy?

SPOTLIGHT
ON DIVERSITY

Racial/Ethnic Disparities in Healthcare

Healthcare in America is facing a serious crisis. Disparities in healthcare include racial, ethnic, and gender differences in 1) the incidence of disease and illness, 2) the quality of medical and diagnostic procedures and treatment service, and 3) the availability and use of health insurance (Smith, 1998). Healthcare and wellness concerns among ethnic minority groups have lacked comprehensive attention, which—among other things—has led to an under-reporting of illnesses and health concerns among member of these communities. The U. S. Department of Health and Human Services begins its latest report on minority health issues with the statement, "There are continuing disparities in the burden of illness and death experienced by African Americans, Hispanic Americans, Asian Americans/Pacific Islanders, and American Indians/Alaska Natives, compared to the U.S. population as a whole (DHHS, 2004, p. 1). Put simply, many diseases often occur much earlier in life, with worse than average symptoms, and higher death rates among members of ethnic minorities.

African Americans
African Americans are more likely than any other ethnic group to suffer from a broad range of physical diseases, according to a Report of the Surgeon General (2004). The eight leading causes of death among African Americans are cardiovascular disease, HIV/AIDS, diabetes, homicide, pneumonia, influenza, chronic pulmonary diseases, and cancer (Anderson & Smith, 2003). Even through diseases of the heart, cancer, and stroke are also among the leading causes for all persons in the United States, African Americans died from these diseases at significantly higher rates than did members of any other racial/ethnic group. The incidence of HIV/AIDS is higher among African Americans than any other ethnic group in America. Although African Americans make up only about 12.5 percent of the U.S. population, they have accounted for more than 40 percent of the AIDS cases diagnosed since the epidemic began (CDC, 2003). AIDS is the leading cause of death among African American men ages 25–44, and during 2000–2003, HIV/AIDS rates for African American females were 19 times the rates for white females and five times the rates for Hispanic females (CDC, 2004).

Overall, African Americans are more likely to develop cancer than are persons of any other racial or ethnic group. They also have highest death rate from cancer (American Cancer Society, 2005a: Jemel et al., 2003; DHHS, 2004). The rate of prostate cancer among African American men is 60 percent higher than in white men, and the death rate is 50 percent higher than for any other racial or ethnic group (Jemel et al., 2003). Recently, researchers found a mutation in a specific gene associated with prostate cancer risks in African American men with a history of the disease in their families (Kittles et al., 2005).

Although their rate of newly diagnosed cases of breast cancer is about 13 percent *lower* than in white women, African American women die of breast cancer more often than do women from any other racial or ethnic group (DHHS, 2004). The higher mortality rate appears to be the result of a twofold delay. Black women delay getting a full diagnosis (for example, a biopsy or genetic counseling) once suspicions are raised, and they typically delay treatment longer than do women of other groups (Armstrong et al., 2005; Bradley, Given, & Roberts, 2002; Gwyn et al., 2004).

Asian Americans

Asian Americans are reported to have good health as compared to other non-white ethnic groups. Their life expectancy is longer than that of any ethnic group in America other than Caucasian Americans. However, stomach cancer, carbon monoxide poisoning, tuberculosis, and leprosy are health risks linked to the Asian American population (American Cancer Society, 2004). In fact, Asian Americans experience four times more tuberculosis than the general population (CDC, 2004). Despite lower cholesterol levels and lower coronary heart disease among Asian Americans, coronary heart disease is the leading cause of death for all Asian Americans. With regard to HIV/AIDS, Asian Americans have the lowest rate of infection of any ethnic group (CDC, 2004).

Hispanic Americans

Of all ethnic groups, Hispanic Americans are least likely to have health insurance or health coverage (Machlin et al., 2000; Zuvekas & Weinick, 1999). However, despite high poverty rates, Hispanics have a lower infant mortality than African Americans. Diabetes is common among middle-aged and older Hispanics (occurring at a rate almost twice as that for non-Hispanic whites of similar age) and this is particularly so among Hispanic women (National Diabetes Information Clearinghouse, 2002). Research data from the American Cancer Society (2003) shows that, compared with other ethnic groups, Hispanics have a higher incidence and mortality rate of stomach, uterine, cervix, liver, and biliary tract (gall bladder and bile duct) cancers.

Conclusion:

Disparities in healthcare and health policies are widespread, occurring across the full spectrum of disease categories and treatment services. There are many reasons for the disparities. They include unequal access to healthcare services, lack of health insurance, difficulty in accessing healthcare services, as well as gaps in income and education. Inequalities in care are also partly explained by cultural differences, such as a reliance on home remedies and a lack of trust in healthcare providers.

PROMOTING HEALTHY BEHAVIORS

In this chapter we have reviewed many statistics. Our motivation in doing so is not have you memorize a large number of large numbers. Rather, we want you to appreciate the enormity of health-related issues that are rooted in people's choices and behaviors. Some personality characteristics affect physical health. The specific traits involved and exactly how they operate are being debated and researched right now. However, we do know that certain behaviors put people at greater risk for physical disease and death. One role of the health psychologist is to help change these potentially dangerous behaviors (Schneiderman et al., 2001).

Helping People to Stop Smoking

Few efforts to change behavior have received as much attention as those meant to discourage people from smoking. The main reason is that smoking is so deadly. The Centers for Disease Control and Prevention tells us (2007b) that a) an estimated 20.8 percent of all adults (45.3 million people) smoke cigarettes in the United States, and that b) cigarette smoking remains the leading preventable cause of death in the United States, accounting for 1 of every 5 deaths (438,000 people) each year. Additionally, "tobacco use is associated with 5 million deaths per year worldwide and is regarded as one of the leading causes of premature death" (Hatsukami, Stead, & Gupta, 2008, p. 2027). The American Cancer Society reports, "Cigarettes kill more Americans than alcohol, car accidents, suicide, AIDS, homicide, and illegal drugs combined" (2005b, p. 1). Smoking provides an increased risk for colon and rectal cancers (Slattery et al., 2003), multiple

sclerosis (Riise, Nortveldt, & Ascherio, 2003), and prostate cancer, particularly in its aggressive forms (Plaskon et al., 2003).

The concern extends beyond smokers to their children. Studies of "secondhand smoke" provide evidence that the children of smokers face increased risk for lung cancer even if they have never smoked. Annually, secondhand smoke causes enough heart disease in non-smokers to kill 62,000 Americans and bring on 200,000 non-fatal heart attacks (American Heart Association, 2000; USDHHS, 2006).

The short of it, of course, is that smoking is a bad thing. It can kill. This is not a new message, nor is it a secret. By now, the facts are common knowledge. Still, tens of millions of people continue to smoke.

Programs to persuade smokers to quit have shown some promise, but quitting is extremely difficult: "Habitual heavy users of heroin and cocaine say it is easier to give up these drugs than to stop smoking" (Grinspoon, 1997). Nearly 70 percent of smokers say they want to quit, and over 40 percent say that they have attempted to quit at least once in the past year (Dunston, 2003). Only five percent of smokers manage to quit on their first try, and almost 80 percent relapse within a year, but after repeated attempts nearly 50 percent of smokers eventually do quit (Bartecchi, MacKenzie, & Schrier, 1995; CDC, 2002). A person who finally gives up smoking permanently has quit, on the average, five times before. Quitters who can cope with other stressors in their lives are significantly more likely to stay off cigarettes than are those who experience additional stress. A good predictor of whether an attempt to stop smoking will be successful is the absence of unpleasant feelings, including anxiety and depression. In fact, when smokers who are about to try quitting are asked about what concerns them, they report worrying about being around others who are smoking, socializing in general, or drinking coffee or alcohol. Actually, in one study, none of these factors was found to be associated with relapse. Only negative affect (depression and anxiety) was (Shiffman et al., 2007). Similarly, many smokers worry about the possibility of significant weight gain if they were to give up their habit, but "heavy smokers tend to have greater body weight than do light smokers or nonsmokers" (Chiolero et al., 2008, p. 801).

Giving up cigarettes takes more than the intellectual insight that smoking is bad for one's health. Being successful at quitting usually requires several factors. The American Council on Science and Health has compiled one list of the success factors (Dunston, 2003, p. 9). Their list includes the following:

Motivation, Desire, Commitment: Successful quitters have their own reasons for quitting. Trying to give up smoking to please someone rarely works. But being married or living with a partner increases the likelihood of success (Lee & Kahende, 2007).

Timing: Giving up an addiction is a disruptive process that takes time to accomplish. Trying to quit smoking in the midst of an important business deal or a difficult family situation can lower the chances of success. The week before final exams is probably not the best time for a college student to try to quit smoking.

Choice of Method: No particular method is right for everyone. What often works best is a combination of individual counseling (Karnath, 2002), support groups (Fiore et al., 2000), and some form of nicotine replacement therapy. Common forms of nicotine replacement therapy include a patch, chewing gum, lozenges, or nasal spray. Social support from nearly any source is helpful. Even advice from the family doctor can make a significant difference (Karnath, 2002).

Repetition: Every smoker should plan on being successful on his or her first attempt. But most smokers will need several attempts. It is as if the smoker learns more each time from the quitting process. Quitting smoking is difficult and can be discouraging. Smokers who want to quit must fight off feelings of discouragement (remember what we said earlier about negative affect making it more difficult to quit).

Psychologists have had some success helping to design programs to get people not to smoke in the first place. These anti-smoking programs have been effective with teenagers in particular (Farrelly et al., 2005; Henriksen et al., 2004; Pierce, 2005; White & Gilpin, 2005). Even campaigns focused on adult smokers seem to have a greater effect on adolescents (White et al., 2003). As more facilities declare themselves "smoke-free environments," the more difficult it is for people to begin or continue smoking. The use of role models and peers to teach specific skills to resist smoking has been successful, particularly when programs focus on the short-term benefits of not smoking, such as freedom from coughing and bad breath and positive factors such as improved appearance. Increasing taxes on cigarettes makes it more expensive to smoke. The greater expense discourages some smokers (Hyland et al., 2005).

Health psychologists' efforts to influence people not to smoke are balanced by the millions of dollars the tobacco industry spends to market their products to young people the world over. For example, in 2000, advertising expenditures for 15 brands of cigarettes in youth-oriented magazines was nearly $70 million, reaching an estimated 80 percent of young people in the United States an average of 17 times each. Between 1990 and 2000 advertising expenditures by foreign companies for cigarette sales in Taiwan increased fourfold (Frieden & Blakemore, 2005; King & Siegel, 2001; Wen et al., 2005).

BEFORE YOU GO ON

9. Why are health psychologists so concerned about smoking, and how are they attempting to reduce the number of smokers?

A Point to Ponder or Discuss

Assume that you are on a committee of your local school system charged with developing a program to keep youngsters between the ages of 10 and 12 from starting to smoke. List some of the factors that will be important determiners of this program's success.

Coping with STDs, HIV, and AIDS

Sexually transmitted diseases (STDs) are contagious diseases usually passed on through sexual contact. They provide an excellent example of a significant health problem directly associated with psychosocial causes. Sexually transmitted diseases affect tens of millions of people—more than 19,000,000 new cases each year in the United States alone. Nearly half of those diagnoses are for young people, ages 15 to 24 (CDC, 2007a; Weinstock, Berman, & Cates, 2004). Sexually transmitted diseases other than HIV/AIDS cost more than $8 billion a year to diagnose and treat. We will begin this final section with a very brief description of a few common STDs, before considering psychological interventions aimed at controlling HIV and AIDS, the deadliest of the STDs.

Chlamydia is caused by a bacterial infection and is usually diagnosed in sexually active persons younger than 35. The incidence of chlamydia is soaring; The Centers for Disease Control and Prevention estimates about three million new cases every year. Symptoms include burning urination in both men and women. Men may experience a penile discharge; women may experience a disruption in their menstrual cycles. Chlamydia usually can be effectively treated within a week with an antibiotic, usually erythromycin.

Gonorrhea is a disease of the young and sexually active. Of the nearly 360,000 cases that will be diagnosed this year, most will be in men between the ages of 20 and 24. After being very stable for the past ten years, gonorrhea infection rates are gradually increasing (Weinstock, Berman, & Cates, 2004). It is a bacterial infection that affects the moist tissue areas around the genitals. A person may be infected with the gonorrhea bacteria and not know it. Undetected infection is particularly common for women, most of whom remain relatively free of symptoms. When symptoms do develop, they are like those experienced with chlamydia: frequent, painful urination; vaginal discharges; and a reddening of the genital area. In men, symptoms include a milky discharge from the penis and painful, frequent urination. Antibiotics are usually successful in treating this STD, although some strains have become resistant to some classes of antibiotic.

Syphilis is caused by the bacterium *spirochete*. If left untreated, the disease may run its course through four known stages, from relatively simple and painless sores all the way to the infection of other, non-sexual organs, and it can lead to death. The prevalence of syphilis is on the increase, with nearly 10,000 new cases can be expected this year in the United States. Treatment for syphilis is penicillin (or tetracycline), and prognosis is related to length of infection. The sooner treatment begins, the better the prognosis.

sexually transmitted diseases (STDs) contagious diseases usually passed on through sexual contact

Genital herpes (herpes type II) is a skin disease that affects the genital area, producing small sores and blisters. It is caused by a virus that was virtually unknown until the mid-1960s. Now genital herpes is the most common STD in the United States—currently afflicting more than 45 million persons. At the moment, herpes has no cure, although medication can reduce the occasionally painful symptoms. A person with genital herpes is most infectious when the sores and blisters are active and erupting. There may be periods during which the infected person remains symptom-free, only to have the reddening and sores recur. There are no life-threatening complications of the disease in males, but genital herpes in females is a significant risk factor for cervical cancer. The herpes virus can be passed along during childbirth, which can cause considerable damage, even death, to the newborn.

As unpleasant—even painful—as sexually transmitted diseases can be, none attract as much public attention as *acquired immune deficiency syndrome, or AIDS*. AIDS is caused by the human immunodeficiency virus, or HIV. HIV is one of the "slow viruses," meaning that there may be a long interval between the initial infection and the onset of serious symptoms (Schneiderman et al., 2001). There are large individual differences in the pace at which the virus has its effects. A faster progression of symptoms is associated with an accumulation of stressful life events, depression, and lack of social support (Leserman et al., 2000). HIV attacks the body's immune system, which normally fights off infections. When his or her immune system becomes sufficiently weakened, an HIV-infected person is said to have AIDS. Someone with AIDS simply does not have the bodily resources to defend against other infections—infections that otherwise might not be life threatening. In other words, patients do not die of AIDS directly, but from other diseases or infections (for example, cancer or pneumonia) against which the body cannot defend.

AIDS was virtually unknown in the United States before 1981. Through 2006, 992,865 persons in the United States had been reported as having AIDS, and an additional 287,954 had HIV infection (but not AIDS) (CDC, 2008b). There may be another 70,000 persons infected with HIV but who are unaware of it (Glynn & Rhodea, 2005; National Institute of Allergy and Infectious Disease, 2003). The United Nations and its World Health Organization claim that the number of people living with HIV/AIDS world-wide is approximately 33.2 million persons, and that more than 25 million people have died of AIDS since 1981 (UNAIDS/WHO, 2007).

HIV almost always enters the body through sexual contact or by the use of contaminated needles in intravenous (IV) drug use. About one infant in three born to an HIV-positive mother will also be infected. In infected persons, concentrations of the virus are highest in the blood and in the semen and/or vaginal fluids.

For those in whom the HIV infection has progressed to AIDS, death within four years is nearly certain. There is no vaccine to prevent it. At the moment, there is no cure for AIDS, but researchers are beginning to be a bit more optimistic about the possibility.

In sub-Saharan Africa, AIDS has become the major killer of adults and children alike. The World Health Organization estimates that more than 1.7 million have died so far, and there is little hope at the moment that this trend will soon be reversed.

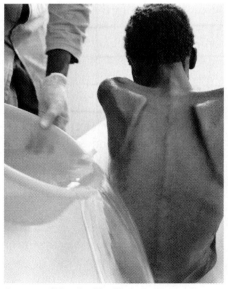

Courtesy of Tom Stoddart/Getty Images.

Some drugs, when taken together in a potent mix called "Highly Active Anti-Retroviral Therapy," or HAART, seem able to at least increase the life span and the quality of life for many diagnosed with HIV (Cohen et al., 2007; Porter et al., 2003). Not surprisingly, given the power of these drugs, their side effects can be significant, ranging from nausea and diarrhea to inflammation of the pancreas and painful nerve damage. Another potential problem with the use of HAART is that, although research continues to confirm its effectiveness as a treatment option for those with HIV/AIDS, it does *not* reduce the chances of transmitting the disease through unprotected sexual behaviors. The concern is that those using the anti-retroviral therapy will continue (or even increase) their unsafe sexual practices. Thus far, that concern does not seem to be realized (Crepaz, Hart, & Marks, 2004; Sarna et al., 2008).

For now, the most reasonable way to reduce the incidence of AIDS is to motivate people to avoid behaviors that put them at risk of infection, such as sharing needles or having unprotected sex. At the very least, sexually active persons should be tested for the HIV infection and should be certain that their partners have been tested as well. Because of the importance of behaviors in transmitting HIV, psychologists can contribute significantly to stopping the spread of the virus. Much has been done, but even more remains to be done: "Behavior change remains the only means for primary prevention of HIV disease. Psychology should take a leading role in efforts to curtail the epidemic, but has not contributed to HIV prevention at a level proportionate to the urgency of the crisis" (Kelly et al., 1993, p. 1023). Attempts to prevent AIDS or to reduce its spread have met with mixed results. Successful interventions are multifaceted, involving education, the changing of attitudes, increasing motivation to engage in safe (or safer) sexual practices, and teaching people the negotiating skills to avoid high-risk situations. Suc-cessful interventions also attend to larger issues, such as the environment in which targeted behaviors occur, the culture in which the audience resides, and marketing.

By and large, most Americans are aware of AIDS, know what causes the disease, and know what can be done to avoid it. Many believed that people would not engage in risky behaviors once they knew the facts about AIDS. The reality has been different: "Unfortunately, the evidence that sex education leads to changes in behaviors intended to prevent AIDS or pregnancy is disappointing" (Helweg-Larsen & Collins, 1997, 23). Even with considerable knowledge about AIDS, few people—teenagers in particular—seem willing to change their sexual practices (Helweg-Larsen & Collins, 1997). Although interventions are often successful at achieving changes in knowledge and motivation, they tend to be less successful in achieving actual behavioral change. Even early changes in motivation decay with time. The most lasting techniques for behavioral change "engage audiences in particular activities, such as role-playing condom use" and use expert intervention facilitators rather than lay community members (Albarracín, Durantini, & Earl, 2006, p. 73; Albarracín et al., 2001).

AIDS is a physical disease, but it has unprecedented psychological complications. Patients diagnosed with HIV who have not yet developed AIDS tend to be more depressed and disturbed than those who have the full-blown and fatal symptoms of the disease. As you might expect, AIDS patients experience significant stress, depression, anger, anxiety, and denial. Individual and group-based psychosocial interventions can significantly reduce the distress associated with a diagnosis of HIV infection. Of particular benefit are interventions that increase the patient's social support network. Such interventions improve the quality of life of HIV/AIDS patients and may even extend survival periods (Schneiderman, 2001).

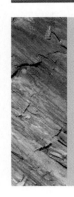

BEFORE YOU GO ON

10. What are some of the most common sexually transmitted diseases (STDs)?
11. What are the causes of AIDS, and what roles can health psychologists play in its prevention and treatment?

A Point to Ponder or Discuss
HIV/AIDS can be prevented to the extent that people abstain from risky behaviors altogether. Are you for or against programs that promote sexual abstinence?

CHAPTER SUMMARY

1. **Define the terms *stress* and *stressor*.**

   Stress is defined as a complex set of reactions made by a person under pressure to adapt. Stress is a response that an individual makes to real or perceived threats to his or her well-being that give rise to physiological reactions and unpleasant feelings like distress and anxiety. Feelings of stress are aroused when an individual is exposed to a *stressor*.

2. **Describe the stressors characterized as frustration, conflict, and life events.**

   Frustration is the blocking or thwarting of goal-directed behaviors. If someone or something in one's environment blocks goal-directed behaviors, environmental frustration is the result. If the source of the frustration is a personal characteristic within the individual, we have personal frustration. *Motivational conflicts* are stressors. They are situations in which we find ourselves faced with difficult choices to make with regard to our motivated behaviors. In an approach-approach conflict, one is faced with two or more attractive (positive) goals and must choose between or among them. In an avoidance-avoidance conflict, a choice must be made between unpleasant (negative) alternatives. In an approach-avoidance conflict, there is one goal under consideration; in some ways that goal is positive, in others it is negative (it attracts and repels at the same time). In a multiple approach-avoidance conflict, a person faces a number of alternatives, each of which has its strengths and its weaknesses, and a choice must be made between or among them.

   Many psychologists argue that *life events*, particularly changes in one's life situation, can act as stressors. *The Social Readjustment Rating Scale* (SRRS) measures stress by having a person indicate recent life-change events. High scores on such scales are associated with an above-average incidence of physical illness. Some psychologists claim that the little hassles of life are more common stressors than large-scale life events. Life-change events do not have to be negative or unpleasant events to act as stressors. *Socioeconomic status* (SES) relates to stress in at least two ways. First, individuals in higher SES brackets are less likely than lower SES individuals to encounter negative life events that can arouse stress. Second, low SES individuals have fewer resources to deal with life events that arouse stress.

3. **Comment on individual differences in how people respond to stressors.**

   People may respond differently to the same stressor. What some find merely challenging, others may find overwhelmingly stressful. Reaction to stressors varies over time: Events that do not seem stressful today may be very stressful tomorrow. Some people are particularly resistant to stressors and have been called "hardy personalities." Such people tend to see difficulties as opportunities, have a sense of being in control of their lives, and be fully engaged in and committed to life.

4. **Describe the stages of Selye's General Adaptation Syndrome.**

   According to Hans Selye, a prolonged stress reaction progresses through three stages, collectively referred to as the *General Adaptation Syndrome* (GAS). The three stages are alarm, resistance, and exhaustion. During the *alarm* stage of the GAS, there are rapid changes in the operation of the sympathetic nervous system, which lead to increases in blood pressure and heart rate and to pupillary dilation, cessation of digestion, and rerouting of blood to body extremities. Adrenaline is dumped into the blood stream, which gets the body ready for action. This stage does not last long, usually for a few hours at the most. If a stressor is persistent, the body enters the *resistance* stage of the GAS. The body continues to fight off the challenges of the stressors. Maintaining high levels of arousal drains the body's resources. If other stressors are encountered, a person is less able to deal with them. Some things that might ordinarily not bother a person become important sources of stress. This added stress further depletes the body's resources. If stress is not reduced in the resistance stage, *exhaustion* may occur. Bodily resources become nearly depleted, and a person runs out of energy to cope with stressors. There may be a psychological and/or physical breakdown.

5. **Briefly summarize both problem-focused and emotion-focused strategies that can help cope with stress.**

In general, the most effective means of dealing with stress is to deal with the stressors that caused it by learning new behaviors that help cope with those stressors. There are two approaches to dealing with stress. One is problem-focused and includes such things as identifying the specific stressor causing stress, removing or minimizing the stressor, reappraising the situation, inoculating against future stressors, and taking time in making difficult decisions. Battling the feelings associated with stress—with what are called emotion-focused approaches—includes learning relaxation techniques, engaging in physical exercise, and seeking social support.

6. **Describe three ineffective, inappropriate reactions to stress.**

Maladaptive reactions to stressors are those that interfere with attempts to change behaviors as a result of experiencing stress. *Fixation* describes a pattern of behaviors in which a person tries repeatedly to deal with stressors, is unsuccessful, but does not try anything new or different. *Aggression* often results from stress, particularly frustration. Although aggression may yield a momentary release of tension, it usually does not remove the original stressor. *Anxiety* is yet another maladaptive response to stress. This general feeling of apprehension and dread is often the aspect of experienced stress that motivates us to do something about it.

7. **What is the relationship, if any, between the Type A behavior pattern and physical health?**

There appears to be a relationship between some personality variables and physical health; that is, some psychological traits put a person at risk for disease. Beginning in the 1950s, evidence accumulated showing a strong positive relationship between a Type A behavior pattern, or TABP (a person who is competitive, achievement-oriented, impatient, easily aroused, often angry or hostile, and who tends to have many projects going at once) and coronary heart disease. The picture, it now seems, is a little less clear, as psychologists seek to identify the "active ingredients" of the TABP. The main personality variables associated with heart disease seem to be anger, hostility, and time-urgency (impatience). These three risk fac-

tors are surely also risk factors for the development of hypertension.

8. **What are some of the components of an unhealthy lifestyle?**

People die for many reasons. Heart disease and cancer account for more than half the deaths in the United States in any given year. Some causes of death are unavoidable; however, many result from risky behaviors. Psychosocial contributors to premature death include behaviors that are simply unhealthy. These unhealthy behaviors include such lifestyle issues as eating too much, exercising too little, smoking, and experiencing stress. Many health psychologists dedicate themselves to helping their clients reduce unhealthy behaviors and live longer, better lives.

9. **Why are health psychologists so concerned about smoking, and how are they attempting to reduce the number of smokers?**

Of the leading causes of death in this country, most could be reduced by behavioral change. Smoking accounts for nearly 440,000 deaths each year in the United States, nearly five million deaths worldwide. Smoking is a major risk factor for cardiovascular disease, cancers, and multiple sclerosis. Health psychologists continue to look for effective means of helping people to stop smoking. Most smokers who do quit have tried to do so several times before. The number of adult smokers in the U. S. is decreasing. Successful quitting takes a motivated, committed person who has chosen a good time to quit (relatively free of other stressors). Those who successfully quit often use a combination of techniques (nicotine replacement therapy, individual counseling, and social support) and are willing to keep trying to quit. Being married or living with a partner and being relatively free of depression and anxiety are predictors of success for smoking cessation. Current anti-smoking efforts try to prevent children and teens from ever starting to smoke in the first place. A promising approach uses other teens as models and as peer teachers.

10. **What are some of the most common sexually transmitted diseases (STDs)?**

A sexually transmitted disease is passed from one person to another through sexual contact. There are over 19 million new cases of STDs each year in the United States. For every one case that is known, there are perhaps two to five others that are not known. One of the most common STDs is *chlamydia*, a bacterial infection of the genitals that results in painful urination and fluid discharge. There are as many as three million new cases each year. *Gonorrhea*, a bacterial infection of the tissues around the genitals, is passed on only by sexual contact. If left untreated, its symptoms increase in severity. Penicillin is an effective treatment. *Syphilis*, a bacterial infection, may progress through four stages as symptoms increase in severity. Left untreated, it may result in death. Again, penicillin is an effective treatment. *Genital herpes*, a viral infection that affects tissue around the genitals, is a very common STD (afflicting over 45 million in the U.S.) and has no known cure. *Acquired immune deficiency syndrome (AIDS)* is a viral infection (HIV) transmitted through the exchange of bodily fluids, usually semen or blood. Once infected, a person may stay symptom-free (but capable of infecting others) in a "carrier state" until the immune system is weakened to the point that AIDS becomes the proper diagnosis. Over 33 million persons worldwide are living with HIV/AIDS, and since 1981, over 25 million people have died of AIDS.

11. **What are the causes of AIDS, and what roles can health psychologists play in its prevention and treatment?**

AIDS is caused by the human immunodeficiency virus (HIV), which enters the body through sexual contact or through the use of contaminated needles. About one in three infants born to an HIV-positive mother will contract the disease. Eventually, HIV attacks the body's immune system, making the body susceptible to a wide range of diseases. Ordinary diseases become life-threatening. Persons with AIDS seldom survive for more than four years after diagnosis. There is no preventative vaccine for HIV at the present time. There are drugs and potent mixtures of drugs (like those available in Highly Active Anti-Retroviral Therapy) that can control the symptoms of AIDS and prolong life, although the side effects of such treatments are often unpleasant at best.

Health psychologists are involved in helping people change their risky sexual behaviors or their IV drug use. Awareness and understanding of the disease have increased markedly, but many at-risk people have made few changes in their sexual practices. More successful programs are those that are multifaceted, doing more than just presenting facts and figures about the prevalence of HIV/AIDS. These programs motivate participants to practice safe sex and arm participants with social or negotiating skills that can be used to avoid high-risk behaviors. Psychologists also help AIDS sufferers (and their friends and families) deal with the emotional aspects of the disease. Psychological interventions—particularly those that provide social support—can improve the quality of life, and even the length of life, of HIV-infected patients.

The Psychological Disorders

12

PREVIEW

Most folks simply do not want to talk about mental illness. Many would rather not think about how common psychological disorders really are. Few of us like hearing that in a given year approximately 30 percent of the adult population will experience a diagnosable mental illness—and that of those, one-quarter will have a "serious" disorder, or that about half of Americans will have a psychological disorder "sometime in their life, with the first onset usually in childhood or adolescence" (Kessler et al., 2005, p. 593). We do not want to hear that "The nation is facing a public crisis in mental healthcare for infants, children and adolescents," or that one in ten children suffers from mental illness severe enough to impair development (Office of the Surgeon General, 2001, p. 10). People who are willing to share the gory details of their abdominal surgery at the dinner table may be unwilling to share that the stress in their lives is unbearable because of the stigma associated with mental illness.

Psychological disorders are common. Some are very dramatic; a few may be devastating. But most are not beyond the experience of any of us. And most can be treated successfully, even cured, if we talk openly about our psychological problems and seek help for them. This chapter provides an overview of the psychological disorders. As students of psychology, perhaps you can help change attitudes about mental illness. The first step is to understand what psychological disorders are.

As we have in previous chapters, we begin by defining a few basic terms. Then we focus on the anxiety disorders. These all-too-common disorders include generalized anxiety disorder, panic disorder, phobia, obsessive-compulsive disorder, and posttraumatic stress disorder. We touch only briefly on the somatoform disorders, which involve some aspect of bodily (somatic) functioning. Next we discuss the dissociative disorders, forms of mental illness that, for some unknown reason, are becoming more common. Then we consider the personality disorders, of which there are many, but we will focus on just one: the antisocial personality disorder. Just as an example of a psychological disorder of childhood, we briefly explore the nature of autism.

It may be unfair to classify some disorders as more debilitating or severe than others. To the person with a disorder, and to those who care about that person, any disorder can seem severe. Nonetheless, the disorders we discuss in the last part of this chapter are generally more disruptive and significantly more discomforting than those covered in the first part.

We begin with a disorder that is much in the news: Alzheimer's type dementia. Alzheimer's is a disease of the brain, the cerebral cortex, in particular. Alzheimer's is commonly associated with the elderly, but is not a product of normal aging. Although the underlying causes of Alzheimer's are physical, its symptoms are psychological.

In most cases, psychologists speaking about "mood disorders" are mostly concerned with depression. Depression is an emotional reaction familiar to all of us. Clearly, one can be depressed without having a psychological disorder of any sort. Sometimes the point at which a normal case of the blues becomes the mood disorder depression is not easily recognized. In many other cases, however, there is no doubt.

We end this chapter with a discussion of schizophrenia, arguably the most devastating of all the psychological disorders. Schizophrenia is an attack on all that makes us human; it has an impact on affect, cognitions, and behavior. It is a disorder that used to be called psychotic—a general term not used as a technical descriptor for over 25 years. The definition of psychotic disorder, however, still fits schizophrenia: a disorder that involves a gross impairment of functioning (difficulty dealing with the demands of everyday life), and a gross impairment in reality testing (a loss of contact with the real world as the rest of us know it).

Courtesy of Bob Thomas/Corbis.

Courtesy of moodboard/Corbis.

What is considered to be abnormal or deviant depends a great deal on context. Behaviors that are "normal" or "appropriate" at a New Year's Eve celebration may be judged to be "abnormal" or "inappropriate" at a church service.

WHAT IS ABNORMAL?

We all have a basic idea of what is meant by such terms as *abnormal, mental illness,* or *psychological disorder.* The more we think about psychological abnormality, however, the more difficult it becomes to define. The concept of abnormal as it is used in psychology is not a simple one. We will use this definition: **Abnormal** refers to maladaptive cognitions, affects, and/or behaviors that are at odds with social expectations and result in distress or discomfort. That is lengthy, but to be complete, our definition must include all these aspects. Let us consider each in turn.

Literally, abnormal means "not of the norm" or "not average." So, behaviors or mental processes that happen to be rare could be considered abnormal; in a literal sense, of course, they are. The problem with this statistical approach is that it would categorize the behaviors of Tiger Woods, Steven Spielberg, Bill Gates, or Katie Curic as abnormal. Statistically, they *are* abnormal. Few others can do what these people do, but, as far as we know, none of them has a psychological disorder. Disorders are not determined by statistical averages alone.

The reactions of people with psychological disorders are *maladaptive.* This is a critical part of our definition. Maladaptive means that the person's thoughts, feelings, and behaviors are such that the person does not function as well as he or she could without the disorder. To be different or strange surely does not mean that someone has

a psychological disorder. A person with a disorder has some impairment, breakdown, or self-defeating interference with his or her growth and functioning (Barlow & Durand, 2009, p. 2).

Our definition reflects that abnormality may show itself in a number of ways. A person with a psychological disorder may experience abnormal *affect,* engage in abnormal *behaviors,* have abnormal *cognitions,* or any combination of these. Here again is our ABCs mnemonic.

Any definition of psychological abnormality should acknowledge social and/or cultural expectations (Wakefield, 1999). What is clearly abnormal and disordered in one culture may be normal or commonplace in another. In some cultures, loud crying and wailing at the funeral of a perfect stranger is considered strange or deviant; in others, this same behavior is common and expected. In some cultures, claiming to have been communicating with dead ancestors would be taken as a sign of mental disturbance; in others, it would be treated as a great gift. Mexican Americans in the Los Angeles area tend to view people with symptoms of schizophrenia as vulnerable and ill, but they explain those symptoms as resulting from "nerves" and from being "sensitive" and assume that recovery is possible. In contrast, Anglo Americans in the same area are more likely to categorize the same people as "crazy," with little or no hope of recovery (NAMHC, 1996). Within any culture, behaviors that are appropriate in one situation may be inappropriate in

abnormal maladaptive affects, behaviors, and/or cognitions that are at odds with social expectations and result in distress or discomfort

another. For example, there is a difference between how Americans behave at a party and at a funeral.

A final point: Psychological disorders involve *discomfort* or *distress*. Psychological disorders cause emotional distress, and individuals with such disorders are often the source of distress and discomfort to others—friends and family who care and worry about them. Another way of thinking about this point is to say that the behaviors, thoughts, or feel-ings associated with a psychological disorder are not what the individual wants to experience. They are beyond the individual's control, and that in itself is distressing (Widiger & Sankis, 2000).

Complex as our definition of abnormal behavior is, there is a reason for each element. Abnormal behaviors or mental processes are maladaptive, at odds with social expectations, and result in distress or discomfort.

BEFORE YOU GO ON

1. How do psychologists define "abnormal"?

A Point to Ponder or Discuss
If you see someone acting odd, even downright bizarre, what would you need to know before deciding the person has a psychological disorder?

Classifying Abnormal Reactions: The DSM Series

Most practicing clinical psychologists do not spend time thinking about what is abnormal in the abstract. However, they do devote themselves to finding out about a person's abnormal reactions and how to most effectively treat that person. In short, practicing clinical psychologists want to give their patients a diagnosis, where **diagnosis** is the act of recognizing a disorder on the basis of specified symptoms. Diagnosis implies that individual disorders can be recognized and rests upon a larger system of classifying abnormal reactions.

Systems of classification are common in science and are not new to psychology. In 1883, Emil Kraepelin (1856–1926) published the first classification scheme for "mental disturbances." He based his system on the idea that each disorder has its own collection of symptoms (a syndrome) and its own biological cause.

diagnosis the act of recognizing a disorder on the basis of specific symptoms

In 1952, the American Psychiatric Association published a system for classifying psychological disorders, the *Diagnostic and Statistical Manual of Mental Disorders (DSM).* The fourth edition (*DSM-IV)* was published in 1994 and the *DSM-IV-TR* (*TR* stands for "text revision") was published in the summer of 2000 (American Psychiatric Association, 2000). For simplicity, we will use the abbreviation DSM-IV to refer to this most recent classification system.

The DSM-IV is the most widely used system of classification in all mental health fields. Indeed, the DSM-IV is a major source of information for this chapter. The DSM-IV lists 297 different diagnostic categories, compared to 265 in the DSM-III, 182 in the DSM-II, and only 106 in the original *Diagnostic and Statistical Manual.*

The DSM-IV is more than just an organized list of disorders in terms of symptoms. Except for cases for which there are known biological factors, the

TABLE 12.1

AXIS	Description	Example
I	Clinical syndrome: the label for a patient's most serious and obvious problem; the issue causing the most distress and impairment	anxiety disorder, mood disorder, schizophrenia
II	Personality disorders and/or mental retardation; long-term, maladaptive patterns causing distress	borderline personality disorder, mild mental retardation
III	General medical disorders relevant to the presented psychological problem	diabetes, cardiovascular disease, hypertension
IV	Psychosocial and environmental problems that contribute to or result from the psychological problem	death of a mate; loss of a job; failure at school
V	Global Assessment of Functioning; a scale from 1–100 rating current adjustment (at work, in social situations) and also for the past year	91–100 = superior; 51–60 = moderate adjustment; 11–20 = a danger of hurting self or others

The multiaxial classification system of the DSM-IV-TR.

manual attempts to avoid any reference to the **etiology**, or causes, of disorders. It is meant to be objective, based on research evidence, described as completely as possible, and theorized as little as possible. Bringing that research evidence up to date was the major reason behind the DSM-IV-TR. The DSM-IV contains more material and references to ethnic and cultural issues than did its predecessors, thanks largely to a three-year effort of the "Group on Culture and Diagnosis," sponsored by the National Institute of Mental Health (DeAngelis, 1994). Introduced with the 1980 revision, the DSM-IV also includes a multiaxial system that asks for information about an individual on five separate axes. (See Table 12.1 for a summary.)

It makes sense to have a classification system for psychological disorders. The major advantage, of course, is communication. People cannot hold a reasonable conversation about a patient's problem if they disagree on the basic definition of the diagnoses appropriate for that patient. If everyone agrees on the DSM-IV's definition, then at least they are using the same term in the same way. Still, classification schemes can cause difficulties.

Problems with Classification and Labeling

Assigning labels to people may be useful for communication, but it can also be dehumanizing. It may be difficult to remember that Sally is a complex and complicated human being with a range of feelings, thoughts, and behaviors, not just a "paranoid schizophrenic." In response to this concern, the DSM-IV refers only to disordered behaviors and to patterns of behaviors, not to disordered people. That is, it refers to paranoid reactions, not to individuals who are paranoid; to persons with anxiety, not anxious persons.

A second problem inherent in classification and labeling is falling into the habit of believing that labels explain behavior. Diagnosing and labeling a pattern of behaviors does not explain those behaviors. It does not tell us why a pattern of behaviors developed or what should be done about them now. How do you know that Bruce has paranoid schizophrenia? Well, he has strange, bizarre, unfounded beliefs about himself and his world, that's why. But why does he have these strange beliefs? Because he

etiology the source or cause of disorders

is a paranoid schizophrenic of course. Rather circular, isn't it? Moreover, labels can create unfortunate, lasting stigmas and negative attitudes. Learning that a person is "psychologically disordered" or is "mentally ill" may cause a wide range of negative reactions, and the label often sticks long after the disorder has been treated and the symptoms are gone.

Another potential problem is **comorbidity**—the occurrence of two or more disorders in the same individual at the same time (Clark et al., 1995). Comorbidity has been described as "the premier challenge facing mental health professionals" (Kendall & Clarkin, 1992, p. 833; Mineka, Watson, & Clark, 1998). The 1994 National Comorbidity Survey found that psychological disorders were much more common than previously believed. This study also suggested that most of the people who experience a disorder in their lifetime (79 percent) will have two or more disorders (Kessler et al., 1994). Comorbidity is even more common in high-risk samples. For example, a study of combat veterans found an average of 3.1 disorders per person (Mellman et al., 1992), and an average of four disorders per person was found in a study of sui-

cidal patients (Rudd et al., 1993). Just as two or more psychological disorders can be present at the same time in the same individual, so can psychological and physical disorders coexist. In July of 2003, the American Psychiatric Association released a statement on this issue. The statement begins, "Mental disorders are medical illnesses and there is growing evidence of the undeniable link between the two" (American Psychiatric Association, 2003, p. 1). For example, depression occurs in 40 to 65 percent of patients who experience a heart attack and in nearly 20 percent of people with coronary artery disease. About 25 percent of all cancer patients also suffer from depression. Both the psychological disorder and the comorbid medical condition must be addressed if the patient is to be treated successfully.

A Word on "Insanity"

In common practice, the terms psychological disorder, mental disorder, and behavior disorder are used interchangeably. However, one term that should be used carefully is insanity. Insanity is not a psychological term. It is a legal term. It relates to problems with psychological functioning, but in a restricted sense. Definitions of **insanity** vary from state to state, but to be judged insane usually requires evidence that a person did not know or fully understand the consequences of his or her actions at a given time, could not discern the difference between right and wrong, and was unable to exercise control over his or her actions at the time a crime was committed. Curiously, the American public has long overestimated the use of an insanity defense in courts of law. The public believes an insanity plea is "used too much"—and the public estimates the defense is used in about 33–43 percent of felony cases. In fact, it is used in less than 1 percent of all felony cases and is successful less than 20 percent of the time, although public estimates of suc-

---

comorbidity the occurrence of two or more disorders in the same individual at the same time

insanity a legal term implying that a person did not fully understand the consequences of his or her actions at a given time, could not discern the difference between right and wrong, and was unable to exercise control over his or her actions at the time a crime was committed

"Insanity" is more of a legal term than a psychological one. It refers to one's mental state at the time a crime was committed, and one's competence to stand trial. In fact, the "insanity defense" is seldom used, and when it is, it is hardly ever successful.

Courtesy of Heide Benser/zefa/Corbis.

cess range from 36–45 percent cases in which it is used (Borum & Fulero, 1999; Melton et al., 2007, pp. 233–235). And, when the insanity defense *is* used successfully, defendants usually spend more time confined to a hospital than they would have been confined to jail (Gracheck, 2006).

A related issue, known as *competence*, has to do with a person's mental state at the time of trial. The central issues are whether a person is in enough control of his or her mental and intellectual functions to understand courtroom procedures and aid in his or her own defense. If not, a person may be ruled "not competent" to stand trial. Most likely, a person who is judged incompetent will be placed into a mental institution until he or she is competent to stand trial.

A Few Cautions

We will consider a variety of psychological disorders in the rest of this chapter. As we do so, please keep in mind all of the following:

1. *"Normal" and "abnormal" are not two distinct categories.* They may be thought of as end points on a dimension that we can use to describe people. However, there is a very large gray area between normal and abnormal in which distinctions get fuzzy. In practice, many psychologists or therapists would agree accurate diagnosis is occasionally as much art as science (Liebert, 2000).

2. *"Abnormal" does not mean dangerous.* Some people with mental disorders may cause harm to themselves or to others, but most people with psychological disorders are not dangerous. Even among persons who have been in jail for violent crimes, those with psychological disorders have no more subsequent arrests than do persons without disorders (Teplin et al., 1994). One large-scale, well-controlled study looked at the violent behaviors of approximately 1,700 patients with psychological disorders one year after they were released from treatment (Steadman et al., 1998). Only two groups of former patients were more likely to engage in violent behaviors than were non-patients: those with personality disorders and those who had a drug-related problem in addition to their psychological disorder. Interestingly, when former patients were violent, they were violent with friends or family members more than 90 percent of the time. All other former patients (the majority) were not more likely to be violent. As David Holmes (2001, p. 546) puts it, ". . . we do not see headlines such as 'PERSON WITH NO HISTORY OF MENTAL ILLNESS COMMITS MURDER,' although, in fact, that situation is more prevalent." On the other hand, individuals with severe mental illness are significantly more likely to be murdered (or be the victims of other violent crimes) compared to members of the general population (Appleby, 2001).

3. *"Abnormal" does not mean bad.* People diagnosed with psychological disorders are not bad or weak people. They may have done bad things, and bad things may have happened to them, but it is certainly not in the tradition of psychology to make moral judgments about patients with disorders.

4. *Most of our depictions of psychological disorders will be made in terms of extreme and obvious cases.* Like physical disorders, psychological disorders occur in mild or moderate forms. Indeed, even two patients with the same diagnosis will differ because they are different people and function differently psychologically.

ANXIETY DISORDERS

Anxiety is a feeling of general apprehension or dread accompanied by predictable physiological changes: increased muscle tension; shallow, rapid breathing; cessation of digestion; increased perspiration; and drying of the mouth. Thus, anxiety involves two levels of reaction: subjective feelings (e.g., apprehension or dread) and physiological responses (e.g., rapid breathing). The unifying symptom of anxiety disorders is felt anxiety. This anxiety often comes with "avoidance behavior" or attempts to resist or avoid any situation that might make the patient anxious.

Anxiety has been described as the most common human emotion (Barlow, 2002; Carter, 2002). Anxiety disorders are the most common psychological disorder in the United States, affecting 19.1 million adults (ages 18–54), with nearly 30 percent of Americans likely to be diagnosed with an anxiety disorder in their lifetime (ADAA, 2003; Kessler et al., 2005). International data suggest that between 8 and 20 percent of children and adolescents have the disorder (Beidel, 2002; Essau, 2002). Percentages of this sort do not convey the enormity of the problem. Millions of people—people like you and me—suffer from anxiety. In this section, we will consider five anxiety disorders: generalized anxiety disorder (GAD), panic disorder, phobic disorder, obsessive-compulsive disorder, and posttraumatic stress disorder.

Generalized Anxiety Disorder (GAD)

The major symptom of **generalized anxiety disorder (GAD)** is distressing, felt anxiety. With this disorder we find unrealistic, excessive, persistent worry. People with generalized anxiety disorder report that their anxiety interferes significantly with their lives and requires heavy medication to control. The DSM-IV adds a new criterion that people with this disorder find it difficult to control their worry or anxiety.

The experienced anxiety of this disorder may be very intense, but it is diffuse, meaning that it is not brought on by anything specific in the person's environment; it just seems to come and go (or come and stay) without reason or warning. People with GAD are usually uneasy and seldom know what is causing their anxiety. Those of us without any sort of anxiety disorder can be anxious from time to time, but we know why we are anxious. Persons with GAD report their major concerns are an inability to relax, tension, difficulty concentrating, feeling frightened, and fear of losing control. GAD brings with it considerable pain. Although people with this disorder often continue to function in social situations and on the job, they are particularly prone to drug and alcohol abuse—the comorbidity problem alluded to earlier (ADAA, 2003).

anxiety a feeling of general apprehension or dread accompanied by predictable physiological changes

generalized anxiety disorder (GAD) distressing, felt anxiety; unrealistic, excessive, persistent worry

Panic Disorder

In the generalized anxiety disorder, the anxiety is *chronic*, meaning that the anxiety is nearly always present, albeit sometimes more so than at other times. For a person suffering from **panic disorder**, the major symptom is more acute—a recurrent, unpredictable, unprovoked onset of sudden, intense anxiety, or a "panic attack." These attacks may last for a few seconds or for hours. Panic attacks are associated with all sorts of physical symptoms—a pounding heart, labored breathing, sweating, trembling, chest pains, nausea, dizziness, and/or numbness and trembling in the hands and feet. As with GAD, no one stimulus brings a panic attack on. The panic attack is unexpected. It just happens. Early in the disorder, nearly 85 percent of patients visit hospital emergency rooms, convinced that they are suffering some life-threatening emergency (Katerndahl & Realini, 1995). The *DSM-IV* points out that panic attacks can occur with other disorders—not just panic disorder. However, patients with panic disorder have a *recurrent pattern* of attacks and a building worry about future attacks.

At some time, 1.5 to 3.5 percent of the U.S. population will experience panic disorder. (That doesn't sound like a large percentage, but it represents four to nine million people!) Interestingly, a study of panic disorder in ten countries found that it occurred at about the same rate in all of the countries (U.S., Canada, Puerto Rico, France, Germany, Italy, Lebanon, Korea, and New Zealand) except Taiwan—which, for some unknown reason, had a rate less than half that of the other countries (Weissman et al., 1997).

The age of onset for panic disorder is usually between adolescence and the mid-20s (Craske & Barlow, 2001; Hayward et al., 1992). Initial panic attacks are often associated with stress, particularly from the loss of an important relationship. Panic disorder can be accompanied by depression, yet another example of comorbidity (Kessler et al., 1998). Comorbidity of depression and panic disorder may explain the higher rates of suicide and attempted suicide for people with panic disorder (20 percent) compared to rates for persons with depression by itself (15 percent) (Johnson et al., 1990; Weissman et al., 1989).

Phobic Disorders

The essential feature of **phobic disorders** (or phobias) is a persistent and excessive fear of some object, activity, or situation that leads a person to avoid that object, activity, or situation. The definition implies two things: the fear is intense enough to be disruptive and fear exists when there is no real or significant threat to give rise to it. The fear is unreasonable, exaggerated, or inappropriate. Did you notice that with this disorder we use the term *fear*, not *anxiety*? What is the difference? In many regards, the two terms (and the two feelings) are the same. The difference is that fear requires an object. One is not just "afraid." One is afraid *of* something. We would say you are afraid of the dark, but we would not say you are anxious of the dark.

panic disorder an acute "attack" of anxiety that is recurrent, unpredictable, unprovoked, sudden, and intense

phobic disorder a persistent and excessive fear of some object, event, or activity that leads to avoidant behaviors

Someone who is claustrophobic and has an intense irrational fear of flying would find traveling by air in a very small plane particularly unnerving.

Courtesy of Push Pictures/Corbis.

Many things are life-threatening or downright frightening. If you drive your car down a steep hill and suddenly realize the brakes are not working, you will probably feel fear. Such a reaction is not phobic because it is not irrational. Similarly, few of us enjoy the company of bees. That we do not like bees and would prefer they not be around us does not mean we have a phobic disorder. Key to a diagnosis is intensity of response. People who have a phobic reaction to bees (called *mellissaphobia*) may refuse to leave the house in the summer for fear of encountering a bee and may become anxious at the buzzing of any insect, fearing it to be a bee. They may become uncomfortable reading a paragraph about bees.

There are many phobias. The two main categories of phobic disorder are *specific phobias* and *social phobias*. Specific phobias involve the fear of animals, the physical environment (storms, heights, water, etc.), blood, injection, injury, or a specific situation (tunnels, elevators, airplanes, etc.). Social phobias

are significant and persistent fears of social or performance situations in which embarrassment may occur. Fear of public speaking or large crowds are social phobias. In one study, 10 percent of respondents reported that public-speaking anxiety significantly interfered with their work, social life, or education, or caused them marked distress (Barlow & Durand, 2002, pp. 131–135; Stein, Walker, & Forde, 1996). Table 12.2 presents a few of the phobic disorders known to psychologists.

For many years researchers assumed that phobias were learned reactions. Stuck in an elevator on a very hot day, Barbara develops claustrophobia. Bitten by a large dog when he was a toddler, Joe now has an intense irrational fear of dogs. The most obvious model for learning phobias was classical conditioning—either by personal experience or by watching someone else go through a trauma. To be sure, learning and experience account for many phobic reactions. However, some people may be genetically predisposed to develop pho-

TABLE 12.2

A sample of phobias: some relatively common (agoraphobia, claustrophobia, pathopobia, nyctophobia, zoohobia), the others quite rare.

THE PHOBIA	IS A FEAR OF
acrophobia	high places
agoraphobia	open spaces
algophobia	pain
astraphobia	lightning and thunder
autophobia	one's self
claustrophobia	small, closed places
hematophobia	blood
monophobia	being alone
mysophobia	dirt or contamination
nyctophobia	the dark
pathophobia	illness or disease
thanatophobia	death and dying
xenophobia	the unknown
zoophobia	animals, in general

bic reactions (Kendler, Myers, & Prescott, 2002). It also follows that people may be more likely to develop phobias to some stimuli (e.g., snakes or heights) than to others (e.g., kittens or sunny days).

In any given year, about 12.5 percent of the population experiences some type of phobic disorder, making it one of the most common of the psychological disorders (Barlow & Durand, 2009, p. 144; Kessler et al., 2005). In some cases, a person with a phobia can avoid the source of fear and the need for treatment. The *prognosis* (the prediction of the future course of a disorder) is good for phobic disorders. That is, therapy is likely to successfully help the phobia sufferer; however, only a small number of those with phobias ever seek professional help (ADAA, 2003).

A commonly treated phobic disorder is **agoraphobia**, which literally means "fear of open places." It is an exaggerated fear of venturing forth into the world alone. People with this disorder avoid crowds, streets, and stores. They establish a safe base for themselves and may, in extreme cases, refuse to leave their homes. Agoraphobia is commonly found in patients with panic disorder (comorbidity again). Although panic disorder can occur without agoraphobia, the two more often occur together (Baker, Patterson, & Barlow, 2002). This comorbidity makes sense, doesn't it? For example, a person with agoraphobia has several panic attacks without a clear cause. As a result, the person finds it increasingly difficult to venture out in the world for fear of another panic attack. In fact, the "open places" of agoraphobia are often the same as activities, situations, or events from which escape might be difficult in the event of a panic attack (Carter, 2002).

Obsessive-Compulsive Disorder (OCD)

The **obsessive-compulsive disorder** (OCD) is an anxiety disorder characterized by a pattern of recurrent obsessions and compulsions. **Obsessions** are ideas

Courtesy of Image Source/Corbis.

A common symptom of obsessive-compulsive disorder (OCD) is "checking behavior." An example would be ritualistically locking a door not once or twice, but exactly 14 times before leaving.

or thoughts that involuntarily and constantly intrude into awareness. Generally speaking, obsessions are groundless thoughts, most commonly about cleanliness (or contamination), violence, disease, danger, or doubt (Grinspoon, 1995). Many of us have experienced mild, obsessive-like thoughts—for example, worrying during the first few days of a vacation if you turned off the stove (Clark & Rhyno, 2005). To qualify as OCD, obsessions must be disruptive; they must interfere with normal functioning. They must be time-consuming and produce anxiety and distress.

Compulsions are constantly intruding, repetitive behaviors. The most commonly reported compulsions are hand-washing, grooming, and counting or checking behaviors, such as checking repeatedly that the door is really locked (Leckman et al., 1997). (See Table 12.3.) Have you ever checked an answer sheet to see that you have really answered all the questions on a test and then checked it again, and again, and again? To do so is compulsive. It serves no real purpose, and it provides no real sense of satisfaction, although it is done very conscientiously to reduce anxiety or stress.

agoraphobia (literally, "fear of open places") an exaggerated fear of venturing forth into the world alone

compulsions constantly intruding, repetitive behaviors that bring no pleasure and are distressing

obsessive-compulsive disorder (OCD) an anxiety disorder characterized by a pattern or recurrent obsessions and compulsions

obsessions ideas or thoughts that involuntarily and constantly intrude on awareness

TABLE 12.3

A few of the more common obsessions and compulsions found in patients with OCR. (From the website of the Obsessive-Compulsive Foundation, www.ocfoundation.org, retrieved July, 2003.)

COMMON OBSESSIONS	COMMON COMPULSIONS
Contamination fears of germs, dirt, etc.	Washing
Imagining having harmed self or others	Repeating
Imagining losing control of aggressive urges	Checking
Intrusive sexual thoughts or urges	Touching
Excessive religious or moral doubt	Counting
Forbidden thoughts	Ordering/arranging
A need to have things "just so"	Hoarding or saving
A need to tell, ask, confess	Praying

| **posttraumatic stress disorder (PTSD)** a disorder that involves distressing symptoms that arise at some time after the experience of a traumatic event

People with OCD recognize that their behaviors serve no useful purpose; they know that the behaviors are unreasonable but cannot stop them. It is as if the person with OCD engages in these compulsive behaviors to prevent some other (even more anxiety-producing) behaviors from taking place.

An obsession or compulsion can exert an enormous influence on a person's life. For example, consider the case of a happily married accountant, the father of three. For reasons he cannot explain, he becomes obsessed with the fear of contracting AIDS. There is no reason for him to be concerned; his sexual activities are entirely monogamous; he has never used drugs; he has never had a blood transfusion. Still, he is overwhelmed with the fear that he will contract this deadly disease. Ritualized, compulsive behaviors are associated with his obsessive thoughts: He washes his hands vigorously at every opportunity and becomes anxious if he cannot change his clothes at least three times a day (all to avoid the dreaded AIDS virus).

Please notice that we are using compulsive in an altogether different way when we refer to someone being a compulsive gambler, a compulsive eater, or a compulsive practical joker. In these cases, the person engaged in habitual patterns of behavior gains pleasure from doing the behaviors. The compulsive

gambler enjoys gambling; the compulsive eater loves to eat. Such people may not enjoy the long-term consequences of their actions, but they enjoy the behaviors themselves.

Obsessive-compulsive disorder is much more common than once believed. It afflicts nearly one of every 200 teenagers (OCD is commonly diagnosed in childhood or adolescence), and as many as five million Americans (Kessler et al., 2005). OCD is one of the few anxiety disorders which occur at about the same rate for males and females.

Posttraumatic Stress Disorder (PTSD)

An anxiety disorder that has been the subject of much public discussion over the past decade is **posttraumatic stress disorder (PTSD)**. This disorder involves distressing symptoms that arise some time after the experience of a highly traumatic event, where trauma is defined by the DSM-IV as an event that meets two criteria: a) the person has experienced, witnessed, or been confronted with an event that involves actual or threatened death or serious injury, and b) the person's response involves intense fear, helplessness, or horror. The disorder was first recognized with the publication of the DSM-III in 1980, considered in response to what appeared to be a significant mental health problem of veterans returning from the Vietnam War. Ironically, the disorder affected only 1.2 percent of Vietnam veterans (compared to 3.7 percent of Korean War veterans and up to ten percent of World War II veterans (Dean, 1997; McNally, 2003).

Three clusters of symptoms further define PTSD: 1) re-experiencing the traumatic event (e.g., flashbacks or nightmares), 2) avoidance of any possible reminders of the event (including people who were there), and 3) increased arousal or "hyper-alertness" (e.g., irritability, insomnia, difficulty concentrating).

The traumatic events that trigger PTSD are many, ranging from natural disasters (e.g., floods or hurricanes), to life-threatening situations (e.g., kidnapping, rape, assault, or combat), to the loss of property (e.g., the house burns down; the car is stolen). Some traumas encompass all of these—think of Hurricane Katrina and the Gulf Coast in the late summer of 2005. Proximity to the worst of a trauma like Hurricane Katrina increases the probability of posttraumatic stress disorder. PTSD among people who lived in downtown metropolitan New Orleans was nearly twice as common as for residents of Alabama, Louisiana and Mississippi affected by the force of the hurricane (Galea et al., 2007).

On the other hand, first-hand experience with trauma is not required for posttraumatic stress syndrome. The disorder has been diagnosed in survivors of the destruction of the World Trade Center buildings on September 11, 2001, in some people who witnessed the attacks from the streets of New York City, and people in some who got "caught up" in the continuous television images of that horrific day and its aftermath.

Estimates of how much PTSD people experience over a lifetime range from about 2 percent of the population (Robb-Nicholson, 1995) to about 8 percent (Kessler et al., 1995). "Nearly half of U. S. adults experience at least one

Courtesy of Dan Anderson/epa/Corbis.

Posttraumatic stress disorder can develop following any kind of traumatic event. It need not be a major, "national" event, like hurricane Katrina. Indeed, "traumas" are in the eye of the beholder.

traumatic event in their lifetimes, yet only 10 percent of women and 5 percent of men develop posttraumatic stress disorder" (Ozer & Weiss, 2004, p. 169). A study of the experience of traumatic events and the development of posttraumatic stress disorder in children (from ages 9, 11, and 12 until they were 16) concluded that nearly two-thirds experienced at least one truly traumatic event, but that very few (fewer than 0.5 percent) met the criteria for PTSD (Copeland et al., 2007). As it happens, the experience of a prior traumatic event does *not*, in itself, increase the risk of developing PTSD with the experience of subsequent trauma (Breslau, Peterson, & Schultz, 2008).

The course of PTSD does not show a predictable pattern of lessening symptoms. Indeed, over a four-year period following diagnosis, symptoms actually increase in number and severity (Port, Engdahl, & Frazier, 2001). Everything else being equal the overall healthcare expenses of women with PTSD were up to 100 percent higher than the healthcare costs for women without the disorder (Walker et al., 2003).

Psychologists often find comorbidity with PTSD. It is commonly associated with alcohol and substance abuse or depression. In fact, the prognosis for posttraumatic stress disorder is related to the extent to which there are comorbid disorders (e.g., alcoholism), the extent to which the patient experienced psychological problems before the traumatic event, and the extent to which social support is available. Some data suggest that higher levels of cognitive ability "protect" against the disorder. This study found that intelligence (measured by a simple IQ test) is a good predictor of which veterans with combat experience are likely to experience PTSD (McNally & Shin, 1995; Silva et al., 2000).

BEFORE YOU GO ON

5. In general, what are the anxiety disorders?
6. Describe each of the following: generalized anxiety disorder, panic disorder, phobic disorder, obsessive-compulsive disorder, and posttraumatic stress disorder.

A Point to Ponder or Discuss
When medical students study diseases, sometimes they develop the symptoms of the diseases they are studying. Do any of the disorders in this section sound like a problem you have had or are having? Do you know where to go to check on your self-diagnosis?

SOMATOFORM DISORDERS

Soma means "body." Hence, the **somatoform disorders** involve physical, bodily symptoms or complaints. They are psychological disorders because there is no known medical or biological cause for the symptoms. We will consider three: two common, hypochondriasis and somatization disorder; the other rare but very dramatic, conversion disorder.

Hypochondriasis and Somatization Disorder

Hypochondriasis is the diagnosis for someone preoccupied with the fear of a serious disease. Persons with this disorder are unusually aware of every ache and pain. They often read popular health magazines and diagnose their own ailments. In reality, they have no medical disorder or disease. Even so, they constantly seek medical attention and are not convinced of their good health despite the best medical opinions.

A man with occasional chest pains, for example, self-diagnoses his condition as lung cancer. Even after many physicians reassure him that his lungs are perfectly fine and that he has no signs of cancer, the man's fears are not put to rest: "They are just trying to make me feel better by not telling me, but they know, as I do, that I have lung cancer and am going to die soon." Hypochondriasis is found equally in men and women (Creed & Barsky, 2004).

It is not difficult to imagine why someone develops hypochondriasis. If a person believes he or she has contracted some terrible disease, three problems might be solved. 1) The person has a way to explain otherwise unexplainable anxiety: "Well, my goodness, if you had lung cancer, you'd be anxious, too." 2) The illness may be used to excuse the individual from activities that he or she finds anxiety producing: "As sick as I am, you don't expect me to go to work, do you?" 3) The illness may be used to gain attention or sympathy: "Don't you feel sorry for me knowing that I have such a terrible disease?"

somatoform disorders psychological disorders that involve physical or bodily symptoms with no known medical or biological cause for the symptoms

hypochondriasis the diagnosis for someone preoccupied with the fear of a serious disease

It is often difficult for mental-health professionals to distinguish hypochondriasis from **somatization disorder**, which is indicated by several recurring, and long-lasting complaints about bodily symptoms for which no physical cause can be found. The subtle difference is that persons with somatization disorder focus primarily on their nonexistent "symptoms," while persons with hypochondriasis focus on some nonexistent underlying "disease" indicated by their symptoms. As reasonable as that may sound, in the real world, there often is considerable overlap between somatization disorder and hypochondriasis (Creed & Barsky, 2004). (Unfortunately, the prognosis for somatization disorder is quite poor. It is most often a lifelong disorder that truly burdens the health-care system (Bell, 1994).

Courtesy of ER Productions/Corbis.

Someone with a somatoform disorder often goes to doctor after doctor, searching for someone to adequately diagnose what they believe to be a serious illness or disease—even when there is no medical evidence of such an illness or disease.

somatization disorder a disorder indicated by several recurring and long-lasting complaints about bodily symptoms for which no physical cause can be found

Conversion Disorder

Conversion disorder is rare (accounting for less than 5 percent of all anxiety disorders). The DSM-IV tells us that it is more common in rural areas or in underdeveloped countries. Indeed, in some cultures, a few of the symptoms of the disorder are considered quite normal. The symptoms of **conversion disorder** are striking. There is a loss or altering of physical function that suggests a physical disorder. The symptoms are not intentionally produced and cannot be explained by any physical disorder. The "loss of functioning" is typically of great significance; paralysis, blindness, and deafness are the classic examples. As difficult as it may be to believe, the symptoms are "real" in the sense that a person cannot feel or move, see, or hear. Again, there is no medical explanation for the symptoms. In some cases, medical explanations run contrary to the symptoms. One type of conversion disorder is *glove anesthesia*, a condition in which the hands lose feeling and become paralyzed from the wrist down. As it happens, it is impossible to have paralysis and loss of feeling in the hands alone. Some

paralysis in the forearm, upper arm, and shoulder must accompany paralysis in the hands because paralysis follows neural pathways.

One remarkable symptom of conversion disorder (which occurs only in some patients) is known as *la belle indifference*—a seemingly inappropriate lack of concern over one's condition. Some persons with conversion disorder seem to feel comfortable with and accepting of their infirmity. They are blind, deaf, or paralyzed and show very little concern.

Conversion disorder is important in psychology's history because it intrigued Sigmund Freud and led him to develop a new method of therapy that we will discuss in the next chapter. Conversion disorder was known to the Greeks, who named it *hysteria*, a label still used from time to time, as in "hysterical blindness." The Greeks believed the disorder was found only in women and was a disorder of the uterus, or *hysterium*, hence the name hysteria. The ancient logic was that the disease would leave the uterus, float through the body, and settle in the eyes, hands, or affected body part. Of course, this ancient logic is no longer considered valid, but the potential sexual basis for the disorder was what initially caught Freud's attention. However, it is true that the disorder is much more common in women than in men (Rosenbaum, 2000).

conversion disorder a disorder in which there is a loss or altering of physical function that suggests a physical disorder; the symptoms are not intentionally produced and cannot be explained by any physical disorder

BEFORE YOU GO ON

7. Compare and contrast hypochondriasis, somatization disorder, and conversion disorder.

A Point to Ponder or Discuss

A very busy family-practice physician sees a female patient who complains of dizziness, headaches, and even minor seizures. In a cursory examination, the physician finds no cause for these symptoms. Is the doctor likely to diagnose a somatoform disorder and simply prescribe anti-anxiety medication? If you think this likely, how might it be changed?

DISSOCIATIVE DISORDERS

dissociative disorders psychological disorders in which a person seeks to escape from some aspects of life or personality seen as the source of stress, discomfort, or anxiety

dissociative fugue amnesic forgetfulness, accompanied by a change of location–seemingly pointless travel

dissociative amnesia the inability to recall important personal information–an inability too extensive to be explained by simple forgetfulness

To *dissociate* means to become separate from or to escape. The underlying theme of the **dissociative disorders** is that a person seeks to escape from some aspect of life or personality seen as the source of stress, discomfort, or anxiety. These disorders can be dramatic, and they have been the subject of novels, movies, and television shows.

Dissociative Amnesia

Dissociative amnesia is the inability to recall important personal information—an inability too extensive to be explained by ordinary forgetfulness. Before the DSM-IV, this disorder was called *psychogenic* amnesia, where psychogenic means "psychological in origin," and amnesia refers to a loss of memory. What is forgotten is usually some traumatic incident and some or all of the experiences that led up to or followed the incident. As you may suspect, there is no medical explanation for the loss of memory. The extent of forgetting associated with dissociative amnesia varies greatly. In some cases of *generalized amnesia*, a person may forget everything; in some cases of *selective amnesia*, a person may "lose" entire days and weeks at a time; in other cases, only specific details of a single incident resist being recalled. Dissociative amnesia is more common in wartime, when traumatic experiences occur more often.

Dissociative Fugue

Occasionally, amnesic forgetfulness is accompanied by a change of location— seemingly pointless travel. For example, a person finds himself in a strange and different place with no reasonable explanation for how he got there. This amnesia and pointless travel is a disorder known as **dissociative fugue**. A typical example is that of Carol, a woman found wandering around the business district of a large eastern city, inappropriately dressed for the cold winds and low temperatures. Her behaviors seemed aimless, and she was stopped by a police officer who asked if he could be of assistance. Carol did not know where she was, so the officer took her to a nearby hospital. She had no memory of where she had been or what she had been doing for the last two weeks. Carol had no idea how she had gotten to the city, which was 350 miles from her home.

In their own ways, dissociative amnesia and fugue disorder are like the somatoform disorders because both kinds of disorders involve escape from stressful situations. In conversion disorders, for example, a person may escape from stress by taking on the symptoms of a major physical disorder. With amnesia and fugue, escape is more literal. People escape by forgetting or they avoid stress by psychologically or physically running away.

Dissociative Identity Disorder

Psychologists still refer to dissociative identity disorder as multiple personality disorder, as it was called before DSM-IV. Please note that a dissociative identity disorder is not the same as schizophrenia. We emphasize the difference because the media consistently create the mistaken impression the two conditions are the same. They are not. Schizophrenia is a different disorder—which we will discuss shortly.

The major symptom of **dissociative identity disorder (DID)** is the existence within the same person of two or more distinct personalities or personality traits. Up to 100 distinct personalities within the same person have been reported, but the average is about 15 (Ross, 1997). The disorder was once rare, but it has become more common for unknown reasons. From the 1920s to 1970, only a handful of cases were reported worldwide; since the 1970s, reported cases have increased astronomically, with thousands reported each year (Ross, 1997; Spanos, 1994). One intriguing finding: the increase in prevalence of DID has occurred only in North America. Multiple personality disorder is seldom diagnosed in France, and it is very rare in Great Britain, Russia, and India. One study in 1990 failed to find even a single case of the disorder in Japan (Spanos, 1994; Takahashi, 1990).

Two or more personalities in the same person is difficult to imagine. Perhaps a contrast would help. We all change our behaviors, and (in a small way) our personalities, depending on our situation. We do not act, think, or feel exactly the same way at school as we do at work, at a party, or at a house of worship. We modify our behaviors to fit the situation. But these changes do not qualify as an identity disorder. What are the differences?

The differences are significant. Someone with a dissociative identity disorder has changes in personality that are dramatic and extreme. They do not slightly alter their behavior; they have two or more distinct personalities, implying a change in underlying consciousness, not just in overt behaviors. Another difference is we change our behaviors in response to situational cues. Someone with DID can change in personalities without warning or provocation. The third major difference involves control. When we change our behaviors, we do so intentionally. Persons with a multiple personality disorder can seldom control or predict which of their personalities are dominant at any one time. Persons diagnosed with DID often have been victims of child abuse or sexual abuse (Putnam et al., 1986; Ross, 1997). The connection between dissociative identity disorder and sexual abuse partially explains the significantly higher incidence of multiple personality disorder in women than in men. Girls and women are much more likely to be sexually or physically abused than are boys and men.

dissociative identity disorder (DID) a disorder characterized by two or more distinct personalities or personality traits within the same person

---

BEFORE YOU GO ON

8. What are the major characteristics of the dissociative disorders?

A Point to Ponder or Discuss

Having multiple personalities would be a convenient defense for a criminal. John's defense might be something like, "I didn't do it; this other, hidden, nasty personality did it." And John could be telling the truth. If you were suspicious, however, how could you determine if the multiple personalities were genuine or not?

PERSONALITY DISORDERS

The psychological disorders we have reviewed so far afflict persons who were normal and undisturbed at one time. In other words, the person did not always exhibit the symptoms of the disorder. This prior state of wellness generally does not exist with personality disorders. **Personality disorders** are long-lasting patterns of perceiving, relating to, and thinking about the environment and oneself that are maladaptive and inflexible and cause either impaired functioning or distress. As we have seen, individual personality is defined by attitudes, behaviors, and traits that persist in many situations over long periods of time. With a personality disorder, the traits and habits that constitute one's personality are inflexible and damaging (Grinspoon, 1996). Personality disorders are usually identifiable by adolescence, but a true diagnosis is not appropriate for anyone younger than 18.

The DSM-IV lists 11 personality disorders (PDs), grouped in three clusters. Cluster I includes disorders in which the person can be characterized as odd or eccentric. People with disorders from this cluster are often difficult to get along with. Cluster II includes disorders in which the person seems overly dramatic, emotional, or erratic, and where behaviors are impulsive. Cluster III includes disorders that add anxiety or fearfulness to the standard criteria for personality disorder. Note that it is only for those personality disorders in Cluster III that we find any reports of fear, anxiety, or depression.

Rather than deal with all of the personality disorders in detail, we will simply describe some of the major characteristics of disorders within each of the three main clusters. Then, we will look at one PD—antisocial personality disorder—in some detail. As we do so, keep in mind that personality disorders generally have long-standing symptoms that usually begin in childhood or adolescence.

personality disorders long-lasting patterns of perceiving, relating to, and thinking about the environment and oneself that are inflexible and maladaptive and cause either impaired functioning or distress

Cluster I: Disorders of Odd or Eccentric Reactions

Paranoid personality disorder—an extreme sensitivity, envy, unjustified suspiciousness, and mistrust of others; the actions of other people are interpreted as deliberately demeaning or threatening. A person with this disorder shows a restricted range of emotional reactivity, is humorless, and rarely seeks help. Example: a person who continually, and without justification, accuses a spouse of infidelity and believes that every wrong number was really a call from the spouse's lover.

Schizoid personality disorder—an inability to form, and an indifference to, interpersonal relationships. A person with schizoid personality disorder appears cold and aloof, and often engages in excessive daydreaming. Example: a person who lives, as she has for years, in a one-room flat in a poor part of town, venturing out only to pick up a social security check and a few necessities at the corner store.

Cluster II: Disorders of Dramatic, Emotional, or Erratic Reactions

Histrionic personality disorder—overly dramatic, reactive, and intensely expressed behaviors. A person with this disorder is emotionally lively, draws attention to himself or herself, and overreacts to matters of little consequence. Example: a woman who spends an inordinate amount of time on her appearance, calls everyone darling, constantly asks for feedback about her looks, describes most of her experiences as wonderful or outstanding even when such an experience is no more than finding a detergent on sale at the grocery store.

Narcissistic personality disorder—grandiose exaggeration of self-importance, a need for attention or admiration, and a tendency to set unrealistic goals. Someone with this personality disorder maintains few lasting relationships and in many ways engages in a "childish" level of behavior. Example: a person who always wants to be the topic of conversation and shows a lack of interest in saying anything positive about anyone else; believes that no one else has ever taken a vacation as stupendous as his or hers, or understood an issue as clearly as he or she does; will do whatever it takes to be complimented.

Cluster III: Disorders Involving Anxiety and Fearfulness

Avoidant personality disorder—an over-sensitivity to the possibility of being rejected by others and an unwillingness to enter into relationships for fear of being rejected. A person with this disorder is devastated by disapproval, but holds out a desire for social relationships. Example: a man with few close friends who almost never dates and talks only to women who are older and less attractive than he is; has worked for years at the same job, never seeking a job change or promotion, rarely speaks in public, and may attend meetings and public gatherings but without actively participating.

Dependent personality disorder—allowing others to dominate and assume responsibility for one's actions, a poor self-image and lack of confidence. A person with this disorder sees himself or herself as stupid and helpless, thus defers to others. Example: a woman frequently abused by her husband; she has from time to time reported the abuse but refuses to take an active role in finding help or treatment, saying it is "her place" to do as he says, and that if she does not please him, it is her fault.

Exactly how many people have personality disorders is hard to determine because personality disorders are difficult to accurately diagnose. Most cases of personality disorder first come to the attention of mental health professionals on referral from the courts (or family members) or because of related problems such as child abuse or alcoholism. What we do find is that while the overall rate of PD may be between 10 percent and 20 percent, the rates of specific disorders are very low (Weissman, 1993). About one-fourth of those with symptoms of a personality disorder fit more than one diagnostic category—another example of comorbidity (Barlow & Durand, 2009; Clark et al., 1995).

The prognosis for the personality disorders is poor. The maladaptive patterns of behavior that characterize personality disorders have usually taken a lifetime to develop. As a result, changing them is very difficult.

An Example: The Antisocial Personality Disorder

The **antisocial personality disorder** is characterized by an exceptional lack of regard for the rights and property of others. Someone with this disorder often engages in impulsive behaviors with little or no regard for the consequences of those behaviors. Diagnosis of this disorder can be difficult because, by definition, symptoms of the disorder include deceit and the manipulation of others: "Lacking in conscience and in feelings for others, they cold-bloodedly take what they want and do as they please, violating social norms and expectations without the slightest guilt or regret" (Hare, 1995, p. 4). People with antisocial PD are sometimes still referred to using the outdated terms "psychopath" or "sociopath." The disorder is included, with the histrionic and the narcissistic personality disorders, in Cluster II in DSM-IV.

Remember, as is the case for all PDs, the antisocial personality disorder is not an appropriate diagnosis for anyone younger than 18. Still, a long history of "getting into trouble" precedes diagnosis in many cases (Donnellan et al., 2005; Johansson, Kerr, & Andershed, 2005). Persons with antisocial personality disorder are impulsive. They change jobs, residences, and relationships frequently. At best, they are irresponsible.

antisocial personality disorder a disorder characterized by an exceptional lack of regard for the rights and property of others, and impulsive behaviors with little or no regard for the consequences of those behaviors

Courtesy of FK Photo/Corbis.

Unfortunately, psychologists often do not get to diagnose someone with antisocial personality disorder until he has had a run-in with the law. And, by far, such diagnoses are much more common for males than for females.

standing characteristic of many people with antisocial personality disorder (Compton et al., 2005; Skodol, Oldham, & Gallaher, 1999). The disorder is much more likely to be diagnosed in males than in females (Paris, 2004). Like many of the other personality disorders, antisocial PD is resistant to treatment because most psychotherapy is designed for people who want to change. Persons with antisocial personality disorder usually enter treatment programs because they have been ordered by a court to do so (Hare, 1995). Court-ordered therapy programs are ineffective for the 25 to 35 percent of spouse abusers who are diagnosed with antisocial PD. Interestingly, persons with antisocial personality disorder do not benefit from punishment; it simply seems to have no effect (Holmes, 2001, p. 352). Another interesting footnote is that alcohol use is a predictive factor in male-to-female intimate partner violence. However, alcohol use is not a predictive factor when the abuser has antisocial personality disorder (Fals-Stewart, Leonard, & Birchler, 2005).

At worst, their behaviors are criminal. A person who has committed a crime does not necessarily have antisocial personality disorder. In fact, many criminals show genuine sadness and remorse over their crimes. If nothing else, they show remorse for the fact that they were caught and punished. Persons with antisocial personality disorder are likely to be indifferent about their crimes, their victims, or even being caught. "Well, that's the way it goes." "He shouldn't have been carrying that much money with him." "A few more months in jail won't bother me much." Persons with antisocial PD make up 15 to 20 percent of the American prison population.

The antisocial personality disorder is much more likely to be found among those who are of low socioeconomic status, live in cities, and have a history of antisocial behaviors beginning before age 10. Substance abuse (including alcohol abuse) is common and a long-

Unlike other personality disorders, it appears that some persons with the disorder have a spontaneous remission of symptoms in their early 40s. In one study prisoners with antisocial personality disorder were most likely to be in prison between the ages of 31 and 35 (90 percent of the sample), and much less likely to be in prison between the ages of 41 and 45 (less than 60 percent of the sample) (Hare et al., 1988). Finally, we should mention that persons with antisocial PD often present themselves in a very positive manner. They appear very self-assured, pleasant, and are willing to say anything to manipulate others. Some become callous street level criminals with boundless capacity for violence without guilt. Others with antisocial PD may be white-collar criminals who swindle with an assured and smooth-talking demeanor but an equal lack of remorse.

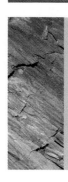

BEFORE YOU GO ON

9. What characterizes the personality disorders?
10. Describe the defining aspects of the antisocial personality disorder.

A Point to Ponder or Discuss

Antisocial personality disorder and substance abuse are correlated. What arguments can you make for a cause-and-effect relationship, and how would you test your hypothesis?

A DISORDER OF CHILDHOOD: AUTISM

There are several psychological disorders that are classified in the DSM-IV as "Disorders Usually First Diagnosed in Infancy, Childhood, or Adolescence," (including learning disorders, attention-deficit disorders, and eating or feeding disorders). None, however, is quite as remarkable or as devastating as **autism**, which is characterized by impaired social interaction, problems with communication, and unusual or severely limited activities and interests (American Psychiatric Association, 2000; Durand, 2004).

Once thought to be a rare disorder, occurring in only 10–15 children of every 10,000, more recent data suggest that estimates of one in every 500 births (with the disorder four times more common among boys than girls) may be too low (Shattuck, 2006). In 2007, the Centers for Disease Control and Prevention reported that autism (and closely related disorders) is now diagnosed in one of every 150 children. The diagnosis of autism is usually made within the first two-and-a-half years of life.

The lack of social interaction by autistic children is striking. Autistic children can seem oblivious to those around them (MacDonald et al., 2006). There are no apparent signs of attachment, even with primary caregivers, and little indication that they have any notion of what others may be thinking or feeling. They just do not seem to understand social cues, such as facial expressions and tone of voice. They often avoid eye contact. Children with autism have great difficulty communicating with others—about one-third never develop language skills (Chan et al., 2005).

Autistic children who are most at risk for language impairment can be identified at a very young age based on predictors known as *joint attention*. This refers to specific behaviors that can be used to follow or direct the attention of another person to an event or object in order to share that interest. This may include behaviors of *pointing* and *directing*, which are often delayed or absent in children with autism. To illustrate "pointing" behavior, consider these examples: 1) a child sees an insect crawling on the ground and points at it so that others may see it as well, and 2) a child who wants a cookie simply points to the cabinet where the cookies are kept in order to signify his or her desire to have one. With respect to "directing" behavior, pre-verbal children can express themselves by grabbing a person by the hand or pushing them in the direction in which they want them to go. These behaviors are important because they are ways in which the child can communicate his or her needs and wants to others. If an autistic child engages in this type of behavior, the chance that they will improve their expressive language is far greater than if the behavior is nonexistent (Anderson et al., 2007).

The behavioral differences of children with autism are also easily recognized.

autism a disorder of childhood characterized by impaired social interactions, problems with communication, and unusual or severely limited activities and interests

Inattention, hyperactivity, and aggression are common in autistic children, and frequently cause significant impairment (Erickson et al., 2007). Behaviors are often repetitive and stereotyped, often just simple rocking and/or twisting about. They show an aversion to being hugged or held. Although they seldom attend to other people they can become preoccupied with inanimate objects, and they clearly prefer that their physical environment remain unchanged in every way—a phenomenon referred to as "insistence on sameness."

You will not be surprised to learn that there is as yet no known cause of autism, although there are some intriguing leads. To be sure, there is a genetic underpinning to the disorder, with probably several specific genes involved (Freitag, 2007; Wickelgren, 2005). There is some evidence that at least a contributing factor to the development of autism may be a viral infection. Researchers are also focusing their attention on the causative influence of environmental toxins and pollutants (Edelson, 2007). Of particular interest—and controversy—is the possibility of mercury poisoning resulting from vaccinations and inoculations that virtually all children receive at the age of about 18 months. Because the onset of autism often occurs at about the time of childhood vaccinations, the hypothesis arose that a preservative ingredient of many such vaccinations—*thimerosal*, which contains trace amounts of the toxin *ethylmercury*—might be a cause of autism. Although the logic of the hypothesis is reasonable, no research data confirmed the hypothesis. In fact, a recent study (Schedcter & Grether, 2008) looked at the prevalence of autism in children from California before and after the ethylmercury was removed from vaccines (in 2004). Removal of the ethylmercury had no discernible affect whatever on the rates of autism in the population studied.

There is no known cure for autism, although there are interventions that can bring about improvement in some symptoms. Highly structured and specifically focused therapy sessions can improve social and language skills in many autistic children. The focused use of *positive behavior support* (immediately and significantly rewarding appropriate behaviors) can bring about meaningful and lasting reductions of inappropriate behaviors. Therapy or counseling for the parents and siblings of a child with autism is useful in helping families cope (Lucyshyn et al., 2007; Myles, 2007). Although there are no medications that impact directly on autistic symptoms, antidepressants and anti-anxiety drugs have been used effectively to treat severe anxiety, depression, and behavioral problems.

Before we go on, we should mention *Asperger's Disorder*, a disorder of childhood very much like a milder form of autism. It, too, is characterized by impaired communication skills (although seldom as severe as in autism), and repetitive patterns of behavior and thought. Children with this disorder usually have IQ scores that are comparable to those of other children. A child with Asperger's disorder shows an obsessive interest in some single object or topic with little sign of interest in anything else (Volkmar, Klin & Schultz, 2005). First discovered in the 1940s, and recognized as a separate disorder in the 1980 DSM, the diagnosis of Asperger's is becoming more and more common.

BEFORE YOU GO ON

11. What are the defining characteristics of autistic disorder?

A Point to Ponder or Discuss
What hypotheses can you generate for why the prevalence rates of childhood autism are so steadily on the increase?

ALZHEIMER'S DEMENTIA

By definition, **dementia** is a condition characterized by the marked loss of intellectual abilities. A person's attention may be intact, but the use of memory is poor and deteriorates. Judgment and impulse control may be adversely affected.

A slow deterioration of intellectual functioning is the most common symptom associated with **Alzheimer's dementia** (AD) (Johnson, Davis, & Bosanquet, 2000). The disease is degenerative (meaning that symptoms get worse with time), resulting in declines in activities of daily living, behavioral disturbances, and reduced cognitive ability (Zurad, 2001). In particular, "difficulty with episodic memory has become known as the hallmark symptom of AD" (Storandt, 2008, p. 198). Problems of recent memory mark the early stages of the disease, "Did I take my pills this morning?" Mild personality changes—apathy, less spontaneity, withdrawal—soon follow. These mild personality changes may result from the attempt to hide one's symptoms from others. Table 12.4 is a summary from the Alzheimer's Association.

A recent reconsideration of the available data on the course of Alzheimer's dementia indicates that there may very well be reliable early indicators (risk factors, if you will) for the development of this disorder. Some of the significant indications for AD include poor attention to an ongoing task (Chen et al., 2005) and difficulties with semantic memory tasks (Storandt, 2008). A pattern of personality changes may also provide early signs of Alzheimer's. These personality changes include such things as increased rigidity, apathy, self-centeredness, and a reduction in inhibitory control (reduced self-restraint) (Balsis, Carpenter, & Storandt, 2005). Physiological risk factors for the development of Alzheimer's dementia virtually mirror those known for cardiovascular disease: obesity (Adlard et al., 2005), high blood pressure, and high levels of cholesterol (Kivipelto, 2006).

dementia a conditioned characterized by the marked loss of intellectual abilities

Alzheimer's dementia (AD) a disorder characterized by a slow deterioration of memory and other intellectual functioning

TABLE 12.4

Ten warning signs of Alzheimer's disease.

NORMAL	POSSIBLE ALZHEIMER'S
1. Temporarily forgetting a colleague's name	Not being able to remember the name later
2. Forgetting the carrots on the stove until the meal is over	Forgetting that a meal was ever prepared
3. Unable to find the right word, but using a fit substitute	Uttering incomprehensible sentences
4. Forgetting for a moment where you're going	Getting lost on your own street
5. Talking on the phone, temporarily forgetting to watch a child	Forgetting a child is present
6. Having trouble balancing a checkbook	Not knowing what the numbers mean
7. Misplacing a wristwatch until steps are retraced	Putting a wristwatch in the sugarbowl
8. Having a bad day	Having rapid mood shifts
9. Gradual change in personality with age	Drastic changes in personality
10. Tiring of housework, but getting back to it	Not knowing or caring that housework needs to be done

Tens of millions of people around the world now suffer from Alzheimer's dementia. Awareness of the disorder was heightened when it was learned that President Ronald Reagan had the disorder. His wife, Nancy, became an outspoken advocate for more monies for Alzheimer's research.

Courtesy of Bettmann/Corbis.

AD was first described in 1907 by Alois Alzheimer and was thought to be an inevitable result of aging (often incorrectly referred to as *senile psychosis*). The symptoms associated with dementia of the Alzheimer's type are not normal, natural, or a necessary part of growing old, but a general acceptance of this reality did not occur until the 1970s. Alzheimer's disease has been diagnosed in persons younger than 65. In such cases, medical professionals call Alzheimer's in patients younger than 65 an early onset form of the disease. But, a body of research suggests that age of onset, by itself, does not define different forms of the disease (Bondareffet et al., 1993; Kukull & Ganguli, 2000).

Alzheimer's is a global phenomenon. Currently, more than 7 million people in North America and Europe have been diagnosed, but an even larger number—perhaps 11 million—suffer from the disorder in developing nations (Farlow, 2000). The incidence of Alzheimer's disease is much higher in industrialized, "Western" countries than in developing, nonindustrialized countries (Hendrie, 1998; 2001). Alzheimer's dementia does become progressively more common with age. In the U.S., it affects one percent of 65-year-olds, but it affects 30 to 35 percent of 85-year-olds (Farlow, 2000). The size of the problem is increasing: "Whatever the current estimates are, all researchers agree that the number of AD cases will probably triple over the next 30 to 40 years" (DeKosky, 2001, p. 1). In 2000, there were 4.5 million persons with AD in the U.S. population. By 2050, the number will reach nearly 13.2 million (Herbert et al., 2003).

Although the symptoms of Alzheimer's disease are psychological, it is a physical disease caused by abnormal changes in brain tissue. As of today, we have no reliable test to diagnose Alzheimer's disease. Alzheimer's is diagnosed with certainty only after an autopsy of the brain. There are several signs which can be used to diagnose Alzheimer's disease: a) a mass of tangles, a spaghetti-like jumble of abnormal protein fibers; b) plaques—waste material, degenerated nerve fibers that wrap around a core of protein; c) the presence of small cavities filled with fluid and debris; d) atrophy—some brain structures are reduced in size (DeKosky, 2001); and e) reduced levels of the neurotransmitter acetylcholine, often implicated in the function of short-term memory (Bartus, 2000). Two cautions are in order: these signs can sometimes be found in a normal brain (seldom more than one at a time, however); and we do not know yet what causes these signs. A recent study reported on the impact of a drug designed to reduce the buildup of amyloid plaques in the brains of patients diagnosed with Alzheimer's (Holmes et al., 2008). What they discovered is perplexing: Compared to patients in the control group, the drug did successfully and significantly reduce the levels of plaques in the brain (determined at autopsy), *but* even these reductions had no discernable effect on the severity or course of the disease.

Scientists are beginning to understand the etiology of Alzheimer's, but are still discussing hypotheses. As noted above, researchers have identified several risk factors for AD, but they do not yet fully understand the causes for the disorder. Scientists know the nerve cells in the brains of Alzheimer's patients start to die off sooner than they should, resulting in the tangles, plaques, and other signs found at autopsy. The crucial unanswered question is how and why do these brain cells die?

As is so often the case with psychological functioning, there is a genetic basis for Alzheimer's disease. There is no doubt that the disease runs in families. A breakthrough occurred in 1993, when a research team at Duke University isolated a gene that might be part of the cause of Alzheimer's dementia. By the summer of 1995, two other genes associated with Alzheimer's were discovered. By 2003, scientists had isolated more than 40 genes with some association with Alzheimer's disease (Schellenberg, D'Souza, & Poorkaj, 2000). Exactly how these genes are connected to Alzheimer's is not yet understood (Hendrie, 2001; Plomin & McGuffin, 2003, pp. 215–216). Two recently published studies (Cheung et al., 2008; Dreses-Werringloer et al., 2008) reported finding a genetic basis for an abnormality in the way that brain cells of Alzheimer's patients process cal-

cium levels. This disruption of the normal role of calcium in the functioning of the brain's neurons may very well be an early indicator for the ultimate development of AD.

Several studies suggest that the frequent participation in cognitively stimulating tasks may actually reduce the risk of Alzheimer's in old age (Hultsch et al., 1999; Wilson & Bennett, 2003). One study followed 469 people 75 or older, for more than five years and tracked how they spent their free time. Cognitively stimulating activities included such things as working crossword puzzles, playing board games or cards, reading, playing musical instruments, and dancing. Participants in these activities generally had a lower risk for Alzheimer's. Participants in physical activities (golf, tennis, bicycling, walking, and the like) did not (Lipton & Katz, 2003). Whether the relationship between cognitive stimulation and Alzheimer's risk is causal or correlational is not yet certain. Researchers would also like to know when in one's life stimulating cognitive activity is most potent for warding off the disorder. Still, simply taking a stimulating college class (like psychology) and learning about new things (like Alzheimer's dementia) may have some hidden benefits.

BEFORE YOU GO ON

12. What is the nature of Alzheimer's dementia?
13. What risk factors have been associated with Alzheimer's disease?

A Point to Ponder or Discuss
If there were a genetic test for Alzheimer's dementia, would you take it? If so, under what conditions?

MOOD DISORDERS

The **mood disorders** (called *affective disorders* until DSM-III-R) clearly demonstrate a disturbance in emotional reactions or feelings. We have to be careful here. Almost all psychological disorders influ-

ence mood or affect. With mood disorders, however, the duration and/or intensity or extreme nature of a person's mood is the major symptom. In this context of disorders, psychologists often distinguish between *mood* and *emotion*. Mood refers to "diffuse, slow-moving feeling states that

mood disorders those disorders that demonstrate a disturbance in emotional reactions or feelings

major depressive disorder a disorder in which a person must have experienced two or more depressive episodes, where such an episode is defined as a period of at least two weeks, during which the person experienced 5 or more of these symptoms: a) depressed or sad mood, b) loss of pleasure or interest in normal activities, c) weight loss or dramatic change in appetite, d) significantly more or less sleep than normal, e) either physical slowness or agitation, f) unusual fatigue or loss of energy, and g) recurrent thoughts of death or suicide

dysthymia a mood disorder that involves recurrent pessimism, low energy level, and low self esteem; a chronic, continual sense of being depressed and sad

bipolar disorder a disorder involving episodes of depression interspersed with episodes of mania

mania an elevated mood with feelings of euphoria or irritability

are weakly tied to objects or situations. By contrast, emotions are quick-moving reactions that occur when organisms encounter meaningful stimuli that call for adaptive responses." (Rottenberg, 2005, p. 167).

Types of Mood Disorders

Listed under the general classification **mood disorder** are several specific disorders differentiated in terms of such criteria as length of episode and severity of symptoms. There is mounting evidence that different varieties of depression (e.g., with or without comorbid anxiety) involve different underlying brain structures or brain circuitry (Davidson et al., 2002; Jacobs, 2004).

Making a diagnosis of **major depressive disorder** can be a challenge. For one thing, a person must have experienced two or more depressive episodes, where such an episode is defined as a period of at least two weeks during which the person experienced five or more of these symptoms nearly every day: a) depressed or sad mood, b) loss of pleasure or interest in normal activities, c) weight loss or dramatic change in appetite, d) significantly more *or* less sleep than normal, e) either physical slowness or agitation, f) unusual fatigue or loss of energy, and g) recurrent thoughts of death or suicide.

Major depression is the leading cause of psychiatric hospitalization (Rottenberg, 2005). This mood disorder is diagnosed about two times more often in women than in men—a ratio that holds across nationalities and ethnic groups (Eaton et al., 2008; Nolen-Hoeksema, 2001). One survey found that in a 12-month time frame, nearly seven percent of their sample met the criteria for major depressive disorder (Kessler et al., 2003; 2005). If this sample accurately reflects the U.S. population, the meaning is plain: over 13 million Americans will suffer major depression in any given year. Moreover, of those diagnosed with major depression, fifteen percent will not have one year free of depressive episodes. Thirty-five percent

will have recurrent episodes, while about half of all patients will recover from their initial episode of major depression and have no further episodes (Eaton et al., 2008). Diagnoses of major depressive disorder are significantly more common for non-Hispanic whites than for African Americans or Caribbean blacks, but the disorder is much more long-lasting for the latter two groups. Additionally, fewer than half of the African Americans (45.0%) and fewer than a quarter (24.3%) of Caribbean blacks who meet the criteria for major depression receive any form of therapy for it (Williams et al., 2007).

Dysthymia [diss-thigh´-me-a´] is essentially a milder, but chronic form of depression. The disorder involves recurrent pessimism, low energy level, and low self-esteem. Whereas major depression tends to occur in a series of extremely debilitating episodes, dysthymia is a more continual sense of being depressed and sad. By definition, the depressed mood must last at least two years—and may last for 20 to 30 years (Akiskal & Cassano, 1997; Klein, Shankman, & Rose, 2006).

For major depression and dysthymia, there need not be an identifiable event or situation that brings on the person's depressed mood. In fact, to feel overwhelmingly depressed upon hearing of a close friend's death is not, in itself, enough to be regarded as a disorder of any sort. We all may feel mild depression from time to time. However, we generally know why we are depressed and have a reasonable expectation of feeling better in the future. With major depressive disorder, however, the depression is significant and is associated with myriad additional symptoms. With dysthymia, the depression lasts (four to five years on average).

In **bipolar disorder**, episodes of depression are interspersed with episodes of mania. Bipolar disorder is often still referred to by its older label, "manic-depression." **Mania** is characterized as an elevated mood with feelings of euphoria or irritability. In a manic state, a person shows increased activity, is more talkative than usual, and seems to get by with less sleep than usual. Mania is a condition that cannot be maintained for long because it is tiring. As is true for depression, mania usually recurs. It seldom occurs as an isolated episode. Nearly 40 percent of those diagnosed as having a manic episode relapse (Mansell & Pedley, 2008; Tohen et al., 1990). People are rarely manic without periods of depression interspersed. In fact, episodes of depression are so common in bipolar disorder, it is often misdiagnosed initially as major depression (Rosa et al., 2008). Approximately 2.5 million Americans suffer from bipolar disorder (Merikangas et al., 2007). For reasons that are not at all clear, the incidence of bipolar disorder has increased significantly in recent years, particularly in youth younger than 19 years old (Moreno et al., 2007).

The Roots of Depression

The answers to the question "What causes depression?" depend largely on where one looks. Most likely, depression is caused by several different but interrelated factors—both biological and psychological. Part of progress toward answers in psychology has been recognition that depression is a disease. One researcher summed up progress in the last century with these words: "When the history of mental illness is written, the twentieth century will be remembered primarily not for its biomedical advances, but as the period when depression (along with the other major psychopathologies) was finally considered to be a disease and not a failure of character or a weakness of will" (Jacobs, 2004, p. 103).

Bipolar mood disorder is not common. A randomly selected person has less than one-half of one percent chance of developing symptoms. The probability rises to 15 percent if a brother, a sister, or either parent had the disorder. For fraternal twins, this percentage is nearly 20 percent if the first twin has the dis-

Courtesy of Mika/zefa/Corbis.

Nearly everyone experiences episodes of depression from time to time, often for good, valid reasons. Major depressive disorder is characterized by inexplicable feelings of sadness and hopelessness, accompanied by a loss of pleasure in common activities.

order. However, if one of a pair of identical twins has bipolar mood disorder, the chance that the other twin will be diagnosed as having the disorder jumps to nearly 70 percent (McGuffin et al., 2003). These increased probabilities are excellent evidence for a genetic, or inherited, predisposition to bipolar mood disorder.

The data are not as striking for the unipolar mood disorder (depression only). Researchers suspect, however, that there is some genetic basis for major depression as well (Kendler et al., 1993). A study of twins confirmed the influence of heredity in major depression and ruled out early childhood experiences as a causative factor. The study found no evidence that growing up at the same time, in the same home with the same parents, in the same neighborhood, or in the same school was related to the development of the symptoms of depression (Kendler et al., 1994).

Genetics seems to be more important in the development of mood disorders in women than in men (Bierut et al., 1999). Researchers have identified a variation of a certain brain-chemistry gene (it plays a role in regulating the neurotransmitter serotonin) that predicts which people are likely to develop depression following a stressful life event (Caspi et al., 2003). Further, stress causes predictable changes in brain chemistry (Ridder et al., 2005). This point gets us to the following model for the development of mood disorders.

We may talk about a genetic basis for depression, but clearly, people do not inherit depression—they inherit genes. What proponents of the **diathesis-stress model** propose is that individuals inherit multiple genes, which may give rise to the tendency or predisposition to express certain behaviors, and that these behaviors are expressed only if activated by stress or trauma. *Diathesis* literally means "a condition which makes someone susceptible to developing a disorder." The proponents of the diathesis-stress model propose that some people have inherited predispositions to develop a depressive disorder when they encounter stress in their lives. Faced with the same or similar stress, a different person may have a diathesis to develop coronary heart disease or gastrointestinal problems. A third person might respond to that same stress with no disease or disorder at all. This interactive explanation applies to all sorts of disorders. Some conditions would require other elements in the environment for a person to become ill. A person may have a genetic predisposition to develop, say, sinus infections, but without exposure to the germs that produce such infections, none will occur. "In any case, in summarizing a large amount of research, it is clear that stressful life events are strongly related to the onset

of mood disorders" (Barlow & Durand, 2009).

Even if researchers knew the site of a gene (or genes) associated with a disorder, they would still want to specify the mechanisms that produce the symptoms of that disorder. For mood disorders, researchers have focused on those neurotransmitters that they believe influence mood directly. Collectively these are called *biogenic amines* and include neurotransmitters such as serotonin, dopamine, and norepinephrine. This research got exciting when it was discovered that reserpine, a drug used to treat high blood pressure, also produced the symptoms of depression. Next, researchers discovered that reserpine lowered the brain's level of norepinephrine, and the search for neurotransmitter involvement in the mood disorders began (Delgado et al., 1994; George et al., 1995). The most effective drugs for treating major depression seem to produce their benefits by blocking the reuptake of serotonin, thus increasing overall levels of the neurotransmitter in the brain (Jacobs, 2004; Manji, Drevets, & Charney, 2001; Sairanen et al., 2005).

Almost certainly in the coming years, neuroscience at the genetic or molecular level will provide more insights about the direct causes of mood disorders—major depression in particular—but psychological, social, and environmental factors (number and severity of stressors, extent of social support, access to adequate diagnosis and care, etc.) will remain factors not to be overlooked.

diathesis-stress model the approach that proposes that individuals inherit multiple genes which may give rise to the predisposition to express certain behaviors, and that these behaviors are expressed only if activated by stress or trauma

BEFORE YOU GO ON

14. What are the mood disorders?
15. What are some of the likely contributing causes in the mood disorders?

A Point to Ponder or Discuss

Suppose that someone becomes deeply depressed over the death of a loved one. Is there a point in time when "normal" depression has lasted too long and becomes abnormal depression? How might the time limits for normal grieving and depression be established?

SCHIZOPHRENIA

Schizophrenia is a diagnosis for what may be several different disorders, which have in common a distortion of reality, a retreat from other people, and disturbances in affect, behavior, and cognition (our ABCs again). To understand the many things that fall into the category of schizophrenia an analogy with cancer will help. If you hear that a friend has cancer, it is certainly not good news. But, how bad the news is depends upon answers to a few questions: "What sort of cancer is it?" "Is it a small spot of skin cancer on the tip of an ear, prostate cancer, breast cancer, pancreatic cancer, brain cancer?" "How aggressive, or fast-spreading, is the cancer?" So it is with schizophrenia, a term so general that it raises many follow-up questions. "Up to this point, investigators have not been able to identify a single factor that characterizes all patients with schizophrenia (Walker et al., 2004, p. 402). Nonetheless, it seems that—by far—measures of cognitive impairment (including tests of attention, memory, language, and reasoning) best distinguish a majority of schizophrenia patients from healthy people (Heinrichs, 2005).

Incidence and Types of Schizophrenia

Schizophrenia (or symptoms typical of the disorder) has ancient roots, going back to at least 2000 BC (Korn, 2001). Schizophrenia is found around the world at the same rate: about 1 percent of the population, but the prognosis for the disorder may differ among countries (Buckley et al., 1996; Kulhara & Chakrabarti, 2001). People in developing countries tend to have a more acute (intense, but short-lived) course—and a better outcome—of the disorder than do people in industrialized nations. In the U. S., schizophrenia accounts for 75 percent of all mental health expenditures. Schizophrenia occurs slightly more frequently in men than in women,

symptoms are likely to show up earlier in males, and males are more likely to be disabled by the disorder and have a higher relapse rate (Aleman, Kahn, & Selten, 2003). There is a substantial gap between the physical health (and mortality) of people with schizophrenia and the general community, and that gap has worsened in recent years (Saha, Chant, & McGrath, 2007).

No matter how we state the statistics, we are talking about very large numbers of people. The prognosis for schizophrenia is not very encouraging. About 25 percent do recover fully from their first episode of the disorder and have no recurrences; in about 50 percent of the cases, there is a pattern of recurrent illness with periods of remission in between, and in the other 25 percent of the cases there are no signs of recovery and there is a long-term deterioration in functioning (Jobe & Harrow, 2005; Torrey, 2001). If treatment begins immediately after an initial episode, the prognosis is better, with as many as 83 percent recovering (Lieberman et al., 1993). As with many physical ailments, the sooner treatment begins, the better the likelihood of recovery.

Researchers have attempted to classify the varieties of schizophrenia in hopes of gaining a better understanding of what causes the disorder and arriving at more effective treatments. Over the years, there have been several attempts to "type" schizophrenia. Recently, a system with divisions based upon positive and negative symptoms has found considerable support among mental health professionals (Andreasen et al., 1995; Buckley et al., 1996; Marsh, 2001).

One dimension of schizophrenia is typified by **negative symptoms**—characterized by a loss of or a decrease in normal functions. They include emotional and social withdrawal, reduced energy and motivation, apathy, and poor attention. The other dimension of schizophrenia is typified by **positive symptoms**, including hallucinations and delusions. **Hallucinations** are false

schizophrenia a psychological disorder characterized by a distortion of reality, a retreat from other people, and disturbances in affect, behavior, and cognition

negative symptoms those characterized by a loss or decrease in normal functions

positive symptoms those characterized by new affects, behaviors, and/or cognitions, including hallucinations and delusions

hallucinations false perceptions—perceiving that which is not there, or failing to perceive that which is

TABLE 12.5	
Classifying schizophrenia on the basis of negative and positive symptoms.	**Schizophrenia with NEGATIVE SYMPTOMS** is characterized by: emotional and social withdrawal, and/or reduced energy and motivation, and/or apathy, and/or poor attention.
	Schizophrenia with POSITIVE SYMPTOMS is characterized by: hallucinations (false perceptions), and/or delusions (false beliefs), and/or disordered thinking and speech, and/or bizarre behaviors, and/or inappropriate affect.

delusions false beliefs—ideas that are firmly held, regardless of evidence to the contrary

perceptions—perceiving that which is not there or failing to perceive that which is. Schizophrenic hallucinations are often auditory, taking the form of "hearing voices inside one's head." **Delusions** are false beliefs, ideas that are firmly held regardless of evidence to the contrary. Delusions of someone with schizophrenia are inconsistent and unorganized. Positive symptoms of schizophrenia also include disordered thinking and speech, bizarre behaviors, and inappropriate affect. Someone displaying these symptoms may say something like, "When you swallow in your throat like a key it comes out, but not a scissors, a robin too, it means spring" (Marengo & Harrow, 1987, p. 654), or the person may giggle and laugh or sob and cry for no apparent reason, or may stand perfectly still for hours at a time. (See Table 12.5.) Of those persons diagnosed with schizophrenia, about 75 percent show positive symptoms, while about 25 percent present negative symptoms (Barlow & Durand, 2009, pp. 470–472).

The usefulness of this negative/positive distinction is that there may be differences in both the causes and the most effective treatment plans for the two types. In brief, the correlates of negative symptoms include enlarged ventricles in the brain, a clearer genetic basis, more severe complications at birth, a lower educational level, poorer adjustment patterns before onset, and a poorer prognosis given the relative ineffectiveness of medications. Correlated with positive symptoms are excesses of the neurotransmitter dopamine, relatively normal brain configuration, severe disruptions in early family life, over-activity and aggressiveness in adolescence, and a relatively good response to treatment (Andreasen et al., 1990; Eaton et al., 1995; McGlashan & Fenton, 1992).

The DSM-IV and its most recent revision characterize schizophrenic subtypes differently. In addition to the positive/negative distinction, the DSM-IV describes schizophrenia as being of one of several sub-types—paranoid, disorganized, catatonic, and undifferentiated. These types are summarized in Table 12.6.

Let us make two things clear. First, as unsettling as these symptoms may be, the average patient with schizophrenia is not the crazed, lunatic often depicted in movies and on television. Day in and day out, the average schizophrenic patient is rather colorless, socially withdrawn, and not at all dangerous. Although there are exceptions to this rule of thumb, it is particularly true when the patient is medicated or in treatment. Their "differentness" may be frightening, but people with schizophrenia are seldom more dangerous than anyone else. Second, when literally translated, schizophrenia means "splitting of the mind." This term was first used by a Swiss psychiatrist, Eugen Bleuler, in 1911. The split that Bleuler was addressing was a split of the mind of the patient from the real world and social relationships as the rest of us experience them. The term has never been used to describe multiple or split personalities of the Jekyll and Hyde variety. Such disorders do occur, but as we have seen, they are classified as dissociative identity disorders.

TABLE 12.6

Types of schizophrenia described in the DSM-IV-TR.

Paranoid Schizophrenia
- absurd, illogical, and changeable delusions, usually of persecution or grandeur, frequently accompanied by vivid hallucinations
- impairment of critical judgment
- erratic and occasionally dangerous behaviors
- usually appears after age 40 and accounts for about 40 percent of all patients with schizophrenia

Disorganized Schizophrenia
- disorganized speech patters
- peculiar mannerisms and bizarre, often obscene behavior
- emotional distortions with inappropriate silliness and laughter
- often found in younger patients and with high prevalence among homeless persons

Catatonic Schizophrenia
- alternating extreme withdrawal and extreme excitement
- tendency to remain motionless for hours–even days
- agitated states involving rapid talking and shouting, and uninhibited, frenzied behaviors
- fewer than 10 percent of schizophrenic cases get this diagnosis

Undifferentiated Schizophrenia
- a rapidly changing mixture of all or most of the primary symptoms of schizophrenia, both positive and negative
- perplexity, confusion, emotional turmoil, depression, fear
- essentially a "catch-all" category for those who do not qualify for one of the types above

BEFORE YOU GO ON

16. What is schizophrenia, and what are some of its variations?

A Point to Ponder or Discuss
Schizophrenia occurs at about the same rate around the world. What does that tell us about its cause or etiology?

The Causes of Schizophrenia

Schizophrenia is a complex family of disorders, and psychologists do not know exactly what causes these disorders, but there several interesting hypotheses.

Schizophrenia has a genetic basis (Buckley et al., 1996; Gottesman, 1991; Torrey, 2001). "Despite the possibility that schizophrenia may be several different disorders, we can safely make one generalization: *Genes are responsible for making some individuals vulnerable to schizophrenia*" (Barlow & Durand, 2009, p. 480). The data may not be as striking as for the mood disorders, but an individual is at a higher risk of being diagnosed with schizophrenia if there is a family history of the disorder. A child of two parents with schizophrenia has about a 40 percent chance of developing the disorder. Schizophrenia occurs at a 30 to 50 percent rate among the identical twins of schizophrenics, but at only a 10 to 15 percent rate in fraternal twins (Grinspoon, 1995; Kety et al., 1994). It is reasonable to say that one may inherit a predisposition to develop schizophrenia, but lest we get too committed to such a hypothesis, consider that 89 percent of persons diagnosed with schizophrenia have no known relative with the disorder (Cromwell, 1993). Still, a number of genes associated with susceptibility for schizophrenia *have* been identified (Kato et al., 2002; Shirts & Nimgaonkar, 2004). Research reveals that genetic liability for schizophrenia "seems to involve multiple genes acting in concert, or numerous single susceptibility genes acting independently" (Walker et al., 2004, p. 408).

Schizophrenia is a disease of the brain, and research has focused upon the role of the neurotransmitter dopamine (Coursey, Alford, & Safarjan, 1997; Maas et al., 1997). Dopamine's role has come to light from several lines of research. We know that amphetamine abuse can lead to many of the symptoms found in schizophrenia. Amphetamines are chemically very similar to dopamine, and actually cause an increase in dopamine levels in the brain. Logic leads researchers to wonder if schizophrenic symptoms (in particular those we have recognized as positive symptoms) are caused by excess amounts of dopamine. Although dopamine is found in all human brains, it is present at high levels in late adolescence, which is when schizophrenia usually first appears. Curiously, measurements of dopamine levels find no significant differences between persons with schizophrenia and persons who are disease-free. Neuroscientists discovered that, although people with schizophrenia have no more dopamine per se, they have significantly more receptor sites for the dopamine that is in their brains. In essence, it is as if there were additional dopamine in their brains (Abi-Dargham et al., 2005; Kestler, Walker, & Vega, 2001).

Support for the dopamine hypothesis also comes from examining the action of drugs that reduce schizophrenic symptoms. Some drugs that ease the symptoms commonly block receptor sites for dopamine in the brain (Snyder, 1980). If reducing the effectiveness of dopamine by blocking its activity at the synapse can control schizophrenic symptoms, might these symptoms have been caused by dopamine (or dopamine receptor sites) in the first place (Schooler & Keith, 1993)?

Many schizophrenia patients, mostly those with negative symptoms, have abnormally large ventricles (cavities or openings that contain cerebrospinal fluid) in their brains (Andreasen et al., 1990b), and evidence suggests a lack of balance between the two hemispheres of the brain (Gur et al., 1987). There are other less dramatic differences between the brains of persons with schizophrenia and those of persons without the disorder. Persons with the disorder tend to have a tissue loss in and around the limbic system (related to the regulation of emotion, and the consolidation of long-term memories), larger crevices in the surface of the cerebral cortex, and a smaller thalamus (the structure that relays information between the cerebral cortex and the rest of the brain) (Schmajuk, 2001; Walker et al., 2004). There is compelling evidence that these changes in the structure of the brain (although subtle at first) appear *before* the diagnosis of schizophrenia is made (Giedd et al., 1999; Pantelis et al., 2003).

As surely as some research supports the idea that schizophrenia is a disease of the brain, other research supports the importance of psychosocial factors in schizophrenia, such as strategies for coping with stress and the availability of social support (Coursey et al., 2000; Marsh, 2001). In some people, the symptoms of schizophrenia remain dormant, or unexpressed, until the individual is subjected to environmental stressors (Gottesman & Bertelsen, 1989). The theory is that some people are genetically prone to develop the symptoms of schizophrenia when they are exposed to stressors. Other people faced with the same type or amount of stress might develop ulcers, major depression, become excessively anxious, or might show no particular symptoms at all.

So it is possible that some life experiences bring on the symptoms of schizophrenia or tend to make those symptoms worse than they would otherwise be. Here we have the *diathesis-stress model* once again.

It was true years ago, and it is still true: "How the environment interacts with genetic risk to trigger the development of schizophrenia remains unknown" (Iacono & Grove, 1993).

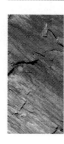

BEFORE YOU GO ON

17. What are some of the factors that have been considered as causes of schizophrenia?

A Point to Ponder or Discuss
How would you react if you learned that one of your classmates was a schizophrenic in treatment?

SPOTLIGHT
ON DIVERSITY

Disorders, Race, and Gender

Psychological disorders are prevalent in the United States. Remember the numbers? Nearly 30 percent of the population in any year, or about 50 percent of the population in their lifetimes, will have a diagnosable psychological disorder. As it happens, mental illnesses affect people from all social and economic classes, religions, cultures and races. Ethnic minorities do *not* exhibit higher rates or greater severity of mental illnesses than non-minorities. However, please note that these statements are made *in general*. Although there may not be any *overall* differences in rates of mental illness across ethnic groups, there may be an unequal distribution of which disorders are more common for different groups. Ethnic minorities *do* encounter greater obstacles in getting adequate care. African Americans, Hispanic Americans, American Indians, and Asian Americans are less likely to receive quality care for psychological disorders than others (Kessler et al., 2005; Satcher, 1999).

Zhang & Snowden (1999), investigating racial gaps in mental health, found that African Americans were more likely to suffer from phobias and somatization disorder and less likely than Caucasians to suffer major depression, dysthymia, and obsessive-compulsive, antisocial personality and anorexia nervosa disorders. Similar results were reported by Lu, Lim, and Mezzich (1995). This study found that the most common idioms of distress experienced by African Americans were in the form of somatization disorder, the expression of mental distress in terms of physical suffering. Interestingly, the "prevalence of major depression has been found to be significantly higher in whites than in African Americans and Mexican Americans" (Riolo et al., 2005, p. 998).

In some cases, the lower socioeconomic status of African Americans places them at higher risk for mental disorders (Chiriboga, Yee, & Jang, 2005; Regier et al., 1993; Riolo et al., 2005). With the added stress caused by poverty, some minorities are more likely to suffer with mental disorders associated with anxiety. Minorities living in poverty are two to three times more likely than the very wealthy to have a mental disorder (Satcher, 1999). On the other hand, a recent study found that "Members of disadvantaged ethnic groups in the United States do not have an increased risk for psychiatric disorders. Members of these groups, however, do tend to have more persistent disorders" (Breslau et al., 2005, p. 317).

Additionally, there are disparities in mental health services and in the treatment of minority groups. African Americans are less likely to seek professional treatment, and when they do, they are more likely to use the emergency room for mental health care. They are also more likely than Caucasians to receive inpatient care (Kunen et al., 2005; Satcher, 1999).

Data from the Surgeon General's report (Satcher, 1999) show that Hispanic Americans suffer from schizophrenia, antisocial behavior, and depression at a rate similar to that of Caucasians. One study (Mukherjee et al., 1983) examined records of patients with bipolar disorder and found that both African American and Hispanic patients were more likely than white patients to be misdiagnosed as having schizophrenia, largely because of cultural and language differences. Certain psychological disorders, such as schizophrenia and mood disorders, are misdiagnosed more often for African Americans and Hispanics than for Caucasians. More research is needed to clarify how cultural and linguistic factors influence diagnoses.

Hispanic adolescents report more suicidal ideation and suicide attempts than young Caucasians and African Americans. Studies have found that Hispanic youths experience more anxiety, delinquency, depression, and drug use than do young whites. In addition, Hispanics and African-American youths run a greater risk that their mental heath problems will go undetected (Borowsky et al., 2000).

Asian Americans report higher distress on various measures of social anxiety and social phobia than any other ethnic group (Norasakkunkit & Kalick, 2002; Okazaki, 1997, 2000, 2002; Okazaki et al., 2002; Sue, Sue, & Ino, 1990) despite the perception that they are well adjusted. In reality, Asian Americans suffer from depression and psychotic disorders at rates equal to or higher than those of Caucasians. Data from the U.S. Surgeon General show us that Asian Americans are significantly less likely than Caucasians to seek outpatient care. Indeed, they seek such care only half as often as do African Americans and Hispanics. Further, Asian Americans are significantly less likely than Caucasians to receive inpatient care.

When American Indians experience psychological disturbance, it is usually depression, posttraumatic stress disorder, or alcohol-related disorders (Beals et al., 1991). According to one study (Robin et al., 1997), American Indians are the ethnic group whose members most often experience situations that can trigger psychological disorders. Researchers theorize that when American Indians experience imbalance in body, mind, or spirit, they may be more likely to become mentally ill because of what they see as a lack of "connectiveness" with the environment (LaFromboise, Berman, & Sohi, 1994). Adolescent American Indians are two to three times more likely to experience suicide ideation than are teenagers of other ethnic groups.

Are there gender differences in the prevalence of psychological disorders? Unquestionably, there are. Men are more likely than women to be diagnosed with some personality disorders (for example, antisocial personality disorder) and are more likely to be substance abusers (Gomel, 1997; Simon, 2002). Most studies of gender differences in mental disorders, however, have focused on the prevalence of depression. As we have noted, major depressive disorder is nearly twice as common among women as men. In any six-month period, 6.6 percent of women, but only 3.5 percent of men are likely to experience an episode of major depression (Nolen-Hoeksema, 2001; Piccinelli & Homen, 1997; Wilhelm et al., 2002). This ratio of 2:1 holds across nationalities and ethnic groups (Papolos & Papolos, 1997). Additionally, depression in women is much more likely to be accompanied by anxiety disorders.

Gender differences exist in the rates of major depression. These differences are well documented, but the unanswered question remains *why*. Almost certainly, the answer will be complex and multifaceted. Let us consider some current thinking on the question.

Susan Nolen-Hoeksema and her colleagues suggest that the personality traits of young female adolescents combined with the stresses of being a teenager produce depression and low self-esteem (Nolen-Hoeksema & Girgus, 1994; Nolen-Hoeksema, Larson, & Grayson, 1999). These researchers contend females are emotionally more dependent on relationships, less assertive, and more inclined to worry about a problem rather than resolving it quickly and decisively, as a male adolescent might. They suggest women's lower social status is detrimental and leads to depression. Nolen-Hoeksema believes that females tend to "over-think" conflicts in their lives (2003). As a result, women work themselves up into a confused emotional state where once-simple solutions become difficult. Nolen-Hoeksema argues women tend to over-think problems because they are perceived as being more sensitive to the feelings of others than men are. This added sensitivity means women work harder to solve personal conflicts without offending anyone (Nolen-Hoeksema, 2003).

Another contributing factor may be puberty. At puberty, girls are more likely than boys to be depressed. The difference in prevalence of depression increases steadily after puberty and into middle adulthood (Ge & Conger, 2003; Wade, Cairney, & Pevalin, 2002; Wichstrom, 1999).

Gender-role identity formation (see Chapter 8) may also play a significant role in why women are more likely than men to develop depression. In large part, becoming depressed (as opposed to reacting to stress in some other way, like alcohol abuse) is simply the reaction *expected* of women (Calvete & Cardensos, 2005; Sachs-Ericsson, 2000; Silverstein & Lynch, 1998).

CHAPTER SUMMARY

1. **How do psychologists define "abnormal"?**

   Within the context of psychological disorders, "abnormal" refers to maladaptive behaviors, cognitions, and/or affect at odds with social expectations; these result in distress or discomfort.

2. **How are psychological disorders classified?**

   The *DSM-IV* is the fourth edition of the *Diagnostic and Statistical Manual of Mental Disorders*, published by the American Psychological Association. The first edition of the *DSM* (as it is commonly referred to) was published in 1952. It is the most widely used classification system for psychological disorders. The DSM-IV spells out criteria for diagnosing disorders on the basis of observable symptoms, and describes five dimensions, or axes, to consider in making a diagnosis.

3. **What are the advantages and disadvantages to having such a system?**

   The major advantage of classifying psychological disorders is that it provides one standard label and cluster of symptoms for each disorder that all mental health practitioners can use; as such, it is a basis for improved communication. It does have its limitations, however. Many persons have more than one disorder at a time, a phenomenon called comorbidity. Schemes of classification can confuse description with explanation; classifying and labeling persons as having psychological disorders may overlook the larger group or society that the individual is part of.

4. **Define *psychological disorder*, *insanity*, and *competence*. Which ones are legal terms?**

   Psychological disorder, *mental disorder*, and *behavior disorder* are all psychological concepts used to label abnormal mental and behavioral conditions. *Insanity* is a legal term. It relates to psychological problems but refers to a defendant's state of mind at the time of a crime. The question of insanity centers on whether a person knew or fully understood the consequences of his or her actions, knew the difference between right and wrong, and could exercise control over his or her actions at the time of a crime. *Competence* is a legal term and refers to a defendant's ability at the time of trial to understand legal proceedings and assist in his or her defense.

5. **In general, what are the anxiety disorders?**

   As a group, anxiety disorders are the most common variety of psychological disorder, and they are characterized by experienced, felt anxiety, usually coupled with attempts to avoid or escape from situations likely to bring on additional anxiety.

6. **Describe each of the following: generalized anxiety disorder, panic disorder, phobic disorder, obsessive-compulsive disorder, and posttraumatic stress disorder.**

   The defining characteristic of *generalized anxiety disorder* is a high level of anxiety that cannot be attributed to any particular source. The anxiety is diffuse and chronic. The defining symptom of a *panic disorder* is a sudden, often unpredictable, attack of intense anxiety, called a panic attack. Such attacks may last for seconds or for hours. There is no particular stimulus that prompts the attack. It has a high rate of comorbidity, often coupled with depression. A *phobic disorder* is typified by an intense, persistent fear of some object, activity, or situation that is in no real sense a threat to the individual's well-being—in brief, an intense, irrational fear. Phobias imply attempts to avoid the phobic object. Most phobias have a reasonably good prognosis. The two categories of phobias are specific and social. Examples of specific phobias are fear of animals, the physical environment (storms, height), blood, injection or injury, or specific situations (tunnels, elevators). Social phobias include fear of social performance, public speaking, and being in large crowds.

   Obsessions are thoughts or ideas that involuntarily and constantly intrude into awareness. They often are pointless or groundless thoughts about cleanliness, violence, disease, danger, or doubt. Compulsions are constantly intruding repetitive behaviors. The most common compulsions are hand washing, grooming, and counting or checking behavior. Obsessions and compulsions are the main symptoms in the *obsessive-compulsive disorder*, or OCD. *Posttraumatic stress disorder*, or PTSD, is an anxiety disorder in which the symptoms of high levels of anxiety, recurrent and disruptive dreams, and recollections of a highly traumatic event (e.g., rape, combat, or natural disaster) occur well after the danger of the event has passed. We often find that persons with PTSD also have alcohol or drug abuse problems or suffer from depression.

7. **Compare and contrast hypochondriasis, somatization disorder, and conversion disorder.**

A *somatoform disorder* involves some physical, bodily symptom or complaint for which there is no known medical or biological cause. In *hypochondriasis*, a person lives in fear and dread of contracting a serious illness or disease when there is no medical evidence for such fears. With *somatization disorder*, the focus is on recurring, long-lasting bodily symptoms for which there is no reasonable medical explanation. In *conversion disorder*, there is an actual loss or alteration in physical functioning—often dramatic, such as blindness or deafness—not under voluntary control, suggesting a physical disorder but without medical basis. This condition, which attracted the attention of Sigmund Freud to mental disorders, is now quite rare.

8. **What are the major characteristics of the dissociative disorders?**

Dissociative disorders are marked by a retreat or escape from (dissociation with) some aspect of one's experience or one's personality. It may be an inability to recall some life event (*dissociative amnesia*), sometimes accompanied by unexplained travel to a different location (*dissociative fugue*). In some cases, aspects of one's personality become so separated that the person suffers from *dissociative identity disorder*, where two or more personalities are found in the same individual. This disorder was once called multiple personality disorder and, for reasons unknown, has become increasingly common in the United States in recent years.

9. **What characterizes the personality disorders?**

Personality disorders (PDs) are enduring patterns of perceiving, relating to, and thinking about the environment and oneself that are inflexible and maladaptive. They are lifelong patterns of maladjustment and may be classified as belonging to one of three groups, or clusters. Cluster I includes those PDs involving odd or eccentric reactions, such as the paranoid and schizoid personality disorders. Cluster II includes disorders of dramatic, emotional, or erratic reactions, such as the narcissistic and histrionic personality disorders. Cluster III includes disorders involving fear and anxiety, such as the avoidant and dependent personality disorders.

10. **Describe the defining aspects of the antisocial personality disorder.**

The diagnosis of antisocial personality disorder fits within the DSM-IV cluster II, "Disorders of dramatic, emotional, or erratic reactions." Persons with this disorder exhibit an exceptional lack of regard for the rights or property of others. Such persons tend to be impulsive and have little or no regard for the consequences of their behaviors. The disorder is much more likely to be found in males, and it is also associated with low socioeconomic status, an urban setting, and a long-standing record of substance abuse. Because people with the antisocial PD show little concern, even for themselves, they tend to come to the attention of psychologists through the courts or by referral from family members.

11. **What are the defining characteristics of autistic disorder?**

Autistic disorder is one of the psychological disorders that is usually diagnosed within 30 months after birth. Its major symptoms include severely impaired social interactions. Children with autism seem oblivious to those around them, even their primary caregivers. There are difficulties in communication, with nearly one-third never developing speech or language skills. Behaviors are often repetitive and stereotyped. They insist on keeping their physical environments unchanged.

12. **What is the nature of Alzheimer's dementia?**

Alzheimer's dementia is a form of degenerative dementia, a loss of intellectual abilities, which becomes progressively worse with age. It is associated with abnormalities in the brain, the formation of tangles and plaques, among other things. It affects over 4.5 million Americans, and as many as 35 percent of persons who are 80 years old and older.

13. **What risk factors have been associated with Alzheimer's disease?**

Although the exact causes for Alzheimer's dementia are not known, there are several risk factors that have been associated with its development. The two main risk factors are age and genetics. Alzheimer's runs in families, and several specific genes have been identified that are hypothesized to play a role in the development of this dementia. Another factor is the presence of a particular protein found in the plaques that may play a causal role. The disease may be related to low levels of the neurotransmitter acetylcholine in the brain. Several lifestyle issues also are relevant. Obesity—particularly in women—is highly associated with Alzheimer's, but cognitively challenging activities may help to ward off the disorder.

14. What are the mood disorders?

In the mood disorders, a disturbance in affect or feeling is the prime, and perhaps only, symptom. Most commonly the disorder involves depression; less commonly we find mania and depression occurring in cycles (*bipolar mood disorder*). Whether the major symptom is depression or mania, there is no reason for the observed mood. *Major depression* affects over 13 million Americans, about twice as many women as men. It involves two or more episodes in which a person experiences sad mood, loss of pleasure, weight loss or change of appetite, physical slowness or agitation, either significantly more or less sleep than usual, unusual fatigue, and/or thoughts of death or suicide. *Dysthymia* involves depression that may be a bit less devastating or debilitating, but which is chronic (lasting for at least two years), involves recurrent feelings of pessimism, low energy levels, and low self-esteem.

15. What are some of the likely causative factors in the mood disorders?

The causes of mood disorders are both biological and psychological and involve an interaction of the two. Mood disorders tend to run in families, so there is most likely a genetic component. However, no specific genes have been identified as causal factors, although recently one gene has been found that predicts which persons are likely to respond to traumatic or stressful events with depression. Attention also has been focused on the role of neurotransmitters that appear to affect mood: serotonin, dopamine, and norepinephrine. Most likely, depression is caused by a combination of genetic factors, biochemical influences, and situational stress. Indeed, the *diathesis-stress model* of the development of disorders (not just mood disorders) proposes that people inherit multiple genes that tend to predispose them to react in certain ways if they are exposed to stress or trauma.

16. What is schizophrenia, and what are some of its variations?

Schizophrenia is a label applied to disorders that involve varying degrees of impairment. It occurs in about 1 percent of the population worldwide, and, in general, is characterized by a distortion of reality, a retreat from others, and disturbances in affect, behavior, and cognition. About 25 percent of those diagnosed with the disorder recover fully from their first episode, while in 50 percent of cases, symptoms are recurrent with periods of remission. In 25 percent of cases, there is no recovery and a deterioration of functioning.

There may be a difference between schizophrenia with positive symptoms and schizophrenia with negative symptoms. Negative symptoms involve a loss of normal functioning, social and emotional withdrawal, reduced energy and motivation, apathy, and poor attention. Positive symptoms are hallucinations (false perceptions) and delusions (false beliefs). Positive symptoms also include disordered thinking, bizarre behavior, and inappropriate affect.

17. What are some of the factors that have been considered as causes of schizophrenia?

Although the causes of schizophrenia are not known, three areas of research have produced hopeful leads: a) There is a genetic predisposition for the disorder. Schizophrenia may not be directly inherited, but it does run in families. b) Research on biochemical correlates of schizophrenia have localized the neurotransmitter dopamine as being involved in the production of schizophrenia-like symptoms, not because of excess dopamine, but excess dopamine receptor sites. c) For some individuals, stressful events may bring on symptoms or make them worse. A reasonable position is that, for some people, environmental events—such as extreme stress—trigger biochemical and structural changes in the brain producing symptoms of schizophrenia—the diathesis-stress model again.

Treatment and Therapy for the Psychological Disorders

13

PREVIEW

As was made clear in the previous chapter, psychological disorders present a major health challenge. As a conservative estimate, 50 million persons need treatment or therapy for mental illness in this country alone. However, over a 12-month period, less than half will receive treatment of any kind for their disorders (Wang et al., 2005). The economic impact of mental disorders is staggering. A recent study found that personal incomes for people with serious psychological disorders were, on average, $16,302 *less* than for comparable individuals without disorders—even with sociodemographic variables controlled. The data from this research indicates that at the level of the American society as a whole, psychological disorders produce a loss of earnings in excess of 193 billion dollars (Kessler et al., 2008).

By their very nature, psychological disorders cause distress, pain, and suffering. What is to be done for the millions afflicted with psychological disorders? The care and treatment of such persons is the subject of this chapter.

Mental illness is not new. Among the earliest written records from the Babylonians, Egyptians, and ancient Hebrews are clear descriptions of what we now refer to as psychological disorders. These civilizations treated individuals with disorders in a way consistent with the prevailing view of what caused those disorders. Just to put this discussion in perspective, we begin with a brief history of the treatment of people with psychological disorders.

Then we discuss treatments that are outside the normal realm of psychologists, called *biomedical treatments*. We will consider three different types: a) surgical procedures to alleviate the symptoms of mental disorders, b) electroconvulsive therapy (often called shock therapy) as a treatment for depression, and c) the use of psychoactive drugs designed to treat psychotic symptoms, depression, or anxiety.

No matter what the specifics, psychotherapy's major goal is to help a person to think, feel, or act more effectively. We will briefly consider the mental health professionals who provide treatment and therapy and comment on what factors to consider when selecting a psychotherapist.

Different types of therapy have different specific sub-goals. We will focus on five varieties of psychotherapy and will see that each approaches therapy from a different perspective. Given their historic significance, we begin by considering psychoanalytic approaches—first Freud's, then more contemporary versions. We then consider humanistic techniques—largely Rogers' client-centered therapy, behavioral techniques (of which there are many), cognitive therapies, and finally, group approaches to psychotherapy. Finally, we consider how to evaluate the different forms of psychotherapy, including a relatively new approach called empirically supported therapies, or EST.

A HISTORICAL PERSPECTIVE

The history of treating psychological disorders in the Western world is not a pleasant one. By today's standards, *therapy*—in the sense of active, humane intervention to improve the condition of persons in psychological distress—does not even seem to be the right term to describe how most disordered persons were dealt with in the past.

The ancient Greeks and Romans believed that individuals who were depressed, manic, irrational, intellectually retarded, or having hallucinations or delusions had offended the gods. In some cases, Greeks and Romans regarded those with disorders as temporarily out of favor with the gods, so their proper places in society could be restored by prayer and religious ritual. More severely disturbed patients were thought to be possessed by evil spirits. Priests tried to exorcise those evil spirits and demons inhabiting the minds and souls of the mentally deranged. Many unfortunates died as a result of their treatment or were killed outright when treatment failed.

There were those in ancient times who had a more reasonable view of psychological disorders. Among them was *Hippocrates* (460–377 B.C.), who believed that mental disorders had physical causes, not spiritual ones. He saw epilepsy as being a disorder of the brain, for example. Some of his views were wrong (e.g., that hysteria is a disorder of the uterus), but at least he tried (albeit without success) to demystify psychological disorders.

During the Middle Ages (1000–1500), the oppression and persecution of the disordered peaked. During this period, most people believed the psychologically disordered were "bad people" under the spell of devils and evil spirits. Those with psychological disorders had brought on their own problems, and their only hope was confessing their evil ways and repenting.

For hundreds of years—well into the eighteenth century—most people thought the mentally ill were in league with the devil or that God was punishing them for their sinful thoughts and deeds. The psychologically disordered were witches who could not be cured except through confession. If a confession was not forthcoming, torture was called for. If torture failed to yield a confession, the psychologically disordered were put to death. Between the fourteenth and mid-seventeenth centuries, an estimated 200,000 to 500,000 "witches" were put to death (Clark, 1997; Ben-Yehuda, 1980). Accurate estimates are difficult, of course, but most persons executed as witches (perhaps 85 percent) were women (Hergenhahn, 2001).

When the disordered (or those who were severely intellectually retarded) were not tortured or put to death, they often were placed in insane asylums. The first insane asylum opened in 1547 in London. It was called St. Mary of Beth-

Courtesy of Corbis.

lehem Hospital and was built to house "fools" and "lunatics." The institution became known as Bedlam (a cockney pronunciation of Bethlehem). Inmates were tortured, poorly fed, or starved to death. To remove the "bad blood" thought to be the cause of their melancholy or delirium, patients were regularly led to bleeding chambers. A small incision was made in a vein in the calf of the leg so that the blood would ooze into leather buckets. There was no professional staff at Bedlam. The "keepers," as they were called, could make extra money by putting their charges on public view; going to see the lunatics of Bedlam became entertainment for the nobility. Inmates who were able were sent into the streets to beg, wearing signs that identified them as "Fools of Bedlam." Even today we use the word "bedlam" to describe a condition of uproar and confusion. It would be comforting to think that Bedlam was an exception, an aberration. It was not. In the eighteenth and nineteenth centuries, similar institutions had become commonplace.

The horrific treatment of the mentally ill and retarded was not simply the action of mean-spirited, violent, nasty people. The treatment persons with psychological disorders received at Bedlam

It is difficult to tell, of course, but estimates are that as many as 200,000 to 500,000 "witches" were put to death between the fourteenth and mid-seventeenth centuries— sometimes following a "trial" such as the one depicted in this painting of a Salem, Massachusetts witch trial. Most of these unfortunates were women, and most probably suffered from a severe psychological disorder.

was what people thought was right and fitting. Perhaps 50 years from now psychologists and their students will look back at our treatment of disordered persons and find it equally ignorant and barbaric.

Against this backdrop of misery and despair, a few enlightened individuals deserve mention. One is **Philippe Pinel** (1745–1826), a French physician who was named director of an insane asylum in Paris. The law of the day required that asylum inmates be chained and confined. On September 2, 1793, Pinel ordered the chains and shackles removed from about 50 of the inmates of his "hospital." He allowed them to move freely about the institution and its grounds. What happened was as surprising to people of that time as it is unsurprising to people of our time: Many patients improved markedly. A few patients were even released from the asylum. Unfortunately, Pinel's "humane therapy," as he called it, did not spread to other asylums. Still, Pinel's unchaining of the insane and his belief in moral treatment for the mentally ill was a beginning.

Benjamin Rush (1745–1813) was the founder of American psychiatry. He published the first American text on mental disorders. Although some of Rush's treatments were crude by today's standards (he believed in bleeding, for example), he was a champion of more humane treatment for the mentally ill. He argued vehemently and successfully, for example, that the mentally ill should not be put on display to satisfy the curiosity of onlookers.

Dorothea Dix (1802–1887) was an American nurse. In 1841 she took a position in a women's prison and was appalled by what she saw there. Among the prisoners were hundreds of women who were mentally retarded or psychologically disordered. Despite her slight stature and her own poor health, she became a vigorous crusader for reform. She traveled across the United States and throughout Europe campaigning for higher standards of care for those in prisons, mental hospitals, and asylums.

Clifford Beers (1876–1943), a graduate of Yale University, had been put in a series of hospitals and asylums. He likely suffered from what we now call bipolar mood disorder. Probably in spite of his treatment rather than because of it, Beers recovered and was released. In 1908, he wrote a book about his experience, *A Mind That Found Itself.* The book became a bestseller; philosopher and psychologist William James and President Theodore Roosevelt were impressed with Beers and his story. The book was read by people in power and played a role in the start of the modern "mental health movement."

Since the early 1900s, progress in providing help for the mentally ill has been slow and unsteady. Over the past 50 years, conditions have improved immeasurably, but there is still a long way to go. Our society still stigmatizes persons with psychological disorders. Indeed, some still believe that people with psychological disorders are weak, sinful, or possessed.

BEFORE YOU GO ON

1. Briefly sketch the history of the treatment of persons with psychological disorders.

A Point to Ponder or Discuss
Why was it difficult for humane treatments, such as Pinel's, to catch on and become widely accepted before the twentieth century?

PSYCHOSURGERY

Psychologists are not medical doctors. As a result, psychologists cannot use medical treatments—performing surgery, administering shock treatments, and prescribing medications requires a medical degree. However, psychologists may recommend a medical treatment or refer a client to the care of a physician or psychiatrist (a person with a medical degree who specializes in mental disorders).

Psychosurgery is the name given to surgical procedures, usually directed at the brain, used to affect psychological reactions. Psychosurgical techniques today are aimed at making rather minimal lesions in the brain.

The surgical destruction of the corpus callosum (in the so-called "split-brain" procedure) is used as a last-chance effort to alleviate symptoms in extreme cases of epilepsy. We discussed this procedure and the insights about brain function that it provides in Chapter 2. Also, small surgical lesions in the limbic system have been effective in reducing or eliminating violent behaviors.

A surgical technique, called a *cingulotomy*, has been used successfully to reduce extreme anxiety and the symptoms of obsessive-compulsive disorders (OCDs). Cingulotomy is a treatment of last resort that involves cutting a bundle of nerve fibers connecting the very front of the frontal lobe with parts of the limbic system (Baer et al., 1995). As a treatment for severe OCD after all other rigorous interventions have proven unsuccessful, it has been used with notable success (Dougherty et al., 2002; Greenberg et al., 2003; Kim et al., 2003). One review of the procedure states, "Many patients are greatly improved after cingulotomy and the complications or side effects are few. Cingulotomy remains an important therapeutic option for disabling psychiatric disease and is probably underutilized." (Cosgrove & Rauch, 2003, p. 225). Surgical techniques are also being used to treat some cases of Parkinson's disease (Cohen et al., 2001; Vastag, 2003).

Of all of the types of psychosurgery, none has ever been used as commonly as a prefrontal lobotomy, or simply, **lobotomy**. This surgery severs the major neural connections between the prefrontal lobes (the area at the very front of the cerebral cortex) and lower brain centers.

The first lobotomy was performed in 1935 by Portuguese psychiatrist Egas Moniz. For developing the procedure, Moniz was awarded the Nobel Prize in 1949. (Ironically, Moniz was then shot by one of his lobotomized patients in 1950. Rendered paraplegic, he was confined to a wheelchair for the rest of his life.) The logic behind a lobotomy is simple: The prefrontal lobes influence the more basic emotional centers low in the brain (e.g., in the limbic system), and severely disturbed patients were thought to have difficulty exercising cerebral cortex control over those lower parts of the brain. Thus, if these areas of the brain were separated surgically, the more depressed, agitated, or violent patients could be brought under control.

Always used as a last resort, the operation often appeared successful. Stories of the changes it produced in chronic

lobotomy a surgical procedure that severs the major neural connections between the prefrontal lobes and lower brain centers

psychosurgery surgical procedures, usually directed at the brain, used to influence psychological functioning

This image of Dr. Walter Freeman performing a prefrontal lobotomy in 1949 hardly conforms to our notion of modern brain surgery. In this "transorbital" procedure, an instrument is inserted below each eyelid and driven up into the brain where connections were severed between the prefrontal cortex and other parts of the brain.

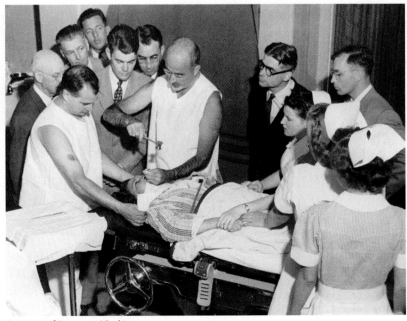

Courtesy of Bettmann/Corbis.

mental patients circulated widely. The November 30, 1942, *Time* magazine called the procedure "revolutionary" and claimed that, "some 300 people in the United States have had their psychoses surgically removed." *Life* magazine, in a graphic photo essay titled "Psychosurgery: Operation to Cure Sick Minds Turns Surgeon's Blade into an Instrument of Mental Therapy," called results "spectacular," claiming that, "about 30 percent of the lobotomized patients were able to return to everyday productive lives" (March 3, 1947, p. 93).

In the 1940s and 1950s, prefrontal lobotomies were performed with regularity. *Time* reported (September 15, 1952) that neurologist Walter Freeman alone was performing about 100 lobotomies a week. It is difficult to estimate how many lobotomies were performed in these two decades, but certainly tens of thousands.

Treating severely disturbed patients had always been difficult, so perhaps we should not be surprised that this relatively simple surgical technique was accepted so widely at first. The procedure was done under local anesthetic in a physician's office and took only ten minutes. An instrument that looks very much like an ice pick was inserted through the eye socket on the nasal side and pushed up into the brain. A few movements of the instrument and the job was done—the lobes were cut loose from the lower brain centers. Within a couple of hours, patients were ready to return to their rooms.

Everyone understood lobotomies could not be reversed. What took longer to realize was that they often brought terrible side effects. Between one and four percent of patients receiving prefrontal lobotomies died. Many who survived suffered seizures, memory loss, an inability to plan ahead, a general listlessness, and loss of affect. Many acted childishly and were difficult to manage within institutions. By the late 1950s, lobotomies had become rare. Contrary to common belief, performing a prefrontal lobotomy is not illegal, although the conditions under which one might even be considered are very restrictive. Prefrontal lobotomies are no longer needed. Psychoactive drugs produce better results more safely and reliably and with fewer side effects.

BEFORE YOU GO ON

2. What is psychosurgery and what is a prefrontal lobotomy?

A Point to Ponder or Discuss
Under what circumstances would you grant permission for an irreversible surgical procedure on a loved one?

ELECTROCONVULSIVE THERAPY

As gruesome as psychosurgery can be, it is less objectionable to many people than **electroconvulsive therapy** (ECT), or shock treatments. Introduced in 1937, ECT involves passing an electric current of between 70 and 150 volts across a patient's head for a fraction of a second. Patients receive a fast-acting anesthetic and a muscle-relaxant drug before the shock is delivered to minimize muscular contractions. Muscular contractions were quite common (and potentially dangerous) in the early days of ECT. The electric shock induces a reaction in the brain not unlike an epileptic seizure; the entire procedure takes about five minutes, and ECT

electroconvulsive therapy (ECT) shock treatments that involve passing an electric current of between 70 and 150 volts across a patient's head for a fraction of a second

patients cannot remember events just before the shock or the shock itself.

At first, ECT was used to calm agitated schizophrenic patients, but mental health professionals learned that ECT works better for patients with major depression and bipolar disorder. For these patients, ECT often alleviates the symptoms of depression and can help relieve other symptoms. In fact, the ECT procedure works best for patients with depression and other symptoms (such as hallucinations or delusions) (Sackeim et al., 2001). It is also effective for patients demonstrating manic symptoms (Fink, 1997). In one study, a group of bipolar patients received electroconvulsive therapy after all available medications failed. All patients in the group responded well to ECT (Brito de Macedo-Soares et al., 2005). For most people with major depression, the treatment of choice is antidepressant medications (see the next section), usually coupled with some form of cognitive-behavioral therapy. However, some patients do not respond well to medications or to psychotherapy. Such patients are said to have *treatment-resistant depression* (or TRD). Rates of treatment-resistant depression are increasing, now estimated to be as high as 40 percent of those diagnosed with depression. "Electroconvulsive therapy (ECT), a safe and effective treatment of severe depression, has been shown to be effective in TRD," with more than half of such patients achieving remission of symptoms (Taylor, 2008, p. 160; Khalid et al., 2008).

Virtually all patients (97 percent) give their consent to the procedure, and negative side effects are rare (Pagnin et al., 2004). The most commonly reported side effects are memory loss and a general mental confusion. The loss of memory that occurs after ECT treatments is almost always for episodic memories, and is relatively short term (lasting only six months or less) and affects memory of prior events that are near the treatment (within the previous six months) rather than earlier (Gardner & O'Conner, 2008; Vamos, 2008). Curiously, patients'

personal accounts of such amnesia are more persistent than are objective measures of such losses (Fraser, O'Carroll, & Ebmeier, 2008). When episodic memory loss does occur, it is much more likely to be for recent public events (knowledge of the world) than for autobiographical, personal memories (Lisanby et al., 2000).

Once they have the procedure, most ECT patients are not afraid of having an electrical shock sent through their brains. Most report that they feel the procedure helped them and they would have it done again (Bernstein et al., 1998). One patient began ECT treatments in 1996 and by 2005 had received 244 "maintenance" treatments. In the four years before her ECT, she had five admissions and spent 29 months in the hospital. Today, her depression is gone, and she has asked to continue maintenance ECT to stay depression-free (Wijkstra & Nolan, 2005). Electroconvulsive therapy is equally effective for patients with mental retardation (Reinblatt, Rifkin, & Freeman, 2004), and the elderly (Little et al., 2004). Gregory Nuttall and his colleagues reviewed the records of 2,279 patients who had received 17,394 ECT treatments and found no permanent injury and that "none of the patients died during or immediately after ECT. There were 18 deaths within 30 days of the final treatment, none related to ECT" (2004, p. 237).

Although ECT is effective, it has a poor reputation among the general population (Dowman, Patel, & Rajput, 2005). The reputation of ECT has been harmed by practices discontinued long ago. In the past, drugs were used to induce the seizures prior to shock therapy. These drug-induced seizures were often so violent they broke bones. Now, drug-induced shock procedures are no longer used. In the past, some patients received hundreds of ECT treatments in a series, and brain damage and permanent memory loss sometimes resulted. Now, no more than a dozen treatments are given in a series, and they are administered no more frequently than every other day.

Administering a shock to just one side of the brain, called a *unilateral ECT*, appears to be a safer and equally effective procedure with fewer side effects. Unilateral ECT works better in the right hemisphere of the cerebral cortex (which is more strongly associated with emotional reactions) than in the left hemisphere (Lisanby et al., 2000; Sackeim et al., 2000).

Why ECT works is not fully understood (Fink, 2000; 2001). Although it must be used with extreme care, ECT is widely used today. The National Institute of Mental Health estimates that 110,000 American patients receive shock treatments each year. Antidepressant medications have reduced the need for ECT, but they are not always successful. Even when they work, drugs often take six to eight weeks. Electroconvulsive therapy can work in a matter of days. Time is no small consideration for patients who are extremely depressed or suicidal.

BEFORE YOU GO ON

3. What is ECT and why is it still being used?

A Point to Ponder or Discuss
What ethical considerations are involved in asking a person with a severe psychological disorder to give his or her informed consent to a procedure like ECT or psychosurgery?

DRUG THERAPY

Chemicals that alter a person's affect, behavior, or cognitions are called **psychoactive drugs**. Using chemicals to improve the condition of the psychologically disordered has been hailed as one of the more significant scientific achievements of the last half of the twentieth century (Snyder, 1984). Three major types of medication are used as therapy: antipsychotic drugs, antidepressant drugs, and antianxiety drugs.

Antipsychotic Drugs

The **antipsychotic drugs** alleviate or eliminate psychotic symptoms, where **psychotic symptoms** signal loss of contact with reality, such as delusions and hallucinations, and a gross impairment of functioning. Inappropriate affect, or total loss of affect, is also a psychotic symptom. Antipsychotic medications are primarily designed to treat schizophrenia, but they are also used to treat

other disorders, including substance abuse. Antipsychotic drugs are also referred to as *neuroleptics*, a term that literally means "to grab hold of the nerves."

The breakthrough in the use of antipsychotic drugs came with the introduction of chlorpromazine in the early 1950s. A French neurosurgeon, Henri Laborit, was looking for a drug that would calm his patients before surgery so that they would recover better afterward. A drug company gave Laborit chlorpromazine. It worked even better than anyone expected. Laborit convinced colleagues to try the drug on their more agitated patients, some of whom were suffering from psychological disorders. The experiments met with great success, and by the late 1950s, the drug was widely used in North America and Europe. Not only did "Laborit's tranquilizer" produce a calm and relaxed state in his patients, but it also significantly reduced psychotic symptoms in other patients.

psychoactive drugs chemicals that alter a person's affects, cognitions, or behaviors

antipsychotic drugs medications designed to alleviate or eliminate psychotic symptoms

psychotic symptoms those that signal loss of contact with reality, such as delusions and hallucinations, and a gross impairment in functioning, inappropriate affect, or loss of affect

The drug revolution had begun. After the success of chlorpromazine, drug companies started the search in earnest for drugs to improve the plight of the mentally ill. Because its side effects tend to be severe, chlorpromazine is seldom used today to treat psychotic symptoms. However many other drugs have been developed that work in essentially the same way—by blocking receptor sites for the neurotransmitter dopamine. These drugs are most effective in treating the positive symptoms of schizophrenia: delusions, hallucinations, and bizarre behaviors.

A newer class of antipsychotic medications, first marketed in the early 1990s and including clozapine and risperidone, block dopamine receptor sites but also have an effect on serotonin synapses. These newer medications are effective on schizophrenia's negative symptoms, such as social withdrawal, as well as its positive ones (Black & Andreasen, 1999). Unfortunately, clozapine and risperidone also have potentially serious side effects, including impairment of the body's immune system. As a result, patients using these drugs must be very carefully monitored.

A researcher at University College London recently reported a meta-analysis and review of studies of the effectiveness of clozapine. Originally, the most glowing assessments for clozapine had come from shorter studies paid for by drug companies and using participants with extreme symptoms. Her conclusions about the drug's effectiveness were less than glowing: "The benefits of clozapine compared with conventional treatment may not be substantial (Moncrieff, 2003, p. 161). Jeffrey Lieberman of Columbia University Medical School and his colleagues reported on a large-scale comprehensive study of antipsychotic medications. The original study involved 1,432 patients at 57 treatment sites and found the newer drugs—although seven to ten times more expensive—were no more effective than older, generic antipsychotics. The one

exception was olanzapine (marketed as *Zyprexa*), but even so, patients experienced dramatic weight gain and a higher risk of diabetes, and 64 percent of patients stopped taking the drug after 18 months (Lieberman et al., 2005). Even more recently, additional data have confirmed that high hopes for this "second generation" of antipsychotic medications were unfounded. They are no more effective than the earlier drugs, and very often lead to a discontinuation because of unpleasant side effects (Kahn et al., 2008).

The antipsychotic drugs have revolutionized the care of psychotic patients, but they are not the ultimate solution for disorders such as schizophrenia. With high dosages or prolonged use, these drugs produce side effects that are unpleasant at best: dry mouth and throat, sore muscles and joints, sedation, sexual impotence, and muscle tremors and involuntary movements. Symptom-free patients released from institutions soon stop using their medication. After the medication stops, the psychotic symptoms resume. One review of 66 studies of 4,365 patients found that relapse was highly associated with sudden withdrawal from antipsychotic medication. Recognizing the unpleasantness and even the danger of the prolonged use of such medications, researchers recommend a slow tapering off of the drugs (Gilbert et al., 1995; Viguera et al., 1997).

Still, the search goes on for effective medications with few or mild side effects. Recently, some hope has arisen for a new type of drug that acts on receptor sites in the brain for an amino acid called *glutamate*, while other approved drugs work to manage dopamine levels. A full set of clinical trials is underway, but early, preliminary trials of this new medication—which has yet to be given a name (it is referred to only as LY2140023)—have been very encouraging, with positive effects on schizophrenic symptoms *and* few serious side effects (Heresco-Levy, 2005; Patil et al., 2007).

Nothing has had a more pro-found impact on the treatment of persons with severe psycho-logical disorders than the intro-duction of psychoactive drugs.

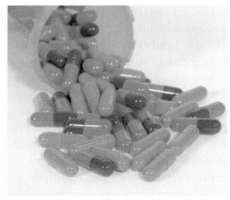

Courtesy of Visuals Unlimited/Corbis.

antidepressant drugs med-ications designed to elevate the mood of persons who are depressed

Antidepressant Drugs

Antidepressant drugs elevate the mood of persons who are depressed. Some antidepressant medications may also be useful in treating disorders other than depression—e.g., panic disorder and generalized anxiety disorder (Rickels et al., 1993). An antidepressant drug that has little or no effect on one person may cause severe, unpleasant side effects in another and yet have markedly benefi-cial effects for a third person. Antide-pressant drugs can elevate the mood of many depressed individuals, but they have no effect on people who are not depressed; antidepressants do not pro-duce a euphoric high for people in a normal or good mood.

There are three classes of antidepres-sant drugs: MAO (monoamine oxidase) inhibitors, tricyclics, and the newer class of antidepressants that act on neuro-transmitter receptor sites (serotonin and norepinephrine). Some of these drugs inhibit the reuptake of serotonin (together, these drugs are known as selective serotonin reuptake inhibitors, or SSRIs). Other newer drugs operate on norepinephrine as well as serotonin.

MAO inhibitors are the oldest of the antidepressant medications. These drugs inhibit the enzyme monoamine oxidase, which normally breaks down levels of serotonin, norepinephrine, and dopamine in the brain. The net result is an increase in these neurotransmitters and elevated mood. MAO inhibitors

can be toxic and difficult to use. They interact badly with foods such as aged cheeses, red wine, and chicken livers. Although they can be very effective, the MAO inhibitors are seldom used these days as a first-line treatment of depres-sion (Hollon, Thase, & Markowitz, 2002). A potentially promising way around MAO inhibitor side effects is the MAO inhibitor patch. Administer-ing the drug through a small patch placed on the upper body can negate all of the usual side effects of MAO inhibitors. In fact, skin irritation around the patch was the only side effect that caused any patients (three of the 177) in the study to withdraw (Bodkin & Amsterdam, 2002).

The tricyclics work to inhibit the reuptake of several neurotransmitters and are generally safer and more effec-tive than the older MAO inhibitors. Tri-cyclics affect the operation of the neurotransmitter serotonin and, to a lesser degree, norepinephrine. Because of the wide range of side effects they can cause, regulating tricyclic medications is difficult. The drugs have an adverse effect on blood pressure and can cause heart rhythm disturbances—both signif-icant concerns for older patients.

Drugs in the SSRI class of antide-pressants are—by far—the most com-monly prescribed medication for depression (Olfson et al., 2002). Although they are seldom more effective than tricyclics, they act faster to relieve symptoms and have fewer side effects. Their main action is to interfere with serotonin reuptake, but they have a sim-ilar effect on other neurotransmitters as well. There are several different selective serotonin reuptake inhibitors. One of the most commonly prescribed is *Prozac*, which was introduced in 1987. Because it is so effective and so safe, Prozac may be over-prescribed to per-sons who are only in a "down" mood, or somewhat sad, rather than genuinely suffering from major depression. Three other commonly prescribed SSRIs are Zoloft, Luvox, and Paxil.

New antidepressant drugs are constantly under development. One recently developed drug, Effexor, for example, targets serotonin levels in the brain but does so more quickly and more precisely than any of the other SSRIs. It also inhibits the reuptake of norepinephrine, thus increasing the levels of this neurotransmitter in the brain (Feighner, 1997). Effexor was approved for use in 1993 and has proven to be effective with few side effects.

One study reported success in treating depression with injections of Botox Toxin A (yes, the same drug that is used by dermatologists to remove "age lines"). The authors of this study reported remarkable results—nine out of the ten patients who received the injections in the "frown lines" of their foreheads were no longer depressed two months after the treatment, and the tenth patient showed some improvement (Finzi & Wassermann, 2006). It is clear that this study has flaws—the small number of participants and the lack of any sort of control group are two. Nonetheless, the reported success of this simple treatment warrants further research.

You might be wondering why there are so many antidepressant drugs that appear to do the same thing. Although the net effect of each may be similar to the others, each produces its effect in a slightly different way. Not everyone responds to the same drug in the same way. What works for one person may not work for another, and actually prescriptions are often made simply on the basis of avoiding unpleasant side effects (Hanson et al., 2005; Zimmerman et al., 2005).

Antidepressant medications typically take two to four weeks to show any effect. Their full effect may take six weeks, and they need to be taken for the long-term to prevent recurrence of the depression. As with the antipsychotics, most antidepressants produce unfortunate side effects in some patients, including intellectual confusion, increased perspiration, and weight gain. Some have been implicated as a cause of heart disease. Some antidepressant drugs also require patients to follow a strict diet and take the medications in the proper amounts on a fairly rigid schedule.

This is an appropriate context in which to mention lithium, or lithium salts, such as lithium carbonate. Lithium salts are referred to as "mood stabilizers" (Maxman, 1991). They have been used with some success in treating major depression but are most useful in controlling the manic stage of bipolar disorders. Lithium treatments are often effective in preventing or reducing manic episodes (Baldessarini & Tondo, 2000; NIMH, 1989; Kahn, 1995). For some patients, the drug has no beneficial effects. It was once believed that prolonged lithium treatments cause kidney failure, convulsions, and other serious reactions, but little data supports such a belief (Schou, 1997).

Unlike antipsychotics, when antidepressants *are* effective, they may actually cure depression rather than just suppress its symptoms. In other words, the changes in mood caused by the drugs may outlast use of the drug itself. Most treatment plans envision gradually reducing the antidepressants as the person breaks free of the depression. For persons with mood disorders who do not respond to drugs presently available, electroconvulsive therapy may be effective. In addition, the pace of innovation in this area means that new drugs are constantly being tested.

Antianxiety Drugs

The **antianxiety drugs** (or tranquilizers) help reduce the felt aspect of anxiety. Some antianxiety drugs, e.g., Miltown or Equanil, are simply muscle relaxants. When muscular tension is reduced, a person usually reports feeling calm and at ease. Benzodiazepines (for example, Librium, Valium, and Xanax) are the other major variety of antianxiety drugs. These are among the most commonly prescribed of all drugs. They increase

antianxiety drugs (tranquilizers) medications designed to help reduce the felt aspect of anxiety

the effectiveness of a neurotransmitter (gamma aminobutyric acid, or GABA) that normally functions in the brain to reduce postsynaptic activity, which in turn inhibits all sorts of reactions. They help anxious people feel less anxious. The action of the benzodiazepines is largely concentrated in areas of the midbrain commonly associated with emotion and reactions to threat (Furmark et al., 2002). Initially, the only negative side effects appear to be a slight drowsiness, blurred vision, and a slight impairment of coordination.

Unfortunately, the tranquilizing effect of the drugs is not long lasting. Patients can fall into a pattern of relying on the antianxiety medications to alleviate even the slightest fears and worries. A far more serious potential side effect is dependency and addiction. A major danger of the antianxiety medications is the very fact that they are so effective. As long as a person can avoid the unpleasant feelings of anxiety simply by taking a pill, that person has little motivation to seek out and deal with the actual cause of the anxiety.

Curiously, antianxiety drugs are much more likely to be prescribed for women, especially women over age 45, than they are for men. This pattern may very well be because physicians tend to see women as more likely to be anxious in the first place (Unger & Crawford, 1992).

BEFORE YOU GO ON

4. What are the antipsychotic medications and how effective are they?
5. What medications are used to treat persons with mood disorders?
6. What are the antianxiety medications and how effective are they?

A Point to Ponder or Discuss
What practical steps can be taken to help patients taking neuroleptic medications to continue to take them in spite of very unpleasant side effects?

WHO PROVIDES PSYCHOTHERAPY?

In the 1980s, a large-scale survey found that only 19 percent of persons with psychological disorders had received psychotherapy within the previous year. In the 1990s, about 25 percent of respondents received treatment for their disorders. In 2004, 41.1 percent of respondents had received treatment for a psychological disorder in the year preceding the survey. More people are seeking treatment, but much still remains to be done to improve the mental health of Americans: "Most people with mental disorders in the United States remain either untreated or poorly treated. Interventions are needed to enhance treatment initiation and quality" (Wang et al., 2005, p. 288).

How can we characterize those people who offer psychotherapy services, the mental professionals? What follows is a list of generalities; these descriptions will not hold true for everyone in a given category. Remember also that some mental health professionals develop specialties within their fields. That is, some therapists specialize in working with children or adolescents, some work primarily with adults, some prefer to work with families, and some devote their efforts to people with substance- and alcohol-abuse problems. With these cautions in mind, the following may be considered psychotherapists:

1. **Clinical psychologists** usually have earned a Ph.D. in psychology from a program that provides applied experience in therapeutic techniques, as well as an emphasis on research. Ph.D. clinicians complete a one-year internship, usually at a mental health center or psychiatric hospital, and have extensive training in psychological testing and assessment. Some clinical psychologists have a Psy.D. (pronounced "sigh-dee"), which is a Doctor of Psychology, rather than the Doctor of Philosophy degree. Psy.D. programs take as long to complete as Ph.D. programs, but they emphasize more practical, clinical work.

2. **Psychiatrists** are medical doctors with a specialty in psychological disorders. In addition to coursework required for an M.D., the psychiatrist does a psychiatric internship (usually one year) and a psychiatric residency (usually three years) in a psychiatric hospital. During the internship and residency, the psychiatrist specializes in the care of the psychologically disturbed. A psychiatrist is the only psychotherapist permitted to use the biomedical treatments. However, a campaign to change the law to allow properly trained Ph.D. psychologists to prescribe medications is slowly making headway in state legislatures (Gutierrez & Silk, 1998; Oliveire-Berry, 2003).

3. **Counseling psychologists** usually have a Ph.D. in psychology. The focus of study (and the required one-year internship) is generally with patients with less-severe psychological problems. For instance, rather than interning in a psychiatric hospital, a counseling psychologist would more likely intern at a university's counseling center.

4. **Licensed professional counselors** have a degree in counselor education (at the master's level) and have met state requirements for a license to practice psychotherapy. Counselors are found in schools and in private practice, but they also work in mental health settings, specializing in family counseling, marriage counseling, and drug abuse counseling.

5. **Psychoanalysts** are clinical psychologists or psychiatrists who have received intensive training (and certification) in the methods of Freudian psychoanalysis.

6. **Clinical social workers** generally have master's degrees, although some earn Ph.D.s in social work. Social workers traditionally provide family and group therapy.

Some professionals with master's degrees in psychology provide psychotherapy, but they cannot advertise themselves as "psychologists" because of certification laws in many states. *Occupational therapists* usually have master's degrees (less frequently bachelor's degrees) in occupational therapy. This course of study includes many psychology classes and internship training in aiding the psychologically and physically handicapped. *Psychiatric nurses* often work in mental hospitals and clinics. In addition to their R.N. degrees, psychiatric nurses have training in the care of mentally ill patients. *Pastoral counseling* is a specialty of those with religious backgrounds and master's degrees in psychology or educational counseling. *Mental health technicians* usually have associate degrees in mental health technology (MHT). MHT graduates seldom provide unsupervised therapy, but they may be involved in the delivery of many mental health services.

Many different professionals offer psychotherapy. How should a person go about choosing a psychotherapist? Many people and agencies can help locate the right mental professional. Let us say that

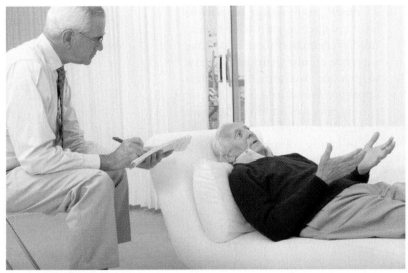

Courtesy of Rolf Bruderer/Corbis.

Ever since early days of psycho-analysis, psychotherapy is rightly thought of as "talk therapy," but careful, active listening by the therapist is crucial.

thing is not to give up. Find help and the sooner the better.

Assume a psychotherapist has been recommended to you and you have made an appointment. How will you know if you have made a wise choice? To be sure, only you can be the judge of that. A few cautions are appropriate here. First, give the therapy and the therapist a chance. By now, you know that psychological problems are seldom simple and easily solved. (In fact, a therapist who suggests that your problem can be easily solved is probably a therapist of whom to be leery). It may take three or four sessions before your therapist has learned (from you) what the exact and real nature of your problem is. Most psychological problems have developed over a long time. An hour or two per week for a week or two cannot be expected to magically make everything right again. Nonetheless, you should expect progress. Very likely, some sessions will be more helpful than others. To expect a miracle cure is to be unreasonable. Therapy with a particular therapist is not always successful. At some point, you may feel that you have given your therapy every opportunity to succeed. If you have been open and honest with your therapist (and yourself) and feel that you are not profiting from your sessions, you should say so. Express your displeasure and/or disappointment. After careful consideration, you should be prepared to change therapists. Starting over again with a new therapist requires time and effort, but occasionally it is the only reasonable option.

Now that we know who may offer psychotherapy and how to go about choosing a therapist, let us consider the different techniques or approaches psychotherapists may use. Summarizing a complex psychotherapeutic approach in a few short paragraphs will not do justice to these techniques. We can only provide some sense or "flavor" of these psychotherapies, while trying not to trivialize them.

you want to locate a therapist for a problem that is bothering you. Where would you turn for help? Do you have any family members or friends who have been in therapy or counseling? What (or whom) do they recommend? If you get little useful information from friends or family, there are many other people you could ask (assuming that your symptoms are not serious, and that time is not critical). You might check with your psychology instructor. He or she may not be a therapist, but your instructor will probably be familiar with the mental health resources of the community. You might also see if your college or university has a clinic or counseling center for students (if nothing else, this is often an inexpensive route to take). You might also check with your family physician. A complete physical examination may turn up some leads about the nature of the problem. You might talk with your rabbi, priest, or minister. Clergy persons commonly deal with people in distress and are usually familiar with community resources. If there is one in your community, call the local mental health center or mental health association. If you think that you may have a problem, the most important

BEFORE YOU GO ON

7. Who may offer psychotherapy and what sorts of issues should be considered when choosing a therapist?

A Point to Ponder or Discuss

A very good friend confides in you that she is having serious adjustment problems. You think that she would profit from seeing a therapist, but she is dead-set against the idea. What do you do now?

SPOTLIGHT
ON DIVERSITY

Psychotherapy and Minority Groups

Psychotherapy is a process whereby mental health professionals seek to help individuals who have psychological disorders or mental health problems. Psychotherapy can take several forms: biomedical therapy, psychosocial therapy, or multi-modal therapy (a combination of the two).

Members of minority groups often fail to seek help and treatment for psychological disorders, and researchers are trying to discover what barriers prevent them from doing so (Alegria, Perez, & Williams, 2003; Balsa & McGuire (2003); Borowsky et al., 2000; Miranda et al., 2005; Wang, Bergland, & Kessler, 2000; Williams & Williams-Morris, 2000). Edward Delgado-Romero and his colleagues reviewed 796 studies of psychotherapy published between 1990 and 1999. Only half reported the racial/ethnic characteristics of the participants, but whites and Asian Americans were over-represented, and African Americans, Hispanics, and Native Americans were significantly under-represented (2005).

African Americans and Hispanics are less likely than Caucasian Americans to seek professional mental health care (Gallo et al., 1995; Wang et al., 2005). Minority group members remain reluctant to seek mental health care even when they can afford it and have adequate health insurance (Padgett et. al., 1994). A report of the Surgeon General of the United States claims that ethnic minorities are less likely to receive needed care, have less access to mental health services, and are more likely than Caucasians to receive poor quality care (U.S. Department of Health & Human Services, 2001). When minority patients try to get care, they often do not receive the best available treatment for depression and anxiety disorders when diagnosed (Harman, Edlund, & Fortney, 2004; Markowitz et al., 2000; Young et al., 2001). Caucasian patients tend to receive antidepressant medication more often than Hispanic patients (Sclar et al., 1999). African Americans are more likely than Caucasians to terminate mental health treatment prematurely (Sue, Zane, & Young, 1994).

Patient attitudes about the mental health service system can keep patients from seeking professional help. Many African Americans, Hispanics, American Indians, and Asian Americans report that they feel alienated, fear the stigma associated with hospitalization for a psychological disorder, fear being labeled, believe they can resolve their own issues, and generally mistrust health professionals due to a history of misdiagnosis and inadequate treatment in minority communities (Balsa, & McGuire, 2003; Sue, 1998; Sussman, Robins, & Earls, 1987; Whaley, 2001). In the United States, "most mental health workers come from middle-class backgrounds and expect their clients to be open, verbal, and psychologically minded. They tend to value verbal, emotional, and behavioral expressiveness" (Koslow & Salett, 1989, p. 3). Members of minority groups—particularly those from non-Western cultures—may not be as open and forthcoming in interacting with a therapist. Cultural and ethnic minorities strongly prefer "ethnically similar" therapists (Coleman et al., 1995; Johnson et al., 2004; Saha et al., 1999). Members of ethnic minorities are likely to seek treatment/therapy informally, from clergy, traditional healers, and family members and friends rather than from mental health professionals (Neighbor & Jackson, 1984; Peifer, Hu, & Vega, 2000).

Members of minority groups have been—and continue to be—inadequately served in their mental health needs. With this knowledge comes the hope that we will do better.

PSYCHOANALYTIC TECHNIQUES

In 1881, Sigmund Freud graduated from the University of Vienna Medical School. From the start, he was interested in what were then called *nervous disorders*. He went to France to study hypnosis, which many claimed to be a worthwhile treatment for such disorders. Freud returned to Vienna not fully convinced of the value of hypnosis, but he and a colleague, Josef Breuer, tried hypnosis to treat conversion reaction ("hysteria" in those days). Both became convinced that hypnosis itself was of little benefit because its effects were temporary (Freud, 1943). Hypnosis, according to Freud, did not allow for an in-depth exploration of the underlying causes for nervous disorder. In fact, Freud illustrated the difference between hypnosis and psychoanalysis in the following way: "The hypnotic therapy endeavors to cover up and as it were to whitewash something going on in the mind, the analytic to lay bare and to remove something. The first works cosmetically, the second surgically" (1943, p. 392).

Freud believed that patients should talk with their analysts about everything relevant to their lives to get at the underlying conflicts causing their symptoms. Freud and Breuer's method became known as the "talking cure," better known as psychoanalysis.

Assumptions and Goals of Freudian Psychoanalysis

Freudian psychoanalysis is based on several assumptions about conflict and the unconscious mind. For Freud, life is often a struggle to resolve conflicts between naturally opposing forces. The biological, sexual, aggressive strivings of the id are often in conflict with the superego, which is associated with being overly cautious and experiencing guilt. The strivings of the id also can be in conflict with the rational, reality-based ego, which may be called upon to mediate between the id and the superego. Anxiety-producing conflicts that go unresolved are repressed—forced out of awareness into the unconscious mind. Conflicts and anxiety-producing traumas of one's childhood are likely to produce symptoms of psychological disturbance later in life.

According to Freud, the way to rid oneself of anxiety is to enter the unconscious; identify the details of the repressed, anxiety-producing conflict; bring it out into the open; and then work to resolve it. The first step is to gain *insight* into the true nature of a patient's problems; only then can *problem solving* begin. Thus, the goals of Freudian psychoanalysis are insight and resolution of repressed conflict. Freudian psychoanalysis is very slow and gradual, because old, repressed experiences tend to be well integrated in a person's current life situation (Kaplan & Sadock, 1991).

Indeed, psychoanalysis with Sigmund Freud was a time-consuming (up to five days per week for as many as ten years!), often tedious process of aided self-examination. The patient talked openly and honestly about all aspects of his or her life, from early childhood memories to dreams of the future. The therapist/analyst interpreted what the patient expressed, always on the lookout for clues to possible repressed conflict. Once repressed conflicts were identified, the patient and the analyst worked together to resolve the conflicts and relieve the anxiety that caused the patient to need psychotherapy. Freudian psychoanalysts used several techniques to uncover repressed conflicts.

Free Association

The technique of **free association** was a standard in psychoanalysis. Patients were to say aloud whatever came into their minds. Sometimes the analyst would provide a word to start the chain of freely flowing associations. To free associate the way Freud wanted was not easy. Many sessions were often required for patients to learn the technique. Patients were not to edit their associations. They were to be completely honest and say whatever popped into consciousness. Many people are uncomfortable, at least initially, sharing their private, innermost thoughts and desires with anyone, much less a

stranger. Here is where the Freudian couch came in. To help his patients relax, Freud would have them lie down, be comfortable, and avoid eye contact with him. The job of the analyst through all of this was to try to interpret the apparently free-flowing verbal responses, always looking for expressions of unconscious desires and conflicts.

Resistance

During the course of psychoanalysis, the analyst listens very carefully to what the patient says. The analyst also listens carefully for what the patient does not say. Freud believed that **resistance**—the unwillingness or inability to discuss freely some aspect of one's life—was a significant process in analysis. Resistance can show itself in many ways, from simply avoiding the mention of some topic, to joking about matters as being inconsequential, to disrupting a session when a particular topic comes up for discussion, to missing appointments altogether.

Say, for example, that over the last six months in psychoanalysis a patient has talked freely about a wide variety of subjects, including early childhood memories and all her family members—all, that is, except her older brother. She has talked about all sorts of private experiences, some of them sexual, some of them pleasant, some unpleasant. But after six months of talking, she has not said anything about her older brother. Her analyst, noting this possible resistance, suggests that during the next visit, he would like to hear about her older brother. Then, for the first time since analysis began, the patient misses her next appointment. She comes to the following appointment, but ten minutes late. The analyst may now suspect a problem with the relationship between the patient and her older brother, a problem that may have begun in childhood and been repressed ever since. Of course, there may be no problem at all, but for psychoanalysis to be successful, potential resistance needs to be broken down and investigated.

resistance in psychoanalysis, the unwillingness or inability to freely discuss some aspect of one's life

free association a technique in psychoanalysis in which patients are to say whatever comes into their minds

In order to get at the contents of his patients' unconscious minds, Freud would interpret their dreams, focusing not only on the content of those dreams as they were reported (manifest content), but also on what those dreams might symbolize (latent content).

transference in psychoanalysis, the process that occurs when the patient unconsciously comes to view and feel about the analyst in much the same way as he or she feels about another important person

Courtesy of Tim Bradley/Getty Images.

Dream Interpretation

Analyzing patient dreams is an important aspect of psychoanalysis. Freud referred to dreams as the "royal road" to the unconscious level of the mind. Freud often trained his patients to recall and record their dreams in great detail. He analyzed dreams at two levels: **manifest content**, the dream as recalled and reported, and **latent content**, the dream as a symbolic representation of the contents of the unconscious. Latent content was usually analyzed to identify some sort of unconscious wish-fulfillment. Symbolism hidden in the latent content of dreams has been one of the most controversial aspects of Freud's theories. Freud believed that true feelings, motives, and desires might be camouflaged in a dream. For example, someone who reports a dream about suffocating under a huge pile of pillows might be expressing feelings about parental over-protectiveness. Someone who dreams about driving into an endless tunnel and becoming lost might be expressing fears or concerns of a sexual nature. The analyst, Freud argued, was to interpret dreams in terms of whatever insights they could provide about the true nature of the patient's unconscious mind.

manifest content the aspects of a dream as recalled and reported

latent content the aspects of a dream seen as symbolic representations of the content of the unconscious mind

Transference

Another controversial aspect of Freudian psychoanalysis is his concept of transference. **Transference** occurs when the patient unconsciously comes to view and feel about the analyst in much the same way he or she feels about another important person in his or her life, usually a parent. As therapy progresses over a long period, the relationship between analyst and patient often becomes a complex and emotional one. If feelings once directed toward someone else of significance are redirected toward the analyst, they are more accessible, more easily observed, and more readily dealt with. Therapists have to guard against letting their own feelings and experiences interfere with their objective interactions with their patients. Failure to do so is called counter-transference.

Post-Freudian Psychoanalysis

Sigmund Freud died in 1939, but psychologists continue to use his approach to psychotherapy. It has been modified (as Freud himself modified it over the years), but it remains true to Freud's basic assumptions.

Early in the twentieth century, Freudian psychoanalysis was the only form of psychotherapy. In the 1940s and 1950s, it was the therapy of choice. Even into the post-WWII era, Freudian psychoanalysis remained dominant because no other alternative presented itself: "Psychoanalytic theory was the dominant force in psychiatry in the postwar period and was embraced by a large number of clinical psychologists. To a certain extent, and for all practical purposes, there was no rival orientation" (Garfield, 1981, p. 176). In recent years, psychoanalysis has become less common, and strict Freudian psychoanalysis has become rare, but some therapists still use it, particularly for patients with "milder disorders" (Gabbard, Gunderson, & Fonagy, 2002, p. 505).

All psychoanalytic approaches share the same basic aims: Therapy must be the uncovering of deep-seated, unconscious conflict, perhaps caused by childhood experiences, and the removal of defenses so that such conflicts can be resolved (Luborsky et al., 1993). How has the Freudian system of therapy evolved since Freud? Probably the most significant change is the concern for shortening the length of analysis. Now therapists talk about time-limited, or short-form, psychoanalytic therapy (Binder, 1993). Today's psychoanalysts take a more active role than did Freud, using interviews and discussions. They rely less on free association. The couch as a requirement is gone. Modern psychoanalysts stress the comfort of the patient, and some patients are more comfortable pacing or sitting than lying on a couch. Modern psychoanalysts spend more time exploring the present. For example, a patient may come for analysis complaining about depression and anger to the point that the analyst believes the patient might commit suicide. The modern psychoanalyst focuses therapy in the here and now, dealing with the patient's current anger and depression until the danger of self-harm has abated. A focus on current feelings and contemporary interpersonal relationships are two distinguishing characteristics of current psychoanalytic therapy (Blagys & Hilsenroth, 2000).

BEFORE YOU GO ON

8. What are the essential features of Freudian psychoanalysis and how is it different today from when Freud practiced it?

A Point to Ponder or Discuss
Do you remember your dreams? Are your dreams in any way symbolic of some content of your unconscious? Can you think of one of your dreams in which that might be the case?

HUMANISTIC TECHNIQUES

There are many different types of *humanistic psychotherapies* and their allied cousins, the *existential therapies*. They all share a concern for self-examination and for personal growth and development. The goal of these therapies is not to uncover deep-seated conflicts but to foster psychological growth and help a person take full advantage of life's opportunities. Based on the premise that people can take charge of themselves and their futures, that they can grow and change, therapy is directed at assisting with these processes. In many regards, this approach may be better suited for someone who does not have a psychological disorder but is simply seeking to be a better person.

Client-centered therapy, also called Rogerian therapy after its founder, Carl Rogers, best typifies the humanistic approach. As its name suggests, the client is the center of the therapeutic interaction. Given his medical training, Freud called the people he dealt with patients. Rogers never used the term "patient," and before his death in 1987, he began using the term "person-centered" rather than "client-centered" to describe his approach to therapy.

In Rogers' view, therapy provides a special opportunity for a person to engage in self-discovery. Another way to express this is to say that a goal of **client-centered therapy** is to help the individual self-actualize—to grow and develop to the best of his or her potential.

What are the characteristics of client-centered therapy? Again, there

client-centered therapy the variety of psychotherapy in which the goal is to help the individual self-actualize; to grow and develop to the best of his or her potential

Gestalt therapy the variety of psychotherapy aimed at assisting a person to integrate thoughts, feelings, and actions; to increase self-awareness, self-acceptance and growth

are variants, but the following ideas characterize a client-centered approach: The focus is on the present, not the past or childhood. The focus is on feelings or affect, not beliefs or cognitions; that is, you are more likely to hear "How do you feel about that?" than "What do you think about that?" The therapist will attempt to reflect, or mirror—not interpret—how a client is feeling (using statements such as, "You seem angry" or "Does that make you feel sad?"). This so-called reflective listening, assessing and reflecting the true nature of a client's feelings, is not easy to do. It requires that the therapist be an active listener and be empathic, or able to understand and share the essence of another's feelings.

Throughout each session, the therapist tries to express *unconditional positive regard*. This is the expression of being accepting and non-critical. "I will not be critical. If that is the way you feel, that is the way you feel. Anything you say in here is okay, so long as you are being honest—not honest with me; that doesn't matter. Are you being honest with yourself?" Most of the positive regard that we get in this world is conditional: If, then. *If* you behave as you should, *then* you will be well thought of. *If* you do what I ask, *then* I will give you a reward.

Gestalt therapy is associated with Fritz Perls (1893–1970) and shares many of the same goals as Rogers' person-centered approach (Perls, 1967, 1971; Perls et al., 1951). Gestalt means (roughly) "whole" or "totality." Thus, the goal of **Gestalt therapy** is to assist a person to integrate his or her thoughts, feelings, and actions—to assist in increasing the person's self-awareness, self-acceptance, and growth. The therapy is aimed at helping the person become aware of his or her whole self—including conflicts and problems—and to begin finding ways to deal with those conflicts and problems.

What we have here is a matter of "getting in touch with one's feelings," acknowledging them as valid, and moving to get on with one's life. Although the focus of Gestalt therapy is the individual, sessions are often convened in small group settings. Clients may be given role-playing exercises and required to play several different parts. They may be asked to act out how they feel in a certain situation and then act out how they wish they could respond.

BEFORE YOU GO ON

9. What are the major features of client-centered and Gestalt therapy?

A Point to Ponder or Discuss
Would you be a good active listener? Give it a try some time, remembering that your job is to reflect and mirror what the speaker is saying while withholding your own opinions and assessments.

BEHAVIORAL TECHNIQUES

There is no one behavior therapy; instead, it is a collection of several techniques. What unites these techniques is that they are "methods of psychotherapeutic change founded on principles of learning established in the psychological laboratory" (Wolpe, 1981, p. 159).

Behavior therapists assume that maladaptive behaviors are learned, and thus they can be unlearned. Behavior therapists use many principles of learning and have applied behavioral techniques to many psychological disorders. In this section, we will list a few applications of learning theory that have become part of behavior therapy.

Systematic desensitization is applying classical conditioning to ease the feelings of anxiety, particularly those associated with phobic disorders. Systematic desensitization is among the first successful applications of learning theory to the treatment of disorders. The technique was introduced by Joseph Wolpe in the late 1950s (1958, 1982), although others had used similar procedures earlier. Systematic desensitization first involves teaching a person to relax totally and then to remain relaxed as he or she thinks about or is exposed to ever-increasing levels of anxiety-producing stimuli. If the person can remain calm and relaxed, that response can be conditioned to replace the person's previous anxious or fearful response.

Obsessive-compulsive disorder (OCD) is usually resistant to psychotherapy. However, a relatively new form of behavior therapy, *exposure and response prevention*, has shown promise as a treatment. In one clinic, patients are exposed to whatever stimulus situation evokes their obsessive thinking or compulsions for two hours a day, five days a week, for three weeks. They are asked to vividly imagine the consequences they fear without engaging in their usual obsessive or compulsive routine; the procedure is also repeated in homework assignments. Next, patients complete a maintenance program of phone calls and clinic visits. For example, a patient who is obsessed with dirt and germs is told to sit on the floor and imagine that she has become ill because of insufficient washing and cleaning. For the first two weeks, she must not wash her hands (at all) and can take a shower for only ten minutes every other day. In the third week, she can wash her hands for 30 seconds, five times a day. No one knows exactly how successful exposure and response prevention programs really are. However, the clinic claims that 75 to 83 percent of the patients who complete the regimen show significant and lasting improvement (Foa, 1995).

Courtesy of Bill Varie/Corbis.

In **aversion therapy**, a stimulus that may be harmful but that produces a "pleasant" response is paired with an aversive, painful stimulus until the original stimulus is avoided. For example, every time a smoker puts a cigarette in her mouth, a painful shock is delivered to her lip. Every time a person takes a drink of alcohol, he gets violently sick to his stomach from a nausea-producing drug. Every time a child molester is shown a picture of a young child, he gets an electric shock.

Aversion therapy does not sound like the sort of thing anyone would agree to. However, many people do volunteer for such treatments for two reasons: First, aversion therapy is very effective at suppressing a specific behavior—at least for a while, and second, volunteers see aversion therapy as the lesser of two evils. (Shocks and nausea are not much fun, but people see continuing their inappropriate, often self-destructive, behaviors as even more dangerous in the long run.) Aversion therapy is not common, and it is rarely effective by itself. It tends to suppress behaviors for only a relatively short time. During that time, therapists often use other techniques to try to bring about a more lasting change in behavior. In other words, aversion therapy is seldom used alone; it is usually used in conjunction with other therapy.

It is sometimes difficult to imagine why someone would agree to aversion therapy. Imagine this scenario: A young man is virtually unable to say "no" to alcohol. Two or three times a week, he drinks so much he passes out in a stupor. There may be many ways to explore why this young man has a problem with alcohol, but it may be more important at first simply to find a way to get him to stop drinking. Aversion therapy may be the answer.

systematic desensitization the technique of applying classical conditioning to ease the feelings of anxiety, particularly those associated with phobic disorders

aversion therapy a form of behavior therapy in which a stimulus that may be harmful but that produces a "pleasant" response is paired with an aversive, painful stimulus until the original stimulus is avoided

contingency management and contingency contracting techniques following the learning principles of operant conditioning in which a person comes, through reinforcement, to appreciate the consequences of his or her behaviors

modeling a form of behavior therapy that involves the acquisition of an appropriate response through the imitation of a model

Contingency management and contingency contracting borrow from the learning principles of operant conditioning. The idea is to have a person appreciate the consequences of his or her behaviors. Appropriate behaviors lead to rewards and the opportunity to do valued things, but inappropriate behaviors do not lead to reinforcement and provide fewer opportunities.

In many cases, these procedures work very well. As operant conditioning would predict, their effectiveness is a function of the extent to which the therapist has control over the situation. If the therapist can manage the control of rewards and punishments (called contingency management,) he or she stands a good chance of modifying the client's behavior. For example, in an institutional setting, if a patient (e.g., a severely disturbed person with schizophrenia) engages in the appropriate response (leaving her room to go to dinner), then the patient gets something she really wants (a chance to watch TV for an extra hour). In an outpatient setting, the therapist tries to arrange the situation so that the client learns to reinforce his or her own behaviors when they are appropriate.

Contingency contracting amounts to establishing a contract with a person so that exhibiting certain behaviors (preparing dinner) results in certain rewards (watching TV). In many cases, contingency contracting involves establishing a *token economy*. What this means is that the person is first taught that some token—a checker, a poker chip, or just a check mark on a pad—can be saved. When enough tokens are accumulated, they are cashed in for something of value to the person. With contracting, the value of a token for a specific behavior is spelled out ahead of time. Contingency contracting works best when the environment of the learner is tightly controlled. For this reason, it works well in institutions and with young children.

Some types of behavior therapy use learning principles other than those from simple conditioning. Introduced by Albert Bandura, **modeling** involves the acquisition of an appropriate response through the imitation of a model. Modeling can be an effective means of learning. In a therapy situation, psychologists can use modeling by having patients watch someone else perform an appropriate behavior and earn a reward for it (called vicarious reinforcement).

Some phobias, particularly those in children, can be overcome with modeling. A child who is afraid of dogs may profit from watching another child (which would be more effective than seeing an adult) enjoying playing with a dog. Modeling is also used in *assertiveness training*. Assertiveness training helps individuals stand up for their rights and express their feelings and opinions. Such training usually includes direct instruction, group discussion, role-playing, and contingency management, but it often uses modeling to teach individuals to express how they feel and what they think in social situations.

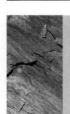

BEFORE YOU GO ON

10. What are some of the techniques that qualify as behavior therapies?

A Point to Ponder or Discuss
For which psychological disorders is behavior therapy least likely to be effective?

COGNITIVE TECHNIQUES

Cognitive therapists believe that what matters most are a client's beliefs, thoughts, perceptions, and attitudes about himself or herself and about the environment (Weinland, 1996). The major principle is that to change how a client feels and acts, therapy should first be directed at changing how that client thinks. The goal of treatment is not only to produce a change in the way the client thinks and behaves, but also to teach the client how those changes were achieved. That is, the goal is not so much to provide a "cure" as it is to develop a strategy that the client can apply to a wide range of contexts and experiences (Hollon, Shelton, & Loosen, 1991). As with the other approaches to psychotherapy, cognitive therapy has several varieties.

Courtesy of Chris Carroll/Corbis.

One of the most effective ways of dealing with depression is cognitive therapy, or cognitive-behavioral therapy. People with depression often have developed some rather irrational beliefs about themselves and the world in which they live. Changing those cognitions and the behaviors that accompany them can be very helpful This is true even if the first line of treatment is antidepressant medication.

cognitive therapists those psychotherapists who believe that what matters most are a client's thoughts, beliefs, perceptions, and attitudes about himself or herself and the environment

Rational-Emotive Therapy

Rational-emotive therapy (RET) (now often rational-emotive behavior therapy) is associated with Albert Ellis (1970, 1991, 1995, 1997). Its basic premise is that psychological problems arise when people try to interpret what happens in the world (a cognitive activity) on the basis of irrational beliefs. Ellis describes the therapy's assumptions: "Rational-emotive therapy (RET) hypothesizes that people largely disturb themselves by thinking in a self-defeating, illogical, and unrealistic manner—especially by escalating their natural preferences and desires into absolutistic, dogmatic musts and commands on themselves, others, and their environmental conditions" (Ellis, 1987, p. 364).

When compared to person-centered techniques, rational-emotive therapy is quite directive. Ellis takes exception with techniques designed to help a person feel better without providing useful strategies by which the person can get better (1991). In rational-emotive therapy, the therapist takes an active role in interpreting a client's system of beliefs

and encourages active change. Therapists often act as role models and make homework assignments that help clients bring their expectations and perceptions in line with reality. Ellis identifies some of the irrational beliefs that lead to psychological problems (1995):

- That one must always do tasks well because of a great desire to perform tasks well
- That one must always have the approval of others due to a strong need for approval
- That one must be loved by everyone for everything done
- That it is better to avoid problems than face them
- That one must always maintain perfect self-control

Cognitive Restructuring Therapy

Although similar in goals to RET, **cognitive restructuring therapy** is less confrontational and direct than RET. Cognitive restructuring theory is associated with Aaron Beck (1976, 1991, 1995).

rational-emotive therapy (RET) a form of cognitive therapy with the basic premise that psychological problems arise when people try to interpret what happens in the world on the basis of irrational beliefs

cognitive restructuring therapy a technique based on the assumption that considerable psychological distress stems from a few, simple, but misguided beliefs (cognitions)

cognitive-behavior therapy (CBT) a form of psychotherapy with the joint focus to a) change the way one has been behaving, and b) change the way one interprets and thinks about the situation in which behavior change is required

Beck's assumption is that considerable psychological distress stems from a few simple, but misguided, beliefs (cognitions). According to Beck, people with disorders (particularly those related to depression, for which cognitive restructuring was first designed) share certain characteristics:

- They tend to have very negative self-images. They do not value themselves or what they do.
- They tend to take a very negative view of life experiences.
- They over-generalize. For example, having failed one test, a person comes to believe that there is no way he or she can do college work, withdraws from school, and looks for a job, even though he or she believes that no one would offer a job to someone who is such a failure and a college dropout.
- They seek out experiences that reinforce their negative expectations. The student in the preceding example may apply for a job as a stockbroker or a law clerk. Lacking even minimal experience, he or she will not be offered either job and, thus, will confirm his or her own worthlessness.
- They tend to hold a rather dismal outlook for the future.
- They tend to avoid seeing the bright side of any experience.

In cognitive restructuring therapy, the patient is given opportunities to test or demonstrate his or her beliefs. The patient and therapist make up a list of hypotheses based on patient beliefs and assumptions and then test these hypotheses. The therapist tries to control the situation so that events do not confirm the patient's negative beliefs. Given the hypothesis "Nobody cares about me," the therapist need find only one person who cares to refute it. The therapist gradually leads the patient to the self-discovery that the negative hypotheses do not stand up to testing in the real world. Cognitive restructuring therapy has proven to be very successful in the treatment of depression, although it has been extended to cover a wide range of psychological disorders (Beck, 1985, 1991; Beck & Freeman, 1990; Zinbarg et al., 1992).

Cognitive-Behavior Therapy (CBT)

This approach combines the essential features of the two approaches that give it its name. **Cognitive-behavior therapy** or **CBT** has a joint focus: Change the way that you have been behaving, and change the way you interpret and think about the situations in which behavior change is required (Dobson & Khatri, 2000). CBT is a little more proactive than simple cognitive therapy, and therapists insist that real behavioral changes follow cognitive changes.

CBT may include determining "problem ownership"—a matter of agreeing on who really has the problem. For example, Cathy is upset because some girls she would like to be friends with are not being very friendly in return. Cathy begins to believe that she is "unworthy" and not a nice person simply because she is scorned by this group. A cognitive-behavior therapist might ask Cathy, "Well, whose problem is this? You're a nice person; you are worthy, but if this snooty little group doesn't think so, that's their problem, not yours." Cathy is challenged not only to change the way she thinks about herself and this group of girls, but also to change her behaviors regarding them. CBT can also be applied to family relationships. For example, Mom and Dad are upset that their 24-year-old son still lives at home, where he does illegal drugs with loud and obnoxious friends. In determining problem ownership, a cognitive-behavior therapist might ask these questions: Whose problem is this? Is this your home? Do you use illegal drugs? Your son is how old? Have you reported him to the police? Can you get him to come to talk with me?"

Sona Dimidjian of the University of Washington and her colleagues studied the relative effectiveness of antidepressant medication, behavior therapy and cognitive therapy in the treatment of patients suffering from major depression (2006). Essentially, they separated out the relative contributions of medication, a cognitive approach to therapy, and *behavioral activation*, which is based on the assumption that the avoidant and withdrawal behaviors of people with depression reduce access to potentially reinforcing situations. Behavioral activation promotes engaging in activities and contexts that may be painful for the short term, but ultimately are reinforc-ing and consistent with the client's long-term goals. All three types of therapeutic intervention were equally effective for clients with low-severity symptoms. For patients who were experiencing a high level of severity, both cognitive therapy and behavioral approaches were superior to using antidepressant medication in terms of the reduction of symptoms, the rates at which clients withdrew from therapy, and the appearance of side effects. Additionally, the behavioral approach of engaging the client in goal setting, self-monitoring, activity scheduling, and problem solving proved more effective than cognitive approaches by themselves.

BEFORE YOU GO ON

11. What are the essential characteristics of the cognitive approaches to psychotherapy?

A Point to Ponder or Discuss
Do you hold any irrational, potentially defeating cognitions? What might they be?

GROUP APPROACHES

Many patients profit from some type of group therapy, and many psychotherapists use the technique. As the name implies, **group therapy** amounts to several people receiving therapy together. If nothing else, group therapy can be less expensive than individual psychotherapy: One therapist can interact with several people at once (Mackenzie, 1997). In standard group therapy, a therapist brings clients together and guides them while they share their feelings and experiences. Most groups are informal, and no particular form of psychotherapy is dominant.

Group therapy has several benefits for the participants, including the awareness that "I'm not the only one with problems." In addition, the sense of support that a participant can get from someone else with problems is sometimes even greater than that afforded by a therapist alone—a sort of "she really knows from experience the hell that I'm going through" logic. And getting involved in helping someone else with a problem is, in itself, therapeutic. Group therapy also teaches participants new, more effective, ways of "presenting" themselves to others (McRoberts, Burlingame, & Hoag, 1998).

A popular group approach is **family therapy**, which focuses on the roles, interdependence, and communication skills of family members. Family therapy often starts after one member of a family enters psychotherapy. After discussing that person's problems for a while, other family members join the therapy sessions. Getting the family members involved in therapy benefits patients with a wide range of disorders,

group therapy an approach to psychotherapy that amounts to several people all having therapy at the same time

family therapy an approach to psychotherapy that focuses on the roles, interdependence, and communication skills of family members

Courtesy of Daly & Newton/Getty Images.

In some instances, group therapy can be very helpful. For one thing, it usually is less expensive than individual sessions with a therapist. It can give a patient the awareness that he or she is not the only person with a problem, and helping someone else who is having difficulties can, in itself, be therapeutic.

including alcoholism, phobias, depression, eating disorders, bipolar disorder, and schizophrenia (Eisler et al., 1997; Feist, 1993; Miklowitz et al., 2003; Pinsof, Wynne, & Hambright, 1996; Schmidt & Asen, 2005).

Two related assumptions underlie a family therapy approach. Family therapists assume that each family member is a part of a system (the family unit), and his or her feelings, thoughts, and behaviors influence the other family members. As a result, a change (even a therapeutic one) in one member of the family system that does not involve the

other members of the family unit will not last long. Unsupported changes are especially short-lived when the initial problem appears to be with a child or adolescent. We say "appears to be" because other family members have at least contributed to the troublesome symptoms of the child or adolescent. A therapist will have a difficult time bringing about significant and lasting change in a child whose parents refuse to become involved in therapy.

Family therapists recognize that some difficulties may arise from improper methods of family communication (Rivett, 1998; Satir, 1967). Quite often, a family member develops false beliefs about the feelings and needs of other family members. The goal of therapy in such cases, then, is to meet with the family in a group setting to foster and encourage open expressions of feelings and desires. For example, it may be very helpful for an adolescent to learn that her parents are upset and anxious about work-related stress and family finances. The adolescent may have assumed all along that her parents yelled at her and at each other because of something *she* was doing. The parents may not have shared their concern over money with the adolescent for fear that it would upset her.

BEFORE YOU GO ON

12. What is "group therapy" and what are its potential benefits?

A Point to Ponder or Discuss
Imagine that you have a problem and have been invited by your therapist to join a group to talk about it. How would you feel about sharing your problem with others?

EVALUATING PSYCHOTHERAPY

Consumer Reports is a popular magazine that each month publishes evaluations of many consumer products and services. It rates refrigerators, VCRs, SUVs,

and baby carriages, among other things. It compares life insurance policies and ranks home security systems. In 1995, *Consumer Reports* published a lengthy ground-breaking article on the effectiveness of various types of psychotherapy. The magazine had never before rated the effectiveness of psychotherapies. Many readers—and many psychologists—responded with surprise, even indignation: "How dare this popular magazine presume to evaluate such a complex, intricate process as psychotherapy?"

Although the *Consumer Reports* study is not without its critics, it has stood up to careful scrutiny very well. It was not the standard, carefully controlled, matched-group experimental design. Instead, its approach was the essence of simplicity: It asked people who had "at any time over the past three years" experienced stress or other emotional problems for which they sought help to take a survey describing their experience. More than 22,000 readers responded. Of those, nearly 3,000 reported having seen a mental health professional (as opposed to friends, clergy, or family doctors).

The conclusion: Patients benefited substantially from psychotherapy. Long-term treatment did considerably better than short-term treatment, and psychotherapy alone did not differ in effectiveness from medication plus psychotherapy. Additionally, no particular type or "brand" of psychotherapy did any better than any other, and no particular type of therapist (e.g., psychologist, psychiatrist, or social worker) was any more effective than any other (Consumer Reports, 1995; Jacobson & Christensen, 1996; Seligman, 1995, 1996; Strupp, 1996).

Difficulties Doing Research on the Effectiveness of Psychotherapy

Evaluating psychotherapy with carefully controlled experiments has proven difficult. Is psychotherapy effective? Compared to what? Is one variety of psychotherapy better than another?

Before we review the data, let us consider just a few of the problems encountered when doing research on the effectiveness of psychotherapy. First, little information is available on how peo-

ple might have responded without treatment. In other words, there is seldom an adequate baseline, or control group, for comparison. Psychologists do know that sometimes there is a spontaneous remission of symptoms. Sometimes people just seem to "get better" without a therapist. To say that people get better "on their own" is seldom literally true—there are many factors that can contribute to improve a person's mental health, even if one is not "officially" in psychotherapy. People may get better because a source of stress is removed—a nagging parent moves out of state, an aggravating boss gets transferred, or an interpersonal relationship begins that provides missing support.

Second, researchers do not agree on what is meant by "recovery," or "cure." These terms take on different meanings depending upon the goal of therapy. For some, recovery or cure means the absence of observable symptoms for a specified period of time. For others, the goal of psychotherapy is something different: the self-report of "feeling better," personal growth, a relatively permanent change in behavior, insight into deep-seated conflicts, or a restructuring of cognitions. In the same vein, who judges whether or not improvement, much less recovery, has occurred? Should the therapist or the client be the judge?

Despite these problems in designing studies to evaluate the outcome of psychotherapy, researchers have done quality studies. Most have focused on the effectiveness of just one technique, and the results have been very positive (Barlow & Lehman, 1996; Clarkin, Pilkonis, & Magruder, 1996; Lipsey & Wilson, 1993; Mueller et al., 1996; Scogin & McElreath, 1994).

General Findings on the Effectiveness of Psychotherapy

Psychotherapy is certainly effective when compared to doing nothing: "By about 1980 a consensus of sorts was reached that psychotherapy, as a generic treatment process, was demonstrably more effective than no treatment" (VandenBos, 1986, p. 111; also see Gelso & Fassinger, 1990; Kingsbury, 1995; Roth & Fonagy, 2004; VandenBos, 1996). Tested over nearly every possible kind of psychological disorder, and without distinguishing one type of treatment from another, psychotherapies produce significant effects. In general, after six months of therapeutic intervention, nearly three-quarters of those persons seeking help from psychotherapists show improvement, and no one type of treatment is significantly more effective than any other (Nathan, Stuart, & Dolan, 2000; Shadish et al., 2000). The authors of one review of research on effectiveness put it this way, "Copious evidence already exists for the proposition that psychotherapy in general is effective for clients in general" (Chamless & Ollendick, 2001, p. 699).

More treatment appears to be better than less treatment, but with most improvement made early on (Hansen, Lambert, & Forman, 2002; Howard et al., 1986). However, in one study, time-limited psychotherapy that actively involved family members in dealing with the problems of children was as effective as therapy that used an unlimited number of sessions (Smyrnios & Kirby, 1993; also see Sechrest & Walsh, 1997). Whether short-term or long-term intervention will be best is often a function of known variables, such as a client's awareness of his or her problems, willingness to change, and the extent to which the client lives in a supportive environment (Steenbarger, 1994).

Research also confirms that the sooner therapy begins, the better the likely outcome (Wyatt & Henter, 1997). Evidence suggests that some therapists are more effective than others, regardless of what type of therapy is practiced (Ackerman & Hilsenroth, 2003; Garfield, 1997; Shaw et al., 1999; Trepka et al., 2004; Wampold & Brown, 2005). A psychotherapist should

be open, warm, and supportive. The qualities of the therapist are important, but so are the qualities of the patient. Regardless of disorder, some people are better patients than others. What makes a good patient? The brighter, the more insightful, and the more motivated to change the patient is, the more effective any therapy.

Empirically Supported Therapies (ESTs)

Despite problems of research design, psychotherapy is effective in treating disorders. It has a "practical significance by almost any reasonable criterion" (Lipsey & Wilson, 1993, p. 1181). But are some psychotherapy techniques more effective in treating certain psychological disorders? For example, isn't short-term behavior therapy better than long-term psychoanalysis for treating a specific phobic disorder?

Researchers continue to try to determine which treatments are most effective for specific disorders. Psychotherapists are, after all, *scientist*-practitioners. Those treatments for specific disorders that are found to be effective are referred to as **empirically supported therapies (ESTs)**. As the name implies, researchers are attempting to find empirical evidence for the effectiveness of some specific therapies in the treatment of some specific disorders. The goal of this effort is to provide accurate information about what works best to practicing psychotherapists. Psychologists and psychiatrists have come together to form task forces to evaluate research and identify empirically supported therapies. These efforts have been successful—at least in the spirit of making a good start—but they also have been controversial (APA Presidential Task Force on Evidence-Based Practice, 2006; Chambless & Ollendick, 2001; Davidson et al., 2004; Davison, 1998; DeRubeis & Crits-Christoph, 1998; Nathan & Gorman, 2002; Norcross, 2002).

empirically supported therapies (ESTs) approaches to psychotherapy for which there is empirical evidence that an approach is effective in the treatment of specific disorders

Each variety of psychotherapy has its strengths and weaknesses. Psychoanalytic approaches can be time-consuming and expensive. Client-centered approaches require an introspective, nondependent client to be most useful. Group approaches may not be useful for clients who need personal attention. Behavioral methods work well with phobic disorders. Cognitive therapies appear to be well suited to patients with depression. Three recent studies demonstrated that 1) short-term cognitive therapy by experienced therapists is as effective, even more effective in many cases, for the relief of moderate to severe depression as are antidepressant drugs, 2) cognitive-behavioral therapy is better at preventing relapse than is short-term use of antidepressants, and 3) cognitive therapy is at least as effective for preventing relapse as is the long-term use of medications (DeRubeis et al., 2005; Hollen et al., 2005; Schatzberg et al., 2005).

A combination of behavioral and cognitive approaches is particularly effective for the obsessive-compulsive disorders. No variety of therapy is effective, by itself, for persons with bipolar disorder or schizophrenia. Many studies indicate that, when the primary treatment option is medical (say, an antipsychotic drug), psychotherapy and medication together yield the best prognosis: "Psychotherapy alone is not a good treatment for schizophrenia, but schizophrenic patients who take antipsychotic drugs can benefit from social skills training and related therapies" (Kingsbury, 1995, p. 8).

One review of empirically supported therapies listed appropriate psychotherapy options for each of dozens of specific disorders. The therapies were deemed appropriate if they were empirically supported in some way. Not all of the associations between disorders and therapies were supported by rigorously controlled experiments, but many were (Chambless & Ollendick, 2001). The review extended the list of empirically supported therapies to those used with children and adolescents. One observation that came from the review was that some disorders, such as depression, seem to benefit from a wide range of therapeutic approaches, while others, such as obsessive-compulsive disorders, seem to benefit most from behavioral or cognitive-behavioral treatments (Beutler, Clarkin, & Bongar, 2000; Nathan & Gorman, 1998).

Why is the search for ESTs controversial? Some therapists worry that if Therapy X is empirically demonstrated to be better than all other therapies for disorder Y, then therapists might be *required* to use that intervention. And just because Therapy X may be "better," that does not mean that a therapist could not have excellent results with a different approach. Let us say that cognitive therapy is found to be a superior treatment for a certain disorder. How can anyone be sure that everyone who uses cognitive therapy does so in the same way? There may be very large differences in how persons who call themselves cognitive therapists, for example, actually conduct a therapy session (Luborsky et al., 2002; Malik et al., 2003). The same logic holds true for the diagnoses. One of psychology's most reliable findings is that there are individual differences—even among people with the same diagnosis. One person diagnosed with depression, for example, might respond to a therapy in quite a different way than someone else with the same diagnosis.

Despite the controversy, ESTs are here to stay. Patients, practitioners, insurance companies, and researchers all have a stake in knowing if some treatments work better than others for specific disorders. The rigorous application of the scientific method to these questions remains the best way to find out. A logical extension of the work on empirically supported therapies is an effort to develop more general guidelines for what is called *Evidence-Based Practice in Psychology (EBPP)*. EBPP "is the integration of the best available research with clinical expertise in the context of patient characteristics, culture, and preferences" (APA Presidential Task Force on Evidence-Based Practice, 2006, p. 273). Research on ESTs starts with a treatment and asks whether it works for a certain disorder. EBPP starts with the patient and asks what research evidence will assist the psychologist in achieving the best possible outcome.

BEFORE YOU GO ON

13. In general, is psychotherapy an effective treatment for psychological disorders?
14. Are any specific therapy techniques better than others? What is the difference between ESTs and EBPP?

A Point to Ponder or Discuss

As a potential consumer of psychotherapy, which would matter more to you: the kind of therapy or the characteristics of the therapist?

CHAPTER SUMMARY

1. **Briefly sketch the history of the treatment of persons with psychological disorders.**

   Psychological disorders are as old as written history. Approaches to treatment have always been consistent with accepted explanations of the causes of such disorders. Early beliefs about mental illness centered on a person being out of favor with the gods. If a person were temporarily out of favor, treatment took the form of prayer and religious rituals. More severely afflicted persons were thought to be possessed by an evil spirit. Treatment involved exorcising the evil spirit. More enlightened scholars of the time believed that there was an underlying physical cause for mental illness, but throughout the Middle Ages, the prevailing belief was that the mentally ill were possessed or under the spell of evil spirits. These individuals were tortured until they confessed their sins. If torture did not yield a confession, the mentally ill person was killed, often by being burned at the stake. Another treatment for the insane was to place them into asylums where conditions were poor at best.

   Philippe Pinel was a French physician who was named director of an asylum in Paris. Pinel ordered that 50 patients be unchained and allowed to move freely about the hospital. This more humane treatment led some patients to get better, a few improving so much they were released from the asylum. Unfortunately, Pinel's humane treatment did not spread to other asylums and did not lead to a widespread reform of treatment for the mentally ill.

   Benjamin Rush published the first text on mental disorders in the United States. He supported humane treatment for the mentally ill. He was successful in curbing the practice of putting the mentally ill on public display. In the late 1800s, Dorothea Dix, a nurse, began a crusade for reform in prisons, mental hospitals, and asylums. Clifford Beers was a former mental patient who wrote a book about his experiences, pointing out that he recovered in spite of his treatment (and not because of it). His book was read by influential people and stimulated the modern "mental health movement."

2. **What is psychosurgery and what is a prefrontal lobotomy?**

   Psychosurgery is any surgical technique (usually directed at the brain) designed to bring about a change in a patient's affects, behaviors, or cognitions. Psychosurgical techniques are irreversible and a treatment of last resort. There are few such operations performed these days, but exceptions include the split-brain procedure as a treatment for epilepsy and the cingulotomy as a treatment for anxiety and obsessive-compulsive disorder. A lobotomy was a commonly used psychosurgical technique for at least two decades. It involved severing the major connections between the prefrontal cortex and lower brain centers. It was first performed in 1935 and became popular thereafter. The theory behind the surgery was that the prefrontal lobes influenced the more basic emotional centers in the lower brain. Often the surgery was successful in reducing a patient's violent emotions. It was used as a measure of last resort because of the potential for serious side effects. Prefrontal lobotomies are no longer performed because other, safer, reversible treatment options are available.

3. **What is ECT and why is it still being used?**

   ECT stands for electroconvulsive, or shock, therapy. In this treatment, a brain seizure is produced with an electric current. Upon regaining consciousness, the patient has no memory of the procedure. Although there may be negative side effects, particularly with prolonged or repeated use, the technique is demonstrably safe and very useful for many patients as a means of reducing or even eliminating severe depression. Although it is not yet clear why ECT has the beneficial results that it does, it is commonly used because it is effective and carries little risk. There is evidence of memory loss for events preceding the treatment, although this side effect is not long-lasting. ECT is particularly useful for those patients who do not respond to antidepressant medications.

4. **What are the antipsychotic medications and how effective are they?**

Antipsychotic drugs are used to reduce or control psychotic symptoms—characterized by a loss of contact with reality and a gross impairment of functioning. These drugs are used primarily to treat schizophrenia. The first antipsychotic drug was *chlorpromazine*, introduced in the 1950s. It was first used as a drug to calm patients before surgery. However, it was found to be effective in treating some patients with mental disorders. By 1956 there were several antipsychotic drugs available. The use of these drugs has steadily increased. Most of these drugs act to block dopamine and relieve positive psychotic symptoms of schizophrenia. One drug, clozapine, reduces the negative psychotic symptoms of schizophrenia. Although these medications are effective, they can have very unpleasant side effects. And although they can reduce or eliminate symptoms, antipsychotic drugs cannot be said to cure a disorder like schizophrenia because symptoms return when a patient stops taking the drugs. Recently, new hope has emerged for an antipsychotic that works not on dopamine levels, but by influencing the amino acid glutamate.

5. **What medications are used to treat persons with mood disorders?**

The three classes of antidepressant drugs are MAO inhibitors, tricyclics, and the newer generation of SSRI drugs. The MAO inhibitors are the oldest. They inhibit monoamine oxidase from metabolizing serotonin, norepinephrine, and dopamine in the brain, leading to elevated mood. These drugs have some potentially serious side effects. Tricyclics were the next drugs to be introduced and have proven to be safer than the MAO inhibitors. A new generation of drugs inhibits the reuptake of serotonin and in some cases, norepinephrine, resulting in elevated mood. Although the SSRI medications are not more effective than the tricyclics, they have fewer side effects and take effect faster. Most antidepressant drugs require from ten to 14 days to take effect and even longer to reach therapeutic levels.

Lithium (or lithium salts) is classified as a mood stabilizer and has been used successfully in treating major depression, but it is most widely used to control bipolar disorder. In addition to controlling symptoms, lithium also reduces the occurrence of future mood disorders and has few serious side effects.

6. **What are the antianxiety medications, and how effective are they?**

The antianxiety drugs include muscle relaxants and benzodiazepines (Librium, Valium, and Xanax, for example). These drugs act on the central nervous system and relieve anxiety. Short-term side effects can include drowsiness, blurred vision, and slight impairment of coordination. The antianxiety drugs tend not to have a long-term effect. A person using these medications can come to over-rely on them because they are so effective. As a result, the person can become dependent and addicted. So long as the antianxiety medications are working, a person may be considerably less motivated to explore the causes of the anxiety that made the medications necessary in the first place.

7. **Who may offer psychotherapy and what sorts of issues should be considered when choosing a therapist?**

Many different mental health professionals can provide psychotherapy. These include clinical psychologists (Ph.D.s or Psy.D.s with graduate training in psychology and a one-year internship), psychiatrists (M.D.s with an internship and residency in a mental hospital), counseling psychologists (Ph.D.s in psychology specializing in less-severe disorders and with an internship in a counseling setting), licensed counselors (perhaps with degrees in education), psychoanalysts (who specialize in Freudian therapy), clinical social workers (usually with a master's degree), and others, including pastoral counselors.

Choosing a therapist can be difficult, but there are many places to turn for assistance in making such a choice. These include friends and family members who've had experience in therapy, psychology faculty members, a campus counseling center, a family physician, a clergy-person, or a local mental health association. It is important to give a therapist a chance, but changing therapists is not always a bad option.

8. **What are the essential features of Freudian psychoanalysis and how is the process different today from when it was practiced by Freud?**

Freudian psychoanalysis is aimed at uncovering repressed conflicts (often developed in childhood) so that they can be resolved. The process involves *free association*, in which the patient says anything and everything that comes to mind, without editing; *resistance*, in which a patient seems unable or unwilling to discuss some aspect of his or her life, which may suggest that the resisted experiences may be anxiety-producing; *dream interpretation*, in which one analyzes both the manifest and the latent content for insights into the nature of the patient's unconscious mind; and *transference*, in which feelings once directed at a significant person in the patient's life become directed toward the analyst. Although its basic principles have remained unchanged since Freud's day, psychoanalysis has evolved since Freud. There is now more effort to shorten the duration of analysis; there is less emphasis on childhood experiences and more concern with the here and now. Present-day analysis is also more involved with current feelings and interpersonal relationships than when it was practiced by Freud.

9. **What are the major features of client-centered and Gestalt therapy?**

Although there are different humanistic approaches, they share a focus on self-examination, personal growth, and development. These therapies focus on factors that foster psychological growth rather than uncovering deep-seated conflicts. A major premise is that the individual can take charge of himself or herself and grow and develop. Client-centered or person-centered therapy, associated with Carl Rogers, is based on the belief that people can control their lives and solve their own problems if they can be helped to understand the true nature of their feelings. Client-centered therapy promotes self-discovery and personal growth. The therapist reflects the client's feelings, focuses on the here and now, and tries to be empathic, actively listening to and relating to the person's feelings. Throughout therapy, the therapist provides unconditional positive regard for the client. Gestalt therapy, associated with Fritz Perls, has many of the same goals as Rogers' person-centered approach, but it is more directive and challenging, striving to integrate a person's thoughts, feelings, and behaviors.

10. **What are some of the techniques that qualify as behavior therapies?**

Behavior therapy is a collection of several techniques that have grown out of laboratory research on basic principles of learning. The main premise of behavior therapy is that maladaptive behaviors are learned, so they can be unlearned. *Systematic desensitization* applies principles of classical conditioning to the treatment of anxiety. In systematic desensitization, a person is taught to

relax totally and then to remain relaxed as he or she thinks about or is exposed to anxiety-producing stimuli. The new relaxation response becomes classically conditioned to the stimulus, replacing the anxiety reaction. *Exposure and response prevention* is a treatment used for obsessive-compulsive disorder. Patients are exposed to the stimulus that evokes obsessive thinking and are then told to imagine the consequences of what they fear without engaging in their usual obsessive or compulsive routine. The procedure is repeated in homework assignments followed by a maintenance program of phone calls and clinic visits. During *aversion therapy*, one stimulus is paired with another aversive, painful stimulus until the original stimulus is avoided. Although unpleasant, individuals still opt for aversion therapy because it is very effective in suppressing behavior and the therapy is seen as better than continuing the original harmful behavior.

Contingency management involves a health professional gaining control over the rewards and punishments that influence a patient's behavior. Patients can be rewarded for productive behaviors and punished for unproductive behaviors. In *contingency contracting*, a contract is established, with a patient specifying those behaviors that will be rewarded and those that will be punished. When enough rewards have been accumulated, they may be traded for something the patient wants. *Modeling* refers to the process of learning behavior by watching and imitating another person (a model). Modeling can be used to treat some disorders, such as phobias. The client is shown a model interacting with a feared stimulus but not exhibiting the fear response. Through a process of observational learning, the patient finds that the feared stimulus is not really dangerous.

11. **What are the essential characteristics of the cognitive approaches to psychotherapy?**

While not denying the importance of a person's affect or behavior, cognitive therapists focus on an individual's thoughts, perceptions, and attitudes. The major premise of cognitive therapy is that if a therapist wants to change how a patient feels, then the therapist has to change how that patient thinks. In addition, the therapist must show the patient how those changes were achieved. *Rational-emotive therapy* (RET) works on the premise that people with problems are operating on irrational assumptions about the world and themselves. RET is directive in its attempts to change people's cognitions. *Cognitive restructuring therapy* is somewhat less directive but is based on the same idea as RET. The underlying premise is that people with psychological disorders have developed negative self-images and negative views (cognitions) about the future. The therapist provides opportunities for the patient to test those negative cognitions and discover that things are not as bad as they may seem. *Cognitive-behavior therapy* (CBT) explicitly combines cognitive and behavioral approaches. In order to make significant, long-lasting changes in a person's cognitions, the person may very well have to make changes in his or her behaviors, and recent evidence suggests that it is this behavior activation that is the most import aspect of the technique.

12. **What is "group therapy" and what are its potential benefits?**

    In group therapy, a number of clients are brought together at the same time under the guidance of a therapist. During group sessions, members share their feelings and experiences. Group meetings are generally informal, and no particular form of psychotherapy is dominant. There are several potential advantages to group therapy. Interpersonal issues may be better understood and dealt with in an interpersonal situation. Participants may learn that they are not the only ones in the world with a problem. Participants may come to appreciate that others face even more difficult problems of the same nature. Participants may benefit from providing support for someone else, and the dynamics of intra-group communication can be analyzed and changed in a group setting. Family therapy is a variety of group therapy based on the assumptions that family members can be seen as part of a system in which one member (and one member's problem) affects all of the others. Family therapists recognize that psychological problems often arise because of faulty communication, and they recognize the importance of communication among family members.

13. **In general, is psychotherapy an effective treatment for psychological disorders?**

    Scientifically evaluating the appropriateness and effectiveness of psychotherapy has been difficult. It is challenging to set up a standard experimental procedure with adequate control groups or baselines against which to compare the outcomes of therapy. It is even more complicated to get consensus on what is meant by recovery—or even significant progress—because the goals of therapy vary from technique to technique. Nonetheless, in general, psychotherapy is effective. It is significantly better than leaving disorders untreated. More treatment tends to be better than less, and some therapists seem to be more effective than others, regardless of the techniques being used. As with physical disorders, the sooner mental disorders are properly diagnosed and treatment begins, the better.

14. **Are any specific therapy techniques better than others? What is the difference between ESTs and EBPP?**

    There are data that suggest that some therapies may be better suited to some clients and to some disorders than they are to others. For example, behavior therapies seem best for treating phobias, and cognitive approaches seem well suited for treating depression. Researchers are making considerable efforts to identify specific empirically supported therapies. Researchers have identified many such therapies, but mental health professionals must take care in applying the findings of this sort of research. A recent move toward *evidence-based practice in psychology* (EBPP) supports integrating the best available scientific research findings with the clinical expertise of therapists, and the characteristics of patients, their culture and their preferences.

Social Psychology

14

PREVIEW

social psychology the field of psychology concerned with how others influence the thoughts, feelings, and behaviors of others, and vice versa

In this chapter, we consider the psychology of people as they really live, interacting with others as social organisms in a social world. **Social psychology** is the field of psychology concerned with how others influence the thoughts, feelings, and behaviors of the individual. Social psychologists focus on the person or the individual in a group setting, and not on the group per se. Group study is more likely to be the focus of sociologists. Because we are social organisms, we are familiar, each in our own way, with many of the concerns of social psychology.

To claim that we are familiar with the concerns of social psychology has certain implications. On the one hand, it means that social psychology is perceived as relevant for all of us because it deals with everyday situations, both immediate (e.g., your personal relationships with friends and family) and more removed (e.g., conflicts in other parts of the world). On the other hand, it means that we are often willing to accept common sense and our own personal experience as the basis for our explanations of social behavior. Although common sense and personal experience may sometimes be valid and may suffice in our everyday lives, they are not acceptable for a scientific approach to understanding social behavior. Social psychology relies on experiments and other scientific methods as sources of knowledge about social behavior.

Over the last 50 years, much of social psychology has taken on a cognitive flavor. That is, social psychologists are attempting to understand social behavior by examining the underlying mental structures and processes (cognitions) reflected in such behavior. A premise of this approach, and this chapter, is that we do not view our social environment solely on the basis of the stimulus information it presents us. Instead, the argument goes, we have developed cognitive structures or processes (e.g., attitudes and schemas)

that influence our interpretation of the world around us. Social psychologists have found that it is not only our conscious cognitive processes that affect social behavior, but there also unconscious processes that play a role as well (as you shall see later in this chapter). "Discovering how people mentally organize and represent information about themselves and others has been a central task of social cognition research" (Berscheid, 1994, p. 84). Social cognition focuses largely on how we come to make sense of the social world in which we live, and how that information influences our social judgments, choices, attractions, and behaviors (Bordens & Horowitz, 2008; Worchel et al., 2000). First, we discuss the notion of building our own social realities, and then we cover three issues of social psychology with a distinctively cognitive flavor: a) attitudes—their nature, formation, and change, b) attributions—coming to understand causes of our behaviors and the behaviors of others, and c) forming and maintaining interpersonal relationships.

For the rest of the chapter, there is a (rather subtle) shift to issues that involve the more direct influence of the social world on our everyday behaviors. The basic questions are simple ones: How do others influence our affects, cognitions, and behaviors? How do we, in turn, influence the affects, cognitions, and behaviors of others? In some cases, the answers are equally straightforward; in other instances, there may be some surprises.

We will begin with the processes of conformity and obedience. They are different processes, to be sure, but they have in common the intent—one way or another—to influence the behaviors of others. Next, we take up bystander apathy and intervention. The focus of research and theory in this field is on helping behaviors. Someone is in need. Other people are in the vicinity. Will they help? Will they turn away? Can psychologists predict which outcome is likely to occur? It is only a small cognitive step to our next issues: social loafing, social facilitation, and decision-making in groups. It is somewhat overly simplistic, but here the research centers on the advantages or disadvantages of working in a group setting, as opposed to working alone.

SOCIAL COGNITION: MAKING SENSE OF THE SOCIAL WORLD

Kurt Lewin, one of the pioneers of social psychology, proposed a model for social psychology claiming that two crucial elements must be understood in order to predict behavior: the person (P) and the environment (E). Lewin stated that, "every psychological event depends on the state of the person and at the same time on the environment, although their relative importance is different in different cases" (1936, p. 12). Thus, Lewin proposed that to understand social behavior, we must understand the interaction between the person (e.g., personality, biases, attitudes, etc.) and the social environment (e.g., the presence of other people, the physical environment, etc.). This conceptualization boils down to the relatively simple formula: $B = \int(PE)$. In words, behavior is a function of the interaction between person variables and environmental variables.

Lewin's model still serves as a foundation for the way in which many social psychologists approach their discipline. However, a lot has happened since 1936, and we now appreciate that a crucial element in understanding social behavior lies in discovering how individuals *think* about and evaluate what happens in their social environment. In other words, it is what you *make* of a situation that determines how you will behave. **Social cognition** describes the processes used to think about and evaluate social situations. We trust that you will recognize here two of the "Key Principles" that we introduced in Chap-

Courtesy of Tim Pannell/Corbis.

Social psychologists focus their efforts on people as they really live—in small groups, be they families, work teams, study groups, or cheerleading squads.

ter 1: *Our experience of the world often matters more than what is in the world,* and *Explanations in psychology often involve INTERACTIONS.*

Let us see how this social cognition works. Imagine you are sitting in class one day and, all of a sudden, the fire alarm rings. What would you do? Would you automatically respond to this environmental signal for danger by getting up and running out of the room? Probably not. It is more likely you would look around you to see how *others* were reacting. You would take into account how your fellow students were responding to the fire alarm. In other words, your evaluation of the situation would depend, in part on how others (fellow students, your instructor) were reacting. This is the essence of social cognition. Based on your evaluation of the situation, you form a *behavioral intention* to act in a certain way (to sit there, or to get up and leave). This crucial process of intervening between the detection of the stimulus and one's ultimate behavior represents an expansion of Lewin's basic model.

In science fiction films and televisions shows, humans are often shown asking for a computer analysis of a given situation. For example, in the classic TV show *Star Trek: The Next Generation,* one character—

social cognition the processes used to think about, understand, and evaluate social situations

naïve realism the tendency for us to believe that we see the world in a more rational, objective way than do others

Lt. Commander Data, an android with supercomputer capabilities—was often approached by other characters who sought Data's analysis of a dangerous situation. Data would respond with cold, hard facts, based on the logical processing of the input he received. The responses he gave were unvarnished and unbiased products of a systematic processing of information. How different might the world be if humans possessed such a capacity?

Unlike Data, humans do not possess the ability to apply cold, hard logic when interpreting most social situations. Instead, our understanding of our social world is colored by our biases and expectations. Here is a classic example: Two sets of football fans watched a football game between Princeton and Dartmouth. During the game, Princeton's "All American" quarterback was injured on a play. Predictably, more Princeton students (55%) believed that the Dartmouth players were intentionally trying to hurt the quarterback, than did Dartmouth students (10%) (Hastroff & Cantril, 1954). This phenomenon is not rare, nor is it simply applicable to sports fans; it permeates how we perceive many situations. Opposing sides to a conflict often see the same event in very different ways. Most Americans view the terrorist attacks of September 11, 2001, as wanton acts of murder. However, these same events are seen as acts of bravery by others. For another example, people can read the same set of documents outlining the credentials of a judicial nominee and come to very different conclusions about that person's fitness to serve. Our ideology, attitudes, prejudices and biases alter our perceptions of objective reality. In essence, each of us views the world through different (sometimes slightly different and sometimes vastly different) lenses. The information filtered through these lenses causes each of us to construct our own version of social reality.

Another remarkable feature of biased social cognitions is that we are often unaware of their influence on our thoughts and behaviors. We believe that we are clearly rational and logical in our perception of the social world. We are more than willing to acknowledge that *others* are biased, but reluctant to do so for ourselves. This is known as *naïve realism* (Ross & Ward, 1995). **Naïve realism** refers to the tendency for us to believe that *we* see the world in a more rational, objective way than do others (Pronin, Gilovich, & Ross, 2004). We are particularly likely to take this position when others disagree with us, all the time believing that others are more susceptible to biased information than we are (Pronin, Lin, & Ross, 2002).

Three related processes underlie naïve realism. First, is the belief that we see the world rationally and objectively, whereas others do not. Second, we assume that if others *are* rational they will also see the world as we do. Third, we assume that if those others do not see the world as we do then either they are not rational and harbor ulterior and bad motives or simply are misinformed (Reeder, Pryor, & Wohl, & Griswell, 2005). In short, we are motivated to see ourselves as free of bias and objective–we have what might fairly be called a "bias blind spot" (Cohen, 2003).

Naive realism has some interesting manifestations. It causes us to believe that we have greater personal insight into the way we think than do others. In one study, for example, college students reported that they "knew themselves better" than their fellow students knew themselves (Pronin et al., 2001). Naïve realism also has implications for understanding political controversies. In our "Red State/Blue State" world, it would appear that there are sharp political divisions between Americans on a wide range of political issues. Some divisions exist. However, the perceived differences among people with opposing viewpoints may be far less than the reality. For example, Farwell and Weiner (2000) found that conservatives and liberals agreed more than they thought they would on how much money should be spent to help the poor. Also, individuals on both sides of the affirmative action debate overestimated the degree of liberalism or conservatism of those on the opposite side (Sherman, Nelson, & Ross, 2003).

The lesson here is, we think, obvious: When people with differing points of view debate or clash, they tend to misperceive their motives and biases. It is easy to dismiss a political opponent as a "bleeding heart liberal" or a "hardhearted conservative" when you overestimate the extremity of your opponent's point of view and believe that you are less biased than they are. We should remind ourselves that each of us has biases that leads to a certain view of the world and one's own subjective reality, which may bear little or no resemblance to either objective reality or to the subjective reality of others.

BEFORE YOU GO ON

1. What do psychologists mean by "social cognitions" and "naïve realism"?
2. What social psychological processes underlie naïve realism?
3. How can biases in social cognition affect interpersonal relationships?

A Point to Ponder or Discuss
What examples of naïve realism can you identify in your own perception of the social world?

THE NATURE OF ATTITUDES

Since the 1920s, a central concern in social psychology has been the nature of attitudes, their formation, and their change. Today, the characterization of attitudes has gone beyond defining a core concern for social psychology. In our world after September 11, 2001, politicians and pundits alike have been asking important questions, such as, "Why do those who wish to do us harm hate us so much?" In fact, according to a Pew Global Attitudes Project survey (2005), attitudes toward the United States remain low in the Muslim countries of Jordan (21% favorable rating), Pakistan (23% favorable rating), and Indonesia (38% favorable rating). The only good news is that in many countries, positive perceptions of the United States have recently improved ever so slightly. The negative attitudes of some extremists around the world have led to horrific acts of violence against Americans and other Western interests. It makes sense that if psychologists could understand the content, origins, and strategies for changing these attitudes, the world might be a safer place.

An **attitude** is a relatively stable disposition used to evaluate an object or event. It is a cognitive summary of experience represented by such attributes as good-bad, pleasant-unpleasant, useful-useless, helpful-harmful (Ajzen, 2001; Ajzen & Fishbein, 2000). An attitude has consequences for influencing a person's feelings, beliefs, and behaviors toward that object or event.

The concept of *evaluation* in this definition refers to a dimension of attitudes that includes such notions as being for or against, or positive or negative. By *disposition* we mean a tendency, or a preparedness, to respond to the object of an attitude (actual responding is not necessary). Note that, by definition, attitudes have objects. We do not have attitudes in general; we have attitudes about objects or events. The word

attitude a relatively stable disposition to evaluate an object or event

implicit attitude an attitude that operates on an unconscious level, beyond our awareness of it affects

attitude is occasionally used differently in common speech. We may hear that someone has a "bad attitude" or "an attitude" in general, as in, "Boy, does he have an attitude!" In psychology, however, an attitude requires an object: that is, a specific object or event attached to the attitude.

Anything can be the object of an attitude, whether it be a person, an event, or an idea. You may have attitudes about this course, the car you drive, democracy, your father, the president, or the fast-food restaurant where you eat lunch. Some of our attitudes are more important than others, of course, but the fact that we have attitudes about so many things is precisely why the study of attitudes is so central in social psychology.

Up until around 10 years ago social psychologists looked at attitudes that existed on a conscious level. That is, it was believed that we are consciously aware of our attitudes and of how they affect behavior. Today, social psychologists know that attitudes exist on two levels of consciousness. An **explicit attitude** works at a conscious level; we are aware of these attitudes and how they

occasionally influence our behaviors. Social psychologists have identified attitudes that do not operate on a conscious level. This type of attitude is an **implicit attitude**, which operates below consciousness, at nearly "gut" level. A special technique is needed to measure implicit attitudes. Instead of asking people about attitudes on a questionnaire (used to measure explicit attitudes), implicit attitudes are measured using the *implicit association test* (Greenwald, McGhee, & Schwartz, 1998). You can try the implicit association test for yourself at *https://implicit.harvard.edu/implicit*.

It is important to understand that implicit and explicit attitudes are two different processes, not just different sides to the same coin (Wilson, Lindsey, & Schooler, 2000). Implicit and explicit attitudes affect behavior differently and under different circumstances. For example, implicit attitudes take over when you are "cognitively busy." That is, when you have a lot on your mind or are thinking about something intensively you are more likely to rely on unconscious implicit attitudes than if your mind is clear (Hofman, Gschwendner, Castelli, & Schmitt, 2008). For example, if you have just had a bad day at work and are thinking about how to solve a particularly difficult problem, you may react negatively to a member of a minority group that you have negative implicit attitudes about. If your mind was not occupied you could bring your reactions to this person under conscious control and be less likely to behave negatively toward him or her (Hofman, et al., 2008). Finally, when you change an explicit attitude you do not simply erase the old attitude from memory and replace it with a new one (Petty, Tormala, Brinol, & Jarvis, 2006). Instead, evidence suggests that the old attitude becomes an implicit attitude and may still affect you on an unconscious level. The new attitude you develop becomes the explicit attitude.

explicit attitude an attitude that works at a conscious level, i.e., we are aware of these attitudes and how they may affect our behaviors

We form attitudes about many of the events and objects in our environments. These attitudes reflect our evaluations. We like watching television, have heard that a certain brand is a good one (and is on sale), so we buy it.

Courtesy of Juice Images/Corbis.

The Components of an Attitude

Although many definitions of an attitude have been proposed over the years, most of them suggest that attitudes have three aspects, or components. These components are affect, behavior, and cognition (which make up the ABCs of attitudes). When the term "attitude" is used in everyday conversation, it is likely that the reference is to the affective component, which consists of our feelings about the attitude object. For example, if you say that you really like iced tea, but do not like lemonade, you are expressing your feelings, or your affect, about these beverages. This emotional aspect is what makes attitudes special and different from other cognitive schemas.

The behavioral component of an attitude consists of our response tendencies toward attitude objects. This component includes our behaviors and intentions to act, should the opportunity arise. Based on your attitude, you would probably order iced tea with your lunch, rather than lemonade. The cognitive component includes all of the information you have relating to an attitude object—both conscious (for explicit attitudes) and unconscious (for implicit attitudes). The cognitive component represents the information storage and organization component of an attitude, making an attitude similar to other information-processing cognitive schemas. You know that iced tea and lemonade are both beverages, you know how they are made, and you know that lemonade is sour. We form a positive attitude toward a beverage because we like the way it tastes (affective), because it is easy to buy (behavioral), and because know it is good for us (cognitive).

Most of the time, the affective, behavioral, and cognitive, components of attitudes are consistent. If we think that classical music is relaxing and we enjoy listening to it, we will buy classical music recordings. If you believe that knowledge of psychology will be an asset in your career and you enjoy your introductory psychology class, you may plan to take more psychology classes in the future. There are occasions, however, when behaviors are not consistent with beliefs and feelings. For example, Rob may have strong, unfavorable beliefs and very negative feelings about someone, yet when he encounters that person at a social event, he smiles, extends his hand, and says something pleasant. In this case, the social situation overpowers the cognitive and affective components of Rob's attitudes. In other words, the components of an attitude may lack consistency, and it is the behavioral component that is most often inconsistent with the other two.

Because our actual behaviors may not reflect true feelings or beliefs, some social psychologists (e.g., Fazio, 2001; Fazio & Olson, 2003) exclude the behavioral component from their definition altogether, reserving the term "attitude" for the basic feelings of like or dislike for the attitudinal object. Others argue that attitude is a two-dimensional concept involving affect and cognition, but not behavior (Ajzen, 2001; Ajzen & Fishbein, 2000). Still others add the notion of a behavior intention—a specific intention to perform a given behavior, whether it is performed or not. For example, you may have a positive attitude toward a particular candidate, yet choose not vote because you did not form an intention to vote. A behavior intention is affected by three things: a) the person's attitude toward a behavior (toward actually voting, for instance), b) normative pressures (are family and friends voting?), and c) the degree to which the person perceives that the behavior will matter (will one vote count?) So, if you think voting is important, all of your friends are voting, and you believe your vote will count, then you will form an intention to vote. Such behavior intentions are better predictors of specific behaviors, like voting, than of one's general political attitudes.

BEFORE YOU GO ON

4. How do social psychologists define attitudes?
5. What are explicit and implicit attitudes and how might they affect your behavior differently?
6. What are the possible components of an attitude, and how are they related?

A Point to Ponder or Discuss

Reflect for a moment on your own collection of attitudes. Can you think of experiences in which an explicit or implicit attitude might have affected your behavior? Can you think of a time when your overt behaviors were inconsistent with how you really felt and what you really thought? If so, why did you behave in such a way?

Where Do Your Attitudes Come From?

As we go through life, we form many attitudes, some of which may stay with us our whole lives (e.g., some religious attitudes, or various marital attitudes, such as monogamy versus polygamy), whereas others are held on a temporary basis (e.g., an attitude toward a political candidate in a particular election, or an attitude about a program on television). Where do attitudes come from? It is safe to say that we are not born with

our attitudes in place. On the other hand, there is evidence for an inherited predisposition to develop some attitudes, but not others (Eaves, Eysenck, & Martin, 1989; Plomin et al., 1990; Tesser, 1993).

People often imitate behaviors that they have seen reinforced in others (called *vicarious reinforcement*). To the extent we perceive others gaining rewards for having and expressing some attitude, we are likely to adopt that attitude ourselves. Advertising that relies on the testimonials of satisfied customers is appealing to this sort of observational learning. It is the stock and trade of many of today's televised "infomercials." The audience is shown a current—and very pleased—consumer of a product or service, and the advertiser hopes that this will lead viewers to develop a favorable evaluation of the product. Obviously, the advertiser is going to show us only those people who are happy with the product. Viewers seldom stop to think about how many people may have used the product or service and are not at all happy with it. (Remember our discussion of pseudoscience in Chapter 1?)

Some attitudes are acquired through the associative process of classical conditioning (see Figure 14.1). Pleasant events (unconditioned stimuli) can be paired with an attitudinal object (conditioned stimulus). As a result of this association, the attitudinal object comes to elicit the same good feeling (a positive evaluation)

Advertising can be thought of as an attempt to get us to form a positive attitude about some product, service, or even some place. Notice that this sign does not just welcome us to Las Vegas, it welcomes us to Fabulous *Las Vegas.*

Courtesy of Beathan/Corbis.

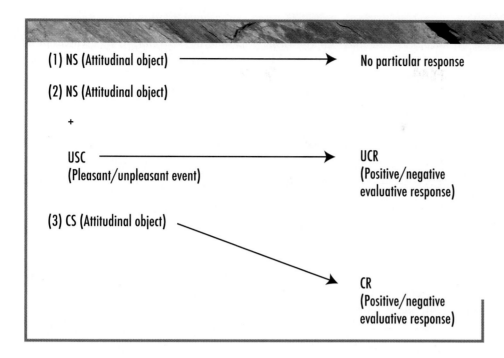

FIGURE 14.1

A schematic diagram of how attitudes may be formed through classical conditioning. At first, the attitudinal object is a neutral stimulus (NS), eliciting no particular response of interest. When it is paired with a stimulus (the unconditional stimulus, or UCS) that naturally produces an evaluative response (the unconditioned response, or UCR) the attitudinal object becomes a conditioned stimulus (CS) that elicits a learned, or conditioned, response (CR).

originally produced by the unconditioned stimulus. The good, pleasant feeling, originally an unconditioned response elicited by a pleasant event, becomes a conditioned response elicited by the attitudinal object. Of course, negative attitudes can be acquired in the same way (Cacioppo et al., 1992).

Some advertising uses conditioning techniques to change attitudes about a product by taking an originally neutral object (the product) and trying to create a positive association for it. For instance, a soft drink advertisement may depict attractive young people having a great time playing volleyball, dancing, or enjoying a concert while drinking that soft drink. The obvious intent is that we will associate the product with good times and having fun. That sports figures often wear brand-name logos or trademarks on their uniforms suggests that manufacturers want us to associate their product with the skills of the athletes we are watching.

Attitudes can also be formed as a result of the direct reinforcement of behaviors consistent with an attitudinal position: in other words, as a matter of operant conditioning. Simple verbal reinforcement (saying "good" or "that's right") when people agree with attitudinal statements leads to the development of attitudes consistent with the position expressed in those statements.

Direct personal experience can mold attitudes. If you continually have an unpleasant experience at some stores, in certain classes, or with a particular group of neighbors, it is likely that you will develop negative evaluations, beliefs, and behavior tendencies toward them. And attitudes tend to be more extreme (whether positive or negative) when they are based on personal experience. For example, no matter what your attitudes about abortion may be, if you have personally experienced the conflicts and decisions involved in the process, your feelings are going to be more intense than those of someone without such experience. One way or another, a veteran is likely to have more intensely felt attitudes about military service than will people who have never been in the military.

In a similar vein, research pioneered by Robert Zajonc tells us that the likelihood of developing positive evaluations of stimuli increases with repeated exposures—he called it the **mere exposure phenomenon**. There are many examples in everyday life. Have you ever downloaded a song that you had not

mere exposure phenomenon the likelihood of developing positive evaluations of stimuli increases with repeated exposures

heard before, assuming you would like it because you had liked all the other recordings made by the performer? The first time you listened to the new song, however, your reaction was lukewarm at best, and you were disappointed with your purchase. Not wanting to feel that you had wasted your money, keep listening to the song on your iPod. In time, more often than not, you would come to realize you liked the song after all—the mere exposure effect. This also commonly happens in our formation of attitudes about other people. Familiarity is more likely to breed attraction than contempt. Although there is evidence that the mere exposure phenomenon is quite real, there remains considerable disagreement about *why* familiarity and repeated interactions breed the formation of positive attitudes. And there are limits. Too much exposure to a stimulus may lead to boredom and devaluation (Bornstein, Kale, & Cornell, 1990).

We also should be mindful of the effects of the news media on attitudes. In our wired, interconnected world there are many sources of news that can potentially shape attitudes (e.g., print media, broadcast news, cable news, Internet blogs, etc.). Exposure to news stories in the media has been found to exert an influence on attitudes toward a range of issues (Wanta, Golan, & Lee, 2004). This is accomplished through **agenda setting**, in which the media tells us which issues we should think about, and how we should think about those issues. Once set, the agenda influences attitudes on the issue that is the target of the agenda.

Agenda setting has recently been conceptualized as comprising two levels. *First-level agenda setting* by the media tells us which issues are important. This is accomplished through the editorial selection of news stories. In short, because there is so much news, editors must select those stories they think are most important and interesting. These are the stories that make the newspapers and nightly news broadcasts. The stories that don't make the cut are largely for-

| agenda setting the phenomena in which the media tells us which issues we should think about, and how we should think about those issues

gotten or relegated to secondary status. *Second-level agenda setting* involves how the media shapes our thinking about an issue based on how the attributes of a story are presented. For example, a political candidate can be portrayed positively by the media if stories highlight his or her positive qualities (e.g., honesty, strength), or negatively if stories portray his or her negative qualities (e.g., secretiveness, dishonesty). The selective presentation of news stories and attributes is at the heart of agenda setting (Wanta, Golan, & Lee, 2004).

There is ample support for the effects of both first-level and second-level agenda setting on attitudes. For example, Wanta, Golan, & Lee (2004) found a positive correlation between the number of media stories about a foreign country and how vital that country was seen to U.S. interests. In general, the greater the number of news stories about a country, the more likely that country was perceived to be of vital interest to our nation. So, the media can be successful in setting the agenda for what is important (first-level). These researchers also found that negative media coverage of a foreign country was related to negative perceived views of that country. Thus, *how* people think was also associated with news coverage (second-level). Interestingly, however, there were not significant correlations for positive and neutral news portrayals and public attitudes. It appears that the negative agenda is more potent than any positive or neutral one.

Agenda setting has also been found to relate to attitudes toward political figures and political issues. Kiousis (2003) found that attitudes about former President Clinton during the Monica Lewinsky scandal were related to news coverage. Media coverage was related to positive attitudes toward Clinton himself, but negatively related to ratings of how well he was doing his job as president. Attitudes toward President Bush and the War in Iraq also appear to be related to news coverage. During late summer, 2005, there was a precipitous drop in support for the president and the war. The Media Research Center reported that during this period, war coverage on the three major network-news broadcasts became increasingly negative (about 50% of Iraq news stories were negative during January and February, compared to 73% during August and September). This trend toward negative coverage of the war was correlated with President Bush's approval rating. As the percentage of negative news stories about Iraq increased, the President's approval rating tended to decline.

Finally, we cannot entirely rule out the role of biology and genetics as origins for our attitudes. Genetics have an indirect effect on our attitudes. Some of our characteristics that have a biological basis predispose us to certain behaviors and attitudes. For example, genetic differences in hearing and taste, could affect our preferences for certain kinds of music or foods (Tesser, 1993). Aggression, which has a genetic component is another example. A person's genetically driven aggressiveness can affect a whole range of attitudes and behaviors, from watching violent TV shows and movies, to hostility toward women or members of other groups, to attitudes toward capital punishment (Oskamp, 1991).

BEFORE YOU GO ON

7. What are some of the factors that influence the formation of attitudes?

A Point to Ponder or Discuss
Relying on your own experience, which of your attitudes do you believe have been formed through classical conditioning, operant conditioning, observational learning, or mere exposure? Which of your attitudes might have formed under the influence of agenda setting by the media?

ATTITUDE CHANGE MECHANISMS

Given the role of learning and experience in forming our attitudes, it is logical to assume that they will undergo changes as we encounter new experiences or learn new things. In fact, our attitudes change as our life experiences change, and sometimes they change in response to direct efforts to change them. Political polls regularly track changes in attitudes about politicians. Based on poll results, political strategists develop photo opportunities and advertisements designed to change attitudes about the candidates. What psychological mechanisms account for attitude change? In this section, we will explore some models of attitude change, beginning with cognitive dissonance theory.

It seems reasonable that a person's attitudes will affect his or her behaviors. It then follows that attitude change will lead to behavior change. In 1957, Leon Festinger proposed the reverse: Attitudes can follow behavior. Festinger's theory involved a concept he called **cognitive dissonance**, which is a negative motivational state that arises when our attitudes, thoughts, and behaviors are out of balance, or inconsistent. Cognitive dissonance arises when we realize (a cognition) that we have behaved in a manner inconsistent (dissonant) with other cognitions. Once dissonance is aroused, we are then motivated to reduce or eliminate it. That is, since cognitive dissonance is a negative motivational state, so we want to eliminate it.

An excellent example of how cognitive dissonance works is found in one of the first demonstrations of the

cognitive dissonance a negative motivational state that arises when our attitudes, thoughts, and behaviors are inconsistent

There are so many good reasons not *to smoke cigarettes that anyone who does so is almost certainly experiencing cognitive dissonance.*

Courtesy of Krista Kennell/Corbis.

phenomenon (Festinger & Carlsmith, 1959). Participants in the research performed an extremely boring task of rotating row after row of small wooden knobs. Following a lengthy knob-turning session, the experimenter explained that the research really had to do with the effects of motivation on such a task. Further, the participant was told that the person in the waiting area was to be the next participant in the project. This person was to be led to believe that the knob-turning task would be interesting, fun, and educational. It was then explained that the experimenter's assistant, who usually told these "lies" to the waiting participant, was absent. Would the participant do this "selling" job? The participant would be paid for his or her help. Nearly all the participants agreed and worked very hard to convince the next participant the project was fun and educational. Weeks later, at the end of the semester, all participants filled out a questionnaire that asked about their reactions to the knob-turning experiment.

The experimental manipulation was a simple one: Some participants were paid $20 for trying to convince the waiting person (who was really not a participant, but was one of the researchers) that the obviously boring task was fun and interesting, whereas others were paid only $1 for convincing the next participant. In all other respects, everyone was treated the same way. Remember that this was the late 1950s, and for college students, $20 was a lot of money. The purpose of the experiment was to determine whether participants changed their attitudes toward the boring task.

At the end of the semester, which participants do you suppose expressed more positive attitudes about the project, the ones paid $20 or those paid $1? Doesn't it seem logical that those college students paid $20 would remember the task as being fun and enjoyable, and would indicate a willingness to participate in similar projects? Festinger and Carlsmith predicted just the opposite. They reasoned that students paid only $1 would feel that their behavior had not been sufficiently justified. They had told a "lie," and had been paid a trivial amount of money for doing so. They would experience a great deal of discomfort—cognitive dissonance would be created. The payment of $1 did not provide sufficient justification for the participants to lie. In essence, Festinger and Carlsmith theorized that participants would conclude: "I lied for a lousy dollar." This is known as the *insufficient justification effect*. Because the participants could not undo the lie, they resolved the dissonance by changing their attitude about the project (to a more positive one) so that it fit better with their behavior—a sort of, "Well, I didn't *really* lie, because the experiment wasn't all *that* bad; it could have been a lot worse; in fact, it was kinda fun at that."

Participants paid $20, on the other hand, had plenty of justification for their actions. Sure, they lied, but they had good reason to do so. As a result, they experienced little cognitive dissonance. They should not be expected to change their attitude about the experiment. "Yeah, I lied, but I got paid 20 bucks." The results of this experiment are presented in Figure 14.2. Seldom do we find differences in an experiment as clear-cut as this one.

Here is another example that most college students find intriguing (Comer & Laird, 1975). Students were led to a small room and told that in the experiment for which they volunteered, they

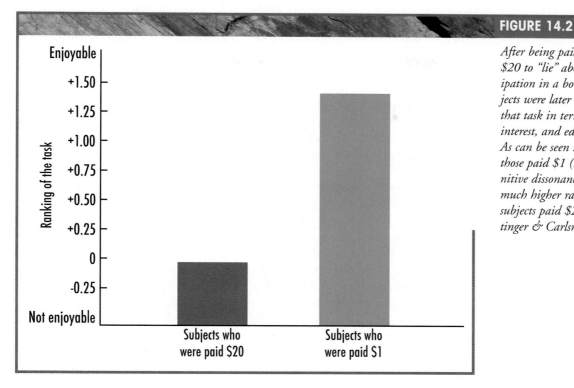

FIGURE 14.2

After being paid either $1 or $20 to "lie" about their participation in a boring task, subjects were later asked to rate that task in terms of enjoyment, interest, and educational value. As can be seen in this graph, those paid $1 (those with cognitive dissonance) gave the task much higher ratings than did subjects paid $20 (from Festinger & Carlsmith, 1959).

were required to eat a large worm. "Yes, that dead worm, there on the table." The students were told that they could refuse to participate if they so chose, and they were given several minutes to decide what they wanted to do. When the experimenter returned, he told the participants that there had been a mistake: the participants were, in fact, able to choose between eating the worm or performing a different, meaningless task. Having taken the time to reduce their dissonance while the experimenter was gone, more than three-quarters of the students formed a favorable attitude toward worm-eating. They chose that option—although they were not actually required to do so. The results of these experiments (and numerous others) suggest that one way to change people's attitudes is to get them to change their behaviors first. Also, there is a clear advantage to offering as little incentive as possible to bring about that change in behavior. Simply "buying someone off" to change his or her behavior may get you *compliance*, but it will not produce the cognitive dissonance needed to bring about lasting attitude *change*.

You should be able to generate many other examples of cognitive dissonance that resulted in an attitude change. Consider those students who changed their attitude about a course, or a discipline, because they were required to take a class in it. For example, as a chemistry major, a student's (quite negative) attitudes about psychology might change because of the dissonance created when he or she is required to take a (very enjoyable and informative) course in introductory psychology.

There are many situations that arouse dissonance, and situations that produce negative consequences are more likely to arouse dissonance than ones that produce positive consequences (Cooper & Scher, 1992). This can be seen as a matter of "Why did I do such a stupid thing? I should have known better than that!"

Dissonance also can be aroused when a person has to make a choice between two mutually exclusive, equally attractive, alternatives. For example, imagine that you have to choose between two jobs. You can only have one of the jobs. Both are equally attractive, but perhaps one is near your favorite city, whereas the other is near to your family. After you make your decision, all of the positive cognitions associated with that job are consistent with your decision. However, all of the positive cognitions you had associated with the job not chosen are inconsistent with your decision. This inconsistency gives rise to *postdecisional dissonance.* How could you reduce that dissonance? Well, changing your decision won't help. That would just shift the source of the dissonance. Instead, most people tend to think of negative things about the not-chosen alternative, and they continue to generate positive cognitions about the chosen alternative. For example, having decided to move to one's favorite city for a job, a person might begin to see being close to family as a drawback (fostering dependency on the family, feeling obligated to attend every family gathering, and so on). Having made the choice, the new employee is likely to discover all sorts of new, fun and exciting opportunities in the chosen city—and with the chosen employer.

Although cognitive dissonance theory has received strong support since it was first proposed, it is clear that the theory cannot account for all attitude-change situations. For example, a person who smokes must surely know that it is unhealthy, yet that person continues to smoke. According to dissonance theory, this should create dissonance and put pressure on the person to change his or her behavior (i.e., stop smoking). But, as many smokers know, that often does not happen. Other proposals have been developed to account for attitude-change situations that cannot be easily explained by dissonance theory.

One alternative to classic dissonance reduction is the Freudian notion of *rationalization.* In our smoking example, for instance, a person may rationalize away the negative aspects of smoking in the face of evidence to the contrary. This rationalization may be expressed in the form of statements such as, "I smoke only 'light' cigarettes," or "Even though smoking may hurt others, it won't hurt me" (called *the illusion of unique invulnerability*). Or a person may find solace in the fact that his or her grandfather smoked three packs of unfiltered cigarettes every day for 80 years, and then died in a scuba diving accident.

Another alternative approach to dissonance theory is *self-affirmation theory,* which states that people may not try to reduce dissonance if they can affirm their self-concept some other way. Self-concept affirmation often takes the form of admitting a weakness (e.g., smoking), while affirming one's strengths in other areas. A smoker, for example, may convince him- or herself that he or she is a good parent, a hard-working businessperson, and a dedicated community supporter. Or even more to the point, "Yes, I smoke, but I work out every single day, and that more than compensates." Such contorted logic may very well reduce the negative affect associated with dissonance (Zimbardo & Leippe, 1992).

Finally, *self-perception theory* suggests that in dissonance-arousing situations, people make careful observations of their behavior, and then try to attribute a cause for that behavior (Bem, 1972). They do so in much the same way they would if they were trying to understand the behavior of someone else. Self-perception theory says that there is no need to rely on dissonance, or any other internal motivational state, and that thought processes replace the motivational aspects of cognitive dissonance. The basic idea is that we form our feelings and our attitudes on the basis of our perceptions of our own behaviors. A person eats a large meal and exclaims, "Boy! I must have been hungry!" This exclamation is a purely cognitive event, not in any way based on any sense of having "felt" hungry. A person paid $1 to lie, aware of what he or she has just done, simply concludes that he or she really must have enjoyed the task.

BEFORE YOU GO ON

8. Briefly describe some of the mechanisms used to explain how attitudes change.

A Point to Ponder or Discuss

The experiments on cognitive dissonance may be called "counter-intuitive" because so many (non-psychology) students fail to accurately predict the results. What are some examples of cognitive dissonance from your own experience?

Attitude Change by Persuasion

A different approach to attitude change focuses on the process of **persuasion**— the application of rational and/or emotional arguments to deliberately convince others to change their attitudes or behavior (Bordens & Horowitz, 2008). The most widely accepted model of persuasion is called the *Yale Communication Model*. According to this classic model (named after Yale University, where the research was done), the ability to persuade someone to change an attitude depends on three factors: the source of the message (who delivers the message), the characteristics of the message (what is said), and the nature of the audience (to whom the message is directed) (Hovland, Janis, & Kelley, 1953). These factors operate to affect internal processes such as attention to, comprehension of, and acceptance of a persuasive message. Change is measured in a person's attitudes, opinions (defined as the verbal expression of an attitude), and overt behavior. In turn, we will explore how the source, message, and audience affect persuasion.

The most important characteristic of the *source* of a persuasive message is the communicator's **credibility**, or believ-ability. Everything else being equal, a high-credibility communicator will be more persuasive than a low-credibility communicator. There are two compo-nents of credibility: expertise and trust-

Courtesy of Digital Vision/Getty Images.

worthiness. *Expertise* refers to the qual-ifications, training, skills, and credentials of the communicator. For example, The Chairman of the Joint Chiefs of Staff for the U.S. military has a high level of expertise in military matters. You would be more impressed by a message com-ing from him about military matters than a message from, say, a private pulled from the ranks or someone with no military experience at all. *Trustwor-thiness* refers to the motivations behind the communicator's attempt to persuade you. Trustworthiness goes to the ques-tion of "Why is this person trying to convince me?" For example, you would

Persuasion is a matter of apply-ing arguments to change their attitudes and their behaviors. Taking the "central route" to attitude change focuses data and evidence for such a change—like voting for candidate "Smith."

persuasion the application of rational and/or emotional argu-ments to deliberately convince others to change their attitudes and/or behaviors

credibility a communicator's believability, reflecting assess-ments of both expertise and trustworthiness

probably trust an automotive review you read in the magazine *Consumer Reports* because they have no vested interest in convincing you to buy one car or over another. On the other hand, you might be less trusting of a review in a magazine that accepts large sums of money from a particular carmaker. In this case, you might question the motives of the reviewer. Interestingly, a communicator who is perceived as arguing against what might appear to be his or her own best interests (for example, a senator representing a tobacco-growing state arguing for strict control of cigarettes) is likely to be perceived as trustworthy.

Although credibility is the most important source characteristic in persuasion, there are others. For example, a pleasant voice and expressive face affect persuasiveness (Burgoon, Birk, & Pfau, 1990). Physical attractiveness also affects the persuasiveness of a communicator (the greater attractiveness, the more the persuasion), the similarity of the communicator to the target of the message, and the communicator's rate of speech (moderately fast delivery enhances persuasion).

How a message is put together can influence the amount of persuasion that occurs. One important message characteristic is the nature of the appeal. In a *rational appeal*, one uses facts and figures. For example, if we want people to stop drinking and driving, we could present statistics concerning the number of alcohol-related traffic accidents and fatalities reported each year. Although rational appeals can be effective, emotional appeals can be even more effective. This is especially true of *fear appeals*, which attempt to persuade through the arousal of the negative emotion, fear. A fear appeal that attempts to persuade people to stop drinking and driving might depict graphic photographs of accident scenes involving drunk drivers.

Fear appeals are generally effective. However, there are four conditions that are necessary for a fear appeal to have its desired effect. First, the appeal must arouse a significant amount of fear. Second, the target of the appeal must believe that the dire consequences depicted in the appeal could happen to him or her. Third, the appeal must include instructions about how to avoid the dire consequences depicted in the appeal (drink only at home; use a designated driver; take a taxi and retrieve your car later). This condition is crucial. If it is not met, then the fear appeal will be ineffective, even if the first two conditions are met. Fourth, the target of the fear appeal must believe that he or she is capable of performing recommended action to avoid the dire consequences.

The target audience of a persuasive appeal also matters. For example, the opinions held by the audience members play a part in persuasion. If a message is very different from the audience members' pre-existing opinions (known as high discrepancy), there is less persuasion than if the message is only moderately different from the pre-existing opinions. This is because the content of the highly discrepant message is likely to be rejected without serious consideration by the audience members. A moderately discrepant message will not be rejected as quickly or as fully as a highly discrepant message, allowing for persuasion to occur. Similarly, if there is too little discrepancy, not much persuasion will occur. In this case, the message may be nothing more than a restatement of the audience's opinion, and little or no persuasion will take place. Whether a given type of message is effective also depends on the audience. For example, rational appeals tend to work best on well-educated audiences who are better able to make sense of the facts and statistics presented. On the other hand, fear appeals work best with less-educated audiences.

The Yale communication model makes a key assumption about the persuasion process: that a person carefully attends to a message, carefully processes the content of the message, and accordingly changes attitudes when the content of the message is accepted. Although this sometimes may be the case, there are situations in which a person can be persuaded even though he or she does not process information in the manner suggested by the model. For example, in a jury case where the evidence was very unclear and verdict came back "not guilty", a juror explained his decision by saying he acquitted because he "didn't like the way the prosecutor ran the show." This juror, who was probably not swayed by unclear evidence, turned to other factors (in this case, the behavior of the prosecutor) as a basis for a decision. Because the Yale model has difficulty accounting for such examples of persuasion, another model has been proposed—the elaboration likelihood model. This model picks up where the Yale model leaves off, but was never intended to replace it.

The **elaboration likelihood model** states that there are two routes to persuasion: the central route and the peripheral route (Petty and Cacioppo, 1986). *Central-route processing* is most likely to occur when an individual is motivated to process the content of a message and can understand the content of the message. In this case, the individual pays close attention to the quality of the message and creates a context for the message, based on pre-existing beliefs and ideas about the issue at hand. A person then uses these ideas to expand and elaborate on the message. Who delivered the message or how it was delivered is not as important as the facts and logic of the message itself. For example, an intelligent, engaged juror who listens carefully to all of the evidence presented during a trial is likely to be persuaded by the strength of the messages (evidence) presented. The individual undergoes a change in his or her underlying attitudes about the issue. Because of this persuasion, once deliberations begin, that attitude will be resistant to change. This juror will have developed a firm belief in the defendant's guilt or innocence. Only new, stronger, persuasive arguments will have a chance to change the juror's mind.

Peripheral-route processing is a matter of being persuaded by factors other than the content of the message. It is most likely to be used when the individual audience member is not motivated or is unable to understand the information contained in the message. Then, factors such as emotion or the communicator's appearance, behavior, and/or demeanor become the driving forces behind the argument's persuasion. The juror who found the defendant not guilty because he did not like the prosecutor's actions or "style" was using peripheral-route processing. Emotional cues are powerful in peripheral-route processing (Petty & Cacioppo, 1986). For example, when using peripheral-route processing, a strong fear appeal is likely to be effective, even if the content of the message is weak (Gleicher & Petty, 1992). Peripheral-route processing often produces attitude change, but because the listener has not carefully processed the message, resulting attitudes tend to be more unstable and easier to change than those based on central-route processing (Kassin, Reddy, & Tulloch, 1990).

It is important to understand that most of us do not use central- or peripheral-route processing in the same way for every situation. We may use central-route processing in one situation and peripheral-route processing in another. Imagine, for example, a juror listening to evidence in a trial. That juror may be fascinated by the testimony of a DNA expert and, as a consequence, will pay close attention to what that witness says. This juror is using central-route processing. However, the juror may be bored by the next witness, who testifies about a bullet's angle of trajectory. In that instance, it is likely the juror will not pay close attention to the content of the message, and will rely more on peripheral-route processing. Additionally, you can use both central and peripheral route processing when processing the same

elaboration likelihood model the point of view that there are two routes to persuasion; the central route and the peripheral route

message. So, while listening to our DNA expert a juror may process some of his testimony centrally (e.g., testimony that is easily understood) and some peripherally (e.g., more difficult or boring testimony). In short, central and peripheral route processing are not mutually exclusive modes of processing. In many persuasion situations, both are used to process a message.

BEFORE YOU GO ON

9. What factors does the Yale communication model suggest are involved in persuading someone to change an attitude?
10. How do the central and peripheral routes play a role in the persuasion process?

A Point to Ponder or Discuss
Someone you care about does not share your attitudes about an issue that it important to you. (It matters not what those attitudes might be.) What sorts of things would you consider as you plan to do all you can to change your friend's attitudes?

PREJUDICE, STEREOTYPES, AND DISCRIMINATION

Clearly, we all have many attitudes about a wide range of things, from the trivial to the profound. Of special interest to social psychologists are those attitudes that people direct toward members of groups other than their own. Unfortunately, history shows us that in many cases people hold negative attitudes toward members of groups perceived to be different from one's own. Social psychologists call these *prejudicial attitudes*. Specifically, **prejudice** is a biased, often negative, attitude toward groups of people.

Note that prejudice is usually thought of as a negative bias against a group of people (e.g., racial prejudice, gender prejudice). However, as the definition suggests, prejudice can also be a positive bias. For example, people often are positively prejudiced toward members of their own racial or religious groups and may give them preferential treatment simply because of their group membership.

Negative prejudicial attitudes, such as sexism and racism, have real and often significant consequences for those who are the targets of such prejudice. For example, groups of people may perform poorly on academic achievement tests simply because prevailing attitudes expect them to perform poorly. (We addressed this issue in Chapter 7, referring to the phenomenon as *stereotype threat*.) Obviously, being the target of prejudice can produce negative emotional consequences. Simply being the butt of prejudice-based jokes leads to negative feelings (Ryan & Kanjorski, 1998). In short, prejudice (even in its most seemingly benign forms) can have some serious negative consequences for its targets.

One important question that social psychologists address is the origin of prejudices. Social psychologists have identified three "roots of prejudice": personality factors, cognitive factors, and social factors. An early personality explanation suggested the individuals with an *authoritarian personality* had a tendency toward prejudice. A person with an authoritarian personality is predisposed to side with authority, has rigid beliefs,

prejudice attitudes that represent a biased, often negative, disposition toward a group of people

resistant to change, and tends to show prejudices against a wide variety of groups. Individuals who are high on the dimensions of agreeableness and openness (traits of the Big Five personality theory) show *low* levels of prejudice (Ekehammar & Akrami, 2003). Another personality dimension associated with prejudice is the **social dominance orientation**. A person with a strong social dominance orientation believes that his or her social group is superior to others (Pratto, Sidanius, Stallworth, & Malle, 1994). Pratto, et al., have found that having a strong social dominance orientation is related to specific prejudices against African Americans and Arabs. Interestingly, social dominance also relates to a more generalized prejudice directed at a wide range of minority groups (Ekehammar, Akrami, Gylje, & Zakrisson, 2004).

Personality factors provide one piece of the puzzle of explaining prejudice. However, such explanations cannot account for the range and scope of prejudice observed. Can we account for every aspect of prejudice by referring to authoritarianism or social dominance? Of course not. This is why social psychologists have explored other roots underlying prejudice. And, as we shall see next these other roots provide stronger explanations for the origins of prejudice than the personality roots just discussed.

The cognitive roots of prejudice include how we think about members of groups other than our own. One important aspect of the cognitive roots of prejudice is that we typically see the world in terms of *in-groups* and *out-groups* (Allport, 1954). An in-group includes members with characteristics similar to our own (race, gender, ethnicity, nationality, for example). We tend to have positive feelings toward members of our in-group. An out-group comprises everyone whom we see as dissimilar to us. In contrast, we generally direct negative feelings and attitudes at members of the out-group, resulting in

Courtesy of Bettmann/Corbis.

an "us versus them" characterization of the world, which fosters prejudice (Allport, 1953). It is important to understand that the tendency to separate our world into in-groups and out-groups is extremely powerful. In fact, we often make this separation based on the most minimal/trivial bases (Tajfel, 1981). Tajfel and his colleagues, for example, have found that people classify themselves into an in-group and others into an out-group after being randomly assigned to meaningless groups (e.g., overestimators or underestimators of the number of dots in an array) and behave differently towards members of the in-group and out-group in a competitive game. Imagine how powerful this effect becomes when you make in-group and out-group distinctions based on relevant social variables such as race, religion, gender or political party affiliation!

Another manifestation of the positive in-group orientation is the belief that members of the in-group are higher in "human essence," or those things that are essential to defining individuals as human beings. Conversely, members of the out-group are seen as "infrahuman," or having less human essence (Vaes et al., 2003). Human

Rosa Parks was an icon of the Civil Rights Movement in this country. She faced prejudice and discrimination head on. At a time when it was illegal for her to do so, she sat at the front of a bus in Montgomery, Alabama, refused to yield her seat to a white patron, and was arrested. It was December 1, 1955, and her actions and her arrest led to a boycott of the Montgomery bus system. In 1999, Rosa Parks was awarded the Congressional Medal of Honor, the highest honor a civilian can receive in the United States. She died on October 24, 2005, at the age of 92.

social dominance orientation the belief that one's own social group is superior to others

essence is seen as including intelligence, unique human emotions, and language (Leyens et al, 2000).

This powerful tendency to separate people into in-groups and out-groups and the corresponding tendency to vilify members of the out-group is related to the kinds of emotions that we associated with members of the in-group and out-group. Identification with the in-group is especially strong when we associate members of the in-group with something good, which carries with it positive emotion (Kessler & Hollbach, 2005). So, if a member of the in-group wins a gold medal at the Olympics or cures a dreaded disease, we tend to feel good about our group and feel a stronger bond with the in-group. Conversely, when a member of the out-group does something bad, which is associated with negative emotions, we are likely to distance ourselves from members of that out-group (Kessler & Hollbach, 2005). So, when a member of an out-group commits a crime or an act of terrorism we are likely to express negative emotions against that person *and* other members of the out-group. And, we use the positive image of the in-group as a standard against which out-groups are judged (Gawronski, Bodenhausen, & Banse, 2005). In short, the way we perceive our in-group goes a long way to determining how we perceive and act towards members of an out-group.

Another important concept in the cognitive explanation of prejudice is the use of stereotypes. A **stereotype** is a rigid set of positive or negative beliefs about a group of people, especially members of an out-group. A stereotype—perhaps based in part on reality or personal experience—leads to a rigid, over-generalized image or schema of members of that group. For example, a person may have a stereotype of NASCAR drivers as being from the South. Whether this is true, in fact, matters little; what matters is that the person develops a rigid belief that

this is the case. Stereotyping is a natural extension of our predisposition to categorize things. We categorize just about everything: A table is a piece of furniture; a dog is a mammal; a snake is not; a car is a means of transportation, and so on. We categorize based on the features we believe objects have. In much the same way, we categorize people into social categories, based on all kinds of features: skin color, gender, religion, occupation, nationality, and so on. We are using a stereotype when we react by saying, "Oh, he's one of those," whatever "those" may be.

The predisposition to categorize people becomes a problem when the features or beliefs we hold about members of a group become rigid (we are unwilling to give them up, even in the face of contrary evidence) and over-generalized (judging a person based on presumed group characteristics, rather than on individual characteristics). For example, if a person believes that women are not able to do a certain job and assumes that all women, regardless of their individual talents, are incapable of doing that job, a stereotype exists because of an over-generalization. We also develop expectations about how a person should behave based on stereotypes, and we often judge another person's behavior based on those stereotypes. For example, you may have a stereotype that older people tend to be out of shape and not fit to compete in certain extreme sporting events. Even though that stereotype is largely based on reality, on the fact that—compared to adults in their early twenties—older people are not as athletically able as they once were, the potential error, of course, is to over-generalize about all older persons. Many are superbly fit and able to compete in all sorts of athletic events. It would be just as errant to stereotype all college professors as absentminded simply because some professors are forgetful.

Like attitudes in general, stereotypes exist on two levels. An **explicit stereotype**

stereotype a rigid set of positive or negative beliefs about a group of people, particularly members of an out-group

explicit stereotype a stereotype of which we are consciously aware and which is under conscious control

is one of which we are consciously aware and which is under conscious control. For example, if a real estate agent deliberately steers an African American couple to houses in a certain neighborhood based on negative beliefs about African Americans and what they might like and not like, an explicit stereotype is at work. An **implicit stereotype** operates on an unconscious level and is activated automatically, without conscious thought (Bargh & Ferguson, 2000; Fazio & Olson, 2003). An implicit stereotype has a more subtle effect on behavior than does an explicit stereotype. For example, a white cab driver may be experiencing the influence of an implicit stereotype if he feels inexplicably uneasy about picking up a racial minority passenger at night. It is important to note, however, that both aspects of implicit stereotypes—automatic activation, and automatic application—must be present to constitute implicit stereotyping (Brauer, Wasel, & Niedenthal, 2000). For example, an implicit stereotype may be automatically activated in a situation (our cab driver's feeling of uneasiness about picking up a minority fare at night), but if the implicit stereotype is not applied or put into action (the cab driver picks up the minority fare, despite his feeling of unease), it does not result in an implicit stereotype.

Before we leave the concept of a stereotype, we need to make one important final point about this concept. Even though we have characterized a stereotype as a primarily cognitive entity, stereotypes also have an emotional component (Jussim, Nelson, Manis, & Soffin, 1995). When we categorize someone based on a stereotype we not only encode information relevant to that categorization into memory. We also encode emotional information as well. That is, stereotypes also include a powerful emotional component as well as the cognitive component. Negative stereotypes carry with them very strong negative emotions. And, research suggests that these negative emotions may actually be more important when judging members of a stereotyped group than the cognitively based information that underlies the stereotype (Jussim, et al., 1995).

Discrimination is the behavioral component of prejudice. Specifically, **discrimination** is biased, often negative, behavior directed at a member of a social group simply because of that person's group membership. If a person does not get a job simply because of her religion, gender, or age, then discrimination has occurred. It is important to note that *discrimination can occur with or without prejudice*. A property owner may not rent apartments to members of a certain ethnic group just because he harbors prejudicial attitudes against them. In this case, discriminatory behavior is clearly tied to underlying prejudicial attitudes. On the other hand, another property owner may not rent to members of that same ethnic group simply because not many of them live in that community or seek apartments to rent. This owner may have no prejudice against the ethnic group; instead, the discriminatory renting results from demographics, rather than prejudice.

The third explanation for prejudice focuses on the social factors that underlie prejudice. Changes in social norms (those unwritten rules that guide social behaviors and social interactions) have led to a reduction in the overt expression of prejudice such as racism. Social psychologists call this overt form of racism *old-fashioned racism*. Research shows a definite trend indicating that old-fashioned racism is no longer socially acceptable. In fact, the trend is in the opposite direction. Data from the *General Social Survey* (1999), for example, shows that between the years 1972 and 1996, whites have increasingly shown positive attitudes toward blacks. Compared to 1972, whites in 1996 were more willing to accept a black president, support laws preventing housing

implicit stereotype a stereotype that operates on an unconscious level and is activated automatically, without conscious thought

discrimination a biased, often negative, behavior directed at a member of a social group simply because of that person's group membership

discrimination, send their children to predominantly black schools, and support changing rules that exclude blacks from social clubs. Good news, indeed.

Do these statistics mean that racism (or other forms of prejudice) is over in the United States? Unfortunately, the answer to this question is "no." Despite the positive changes in racial attitudes and less old-fashioned racism, racism and other forms of prejudice still exist on a more subtle level. Social psychologists have noted that, even though overt expressions of prejudice are no longer prevalent, prejudicial attitudes and stereotypes still manifest themselves in less-obvious ways. This form of prejudice is called modern racism. **Modern racism** is racism that is not expressed openly, as in the past, but, rather, is manifested in an uncertainty in feelings and behaviors toward minorities. For example, a modern racist might freely and openly declare that racism is bad, but at the same time subscribe to ideas that "minorities are pushing too hard, too fast, and into places where they are not wanted" (McConahay, 1986, p. 93). A modern racist might declare that he or she is thrilled that Barack Obama can become a candidate for President of the United States, but would vote for nearly anyone who ran against him in a national election.

Another concept similar to that of modern racism is *aversive racism*

(Dovidio & Gaertner, 2000; Dovidio, Kawakami, & Gaertner, 2002). Nonprejudiced individuals who hold egalitarian attitudes may show this form of prejudice. This contemporary form of racism (and prejudice, more generally) is expressed in subtle ways. Even though aversive racism is less overt, it can impact the life of a minority person just as much as old-fashioned racism could. In an experiment that demonstrated aversive racism participants (48 white males and 64 white females) evaluated job candidates for a position at a counseling center. The candidate was portrayed alternately as having strong, weak, or ambiguous (mixed) qualifications, and as being black or white. The white participants rated the white and black candidates equally when the credentials were strong or weak. However, when the credentials were ambiguous, the white participants rated the white candidate more highly than the black candidate. When asked whether to recommend a candidate for the position, the white candidate with ambiguous credentials was more likely to be recommended than the black candidate with the same credentials. So, as long as the credentials were clearly good or bad, black and white candidates fared the same. However, aversive racism manifested itself when the credentials were ambiguous (Dovidio & Gaertner, 2000).

modern racism a variety of racism that is not expressed openly, as in the past, but rather is manifested in an uncertainty in feelings and behaviors directed toward others

BEFORE YOU GO ON

11. What are prejudice, stereotypes, and discrimination, and how are they related?
12. How are in-groups and out-groups used to define the social world and what are the consequences of this type of thinking?
13. How do implicit and explicit stereotypes influence they way we think about others and behave toward them?

A Point to Ponder or Discuss
We have made the point that dividing the world into in-groups and out-groups has serious implications for how we think about and act toward others. Find an example from current events or history that illustrates how making the distinction between in-groups and out-groups has led to or sustained prejudice and contributed to discrimination (or worse).

SPOTLIGHT
ON DIVERSITY

Attitudes Toward People with Disabilities

Nearly 50 million Americans in the civilian, noninstitutionalized population have one or more physical or mental disabilities. About 2.5 million veterans received compensation for service-related disabilities between 1990 and 2003 (U.S. Census Bureau, 2005). The Centers for Disease Control and Prevention (CDC) reports that one in five working adults has a disability (CDC, 2001). A critical factor that separates people with disabilities from other minority groups is that anyone may join at any time. Indeed, the largest segment of the population with disabilities is the elderly, most of whom are taking on the status of disabled for the first time.

The United States Census Bureau considers a person to have a disability "if he or she has difficulties performing certain functions (seeing, hearing, talking, walking, climbing stairs, and lifting and carrying), or has difficulty performing activities of daily living, or has difficulty with certain social roles (in children, doing schoolwork; in adults, working at a job or around the house). A person who is unable to perform one or more activities, or who uses an assistive device to get around, or who needs assistance from another person to perform basic activities is considered to have a severe disability" (2005). Additionally, disabilities fall into four categories: physical (requiring the use of wheelchairs, crutches, canes, braces, and the like), mental (displaying problems with learning, memory, or concentration), emotional/behavioral (exhibiting withdrawal, depression, or aggression), and sensory (having severe impairment in seeing or hearing).

Sadly, persons with disabilities often have to cope with more than just the difficulties that their disabilities present; they face negative stereotypes, discrimination, and uncharitable behaviors. This remains the case, despite federal and state laws prohibiting discrimination, and the activism of such groups as the *Independent Living Movement, American Association of People with Disabilities,* the *Human Rights Education Associates,* and the *Disability Rights Movement.*

Stereotypes are at the core of negative attitudes toward people with disabilities, and these stereotypes appear to develop early. According to Robert Funk (1987), the inferior economic and social status of disabled persons has been viewed as an inevitable consequence of the physical and mental differences imposed by disability. Funk's argument is that people often view disabled people as incompetent, and also assume that people with physical disabilities are mentally impaired. Clearly, such attitudes can have adverse effects on the social, emotional, and psychological well-being of disabled people. Rhoda Olkin is a psychotherapist and a woman with a disability. Part of her message is that individuals who are not part of the mainstream population—like those who have a disability—are traditionally seen as inferior. They are viewed as not merely different, but as damaged, not quite whole (Lorde, 1984). In addition, people with disabilities have few positive role models and experience limited positive images in the arts and the media (Olkin, 1999). In their text *Counseling Diverse Populations,* Atkinson and Hackett (2004) argue that American society predominantly views disabled people as burdens, rather than as productive members of society.

Katherine D. Seelman of the University of Pittsburgh serves as a Board Member of the Society for Disability Studies. She suggests that disability can be viewed from the perspective of four (occasionally interacting) models that provide the foundation of misperceptions and stereotypes (Seelman, 2001; Seelman & Sweeney, 1995). Her four models are detailed below:

The Traditional Model is based on reflections of cultural and religious views and practices. This model places people with disabilities on a continuum from human to nonhuman. Objective, scientific methods are simply not associated with this approach. In the extreme, a manifestation of the Traditional Model is the practice of infanticide and the rejection of disabled infants' humanity. Consistent with this model is the view that the roles assumed by people with disabilities within a given culture range from participant to pariah (Barnes & Mercer, 2003).

The Medical Model views disabled people as passive receivers of service, with their physical or mental impairment as the source of the problem. This vision results in a society that tends to segregate and separate, creating "special needs" facilities away from the mainstream of community life. The personal (or social) perspective of people with disabilities is routinely ignored in this model.

The Social Model sees handicapped people as disabled by society. In this view, the impairment is not in itself a problem, even though it may produce a need for a different set of living requirements. Rather, society's insistence on segregation in education and services, and the inaccessibility of buildings, transportation, and the like, results in a general prejudice against an integrated community life for disabled people.

The Integrative Model is a broad knowledge-based model that ranges from medicine to research findings, and is informed by the experience of people with disabilities themselves. According to Seelman (2001), the Integrative Model is "under construction," and perceives people with disabilities functioning in many roles, including citizen and patient, among others. Perhaps the major difference between this approach and the others is the vision of the disabled person as a *participant* in the determination of not only what is best for him or her, but for society as a whole.

Negative stereotypes and exclusionary practices affecting people with disabilities have a crippling effect—despite legislation to protect the legal rights of disabled persons and to mandate equal opportunity to employment, education, and public accommodations. When society's stereotypes and attitudes change so that people with disabilities can be seen as productive citizens, and when society's focus is on inclusion, rather than segregation, perhaps the needs for legislation will be lessened (Favazza, Phillipsen, & Kumar, 2000; Royal & Roberts, 1987; Shapiro, 1999).

ATTRIBUTION PROCESSES

We have discussed how social cognition help us make sense of the social context in which we live. **Attribution theory** is an excellent example of the work done by some social psychologists in this area. Such psychologists are interested in understanding the cognitions we use when we try to explain the causes or

sources of our own or others' behavior (Jones, 1990). Attribution theory has been a major theory of motivation for the past 30 years (Eccles & Wigfield, 2002). The main issue boils down to the question, "Do we tend to attribute the behaviors or events we observe in the world around us to internal or external sources, that is, to personal dispositions, or to environmental factors?"

attribution theory the attempt to understand the cognitions we use when we try to explain the causes or sources of our own and other people's behaviors

Internal and External Attributions

An **internal attribution** explains the source of a person's behavior in terms of a person's characteristic—a personality trait or disposition (for this reason, internal attributions are often called dispositional attributions). For example, if you have a friend who is chronically late, you might conclude that tardiness is a personal characteristic of this individual. There is just something about this friend's personality that tends to make him late for nearly everything. By drawing this inference, you have made an internal attribution. An **external attribution** explains a person's behavior in terms of a person's situation or context (often called situational attributions). For example, if you have a friend who is hardly ever late, you may make an external attribution if he is late once or twice by assuming that his alarm clock failed to go off, or that he got caught in heavy traffic.

We tend to rely on different types of information when making judgments about the sources of behavior. Imagine, for example, that your friend is late only when he is supposed to be at work. As far as you know, he is not late any other time. That information is useful because of its *distinctiveness* (lateness shows up only when he's dealing with work). As a result, you may take it as a signal of problems in the workplace. A second source of information is *consistency*, or how regular is the behavior pattern is observed. For example, if your friend is always late for work, he exhibits a consistent pattern of behavior, compared with someone who is late only occasionally. The final source of information is *consensus*—a question of what other people do in the same situation. If nobody else is consistently late for work, then consensus is low. If almost everyone is also late for work, then consensus is high. Compared to the other two types of assessment, consensus information tends to be underused.

Using information about distinctiveness, consensus, and consistency is important in determining the kinds of attributions we make about our own behaviors and about the behaviors of others (Kelley, 1967, 1973, 1992). The manner in which the sources of information interact determines the type of attribution you make. High consensus (everyone else is late for work), high consistency (my friend is always late), and high distinctiveness (my friend is only late for work) lead to an external attribution, e.g., it must be something about the job situation that is causing the lateness. (Perhaps the boss doesn't care if people are late for work.) On the other hand, low consensus (nobody else is late for work), high consistency (my friend is always late for work), and low distinctiveness (my friend is late for just about anything: golf games, dates, etc.) lead to an internal attribution, e.g., some characteristic of your friend causes him to be late.

Depending upon our interest, there may be two different processes involved in making attributions, (Krull & Erickson, 1995). Which attribution we use may reflect the focus of our concern or interest at the time. In some circumstances we may use a trait inference process. This is likely to be the case when we want to know about a particular person ("Just what kind of a guy is he?"). In this instance we might: a) note the person's behavior, b) draw an inference about the presence of a trait that led to the behavior, and c) revise or modify our inference or attribution as we consider the situation more fully. On the other hand, we may use a situational inference process. In that situation, our focus has shifted, and we may want to know about a particular situation ("Just what kind of a party is this?"). In this case, we reverse steps b) and c). First, a) we note a person's behavior then b) we infer that the situation has caused this behavior, and c) we revise or modify our inferences on the basis of what we know or discover about the person we observed.

internal attribution an explanation of the source of a person's behavior in terms of the person's characteristics–personality traits or dispositions

external attribution an explanation of the source of a person's behavior in terms of the situation or context in which the behavior occurs

Courtesy of Leland Bobbé/Corbis.

We see someone helping to remove litter from a public area and—given the fundamental attribution error—are likely to imagine that he or she is an active environmentalist in all regards.

The Accuracy of Attributions

As we gain experience in our social environments, we get rather good at understanding why people do what they do—and why we behave as we do. Nonetheless, it is obvious that we often err in our attributions. In many cases, such errors are of little consequence. Occasionally, however, misattributing someone's motivation can cause serious difficulties. Social psychologists can tell us quite a bit about attribution errors.

In general terms, we make attribution errors because of pre-existing cognitive biases that influence our judgments of causality. An example of such a bias is the **fundamental attribution error**—the general tendency to favor internal, personal attributions for behaviors, rather than to favor external, situational explanations (Jones, 1979). For example, if we see a man pick up a wallet that was dropped on the pavement and race half a block to return it to its owner, we might say to ourselves, "Now there's an honest man." (And, we might predict

that he will act honestly in a variety of situations.) The truth might be, however, that the fellow returned the wallet only because he knew that we saw him pick it up. If no one else was around, the wallet might not have been returned. Again, the fundamental attribution error is the tendency to disregard, or discount, situational factors in favor of internal, dispositional factors when we make inferences about the causes of behaviors. As it happens, the fundamental attribution error can be a powerful bias. Even when we are told of situational factors that determined someone's behaviors, we are likely to stick to our belief that what we saw had to do with the person and not the situation. For example, if we read a position paper in favor of gun-control legislation, we may jump to conclusions about the person who wrote the paper. Curiously, if we are then told that the paper was written only as an assignment and does not reflect the writer's actual feelings about gun control, we probably will hold on to our internal attribution, thinking something like "If she didn't really feel that way, she could not have written such a good paper." (McClure, 1998).

Many attribution biases, such as the fundamental attribution error, may be more common in Western cultures (Choi, Nisbett, & Norenzayan, 1999; Morris & Peng, 1998; Norenzayan & Nisbett, 2000). East Asians, for example, are more likely to be affected by situational information when making predictions about other's behaviors Norenzayan, Choi, & Nisbett, 2002). People from India also tend to make fewer dispositional attributions than Americans (Millen 1984). Indians are more likely than Americans to explain behavior in terms of the situation or the environment than in terms of personality traits, abilities, or inabilities.

There are several biases that lead us to make incorrect attributions about others or ourselves. One is **the just world**

---

fundamental attribution error the general tendency to favor internal, personal, attributions rather than favoring external, situational explanations

just world hypothesis an error in which people believe that we live in a world where good things happen to good people and bad things happen to bad people

hypothesis, in which people believe that we live in a world where good things happen only to good people, and bad things happen only to bad people (Lerner, 1965). It is a sort of "everybody gets what they deserve" mentality. We see this bias (or fallacy) when we hear people claim that victims of rape "asked for it by the way they dressed and acted." In fact, even the victims of rape sometimes engage in self-blame in an attempt to understand the random nature of the crime (Arata & Burkhart, 1998; Montada & Lerner, 1998).

Another bias that affects our attributions is the **self-serving bias**. It occurs when we attribute successes–or positive outcomes–to personal, internal sources, and failures–or negative outcomes–to situational, external sources (Harvey & Weary, 1984; Miller & Ross, 1975). We tend to think that we do well because we are able, talented, and hardworking. However, when we do poorly, we tend to hold someone or something else responsible for our failure. For example, if we are happy with the results of painting a room, we might say, "Boy, I did a great job painting that room!" But if we are unhappy with the results, we might say, "That room turned out shoddy because the paint was cheap and the brush was old." The process is at work in our social groups, as well. If someone in our group (be it ethnic, cultural, social, or gender) succeeds, we are likely to attribute that success to an internal, personal effort or ability. If someone outside our group succeeds, we are likely to attribute that success to the situation (Finchilescu, 1994). Some cognitive theorists argue that depression often can be explained as a failure to apply the self-serving bias. That is, some people get into the habit of blaming themselves for failures and negative outcomes, regardless of where the real blame resides and regardless of whether there even is any blame to attribute. The self-serving bias is also in operation as individuals work

toward establishing close relationships with others. In this variety, we see what is called *self-presentation* (Rusbult & Van Lange, 2003). It amounts to purposively presenting one's self in a (hopefully) favorable way, even if doing so is deceptive (Leary, 2001; Tice et al., 1995). When Rick (who would really much rather go camping in the mountains) professes to Gayle his love of vacationing at the beach, Rick is displaying a self-presentation bias. Such distortions are much more likely to occur early in a relationship's formation.

Yet another attribution error is the **actor-observer bias** (Jones & Nisbett, 1971; Monson & Snyder, 1977). This is a discrepancy between the way we explain our behaviors (as actor) and the way we explain someone else's (as observer). Generally, we use external attributions when we talk about why we do things. When we explain someone else's behaviors, we are more likely to use internal attributions and refer to characteristics of the person: e.g., "I took that class because the instructor is excellent," versus "He took that class because he's so lazy"; "I am dating Trevor because he's so caring and considerate," versus "She's dating him only because she wants to be seen with an athlete"; "I went there because the rates were lower than anyplace else," versus "He went there because he wanted to show off." That we explain our own behaviors differently than we explain the behaviors of others is not surprising. For one thing, we have more information about ourselves (and our own past experiences) than we do about anyone else. In fact, the more information we have about someone, the less likely we are to use internal attributions to explain his or her behaviors. And, in any case, the actor gets a different view of what is happening than does the observer; that is, actors and observers attempt to attribute the causes of behavior on the basis of different information.

self-serving bias occurs when we attribute successes (positive outcomes) to personal, internal sources, and failures (negative outcomes) to situational, external sources

actor-observer bias a discrepancy between the way we explain our behaviors (as actor) and the way we explain someone else's (as observer)

INTERPERSONAL ATTRACTION

In the context of social cognition, we now turn to the topic of **interpersonal attraction**—a positive, favorable, and powerful attitude toward another person. Interpersonal attraction reflects the extent to which someone has formed positive feelings and beliefs about another person and is prepared to act on those affects and cognitions.

Theories of Interpersonal Attraction

Social psychologists have put forth several theoretical models to account for interpersonal attraction. Here we briefly review four such theories.

The simplest is the **reinforcement-affect model** (Clore & Byrne, 1974; Lott & Lott, 1974). This approach states that we are attracted to (have positive attitudes toward) people whom we associate with rewarding experiences. It also follows that we tend not to be attracted to those we associate with punishment. One implication of this viewpoint is that you will like your instructor, and seek him or her out for future classes, if you get (or earn) a high grade in his or her class.

Another popular—and classic—theory of interpersonal attraction is **social exchange theory** (Kelley & Thibault,

1978; Thibault & Kelley, 1959). According to this approach, what matters most is a comparison of the costs and benefits of establishing or maintaining a relationship. Leslie may judge John to be attractive, but feel that entering into a relationship with him is not worth the grief she would get from friends and family, who believe that John is lazy and untrustworthy. On the other hand, if Leslie has recently gone through a series of failed relationships with other men who were not physically attractive, she might take a chance on John, judging (in her frustration) that he is worth it. This theory takes into account a series of comparative judgments made in social situations. Being attracted to someone else is not just a matter of asking, "Is this a good thing?" It is more a matter of considering, "Is the reward I might get from this relationship worth the potential cost, and what other alternatives exist at the moment?"

A third approach to interpersonal attraction is equity theory, which is really more an extension of social exchange theory, than a departure from it (Greenberg & Cohen, 1982). **Equity theory** considers the appraisal of rewards and costs for both parties of a social relationship. You may feel a relationship is worth the effort you have been putting into it, for example, but if your relationship partner does not feel the same, the relationship is in danger. Likewise, if one person feels that he or she is getting

---

interpersonal attraction
a positive, favorable, and powerful attitude toward another person

reinforcement-affect model
the position that we are attracted to people with whom we associate rewarding experiences

equity theory a position that considers the appraisal of rewards and costs for both parties of a social relationship

social exchange theory
the position that, with regard to interpersonal attraction, what matters most is a comparison of costs and benefits of establishing or maintaining a relationship

more from a relationship than is deserved (on the basis of costs and rewards), the relationship is not equitable and is in jeopardy. What matters is that both (or all) members of a relationship feel they are getting a fair deal (equity). The best relationships are those in which all members receive an equal ratio of rewards to costs.

Another approach to understanding interpersonal relationships is based on feelings or affect more than on cognitions. This model is referred to as **attachment theory** (Berseheid, 1994; Waters et al., 2000). It suggests that interpersonal relationships can be classified into one of three types—secure, avoidant, or anxious/ambivalent—depending on the attitudes one has about such relationships (from Shaver, Hazan, & Bradshaw, 1988, p. 80):

Secure: "I find it relatively easy to get close to others, and am comfortable depending on them and having them depend on me. I don't often worry about being abandoned or about someone getting too close to me."

Avoidant: "I am somewhat uncomfortable being close to others; I find it difficult to trust them completely, and difficult to allow myself to depend on them. I get nervous when anyone gets too close, and partners often want me to be more intimate than I feel comfortable being."

Anxious/ambivalent: "I find that others are reluctant to get as close as I would like to be. I often worry that my partner doesn't really love me or won't stay with me. I want to merge completely with another person, and this desire sometimes scares people away."

One of the things that makes attachment theory appealing is evidence that suggests a person's attachment style is remarkably stable throughout their life (Waters et al., 2000). It may be that the types of interpersonal relationships we form as adults, are influenced by the types of attachments we developed as young children.

Finally, we should remind you of a point we discussed in the context of mate selection: Few people enter into relation-

Courtesy of Cultura/Corbis.

ships having carefully considered all of the factors these models imply. That is, assessments of reinforcement, exchange, or equity value are seldom made at a conscious level; and it is unlikely we purposely seek out relationships that mirror those we had in childhood.

Factors Affecting Interpersonal Attraction

Having reviewed four general models of interpersonal attraction, let us now look at some empirical evidence. What tends to determine your attraction to someone? What factors provide those rewards, or positive reward/cost ratios, that serve as the basis for strong relationships? We'll consider four common determinants of attraction: reciprocity, proximity, physical attractiveness, and similarity.

Reciprocity, our first principle, is perhaps the most obvious: We tend to value and like people who like and value us (Backman & Secord, 1959; Curtis & Miller, 1986). We noted when discussing operant conditioning that the attention of others can be a powerful reinforcer. This is particularly true if the attention is positive, supportive, or affectionate. The value of someone else caring for us is particularly strong when that someone else initially seemed to

There are many reasons why people are likely to be attracted to each other, and similarity—including similarity in physical attractiveness—is a powerful one.

attachment theory the position that interpersonal relationships can be classified into one of three types: secure, avoidant, or anxious/ambivalent, depending upon the attitudes one has about that relationship

have neutral or negative attitudes toward us. In other words, we are most attracted to people who like us now, but who didn't originally.

Our second principle, *proximity,* suggests that physical closeness can yield attraction. Sociologists, as well as your own experience, will tell you that people tend to establish friendships (and romances) with others with whom they have grown up, worked, or gone to school. Residents of apartments or dormitories, for example, tend to become friends with residents living closest to them (Festinger et al., 1950). Being around others gives us the opportunity to discover who does and doesn't provide the interpersonal rewards we seek in friendship.

The Internet has forced psychologists to reconsider the definition of proximity. Physical closeness is becoming less important as it becomes more possible to communicate with someone halfway around the world as if he or she were right next door. The Internet brings people close together interpersonally and psychologically, if not physically. Research shows that people do use the Internet to form close personal relationships (McCown, Fischer, Page, & Homant, 2001) and that these relationships are as important and as stable offline, face-to-face relationships (McKenna, Green, & Gleason, 2002). We should note that there are differences between Internet and face-to-face relationships. One study, for example, found that traditional, face-to-face relationships were more interdependent and showed greater depth and breadth of communication than Internet relationships (Chan & Cheng, 2004). Additionally, traditional, face-to-face relationships are associated with low levels of social loneliness (associated with having friends and meaningful relationships) and emotional loneliness (an empty feeling associated with a lack of intimate relationships), whereas Internet relationships are associated with low levels of social loneliness but higher levels of emotional loneliness (Moody, 2001). So, the Internet may enhance social interaction while decreasing emotional well-being (Moody, 2001).

Physical attractiveness is a factor that has an important effect on interpersonal attraction and mate selection. Social psychologists have consistently found evidence of an "attractiveness bias," predicting that people form more positive attributions about attractive individuals. But, what exactly constitutes physical attractiveness? Granted, a great deal of attractiveness is "in the eye of the beholder," but there is some regularity to the quality we call attractiveness. Male attractiveness is most closely tied to the waist-to-chest ratio, yielding an inverted triangle shape. Females tend to find men who have broad shoulders and a narrow waist attractive (Maisey et al, 1999). Female attractiveness is tied to two factors: Body mass index (BMI) and waist-to-hip ratio (WHR). Normal weight women (with lower BMIs) are generally seen as more attractive than overweight women (with higher BMIs). In addition, women with lower WHRs typically are rated as more attractive (Weeden & Sabini, 2005). Characteristics that define physical attractiveness may be fairly consistent across cultures. For example, Gitter, Lomranz, and Saxe (1982) investigated how American and Israeli men and women evaluated people with various body shapes and found that men and women from both cultures rated individuals with large, protruding waistlines as the most unattractive. And, believe it or not, individuals from nine cultures agreed that small feet on women and average-sized feet on men helped define physical attractiveness (Fessler et al., 2005). Facial symmetry is another factor contributing to the perception of physical attractiveness (Cardenas & Harris, 2006). Generally, the more symmetrical the face, the more attractive it is perceived to be. An asymmetrical facial configuration is not only associated with lower ratings of physical attractiveness, but also with perceived negative characteristics such as neuroticism and being less agreeable as a person (Noor & Evans, 2003).

The power of physical attractiveness in the context of dating was demonstrated experimentally in a classic study directed by Elaine Walster (Walster et al., 1966). University of Minnesota freshmen completed several psychological tests as part of an orientation program. Students were then randomly paired with dates for an orientation dance, during which they took a break and evaluated their assigned partners. The researchers hoped to uncover intricate and subtle facts about interpersonal attraction, such as which personality traits might mesh to produce interest and closeness. As it turned out, none of these psychological factors was important. The impact of physical attractiveness was so powerful that it wiped out all other effects. For men and for women, the more physically attractive their date, the more they liked that date and the more they wanted to date her or him again. Many studies of physical attractiveness have followed Walster's lead. Some gave participants a chance to pick a date from a group of several potential partners (using descriptions or pictures). Not surprisingly, participants almost always selected the most attractive person to be their date (Reis et al., 1980).

One recent study suggests that physical attractiveness may be a more powerful factor for males than for females (Todd, et al., 2007). These researchers used a speed dating session where participants have "mini dates" with as many as 30 people in succession, with each "date" lasting only three to seven minutes. After each date, they check a box to indicate whether they want to see that person again. Before the session began, most participants said that they were looking for someone whose values and interests were similar to their own. However, during the speed dating session, men chose women who were physically attractive while women were drawn to wealth and security.

We seldom have the luxury of asking for a date without the possibility of being turned down. When experiments added the possibility of rejection, an interesting effect emerged: People no longer chose the most attractive candidate, but selected partners whose level of physical attractiveness was more similar to their own. This is called the **matching phenomenon**, and it occurs in both physical attractiveness and social status. Even when we consider relationships between or among friends of the same sex, we find that they tend to be similar when rated for physical attractiveness. Thus, our fourth determinant of interpersonal attraction is *similarity*. Simply put, the more similar another person is to you, the more you will tend to like that person, and the more likely you are to believe that person likes you. We also tend to be repelled, or put off, by persons we believe to be dissimilar to us. Opposites may occasionally attract, but similarity is probably the glue that holds together romances and friendships over time. A recent study (Lee et al., 2008) has confirmed the power of similarity as a factor in forming relationships. As valued as physical attractiveness may be for someone choosing a dating or mating partner, the overriding tendency is for people to choose others of essentially the same level of attractiveness for a partner (e.g., Todd et al, 2007). Moreover, when less attractive individuals choose a less attractive person for dating, they know very well what they are doing. When less attractive people "accept less attractive others as dating partners, they do not delude themselves into thinking that these less attractive others are, in fact, more physically attractive than they really are" (Lee et al., 2008, p. 675).

Why is similarity so important? Similarity enhances attraction because, through a process of *social comparison*, we can have our attitudes and beliefs verified by others. Such verification is immensely rewarding.

Recall that the reinforcement-affect model tells us that we like things that are associated with reward. So the rewards we derive from others verifying our attitudes serves to strengthen our attraction to those people. Similarity

matching phenomenon the observation that people select partners whose level of physical attractiveness is similar to their own

also enhances attraction because we believe that we can predict how a similar person will act in social situations. This predictability is rewarding and, thus, enhances attraction. Finally, we are likely to believe that people who are similar to us will like us back—again, a source of interpersonal reward. Being liked by another person is, for most of us, very rewarding.

BEFORE YOU GO ON

18. Briefly describe four theories of interpersonal attraction.
19. Summarize some of the factors known to influence such attraction.

A Point to Ponder or Discuss
Reflecting on those persons to whom you are most attracted, which theory, or which factors affecting interpersonal attraction, do you feel are most relevant to your choices?

CONFORMITY

One of the most direct forms of social influence occurs when we modify our behavior, under perceived pressure to do so, to make it consistent with the behavior of others, a process referred to as **conformity**. Although we often think of conformity in a negative way, it is natural and often desirable. Conformity helps make social behaviors efficient and, at least to a degree, predictable.

When he began his research on conformity, Solomon Asch believed that people were not terribly susceptible to social pressure in situations that are clear-cut and unambiguous. Asch thought an individual would behave independently of group pressure when there was little doubt that his or her own judgments were accurate. He developed an interesting technique for testing his hypothesis (Asch, 1951, 1956).

A participant in Asch's experiments joined a group seated around a table. In the original study, the group consisted of seven people. Unknown to the participant, six of the people in the group were confederates of the experimenter; they were "in" on what was happening. The real participant was told that the study dealt with the ability to make perceptual judgments. The participant had

to do nothing more than decide which of three lines was the same length as a standard line (Figure 14.3). The experimenter showed each set of lines to the group and collected responses, one by one, from each member of the group. There were 18 sets of lines to judge, and the real participant was always the last one to respond.

Each judgment involved clearly unambiguous stimuli: The correct answer was obvious. On 12 of the 18 trials, however, the confederates gave a unanimous, but incorrect, answer. What would the "real" participants do? How would they resolve this conflict? Their eyes were telling them what the right answer was, but the group was saying something else.

The results of his first study surprised even Asch. When confederates gave wrong answers, conformity occurred 37 percent of the time. That is, the participants responded with an incorrect answer, agreeing with the majority on more than one-third of the trials. Moreover, three-quarters of Asch's participants conformed to the group pressure at least once.

Based on post-experimental interviews, Asch determined that participants conformed or remained independent for a variety of reasons. He categorized par-

conformity the modification of behavior, under perceived pressure to do so, to make it consistent with the behavior of others

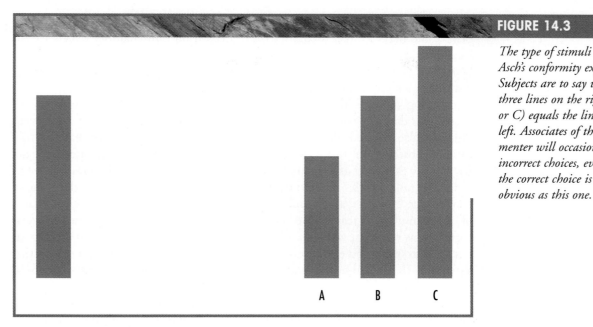

FIGURE 14.3

The type of stimuli used in Asch's conformity experiments. Subjects are to say which of the three lines on the right (A, B, or C) equals the line on the left. Associates of the experimenter will occasionally make incorrect choices, even though the correct choice is always as obvious as this one.

ticipants as yielding or independent. He found that some participants, although very few, yielded because they had come to accept the majority's judgments as correct. Most participants yielded because they did not have adequate confidence in their own judgments. Some yielded because they did not want to appear to be defective in the eyes of the confederates. These individuals knew the majority was wrong, but went along anyway. Independent participants also fell into three categories. Some people in the study remained independent because they knew the majority was wrong and had adequate confidence in their own judgments. Others maintained their independence because they felt a strong personal need to do so. These individuals might be called non-conformists, or even anti-conformists. The final group of independent participants remained independent simply because they wanted to perform well on the task. This latter reason for being independent has been noted by other researchers, who also claim that the appearance of accountability supports independence. That is, not only do some people want to do well on a task, but they also will stay independent in their judgments if they feel that they will

be held accountable in any way for their performance (Cialdini & Goldstein, 2004; Quinn & Schlenker, 2002).

In subsequent studies, Asch tried several variations of his original procedure. In one experiment, he varied the size of the unanimous, incorrect majority. As you might expect, the level of conformity increased as the size of the majority increased, leveling off at three or four people (Asch, 1956; Knowles, 1983). Participants gave incorrect judgments only 4 percent of the time when just one other incorrect judgment preceded their own. In another experiment, Asch found that participants gave an erroneous judgment only 10 percent of the time when only one dissenter among the six confederates voiced an accurate judgment before the participants gave theirs. In other words, when the participants had any social support for what their eyes had told them, they tended to trust their own judgment. This is known as the *true partner effect*. If the true partner withdrew his or her support, conformity returned to its previous rate.

Several factors have been found to affect the amount of conformity observed. If you believe that the majority facing you is highly competent, you are more likely to conform than if you believe the majority is less competent. Imagine participating in this study and being told that all the participants were draftsmen or engineers and that you were filling in for someone who was absent that day. The nature of the stimulus task also affected the level of conformity observed in this experiment. Remember that Asch used a simple line judgment task, which had a clearly correct answer. However, as the ambiguity of the stimulus increases, conformity increases, as well. The *autokinetic effect* is a good example of a truly ambiguous situation. In an otherwise darkened room, a pinpoint source of light appears to move. It is a very compelling illusion, one you can easily demonstrate for yourself. In a conformity task, participants are asked to estimate the direction and extent of the light's movement. Just one other person saying, "Oh look; there it goes to the left—about three feet" will prompt significant agreement. In fact, Sherif (1936) found a 70 percent conformity rate in just such an experiment. When attitude items are used for which there is no clear "correct" answer, conformity rates also approach 70 percent (Crutchfield, 1955).

In the classic film *Twelve Angry Men* a juror played by Henry Fonda was convinced that the defendant in a trial was innocent. His eleven fellow jurors believed just the opposite. As the story unfolds, Fonda convinces the other jurors, one by one, that the defendant is actually innocent, and the jury eventually finds the defendant not guilty. In this film, Fonda's character acts in a manner opposite of what we would predict from Asch's conformity research. He should have conformed to the overwhelming pressure of the majority. As it happens, in real life, with an 11:1 split in favor of guilt, the likelihood of conviction is close to 100 percent (Kalven & Zeisel, 1966). Does this mean that a minority can never influence a majority? Not really, as we shall see next.

While American social psychologists focused on how majority effects work, European social psychologists studied minority influence. Moscovici, Lage and Naffrechoux (1969) conducted an experiment that was very similar to Asch's. In this experiment, however, things were reversed. Instead of the majority being confederates of the experimenter, the minority was made up of two confederates. It was the minority that made errors on critical trials. The researchers found that the incorrect minority influenced real participants in the minority on 8.42 percent of the critical trials, compared to only .025 percent of control trials. Later research has confirmed that a minority can influence a majority, especially if some conditions are met. First, the minority must be consistent in its position (as Henry Fonda portrayed in *Twelve Angry Men*). Consistent minorities are likely to be viewed as less willing to compromise their position (Wolf, 1979). Second, although the minority must be consistent, they also must be flexible and willing to consider the arguments made by the majority (Mugny, 1975). An inflexible, intransigent minority causes the majority to dig in their heels. Third, the minority will be most effective if they adopt a "negotiating style" in which they show willingness to compromise.

You will not be surprised to learn that there are predictable cultural differences in the conformity to group pressures. In those cultures characterized as *collectivist*, in which the individual normally serves the group rather than self (largely Asian, and many Middle-Eastern cultures), conformity scores are much higher than in Western, *individualistic* cultures (e.g., Bond & Smith, 1996).

Conformity involves yielding to the perceived pressure of a group. In most cases, it is assumed, group members are peers, or at least similar to the conformer. When someone yields to the pressure of a perceived authority, the result is obedience. It is to this issue we turn next.

BEFORE YOU GO ON

20. What is conformity, and how was it demonstrated by Solomon Asch?

A Point to Ponder or Discuss
In what sorts of social situations does conformity tend to lead to negative outcomes, and in what situations might it lead to positive outcomes?

OBEDIENCE TO AUTHORITY

Adolph Eichmann, considered to be the "architect" of the Holocaust during World War II, was captured by Israeli agents in 1961. He was brought to Israel, and placed on trial for crimes against humanity. Eichmann's principal defense was that he was only a mid-level officer, a simple administrator, who was "just following orders." It was his contention that he organized the trainloads of Jews sent to concentration camps and the gas chambers at the behest of individuals who had the power to inflict punishment if he did not obey their orders. Is "just following orders" a legitimate excuse? As we saw in the section on attribution, our predisposition is to attribute such behaviors internally. As a result, in the minds of many, Eichmann becomes an inhuman monster, not a human being caught up in a highly unusual social situation. Which is it? Was Eichmann an evil monster, or a victim of circumstances?

This question intrigued Yale University social psychologist Stanley Milgram (1933–1984). Milgram had been a student of Solomon Asch and was interested in the conditions that lead to conformity. The participants in Asch's studies took the experimental procedures seriously, but consequences of either conforming or maintaining independence were rather trivial. At worst, they might have experienced some discomfort as a result of voicing independent judgments. There were no external rewards or punishments for their behavior, and there was no one telling them how to respond. Milgram went beyond Asch's procedure to see if an ordinary person placed in an extraordinary situation would obey an authority figure and inflict pain on an innocent victim. Milgram's research, conducted in the early 1960s, has become among the most famous and controversial in all of psychology. His experiments pressured participants to comply with the demands of an authority figure. Those demands were both unreasonable and troubling (Milgram, 1963, 1965, 1974).

All of Milgram's studies involved the same procedure. Participants arrived at the laboratory to find they would be participating with a second person (a confederate of the experimenter). The experimenter explained that the research

Obedience to authority is not always a bad thing. Although there are clear limits, the military relies on the process of following orders.

Courtesy of Leif Skoogfors/Corbis.

dealt with the effects of punishment on learning and that one participant would serve as a "teacher," while the other would act as a "learner." The roles were assigned by a rigged drawing in which the actual participant was always assigned the role of teacher, while the confederate was always the learner. The participant watched as the learner was taken into a room and wired to electrodes to be used for delivering punishment in the form of electric shocks.

After the teacher received a sample shock of 45 volts, just to see what the shocks felt like, the teacher received his instructions. He was to read to the learner a list of four pairs of words. The teacher was then to read the first word of one of the pairs, and the learner was to supply the second word. The teacher sat in front of a rather imposing electric "shock generator" that had 30 switches. From left to right, the switches increased by increments of 15 volts, ranging from 15 to 450 volts. Labels were printed under the switches, ranging from "Slight" to "Moderate" to "Extreme Intensity" to "Danger: Severe Shock." The label at the 450-volt end read "XXX."

As the task proceeded, the learner periodically made errors according to a prearranged schedule. The teacher had been instructed to deliver an electric shock for every incorrect answer. With each error, the teacher was to move up the scale of shocks, giving the learner a more potent shock with each new mistake. (The learner, remember, was part of the act, and no one was actually receiving any shocks.)

When the teacher hesitated or questioned whether he should continue, the experimenter was ready with a verbal prod, "Please continue," or "The experiment requires that you continue." If the participant protested, the experimenter became more assertive and offered an alternative prod, such as, "You have no choice; you must go on."

Milgram was astonished by the results of his study, and the results still amaze us. Twenty-six of Milgram's 40 participants—65 percent—obeyed the demands of the experimenter and went all the way to the highest shock, closing all the switches. In fact, no participant stopped prior to the 300-volt level, the point at which the learner pounded on the wall in protest. One later variation of this study added vocal responses from the learner, who delivered an increasingly stronger series of demands to be let out of the experiment. The level of obedience in this study was still unbelievably high, as 25 of 40 participants—62.5 percent— continued to administer shocks to the 450-volt level. As shown in Figure 14.4, the level of obedience decreased as the distance between the "teacher" and

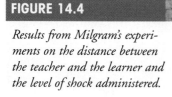

FIGURE 14.4

Results from Milgram's experiments on the distance between the teacher and the learner and the level of shock administered.

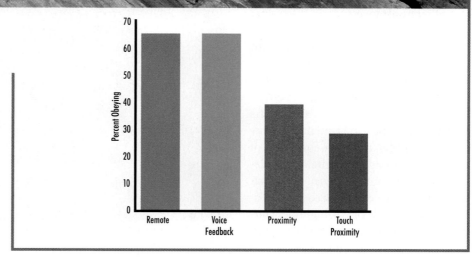

"learner" decreased. Obedience dropped when the teacher and learner were in the same room (proximity). The lowest levels of obedience were observed when the teacher was required to physically force the learner's hand onto a shock plate device (touch proximity).

The behavior of Milgram's participants indicated that they were concerned about the learner. All participants claimed that they experienced genuine and extreme stress in this situation. Some fidgeted, some trembled, many perspired profusely. Several giggled nervously. In short, the people caught up in this situation showed obvious signs of conflict and anxiety. Nonetheless, they continued to obey the orders of the experimenter, even though they had good reason to believe they might be harming the learner. A reanalysis of audiotapes made during Milgram's study was conducted in 2000 (Rochat, Maggioni, & Modigliana, 2000). This study suggested that participants were much more concerned about the learner than even Milgram may have believed. The researchers heard protests from teachers and defiant resistance to continuing, fairly early in the shock-generation process. Even by the 150-volt level of shock, nearly half of the teachers stopped to check with the experimenter to be reassured that they were doing the right thing.

Milgram's first study was performed with male participants, ranging in age from 20 to 50. A replication with adult women produced precisely the same results: 65 percent obeyed fully. Other variations of the procedure uncovered several factors that could reduce the amount of obedience. Putting the learner and teacher in the same room or having the experimenter deliver orders over the telephone, rather than in person, reduced levels of obedience markedly. When the shocks were to be delivered by a team made up of the participant and two confederates who refused to give the shocks, full-scale obedience dropped to only 10 percent. Obedience also was extremely low if there were conflicting authority figures, one urging the teacher to continue delivering shocks and the other urging the participant to stop. When given the choice, participants obeyed the authority figure who said to stop.

Although Milgram's first study on obedience was published more than 45 years ago, couple of recent studies have replicated his results and provided a few additional insights. A re-analysis of Milgram's data by Dominic Parker of Ohio State University (2008) tells us that of those participants who were disobedient and stopped administering shocks, most did so when shock levels reached the 150-volt level—when the "learner" began to protest, with statements such as, "Stop, let me out! I don't want to do this anymore." It was at this point that some participants perceived the learner's right to terminate the experiment, as overriding the experimenter's orders to continue. Once past the 150-volt level, however, the learner's escalating expressions of pain had little effect. Those who continued felt that the responsibility for the learner's condition was then the experimenter's and not theirs. A partial replication of Milgram's basic experimental design (shock levels never exceeded the 150-volt level) found (virtually) the same obedience/disobedience rates as reported by Milgram (Burger, 2008). This was true in the replication even though learners were repeatedly and explicitly told that they could leave the study at any time. In addition, participants were aware that the experimenter had given this same assurance to the confederate/learner.

Attribution Errors and a Word of Caution

Upon learning about these distressing results, many people tend to think of Milgram's obedient participants as unfeeling, unusual, or even downright cruel and sadistic people. Nothing could be further from the truth. The participants were truly troubled by what was happening. If you thought

Milgram's participants must be strange or different, perhaps you were a victim of the *fundamental attribution error*. You were willing to attribute the participants' behaviors to internal personality characteristics, instead of recognizing the powerful situational forces at work. It is on this point that several have noted a significant difference between the participants in Milgram's research and the behaviors of many people involved in the Holocaust. Whereas all of Milgram's participants were emotionally and attitudinally in opposition to the orders they were given, many of the Holocaust atrocities were committed willingly, even eagerly (Berkowitz, 1999; Goldhagen, 1996).

Attributing evil personality characteristics to Milgram's teachers is particularly understandable in light of the unexpected nature of the results. Commenting on this research, psychologists have suggested that perhaps the most significant aspect of Milgram's findings is that they are so surprising. Milgram asked people, including a group of psychiatrists and a group of ministers, to predict what *they* would do under these circumstances, and asked them to predict how far others would go before refusing the authority. Respondents predicted very little obedience, expecting practically no one to proceed all the way to the final switch on the shock generator.

In terms of attributing causes to obedient behaviors, consider some research on obedience in the cockpit of airliners (Turnow, 2000). The captain of an aircraft is a person of authority, and what he or she says or does during a flight is seldom questioned or challenged. This nearly blind obedience to the authority of the pilot, however, may lead to disaster. Turnow's report concluded that the failure of non-flying crew members (e.g., the co-pilot) to monitor and challenge an error made by the pilot occurs in about 80 percent of all airline accidents! No one in this

scenario is likely to be viewed as evil. In fact, "most organizations would cease to operate efficiently if deference to authority were not one of the prevailing norms" (Cialdini & Goldstein, 2004, p. 596). Unfortunately, this accepted norm of "following orders" is so well entrenched in some organizations that orders are regularly carried out by subordinates with little regard for possible negative ethical consequences (Ashford & Anand, 2003; Darley, 2001; Peterson & Dietz, 2000).

Does this discussion mean that all acts of obedience that harm others are due to situational circumstances and not to internal characteristics of the perpetrator? No, it doesn't. Social psychologists have recently started exploring the concept of evil and some have concluded that there are instances of obedient behavior that are driven by internal motives more than circumstances (Calder, 2003). For example, Zimbardo (2004) defines evil as "intentionally behaving, or causing others to act, in ways that demean, dehumanize, harm, destroy or kill innocent people" (p. 22). Under this definition, a wide range of behaviors including terrorism, genocide, and even corporate misdeeds could be considered evil (Zimbardo, 2004). It may be that an individual carries out an evil act (e.g., genocide) because of an evil character, whereas others do so at the behest of others. Todd Calder (2003) makes an interesting distinction between two types of individuals who carry out evil deeds. *Moral monsters* are individuals who carry out evil deeds on their own without direction from anyone else. Moral monsters are driven more internally than by external circumstances. *Moral idiots* are individuals who perform evil deeds in response to directions or orders from someone else. These people may have a legitimate claim to "just following orders," a common defense of those who are called to account for their evil deeds.

A Reminder about Ethics in Research

In reading about Milgram's research, it should have occurred to you that putting people in such a stressful situation could be considered ethically objectionable. Milgram, himself, was concerned with the welfare of his participants, and he took great care to debrief them fully after each session. He informed them that they had not really administered any shocks, and explained why deception had been used. It is, of course, standard practice in psychological experiments to conclude the session by disclosing the true purpose of the study and alleviating any anxiety that might have arisen.

Milgram reported that, after debriefing, the people in his studies were not upset at having been deceived. Their principal reaction was one of relief when they learned that no electric shock had been used. Milgram indicated that a follow-up study done a year later with some of the same participants showed no long-term adverse effects had been created by his procedure. Despite his precautions, Milgram was severely criticized for placing people in such an extremely stressful situation. One of the effects of his research was to establish in the scientific community a higher level of awareness of the need to protect the wellbeing of human research participants.

BEFORE YOU GO ON

21. What do social psychologists mean by "obedience," and how was such obedience demonstrated in the laboratory by Milgram?
22. How can we account for "evil" deeds that we have seen carried out throughout history? Are these deeds perpetrated by evil people or are those people victims of circumstances?

A Point to Ponder or Discuss

If you can find people who have not heard of Milgram's study, describe to them the procedures that were used, and ask them to estimate how many "teachers" they think would administer the highest level of shock. How do your results compare with Milgram's?

BYSTANDER INTERVENTION

On March 13, 1964, a New York City cocktail waitress, Kitty Genovese, was brutally murdered in front of her apartment building as she returned from work about 3:30 in the morning. Her assailant was Winston Moseley, whose only motivation that night was to kill a woman. What made this murder so noteworthy was that around 38 of Genovese's neighbors were aware of what was happening to her over the course of about an hour.

Although most of the "witnesses" did not actually see what was happening, they were aware of it. And, some did directly witness her being stabbed. It is astonishing to think that a young woman was brutally slain and nobody came to her aid. This tragic event stimulated public concern and sparked much commentary in the media. People wondered how all those witnesses could have shown such a lack of concern for another human being. *Apathy* and *alienation* were terms used to describe what had happened. The Kitty Genovese case was certainly not the first such incident of bystanders watching without intervening, nor was it the last. What makes it special—what gets it into psychology textbooks—is that the *New York Times* story of the Genovese murder caught the attention of Bibb Latané and John Darley, two social psychologists who, at the time, were at universities in New York City.

They were not satisfied that terms such as *bystander apathy* or *alienation* adequately explained what happened in the Genovese case. They were not willing to attribute people's failure to help to internal, dispositional, or personality factors. They were convinced that situational factors made such events possible. Latané and Darley (1970) pointed out that there were logical reasons to explain why people would not offer help in an emergency. Emergencies tend to happen quickly and without warning. Except for medical technicians, firefighters, and a few other select categories of individuals, people are not prepared to deal with emergencies when they arise. In fact, one good predictor of who will intervene in an emergency is that person's previous experience with a similar emergency situation (Cramer et al., 1988).

A Cognitive Model of Bystander Intervention

Latané and Darley (1968) suggested that a series of cognitive events must occur before a bystander can intervene in an emergency (Figure 14.5). First, the bystander must *notice* what is going on. A window-shopper who fails to see someone collapse on the opposite side of the street cannot be expected to rush over and offer assistance. Second, if a bystander does notice something happen, he or she must *label* the situation as an emergency (perhaps the person who collapsed is simply drunk or tired and not really having a stroke or a heart attack). Third, the bystander must make the *decision* that it is his or her (and not someone else's) responsibility to do something.

Even after these conditions are met—the bystander noticed something happening, labeled the situation as one calling for action, and assumed responsibility for helping—he or she must still decide what form of assistance to offer. Should he or she try to give first aid? Should he or she try to find the nearest telephone, or simply start shouting for

FIGURE 14.5

Some of the decisions and outcomes involved as a bystander considers intervening in an emergency situation (Latané & Darley, 1968).

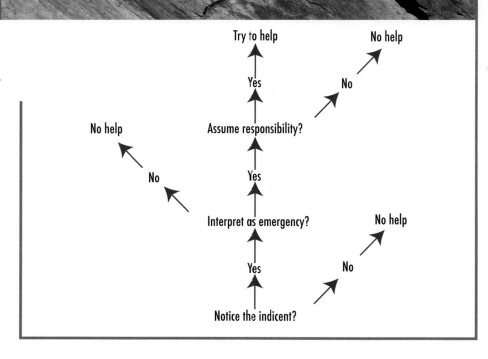

help? As a final step, the person must decide how to *implement* the decision to act. What is the best first aid under these circumstances? Just where can help be found? Thus, we can see that intervening on behalf of someone else in a social situation involves a series of cognitive choices.

A negative outcome at any of these steps will lead to a decision not to offer assistance. When one considers the cognitive events necessary for helping, it becomes apparent that the deck is stacked against the victim in an emergency when bystanders are present. Interestingly, bystanders need not be physically present for the bystander effect to occur. Just having someone imagine that there are bystanders present can suppress helping (Garcia, Weaver, Moskowitz, & Darley, 2002). The bystander effect also can be found to occur in Internet chat rooms (Markey, 2000)! Perhaps we should be surprised that bystanders *ever* offer to help.

Social psychologists refer to the suppression of helping when bystanders are present at an emergency situation as the **bystander effect**. It has been found to be one of the most consistent and powerful phenomena discovered by social psychologists. Why does the bystander effect occur? We shall explore possible explanations next.

Processes That Inhibit Helping Behaviors

Audience inhibition refers to the tendency to be hesitant about doing things in front of others, especially strangers. We tend to be concerned about how others will evaluate us. In public, no one wants to do anything that might appear to be improper, incompetent, or silly. The bystander who intervenes risks embarrassment if he or she blunders, and that risk increases as the number of people present increases. Those people who are sensitive to becoming embarrassed in public are most likely to be inhibited (Tice & Baumeister, 1985).

Emergencies tend to be ambiguous (e.g., Is the man who collapsed on the street ill, or is he drunk? Is the commotion in a neighboring apartment an assault, or a family quarrel that's a little out of hand?) When social reality is not clear, we often turn to others for clues. While getting information from others, a person will probably try to remain calm, cool, and collected, acting as if there is no emergency. Everyone else, of course, is doing the very same thing, showing no outward sign of concern. The result is that each person is led by the others to think that the situation is really not an emergency after all, a phenomenon called pluralistic ignorance (Miller & McFarland, 1987). **Pluralistic ignorance** is the belief on the part of the individual that only he or she is confused and does not know what to do in an emergency, whereas everyone else is standing around doing nothing for a good reason. The group becomes paralyzed by a type of conformity—conformity to the inaction of others.

This process was demonstrated in a classic experiment by Latané and Darley (1968, 1970). Columbia University students reported to a campus building to participate in an interview. They were sent to a waiting room and asked to fill out some forms. As they did so, smoke began billowing out through a wall vent. After six minutes (at which time the procedure was ended if the "emergency" had not been reported), there was enough smoke in the room to interfere with breathing and prevent seeing across the room.

When participants were alone in the waiting room, 75 percent of them came out to report the smoke. When two passive confederates were in the room with the participant, only 10 percent responded. Those from the groups who failed to make a report came up with all sorts of explanations for the smoke: steam, vapors from the air conditioner, smog introduced to simulate an urban environment, even "truth gas." Participants who were unresponsive had been led by the inaction of

pluralistic ignorance the belief on the part of an individual that only he or she is confused and does not know what to do in an emergency, whereas everyone else is standing around doing nothing for good reason

bystander effect the suppression of helping when bystanders are present at an emergency situation

audience inhibition the tendency to be hesitant about doing things in front of others, especially strangers

others to conclude almost anything but the obvious—that something was very wrong. In the Kitty Genovese murder, it was clear that an emergency was in progress. After all she did shout things such as "Oh, my God, he stabbed me! Please help me! Please help me!" and "I'm dying! I'm dying!" Her cries left very little ambiguity about what was happening. Further, witnesses in the Genovese case were not in a face-to-face group that would allow social influence processes such as pluralistic ignorance to operate. Latané and Darley suggested that a third process is necessary to complete the explanation of bystander behavior.

A single bystander in an emergency situation has to bear the full responsibility of offering assistance, but a witness who is part of a group shares that responsibility with other onlookers. The greater the number of people present, the smaller is each individual's perceived obligation to intervene, a process referred to as **diffusion of responsibility**.

Incidentally, diffusion of responsibility comes in forms much less serious in their implications. Those of you with a few siblings can probably recall times at home when the telephone rang five or six times before anyone made a move to answer it, even though the entire family was home at the time. Some of you probably have been at parties where the doorbell went unanswered with everyone thinking that "someone else" would get it.

The *diffusion of responsibility* is generally considered to be one of the best explanations for the bystander effect. However, it need not always occur for the bystander effect to develop. In some cases, help can be suppressed if the bystanders assume that a *category relationship* exists between the parties involved in an incident (Levine, 1999). A **category relationship** means that parties involved in a social situation are perceived to belong together in some way (e.g., siblings, boyfriend-girlfriend). When a category relationship is assumed, people are less willing to intervene than when such

a relationship is not assumed (Shotland & Straw, 1976).

Mark Levine (1999) maintains that what happened to Kitty Genovese can be accounted for (in part) by witnesses assuming that Genovese and her attacker had previously formed a category relationship. In fact, some of the witnesses expressed the sentiment that, "We thought it was a lover's quarrel." When a category relationship is believed to exist, a powerful social norm is activated: We don't stick our noses in the business of others.

Social psychologists have also looked at bystander intervention from the perspective of bystander empathy and altruism. Others have been quick to point out that situational factors interact with the bystander's individual characteristics to affect helping. For example, true caring for a victim may motivate us to provide help (Batson 1987, 1990; Batson et al., 1997; Batson et al., 1999). This caring is rooted in an emotional state called **empathy**, a compassionate understanding of how the person in need feels. If someone needs our help, feelings of empathy might include sympathy, pity, and sorrow. Batson suggests that empathy may lead to altruistic acts. According to this **empathy-altruism hypothesis**, empathy is one reason for helping those in need. However, it is not the only reason. You might be motivated to help a person in need to relieve the personal distress associated with not helping. This motive for helping is called *egoism*. For example, if you saw a motorist stranded on the side of the road and said to yourself, "I'd better do something, or I'll feel terrible all day," your helping is designed to relieve your own distress, not the distress of the victim. So, empathy is focused on the victim's distress and suffering, whereas egoism is focused on your own distress and suffering.

A Final Note on the Bystander Effect

We have made the case that the bystander effect is a powerful and per-

---

diffusion of responsibility the observation that the greater the number of people present, the smaller is each individual's perceived obligation to intervene

empathy a compassionate understanding of how a person in need is feeling

empathy-altruism hypothesis the proposal that empathy is one reason for helping those in need

category relationship the situation in which the parties involved in a social interaction are perceived to belong together in some way

vasive social phenomenon. However, are there any circumstances in which the bystander effect does not occur, or where the presence of bystanders actually can facilitate helping? It turns out that the answer is "yes"—if the situation is potentially dangerous (Fischer, Greitemeir, Pollozek, & Frey, 2006). Fischer, et al. found the usual bystander effect (inhibition of helping when bystanders were present) in a low-danger helping situation. However, when help was dangerous (stopping a large, thug-like male from harming a woman), the presence of bystanders facilitated helping. Finally, the bystander effect is less likely to occur when a clearly defined social norm is violated, such as if someone litters in a public park in front of a group of bystanders (Chekroun & Brauer, 2001).

BEFORE YOU GO ON

23. What are some of the factors that predict whether someone in need will be given assistance from bystanders?

A Point to Ponder or Discuss
To what extent have you observed the bystander effect on your campus? When there is a campus-wide election, what percentage of the student body actually votes? Is any of this preceding discussion relevant to that issue?

SOCIAL LOAFING AND FACILITATION

A well-researched variety of social influence is **social loafing**—a tendency to work less (to decrease individual effort) as the size of the group in which one works becomes larger. In a classic study of the phenomenon, Latané, Williams, and Harkins (1979) had participants shout or clap as loudly as possible, either in groups or alone. If people were led to believe that their performance could not be identified, they invested less effort in the task as group size increased. Other studies have used different, more cognitive tasks, such as evaluating poetry. The results tend to be consistent: When people can hide in the crowd, their effort (and, hence, productivity) declines.

That the extent of social loafing is tied to an individual's anonymity in a group setting has been verified by several studies of problem solving or brainstorming (Levine & Moreland, 1990; Markey, 2000; McKinlay, Proctor, & Dunnett, 1999; Shepard et al., 1996). Such studies consistently show that individual effort is greater in real, face-to-face groups than it is in "nominal groups" in which individuals work at their own computer stations, participating with others on some common task. Loafing is reduced to the extent that others in the group can monitor the inputs and behaviors of each individual.

Not surprisingly, social loafing is positively correlated with fatigue. Although performance usually can be expected to diminish as one tires, fatigue increases social loafing (that is, decreases effort) to a greater extent when individuals work in a group setting (Hoeksema-van Orden, Gaillard, & Buunk, 1998). Social loafing occurs even in 3- to 5- year-old preschool children (engaged in the task of pumping up balloons). This is true, however, only for those preschoolers who are mentally able to reason about the perception of others and their beliefs (Carl et al., 2003).

social loafing the tendency to work less (to decrease individual effort) as the size of the group in which one works becomes larger

Courtesy of Michael Prince/Corbis.

The notion of "social loafing" is not a new one in social psychology. Social loafing refers to the tendency to decrease one's efforts when working on a task as the size of the group in which one is working gets larger.

| **social facilitation** the process that occurs when the presence of others improves an individual's performance on some task

Although social loafing is a widespread phenomenon, it is not always predicted when one works in a group setting. Remember our discussions of cultures and the exhibition of collectivist or individualist characteristics? Social loafing is significantly less likely in those collectivist cultures—such as in many Asian countries—that place a high value on participation in group activities (Kerr & Tinsdale, 2004; Worchel, et al., 1998). In individualist cultures, such as the United States and most Western countries, social loafing can be nearly eliminated if group members believe their effort is special and required for the group's success, or they believe their performance can be identified and evaluated individually. Loafing also reduces when individuals within the group find a task interesting or they get personally involved in the task at hand (Smith et al., 2001). Indeed, there are situations in which social influence actually facilitates behavior.

Well over 100 years ago, psychologist Norman Triplett observed that bicycle riders competing against other cyclists outperformed those racing against a clock. He then performed what is considered the first laboratory experiment in social psychology (Triplett, 1898). Triplett had children wind a fishing reel as rapidly as they could. They engaged in this task either alone or alongside another child doing the same thing. Just as he had noticed in his records of bicycle races, Triplett found that the children worked faster when another child was present. Such an effect occurs not only when working with co-actors (others engaged in the same task), but also when performing before an audience. For example, joggers, both male and female, pick up the pace and run faster when going past a person sitting on a park bench (Worringham & Messick, 1983). When the presence of others improves an individual's performance on some task, **social facilitation** has occurred.

Numerous studies of this phenomenon were performed early in the twentieth century, with a puzzling inconsistency in results. Sometimes social facilitation would occur, but on other occasions, the opposite would happen. Sometimes people performed more poorly in the presence of others than they did alone, a reaction that social psychologists call *social interference*. The inconsistency in these findings was so bewildering that most social psychologists eventually gave up investigating social facilitation.

In 1965, Robert Zajonc resurrected the topic of social facilitation by providing a plausible interpretation for the lack of consistency in social facilitation effects. In his examination of the research, Zajone noticed that social facilitation occurred whenever the behavior under study was simple, routine, or very well learned (for example, bicycle riding or winding line on a fishing reel). Social interference tended to occur whenever the behavior involved was complex or not well learned. Zajonc's insight was that the presence of others creates increased arousal, which in turn energizes the dominant (most likely) response under the circumstances. When a dominant response is the correct one, as with a simple, well-practiced task, facilitation occurs. When the dominant response is incorrect, as with a complex task or one with which we have had little practice, the result is interference (Levine et al., 1993).

You may have experienced this effect yourself if you have ever tried a sport totally new to you. Whereas skilled athletes often perform better in front of audiences, most novices tend to do better alone. You may have experienced—as a novice, that is—the frustration of failing to make contact with a golf ball or tennis ball when there are others standing nearby, watching you.

In conclusion, we may safely assume that social interference and social loafing are more common than social facilitation. Although there are occasions in which coworkers or an audience may enhance individual performance, the presence of others is more likely to inhibit it.

BEFORE YOU GO ON

24. What are social loafing and social facilitation, and under what circumstances are they likely to occur?

A Point to Ponder or Discuss
A teacher believes in the value of having small groups of students work together on some class projects. What can she do to prevent some students from engaging in social loafing and letting other students do most of the work?

DECISION MAKING IN GROUPS

Many of the decisions we face in our daily lives are made within group settings. Committees, boards, family groups, and group projects for a class are only a few examples. There is logic in the belief that group efforts to solve problems should be superior to individual efforts. Having more people available should mean having more talent and knowledge available. It also seems logical that the cohesiveness of the group would contribute to a more productive effort (for some groups and some problems, this is exactly the case). But, we know better than to assume that just because a conclusion is logical, it is true.

Decades of research have shown us that groups can, and often do, outperform individuals. Here is a partial list of what we know about group decision making:

- Groups outperform the average individual in the group mainly because groups recognize a correct answer to a problem faster, reject an incorrect answer, and have better memory systems than the average individual.
- Groups comprising high-quality members perform better than groups with low-quality members.
- As you increase the size of the group, you increase the resources available to the group. However, you also increase process loss (loss of productivity due to faulty group interaction). Additionally, in larger groups, you get even less member participation than in smaller groups.
- When the problem a group must solve involves a great deal of interaction, interpersonal cohesiveness (how much members like each other) and task-based cohesiveness (mutual respect for skills and abilities) increase productivity. When a problem does not require much interaction, task-based cohesiveness increases productivity, but interpersonal cohesiveness does not.

Although it is generally true that groups outperform individuals, there are some liabilities attached to using groups to make decisions. In this section, we consider two aspects of group decision making that can lead to low-quality decisions.

Group Polarization

When he was an MIT graduate student in industrial management, James Stoner gave participants in his study a series of dilemmas to consider (Stoner, 1961). Participants were to decide how much risk a fictitious character in a dilemma should take. One dilemma, for example, involved a star quarterback who had to choose a late play in an important game with an archrival. One choice—a simple play, likely to succeed—would lead to a tie score, whereas the other choice—a very risky play with only a slim hope of success—would lead to certain victory. Much to his surprise, Stoner found that the decisions rendered by the groups were much riskier than those formed by the individual group members prior to joining the group discussions. Stoner called this move away from conservative solutions a *risky shift*. For example, doctors, if asked individually, might claim that a patient's problem (whatever it might be) could be handled with medication and a change in diet. If these same doctors were to jointly discuss the patient's situation, they might conclude that a new and potentially dangerous (risky) surgical procedure was necessary.

Several hundred experimental studies later, psychologists now know that this effect also occurs in the opposite direction, a *cautious shift* (Levine & Moreland, 1990; Moscovici et al., 1985). In other words, a risky shift is a general **group polarization effect** in which group participation makes an individual's reactions more extreme, or polarized. Group discussion usually leads to an enhancement of the group members' preexisting beliefs and attitudes. One explanation for group polarization is that open discussion gives group members an opportunity to hear persuasive arguments not previously considered, leading to a strengthening of their original attitudes (Isenberg, 1986). Another possibility is that, after comparing attitudinal positions with one another, some group members feel pressure to "catch up" with group members who have more extreme attitudes.

Groupthink

Irving Janis (1972, 1983a) has described a related phenomenon of influence he calls **groupthink**, an excessive concern for reaching a consensus in group decision making to the extent that critical evaluations are withheld. Janis maintains that this style of thinking emerges when group members are so interested in maintaining harmony within the group that differences of opinion or alternative courses of action are suppressed. Janis maintained that groupthink is most likely to occur in cohesive groups.

Janis (1972) identified eight common indicators of groupthink that lead to bad group decisions:

1. *An illusion of invulnerability:* Group members believe that nothing can harm them, which leads to excessive optimism.
2. *Rationalization:* Rather than realistically evaluating information, group members collectively rationalize away damaging information.
3. *Unquestioned belief in the group's inherent morality:* The group sees itself on the side of what is right and just. This leads group members to ignore the moral implications and consequences of their actions.
4. *Stereotyped views of the enemy:* The "enemy" is characterized as too weak or stupid to put up any meaningful resistance to the group's planned course of action,
5. *Conformity pressures:* Direct pressure is placed on any group member who dissents from the group's consensus of action.

groupthink an excessive concern for reaching consensus in group decision-making to the extent that critical evaluations are withheld

group polarization effect the phenomenon in which group participation makes an individual's reactions more extreme or polarized

6. *Self-censorship:* Due to conformity pressure, individual group members remain silent because of the potential consequences.

7. *An illusion of unanimity:* Because of self-censorship, the group suffers the illusion that everyone agrees with the course of action being planned by the group.

8. *Emergence of self-appointed mind-guards:* Self-appointed "mind-guards" emerge to protect the group from damaging outside information. These people intercept potentially damaging information and don't pass it along to the group.

Janis analyzed the decision-making process involved in several key historical events—such as the bombing of Pearl Harbor military response, the Bay of Pigs invasion, and the Challenger explosion—in terms of groupthink. He found that such situations involved three common factors: a cohesive, decision-making group that was relatively isolated from outside judgments; a directive leader who supplied pressure to conform to his position; and an illusion of unanimity (see also, McCauley, 1989).

Generally, Janis' groupthink hypothesis has weathered the test of time. However, some research suggests that group cohesiveness may not be as crucial to the emergence of groupthink as Janis originally believed (Kerr & Tindale, 2004). Directive leadership and consensus seeking, which make groups more concerned with enhancing morale and reaching agreement, than with attaining

Courtesy of moodboard/Corbis.

quality decisions, are important precursors of groupthink (Tetlock, Peterson, McGuire, Chang, & Feld, 1992). Finally, Gerald Whyte (1989) has proposed that group polarization, risk-taking, and the potential for a fiasco occur when a group frames its decision in terms of potential failure. Whyte suggests that when a group frames possible outcomes in terms of potential failure, the group is more likely to make a risky decision. Working in an environment that favors risky decisions enhances the likelihood of a disastrous group decision. There also is good evidence that time pressure—or the perception of time pressure—increases the likelihood to seek consensus and solution, whether the solution is a good one or not (Kelly, Jackson, & Huston-Comeaux, 1997).

Some decisions are better made by groups than by individuals. However, there are some pitfalls to avoid. One of the most common is the group polarization effect, in which an individual's beliefs and reactions become more extreme than they would be if the person thought through the issue alone.

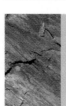

BEFORE YOU GO ON

25. What are some of the factors known to influence decision making within groups?

A Point to Ponder or Discuss
If psychologists have such a clear idea of why some decisions made by groups are—at best—overly risky, why do groups continue to make such errors?

CHAPTER SUMMARY

1. **What do psychologists mean by "social cognitions" and "naïve realism"?**

   Social psychology is the field of psychology concerned with how others influence the thoughts, feelings, and behaviors of the individual. Social psychologists accept the premise that we do not view our social environment solely on the basis of the stimulus information that it presents to us, but that we have developed cognitive structures or processes (e.g., attitudes and schemas) that influence our interpretation of the world around us. *Naïve realism* is the term used to describe the phenomenon wherein we tend to believe *we* see the world in a more rational, objective way than others do.

2. **What social psychological processes underlie naïve realism?**

   First, is the belief that we see the world rationally and objectively, while others do not. Second, we assume that if others are rational, they will see the world as we do. Third, if other do not see the world as we do, then either they are irrational or harbor ulterior and bad motives or they simply are misinformed.

3. **How can biases in social cognition affect interpersonal relationships?**

   Consistent with a basic psychological principle introduced in Chapter 1, our perceptions (and cognitions in general) of our social world (including our interpersonal relationships are often more influential that any sort of objective reality concerning our social world. Additionally, our ideology, attitudes, prejudices and biases alter our perceptions of objective reality. In essence, each of us views the world through different lenses to construct our own versions of social reality.

4. **How do social psychologists define *attitude*?**

   Social psychologists define *attitudes* as relatively stable evaluative dispositions (positive or negative) directed toward some object or event.

5. **What are explicit and implicit attitudes and how might they affect your behavior differently?**

   Explicit attitudes work at a conscious level. We are aware of these attitudes and how they may influence our behaviors. Implicit attitudes oper-

ate at levels below conscious awareness. They tend to operate when we are actively engaged in other—distracting—cognitive tasks.

6. **What are the possible components of an attitude, and how are they related?**

   An attitude consists of feelings (affects), behaviors, and beliefs (cognitions). Although the affective and cognitive components of attitudes are often consistent with each other, they may be inconsistent with behavior, largely because behavior is influenced by so many situational variables. Because of the possible inconsistency of other attitude components and behaviors, some psychologists have argued that a significant component of an attitude is not actual, overt behavior, as such, but behavior intention.

7. **What are some of the factors that influence the formation of attitudes?**

   Attitudes may be acquired through classical conditioning: After positive or negative experiences are associated with an attitudinal object, the object itself comes to produce a positive or negative evaluation. Attitudes may develop as a result of direct reinforcement (operant conditioning), or they may be formed when they are vicariously reinforced (observational learning). Although there may be some genetic predisposition to develop some attitudes and not others, most attitudes clearly are a reflection of a person's experiences. In fact, simple, repetitive exposure to an object (or person) leads to the formation of positive attitudes—the mere exposure phenomenon. The media may also be influential in the formation of attitudes through *agenda setting*, first by deciding which issues to cover (*first-level*) and by presenting issues—including stories about newsworthy people—in either a positive or negative way (*second-level*). Also, one's genetic constitution may predispose us to develop some attitudes and not others.

8. **Briefly describe some of the mechanisms used to explain how attitudes change.**

   Just as attitude formation is mostly a matter of experience, so is attitude change. One well-supported approach to attitude change proposes that a change of attitude occurs to reduce a negative motivational state called cognitive dissonance. *Cognitive dissonance* emerges whenever there is inconsistency between our cognitions (thoughts), attitudes, and behavior. Once dissonance is aroused, we are motivated to reduce or eliminate it. For example, the insufficient justification effect occurs when we behave in an inconsistent way and we lack sufficient reason for our behavior. Dissonance also is aroused when a person is forced to make a choice between two mutually exclusive, equally attractive alternatives. It is usually resolved by developing negative cognitions concerning the alternative that was not chosen. *Self-perception theory* was developed to account for attitude change that occurs when cognitive dissonance seems an inappropriate explanation. The theory proposes that we observe our behavior and then look for reasons why we might have behaved in the demonstrated manner. In some cases, dissonance does not motivate attitude change because people can bolster their self-esteem in other ways—a process called self-affirmation theory.

9. **What factors does the Yale communication model suggest are involved in persuading someone to change an attitude?**

    Persuasion is the application of rational and/or emotional arguments to convince others to change their attitudes. The *Yale communication model* is the most widely accepted model of persuasion. The three factors outlined by this model are the source of a persuasive message (who delivers the message), the characteristics of the message, and the nature of the audience. A communicator's credibility, or believability, is an important factor in determining attitude change. *Credibility* is made up of two components: expertise (the qualifications of the source), and trustworthiness (the motivation of the source). All other things being equal, a communicator with high credibility is more persuasive than one with low credibility. In addition to credibility, the *attractiveness* of the communicator and his or her perceived similarity to the audience affect persuasion. Discrepancy refers to the difference between the initial position of the audience and the content of a persuasive message. Too much or too little discrepancy leads to little or no attitude change. A moderate amount of discrepancy leads to the most persuasion. Fear appeals are effective in producing attitude and behavior change when three conditions are met: 1) the fear aroused must be quite high; 2) the target of the message must believe that the dire consequences

depicted in the appeal could happen, and 3) specific instructions must be given on how to avoid the dire consequences. Without this third factor, a fear appeal will not work, even if the first two conditions are met.

10. **How do central and peripheral routes play a role in the persuasion process?**

    The *elaboration likelihood model* was proposed to account for situations in which persuasion occurs even in the absence of the careful processing of a persuasive message. According to the model, messages can be processed along either a *central route* (involving careful processing of the content of the message) or a peripheral route (where the content of the message is not carefully considered, but cues—like the attractiveness of the communicator—become important). A message will be processed along the central route if the audience can understand the message and is motivated to process it. Otherwise, the message will be processed along the *peripheral route*. Attitude change brought about by central processing is more enduring than change brought about by peripheral processing.

11. **What are prejudice, stereotypes, and discrimination, and how are they related?**

    A *prejudice* is an attitude about another person based solely on his or her membership in some group. Prejudices are usually negative. They lead to expectations of behaviors, based solely on group membership. *Stereotypes* are rigid beliefs about members of a group that lead to over-generalized schemas or images of group members. It is a matter of over-categorization based on a small set of characteristics. Like attitudes, stereotypes may be explicit or implicit. *Discrimination* is the behavioral outcome of prejudice or stereotyping. It is a matter of actually acting toward someone based on his or her group membership. That is how these three concepts are related: Each uses group membership, rather than the characteristics of the individual, as a basis of action and reaction.

12. **How are in-groups and out-groups used to define the social world, and what are the consequences of this type of thinking?**

    In-groups include those people with characteristics similar to our own (e.g., race, gender, ethnicity, nationality and the like), toward whom we tend to have positive feelings. Out-groups comprise everyone we see as dissimilar to ourselves, and toward whom we have negative feelings. People tend to see members of their in-groups as in many ways "superior" all who are members of out-groups. When members of our in-groups do something positive, we feel good about that, and when members of out-groups do something bad, we tend to express negative emotions about those members and all others of the out-group.

13. **How do implicit and explicit stereotypes influence the way we think about others and behave toward them?**

In general, a stereotype is a rigid set of positive or negative beliefs about a group of people, especially out-group members. We develop expectations based on our stereotypes and often judge others on the basis of our stereotypes. Explicit stereotypes are those of which we are consciously aware. Implicit stereotypes operate on an unconscious level and are activated automatically, without conscious thought.

14. **What do social psychologists mean by "attributions?"**

Attributions are cognitions we use to explain the sources of the behaviors we see in our social worlds.

15. **Distinguish between internal and external attributions.**

Internal attributions identify the source of behavior as within the person; they are also called dispositional attributions. *External attributions* find the source of behaviors to be outside the person; they are also called situational attributions.

16. **What are the three sources of information used to make attributions and how do they lead to internal or external attribution?**

Forming attributions about others usually involves the combination of three types or sources of information. *Distinctiveness* refers to the extent to which a behavior is different from other behaviors of the individual. *Consistency* is a matter of how frequent or regular a particular pattern of behavior happens to be. *Consensus* describes the extent to which other people engage in the same (or similar) pattern of behavior in the same (or similar) situation. High consensus, high consistency, and high distinctiveness lead to external attributions. Low levels of consistency, consensus and distinctiveness lead to internal attributions.

17. **What are some of the errors that occur in the attribution process?**

The *fundamental attribution error* leads people to overuse internal, or personal, attributions when explaining behaviors. It is most common in Western cultures. Those who hold to the *just world hypothesis* are likely to believe that good things happen only to good people and that bad things happen only to bad people, who in some way deserve their misfortune. With *self-serving bias*, we attribute our successes to our own efforts and actions, and our failures to other, external factors. The *actor-observer* bias is the tendency to use external attributions to explain the behaviors of ourselves (actor), and internal attributions to explain the behaviors of others (observer).

18. **Briefly describe four theories of interpersonal attraction.**

The *reinforcement model* of interpersonal attraction claims that we are attracted to those persons we associate with rewards, or reinforcers. The *social exchange model* adds cost to the equation, claiming that what matters in interpersonal relationships is the ratio of the benefits received to the costs invested in that relationship. The *equity model* suggests that both or all members of a relationship assess a benefit/cost ratio, and the best, most stable, relationships are those in which the ratio is nearly the same (equitable) for both or all parties, no matter what the value of the benefits for any one member of the relationship. *Attachment theory* tells us that there are only a few relationship styles, and that each individual is consistent over his or her lifetime in the style used when relating to others.

19. **Summarize some of the factors known to influence such attraction.**

The principle of *reciprocity* states that we tend to like people who like us back. This is the most straightforward example of interpersonal attraction, and is based on a system of rewards. *Proximity* promotes attraction, in part, by means of the mere exposure effect: Being near another person on a frequent basis gives us the opportunity to see what that other person has to offer. Recently, because of Internet use, psychologists have had to extend proximity to mean more than physical, face-to-face closeness. We also tend to be attracted to people we judge *physically attractive*. Finally, the principle of *similarity* suggests that we tend to be attracted to those we believe to be similar to ourselves.

20. What is conformity, and how was it demonstrated by Solomon Asch?

Conformity is a social influence process in which behavior is modified in response to perceived pressure from others so that the behavior becomes consistent with that of others. Conformity is often thought of in negative terms, but conformity helps make social behavior efficient and predictable. In Asch's studies, people made judgments about unambiguous perceptual stimuli: the length of lines. During some trials, confederates gave judgments that were clearly incorrect, before the actual participant had a chance to respond. Although there were situations in which yielding to perceived group pressure could be lessened, many of Asch's participants followed suit and conformed. Some, but very few, participants conformed because they accepted that the majority was correct in its judgments. A second group, making up the largest group of yielding participants, conformed because they had little confidence in their own judgments. The final group of yielding participants conformed because they didn't want to appear defective to others.

Several factors affect conformity rates. Conformity increases as the size of the majority increases—up to a point. Then it levels off. The more competent the majority is perceived to be, the greater the conformity. If the person holding the minority opinion perceives himself or herself to be competent, conformity decreases. Conformity increases if an ambiguous task is used. There is a small gender difference, with women conforming more often than men, when a male is the experimenter or when group pressure is involved. There are also cultural and sociopolitical climate relationships that affect conformity rates.

21. What do social psychologists mean by "obedience," and how was such obedience demonstrated in the laboratory by Milgram?

Obedience means complying with the demands of an authority figure, even if such compliance is against one's better judgment. Participants in Milgram's experiments were led to believe they were administering more and more potent shocks to another person in a learning task. When they hesitated to deliver shocks, an authority figure, the experimenter, prodded them to continue. All participants obeyed to some degree, and nearly two-thirds delivered what they thought was the most intense shock, even over the protests of the learner. Those who obeyed in Milgram's experiments were neither cruel nor inhumane. Rather, the experimenter created a powerful social situation that made it difficult to refuse the authority figure's orders. Milgram found that gender was not related to obedience rates. However, as Milgram moved the teacher and learner closer together (in the same room), obedience dropped. The lowest rate of obedience was observed when the teacher actually had to touch the learner to give him a shock. When the experiment was conducted with a group administering the shocks, and two group members refused to continue, obedience also was reduced. Having the experimenter leave the room and deliver orders by telephone, or adding another authority figure, who told the participant to stop the experiment, also reduced obedience.

22. How can we account for "evil" deeds that we have seen carried out throughout history? Are these deeds perpetrated by evil people or are those people victims of circumstances?

There is little doubt that evil, defined as intentionally behaving, or causing others to act, in ways that demean, dehumanize, harm, destroy or kill innocent people, occurs in our social world all too frequently. Sometimes these acts do reflect obedience in the sense that Milgram demonstrated in his experiments, circumstances when people do evil things in response to pressure form others. Psychologists are also coming to posit that there are people who may be said to have an "evil character." So-called *moral monsters* carry out evil deeds without direction from anyone else. Those people who carry out evil deeds in response to directions or orders from someone else are referred to as *moral idiots.*

23. What are some of the factors that predict whether someone in need will be given assistance from bystanders?

Darley and Latané proposed that a person must pass through a series of cognitive events before he or she will help someone in need. First, a bystander must notice the emergency. Second, the bystander must label the situation. Third, the bystander must assume responsibility for helping. Fourth, the bystander must decide how to help. Finally, the bystander must implement the decision to help. A negative decision at any point will result in no help being offered.

The likelihood that someone will intervene on behalf of another in an emergency is lessened as a function of how many others (bystanders) are present at the time. (And, it is the perception of others being present, not actual face-to-face contact, that matters here.) The greater the number of bystanders present, the less likely a person in need will receive help. This is known as the *bystander effect*. Several factors have been proposed to account for this phenomenon. *Audience inhibition* is the term used to describe the hesitancy to intervene in front of others, perhaps out of fear of embarrassing oneself. *Pluralistic ignorance* occurs when others lead someone to think (by their inactivity) that nothing is wrong in an ambiguous emergency situation. *Diffusion of responsibility* causes a member of a group to feel less obligated to intervene (less responsible) than if he or she were alone. Each of these processes tends to discourage helping, and they more likely to operate as the number of persons present increases. There are two forces that can motivate altruism: empathy and egoism. Empathy is an emotional state in which a person feels the suffering of a victim in need. Helping based on empathy is focused on relieving the suffering of the victim. Egoism motivates a person to help to avoid personal displeasure. The *empathy-altruism hypothesis* suggests that empathy is one important factor in motivating altruism.

24. **What are social loafing and social facilitation, and under what circumstances are they likely to occur?**

Social loafing occurs when one is less likely to invest full effort and energy in the task at hand as a member of a group than he or she would if working alone (at least in Western, individualist cultures). Data suggest that as group size increases, social loafing increases. Being able to "hide" in a group and go unnoticed also increases the social loafing effect. On the other hand, when tasks are simple or well-rehearsed, performance may be enhanced, a process called *social facilitation*. When tasks are difficult, complex, or unrehearsed, the presence of others is likely to have a negative effect on performance.

25. **What are some of the factors known to influence decision-making within groups?**

Groups often outperform the average individual because groups recognize a correct answer faster, reject an incorrect answer faster, and have better (or at least larger) memory systems than the average person. Groups with high-quality members perform better than groups with low-quality members. Increasing group size increases resources available to the group, but it also increases process loss. In larger groups, member participation is less even than in smaller groups. Interpersonal cohesiveness and task-based cohesiveness enhance group performance when a problem requires a great deal of interaction.

Although there are advantages to problem solving in a group setting, there are also liabilities. *Group polarization* (originally known as the risky shift) is the tendency for a group discussion to solidify and enhance pre-existing attitudes. *Groupthink* is an excessive concern for reaching a consensus at the expense of carefully considering alternative courses of action. Groupthink has been found to contribute to bad group decisions. Irving Janis identified eight symptoms of groupthink: An illusion of invulnerability, rationalization, an unquestioned belief in the group's morality, stereotyped views of the enemy, conformity pressures, self-censorship, an illusion of unanimity, and the emergence of self-appointed "mindguards."

Glossary

abnormal maladaptive affects, behaviors, and/or cognitions that are at odds with social expectations and result in distress or discomfort

absolute threshold the physical intensity of a stimulus that a person reports detecting 50 percent of the time

accommodation according to Piaget, the process that allows a child to modify his or her schemas in order to account for new objects or experiences (or to create new schemas)

accommodation (in vision) the process of the changing of the shape of the lens by the ciliary muscles to focus images on the retina

acquisition the stage of classical conditioning during which the CS and the UCS are paired and the strength of the CR increases

action potential the electrical charge that results when the ions within the neuron become more positive than the ions within the neuron (about + 40 mV)

actor-observer bias a discrepancy between the way we explain our behaviors (as actor) and the way we explain someone else's (as observer)

adaptation according to Piaget, the process of developing the appropriate schemas to meet the demands of the environment

adolescence a developmental period of transition from the dependence of childhood to the independence of adulthood, beginning at puberty and lasting through the teen years—the second decade of life

adrenal glands secrete a variety of hormones into the bloodstream that are very useful in terms of stress, danger or threat

affect one's feelings, moods, or emotions

ageism discrimination and/or prejudice against a group or an individual solely on the basis of age

agenda setting the phenomena in which the media tells us which issues we should think about, and how we should think about those issues

aggression any behavior intended to inflict physical and/or psychological harm to another organism or the symbol of that organism

agoraphobia (literally, "fear of open places") an exaggerated fear of venturing forth into the world alone

algorithm a strategy that, if correctly applied, guarantees a solution to a problem eventually

all-or-none principle the observation that a neuron either fires or it doesn't

Alzheimer's dementia (AD) a disorder characterized by a slow deterioration of memory and other intellectual functioning

anorexia nervosa an eating disorder characterized by an inability (or refusal) to maintain one's body weight

anterograde (forward-acting) amnesia the inability to form memories of events that happen after the onset of the amnesia

antianxiety drugs (tranquilizers) medications designed to help reduce the felt aspect of anxiety

antidepressant drugs medications designed to elevate the mood of persons who are depressed

antipsychotic drugs medications designed to alleviate or eliminate psychotic symptoms

antisocial personality disorder a disorder characterized by an exceptional lack of regard for the rights and property of others, and impulsive behaviors with little or no regard for the consequences of those behaviors

anxiety a feeling of general apprehension or dread accompanied by predictable physiological changes

approach-approach conflict a situation in which an organism is caught between two or more alternatives and each of them is positive, or potentially reinforcing

approach-avoidance conflict a situation in which a person is faced with only one goal and would like to reach that goal, but at the same time would like not to

aqueous humor the material that provides nourishment to the cornea and other structures at the front of the eye

arousal one's overall level of activation or excitement

assimilation according to Piaget, a process that occurs when a child incorporates new information into an existing schema

association areas regions of the cerebral cortex where sensory input is integrated with motor responses and where cognitive functions, such as memory, problem solving and thinking occur

atonia a period of muscular immobility

attachment a strong and reciprocal emotional bond or relationship between a child and his or her primary caregiver

attachment theory the position that interpersonal relationships can be classified into one of three types: secure, avoidant, or anxious/ambivalent, depending upon the attitudes one has about that relationship

attitude a relatively stable disposition to evaluate an object or event

attribution theory the attempt to understand the cognitions we use when we try to explain the causes or sources of our own and other people's behaviors

audience inhibition the tendency to be hesitant about doing things in front of others, especially strangers

autism a disorder of childhood characterized by impaired social interactions, problems with communication, and unusual or severely limited activities and interests

autonomic nervous system (ANS) the system involved in activating the smooth muscles, such as those of the stomach, intestines, and glands

availability heuristic the assumption that things that readily come to mind are more common than are things that do not come to mind so readily

aversion therapy a form of behavior therapy in which a stimulus that may be harmful but that produces a "pleasant" response is paired with an aversive, painful stimulus until the original stimulus is avoided

avoidance conditioning a process in which an organism learns to get away from (avoid) a painful, noxious, aversive situation before it occurs

avoidance-avoidance conflict a situation in which a person is faced with several alternatives, each of them negative or in some way punishing

axon a long protuberance extending from the neuron's cell body that carries neural impulses to other neurons, muscles, or glands

axon terminal a branching series of bare end points where an axon ends

basal ganglia lower brain centers that are involved in the planning, initiating, and coordinating of large, slow movements

baseline designs techniques of arranging conditions so that each participant serves in both the experimental and in the control group conditions

behavior what organisms do—their actions and reactions

behavior genetics the discipline that studies the effects of genes on psychological functioning

behavioral observation a method of drawing conclusions about someone's personality on the basis of observations of his or her behaviors

behaviorism the approach to psychology, first associated with Watson, that claims psychology should give up the study of the mind and focus on observable behaviors

biological approach (to personality) focuses on biological, physiological, and genetic mechanisms to describe and explain personality

bipolar disorder a disorder involving episodes of depression interspersed with episodes of mania

blind spot the place at which nerve impulses from the rods and cones, having passed through many layers of cells, leave the eye

bottom-up processing a process that occurs when what we perceive is determined in large extent by the bits and pieces of information we receive from our senses

brightness constancy the process that causes familiar objects to be perceived with their usual brightness, regardless of the actual amount or type of light under which they are viewed

bulimia nervosa an eating disorder characterized by episodes of binge eating followed by purging—usually self-induced vomiting or the use of laxatives to rapidly rid the body of just-eaten food

bystander effect the suppression of helping when bystanders are present at an emergency situation

case history a method in which one person—or a small group of persons—is studied in depth, often over a long period of time

category relationship the situation in which the parties involved in a social interaction are perceived to belong together in some way

cell body the largest concentration of mass in the neuron, containing the nucleus of the cell

central nervous system (CNS) all neurons and supporting cells found in the spinal cord and brain

cerebellum the lower brain center that smoothes and coordinates rapid bodily movements cerebral cortex the large, convoluted outer portion of the brain that makes us uniquely human, giving us our abilities to think, reason, and use language

chemical ions chemical particles that carry a small electrical charge, either positive (+) or negative (−)

chunk the representation in memory of a meaningful unit of information

ciliary muscles powerful muscles that expand or contract to reflexively change the shape of the lens to focus an image on the retina

classical conditioning a learning process in which a neutral stimulus is paired with a stimulus that reliably elicits an unconditioned response

client-centered therapy the variety of psychotherapy in which the goal is to help the individual self-actualize; to grow and develop to the best of his or her potential

closure the process by which we tend to fill in gaps or spaces in our perceptual world

cochlea the snail-like structure of the inner ear that contains the receptor cells for hearing

cognitions mental events; such as perception, beliefs, thoughts, ideas, and memories

cognitive dissonance a motivating state of tension or discomfort that exists when we hold or are aware of inconsistent ideas, beliefs, or cognitions

cognitive map a mental picture or representation of the physical environment, noting specific landmarks when possible

cognitive restructuring therapy a technique based on the assumption that considerable psychological distress stems from a few, simple, but misguided beliefs (cognitions)

cognitive therapists those psychotherapists who believe that what matters most are a client's thoughts, beliefs, perceptions, and attitudes about himself or herself and the environment

cognitive-behavior therapy (CBT) a form of psychotherapy with the joint focus to a) change the way one has been behaving, and b) change the way one interprets and thinks about the situation in which behavior change is required

color constancy the process that allows one to perceive the color of a familiar object as constant, despite changing lighting conditions

common fate the tendency to group together in the same figure those elements of a scene that appear to move together in the same direction and at the same speed

comorbidity the occurrence of two or more disorders in the same individual at the same time

compulsions constantly intruding, repetitive behaviors that bring no pleasure and are distressing

concepts mental categories or classes into which we place the events and objects that we experience

concrete operations stage Piaget's stage of cognitive development (7 to 11 years) in which children begin to develop many new concepts and show that they can manipulate those concepts

confirmation bias the notion that we tend to select from among several options the one that best fits with what we have suspected to be true for some time

conformity the modification of behavior, under perceived pressure to do so, to make it consistent with the behavior of others

conscious the level of consciousness containing ideas, memories, feelings, or motives of which we are actively aware

consciousness the subjective awareness of the environment and of one's own mental processes

conservation the awareness that changing the form or appearance of something does not change what it really is

contingency management and contingency contracting techniques following the learning principles of operant conditioning in which a person comes, through reinforcement, to appreciate the consequences of his or her behaviors

continuity (or good continuation) a process that operates when we see things as ending up consistent with the way they began

continuous reinforcement (CRF) schedule a procedure in which each and every desired response is reinforced after it occurs

control group participants in an experiment who receive a zero level of the independent variable

conventional morality Kohlberg's stage of moral development in which moral judgments are based on an accepted social convention

convergence a cue to 3-dimensionality that occurs when our eyes turn toward each other when we view something close

convergent thinking the process of taking many ideas or bits of information and attempting to reduce them to a simple solution

conversion disorder a disorder in which there is a loss or altering of physical function that suggests a physical disorder; the symptoms are not intentionally produced and cannot be explained by any physical disorder

cornea the tough, round, virtually transparent outer shell of the eye that begins focusing light waves

corpus callosum the structure that richly interconnects the two hemisphere of the cerebral cortex

correlation coefficient a number with a value between +1.00 and −1.00 that tells us about the nature and the extent of a relationship between the variables that have been measured

correlational research a scientific method seeking associations between variables that are observed and measured, but not manipulated

credibility a communicator's believability, reflecting assessments of both expertise and trustworthiness

cross laterality the process of nerve fibers crossing from one side of the body to the opposite side of the brain

CT scan (computed tomography) the procedure for taking a series of thousands of X-ray pictures of the brain from many angles

dark adaptation the process in which the visual receptors become more sensitive with time spent in the dark

death instincts (thanatos) opposed to life instincts, inborn impulses that are largely directed at destruction and aggression

decibel scale a scale of sound intensity measuring perceived loudness

declarative memory (explicit memory) memory systems from which information can be readily retrieved

deductive reasoning mental processes that lead to specific conclusions based on a small number of general principles

defense mechanisms unconsciously applied techniques that protect the conscious self (ego) against strong feelings of anxiety

delusions false beliefs—ideas that are firmly held, regardless of evidence to the contrary

dementia a conditioned characterized by the marked loss of intellectual abilities

dendrites protuberances that reach out to receive messages, or neural impulses, from other nearby neurons

denial a defense mechanism in which a person refuses to acknowledge the realities of an anxiety-producing situation

dependent variable (or "dependent measure") a measure of the behavior of the participants in an experiment

depressants psychoactive drugs that reduce awareness of external stimuli, slow bodily functioning, and decrease levels of overt behavior

deviation IQ a numerical estimate of intelligence that uses established group norms and allows for comparing intelligence scores across age and gender groups

diagnosis the act of recognizing a disorder on the basis of specific symptoms

diathesis-stress model the approach that proposes that individuals inherit multiple genes which may give rise to the predisposition to express certain behaviors, and that these behaviors are expressed only if activated by stress or trauma

difference threshold the minimum difference between stimuli that is detected 50 percent of the time

diffusion of responsibility the observation that the greater the number of people present, the smaller is each individual's perceived obligation to intervene

discrimination a biased, often negative, behavior directed at a member of a social group simply because of that person's group membership

discrimination learning a process in classical conditioning in which an organism learns to discriminate between different stimuli, emitting a CR in response to some stimuli, but not to others

discrimination training in operant conditioning, a matter of differential reinforcement—responses made to appropriate stimuli are reinforced, while responses made to inappropriate stimuli are not reinforced

displacement the defense mechanism that involves redirecting aggression at a substitute person or object rather than expressing it directly

dissociative amnesia the inability to recall important personal information—an inability too extensive to be explained by simple forgetfulness

dissociative disorders psychological disorders in which a person seeks to escape from some aspects of life or personality seen as the source of stress, discomfort, or anxiety

dissociative fugue amnesic forgetfulness, accompanied by a change of location—seemingly pointless travel

dissociative identity disorder a disorder characterized by two or more distinct personalities or personality traits within the same person

divergent thinking the process of starting with one idea and generating from it a number of new ones

drive a state of tension, arousal, or activation—aimed at satisfying a need

dualism associated with Descartes, the position that humans posses more than just a body; they have a mind

dysthymia a mood disorder that involves recurrent pessimism, low energy level, and low self esteem; a chronic, continual sense of being depressed and sad

ego the part of the personality that develops through one's experiences with reality; the rational, reasoning part of our personalities

elaboration likelihood model the point of view that there are two routes to persuasion; the central route and the peripheral route

elaborative rehearsal the process of moving information into long-term memory by thinking about it, organizing it, forming images of it, and making it meaningful—relating it to something already in LTM

electroconvulsive therapy (ECT) shock treatments that involve passing an electric current of between 70 and 150 volts across a patient's head for a fraction of a second

electroencephalograms (EEGs) recordings of the electrical activity of the brain

electroencephalograph (EEG) an instrument that measures and records the electrical activity of the brain

electromyogram (EMG) a record of a muscle's activity, tone, or state of relaxation

embryonic stage the period of development during which the embryo develops at a rapid rate, and all of the organ systems of the body are laid in place—lasts about 6 weeks

emotion an experience that includes a subjective feeling, a cognitive interpretation, a physiological reaction, and a behavioral expression

emotion-focused strategies techniques that deal with how one feels and how to change the way one feels when dealing with stress and stressors

empathy a compassionate understanding of how a person in need is feeling

empathy-altruism hypothesis the proposal that empathy is one reason for helping those in need

empirically supported therapies (ESTs) approaches to psychotherapy for which there is empirical evidence that an approach is effective in the treatment of specific disorders

empiricists those who credit experience and observation as the source of mental life

encoding specificity principle the assertion that how one retrieves information depends upon how it was encoded in the first place

encoding the process of putting information into memory, or forming cognitive representations of experiences

endocrine system a network of glands that affects behavior by secreting chemicals called hormones

epigenetics a complex biochemical system, above the level of one's DNA code that can affect the expression of genetically influenced traits

episodic memory the type of LTM in which memories of life events and experiences are stored

equity theory a position that considers the appraisal of rewards and costs for both parties of a social relationship

escape conditioning a process in which an organism learns to get away from (escape) a painful, noxious, aversive situation once in it

etiology the source or cause of disorders

excitatory the name of the process in which neurotransmitter chemicals are released from the vesicles, cross the synaptic cleft, and stimulate the next neuron to fire

experiment a series of operations used to investigate whether changes in one variable cause measurable changes in another variable, while all other variables are controlled or eliminated

experimental group participants in an experiment exposed to some value of the independent variable

experimental research a scientific method in which investigators manipulate a variable (or more than one) and look for a relationship between those manipulations and changes in the value of some other variable

explicit attitude an attitude that works at a conscious level, i.e., we are aware of these attitudes and how they may affect our behaviors

explicit stereotype a stereotype of which we are consciously aware and which is under conscious control

external attribution an explanation of the source of a person's behavior in terms of the situation or context in which the behavior occurs

extinction in operant conditioning, the decrease in the rate of a response that occurs as reinforcers are withheld

extinction the stage of classical conditioning in which the strength of the CR decreases with repeated presentations of the CS alone

extraneous variables those factors, other than the independent variable, that can influence the dependent variable of an experiment and need to be controlled or eliminated

family therapy an approach to psychotherapy that focuses on the roles, interdependence, and communication skills of family members

fantasy the defense mechanism that provides escape from anxiety through imagination or daydreaming

fetal alcohol syndrome (FAS) a problem in which smaller babies with retarded growth, poor coordination, poor muscle tone, and intellectual retardation result when the mother consumes alcohol during pregnancy

fetal stage the period of development during which the organs of the body continue to increase in complexity and size, and also begin to function—includes months 3 through 9

field experiments those done, not in a laboratory, but in the "real world"

figure-ground relationship the name for the process in which those stimuli that are attended to and grouped together are figures, and all the rest is ground

fixed interval (FI) schedule a procedure in which time is divided into set (fixed) intervals, and after each interval, a reinforcer is delivered when the next appropriate response occurs

fixed ratio (FR) schedule a procedure in which one establishes (fixes) a ratio of reinforcers to responses

formal operations stage Piaget's stage of cognitive development (12 and older) characterized by the logical manipulation of abstract, symbolic concepts

fovea the place in the retina where visual acuity is best in daylight or in reasonably high levels of illumination

free association a technique in psychoanalysis in which patients are to say whatever comes into their minds

frustration the blocking or thwarting of goal-directed behavior

frustration-aggression hypothesis the claim (now discredited) that frustration can produce several different reactions, including aggression, but that aggression was always caused by frustration

functional fixedness a type of mental set; the inability to discover an appropriate new use for an object because of experience using the object for some other purpose

functional magnetic resonance imaging (fMRI) a technique that allows for the measurement of molecules of blood in the brain, taken as an indicator of neural activity

functionalism the approach to psychology that focuses on the mind, but emphasizes its adaptive functions

fundamental attribution error the general tendency to favor internal, personal, attributions rather than favoring external, situational explanations

gender one's sense of maleness or femaleness

General Adaptation Syndrome the most widely accepted description of the physiological reactions to chronic stressors, including alarm, resistance, and exhaustion stages

generalization in operant conditioning, a process in which responses conditioned in the presence of specific stimuli also appear in the presence of other, similar stimuli

generalization (in experiments) the ability to apply results beyond the restrictive conditions of an experimental setting

generalized anxiety disorder (GAD) distressing, felt anxiety; unrealistic, excessive, persistent worry

generativity a concern for family and for a person's impact on future generations

germinal stage the period of development that lasts from the time of fertilization until the blastocyst implants itself into the uterus—about 2 weeks

gestalt psychology the approach to psychology that focuses on perception, concerned with how we select and organize information form the outside world

Gestalt therapy the variety of psychotherapy aimed at assisting a person to integrate thoughts, feelings, and actions; to increase self-awareness, self-acceptance and growth

g-factor according to Spearman, one's general, overall intelligence

grammar the formal expression of the syntax of a language

group polarization effect the phenomenon in which group participation makes an individual's reactions more extreme or polarized

group therapy an approach to psychotherapy that amounts to several people all having therapy at the same time

groupthink an excessive concern for reaching consensus in group decision making to the extent that critical evaluations are withheld

gustation the technical term for the sense of taste

habituation a simple form of learning in which an organism comes to disregard a stimulus of little or no consequence

hallucinations false perceptions—perceiving that which is not there, or failing to perceive that which is

hallucinogens psychoactive drugs with unpredictable effects on consciousness, including the formation of hallucinations

heuristic an informal, rule-of-thumb strategy of generating and testing problem solutions

homeostasis a state of balance or equilibrium among internal physiological processes

homosexuality sexual arousal and attraction to members of the same sex

humanistic psychology the approach to psychology that takes the position that the individual, or self, should be of central concern

hypnosis an altered state of consciousness characterized by a) a marked increase in suggestibility, b) a focusing of attention, c) an exaggerated use of imagination, d) an unwillingness or inability to act on one's own, and e) an unquestioning acceptance of distortions of reality

hypochondriasis the diagnosis for someone preoccupied with the fear of a serious disease

hypothesis a tentative explanation of a phenomenon that can be tested and either supported or rejected

id the totally inborn portion of personality, residing in the unconscious; it is through the id that basic instincts are expressed

idealistic principle the basis of operation of the superego—to promote what is good or right, regardless of pressure from the id

identity crisis the struggle to define and integrate the sense of who one is, what one is to do in life, and what one's attitudes, beliefs, and values should be

illusions experiences in which our perceptions are at odds with reality

implicit attitude an attitude that operates on an unconscious level, beyond our awareness of it affects

implicit stereotype a stereotype that operates on an unconscious level and is activated automatically, without conscious thought

incentives the end states, or goals, of behaviors that organisms are motivated to attain

independent variable the variable in an experiment that the experimenter manipulates

inductive reasoning mental processes that lead to a likely general conclusion based upon separate, specific facts and observations

inferiority complex (according to Adler) the feeling that we are less able than others to solve life's problems and get along in the world

information processing the means by which we find out about the world, make judgments about it, learn from it, and remember what we have learned

inhibitory the name of the process in which neurotransmitters flood across the synaptic cleft, bind to receptor sites, and prevent the next neuron from firing

insanity a legal term implying that a person did not fully understand the consequences of his or her actions at a given time, could not discern the difference between right and wrong, and was unable to exercise control over his or her actions at the time a crime was committed

insomnia the inability to fall asleep or stay asleep when one wants to

instincts unlearned, complex patterns of behavior that occur in the presence of certain stimuli

intelligence the capacity of an individual to understand the world and his or her resourcefulness to cope with its challenges

interactive dualism Descartes' position that the mind and body are separate entities and interact or influence each other; knowing the body provides knowledge of the mind

internal attribution an explanation of the source of a person's behavior in terms of the person's characteristics—personality traits or dispositions

interneurons those within the central nervous system

interpersonal attraction a positive, favorable, and powerful attitude toward another person

interview a method that yields data of what people say about themselves, rather than what they do

IQ a numerical estimate of intelligence found by dividing one's mental age (MA) by his or her actual chronological age (CA), and then multiplying by 100

iris the colored part of the eye that can expand or contract depending upon the intensity of light striking the eye

just noticeable difference (jnd) the amount of change in a stimulus that makes it just detectably difference from what it was

just world hypothesis an error in which people believe that we live in a world where good things happen to good people and bad things happen to bad people

kinesthetic sense the sense that informs us about body position with receptors in joints, muscles, and tendons

language a large collection of arbitrary symbols that have a common shared significance for a language-using community, and that follow certain rules of combination

latent content the aspects of a dream seen as symbolic representations of the content of the unconscious mind

latent learning a "hidden" learning that is not shown in behavior until it is reinforced (until there is a reason for doing so)

law of effect responses are acquired when followed by a "satisfying state of affairs, an if responses are not followed by a satisfying state of affairs, or lead to "discomfort," an organism will tend not make that response again

learned helplessness a phenomenon of learning that there is no escape from a punishing situation or stimulus and passively giving in to it without resistance

learning a process demonstrated by a relatively permanent change in behavior that occurs as the result of practice or experience

lens a flexible structure that changes its shape in order to focus images on the back of the eye

libido the driving force of the id; the sexual/sensual energy by which the id operates

life instincts (eros) impulses for survival, including those that motivate sex, hunger, and thirst limbic system a collection of small structures in the center of the brain involved in emotionality and memory formation

lobotomy a surgical procedure that severs the major neural connections between the prefrontal lobes and lower brain centers

loneliness a subjective psychological state in which there is a discrepancy between relationships we would like to have and those that we actually have

long-term memory (LTM) that level or store of memory that holds large amounts of information for long periods of time

maintenance rehearsal the simple repetition of the information already in STM in an effort to keep it there

major depressive disorder a disorder in which a person must have experienced two or more depressive episodes, where such an episode is defined as a period of at least two weeks, during which the person experienced 5 or more of these symptoms: a) depressed or sad mood, b) loss of pleasure or interest in normal activities, c) weight loss or dramatic change in appetite, d) significantly more or less sleep than normal, e) either physical slowness or agitation, f) unusual fatigue or loss of energy, and g) recurrent thoughts of death or suicide

mania an elevated mood with feelings of euphoria or irritability

manifest content the aspects of a dream as recalled and reported

matching phenomenon the observation that people select partners whose level of physical attractiveness is similar to their own

meaningfulness the extent to which to-be-remembered items elicit existing associations in memory

mechanism associated with Descartes, the notion that if the body consists essentially of tubes, gears, valves, and fluids, its operation must be subject to physical laws, and those laws can be discovered

meditation a self-induced state of altered consciousness characterized by a focusing of attention and relaxation

medulla the lower brain center that controls such functions as coughing, sneezing, respiration, heart function, and reflexive eye movements

memory a set of systems involved in the acquisition, storage, and retrieval of information

menarche the first menstrual period, indicative of the beginning of puberty in females

mental retardation a disability characterized by significant limitations both in intellectual functioning and in adaptive behavior as expressed in conceptual, social, and practical adaptive skills

mental set the cognitive process of being psychologically ready or predisposed to perceive something

mere exposure phenomenon the likelihood of developing positive evaluations of stimuli increases with repeated exposures

meta-analysis a statistical procedure of combining the results of many studies to see more clearly the relationship(s), if any, between or among variables

method of loci the mnemonic technique in which the learner imagines a familiar location and "places" the material to be retrieved in various places throughout that location in a sensible order

Minnesota Multiphasic Personality Inventory (MMPI) a paper-and-pencil personality test that measures several personality dimensions with the same set of (567) items

mnemonic devices techniques that aid retrieval by helping one to organize and add meaningfulness to new material

Modal Memory Model a way of looking at memory, i.e., that information is processed through three distinct memory storage systems: sensory memory, short-term memory (STM), and long-term memory (LTM)

modeling a form of behavior therapy that involves the acquisition of an appropriate response through the imitation of a model

modern racism a variety of racism that is not expressed openly, as in the past, but rather is manifested in an uncertainty in feelings and behaviors directed toward others

mood disorders those disorders that demonstrate a disturbance in emotional reactions or feelings

morphemes the smallest units of meaning in a spoken language—a collection of phonemes that mean something

motivation the process that arouses, directs, and maintains behaviors

motor areas those parts of the cerebral cortex in which most voluntary movement is initiated

motor neurons those that carry impulses away from the spinal cord and brain to muscles and glands

multiple approach-avoidance conflict a situation in which an individual is faced with a number of alternatives, each one of which is at the same time and in some way both positive and negative

myelin a white substance composed of fat and protein that covers, insulates, and protects about half of the axons in an adult's nervous system

naïve realism the tendency for us to believe that we see the world in a more rational, objective way than do others

narcolepsy the sleep disorder that involves going to sleep, even during the day, without any intention of doing so

narrative chaining the process that aids retrieval by the weaving of unorganized materials into a meaningful story

naturalistic observation the method of systematically watching behaviors as they occur naturally, with a minimum involvement of the observer

need a lack or shortage of some biological essential required for survival

need for affiliation the need to be with others, to work with others toward the same ends, and to form friendships and associations

need for intimacy the need to form and maintain close affectionate relationships

need for power the need to be in control, to be in charge of both the situation and of others

need to achieve (nAch) the acquired need to meet or exceed some standard of excellence in one's behaviors

negative correlation coefficient a value between 0.00 and −1.00 that tells us that as values of one variable increase, the values of the other variable decrease

negative reinforcer a stimulus that increases (or maintains) the rate of a response that precedes it removal

negative symptoms those characterized by a loss or decrease in normal functions

neonate the name given to a newborn

neural impulse a rapid, reversible change in the electrical charge within and outside a neuron

neural threshold the minimum level of stimulation required to get a neuron to fire

neurogenesis the term used to describe the production of functioning neurons after birth

neuron the microscopically small cell that transmits information in the form of nerve impulses from one part of the body to another

neuroscientists scientists concerned with the development, structure, function, chemistry, pharmacology, and pathology of the nervous system

nondeclarative memory (procedural memory) the type of LTM in which well-learned chains of responses are stored

object permanence the awareness that objects still exist even if they cannot be seen and that their reappearance is anticipated

observer bias a problem that arises when an observer's own motives, expectations, and previous experiences interfere with the objectivity of the observations being made

obsessions ideas or thoughts that involuntarily and constantly intrude on awareness

obsessive-compulsive disorder (OCD) an anxiety disorder characterized by a pattern or recurrent obsessions and compulsions

olfaction the technical term for the sense of smell

operant a behavior or behaviors an organism uses to interact with its environment in order to produce certain effects

operant conditioning a form of learning that changes the rate or probability of responses on the basis of the consequences that result from those responses

operational definition a definition of concepts in terms of the procedures used to measure or create those concepts

opponent-process theory a theory of color vision proposing that color vision works by means of three pairs of mechanisms that respond to different wavelengths of light: a blue-yellow processor, a red-green processor, and a black-white processor

optic chiasma where fibers in the optic nerve get directed to the occipital lobe

optic nerve the collection of neurons that leaves the eye and starts back toward other parts of the brain

orienting reflex a simple, unlearned response of attending to a new or unusual stimulus

overlearning the process of practicing or rehearsing information over and above what is necessary to learn it

panic disorder an acute "attack" of anxiety that is recurrent, unpredictable, unprovoked, sudden, and intense

parasympathetic division (of the ANS) is active when we are relaxed and quiet

Parkinson's disease a disorder involving the basal ganglia in which the most noticeable symptoms are impairment of movement and involuntary tremors

perception the process that involves the selection, organization, and perception of stimuli

peripheral detail aspects of the environment that do not draw our attention and make up our perceptual background

peripheral nervous system (PNS) all neurons not in the CNS; the nerve fibers in our arms, legs, face, torso, intestines, and so on

personality those affects, behaviors, and cognitions of individuals that characterize them in a number of situations over time

personality disorders long-lasting patterns of perceiving, relating to, and thinking about the environment and oneself that are inflexible and maladaptive and cause either impaired functioning or distress

persuasion the application of rational and/or emotional arguments to deliberately convince others to change their attitudes and/or behaviors

PET scan (positron emission tomography a scanning techniques that provides insights about the functions of the intact brain

pheromones chemicals that produce distinctive odors that may be related to attracting members of the opposite sex

phobic disorder an intense, irrational fear of an object or event that leads a person to avoid contact with it

phonemes the individual speech sounds of a language

pinna the outer ear

pituitary gland the master gland, reflecting its direct control over the activity of many other glands in the endocrine system

placebo something given to participants that has no identifiable effect on the dependent variable

pleasure principle the basis of operation of the id—to find satisfaction for basic pleasurable impulses

pluralistic ignorance the belief on the part of an individual that only he or she is confused and does not know what to do in an emergency, whereas everyone else is standing around doing nothing for good reason

point of viability that time at which the fetus could survive if it were born

pons a relay station, or bridge, relaying sensory messages from the spinal cord and the face to higher brain centers, and relaying motor impulses from higher centers in the brain down to the rest of the body

positive correlation coefficient a value between 0.00 and +1.00 that tells us that as values of one variable increase, the values of the other variable increase as well

positive reinforcer a stimulus given to an organism after a response is made that increases (or maintains) the rate of that response

positive symptoms those characterized by new affects, behaviors, and/or cognitions, including hallucinations and delusions

positive test strategy the procedure that claims that if something works, one should not drop it to try something else that might work better

postconventional morality Kohberg's stage of moral development in which moral reasoning at this highest level reflects complex, internalized standards

posttraumatic stress disorder (PTSD) a disorder that involves distressing symptoms that arise at some time after the experience of a traumatic event

pragmatics the study of how language is related to the social context in which it occurs

preconscious the level of consciousness containing aspects of our experience of which we are not conscious at the moment, but that easily can be brought into awareness

preconventional morality Kohlberg's stage of moral development in which moral reasoning is mostly concerned about the rewards and punishments that come from breaking a rule

prejudice attitudes that represent a biased, often negative, disposition toward a group of people

prenatal period the time from conception to birth

preoperational stage Piaget's stage of cognitive development (2 to 7 years) in which a child's thinking is self-centered, or egocentric

primary reinforcers those that do not require previous experience to be effective; they are related to an organism's survival and usually are physiological or biological in nature

proactive interference the process that occurs when previously learned material inhibits the retrieval of more recently learned material

problem a situation that exists when there is a discrepancy between one's present state and one's perceived goal state and no readily apparent way to get from one to the other

problem-focused strategies techniques that deal with finding the underlying situation that is causing one's stress and taking steps to deal with it

problem-solving strategy a systematic plan for generating possible solutions to a problem that can be tested to see if they are correct

projection seeing one's own unacceptable, anxiety-producing thoughts, motives, or traits in others

projective technique an assessment device that asks a person to respond to ambiguous stimuli

prototypes members of a category that typify or best represent the category to which they belong

proximity the observation that events occurring close together in space or time are perceived as belonging together and being part of the same figure

pseudoscience a set of ideas based on theories put forth as scientific when they are not

psychiatry the field of medicine that studies, diagnoses, and treats mental disorders

psychoactive drugs chemicals that alter a person's affects, cognitions, or behaviors psychoanalytic psychology associated with Freud, the approach to psychology that emphasizes innate strivings and the unconscious mind

psychological test an objective, standardized, measure of a sample of behavior

psychology the science that studies behavior and mental processes

psychophysics the study of relationships between the physical attributes of stimuli and the psychological experiences they produce

psychosurgery surgical procedures, usually directed at the brain, used to influence psychological functioning

psychotic symptoms those that signal loss of contact with reality, such as delusions and hallucinations, and a gross impairment in functioning, inappropriate affect, or loss of affect

puberty the onset of sexual maturity and the ability to reproduce

punishment in operant conditioning, a process that occurs when a stimulus delivered to an organism decreases the rate of probability of the response that preceded it

pupil the opening through which light enters the eye

random assignment a procedure by which each participant in a research program has an equal chance of being assigned to any of the groups in an experiment

rapid eye movements (REM) times when a sleeping person's eyes move quickly under his or her closed eyelids; associated with dreaming

rational-emotive therapy (RET) a form of cognitive therapy with the basic premise that psychological problems arise when people try to interpret what happens in the world on the basis of irrational beliefs

rationalization making up excuses for one's behaviors, rather than facing their (anxiety-producing) causes or consequences

reality principle the basis of operation of the ego—to find satisfaction for the id, but in ways that are reasonable and rational

reasoning the process of reaching conclusions that are based either on a set of general (cognitive) principles, or on an assortment of acquired facts and observations

recall the process that occurs when someone produces information to which he or she has been previously exposed

receptor sites special places on a neuron where neurotransmitters can be received

recognition the process in which someone is asked to identify material previously experienced

reconstructive memory the notion that we store only features of what has been experienced and then retrieve those features and construct a meaningful story about what was encoded and stored

refractory period the brief time during which a neuron, having just fired, cannot fire again

regression a return to earlier, more primitive, childish levels of behavior that were once effective in securing desired outcomes

reinforcement the process of increasing the rate or probability of a response

reinforcement-affect model the position that we are attracted to people with whom we associate rewarding experiences

reinforcer the actual stimulus used in the process of reinforcement that increases the rate or probability of a response

relearning the change in performance that occurs when a person is required to learn material for a second time

reliability the extent to which a test produces the same or highly similar results across similar testing situations

representativeness heuristic the assumption that judgments about the most prototypic member of a category will hold for all members of that category

repressed memory a stored memory that so disturbs a person that he or she pushes it deep into the unconscious and can no longer retrieve it readily

repression the most basic defense mechanism—referred to as motivated forgetting

resistance in psychoanalysis, the unwillingness or inability to freely discuss some aspect of one's life

resting potential the tension that results from the positive and negative ions' attraction to each other (about −70 mV)

reticular formation an ill-defined collection of nerve fibers involved in one's level of activation or arousal

retina the place where vision begins to take place; where light wave energy is transduced into neural energy

retinal disparity a binocular cue to depth caused by the fact that when we look at a nearby 3-dimensional object, each eye gets a somewhat different view of it

retrieval the process of finding and moving information out of memory for use

retroactive interference the process of inhibiting the retrieval of learned material by the acquisition of information learned after the to-be-remembered information

retrograde (backward-acting) amnesia the loss of memories of events that occurred before the onset of the amnesia

reuptake the process by which neurotransmitters are reabsorbed by the membrane of the neuron from which they came rods/cones the photo-receptor cells (transducers) found in the retina

salient detail an aspect or detail of the environment that captures our attention

sample a subset, or portion, of a larger group (population) that has been chosen for study

schema (in human memory) an internal, organized knowledge system stored in long-term memory

schemas according to Piaget, integrated mental representations that children construct to make sense of the world

schizophrenia a psychological disorder characterized by a distortion of reality, a retreat from other people, and disturbances in affect, behavior, and cognition

science a discipline that demonstrates a) an organized body of knowledge (a set of scientific laws), and 2) the use of scientific methods

scientific methods techniques of acquiring knowledge that involve observing phenomena, formulating hypotheses about them, making additional observations, and refining and re-testing hypotheses

secondary drives those drives that are derived from learning experiences

secondary reinforcers a conditioned, acquired, or learned reinforcer

self-serving bias occurs when we attribute successes (positive outcomes) to personal, internal sources, and failures (negative outcomes) to situational, external sources

semantic memory the type of long-term memory in which vocabulary, simple concepts, and rules are stored

semantics the study of meaning

sensation the action of detecting external stimuli and converting those stimuli into nervous system activity

sense receptors the specialized neural cells in the sense organs that change physical energy into neural impulses

sensorimotor stage Piaget's stage of cognitive development (birth to 2 years) in which children discover by sensing (sensori-) and by doing (motor)

sensory adaptation what occurs when our sensory experience decreases with continued exposure to a stimulus

sensory areas those parts of the cerebral cortex that receive impulses from the senses

sensory memory a variety of memory that stores large amounts of information for brief periods (a few seconds or less)

sensory neurons those that carry impulses toward the brain or spinal cord

sexually transmitted diseases (STDs) contagious diseases usually passed on through sexual contact

s-factors according to Spearman, a collection of a person's specific cognitive skills

shape constancy the perception that objects maintain their shape, even though the retinal image they cast may change

shaping the process of reinforcing successive approximations of a response one ultimately wants to operantly condition

short-term memory (STM) a level, or store in memory with a limited capacity and, without the benefit of rehearsal, a brief duration

signal detection theory the position that stimulus detection is a decision-making process of determining if a signal exists against a background of noise

similarity the observation that stimuli that are alike or share properties tend to be grouped together in our perceptions

size constancy the tendency to see objects as unchanging in size, regardless of the size of the retinal image that they produce

sleep apnea patterns of sleep during which breathing stops entirely

social cognition the processes used to think about, understand, and evaluate social situations

social dominance orientation the belief that one's own social group is superior to others

social exchange theory the position that, with regard to interpersonal attraction, what matters most is a comparison of costs and benefits of establishing or maintaining a relationship

social facilitation the process that occurs when the presence of others improves an individual's performance on some task

social learning theory associated with Bandura, the position that learning often takes place through the observation and imitation of models

social loafing the tendency to work less (to decrease individual effort) as the size of the group in which one works becomes larger

social psychology the field of psychology concerned with how others influence the thoughts, feelings, and behaviors of others, and vice versa

socioeconomic status (SES) a measure that reflects income, educational level, and occupation

somatic nervous system those neurons that are outside the CNS, serve the skeletal muscles and pick up impulses from our sense receptors

somatization disorder a disorder indicated by several recurring and long-lasting complaints about bodily symptoms for which no physical cause can be found

somatoform disorders psychological disorders that involve physical or bodily symptoms with no known medical or biological cause for the symptoms

spanking a form of punishment that is physically non-injurious, intended to modify behavior, and administered with an opened hand to the extremities or buttocks

spinal reflexes simple, automatic behaviors that occur without the conscious, voluntary action of the brain

split-brain procedure a surgical technique that destroys the corpus callosum's connections between the two hemisphere of the cerebral cortex

spontaneous recovery in operant conditioning, the automatic return of an extinguished response following a rest interval

spontaneous recovery the stage of classical conditioning that occurs after extinction and following a rest interval in which the extinguished CR automatically reappears in response to the CS

stereotype a rigid set of positive or negative beliefs about a group of people, particularly members of an out-group

stimulants psychoactive drugs that stimulate or activate and organism, producing a heightened state of arousal and elevation of mood

stimulus generalization a process in classical conditioning in which a conditioned response is elicited by stimuli similar to the original CS

storage the process of holding encoded information in memory

stress a complex set of reactions made by an individual under pressure to adapt

stressor the source of stress

structuralism Wundt's approach to psychology, committed to describing the structures of the mind and their operation

subjective contours a perceptual phenomenon in which arrangements of lines and patterns enable us to "see" figures that are not actually there

sublimation a defense mechanism involving the repression of unacceptable sexual or aggressive impulses and allowing them to surface in socially acceptable behaviors that are not openly sexual or aggressive

subliminal perception the process of perceiving and responding to stimuli presented at levels that are below one's absolute threshold of conscious processing

superego one's sense of morality or conscience, reflecting one's internalization of society's rules

survey a data collection method of systematically asking a large number of persons the same question or set of questions

sympathetic division the component of the ANS that is actively involved in states of emotionality

synapse the location at which a neural impulse is relayed from one neuron to another

synaptic cleft a microscopically small gap between the axon terminal and the dendrites (or cell body) of another neuron

syntax the rules that govern how sentences are formed or structured in a language

systematic desensitization a process for treating phobias in which the goal is to gradually teach (through classical conditioning) a patient to associative positive feelings and relaxation with a previously feared stimulus

taste buds the receptor cells for taste, located in the tongue

test norms results of a test taken by a large group of people whose scores are used to make comparisons

thalamus a relay station for impulses to and from the cerebral cortex

theory an organized collection of testable ideas used to describe and explain a particular subject matter

thinking a term referring to cognitive processes that build on existing cognitions—perceptions, ideas, experiences, and memories

thyroid gland regulates the pace of the body's functioning—the rate at which oxygen is used and the rate of body function and growth

timbre the psychological quality or character of sound that reflects its degree of purity

top-down processing a process that occurs when what one selects and and perceives depends largely on what the perceiver already knows

trait (personality) any distinguishable, relatively enduring way in which one individual differs from others

transducer a mechanism that converts energy from one form into another

transference in psychoanalysis, the process that occurs when the patient unconsciously comes to view and feel about the analyst in much the same way as he or she feels about another important person

trichromatic theory a theory of color vision proposing that the eye contains three (tri) distinct receptors for color (chroma)

type A behavior pattern (TABP) characterizes a person who is competitive, achievement-oriented, impatient, who typically works at many tasks at the same time, is easily aroused, and prone to hostility and anger

unconscious the level of consciousness containing cognitions, feelings, or motives that are not available at the conscious or preconscious level

validity the extent to which a test actually measures what it claims to be measuring

variable interval (VI) schedule a schedule in which one randomly varies the time interval between reinforcers

variable ratio (VR) schedule a schedule in which one varies (changes) the ratio of reinforcers to responses

vesicles incredibly small containers that hold complex chemicals called neurotransmitters

vestibular sense the sense that tells us about balance, where we are in relation to gravity, and about acceleration or deceleration

vicarious reinforcement/vicarious punishment learning about the consequences of one's own behaviors by observing what happens to someone else who engages in those behaviors

vitreous humor the thick fluid in the center of the eye (behind the lens) with the major function of keeping the eyeball spherical

vomeronasal organ (VNO) the primary organ involved in the detection of pheromones

white light a light of the lowest possible saturation, consisting of a random mixture of wavelengths

zygote the first new cell resulting from conception

References

AADA (Anxiety Disorders Association of America). (2003). *Statistics and facts about anxiety disorders.* Silver Spring, MD: Author.

AAHSA, American Association of Homes and Services for the Aging. (2003). *Nursing home statistics.* From the AAHSA website at www.aahsa.org.

AAMR. (2002). *Mental retardation: Definition, classification, and systems of supports.* Washington, DC: American Association of Mental Retardation.

AARP. (1993). Census Bureau ups 65+ population estimates. *AARP Bulletin,* **34,** p. 2.

——. (1995). Negative stereotypes still plague older workers on the job. *AARP Bulletin,* **36,** April, p. 3.

——. (2005). *AARP Massachusetts end of life survey: Research report.* Boston: AARP Massachusetts.

Abel, E. L. (1981). Behavioral teratology. *Psychological Bulletin,* **90,** 564–581.

——. (1984). *Fetal alcohol syndrome and fetal alcohol effects.* New York: Plenum.

Abi-Dargham, A., Guo, N., Narendran, R., Hwang, D., Ekelund, J., Guillan, O., Martinez, D., Frankle, G., & Laruelle, M. (2005). Prefrontal dopamine transmission in schizophrenia: Is D1 receptor a relevant biomarker? *Behavioural Pharmacology,* **16** (Supplement 1:S13).

Abrams, R. L., & Greenwald, A. G. (2000). Parts outweigh the whole (word) in unconscious analysis of meaning. *Psychological Science,* **11,** 118-124.

Abravanel, E. & Sigafoos, A. D. (1984). Exploring the presence of imitation during early infancy. *Child Development,* **55,** 381–392.

Ackerman, P. L., & Kanfer, R. (1993). Integrating laboratory and field study for improving selection: Development of a battery for predicting air traffic controller success. *Journal of Applied Psychology,* **78,** 413–432.

Ackerman, S. J., & Hilsenroth, M. J. (2003). A review of therapist characteristics and techniques positively impacting on the therapeutic alliance. *Clinical Psychology Review,* **23,** 1–33.

Adame, D. E., Johnson, T. C., & Cole, S. P. (1989). Physical fitness, body image, and locus of control in college freshmen men and women. *Perceptual and Motor Skills,* **68,** 400-402.

Adams, J. L. (1974). Conceptual blockbusting. Stanford, CA: Stanford Alumni Association. Cited in A. L. Glass, K. J. Holyoak, & J. L. Santa (1979), *Cognition.* Reading, MA: Addison-Wesley.

Adams, J. S. (1965). Inequity in social exchange. In L. Berkowitz (Ed.), *Advances in experimental social psychology.* New York: Academic Press.

Adams, L. A., & Rickert, V. I. (1989). Reducing bedtime tantrums: Comparison between positive routines and graduated extinctions. *Pediatrics,* **84,** 756–761.

Adams, R. J., & Courage, M. L. (1998). Human newborn color vision: Measurement with chromatic stimuli varying in excitement purity. *Journal of Experimental Child Psychology,* **67,** 22–34.

Adams, R. M. (1992). The "hot hand" revisited: Successful basketball shooting as a function of inter-shot interval. *Perceptual and Motor Skills,* **74,** 934.

——. (1995). Momentum in the performance of professional tournament pocket billiards players. *International Journal of Sport Psychology,* **26,** 580–587.

Adelmann, P. K., & Zajonc, R. B. (1989). Facial efference and the experience of emotion. *Annual Review of Psychology,* **40,** 249–280.

Adelson, B. (1984). When novices surpass experts: The difficulty of a task may interfere with expertise. *Journal of Experimental Psychology,* **10,** 483–495.

Adlard, P. A., Perreau, V. M., Pop, V., & Cotman, C. W. (2005). Voluntary exercise decreases amyloid load in a transgenic model of Alzheimer's disease. *Journal of Neuroscience,* **25,** 4217-4221.

Adler, N., & Matthews, K. (1994). Health psychology: Why do some people get sick and some stay well? *Annual Review of Psychology,* **45,** 229–259.

Adler, N. E., Boyce, T., Chesney, M. A., Cohen, S., Folkman, S., Kahn, R. L., & Syme, S. L. (1994). Socioeconomic status and health: The challenge of the gradient. *American Psychologist,* **49,** 15–24.

Adler, N. E., Marmot, M., McEwen, B. S., & Stewart, J. (1999). *Socioeconomic status and health in industrialized nations.* New York: New York Academy of Science.

Adler, N. E., Ozer, E. J., & Tschann, J. (2003). Abortion among adolescents. *American Psychologist,* **58,** 211–217.

Adler, N. E., & Stone, G. (1984). Psychology in the health system. In J. Ruffini (Ed.), *Advances in medical social science.* New York: Gordon & Breach.

Adler, T. (1989). Cocaine babies face behavior deficits. *APA Monitor,* **20**, 14.

——. (1990). Does the "new" MMPI beat the "classic"? *APA Monitor,* **21**, 18–19.

Adrogué, H. J., & Madias, N. E. (2000). Hypernatremia. *New England Journal of Medicine,* **342**, 1493–1499.

Agnew, H. W., Webb, W. W., & Williams, R. L. (1964). The effects of stage 4 sleep deprivation. *Electroencephalography and Clinical Neurophysiology,* **17**, 68–70.

Agnieszka, N. (2003). Gender differences in vivid memories. *Sex Roles,* **49**, 321-331.

Aiello, R. R., & Aiello, T. D. (1974). The development of personal space: Proxemic behavior of children 6 through 16. *Human Ecology,* **2**, 177–189.

Ainsworth, M. D. S. (1979). Infant-mother attachment. *American Psychologist,* **34**, 932–937.

——. (1989). Attachments beyond infancy. *American Psychologist,* **44**, 709–716.

Ajzen, I. (2001) Nature and operation of attitudes. *Annual Review of Psychology,* **52**, 27–58.

——. (2000). Attitudes and the attitude-behavior relation: Reasoned and automatic processes. In W. Stroebe & M. Hewstone (Eds.), *European Review of Social Psychology.* Chicester, England: Wiley.

Akan, G. E., & Grilo, C. M. (1995). Sociocultural influences on eating attitudes and behaviors, body image, and psychological functioning: A comparison of African-American, Asian-American, and Caucasian college women. *International Journal of Eating Disorders,* **18**, 181–187.

Akiskal, H. S., & Cassano, G. B. (Eds.). (1997). *Dysthymia and the spectrum of chronic depressions.* New York: Guilford Press.

Alain, C., Woods, D. L., & Knight, R. T. (1998). A distributed cortical network for auditory sensory memory in humans. *Brain research,* **812**, 23–37.

Alba, J. W., & Hasher, L. (1983). Is memory schematic? *Psychological Bulletin,* **93**, 201–231.

Albarracín, D., Durantini, M. R., & Earl, A. (2006). Empirical and theoretical conclusions of an analysis of outcomes of HIV-prevention interventions. *Current Directions in Psychological Science,* **15**, 73–78.

Albarracín, D., Johnson, B. T., Fishbein, M., & Muellerleile, P. (2001). Reasoned action and planned behavior as models of condom use: A meta-analysis. *Psychological Bulletin,* **127**, 142–161.

Albert, D. J., Petrovic, D. M., & Walsh, M. L. (1989). Competitive experience activates testosterone-dependent social aggression toward unfamiliar males. *Physiology and Behavior,* **45**, 723–727.

Alden, P., & Heap, M. (1998). Hypnotic pain control: Some theoretical and practical issues. *International Journal of Clinical and Experimental Hypnosis,* **46**, 62–76.

Alegria, M., Perez, D., & Williams, S. (2003). The role of public policies in reducing mental health status disparities for people of color. *Health Affairs,* **22**, 51-64.

Aleman, A., Kahn, R. S., & Selton, J. (2003). Sex differences in the risk for schizophrenia. *Archives of General Psychiatry,* **60**, 565–571.

Alexander, G. M. (2003). An evolutionary perspective of sex-typed toy preferences: Pink, blue and the brain. *Journal of Sexual Behavior,* **32**, 7–14.

Alexander, G. M., & Hines, M. (2002). Sex differences in response to children's toys in nonhuman primates (Cercopithecus aethiops sabaeus). *Evolution and Human Behavior,* **23**, 467–479.

Alexander, K. W., Quas, J. A., Goodman, G. S., Ghetti, S., Edelstein, R. S., Redlich, A. D., Corden, I. M., Jones, D. P. H. (2005). Traumatic implact predicts long-term memory for documented child sexual abuse. *Psychological Science,* **16**, 33–40.

Allen, J. L., Walker, L. D., Schroeder, D. A., & Johnson, D. E. (1987). Attributions and attribution-behavior relations: The effect of level of cognitive development. *Journal of Personality and Social Psychology,* **52**, 1099–1109.

Allen, M. G. (1976). Twin studies of affective illness. *Archives of General Psychiatry,* **33**, 1476–1478.

Alley, D., Suthers, K., & Crimmins, E. (2007). Education and cognitive decline in older Americans. *Research on Aging,* **29**, 73–94.

Allport, G. (1954). *The nature of prejudice.* Reading, MA: Addison-Wesley.

Allport, G. W. (1961). *Pattern and growth in personality.* New York: Holt, Rinehart & Winston.

Almeida, D. M. (2005). Resilience and vulnerability to daily stressors assessed via diary methods. *Current Directions in Psychological Science,* **14**, 64-68.

Altman, I. (1975). *The environment and social behavior.* Monterey, CA: Brooks/Cole.

Amabile, T. M. (1985). Motivation and creativity. *Journal of Personality and Social Psychology,* **48**, 393–399.

——. (2001). Beyond talent: John Irving and the passionate craft of creativity. *American Psychologist,* **56**, 333–336.

Amaro, H. (1995). Love, sex, and power: Considering women's realities in HIV prevention. *American Psychologist,* **50**, 437–447.

Ambuel, B. (1995). Adolescents, unintended pregnancy, and abortion: The struggle for a compassionate social policy. *Current Directions in Psychological Science,* **4**, 1–5.

American Academy of Sleep Medicine. (2001). *Sleep hygiene tips.* Downloaded from the World Wide Web, January 31, 2001. http://www.asda.org/.

American Association of Retired Persons. (1997). *A Profile of Older Americans 1997.* Downloaded from the World Wide Web, January 30, 2001. http://research.aarp.org/general/profile97.html#living.

American Automobile Association. (1997). *Road rage on the rise, AAA foundation reports.* [On-line]. Available: http://webfirst.com/aaa/text/roadrage.htm.

American Cancer Society. (2000). *1998 Facts and figures: Tobacco use.* American Cancer Society.

——. (2003). *Cancer facts & figures for Hispanics/Latinos 2003-2005.* Atlanta: American Cancer Society.

——. (2004). *Cancer facts & figures 2004.* Atlanta: American Cancer Society.

——. (2005a). *Cancer facts & figures 2005.* Atlanta: American Cancer Society.

——. (2005b). *Cancer facts & figures for African Americans 2005-2006.* Atlanta: American Cancer Society.

American Diabetes Association. (2001). *The Dangerous Toll of Diabetes.* Downloaded from the World Wide Web, January 30, 2001. http://www.diabetes.org/ada/facts.asp#youth.

American Heart Association. (2000). *Cigarette smoking and cardiovascular diseases.* American Heart Association.

American Psychiatric Association. (1987). *Diagnostic and statistical manual of mental disorders (3rd rev. ed.).* Washington, DC: American Psychiatric Association.

——. (1994). *Diagnostic and statistical manual of mental disorders (4th ed.).* Washington, DC: American Psychiatric Association.

——. (1997). Practice guidelines for the treatment of patients with schizophrenia. *American Journal of Psychiatry,* **154**, Supplement, 1–63.

——. (2000). *Diagnostic and statistical manual of mental disorders, Fourth Edition Text Revision (DSM-IV-TR).* Washington: American Psychiatric Association.

——. (2003). *Coexisting severe mental disorders and physical illness-Statement by the American Psychiatric Association.* Release No. 03-31 (July 7, 2003).

American Psychological Association. (2002). Data retrieved February 10, 2002, from http://apa.org.

——. (2002). Ethical principles of psychologists and code of conduct. *American Psychologist,* **57**, 1060–1073.

——. (1992). Ethical principles of psychologists and code of conduct. *American Psychologist,* **47**, 1597–1611.

American Psychological Society. (2002). Data retrieved February 10, 2002, from http://psychologicalscience.org.

American Sleep Apnea Association. (2001). *Information about sleep apnea: Sleep apnea defined.* Downloaded from the World Wide Web, February 1, 2001. http://www.sleepapnea.org/eninfo.html#defined.

American Social Health Association. (2001). *Facts and answers about STDs.* Research Triangle Park, NC: American Social Health Association.

Amoore, J. E. (1970). *Molecular basis of odor.* Springfield, IL: Thomas.

Anastasi, A. (1988). *Psychological testing (6th ed.).* New York: Macmillan.

Anderman, E. M., Austin, A. C., & Johnson, D. M. (2001). The development of goal orientation. In A. Wigfield and J. S. Eccles (Eds.), *The development of achievement motivation.* San Diego, CA: Academic Press.

Anderson, B. L. (1997). Psychological interventions for individuals with cancer. *Clinician's Research Digest; Supplemental Bulletin* **16**, July, 1997.

Anderson, C. A. (1987). Temperature and aggression: Effects on quarterly, yearly, and city rates of violent and nonviolent crime. *Journal of Personality and Social Psychology,* **52**, 1161–1173.

——. (1989). Temperature and aggression: Ubiquitous effects of heat on occurrence of human violence. *Psychological Bulletin,* **106**, 74–96.

Anderson, C. A., & Anderson, D. C. (1984). Ambient temperature and violent crime: Tests of the linear and curvilinear hypotheses. *Journal of Personality and Social Psychology,* **46**, 91–97.

Anderson, C. A., & Bushman, B. J. (2002). Human aggression. *Annual Review of Psychology,* **53**, 27–51.

Anderson, C. A., & Dill, K. E. (2000). Video games and aggressive thoughts, feelings, and behavior in the laboratory and in life. *Journal of Personality and Social Psychology,* **78**, 772–790.

Anderson, C. A., & Morrow, M. (1995). Competitive aggression without interaction: Effects of competitive versus cooperative instructions on aggressive behavior in video games. *Personality and Social Psychology Bulletin,* **21**, 1020–1030.

Anderson, D. K., Lord, C., Risi, S., DiLavore, P. S., Shulman, C., Thurm, A., et al. (2007). Patterns of growth in verbal abilities among children with autism spectrum disorder. *Journal of Consulting and Clinical Psychology,* **75**, 594–604.

Anderson, J. R. (1980). *Cognitive psychology and its implications.* San Francisco: Freeman.

——. (1987). Skill acquisition: Compilation of weak-method problem solutions. *Psychological Review,* **94**, 192–210.

Anderson, R., & Nida, S. A. (1978). Effect of physical attractiveness on opposite- and same-sex evaluations. *Journal of Personality,* **46**, 401–413.

Anderson, R. C., & Pichert, J. W. (1978). Recall of previously unrecallable information following a shift in perspective. *Journal of Verbal Learning and Verbal Behavior,* **17**, 1–12.

Anderson, R. N., & Smith, B. L. (2003). Deaths: Leading causes for 2001. *National Vital Statistics Reports,* **52**, 27-33.

Andreasen, N. C. (1982). Negative versus positive schizophrenia: Definition and validation. *Archives of General Psychiatry,* **39**, 789–794.

Andreasen, N. C., Arndt, S., Alliger, R., Miller, D., & Flaum, M. (1995). Symptoms of schizophrenia: Methods, meanings, and mechanisms. *Archives of General Psychiatry,* **52**, 341–351.

Andreasen, N. C., Ehrhardt, J. C., Swayze, V. W., Alliger, R. J, Yuh, W. T. C., Cohen, G., & Ziebell, S. (1990a). Magnetic resonance imaging of the brain in schizophrenia. *Archives of General Psychiatry,* **47**, 35–44.

Andreasen, N. C., Flaum, M., Swayze, V. W., Tyrrell, G., & Arndt, S. (1990). Positive and negative symptoms in schizophrenia. *Archives of General Psychiatry,* **47**, 615–621.

Andreasen, N. C., Olsen, S. A., Dennert, J. W., & Smith, M. R. (1982). Ventricular enlargement in schizophrenia: Definition and prevalence. *American Journal of Psychiatry,* **139**, 292–296.

Andrews, R. J. (1963). Evolution of facial expression. *Science,* **142**, 1034–1041.

Angoff, W. H. (1988). The nature-nurture debate, aptitudes, and group differences. *American Psychologist,* **43**, 713–720.

Anisfeld, M. (1984). *Language development from birth to three.* Hillsdale, NJ: Erlbaum.

Anisman, H., & Zacharko, R. M. (1982). Depression: The predisposing influence of stress. *The Behavioral and Brain Sciences,* **5**, 89–137.

Anshel, M. H. (1996). Effect of chronic aerobic exercise and progressive relaxation on motor performance and affect following acute stress. *Behavioral Medicine,* **21**, 186–196.

Anthony, M. V. (2002). Concepts of consciousness, kinds of consciousness, meanings of "consciousness." *Philosophical Studies*, **109**, 1–16.

Antoni, M. H., & Lutgendorf, S. (2007). Psychosocial factors and disease progression in cancer. *Current Directions in Psychological Science*, **16**, 42–46.

APA Presidential Task Force on Evidence-Based Practice. (2006). Evidence-based practice in Psychology. *American Psychologist*, **61**, 271–285.

Appleby, L. (2001). Mentally ill at risk for dying of unnatural causes. *The Lancet*, **358**, 2110–2112.

Arata, C. M., & Burkhart, B. R. (1998). Coping appraisals and adjustment to nonstranger sexual assault. *Violence Against Women*, **4**, 224–239.

Archer, S. L., & Waterman, A. S. (1988). Psychological individuation: Gender differences or gender neutrality? *Human Development*, **31**, 65-81.

Arendt, J., & Skene, D. J. (1997). Efficacy of melatonin treatment in jet lag, shift work, and blindness. *Journal of Biological Rhythms*, **12**, 604–617.

Arias, E., Anderson, R. N., Kung, H., Murphy, S. L., & Kochanek, K. D. (2003). Deaths: Final Data for 2001. *National Vital Statistics Reports*, **52**, 1–116.

Armas, G. C. (2003). Worldwide population aging. In H. Cox (Ed.), *Annual editions: Aging*. Guilford, CT: McGraw-Hill.

Armstrong, D. (1981). *The nature of the mind*. Ithaca, NY: Cornell University Press.

——. (1999). *The mind-body problem: An opinionated introduction*. Boulder, CO: Westview Press.

Armstrong, K., Micco, E., Carney, A., Stopfer, J., & Putt, M. (2005). Racial differences in the use of BRCA1/2 testing among women with a family history of breast or ovarian cancer. *Journal of the American Medical Association*, **293**, 1729-1736.

Armstrong, T. (1987). *In their own way: Discovering and encouraging your child's personal learning style*. Los Angeles: Jeremy P. Tarcher.

Arneill, A. B., & Devlin, A. S. (2002). Perceived quality of care: The influence of the waiting room environment. *Journal of Environmental Psychology*, **22**, 345–360.

Arnold, M. (1960). *Emotion and personality: Volume 1. Psychological aspects*. New York: Columbia University Press.

Arnot Ogden Medical Center. (1998a). *Frequently asked questions-viagra* [On-line]. Available: http://external.aomc.org/HOD2/general/viagraFAQ.html.

——. (1998b). *Synopsis of fatal outcome reports submitted to the FDA regarding viagra use* [On-line]. Available: http://external.aomc.org/HOD2/general/viagraFORs.html.

Aronson, E., Turner, J. A., & Carlsmith, J. M. (1963). Communicator credibility and communication discrepancy as a determinant of opinion change. *Journal of Abnormal and Social Psychology*, **67**, 31–36.

Aronson, E., Wilson, T. D., & Akert, R. M. (2005). *Social psychology (5th edition)*. Upper Saddle River, NJ: Prentice-Hall.

Aronson, J., Lustina, M. J., Good, C., Keough, K., Steele, C. M., & Brown, J. (1999). When white men can't do math: Necessary and sufficient factors in stereotype threat. *Journal of Experimental Social Psychology*, **35**, 29-46.

Aronson, J., Quinn, D., & Spencer, S. (1998). Stereotype threat and the academic underperformance of minorities and women. In J. Swim & C. Stangor (Eds.), *Prejudice: The target's perspective*. New York: Academic Press, 85-103.

Arvey, R. D., & Campion, J. E. (1982). The employee interview: A summary and review of recent research. *Personnel Psychology*, **35**, 281–322.

Arvey, R. D., Miller, H. E., Gould, R., & Burch, P. (1987). Interview validity for selecting sales clerks. *Personnel Psychology*, **40**, 1–12.

Asch, S. E. (1951). The effects of group pressure upon the modification and distortion of judgment. In H. Guetzkow (Ed.), *Groups, leadership, and men*. Pittsburgh: Carnegie Press.

——. (1956). Studies of independence and conformity: I. A minority of one against a unanimous majority. *Psychological Monographs: General and Applied*, **70** (Whole No. 416), 1–7.

Aserinsky, E., & Kleitman, N. (1953). Regularly occurring periods of eye mobility and concomitant phenomena during sleep. *Science*, **18**, 273–274.

Ashby, F. G., & Maddox, W. T. (2005). Human category learning. *Annual Review of Psychology*, **56**, 149-178.

Ashford, B. E., & Anand, V. (2003). The normalization of corruption in organizations. In B. M. Staw, & R. M. Kramer (Eds.), *Research in organizational behavior, Vol. 25*. Greenwich, CT: JAI Press.

Ashmore, R. D. (1990). Sex, gender, and the individual. In L. A. Pervin (Ed.), *Handbook of personality*. New York: Guilford.

Ashton, C., Whitworth, G. C., Seldomridge, J. A., Shapiro, P. A., Weinberg, A. D., & Michler, R. E. (1997). Self-hypnosis reduces anxiety following coronary artery bypass surgery: A prospective, randomized trial. *Journal of Cardiovascular Surgery*, **38**, 69-75.

Aspinwall, L. G. (2003). Proactive coping, well-being, and health. In N. J. Smelser, & P. B. Baltes (Eds.), *The international encyclopedia of the social and behavioral sciences*. Oxford: Elsevier.

Aspinwall, L. G., & Staudinger, U. M. (Eds.). (2003). *A psychology of human strengths: Fundamental questions and future directions for a positive psychology*. Washington, DC: The American Psychological Association.

Aspinwall, L. G., & Taylor, S. E. (1997). A stitch in time: Self-regulation and proactive coping. *Psychological Bulletin*, **121**, 417-436.

——. (1992). Modeling cognitive adaptation: A longitudinal investigation of the impact of individual differences and coping on college adjustment and performance. *Journal of Personality and Social Psychology*, **63**, 989–1003.

Atkinson, J. W., & Feather, N. T. (1966). *A theory of achievement motivation*. New York: Wiley.

Atkinson, J. W., & Litwin, G. H. (1960). Achievement motive and test anxiety conceived as motive to approach success and motive to avoid failure. *Journal of Abnormal and Social Psychology*, **60**, 27–36.

Atkinson, R. C. (1975). Mnemotechnics in second-language learning. *American Psychologist*, **30**, 821–828.

Atkinson, R. C., & Shiffrin, R. M. (1968). Human memory: A proposed system and its control processes. In K. W. Spence & J. T. Spence (Eds.), *The psychology of learning and motivation: Advances in research and theory*. New York: Academic Press.

Atwood, M. E., & Polson, P. G. (1976). A process model for water jug problems. *Cognitive Psychology*, **8**, 191–216.

Auletta, K. (1984). Children of children. *Parade Magazine*, **17**, 4–7.

Auyeung, P., & Sands, J. (1997). A cross-cultural study of the learning styles of accounting students. *Accounting and Finance*, **36**, 261–274.

Axelrod, S., & Apsche, J. (1983). *The effects of punishment on human behavior*. New York: Academic Press.

Azrin, N. H., & Holz, W. C. (1966). Punishment. In W. K. Honig (Ed.), *Operant behavior: Areas of research and application*. Englewood Cliffs, NJ: Prentice-Hall.

Azumi, K., & McMillan, C. J. (1976). Worker sentiment in the Japanese factory: Its organizational determinants. In L. Austin (Ed.), *Japan: The paradox of progress*. New Haven, CT: Yale University Press.

Azzopardi, P., & Cowey, A. (1997). Is blindsight like normal, near-threshold vision? *Proceedings of the National Academy of Sciences*, **94**, 14190-14194.

Baars, B. J. (2003). Some good things about Crick and Koch's "Framework for consciousness." *Science & Consciousness Review*, **3**, http://psych.pomona.edu/scr/editorials/20030303.html.

Baarschers, W. H. (2005). The elixir of life: Green tea or red wine? *Skeptical Inquirer*, **29**, 30-33.

Babor, T. F., Berglas, S., Mendelson, J. H., Ellinboe, J., & Miller, K. (1983). Alcohol, effect and the disinhibition of behavior. *Psychopharmacology*, **80**, 53–60.

Bach, M., & Poloschek, C. M. (2006). Optical illusions. *Visual Neuroscience*, **6**, 20–21.

Bachorowski, J., & Owren, M. J. (1995). Vocal expression of emotion: Acoustic properties of speech are associated with emotional intensity and context. *Psychological Science*, **6**, 219–224.

Backman, C. W., & Secord, P. F. (1959). The effect of perceived liking on interpersonal attraction. *Human Relations*, **12**, 379–384.

Badawy, A. (1998). Alcohol, aggression and serotonin: Metabolic aspects. *Alcohol and Alcoholism*, **33**, 66–72.

Baddeley, A. (1998). *Human Memory: Theory and Practice (Revised Edition)*. Boston: Allyn & Bacon.

——. (1990). *Human memory: Theory and practice*. Boston: Allyn & Bacon.

——. (1992). Working memory. *Science*, **25**, 556–559.

Baddeley, A. D. (1982). Domains of recollection. *Psychological Review*, **89**, 708–729.

Baddeley, A. D. (2001). Is working memory still working? *American Psychologist*, **56**, 851–864.

Baer, L., Rauch, S. L., Ballantine, T., Martoza, R., Cosgrove, R., Cassem, E., et al. (1995). Cingulotomy for intractable obsessive-compulsive disorder. *Archives of General Psychiatry*, **52**, 384–392.

Bagozzi, R. P., & Burnkrant, R. E. (1979). Attitude organization and the attitude-behavior relationship. *Journal of Personality and Social Psychology*, **37**, 913–929.

Bahrick, H. P. (1984). Semantic memory content in perma-store. *Journal of Experimental Psychology: General*, **13**, 1–29.

Bailey, D., Taylor, S. P. (1991). Effects of alcohol and aggressive disposition on human physical aggression. *Journal of Research in Personality*, **25**, 334–342.

Bailey, J. M., & Pillard, R. C. (1991). A genetic study of male sexual orientation. *Archives of General Psychiatry*, **48**, 1089–1096.

Bair, J. S., Sampson, P. D., Barr, H. M., Conner, P. D., & Streissguth, A. P. (2003). A 21-year longitudinal analysis of the effects of prenatal alcohol exposure on young adult drinking. *Archives of General Psychiatry*, **60**, 377–385.

Baker, S. L., Patterson, M. D., & Barlow, D. H. (2002). Panic disorder and agoraphobia. In M. M. Antony & D. H. Barlow (Eds.), *Handbook of assessment and treatment planning for psychological disorders (2nd ed)*. New York: Guilford Press.

Baldessarini, R. J., & Tondo, L. (2000). Does lithium treatment still work? *Archives of General Psychiatry*, **57**, 187–190.

Baldwin, M. W. (1992). Relational schemas and the processing of social information. *Psychological Bulletin*, **112**, 461–484.

Baley, S. (1985). The legalities of hiring in the 80s. *Personnel Journal*, **64**, 112–115.

Ballenger, J. C. (1989). Toward an integrated model of panic disorder. *American Journal of Orthopsychiatry*, **9**, 284–293.

Balleyguier, G., & Melhuish, E. C. (1996). The relationship between infant day care and socio-emotional development with French children. *European Journal of Psychology of Education*, **11**, 193–199.

Balsa, A., & McGuire, T. G. (2003). Prejudice, clinical uncertainty and stereotyping as sources of health disparities. *Journal of Health Economics*, **8**, 89-116.

Balsis, S., Carpenter, B. D., & Storandt, M. (2005). Personality change precedes clinical diagnosis of dementia of the Alzheimer type. *Journal of Gerontology: Psychological Sciences*, **60B**, P98–P101.

Baltes, M. M. (1995). Dependency in old age: Gains and losses. *Current Directions in Psychological Science*, **4**, 14–19.

Bamberg, S. (2003). How does environmental concern influence specific environmentally related behaviors? A new answer to an old question. *Journal of Environmental Psychology*, **23**, 21–32.

Bandura, A. (1965). Influence of models' reinforcement contingencies on the acquisition of imitative responses. *Journal of Personality and Social Psychology*, **1**, 589–595.

——. (1971). An analysis of modeling processes. In A. Bandura (Ed.), *Psychological modeling*. New York: Lieber-Atherton.

——. (1974). Behavior theory and the models of man. *American Psychologist*, **29**, 859–869.

——. (1976). Modeling theory: Some traditions, trends and disputes. In W. S. Sahakian (Ed.), *Learning: Systems, models, and theories*. Skokie, IL: Rand McNally.

——. (1977). *Social learning theory*. Englewood Cliffs, NJ: Prentice-Hall.

——. (1978). The self-system in reciprocal determinism. *American Psychologist*, **33**, 344–358.

——. (1982). Self-efficacy mechanism in human agency. *American Psychologist*, **37**, 122–147.

——. (1999). Social cognitive theory of personality. In D. Cervone, & Y. Shoda, (Eds.), *The coherence of personality: Social-cognitive bases of consistency, variability, and organization*. New York: Guilford.

——. (2001a). Social cognitive theory: An agentic perspective. *Annual Review of Psychology*, **52**, 1–26.

——. (2001b). *On shaping one's future: The primacy of human agency.* Paper presented at the annual meeting of The American Psychological Society, Toronto, June 14, 2001.

Bandura, A., Barbaranelli, C., Caprara, G. V., & Pastorelli, C. (2001). Self-efficacy beliefs as shapers of children's aspirations and career trajectories. *Child Development, 72,* 187–206.

Bandura, A., Ross, D., & Ross, S. A. (1963). Imitation of film-mediated aggressive models. *Journal of Abnormal and Social Psychology,* **66,** 3–11.

Bar, M., & Biederman, I. (1998). Subliminal visual priming. *Psychological Science,* **9,** 464–469.

Barber, B. K. (1996). Parental psychological control: Revisiting a neglected construct. *Child Development,* **67,** 3296-3319.

Barber, N. (1998). *Parenting: Roles, styles, outcomes.* New York: Nova Science Publishers.

Barber, T. F. X. (1972). Suggested (hypnotic) behavior: The trace paradigm vs. an alternative paradigm. In E. Fromm & R. E. Shorr (Eds.), *Hypnosis: Research developments and perspectives.* Chicago: Aldine-Atherton.

Barber, T. X. (2000). A deeper understanding of hypnosis: Its secrets, its nature, its essence. *American Journal of Clinical Hypnosis,* **42,** 208–272.

Barber, T. X., Spanos, N. P., & Chaves, J. F. (1974). *Hypnosis: Imagination and human potentialities.* New York: Pergamon Press.

Bard, P. (1934). The neurohormonal basis of emotional reactions. In C. A. Murchison (Ed.), *Handbook of general experimental psychology.* Worchester, MA: Clark University Press.

Barefoot, J. C., Dahlstrom, W. D., & Williams, R. B. (1983). Hostility, CHD incidence, and total mortality: A 25-year follow-up study of 255 physicians. *Psychosomatic Medicine,* **45,** 59–63.

Bargh, J. A., & Ferguson, M. J. (2000). Beyond behaviorism: On the automaticity of higher mental processes. *Psychological Bulletin,* **126,** 925–945.

Barinaga, M. (1991). Is homosexuality biological? *Science,* **253,** 956–957.

——. (1995). "Obese" protein slims mice. *Science,* **269,** 475–476.

——. (1996). Developmental neurobiology: Guiding neurons to the cortex. *Science,* **274,** 1100–1101.

Barker, R. (1968). *Ecological psychology.* Stanford, CA: Stanford University Press.

Barlow, D. H. (2002). *Anxiety and its disorders: The nature and treatment of anxiety and panic (2nd ed.).* New York: Guilford Press.

Barlow, D. H., & Durand, V. M. (2002). *Abnormal psychology: An integrative approach.* Belmont, CA: Wadsworth.

——. (2009). *Abnormal psychology: An integrative approach.* Belmont, CA: Wadsworth.

Barlow, D. H. & Lehman, C. L. (1996). Advances in the psychosocial treatment of anxiety disorders: Implications for National Health Care. *Archives of General Psychiatry,* **53,** 727–735.

Barnes, C., & Mercer, G. (2003). *Disability.* Cambridge, UK: Polity Press.

Barnett, R. C., & Hyde, J. S. (2001). Women, men, work, and family: An expansionist theory. *American Psychologist,* **56,** 781–796.

Barnett, R. C., Marshall, N. L., Raudenbush, S. W., & Brennan, R. T. (1993). Gender and the relationship between job experiences and psychological distress: A study of dual-earner couples. *Journal of Personality and Social Psychology,* **64,** 794–806.

Barnier, A. J., & McConkey, K. M. (2004). Defining and identifying the highly hypnotizable person. In M. Heap, R. J. Brown, & D. A. Oakley (Eds.), *High hypnotizability: Theoretical, experimental and clinical issue.* (pp. 30–60). New York: Brunner Rutledge.

Baron, M., Freimer, N. F., Risch, N., Lerer, B., Alexander, J. R., et al. (1993). Diminished support for linkage between manic depressive illness and X-chromosome markers in three Israeli pedigrees. *Natural Genetics,* **3,** 49–55.

Baron, R. A. (1999). Social and personal determinants of workplace aggression: Evidence for the impact of perceived injustice and the Type A behavior pattern. *Aggressive Behavior,* **25,** 281–296.

Baron, R. A., & Ransberger, V. M. (1978). Ambient temperature and the occurrence of collective violence: The "long hot summer" revisited. *Journal of Personality and Social Psychology,* **36,** 351–360.

Barr, H. M., Streissguth, A. P., Darby, B. L., & Sampson, P. D. (1990). Prenatal exposure to alcohol, caffeine, tobacco, and aspirin: Effects on fine and gross motor performance in 4-year-old children. *Developmental Psychology,* **26,** 339–348.

Barrett, G. V., & Depinet, R. L. (1991). A reconsideration of testing for competence rather than for intelligence. *American Psychologist,* **46,** 1012–1024.

Barrett, L. F. (2006). Are emotions natural kinds? *Perspectives on Psychological Science,* **2,** 28–58.

Barron, F., & Harrington, D. M. (1981). Creativity, intelligence, and personality. *Annual Review of Psychology,* **32,** 439–476.

Barsalou, L. W. (1983). Ad hoc categories. *Memory and Cognition,* **11,** 211–227.

——. (1989). Intra-concept similarity and its implications for inter-concept similarity. In S. Vosniadou & A. Ortony (Eds.), *Similarity and analogical reasoning.* New York: Cambridge University Press.

Bartecchi, C. E., MacKenzie, T. D., & Schrier, R. W. (1995). The global tobacco epidemic. *Scientific American* (May).

Bartlett, F. C. (1932). *Remembering.* Cambridge: Cambridge University Press.

Bartoshuk, L. M., & Beauchamp, G. K. (1994). Chemical senses. *Annual Review of Psychology,* **45,** 419–449.

Bartus, R. T. (2000). On neurodegenerative diseases, models, and treatment strategies: lessons learned and lessons forgotten a generation following the cholinergic hypothesis. *Experimental Neurology,* **163,** 495–529.

Bartus, R. T., Dean, R. L., Beer, B., & Lippa, A. S. (1982). The cholinergic hypothesis of geriatric memory dysfunction. *Science,* **217,** 408–417.

Bassi, L. J., & Van Buren, M. E. (1999). *The 1999 ASTD state of the industry report.* Alexandria, VA: The American Society for Training and Development.

Batson, C. D. (1987). Prosocial motivation: Is it ever truly altruism? In L. Berkowitz (Ed.), *Advances in experimental social psychology (Vol. 20).* New York: Academic Press.

——. (1990a). How social an animal: The human capacity for caring. *American Psychologist,* **45,** 336–346.

——. (1990b). Good samaritans-or priests and Levites? *Personality and Social Psychology Bulletin,* **16,** 758–768.

Batson, C. D., Nadia, A., Jodi, Y., Bedell, S. J., & Johnson, J. W. (1999). Two threats to the common good: Self-interest and empathy-induced altruism. *Personality and Social Psychology Bulletin, 25*, 3–16.

Batson, C. D., Sager, K., Garst, E., Kang, M., Rubchinsky, M., & Dawson, K. (1997). Is empathy-induced helping due to self-other merging? *Journal of Personality and Social Psychology, 73*, 495–509.

Batterham, R. L., Cohen, M. A., Ellis, S. M., Le Roux, C. W., Withers, D. J., Frost, G. S., Ghatei, M. A., & Bloom, S. R. (2003). Inhibition of food intake in obese subjects by peptide YY3-36. *The New England Journal of Medicine, 349*, 941–948.

Baum, A., & Grunberg, N. E. (1991). Gender, stress, and health. *Health Psychology, 10*, 80–85.

Baumeister, R. F. (1985). The championship choke. *Psychology Today, 19*, 48–52.

——. (2000). Gender differences in erotic plasticity. *Psychological Bulletin, 126*, 347–374.

Baumeister, R. F., & Steinhilber, A. (1984). Paradoxical effects of supportive audiences on performanceunder pressure: The home field disadvantage in sports championships. *Journal of Personality and Social Psychology, 47*, 85–93.

Baumeister, R. F., Campbell, J. D., Krueger, J. I., & Vohs, K. D. (2003). Does high self-esteem cause better performance, interpersonal success, happiness, or healthier lifestyles? *Psychological Science in the Public Interest, 4*, (Whole No. 1).

——. (2005). Exploding the self-esteem myth. *Scientific American*, January, downloaded from www.SCIENTIFICAMERICAN.com August 22, 2005.

Baumeister, R. F., Catanese, K. R., & Vohs, K. D. (2001). Is there a gender difference in strength of sex drive? *Personality and Social Psychology Review, 5*, 242–273

Baumeister, R. F., Dale, K., & Sommer, K. L. (1998). Freudian defense mechanisms and empirical findings in modern social psychology: reaction formation, projection, displacement, undoing, isolation, sublimation, and denial. *Journal of Personality, 66*, 1081–1124.

Baumrind, D. (1971). Current patterns of parental authority. *Developmental Psychology Monograph, Part 2, 4*, 1-103.

——. (1989). Rearing competent children. In W. Damon (Ed.), *Child development today and tomorrow* (pp. 349-378). San Fransisco: Jossey-Bass.

——. (1991). The influence of parenting style on adolescent competence and substance use. *Journal of Early Adolescence, 11*, 56-95.

Baumrind, D., Larzelere, R. E., & Cowan, P. A. (2002). Ordinary physical punishment: Is it harmful? Comment on Gershoff (2002). *Psychological Bulletin, 128*, 580–589.

Bausbaum, A. I., & Levine, J. D. (1991). Opiate analgesia: How central is a peripheral target? *New England Journal of Medicine, 325*, 1168–1169.

Bayley, N. & Schaefer, E. S. (1964). Correlations of maternal and child behaviors with the development of mental abilities: Data from the Berkeley Growth Study. *Monographs of the Society for Research in Child Development, 29*, 1–80.

Beals, J., Manson, S. M., et al. (1991). Factorial structure of the Center for Epidemiologic Studies Depression Scale among American Indian college students. *Psychological Assessment, 3*, 623-627.

Bearman, P. S., & Bruckner, H. (2002). Opposite-sex twins and same-sex attraction. *Journal of Sociology, 107*, 1179-1205.

Beatty, J. (1995). *Principles of behavioral neuroscience.* Chicago: Brown & Benchmark.

Beauquis, J., Saravia, F., Coulaud, J., Roig, P., Dardenne, M., Homo-Delarche, F., & De Nicola, A. (2008). Prominently decreased hippocampal *neurogenesis* in a spontaneous model of type 1 diabetes, the nonobese diabetic mouse. *Experimental Neurology, 210*, 359–367.

Beauvais, F., Oetting, E. R., Wolf, W., & Edwards, R. W. (1989). American Indian youth and drugs: 1975–1987, a continuing problem. *American Journal of Public Health, 79*, 634–636.

Beck, A. T. (1967). *Depression: Clinical, experimental, and theoretical aspects.* New York: HarperCollins.

——. (1976). *Cognitive therapy and the emotional disorders.* New York: International University Press.

——. (1991). Cognitive therapy: A 30-year retrospective. *American Psychologist, 46*, 368–375.

——. (1995). *Cognitive therapy: Basics and beyond.* New York: Guilford.

Beck, A. T., & Emery, G. (1985). *Anxiety disorders and phobias: A cognitive perspective.* New York: Basic Books.

Beck, A. T., & Freeman, A. (1990). *Cognitive therapy of personality disorders.* New York: Guilford.

Bednar, J. A., & Miikkulainen, R. (2002). Neonatal learning of faces: Interactions between genetic and environmental inputs. In W. Gray & C. Schunn (Eds.), *Proceedings of the 24th Annual Conference of the Cognitive Science Society* (pp. 107-112). Hillsdale, NJ: Erlbaum.

Bee, H. (1992). *The developing child (6th ed.).* New York: HarperCollins.

——. (1995). *The developing child (7th ed.).* New York: HarperCollins.

——. (1996). *The journey of adulthood (Third Edition).* Upper Saddle River, NJ: Prentice Hall.

Beekman, M. (2002). Pheromone Reception: When in doubt, mice mate rather than hate. *Science, 295*, 782.

Beer, M., & Walton, A. E. (1987). Organization change and development. *Annual Review of Psychology, 38*, 339–367.

Beidel, D. C. (2002). Childhood anxiety disorders. *Clinician's Research Digest: Supplemental Bulletin 27*, Nov., pp. 1–2.

Bekerian, D. A. (1993). In search of the typical eyewitness. *American Psychologist, 48*, 574–576.

Bell, I. R. (1994). Somatization disorder: Healthcare costs in the decade of the brain. *Biological Psychiatry, 35*, 81–83.

Bell, N. (1991). *Visualizing and verbalizing for language comprehension and thinking.* Paso Robles, CA: NBI Publications.

Bellack, A. S. (1986). Schizophrenia: Behavior therapy's forgotten child. *Behavior Therapy, 17*, 199–214.

Bellack, A. S., & Mueser, K. T. (1986). A comprehensive treatment program for schizophrenia and chronic mental illness. *Community Mental Health Journal, 22*, 175–189.

Belsher, G., & Costello, C. G. (1988). Relapse after recovery from unipolar depression: A critical review. *Psychological Bulletin, 104*, 84–96.

Belsky, J. (1990). The "effects" of infant day care reconsidered. In N. Fox & G. G. Fein (Eds.), *Infant day care: The current debate*. Norwood, NJ: Ablex.

Belsky, J., Lang, M. E., & Rovine, M. (1985). Stability and change in marriage across the transition to parenthood: A second study. *Journal of Marriage and the Family, 47*, 855–865.

Belsky, J., Steinberg, L., & Draper, P. (1991). Childhood experience, interpersonal development, and reproductive strategy: An evolutionary theory of socialization. *Child Development, 62*, 647-670.

Beltramini, A. U., & Hertzig, M. E. (1983). Sleep and bedtime behavior in preschool-aged children. *Pediatrics, 71*, 153–158.

Bem, D. J. (1972). Self-perception theory. In L. Berkowitz (Ed.), *Advances in experimental social psychology (Vol. 6)*. San Diego: Academic Press.

Bem, S. (1981). Gender schema theory: A cognitive account of sex typing. *Psychological Review, 88*, 354–364.

Bem, S. L. (1993). *The lenses of gender: Transforming the debate on sexual inequality*. New Haven, CT: Yale University Press.

Benbow, C. P. (1987). Possible biological correlates of precocious mathematical reasoning ability. *Trends in Neuroscience, 10*, 17–20.

——. (1990). Gender differences: Searching for facts. *American Psychologist, 45*, 988.

Benbow, C. P., Lubinski, D., Shea, D. L., & Eftekhari-Sanjani, H. (2000). Sex differences in mathematical reasoning ability at age 13: Their status 20 years later. *Psychological Science, 11*, 474–480.

Benenson, J. F., & Heath, A. (2006). Boys withdraw from one-on-one interactions, whereas girls withdraw more in groups. *Developmental Psychology, 42*, 272–282.

Benjet, C., & Kazdin, A. E. (2003). Spanking children: The controversies, findings, and new directions. *Clinical Psychology Review, 23*, 197–224.

Bennett, T. L. (1982). *Introduction to physiological psychology*. Monterey, CA: Brooks/Cole.

Bennett, W. (1980). The cigarette century. *Science, 80*, 36–43.

Ben-Porath, Y. S., & Butcher, J. N. (1989). The comparability of MMPI and MMPI-2 scales and profiles. *Psychological Assessment, 1*, 345–347.

Benson, E. (2002). Pheromones, in context. *Monitor on Psychology, 33*, 46-48.

Ben-Yehuda, N. (1980). The European witch craze. *American Journal of Sociology, 86*, 1–31.

Berenbaum, S. A., & Hines, M. (1992). Early androgens are related to childhood sex-typed toy preferences. *Psychological Science, 3*, 203–206.

Berghuis, J. P., & Stanton, A. L. (2002). Adjustment to a dyadic stressor: A longitudinal study of coping and depressive symptoms in infertile couples over an insemination attempt. *Journal of Consulting and Clinical Psychology, 70*, 433-438.

Berkowitz, H. (1994). U.S. Firms Trip Over Their Tongues in Wooing the World. *The Journal Gazette*, June 21, Fort Wayne, IN.

Berkowitz, L. (1978). Whatever happened to the frustration-aggression hypothesis? *American Behavioral Scientist, 21*, 691–708.

——. (1982). Aversive conditions as stimuli to aggression. *Advances in Experimental Social Psychology, 15*, 249–288.

——. (1989). Frustration-aggression hypothesis: Examination and reformulation. *Psychological Bulletin, 106*, 59–73.

——. (1990). On the formation and regulation of anger and aggression. *American Psychologist, 45*, 494–503.

——. (1993). Pain and aggression: Some findings and implications. *Motivation and Emotion, 17*, 277–293.

——. (1997). On the determinants and regulation of impulsive aggression. In S. Feshbach & J. Zagrodzia (Eds.), *Aggression: Biological, developmental and social perspectives*. (pp. 187-211). New York: Plenum.

——. (1999). Evil is more than banal: Situationism and the concept of evil. *Personality and Social Psychology Review, 3*, 246-253.

Berkowitz, L., & Harmon-Jones, E. (2004). Toward an understanding of the determinants of anger. *Emotion, 4*, 107-130.

Berlyne, D. E. (1960). *Conflict, arousal, and curiosity*. New York: McGraw-Hill.

——. (1971). *Aesthetics and psychobiology*. Englewood Cliffs, NJ: Prentice-Hall.

Bernstein, H. J., et al. (1998). Patient attitudes about ECT after treatment. *Psychiatric Annals, 28*, 524–527.

Bernstein, I. (1978). Learned taste aversion in children receiving chemotherapy. *Science, 200*, 1302–1303.

Bernstein, R. (1981). The Y chromosome and primary sexual differentiation. *Journal of the American Medical Association, 245*, 1953–1956.

Berrettini, W. H., Golden, L. R., Gelernter, J., Gejman, P. V., Gershon, E. S., & Datera-Wadleigh, S. (1990). X-chromosome markers and manic-depressive illness. *Archives of General Psychiatry, 47*, 366–374.

Berry, J., Poortinga, Y., Segall, M., & Dasen P. (1992). *Cross-cultural psychology: Research and applications*. New York: Cambridge University Press.

Berscheid, E. (1994). Interpersonal relationships. *Annual Review of Psychology, 45*, 79–129.

Bertenthal, B. I., & Campos, J. J. (1989). A systems approach to the organizing effects of self-produced locomotion during infancy. In C. Rovee-Collier & L. P. Lipsett (Eds.), *Advances in infancy research*. Norwood, NJ: Ablex.

Beutler, L. E., Clarkin, J., & Bongar, B. (2000). *Guidelines for the systematic treatment of the depressed patient*. Oxford, UK: Oxford University Press.

Beutler, L. E., Crago, M., & Arizmendi, T. G. (1986). Therapist variables in psychotherapy process and outcome. In S. L. Garfield & A. E. Bergin (Eds.), *Handbook of psychotherapy and behavior change (3rd ed.)*. New York: Wiley.

Beyer, S. (1990). Gender differences in the accuracy of self-evaluation and performance. *Journal of Personality and Social Psychology, 59*, 960–970.

Bhawuk, D. P. S., & Brislin, R. (1992). The measurement of intercultural sensitivity using the concepts of individualism and collectivism. *International Journal of Intercultural Relations, 16*, 413–436.

Bieman-Copland, S., Ryan, E. B., & Cassano, J. (1998). Responding to the challenges of late life. In D. Pushkar, W. M. Bukowski, A. E. Schwartzman, D. M. Stack, & D. R. White (Eds.), *Improving competence across the lifespan: Building interventions based on theory and research* (pp. 141–157). New York: Plenum.

Bierut, L. J., Heath, A. C., Bucholz, K. K., Dinwiddie, S. H., Madden, P. A., Statham, D. J., Dunne, M., & Martin, N. G. (1999). Major depressive disorder in a community-based twin sample: Are there different genetic and environmental contributions for men & women? *Archives of General Psychiatry, 56*, 557–563.

Billy, J. O. G., Tanfer, K., Grady, W. R., & Klepinger, D. H. (1993). The sexual behavior of men in the United States. *Family Planning Perspectives, 25*, 52–60.

Binder, J. L. (1993). Research findings on short-term psychodynamic therapy techniques. *Directions in Clinical Psychology, 3*, 10.3–10.13.

Birdwhistell, R. L. (1952). *Introduction to kinesics.* Louisville, KY: University of Louisville Press.

Birren, F. (1952). *Your color and yourself.* Sandusky, OH: Prang.

Bjorklund, A., Dunnett, S. B., & Stenevi, U. (1980). Reinnervation of the denervated striatum by substantia nigra transplants: Functional consequences as revealed by pharmacological and sensorimotor testing. *Brain Research, 199*, 307–333.

Bjorklund, D. F. (2000). *Children's thinking: Developmental function and individual differences (3rd ed.).* Belmont, CA: Wadsworth.

Black, D. W., & Andreasen, N. C. (1999). Schizophrenia, schizophreniform disorder, and delusional (paranoid) disorders. In R. E. Hales, S. C. Yudofsky, & J. A. Talbott (Eds.), *Textbook of psychiatry (3rd ed.).* Washington, DC: American Psychiatric Press.

Blagys, M. D., & Hilsenroth, M. J. (2000). Distinctive features of short-term psychodynamic-interpersonal psychotherapy: A review of the comparative psychotherapy process literature. *Clinical Psychology: Science and Practice, 7*, 167–188.

Blair, E. (2003). Culture and leadership: Seven key points for improved safety performance. *Professional Safety, 48(6)*, 18–22.

Blair, P. S., & Fleming, P. J. (1996). Smoking and the sudden infant death syndrome: Results from 1993-5 case-control study for confidential inquiry into stillbirths and deaths in infancy. *British Medical Journal, 313*, 195–198.

Blakemore, S. (2001). State of the art—the psychology of consciousness. *The Psychologist, 14*, 522-525.

Blanchard, D. C., & Blanchard, R. J. (1984). Affect and aggression: An animal model applied to human behavior. In R. J. Blanchard & D. C. Blanchard (Eds.), *Advances in the study of aggression (Volume 1).* New York: Academic Press.

——. (1988). Ethoexperimental approaches to the biology of emotion. *Annual Review of Psychology, 39*, 43–68.

Blaney, P. H. (1986). Affect and memory: A review. *Psychological Bulletin, 99*, 229–246.

Blashfield, R. K., & Breen, M. J. (1989). Face validity of the DSM-III-R personality disorders. *American Journal of Psychiatry, 146*, 1575–1579.

Blass, E. M., Ganchow, J. R., & Steiner, J. E. (1984). Classical conditioning in newborn human infants 2-48 hours of age. *Infant Behavior and Development, 7*, 223–235.

Bleier, R., Houston, L., & Byne, W. (1987). Can the corpus callosum predict gender, age, handedness, or cognitive differences? *Trends in Neuroscience, 9*, 391–394.

Bloch, D., & Simon, R. (Eds.). (1982). *The strength of family therapy: Selected papers of Nathan Ackerman.* New York: Brunner/Mazel.

Block, J. (1965). *The challenge of response sets.* Englewood Cliffs, NJ: Prentice-Hall.

Bloom, B. L. (1997). *Planned short-term psychotherapy (2nd Edition).* Boston: Allyn & Bacon.

Bloom, F. E., Lazerson, A., & Hotstadter, L. (1985). *Brain, mind, and behavior.* San Francisco: Freeman.

Bloom, S. (2003). The fat controller. *New Scientist, 179*, 38–42.

Blum, J. E., Jarvik, L. F., & Clark, E. T. (1970). Rate of change on selective tests of intelligence: A twenty-year longitudinal study. *Journal of Gerontology, 25*, 171–176.

Bodick, N. C., Offen, W. W., Levey, A., et al. (1997). Effects of xanomelin, a selective muscarinic receptor agonist, on cognitive function and behavioral symptoms in Alzheimer disease. *Archives of Neurology, 54*, 465–473.

Bodkin, J. A., & Amsterdam, J. D. (2002). Transdermal selgiline in major depression: A double-blind, placebo-controlled, parallel-group study in outpatients. *The American Journal of Psychiatry, 159*, 1869–1875.

Bolles, R. C. (1970). Species-specific defense reactions and avoidance learning. *Psychological Review, 7*, 32–48.

——. (1972). Reinforcement, expectancy, and learning. *Psychological Review, 79*, 394–409.

Bond, R., & Smith, P. B. (1996). Culture and conformity: A meta-analysis of studies using Asch's (1952b, 1956) line judgment task. *Psychological Bulletin, 119*, 111–137.

Bond, T. J., Galinsky, E., & Swanberg, J. E. (1998). *The 1997 national study of the changing workforce.* New York: Families and Work Institute.

Bondareff, W., Mountjoy, C. Q., Wischik, C. M., Hauser, D. L., LaBree, L. D., & Roth, M. (1993). Evidence of subtypes of Alzheimer's disease and implications for etiology. *Archives of General Psychiatry, 50*, 350–356.

Booth, A., Johnson, D. R., Granger, D. A., Crouter, A. C., & McHale, S. (2003). Testosterone and child and adolescent adjustment: The moderating role of parent-child relationships. *Developmental Psychology, 39*, 85-98.

Bootzin, R. R., & Accella, J. R. (1984). *Abnormal psychology: Current perspectives (4th ed.).* New York: Random House.

Bootzin, R. R., & Rider, S. P. (1997). Behavioral techniques and biofeedback for insomnia. In M. R. Pressman & W. C. Orr (Eds.), *Understanding sleep: The evaluation and treatment of sleep disorders.* Washington, D. C.: American Psychological Association.

Boraod, J. C. (1992). Interhemispheric and introhemispheric control of emotion: A focus on unilateral brain damage. *Journal of Consulting and Clinical Psychology, 60*, 339–348.

Borbely, A. (1986). *Secrets of sleep.* New York: Basic Books.

Bordens, K. S., & Abbott, B. B. (1991). *Research design and methods: A process approach.* Mountain View, CA: Mayfield.

——. (2008). *Research design and methods: A process approach (7th edition).* New York: McGraw Hill.

——. (1999). *Research design and methods: A process approach (4th Edition).* Mountain View, CA: Mayfield Publishing Company.

Bordens, K. S., & Horowitz, I. A. (2002). *Social psychology.* Mahwah, NJ: Lawrence Erlbaum Associates.

Bornstein, R. F., Kale, A. R., & Cornell, K. R. (1990). Boredom as a limiting condition of the mere exposure effect. *Journal of Personality and Social Psychology, 58*, 791–800.

Borowsky, S. J., Rubenstein, L. V., Meredith, L. S., Camp, P., Jackson-Triche, M., & Wells, K. B. (2000). Who is at risk of nondetection of mental health problems in primary care? *Journal of General Internal Medicine, 15*, 381-388.

Borum, R., & Fulero, S. M. (1999). Empirical research on the insanity defense and attempted reforms: Evidence toward informed policy. *Law and Human Behavior, 23*, 117–135.

Botto, L. D., Erickson, J. D., Mulinare, J., Lynberg, M. C., & Liu, Y. (2002). Maternal fever, multivitamin use and selected birth defects: Evidence of interaction? *Epidemiology, 13*, 485–488.

Bouchard, C., Tremblay, A., Després, J., et al. (1990). The response to long-term overfeeding in identical twins. *The New England Journal of Medicine, 322*, 1477–1482.

Bourne, L. E. (1992). Cognitive psychology: A brief overview. *Psychology Science Agenda, 5(5)*, 5, 20.

Bourne, L. E., Dominowski, R. L., & Loftus, E. F. (1983). *Cognitive process.* Englewood Cliffs, NJ: Prentice-Hall.

Bousfield, W. A. (1953). The occurrence of clustering in the free recall of randomly arranged associates. *Journal of General Psychology, 49*, 229–240.

Boutla, M., Supalla, T., Newport, E. L., & Bavelier, D. (2004). Short-term memory span: Insights from sign language. *Nature: Neuroscience, 7*, 997–1002.

Bower, G. H. (1970). Imagery as a relational organizer in associative learning. *Journal of Verbal Learning and Verbal Behavior, 9*, 529–533.

——. (1972). Mental imagery and associative learning. In L. W. Gregg (Ed.), *Cognition in learning and memory.* New York: Wiley.

——. (1981). Mood and memory. *American Psychologist, 36*, 129–148.

Bower, G. H., & Clark, M. C. (1969). Narrative stories as mediators for serial learning. *Psychonomic Science, 14*, 181–182.

Bower, G. H., & Mayer, J. D. (1989). In search of mood-dependent retrieval. *Journal of Social Behavior and Personality, 4*, 133–168.

Bower, G. H., & Springston, F. (1970). Pauses as recoding points in letter series. *Journal of Experimental Psychology, 83*, 421–430.

Bower, T. G. R., Broughton, J. M., & Moore, M. K. (1971). Infant responses to approaching objects: An indicator of response to distal variables. *Perception and Psychophysics, 9*, 193–196.

Bowers, J. S., & Schacter, D. L. (1990). Implicit memory and test awareness. *Journal of Experimental Psychology: Learning, Memory, and Cognition, 16*, 404–416.

Bowlby, J. (1982). *Attachment and loss: Vol. 1. Attachment (2nd ed.).* New York: Basic Books.

Bowling, A. (2000). A good death: Research on dying is scanty. *British Medical Journal, 320*, 1205–1206.

Boykin, W. (1983). On task performance and African-American children. In U. R. Spencer (Ed.), *Achievement and achievement motives* (pp. 324-371). Boston: W. H. Freeman.

Brackett, M. A., Mayer, J. D., & Warner, R. M. (2004). Emotional Intelligence and the prediction of behavior. *Personality and Individual Differences, 36*, 1387–1402.

Bradbard, M. R., & Endsley, R. C. (1983). The effects of sex-typed labelling on preschool children's information seeking and retention. *Sex Roles, 9*, 247–260.

Bradley, C. J., Given, C. W., & Roberts, C. (2002). Race, socioeconomic status, and breast cancer treatment and survival. *Journal of the National Cancer Institute, 94*, 490-496.

Bradley, R. H., & Corwyn, R. F. (2002). Socioeconomic status and child development. *Annual Review of Psychology, 53*, 371–399.

Bradshaw, J. L., & Nettleton, N. C. (1983). *Human cerebral asymmetry.* Englewood Cliffs, NJ: Prentice-Hall.

Braffman, W., & Kirsch, I. (1999). Imaginative suggestibility and hypnotizability: An empirical analysis. *Journal of Personality and Social Psychology, 77*, 578–587.

Brandon, T. H. (1994). Negative affect as motivation to smoke. *Current Directions in Psychological Sciences, 3*, 33–37.

Bransford, J. D., & Johnson, M. K. (1972). Contextual prerequisites for understanding: Some investigations of comprehension and recall. *Journal of Verbal Learning and Verbal Behavior, 11*, 717–720.

Bratic, E. B. (1982). Healthy mothers, healthy babies coalition. *Prevention, 97*, 503–509.

Brauer, M., Wasel, W., Niedenthal, P. (2000). Implicit and explicit components of prejudice. *Review of General Psychology, 4*, 79–101.

Braun, K. A., Ellis, R., & Loftus, E. F. (2002). Make my memory: How advertising can change our memories of the past. *Psychology and Marketing, 19*, 1-23.

Braun, P., Kochansky, G., Shapiro, R., Greenberg, S., Gudeman, J. E., Johnson, S., & Shore, M. (1981). Overview: Deinstitutionalization of psychiatric patients, a critical review of outcome studies. *American Journal of Psychiatry, 138*, 736–749.

Bray, D. W., Campbell, R. J., & Grant, D. L. (1974). *Formative years in business: A long-term AT&T study of managerial lives.* New York: Wiley.

Bregman, J., Dykens, E. Watson, M., & Leckman, J. (1987). Fragile X syndrome: Variability in phenotype expression. *Journal of the American Academy of Child and Adolescent Psychiatry, 26*, 463–471.

Brehm, J. W., & Self, E. A. (1989). The intensity of motivation. *Annual Review of Psychology, 40*, 109–131.

Breier, A., Schreiber, J. L., Dyer, J., & Pickar, D. (1991). National Institute of Mental Health longitudinal study of chronic schizophrenia: Prognosis and predictors of outcome. *Archives of General Psychiatry, 48*, 239–246.

Breslau, J., Kendler, K. S., Su, M., Gaxiola-Aguilar, S., & Kessler, R. C. (2005). *Psychological Medicine, 35*, 317-327.

Breslau, N., Peterson, E., & Schultz, L. R. (2008). A second look a prior trauma and the posttraumatic stress disorder effects of subsequent trauma. *Archives of General Psychiatry, 65*, 431–437.

Brett, J. F., Brief, A. P., Burke, M. J., George, J. M., & Webster, J. (1990). Negative affectivity and the reporting of stressful events. *Health Psychology, 9*, 57–68.

Brewer, J. B., Zhao, Z., Desmond, J. E., Glover, G. H., & Gabrieli, J. D. E. (1998). Making memories: Brain activity that predicts how well visual experience is remembered. *Science, 281*, 1185–1187.

Brewer, W. F., & Nakamura, G. V. (1984). The nature and function of schemas. In R. S. Wyler and T. K. Sroll (Eds.), *Handbook of social cognition*. Hillsdale, NJ: Erlbaum.

Brief, A. P., & Weiss, H. M. (2002). Organizational behavior: Affect in the workplace. *Annual Review of Psychology*, **53**, 279–307.

Brinkerhoff, R. O. (1989). *Evaluating training programs in business and industry*. San Francisco: Jossey-Bass.

Brislin, R. W. (1990). *Applied cross-cultural psychology*. Newbury Park, CA: Sage.

——. (1993). *Understanding culture's influence on behavior*. Fort Worth, TX: Harcourt Brace.

Brita de Macedo-Soares, M., Moeno, R. A., Rigonatti, S. P., & Lafer, B. (2005). Efficacy of electroconvulsive therapy in treatment-resistant bipolar disorder: A case series. *The Journal of ECT*, **21**, 31-34.

Brod, M., Stewart, A. L., Sands, L., & Walton, P. (1999). Conceptualization and measurement of quality of life in dementia: The Dementia Quality of Life Instrument (DQoL). *The Gerontologist*, **39**, 25–35.

Brody, E. M. (1981). Women in the middle and family help to older people. *Gerontologist*, **21**, 471–480.

——. (1985). Parent care as a normative family stress. *Gerontologist*, **25**, 19–29.

Brody, N. (1992). *Intelligence (2nd edition)*. New York: Academic Press.

Brown, D., Scheflin, A. W., & Hammond, D. C. (1998). *Memory, trauma treatment, and the law*. New York: Norton.

Brown, J. (1958). Some tests of the decay theory of immediate memory. *Quarterly Journal of Experimental Psychology*, **10**, 12–21.

Brown, J. I. (1973). *The Nelson-Denny reading test*. Boston: Houghton Mifflin.

Brown, R., & Kulik, J. (1977). Flashbulb memories. *Cognition*, **5**, 73–99.

Brown, R., & McNeill, D. (1966). The tip-of-the-tongue phenomenon. *Journal of Verbal Learning and Verbal Behavior*, **5**, 325–337.

Browne, M. A., & Mahoney, M. J. (1984). Sport psychology. *Annual Review of Psychology*, **35**, 605–626.

Brownell, K. D. (1993). Whether obesity should be treated. *Health Psychology*, **12**, 339–341.

——. (2002). The environment and obesity. In C. G. Fairburn & K. D. Brownell (Eds.), *Eating disorders and obesity: A comprehensive handbook (2nd ed.)*. New York: Guilford Press.

Brownell, K. D., & Rodin, J. (1994). The dieting maelstrom: Is it possible and advisable to lose weight? *American Psychologist*, **49**, 781–791.

Bruch, H. (1980). Preconditions for the development of anorexia nervosa. *American Journal of Psychoanalysis*, **40**, 169–172.

Bruner, J. S. & Goodman, C. C. (1947). Value and need as organizing factors in perception. *Journal of Abnormal and Social Psychology*, **42**, 33–44.

Bruner, J. S., Goodnow, J. J., & Austin, G. A. (1956). *A study of thinking*. New York: Wiley.

Buck, R. (1980). Nonverbal behavior and the theory of emotion: The facial feedback hypothesis. *Journal of Personality and Social Psychology*, **38**, 811–824.

——. (1985). Prime theory: An integrated view of motivation and emotion. *Psychological Review*, **92**, 389–413.

——. (1999). The biological affects: A typology. *Psychological Review*, **106**, 301–336.

Buckley, P. F., Buchanan, R. W., Schulz, S. C., & Tamminga, C. A. (1996). Catching up on schizophrenia. *Archives of General Psychiatry*, **53**, 456–462.

Buckout, R. (1975). Nearly 2000 witnesses can be wrong. *Social Action and the Law*, **2**, 7.

Bullock, W. A., & Gilliland, K. (1993). Eysenck's arousal theory of introversion-extraversion: A converging measures investigation. *Journal of Personality and Social Psychology*, **64**, 113–123.

Bunde, J., & Suls, J. (2006). A quantitative analysis of the relationship between the Cook-Medley hostility scale and traditional coronary artery disease risk factors. *Health Psychology*, **25**, 493–500.

Burchinal, M. R., Roberts, J. E., Riggins, R. Jr., Zisel, S. A., Neebe, E., & Bryant, D. (2000). Relating quality of center-based care to early cognitive and language development longitudinally. *Child Development*, **71**, 339–357.

Bureau of Justice Statistics (1999). *Sourcebook for criminal justice statistics, 1999* (Table 4.8, p. 347). Downloaded from the World Wide Web, January 30, 2001. http://www.albany.edu/sourcebook/1995/toc_4html.

——. (2003). *Contacts between police and the public: Findings from the 2002 National Survey*. Washington, DC: U.S. Department of Justice.

Burger, J. M. (2000). *Personality (Fifth Edition)*. Belmont, CA: Wadsworth.

——. (2008). Replicating Milgram: Would people still obey today? *American Psychologist* (in press).

Burgoon, J. K., Birk, T., & Pfau, M. (1990). Non-verbal behaviors, persuasion, and credibility. *Human Communication Research*, **17**, 140–169.

Burisch, M. (1984). Approaches to personality inventory construction. *American Psychologist*, **39**, 214–227.

Burke, R. J., & Greenglass, E. R. (2001). Hospital restructuring, work-family conflict and psychological burnout among nursing staff. *Community, Work, and Family*, **4**, 49–62.

Bushman, B. J., & Anderson, C. A. (2001). Media violence and the American public: Scientific facts versus media misinformation. *American Psychologist*, **56**, 477–489.

Bushman, B. J., & Cooper, H. M. (1990). Effects of alcohol on human aggression: An integrative research review. *Psychological Bulletin*, **107**, 341–354.

Buss, A. H. (1966). *Psychopathology*. New York: Wiley.

Buss, D. M. (1984). Evolutionary biology and personality psychology. *American Psychologist*, **39**, 1135–1147.

——. (1989). Personality as traits. *American Psychologist*, **44**, 1378–1388.

Buss, D. M., Abbott, M., Angleitner, A., Asherian, A., Biaggio, A., Blanco-Villasenor, A., et al. (1990). International preferences in mate selection: A study of 37 cultures. *Journal of Cross-Cultural Psychology*, **21**, 5–47.

Buss, D. M., & Barnes, M. (1986). Preferences in human mate selection. *Journal of Personality and Social Psychology*, **50**, 559–570.

Buss, D. M., & Plomin, R (1984). *Temperament: Early developing personality traits*. Hillsdale, NJ: Lawrence Erlbaum.

Butler, R., & Emr, M. (1982). SDAT research: Current trends. *Generations*, **7**, 14–18.

Butler, R., & Lewis, M. (1981). *Aging and mental health*. St. Louis: Mosby.

Byne, W., Lasco, M. S., Kemether, E., Edgar, M. A., Morgello, S., Jones, L. B., & Tobet, S. (2000). The interstitial nuclei of the human anterior hypothalamus: An investigation of sexual variation in volume and cell size, number and density. *Brain Research*, **856**, 254–258.

Byrd, K. R. (1994). The narrative reconstruction of incest survivors. *American Psychologist*, **49**, 439–440.

Byrne, P., Jones, S., & Williams, R. (2004). The association between cannabis and alcohol use and the development of mental disorder. *Current Opinion in Psychiatry*, **17**, 255-261.

Cabeza, R., & Nyberg, L. (2000). Imaging cognition II: An empirical review of 275 PET and fMRI studies. *Journal of Cognitive Neuroscience*, **12**, 1-47.

Cacioppo, J. T., Marshall-Goodell, B. S., Tassinary, L. G., & Petty, R. E. (1992). Rudimentary determinants of attitudes: Classical conditioning is more effective when prior knowledge about the attitude stimulus is low than high. *Journal of Experimental Social Psychology*, **28**, 207–233.

Cacioppo, J. T., & Petty, R. E. (1989). Effects of message repetition on argument processing, recall, and persuasion. *Basic Applied Social Psychology*, **10**, 3–12.

Cahill, L., Uncapher, M., Kilpatrick, L., Alkire, M. T., & Turner, J. (2004). Sex-related hemispheric lateralization of amygdala function in emotionally influenced memory: An fMRI investigation. *Learning and Memory*, **11**, 261-266.

Cahn, B. R., & Polich, J. (2006). Meditation states and traits: EEG, ERP, and neuroimaging studies. *Psychological Bulletin*, **132**, 180–211.

Cairns, E., McWhirter, L., Duffy, U., & Barry, R. (1990). The stability of self-concept in late adolescence: Gender and situational effects. *Personality and Individual Differences*, **11**, 937-944.

Calder, T. (2003). The apparent banality of evil: The relationship between evil acts and evil character. *Journal of Social Philosophy*, **34**, 364–376.

Calhoun, J. B. (1962). Population density and social pathology. *Scientific American*, **206**, 139–148.

Calsyn, D. A., Saxon, A. J., Freeman, G., & Whittaker, S. (1992). Ineffectiveness of AIDS education and HIV antibody testing in reducing high-risk behaviors among injection drug users. *American Journal of Public Health*, **82**, 573–575.

Calvete, E., & Cardenoso, O. (2005). Gender differences in cognitive vulnerability to depression and behavior problems in adolescence. *Journal of Abnormal Child Psychology*, **33**, 179-192.

Campbell, J. P. (1988). Training design for performance improvement. In J. P. Campbell & R. J. Campbell (Eds.), *Productivity in organizations*. San Francisco: Jossey-Bass.

Campbell, J. P., McHenry, J. J., & Wise, L. L. (1990). Modeling job performance in a population of jobs. *Personnel Psychology*, **43**, 313–333.

Campfield, L. A., Smith, F. J., Guisez, Y., Devos, R., & Burn, P. (1995). Recombinant mouse OB protein: Evidence for a peripheral signal linking adiposity and central neural networks. *Science*, **269**, 546–549.

Campion, M. A., Palmer, D. K., & Campion, J. E. (1997). A review of structure in the selection interview. *Personnel Psychology*, **50**, 655–702.

——. (1998). Structuring employment interviews to improve reliability, validity, and users' reactions. *Current Directions in Psychological Science*, **7**, 77–82.

Campos, J. J. Heart rates: A sensitive tool for the study of emotional development. In L. Lipsett (Ed.), *Developmental psychobiology: The significance of infancy*. Hillsdale, NJ: Erlbaum.

Campos, J. J., Hiatt, S., Ramsey, D., Henderson, C., & Svejda, M. (1978). The emergence of fear on the visual cliff. In M. Lewis & L. A. Rosenbaum (Eds.), *The development of affect*. New York: Plenum.

Canetti, L., Kanyas, K., Lerer, B., Latzer, Y., & Bachar, E. (2008). Anorexia nervosa and parental bonding: the contribution of parent–grandparent relationships to eating disorder psychopathology. *Journal of Clinical Psychology*, **64**, 703–716.

Canli, T., Desmond, J. E., Zhao, Z., & Gabrieli, J. D. E. (2002). Sex differences in the neural basis of emotional memories. *Proceedings of the National Academy of Sciences*, **99**, 10789–10795.

Canli, T., Zhao, Z., Bewer, J., Gabrieli, J. D., & Cahill, L. (2000). Event-related activation in the human amygdala associated with later memory for individual emotional experience. *Journal of Neuroscience*, **20**, RC99.

Cannon, T. D., Mednick, S. A., & Parnas, J. (1990). Antecedents of predominantly negative- and predominantly positive-symptom schizophrenia in a high-risk population. *Archives of General Psychiatry*, **47**, 622–632.

Cannon, W. B. (1927). The James-Lange theory of emotions: A critical examination and an alternative theory. *American Journal of Psychology*, **39**, 106-124.

——. (1932). *The wisdom of the body*. New York: Norton.

——. (1934). Hunger and thirst. In C. Murchinson (Ed.), *Handbook of experimental psychology* (pp. 247-263). Worchester, MA: Clark University Press.

Cantor, N., & Kihlstrom, J. F. (1989). Social intelligence and cognitive assessments of personality. In R. S. Wyer & T. K. Srull (Eds.), *Advances in social cognition, volume II: Social intelligence and cognitive assessments of personality*. Hillsdale, NJ: Lawrence Erlbaum.

Cantor, N., & Langston, C. A. (1989). Ups and downs of life tasks in a life transition. In L. A. Pervin (Ed.), *Goal concepts in personality and social psychology*. Hillsdale, NJ: Lawrence Erlbaum Associates.

Caplan, N. (1989). *The boat people and achievement in America: A study of family life, hard work, and cultural values*. Ann Arbor: University of Michigan Press.

Cardenas, R. A., & Harris, L. J. (2006). Symmetrical decorations enhance the attractiveness of faces and abstract designs. *Evolution and Human Behavior, 27,* 1–18.

Carl, L., Sheppard, J., Thornton, B., & Thompson, R. B. (2003). *Social loafing and the theory of mind: Diminished individual effort in a group as a developmental function of the ability to reason about other's beliefs and intentions.* International Conference on Statistics, Combinatorics and Related Areas. Portland, ME, Oct. 3–5.

Carlson, N. R. (1991). *Physiology of behavior (4th ed.).* Boston: Allyn & Bacon.

——. (1998). *Physiology of behavior (6th ed.).* Boston: Allyn & Bacon.

Carnegey, N. L., Anderson, C. A., & Bartholow, B. B. (2007). Media violence and social neuroscience: New questions and new opportunities. *Current Directions in Psychological Science, 16,* 178–182.

Carone, B. J., Harrow, M., & Westermeyer, J. F. (1991). Posthospital course and outcome in schizophrenia. *Archives of General Psychiatry, 48,* 247–253.

Carpenter, S. (2001) Sleep deprivation may be undermining teen health. *Monitor on Psychology,* October, 2001, 42–45.

Carroll, K. M. (2003). *A Cognitive-Behavioral Approach: Treating Cocaine Addiction.* Washington, DC: National Institute on Drug Abuse.

Carson, R. C. (1989). Personality. *Annual Review of Psychology, 40,* 227–248.

Carson, R. L. (1962). *Silent Spring.* Boston: Houghton Mifflin.

Carson, T. P., & Carson, R. C. (1984). The affective disorders. In H. E. Adams & P. B. Sutker (Eds.), *Comprehensive handbook of psychpathology.* New York: Plenum.

Carter, M. M. (2002). Uncontrolled anxiety: Understanding panic disorder with agoraphobia. *Family Therapy Magazine,* Sept./Oct., pp. 32–38.

Caruso, D. A. (1996). Maternal employment status, mother-infant interaction, and infant development in day care and non-day care groups. *Child and Youth Care Forum, 25,* 125–134.

Carver, C. S. & Scheier, M. F. (1999). Optimism. In C. R. Snyder (Ed.), *Coping: The psychology of what works,* pp. 182–204. New York: Oxford University Press.

CASA (The National Center on Addiction and Substance Abuse at Columbia University). (2003). *National survey of American attitudes on substance abuse VIII: Teens and parents.* New York: Author.

Cash, T. F., & Kilcullen, R. N. (1985). The eye of the beholder: Susceptibility to sexism and beautyism in the evaluation of managerial applicants. *Journal of Applied Social Psychology, 15,* 591–605.

Caspi, A. (2000). The child is father of the man: Personality continuities from childhood to adulthood. *Journal of Personality and Social Psychology, 78,* 158–172.

Caspi, A., Roberts, B. W., & Shiner, R. L. (2005). Personality development: Stability and change. *Annual Review of Psychology, 56,* 453–485.

Caspi, A., Sugden, K., Moffitt, T. E., Taylor, A., Craig, I. W., et al. (2003). Influence of life stress on depression: Moderation by a polymorphism in the 5-HTT gene. *Science, 301,* 291–293.

Castro-Fornieles, J., et al. (2007). Self-oriented perfectionism in eating disorders. *International Journal of Eating Disorders, 40,* 562–568.

Cattell, R. (1963). Theory of fluid and crystallized intelligence: A critical experiment. *Journal of Educational Psychology, 54,* 1–22.

Cattell, R. B. (1973). *Personality and mood by questionnaire.* San Francisco: Jossey-Bass.

——. (1979). *The structure of personality in its environment.* New York: Springer.

Cavaliere, F. (1995). APA and CDC join forces to combat illness. *The APA Monitor, 26,* 1, 13.

Cavanaugh, J. C., & Blanchard-Fields, F. (2002). *Adult development and aging.* Belmont, CA: Wadsworth.

CDC (Centers for Disease Control and Prevention). (1991). Body-weight perceptions and selected weight-management goals and practices of high school students—United States, 1990. *Mortality and Morbidity Weekly Report, 40,* 741-750.

——. (1993). *Past month smokeless tobacco use among boys, grades 9–12—United States, 1993.* Downloaded from the World Wide Web, January 31, 2001. http://www.cdc.gov/tobacco/research_data/spit/sltboys.htm.

——. (1999). *Youth Risk Behavior Surveillance—United States, 1999.* Downloaded from the World Wide Web, January 31, 2001. http://www.cdc.gov/mmwr/preview/mmwrhtml/ss4905a1.htm.

——. (1999a). *Youth Risk Behavior Surveillance—United States, 1999: State and Local Youth Risk Behavior Surveillance System Coordinators.* Downloaded from the World Wide Web, January 30, 2001. http://www.cdc.gov/mmwr/preview/mmwrhtml/ss4095a1.htm.

——. (1999b). *Tobacco advertising and promotion fact sheet.* Downloaded from the World Wide Web, January 30, 2001. http://www/cdc.gov/tobacco/sgr/sgr_2000/TobaccoAdvertising.pdf.

——. (2000). *Reducing children's use of tobacco: Fact sheets.* Downloaded from the World Wide Web, January 30, 2001. http://www.cdc.gov/tobacco/youth.htm.

——. (2001). Prevalence of disabilities and associated health conditions in adults—United States, 1999. *MMWR, 50,* 120-125.

——. (2003). Diagnoses of HIV/AIDS—32 sites, 2000-2003. *Morbidity and Mortality Weekly Report, 53,* 1106-1110.

——. (2003). *Teen Births.* From the website of The National Center for Health Statistics. www.cdc.gov/nchs/fastats/teenbrth.htm.

——. (2004). *HIV/AIDS surveillance report, 2003 (Vol. 15).* Atlanta: U.S. Department of Health and Human Services.

——. (2005). *National Vital Statistics Reports (Vol. 53).* From the website of the National Center for Health Statistics www.cdc.gov/nchs/deaths.htm. Centers for Disease Control and Prevention (1996, August). *Medical and lifestyle risk factors affecting fetal mortality. Series 20 (31),* U.S. Department of Health and Human Services.

——. (2002). Cigarette smoking among adults—United States, 2000. *Morbidity and Mortality Weekly Report, 51,* 642–645.

——. (2003). *Targeting tobacco use: The nation's leading cause of death, 2003.* Washington, DC: Department of Health and Human Services.

——. (2003). *Tobacco Information and Prevention Source (TIPS)*. Washington, DC: National Center for Chronic Disease Prevention and Health Promotion.

——. (2004). Smoking during pregnancy—United States 1990–2002. Retrieved on May 22, 2004 from http://www.cdc.gov/mmwr/preview/mmwrhtml/mm5339a1.htm.

——. (2005a). *What is the prevalence of overweight and obesity among US adults?* Downloaded on October 25, 2005 from www.cdc.gov/nccdphp/dnpa/obesity/faq.htm#adults.

——. (2005b). *Genetic polymorphisms and Quantitative Trait Loci (QTLs) associated with specific obesity sub-phenotypes.* Downloaded on October 25, 2005 from www.cdc.gov/genomics/info/perspectives/files/obesomim.htm

——. (2007). Prevalence of autism spectrum disorders: Autism and developmental disabilities monitoring network, six sites, United States, 2000. Surveillance summaries, 2002. *Morbidity and Mortality Weekly Report (MMWR)*, **56**, 1–11.

——. (2007a). *Trends in reportable sexually transmitted diseases in the United States, 2006.* Hyattsville, MD: U. S. Department of Health and Human Services. [Also available on the Internet at www.cdc.gov/std/stats/trends2006.htm]

——. (2007b). Adult cigarette smoking in the United States: Current estimates. *Smoking & Tobacco Use: Fact Sheet.* Hyattsville, MD: U. S. Department of Health and Human Services.

——. (2008a). Deaths: Final data for 2005. *National Vital Statistics Reports,* **56**, April 24, 2008.

——. (2008b). *HIV/AIDS surveillance report, 2006* (vol. 18). Atlanta: U. S. Department of Health and Human Services.

——. (2008a). Overweight and obesity: Introduction. Downloaded on September 7, 2008 from http://www.cdc.gov/nccdphp/dnpa/obesity/index.htm

——. (2008b). Overweight and obesity: Childhood overweight. Downloaded on September 7, 2008 from http://www.cdc.gov/nccdphp/dnpa/obesity/childhood/index.htm

——. (2008c). Overweight and obesity: Overweight prevalence. Downloaded on September 7, 2008 from http://www.cdc.gov/nccdphp/dnpa/obesity/childhood/prevalence.htm

——. (2008c). Overweight and obesity: Contributing factors. Downloaded on September 7, 2008 from http://www.cdc.gov/nccdphp/dnpa/obesity/contributing_factors.htm.

Ceci, S. J. (1994, May 5–7). *Children's testimony: How reliable is it?* Invited address, Midwestern Psychological Association, Chicago, IL.

Ceci, S. J., & Bruck, M. (1996). *Jeopardy in the courtroom: A scientific analysis of children's testimony.* Washington, D.C.: American Psychological Association.

Cefalo, R. C. (1996). Prevention of neural tube defects. In J. A. Kuller, N. C. Cheschier, & R. C. Cefalo (Eds.), *Prenatal diagnosis and reproductive genetics* (pp. 2-9). St. Louis: Mosbey Press.

Cell Medicine (2008). Stem cell therapy for Parkinson's Disease. Retrieved May 14, 2008 from http://www.cellmedicine.com/parkinsonsdisease.asp.

Centerwall, B. S. (1992). Television and violence: The scale of the problem and where to go from here. *Journal of the American Medical Association,* **267**, 3059–3063.

Cepeda, N. J., Pashler, H., Vul, E., Wixsted, T. J., & Rohrer, D. (2006). Distributed practice in verbal recall tasks: A review and quantitative synthesis. *Psychological Bulletin,* **132**, 354–380.

Cermak, L. S., & Craik, F. I. M. (Eds.). (1979). *Levels of processing in human memory.* Hillsdale, NJ: Erlbaum.

Cernoch, J. M., & Porter, R. H. (1985). Recognition of maternal axillary odors by infants. *Child Development,* **56**, 1593–1598.

Chagnon, N. A. (1983). *Yanomamö: The fierce people (3rd ed.).* New York: Holt, Rinehart & Winston.

Chalmers, D. J. (1995). The puzzle of conscious experience. *Scientific American,* **273**, 62-68.

Chambless, D. L., & Ollendick, T. H. (2001). Empirically supported psychological interventions: Controversies and evidence. *Annual Review of Psychology,* **52**, 685–716.

Chan, A. S., Cheung, J., Leung, W. W. M., Cheung, R., & Cheung, M. (2005). Verbal expression and comprehension deficits in young children with autism. *Focus on Autism and Other Developmental Disabilities,* **20**, 117–124.

Chan, D. K-S., & Cheng, G. H-L. (2004). A comparison of offline and online friendship qualities at different stages of relationship development. *Journal of Social and Personal Relationships,* **21**, 305–320.

Chandola, T., Brunner, E., & Marmot, M. (2006). Chronic stress at work and the metabolic syndrome: Prospective study. *British Medical Journal,* **332**, 521–525.

Chandrashekar, J., Hoon, M. A., Ryba, N. J., & Zuker, C. S. (2006). The receptors and cells for mammalian taste. *Nature,* **444**, 288–294.

Changizi, M. A., & Widders, D. (2002). Latency correction explains the classical geometric illusions. *Perception,* **31**, 1241–1262.

Changizi, M. A., Hsieh, A., Nijhawan, R., Kanai, R., & Shimojo, S. (2008). Perceiving the present and a systematization of Illusions. *Cognitive Science: A Multidisciplinary Journal,* **32**, 459–503.

Chao, R. K. (1994). Beyond parental control and authoritarian parenting style: Understanding Chinese parenting through the cultural notion of training. *Child Development,* **65**, 1111-1119.

——. (1996). Chinese and European-American mothers' beliefs about the role of parenting in children's school success. *Journal of Cross-cultural Psychology,* **27**, 403-421.

Chao, R. K., & Sue, S. (1996). Chinese parental influence and their children's success: A paradox in the literature on parenting styles. In S. Lau (Ed.), *Youth and child development in Chinese societies.* Hong Kong: Chinese University of Hong Kong.

Charney, D. S., Deutch, A. Y., Krystal, J. H., Southwick, S. M., & Davis, M. (1993). Psychobiological mechanisms of posttraumatic stress disorder. *Archives of General Psychiatry,* **50**, 294–305.

Chase, W. G., & Simon, H. A. (1973). The mind's eye in chess. In W. G. Chase (Ed.), *Visual information processing.* New York: Academic Press.

Chasnoff, I. J., Griffith, D. R., MacGregor, S., Dirkes, K., & Burns, K. (1989). Temporal patterns of cocaine use in pregnancy. *Journal of the American Medical Association*, **261**, 1741–1744.

Chaudhari, N., Landin, A. M., & Roper, S. D. (2000). A metabotropic glutamate receptor variant functions as a taste receptor. *Nature: Neuroscience*, **3**, 113–119.

Chekroun, P., & Brauer, M. (2001). The bystander effect and social control behavior: The effect of the presence of others on people's reactions to norm violations. *European Journal of Social Psychology*, **32**, 853–867.

Chen, P., Ratcliff, G., Belle, S. H., Cauley, J. A., Dekosky, S. T., & Ganguli, M. (2001). Patterns of cognitive decline in presymptomatic Alzheimer disease. *Archives of General Psychiatry*, **58**, 853–858.

Cherney, I. D., & Ryalls, B. O. (1999). Gender-linked differences in the incidental memory of children and adults. *Journal of Experimental Child Psychology*, **72**, 305–328.

Cheung, K-H., Shineman, D., Müller, M., Cárdenas, C., Mei, L., Yang, J., Tomita, T., Iwatsubo, T., Lee, V. M.-Y, & Foskett, K. (2008). Mechanism of Ca^{2+} disruption in Alzheimer's disease by presenilin regulation of InsP$_3$ channel gating. *Neuron*, **58**, 871–883.

Chi, M. T. H., & Glaser, R. (1985). Problem solving ability. In R. J. Sternberg (Ed.), *Advances in the psychology of human intelligence*. San Francisco: Freeman.

Chilman, C. S. (1980). Parent satisfactions, concerns, and goals for their children. *Family Relations*, **29**, 339–346.

——. (1983). *Adolescent sexuality in a changing American society: Social and psychological perspectives for the human services profession (2nd ed.)*. New York: Wiley.

Chiolero, A., Fach, D., Paccaud, F., & Cornuz, J. (2008). Consequences of smoking for body weight, body fat distribution, and insulin resistance. *American Journal of Clinical Nutrition*, **87**, 801–809.

Chiriboga, D. A., Yee, B. W. K., & Yang, Y. (2005). Minority and cultural issues in late-life depression. *Clinical Psychology: Science and Practice*, **12**, 358-363.

Chisholm, J. F. (1999). The sandwich generation. *Journal of Social Distress and the Homeless*, **8**, 177–191.

Chiu, C., & Hong, Y. (2005). Cultural competence: Dynamic processes. In A. Elliot & C. S. Dweck (Eds.), *Handbook of motivation and competence*, (pp. 489-505). New York: Guilford.

Chodosh, J., Ferrell, B. A., Shekelle, P. G., & Wenger, N. S. (2001). Quality indicators for pain management in vulnerable elders. *Annals of Internal Medicine*, **135**, 731-735.

Choi, I., Nisbett, R. E., & Norenzayan, A. (1999). Causal attribution: Variation and universality. *Psychological Bulletin*, **125**, 47–63.

Chomsky, N. (1957). *Syntactic structures*. The Hague: Mouton.

Chrisjohn, R. D., & Peters, M. (1989). The right-brained Indian: Fact or fiction? *Journal of American Indian Education*, **28**, 77-83.

Christiansen, K., & Knussmann, R. (1987). Androgen levels and components of aggressive behavior in men. *Hormones & Behavior*, **21**, 170–180.

Chubb, N. H., Fertman, L. I., & Ross, J. L. (1997). Adolescent self-esteem and locus of control: A longitudinal study of gender and age differences. *Adolescence*, **32**, 113-129.

Cialdini, R. B. (2003). Crafting normative messages to protect the environment. *Current Directions in Psychological Science*, **12**, 105–109.

Cialdini, R. B., & Goldstein, N. J. (2004). Social influence: Compliance and conformity. *Annual Review of Psychology*, **55**, 591-621.

Cialdini, R. B., Reno, R. R., & Kallgren, C. A. (1990). A focus theory of normative conduct: Recycling the concept of norms to reduce littering in public places. *Journal of Personality and Social Psychology*, **58**, 1015–1026.

Ciarrochi, J. V., Chan, A. Y. C., & Caputi, P. (2000). A critical evaluation of the emotional intelligence construct. *Personality and individual differences*, **28(3)**, 539–561.

CIBA-GEIGY. (1991). *OCD: When a habit isn't just a habit*. Pine Brook, NJ: CIBA-GEIGY Corporation.

Cinciripini, P. M., Cinciripini, L. G., Wallfisch, A., Haque, W., & Van Vunakis, H. (1996). Behavior therapy and the transdermal nicotine patch: Effects on cessation outcome, affect, and coping. *Journal of Consulting and Clinical Psychology*, **64**, 314–323.

Clark, C. W. (1997). The witch craze in 17th century Europe. In W. G. Bringmann, H. E. Lück, R. Miller, & C. E. Early (Eds.), *A pictorial history of psychology*. Carol Stream, IL: Quintessence Publishing.

Clark, D. A., & Ryhno, S. (2005). Unwanted intrusive thoughts in nonclinical individuals: Implications for clinical disorders. In D. A. Clark (Ed.). *Intrusive thoughts in clinical disorders* (pp. 1–29). New York: Guilford.

Clark, K. B., & Clark, M. P. (1939). The development of consciousness of the self and the emergence of racial identification in Negro preschool children. *Journal of Social Psychology*, **10**, 591-599.

——. (1947). Racial identification and preference in Negro children. In T. M. Newcomb & E. L. Hartley (Eds.), *Readings in social psychology*. New York: Holt, Rinehart & Winston.

Clark, L. A., Watson, D., & Reynolds, S. (1995). Diagnosis and classification of psychopathology: Challenges to the current system and future directions. *Annual Review of Psychology*, **46**, 121–153.

Clarkin, J. F., Pilkonis, P. A., & Magruder, K. M. (1996). Psychotherapy of depression: Implications for reform of the health care system. *Archives of General Psychiatry*, **53**, 717–723.

Clarkson-Smith, L., & Hartley, A. A. (1989). Relationships between physical exercise and cognitive abilities in older adults. *Psychology and Aging*, **4**, 183–189.

Clay, R. A. (2002). A renaissance for humanistic psychology. *Monitor on Psychology*, **33** (September), 42–43.

——. (2002, April). Overcoming barriers to pain relief. *Monitor on Psychology*, **33**, 58–60.

Cleary, L. M., & Peacock, T. D. (1999). *Collected wisdom: American Indian education*. Boston: Allyn & Bacon.

Clifford, M. M., & Hatfield, E. (1973). The effect of physical attractiveness on teacher expectation. *Sociology of Education*, **46**, 248–258.

Clinton, J. J. (1992). Acute pain management can be improved. *Journal of the American Medical Association*, **267**, 2580.

Clore, G. L., & Byrne, D. (1974). A reinforcement-affect model of attraction. In T. L. Huston (Ed.), *Foundations of interpersonal attraction*. New York: Academic Press.

Coccaro, E. F., Kavoussi, R. J., & McNamee, B. (2000). Central neurotransmitter function in criminal aggression. In D. H. Fishbein, Ed, *The science, treatment, and prevention of antisocial behaviors*. (pp. 6-1–6-16). Kingston, NJ: Civic Research Institute.

Cohen, C. B., Dressor, R., Lanza, R. P., Cibelli, J. B., et al. (2001). Ethical issues in embryonic stem cell research. *Journal of the American Medical Association*, **285**, 1439.

Cohen, G. D. (1980). *Fact sheet: Senile dementia (Alzheimer's disease), [No. ADM 80-929]*. Washington, DC: Center for Studies of the Mental Health of the Aging.

Cohen L. & Dehaene, S. (2000). Calculating without reading: Unsuspected residual abilities in pure alexia. *Cognitive Neuropsychology*, **17**, 563-583.

Cohen, M. S., Gay, C., Kashuba, A. D. M., Blower, S., & Paxton, L. (2007). Narrative review: Antiretroviral therapy to prevent the sexual transmission of HIV-1. *Annals of Internal Medicine*, **146**, 591–601.

Cohen, R. J., Montague, P., Nathanson, L. S., & Swerdlik, M. E. (1988). *Psychological testing: An introduction to tests and measurement*. Mountain View, CA: Mayfield Publishing Company.

Cohen, S. (1996). Psychological stress, immunity, and upper respiratory infections. *Current Directions in Psychological Science*, **5**, 85–90.

Cohen, S., & Lichtenstein, E. (1990). Perceived stress, quitting smoking, and smoking relapse. *Health Psychology*, **9**, 466–478.

Cohen, S., & Pressman, S. D. (2006). Positive affect and health. *Current Directions in Psychological Science*, **15**, 122–125.

Cohen, S., & Williamson, G. M. (1991). Stress and infectious disease in humans. *Psychological Bulletin*, **109**, 5–24.

Cohen, S., Doyle, W. J., Skoner, D. P., Fireman, P., Gwalyney, J., & Newsom, J. (1995). State and trait negative affect as predictors of objective and subjective symptoms of respiratory viral infections. *Journal of Personality and Social Psychology*, **68**, 159–169.

Cohen, S., Evans, G. W., Krantz, D. S., Stokols, D., & Kelly, S. (1980). Aircraft noise and children: Longitudinal and cross-sectional evidence on the adaptation to noise and the effectiveness of noise abatement. *Journal of Personality and Social Psychology*, **40**, 331–345

Cohen, S., Evans, G. W., Stokols, D., & Krantz, D. S. (1986). *Behavior, health, and environmental stress*. New York: Plenum.

Cohen, S., Lichtenstein, E., Prochaska, J. O., Rossi, J. S., Gritz, E. R., Carr, C. R., et al. (1989). Debunking myths about self-quitting: Evidence from 10 prospective studies of persons who attempt to quit smoking by themselves. *American Psychologist*, **44**, 1355–1365.

Colby, A., & Kohlberg, L. (1984). Invariant sequence and internal consistency in moral judgment stages. In W. M. Kurtines & J. L. Gewitz (Eds.), *Morality, moral behavior, and moral development*. New York: Wiley.

Cole, J. O. (1988). Where are those new antidepressants we were promised? *Archives of General Psychiatry*, **45**, 193–194.

Cole, K. N., Mills, P. E., Dale, P. S., & Jenkins. J. R. (1991). Effects of preschool integration for children with disabilities. *Exceptional Children*, **58**, 36–45.

Cole, R. E. (1979). *Work, mobility, and participation*. Berkeley: University of California Press.

Coleman, H. L. K., Wampold, B. E., & Casali, S. L. (1995). Ethnic minorities' ratings of ethnically similar and European-American counselors: A meta-analysis. *Journal of Counseling Psychology*, **42**, 55–64.

Coles, R., & Stokes, G. (1985). *Sex and the American teenager*. New York: HarperCollins.

Collins, A. M., & Quillian, M. R. (1960). Retrieval time from semantic memory. *Journal of Verbal Learning and Verbal Behavior*, **8**, 240–247.

Collins, W. A., & Gunnar, M. R. (1990). Social and personality development. *Annual Review of Psychology*, **41**, 387–416.

Collins, W. A., Maccoby, E. E., Steinberg, L., Hetherington, E. M., & Bornstein, M. H. (2000). Contemporary research on parenting. *American Psychologist*, **55**, 218–232.

Comer, R., & Laird, J. D. (1975). Choosing to suffer as a consequence of expecting to suffer: Why do people do it? *Journal of Personality and Social Psychology*, **32**, 92–101.

Committee on Health and Behavior; National Institute of Medicine. (2001). *Health and behavior: The interplay of biological, behavioral, and societal influences*. Washington, DC: National Academy Press.

Committee on Lesbian and Gay Concerns. (1991). Avoiding heterosexual bias in language. *American Psychologist*, **46**, 973–974.

Compas, B. E., Hinden, B. R., & Gerhardt, C. A. (1995). Adolescent development: Pathways and processes of risk and resilience. *Annual Review of Psychology*, **46**, 265–293.

Compton, J., van Amelsvoort, T., & Murphy, D. (2001). HRT and its effect on normal ageing of the brain and dementia. *British Journal of Clinical Pharmacology*, *52*, 647–653.

Compton, W. M., Conway, K. P., Stinson, F. S., Colliver, J. D., & Grant, B. F. (2005), Prevalence, correlates, and comorbidity of DSM-IV antisocial personality syndromes and alcohol and specific drug use disorders in the United States: Results from the national epidemiologic survey on alcohol and related conditions. *Journal of Clinical Psychiatry*, **66**, 677-685.

Condon, J. (1984). *With respect to the Japanese*. Yarmouth, ME: Intercultural Press.

Condry, J., & Condy, S. (1976). Sex differences: A study of the eye of the beholder. *Child Development, 47*, 812–819.

Conference Board, The. (2003). *Special consumer survey report: Job satisfaction—September 2003*. Washington, DC: The Conference Board, Inc.

Conger, J. J. (1991). *Adolescence and youth (4th ed.)*. New York: HarperCollins.

Conger, J. J., & Peterson, A. C. (1984). *Adolescence and youth: Psychological development in a changing world*. New York: HarperCollins.

Conklin, C. A. (2006). Environments as cues to smoke: Implications for human extinction-based research and treatment. *Experimental and Clinical Psychopharmacology*, **14**, 12–19.

Conrad, R. (1963). Acoustic confusions and memory span for words. *Nature*, **197**, 1029–1030.

——. (1964). Acoustic confusions in immediate memory. *British Journal of Psychology*, **55**, 75–84.

Consumer Reports. (1995, November). *Mental health: Does therapy help?*, 734–739.

Cooper, D. (1998). *Improving safety culture*. Chichester, UK: Wiley.

Cooper, J., & Croyle, R. T. (1984). Attitudes and attitude change. *Annual Review of Psychology*, **35**, 395–426.

Cooper, J., & Scher, S. J. (1992). Actions and attitudes: The role of responsibility and aversive consequences in persuasion. In T. Brock & S. Shavitt (Eds.), *The psychology of persuasion*. San Francisco: Freeman.

Cooper, J. R., Bloom, F. E., & Roth, R. E. (1996). *The biochemical basis of neuropharmacology (Seventh Edition)*. New York: Oxford University Press.

Cooper, L., & Fazio, R. H. (1984). A new look at cognitive dissonance theory. In L. Berkowitz (Ed.), *Advances in experimental social psychology (Vol. 17)*. San Diego: Academic Press.

Cooper, L. A., & Shepard, R. N. (1973). Chronometric studies of the rotation of mental images. In W. G. Chase (Ed.), *Visual information processing*. New York: Academic Press.

Cooper, M. D. (2002). Safety culture: A model for understanding and quantifying a difficult concept. *Professional Safety*, **47**(6), 30–36.

Cooper, M. K., Porter, J. A., Young, K. E., & Beachy, P. A. (1998). Teratogen-mediated inhibition of target tissue response to Shh signaling. *Science*, **280**, 1603–1607.

Copeland, W. E., Keeler, G., Angold, A., & Costello, E. J. (2007). Traumatic events and posttraumatic stress in childhood. *Archives of General Psychiatry*, **64**, 577–584.

Corballis, P. M., Funnell, M. G., & Gazzaniga, M. S. (2002). Hemispheric asymmetries for simple visual judgments in the split brain. *Neuropsychologia*, **40**, 401-410.

Cordua, G. D., McGraw, K. O., & Drabman, R. S. (1979). Doctor or nurse: Children's perception of sex typed occupations. *Child Development*, **50**, 590–593.

Cornblatt, B. A., & Erlenmeyer-Kimling, L. (1985). Global attention deviance as a marker of risk for schizophrenia: Specificity and predictive validity. *Journal of Abnormal Psychology*, **94**, 470–486.

Cornelius, R. R. (1996). *The science of emotion: Research and tradition in the psychology of emotion*. Upper Saddle River, NJ: Prentice Hall.

Cosgrove G. R., & Rauch, S. L. (2003). Stereotactic cingulotomy. *Neurosurgery Clinics of North America*, **14**, 225-235.

Costa, L. G., Aschner, M., Vitalone, A., Syversen, T., & Soldin, O. P. (2004). Developmental neuropathology of environmental agents. *Annual Review of Pharmacology and Toxicology*, **44**, 87-110.

Costa, P. T., & McCrae, R. R. (1980). Still stable after all these years: Personality as a key to some issues in adulthood and old age. In P. B. Baltes & O. G. Brim, Jr. (Eds.), *Life-span development and behavior*. New York: Academic Press.

Costello, C. G. (1982). Fears and phobias in women: A community study. *Journal of Abnormal Psychology*, **91**, 280–286.

Coté, T. R., Biggar, R. J., & Dannenberg, A. L. (1992). Risk of suicide among persons with AIDS: A national assessment. *Journal of the American Medical Association*, **268**, 2066–2068.

Couce, M. E., Burguera B., Parisi J. E., Jensen M. D., & Lloyd R. V. (1997). Localization of leptin receptor in the human brain. *Neuroendocrinology*, **66**, 145–50.

Coulter, W. A., & Morrow, H. W. (Eds.). (1978). *Adaptive behavior: Concepts and measurements*. New York: Grune & Stratton.

Council, J. R. (1993). Context effects in personality research. *Current Directions in Psychological Science*, **2**, 3–34.

Council, J. R., & Green, J. P. (2004). Examining the absorption-hypnotizability link: The role of acquiescence and consistentcy motivation. *International Journal of Clinical and Experimental Hypnosis*, **52**, 364–377.

Coursey, R. D., Alford, J., & Safarjan, B. (1997). Significant advances in understanding and treating serious mental illness. *Professional Psychology: Research and Practice*, **28**, 205–216.

Coursey, R. D., Gearon, J., Bradmiller, M. A., Ritsher, J., Keller, A., & Selby, P. (2000). A psychological view of people with serious mental illness. In F. J. Frese (Ed.), *The role of organized psychology in the treatment of the seriously mentally ill*. San Fransisco: Jossey-Bass.

Cowan, G., & Avants, S. K. (1988). Children's influence strategies: Structure, sex differences, and bilateral mother-child influences. *Child Development*, **59**, 1303–1313.

Cowan, N. (1984). On short and long auditory stores. *Psychological Bulletin*, **96**, 341–370.

——. (1993). Activation, attention, and short-term memory. *Memory and Cognition*, **21**, 162–167.

——. (1994). Mechanisms of verbal short-term memory. *Current Directions in Psychological Science*, **3**, 185–189.

——. (2001). The magical number 4 in short-term memory: A reconsideration of mental storage capacity. *Behavioral and Brain Sciences*, **24**, 87–114.

——. (2005). *Working memory capacity*. New York: Psychology Press.

Cowan, N., & Davidson, G. (1984). Salient childhood memories. *Journal of Genetic Psychology*, **145**, 101-107.

Cowan, W. M. (1979). The development of the brain. *In The brain*. San Francisco: Freeman.

Cox, R. H. (1990). *Sport psychology: Concepts and applications*. Dubuque, IA: Brown.

Coyle, J. T., Price, D. L., & DeLong, M. H. (1983). Alzheimer's disease: A disorder of central cholinergic innervation. *Science*, **219**, 1184–1189.

Coyne, J. C., & Downey, G. (1991). Social factors and psychopathology: Stress, social support, and coping processes. *Annual Review of Psychology*, **42**, 401–425.

Coyne, J. C., Pepper, C. M., & Flynn, H. (1999). Significance of prior episodes of depression in two patient populations. *Journal of consulting and Clinical Psychology*, **67**, 76–81.

Cozby, P. C. (1973). Self-disclosure: A literature review. *Psychological Bulletin*, **79**, 73–91.

Craik, F. I. M. (1970). The fate of primary memory items in free recall. *Journal of Verbal Learning and Verbal Behavior*, **9**, 143–148.

Craik, F. I. M., & Lockhart, R. S. (1972). Levels of processing: A framework for memory research. *Journal of Verbal Learning and Verbal Behavior*, **11**, 671–684.

Craik, F. I. M., & Tulving, E. (1975). Depth of processing and the retention of words in episodic memory. *Journal of Experimental Psychology: General*, **104**, 268–294.

Cramer, P. (2000). Defense mechanisms in psychology today: Further processes for adaptation. *American Psychologist*, **55**, 637–646.

Cramer, R. E., McMaster, M. R., Bartell, P. A., & Dragna, M. (1988). Subject competence and minimization of the bystander effect. *Journal of Applied Social Psychology*, **18**, 1133–1148.

Craske, M. G., & Barlow, D. H. (2001). Panic disorder and agoraphobia. In D. H. Barlow (Ed.), *Clinical handbook of psychological disorders (3rd ed.)*. New York: Guilford Press.

Creed, F., & Barsky, A. (2004). A systematic review of the epidemiology of somatization disorder and hypochondriasis. *Journal of Psychosomatic Research*, **56**, 391–408.

Creekmore, C. R. (1984). Games athletes play. *Psychology Today*, **19**, 40–44.

——. (1985). Cities won't drive you crazy. *Psychology Today*, **19**, 46–53.

Creeley, C. E., & Kelemen, W. L. (2003). State-dependent memory effects using caffeine and placebo do not extend to metamemory. *Journal of General Psychology*, **130**, 70–86.

Crepaz, N., Hart, T. A., & Marks, G. (2004). Highly active antiretroviral therapy and sexual risk behavior. *The Journal of the American Medical Association*, **292**, 224–236.

Crews, D. J., & Landers, D. M. (1987). A meta-analytic review of aerobic fitness and reactivity to psychosocial stressors. *Medicine and Science in Sport and Exercise*, **19**, 114–120.

Crick, F., & Koch, C. (1998). Consciousness and neuroscience. *Cerebral Cortex*, **8**, 97–107.

——. (2000). The unconscious homunculus. In T. Metzinger (Ed.), *The neural correlates of consciousness*. Cambridge, MA: MIT Press.

——. (2003). A framework for consciousness. *Nature Neuroscience*, **6**, 119–126.

Critchley, H. D., Wiens, S., Rotshtein, P., Ohman, A., & Dolan, J. D. (2004). Neural systems supporting interoceptive systems. *Nature: Neuroscience*, **7**, 189-1056.

Crocker, J., Luhtanen, R., Blaine, B., & Broadnax, S. (1994). Collective self-esteem and psychological well-being among, white, black, and Asian college students. *Personality and Social Psychology Bulletin*, **20**, 503-513.

Crocker, J., Major, B., & Steele, C. (1998). Social stigma. In S. Friske, D. Gilbert, & G. Lindzey (Eds.), *Handbook of social psychology, vol. 2*, pp. 504-553. Boston: McGraw-Hill.

Crombag, H. S., & Robinson, T. E. (2004). Drugs, environment, brain, and behavior. *Current Directions in Psychological Science*, **13**, 107-111.

Cromwell, R. L. (1993). Searching for the origins of schizophrenia. *Psychological Science*, **4**, 276–279.

Crow, T. J. (1980). Molecular pathology of schizophrenia: More than one disease process? *The British Medical Journal*, **280**, 66–68.

Crowder, R. G. (1993). Short-term memory: Where do we stand? *Memory and Cognition*, **2**, 142–145.

Crutchfield, R. S. (1955). Conformity and character. *American Psychologist*, **10**, 191–198.

Cruz, A. & Green, B. J. (2000). Thermal stimulation of taste. *Nature*, **403**, 889–892.

Cuellar, N. G. (2005). Hypnosis for pain management in the older adult. *Pain Management Nursing*, **6**, 105-111.

Culbertson, J. L., & Edmonds, J. E. (1996). Learning disabilities. In R. L. Adams, O. A. Parsons, J. L. Culbertson, & S. J. Nixon (Eds.), *Neuropsychology for clinical practice: Etiology, assessment, and treatment of common neurological disorders* (pp. 331-408). Washington, DC: American Psychological Association.

Culbertson, W. C. (2001). Learning and neuropsychiatric disorders of childhood. In E. A. Zillmer & M. V. Spiers (Eds.), *Principles of neuropsychology* (pp. 260-294). Belmont, CA: Wadsworth.

Cummings, B. J., Uchida, N., Tamaki, S. J., Salazar, D. L., Hooshmand, M., Summers, R., Gage, F. H., & Anderson, A. J. (2005). *Proceedings of the National Academy of Sciences*, **102**, 14069-14074.

Curtis, R. C., & Miller, K. (1986). Believing another likes or dislikes you: Behaviors making the beliefs come true. *Journal of Personality and Social Psychology*, **51**, 284–290.

Cusumano, D. L., & Thompson, J. K. (2001). Media influence and body image in 8–11-year-old boys and girls: A preliminary report on the Multidimensional Media Influence Scale. *International Journal of Eating Disorders*, **29**, 37–44.

Cutler, W.B., Friedmann, E., & McCoy, N. L. (1998). Pheromonal influences on sociosexual behavior. *Archives of Sexual Behavior*, **27**, 1–13.

Cutler, W. B., Preti, G., Krieger, A., Huggins, G. R., Ramon Garcia, C., & Lawley, H. J. (1986). Human axillary secretions influence women's menstrual cycles: The role of donor extract from men. *Hormones and Behavior*, **20**, 463–473.

Cutmore, T. H. S., Hine, T. J., Maberly, K. J. Langford, N. M., & Hawgood, G. (2000). Cognitive and gender factors influencing navigation in a virtual environment. *International Journal of Human-Computer Studies*, **53**, 223–249.

Dabs, J. M., Carr, T. S., Frady, R. L., & Riad, J. K. (1995). Testosterone, crime, and misbehavior among 692 male prison inmates. *Personality and Individual Differences*, **19**, 627-633.

Dabbs, J. M., Jr., Strong, R., & Milun, R. (1997). Exploring the mind of testosterone: A beeper study. *Journal of Research in Personality*, **31**, 577–587.

Dadler, H., & Gustavson, P. (1992). Competition by effective management of cultural diversity in the case of international construction projects. *International Studies of Management and Organizations*, **22**, 81–93.

Damasio, A. R. (1997). Toward a neuropathology of emotion and mood. *Nature*, **386**, 769–770.

Damasio, A. R., Grabowski, T. J., Bechara, A., Damasio, H., Ponto. L. L. B., Parviza, J., & Hichwa, R. D. (2000). Subcortical and cortical brain activity during the feeling of self-generated emotions. *Nature: Neuroscience*, **3**, 1049-1056.

Daniel, T. C. (1990). Measuring the quality of the natural environment: A psychophysical approach. *American Psychologist*, **45**, 633–637.

Daniels, S. R., Arnett, D. K., Eckel, R. H., Gidding, S. S., Hayman, L. L., et al. (2005). Overweight in children: Pathophysiology, consequences, prevention, and treatment. *Circulation, 111,* 1999-2012.

Danmiller, J. L., & Stephens, B. R. (1988). A critical test of infant pattern preference models. *Child Development, 59,* 210–216.

Darley, J. M. (2001). The dynamics of authority in organizations. In J. M. Darley, D. M. Messick, & T. R. Tyler (Eds.), *Social influences on ethical behaviors in organizations* (pp. 37-52). Mahwah, NJ: Erlbaum.

Darley, J. M., & Fazio, R. H. (1980). Expectancy confirmation processes arising in the interaction sequence. *American Psychologist, 35,* 861–866.

Darley, J. M., & Schultz, T. R. (1990). Moral rules: Their content and acquisition. *Annual Review of Psychology, 41,* 525–556.

Darling, C. A., & Davidson, J. K. (1986). Coitally active university students: Sexual behaviors, concerns, and challenges. *Adolescence, 21,* 403–419.

Darling, N., & Steinberg, L. (1993). Parenting style as context: An integrative model. *Psychological Bulletin, 113,* 487-496.

Darwin, C. T., Turvey, M. T., & Crowder, R. G. (1972). An auditory analogue of the Sperling partial report procedure: Evidence for brief auditory storage. *Cognitive Psychology, 3,* 255–267.

Das, J. P., Kirby, J., & Jarman, R. F. (1992). Simultaneous and successive synthesis: An alternative model for cognitive abilities. *Psychological Bulletin, 82,* 87-103.

Daubman, K. A., Heatherinton, L., & Ahn, A. (1992). Gender and the self-presentation of academic achievement. *Sex Roles, 27,* 187–204.

Davidoff, J. B. (1975). *Differences in visual perception: The individual eye.* New York: Academic Press.

Davidson, G. C. (1998). Being bolder with the Boulder Model: The challenge of education and training in empirically supported treatments. *Journal of Consulting and Clinical Psychology, 66,* 163–167.

Davidson, J. M., Smith, E. R., Rodgers, C. H., & Bloch, G. J. (1968). Relative thresholds of behavioral and somatic responses to estrogen. *Physiology and Behavior, 3,* 227–229.

Davidson, J. R. T., Hughs, D. C., George, L. K., & Blazer, D. G. (1994). The boundary of social phobia: Exploring the threshold. *Archives of General Psychiatry, 51,* 975–983.

Davidson, K. W., Trudeau, K. J., Ockene, J. K., Orleans, C. T., & Kaplan, R. M. (2004). A primer on current evidence-based review systems and their implications for behavioral medicine. *Annals of Behavioral Medicine, 28,* 226-238.

Davidson, R. J., Gray, J. A., LeDoux, J. E., Levenson, R. W., Panksepp, J., & Ekman, P. (1994). Is there emotion-specific physiology? In P. Ekman & Davidson, R. J. (Eds.), *The nature of emotion: Fundamental questions. Series in affective science* (pp. 235-262). London, Oxford University Press.

Davidson, R. J., Pizzagalli, D., Nitschke, J. B., & Putnam, K. (2002). Depression: Perspectives from affective neuroscience. *Annual Review of Psychology, 53,* 545–574.

Davidson, R. J., Pizzagalli, J. B., Nitschke, J. B., & Putnam, K. (2002). Depression: Perspectives from affective neuroscience. *Annual Review of Psychology, 53,* 545–574.

Davies, M., Stankov, L., & Roberts, R. D. (1998). Emotional intelligence: In search of an elusive construct. *Journal of Personality and Social Psychology, 75(4),* 989–1015.

Davis, K. L., Mohs, R. C., Marin, D., et al. (1999). Cholinergic markers in elderly patients with early signs of Alzheimer disease. *Journal of the American Medical Association, 281,* 1401–1406.

Davis, L. E., & Cherns, A. B. (1975). *The quality of working life: Vol. I. Problems, prospects and the state of the art.* New York: Free Press.

Davis, P. (1999). Gender differences in autobiographical memory for childhood emotional experiences. *Journal of Personality and Social Psychology, 76,* 498-510.

Davison, G. C., & Neale, J. M. (1998). *Abnormal Psychology (7th ed.).* New York: John Wiley.

DeAngelis, T. (1989). Behavior is included in report on smoking. *APA Monitor, 20,* 3–4.

——. (1994). Ethnic-minority issues recognized in DSM-IV. *APA Monitor,* November, p. 36.

deBoer, C. (1978). The polls: Attitudes toward work. *Public Opinion Quarterly, 42,* 414–423.

DeBono, K. G., & Harnish, R. J. (1988). Source expertise, source attractiveness, and the processing of persuasive information: A functional approach. *Journal of Personality and Social Psychology, 55,* 541–546.

DeCasper, A. J., Lecanuet, J. P., Busnel, M. C., Deferre-Granier, C., & Maugeais, R. (1994). Fetal reactions to recurrent maternal speech. *Infant Behavior and Development, 17,* 159–164.

de Cuevas, J. (1990, September/October). "No, she holded them loosely." *Harvard Magazine,* pp. 60–67.

Deadwyler, S. A., & Hampson, R. E. (2004). Differential but complementary mnemonic functions of the hippocampus and subiculum. *Neuron, 42,* 465–476.

Dean, E. T., Jr. (1997). *Shook over hell: Posttraumatic stress, Vietnam and the Civil War.* Cambridge, MA: Harvard University Press.

Deary, I. J., Strand, S., Smith, P., & Fernandes, C. (2007). Intelligence and educational achievement. *Intelligence, 35,* 13–21.

Deffenbacher, J. L. (1988). Some recommendations and directions. *Counseling Psychology, 35,* 234–236.

DeGroot, A. D. (1965). *Thought and chance in chess.* The Hague: Mouton.

——. (1966). Perception and memory versus thought: Some old ideas and recent findings. In B. Kleinmuntz (Ed.), *Problem solving.* New York: Wiley.

DeJarlais, D. C., & Friedman, S. R. (1988). The psychology of preventing AIDS among intravenous drug users: A social learning conceptualization. *American Psychologist, 43,* 865–870.

DeKosky, S. T. (2001). Epidemiology and pathophysiology of Alzheimer's disease. *Clinical Cornerstone, 3,* 15–26.

De la Chica, R. A., Ribas, I., Giraldo, J., Egozcue, J., & Fuster, C. (2005). Chromosomal instability in amniocytes from fetuses of mothers who smoke. *Journal of the American Medical Association, 293,* 1212-1222.

Delahoussaye, M. (2002). The perfect learner: An expert debate onlearning styles. *Training, 39,* 28–36.

Delaney-Black, V., Covington, C., Nordstrom, B., Ager, J., Janisse, J., Hannigan, J., Chiodo, L., & Sokol, R. J. (2004). Prenatal cocaine: Quantity of exposure and gender moderation. *Journal of Developmental and Behavioral Pediatrics*, **25**, 254-263.

Delaney-Black, V., Covington, C., Templin, T., Ager, J., Nordstrom-Klee, B., Martier, S., Leddick, L., Czerwinski, R. H., & Sokol, R. J. (2000). Teacher assessed behavior of children prenatally exposed to cocaine. *Pediatrics*, **106**, 782–791.

Delgado, P. L., Price, L. H., Miller, H. L., Salomon, R. M., et al. (1994). Serotonin and the neurobiology of depression: Effects of tryptophan depletion in drug-free depressed patients. *Archives of General Psychiatry*, **51**, 865–874.

Delgado-Romero, E. A., Galván, N., Maschino, P., & Rowland, M. (2005). Race and ethnicity in empirical counseling and counseling psychology research: A 10-year review. *The Counseling Psychologist*, **33**, 419-448.

Dellas, M., & Jernigan, L. P. bv (1987). Occupational identity status development, gender comparisons, and internal-external locus of control in first-year Air Force cadets. *Journal of Youth and Adolescence*, **16**, 587-600.

DeLongis, A., Folkman, S., & Lazarus, R. S. (1988). The impact of daily stress on health and mood: Psychological and social resources as mediators. *Journal of Personality and Social Psychology*, **54**, 486–495.

Dembroski, T. M., MacDougall, J. M., Williams, R. B., Haney, T. I., & Blumenthal, J. A. (1985). Components of Type A, hostility, and anger in relationship to angiographic findings. *Psychosomatic Medicine*, **47**, 219–233.

Dement, W. C. (1974). *Some must watch while some must sleep*. San Francisco: Freeman.

Department of Justice (2000*). 1999 Annual report on drug use among adult and juvenile arrestees*. Washington, DC: Department of Justice.

De Radd, B. (1998). Five big, Big Five issues. *European Psychologist*, **3(2)**, 113–124.

Deregowski, J. B. (1972). Pictorial perception and culture. *Scientific American*, **227**, 82-88.

——. (1973). Illusion and culture. In R. L. Gregory & G. H. Gombrichs (Eds.), *Illusion in nature and art*. New York: Scribner's, 161–192.

Derlega, V. J., Winstead, B. A., & Jones, W. H. (1991). *Personality: Contemporary theory and research*. Chicago: Nelson-Hall.

DeRubeis, R. J. & Crits-Christoph, P. (1998). Empirically supported individual and group psychotherapy treatments for adult mental disorders. *Journal of Consulting and Clinical Psychology*, **66**, 37–52.

DeRubeis, R. J., Hollen, S. D., Amsterdam, J. D., Shelton, R. C., Salomon, R. M., et al. (2005). Cognitive therapy vs medications in the treatment of moderate to severe depression. *Archives of General Psychiatry*, **62**, 409-416.

De Schipper, J. C., Tavecchio, L. W. C, & Van Ijendoorn, M. H. (2008). Children's attachment relationships with daycare caregivers: Associations with positive caregiving and the child's temperament. *Social Development*, doi:10.1111/j.1467–9507.2007.00448.x.

D'Esposito, M., Zorahn, E., & Aguirre, G. K. (1999). Event-related functional MRI: Implications for cognitive psychology. *Psychological Bulletin*, **125**, 155-164.

Detterman, D. K., & Thompson, L. A. (1997). What is so special about special education? *American Psychologist*, **52**, 1082–1090.

Deutsch, J. A. (1973). The cholinergic synapse and the site of memory. In J. A. Deutsch (Ed.), *The physiological basis of memory*. New York: Academic Press.

de Waal, F. B. M. (1999). The end of nature versus nurture. *Scientific American*, **281**, 94–99.

——. (2002). Evolutionary psychology: The wheat and the chaff. *Current Directions in Psychological Science*, **11**, 187–191.

DHHS. (2004). *HHS fact sheet: Minority health disparities at a glance*. Washington, DC: U.S. Department of Health and Human Services.

Diamond, L. M. (2000). Sexual identity, attractions, and behavior among young sexual-minority women over a 2-year period. *Developmental Psychology*, **36**, 241–250.

Diamond, M., & Karlen, A. (1980). *Sexual decisions*. Boston: Little, Brown.

Diamond, M. C., Lindner, B., Johnson, R., Bennett, E. L., & Rosenzweig, M. R. (1975). Differences in occipital cortical synapses from environmentally enriched, impoverished, and standard colony rats. *Journal of Neuroscience Research*, **1**, 109–119.

Dibble, K. (1995). Hearing loss & music. *Journal of the Audio Engineering Society*, **43(4)**, 251–266.

Dick, D. M., Rose, R. J., Viken, R. J., & Kaprio, J. (2000). Pubertal timing and substance use between and within families across late adolescence. *Developmental Psychology*, **36**, 180–189.

Diener, E. & Seligman, M. E. P. (2002). Very happy people. *Psychological Science*, **13(1)**, 81–84.

Digman, J. M. (1990). Personality structure: Emergence of the five-factor model. *Annual Review of Psychology*, **41**, 417–440.

Dijksterhuis, A. (2004). Think different: The merits of unconscious thought in preference development and decision making. *Journal of Personality and Social Psychology*, **87**, 586–598.

Dijksterhuis, A., & Meurs, T. (2006). Where creativity resides: The generative power of unconscious thought. *Consciousness and Cognition*, **15**, 135–146.

Dijksterhuis, A., & Nordgren, L. F. (2006). A theory of unconscious thought. *Perspectives on Psychological Science*, **1**, 95–109.

Dijksterhuis, A., Bos, M. W., Nordgren, L. F., & van Baaren, R. B. (2006). On making the right choice: The deliberation-without-intention effect. *Science*, **311**, 1005–1007.

Dill, J., & Anderson, C. A. (1995). Effects of justified and unjustified frustration on aggression. *Aggressive Behavior*, **21**, 359–369.

DiMatteo, M. R., & Friedman, H. S. (1988). *Social psychology and medicine*. Cambridge, MA: Oeleschlager, Gunn & Hain.

Dimidjian, S., Hollen, S. D., Dobson, K. S., Schmaling, K. B., Kohlenberg, R. J., Addis, M. E., et al. (2006). Randomized trial of behavioral activation, cognitive therapy, and antidepressant medication in the acute treatment of adults with major depression. *Journal of Consulting and Clinical Psychology*, **74**, 658–670.

Dion, K. K. (1972). Physical attractiveness and evaluation of children's transgressions. *Journal of Personality and Social Psychology*, **24**, 207–213.

Dion, K. K., Berscheid, E., & Walster (Hatfield), E. (1972). What is beautiful is good. *Journal of Personality and Social Psychology*, **24**, 285–290.

Dixon, N. F. (1981). *Preconscious processing*. New York: Wiley.

Dobson, K. S. (1988). *Handbook of cognitive-behavioral therapies*. New York: Guilford.

Dobson, K. S., & Khatri, N. (2000). Cognitive therapy: Looking backward, looking forward. *Journal of Clinical Psychology*, **56**, 907–923.

Dogil, G., Ackermann, H., Grodd, H., Haider, H., Kamp, H., Mayer, J., Riecker, A., & Wildgruber, D. (2002). The speaking brain: A tutorial introduction to fMRI experiments in the production of speech, prosody, and syntax. *Journal of Neurolinguistics*, **15**, 59–90.

Doktor, R. H. (1982). A cognitive approach to culturally appropriate HRD programs. *Training and Development Journal*, **36**, 32–36.

Dolinoy, D. C., Weidman, J. R., Waterman, R. A., & Jirtle, R. L. (2006). Maternal genistein alters coat color and protects A^vy mouse offspring from obesity by modifying the fetal epigonome. *Environmental Health Perspectives, 114*, 567–572.

Doll, R., & Peto, R. (1981). *The causes of cancer*. New York: Oxford University Press.

Dollard, J., Doob, L., Miller, N., Mowrer, O. H., & Sears, R. R. (1939). *Frustration and aggression*. New Haven, CT: Yale University Press.

Domjan, M. (1987). Animal learning comes of age. *American Psychologist*, **42**, 556–564.

——. (2005). Pavlovian conditioning: A functional perspective. *Annual Review of Psychology*, **56**, 179–206.

Donnellan, M. B., Trzesniewski, K. H., Robins, R. W., Moffitt, T. E., & Caspi, A. (2005). Low self-esteem is related to aggression, anti-social behavior, and delinquency. *Psychological Science*, **16**, 328–335.

Donnenberg, G. R., & Hoffman, L. W. (1988). Gender differences in moral development. *Sex Roles*, **18**, 701–717.

Donnerstein, E. (2005). *Media violence and children: What do we know? What do we do?* Paper presented at the 27th National Institute on the Teaching of Psychology, St. Petersburg Beach, FL, January 2–5.

Dornbusch, S. M., Ritter, P. L., Leiderman, P. H., Roberts, D. F., & Fraleigh, M. J. (1987). The relation of parenting style to adolescent school performance. *Child Development*, **58**, 1244-1257.

Dotterer, A. M., Hoffman, L., Crouter, A. C., & McHale, S. M. (2008). A longitudinal examination of the bidirectional links between academic achievement and parent-adolescent conflict. *Journal of Family Issues, 29*, 762–779.

Doty, R. Y. (1986). Gender and endocrine-related influences on human olfactory perception. In H. Meiselman & R. S. Rivlin (Eds.), *Clinical measurement of taste and smell*. New York: Macmillan.

Dougherty, D. D., Baer, L., Cosgrove, G. R., Cassem, E. H., Price, B. H., Nierenberg, A. A., Jenike, M. A., & Rauch, S, L. (2002). Prospective long-term follow-up of 44 patients who received cingulotomy for treatment-refractory obsessive-compulsive disorder. *The American Journal of Psychiatry*, **159**, 269–275.

Douglass, H. M., Moffitt, T. E., Dar, R., McGee, R., & Silva, P. (1995). Obsessive-compulsive disorder in a birth cohort of 18-year-olds: Prevalence and predictors. *Journal of the American Academy of Child and Adolescent Psychiatry*, **34**, 1424–1431.

Dovidio, J. F., Allen, J. L., & Schroeder, D. A. (1990). Specificity of empathy-induced helping: Evidence for altruistic motivation. *Journal of Personality and Social Psychology*, **59**, 249–260.

Dovidio, J. F., & Gaertner, S. L. (2000). Aversive racism and selection decisions: 1989 and 1999. *Psychological Science*, **11**, 315–319.

Dovidio, J. F., Kawakami, K., & Gaertner, S. L. (2002). Implicit and explicit prejudice and interracial interactions. *Journal of Personality and Social Psychology*, **82**, 62–68.

Doweiko, H. E. (1993). *Concepts of chemical dependency (2nd ed.)*. Pacific Grove, CA: Brooks/Cole.

Dowman, J., Patel, A., & Rajput, K. (2005). Electroconvulsive therapy: Attitudes and misconceptions. *The Journal of ECT*, **21**, 84–87.

Dragan, W., & Oniszczenko, W. (2006). Association of a functional polymorphism in the serotonin transporter gene with personality traits in females in a polish population. *Neuropsychobiology*, **54**, 45–50.

Dreses-Werringloer, U., Lambert, J-C., Vingtdeux, V., Zhao, H., Vais, H., Siebert, A., Jain, A., Koppel, J. et al. (2008). A polymorphism in CALHM1 influences Ca^{2+} homeostasis, Aβ levels, and Alzheimer's disease risk. *Cell, 133*, 1149–1161.

Drews, C. D., & Murphy, C. C. (1996). The relationship between idiopathic mental retardation and maternal smoking during pregnancy. *Pediatrics*, **97**, 547–553.

Driskell, J. E., & Johnston, J. H. (1998). Stress exposure training. In Cannon-Bowers, J. A., & Salas, E. (Eds.), *Making decisions under stress: Implications for individual and team training*. Washington, DC: American Psychological Association.

Duffy, E. (1962). *Activation and behavior*. New York: Wiley.

Duncan, J. (1985). Two techniques for investigating perception without awareness. *Perception and Pychophysics*, **38**, 296–298.

Dunker, K. (1945). On problem solving. *Psychological Monographs, 58* (Whole No. 27).

Dunn, R., & Dunn, K. (1992). *Teaching elementary students through their individual learning styles*. Boston: Allyn & Bacon.

——. (1993). *Teaching secondary students through their individual learning styles: Practical approaches for grades 7-12*. Boston: Allyn & Bacon.

Dunn, R., Griggs, S., & Price, G. (1993). Learning styles of Mexican-American and Anglo-American elementary-school students. *Journal of Multicultural Counseling and Development*, **21**, 237-247.

Dunnette, M. D., & Borman, W. C. (1997). Personnel selection and classification systems. *Annual Review of Psychology*, **30**, 477–525.

Dunston, A. (2003). *Kicking butts in the twenty-first century: What modern science has learned about smoking cessation*. New York: The American Council on Science and Health.

Durand, V. M. (2004). Past, present and emerging directions in education. In D. Zager (Ed.), *Autism: Identification, education, and treatment (3rd edition)*. Hillsdale, NJ: Erlbaum.

Durand, V. M. & Barlow, D. H. (2000). *Abnormal psychology: An introduction*. Belmont, CA: Wadsworth.

Dweck, C. S. (1986). Motivational processes affecting learning. *American Psychologist,* **41**, 1040–1048.

Eagly, A. H. (1987). *Sex differences in social behavior: A social-role interpretation.* Hillsdale, NJ: Lawrence Erlbaum Associates.

——. (1995). The science and politics of comparing women and men. *American Psychologist,* **50**, 145–158.

Eagly, A. H., & Steffen, V. J. (1986). Gender and aggressive behavior: A meta-analytic review of the social psychological literature. *Psychological Bulletin,* **100**, 309–330.

Eagly, A. H., Wood, W., & Fishbaugh, L. (1981). Sex differences in conformity: Surveillance by the group as a determinant of male conformity. *Journal of Personality and Social Psychology,* **40**, 384–394.

Eaker, E. D., Packard, B., Wenger, N. K., et al. (1988). Coronary heart disease in women. *American Journal of Cardiology,* **61**, 641–644.

Eaker, E. D., Pinsky, J., & Castelli, W. P. (1992). Myocardial infarction and coronary death among women: Psychosocial predictors from a 20-year follow-up on women in the Framingham study. *American Journal of Epidemiology,* **135**, 854–864.

Early, P. C. (1986). Supervisors and shop stewards as sources of contextual information in goal-setting: A comparison of the U.S. with England. *Journal of Applied Psychology,* **71**, 111–118.

——. (1989). Social loafing and collectivism: A comparison of the United States and the People's Republic of China. *Administrative Science Quarterly,* **34**, 555–581.

Eating Disorders Association (1999). *Anorexia nervosa.* Retrieved on June 19, 2001 from the World Wide Web: http://www.uq.net.au/eda/documents/anorexia.html.

Eaton, W. O., & Enns, L. R. (1986). Sex differences in human motor activity level. *Psychological Bulletin,* **100**, 19–28.

Eaton, W. W., Anthony, J. C., Gallo, J., Cai, G., et al. (1997). Natural history of diagnostic interview schedule/DSM-IV major depression: The Baltimore Epidemiological Catchment Area follow-up. *Archives of General Psychiatry,* **54**, 993–999.

Eaton, W. W., Shao, H., Nestadt, G., Lee, B. H., Bienvenu, O. J., & Zandi, P. (2008). Population-based study of first onset and chronicity in major depressive disorder. *Archives of General Psychiatry,* **65**, 513–520.

Eaton, W. W., Thara, R., Federman, B., Melton, B., & Liang, K. (1955). Structure and course of positive and negative symptoms in schizophrenia. *Archives of General Psychiatry,* **52**, 127–134.

Eaves, L. J., Eysenck, H. J., & Martin, N. G. (1989). *Genes, culture, and personality: An empirical approach.* San Diego, CA: Academic Press.

Ebbinghaus, H. E. (1885/1964). *Memory: A contribution to experimental psychology.* New York: Dover.

Ebstein, R. P., Novick, O., Umansky, R., Priel, B., et al. (1996). Dopamine D4 Receptor (D4DR) Exon III polymorphism associated with the human personality trait of novelty seeking. *Nature Genetics,* **12**, 78–80.

Eccles, J., Wigfield, A., Harold, R. D., & Blumenfeld, P. (1993). Age and gender differences in children's self- and task perceptions during elementary school. *Child Development,* **64**, 830–847.

Eccles, J. S., & Wigfield, A. (2002). Motivational beliefs, values, and goals. *Annual Review of Psychology,* **53**, 109–132.

Edleson, S. M. (2007). Overview of autism. From the website of the Autism research Institute, www.autism.com. Downloaded March 4, 2008.

Edmands, M. S. (1993). Caring for students with eating disorders on college and university campuses. *Advances in Medical Psychotherapy,* **6**, 59–75.

Edwards, C. P. (1977). The comparative study of the development of moral judgment and reasoning. In R. L. Munroe, R. Munroe, & B. B. Whiting (Eds.), *Handbook of cross-cultural human development.* New York: Garland.

——. (1981). The development of moral reasoning in cross-cultural perspective. In R. H. Munroe, R. L. Munroe, & B. B. Whiting (Eds.), *Handbook of cross-cultural human development.* New York: Garland.

Edwards, L. K., & Edwards, A. L. (1991). A principal components analysis of the Minnesota Multiphasic Personality Inventory Factor Scales. *Journal of Personality and Social Psychology,* **60**, 766–772.

Egeland, J. A., Gerhard, D. S., Pauls, D. L., Suddex, J. N., Kidd, K. K., Allen, C. R., Hostetter, A. M., & Housman, D. E. (1987). Bipolar affective disorders linked to DNA markers on chromosome 11. *Nature,* **325**, 783–787.

Egeth, H. E. (1993). What do we not know about eyewitness identification? *American Psychologist,* **48**, 577–580.

Eich, E. (1995). Searching for mood dependent memory. *Psychological Science,* **6**, 67–75.

Eich, E., MacCauley, D., & Ryan, L. (1994). Mood dependent memory for events of the personal past. *Journal of Experimental Psychology: General,* **123**, 201–215.

Eich, J. E., Weingartner, H., Stillman, R. C., & Gillan, J. C. (1975). State-dependent accessibility of retrieval cues in the retention of a categorized list. *Journal of Verbal Learning and Verbal Behavior,* **14**, 408–417.

Eichenbaum, H., & Fortin, N. (2003). Episodic memory and the hippocampus: It's about time. *Current Directions in Psychological Science,* **12**, 53–57.

Eisenberg, N. & Lennon, R. (1983). Sex differences in empathy and related capacities. *Psychological Bulletin,* **94**, 100–131.

Eisenberg, N., Zhou, Q., Spinrad, T. L., Valiente, C., Fabes, R. A., & Liew, J. (2005). Relations among positive parenting, children's effortful control, and externalizing problems: A three-wave longitudinal study. *Child Development,* **76**, 1055-1071.

Eisler, I., Dare, C., Russell, G. F. M., Szmukler, G., le Grange, D., & Dodge, E. (1997). Family and individual therapy in anorexia nervosa: A five-year follow-up. *Archives of General Psychiatry,* **54**, 1025–1030.

Ekehammar, B., Akrami, N., Gylje, M., & Zakrisson, I. (2004). What matters most to prejudice: Big five personality, social dominance orientation, or right-wing authoritarianism? *European Journal of Personality,* **18**, 463-482.

Ekman, P. (1972). Universals and cultural differences in facial expression of emotion. In J. K. Cole (Ed.), *Nebraska symposium on motivation.* Lincoln: University of Nebraska Press.

——. (1973). Cross-cultural studies in facial expression. In P. Ekman (Ed.), *Darwin and facial expressions: A century of research in review.* New York: Academic Press.

——. (1992). Facial expression and emotion: New findings, new questions. *Psychological Science, 3,* 34–38.

——. (1992a). An argument for basic emotions. *Journal of Cognition and Emotion, 6,* 169–200.

——. (1993). Facial expression and emotion. *American Psychologist, 48,* 384–392.

Ekman, P., & Friesen, W. V. (1971). Constants across cultures in the face and emotion. *Journal of Personality and Social Psychology, 17,* 124–129.

Ekman, P., Friesen, W. V., O'Sullivan, M., Diacoyanni-Tarlatzis, I., Krause, R., et al. (1987). Universal and cultural differences in the judgment of facial expressions of emotion. *Journal of Personality and Social Psychology, 53,* 712–717.

Ekman, P., Levenson, R. W., & Friesen, W. V. (1983). Autonomic nervous system activity distinguishes among emotions. *Science, 221,* 1208–1210.

Eley, T. C., Lichenstein, P., & Stevenson, J. (1999). Sex differences in the etiology of aggressive and nonaggressive antisocial behavior: Results from two twin studies. *Child Development, 70,* 155-168.

Elfenbein, H. A., & Ambady, N. (2002). On the universality of cultural specificity of emotional recognition. *Psychological Bulletin, 128,* 203–235.

Elliott, A., & Church, M. (1997). A hierarchical model of approach and avoidance achievement motivation. *Journal of Personality and Social Psychology, 72,* 218–232.

Ellis, A. (1970). *Reason and emotion in psychotherapy.* Secaucus, NJ: Stuart.

——. (1973). *Humanistic psychotherapy: The rational-emotive approach.* New York: McGraw-Hill.

——. (1987). The impossibility of achieving consistently good mental health. *American Psychologist, 42,* 364–375.

——. (1991). How can psychological treatment aim to be briefer and better? The rational-emotive approach to brief therapy. In K. N. Anchor (Ed.), *Handbook of medical psychotherapy.* Toronto: Hogrefe & Huber.

——. (1995). Rational emotive behavior therapy. In R. J. Corsini & D. Wedding (Eds.), *Current psychotherapies, Fifth Edition.* (pp. 162-196). Itasca, IL: Peacock.

——. (1997). Using rational emotive behavior therapy techniques to cope with disability. Professional psychology: *Research and Practice, 28,* 17–22.

Ellis, B. J., & Garber, J. (2000). Psychosocial antecedents of variation in girls' pubertal timing: Maternal depression, stepfather presence, and marital and family stress. *Child Development, 71,* 485-501.

Ellis, B. J., McFayden-Ketchum, S., Dodge, K. A., Pettit, G. S., & Bates, G. E. (1999). Quality of early family relationships and individual differences in the timing of pubertal maturation in girls: A longitudinal test of the evolutionary model. *Journal of Personality and Social Psychology, 77,* 387-401.

Ellis, C. M., Lemmens, G., & Parkes, J. D. (1996). Melatonin and insomnia. *Journal of Sleep Research, 5,* 61–65.

Ellis, L., & Ames, M. A. (1987). Neurohormonal functioning and sexual orientation: A theory of homosexuality-heterosexuality. *Psychological Bulletin, 101,* 233–258.

Elovainio, M., Kivimaeki, M., Sreen, M., & Kalliomaeki-Levanto, T. (2000). Organizational and individual factors affecting mental health and job satisfaction. *Journal of Occupational Health Psychology, 5,* 269–277.

ElSohly, M. A., Ross, S. A., Mehmedic, Z, Arafat, R., Yi, B., & Banahan, B. (2000). Potency trends of delta-9-THC and other cannabinoids in confiscated marijuana from 1980-1997. *Journal of Forensic Sciences, 45,* 24–30.

Endler, N. S., Cox, B. J., Parker, J. D. A., & Bagby, R. M. (1992). Self-reports of depression and state-trait-anxiety: Evidence for differential assessment. *Journal of Personality and Social Psychology, 63,* 832–838.

Epel, E. S., Blackburn, E. H., Lin, J., Dhabhar, F. S., Adler, N. E., Morrow, J. D., & Cawthon, R. M. (2004). Accelerated telomere shortening in response to life stress. *Proceedings of the National Academy of Sciences, 101,* 17312-17315.

Epstein, L. H., & Cluss, P. A. (1982). A behavioral medicine perspective on adherence to long-term medical regimes. *Journal of Consulting and Clinical Psychology, 50,* 950–971.

Epstein, S. (1979). The stability of behavior: On predicting most of the people much of the time. *Journal of Personality and Social Psychology, 37,* 1097–1126.

Erdelyi, M. H. (1992). Psychodynamics and the unconscious. *American Psychologist, 47,* 784–787.

Erel, O., Oberman, Y., & Yirmiya, N. (2000). Maternal versus nonmaternal care and seven domains of child development. *Psychological Bulletin, 126,* 727–747.

Erez, M., & Early, P. C. (1987). Comparative analysis of goal-setting strategies across cultures. *Journal of Applied Psychology, 72,* 658–665.

——. (1993). *Culture, self-identity, and work.* New York: Oxford University Press.

Erez, M., & Zidon, I. (1984). Effect of goal acceptance on the relationship of goal difficulty to performance. *Journal of Applied Psychology, 69,* 69–78.

Erickson, C. A., Posey, D. J., Stigler, K. A., & McDougle, C. J. (2007). Pharmacotherapy of autism and related disorders. *Psychiatric Annals, 37,* 490–500.

Ericsson, K. A., & Chase, W. G. (1982). Exceptional memory. *American Scientist, 70,* 607–615.

Erikson, E. H. (1963). *Childhood and society.* New York: Norton.

——. (1965). *The challenge of youth.* Garden City, NY: Doubleday (Anchor Books).

——. (1968). *Identity: Youth and crisis.* New York: Norton.

Eriksson, P. S., Perfilieva, E., Bjork-Eriksson, T., Alborn, A., Nordborg, C., Peterson, D. A., & Gage, F. A. (1998). Neurogenesis in the adult hippocampus. *Nature Medicine, 4,* 1313-1317.

Erlenmeyer-Kimling, L. (1968). Studies on the offspring of two schizophrenic parents. In D. Rosenthal & S. S. Kety (Eds.), *The transmission of schizophrenia*. Elmsford, NY: Pergamon Press.

Erowid (2001). *MDMA basics*. Downloaded from the World Wide Web, February 1, 2001.http://www.erowid.org/chemicals/mdma/mdma_basics.shtml.

Espie, C. A. (2002). Insomnia: Conceptual issues in the development, persistence, and treatment of sleep disorder in adults. *Annual Review of Psychology, 53*, 215–243.

Espie, C. A., Inglis, S. I., Tessier, S., & Harvey, L. (2001). The clinical effectiveness of cognitive behavior therapy for chronic insomnia: Implication and evaluation of a sleep clinic in general medical practice. *Behavioral Research and Therapy, 39*, 45-60.

Essau, C. A. (200). Frequency, comorbidity and psychosocial impairment of anxiety disorders in German adolescents. *Journal of Anxiety Disorders, 14*, 263–279.

Estelles, J., Rodriguez-Arias, M., Maldonado C., Aguilar, M. A., & Minarro, J. (2005). Prenatal cocaine exposure alters spontaneous and cocaine-induced motor and social behaviors. *Neurotoxicology and Teratology, 27*, 449-457.

Etaugh, C. (1980). Effects of nonmaternal care on children. *American Psychologist, 35*, 309–316.

Euling, S. Y., Selevan, S. G., Pescovitz, O. H., & Skakkeback, N. E. (2008). Role of environmental factors in the timing of puberty. *Pediatrics, 121*, S167–S171.

Evans, G. W., & Howard, R. B. (1973). Personal space. *Psychological Bulletin, 80*, 334–344.

Evans, G. W. & Lepore, S. J. (1993). Nonauditory effects of noise on children. *Children's Environment, 10*, 31–51.

Evans, G. W., Bullinger, M., & Hygge, S. (1998). Chronic noise exposure and physiological response. *Psychological Science, 9*, 75–77.

Evans, G. W., Hygge, S., & Bullinger, M. (1995). Chronic noise and psychological stress. *Psychological Science, 6*, 333–338.

Evans, R. I., Rozelle, R. M., Maxwell, S. E., Raines, B. E., et al. (1981). Social modeling films to deter smoking in adolescents: Results of a three-year field investigation. *Journal of Applied Psychology, 66*, 399–414.

Eveleth, P., & Tanner, J. (1978). *Worldwide variations in human growth*. New York: Cambridge University Press.

Everson, S. A., Kauhanen, J., Kaplan, G. A., Goldberg, D. E., Julkunen, J., et al. (1997). Hostility and increased risk of mortality and acute myocardial infarction: The mediating role of behavioral risk factors. *American Journal of Epidemiology, 146*, 142–152.

Eysenck, H. J. (1941). A critical and experimental study of color preferences. *American Journal of Psychology, 54*, 385-394.

Eysenck, H. J. (1952). The effects of psychotherapy: An evaluation. *Journal of Consulting Psychology, 16*, 319–324.

——. (1960). *Behavior therapy and neurosis*. London: Pergamon.

——. (1967). *The biological basis of personality*. Springfield, IL: Charles C. Thomas.

——. (1982). *Personality, genetics, and behavior: Selected papers*. New York: Praeger.

——. (1990). Biological dimensions of personality. In L. A. Pervin (Ed.), *Handbook of personality: Theory and research*. New York: Guilford.

Ezzati, M., & Lopez, A. D. (2003). Estimates of global mortality attributable to smoking in 2000. *Lancet, 362*, 847–852.

Fackelman, K. A. (1992). Anatomy of Alzheimer's: Do immune proteins help destroy brain cells? *Science News, 142*, 394–396.

Fadiman, J., & Frager, R. (1994). *Personality and personal growth (3rd ed.)*. New York: HarperCollins.

Fagan, J. F., & Singer, L. T. (1979). The role of single feature differences in infant recognition of faces. *Infant Behavior and Development, 2*, 39–45.

Fahn, S. (1992). Fetal-tissue transplants in Parkinson's disease. *New England Journal of Medicine, 327*, 1589–1590.

Fairburn, C. G., & Wilson, G. T. (Eds.). (1993). *Binge eating: Nature, assessment and treatment*. New York: Guilford.

Fairburn, C. G., Cooper, Z., Doll, H. A., Norman, P., & O'Connor, M. (2000). The natural course of bulimia nervosa and binge eating disorder in young women. *Archives of General Psychiatry, 57*, 659-665.

Fairburn, C. G., Jones, R., Peveler, R. C., Hope, R. A., & O'Conner, M. (1993). Psychotherapy and bulimia nervosa. *Archives of General Psychiatry, 50*, 419–428.

Fairburn, C. G., Norman, P. A., Welch, S. L., O'Conner, M. E., Doll, H. A., & Peveler, R. C. (1995). A prospective study of outcome in bulimia nervosa and the long-term effects of three psychological treatments. *Archives of General Psychiatry, 52*, 304–312.

Falbo, T., & Peplau, L. A. (1980). Power strategies in intimate relationships. *Journal of Personality and Social Psychology, 38*, 618–628.

Fallon, A. (1990). Culture in the mirror: Sociocultural determinants of body-image. In T. F. Cash, & T. Pruzinsky. (Eds.), *Body images: Development, deviance and change*. New York: Guilford.

Falloon, I., Roncone, R., Malm, U., & Coverdale, J. (1998). Effective and efficient treatment strategies to enhance recovery from schizophrenia: How much longer will people have to wait before we provide them? *Psychiatric Rehabilitation Skills, 2*, 107–127.

Fals-Stewart, W., Leonard, K. E., & Birchler, G. R. (2005). The occurrence of male-to-female intimate partner violence on days of men's drinking: The moderating effects of antisocial personality disorder. *Journal of Consulting and Clinical Psychology, 73*, 239–248.

Fantz, R. L. (1961). The origin of form perception. *Scientific American, 204*, 66–72.

——. (1963). Pattern vision in newborn infants. *Science, 140*, 296–297.

Farace, E. & Alves, W. (2000). Do women fare worse: A metaanalysis of gender differences in traumatic brain injury outcome. *Journal of Neurosurgery, 93*, 539-545.

Farlow, M. R. (2000). *Therapeutic advances for Alzheimer's disease and other dementias*. The Medical Education Collaborative. Golden, Colorado.

Farooqi, I. S., Keough, J. M., Yeo, G. S. H., Lank, E. J., Cheetham, T., & O'Rahilly, S. (2003). Clinical spectrum of obesity mutations in the melanacortin 4 receptor gene. *The New England Journal of Medicine, 348*, 1085–1095.

Farrell, M. P., & Rosenberg, S. D. (1981). *Men at midlife*. Boston: Auburn House.

Farrelly, M. C., Davis, K. C., Haviland, M. L., Messeri, P., & Healton, C. G. (2005). Evidence of a dose-response relationship between "truth" antismoking ads and youth smoking prevalence. *American Journal of Public Health, 95*, 425-431.

Farwell, L. & Weiner, B. (2000). Bleeding hearts and the heartless: Popular perceptions of liberal and conservative ideologies. *Personality and Social Psychology Bulletin,* **26**, 845-852.

Fast, J. (1970). *Body language.* New York: M. Evans.

Favazza, P. C., Phillipsen, L., & Kumar, P. (2000). Measuring and promoting acceptance of young children with disabilities. *Exceptional Children,* **66**, 491-508.

Fazio, R. H. (2001). On the automatic activation of associated evaluations: An overview. *Cognition and Emotion,* **15**, 115–141.

Fazio, R. H., & Olson, M. A. (2003). Implicit measures in social cognition research: Their meaning and use. *Annual Review of Psychology,* **54**, 297–327.

Feeney, J. A., & Noller, P. (1990). Attachment style as a predictor of adult romantic relationships. *Journal of Personality and Social Psychology,* **58**, 281–291.

Feighner, J. P. (1997). Are the new antidepressants Venlafaxine and Nefazodone really different? *The Harvard Mental Health Letter,* **13(8)**, p. 8.

Fein, G. G., Schwartz, P. M., Jacobson, S. W., & Jacobson, J. L. (1983). Environmental toxins and behavior development. *American Psychologist,* **38**, 1188–1197.

Feingold, A. (1995). The additive effects of differences in central tendency and variability are important in comparisons between groups. *American Psychologist,* **50**, 5–13.

Feist, S. C. (1993). Marriage and family therapy: Theories and applications. *Directions in Clinical Psychology,* **3**, 4.3–4.24.

Felder, R. M., & Brent, R. (2005). Understanding student differences. *Journal of Engineering Education,* **94**, 57–72.

Feldman, S. S., & Elliott, G. R. (Eds.). (1990). *At the threshold: The developing adolescent.* Cambridge, MA: Harvard University Press.

Felson, R. B. (2002). *Violence and gender reexamined.* Washington, DC: American Psychological Association.

Feng, A. S. & Ratnam, R. (2000). Neural basis of hearing in real-world situations. *Annual Review of Psychology,* **51**, 699–725.

Fenker, R. M., & Lambiotte, J. G. (1987). A performance enhancement program for a college football team: One incredible season. *The Sport Psychologist,* **1**, 224–236.

Fermüller, C., & Malm, H. (2004). Uncertainty in visual processes predicts geometrical optical illusions. *Vision Research,* **44**, 727–749.

Feshbach, S., Weiner, B., & Bohart, A. (1996). *Personality (4th ed.).* Lexington, MA: D. C. Heath & Co.

Festinger, L. (1957). *A theory of cognitive dissonance.* Stanford, CA: Stanford University Press.

Festinger, L., & Carlsmith, J. M. (1959). Cognitive consequences of forced compliance. *Journal of Abnormal and Social Psychology,* **58**, 203–210.

Festinger, L., Riecken, H. W., & Schachter, S. (1993). When prophecy fails. In A. Pines & C. Maslach (Eds.), *Experiencing social psychology: readings and projects (Third Edition).* New York: McGraw Hill.

Festinger, L., Schachter, S., & Back, K. (1950). *Social processes in informal groups: A study of human factors in housing.* New York: HarperCollins.

Fiedorowicz, C., Benezra, E., MacDonald, W., McElgunn, B., & Wilson, A. (2001). Neurobiological basis of learning disabilities: An update. *Learning Disabilities: A Multidisciplinary Journal,* **11**, 61–74.

Field, A. E., Colditz, G. A., & Peterson, K. E. (1997). Racial/ethnic and gender differences in concern with weight and in bulimic behaviors among adolescents. *Obesity Research,* **5**, 447-454.

Finchilescu, G. (1994). Intergroup attributions in minimal groups. *Journal of Social Psychology,* **2**, 1–3.

Fink, M. (1997). What is the role of ECT in the treatment of mania? *The Harvard Mental Health Letter,* June, p. 8.

——. (2000). Electroshock revisited. *American Scientist,* **88**, 162–167.

——. (2001). Convulsive therapy: A review of the first 55 years. *Journal of Affective Disorders,* **63**, 1–15.

Finnegan, L. P. (1982). Outcome of children born to women dependent upon narcotics. In B. Stimmel (Ed.), *The effects of maternal alcohol and drug abuse on the newborn.* New York: Haworth.

Finzi, E., & Wasserman, E. (2006). Treatment of depression with Botulinum Toxin A: A case series. *Dermatologic Surgery,* **32**, 645.

Fiore, M. C., Bailey, W. C., Cohen, S. J., Dorfman, S. F., Goldstein, M. G., et al. (2000). *Treating tobacco use and dependence: Clinical practice guideline.* Rockville, MD: U.S. Department of Health and Human Services, Public Health Service.

Fiore, M. C., Novotny, T. E., Pierce, J. P., Hatzlandreu, E. J., Patel, K. M., & Davis, R. M. (1989). Trends in cigarette smoking in the United States: The changing influence of gender and race. *Journal of the American Medical Association,* **261**, 49–55.

Firestein, S. (2001). How the olfactory system makes sense of scents. *Nature,* **413**, 211–218.

Fischer, P., Greitemeir, T., Pollozek, F., & Frey, D. (2006). The unresponsive bystander: Are bystanders more responsive in dangerous emergencies? *European Journal of Social Psychology,* **36**, 267–278.

Fischhoff, B. (1990). Psychology and public policy: Tool or toolmaker? *American Psychologist,* **45**, 647–653.

Fishbein, M., & Ajzen, I. (1975). *Belief, attitude, intention, and behavior: An introduction to theory and research.* Reading, MA: Addison-Wesley.

Fisher, A. C. (1977). Sport personality assessment: Facts, fallacies, and perspectives. *Motor Skills: Theory into Practice,* **1**, 87–97.

Fisher, S. & Greenberg, R. P. (1977). *The scientific credibility of Freud's theories and therapy.* New York: Basic Books.

Fishman, J. (1987). Type A on trial. *Psychology Today,* **21**, 42–50.

Fiske, S. T., & Glick, P. (1995). Ambivalence and stereotype cause sexual harassment. *Journal of Social Issues,* **51**, 97–115.

Fitzgerald, L. (1993). Sexual harassment: Violence against women in the workplace. *American Psychologist,* **48**, 1070–1076.

Fitzgibbon, M. L., Blackman, L. R., & Avellone, M. E. (2000). The relationship between body image discrepancy and body mass index across ethnic groups *Obesity Research,* **8**, 582-589.

Fitzgibbon, M. L., Spring, B., Avellone, M. E., Blackman, L. R., Pingetore, R., & Stolley, M. R. (1998). Correlates of binge eating in Hispanic, black, and white women. *International Journal of Eating Disorders,* **24**, 43-52.

Flack, W. F., Laird, J. D., & Cavallaro, L. A. (1999). Separate and combined effects of facial expressions and bodily posture on emotional feelings. *European Journal of Social Psychology, 29*, 203-217.

Flament, M. F., Rapoport, J. L., Berg, C. J., Sceery, W., Kilts, C., Mellstrom, B., & Linnoila, M. (1985). Clomipramine treatment of childhood obsessive-compulsive disorder: A double-blind study. *Archives of General Psychiatry, 42*, 977–983.

Flament, M. F., Whitaker, A., Rapoport, J. L., Davies, M., Berg, C. Z., Kalikow, K., Sceery, W., & Shaffer, D. (1988). Obsessive-compulsive disorder in adolescence: An epidemiologic study. *Journal of the American Academy of Child and Adolescent Psychiatry, 27*, 289–296.

Flavell, J. H. (1977). *Cognitive development.* Englewood Cliffs, NJ: Prentice Hall.

——. (1982). On cognitive development. *Child Development, 53*, 1–10.

Flegal, K. M., Carroll, M. D., Ogden, C. L., & Johnson, C. L. (2002). Prevalence and trends in obesity among US adults 1999-2000. *The Journal of the American Medical Association, 288*, 1723-1727.

Fleishman, E. A., & Mumford, M. D. (1991). Evaluating classifications of job behavior: A construct of the ability requirement scales. *Personnel Psychology, 44*, 523–575.

Flexser, A. J., & Tulving, E. (1982). Priming and recognition failure. *Journal of Verbal Learning and Verbal Behavior, 21*, 237–248.

Flynn, J. P., Vanegas, H., Foote, W., & Edwards, S. (1970). Neural mechanisms involved in a cat's attack on a rat. In R. E. Whalen, R. F. Thompson, M. Verzeano, & N. M. Weinberger (Eds.), *The neural control of behavior.* New York: Academic Press.

Foa, E. B. (1995). How do treatments for obsessive-compulsive disorder compare? *The Harvard Mental Health Letter, 12*, 8.

Foa, E. B., & Riggs, D. S. (1995). Posttraumatic stress disorder following assault: Theoretical considerations and empirical findings. *Current Directions in Psychological Science, 4*, 61–65.

Foerch, C., Misselwitz, B., Sitzer, M., Berger, K., Steinmetz, H., & Neumann-Haeflin, T. (2005). Difference in recognition of right and left hemispheric stroke. *The Lancet, 366*, 392-393.

Folkman, S. (1984). Personal control and stress and coping processes: A theoretical analysis. *Journal of Personality and Social Psychology, 46*, 839–852.

Folkman, S., & Lazarus, R. S. (1985). If it changes it must be a process: Study of emotion and coping during three stages of a college exam. *Journal of Personality and Social Psychology, 48*, 150-170.

Folkman, S. & Moskowitz, J. T. (2000). Stress, positive emotion, and coping. *Current Directions in Psychological Science, 9*, 115–118.

——. (2004). Coping: Pitfalls and promise. *Annual Review of Psychology, 55*, 745-774.

Folstein, S. E., & Rutter, M. L. (1977). Genetic influences and infantile autism. *Nature, 265*, 726–728.

——. (1988). Autism: Familial aggregation and genetic implications. *Journal of Autism and Development Disorders, 18*, 3–30.

Fontenot, N. A. (1993). Effects of training in creativity and creative problem finding upon business people. *Journal of Social Psychology, 133*, 11–22.

Food and Drug Administration. (1995). FDA says tobacco and nicotine are drugs. *Federal Register, 60*. Downloaded from the World Wide Web, January 31, 2001. http://www.wellweb.com/SMOKING/fdadrug.htm.

Ford, C. E., Wright, R. A., & Haythornwaite, J. (1985). Task performance and magnitude of goal valence. *Journal of Research in Personality, 19*, 253–260.

Ford, M. R., & Lowery, C. R. (1986). Gender differences in moral reasoning: A comparison of justice and care orientations. *Journal of Personality and Social Psychology, 4*, 777–783.

Ford-Gilboe, M., & Cohen, J. A. (2000). Hardiness: A model of commitment, challenge, and control. In V. R. Rice (Ed.), *Handbook of stress, coping, and health.* Thousand Oaks, CA: Sage.

Fortner, B. V., & Neimeyer, R. A. (1999). Death anxiety in older adults: A quantitative review. *Death Studies, 23*, 387–411.

Foster, S. E., Vaughan, R. D., Foster, W. H., & Califano, J. A. (2003). Alcohol consumption and expenditures for underage drinking and adult excessive drinking. *Journal of the American Medical Association, 289*, 989–995.

Foulkes, D. (1966). *The Psychology of Sleep.* New York: Charles Scribner.

Fowler, C. A., Wolford, G., Slade, R., & Tassinary, L. (1981). Lexical access with and without awareness. *Journal of Experimental Psychology: General, 110*, 341–362.

Fowler, R. D. (1992). Report to the Chief Executive Officer: A year of building for the future. *American Psychologist, 47*, 876–883.

Fowles, D. G. (1990). *A profile of older Americans: 1989.* Washington, DC: American Association of Retired Persons.

Fox, R., Aslin, R. N., Shea, S. L., & Dumais, S. T. (1980). Stereopsis in human infants. *Science, 207*, 323–324.

Fraley, R. C. (2002). Attachment stability from infancy to adulthood: Meta-analysis and dynamic modeling of developmental mechanisms. *Personality and Social Psychology Review, 6*, 123–151.

France, K. G. (1992). Behavior characteristics and security in sleep-disturbed infants treated with extinction. *Journal of Pediatric Psychology, 17*, 467–475.

France, K. G., & Hudson, S. M. (1993). Management of infant sleep disturbance: A review. *Clinical Psychology Review, 13*, 635–647.

Franco, P., Groswasser, J., Hassid, S., Lanquart, J. P., Scaillet, S., & Kahn, A. (1999). Prenatal exposure to cigarette smoking is associated with a decrease in arousal in infants. *Journal of Pediatrics, 135*, 34–38.

Frank, D. A., & McCarten, K. M. (1999). Level of in utero cocaine exposure and neonatal ultrasound findings. *Pediatrics, 104*, 1101–1105.

Frank, E., Kupfer, D. J., Perel, J. M., Cornes, C., Jarrett, D. B., et al. (1990). Three-year outcomes for maintenance therapies in recurrent depression. *Archives of General Psychiatry, 47*, 1093–1099.

Frankenburg, W. K., & Dodds, J. B. (1967). The Denver Developmental Screening Test. *Journal of Pediatrics, 71*, 181–191.

Franklin, V. P., Hale, J. E., & Bailey, W. A. (2001). *Learning while Black: Creating educational excellence for African-American children.* Baltimore: Johns Hopkins University Press.

Fraser, L. M., O'Carroll, R. E., & Ebmeier, K. P. (2008). The effect of electroconvulsive therapy on autobiographical memory: A systematic review. *The Journal of ECT*, **24**, 10–17.

Frasure-Smith, N., & Lespérance, F. (2005). Depression and coronary heart disease: Complex synergism of mind, body, and environment. *Current Directions in Psychological Science*, **14**, 39-43.

Frazier, T. M., David, G. H., Goldstein, H., & Goldberg, I. D. (1961). Cigarette smoking and prematurity. *American Journal of Obstetrics and Gynecology*, **81**, 988–996.

Frederickson, P. A. (1987). The relevance of sleep disorders medicine to psychiatric practice. *Psychiatric Annals*, **17**, 91–100.

Free, M. L., & Oei, T. P. S. (1989). Biological and psychological processes in the treatment and maintenance of depression. *Clinical Psychology Review*, **9**, 653–688.

Freitag, C. M. (2007). The genetics of autistic disorders and its clinical significance: A review of the literature. *Molecular Psychiatry*, **12**, 2–22.

Freed, C. R., Breeze, R. E., Rosenberg, N. L., et al. (1992). Survival of implanted fetal dopamine cells and neurologic improvement 12 to 46 months after transplantation for Parkinson's disease. *New England Journal of Medicine*, **327**, 1549–1555.

Freedman, D. X. (1984). Psychiatric epidemiology counts. *Archives of General Psychiatry*, **41**, 931–934.

Freedman, J. L. (1975). *Crowding and behavior*. New York: Viking Press.

French, C. C., & Richards, A. (1993). Clock this! An everyday example of schema-driven error in memory. *British Journal of Psychology*, **84**, 249–253.

Freud, A. (1958). *Adolescence: Psychoanalytic study of the child*. New York: Academic Press.

Freud, S. (1900). The interpretation of dreams. In J. Strachey (Ed.), *The complete psychological works of Sigmund Freud*. London: Hogarth Press.

——. (1900a). *The interpretation of dreams (3rd ed)* (A. A. Brill, Trans). Retrieved October 5, 2000, from the World Wide Web: http://www.yorku.ca/dept/psych/ classics/Freud/Dreams/ index.htm.

——. (1900b/1952). *On dreams* (J. Starchey, Trans.). New York: W. W. Norton.

——. (1910). The origin and development of psychoanalysis. *American Journal of Psychology*, **21**, 181–218. Retrieved October 5, 2000, from the World Wide Web: http://www. yorku.ca/dept/psych/classics/Freud/Origin/ index.htm.

——. (1933). *New introductory lectures on psychoanalysis: Standard edition*. New York: Norton.

——. (1943). *A general introduction to psychoanalysis*. Garden City, NY: Garden City Publishing.

Fribourg, S. (1982). Cigarette smoking and sudden infant death syndrome. *Journal of Obstetrics and Gynecology*, **142**, 934–941.

Fried, P. A. (1993). Prenatal exposure to tobacco and marijuana: Effects during pregnancy, infancy, and early childhood. *Clinical Obstetrics and Gynecology*, **36**, 319–337.

Fried, P. A., & Watkinson, B. (2000). Visuoperceptual functioning differs in 9 to 12-year olds prenatally exposed to cigarettes and marijuana. *Neurotoxicology and Teratology*, **22**, 11–20.

Frieden, T. R., & Blakeman, D. E. (2005). The dirty dozen: 12 myths that undermine tobacco control. *American Journal of Public Health*, **95**, 1500-1505.

Friedman, A., & Pines, A. (1991). Sex differences in gender related childhood memories. *Sex Roles*, **25**, 25-32.

Friedman, H. S., & Booth-Kewley, S. (1987). The "disease-prone personality": A meta-analytic review of the construct. *American Psychologist*, **42**, 539–555.

Friedman, H. S., Tucker, J. S., Schwartz, J. E., Tomlinson-Keasey, C., Martin, L. R., Wingard, D. L., & Cirqui, M. H. (1995). Psychosocial and behavioral predictors of longevity: The aging and death of the "Termites." *American Psychologist*, **50**, 69–78.

Friedman, J. M. (2000). Obesity in the new millennium. *Nature*, **404**, 632–634.

Friedman, J. M., & Polifka, J. E. (1996). *The effects of drugs on the fetus and nursing infant*. Baltimore: Johns Hopkins University Press.

Friedman, M., & Rosenman, R. (1959). Association of specific overt behavior patterns with blood and cardiovascular findings. *Journal of the American Medical Association*, **169**, 1286.

Friedman, M. I., & Stricker, E. M. (1976). The physiological psychology of hunger: A physiological perspective. *Psychological Review*, **83**, 409–431.

Friedman, S. (1972). Habituation and recovery of visual response in the alert human newborn. *Journal of Experimental Child Psychology*, **13**, 339–349.

Friedman, S., & Schonberg, S. K. (1996). Consensus statements. *Pediatrics*, **98**, 853.

Friston, K. J. (2005). Models of brain function in neuroimaging. *Annual Review of Psychology*, **56**, 57-87.

Frost, J. A., Binder, J. R., Springer, J. A., Hameke, T. A., et al. (1999). Language processing is strongly left lateralized in both sexes: Evidence from functional MRI. *Brain*, **122**, 199–208.

Fuchs, L. S. & Fuchs, D. (2002). Mathematical problem-solving profiles of students with mathematics disabilities with and without comorbid reading disabilities. *Journal of Learning Disabilities*, **35**, 563-573.

Fujita, F., Diener, E., & Sandvik, E. (1991). Gender differences in the negative affect of well-being: The case for emotional intensity. *Journal of Personality and Social Psychology*, **61**, 427-434.

Funder, D. C. (1995). On the accuracy of personality judgments: A realistic approach. *Psychological Review*, **102**, 652–670.

——. (1996). *The Personality Puzzle*. New York: W. W. Norton.

——. (2001a). Personality. *Annual Review of Psychology*, **52**, 197–221.

——. (2001b). *The personality puzzle (2nd Ed.)*. New York: Norton.

——. (2007). *The personality puzzle (4th edition)*. New York: W. W. Norton.

Funk, R. (1987). Disability rights: From caste to class in the context of civil rights. In A. Gartner & T. Joe (Eds.), *Images of the disabled, disabling images*. (pp. 7-30). New York: Praeger.

Furmack, T., Tillfors, M., Marteinsdottir, I., Fisher, H., Pissiota, A., Långström, B., & Fredrikson, M. (2002). Common changes in cerebral blood flow in patients with social phobia treated with citalopram or cognitive-behavioral therapy. *Archives of General Psychiatry*, **59**, 425–433.

Furstenberg, F. F., Brooks-Gunn, J., & Chase-Lansdale, L. (1989). Teenaged pregnancy and childbearing. *American Psychologist*, **44**, 313–320.

Furumoto, L., & Scarborough, E. (1986). Placing women in the history of psychology: The first American women psychologists. *American Psychologist*, **41**, 35–42.

Gabrena, W., Wang, Y., Latané, B. (1985). Social loafing on an optimizing task: Cross-cultural differences among Chinese and Americans. *Journal of Cross-cultural Psychology*, **16**, 223–242.

Gabrieli, J. D. E. (1998). Cognitive neuroscience of memory. *Annual Review of Psychology*, **48**, 87–115.

Gage, F. H. (2002). Neurogenesis in the adult brain. *The Journal of Neuroscience*, **22**, 612-613.

Gagné, G. G., Jr., Furman M. J., Carpenter, L. L., & Price, L. H. (2000). Efficacy of continuation ECT and antidepressant drugs compared to long-term antidepressants alone in depressed patients. *American Journal of Psychiatry*, **157**, 1969–1965.

Galanter, E. (1962). Contemporary psychophysics. In R. Brown et al. (Eds.), *New directions in psychology*. New York: Holt, Rinehart & Winston.

Galbaud du Fort, G., Newman, S. C., & Bland, R. C. (1993). Psychiatric comorbidity and treatment seeking: Sources of selection bias in the study of clinical populations. *Journal of Nervous and Mental Disorders*, **181**, 467–474.

Galea, S., Brewin, C. R., Gruber, M., Jones, R. T., King, D. W., King, L. A., McNally, R. J., Ursana, R. J., Petukhova, M., & Kessler, R. C. (2007). Exposure to hurricane-related stressors and mental illness after Hurricane Katrina. *Archives of General Psychiatry*, **64**, 1427–1434.

Gallacher, J. E. J., Yarnell, J. W. G., Elwood, P. C., & Stansfeld, S. A. (2003). Is Type A behavior really a trigger for coronary heart disease events? *Psychosomatic Medicine*, **65**, 339–346.

Gallagher, J. J., & Ramey, C. T. (1987). *The malleability of children*. Baltimore: Paul H. Brooks.

Gallo, V., & Robinson, P. R. (2000). Is there a homosexual brain? *Gay & Lesbian Review Worldwide*, **7**, 12-16.

Gallup Organization. (1995). *Disciplining children in America: A Gallup poll report*. Princeton, NJ: Author.

Gallup Poll Organization. (1999). *Racial profiling is seen as widespread, particularly among young Black men*. Princeton, NJ: Gallup Poll Organization.

Galton, F. (1865). Heredity, talent and character. Retrieved on August 28, 2008, from http://psychclassics.yorku.ca/Galton/talent.htm.

——. (1879). *Hereditary genius: An inquiry into its laws and consequences*. Englewood Cliffs, NJ: Prentice-Hall.

Gans, J. E., & Blyth, D. A. (1990). *American adolescents: How healthy are they?* AMA Profiles of Adolescent Health series. Chicago: American Medical Association.

Garbarino, J. (1985). *Adolescent development: An ecological perspective*. Columbus, OH: Merrill.

Garcia, J., Ervin, F. R., & Koelling, R. A. (1966). Learning with prolonged delay of reinforcement. *Psychonomic Science*, **5**, 121–122.

Garcia, S. M., Weaver, K., Moskowitz, G. D., & Darley, J. M. (2002). Crowded minds: The implicit bystander effect. *Journal of Personality and Social Psychology*, **83**, 843–853.

Garde, M. M., & Cowey, A. (2000) Deaf hearing: Unacknowledged detection of auditory stimuli in a patient with cerebral deafness. *Cortex*, **36**, 71–80.

Gardner, B. T., & O'Conner, D. W. (2008). A review of the cognitive effects of electroconvulsive therapy in older adults. *The Journal of ECT*, **24**, 68–80.

Gardner, H. (1983). *Frames of mind: The theory of multiple intelligences*. New York: Basic Books.

——. (1993a). *Multiple intelligences: The theory in practice*. New York: Basic Books.

——. (1993b). *Creating minds*. New York: Basic Books.

——. (2003). *Multiple intelligences after twenty years*. Invited address presented at the American Educational Research Association meeting, Chicago, Illinois, April 21, 2003.

——. (2003b). Three distinct meanings of intelligence. In R. Sternberg et al. (Eds.), *Models of intelligence for the new millennium*. Washington, DC: American Psychological Association.

Gardner, H., & Hatch, T. (1989). Multiple intelligences go to school: Educational implications of the theory of multiple intelligences. *Educational Researcher*, **18**, 6.

Gardner, M. (1993). The false memory syndrome. *Skeptical Inquirer*, **17**, 370–375.

Garfield, S. L. (1981). Psychotherapy: A 40-year appraisal. *American Psychologist*, **36**, 174–183.

Garfield, S. L. (1997). The therapist as a neglected variable in psychotherapy research. *Clinical Psychology: Science and Practice*, **4(1)**, 40–43.

Garner, D. M., Olmsted, M. P., Davis, R., Rockert, W., Goldbloom, D., & Eagle, M. (1990). The association between bulimic symptoms and reported psychopathology. *International Journal of Eating Disorders*, **9**, 1–15.

Garry, M., & Loftus, E. F. (1994). Repressed memories of childhood trauma: Could some of them be suggested? *USA Today*, January, 22, 82–84.

Gaugler, B. B., Rosenthal, D. B., Thornton, G. C., & Bentson, C. (1987). Meta-analysis of assessment center validity. *Journal of Applied Psychology*, **72**, 493–511.

Gawronski, B., Bodenhausen, G. V., & Banse, R. (2005). We are, therefore they aren't: Ingroup construal as a standard of comparison for outgroup judgments. *Journal of Experimental Social Psychology*, **41**, 515–526.

Gay, M. C., Philippot, P., Luminet, O. (2002). Differential effectiveness of psychological interventions for reducing osteoarthritis pain: A comparison of Erikson hypnosis and Jacobson relaxation. *European Journal of Pain*, **6**, 1-16.

Gazzaniga, M. S. (1998). The split brain revisited. *Scientific American*, July, 50–55.

Gazzaniga, M. S., & Ledoux, J. E. (1978). *The integrated mind*. New York: Plenum.

Gazzaniga, M. S., Ivry, R. B., & Mangun, G. R. (2002). *Cognitive neuroscience: The biology of the mind (2nd ed.)*. New York: W. W. Norton.

Ge, X., & Conger, R. D. (2003). Pubertal transition, stressful life events, and the emergence of gender differences in adolescent depressive symptoms. *Developmental Psychology*, **37**, 1-20.

Ge, X., Conger, R. D., & Elder, G. H., Jr. (1996). Coming of age too early: Pubertal influences on girls' vulnerability to psychological distress. *Child Development*, **67**, 3386–4000.

Gearing, R. E., McNeill, T., & Lozier, F. A. (2005). Father involvement and fetal alcohol spectrum disorder: Developing best practices. *Journal of FAS International*, **3**, 1-11.

Gebbard, G. O., Gunderson, J. G., & Fonagy, P. (2002). The place of psychoanalytic treatments within psychiatry. *Archives of General Psychiatry*, **59**, 505–510.

Gefou-Madianou, D. (1992). *Alcohol, gender and culture*. New York: Routledge, Chapman Hall.

Geller, E. S. (1985). The behavior change approach to litter management. *Journal of Resource Management*, **14**, 117–122.

——. (1986). Prevention of environmental problems. In B. A. Edelstein & L. Michelson (Eds.), *Handbook of prevention*. New York: Plenum.

——. (1989). Applied behavioral analysis and social marketing: An integration to preserve the environment. *Journal of Social Issues*, **45**, 17–36.

——. (1992). It takes more than information to save energy. *American Psychologist*, **47**, 814–815.

Geller, E. S., & Lehman, G. R. (1986). Motivating desirable waste management behavior: Applications of behavioral analysis. *Journal of Resource Management*, **15**, 58–68.

Geller, E. S., & Nimmer, J. G. (1985). *Social marketing and applied behavior analysis: An integration for quality of life intervention*. Blacksburg: Virginia Polytechnic Institute and State University.

Geller, E. S., Bruff, C. D., & Nimmer, J. G. (1985). "Flash for life": Community-based prompting for safety belt promotion. *Journal of Applied Behavioral Analysis*, **18**, 309–314.

Geller, E. S., Rudd, J. R., Kalsher, M. J., Sreff, F. M., & Lehman, G. R. (1987). Employer-based programs to motivate safety belt use: A review of short-term and long-term effects. *Journal of Safety Research*, **18**, 1–17.

Geller, E. S., Winett, R. A., & Everett, P. B. (1982). *Preserving the environment: New strategies for behavior change*. New York: Pergamon Press.

Gellhorn, E. (1964). Motion and emotion: The role of proprioception in the physiology and pathology of the emotions. *Psychological Review*, **71**, 457–472.

Gelman, D., Doherty, S., Joseph, N., & Carroll, G. (1987, Spring). How infants learn to talk. *Newsweek: On Health*.

Gelso, C. J., & Fassinger, R. E. (1990). Counseling psychology: Theory and research on interventions. *Annual Review of Psychology*, **41**, 355–386.

Gemberling, G. A., & Domjan, M. (1982). Selective associations in one-day-old rats: Taste toxicosis and texture-shock aversion learning. *Journal of Comparative and Physiological Psychology*, **96**, 105–113.

Gendel, E. S., & Bonner, E. J. (1988). Sexual dysfunction. In H. H. Goldman (Ed.), *Review of general psychiatry (2nd ed.)*, Norwalk, CT: Appleton and Lange.

General Social Survey. (1999). Retrieved January 8, 2001, from http://www.icpsr.umich.edu/GSS99/home.htm.

George, L. (1992). Acupuncture: Drug free pain relief. *American Health*, **11**, 45.

George, M. S., Ketter, T. A., Parekh, P. I., Horwitz, B., Herscovitch, P., & Post, R. M. (1995). Brain activity during transient sadness and happiness in healthy women. *American Journal of Psychiatry*, **152**, 341–351.

Gera, G., Avanzini , P., Zaimovic, A., Sartori, R., Bocchi, C., Timpano, M., Zambelli, U., Delsignore, R., Gardini, F., Talarico, E., & Brambilla, F. (1999). Neurotransmitters, neuroendocrine correlates of sensation-seeking temperament in normal humans. *Neuropsychobiology, 39*, 207–213.

Geracioti, T. D., & Liddle, R. A. (1988). Impaired cholecystokinin secretion in bulimia nervosa. *New England Journal of Medicine*, **319**, 683–688.

Gerbert, B., & Maguire, B. (1989). Public acceptance of the Surgeon General's brochure on AIDS. *Public Health Report*, **104**, 130–133.

Gernsbacher, M. A., & Kaschak, M. P. (2003). Neuroimaging studies of language production and comprehension. *Annual Review of Psychology*, **54**, 91–114.

Gershoff, E. T. (2002). Parental corporal punishment and associated child behaviors and experiences: A meta-analytic and theoretical review. *Psychological Bulletin*, **128**, 539–579.

Gerow, J. R., & Murphy, D. P. (1980). The validity of the Nelson-Denny Reading Test as a predictor of performance in introductory psychology. *Educational and Psychological Measurement*, **40**, 553–556.

Gibson, E. J. (1987). Introductory essay: What does infant perception tell us about theories of perception? *Journal of Experimental Psychology: Perception and Performance*, **13**, 515–523.

——. (1988). Exploratory behavior in the development of perceiving, acting, and the acquiring of knowledge. *Annual Review of Psychology*, **39**, 1–41.

Gibson, E. J., & Walk, R. D. (1960). The visual cliff. *Scientific American*, **202**, 64–71.

Giedd, J. N., Jeffries, N. O., Blumenthal, J., Castellanos, F. X., Vaitzis, A. C., et al., (1999). Childhood-onset schizophrenia: Progressive brain changes during adolescence. *Biological Psychiatry*, **46**, 892-898.

Gila, A., Castro, J., Toro, J., & Salamero, M. (1998). Subjective body-image dimensions in normal and anorexic adolescents. *British Journal of Medical Psychology, 71,* 175–84.

Gilbert, P. A., Harris, M. J., McAdams, L. A., & Jeste, D. (1995). Neuroleptic withdrawal in schizophrenic patients. *Archives of General Psychology, 52,* 173–188.

Gillick, M. (2000). *Lifelines: Living longer, growing frail, taking heart.* New York: W. W. Norton & Company.

Gilligan, C. (1982). *In a different voice: Psychological theory and women's development.* Cambridge, MA: Harvard University Press.

——. (1993). Adolescent development reconsidered. In A. Garrod (Ed.), *Approaches to moral development: New research and emerging themes.* New York: Teachers College Press.

Gilliland, H. (1999). *Teaching the Native American.* Dubuque, IA: Kendall Hunt.

Gilovich, T., Vallone, R., & Tversky, A. (1985). The hot hand in basketball: On the misperception of random sequences. *Cognitive Psychology, 17,* 295–314.

Gilvarry, E. (2000). Substance use in young people. *Journal of Child Psychology, 41,* 55-80.

Giron, S. T., Wang, H. X., Bernsten, C., Thorslund, M., Winblad, B., & Fastbom, J. (2001). The appropriateness of drug use in an older nondemented and demented population. *Journal of the American Geriatrics Society, 49,* 277–283.

Gitter, G. A., Lomranz, J., & Saxe, L. (1982). Factors affecting perceived attractiveness of male physiques by American and Israeli students. *Journal of Psychology, 118,* 167-175.

Gladue, B. A. (1994). The biopsychology of sexual orientation. *Current Directions in Psychological Science, 3,* 150–154.

Gladue, B. A., Green, R., & Hellman, R. E. (1984). Neuroendocrine response to estrogen and sexual orientation. *Science, 225,* 1496–1499.

Glanz, K. (1997). Behavioral research contributions and needs in cancer prevention and control: Dietary change. *Preventative Medicine, 26,* S43–S55.

Glanz, K., Lew, R., Song, V., & Cook, V. A. (1999). Factors associated with skin cancer prevention practices in a multiethnic population. *Health Education and Behavior, 26,* 44–59.

Glaser, R. (1984). Education and thinking. *American Psychologist, 39,* 93–104.

Glasgow, R. E., & Lichtenstein, E. (1987). Long-term effects of behavioral smoking cessation interventions. *Behavior Therapy, 18,* 297–324.

Glass, A. L., Holyoak, K. J., & Santa, J. L. (1979). *Cognition.* Reading, MA: Addison-Wesley.

Glass, D. C., & Singer, J. E. (1972). *Urban stress.* Hillsdale, NJ: Erlbaum.

Glass, D. C., Singer, J. E., & Friedman, L. N. (1969). Psychic cost of adaptation to an environmental stressor. *Journal of Personality and Social Psychology, 12,* 200–210.

Gleaves, D. H. (1994). On "the reality of repressed memories." *American Psychologist, 49,* 440–441.

Gleicher, F. & Petty, R. E. (1992). Expectations of reassurance influence the nature of fear-stimulated attitude change. *Journal of Experimental Social Psychology, 28,* 86–100.

Glenn, N. D. (1990). Quantitative research on marital quality in the 1980s: A critical review. *Journal of Marriage and the Family, 52,* 818–831.

Glenn, N. D., & Weaver, C. N. (1981). The contribution of marital happiness to global happiness. *Journal of Marriage and the Family, 43,* 161–168.

Glick, I. D., & Berman, E. M. (2000). Gay and lesbian couples. In I. D. Glick, E. M. Berman, J. F. Clarkin, & D. S. Rait (Eds.), *Marital and family therapy* (pp. 453-472). Washington, DC: American Psychiatric Press.

Gluck, M. A., & Myers, C. E. (1995). Representation and association in memory: A neurocomputational view of hippocampal function. *Current Directions in Psychological Science, 4,* 23–29.

Glucksberg, S., & Danks, J. H. (1975). *Experimental Psycholinguistics: An introduction.* New York: Lawrence Erlbaum Associates.

Glynn, M., & Rhodes, P. (2005). *Estimated HIV prevalence in the United States at the end of 2003.* Atlanta: National HIV Prevention Conference.

Golbin, J. M., Somers, V. K., & Caplpes, S. M. (2008). Obstructive sleep apnea, cardiovascular disease, and pulmonary hypertension. *Proceedings of the American Thoracic Society 5,* 200–206.

Gold, S. N., Hughes, D., & Hohnecker, L. (1994). Degrees of repression of sexual abuse memories. *American Psychologist, 49,* 441–442.

Goldberg, L. R. (1993). The structure of phenotypic personality traits. *American Psychologist, 48,* 26–34.

Goldhagen, D. J. (1996). *Hitler's willing executioners: Ordinary Germans and the Holocaust.* New York: Knopf.

Goldsmith, H. H., & Harman, C. (1994). Temperament and attachment; individuals and relationships. *Current Directions in Psychological Science, 3,* 53–57.

Goldstein, E. B. (1999). *Sensation and Perception, Fifth Edition.* Pacific Grove, CA: Brooks/Cole.

——. (2002). *Sensation and perception (6th ed.).* Pacific Grove, CA: Wadsworth.

Goldstein, I. L. (1986). *Training in organizations.* Monterey, CA: Brooks/Cole.

——. (1989). *Training and development in organizations.* San Francisco: Jossey-Bass.

Goleman, D. (1995). *Emotional intelligence.* New York: Bantam.

Goleman, O. (1980). 1,528 little geniuses and how they grew. *Psychology Today, 14,* 28–53.

Golub, M. S., Coollman, G. W., Foster, P. M. D., Kimmel, C. A., Rajpert-De Meyts, E., Reiter, E. O., Sharpe, R. M., Skakkeback, N. E., & Toppari, J. (2008). Public health implications of altered puberty timing. *Pediatrics, 121,* S218–S230.

Gomel, M. K. (1997). *Nations for mental health: A focus on women.* Geneva: World Health Organization.

Gómez-Jacinto, L, & Hombrados-Mendietta, I. (2002). Multiple effects of community and household crowding. *Journal of Environmental Psychology, 22,* 233–246.

Gooden, D., & Baddeley, A. D. (1975). Context-dependent memory in two natural environments: On and under water. *British Journal of Psychology, 66*, 325–331.

Goodman, G. S., Ghetti, S., Quas, J. A., Edelstein, R. S., Alexander, K. W., Redlich, A. D., Cordon, I. M., & Jones, D. P. H. (2003). A prospective study of memory for child sexual abuse: New findings relevant to the repressed-memory controversy. *Psychological Science, 14*, 113–118.

Gordon, C. T., State, R. C., Nelson, J. E., Hamburger, S. D., & Rapoport, J. L. (1993). A double-blind comparison of clomipramine, desipramine, and placebo in the treatment of autistic disorder. *Archives of General Psychiatry, 50*, 441–447.

Gore, S. V. (1999). African-American women's perceptions of weight: Paradigm shift for advanced practice. *Holistic Nursing Practices, 13*, 71-79.

Gorenstein, E. E. (1984). Debating mental illness. *American Psychologist, 39*, 50–56.

Gotlib, I. H. & Krasnoperova, E. (1998). Biased information processing as a vulnerability factor for depression. *Behavior Therapy, 29*, 603–617.

Gottesman, I. I. (1991). *Schizophrenia genesis: The origins of madness.* New York: W. H. Freeman.

——. (2001). Psychopathology through a life span-genetic prism. *American Psychologist, 56*, 867-878.

Gottesman, I. I., & Bertelsen, A. (1989). Confirming unexpressed genotypes for schizophrenia. *Archives of General Psychiatry, 46*, 867–872.

Gottesman, I. I., & Shields, J. (1982). *Schizophrenia: The epigenetic puzzle.* Cambridge, UK: Cambridge University Press.

Gottfredson, L. S. (2004). Intelligence: Is is the epidemiologist's "fundamental cause" of social class inequalities in health? *Journal of Personality and Social Psychology, 86*, 174–199.

Gottfredson, L. S., & Deary, I. J. (2004). Intelligence predicts health and longevity, but why? *Current Directions in Psychological Science, 13*, 1–4.

Gottlieb, B. H. (1981). *Social networks and social support.* Beverly Hills, CA: Sage.

Gottlieb, G. (1970). Conceptions of prenatal development. In L. R. Aronson, E. Robach, D. S. Lehrman, & J. S. Rosenblatt (Eds.), *Development and evolution of behavior.* San Francisco: Freeman.

Gottman, J. (1994). Why marriages fail. *Networker, 18*, 41–48.

Goya, R. L., Tyers, P., & Barker, R. A. (2008). The search for curative cell therapy in Parkinson's disease. *Journal of the Neurological Sciences, 265*, 32–42.

Gracely, R. H., Lynch, S., & Bennett, G. J. (1991). *The central process responsible for A_LTM-medicated allodynia in some patients with RSD is sensitive to perfusion of the microenvironment of nociceptor terminals.* Paper presented at the 21st Annual Meeting of the Society for Neuroscience. New Orleans.

Gracheck, J. E. (2006). The insanity defense in the twenty-first century: How recent United States Supreme Court case law can improve the system. *Indiana Law Journal, 81*, 1479–1501.

Grady, C. L., McIntosh, A. R., Horowitz, B., Maisog, J. M., Ungerleider, L. G., Mentis, M. J., Pietrini, P., Schapiro, M. B., & Haxby, J. V. (1995). Age-related reductions in human recognition memory due to impaired encoding. *Science, 269*, 218–221.

Graf, P., & Mandler, G. (1984). Activation makes words more accessible, but not necessarily more retrievable. *Journal of Verbal Learning and Verbal Behavior, 23*, 553–568.

Gray-Little, B., & Hafdahl, A. R. (2000). Factors influencing racial comparisons of self-esteem: A quantitative review. *Psychological Bulletin, 126*, 26–54.

Graziano, A. M., & Raulin, M. L. (1993). *Research methods: A process of inquiry.* New York: HarperCollins.

Green, D. M., & Swets, J. A. (1966). *Signal detection theory and psychophysics.* New York: Wiley.

Green, K. S. (1995). Blue versus periwinkle: Color identification and gender. *Perceptual and Motor Skills, 80*, 21-32.

Greenberg, B. D., Price, L. H., Rauch, S. L., Friehs, G., Noren, G., Malone, D., et al., (2003). Neurosurgery for intractable obsessive-compulsive disorder and depression: Critical issues. *Neurosurgery Clinics of North America, 14*, 199-212.

Greenberg, J., & Cohen, R. L. (1982). *Equity and justice in social behavior.* New York: Academic Press.

Greenberg, L. S., & Safran, J. D. (1989). Emotion in psychotherapy. *American Psychologist, 44*, 19–29.

Greene, J., & Haidt, J. (2002). How (and where) does moral judgment work? *Trends in Cognitive Sciences, 6*, 517-523.

Greengard, P. (2001). The neurobiology of slow synaptic transmissions. *Science, 294*, 1024-1030.

Greeno, J. G. (1978). Natures of problem-solving abilities. In W. K. Estes (Ed.), *Handbook of learning and cognitive processes (Vol. 5).* Hillsdale, NJ: Erlbaum.

——. (1989). A perspective on thinking. *American Psychologist, 44*, 134–141.

Greenough, W. T. (1984). Structural correlates of information storage in mammalian brain. *Trends in Neurosciences, 7*, 229–233.

Greenwald, A. G., Klinger, M. R., & Schuh, E. S. (1994). Activation by marginally perceptible ("subliminal") stimuli: Dissociation of unconscious from conscious cognition. *Journal of Experimental Psychology: General, 125*, 22–42.

Greenwald, A. G., Spangenberg, E. R., Pratkais, A. R., & Eskenazi, J. (1991). Double-blind tests of subliminal self-help audio tapes. *Psychological Science, 2*, 119–122.

Greer, S. (1964). Study of parental loss in neurotics and sociopaths. *Archives of General Psychiatry, 11*, 177–180.

Gregory, R. J. (1999). *Foundations of intellectual assessment.* Boston: Allyn and Bacon.

Gregory, R. L. (1977). *Eye and brain: The psychology of seeing (3rd ed.)* New York: New World Library.

Gregory, W. L., Mowen, J. C., & Linder, D. E. (1978) Social psychology and plea bargaining: Applications, methodology, and theory. *Journal of Personality and Social Psychology, 36*, 1521–1530

Grewald, D., & Salovey, P. (2005). Feeling smart: The science of emotional intelligence. *American Scientist, 93*, 330–339.

Grice, G. R. (1948). The relation of secondary reinforcement to delayed reward in visual discrimination learning. *Journal of Experimental Psychology, 38*, 1–16.

Grinspoon, L. (1977). *Marijuana reconsidered (2nd ed.)*. Cambridge, MA: Harvard University Press.

—— (Ed.). (1995). Obsessive-compulsive disorder-Part I. *The Harvard Mental Health Letter*, **12**, 1–3.

——. (1995). Schizophrenia update-Part I. *The Harvard Mental Health Letter*, **11**, 1–4.

—— (Ed.). (1996). Personality disorders: The anxious cluster—Part I. *The Harvard Mental Health Letter*, **12(8)**, 1–3.

—— (Ed.). (1997). Mood disorders: An overview—Part I. *The Harvard Mental Health Letter*, **14(6)**, 1–4.

—— (Ed.). (1997). Nicotine dependence—Part I. *The Harvard Mental Health Letter*, **13(11)**,1–4.

—— (Ed.). (1998). Mood disorders: An overview—Part II. *The Harvard Mental Health Letter*, **14(7)**, 1–5.

Grob, C., & Dobkin de Rois, M. (1992). Adolescent drug use in cross-cultural perspective. *Journal of Drug Issues*, **22**, 121–138.

Gross, C. G. (2000). Neurogenesis in the adult brain: Death of a dogma. *Nature Reviews: Neuroscience*, **1**, 67-73.

Gross, R. T., & Duke, P. M. (1980). The effect of early and late maturation on adolescent behavior. *The Pediatric Clinics of North America*, **27**, 71–77.

Grundy, S. M. (1999). Primary prevention of coronary heart disease. Integrating risk assessment with intervention. *Circulation*, **100**, 988–998.

Grych, J. H., & Clark, R. (1999). Maternal employment and development of the father-infant relationship in the first year. *Developmental Psychology*, **35**, 893–903.

Guilford, J. P. (1959a). *Personality*. New York: McGraw-Hill.

Guilford, J. P. (1967). *The nature of human intelligence*. New York: McGraw-Hill.

——. (1988). Some changes in the structure-of-intellect model. *Educational and Psychological Measurement*, **48**, 1–4.

Gur, R. E., Resnick, S. M., Alavi, A., Gur, R. C., Caroff, S., Dann, R., et al. (1987). Regional brain function in schizophrenia. *Archives of General Psychiatry*, **44**, 119–125.

Gureje, O., Von Korff, M., Simon, G. E., & Gater, R. (1998). Persistent pain and well-being: A World Health Organization study in primary care. *Journal of the American Medical Association*, **280**, 147–151.

Gurman, A. S., Kniskern, D. P., & Pinsof, W. M. (1986). Research on the process and outcome of marital and family therapy. In S. L. Garfield & A. E. Bergin (Eds.), *Handbook of psychotherapy and behavior change (3rd ed.)*. New York: Wiley.

Gustafson, D., Rothenberg, E., Blennow, K., Steen, B., & Skoog, I. (2003). An 18-year follow-up of overweight and risk of Alzheimer Disease. *Archives of Internal Medicine*, **163**, 1524–1528.

Gustafson, R. (1990). Wine and male physical aggression. *Journal of Drug Issues*, **20**, 75–87.

Guthrie, R. V. (1976/2004). *Even the rat was white: A historical view of psychology*. Boston: Allyn and Bacon.

Gutierrez, P. M. & Silk, K. R. (1998). Prescription privileges for psychologists: A review of the psychological literature. *Professional Psychology: Research and Practice*, **29**, 213–222.

Guttentag, R. E., Ornstein, P. A., & Seimans, L. (1987). Children's spontaneous rehearsal: Transitions in strategy acquisition. *Cognitive Development*, **2**, 307–326.

Guttmacher, A. E., & Collins, F. S. (2003). Welcome to the genomic era. *New England Journal of Medicine*, **349**, 996–998.

Guyton, A.C. (1972). *Organ physiology: Structure and function of the nervous system*. Philadelphia: W. B. Saunders.

Gwyn, K., Bondy, M. L., Cohen, D. S., Lund, M. J., Liff, J. M., Flagg, E. W., Brinton, L. A., Eley, J. W., & Coates, R. J. (2004). Racial differences in diagnosis, treatment, and clinical delays in a population-based study of patients with newly diagnosed breast carcinoma. *Cancer*, **100**, 1595-1604.

Haaf, R. A., & Brown, C. J. (1976). Infants' response to face-like patterns: Developmental changes between 10 and 15 weeks of age. *Journal of Experimental Child Psychology*, **22**, 155–160.

Habermas, T., & Bluck, S. (2000). Getting a life: The emergence of the life story in adolescence. *Psychological Bulletin*, **126**, 748–769.

Haight, J. M. (2003). Human error and the challenge of an aging workforce: Considerations for improving workplace safety. *Professional Safety*, **48(12)**, 18–24.

Haist, F., Shimamura, A. P., & Squire, L. R. (1992). On the relationship between recall and recognition memory. *Journal of Experimental Psychology: Learning, Memory and Cognition*, **18**, 691–702.

Hake, D. F., & Foxx, R. M. (1978). Promoting gasoline conservation: The effects of reinforcement schedules, a leader, and self-recording. *Behavior Modification*, **2**, 339–369.

Halaas, J. L., Gajiwala, K. S., Maffei, M., Cohen, S. L., Chait, B. T., et al. (1995). Weight-reducing effects of the plasma protein encoded by the obese gene. *Science*, **269**, 543–546.

Halberstadt, A. G., & Saitta, M. B. (1987). Gender, nonverbal behavior, and perceived dominance: A test of the theory. *Journal of Personality and Social Psychology*, **53**, 257–272.

Hall, C. S. (1954). *A primer of Freudian psychology*. New York: Mentor.

Hall, E. D., Gibson, T. R., & Pavel, K. M. (2005). Lack of gender differences in post-traumatic neurodegeneration in the mouse controlled cortical impact injury model. *Journal of Neurotrauma*, **22**, 669-679.

Hall, E. T. (1966). *The hidden dimension*. Garden City, NY: Doubleday.

Hall, G. S. (1904). *Adolescence*. Englewood Cliffs, NJ: Prentice-Hall.

Hall, J. A. (1978). Gender effects in decoding nonverbal cues. *Psychological Bulletin*, **85**, 845–857.

Hall, W. G., & Oppenheim, R. W. (1987). Developmental psychology. *Annual Review of Psychology*, **38**, 91–128.

Halpern, D. F. (1997). Sex differences in intelligence: Implications for education. *American Psychologist*, **52**, 1091–1102.

——. (2004). A cognitive-process taxonomy for sex differences in cognitive abilities. *Current Directions in Psychological Science*, **13**, 135–139.

Halpern, D. F., Benbow, C. P., Geary, D. C. Gur, R. C., Hyde, J. S., & Gernsbacher, M. A. (2007). The science of sex differences in science and mathematics. *Psychological Science in the Public Interest*, **8**, 1–51.

Hamburg, D. A. (1992). *Today's children: Creating a future for a generation in crisis.* New York: New York Times Books.

Hamel, M., Gallagher, S., & Soares, C. (2001). The Rorschach: Here we go again. *Journal of Forensic Psychology Practice,* **1,** 79–87.

Hamer, D. H., Hu, S., Magnuson, V. L., Hu, N., & Pattatucci, A. M. L. (1993). A linkage between DNA markers on the X chromosome and male sexual orientation. *Science,* **261,** 321–327.

Hammann, S. (2005). Sex differences in the responses of the human amygdala. *The Neuroscientist,* **11,** 288-293.

Han, S. K., & Moen, P. (1999). Clocking out: Temporal patterning of retirement. *American Journal of Sociology,* **105,** 191–236.

Hansen, N. B., Lambert, M. J., & Forman, E. M. (2002). The psychotherapy dose-response effect and its implications for treatment delivery services. *Clinical Psychology Science and Practice,* **9,** 329–343.

Hansen, R. A., Gartlehner, G., Lohr, K. N., Gaynes, B. N., & Carey, T. S. (2005). Efficacy and safety of second-generation antidepressants in the treatment of major depressive disorder. *Annals of Internal Medicine,* **143,** 415-426.

Hansen, W. B., Hahn, G. L., & Wolkenstein, J. (1990). Perceived personal immunity: Beliefs about susceptibility to AIDS. *Journal of Sex Research,* **27,** 622–628.

Harding, C. M. (1988). Course types in schizophrenia: An analysis of European and American studies. *Schizophrenia Bulletin,* **14,** 633–642.

Hare, R. D. (1970). *Psychopathology: Theory and research.* New York: Wiley.

——. (1995). Psychopaths: New trends in research. *The Harvard Mental Health Letter,* **12,** 4–5.

Hare, R. D., McPherson, L. M., & Forth, A. E. (1988). Male psychopaths and their criminal careers. *Journal of Consulting and Clinical Psychology,* **56,** 710–714.

Harkins, S. G., & Petty, R. E. (1983). Social context effects in persuasion: The effects of multiple sources and multiple targets. In P. B. Paulus (Ed.), *Basic group processes.* New York: Springer-Verlag.

Harlow, H. F. (1932). Social facilitation of feeding in the albino rat. *Journal of Genetic Psychology,* **41,** 211–221.

——. (1959). Love in infant monkeys. *Scientific American,* **200,** 68–74.

Harlow, H. F., Harlow, M. K., & Suomi, S. J. (1971). From thought to therapy: Lessons from a private library. *American Scientist,* **59,** 536–549.

Harman, J. S., Edlund, M. J., & Fortney, J. C. (2004). Disparities in the adequacy of depression treatment in the United States. *Psychiatric Services,* **55,** 1379-1385.

Harnack, L. J., Jeffery, R. W., & Boutelle, K. N. (2000). Temporal trends in energy intake in the United States: An ecological perspective. *American Journal of Clinical Nutrition,* **71,** 1478–1484.

Harris, B. (1979). What ever happened to Little Albert? *American Psychologist,* **34,** 151–160.

Harris, D. V. (1973). *Involvement in sport: A somatopsychic rationale for physical activity.* Philadelphia: Lea & Febiger.

Harris, J. R. (1998). *The nurture assumption: Why children turn out the way they do.* New York: Free Press.

——. (1999). How many environments does a child have? *Harvard Education Letter,* **15,** 8.

Harris, L., & Associates. (1975, 1981, 1983). *The myth and reality of aging in America.* Washington, DC: The National Council on Aging.

Harris, M. M. (1989). Reconsidering the employment interview: A review of recent literature and suggestions for future research. *Personnel Psychology,* **42,** 691–726.

Harris, T. C. (2003). *An instructor's guide for introducing industrial-organizational psychology.* Society for Industrial and Organizational Psychology, Inc., from www.siop.org.

Harrison, G., Andrews, J., & Saklofske, D. (2003). Current perspectives on cognitive learning styles. *Education Canada,* **43,** 44–47.

Hassett, J. M., Siebert, E. R., & Wallen, K. (2004). Sexually differentiated toy preferences in Rhesus monkeys. Paper presented at the Annual Meeting of the Society for Behavioral Neuroendicrinology, July 26–30, Lisbon, Portugal.

Hartman, S., Grigsby, D. W., Crino, M. D., & Chokar, J. (1986). The measurement of job satisfaction by action tendencies. *Educational and Psychological Measurement,* **46,** 317–329.

Hartup, W. W. (1989). Social relationships and their developmental significance. *American Psychologist,* **44,** 120–126.

Haruki, T., Shigehisa, T., Nedate, K., Wajima, M., & Ogawa, R. (1984). Effects of alien-reinforcement and its combined type of learning behavior and efficacy in relation to personality. *International Journal of Psychology,* **19,** 527–545.

Harvey, J. H., & Weary, G. (1984). Current issues in attribution theory. *Annual Review of Psychology,* **35,** 427–459.

Harvey, R. J., & Wilson, M. A. (2000). Yes Virginia, there is an objective reality in job analysis. *Journal of Organizational Behavior,* **21,** 829–854.

Hastie, R., & Park, B. (1986). The relationship between memory and judgment depends on whether the judgment task is memory-based or on-line. *Psychological Review,* **93,** 258–268.

Hastorf, A. H., & Cantril, H. (1954). They saw a game: A case study. *Journal of Abnormal and Social Psychology,* **49,** 129–134.

Hatfield, E., & Sprecher, S. (1986). *Mirror, mirror… The importance of looks in everyday life.* Albany: State University of New York Press.

Hatsukami, D. K., Stead, L. F., & Gupta, P. C. (2008). Tobacco addiction. *The Lancet,* **371,** 2027–2038.

Haugh, S. S., Hoffman, C. D., & Cowen, G. (1980). The eye of the young beholder: Sex typing of infants by young children. *Child Development, 51,* 598–600.

Havighurst, R. J. (1972). *Developmental tasks and education (3rd ed.).* New York: McKay.

Hayduk, L. A. (1983). Personal space: Where we now stand. *Psychological Bulletin,* **94,** 293–335.

Hayes, C. D. (1987). *Risking the future (Vol. 1).* Washington, DC: National Academy Press.

Hayes, J., & Allinson, C. H. (1988). Cultural differences in the learning styles of managers. *Management International Review,* **28,** 75–80.

Hayman, C. A. G., & Tulving, E. (1989). Contingent dissociation between recognition and fragment completion: The method of triangulation. *Journal of Experimental Psychology: Learning, Memory, and Cognition, 15*, 220–224.

Haynes, S. G., McMichael, A. J., & Tyroler, H. A. (1978). Survival after early and normal retirement. *Journal of Gerontology, 33*, 872–883.

Hays, K. F. (1995). Putting sports psychology into (your) practice. *Professional Psychology: Research and Practice, 26*, 33–40.

Hayward, C., Killan, J. D., Hammer, L. D., Litt, I. F., Wilson, D. M., Simmonds, B., & Taylor, C. B. (1992). Pubertal stage and panic attack history in sixth- and seventh-grade girls. *American Journal of Psychiatry, 149*, 1239–1243.

Hebb, D. O. (1955). Drives and the C.N.S. (conceptual nervous system). *Psychological Review, 62*, 243–254.

Hedges, L. V., & Newell, A. (1995). Sex differences in mental test scores, variability, and numbers of high-scoring individuals. *Science, 269*, 41–45.

Heffernan, J. A., & Albee, G. W. (1985). Prevention perspectives. *American Psychologist, 40*, 202–204.

Hegarty, J. D., Baldessarini, R. J., Tohen, M., Waternaux, C., & Oepen, G. (1994). One hundred years of schizophrenia: A meta-analysis of the outcome literature. *The American Journal of Psychiatry, 151*, 1409–1416.

Heidbreder, E. (1946). The attainment of concepts. *Journal of General Psychology, 24*, 93–108.

Heinrichs, R. W. (1993). Schizophrenia and the brain: Conditions for a neuropsychology of madness. *American Psychologist, 48*, 221–233.

——. (2005). The primacy of cognition in schizophrenia. *American Psychologist, 60*, 229-242.

Hellige, J. B. (Ed.). (1983). *Cerebral hemisphere asymmetry: Method, theory, and application.* New York: Praeger.

——. (1990). Hemispheric asymmetry. *Annual Review of Psychology, 41*, 55–80.

Helms, J. E. (1990). *Black and White racial identity: Theory, research, and practice.* New York: Greenwood Press.

——. (1992). Why is there no study of cultural equivalence in standardized cognitive ability testing? *American Psychologist, 47*, 1083–1101.

Helweg-Larsen, M., & Collins, B. E. (1997). A social psychological perspective on the role of knowledge about AIDS in AIDS prevention. *Current Directions in Psychological Science, 6*, 23–26.

Helzer, J. E., Robins, L. N., & McEnvoy, L. (1987). Posttraumatic stress disorder in the general population. *New England Journal of Medicine, 317*, 1630–1634.

Hemmingway, H., & Marmot, M. (1999). Psychosocial factors in the aetiology and prognosis of coronary heart disease: Systematic review of prospective cohort studies. *British Medical Journal, 318*, 1460–1467.

Hendrie, H. C. (1998). Epidemiology of dementia and Alzheimer disease. *American Journal of Geriatric Psychiatry, 6*, S3–S18.

——. (2001). Exploration of environmental and genetic risk factors for Alzheimer's disease: The value of cross-cultural studies. *Current Directions in Psychological Science, 10*, 98–101.

Henley, T. B., Johnson, M. G., Jones, E. M., & Herzog, H. A. (1989). Definitions of psychology. *The Psychological Record, 39*, 143–152.

Hennessey, B. A., & Amabile, T. M., (1988). The conditions of creativity. In R. J. Sternberg (Ed.), *The nature of creativity.* New York: Cambridge University Press.

Hennessy, J., & Melhuish, E. C. (1991). Early day care and the development of school-age children. *Journal of Reproduction and Infant Psychology, 9*, 117–136.

Henriksen, L., Feighery, E. C., Schleicher, N. C., Haladjian, H. H., & Fortmann, S. P. (2004). Reaching youth at the point of sale: Cigarette marketing is more prevalent in stores where adolescents shop frequently. *Tobacco Control, 13*, 315-318.

Herald, M. M., & Tomaka, J. (2002). Patterns of emotion-specific behavior, coping, and cardiovascular reactions during an ongoing emotional episode. *Journal of Personality and Social Psychology, 83*, 434-450.

Herek, G. M., & Glunt, E. K. (1988). An epidemic of stigma: Public reactions to AIDS. *American Psychologist, 43*, 886–891.

Heresco-Levy, U., Javittd, D. C., Ebstein, R., Vass, A., Lichtenberg, P., Bar, G., Catinari, S., & Ermilov, M. (2005). D-serine efficacy as add-on pharmacotherapy to risperidone and olanzapine for treatment-refractory schizophrenia. *Biological Psychiatry, 57*, 577–585.

Hergenhahn, B. R. (2001). *An introduction to the history of psychology (4th ed.).* Belmont, CA: Wadsworth.

Herlitz, A., & Yonker, J. E. (2002). Sex differences in episodic memory: The influence of intelligence. *Journal of Clinical and Experimental Neuropsychology, 24*, 107-114.

Herlitz, A., Nilsson, L. G., & Backman, L. (1997). Gender differences in episodic memory. *Memory and Cognition, 25*, 801- 811.

Hershberger, S. L. (2001). Biological factors in the development of sexual orientation. In A. D'Augelli, & C. Patterson (Eds). *Lesbian, gay, and bisexual identities and youth: Psychological perspectives.* (pp. 27-51). New York, NY, US: Oxford University Press.

Heshka, S., & Nelson, Y. (1972). Interpersonal speaking distance as a function of age, sex, and relationship. *Sociometry, 35*, 491–498.

Hesse-Biber, S. (1996). *Am I thin enough yet? The cult of thinness and the commercialization of identity.* New York: Oxford University Press.

Hetherington, E. M., & Parke, R. D. (1999). *Child Psychology: A contemporary viewpoint (Fifth Edition).* Boston: McGraw Hill.

Hew, T. D., Chorley, J. N., Cianca, J. C., & Divine, J. G. (2003). The incidence, risk factors and clinical manifestations of hypernatremia in marathon runners. *Clinical Journal of Sports Medicine, 13*, 41–47.

HHS. (2001). *Substance abuse—A national challenge: Prevention, treatment and research at HHS.* Washington, DC: U.S. Department of Health and Human Services.

——. (2002). *HHS news: 2002 monitoring the future survey shows decrease in use of marijuana, club drugs, cigarettes and tobacco.* Washington, DC: U.S. Department of Health and Human Services.

——. (2002). *Substance abuse—A national challenge: Prevention, treatment and research at HHS.* Washington, DC: U.S. Department of Health and Human Services.

Higgins, E. T, & Bargh, J. A. (1987). Social cognition and social perception. *Annual Review of Psychology*, **38**, 369–426.

Hilgard, E. R. (1975). Hypnosis. *Annual Review of Psychology*, **26**, 19–44.

——. (1978, January). Hypnosis and consciousness. *Human Nature*, pp. 42–49.

Hilgard, E. R. (1992). Divided consciousness and dissociation. *Consciousness and Cognition*, **1**, 16–31.

Hilgard, E. R., & Hilgard, J. R. (1975*). Hypnosis in the relief of pain*. Los Altos, CA: W. Kaufman.

Hill, C. A. (1997). The distinctiveness of sexual motives in relation to sexual desire and desirable partner attributes. *Journal of Sex Research*, **34**, 139–153.

Hill, C. A., & Preston, L. K. (1996). Individual differences in the experience of sexual motivation: Theory and measurement of dispositional sexual motives. *Journal of Sex Research*, **33**, 27–45.

Hill, J. O., & Peters, J. C. (1998). Environmental contributions to the obesity epidemic. *Science*, **280**, 1371–1374.

Hill, J. O., Wyatt, H. R., Reed, G. W., & Peters, J. C. (2003). Obesity and the environment: Where do we go from here? *Science*, **299**, 853–855.

Hill, W. F. (1985). *Learning: A survey of psychological interpretations (4th ed.)*. New York: HarperCollins.

Hilliard, A. G. (2001). Race, identity, hegemony, and education: What do we do now? In W. H. Watkins, J. H. Lewis, & V. Chou (Eds.), *Race and education: The roles of history and society in educating African-American students*. (pp. 7-33). Boston: Allyn & Bacon.

Hillier, L. W., Graves, T. A., Fulton, R. S., Pepin, K. H., Minx, P., et al. (2005). Generation and annotation of the DNA sequences of human chromosomes 2 and 4. *Nature*, **434**, 724-731.

Hoaken, P. N. S., Giancola, P. R., & Pihl, R. O. (1998). Executive cognitive functions as mediators of alcohol-related aggression. *Alcohol and Alcoholism*, **33**, 47–54.

Hobfoll, S. E. (1988). *The ecology of stress*. Washington, DC: Hemisphere.

Hobson, J. A. (1977). The reciprocal interaction model of sleep cycle control: Implications for PGO wave generation and dream amnesia. In R. R. Drucker-Colin & J. L. McGaugh (Eds.), *Neurobiology of sleep and memory*. New York: Academic Press.

——. (1988). *The dreaming brain*. New York: Basic Books.

——. (1988). *The dreaming brain: How the brain creates both the sense and nonsense of dreams*. New York: Basic Books.

——. (1994). *The chemistry of conscious states: How the brain changes its mind*. Boston: Little Brown.

——. (1995). *Sleep*. New York: Scientific American Library.

Hobson, J. A., & McCarley, R. W. (1977). The brain as a dream-state generator: An activation-synthesis hypothesis of the dream process. *American Journal of Psychiatry*, **134**, 1335–1368.

Hoeft, F., Watson, C. L., Kesler, S. R., Bettinger, K. E., & Reiss, A. L. (2008). Gender differences in the mesocorticolimbic system during computer game play. *Journal of Psychiatric Research*, *42*, 252–258.

Hoek, H. W. (1995). The distribution of eating disorders. In K. D. Brownell & C. G. Fairburn (Eds.), *Eating disorders: A comprehensive handbook*. New York: Guilford Press.

Hoeksema-van Orden, C. Y. D., Gaillard, A. W. K., & Buunk, B. (1998). Social loafing under fatigue. *Journal of Personality and Social Psychology*, **75**, 1179–1190.

Hofferth, S. L., & Hayes, C. D. (Eds.). (1987). *Risking the future: Adolescent sexuality, pregnancy, and childbearing*. Washington, DC: National Academy Press.

Hoffman, L. W. (2003). Methodological issues in studies of SES, parenting, and child development. In M. H. Bornstein & R. H. Bradley (Eds.), *Socioeconomic status, parenting, and child development* (pp. 125-143). Hillsdale, NJ: Erlbaum.

Hoffmann, R. F. (1978). Developmental changes in human infant visual-evoked potentials to patterned stimuli recorded at different scalp locations. *Child Development*, **49**, 110–118.

Hofman, W., Gschwendner, T, Castelli, L., & Schmitt, M. (2008). Implicit and explicit attitudes and interracial interaction: The moderating role of situationally available control resources. *Group Processes & Intergroup Relations*, **11**, 69–87.

Hogan, J. (1989). Personality correlates of physical fitness. *Journal of Personality and Social Psychology*, **56**, 284–288.

Hogan, R., & Nicholson, R. A. (1988). The meaning of personality test scores. *American Psychologist*, **43**, 621–626.

Hogan, R., & Roberts, B. W. (2004). A socioanalytic model of maturity. *Journal of Career Assessment*, **12**, 207-217.

Hogg, M. A., & Hains, S. C. (1998). Friendship and group identification: a new look at the role of cohesiveness in groupthink. *European Journal of Social Psychology*, **28**, 323-341.

Hohlstein, L. A., Smith, G. T., & Atlas, J. G. (1998). An application of expectancy theory to eating disorders: Development and validation of measures of eating and dieting expectancies. *Psychological Assessment*, **10**, 49–58.

Hollander, E., DeCaria, C. M., Nitescu, A., Gully, R., Suckow, R. F., et al. (1992). Serotonergic function in obsessive-compulsive disorder. *Archives of General Psychiatry*, **49**, 21–28.

Hollingworth, L. S. (1914). Variability as related to sex differences in achievement: A critique. Retrieved May 6, 2008 from http://psychclassics.yorku.ca/ Hollingworth/sexdiffs.htm.

Hollis, J. F., Connett, J. E., Stevens, V. J., & Greenlick, M. R. (1990). Stressful life events, Type A behavior, and the prediction of cardiovascular and total mortality over six years. *Journal of Behavioral Medicine*, **13**, 263–281.

Hollis, K. L. (1997). Contemporary research on Pavlovian conditioning: A "new" functional analysis. *American Psychologist*, **52**, 956–965.

Hollon, S. D., DeRubeis, R. J., Shelton, R. C., Amsterdam, J. D., Salomon, R. M., O'Reardon, J. P., et al. (2005). Prevention of relapse following cognitive therapy vs medications in moderate to severe depression. *Archives of General Psychiatry*, **62**, 417-422.

Hollon, S. D., Shelton, R. C., & Loosen, P. T. (1991). Cognitive therapy and pharmacotherapy for depression. *Journal of Consulting and Clinical Psychology*, **59**, 88–99.

Hollon, S. D., Thase, M. E., & Markowitz, J. C. (2002). Treatment and prevention of depression. *Psychological Science in the Public Interest: A Supplement to Psychological Science, 3,* 38–77.

Holman, B. L., & Tumeh, S. S. (1990). Single-photon emission computed tomography (SPECT): Applications and potential. *Journal of the American Medical Association, 263,* 561–564.

Holmes, C., Bosche, D., Wilkinson, D., Yadegarfar, G., Hopkins, V., Bayer, A., Jones, R. W., Bullock, R. Love, S., et al. (2008). Long-term effects of Aβ$_{42}$ immunisation in Alzheimer's disease: Follow-up of a randomized, placebo-controlled phase I trial. *The Lancet, 372,* 216–223.

Holmes, D. (1994). *Abnormal psychology (2nd ed.).* New York: HarperCollins.

Holmes, D. S. (1984). Meditation and somatic arousal reduction: A review of the experimental evidence. *American Psychologist, 39,* 1–10.

——. (1985). To meditate or simply rest, that is the question: A response to the comments of Shapiro. *American Psychologist, 40,* 722–725.

——. (1987). The influence of meditation versus rest on physiological arousal: A second examination. In M. West (Ed.), *The psychology of meditation.* Oxford: Oxford University Press.

——. (2001). *Abnormal psychology, Fourth Edition,* (p. 239). Boston: Allyn & Bacon.

Holmes, T. S., & Holmes, T. H. (1970). Short-term intrusions into the life-style routine. *Journal of Psychosomatic Research, 14,* 121–132.

Holyoak, K. J., & Spellman, B. A. (1993). Thinking. *Annual Review of Psychology, 44,* 265–315.

Hood, R. D. (1990). Paternally mediated effects. In R. D. Hood (Ed.), *Developmental toxicology: Risk assessment and the future.* New York: Van Nostrand Reinhold.

Hoppock, R. (1935). *Job satisfaction.* New York: HarperCollins.

Horn, J., & Anderson, K. (1993). Who in America is trying to lose weight? *Annals of Internal Medicine, 119,* 672–676.

Horn, J. L. (1976). Human abilities: A review of research and theories in the early 1970s. *Annual Review of Psychology, 27,* 437–485.

——. (1982). The aging of human abilities. In J. Wolman, (Ed.), *Handbook of developmental psychology.* Englewood Cliffs, NJ: Prentice-Hall.

——. (1985). Remodeling old models of intelligence. In B. B. Wolman (Ed.), *Handbook of intelligence.* New York: Wiley.

Horn, J. L., & Cattell, R. B. (1966). Refinement and test of the theory of fluid and crystallized intelligence. *Journal of Educational Psychology, 57,* 253–276.

Horne, J. A. (1988). *Why we sleep: The function of sleep in humans and other mammals.* Oxford: Oxford University Press.

Horner, M. S. (1969). Women's will to fail. *Psychology Today, 3,* 36.

Horowitz, F. D., & O'Brien, M. (Eds.). (1985). *The gifted and talented: Developmental perspectives.* Washington, DC: American Psychological Association.

Horowitz, I. A., & Bordens, K. S. (1995). *Social psychology.* Mountain View, CA: Mayfield Publishing Company.

Hostetler, A. J. (1987). Alzheimer's trials hinge on early diagnosis. *APA Monitor, 18,* 14–15.

Hough, L. M., & Oswald, F. L. (2000). Personnel selection. *Annual Review of Psychology, 51,* 631–664.

Houston, B. K., & Vavak, C. R. (1991). Cynical hostility: Developmental factors, psycho-social correlates, and health behaviors. *Health Psychology, 10,* 9–17.

Houston, J. P. (1986). *Fundamentals of learning and memory (3rd ed.).* New York: Harcourt Brace Jovanovich.

Houston, L. N. (1990). *Psychological principles and the black experience.* New York: University Press of America.

Hovland, C. I., & Weiss, W. (1951). The influence of source credibility on communication effectiveness. *Public Opinion Quarterly, 15,* 635–650.

Hovland, C. I., Janis, I. L., & Kelley, H. H. (1953). *Persuasion and communication.* New Haven, CT: Yale University Press.

Howard, K. I., Kopata, S. M., Krause, M. S., & Orlinsky, D. E. (1986). The dose-effect relationship in psychotherapy. *American Psychologist, 41,* 159–164.

Howe, M. L. (2000). *The fate of early memories: Developmental science and the retention of childhood experiences.* Washington, DC: American Psychological Association.

——. (2003). Memories from the cradle. *Current Directions in Psychological Science, 12,* 62–65.

Howell, W. C., & Dipboye, R. L. (1982). *Essentials of industrial and organizational psychology.* Homewood, IL: Dorsey Press.

Howes, C. (1990). Can the age of entry into child care and the quality of child care predict adjustment in kindergarten? *Developmental Psychology, 26,* 292–303.

Hubel, D. H., & Wiesel, T. N. (1979). Brain mechanisms of vision. *Scientific American, 241,* 150–162.

Hudson, W. (1960). Pictorial depth perception in subcultural groups in Africa. *Journal of Social Psychology, 52,* 183-208.

Hudspeth, A. J. (1997). How hearing happens. *Neuron, 19,* 947–950.

Huesmann, L. R. (1986). Psychological processes promoting the relationship between exposure to media violence and aggression. *Journal of Social Issues, 42,* 125–139.

Huesmann, L. R., & Malamuth, N. (1986). Media violence and antisocial behavior: An overview. *Journal of Social Issues, 42,* 1–6.

Hughes, F. P., & Noppe, L. D. (1985). *Human development.* St. Paul, MN: West.

Hughes, J., Smith, T. W., Kosterlitz, H. W., Fothergill, L. A., Morgan, G. A., & Morris, H. R. (1975). Identification of two related peptides from the brain with potent opiate agonist activity. *Nature, 258,* 577–579.

Hughes, J. R., Gust, S. W., & Pechacek, T. F. (1987). Prevalence of tobacco dependence and withdrawal. *American Journal of Psychiatry, 144,* 205–208.

Hugick, L., & Leonard, J. (1991). Despite increasing hostility, one in four Americans still smokes. *Gallup Poll Monthly, 315,* 2–10.

Hui, C. H. (1990). Work attitudes, leadership styles, and managerial behaviors in different cultures. In R. W. Brislin (Ed.), *Applied cross-cultural psychology*. Newbury Park, CA: Sage.

Hulin, C. L., & Smith, P. C. (1964). Sex differences in job satisfaction. *Journal of Applied Psychology*, **48**, 88–92.

Hull, C. L. (1943). *Principles of behavior*. Englewood Cliffs, NJ: Prentice-Hall.

Hultsch, D., Hertzog, C., Small, B., & Dixon, R. (1999). Use it or lose it: Engaged lifestyle as a buffer of cognitive decline in aging? *Psychology and Aging*, **14**, 245–263.

Hunt, E., & Carlson, J. (2007). Considerations relating to the study of group differences in intelligence. *Perspectives on Psychological Science*, **2**, 194–213.

Hunt, M. (1987, August 30). Navigating the therapy maze. *The New York Times Magazine*, pp. 28–31, 37, 44, 46, 49.

Hunter, J. E. (1986). Cognitive ability, cognitive aptitudes, job knowledge, and job performance. *Journal of Vocational Behavior*, **29**, 340–362.

Hunter, J. E., & Hunter, R. F. (1984). Validity and utility of alternative predictors of job performance. *Psychological Bulletin*, **96**, 72–98.

Hunter, S., & Sundel, M. (Eds.). (1989). *Midlife myths*. Newbury Park, CA: Sage.

Huselid, R. F., & Cooper, M. L. (1992). Gender roles as mediators of sex differences in adolescent alcohol use and abuse. *Journal of Health and Social Behavior*, **33**, 348-362.

Huston, A. C. (1985). The development of sex-typing: Themes from recent research. *Developmental Review*, **5**, 1–17.

Hyde, J. S. (1984). How large are gender differences in aggression? A developmental meta-analysis. *Developmental Psychology*, **20**, 697–706.

——. (1986). *Understanding human sexuality (3rd ed.)*. New York: McGraw-Hill.

——. (1994a). *Understanding human sexuality (5th ed.)*. New York: McGraw-Hill.

——. (1994b). Can meta-analysis make feminist transformations in psychology? *Psychology of Women Quarterly*, **18**, 451–462.

——. (2005). The gender similarities hypothesis. *American Psychologist*, **60**, 581–592.

Hyde, J. S., Lindberg, S. M., Linn, M. C., Ellis, A. B., & Williams, C. C. (2008). Diversity: Gender similarities characterize math performance. *Science*, **321**, 494–495.

Hyland, A., Bauer, J. E., Li, Q., Abrams, S. M., Higbee, C., Peppone, L., & Cummings, K. M. (2005). Higher cigarette prices influence cigarette purchase patterns. *Tobacco Control*, **14**, 86-92.

Iacono, W. G., & Grove, W. M. (1993). Schizophrenia reviewed: Toward an integrative genetic model. *Psychological Science*, **4**, 273–276.

Iaffaldano, M. T., & Muchinsky, P. M. (1985). Job satisfaction and job performance: A meta-analysis. *Psychological Bulletin*, **97**, 251–273.

Iervolino, A. C., Hines, M., Golomok, S. E., Rust, J., & Plomin, R. (2005). Genetic and environmental influences on sex-typed behavior during the preschool years. *Child Development, 76*, 826–840.

Ilgen, D. R., & Klein, H. J. (1989). Organizational behavior. *Annual Review of Psychology*, **40**, 327–351.

Impett, E., & Peplau, L. A. (2003). Sexual compliance: Gender, motivational, and relationship perspectives. *Journal of Sex Research*, **40**, 87–100.

Infante-Rivard, C., Fernandez, A., Gauthier, R., David, M., & Rivard, G. (1993). Fetal loss associated with caffeine intake before and during pregnancy. *Journal of the American Medical Association*, **270**, 2940–2943.

Irvine, J., Garner, D. M., Craig, H. M., & Logan, A. G. (1991). Prevalence of Type A behavior in untreated hypertensive individuals. *Hypertension*, **18**, 72–78.

Isabella, R. A., & Belsky, J. (1991). Interactional synchrony and the origins of inant-mother attachments: A replication study. *Child Development*, **62**, 373–384.

Isen, A. M. (1999). Positive affect and creativity. In S. Russ (Ed.), *Affect, creative experience, and psychological adjustment*. Philadelphia: Bruner/Mazel.

Isenberg, D. J. (1986). Group polarization: A critical review and meta-analysis. *Journal of Personality and Social Psychology*, **50**, 1141–1151.

Iso-Ahola, S. E., & Blanchard, W. J. (1986). Psychological momentum and competitive sport performance: A field study. *Perceptual and Motor Skills*, **62**, 763–768.

Istvan, J. (1986). Stress, anxiety, and birth outcomes: A critical review of the evidence. *Psychological Bulletin*, **100**, 331–348.

Itika, P. R., Watkins, M. L., Mulinare, J., Moore, C. A., & Liu, Y. (2001). Maternal multivitamin use and oralfacial clefts in offspring. *Teratology*, **63**, 79–86.

Ito, T. A., Miller, N., & Pollack, V. E. (1996). A meta-analysis on the moderating effects of inhibitory cues, triggering events, and self-focused attention. *Psychological Bulletin*, **120**, 60–82.

Izard, C. E. (1972). *Patterns of emotion: A new analysis of anxiety and aggression*. New York: Academic Press.

——. (1993). Four systems for emotional activation: Cognitive and metacognitive processes. *Psychological Review*, **100**, 68–90.

Izard, C. E. (2007). Basic emotions, natural kinds, emotion schemas, and a new paradigm. *Perspectives in Psychological Science*, **2**, 260–280.

Jackaway, R., & Teevan, R. (1976). Fear of failure and fear of success: Two dimensions of the same motive. *Sex Roles*, **2**, 283–294.

Jacklin, C. N. (1989). Female and male: Issues of gender. *American Psychologist*, **44**, 27–133.

Jacklin, C. N., & Maccoby, E. E. (1978). Social behavior at 33 months in same-sex and mixed-sex dyads. *Child Development*, **49**, 557–569.

Jackson, D. N., & Rushton, J. P. (2005). Males have greater *g*: Sex differences in general mental ability from 100,000 17- to 18-year-olds on the Scholastic Assessment Test. *Intelligence*, **34**, 479–486.

Jackson, S. A. (2000). Joy, fun, and flow state in sport. In Y. L. Hanin (Ed.)., *Emotions in sport.* Champaign, IL: Human Kinetics.

Jacob, S., McClintock, M. K., Zelano, B., & Ober, C. (2002). Paternally inherited HLA alleles are associated with women's choice of male odor. *Nature Genetics, 30,* 175-179.

Jacobs, B. L. (1987). How hallucinogenic drugs work. *American Scientist, 75,* 386–392.

——. (2004). Depression: The brain finally gets into the act. *Current Directions in Psychological Science, 13,* 103-106.

Jacobs, B. L., & Trulson, M. E. (1979). Mechanisms of action of LSD. *American Scientist, 67,* 396–404.

Jacobson, D. S. (1984). Neonatal correlates of prenatal exposure to smoking, caffeine, and alcohol. *Infant Behavior and Development, 7,* 253–265.

Jacobson, N. S. & Christensen, A. (1996). Studying the effectiveness of psychotherapy: How well can clinical trials do the job? *American Psychologist, 51,* 1031–1039.

Jacoby, L. L., & Dallas, M. (1981). On the relationship between autobiographical memory and perceptual learning. *Journal of Experimental Psychology: General, 3,* 306–340.

Jaffe, M. L. (1998). *Adolescence.* New York: John Wiley & Sons.

James, L. (1998a). *Dr. Driving's world road rage survey: USA & Canada men/women contrasts* [On-line]. Available: http://www.aloha.net/~dyc/surveys/mf.html.

——. (1998b). *Dr. Driving's world road rage survey: USA & Canada age contrasts* [On-line]. Available: http://www.aloha.net/~dyc/survey/age.html.

——. (1998c). *Principles of Driving Psychology (Chapter 11).* [On-line]. Available: http://www.aloha.net/~dyc/ch11.thml.

——. (1998d). *Congressional testimony by Dr. Leon James* [On-line]. Available: http://www.aloha.net/~dyc/testimony.html#Heading5.

James, W. (1884). *What is an emotion?* Downloaded on October 14, 2005 from http://psychclassics.yorku.ca/james/emotion.htm,

——. (1890). *Principles of psychology.* New York: Holt, Rinehart & Winston.

——. (1892). *Psychology: Briefer course.* New York: Holt, Rinehart & Winston.

——. (1904). Does consciousness exist? *Journal of Philosophy, 1,* 477–491.

Jameson, K. A., Highnote, S. M., & Wasserman, L. M. (2001). Richer color experience in observers with multiple opsin genes. *Psychonomic Bulletin and Review, 8,* 244-261.

Jang, K. L., Livesley, W. J., & Vernon, P. (1996). Heritability of the big five personality dimensions and their facets: A twin study. *Journal of Personality, 64,* 577–591.

Janis, I. L. (1972). *Victims of groupthink.* Boston: Houghton Mifflin.

——. (1983a). *Groupthink: Psychological studies of policy decisions and fiascoes (2nd ed.).* Boston: Houghton Mifflin.

——. (1983b). The role of social support in adherence to stressful decisions. *American Psychologist, 38,* 143–160.

Janoff-Bulman, R. (1979). Characterological versus behavioral self-blame: Inquiries into depression and rape. *Journal of Personality and Social Psychology, 37,* 1798–1809.

Janssen, E., & Everaerd, W. (1993). Determinants of male sexual arousal. *Annual Review of Sex Research, 24,* 211–245.

Jaroff, L. (1993). Lies of the mind. *Time,* November 29, 52–59.

Jastrow, J. (1897). The popular aesthetics of color. *Popular Science Monthly, 50,* 361-368.

Jeanneret, P. R., Andberg, M. M., Camara, W. J., Denning, D. L., Kehoe, J. F., Sackett, P. R., Tippins, N. T., et al. (2003). *Principles for the validation and use of personnel selection procedures.* Bowling Green, OH: The Society for Industrial and Organizational Psychology.

Jemal, A., Murray, T., Samuels, A., Ghafoor, A., Ward, E., & Thun, M. J. (2003). Cancer statistics: 2003. *CA: A Cancer Journal for Clinicians, 53,* 5-26.

Jenike, M. A., Baer, L., Ballentine, H. T., Martuza, R. L., Tynes, S., Giriunas, L., Buttolph, M. L., & Cassem, N. H. (1991). Cingulotomy for refractory obsessive-compulsive disorder: A long-term follow-up of 33 patients. *Archives of General Psychiatry, 48,* 548–555.

Jenkins, C. D. (1976). Recent evidence supporting psychological and social risk factors for coronary disease. *New England Journal of Medicine, 294,* 1033–1038.

Jenkins, J. G., & Dallenbach, K. M. (1924). Oblivescence during sleep and waking. *American Journal of Psychology, 35,* 605–612.

Jessor, R. (1993). Successful adolescent development among youth in high-risk settings. *American Psychologist, 48,* 117–126.

Jo, E. (1994). Combining physical sensations and ideas in the construction of emotional experiences. *Dissertation Abstracts International Section B: The Sciences and Engineering, 54(7-B),* 3900.

Jobe, T. H., & Harrow, M. (2005). Long-term outcomes of patients with schizophrenia: A review. *Canadian Journal of Psychiatry, 50,* 892–900.

Johansson, P., Kerr, M., & Andershed, H. (2005). Linking adult psychopathy with childhood hyperactivity-impulsivity-attention problems and conduct problems through retrospective self-reports. *Journal of Personality Disorders, 19,* 94-101.

John, O. P., & Srivastava, S. (1999). The big five trait taxonomy: History, measurement, and theoretical perspectives. In L. A. Pervin & O. P. John (Eds.), *Handbook of personality.* (pp. 102-138). New York: Guilford Press.

Johns, G. (1997). Contemporary research on absence from work: Correlates, causes, and consequences. In C. L. Cooper & I. T. Robertson (Eds.), *International review of industrial and organizational psychology (Vol. 12).* Chichester, UK: Wiley.

Johns, M., Schmader., T., & Martens, A. (2005). Knowing is half the battle: Teaching stereotype threat as a means of improving women's math performance. *Psychological Science, 16,* 175–179.

Johnson, E. H. (1978). Validation of concept-learning strategies. *Journal of Experimental Psychology, 107,* 237–265.

Johnson, J., Weissman, M. M., & Klerman, G. L. (1990). Panic disorder, comorbidity, and suicide attempts. *Archives of General Psychiatry, 47,* 805–808.

Johnson, L., Bachman, J., & O'Malley, P. (1997). *Monitoring the future*. Ann Arbor, MI: Institute for Social Research.

Johnson, M. K., & Hasher, L. (1987). Human learning and memory. *Annual Review of Psychology, 38*, 631–668.

Johnson, N., Davis, T., & Bosanquet, N. (2000). The epidemic of Alzheimer's disease: How can we manage the costs? *Pharmoeconomics, 18*, 215–223.

Johnson, R. L., Saha, S., Arbelaez, J. J., Beach, M. C., & Cooper, L. A. (2004). Racial and ethnic differences in patient perceptions of bias and cultural competence in health care. *Journal of General Internal Medicine, 19*, 101-110.

Joint statement on the impact of entertainment violence on children: Congressional Public Health Summit. (2000, July 26). Retrieved July 1, 2003 from http://www.senate.gov/~brownback/violence1.pdf.

Jones, E. E. (1979). The rocky road from acts to dispositions. *American Psychologist, 34*, 107–117.

——. (1990). *Interpersonal perception*. New York: Macmillan.

Jones, E. E., & Nisbett, R. E. (1971). *The actor and the observer: Divergent perceptions of behavior*. Morristown, NJ: General Learning Press.

Jones, K. L., Smith, D. W., Ulleland, C. N., & Streissgoth, A. P. (1973). Patterns of malformation in offspring of chronic alcoholic mothers. *Lancet, 3*, 1267–1271.

Jones, M. C. (1924). A laboratory study of fear: The case of Peter. *Pedagogical Seminary, 31*, 308–315.

——. (1957). The careers of boys who were early or late maturing. *Child Development, 28*, 113–128.

Jonides, J., Lacey, S. C., & Nee, D. E. (2005). Processes of working memory in mind and brain. *Current Directions in Psychological Science, 14*, 2-5.

Jonides, J., Lewis, R. L., Nee, D. E., Lustig, C. A., Berman, M. G., & Moore, K. S. (2008). The mind and brain of short-term memory. *Annual Review of Psychology, 59*, 193–224.

Jordan, B. K., Marmar, C. R., Fairbank, J. A., Schlenger, W. E., Kulka, R. A., Hough, R. L., & Weiss, D. S. (1992). Problems in families of male Vietnam veterans with posttraumatic stress disorder. *Journal of Consulting and Clinical Psychology, 60*, 916–926.

Jordan, J., Kaplan, A., Miller, J., Striver, I., & Surrey, J. (1991). *Women's growth in connection*. New York: Guilford.

Journal of the American Medical Association (1995). Editorial. *The Brown and Williamson Documents: Where do we go from here?* July 19, 274, 256–258.

Joyce, P. R., & Paykel, E. S. (1989). Predictors of drug response in depression. *Archives of General Psychiatry, 46*, 89–99.

Juengst, E., & Fossel, M. (2000). The ethics of embryonic stem cells; now and forever—cells without end. *Journal of the American Medical Association, 284*, 3180–3184.

Julien, R. M. (1988). *A primer of drug addiction (5th ed.)*. New York: Freeman.

——. (1995). *A primer of drug action, (7th ed.)*. New York: W. H. Freeman.

Jussim, L., Nelson, T. E., Manis, M., & Soffin, S. (1995). Prejudice, stereotypes, and labeling effects: Sources of bias in person perception. *Journal of Personality and Social Psychology, 68*, 228–246.

Kacmar, K. M., & Ferris, G. R. (1989). Theoretical and methodological considerations in the age-job satisfaction relationship. *Journal of Applied Psychology, 74*, 201–207.

Kagan, J. (1988). The meanings of personality predicates. *American Psychologist, 43*, 614–620.

Kagan, J., Resnick, J. S., & Snidman, N. (1988). Biological bases of childhood shyness. *Science, 240*, 167–171.

Kagan, S. (1986). Cooperative learning and sociocultural factors in schooling. In California Department of Education. *Beyond language: Social and cultural factors in schooling language minority students* (pp. 231-298). Los Angeles: Evaluation, Dissemination, and Assessment.

Kahane, P., Hoffman, D., Minotti, L., & Berthoz, A. (2003). Reappraisal of the human vestibular cortex by cortical electrical stimulation. *Annals of Neurology, 54*, 615-624.

Kahn, D. A. (1995). New strategies in bipolar disorder: Part II. Treatment. *Journal of Practical Psychiatry and Behavioral Health, 3*, 148–157.

Kahn, R. S., Fleishhacker, W. W., Boter, H., Davidson, M., Vergouwe, Y., Keet, I. P. M., Gheorghe, M. D., Rybakowski, J. K., et al. (2008). Effectiveness of antipsychotic drugs in first-episode schizophrenia and schizophreniform disorder: An open randomized clinical trial. *The Lancet, 371*, 1085–1097.

Kahn, S., Zimmerman, G., Csikzentmihalyi, M., & Getzels, J. W. (1985). Relations between identity in young adulthood and intimacy at midlife. *Journal of Personality and Social Psychology, 49*, 1316–1322.

Kahneman, D., & Tversky, A. (1973). On the psychology of prediction. *Psychological Review, 80*, 237–251.

——. (1979). On the interpretation of intuitive probability: A reply to Jonathan Cohen. *Cognition, 7*, 409–411.

——. (1984). Choices, values, and frames. *American Psychologist, 39*, 341–350.

Kalat, J. W. (1984). *Biological psychology (2nd ed.)*. Belmont, CA: Wadsworth.

Kalish, R. A. (1982). *Late adulthood: Perspectives on human development*. Monterey, CA: Brooks/Cole.

——. (1985). The social context of death and dying. In R. H. Binstock & E. Shanas (Eds.), *Handbook of aging and the social sciences (Second Edition)*. New York: Van Nostrand-Reinhold.

Kallgren, C. A., Reno, R. R., & Cialdini, R. B. (2000). A focus theory of normative conduct: When norms do and do not affect behavior. *Personality and Social Psychology Bulletin, 26*, 1002–1012.

Kaltiala-Heino, R., Kosunen, E., & Rimpela, M. (2003). Pubertal timing, sexual behaviour and self-reported depression in middle adolescence. *Journal of Adolescence, 26*, 531–545.

Kalven, H., & Zeisel, H. (1966). *The American jury*. Boston: Little Brown.

Kamin, L. (1968). Attention-like processes in classical conditioning. In M. Jones (Ed.), *Miami symposium on the prediction of behavior: Aversive stimulation*. Miami: University of Miami Press.

——. (1969). Predictability, surprise, attention, and conditioning. In R. Church & B. Campbell (Eds.), *Punishment and aversion behaviors*. Englewood Cliffs, NJ: Prentice-Hall.

Kamiya, J., Barber, T. X., Miller, N. E., Shapiro, D., & Stoyva, J. (1977). *Biofeedback and self-control*. Chicago: Aldine.

Kanazawa, S. (2001). Why father absence might precipitate early menarch: The role of polygyny. *Evolution and Human Behavior*, **22**, 329-334.

Kane, J. (1989). The current status of neuroleptics. *Journal of Clinical Psychiatry*, **50**, 322–328.

Kann, L., Kinchen, S. A., Williams, B. I., Ross, J. G., Lowry, R., Grunbaum, J. A., & Kolbe, L. J. (2000). Youth risk behavior surveillance: United States, 1999. *Morbidity and Mortality Weekly*, **49**, 1-104.

Kanner, A. D., Coyne, J. C., Schaefer, C., & Lazarus, R. S. (1981). Comparison of two modes of stress measurement: Daily hassles and uplifts versus major life events. *Journal of Behavioral Medicine*, **4**, 1–39.

Kanner, L. (1943). Autistic disturbances of affective contact. *Nervous Child*, **2**, 217–250.

Kaplan, G. M. (1991). The use of biofeedback in the treatment of chronic facial tics: A case study. *Medical Psychotherapy*, **4**, 71–84.

Kaplan, H. S. (1974*). The new sex therapy: Active treatment of sexual dysfunction*. New York: Quadrangle.

——. (1975). *The illustrated manual of sex therapy*. New York: Quadrangle.

Kaplan, H. S., & Sadock, B. J. (1991). *Synopsis of psychiatry*. Baltimore: Williams & Wilkins.

Kaplan, R. M. (1984). The connection between clinical health promotion and health status. *American Psychologist*, **39**, 755–765.

Kaplan, R. M., & Saccuzzo, D. P. (1989). *Psychological testing (2nd ed.)*. Monterey, CA: Brooks/Cole.

——. (2001). *Psychological testing: Principles, applications, and issues (5th edition)*. Belmont, CA: Wadsworth.

Kaplan, S. (1987). Aesthetics, affect and cognition: Environmental preference from an evolutionary perspective. *Environment and Behavior*, **19**, 3–32.

Kaplowitz, P. B. (2008). Link between body fat and the timing of puberty. *Pediatrics*, **121**, S208–S211.

Karnath, B. (2002). Smoking cessation. *The American Journal of Medicine*, **112**, 399–405.

Karney, B. R., & Bradbury, T. N. (1995). The longitudinal course of marital quality and stability: A review of theory, method, and research. *Psychological Review*, **118**, 3–34.

Karou, S. J., & Williams, K. D. (1993). Social loafing: A meta-analytic review and theoretical integration. *Journal of Personality and Social Psychology*, **65**, 681–706.

Karoum, F., Karson, C. N., Bigelow, L. B., Lawson, W. B., & Wyatt, R. J. (1987). Preliminary evidence of reduced combined output of dopamine and its metabolites in chronic schizophrenia. *Archives of General Psychiatry*, **44**, 604–607.

Kassin, S. M., Ellsworth, P. C., & Smith, V. L. (1989). The "general acceptance" of psychological research on eyewitness testimony: A survey of experts. *American Psychologist*, **44**, 1089–1098.

Kassin, S. M., Reddy, M. E., & Tulloch, W. G. (1990). Juror interpretations of ambiguous evidence: The need for cognition, presentation order, and persuasion. *Law and Human Behavior*, **14**, 43–56.

Kassin, S. M., Tubb, V. A., Hosch, H. M., & Memon, A. (2001). On the "general acceptance" of eyewitness testimony research: A new survey of the experts. *American Psychologist*, **56**, 405–416.

Kastenbaum, R., & Costa, P. (1977). Psychological perspectives on death. *Annual Review of Psychology*, **28**, 225–249.

Katerndahl, D. A., & Realini, J. P. (1995). Where do panic attack sufferers seek care? *Journal of Family Practice*, **40**, 237–243.

Kato, C., Petronis, A., Okazaki, Y., Tochigi, M., Umekage, T., & Sasaki, T. (2002). Molecular genetic studies of schizophrenia: Challenges and insights. *Neuroscience Research*, **43**, 295-304.

Katzell, R. A., & Thompson, D. E. (1990). Work motivation: Theory and practice. *American Psychologist*, **45**, 144–153.

Katzman, R. (1987). Alzheimer's disease. *New England Journal of Medicine*, **314**, 964–973.

Kaufmann, W. E., & Reiss, A. L. (1999). Molecular and cellular genetics of fragile X syndrome. *American Journal of Medical Genetics*, **88**, 11–24.

Kaya, N., & Weber, M. J. (2003). Cross-cultural differences in the perception of crowding and privacy regulation: American and Turkish students. *Journal of Environmental Psychology*, **23**, 301–309.

Kaye, W. (2008). Neurobiology of anorexia and bulimia nervosa. *Physiology and Behavior*, **94**, 121–135.

Kazdin, A. E., & Benjet, C. (2003). Spanking children: Evidence and issues. *Current Directions in Psychological Science*, **12**, 99–103.

Kazdin, A. E. & Mazurick, J. L. (1994). Dropping out of child psychotherapy: Distinguishing early and late dropouts over the course of treatment. *Journal of Consulting and Clinical Psychology*, **62**, 1069-1074.

Kazdin, A. E., Esveldt-Dawson, K., French, N. H., & Unis, A. S. (1987). Problem-solving skills training and relationship therapy in the treatment of antisocial child behavior. *Journal of Consulting and Clinical Psychology*, **55**, 76–85.

Keating, D. P. (1980). Thinking processes in adolescents. In J. Adelson (Ed.), *Handbook of adolescent psychology*. New York: Wiley.

Keck, P. (2001). *"Update on treatment advances in bipolar disorder."* Presented at the Fourth Annual Symposium sponsored by NARSAD, the National Alliance for Research on Schizophrenia and Depression. January 20, Sarasota, FL.

Keefe, F. J., Abernathy, A. P., & Campbell, L. C. (2005). Psychological approaches to understanding and treating disease-related pain. *Annual Review of Psychology*, **56**, 601-630.

Keefe, F. J., & France, C. R. (1999). Pain: Biopsychosocial mechanisms and management. *Current Directions in Psychological Science*, **8**, 137-140.

Keefe, J. W. (1979). *Learning style overview, student learning style; Diagnosing and prescribing programs*. Reston, VA: National Association of Secondary School Principals.

Keefe, S. J., Abernethy, A. P., & Campbell, L. C. (2004). Psychological approaches to understanding and treating disease-related pain. *Annual Review of Psychology*, **56**, 601-630.

Keesey, R. E., & Powley, T. L. (1975). Hypothalamic regulation of body weight. *American Scientist*, **63**, 558–565.

——. (1986). The regulation of body weight. *Annual Review of Psychology*, **37**, 109–133.

Keeton, B. (2003). Identity crisis. *The Health Psychologist*, **25**, 4.

Kelley, H. H. (1967). Attribution theory in social psychology. In D. Levine (Ed.), *Nebraska symposium on motivation*. Lincoln: University of Nebraska Press.

——. (1973). The process of causal attribution. *American Psychologist*, **28**, 107–128.

——. (1992). Common-sense psychology and scientific psychology. *Annual Review of Psychology*, **43**, 1–24.

Kelley, H. H., & Thibault, J. W. (1978). *Interpersonal relations: A theory of interdependence*. New York: Wiley.

Kelley, K. (1985). Sex, sex guilt, and authoritarianism: Differences in responses to explicit heterosexual and masturbatory slides. *The Journal of Sex Research*, **21**, 68–85.

Kelly, G. A. (1964). Man's construction of his alternatives. In E. A. Southwell & M. Merbaum (Eds.), *Personality: Readings in theory and research*. Belmont, CA: Wadsworth.

Kelly, G. F. (1995). *Sexuality today: The human perspective*. Madison, WI: Brown & Benchmark.

Kelly, J. A., Kalichman, S. C., Kauth, M. R., Kilgore, H. G., Hood, H. V., et al. (1991). Situational factors associated with AIDS risk behavior lapses and coping strategies used by gay men who successfully avoid lapses. *American Journal of Public Health*, **81**, 1335–1338.

Kelly, J. A., Murphy, D. A., Sikkema, K. J., & Kalichman, S. C. (1993). Psychological interventions to prevent HIV infection are urgently needed. *American Psychologist*, **48**, 1023–1034.

Kelly, J. A., & St. Lawrence, J. S. (1988). *The AIDS health crisis*. New York: Plenum.

Kelly, J. A., St. Lawrence, J. S., Hood, H. V., & Brasfield, T. L. (1989). Behavior intervention to reduce AIDS risk activities. *Journal of Consulting and Clinical Psychology*, **57**, 60–67.

Kelly, J. R., Jackson, J. W., & Huston-Comeaux, S. L. (1997). The effects of time pressure and task differences on influence modes and accuracy in decision-making groups. *Personality and Social Psychology Bulletin*, **23**, 10–22.

Kelner, K., & Helmuth, L. (2003). Obesity—what is to be done? *Science*, **299**, 845.

Kemper, K. A., Sargent, R. C., Drane, J. W., Valois, R. F., & Hussey, J. R. (1994). Black and white females' perceptions of ideal body size and social norms. *Obesity Research*, **2**, 117-126.

Kempermann, G. (2002). Why new neurons? Possible functions for adult hippocampal neurogenesis. *Journal of Neuroscience*, **22**, 635–638.

Kempermann, G., & Gage, F. H. (1999). New nerve cells for the adult brain. *Scientific American*, **280**, 48-53 (May).

Kendall, P. C., & Clarkin, J. F. (1992). Introduction to special section: Comorbidity and treatment implications. *Journal of Consulting and Clinical Psychology*, **60**, 833–834.

Kendler, K. S., & Gruenberg, A. M. (1982). Genetic relationship between paranoid personality disorder and the "schizophrenic" spectrum disorders. *American Journal of Psychiatry*, **139**, 1185–1186.

Kendler, K. S., Gruenberg, A. M., & Kinney, D. K. (1994). Independent diagnoses of adoptees and relatives as defined by the DSM-III-R in the Provincial and National Samples of the Danish Adoption Study of Schizophrenia. *Archives of General Psychiatry*, **51**, 456–468.

Kendler, K. S., Myers, J., & Prescott, C. A. (2002). The etiology of phobias: An evaluation of the stress-diathesis model. *Archives of General Psychiatry*, **59**, 242–248.

Kendler, K. S., Neale, M. C., Kessler, R. C., Heath, A. C., & Eaves, L. J. (1993). A longitudinal twin study of 1-year prevalence of major depression in women. *Archives of General Psychiatry*, **50**, 843–852.

Kendler, K. S., Walters, E. E., Truett, K. R., et al. (1994). Sources of individual differences in depressive symptoms: Analysis of two samples of twins and their families. *American Journal of Psychiatry*, **51**, 1605–1614.

Kendrick, D. T., & Funder, D. C. (1988). Profiting from controversy: Lesson from the person-situation debate. *American Psychologist*, **43**, 23–34.

——. (1991). The person-situation debate: Do personality traits really exist? In V. J. Derlega et al. (Eds.), *Personality: Contemporary theory and research*. Chicago: Nelson-Hall.

Kentridge, R. W., & Heywood, C. A. (1997). Residual vision in multiple retinal locations within a scotoma: Implications for blindsight. *Journal of Cognitive Neuroscience*, **9**, 191. Retrieved from the World Wide Web October 5, 2000, http://ehostvgw15.epnet.com/.

——. (1999). The status of blindsight: Near-threshold vision, islands of cortex and the Riddoch phenomenon. *Journal of Consciousness Studies*, **6**, 3–11.

Kermis, M. D. (1984). *The psychology of human aging*. Boston: Allyn & Bacon.

Kerr, N. L., & Tindale, R. S. (2004). Group performance and decision making. *Annual Review of Psychology*, **55**, 623-655.

Kershner, J. R., & Ledger, G. (1985). Effect of sex, intelligence, and style of thinking on creativity: A comparison of gifted and average IQ children. *Journal of Personality and Social Psychology*, **48**, 1033–1040.

Kessler, R. C., Berglund, P., Demler, O., Jin, R., & Walters, E. E. (2005). Lifetime prevalence and age-of-onset distributions of DSM-IV disorders in the National Comorbidity Survey Replication. *Archives of General Psychiatry*, **62**, 593-602.

Kessler, R. C., Berglund, P., Demler, O., Jin, R., Koretz, D., et al. (2003). The epidemiology of major depressive disorder: Results from the National Comorbidity Survey Replication (NCS-R). *Journal of the American Medical Association*, **289**, 3095–3105.

Kessler, R. C., Chiu, W. T., Demler, O., & Walters, E. E. (2005). Prevalence, severity, and comorbidity of 12–month DSM-IV disorders in the National Comorbidity Survey replication. *Archives of General Psychiatry*, **62**, 617–627.

Kessler, R. C., Heeringa, S., Lakoma, M. D., Petukhova, M., Rupp, A. E., Schoenbaum, M., Wang, P. S., & Zaslavsky, A. M. (2008). Individual and societal effects of mental disorders on earnings in the United States: Results from the National Comorbidity Survey Replication. *American Journal of Psychiatry*, **165**, 703–711.

Kessler, R. C., McGonagle, K. A., Zhao, S., Nelson, C. P., et al. (1994). Lifetime and 12-month prevalence of DSM-III-R psychiatric disorders in the United States: Results from the National Comorbidity Survey. *Archives of General Psychiatry*, **51**, 18–19.

Kessler, R. C., Sonnega, A., Bromet, E., Hughes, M., & Nelson, C. B. (1995). Popsttraumatic stress disorder in the National Comorbidity Survey. *Archives of General Psychiatry*, **52**, 1048–1060.

Kessler, R. C., Stang, P. E., Wittchen, H. U., & Ustun, T. B. (1998). Lifetime panic-depression comorbidity in the National Comorbidity Survey. *Archives of General Psychiatry*, **(55)** 9, 801–808.

Kessler, T., & Hollbach, S. (2005). Group-based emotions as determinants of ingroup identification. *Journal of Experimental Social Psychology*, **41**,677–685.

Kestler, L. P., Walker, E., & Vega, E. M. (2001). Dopamine receptors in the brains of schizophrenia patients: A meta-analysis of the findings. *Behavioural Pharmacology*, **12**, 355-371.

Kett, J. F. (1977). *Rites of passage: Adolescence in America from 1790 to the present.* New York: Basic Books.

Kety, S. S., Wender, P. H., Jacobsen, B., Ingraham, L. J., Jansson, L., Faber, B., & Kinney, D. K. (1994). Mental illness in the biological and adoptive relatives of schizophrenic adoptees. *Archives of General Psychiatry*, **51**, 442–455.

Key, M. R. (1975). *Male/female language.* Metuchen, NJ: Scarecrow Press.

Key, S. W., & Marble, M. (1996). NIH panel seeks to curb use. *Cancer Weekly Plus* (August-September), 19–21.

Khalid, H., Atkins, M., Tredjet, J., Giles, M., Champney-Smith, K., & Kirov, G. (2008). The effectiveness of electroconvulsive therapy in treatment-resistant depression: A naturalistic study. *The Journal of ECT*, **24**, 41–145.

Kientzle, M. J. (1946). Properties of learning curves under varied distributions of practice. *Journal of Experimental Psychology*, **36**, 187–211.

Kiester, E. (1984a). The playing fields of the mind. *Psychology Today*, **18**, 18–24.

——. (1984b). The uses of anger. *Psychology Today*, **18**, 26.

Kiester, E., Jr. (1980). Images of the night: The physiological roots of dreaming. *Science 80*, **1**, 36–43.

Kim, C. H., Chang, J. W., Koo, M. S., Kim, J. W., Suh, H. S., Park, I. H., & Lee, H. S. (2003). Anterior cingulotomy for refractory obsessive-compulsive disorder. *Acta Psychiatrics Scandinavia*, **107**, 283-290.

Kim, J. E., & Moen, P. (1999). *Work/retirement transitions and psychological well-being in late midlife.* Life Course Center Working Paper (No. 99–10). Ithaca, NY: Cornell University.

——. (2001). Is retirement good or bad for subjective well-being? *Current Directions in Psychological Science*, **10**, 83–86.

Kim, K., & Smith, P. K. (1998). Childhood stress, behavioral symptoms and mother-daughter pubertal development. *Journal of Adolescence*, **21**, 231–240.

Kimball, M. M. (1989). A new perspective on women's math achievement. *Psychological Bulletin*, **105**, 198–214.

Kimble, G. A. (1981). Biological and cognitive constraints on learning. In L. Benjamin (Ed.), *The G. Stanley Hall Lecture Series (Vol. 1).* Washington, DC: American Psychological Association.

Kimble, G. A. (1989). Psychology from the standpoint of a generalist. *American Psychologist*, **44**, 491-499.

Kimmel, D. C. (1988). Ageism, psychology, and public policy. *American Psychologist*, **43**, 175–178.

King, C., & Siegel, M. (2001). The Master Settlement Agreement with the tobacco industry and cigarette advertising in magazines. *The New England Journal of Medicine*, **345**, 504-511.

King, M., Murray, M. A., & Atkinson, T. (1982). Background, personality, job characteristics, and satisfaction with work in a national sample. *Human Relations*, **35**, 119–133.

King, M. J., Zir, L. M., Kaltman, A. J., & Fox, A. C. (1973). Variant angina associated with angiographically demonstrated coronary artery system spasm and REM sleep. *American Journal of Medical Science*, **265**, 419–422.

Kingsbury, S. J. (1995). Where does research on the effectiveness of psychotherapy stand today? *The Harvard Mental Health Letter*, **12(3)**, 8.

Kinsbourne, M. (1982). Hemispheric specialization and the growth of human understanding. *American Psychologist*, **37**, 411–420.

Kinsella, K. (1995). Understanding and empowering diverse learners in the ESL classroom. In J. Reid (Ed.), *Learning styles in the ESL/EFL classroom* (pp. 170-194). Boston: Hienle & Hienle.

Kinsey, A. C., Pomeroy, W. B., & Martin, C. E. (1948). *Sexual behavior in the human male.* Philadelphia: Saunders.

Kinsey, A. C., Pomeroy, W. B., Martin, C. E., & Gebhard, P. H. (1953). *Sexual behavior in the human female.* Philadelphia: Saunders.

Kirby, D. A., & Verrier, R. L. (1989). Differential effects of sleep stage on coronary hemodynamic function during stenosis. *Physiology and Behavior*, **45**, 1017–1020.

Kirkpatrick, D. L. (1976). Evaluation of training. In R. L. Craig (Ed.), *Training and development handbook (2nd ed.).* New York: McGraw-Hill.

Kirsch, I. (2000). The response set theory of hypnosis. *American Journal of Clinical Hypnosis*, **42**, 274–292.

Kirsch, I., & Braffman, W. (2001). Imaginative suggestibility and hypnotizability. *Current Directions in Psychological Science,* **10**, 57–61.

Kirscht, J. P. (1983). Preventive health behavior: A review of research and issues. *Health Psychology*, **2**, 277–301.

Kitayama, S., Markus, H. R., Matsumoto, H., & Norasakkunkit, V. (1997). Individual and collective processes in the construction of the self: Self-enhancement in the United States and self-criticism in Japan. *Journal of Personality and Social Psychology*, **72**, 1245–1267.

Kittles, R. A., Boffoe-Bonnie, A., Moses, T., Robbins, C., Ahaghotu, C., Huusko, P., et al. (2002). A common nonsense mutation in EphB2 is associated with prostate cancer risk in African American men with a positive family history. *Journal of Medical Genetics*, September 9, downloaded 9/29/05 from http://bmg.bmjjournals.com.

Kivipelto, M., Ngandu, T., Laatikainen, T., Winblad, B., Soininen, H., & Tuomilehto, J. (2002). Risk score for the prediction of dementia risk in 20 years among middle aged people: A longitudinal, population-based study. *Lancet Neurology*, **5**, 735–741.

Klauer, S. D., Dingus, T. A., Neale, V. L., Sudweeks, J. D., & Ramsey, D. J. (2006). *The impact of driver inattention on near-crash/crash risk: An analysis using the 100-car naturalistic driving study data*. Springfield, VA: National Technical Information Service. [Also available as a pdf file at www.nhsta.dot.gov]

Klayman, J., & Ha, Y-W. (1987). Confirmation, disconfirmation, and information in hypothesis testing. *Psychological Review*, **94**, 211–228.

Klein, D. N., Shankman, S., & Ross, S. (2006). Ten-year prospective follow-up study of the naturalistic course of dysthymic disorder and double depression. *American Journal of Psychiatry*, **163**, 872–880.

Kleitman, N. (1963a). Patterns of dreaming. *Scientific American*, **203**, 82–88.

——. (1963b). *Sleep and wakefulness*. Chicago: University of Chicago Press.

Klepinger, D. H., Billy, J. O. G., Tanfer, K., & Grady, W. R. (1993). Perceptions of AIDS risk and severity and their association with risk-related behavior among U.S. men. *Family Planning Perspectives*, **25**, 74–82.

Klerman, G. L. (1990). Treatment of recurrent unipolar major depressive disorder. *Archives of General Psychiatry*, 47, 1158–1162.

Kling, K. C., Hyde, J. S., Showers, C. J., & Buswell, B. N. (1999). Gender differences in self-esteem: A meta-analysis. *Psychological Bulletin*, **125**, 470-500.

Klump, K., McGue, M., & Iacono, W. G. (2000). Age differences in genetic and environmental influences on eating attitudes and behaviors in preadolescent and adolescent female twins. *Journal of Abnormal Psychology*, **109**, 239-251.

Knapp, S., & VandeCreek, L. (1989). What psychologists need to know about AIDS. *The Journal of Training and Practice in Professional Psychology*, **3**, 3–16.

Knittle, J. L. (1975). Early influences on development of adipose tissue. In G. A. Bray (Ed.), *Obesity in perspective*. Washington, DC: U.S. Government Printing Office.

Knowles, E. S. (1983). Social physics and the effects of others: Tests of the effects of audience size and distance on social judgments and behavior. *Journal of Personality and Social Psychology*, **45**, 1263–1279.

Knowlton, R. C. (2003). Magnetoencephalography: Clinical application in epilepsy. *Current Neurology and Neuroscience Reports*, **3**, 341-348.

Knowlton, R. C., Shih, J. (2004). Magnetoencephalography in epilepsy. *Epilepsia*, **45**, Suppl. 4, 61-71.

Knox, P. L., Fagley, N. S., & Miller, P. M. (2004). Care and justice moral orientation among African American college students. *Journal of Adult Development*, *11*, 41–45.

Kobasa, S. C. (1979). Stressful life events, personality, and health: An inquiry into hardiness. *Journal of Personality and Social Psychology*, **37**, 1–11.

Kobasa, S. C. (1982). The hardy personality: Toward a social psychology of stress and health. In G. S. Sanders & J. Suls (Eds.), *Social psychology of health and illness*. Hillsdale, NJ: Erlbaum.

Kobasa, S. C. (1987). Stress responses and personality. In R. C. Barnette, L. Beiner, & G. K. Baruch (Eds.), *Gender and stress*. New York: Free Press.

Kocel, K. M. (1977). Cognitive abilities: Handedness, familial sinistrality, and sex. *Annals of the New York Academy of Sciences*, **299**, 233–243.

Kochanek, K. D., Maurer, J. D., & Rosenberg, H. M. (1994). Causes of death contributing to changes in life expectancy: United States, 1984C1989. *Vital and Health Statistics*, **20**, 1–35.

Koegel, R., Openden, D., & Koegel, L. (2004). A systematic desensitization paradigm to treat hypersensitivity to auditory stimuli in children with autism in family contexts. *Research and Practice for Persons with Severe Disabilities*, *29*, 122–134.

Koestler, A. (1964). *The act of creation*. New York: Macmillan.

Koger, S. M., Schettler, T., & Weiss, B. (2005). Environmental toxicants and developmental disabilities: A challenge for psychologists. *American Psychologist*, **60**, 243-255.

Kohlberg, L. (1963). Moral development and identification. In H. W. Stevenson (Ed.), *Child psychology*. Chicago: University of Chicago Press.

——. (1969). *Stages in the development of moral thought and action*. New York: Holt, Rinehart & Winston.

——. (1981). *Philosophy of moral development*. New York: HarperCollins.

——. (1985). *The psychology of moral development*. New York: HarperCollins.

Köhler, W. (1969). *The task of Gestalt psychology*. Princeton, NJ: Princeton University Press.

Kolata, G. (1987). What babies know, and noises parents make. *Science*, *237*, 726.

Kolb, B. (1989). Brain development, plasticity, and behavior. *American Psychologist*, **44**, 1203–1212.

Kolb, F. C., & Braun, J. (1995). Blindsight in normal observers. *Nature*, *377*, 336. Retrieved from the World Wide Web on October 5, 2000, http://ehostvgw15.epnet.com/.

Korchin, S. J., & Scheldberg, D. (1981). The future of clinical assessment. *American Psychologist*, **36**, 1147–1158.

Korn, M. L. (2001). Historical roots of schizophrenia. *Psychiatry Clinical Management*, **5**, 1–31.

Koslow, D. R., & Salett, E. P. (1989). *Crossing cultures in mental health*. Washington, DC: SIETAR International.

Kosslyn, S. M. (1987). Seeing and imagining in the cerebral hemispheres: A computational approach. *Psychological Review*, **94**, 148–175.

Kouider, S., & Dupoux, E. (2005). Subliminal speech priming. *Psychological Science*, **16**, 617.

Kraepelin, E. (1883). *Compendium der psychiatrie*. Leipzig: Abel.

Kramer, B. A. (1985). The use of ECT in California, 1977-1983. *The American Journal of Psychiatry*, **142**, 1190–1192.

Krantz, D. S., & McCeney, M. K. (2002). Effects of psychological and social factors on organic disease: A critical assessment of research on coronary heart disease. *Annual Review of Psychology, 53*, 341-369.

Krantz, D. S., Grunberg, N. E., & Braum, A. (1985). Health psychology. *Annual Review of Psychology, 36*, 349–383.

Krätzig, G. P., & Arbuthnott, K. D. (2006). Perceptual learning style and learning proficiency: A test of the hypothesis. *Journal of Educational Psychology, 98*, 238–246.

Krebs, D. L. (2000). The evolution of moral dispositions in the human species. *Annals of the New York Academy of Sciences, 907*, 132–148.

Kreutzer, J. S., Schneider, H. G., & Myatt, C. R. (1984). Alcohol, aggression, and assertiveness in men: Dosage and expectancy effects. *Journal of Studies on Alcohol, 45*, 275–278.

Krueger, J. M., & Obal, F. (1993). A neuronal group theory of sleep function. *Journal of Sleep Research, 2*, 63–69.

Krueger, W. C. F. (1929). The effect of overlearning on retention. *Journal of Experimental Psychology, 12*, 71–78.

Krull, D. S., & Erickson, D. J. (1995). Inferential hopscotch: How people draw social inferences from behavior. *Current Directions in Psychological Science, 4*, 35–38.

Krupat, E. (1985). *People in cities: The urban environment and its effects.* New York: Cambridge University Press.

Kübler-Ross, E. (1969). *On death and dying.* New York: Macmillan.

——. (1981). *Living with death and dying.* New York: Macmillan.

Kukull, W. A., & Ganguli, M. (2000). Epidemiology of dementia: Concepts and overview. In S. T. DeKosky (Ed.), *Dementia.* Philadelphia: W. B. Saunders.

Kulhara, P., & Chakrabarti, S. (2001). Culture and schizophrenia and other psychotic disorders. *Psychiatric Clinics of North America, 24*, 449-464.

Kulis, S., Marsiglia, F. F., & Hecht, M. E. (2002). Gender labels and gender identity as predictors of drug use among ethnically diverse middle school students. *Youth and Society, 33*, 442-475.

Kumanyika, S., Wilson, J. F., & Guilford-Davenport, M. (1993). Weight-related attitudes and behaviors of black women *Journal of the American Dietetic Association, 93*, 416-422.

Kumar, S. (2001). Crowding and violence on psychiatric wards: Explanatory models. *Canadian Journal of Psychiatry, 46*, 433–437.

Kunen, S., Niederhauser, R., Smith, P. O., Morris, J. A., & Marx, B. D. (2005). Race disparities in psychiatric rates in emergency departments. *Journal of Consulting and Clinical Psychology, 73*, 116-126.

Labov, W. (1973). The boundaries of words and their meaning. In C. J. N. Bailey & R. W. Shuy (Eds.), *New ways of analyzing variations in English.* Washington, DC: Georgetown University Press.

Labroo, A. A., Dhar, R., & Schwartz, N. (2008). Of frog wines and frowning watches: Semantic priming, fluency, and brand evaluation. *Journal of Consumer Research, 34*, 819–831.

Lackner, J. R., & DiZio, P. (2005). Vestibular, proprioceptive, and haptic contributions to spatial orientations. *Annual Review of Psychology, 56*, 115-147.

LaFromboise, T. D., Berman, J. S., & Sohi, B. K. (1994). American Indian women. In L. Comas-Diaz & B. Greene (Eds.), *Women of color: Integrating ethnic and gender identities in psychotherapy.* (pp. 30-71). New York: Guilford.

Laird, J. (1984). The real role of facial response in the experience of emotion: A reply to Tourangeau and Ellsworth, and others. *Journal of Personality and Social Psychology, 47*, 909–917.

Laird, J. M. A., & Bennett, G. J. (1991). *Dorsal horn neurons in rats with an experimental peripheral mononeuropathy.* Paper presented at the 21st Annual Meeting of the Society for Neuroscience, New Orleans.

Lakoff, R. (1975). *Language and women's place.* New York: HarperCollins.

Lam, D. A., & Miron, J. A. (1995). Seasonality of births in human populations. *Social Biology, 38*, 51–78.

Lamb, M. E. (1977). Father-infant and mother-infant interaction in the first year of life. *Child Development, 48*, 167–181.

——. (1979). Paternal influences and the father's role: A personal perspective. *American Psychologist, 34*, 938–943.

——. (1998). Nonparental child care: Context, quality, correlates, and consequences. In W. Damon (Series Ed.) & I. E. Sigel & K. A. Renniger (Vol. Eds.), *Handbook of child psychology: Vol. 4. Child psychology in practice* (5th ed., pp. 73–133). New York: John Wiley.

——. (Ed.). (2004). *The role of fathers in child development (4ᵗʰ ed.)* Hoboken, NJ: Wiley.

Lamb, M. E., & Sternberg, K. J. (1990). Do we really know how day care affects children? *Journal of Applied Developmental Psychology, 11*, 499.

Lamborn, S., Mounts, N. S., Steinberg. L., & Dornbusch, S. (1991). Patterns of competence and adjustment among adolescents from authoritative, authoritarian, indulgent, and neglectful families. *Child Development, 62*, 1049-1065.

Landhuis, C. E., Poulton, R., Welch, D., & Hancox, R. J. (2007). Does childhood television viewing lead to attention problems in adolescence? Results from a prospective longitudinal study. *Pediatrics, 120*, 532–537.

Landers, D. M. (1982). Arousal, attention, and skilled performance: Further considerations. *Quest, 33*, 271–283.

Landers, S. (1987). Panel urges teen contraception. *APA Monitor, 18*, 6.

Landy, F. J. (1989). *Psychology of work behavior (2nd ed.).* Homewood, IL: Dorsey Press.

Landy, F. J., Shankster, L. J., & Köhler, S. S. (1994). Personnel selection and placement. *Annual Review of Psychology, 45*, 261–296.

Lanetto, R. (1980). *Children's conceptions of death.* New York: Springer.

Lang, C., Barco, A., Zablow, L., Kandel, E. R., Siegelbaum, S. A., & Zakharenko, S. (2004). Transient expansion of synaptically connected dendritic spines upon induction of hippocampal long-term potentiation. *Proceedings of the National Academy of Sciences, 101*, 16665–16670.

Lang, P. J. (1985). The cognitive psychophysiology of emotion: Fear and anxiety. In A. H. Tuma & J. D. Maser (Eds.), *Anxiety and the anxiety disorders.* Hillsdale, NJ: Erlbaum.

Langer, S. K. (1951). *Philosophy in a new key.* New York: New American Library.

Langston, J. W. (2005). The promise of stem cells in Parkinson disease. *Journal of Clinical Investigation,* **115,** 23-25.

Laplace, A. C., Chermack, S. T., & Taylor, S. P. (1994). Effects of alcohol and drinking experience on human physical aggression. *Personality and Social Psychology Bulletin,* **20,** 439–444.

Larson, R., & Ham, M. (1993). Stress and "storm and stress" in early adolescence: The relationship of negative events with dysphoric affect. *Developmental Psychology,* **29,** 130–140.

Larson, R., & Lampman-Petraitis, R. (1989). Daily emotional states as reported by children and adolescents. *Child Development,* **60,** 1250–1260.

Lashley, K. S. (1950). In search of the engram. *Symposia for the Society for Experimental Biology,* **4,** 454–482.

Lasky, R. E., & Kallio, K. D. (1978). Transformation rules in concept learning. *Memory and Cognition,* **6,** 491–495.

Latané, B. (1981). The psychology of social impact. *American Psychologist,* **36,** 343–356.

Latané, B., & Darley, J. M. (1968). Group inhibition of bystander intervention in emergencies. *Journal of Personality and Social Psychology,* **10,** 215–221.

———. (1970). *The unresponsive bystander: Why doesn't he help?* Englewood Cliffs, NJ: Prentice-Hall.

Latané, B., & Nida, S. (1981). Ten years of research on group size and helping. *Psychological Bulletin,* **89,** 308–324.

Latané, B., Williams, K., & Harkins, S. (1979). Many hands make light work: The causes and consequences of social loafing. *Journal of Personality and Social Psychology,* **37,** 822–832.

Latham, G. P. (1988). Human resource training and development. *Annual Review of Psychology,* **39,** 545–582.

Lattal, K. A. (1992). B. F. Skinner and psychology: Introduction to the special issue. *American Psychologist,* **47,** 1269–1272.

Laumann, E. O., Michael, R., Michael, S., & Gagnon, J. (1994). *The social organization of sexuality.* Chicago: University of Chicago Press.

Laumann, E. O., Paik, A., & Rosen, R. C. (1999). Sexual dysfunction in the United States: Prevalence and predictors. *Journal of the American Medical Association,* **281,** 537–544.

Lavie, P. (2007). Insomnia and sleep-disordered breathing. *Sleep Medicine,* **8,** Supplement 4: S21–25.

Law, M., & Wald, N. (1999). Why heart disease mortality is low in France: The time-lag explanation. *British Medical Journal,* **318,** 471-480.

Lawler, E. E. (1982). Strategies for improving the quality of work life. *American Psychologist,* **37,** 486–493.

Lawrence, E., Rothman, A. D., Cobb, R. J., Rothman, M. T., & Bradbury, T. N. (2008). Marital satisfaction across the transition to parenthood. *Journal of Family Psychology, 22,* 41–50.

Lazarus, R. S. (1981). Little hassles can be hazardous to your health. *Psychology Today,* **15,** 58–62.

———. (1991a). Cognition and motivation in emotion. *American Psychologist,* **46,** 352–367.

———. (1991b). Progress on a cognitive-motivational-relational theory of emotion. *American Psychologist,* **46,** 819–834.

———. (1991c). *Emotion and adaptation.* New York: Oxford University Press.

———. (1993). From psychological stress to the emotions: A history of changing outlooks. *Annual Review of Psychology,* **44,** 1–21.

———. (2000). Toward better research on stress and coping. *American Psychologist,* **55,** 665–673.

Lazarus, R. S., & Folkman, S. (1984). *Stress, appraisal, and coping.* New York: Springer.

Leadership Conference on Civil Rights Education Fund. (2003). *Wrong then, wrong now: Racial profiling before and after September 11, 2001.* Downloaded November 8, 2005 from www.civilrights.org/publications/reports/racial_profiling/racial_profiling_report.pdf.

Leahey, T. H., & Harris, R. J. (1989). *Human learning (2nd ed.).* Englewood Cliffs, NJ: Prentice-Hall.

Leary, M. (1983). *Understanding social anxiety: Social, personality, and clinical perspectives: Volume 153,* Sage library of social research. Beverly Hills, CA: Sage.

Leary, M. R. (2001). The self we know and the self we show: Self-esteem, self-preservation, and the maintenance of interpersonal relationships. In G. J. O. Fletcher, & M. S. Clark (Eds.), *Blackwell handbook of social psychology.* Oxford, UK: Blackwell.

Leather, P., Beale, D., & Sullivan, L. (2003). Noise, psychosocial stress and their interaction in the workplace. *Journal of Environmental Psychology,* **23,** 213–233.

Leckman, J. F., Grice, D. E., Boardman, J., Zhang, H., Vitali, A., Bondi, C., Alsobrook, J., Peterson, B. S., Cohen, D. J., Pauls, D. L. (1997). Symptoms of obsessive-compulsive disorder. *American Journal of Psychiatry,* **154,** 911–917.

LeDoux, J. E. (1995). Emotion: Clues from the brain. *Annual Review of Psychology,* **46,** 209–235.

Lee, C-W., & Kahende, J. (2007). Factors associated with successful smoking cessation in the United States, 2000. *American Jornal of Public Health,* **97,** 1503–1509.

Lee, E. (1997). Overview: The assessment and treatment of Asian American families. In E. Lee (Ed.), *Working with Asian Americans: A guide for clinicians* (p. 3-36). New York: Guilford Press.

Lee, I. M., Manson, J. E., Hennekens, C. H., & Paffenbarger, R. S. (1993). Body weight and mortality: A 27-year follow-up of middle-aged men. *Journal of the American Medical Association,* **270,** 2823–2828.

Lee, J. M., Appugliese, D., Kaciroti, N., Corwyn, R. F., Bradley, R. H., & Lumeng, J. C. (2006). Weight status in young girls and the onset of puberty. *Pediatrics,* **119,** 624–630.

Lee, L., Loenstein, G., Ariely, D., Hong, J., & Young, J. (2008). If I'm not hot, are you hot or not?: Physical-attractiveness evaluations and dating preferences as a function of one's own attractiveness. *Psychological Science,* **19,** 669–677.

Lee, T. S., & Nguyen, M. (2001). Dynamics of subjective contour formation in the early visual cortex. *Proceedings of the National Academy of Scinces,* **98,** 1907–1911.

Leeming, F. C. (2004). The exam-a-day procedure improves performance in psychology classes. *Teaching of Psychology,* **29,** 210–212.

Leger, D. W. (1992). *Biological foundations of behavior: An integrative approach.* New York: HarperCollins.

Lehman, D. R., Chiu, Chi-yue, & Schaller, M. (2004). Psychology and culture. *Annual Review of Psychology,* **55,** 689-714.

Leigh, J. P., Markowitz, S. B., Fahs, M., Shin, C., & Landrigan, P. J. (1997). Occupational injury and illness in the United States: Estimates of costs, morbidity, and mortality. *Archives of Internal Medicine, 157,* 1557–1568.

Leinders-Zufall, T., Lane, A., Puche, A. C., Ma, W., et al. (2000). Ultrasensitive pheromone detection by mammalian vomeronasal neurons. *Nature, 405,* 792–796.

Lemieux, P., McKelvie, S. J., & Stout, D. (2003). Self-reported hostile aggression in contact athletes, no contact athletes, and non-athletes. *Athletic Insight.* From www.athleticinsight.com/Vol4Iss3/SelfReportedAggression.htm.

Leming, M. R., & Dickinson, G. E. (2002). *Understanding dying, death, and bereavement (5th ed.).* Fort Worth, TX: Harcourt College Publishers.

Lempers, J. D., Flavell, E. R., & Flavell, J. H. (1977). The development in very young children of tactile knowledge concerning visual perception. *Genetic Psychology Monographs, 95,* 3–53.

Lenneberg, E. H., Rebelsky, F. G., & Nichols, I. A. (1965). The vocalizations of infants born to deaf and hearing parents. *Human Development, 8,* 23–27.

Leon, G. R., & Roth, L. (1977). Obesity: Psychological causes, correlations and speculations. *Psychological Bulletin, 84,* 117–139.

Lerman, C., Rimer, B., & Glynn, T. (1997). Priorities in behavioral research in cancer prevention and control. *Preventative Medicine, 26,* S3–S9.

Lerner, M. J. (1965). The effect of responsibility and choice on a partner's attractiveness following failure. *Journal of Personality, 33,* 178–187.

Lerner, R. M. (1978). Nature, nurture, and dynamic interactionism. *Human Development, 21,* 1–20.

——. (1988). Early adolescent transitions: The lore and laws of adolescence. In M. D. Levine & E. R. McAnarney (Eds.), *Early adolescent transitions.* Lexington, MA: Lexington Books.

Leserman, J., Petitto, J. M., Golden, R. N., Gaynes, B. N., Gu, H., & Perkins, D. O. (2000). The impact of stressful life events, depression, social support, coping and cortisol on progression to AIDS. *American Journal of Psychology, 57,* 1221–1228.

Levant, R. F. (2005). A giant has fallen. *Monitor on Psychology, 36,* 5.

LeVay, S. (1991). A difference in hypothalamic structure between heterosexual and homosexual men. *Science, 253,* 1034–1037.

Leventhal, H., & Cleary, P. D. (1980). The smoking problem: A review of the research and theory in behavioral risk modification. *Psychological Bulletin, 88,* 370–405.

Levine, H. Z. (1983). Safety and health programs. *Personnel, 3,* 4–9.

Levine, J. M., & Moreland, R. L. (1990). Progress in small group research. *Annual Review of Psychology, 41,* 585–634.

Levine, L. J., & Bluck, S. (2004). Painting with broad strokes: Happiness and the malleability of event memory. *Cognition and Emotion, 18,* 559-574.

Levine, M. (1999). Rethinking bystander nonintervention: Social categorization and the evidence of witnesses at the James Bulger murder trial. *Human Relations, 52,* 1133-1155.

Levine, M., Toro, P. A., & Perkins, D. V. (1993). Social and community interventions. *Annual Review of Psychology, 44,* 525–558.

Levine, M. F., Taylor, J. C., & Davis, L. E. (1984). Defining quality of work life. *Human Relations, 37,* 81–104.

Levine, M. W., & Shefner, J. M. *Fundamentals of sensation and perception (2nd ed.).* Pacific Grove, CA: Brooks/Cole.

Levine, S. C., Vasilyeva, M., Lourenco, S. F., Newcobe, & Hottenlocher (2005). Socioeconomic status modifies the sex difference in special skills. *Psychological Science, 11,* 841-845.

Levinson, D. J. (1978). *The seasons of a man's life.* New York: Ballantine Books.

——. (1986). A conception of adult development. *American Psychologist, 41,* 3–13.

Levinson, D. J., Darrow, C. M., Klein, E. B., Levinson, M. H., & McKee, B. (1974). *The seasons of a man's life.* New York: Knopf.

Levinthal, C. F. (1983). *Introduction to physiological psychology (2nd ed.).* Englewood Cliffs, NJ: Prentice-Hall.

Levitt, M. J., Guacci-Franco, N., & Levitt, J. L. (1993). Convoys of social support in childhood and early adolescence: Structure and function. *Developmental Psychology, 29,* 811-818.

Lewin, K. (1936). *Principles of topographic psychology.* New York: McGraw Hill.

Lewinsohn, P. M. & Clard, G. N. (1999). Psychological treatments for adolescent depression. *Clinical Psychology Review, 19,* 329-342.

Lewinsohn, P. M., Zeiss, A. M., & Duncan, E. M. (1989). Probability of relapse after recovery from an episode of depression. *Journal of Abnormal Psychology, 98,* 107–116.

Lewis, B. A., Singer, L. T., Short, E. J., Minnes, S., Arendt, R., Weishampel, P., Klein, N., & Min, M. O. (2004). Four-year language outcomes of children exposed to cocaine in utero. *Neurotoxicology and Teratology, 26,* 617-627.

Ley, B. W. (1985). Alcohol problems in special populations. In J. H. Mendelson & N. K. Mello (Eds.), *The diagnosis and treatment of alcoholism (2nd ed.).* New York: McGraw-Hill.

Ley, P. (1977). Psychological studies of doctor-patient communication. In S. Rachman (Ed.), *Contributions to medical psychology (Vol. 1).* Elmsford, NY: Pergamon Press.

Leyens, J. P., Paladino, M. P., Rodriguez, R. T., Vaes, J., Demoulin, S., Rodriguez, A. P., & Gaunt, R. (2000). The emotional side of prejudice: The attribution of secondary emotions to ingroups and outgroups. *Personality and Social Psychology Review, 4,* 186–197.

Li, J. (2003). U.S. and Chinese cultural beliefs about learning. *Journal of Educational Psychology, 95,* 258-267.

——. (2004). Mind or virtue: Western and Chinese beliefs about learning. *Current Directions in Psychological Science, 14,* 190-194.

Liben, L. S., & Signorella, M. L. (1993). Gender-schematic processing in children: The role of initial interpretations of stimuli. *Developmental Psychology, 29,* 141–149.

Libman, E., Creti, L., Amsel, R., Brender. W., & Fichten, C. S. (1997). What do older good and poor sleepers do during periods of nocturnal wakefulness? The sleep behaviors scale: 60+. *Psychology and Aging, 12,* 170–182.

Lidz, T. (1973). *The origin and treatment of schizophrenic disorders.* New York: Basic Books.

Lieberman, J. A., Stroup, S., McEvoy, J. P., Swartz, M. S., Rosenheck, R. A., Perkins, D. O., Keefe, R. S. E., et al. (2005). Effectiveness of antipsychotic drugs in patients with chronic schizophrenia. *The New England Journal of Medicine, 353*, 1209-1223.

Lieberman, M. A. (1983). The effects of social support on response to stress. In L. Goldbert & D. S. Breznitz (Eds.), *Handbook of stress management.* New York: Free Press.

Liebert, D. T. (2000). Personal communication.

Light, K. C. (1997). Stress in employed women: A woman's work is never done if she's a working mom. *Psychosomatic Medicine, 59*, 360–361.

Lightman, S. W., Pisarska, K., Berman, E. R., Pestone, M., et al. (1992). Discrepancy between self-reported and actual caloric intake in obese subjects. *New England Journal of Medicine, 327*, 1893–1898.

Lilienfeld, S. O. (1999). Projective measures of personality and psychopathology: How well do they work? *Skeptical Inquirer, 23*, 32–39.

——. (2005). The 10 commandments of helping students science from pseudoscience in psychology. Retrieved May 6, 2008 from http://www.psychologicalscience.org/observer/getArticle.cfm?id=1843.

Lilienfeld, S. O., Wood, J. M., & Gard, H. N. (2000). The scientific status of projective techniques. *Psychological Science in the Public Interest, 1*, 27–66.

Lin, E., & Kleinman, A. (1988). *Psychotherapy and clinical course of schizophrenia: A cross-cultural Perspective,* 555–567.

Lin, T. R., Dobbins, G. H., & Farh, J. L. (1992). A field study of race and similarity effects on interview ratings in conventional and situational interviews. *Journal of Applied Psychology, 77*, 363–371.

Lincoln, J. R., & Kalleberg, A. L. (1985). Work organization and workforce commitment: A study of plants and employees in the U.S. and Japan. *American Sociological Review, 50*, 738–760.

Linden, W., & Moseley, J. V. (2006). The efficacy of behavioral treatments for hypertension. *Applied Psychophysiology and Biofeedback, 31*, 51–63.

Lindfors, K., Elovainio, M., Wickman, S., Vuorinen, R., Sinkkonen, J., Dunkel, L., & Raappana, A. (2007). Brief Report: The role of ego development in psychosocial adjustment among boys with delayed puberty. *Journal of Research on Adolescence, 17*, 601–612.

Lindholm T., & Christianson, S. A. (1998). Gender effects in eyewitness accounts of a violent crime. *Psychology, Crime and Law, 4*, 323-339.

Lindley, A. A., Gray, R. H., Herman, A. A., & Becker, S. (2000). Maternal cigarette smoking during pregnancy and infant ponderal index at birth in the Swedish medical birth register, 1991–1992. *American Journal of Public Health, 90*, 420–423.

Lindsay, D. S., Hagen, L., Read, J. D., Wade, K. A., & Garry, M. (2004). True photographs and false memories. *Psychological Science, 15*, 149-154.

Lindsley, D. B., Bowden, J., & Magoun, H. W. (1949). Effect upon EEG of acute injury to the brain stem activating system. *Electroencephalography and Clinical Neurophysiology, 1*, 475–486.

Link, S. W. (1995). Rediscovering the past: Gustav Fechner and signal detection theory. *Psychological Science, 5*, 335–340.

Linn, M. C., & Peterson, A. C. (1985). Emergence and characterization of sex differences in spatial ability: A meta-analysis. *Child Development, 56*, 1479–1498.

Liossi, C, & Hatira, P. (2003). Clinical hypnosis in the alleviation of procedure-related pain in pediatric oncology patients. *International Journal of Clinical and Experimental Hypnosis, 51*, 4-28.

Lipsey, M. W., & Wilson, D. B. (1993). The efficacy of psychological, educational, and behavioral treatment: Confirmation from meta-analysis. *American Psychologist, 48*, 1181–1209.

Lisanby, S. H., Maddox, J. H., Prudic, J. & Sackeim, H. A. (2000). The effects of electroconvulsive therapy on memory of autobiographical and public events. *Archives of General Psychiatry, 57*, 581–590.

Liston, C., & Kagan, J. (2002). Brain development: Memory enhancement in early childhood. *Nature, 419*, 896.

Little, J. D., Akins, M. R., Munday, J., Lyall, G., Chubb, G., & Orr, M. (2004). Bifrontal electroconvulsive therapy in the elderly: A two-year study. *The Journal of ECT, 20*, 139-141.

Locke, E. A. (1968). Toward a theory of task motivation and incentives. *Organizational Behavior and Human Performance, 3*, 157–189.

——. (1976). The nature and causes of job satisfaction. In M. D. Dunnette (Ed.), *Handbook of industrial and organizational psychology.* Skokie, IL: Rand McNally.

Locke, E. A., & Latham, G. P. (1984). *Goal setting: A motivational technique that works.* Englewood Cliffs, NJ: Prentice-Hall.

Locke, E. A., Shaw, K. N., Saari, L. M., & Latham, G. (1981). Goal-setting and task performance: 1969–1980. *Psychological Bulletin, 90*, 124–152.

Lockhard, J. S., & Paulus, D. L. (Eds.). (1988). *Self-deception: An adaptive mechanism?* Englewood Cliffs, NJ: Prentice-Hall.

Lockyer, L., & Rutter, M. L. (1969). A five- to fifteen-year follow-up study of infantile psychosis. *British Journal of Psychiatry, 115*, 865–882.

Loehlin, J. C. (1992). *Genes and environment in personality development.* Newbury Park, CA: Sage.

Loftus, E. (2003). *Illusions of memory.* Presentation at The 25th Annual National Institute on the Teaching of Psychology. St. Petersburg Beach, FL, January 3.

Loftus, E. F. (1979a). *Eyewitness testimony.* Cambridge, MA: Harvard University Press.

——. (1979b). The malleability of human memory. *American Scientist, 67*, 312–320.

——. (1984). The eyewitness on trial. In B. D. Sales & A. Elwork (Eds.), *With liberty and justice for all.* Englewood Cliffs, NJ: Prentice-Hall.

——. (1991). The glitter of everyday memory … and the gold. *American Psychologist, 46*, 16–18.

——. (1993a). The reality of repressed memories. *American Psychologist, 48*, 518–53?.

——. (1994). The repressed memory controversy. *American Psychologist, 49,* 443–445.

——. (1997). Researchers are showing how suggestion and imagination can create memories of events that did not actually occur. *Scientific American,* (September), 71–75.

——. (2003). Make-believe memories. *American Psychologist, 58,* 864-873.

——. (2004). Memories of things unseen. *Current Directions in Psychological Sciences, 13,* 145-147.

Loftus, E. F., & Klinger, M. R. (1992). Is the unconscious smart or dumb? *American Psychologist, 47,* 761–765.

Loftus, E. F., Loftus, G. R., & Messo, J. (1987). Some facts about weapon focus. *Law and Human Behavior, 11,* 55–62.

Loftus, E. F., Miller, D. G., & Burns, H. J. (1978). Semantic integration of verbal information into a visual memory. *Journal of Experimental Psychology: Human Learning and Memory, 4,* 19–31.

Loftus, E. F., Schooler, J. W., & Wagenaar, W. A. (1985). The fate of memory: Comment on McCloskey & Zaragoza. *Journal of Experimental Psychology: General, 114,* 375–380.

Loftus, E. F., & Zanni, G. (1975). Eyewitness testimony: The influence of wording on a question. *Bulletin of the Psychonomic Society, 5,* 86–88.

Londerville, S., & Main, M. (1981). Security of attachment and compliance in maternal training methods in the second year of life. *Developmental Psychology, 17,* 289–299.

London, M., & Moore, E. M. (1999). Continuous learning. In D. R. Ilgen & E. D, Pulakos (Eds.), *The changing nature of performance.* San Francisco, CA: Jossey-Bass.

Long, P. (1986). Medical mesmerism. *Psychology Today, 20(1),* 28–29.

Lonner, W. J. (1980). The search for psychological universals. In H. C. Triandis & W. W. Lambert (Eds.), *Handbook of cross-cultural psychology (Vol. I).* Boston: Allyn & Bacon.

Loo, R. (2002). A meta-analytic examination of Kolb's learning style preferences among business majors. *Journal of Education for Business, 77,* 252–256.

Lopez-Jimenez, F., Sert, F. H., & Somers, G. A. (2008). Obstructive sleep apnea: Implications for cardiac and vascular disease. *Chest, 133,* 793–804.

Lord, C. G. (1980). Schemas and images as memory aids. *Journal of Personality and Social Psychology, 38,* 257–269.

Lorde, A. (1984). Age, race, class, and sex: Women redefining different. In A. Lorde (Ed.), *Sister outsider.* Freedom, CA: The Crossing Press.

Lorenz, K. (1969). *On aggression.* New York: Bantam Books.

Lott, A. J., & Lott, B. E. (1974). The role of reward in the formation of positive interpersonal attitudes. In T. L. Huston (Ed.), *Foundations of interpersonal attraction.* New York: Academic Press.

Lovaas, O. I. (1987). Behavioral treatment and normal educational and intellectual functioning in young autistic children. *Journal of Consulting and Clinical Psychology, 55,* 3–9.

Lovaas, O. I., & Smith, P. (1988). Intensive behavioral treatment for young autistic children. In B. Lahey & A. Kazdin (Eds.), *Advances in clinical child psychology (Vol. 2).* New York: Plenum.

Loyd, D., & Murphy, A. (2006). Sex differences in the anatomical and functional organization of the midbrain periaqueductal gray-rostal ventromedial medullary pathway. *Neurology. 496,* 723–738.

Lozada, C. J., Altman, R. D. (2001) Management of osteoarthritis. In W. J. Koopman (Ed.), *Arthritis and Allied Conditions: A Textbook of Rheumatology (14th ed.)* Philadelphia: Lippincott Williams & Wilkins, 2246-2258.

Lozoff, B. (1989). Nutrition and behavior. *American Psychologist, 44,* 231–236.

Lu, F. G., Lim, R. F., & Mezzich, J. E. (1995). Issues of assessment and diagnosis of culturally diverse individuals. In J. Oldham & M. Riba (Eds.), *Review of Psychiatry, 14,* 477-510. Washington, DC: American Psychiatric Press.

Lubin, B., Larsen, R. M., & Matarazzo, J. D. (1984). Patterns of psychological test usage in the United States: 1935-1982. *American Psychologist, 39,* 451–454.

Luborsky, I., Barber, J. P., & Beutler, L. (Eds.). (1993). Curative factors in dynamic psychotherapy. *Journal of Consulting and Clinical Psychology, 61,* 539–610.

Luborsky, L., Rosenthal, R., Diguer, L., Andrusyna, T. P., Berman, J. S., Levitt, J. T., et al. (2002). The dodo bird verdict is alive and well—mostly. *Clinical Psychology Science and Practice, 9,* 2–12.

Lucas, E. A., Foutz, A. S., Dement, W. C., & Mittler, M. M. (1979). Sleep cycle organization in narcoleptic and normal dogs. *Physiology and Behavior, 23,* 325–331.

Lucas, R. E., & Fujita, F. (2000). Factors influencing the relation between extroversion and pleasant affect. *Journal of Personality and Social Psychology, 79,* 1039–1056.

Lucyshyn, J. M., Albin, R. W., Horner, R. H., Mann, J. C., Mann, J. A., & Wadsworth, G. (2007). Family implementation of positive behavior support for a child with autism: Longitudinal, single-case, experimental, and descriptive replication and extension. *Journal of Positive Behavior Interventions, 9,* 131–150.

Lugaresi, E., R., Montagna, P., Baruzzi, A., Cortelli, P., Lugaresi, A., Tinuper, P., Zucconi, M., & Gambetti, P. (1986). Fatal familial insomnia and dyautonomia with selective degeneration of the thalamic nuclei. *New England Journal of Medicine, 315,* 997–1003.

Luh, C. W. (1922). The conditions of retention. *Psychological Monographs (Whole No. 142).*

Luo, M., Fee, M. S., & Katz, L. C. (2003). Encoding pheromonal signals in the accessory olfactory bulb of behaving mice. *Science, 299,* 1196–1201.

Lynn, R. (2006). *Race differences in intelligence: An evolutionary analysis.* Augusta, GA: Washington Summit Books.

Lykken, D. T. (1957). A study of anxiety in sociopathic personality. *Journal of Abnormal and Social Psychology, 55,* 6–10.

Lykken, D. T. (1982). Fearlessness: Its carefree charm and deadly risk. *Psychology Today, 16,* 20–28.

Lykken, D. T., McGue, M., Tellegen, A., & Bouchard, T. J., Jr. (1992). Emergenesis: Genetic traits that may not run in families. *American Psychologist, 47*, 1565–1577.

Lynch, G., & Baudry, M. (1984). The biochemistry of memory: A new and specific hypothesis. *Science, 224*, 1057–1063.

Lyness, S. A. (1993). Predictors of differences between Type A and B individuals in heart rate and blood pressure reactivity. *Psychological Bulletin, 114*, 266–295.

Lynn, R. (1977). The intelligence of the Japanese. *Bulletin of the British Psychological Society, 30*, 69–72.

Lynn, S. J., & Rhue, J. W. (1986). The fantasy-prone person: Hypnosis, imagination, and creativity. *Journal of Personality and Social Psychology, 51*, 404–408.

Lynskey, M. T., Heath, A. C., Bucholz, K. K., Slutske, W. S., et al. (2003). Escalation of drug use in early-onset cannabis users vs co-twin controls. *Journal of the American Medical Association, 289*, 427–433.

Lytton, H., & Romney, D. M. (1991). Parents' differential socialization of boys and girls: A meta-analysis. *Psychological Bulletin, 109*, 267–296.

Maas, J. W., Bowden, C. I., Miller, A. L., Javors, M. A., Funderburg, L. G., Berman, N., & Weintraub, S. T. (1997). Schizophrenia, psychosis, and cerebral spinal fluid homovanillic acid concentrations. *Schizophrenia Bulletin, 23*, 147–154.

Maccoby, E. (2000). Parenting and its effects on children: On reading and misreading behavior genetics. *Annual Review of Psychology, 51*, 1–27.

Maccoby, E. E. (1988). Gender as a social category. *Developmental Psychology, 24*, 755–765.

——. (1990). Gender and relationships: A developmental account. *American Psychologist, 45*, 513–520.

Maccoby, E. E., & Jacklin, C. N. (1974). *The psychology of sex differences.* Stanford, CA: Stanford University Press.

——. (1980) Sex differences in aggression: A rejoinder and reprise. *Child Development, 51*, 964–980.

——. (1987). Gender segregation in childhood. In E. H. Reese (Ed.), *Advances in child development and behavior (Vol. 23).* New York: Academic Press.

Maccoby, E. E., & Martin, J. A. (1983). Socialization in the context of the family: Parent-child interaction. In P. H. Mussen and E. M. Hetherington (Eds.), *Handbook of child psychology: Vol. 4. Socialization, personality, and social development* (pp. 1-101). New York: Wiley.

MacDonald, R., Anderson, J. Dube, W. V., Geckeler, A., Green, G., et al. (2006). Behavioral assessment of joint attention: A methodological report. *Research in Developmental Disabilities, 27*, 138–150.

Mace, N. L., & Rabins, P. V. (1981). *The 36-hour day.* Baltimore: Johns Hopkins University Press.

Machlin, S., Cohen, J., Zuvekas, S., & Thorpe, J. (2000). *Per capita health care expenses, 1996.* Rockville, MD: Agency for Health Care Research and Quality.

MacIvor, M. (1999). Redefining science education for aboriginal students. In M. Battiste & J. Barman (Eds.), *First Nation's education in Canada: The circle unfolds* (pp. 73-98). Vancouver: University of British Columbia Press.

Mack, A., & Rock, I. (1998). *Inattentional blindness.* Cambridge, MA: MIT Press.

Mackenzie, B. (1984). Explaining race differences in IQ: The logic, the methodology, and the evidence. *American Psychologist, 39*, 1214–1233.

MacKenzie, K. R. (1997). *Time-managed group psychotherapy: Effective clinical applications.* Washington, DC: American Psychiatric Press.

Mackintosh, N. J. (1975). A theory of attention: Variations in the associability of stimuli with reinforcement. *Psychological Review, 82*, 276–298.

——. (1986). The biology of intelligence? *British Journal of Psychology, 77*, 1–18.

Mackowiak, P. A., Wasserman, S. S., & Levine, M. M. (1992). A critical appraisal of 98.6F, the upper limit of the normal body temperature, and other legacies of Carl Reinhold August Wunderlich. *Journal of the American Medical Association, 268*, 1578–1580.

MacMillan, J., & Kofoed, L. (1984). Sociobiology and antisocial personality: An alternative perspective. *Journal of Mental Disorders, 172*, 701–706.

Maertens, M., Pollmann, S., Hanke, M., Mildner, T., & Möller, H. E. (2008). Retinotropic activation in response to subjective contours in primary visual cortex. *Frontiers in Human Neuroscience, 2*, doi:10.3389/neuro.09.002.2008.

Maestripieri, D., Roney, J. R., DeBias, N., Durante, K. M., & Spaepen, G. M. (2004). Father absence, menarche and interest in infants among adolescent girls. *Developmental Science, 7*, 560-566.

Magee, W. J., Eaton, W. W., Wittchen, H., McGonagle, K. A., & Kessler, R. C. (1996). Agoraphobia, simple phobia, and social phobia in the National Comorbidity Survey. *Archives of General Psychiatry, 53*, 159–168.

Magid, K. (1988). *High Risk: Children Without a Conscience.* New York: Bantam.

Magsud, M. (1979). Resolution and moral dilemmas by Nigerian secondary school pupils. *Journal of Moral Education, 7*, 40–49.

Maharishi, Mahesh Yogi. (1963). *The science of living and art of being.* London: Unwin.

Maier, N. R. F. (1931). Reasoning in humans: II. The solution of a problem and its appearance in consciousness. *Journal of Experimental Psychology, 105*, 181–194.

Maisey, R. M., Vale, E. L. E., Cornelissen, P. L., & Tovee, M. J. (1999). Characteristics of male attractiveness for women. *Lancet, 353*, 1500.

Major, B., & O'Brien, L. T. (2005). The social psychology of stigma. *Annual Review of Psychology, 56*, 393-421.

Malatesta, C. A., & Isard, C. E. (1984). The ontogenesis of human social signals: From biological imperative to symbol utilization. In N. A. Fox & R. J. Davidson (Eds.), *The psychobiology of affective development.* Hillsdale, NJ: Erlbaum.

Malik, M. L., Beutler, L. E., Alimohamed, S., Gallagher-Thompson, D., & Thompson, L. (2003). Are all cognitive therapies alike? A comparison of cognitive and noncognitive therapy process and implications for the application of empirically supported treatments. *Journal of Consulting and Clinical Psychology, 71*, 150–158

Mandiyan, V. S., Coats, J. K., & Shah, N. M. (2005). Deficits in sexual and aggressive behaviors in Cnga2 mutant mice. *Nature: Neuroscience, 1*, 1660–1662.

Mandler, G. (1980). Recognizing: The judgment of previous occurrence. *Psychological Review, 87*, 252–271.

Mania, K., Robinson, A., & Brandt, K. R. (2005). The effect of memory schemas on object recognition in visual environments. *Presence, 14*, 606–615.

Manji, H. K., Drevets, W. C., & Charney, D. S. (2001). The cellular neurobiology of depression. *Nature Medicine, 7*, 541-547.

Mann, J. M., Tarantola, D. J. M., & Netter, T. W. (Eds.). (1992). *AIDS in the world.* Cambridge, MA: Harvard University Press.

Manning, M. L. (1983). Three myths concerning adolescence. *Adolescence, 18*, 823–829.

Mansell, W., & Pedley, R. (2008). The ascent into mania: A review of psychological processes associated with the development of manic symptoms. *Clinical Psychology Review, 28*, 494–520.

Marcia, J. E. (1980). Identity in adolescence. In J. H. Flavell & E. K. Markman (Eds.), *Handbook of adolescent psychology,* New York: John Wiley.

Marengo, J. T., & Harrow, M. (1987). Schizophrenic thought disorder at follow-up. *Archives of General Psychiatry, 44*, 651–659.

Markay, P. M. (2000). Bystander intervention in computer-mediated communication. *Computers in Human Behavior, 16*, 183–188.

Markman, A. B., & Genter, D. (2001). Thinking. *Annual Review of Psychology, 52*, 223–247.

Markowitz, J. C., Spielman, L. A., Sullivan, M., & Fishman, B. (2000). An exploratory study of ethnicity and psychotherapy outcome among HIV-positive patients with depressive symptoms. *Journal of Psychotherapy Practice and Research, 9*, 226-231.

Markowitz, J. S., Weissman, M. M., Ouellete, R., Lish, J. D., & Klerman, G. L. (1989). Quality of life in panic disorder. *Archives of General Psychiatry, 46*, 984–992.

Marks, I. M. (1986). Epidemiology of anxiety. *Social Psychiatry, 21*, 167–171.

Marschark, M., Richmond, C. L., Yuille, J. C., & Hunt, R. R. (1987). The role of imagery in memory: On shared and distinctive information. *Psychological Bulletin, 102*, 28–41.

Marsh, D. T. (2001). Understanding schizophrenia. *AAMFT Clinical Update, 3*, 1–6.

Marshall, G. D., & Zimbardo, P. G. (1979). Affective consequences of inadequately explained physiological arousal. *Journal of Personality and Social Psychology, 37*, 970-988.

Marshall, J., Marquis, K. H., & Oskamp, S. (1971). Effects of kind of question and atmosphere of interrogation on accuracy and completeness of testimony. *Harvard Law Review,* 1620–1643.

Marsiglia, F. F., Kulis, S., Hecht, M. E., & Sills, S. (2004). Ethnic self-identification and ethnic identity as predictors of drug norms and drug use among pre-adolescents in the Southwest. *Substance Use and Misuse, 39*, 1061-1094.

Martin, B. J. (1986). Sleep deprivation and exercise. In K. B. Pandolf (Ed.), *Exercise and sport sciences review.* New York: Macmillan.

Martin, C. L. (1991). The role of cognition in understanding gender effects. In H. W. Reese (Ed.), *Advances in child development and behavior (Vol. 23).* New York: Academic Press.

Martin, R. J., White, B. D., & Hulsey, M. G. (1991). The regulation of body weight. *American Scientist, 79*, 528–541.

Martin, S. (2002). Thwarting terrorism. *Monitor on Psychology, 33* (January), 28–29.

Martindale, C. (1981). *Cognition and consciousness.* Homewood, IL: Dorsey Press.

Marx, J. (2003). Cellular warriors in the battle of the bulge. *Science, 299*, 846–849.

Marziali, E. (1984). Prediction of outcome of brief psychotherapy from therapist interpretive interactions. *Archives of General Psychiatry, 41*, 301–304.

Maslach, C. (1979). The emotional consequences of arousal without reason. In C. E. Izard (Ed.), *Emotions in personality and psychopathology.* New York: Plenum.

——. (2003). Job burnout: New directions in research and intervention. *Current Directions in Psychological Science, 12*, 189–192.

Maslach, C., Schaufeli, W. B., & Leiter, M. P. (2001). Job burnout. *Annual Review of Psychology, 52*, 397–422.

Maslow, A. H. (1943). A theory of human motivation. *Psychological Review, 50*, 370–396.

——. (1954). *Motivation and personality.* New York: Harper.

——. (1970). *Motivation and personality. (2nd ed.).* New York: HarperCollins.

Massaro, D. W. (1975). *Experimental psychology and information processing.* Skokie, IL: Rand McNally.

Masters, M. S., & Sanders, B. (1993). Is the gender difference in mental rotation disappearing? *Behavior Genetics, 23*, 337–341.

Masters, W., & Johnson, V. (1979). *Homosexuality in perspective.* Boston: Little, Brown.

Masters, W., Johnson, V., & Kolodny, R. C. (1987). *Human sexuality (3rd ed.).* Glenview, IL: Scott, Foresman/Little, Brown.

Masters, W. H., Johnson, V. E., & Kolodny, R. C. (1992). *Human sexuality (4th ed.).* New York: HarperCollins.

Matarazzo, J. D. (1980). Behavioral health and behavioral medicine: Frontiers for a new health psychology. *American Psychologist, 35*, 807–817.

——. (1990). Psychological assessment versus psychological testing: Validation from Binet to the school, clinic, and courtroom. *American Psychologist, 45*, 999–1017.

Mathews, A., & MacLeod, C. (1994). Cognitive approaches to emotion and emotional disorders. *Annual Review of Psychology, 45*, 25–50.

Matlin, M. W. (1983). *Perception.* Boston: Allyn & Bacon.

Matsumoto, D. (1987). The role of facial response in the experience of emotion: More methodological problems and a meta-analysis. *Journal of Personality and Social Psychology, 52*, 769–774.

Matsunaga, H., Kiriike, N., Iwasaki, Y., Miyata, A., & Matsui, T. (2000). Multi-impulsivity among bulimic patients in Japan. *International Journal of Eating Disorders, 27*, 348-352.

Matthews, K. A. (1982). Psychological perspectives on the Type A behavior pattern. *Psychological Bulletin, 91*, 293–323.

——. (1988). Coronary heart disease and Type A behavior: Update on an alternative to the Booth-Kewley and Friedman (1987) quantitative review. *Psychological Bulletin,* **104**, 373–380.

Matthews, K. A., & Gump, B. B. (2002). Chronic work stress and marital dissolution increase risk of posttrial mortality in men from the Multiple Risk Factor Intervention Trial. *Archives of Internal Medicine,* **162**, 309–315.

Matthews, K. A., Shumaker, S. A., Bowen, D. J., Langer, R. D., et al., (1997). Women's Health Initiative: Why now? What is it? What's new? *American Psychologist,* **52**, 101–116.

Mattson, S. N., Barron, S., & Riley, E. P. (1988). The behavioral effects of prenatal alcohol exposure. In K. Kuriyama, A. Takada, & H. Ishii (Eds.), *Biomedical and social aspects of alcohol and alcoholism.* Tokyo: Elsevier.

Maxhom, J. (February 12, 2000). Nicotine addiction. *British Medical Journal,* 391–392.

Maxman, J. S. (1991). *Psychotropic drugs: Fast facts.* New York: Norton.

Mayer, J. D., & Geher, G. (1996). Emotional intelligence and the identification of emotion. *Intelligence,* **22(2)**, 89–114.

Mayer, J. D., & Salovey, P. (1995). Emotional intelligence and the construction and regulation of feelings. *Applied and Preventative Psychology,* **4(3)**, 197–208.

——. (1997). What is emotional intelligence? In P. Salovey, D. J. Sluyter, et. al. (Eds.), *Emotional development and emotional intelligence: Educational implications* (pp. 3–34). New York: Basicbooks.

Mayer, R. E. (1983). *Thinking, problem solving, cognition.* San Francisco: Freeman.

——. (2004). Teaching of subject matter. *Annual Review of Psychology,* **55**, 715-744.

Mayo, E. (1933). *The human problems of an industrial civilization.* Cambridge, MA: Harvard University Press.

McAdams, D. P. (1989). *Intimacy.* New York: Doubleday.

——. (1990). *The person: An introduction to personality psychology.* San Diego: Harcourt, Brace, Jovanovich.

——. (2000). *The person: An integrated introduction to personality psychology.* New York: Harcourt.

McAdams, D. P., & Pals, J. L. (2006). A new big five: Fundamental principles for an integrative science of personality. *American Psychologist,* **61**, 204–217.

McAdoo, W. G., & DeMyer, M. K. (1978). Personality characteristics of parents. In M. Rutter & E. Schopler (Eds.), *Autism: A reappraisal of concepts and treatment.* New York: Plenum.

McAndrew, F. T. (2002). New evolutionary perspectives on altruism: Multilevel-selection and costly-signaling theories. *Current Directions in Psychological Science,* **11(2)**, 79–82.

McAngus-Todd, N.P. & Cody, F. W. (2000). Vestibular responses to loud dance music: A physiological basis of the "rock and roll threshold?" *Journal of the Acoustical Society of America,* **107(1)**, 496–500.

McCann, I. L., & Holmes, D. S. (1984). Influence of aerobic exercise on depression. *Journal of Personality and Social Psychology,* **46**, 1142–1147.

McCardle, P., Scarborough, H. S., & Catts, H. W. (2001). Predicting, explaining, and preventing children's reading difficulties. *Learning Disabilities Research & Practice,* **16**, 230-239.

McCarley. R. W., & Hobson, J. A. (1981). REM sleep dreams and the activation-synthesis hypothesis. *American Journal of Psychiatry,* **138**, 904–912.

McCarthy, B. W., Ryan, M., & Johnson, F. (1975). *Sexual awareness.* San Francisco: Boyd & Fraser.

McCaul, K. D., Veltum, L. G., Boyechko, V., & Crawford, J. J. (1990). Understanding attributions of victim blame for rape: Sex, violence, and foreseeability. *Journal of Applied Social Psychology,* **20**, 1–26.

McCauley, C. (1989). The nature of social influence in groupthink: Compliance and internalization. *Journal of Personality and Social Psychology,* **57**, 250–260.

McClelland, D. C. (1958). Risk-taking in children with high and low need for achievement. In J. W. Atkinson (Ed.), *Motives in fantasy, action, and society.* New York: Van Nostrand Reinhold.

——. (1973). Testing for competence rather than for "intelligence." *American Psychologist,* **28**, 1–14.

——. (1982). The need for power, sympathetic activation, and illness. *Motivation and Emotion,* **6**, 31–41.

——. (1985). *Human motivation.* Glenview, IL: Scott, Foresman.

——. (1993). Intelligence is not the best predictor of job performance. *Current Directions in Psychological Science,* **2**, 5–6.

McClelland, D. C., & Winter, D. G. (1969). *Motivating economic development.* New York: Free Press.

McClelland, D. C., Atkinson, J. W., Clark, R. A., & Lowell, E. L. (1953). *The achievement motive.* Englewood Cliffs, NJ: Prentice-Hall.

McClintock, M. K. (1971). Menstrual synchrony and suppression. *Nature,* **229**, 244–245.

——. (1979). Estrous synchrony and its mediation by airborne chemical communication. *Hormones and Behavior,* **10**, 264.

McCloskey, M., & Egeth, H. (1983). Eyewitness identification: What can a psychologist tell a jury? *American Psychologist,* **38**, 550–563.

McCloskey, M., Wible, C., & Cohen, N. J. (1988). Is there a special flashbulb-memory mechanism? *Journal of Experimental Psychology: General,* **117**, 171–181.

McClure, J. (1998). Discounting causes of behavior: Are two reasons better than one? *Journal of Personality and Social Psychology,* **74**, 7–20.

McConahay, J. G. (1986). Modern racism, ambivalence, and the modern racist scale. In J. F. Dovidio & S. L. Gaertner (Eds.), *Prejudice, discrimination, and racism.* San Diego, CA: Academic Press.

McCown, J. A., Fischer, D., Page, R., & Homant, M. (2001). Internet relationships: People who meet people. *CyberPsychology and Behavior,* **4**, 593–596.

McCrae, R. (1984). Situational determinants of coping responses: Loss, threat, and challenge. *Journal of Personality and Social Psychology,* **46**, 919–928.

McCrae, R. R., & Costa, P. T. (1984). *Emerging lives, enduring dispositions: Personality in adulthood.* Boston: Little, Brown.

——. (1986). Clinical assessment can benefit from recent advances in personality psychology. *American Psychologist, 41,* 1001–1002.

——. (1987). Validation of the five-factor model of personality across instruments and observers. *Journal of Personality and Social Psychology, 52,* 81–90.

——. (1994). The stability of personality: Observations and evaluations. *Current Directions in Psychological Science, 3,* 173–175.

——. (1997). Personality trait structure as a human universal. *American Psychologist, 52(5),* 509–516.

McCrae, R. R., & Costa, P. T., Jr. (1990). *Personality in adulthood.* New York: Guilford.

——. (1999). A five-factor theory of personality. In L. A. Pervin & O. P. John (Eds.), *Handbook of personality (2nd ed.).* New York: Guilford.

McCrae, R. R., & John, O. P. (1992). An introduction to the five-factor model and its applications. *Journal of Personality, 60,* 175–215.

McDougall, W. (1908). *An introduction to social psychology.* London: Methuen.

McElree, B. (2001). Working memory and focal attention. *Journal of Experimental Psychology: Learning, Memory, & Cognition, 27,* 817–835.

McEvoy, G. M., & Beatty, R. W. (1989). Assessment centers and subordinate appraisals of managers: A seven-year examination of predictive validity. *Personnel Psychology, 42,* 37–52.

McGaugh, J. L. (1983). Hormonal influences on memory. *Annual Review of Psychology, 34,* 297–323.

McGee, M. G. (1979). Human spatial abilities: Psychometric studies and environmental, genetic, hormonal, and neurological influences. *Psychological Bulletin, 86,* 889–918.

McGehee, D. S., Heath, M. J. S., Gelber, S., Devay, P., & Role, L. W. (1995). Nicotine enhancement of fast excitatory synaptic transmission in CNS by presynaptic receptors. *Science, 269,* 1692–1696.

McGeoch, J. A., & McDonald, W. T. (1931). Meaningful relation and retroactive inhibition. *American Journal of Psychology, 43,* 579–588.

McGillicuddy-De Lisi, A. V., Sullivan, B., & Hughes, B. (2003). The effects of interpersonal relationship and character gender on adolescents' resolutions of moral dilemmas. *Applied Developmental Psychology, 23,* 655–669.

McGinnis, J. M. (1985). Recent history of federal initiatives in prevention policy. *American Psychologist, 40,* 205–212.

McGinnis, J. M., & Foege, W. H. (1993). Actual causes of death in the United States. *Journal of the American Medical Association, 270,* 2207–2212.

McGlashen, T. H., & Fenton, W. S. (1992). The positive-negative distinction in schizophrenia: Review of natural history indicators. *Archives of General Psychiatry, 49,* 63–72.

McGlone, J. (1977). Sex differences in the cerebral organization of verbal functions in patients with unilateral lesions. *Brain, 100,* 775–793.

——. (1978). Sex differences in functional brain asymmetry. *Cortex, 14,* 122–128.

——. (1980). Sex differences in human brain asymmetry: A critical survey. *The Behavioral and Brain Sciences, 3,* 215-227.

McGrath, E., Keita, G. P., Strickland, B., & Russo, N. F. (Eds.). (1990). *Women and depression: Risk factors and treatment issues.* Washington, DC: American Psychological Association.

McGraw, K. O. (1987). *Developmental psychology.* San Diego: Harcourt Brace Jovanovich.

McGue, M., & Lykken, D. T. (1992). Genetic influence on risk of divorce. *Psychological Science, 3,* 368–373.

McGuffin, P., Rijsdijk, F., Andrews, M., Sham, P., Katz, R., & Cardno, A. (2003). The heritability of bipolar affective disorder and the genetic relationship to unipolar depression. *Archives of General Psychiatry, 60,* 497–502.

McGuffin, P., Riley, B., & Plomin, R. (2001). Toward behavioral genomics. *Science, 291,* 1232-1249.

McGuire, W. J. (1985). Attitudes and attitude change. In G. Lindzey & E. Aronson (Eds.), *Handbook of social psychology.* New York: Random House.

McHale, S. M., Updegruff, K. A., Helms-Erikson, H., & Crouter, A. C. (2001). Sibling influences on gender development in middle childhood and early adolescence: A longitudinal study. *Developmental Psychology, 37,* 115–125.

McInnis, J. H., & Shearer, J. K. (1964). Relationship between color choices and selected preferences for the individual. *Journal of Home Economics, 56,* 181-187.

McKenna, K., Green, A., & Gleason, M. (2002). Relationship formation on the Internet: What's the big attraction? *Journal of Social Issues, 58,* 9–31.

McKenna, M. C., Zevon, M. A., Corn, B., & Rounds, J. (1999). Psychosocial factors and the development of breast cancer: A meta-analysis. *Health Psychology, 18,* 520–531.

McKim, W. A. (1986). *Drugs and behavior.* Englewood Cliffs, NJ: Prentice-Hall.

McKinlay, A., Proctor, R., & Dunnett, A. (1999). *An investigation of social loafing and social compensation in computer-supported cooperative work.* Proceedings of the international ACM SIGGROUP conference on supporting group work, Phoenix, AZ, Nov. 14–17.

McLeod, J. D., & Kessler, R. C. (1990). Socioeconomic status and differences in vulnerability to undesirable life events. *Journal of Health and Social Behavior, 31,* 162–172.

McLeod, M. D., & Ellis, H. D. (1986). Modes of presentation in eyewitness testimony research. *Human Learning Journal of Practical Research and Applications, 5,* 39–44.

McMahon, J., Garner, J., Davis, R., & Kraus, A. (2002). *How to correctly collect and analyze racial profiling data: Your reputation depends on it!* Washington, DC: Government Printing Office.

McNally, R. J. (2003). Progress and controversy in the study of posttraumatic stress disorder. *Annual Review of Psychology, 54,* 229–252.

——. (2003). Recovering memories of trauma: A view from the laboratory. *Current Directions in Psychological Science, 12,* 32–35.

——. (2003). *Remembering trauma.* Cambridge, MA: Belknap Press/Harvard University Press.

McNally, R. J. & Shin, L. M. (1995). Association of intelligence with severity of posttraumatic stress disorder symptoms in Vietnam combat veterans. *American Journal of Psychiatry, 152,* 936–938.

McRoberts, C., Burlingame, G. M., & Hoag, M. J. (1998). Comparative efficacy of individuals and group psychotherapy. *Group dynamics, 2,* 101–117.

Meara, E. R., Richards, S., & Cutler, D. M. (2008). The gap gets bigger: Changes in mortality and life expectancy by education, 1981–2000. *Health Affairs, 27,* 350–360.

Medin, D. L. (1989). Concepts and concept structure. *American Psychologist, 44,* 1469–1481.

Mednick, M. T. (1989). On the politics of psychological constructs: Stop the bandwagon, I want to get off. *American Psychologist, 44,* 1118–1123.

Mednick, M. T. S. (1979). The new psychology of women: A feminist analysis. In J. E. Gullahorn (Ed.), *Psychology and women: In transition.* New York: Wiley.

Mednick, S. A., Moffitt, T. E., & Stack, S. (1987). *The causes of crime: New biological approaches.* New York: Cambridge University Press.

Meer, J. (1986). The reason of age. *Psychology Today, 20,* 60–64.

Meichenbaum, D. (1977). *Cognitive-behavior modification: An integrative approach.* New York: Plenum.

Meichenbaum, D., & Turk, D. C. (1987). *Facilitating treatment adherence.* New York: Plenum.

Mellman, T. A., Randolph, C. A., Brawman-Mintzer, O., Fores, L. P., & Milanes, F. J. (1992). Phenomenology and course of psychiatric disorders associated with combat-related post-traumatic stress disorder. *American Journal of Psychiatry, 149,* 1568–1574.

Melton, G. B., Petrila, J., Poythress, N. G., & Slobogin, C. (2007). *Psychological evaluation for the courts: A handbook for mental health professionals and lawyers.* New York: Guilford.

Meltzoff, A. N. (1995). Understanding the intentions of others: Re-enactment of intended acts by 18-month-old children. *Developmental Psychology, 31,* 838–850.

Meltzoff, A. N., & Moore, M. K. (1977). Imitation of facial and manual gestures by human neonates. *Science, 198,* 75–78.

——. (1983). Newborn infants imitate adult facial gestures. *Child Development, 54,* 702–709.

——. (1989). Imitation in newborn infants: Exploring the range of gestures imitated and the underlying mechanism. *Developmental Psychology, 25,* 954–962.

Melzack, R. (1973). *The puzzle of pain.* Baltimore: Penguin Books.

——. (1999). From the gate to the neuromatrix. *Pain (Supplement No. 6),* 121-126.

Melzack, R., & Wall, P. D. (1965). Pain mechanisms: A new theory. *Science, 150,* 971–979.

Memon, T., Morris, M. W., Chiu, C., & Hong, Y. (1999). Culture and the construal of agency: Attribution to individual versus group dispositions. *Journal of Personality and Social Psychology, 76,* 701-717.

Mendelson, W. B. (1997). Efficacy of melatonin as a hypnotic agent. *Journal of Biological Rhythms, 12,* 651–657.

Mercader, J. M., et al. (2008). Altered brain-derived neurotrophic factor blood levels and gene variability are associated with anorexia and bulimia. *Genes, Brain, & Behavior, 6,* 706–716.

Meredith, N. (1986). Testing the talking cure. *Science 86, 7(5),* 30–37.

Merikangas, K. R., Akiskai, H. S., Angst, J., Greenberg, P. E., Hirschfield, R. M. A., Petukova, M., & Kessler, R. C. (2007). Lifetime and 12-month prevalence of bipolar spectrum disorder in the National Comorbidity Survey Replication. *Archives of General Psychiatry, 64,* 543–552.

Merikle, P. M., & Daneman, M. (1998). Psychological investigations of unconscious perception. *Journal of Consciousness Studies, 5,* 5–18.

Mervis, J. (1986). NIMH data points the way to effective treatment. *APA Monitor, 17,* 1, 13.

Metcalf, J. (1990). Composite holographic associative recall model (CHARM) and blended memory in eyewitness testimony. *Journal of Experimental Psychology: General, 119,* 145–160.

Metcalfe, J., & Wiebe, D. (1987). Intuition and insight and noninsight problem solving. *Memory and Cognition, 15,* 238–246.

Metcalfe, J., Funnell, M., & Gazzaniga, M. S. (1995). Right-hemisphere memory superiority: Studies of a split-brain patient. *Psychological Science, 6,* 157–164

Mezey, E., Key, S., Vogelsang, G., Szalayova, I., Lange, G. D., & Crain, B. (2003). Transplanted bone marrow generates new neurons in human brains. *Proceedings of the National Academy of Sciences, 100,* 1364-1369.

Michael, R. T., Gagnon, J. H., Laumann, E. O., & Kolata, G. (1994). *Sex in America: A definitive study.* Boston: Little, Brown.

Mick, E., Biederman, J., Faraone, S. V., Sayer, J., & Kleinman, S. (2002). Case-control study of attention-deficit hyperactivity disorder and maternal smoking, alcohol use, and drug use during pregnancy. *Journal of the American Academy of Child and Adolescent Psychiatry, 41,* 378–385.

Middlemist, R. D., & Peterson, R. B. (1976). Test of equity theory by controlling for comparison of workers' efforts. *Organizational Behavior and Human Performance, 15,* 335–354.

Midgley, C., Kaplan, A., & Middleton, M. (2001). Performance-approach goals: Good for what, for whom, under what conditions, and at what cost? *Journal of Educational Psychology, 93,* 77–86.

Miklowitz, D. J., George, E. L., Richards, J. A., Simoneau, T. L., & Suddath, R. L. (2003). A randomized study of family-focused psychoeducation and pharmacotherapy in the outpatient management of bipolar disorder. *Archives of General Psychiatry, 60,* 904–912.

Milekic, M. H., Brown, S. D., Castellini, C., & Albernini, C. M. (2006). Persistent disruption of an established morphine conditioned place preference. *The Journal of Neuroscience, 26,* 3010–3020.

Milgram, S. (1963). Behavioral studies of obedience. *Journal of Abnormal and Social Psychology, 67,* 371–378.

——. (1965). Some conditions of obedience and disobedience to authority. *Human Relations, 18,* 57–76.

——. (1970). The experience of living in cities. *Science, 167,* 1461–1468.

——. (1974). *Obedience to authority.* New York: HarperCollins.

——. (1977). *The individual in a social world.* Reading, MA: Addison-Wesley.

Miller, D. T., & McFarland, C. (1987). Pluralistic ignorance: When similarity is interpreted as dissimilarity. *Journal of Personality and Social Psychology, 53*, 298–305.

Miller, D. T., & Ross, M. (1975). Self-serving biases in the attribution of causality: Fact or fiction? *Psychological Bulletin, 82*, 213–225.

Miller, J. G. (1984). Culture and the development of everyday social explanation. *Journal of Personality and Social Psychology, 46*, 961–978.

Miller, K. J., Gleaves, D. H., Hirsch, T. G., Green, B. A., Snow, A. C., & Corbett, C. C. (2000). Comparisons of body image dimensions by race/ethnicity and gender in a university population. *International Journal of Eating Disorders, 27*, 310-316.

Miller, N. E. (1941). The frustration-aggression hypothesis. *Psychological Review, 48*, 337–342.

——. (1944). Experimental studies of conflict. In J. M. Hunt (Ed.), *Personality and the behavior disorders.* New York: Ronald Press.

——. (1983). Behavioral medicine: Symbiosis between laboratory and clinic. *Annual Review of Psychology, 34*, 1–31.

Miller, R. C., & Berman, J. S. (1983). The efficacy of cognitive behavior therapies: A quantitative review of the research evidence. *Psychological Bulletin, 94*, 39–53.

Miller, W. R. (1992). Client/treatment matching in addictive behaviors. *The Behavior Therapist, 15*, 7–8.

Millstein, S. G. (1989). Adolescent health: Challenges for behavioral scientists. *American Psychologist, 44*, 837–842.

Millstein, S. G., Peterson, A. C., & Nightingate, E. O. (Eds.). (1993). *Promoting the health of adolescents: New directions for the twenty-first century.* New York: Oxford University Press.

Milner, B., Corkin, S., & Teuber, H. L. (1968). Further analysis of the hippocampal amnesic syndrome: 14-year follow-up study of H. M. *Neuropsychologica, 6*, 215–234.

Minami, H., & Dallenbach, K. M. (1946). The effect of activity upon learning and retention in the cockroach. *American Journal of Psychology, 59*, 682–697.

Mineka, S., Watson, D., & Clark, L. A. (1998). Comorbidity of anxiety and unipolar mood disorders. *Annual Review of Psychology, 49*, 377–412.

Minton, H. L. (2000). Psychology and gender at the turn of the century. *American Psychologist, 55*, 613-615.

Minuchin, S., & Fishman, H. C. (1981). *Family therapy techniques.* Cambridge, MA: Harvard University Press.

Miranda, J., Bernard, G., Lau, L., Kohn, L., Hwang, W., & LaFramboise, T. (2005). State of the science on psychological interventions for ethnic minorities. *Annual Review of Clinical Psychology, 1*, 113-142.

Mirin, S. M., Weiss, R. D., & Greenfield, S. F. (1991). Psychoactive substance abuse disorders. In A. J. Galenberg, E. L. Bassuk, & S. C. Schoonover (Eds.), *The practitioner's guide to psychoactive drugs.* New York: Plenum.

Mischel, W. (1968). *Personality and assessment.* New York: Wiley.

——. (1973). Toward a cognitive social learning reconceptualization of personality. *Psychological Review, 80*, 252–283.

——. (1979). On the interface of cognition and personality. *American Psychologist, 34*, 740–754.

——. (1981). *Introduction to personality (3rd ed.).* New York: Holt, Rinehart & Winston.

——. (1999). Personality coherence and dispositions in a cognitive-affective personality system (CAPS) approach. In D. Cervone, & Y. Shoda (Eds.), *The coherence of personality: Social-cognitive bases of consistency, variability, and organization.* New York: Guilford.

——. (2004). Toward an integrative science of the person. *Annual Review of Psychology, 55*, 1-22.

Mischel, W. (2004). Toward an integrative science of the person. *Annual Review of Psychology, 55*, 1–22.

Mischel, W., & Peake, P. K. (1982). Beyond déja vu in the search for cross-situational consistency. *Psychological Review, 89*, 730–755.

Mischel, W., & Shoda, Y. (1998). Reconciling processing dynamics and personality dispositions. *Annual Review of Psychology, 49*, 229–258.

Mischel, W., Shoda, Y., & Mendoza-Denton, R. (2002). Situation-behavior profiles as a locus of consistency in personality. *Current Directions in Psychological Science, 11*, 50–54.

Mischel, W., Shoda, Y., & Smith, R. E. (2004). *Introduction to personality: Toward an integration.* New York: Wiley.

Mishkin, M., & Appenzeller, T. (1987). The anatomy of memory. *Scientific American, 256*, 80–89.

Mitchell, D. B. (2006). Nonconscious priming after 17 years: Invulnerable implicit memory? *Psychological Science, 17*, 925–929.

Mitchell, M. & Jolley, J. (2001). *Research Design Explained, 4th edition,* Belmont, CA: Thomson/Wadsworth.

Mitler, M. M., Miller, J. C., Lipsitz, J. J., & Walsh, J. K. (1997). The sleep of long-haul truck drivers. *New England Journal of Medicine, 337*, 755–761.

Mobley, W. H. (1977). Intermediate linkages in the relationship between job satisfaction and employee turnover. *Journal of Applied Psychology, 62*, 237–240.

Moen, P., Kim, J. E., & Hofmeister, H. (2001). Couples' work/retirement transitions, gender, and marital status. *Social Psychology Quarterly, 64*, 55–71.

Moffitt, T. E., Caspi, A., & Rutter, M. (2005). Strategy for investigating interactions between measured genes and measured environments. *Archives of General Psychiatry, 62*, 473-481.

Mohr, C., Binkofski, F., Erdmann, C., Buchel, C., & Helmchen, C. (2005). The anterior cingulated cortex contains distinct areas dissociating external from self-administered stimulation: A parametric fMRI study. *Pain, 114*, 347–357.

Moll, L. C., & Diaz, S. (1987). A socio-cultural approach to the study of Hispanic children. In A. A. Allen (Ed.), *Library services for Hispanic children: A guide* (pp. 12-26). Phoenix, AZ: Oryx Press.

Monastersky, R. (2003). Whence wine? Blending chemistry and archeology, a researcher tracks the origins of grape fermentation. *The Chronicle of Higher Education,* August 15, pp. A16–A18.

Moncher, M. S., Holden, G. W., & Trimble, J. E. (1990). Substance abuse among Native American youth. *Journal of Consulting and Clinical Psychology, 58*, 408–415.

Moncrieff, J. (2003). Clozapine vs. conventional antipsychotic drugs for treatment-resistant schizophrenia: A re-examination. *The British Journal of Psychiatry*, **183**, 161–166.

Money, J. (1987). Sin, sickness, or status? Homosexual gender identity and psychoneuroendocrinology. *American Psychologist*, **42**, 384–399.

Monson, T. C., & Snyder, M. (1977). Actors, observers, and the attribution process. *Journal of Experimental Social Psychology*, **13**, 89–111.

Montada, L., & Lerner, M. (Eds.). (1998). *Responses to victimizations and belief in a just world.* New York: Plenum.

Montgomery, G. H., DuHamel, K. N., & Redd, W. H. (2000). A meta-analysis of hypnotically induced analgesia: How effective is hypnosis? *International Journal of Clinical and Experimental Hypnosis*, **48**, 138–153.

Montgomery, G. H., Weltz, C. R., Seltz, M., & Bovbjerg, D. H. (2002). Brief presurgery hypnosis reduces distress and pain in excisional breast biopsy patients. *International Journal of Clinical and Experimental Hypnosis*, **50**, 17-32.

Montgomery, M. R., Stren, R., Cohen, B., & Reed, H. E. (Eds.). (2003). *Cities transformed: Demographic change and its implications in the developing world.* Washington, DC: Academic Press.

Moody, E. J. (2001). Internet use and its relationship to loneliness. *CyberPsychology and Behavior*, **4**, 393–401.

Moon, C., & Fifer, W. P. (1990). Syllables as signals for 2-day old infants. *Infant Behavior and Development*, **13**, 377–390.

Moore, K. (1992). *Facts at a glance.* Washington, DC: Childtrends.

Moore, K. L. & Persaud, T. V. (2002). *Before we are born: Essentials of embryology and birth defects.* Philadelphia: W. B. Saunders.

Moore, T. H. M., Zammit, S., Lingford-Hughes, A., Barnes, T. R. E., Jones, P. B., Burke, M., & Lewis, G. (2007). Cannabis use and risk of psychotic or affective mental health outcomes: A systematic review. *The Lancet*, **370**, 319–328.

Moorecroft, W. H. (1987). An overview of sleep. In J. Gackenback (Ed.), *Sleep and dreams.* New York: Garland.

——. (1989). *Sleep, dreaming, and sleep disorders.* Latham, MD: University Press of America.

Moran, J. S., Janes, H. R., Peterman, T. A., & Stone, K. M. (1990). Increase in condom sales following AIDS education and publicity, United States. *American Journal of Public Health*, **80**, 607–608.

Moreno, C., Laje, G., Blanco, C., Jiang, H., Schmidt, A., & Olfson, M. (2007). National trends in the outpatient diagnosis and treatment of bipolar disorder in children. *Archives of General Psychiatry*, **64**, 1032–1039.

Morgan, C. T. (1961). *Introduction to psychology.* New York: McGraw Hill.

Morgan, W. P. (1980). The trait psychology controversy. *Research Quarterly for Exercise and Sport*, **51**, 50–76.

Moriceau, S., & Sullivan, R. M. (2004). Unique neural circuitry for neonatal olfactory learning. *The Journal of Neuroscience*, **24**, 1182–1189.

Morris, C. W. (1946). *Signs, language, and behavior.* Englewood Cliffs, NJ: Prentice-Hall.

Morris, L. A., & Halperin, J. (1979). Effects of written drug information on patient knowledge and compliance: A literature review. *American Journal of Public Health*, **69**, 47–52.

Morris, M., & Peng, K. (1994). Culture and cause: American and Chinese attributions for social and physical events. *Journal of Personality and Social Psychology*, **67**, 949–971.

Morrison, D. M. (1985). Adolescent contraceptive behavior: A review. *Psychological Bulletin*, **98**, 538–568.

Moruzzi, G. (1975). The sleep-wake cycle. *Reviews of Psychology*, **64**, 1–165.

Moruzzi, G., & Magoun, H. W. (1949). Brain stem reticular formation and activation of the EEG. *Electroencephalography and Clinical Neurophysiology*, **1**, 455–473.

Moscovici, S., Lage, E., & Naffrechoux, M. (1969). Influences of a consistent minority on the response of a majority in a color perception task. *Sociometry*, **32**, 365–380.

Moscovici, S., Mugny, G., & Van Avermaet, E. (1985). *Perspectives on minority influence.* New York: Cambridge University Press.

Mowday, R. T. (1983). Equity theory prediction of behavior in organizations. In R. M. Steers & L. W. Porter (Eds.), *Motivation and work behavior (3rd ed.).* New York: McGraw-Hill.

Mshelia, A. Y., & Lapidus, L. B. (1990). Depth picture perception in relation to cognitive style and training in non-Western children. *Journal of Cross-Cultural Psychology*, **21**, 414–433.

Muchinsky, P. M., & Tuttle, M. L. (1979). Employee turnover: An empirical and methodological assessment. *Journal of Vocational Behavior*, **14**, 43–77.

Mueller, T. I., Keller, M. B., Leon, A. C., Solomon, D. A., Shea, M. T., Coryell, W., & Endicott, J. (1996). Recovery after 5 years of unremitting major depressive disorder. *Archives of General Psychiatry*, **53**, 794–799.

Mugny, G. (1975). Negotiations, image of the other and the process of minority influence. *European Journal of Social Psychology*, **5**, 209-228.

Mukherjee, S., Shukla, S., Woodle, J., Rosen, A. M., & Olarte, S. (1983). Misdiagnosis of schizophrenia and bipolar patients: A multiethnic comparison. *American Journal of Psychiatry*, **140**, 1571-1574.

Mulac, A., Incontro, C. R., & James, M. R. (1985). Comparison of gender-linked language effect and sex role stereotypes. *Journal of Personality and Social Psychology*, **49**, 1098–1109.

Mulholland, A. M., & Mintz, L. B. (2001). Prevalence of eating disorders among African American women. *Journal of Counseling Psychology*, **48**, 111–116.

Mumford, M. D., Uhlman, C. E., & Kilcullen, R. N. (1992). The structure of life history: Implications for the construct validity of background data scales. *Human Performance*, **5**, 109–137.

Munn, N. L. (1956). *Introduction to psychology.* Boston: Houghton Mifflin.

Murdoch, D. D., & Pihl, R. O. (1988). The influence of beverage type on aggression in males in the natural setting. *Aggressive Behavior*, **14**, 325–335.

Murphy, S. L. (2000). Deaths: Final data for 1998. *National Vital Statistics Reports,* **48**(11), July 24, 2000.

Murray, B. (2002). What a recovering nation needs from behavioral science. *Monitor on Psychology,* **33** (February), 30–33.

Murray, D. J. (1983). *A history of Western psychology.* Englewood Cliffs, NJ: Prentice-Hall.

Murray, D. M., Johnson, C. A., Leupker, R. R., & Mittlemark, M. B. (1984). The prevention of cigarette smoking in children: A comparison of four strategies. *Journal of Applied Social Psychology,* **14**, 274–288.

Murray, H. A. (1938). *Explorations in personality.* New York: Oxford University Press.

Myles, B. S. (2007). Teaching students with autism spectrum disorders. *Remedial and Special Education,* **28**, 130–131.

Nakamura, J., & Csikszentmihalyi, M. (2001). Catalytic creativity: The case of Linus Pauling. *American Psychologist,* **56**, 337–341.

Nakao, M., Yano, E., Nomura, S., & Kuboki, T. (2003). Blood pressure lowering effects of biofeedback treatment in hypertension: A meta-analysis of randomized controlled trials. *Hypertension research,* **26**, 37–46.

NAMHC [Basic Behavioral Science Task Force of the National Advisory Mental Health Council]. (1996). Basic Behavioral Science Research for Mental Health: Sociocultural and environmental processes. *American Psychologist,* **51**, 722–731.

Namir, S., Wolcott, D. L., Fawzy, F. I., & Alumbaugh, M. J. (1987). Coping with AIDS: Psychological and health implications. *Journal of Applied Social Psychology,* **17**, 309–328.

Nash, M. (1987). What, if anything, is regressed about hypnotic age regression? *Psychological Bulletin,* **102**, 42–52.

Nathan, P. E., & Gorman, J. M. (Eds.). (1998). *A guide to treatments that work.* New York: Oxford University Press.

——. (Eds.). (2002). *A guide to treatments that work (2nd ed.).* New York: Oxford University Press.

Nathan, P. E., Stuart, S. P., & Dolan, S. L. (2000). Research of psychotherapy efficacy and effectiveness: Between Scylla and Charibdis. *Psychological Bulletin,* **126**, 964–981.

National Academy of Sciences, National Research Council. (1989). *Diet and health: Implications for reducing chronic disease risk.* Washington, DC: National Academy Press.

National Association of Anorexia Nervosa and Associated Disorders. (2001). *Facts about eating disorders.* Retrieved on June 19, 2001 from the World Wide Web: http://www.anad.org/ facts.htm.

National Eating Disorders Association. (2003). *Statistics: Eating disorders and their precursors.* Available at: http://www.nationaleatingdisorders.org.

——. (2005). *Facts for activists (or anyone).* Downloaded on October 25, 2005 from www.nationaleatingdisorders.org/p.asp?WebPage_ID=286&Profile_ID=95634.

——. (2008). Facts and statistics. Downloaded on September 7, 2008 from http://www.nationaleatingdisorders.org/information-resources/general-information.php#facts-statistics.

National Highway Traffic Safety Administration (NHTSA). (2003). *National survey of distracted and drowsy driving attitudes and behaviors: 2002.* Washington, DC: NATSA.

National Institute of Allergy and Infectious Diseases. (2003). *HIV infection and AIDS: An overview, June 2003.* Bethesda, MD: National Institutes of Health.

National Institute of Mental Health (NIMH). (1981). *Depressive disorders: Causes and treatment (DHEW Publication No. ADM 81–108).* Washington, DC: U.S. Government Printing Office.

——. (1984). The NIMH epidemiologic catchment area program. *Archives of General Psychiatry,* **41**, 931–1011.

——. (1989). *Information on lithium.* Rockville, MD: U.S. Department of Health and Human Services.

——. (1990). *Bipolar disorder: Manic-depressive illness.* Washington, DC: U.S. Government Printing Office.

——. (1991). *Information about D/Art and depression.* Rockville, MD: U.S. Department of Health and Human Services.

——. (1993). The NIMH epidemiologic catchment area program. *Archives of General Psychiatry,* 50.

National Institute on Drug Abuse. (1987). *National household survey on drug abuse: Population estimates 1985.* Rockville, MD.

——. (1999a). *Ecstacy.* Downloaded from the World Wide Web, February 1, 2001. http://www.nidanih.giv/Infofax/ecstacy.html.

——. (1999a). *Marijuana.* Downloaded from the World Wide Web, February 1, 2001. http://www.nida.nih.gov/Infofax/marijuana.html.

——. (2001). *MDMA/Ecstasy research: Advances, challenges, future directions: A scientific conference.* Washington, DC: National Institutes of Health.

——. (2003). *Research report series—marijuana abuse.* Washington, DC: National Institutes of Health.

——. (2005). *NIDA InfoFacts: Methamphetamine* Downloaded from www.drugabuse.gov on November 3, 2005.

——. (2006). *MDMA (Ecstasy) abuse. Technical Report No. 06–4728.* Rockwell, MD National Institute on Drug Abuse.

National Institutes of Health, Review Panel on Coronary Prone Behavior and Coronary Heart Disease. (1981). Coronary-prone behavior and coronary heart disease: A critical review. *Circulation,* **63**, 1199–1215.

National Multiple Sclerosis Society. (2003) *Just the facts: 2001—2002,* revised, January 8, 2003. New York: National Multiple Sclerosis Society.

——. (2005). *Just the facts: 2004-2005.* New York: National Multiple Sclerosis Society.

——. (2007). National MS society raises concerns that recent NIH study underestimates number of people with MS in the U.S. Retrieved on May 14, 2008 from http://www.nationalmssociety.org/news/news-detail/index.aspx?nid=141.

——. (2008). Treatments. Retrieved on May 14, 2008 from http://www.nationalmssociety.org/about-multiple-sclerosis/treatments/index.aspx.

NCHS (National Center for Health Statistics). (2003). *National vital statistics report (Vol. 51).* Hyattsville, MD: Author.

——. (2003). *Overweight prevalence.* Centers for Disease Control. Available at: http://www.cdc.gov/nchs.

NDMDA (National Depressive and Manic-Depressive Association). (1996). *Depressive illness: The medical facts, the human challenge.* New York: The National Depressive and Manic Depressive Association.

Nee, D. E., Berman, M. G., Moore, K. S., & Jonides, J. (2008). Neuroscientific evidence about the distinction between short- and long-term memory. *Current Directions in Psychological Science, 17*, 102–106.

Neighbors, H. W., & Jackson, J. S. (1984). The use of informal and formal help: Four patterns of illness behavior in the Black community. *American Journal of Community Psychology, 12*, 629-644.

Neisser, U. (1976). *Cognition and reality: Principles and implications of cognitive psychology.* San Francisco: W. H. Freeman.

——. (1982). *Memory observed.* San Francisco: Freeman.

——. (1991). A case of misplaced nostalgia. *American Psychologist, 46*, 34–36.

Nelson, G. (1995). Cultural differences in learning styles. In J. Reid (Ed.), *Learning styles in the ESL/EFL classroom* (pp. 3-18). Boston: Heinle & Heinle.

Nelson, G., Chandrashekar, J., Hoon, M. A., Feng, L., Zhao, G., Ryba, N. J. P., & Zuker, C. S. (2002). An amino-acid taste receptor. *Nature, 416*, 199–202.

Nelson, K. (1993). The psychological and social origins of autobiographical memory. *Psychological Science, 4*, 7–14.

Nemeth, C. (1986). Differential contributions of majority and minority influence. *Psychological Review, 93*, 23–32.

Neugarten, B. L., & Neugarten, D. A. (1986). Changing meanings of age in the aging society. In A. Piter & L. Bronte (Eds.), *Our aging society: Paradox and promise.* New York: Norton.

——. (1989). Policy issues in an aging society. In M. Storandt & G. R. VandenBos (Eds.), *The adult years: Continuity and change.* Washington, DC: American Psychological Association.

Newby, R. W. (1987). Contextual areas in item recognition following verbal discrimination learning. *Journal of General Psychology, 114*, 281–287.

Newcomb, M. D., & Bentler, P. M. (1989). Substance abuse among children and teenagers. *American Psychologist, 44*, 242–248.

Newcomb, N., & Dubas, J. S. (1987). Individual differences in cognitive ability: Are they related to timing of puberty? In R. M. Lerner & T. T. Foch (Eds.), *Biological-psychosocial interactions in early adolescence: A life-span approach.* Hillsdale, NJ: Erlbaum.

Newcombe, N. S. (2002).The nativist-empiricist controversy in the context of recent research on spatial and quantitative development. *Psychological Science, 13*, 395–401.

Newman, B. M., & Newman, P. R. (1984). *Development through life: A psychosocial approach.* Homewood, IL: Dorsey Press.

NHGRI (National Human Genome Research Institute). (2005). *About the National Genome Research Institute.* Downloaded from the Internet www.genome.gov on September 12, 2005.

NHSDA. (2002). *Results from the 2001 National Household Survey on Drug Abuse: Volume II.* Rockville, MD: SAMHSA.

Ni, H., Schiller, J., Hao, C., Cohen, R. A., & Barnes, P. (2003). *Early release of selected estimates based on data from the first quarter 2003 National Health Interview Survey.* National Center for Health Statistics. Available at: http://www.cdc.gov/nchs/nhis.htm.

NICHD (Early Child Care Research Network). (1997). The effects of infant child care on infant-mother attachment security: Results of the NICHD study of early child care. *Child Development, 68*, 860–879.

NICHD (National Institute on Child Health and Human Development). (2002). Child-care structure —> process —> outcome: Direct and indirect effects of child-care quality on young children's development. *Psychological Science, 13*, 199–206.

Nickerson, R. S., & Adams, M. J. (1979). Long-term memory for a common object. *Cognitive Psychology, 11*, 287–307.

Nigg, J. T., & Goldsmith, H. H. (1994). Genetics of personality disorders: Perspectives from personality and psychopathology research. *Psychological Bulletin, 115*, 346–380.

Nijhawan, R. (2002). Neural delays, visual motion and the flash-lag effect. *Trends in Cognitive Science, 6*, 387–393.

Nilsson, K., Sundbom, E., & Hägglöf, B. (2008). A longitudinal study of perfectionism in adolescent onset anorexia nervosa-restricting type. *European Eating Disorders Review, 16*, 386–394.

Nisan, M., & Kohlberg, L. (1982). Universality and variation in moral judgement: A longitudinal and cross-sectional study in Turkey. *Child Development, 53*, 865–876.

Nisbett, R. E. (1972). Hunger, obesity, and the ventromedial hypothalamus. *Psychological Review, 79*, 433–453.

——. (1980). The trait construct in lay and professional psychology. In L. Festinger (Ed.), *Retrospections on Social Psychology.* New York: Oxford University Press.

Noakes, T. D. (2003). Overconsumption of fluids by athletes. *British Journal of Medicine, 327*, 113–114.

Nolen-Hoeksema, S. (2001). Gender differences in depression. *Current Directions in Psychological Sciences, 10*, 173–176.

——. (2003). *Women who think too much: How to break free of overthinking and reclaim your life.* New York: Holt.

Nolen-Hoeksema, S., & Girgus, J. S. (1994). The emergence of gender differences in depression during adolescence. *Psychological Bulletin, 115*, 424-443.

Nolen-Hoeksema, S., Larson, J., & Grayson, C. (1999). Explaining the gender difference in depressive symptoms. *Journal of Personality and Social Psychology, 77*, 1061-1072.

Noor, F., & Evans, D. C. (2003). The effect of facial symmetry on perceptions of personality and attractiveness. *Journal of Research in Personality, 37*, 339–347.

Norasakkunkit, V., & Kalick S. M. (2002). Culture, ethnicity, and emotional distress measures: The role of self-construal and self-enhancement. *Journal of Cross-Cultural Psychology, 33*, 56-70.

Norcross, J. C. (1986). *Handbook of eclectic psychotherapy.* New York: Brunner/Mazel.

——. (Ed.). (2002). *Psychotherapy relationships that work.* New York: Oxford University Press.

Norenzayan, A., Choi, I., & Nesbitt, R. E. (2002). Cultural similarities and differences in social inference: Evidence from behavioral predictions and lay theories of behavior. *Personality and Social Psychology Bulletin, 28*, 109-120.

Norenzayan, A., & Nisbett, R. E. (2000). Culture and causal cognition. *Current Directions in Psychological Science, 9*, 132–135.

Norman, G. R., Brooks, L. R., & Allen, S. W. (1989). Recall by expert medical practitioners and novices as a record of processing attention. *Journal of Experimental Psychology: Learning, Memory, and Cognition, 15*, 1166–1174.

Northeastern University. (2005). *Racial profiling data collection resource center*. Downloaded November 9, 2005 from: www.racialprofil-inganaysis.neu.edu/background/jurisdictions.php.

Noyes, R., Reich, J., Christiansen, J., Suelzer, M., Pfohl, B., & Coryell, W. A. (1990). Outcome of panic disorder. *Archives of General Psychiatry*, **47**, 809–818.

Nuby, J. F., & Oxford, R. L. (1997). Learning style preference of Native American and African American students as measured by the MBTI. *Journal of Psychological Type*, **26**, 1-15.

Nuby, J. F., Ehle, M. A., & Thrower, E. (2001). Culturally responsive teaching as related to the learning styles of Native American students. In J. Nyowe & S. Abadullah (Eds.), *Multicultural education: Diverse perspectives* (pp. 231-271). Victoria, BC: Strafford Publishing.

Nuttall, G. A., Bowersox, M. R., Douglass, S. B., McDonald, J., Rasmussen, L. J., Decker, P. A., Oliver, W. C., & Rasmussen, K. G. (2004). Morbidity and mortality in the use of electroconvulsive therapy. *The Journal of ECT*, **20**, 237-241.

O'Connell, M. H., & Russo, A. N. (Eds.). (2001). *Models of achievement: Reflections of eminent women in psychology*. New York: Columbia University Press.

O'Conner, E. M. (2001). An American psychologist. *Monitor on Psychology*, **10**, November. Downloaded from http://www.apa.org/monitor/nov01/american.html.

Oden, G. C. (1987). Concept, knowledge, and thought. *Annual Review of Psychology*, **38**, 203–227.

Oden, M. H. (1968). The fulfillment of promise: 40-year follow-up of the Terman gifted group. *Genetic Psychology Monographs*, **77(1)**, 3–93.

Oesterman, K., Bjoerkqvist, K., Lagerspetz, K. M. J., Kaukiainen, A., Landau, S. F., et al. (1998). Cross-cultural evidence of female indirect aggression. *Aggressive Behavior*, **24**, 1–8.

Oetting, E. R., & Beauvais, F. (1987). Peer cluster theory, socialization characteristics and adolescent drug use: A path analysis. *Journal of Counseling Psychology*, **34**, 205–213.

——. (1990). Adolescent drug use: Findings of national and local surveys. *Journal of Consulting and Clinical Psychology*, **58**, 385–394.

Offer, D., & Offer, J. (1975). *From teenage to young manhood: A psychological study*. New York: Basic Books.

Office of the Surgeon General. (2001). *Report of the Surgeon General's Conference on Children's Mental Health: A national agenda*. Washington, DC: Department of Health and Human Services.

Offord, D. R., Boyle, M. H., Szatmari, P., Rae-Grant, N. I., Links, P. S., et al. (1987). Ontario child health study. *Archives of General Psychiatry*, **44**, 832–836.

Ogata, S. N., Silk, K. R., Goodrich, S., Lohr, N. E., & Hill, E. M. (1990). Childhood sexual and physical abuse in patients with borderline personality. *American Journal of Psychiatry*, **147**, 1008–1013.

Ogilvie, B. C., & Howe, M. A. (1984). Beating slumps at their game. *Psychology Today*, **18**, 28–32.

Ogle, L., Sen., A., Pahlke, E., Jocelyn, L., Kostberg, D., Roey, S. & Williams, T. (2003). *International comparisons in fourth-grade reading literacy: Findings from the Progress in International Literacy Study (PIRLS) of 2001 (NCES 2003–073)*. Washington, DC: U. S. Government Printing Office.

Ohbuchi, K., & Kamgara, T. (1985). Attacker's intent and awareness of outcome, impression management and retaliation. *Journal of Experimental Social Psychology*, **21**, 321–330.

Okazaki, S. (1997). Sources of ethnic differences between Asian American and White American college students on measures of depression and social anxiety. *Journal of Abnormal Psychology*, **106**, 52-60.

——. (2000). Asian American and White American differences on affective distress symptoms: Do symptom reports differ across reporting methods? *Journal of Cross-Cultural Psychology*, **31**, 603-625.

——. (2002). Self-other agreement on affective distress scales in Asian Americans and White Americans. *Journal of Counseling Psychology*, **49**, 428-437.

Okazaki, S., Liu, J. F., Longworth, S. L., & Minn, J. Y. (2002). Asian American-white American differences in expressions of social anxiety: A replication and extension. *Cultural Diversity and Ethnic Minority Psychology*, **8**, 234-247.

Olfson, M., & Pincus, H. A. (1994). Outpatient psychotherapy in the United States, I: Volume, costs, and user characteristics. *American Journal of Psychiatry*, **151**, 1281–1288.

Olfson, M., Marcus, S. C., Druss, B., Elinson, L., Tanielian, T., & Pincus, H. A. (2002). National trends in the outpatient treatment of depression. *Journal of the American Medical Association*, **287**, 203–209.

Olio, K. A. (1994). Truth in memory. *American Psychologist*, **49**, 442–443.

Oliveire-Berry, J. (2003). RxP: The heart of the matter. *Monitor on Psychology*, **34**, 63.

Olkin, R. (1999). *What psychotherapists should know about disability*. New York: The Guilford Press.

Olson, I. R., Rao, H., Moore, K. S., Wang, J., Detra, J. A., & Aguirre, G. K. (2006). Using perfusion fMRI to measure continuous changes in neural activity with learning. *Brain and Cognition*, **60**, 262–271.

Olton, D. S. (1978). Characteristics of spatial memory. In S. H. Hule, H. F. Fowler, & W. K. Honig (Eds.), *Cognitive processes in animal behavior*. Hillsdale, NJ: Erlbaum.

——. (1979). Mazes, maps, and memory. *American Psychologist*, **34**, 583–596.

Opalic, P. (1989). Existential and psychopathological evaluation of group psychotherapy of neurotic and psychotic patients. *International Journal of Group Psychotherapy*, **39**, 389–422.

Orlebeke, J. F., Knol, D. L., & Verhulst, F. C. (1999). Child behavior problems increased by maternal smoking during pregnancy. *Archives of Environmental Health*, **54**, 15–19.

Ornstein, P. A., Gordon, B. N., & Baker-Ward, L. E. (1992). Children's memory for salient events: Implications for testimony. In M. L. Howe, C. L. Brainerd, & V. F. Reyna (Eds.), *Development of long-term retention*. New York: Springer-Verlag.

Ornstein, P. A., Naus, M. J., & Liberty, C. (1975). Rehearsal and organizational processes in childhood memory. *Child Development*, **46**, 818–830.

Ortony, A., & Turner, T. J. (1990). What's basic about basic emotions? *Psychological Review*, **97**, 315–331.

Ortony, A., Clore, G. L., & Collins, A. (1988). *The cognitive structure of emotions.* New York: Cambridge University Press.

Oskamp. S. (1991). *Attitudes and opinions* (2nd ed.). New York, Prentice-Hall.

Ospina, M. B., Bond, K., Karkhanen, M., Tjosvold, B., Vandermeer, B., Liang, Y., Bialy, L., Hooton, N., Buscemi, N., Dryden, D. M., & Klassen, T. P. (2007). *Meditation practices for health: State of the research.* (Publication No. 07–E010.) Rockville, MD: Agency for Healthcare Research and Quality.

Ostovich, J. M., & Sabini, J. (2005). Timing of puberty and sexuality in men and women. *Archives of Sexual Behavior*, **34**, 197-206.

Ouis, D. (2001). Annoyance from road traffic noise: A review. *Journal of Environmental Psychology*, **21**, 101–120.

Ozer, D. J., & Reise, S. P. (1994). Personality assessment. *Annual Review of Psychology*, **45**, 357–388.

Ozer, E. J., & Weiss, D. S. (2004). Who develops posttraumatic stress disorder? *Current Directions in Psychological Science*, **13**, 169-172.

Packer, D. J. (2008). Identifying systematic disobedience in Milgram's obedience experiments: A meta-analytic review. *Perspectives on Psychological Science*, **3**, 301–304.

Padgett, D. K., Patrick, C., Burns, B. J., & Schesinger, H. J. (1994). Ethnicity and the use of outpatient mental health services in a national insured population. *American Journal of Public Health*, **84**, 222-226.

Pagnin, D., de Queiroz, V., Pini, S., & Cassano, G. B. (2004) Efficacy of ECT in depression: A meta-analytic review. *The Journal of ECT*, **20**, 13-20.

Pagoto, S. L., Kozac, A. T., Spates, C. R., & Spring, B. (2006). Systematic desensitization for an older woman with a severe specific phobia: An application of evidence-based practice. *Clinical Gerontologist*, **30**, 89–98.

Paivio, A. (1971). *Imagery and verbal processes.* New York: Holt, Rinehart & Winston.

——. (1981). *Mental representations: A dual coding approach.* New York: Oxford University Press.

——. (1986). *Mental representations: A dual coding approach.* New York: Oxford University Press.

Palmer, R. K. (2007). The pharmacology and signaling of bitter, sweet, and umami taste sensing. *Molecular Interventions*, **7**, 87–98.

Paludi, M. A., & Gullo, D. F. (1986). The effect of sex labels on adults' knowledge of infant development. *Sex Roles*, **16**, 19–30.

Pandey, J. (1990). The environment, culture, and behavior. In R. W. Brislin (Ed.), *Applied cross-cultural psychology.* Newbury Park CA: Sage.

Pandey, S. (1999). Role of perceived control in coping with crowding. *Psychological Studies*, **44**, 86–91.

Pang, V. O., & Cheng, L. L. (1998). *Struggling to be heard: The unmet needs of Asian-Pacific children.* Albany: University of New York Press.

Pantelis, C., Velakoulis, D., McGorry, P. D., Wood, S. J., Suckling, J., et al. (2003). Neuroanatomical abnormalities before and after onset of psychosis: A cross-sectional and longitudinal comparison. *Lancet*, **361**, 281-288.

Papilia, D. E., Camp, C. J., & Feldman, R. D. (1996). *Adult development and aging.* New York: McGraw-Hill.

Paris, J. (2004). Gender differences in personality traits and disorders. *Current Psychiatric Reports*, **6**, 71-74.

Park, C. C., & Chi, M. M. (1999). *Asian-American education: Prospects and challenges.* Westport, CN: Bergin & Harvey.

Parke, R. D., & Tinsley, B. J. (1987). Family interaction in infancy. In J. D. Osofsky (Ed.), *Handbook of infant development (2nd ed.).* New York: Wiley.

Parker, E. S., Birnbaum, I. M., & Noble, E. P. (1976). Alcohol and memory: Storage and state dependency. *Journal of Verbal Learning and Verbal Behavior*, **15**, 691–702.

Parra, J., Kalitzin, S. N., da Silva, F.H. (2004). Magnetoencephalography: An investigational tool or a routine clinical technique? *Epilepsy and Behavior*, **5**, 277-285.

Parrott, A. C., Lees, A., Garnham, N. J., Jones, M., & Wesnes, K. (1998). Cognitive performance in recreational users of MDMA or 'ecstasy': Evidence for memory deficits. *Journal of Psychopharmacology*, **12**, 79–83.

Parson, A. (1993). Getting the point. *Harvard Health Letter*, **18**, 6–9.

Pate, J. E., Pumariega, A. J., Hester, C., & Garner, D. M. (1992). Cross-cultural patterns in eating disorders: A review. *Journal of the American Academy of Child and Adolescent Psychiatry*, **31**, 802–809.

Pates, J., Oliver, R., & Maynard, I. (2001). The effects of hypnosis on flow states and golf putting performance. *Journal of Applied Sport Psychology*, **9**, 341–354.

Patil, S. T., Zhang, L., Marenyi, F., Lowe, S. L., Jackson, K. A., Andreev, B. V., Avedisova, A. S., Bardenstein, L. M., Gurovich, I. Y., et al. (2007). Activation of mGlu2/3 receptors as a new approach to treat schizophrenia: A randomized Phase 2 clinical trial. *Nature Medicine*, **13**, 1102–1107.

Patton, G. C., McMorris, B. J., Toumbourou, J. W., Hemphill, S. A., Donath, S., & Catalano, R. F. (2004). Puberty and the onset of substance use and abuse. *Pediatrics*, **114**, e300-e306.

Paulus, D. L., & Bruce, M. N. (1992). The effect of acquaintanceship on the validity of personality impressions: A longitudinal study. *Journal of Personality and Social Psychology*, **63**, 816–824.

Pauly, I. B., & Goldstein, S. G. (1970, November). Prevalence of significant sexual problems in medical practice. *Medical Aspects of Human Sexuality*, pp. 48–63.

Paunonen, S. P., Jackson, D. N., Trzebinski, J., & Fosterling, F. (1992). Personality structures across cultures: A multimethod evaluation. *Journal of Personality and Social Psychology*, **62**, 447–456.

Paunonen, S. V., & Jackson, D. N. (2000). What is beyond the big five? Plenty! *Journal of Personality*, **68**, 821–835.

Pavlov, I. (1927). *Conditioned reflexes.* New York: Oxford University Press.

——. (1928). *Lectures on conditioned reflexes: The higher nervous activity of animals (Vol. I)* (H. Gantt, Trans.). London: Lawrence and Wishart.

Pavlovich, M., & Greene, B. F. (1984). A self-instructional manual for installing low-cost/no-cost weatherization material: Experimental validation with scouts. *Journal of Applied Behavior Analysis, 17*, 105–109.

Pawaskar, M. D., Joish, V. N., Camacho, F. T., Rasu, R. S., & Balkrishnan, R. (2006). The influence of co-morbidities on prescribing pharmacotherapy for insomnia: Evidence from US national outpatient data 1955–2004. *Journal of Medical Economics, 11*, 41–56.

Pawlicki, R. E., & Heitkemper, T. (1985). Behavioral management of insomnia. *Journal of Psychosocial Nursing, 23*, 14–17.

Payne, J. W., Bettman, J. R., & Johnson, E. J. (1992). Behavioral decision research: A constructive processing perspective. *Annual Review of Psychology, 43*, 87–131.

Peabody, D., & Goldberg, L. R. (1989). Some determinants of factor structures from personality trait descriptors. *Journal of Personality and Social Psychology, 57*, 552–567.

Pearce, J. M., & Bouton, M. E. (2001). Theories of associative learning in animals. *Annual Review of Psychology, 52*, 111–139.

Pearson, J. C., Turner, L. H., & Todd-Mancillas, W. (1991). *Gender and communication (2nd ed.).* Dubuque, IA: Brown.

Pederson, D. R., Morgan, G., Sitko, C., Campbell, K., Ghesquire, K., & Acton, H. (1990). Maternal sensitivity and the security of infant-mother attachment: A Q-sort study. *Child Development, 61*, 1974–1983.

Pederson, W. C., Gonzales, C., & Miller, N. (2000). The moderating effect of trivial triggering provocation on displaced aggression. *Journal of Personality and Social Psychology, 78*, 913–927.

Peifer, K. L., Hu, T. W., Vega, W. A. (2000). Help seeking by persons of Mexican origin with functional impairments. *Psychiatric Services, 51*, 1293-1298.

Pelleymounter, M. A., Cullen, M. J., Baker, M. B., Hecht, R., Winters, D., Boone, T., & Collins, F. (1995). Effects of the obese gene product on body weight regulation in ob/ob mice. *Science, 269*, 540–543.

Penfield, W. (1975). *The mystery of the mind.* Princeton, NJ: Princeton University Press.

Penfield, W., & Rasmussen, T. (1950). *The cerebral cortex of man.* New York: Macmillan.

Penner, L. A., Dovidio, J. F., Piliavin, J. A., & Schroeder, D. A. (2005). Prosocial behavior: Multilevel perspectives. *Annual Review of Psychology, 56*, 365-392.

Pennisi, E. (2001). Behind the scenes of gene expression. *Science, 293,* 1064–1068.

Peplau, L. A. (2003). Human sexuality: How do men and women differ? *Current Directions in Psychological Science, 12*, 37–40.

Peplau, L. A., & Perlman, D. (1982). Perspectives on loneliness. In L. A. Peplau & D. Perlman (Eds.), *Loneliness: A sourcebook of current theory, research and therapy.* New York: John Wiley.

Perez H., Vignoles, M., Laufer, N., Schvachsa, N., Dolcini, G., Coll, P., Lattner, J., Rolon, M., Salomon, H., & Cahn, P. (2006). *Postpartum interruption of a triple drug regimen containing nevirapine for prevention of mother-to-child HIV transmission does not select the K103N mutation.* Paper presented at the 13th Conference on Retroviruses and Opportunistic Infections, Denver, February 5-8. Downloaded on February 12, 2006, from http://www.retroconference.org:8888/2006/Abstracts/26407.HTM.

Perlis, M. L., Smith, M. T., & Pigeon, W. R. (2005). Etiology and pathophysiology of insomnia. In M. H. Kryger, T. Roth, & W. C. Dement (Eds), *Principles and practice of sleep medicine* (pp. 714-725). New York: Elsevier.

Perls, F. S. (1967). *Group vs. individual psychotherapy. ECT: A Review of General Semantics, 34*, 306–312.

——. (1971). *Gestalt therapy verbatim.* New York: Bantam Books.

Perls, F. S., Hefferline, R. F., & Goodman, P. (1951). *Gestalt therapy.* New York: Julien Press.

Pervin, L. A., & John, O. P. (2001). *Personality: Theory and Research (8th ed.).* New York: John Wiley.

Peterson, A. C., & Ebata, A. T. (1987). Developmental transitions and adolescent problem behavior: Implications for prevention and intervention. In K. Hurrelmann (Ed.), *Social prevention and intervention.* New York: de Gruyter.

Peterson, L. E., & Dietz, J. (2000). Social discrimination in a personnel selection context: The effects of an authority's instruction to discriminate and followers' authoritarianism. *Journal of Applied Social Psychology, 30*, 206-220.

Peterson, L. R., & Peterson, M. J. (1959). Short-term retention of individual verbal items. *Journal of Experimental Psychology, 58*, 193–198.

Petty, R. A., Tormala, Z. L., Brinol, P., & Jarvis, W. B. G. (2006). Implicit ambivalence from attitude change: An expiration of the PAST model. *Journal of Personality and Social Psychology, 90(1),* 21–41.

Petty, R. E. & Cacioppo, J. T. (1986). *Communication and persuasion.* New York: Springer-Verlag.

——. (1986). The elaboration likelihood model of persuasion. *Advances in Experimental Social Psychology, 19*, 123–205.

Petty, R. E., Harkins, S. G., Williams, K. D., & Latané, B. (1977). The effects of group size on cognitive effort and evaluation. *Personality and Social Psychology Bulletin, 3*, 579–582.

Petty, R. E., Ostrow, T. M., & Brock, T. C. (1981). *Cognitive responses in persuasive communications: A text in attitude change.* Hillsdale, NJ: Erlbaum.

Petty, R. E., Wells, G. L., & Brock, T. C. (1976). Distraction can enhance or reduce yielding to propaganda: Thought disruption versus effort justification. *Journal of Personality and Social Psychology, 34*, 874–884.

Pew Global Attitudes Project. (2005). *U.S. Image Up Slightly, But Still Negative: American Character Gets Mixed Reviews.* Downloaded on November 16, 2005 from http://pewglobal.org/reports/display.php?PageID=800.

Pewewardy, C. (2002). Learning styles of American Indian/Alaska Native students: A review of the literature and implications for practice. *Journal of American Indian Education, 41*, 22-56.

Phares, V., & Compas, B. E. (1993). Fathers and developmental psychopathology. *Current Directions in Psychological Science, 2*, 162–165.

Phares, V., Fields, S., Kamboukos, D., & Lopez, E. (2005). Comment: Still looking for Poppa. *American Psychologist, 60*, 735-736.

Phillips, D., McCartney, K., & Scarr, S. (1987). Child-care quality and children's social development. *Developmental Psychology, 23*, 537–543.

Phinney, J. S., Cantu, C. L., & Kurtz, D. A. (1997). Ethnic and American identity as predictors of self-esteem among African-Americans. *Journal of Youth and Adolescence,* **26,** 165–185.

Piaget, J. (1932/1948). *The moral judgment of the child.* New York: Free Press.

——. (1952). *The origins of intelligence in children.* New York: W. W. Norton.

——. (1954). *The construction of reality in the child.* New York: Basic Books.

——. (1967). *Six psychological studies.* New York: Random House.

Piccinelli, M., & Homen, F. G. (1997). *Gender differences in the epidemiology of affective disorders and schizophrenia.* Geneva: World Health Organization.

Pierce, J. P., White, M. M., & Gilpin, E. A. (2005). Adolescent smoking decline during California's tobacco control programme. *Tobacco Control,* **14,** 207-212.

Pihl, R. O., & Peterson, J. B.(1993). Alcohol, serotonin and aggression. *Alcohol Health and Research World,* **17,** 113–117.

Pihl, R. O., & Zacchia, C. (1986). Alcohol and aggression: A test of the affect-arousal hypothesis. *Aggressive Behavior,* **12,** 367–375.

Pihl, R. O., Peterson, J. B., & Lau, M. A. (1993). A biosocial model of the alcohol-aggression relationship. *Journal of Studies on Alcohol,* **54,** 128–140.

Pihl, R. O., Smith, M. & Farrell, B. (1984). Alcohol and aggression in men: A comparison of brewed and distilled beverages. *Journal of Alcohol Studies,* **45,** 278–282.

Pillemer, D. B., & White, S. H. (1989). Childhood events recalled by children and adults. In H. W. Reese (Ed.), *Advances in child development and behavior (Vol. 21).* New York: Academic Press.

Pillemer, D. B., Wink, P., DiDonato, T. E., & Sanborn, R. L. (2003). Gender differences in autobiographical memory styles of older adults. *Memory,* **11,** 525-532.

Pinder, C. C. (1998). *Work motivation in organizational behavior.* Upper Saddle River, NJ: Prentice-Hall.

Piner, K. E., & Kahle, L. R. (1984). Adapting to the stigmatizing label of mental illness: Foregone but not forgotten. *Journal of Personality and Social Psychology,* **47,** 805–811.

Pinsof, W. M., Wynne, L. C., & Hambright, A. B. (1996). The outcomes of couple and family therapy. *Psychotherapy,* **33,** 321–331.

Piotrowski, C., Belter, R. W., & Keller, J. W. (1998). The impact on "managed care" on the practice of psychological testing: Preliminary findings. *Journal of Personality Assessment,* **70,** 441–447.

Planalp, S. (1999). *Communicating emotion: Social, moral, and cultural processes.* Cambridge, UK: Cambridge University Press.

Plaskon, L. A., Penson, D. F., Vaughan, T. L., & Stanford, J. L. (2003). Cigarette smoking and risk of prostate cancer in middle-aged men. *Cancer Epidemiology, Biomarkers and Prevention,* **12,** 604–609.

Plassman, B. L., Langa, K. M., Fisher, G. G., Heeringa, S. G., Weir, D. R., Ofstedal, M. B., Burke, J. R., Hurd, M. D., et al. (2008). Prevalence of cognitive impairment without dementia in the United States. *Annals of Internal Medicine,* **148,** 427–434.

Plawin, P., & Suied, M. (1988, December). Can't get no satisfaction. *Changing Times,* p. 106.

Plomin, R. (1988). The nature and nurture of cognitive abilities. In J. Sternberg (Ed.), *Advances in the psychology of human intelligence (Vol. 4).* Hillsdale, NJ: Erlbaum.

——. (1989). Environment and genes: Determinants of behavior. *American Psychologist,* **44,** 105–111.

——. (1990). *Nature and nurture: An introduction to behavioral genetics.* Pacific Grove, CA: Brooks/Cole.

Plomin, R., & McGuffin, P. (2003). Psychopathology in the postgenomic era. *Annual Review of Psychology,* **54,** 205–228.

Plomin, R. Chipuer, H. M., & Loehlin, J. C. (1990). Behavioral genetics and personality. In L. Pervin (Ed.), *Handbook of personality: Theory and research.* New York: Guilford.

Plomin, R., Corley, R., DeFries, J. C., & Fulker, D. W. (1990). Individual differences in television viewing in early childhood: Nature as well as nurture. *Psychological Science,* **1,** 371–377.

Plomin, R., DeFries, J. C., & Fulker, D. W. (1988). *Nature and nurture during infancy and early childhood.* New York: Cambridge University Press.

Plomin, R., Defries, J. C., Craig, I. W., & McGuffin, P. (2003). *Behavioral genetics in the post-genomic era.* Washington, DC: American Psychological Association.

Plutchik, R. (1980a). *Emotion: A psychoevolutionary synthesis.* New York: HarperCollins.

——. (1980b, February). A language for the emotions. *Psychology Today,* pp. 68–78.

——. (1994). *The psychology and biology of emotion.* New York: HarperCollins.

Pola, J., & Martin, L. (1977). Eye movements following autokinesis. *Bulletin of the Psychonomic Society,* **10,** 397–398.

Polivy, J., & Herman, C. P. (2002). Causes of eating disorders. *Annual Review of Psychology,* **53,** 187–213.

Pollack, H., Lantz, P. M., & Frohna, J. G. (2000). Maternal smoking and adverse birth outcomes among singletons and twins. *American Journal of Public Health,* **90,** 395–400.

Pollio, H. R. (1974). *The psychology of symbolic activity.* Reading, MA: Addison-Wesley.

Pool, R. (1993). Evidence for homosexuality gene. *Science,* **261,** 291–292.

Pope, H. G., & Hudson, J. I. (1986). Antidepressant therapy for bulimia: Current status. *Journal of Clinical Psychiatry,* **47,** 339–345.

Pope, H. G., Gruber, A. J., Hudson, J. I., Huestis, M. A., & Yurgelin-Todd, D. (2001). Neuropsychological performance in long-term cannabis users. *Archives of General Psychiatry,* **58,** 909–915.

Pope, H. G., Hudson, J. I., Jonas, J. M., & Yurgelun-Todd, D. (1985). Antidepressant treatment of bulimia: A two-year follow-up study. *Journal of Clinical Psychopharmacology,* **5,** 320–327.

Pope, H. G., Yurgelun-Todd, D. (1996). The residual cognitive effects of heavy marijuana use in college students. *Journal of the American Medical Association,* **275,** 521–527.

Port, C. L., Engdahl, B., & Frazier, P. (2001). A longitudinal and retrospective study of PTSD among older prisoners of war. *American Journal of Psychiatry*, **158**, 1474–1479.

Porter, K., Walker, A. S., Bhaskaren, K., Babiker, A. G., Darbyshire, J. H., & Pezzoti, P. (2003). Determinants of survival following HIV-1 seroconversion after the introduction of HAART. *The Lancet*, **362**, 1267–1274.

Porter, L. W., & Steers, R. M. (1973). Organizational, work, and personal factors in employee turnover and absenteeism. *Psychological Bulletin*, **80**, 151–176.

Posner, M. I. (1973). *Cognition: An introduction*. Glenview, IL: Scott, Foresman.

Posner, M. I., & Keele, S. W. (1968). On the genesis of abstract ideas. *Journal of Experimental Psychology*, **77**, 353–363.

——. (1970). Retention of abstract ideas. *Journal of Experimental Psychology*, **83**, 304–308.

Post, R. B., & Leibowitz, H. W. (1985). A revised analysis of the role of efference in motion perception. *Perception*, **14**, 631–643.

Powell, A. D., & Kahn, A. S. (1995) Racial differences in women's desires to be thin *International Journal of Eating Disorders*, **17**, 191–195.

Powell, L. H., Shaker, L. A., Jones, B. A., Vaccarino, L. V., et al. (1993). Psychosocial predictors of mortality in 83 women with premature acute myocardial infarction. *Psychosomatic Medicine*, **55**, 221–225.

Powers, S. I., Hauser, S. T., & Kilner, L. A. (1989). Adolescent mental health. *American Psychologist*, **44**, 200–208.

Pratto, F., Sidanius, J., Stallworth, L. M., & Malle, B. F. (1994). Social dominance orientation: A personality variable predicting social and political attitudes. *Journal of Personality and Social Psychology*, **67**, 741-763.

Pressley, M., Levin, J. R., & Delaney, H. D. (1982). The mnemonic keyword method. *Review of Educational Research*, **52**, 61–91.

Pressman, S. D., & Cohen, S. (2005). Does positive affect influence health? *Psychological Bulletin*, **131**, 925–971.

Price-Williams, D. R., Gordon, W., & Ramirez, M. (1969). Skill and conservation. *Developmental Psychology*, **1**, 769.

Prior, M., & Wherry, J. S. (1986). Autism, schizophrenia, and allied disorders. In H. C. Quay & J. S. Wherry (Eds.), *Psychopathological disorders of childhood (3rd ed.)*. New York: Wiley.

Pronin, E., Gilovich, T., & Ross, L. (2004). Objectivity in the eye of the beholder: Divergent perceptions in self versus others. *Psychological Bulletin*, **111**, 781-799.

Pronin, E., Kruger, J., Savitsky, K., & Ross, L. (2001). You don't know me, but I know you: The illusion of asymmetric insight. *Journal of Personality and Social Psychology*, **81**, 639-656.

Pronin, E., Lin, D. Y., & Ross, L. (2002). The bias blind spot: Perceptions of bias in self versus others. *Personality and Social Psychology Bulletin*, **28**, 369-381.

Pugh, K. R., Menci, W. E., Jenner, A. R., Lee, R. N., Katz, L., Frost, S. J., Shaywitz, S. E., & Shaywitz, B. A. (2002). Neuroimaging studies of reading development and reading disability. *Learning Disabilities Research & Practice*, **16**, 479-492.

Punjabi, N. M. (2008). The epidemiology of adult obstructive sleep apnea. *The Proceedings of the American Thoracic Society*, **5**, 136–143.

Putnam, F. W. (1989). *Diagnosis and treatment of multiple personality disorder*. New York: Guilford Press.

Putnam, F. W., Guroff, J. J., Silberman, E. K., Barban, L., & Post, R. M. (1986). The clinical phenomenology of multiple personality disorder: Review of 100 recent cases. *Journal of Clinical Psychology*, **47**, 285–293.

Pyle, R. L., Mitchell, J. E., & Eckert, E. D. (1981). Bulimia: Report of 34 cases. *Journal of Clinical Psychiatry*, **42**, 60–64.

Pyle, R. L., Mitchell, J. E., Eckert, E. D., Hatsukami, D. K., Pomeroy, C., & Zimmerman, R. (1990). Maintenance treatment and 6-month outcome for bulimic patients who respond to initial treatment. *American Journal of Psychiatry*, **147**, 871–875.

Pynes, J., & Bernardin, H. J. (1989). Predictive validity of an entry-level police officer assessment center. *Journal of Applied Psychology*, **74**, 831–833.

Quadrel, M. J., Fishhoff, B., & Davis, W. (1993). Adolescent (in)vulnerability. *American Psychologist*, **48**, 102–116.

Quay, H. C. (1965). Psychopathic personality as pathological sensation seeking. *American Journal of Psychiatry*, **122**, 180–183.

Quick, H. E., & Moen, P. (1998). Gender, employment, and retirement quality: A life course approach to the differential experiences of men and women. *Journal of Occupational Health Psychology*, **3**, 44–64.

Quina, K., Wingard, J. A., & Bates, H. G. (1987). Language style and gender stereotypes in person perception. *Psychology of Women Quarterly*, **11**, 111–222.

Quinn, A., & Schlenker, B. R. (2002). Can accountability produce independence? Goals as determinants of the impact of accountability on conformity. *Personality and Social Psychology Bulletin*, **28**, 472-483.

Radeloff, D. J. (1990). Role of color perception of attractiveness. *Perceptual and Motor Skills*, **71**, 151-160.

Radziszewska, B., Richardson, J. L., Dent, C. W., & Flay, B. R. (1996). Parenting style and adolescent depressive symptoms, smoking, and academic achievement: Ethnic, gender, and SES differences. *Journal of Behavioral Medicine*, **19**, 289-305.

Raine, A., Venables, P. H., & Williams, M. (1990). Relationship between central and autonomic measures of arousal at age 15 years and criminality at age 24 years. *Archives of General Psychiatry*, **46**, 1003–1007.

Ramirez, D., McDevitt, J., & Farrell, A. (2000). *A resource guide on racial profiling data collection systems: Promising practices and lessons learned*. Washington, DC: U.S. Department of Justice.

Ramirez, M., & Castaneda, A. (1974). *Cultural democracy, cognitive development, and education*. New York: Academic Press.

Raskin, N. J. & Rogers, C. R. (1995). Person-centered therapy. In J. J. Corsini & D. Wedding (Eds.), *Current psychotherapies, Fifth edition* (pp. 128–161). Itasca, IL: Peacock.

Rattner, A. (1988). Convicted but innocent: Wrongful conviction in the criminal justice system. *Law and Human Behavior*, **12**, 283–294.

Ray, O. S., & Ksir, C. (1987). *Drugs, society, and human behavior*. St. Louis: Mosby.

Reason, J. T., & Lucas, D. (1984). Using cognitive diaries to investigate naturally-occurring memory blocks. In J. E. Harris, & P. E. Morris (Eds.), *Everyday memory: Actions and absent mindedness.* London: Academic Press.

Regan, P. C., & Berscheid, E. (1999). Lust: What we know about human sexual desire. Thousand Oaks, CA: Sage.

Regier, D. A., Narrow, W. E., Rae, D. S., Manderscheid, R. W., Locke, B. Z., & Goodwin, F. K. (1993). The de facto US mental and addictive disorders service system: Epidemiological catchment area prospective 1-year revalence rates of disorders and services. *Archives of General Psychiatry,* **50**, 85-94.

Reich, D. A. (2004). What you expect is not always what you get: The roles of extremity, optimism, and pessimism in the behavioral confirmation process. *Journal of Experimental Social Psychology,* **40**, 199–215.

Reich, J. (1986). The epidemiology of anxiety. *The Journal of Nervous and Mental Disease,* **174**, 129–136.

Reichenberg, A., Gross, R., Weiser, M., Bresnahan, N. N., Silverman, J., Harlap, S., Rabinowitz, J., et al. (2006). Advancing paternal age and autism. *Archives of General Psychiatry,* **63**, 1026–1032.

Reilly, R. R., & Chao, G. T. (1982). Validity and fairness of some alternative employee selection procedures. *Personnel Psychology,* **35**, 1–62.

Reinblatt, S. P., Rifkin, A., & Freeman, J. (2004). The efficacy of ECT in adults with mental retardation experiencing psychiatric disorders. *The Journal of ECT,* **20**, 208-212.

Reinisch, J. M., & Sanders, S. A. (1992). Effects of prenatal exposure to diethylstilbestrol (DES) on hemispheric laterality and spatial ability in human males. *Hormones and Behavior,* **26**, 62–75.

Reis, H. T., Nezlek, J., & Wheeler, L. (1980). Physical attractiveness in social interaction. *Journal of Personality and Social Psychology,* **38**, 604–617.

Reitzes, D. C., Multran, E. J., & Fernandez, M. E. (1998). The decision to retire: A career perspective. *Social Science Quarterly,* **79**, 607–619.

Renaud, S., & de Lorgeril, M. (1992). Wine, alcohol, platelets, and the French paradox for coronary heart disease. *The Lancet,* **339**, 1523–1526.

Reneman, L., Lavalaye, J., Schmand, B., de Wolff, F. A., van den Brink, W., den Heeten, G. J., & Booij, J. (2001). Cortical serotonin transporter density and verbal memory in individuals who stopped using 3,4-methylenedioxymethamphetamine (MDMA or "Ecstasy"). *Archives of General Psychiatry,* **58**, 901–906.

Rensink, R. A. (2002). Change detection. *Annual Review of Psychology,* **53**, 245–277.

Rensink, R. A., O'Regan, J. K., & Clark, J. J. (1997). To see or not to see: The need for attention to perceive changes in scenes. *Psychological Science,* **8**, 368–373.

Rescorla, R. A. (1968). Probability of shock in the presence and absence of CS in fear conditioning. *Journal of Comparative and Physiological Psychology,* **66**, 1–5.

——. (1987). A Pavlovian analysis of goal-directed behavior. *American Psychologist,* **42**, 119–129.

——. (1988). Pavlovian conditioning: It's not what you think it is. *American Psychologist,* **43**, 151–160.

——. (2000). Associative changes with a random CS-US relationship. *Quarterly Journal of Experimental Psychology,* **53B**, 325-340.

Rescorla, R. A., & Wagner, A. R. (1972). A theory of Pavlovian conditioning: Variations in the effectiveness of reinforcement and non-reinforcement. In A. H. Black & W. F. Prokasy (Eds.), *Classical conditioning II: Current research and theory.* Englewood Cliffs, NJ: Prentice-Hall.

Resnick, H. D., Kilpatrick, D. G., Dansky, B. S., Saunders, B. E., & Best, C. L. (1993). Prevalence of civilian trauma and posttraumatic stress disorder in a representative national sample of women. *Journal of Consulting and Clinical Psychology,* **61**, 984–991.

Resnick, L. B. (1987). *Education and learning to think.* Washington, DC: National Academy Press.

Reveley, M. A., Reveley, A. M., & Baldy, R. (1987). Left cerebral hemisphere hypodensity in discordant schizophrenic twins. *Archives of General Psychiatry,* **44**, 624–632.

Revelle, W. (1987). Personality and motivation: Sources of inefficiency in cognitive performance. *Journal of Research in Personality,* **21**, 436–452.

Revulsky, S. H., & Garcia, J. (1970). Learned associations over long delays. In G. H. Bower & J. T. Spence (Eds.), *The psychology of learning and motivation (Vol. 4).* New York: Academic Press.

Reynolds, A. G., & Flagg, P. W. (1983). *Cognitive psychology.* Boston: Little, Brown.

Reynolds, B. A., & Weiss, S. (1992). Generation of neurons and astrocytes from isolated cells of the adult mammalian nervous system. *Science,* **225**, 1707–1710.

Reynolds, R., & Brannick, M. T. (2001). Is job analysis doing the job? Extending job analysis with cognitive task analysis. *The Industrial-Organizational Psychologist,* **39**, from www.siop.org/tip/backissues.

Rhodes, S. R. (1983). Age-related differences in work attitudes and behaviors: A review and conceptual analysis. *Psychological Bulletin,* **93**, 328–367.

Rhyne, D. (1981). Bases of marital satisfaction among men and women. *Journal of Marriage and the Family,* **43**, 941–954.

Richardson, D. R., Vandenberg, R. J., & Humphries, S. A. (1986). Effect of power to harm on retaliative aggression among males and females. *Journal of Research in Personality,* **20**, 402–419.

Richardson, J. D. (1991). Medical causes of male sexual dysfunction. *Medical Journal of Australia,* **155**, 29–33.

Rickels, K., Downing, R., Schweizer, E., & Hassman, H. (1993). Antidepressants for the treatment of generalized anxiety disorder. *Archives of General Psychiatry,* **50**, 884–895.

Rickert, V. I., Vaughn, I., & Johnson, C. (1988). Reducing nocturnal awakenings and crying episodes in infants and young children: A comparison between scheduled awakenings and systematic ignoring. *Pediatrics,* **81**, 203–212.

Ridder, S., Chourbaji, S., Hellweg, R., Urani, A., Zacher, C., Schmid, W., Zink, M., et al. (2005). *The Journal of Neuroscience*, **25**, 6243-6250.

Riggio, R. E. (2002). *Introduction to industrial organizational psychology (4th Ed.)* New York: Prentice-Hall.

Rigotti, N. A., Lee, J. E., & Wechsler, H. (2000). US college students' use of tobacco products. *Journal of the American Medical Association*, **284**, 699–705.

Riise, T., Nortvedt, M. W., & Ascherio, A. (2003). Smoking is a risk factor for multiple sclerosis. *Neurology*, **61**, 1122–1124.

Rinberg, D. & Davidowitz, H. (2000). Insect perception: Do cockroaches 'know' about fluid dynamics? *Nature*, **405**, 756–757.

Riolo, S. A., Nguyen, T. A., Greden, J. F., & King, C. A. (2005). Prevalence of depression by race/ethnicity: Findings from the National Health and Nutrition Examination Survey III. *American Journal of Public Health*, **95**, 998-1000.

Rist, M. C. (1990). Crack babies in school. *Education Digest*, **55**, 30–33.

Rivett, M. (1998). The family therapy journals in 1997: A thematic review. *Journal of Family Therapy*, **20**, 423–430.

Roberts, G. W., Banspach, S. W., & Peacock, N. (1997). Behavioral scientists at the Centers for Disease Control and Prevention: Evolving and integrated roles. *American Psychologist*, **52**, 143–146.

Robin, R. W., Chester, B., Rasmussen, J. K., Jaranson, J. M., & Goldman, D. (1997). Prevalence, characteristics, and impact of childhood sexual abuse in a Southwestern American Indian tribe. *Child Abuse and Neglect*, **21**, 769-787.

Robins, L. N., Helzer, J. E., Weissman, M. M., Orvaschel, H., Guenberg, E., Burke, J. D., & Regier, D. A. (1984). Lifetime prevalence of specific psychiatric disorders in three sites. *Archives of General Psychiatry*, **41**, 949–958.

Robins, R. W., & Trzesniewski, K. H. (2005). Self-esteem development across the lifespan. *Current Directions in Psychology*, **14**, 158–162.

Robinson, T. E., & Berridge, K. C. (2003). Addiction. *Annual Review of Psychology*, **54**, 25–53.

Robles, T. F., Glaser, R., & Kiecolt-Glaser, J. K. (2005). A new look at chronic stress, depression, and immunity. *Current Directions in Psychological Science*, **14**, 111-115.

Rochat, F., Maggioni, O., & Modgiliani, A. (2000). The dynamics of obeying and opposing authority: A mathematical model In T. Blass (Ed.), *Obedience to authority: Current perspectives on the Milgram paradigm*. Mahwah, NJ: Lawrence Erlbaum.

Rock, I. (1986). The description and analysis of object and event perception. In K. R. Boff, L. Kaufman, & J. P. Thomas (Eds.), *Handbook of perception and human performance: Vol. 2. Cognitive processes and performance*. New York: Wiley.

Rodgers, W. L., Ofstedal, M. B., & Herzog, A. R. (2003). Trends in scores on tests of cognitive ability in the elderly U. S. population, 1993–2000. *The Journal of Gerontology*, **58**, S338–S346.

Rodin, J. (1976). Crowding, perceived choice and response to controllable and uncontrollable outcomes. *Journal of Experimental Social Psychology*, **12**, 564–578.

——. (1981). Current status of the internal-external hypothesis of obesity: What went wrong? *American Psychologist*, **36**, 361–372.

——. (1993). Cultural and psychosocial determinants of weight concerns. *Annals of Internal Medicine*, **119**, 643–645.

Rodin, J., & Salovey, P. (1989). Health psychology. *Annual Review of Psychology*, **40**, 533–579.

Roediger, H. L. (1990). Implicit memory: Retention without remembering. *American Psychologist*, **45**, 1043-1056.

Roediger, H. L., III, & Karpicke, J. D. (2006a). The power of testing memory: Basic research and implications for educaitonal practice. *Perspectives on Psychological Science*, **1**, 181–210.

——. (2006b). Test enhanced learning: Taking memory tests improves long-term retention. *Psychological Science*, **17**, 249–255.

Rogers, C. R. (1959). A theory of therapy, personality, and interpersonal relationships as developed in the client-centered framework. In S. Koch (Ed.), *Psychology: A study of science*. New York: McGraw Hill.

Rohrer, D., & Pashler, H. (2007). Increasing retention without increasing study time. *Current Directions in Psychological Science*, **16**, 183–186.

Rohrer, D., Taylor, K., Pashler, H., Wixted, J. T., & Cepeda, N. J. (2005). The effect of overlearning on long-term retention. *Applied Cognitive Psychology*, **19**, 361–374.

Roid, G. (2003). *Stanford-Binet Intelligence Scales (5th ed.)*. Itasca, IL: Riverside Publishing.

Rollins, B. C., & Feldman, H. (1970). Marital satisfaction over the family life cycle. *Journal of Marriage and the Family*, **32**, 20–27.

Rolls, B. J., Federoff, I. C., & Guthrie, J. F. (1991). Gender differences in eating behavior and body weight regulation. *Health Psychology*, **10**, 133–142.

Rolls, E. T. (2000). Memory systems in the brain. In S. T. Fiske, D. L. Schacter, & C. Zahn-Waxler, (Eds.), *Annual review of psychology (volume 52)* (pp. 599–630). Palo Alto, CA: Annual Reviews.

Rorschach, H. (1921). *Psychodiagnostics*. Bern: Huber.

Rosa, A. R., Andreazza, A. C., Kunz, M., Gomes, F., Santin, A., Sanchez-Moreno, J., Colom, F., Vieta, E., & Kapczinski, F. (2008). Predominant polarity in bipolar disorder: Diagnostic implications. *Journal of Affective Disorders*, **107**, 45–51.

Rosch, E. (1973). Natural categories. *Cognitive Psychology*, **4**, 328–350.

——. (1975). Cognitive representations of semantic categories. *Journal of Experimental Psychology: General*, **104**, 192–253.

——. (1978). Principles of categorization. In E. Rosch & B. B. Lloyds (Eds.), *Cognition and categorization*. Hillsdale, NJ: Erlbaum.

Rosenblum, L. (2008). Unobtrusive hybrid car "noise" being developed. *The Fort Wayne Journal Gazette*, May 8, 2008, p. 13A. [Note: A copy of H.R. 5734 is available at http://Thomas.loc.gov/cgi-bin/query/C?c110:/temp/~c11009KQ1un]

Rosenbaum, M. (2000). Psychogenic seizures—why women? *Psychosomatics*, **41**, 147–149.

Rosenman, R. H., Brand, R. J., Jenkins., C. D., Friedman, M., Straus,. R., & Wurm, M. (1975). Coronary heart disease in the Western Collaborative Group Study: Final follow-up experience of 8 1/2 years. *Journal of the American Medical Association*, **233**, 872–877.

Rosenthal, D. (1970). *Genetics of psychopathology*. New York: McGraw-Hill.

Rosenthal, R. & DiMatteo, M. R. (2001). Meta-analysis: Recent developments in quantitative methods for literature reviews. *Annual Review of Psychology*, **52**, 59–82.

Rosenzweig, M. R. (1922). Psychological science around the world. *American Psychologist*, **47**, 718–722.

Rosenzweig, M. R., Bennett, E. L., & Diamond, M. C. (1972). Brain changes in response to experiences. *Scientific American*, **226**, 22–29.

Rosenzweig, M. R., Leiman, A. L., & Breedlove, S. M. (1996). *Biological psychology*. Sunderland, MA: Sinauer Associates.

Rosnow, R. L., Skleder, A. A., & Rind, B. (1995). Reading other people: A hidden cognitive structure? *The General Psychologist*, **31**, 1–10.

Ross, C. A. (1989). *Multiple personality disorder: Diagnosis, clinical features, and treatment*. New York: Wiley.

——. (1997). *Dissociative identity disorder*. New York: Wiley.

Ross, D., Read, J. D., & Toglia, M. P. (Eds.). (1993). *Eyewitness testimony: Current trends and developments*. New York: Cambridge University Press.

Ross, L. D., & Ward, A. (1995). Psychological barriers to dispute resolution. In M. Zanna (Ed.), *Advances in experimental social psychology* (Volume 27, pp. 255-304). San Diego, CA: Academic Press.

Rossi, A. S. (1980). Aging and parenthood in the middle years. In P. B. Baltes & O. G. Brim, Jr. (Eds.), *Lifespan development and behavior (Vol. III)*. New York: Academic Press.

Roth, A., & Fonagy, P. (2004). *What works for whom? A critical review of psychotherapy research* (2nd edition). New York: Guilford Press.

Roth, E. M., & Shoben, E. J. (1983). The effect of context on the structure of categories. *Cognitive Psychology*, **15**, 346–378.

Rothbart, M. K., Ahadi, S. A., & Evans, D. E. (2000). Temperament and personality: Origins and outcomes. *Journal of Personality and Social Psychology*, **78**, 122–135.

Rothbaum, B. O., Foa, E. B., Murdock, T., Riggs, D., & Walsh, W. (1992). A prospective examination of post-traumatic stress disorder in rape victims. *Journal of Traumatic Stress*, **5**, 455–475.

Rothstein, H. R., Schmidt, F. L., Erwin, F. W., Owens, W. A., & Sparks, C. P. (1990). Biographical data in employment selection: Can validities be made generalizable? *Journal of Applied Psychology*, **75**, 175–184.

Rottenberg, J. (2005). Mood and emotion in major depression. *Current Directions in Psychological Science*, **14**, 167-170.

Rotter, J. B. (1954). *Social learning and clinical psychology*. Englewood Cliffs, NJ: Prentice-Hall.

——. (1966). Generalized expectancies for internal versus external control of reinforcement. *Psychological Monographs*, **80**, (Whole No. 609).

Rotton, J., & Frey, J. (1985). Air pollution, weather, and violent crimes: Concomitant analysis of archival data. *Journal of Personality and Social Psychology*, **49**, 1207–1220.

Rovee-Collier, C. K. (1984). The ontogeny of learning and memory in infancy. In R. Kail & N. E. Spear (Eds.), *Comparative perspectives on the development of memory*. Hillsdale, NJ: Lawrence Erlbaum Associates.

Rowe, D. C. (1981). Environmental and genetic influences on dimensions of perceived parenting: A twin study. *Developmental Psychology*, **17**, 203–208.

——. (1987). Resolving the person-situation debate. *American Psychologist*, **42**, 218–227.

——. (2005). Under the skin: On the impartial treatment of genetic and environmental hypotheses of racial differences. *American Psychologist*, **60**, 60–70.

Rowe, J. W., & Kahn, R. L. (1987). Human aging: Usual and successful. *Science*, **237**, 143–149.

Royal, G. P., & Roberts, M. C. (1987). Students' perceptions of and attitude toward disabilities: A comparison of twenty conditions. *Journal of Clinical Child Psychology*, **16**, 122-132.

Rozanski, A., Blementhal, J. A., & Kaplan, J. (1999). Impact of psychological factors on the pathogenesis of cardiovascular disease and implications for therapy. *Circulation*, **99**, 2192–2217.

Rozin, P., Fischler, C., Imada, S., Sarubin, A., & Wrzesniewski, A. (1999). Attitudes to food and the role of food in life: Comparisons of Flemish Belgium, France, Japan, and the United States. *Appetite*, **33**, 163–180.

Rozin, P., Kabnick, K., Pete, E., Fischler, C., & Shields, C. (2003). The ecology of eating: Smaller portion sizes in France than in the United States help explain the French paradox. *Psychological Science*, **14**, 450–454.

Ruback, R. B., & Pandey, J. (1988). *Crowding and perceived control in India*. Unpublished manuscript, cited in J. Pandet (1990).

Rubin, D. C., & Kontis, T. C. (1983). A schema for common cents. *Memory and Cognition*, **11**, 335–341.

Rudd, M. D., Dahm, P. F., & Rajab, M. H. (1993). Diagnostic comorbidity in persons with suicidal ideation and behavior. *American Journal of Psychiatry*, **150**, 928–934.

Runco, M. A. (2004). Creativity. *Annual Review of Psychology*, **55**, 657-687.

Rusbult, C. E., & Van Lange, P. A. M. (2003). Interdependence, interaction, and relationships. *Annual Review of Psychology*, **54**, 351–375.

Rushton, J. P. (1988). Race differences in behavior: A review and evolutionary analysis. *Personality and Individual Differences*, **9**, 1009–1024.

Rushton, J. P., & Jensen, A. R. (2005). Thirty years of research on race differences in cognitive ability. *Psychology, Public Policy, and Law*, **11**, 235–294.

Rushton, J. P., Fulker, D. W., Neale, M. C., Nias, D. K. B., & Eysenck, H. J. (1986). Altruism and aggression: The heritability of individual differences. *Journal of Personality and Social Psychology*, **50**, 1192–1198.

Russell, J. A. (2003). Core affect and the psychological construction of emotion. *Psychological Review*, **110**, 145172.

Russell, J. A., Bachorowski, J., & Fernández-Dols, J. (2003). Facial and vocal expressions of emotion. *Annual Review of Psychology*, **54**, 329–349.

Rutter, M., & Schopler, E. (1987). Autism and pervasive developmental disorders: Concepts and diagnostic uses. *Journal of Autism and Developmental Disorders, 17,* 159–186.

Rutter, M., Graham, P., Chadwick, O., & Yule, W. (1976). Adolescent turmoil: Fact or fiction? *Journal of Child Psychology and Psychiatry, 17,* 35–56.

Ruys, K. I., Dijksterhuis, A., & Corneille, O. (2008). On the (mis)categorization of unattractive brides and attractive prostitutes: Extending evaluative congruency to social category activation. *Experimental Psychology, 55,* 182–188.

Ruys, K. L., & Stapel, D. A. (2008a). The secret life of emotions. *Psychological Science, 19,* 385–391.

——. (2008b). Emotion elicitor or emotion messenger? Subliminal priming reveals two faces of facial expressions. *Psychological Science, 19,* 593–600.

Ryan, A. M. (2003). Defining ourselves: I-O psychology's identity quest. *The Industrial-Organizational Psychologist, 41,* 21–33.

Ryan, E. D., & Kovacic, C. R. (1966). Pain tolerance and athletic participation. *Journal of Personality and Social Psychology, 22,* 383–390.

Ryan, K. M., & Kanjorski, J. (1998). The enjoyment of sexist humor, rape attitudes, and relationship aggression in college students. *Sex Roles, 38,* 743–756.

Saal, F. E., & Knight, P. A. (1988). *Industrial/organizational psychology.* Monterey, CA: Brooks/Cole.

Saari, L. M., Johnson, T. R., McLaughlin, S. D., & Zimerle, D. M. (1988). A survey of management training and education practices in U.S. companies. *Personnel Psychology, 41,* 731–743.

Sachdev, P., Hay, P., & Cummings, S. (1992). Psychosurgical treatment of obsessive-compulsive disorder. *Archives of General Psychiatry, 49,* 582–583.

Sachdev, P., Mondraty, N., Wen, W., & Guilford, K. (2008). Brains of anorexia nervosa patients process self-images differently from non-self-images: An fMRI study. *Neuropsychologia, 46,* 2161–2168.

Sachs-Ericsson, N. (2000). Gender, social roles, and suicidal ideation and attempts in a general population sample. In T. Joiner & M. D. Rudd (Eds.), *Suicide science: Expanding the boundaries* (pp. 201-220). Boston: Kluwer Academic Press.

Sack, R.L., & Lewy, A.J. (1997). Melatonin as a chronobiotic: Treatment of circadian desynchrony in night workers and the blind. *Journal of Biological Rhythms, 12,* 595–603.

Sackeim, H. A. (1985). The case for ECT. *Psychology Today, 19,* 36–40.

Sackeim, H. A., Haskett, R. F., Mulsant, B. H., Thase, M. E., Mann, J. J., Pettinati, H. M., Greenberg, R. M., Crowe, R. R., Cooper, T. B., & Prudic, J. (2001). Continuation pharmacotherapy in the prevention of relapse following electroconvulsive therapy: A randomized control trial. *Journal of the American Medical Association, 14,* 1299–1307.

Sackeim, H. A., Luber, B., Katzman, G. P., Moeller, J. R., Prudic, J., Devanand, D. P., & Nobler. (1996). The effects of electroconvulsive therapy on quantitative electroencephalograms: Relationship to clinical outcome. *Archives of General Psychiatry, 53,* 814–824.

Sackeim, H. A., Prudic, J., Devanand, D. P., Nobler, M. S., Lisanby, S. H., Peyser, S., Fitzsimons, L., Moody, B. J., & Clark, J. (2000). A prospective, randomized, double-blind comparison of bilateral and right unilateral electroconvulsive therapy at different stimulus intensities. *Archives of General Psychiatry, 57,* 425–434.

Sackett, P. R., Hardison, C. M., & Cullen, M. J. (2004). On interpreting stereotype threat as accounting for African American—White differences on cognitive tests. *American Psychologist, 59,* 7-13.

Sadalla, E. K., & Oxley, D. (1984). The perception of room size. The rectangularity illusion. *Environment and Behavior, 16,* 394–405.

Saegert, S., & Winkel, G. H. (1990). Environmental psychology. *Annual Review of Psychology, 41,* 441–477.

Saha, S., Chant, D., & McGrath, J. (2007). A systematic review of mortality in schizophrenia: Is the difference in the mortality gap worsening over time? *Archives of General Psychiatry, 64,* 1123–1131.

Saha, S., Komaromy, M., Koepsell, T. D., & Bindman, A. B. (1999). Patient-physician racial concordance and the perceived quality and use of health care. *Archives of Internal Medicine, 159,* 997-1004.

Sairanen, M., Lucas, G., Ernfors, P., Castrén, M., & Castrén, E. (2005). Brain-derived neurotropic factor and antidepressant drugs have different but coordinated effects on neuronal turnover, proliferation, and survival in the adult dentrate gyrus. *The Journal of Neuroscience, 25,* 1089-1094.

Salapatek, P. (1975). Pattern perception in early infancy. In L. B. Cohen & P. Salapatek (Eds.), *Infant perception: From sensation to cognition.* New York: Academic Press.

Salas, E., & Cannon-Bowers, J. A. (2001). The science of training: A decade of progress. *Annual Review of Psychology, 52,* 471–499.

Salovey, P., & Grewald, D. (2005). The science of emotional intelligence. *Current Directions in Psychological Science, 14,* 281–285.

Salovey, P., & Mayer, J. D. (1994). Some final thoughts about personality and intelligence. In R. J. Sternberg (Ed.), *Personality and intelligence* (pp. 303–318). New York: Cambridge University Press.

Salthouse, T. A. (2001). Attempted decomposition of age-related influences on tests of reasoning. *Psychology and Aging, 16,* 251-263.

——. (2003). Interrelations of aging, knowledge, and cognitive performance. In U. Standinger & U. Lindenberger (Eds.), *Understanding human development: Lifespan psychology in exchange with other disciplines* (pp. 265-287). Berlin, Germany: Kluwer Academic.

——. (2004). What and when of cognitive aging. *Current Directions in Psychological Science, 13,* 140-144.

Salthouse, T. A., & Ferrer-Caja, E. (2003). What needs to be explained to account for age-related effects on multiple cognitive variables? *Psychology and Aging, 18,* 91-110.

Sameroff, A. J., & Cavanaugh, P. J. (1979). Learning in infancy: A developmental perspective. In J. D. Osofsky (Ed.), *Handbook of infant development.* New York: Wiley.

SAMSHA (Substance Abuse and Mental Health Services Administration). (2003). *National survey on drug use and health — 2003.* Washington, DC: U.S. Department of Health and Human Services.

——. (2005). *Methamphetamine use, abuse, and dependence: 2002, 2003, 2004.* Washington, DC: U.S. Department of Health and Human Services.

——. (2005). *National survey on drug use and health—2005*. Washington, DC: U.S. Department of Health and Human Services.

Samuelson, F. J. B. (1980). Watson's Little Albert, Cyril Burt's twins, and the need for a critical science. *American Psychologist*, **35**, 619–625.

Sanchez, I. M. (2000). Motivating and maximizing learning in minority classrooms. *New Directions for Community Colleges*, **28**, 35-44.

Sandler, J., Dare, C., & Holder, A. (1992). *The patient and the analyst: The basis of the psychoanalytic process (2nd ed.)*. Madison, CT: International University Press.

Sands, L. P., Terry, H., & Meredith, W. (1989). Change and stability in adult intellectual functioning assessed by Wechsler item responses. *Psychology and Aging*, **4**, 79–87.

Sanua, V. D. (1987). Standing against an established ideology: Infantile autism, a case in point. *Clinical Psychology*, **4**, 96–110.

Sapolsky, R. (2005). Sick of poverty. *Scientific American*, **293**, 92–99.

Sarkus, D. J. (2003). Safety and psychology: Where do we go from here? *Professional Safety*, **48(1)**, 18–25.

Sarna, A., Luchters, S. M. F., Geibel, S., Kaai, S., Munyao, P., Shikely, K. S., Mandaliya, K., van Dam, J., & Temmerman, M. (2008). Sexual risk behavior and HAART: A comparative study of HIV-infected persons on HAART and on preventive therapy in Kenya. *International Journal of STD & AIDS*, **19**, 85–89.

Satcher, D. (1999). *Mental health: A report of the Surgeon General*. Paper presented at the annual meeting of the NAACP, New Orleans, LA.

Satir, V. (1967). *Conjoint family therapy*. Palo Alto, CA: Science and Behavior Books.

Saunders, N. A., & Sullivan, C. E. (Eds.). (1994). *Sleep and breathing (2nd ed.)*. New York: Marcel Dekker.

Sauser, W. J., & York, C. M. (1978). Sex differences in job satisfaction: A reexamination. *Personnel Psychology*, **31**, 537–547.

Savazzi, S., Fabri, M., Rubboli, G., Paggi, A., Tassinari, C. A., Marzi, C. A. (2007). Interhemispheric transfer following callosotomy in humans: Role of the superior colliculus. *Neuropsychologia, 45*, 2417–2427.

Savic, I., Berglund, H., Gulyas, B., & Roland, P. (2001). Smelling of odorous sex hormone-like compounds causes sex-differentiated hypothalamic activations in humans. *Neuron, 31*, 661-668.

Sawyer, T. F. (2000). Francis Cecil Sumner: His views and influence on African American higher education. *History of Psychology*, **3**, 122-141.

Saxe, R., Carey, S., & Kanwisher, N. (2004). Understanding other minds: Linking developmental psychology and functional neuroimaging. *Annual Review of Psychology*, **55**, 87-124.

Scarborough, E., & Furumoto, L. (1987). *Untold lives: The first generation of American women psychologists*. New York: Columbia University Press.

Scarr, S., & Eisenberg, M. (1993). Child care research: Issues, perspectives, and results. *Annual Review of Psychology*, **44**, 613–644.

Scarr, S., & Kidd, K. K. (1983). Developmental behavior genetics. In P. H. Mussen (Ed.), *Handbook of child psychology, Vol. 2: Infancy and developmental psychobiology*. New York: Wiley.

Schachter, S. (1971). Some extraordinary facts about obese humans and rats. *American Psychologist*, **26**, 129–144.

Schachter, S., & Gross, L. P. (1968). Manipulated time and eating behavior. *Journal of Personality and Social Psychology*, **1**, 98–106.

Schachter, S., & Singer, J. E. (1962). Cognitive, social, and physiological determinants of emotional state. *Psychological Review*, **69**, 379–399.

Schacter, D. L. (1996). *Searching for memory: The brain, mind and the past*. New York: Basic Books.

Schacter, D. L., Norman, K. A., & Koutstaal, W. (1998). The cognitive neuroscience of constructive memory. *Annual Review of Psychology*, **48**, 289–318.

Schaffer, H. R., & Emerson, P. E. (1964). The development of social attachments in infancy. *Monographs for the society for research in child development, 29, Serial 94*.

Schaie, K. W. (1996). Intellectual functioning in adulthood. In J. E. Birren & K. W. Schaie (Eds.), *Handbook of the psychology of aging* (4th ed., pp. 266-286). San Diego: Academic Press.

Schaie, K. W., & Willis, S. L. (1986). *Adult development and aging (2nd ed.)*. Boston: Little, Brown.

Schall, J. D. (2004). On building a bridge between brain and behavior. *Annual Review of Psychology*, **55**, 23-50.

Scharf, B. (1978). Loudness. In E. C. Carterette & M. P. Friedman (Eds.), *Handbook of perception*. New York: Academic Press.

Scharli, H., & Harman, A. M. (1999) Residual vision in a subject with damaged visual cortex. *Journal of Cognitive Neuroscience, 11, 502*. Retrieved from the World Wide Web October 5, 2000, http://ehostvgw15.epnet.com/.

Scharli, H., Harman, A. M., &. Hogben, J. H. Blindsight in subjects with homonymous visual field defects. Journal of Cognitive *Neuroscience, 11*, 52. Retrieved from the World Wide Web on October 5, 2000, http://ehostvgw15.epnet.com/.

Schatzberg, A. F., Rush, A. J., Arnow, B. A., Banks, P. L. C., Blalock, J. A., Borian, F. E., et al. (2005). Chronic depression: Medication (nefazodone) or psychotherapy (CBASP) is effective when the other is not. *Archives of General Psychiatry*, **62**, 513-520.

Schau, C. G., Kahn, L., Diepold, J. H., & Cherry, F. (1980). The relationships of parental expectations and preschool children's verbal sex typing to their sex-typed toy play behavior. *Child Development*, **51**, 266–270.

Shaywitz, S. E., Shaywitz, B. A., Pugh, K. R., Fulbright, R. K., Constable, R. T., et al. (1998). *Proceedings of the National Academy of Sciences*, **95**, 2636-2641.

Schechter, R., & Grether, J. K. (2008). Continuing increases in autism reported to California's Developmental Services System. *Archives of General Psychiatry*, **65**, 19–24.

Scheck, B., Neufeld, P., & Dwyer, J. (2000). *Actual innocence*. New York: Doubleday.

Sheer, D. E. (1961). *Electrical stimulation of the brain*. Austin: University of Texas Press.

Scheerer, M. (1963). Problem solving. *Scientific American*, **208**, 118–128.

Scheff, T. J., & Fearon, D. (2004). Cognition and emotion? The dead end in self-esteem research. *Journal of the Theory of Social Behavior, 34*, 73-90.

Scheier, M. F., & Carver, C. S. (1992). Effects of optimism on psychological and physical well-being: Theoretical overview and empirical update. *Cognitive Therapy and Research,* **16,** 206–228.

——. (1993). On the power of positive thinking: The benefits of being optimistic. *Current Directions in Psychological Science,* **2,** 26–30.

Schellenberg, G. D., D'Souza, I., & Poorkaj, P. (2000). The genetics of Alzheimer's disease. *Current Psychiatry Reports,* **2,** 158–164.

Scher, S. J., & Cooper, J. (1989). Motivational basis of dissonance: The singular role of behavioral consequences. *Journal of Personality and Social Psychology,* **56,** 899–906.

Scherer, K. R. (1984). On the nature and function of emotion: A component process approach. In K. R. Scherer, & P. Ekman (Eds.), *Approaches to emotion* (pp. 293-317). Hillsdale, NJ: Lawrence Erlbaum Associates.

——. (1986). Vocal affect expression: A review and model for future research. *Psychological Bulletin,* **99,** 143–165.

——. (1999). On the sequential nature of appraisal processes: Indirect evidence from a recognition task. *Cognition and Emotion,* **13,** 763-793.

Schiff, B. B., & Lamon, M. (1989). Inducing emotion by unilateral contraction of facial muscles: A new look at hemispheric specialization and the experience of emotion. *Neuropsychologia,* **27,** 923–925.

Schiffer, F., Stinchfield, Z., & Pascual-Leone, A. (2002). Prediction of clinical response to transcranial magnetic stimulation for depression by baseline lateral visual-field stimulation. *Neuropsychiatry, Neuropsychology, and Behavioral Neurology,* **15,** 18–27.

Schiffman, H. R. (1990). *Sensation and perception: An integrated approach.* New York: Wiley.

Schiller, J. S., Martinez, M., & Barnes, P. (2005). *Early release of selected estimates based on data from the January-March 2005 National Health Interview.* Hyattsville, MD: National Center for Health Statistics.

Schilt, T., de Win, M. M. L., Koeter, M., Jager, G., Korf, D. J., van den Brink, W., & Schmand, B., (2007). Cognition in novice ecstasy users with minimal exposure to other drugs: A prospective cohort study. *Archives of General Psychiatry,* **64,** 728–736.

Schmader, T., & Johns, M. (2003). Converging evidence that stereotype threat reduces working memory capacity. *Journal of Personality and Social Psychology,* **85,** 440-452.

Schmajuk, N. A. (2001). Hippocampal dysfunction in schizophrenia. *Hippocampus,* **11,** 599-613.

Schmidt, F. L. (1992). What do data really mean? Research findings, meta-analysis, and cumulative knowledge in psychology. *American Psychologist,* **47,** 1173–1181.

Schmidt, F. L., & Hunter, J. E. (1993). Tacit knowledge, practical intelligence, general mental ability, and job knowledge. *Current Directions in Psychological Science,* **2,** 8–9.

Schmidt, U., & Asen, E. (2005). Editorial: Does multi-family day treatment hit the spot that other treatments cannot reach? *Journal of Family Therapy,* **27,** 101-103.

Schmitt, H. N., Schneider, J. R., & Cohen, S. A. (1990). Factors affecting validity of a regionally administered assessment center. *Personnel Psychology,* **43,** 1–12.

Schmitt, N., & Robertson, I. (1990). Personnel selection. *Annual Review of Psychology,* **41,** 289–319.

Schmitt, R. C. (1966). Density, health, and social disorganization. *American Institute of Planners Journal,* **32,** 38–40.

Schneider, R. H., Alexander, C. N., Staggers, F., Rainforth, M., Salerno, J. W., Hartz, A., Arndt, S., Barnes, V. A., & Nidich, S. (2005). Long-term effects of stress reduction on mortality in persons > or = 55 years of age with systemic hypertension. *American Journal of Cardiology,* **95,** 1060–1064.

Schneiderman, N. (2004). Psychosocial, behavioral, and biological aspects of chronic diseases. *Current Directions in Psychological Science,* **13,** 247-251.

Schneiderman, S., Antoni, M. H., Saab, P. G., & Ironson, G. (2001). Health psychology: Psychosocial and biobehavioral aspects of chronic disease management. *Annual Review of Psychology,* **52,** 555–580.

Schooler, N. R., & Keith, S. J. (1993). The clinical research base for the treatment of schizophrenia. *Psychopharmacology Bulletin,* **29,** 431–446.

Shors, T. J., Miesegaes, G., Beylin, A., Zhao, M., Rydel, T., & Gould, E. (2001). Neurogenesis in the adult is involved in the formation of trace memories. *Nature,* **410,** 372-376.

Schou, M. (1997). Forty years of lithium treatment. *Archives of General Psychiatry,* **54,** 9–13.

Schraagen, J. M., Chipman, S. F., & Shalin, V. L. (Eds.). (2000). *Cognitive task analysis.* Mahwah, NJ: Erlbaum.

Schroeder, S. R., Schroeder, C. S., & Landesman, S. (1987). Psychological services in educational settings to persons with mental retardation. *American Psychologist,* **42,** 805–808.

Schrores, M., Prigot, J., & Fagan, J. (2007). The effect of a salient odor context on memory retrieval in young infants. *Infant Behavior and Development, 30,* 685–689.

Schultz, D. P., & Schultz, S. E. (1990). *Psychology and industry today.* New York: Macmillan.

——. (1998). *Psychology and work today: An introduction to industrial and organizational psychology (7th ed.).* Belmont, CA: Wadsworth.

Schultz, R., & Decker, S. (1985). Long-term adjustment to physical disability: The role of social support, perceived control and self-blame. *Journal of Personality and Social Psychology,* **48,** 1162–1172.

Schutte, N. S., Malouff, J. M., Hall, L. E., Haggerty, D. J., Cooper, J. T., Golden, C. J., & Dornheim, L. (1998). Development and validation of a measure of emotional intelligence. *Personality and Individual Differences,* **25(2),** 167–177.

Schwartz, A. E. (1984). Earliest memories: Sex-differences in the meaning of experience. *Imagination, Cognition, and Personality,* **4,** 43–52.

Schwartz, P. (1983). Length of day-care attendance and attachment behavior in eighteen-month-old infants. *Child Development,* **54,** 1073–1078.

Sclar, D. A., Robinson, L. M., Skaer, T. L., & Galin, R. S. (1999). Ethnicity and the prescribing of antidepressant pharmacotherapy. *Harvard Review of Psychiatry,* **7,** 29-36.

Scogin, F., & McElreath, L. (1994). Efficacy of psychosocial treatments for geriatric depression: A quantitative review. *Journal of Consulting and Clinical Psychology,* **62,** 69–74.

Scott, K. G., & Carran, D. T. (1987). The epidemiology and prevention of mental retardation. *American Psychologist, 42*, 801–804.

Scott, M. D., & Pelliccioni, L., Jr. (1982). *Don't choke: How athletes become winners.* Englewood Cliffs, NJ: Prentice-Hall.

Sears, P. S., & Barbee, A. H. (1977). Career and life satisfaction among Terman's gifted women. In J. Stanley et al. (Eds.), *The gifted and the creative: Fifty year perspective.* Baltimore: Johns Hopkins University Press.

Sechrest, L. & Walsh, M. (1997). Dogma or data: Bragging rights. *American Psychologist, 52*, 536–540.

Seegall, M. H., Campbell, D. T., & Herskovits, M. J. (1966). *The influence of culture on visual perception.* Indianapolis: Bobbs-Merrill.

Seelman, K. D. (2001). Science and technology: Is disability a missing factor? In K. D. Seelman, G. Albrecht, & M. Bury (Eds.), *Handbook of disability studies.* Thousand Oaks, CA: Sage.

Seelman, K. D. & Sweeney, S. (1995). The changing universe of disability. *American Rehabilitation, 21*, 2-13.

Segall, M., Dasen, P., Berry, J., & Poortinga, Y. (1990). *Human behavior in global perspective.* Elmsford, NY: Pergamon.

Segall, M. H., Campbell, D. T., & Herskovits, M. J. (1966). *The influence of culture on visual perception.* Indianapolis: Bobbs-Merrill.

Segall, M. H., Lonner, W. J., & Berry, J. W. (1998). Cross-cultural psychology as a scholarly discipline: On the flowering of culture in behavioral research. *American Psychologist, 53*, 1101–1110.

Seghier, M. L., Lazeyras, F., Vuileumier, P., Schnider, A., & Carota, A. (2005). Functional magnetic resonance imaging and diffusion tensor imaging in a case of central poststroke pain. *Journal of Pain, 6*, 208–212.

Seid, R. (1989). *Never too thin: Why women are at war with their bodies.* New York: Prentice Hall.

Seidlitz, L., & Diener, E. (1998). Sex differences in the recall of affective experiences. *Journal of Personality and Social Psychology, 74*, 262–271.

Seligman, M. E. P. (1975). *Helplessness: On depression development and death.* San Francisco: Freeman.

——. (1991). *Learned optimism.* New York: Norton.

——. (1995). The effectiveness of psychotherapy: The Consumer Reports study. *American Psychologist, 50*, 965–974.

——. (1996). Long-term psychotherapy is highly effective: The Consumer Reports study. *The Harvard Mental Health Letter, 13(1)*, 5–7.

Selkoe, D. J. (1990). Deciphering Alzheimer's disease: The amyloid precursor protein yields new clues. *Science, 248*, 1058.

Selye, H. (1974). *Stress without distress.* Philadelphia: Lippincott.

——. (1976). *The stress of life.* New York: McGraw-Hill.

Sennecker, P., & Hendrick, C. (1983). Androgyny and helping behavior. *Journal of Personality and Social Psychology, 45*, 916–925.

Serbin, L. A., Sprafkin, C., Elman, M., & Doyle, A. B. (1984). The early development of sex differentiated patterns of social influence. *Canadian Journal of Social Science, 14*, 350–363.

Serpell, R., & Deregowski, J. B. (1980). The skill of pictorial perception: An interpretation of cross-cultural evidence. *International Journal of Psychology, 15*, 145–180.

Shade, B. (1992). Is there an African-American cognitive style? An exploratory study. In A. K. Burlew, W. Banks, H. McAdoo, & D. Azibo (Eds.), *African-American psychology: Theory, research, and practice* (pp. 256-259). Newbury Park, CA: Sage.

Shadish, W. R. (1984). Policy research: Lessons from the implementation of deinstitutionalization. *American Psychologist, 39*, 725–738.

Shadish, W. R., Montgomery, L. M., Wilson, P., Wilson, M. R., Bright, I., & Okwumabua, T. (1993). Effects of marital and family psychotherapies: A meta-analysis. *Journal of Consulting and Clinical Psychology, 61*, 992–1002.

Shadish, W. R., Navarro, A. M., Matt, G. E., & Phillips, G. (2000). The effects of psychological therapies under clinically representative conditions: A meta-analysis. *Psychological Bulletin, 126*, 512–529.

Shadmehr, R., & Holcomb, H. H. (1997). Neural correlates of motor memory consolidation. *Science, 277*, 821-825.

Shafer, M., & Crichlow, S. (1996). Antecedents of groupthink: A quantitative study. *Journal of Conflict Resolution, 40*, 415-435.

Shaffer, D. R. (2000). *Social and personality development (4th ed.).* Belmont, CA: Wadsworth.

——. (2002). *Developmental psychology: Childhood & Adolescence (6th ed.).* Belmont, CA: Wadsworth.

Shaffer, D. R., & Kipp, K. (2007). *Developmental psychology: Childhood and adolescence.* Belmont, CA: Wadsworth.

Shaffer, G. S., Saunders, V., & Owens, W. A. (1986). Additional evidence for the accuracy of biographical data: Long-term retest and observer ratings. *Personnel Psychology, 39*, 791–809.

Shaffer, M. (1982). *Life after stress.* New York: Knopf.

Shalizi, Z. (2003). *World development report 2003: Sustainable development in a dynamic world.* Washington, DC: World Bank Group.

Shapiro, A. (1999). *Everybody belongs: Changing negative attitudes toward classmates with disabilities.* New York: Garland Press.

Shapiro, D. H., Jr. (1985). Clinical use of meditation as a self-regulation strategy: Comment on Holmes's conclusions and implications. *American Psychologist, 40*, 719–722.

Shattuck, P. T. (2006). The contribution of diagnostic substitution to the growing administrative prevalence of autism in U.S. special education. *Pediatrics, 117*, 1028–1037.

Shaver, P., Hazan, C., & Bradshaw, D. (1988). Love as attachment: The integration of three behavioral systems. In R. J. Sternberg & M. L. Barnes (Eds.), *The psychology of love.* New Haven, CT: Yale University Press.

Shaw, B. F., Elkin, I., Yamaguchi, J., Olmsted, M., Vallis, T. M., et al. (1999). Therapist competence ratings in relation to clinical outcome in cognitive therapy of depression. *Journal of Consulting and Clinical Psychology, 67*, 837–846.

Shaywitz, B. A., Shaywitz, S. E., Pugh, K. R., Constable, R. T., Skudlarski, P., Fulbright, R. K., et al. (1995). Sex differences in the functional organization of the brain for language. *Nature, 373*, 607–609.

Shedler, J., & Block, J. (1990). Adolescent drug use and psychological health: A longitudinal study. *American Psychologist, 45*, 612–630.

Sheehan, P. W., & Statham, D. (1989). Hypnosis, the timing of its introduction, and acceptance of misleading information. *Journal of Abnormal Psychology, 93*, 170–176.

Sheehan, P. W., Green, V., & Truesdale, P. (1992). Influence of rapport on hypnotically induced pseudomemory. *Journal of Abnormal Psychology, 101*, 690–700.

Sheehan, P. W., Statham, D., Jamison, G. A., Ferguson, S. (1991). Ambiguity in suggestion and the occurrence of pseudomemory in the hypnotic interview. *Australian Journal of Clinical and Experimental Hypnosis*, **19**, 1–18.

Sheer, D. E. (Ed.). (1961). *Electrical stimulation of the brain.* Austin: University of Texas Press.

Shekelle, B., Hulley, S. B., Neaton, J. D., Billings, J. H., Borhani, N. O., et al. (1985). The MRFIT behavior pattern study II: Type A behavior and the incidence of coronary heart disease. *American Journal of Epidemiology*, **122**, 559–570.

Shekelle, R. B., Gale, M. E., & Norvis, M. (1985). Type A scores (Jenkins Activity Survey) and risk of recurrent coronary heart disease in the Aspirin Myocardial Infarction Study. *American Journal of Cardiology*, **56**, 221–225.

Shepard, M. M., Briggs, R. O., Reinig, B. A., Yen, J., & Nunamaker, J. (1996). Invoking social comparison to improve electronic brainstorming: Beyond anonymity. *Journal of Management Information Systems*, **12**, 155–170.

Sheridan, C. L., & Smith, L. K. (1987). Toward a comprehensive scale of stress assessment: Norms, reliability, and validity. *International Journal of Psychometrics*, **34**, 48–54.

Sheridan, K., Humfleet, G., Phair, J., & Lyons, J. (1990). The effects of AIDS education on the knowledge and attitudes of community leaders. *Journal of Community Psychology*, **18**, 354–360.

Sherif, M. (1936). *The Psychology of Social Norms.* New York: Harper & Row.

Sherman, D. K., Nelson, L. D., & Ross, L. D. (2003). Naïve realism and affirmative action: Adversaries are more similar than they think. *Basic and Applied Social Psychology*, **25**, 275-289.

Sherman, R. T., & Thompson, R. A. (1990). *Bulimia: A guide for family and friends.* Lexington, MA: Lexington Books.

Shertzer, B. (1985). *Career planning (3rd ed.).* Boston: Houghton Mifflin.

Shiffman, L. B., Fischer, L. B., Zettler-Segal, M., & Benowitz, N. L. (1990). Nicotine exposure among nondependent smokers. *Archives of General Psychiatry*, **47**, 333–340.

Shiffman, S. (1992). Relapse process and relapse prevention in addictive behaviors. *The Behavior Therapist*, **15**, 99–111.

Shiffman, S., Balabanis, M. H., Gwaltney, C. J., Paty, J. A., Gnys, M., Kassel, J. D., et al. (2007). Prediction of lapse from associations between smoking and situational antecedents assessed by ecological assessment. *Drug and Alcohol Dependence*, **91**, 159–168.

Shimamura, A. P. (1986). Priming effects in amnesia: Evidence for a dissociable memory function. *Quarterly Journal of Experimental Psychology*, **38A**, 619–644.

Shipley, T. (1961). *Classics in psychology.* New York: Philosophical Library.

Shippee, G., & Gregory, W. L. (1982). Public commitment and energy conservation. *American Journal of Community Psychology*, **10**, 81–93.

Shirley, M. C., Matt, D. A., & Burish, T. G. (1992). Comparison of frontalis, multiple muscle site, and reactive muscle site feedback in reducing arousal under stressful and nonstressful conditions. *Medical Psychotherapy*, **5**, 133–148.

Shirts, B. H., & Nimgaonkar, V. (2004). The genes for schizophrenia: Finally a breakthrough? *Current Psychiatry Reports*, **6**, 303-312.

Shocat, T., Umphress, J., Isreal, A. G., & Ancoli-Isreal, S. (1999). Insomnia in primary care patients. *Sleep*, **22** (Supplement No. 2), S359–365.

Shotland, R. L., & Straw, M. K. (1976). Bystander response to an assault: When a man attacks a woman. *Journal of Personality and Social Psychology*, **34**, 990-999.

Shulman, H. G. (1971). Similarity effects in short-term memory. *Psychological Bulletin*, **75**, 399–415.

——. (1972). Semantic confusion errors in short-term memory. *Journal of Verbal Learning and Verbal Behavior*, **11**, 221–227.

Shweder, R. A., & Sullivan, M. A. (1993). Cultural psychology: Who needs it? *Annual Review of Psychology*, **44**, 497–523.

Sibai, B. M., Caritis, S. N., Thom, E., Klebanoff, M., McNellis, D., et al. (1993). Prevention of preeclampsia with low-dose aspirin in healthy, nulliparous pregnant women. *New England Journal of Medicine*, **329**, 1213–1218.

Siegel, J. M. (2004). Hypocretin (orexin): Role in normal behavior and neuropathology. *Annual Review of Psychology*, **55**, 125-148.

Siegel, S. (1984). Pavlovian conditioning and heroin overdose: Reports by overdose victims. *Bulletin of the Psychonomic Society*, **22**, 428–430.

Siegel, S. (2005). Drug tolerance, drug addiction, and drug anticipation. *Current Directions in Psychological Science*, **14**, 296–300.

Siegel, S., & Ramos, B. M. C. (2002). Applying laboratory research: Drug anticipation and the treatment of drug addiction. *Experimental and Clinical Psychopharmacology*, **10**, 162-183.

Siegel, S., Baptista, M. A. S., Kim, J. A., McDonald, R. V., & Weise-Kelly, L. (2000). Pavlovian psychopharmacology: The associative basis of tolerance. *Experimental and Clinical Psychopharmacology*, **8**, 276-293

Siegler, R. S. (1983). Five generalizations about cognitive development. *American Psychologist*, **38**, 263–277.

——. (1989). Mechanisms of cognitive development. *Annual Review of Psychology*, **40**, 353–379.

Signorella, M. L., Bigler, R. S., & Liben, L. S. (1997). A meta-analysis of children's memories for own-sex and other-sex information. *Journal of Applied Developmental Psychology*, **18**, 429–445.

Silber, M. H. (2005). Chronic insomnia. *New England Journal of Medicine*, **353**, 803-810.

Silva, J. M., Hardy, C. J., & Crace, R. K. (1988). Analysis of momentum in intercollegiate tennis. *Journal of Sport and Exercise Psychology*, **10**, 346–354.

Silva, R. R., Alpert, M., Munoz, D. M., Singh, S., Matzner, F., & Dummitt, S. (2000). Stress and vulnerability to posttraumatic stress disorder in children and adolescents. *American Journal of Psychiatry*, **157**, 1229–1235.

Silverstein, B., & Lynch, A. D. (1998). Gender differences in depression: The role played by paternal attitudes of male superiority and maternal modeling of gender-related limitations. *Sex Roles*, **38**, 609-615.

Simkins-Bullock, J. A., & Wildman, B. G. (1991). An investigation into the relationships between gender and language. *Sex Roles*, **24**, 149–160.

Simon, D. (1990). Men as success objects and women as sex objects: A study of personal advertisements. *Sex Roles*, **23**, 43-50.

Simon, H. A. (1990). Invariants of human behavior. *Annual Review of Psychology*, **41**, 1–19.

Simon, R. W. (2002). Revising the relationship among gender, marital status, and mental health. *American Journal of Sociology*, **107**, 1065–1096.

Simon, S. I., & Carrillo, R. A. (2002). Improving safety performance through cultural intervention. In R. W. Lack (Ed.), *Safety, health, and asset protection: Management essentials*. Boca Raton, FL: CRC Press.

Simoni-Wastila, R. (1998). Gender and psychotropic drug use. *Medical Care*, **36**, 88-94.

Simonton, D. K. (1984). *Genius, creativity, and leadership*. Cambridge, MA: Harvard University Press.

——. (1997). Creative productivity: A predictive and explanatory model of career trajectories and landmarks. *Psychological Review*, **104**, 66–89.

Simos, P. G., Breier, J. I., Fletcher, J. M., Bergman, E., & Papanicolaou, A. C. (2000). Cerebral mechanisms involved in word reading in dyslexic children: A magnetic source imaging approach. *Cerebral Cortex*, **10**, 809-816.

Sims, E. A. H. (1990). Destiny rides again as twins overeat. *New England Journal of Medicine*, **322**, 1522–1523.

Sinai, M. J., Ooi, T. L., & He, Z, J. (1998). Terrain influences the accurate judgment of distance. *Nature*, **395**, 497–500.

Sinton, C. M., Fitch, T. E., & Gershenfeld, H. K. (1999). The effects of leptin on REM sleep and slow wave delta in rats are reversed by food deprivation. *Journal of Sleep Research*, **8**, 197–203.

Sivertsen. B., Omvik, S., Paliesen, S., Bjorvatn, B., Havik, O. D., Kvale, G., Nielsen, G. H., & Nordhus, I. H. (2006). Cognitive behavioral therapy vs Zopicione for treatment of chronic primary insomnia in older adults. *Journal of the American Medical Associaiton*, **295**, 2851–2858.

Skinner, B. F. (1938). *The behavior of organisms: A behavioral analysis*. Englewood Cliffs, NJ: Prentice-Hall.

——. (1956). A case history in the scientific method. *American Psychologist*, **11**, 221–233.

——. (1957). *Verbal behavior*. Englewood Cliffs, NJ: Prentice-Hall.

——. (1983). Intellectual self-management in old age. *American Psychologist*, **38**, 239–244.

——. (1984). *A matter of consequence*. New York: Knopf.

——. (1987). What ever happened to psychology as the science of behavior? *American Psychologist*, **42**, 780–786.

——. (1989). The origins of cognitive thought. *American Psychologist*, **44**, 13–18.

——. (1990). Can psychology be a science of mind? *American Psychologist*, **45**, 1206–1210.

Skodol, A. E., Oldham, J. M., & Gallaher, P. E. (1999). Axis II comorbidity of substance use disorders among patients referred for treatment of personality disorders. *American Journal of Psychiatry*, **156**, 733–738.

Slater, A., Morison, V., Town, C., & Rose, D. (1985). Movement perception and identity constancy in the newborn baby. *British Journal of Developmental Psychology*, **3**, 211–220.

Slater, J. M., Guthrie, B. J., & Boyd, C. J. (2001). A feminist theoretical approach to understanding health of adolescent females. *Journal of Adolescent Health*, **28**, 443-449.

Slattery, M. L., Edwards, S., Curtin, K., Schaffer, D., & Neuhausen, S. (2003). Associations between smoking, passive smoking, GSTM-1, NAT2, and rectal cancer. *Cancer Epidemiology, Biomarkers and Prevention*, **12**, 882–889.

Small, B. J., Hertzog, C., Hultsch, D. F., & Dixon, R. A. (2003). Stability and change in adult personality over 6 years: Findings from the Victoria Longitudinal Study. *The Journals of Gerontology Series B: Psychological Sciences and Social Sciences*, **58**, 166-176.

Small, J. G., Klapper, M. H., Kellams, J. J., Miller, M. J., Milstein, V., Sharpley, P. H., & Small, I. F. (1988). Electroconvulsive treatment compared with lithium in the management of manic states. *Archives of General Psychiatry*, **45**, 727–732.

Smalley, S. L. (1991). Genetic influences in autism. *Psychiatric Clinics of North America*, **14**, 125–139.

Smetna, J. G., & Gaines, C. (1999). Adolescent-parent conflict in middle-class African-American families. *Child Development*, **70**, 1447–1463.

Smetna, J. G., Killen, M., & Turiel, E. (1991). Children's reasoning about interpersonal and moral conflicts. *Child Development*, **62**, 629–644.

Smith, A. P. & Jones, D. M. (1992). Noise and performance. In D. M. Jones & A. P. Smith (Eds.), *Handbook of human performance (Vol. 1)*. London: Academic Press.

Smith, B. N., Kerr, N. A., Markus, M. J., & Stasson, M. F. (2001). Individual differences in social loafing: Need for cognition as a motivator in collective performance. *Group Dynamics*, **5**, 150-158.

Smith, C. P. (Ed.). (1992). *Motivation and personality: Handbook of thematic content analysis*. Cambridge: Cambridge University Press.

Smith, D. (1987). Conditions that facilitate the development of sport imagery training. *The Sport Psychologist*, **1**, 237–247.

——. (2002). Sleep psychologists in demand. *Monitor on Psychology*, October, 2001, 36–39.

Smith, D. B. (1998). Addressing racial inequalities in health care: Civil rights monitoring and report cards. *Journal of Health Politics, Policy and Law*, **23**, 75-105.

Smith, D. E., Thompson, J. K., Raczynski, J. M., & Hilner, J. E. (1999). Body image among men and women in a biracial cohort: The CARDIA study. *International Journal of Eating Disorders*, **25**, 71-82.

Smith, G. B., Schwebel, A. I., Dunn, R. L., & McIver, S. D. (1993). The role of psychologists in the treatment, management, and prevention of chronic mental illness. *American Psychologist*, **48**, 966–971.

Smith, K. (2007). Brain waves reveal intensity of pain. *Nature*, **450**, 329.

Sobel, K. V., & Blake, R. (2003). *Vision Research*, **43**, 1533–1540.

Smith, M. L., Glass, G. V., & Miller, T. I. (1980). *The benefits of psychotherapy*. Baltimore: Johns Hopkins University Press.

Smith, P. C. (1976). Behavior, results, and organizational effectiveness: The problem of criteria. In M. D. Dunnette (Ed.), *Handbook of industrial and organizational psychology*. Skokie, IL: Rand McNally.

Smith, S. (1979). Remembering in and out of context. *Journal of Experimental Psychology: Human Learning and Memory*, **5**, 460–471.

——. (2003). The top 10 ways to improve safety management. *Occupational Hazards*. From www.occupationalhazards.com.

Smith, T. W. (1992). Hostility and health: Current status of a psychosomatic hypothesis. *Health Psychology*, **11**, 139–150.

Smither, R. D. (1994). *The psychology of work and human performance.* New York: HarperCollins.

Smyrnios, K. X., & Kirkby, R. J. (1993). Long-term comparison of brief versus unlimited psychodynamic treatments with children and their parents. *Journal of Consulting and Clinical Psychology, 61,* 1020–1027.

Snarey, J. (1987). A question of morality. *Psychology Today, 21,* 6–8.

Snarey, J. R., Reimer, J., & Kohlberg, L. (1985). Development of social-moral reasoning among kibbutz adolescents: A longitudinal cross-sectional study. *Developmental Psychology, 21,* 3–17.

Snow, M. E., Jacklin, C. N., & Maccoby, E. E. (1983). Sex-of-child differences in father-child interaction at one year of age. *Child Development, 54,* 227–232.

Snyder, S. H. (1984, November). Medicated minds. *Science 84,* pp. 141–142.

Snyderman, M., & Rothman, S. (1987). Survey of expert opinion on intelligence and aptitude testing. *American Psychologist, 42,* 137–144.

Sobal, J., & Stunkard, A. J. (1989). Socioeconomic status and obesity: A review of the literature. *Psychological Bulletin, 105,* 260–275.

Sobel, K. V., & Blake, R. (2003). *Vision Research, 43,* 1533–1540.

Soldo, T., Blank, I., & Hofmann, T. (2003). (+)-(S)-Alapyridaine—A general taste enhancer? *Chemical Senses, 28,* 371–379.

Soloman, R. C. (2003). *What is an emotion? Classic and contemporary reading (2nd edition).* New York: Oxford University Press.

Solowij, N., Stephens, R. S., Roffman, R. A., Babor, T., Kadden, R., et al. (2002). Cognitive functioning of long-term heavy cannabis users seeking treatment. *Journal of the American Medical Association, 287,* 1123–1131.

Somerfield, M. R. & McCrae, R. R. (2000). Stress and coping research: Methodological challenges, theoretical advances, and clinical applications. *American Psychologist, 55,* 620–625.

Somers, V. K., Dyken, M. E., Mark, A. L., & Abboud, F. M. (1993). Sympathetic-nerve activity during sleep in normal subjects. *The New England Journal of Medicine, 328,* 303–307.

Sommer, R. (1969). *Personal space: The behavioral basis of designs.* Englewood Cliffs, NJ: Prentice-Hall.

Sood, B., Delany-Black, V., Covington, C., Nordstrom-Klee, B., Ager, J., Templin, T., Janisse, J., Martier, S., & Sokol, R. J. (2001). Prenatal alcohol exposure and childhood behavior at age 6 to 7 years: I. Dose-response effect. *Pediatrics, 108,* e34.

Sorensen, J. L., Wermuth, L. A., Gibson, D. R., Choi, K., et al. (1991). *Preventing AIDS in drug users and their sexual partners.* New York: Guilford.

Spanos, N. P. (1994). Multiple identity enactments and multiple personality disorder: A socoiocognitive perspective. *Psychological Bulletin, 116,* 143–165.

Spanos, N. P., & Barber, T. F. S. (1974). Toward convergence in hypnosis research. *American Psychologist, 29,* 500–511.

Spanos, N. P., Menary, E., Gabora, N. J., DuBreuil, S. C., & Dewhirst, B. (1991). Secondary identity enactments during past-life regression: A sociocognitive perspective. *Journal of Personality and Social Psychology, 61,* 308–320.

Spear, N. E., Miller, J. S., & Jagielo, J. A. (1990). Animal learning and memory. *Annual Review of Psychology, 41,* 169–211.

Spearing, M. (2001). *Eating disorders: Facts about eating disorders and the search for solutions.* Washington, DC: National Institute of Mental Health.

Spearman, C. (1904). "General intelligence" objectively determined and measured. *American Journal of Psychology, 15,* 201–293.

Speck, O., Ernst, T., Braun, J., Koch, C., Miller, E., & Chang, L. (2000). Gender differences in the functional organization of the brain for working memory. *Neuroreport, 11,* 2581-2585.

Spencer, D. D., Robbins, R. J., Naftolin, F., et al. (1992). Unilateral transplantation of human fetal mesencephalic tissue into the caudate nucleus of patients with Parkinson's disease. *New England Journal of Medicine, 327,* 1541–1548.

Sperling, G. (1960). The information available in brief visual presentation. *Psychological Monographs, 74* (Whole No. 498).

——. (1963). A model for visual memory tasks. *Human Factors, 5,* 19–31.

Sperry, R. (1968). Hemispheric disconnection and unity in conscious awareness. *American Psychologist, 23,* 723–733.

——. (1982). Some effects of disconnecting the cerebral hemispheres. *Science, 217,* 1223–1226.

Spillman, B. C., & Pezzin, L. E. (2000). Potential and active family caregivers: Changing networks and the "sandwich generation." *Milbank Quarterly, 78,* 347–374.

Sprecher, S., Sullivan, Q., & Hatfield, E. (1994). Mate selection preferences: Gender differences examined in a national sample. *Journal of Personality and Social Psychology, 66,* 1074-1080.

Springer, J. P., & Deutsch, G. (1981). *Left brain, right brain.* San Francisco: Freeman.

Squire, L. R. (1992). Memory and the hippocampus: A synthesis from findings with rats, monkeys, and humans. *Psychological Review, 99,* 195–231.

Squire, L. R., & Slater, P. C. (1978). Bilateral and unilateral ECT: Effects on verbal and nonverbal memory. *American Journal of Psychiatry, 135,* 1316–1320.

Squire, L. R., Knowlton, B., & Mussen, G. (1993). The structure and organization of memory. *Annual Review of Psychology, 44,* 453–495.

Squire, S., & Stein, A. (2003). Functional MRI and parental responsiveness: An avenue into parental psychopathology and early parent-child interactions? *The British Journal of Psychiatry, 183,* 481-483.

Staddon, J. E. R., & Cerutti, D. Y. (2003). Operant conditioning. *Annual Review of Psychology, 54,* 115–144.

Stahl, S. A. (1999, Fall). Different strokes for different folks? A critique of learning styles. *American Educator,* 1–5.

Stall, R. D., Coates, T. J., & Huff, C. (1988). Behavioral risk reduction of HIV infection among gay and bisexual men: A review of results from the United States. *American Psychologist, 43,* 878–885.

Standing, L. (1973). Learning 10,000 pictures. *Quarterly Journal of Experimental Psychology, 25,* 207–222.

Standing, L., Canezio, J., & Haber, R. N. (1970). Perception and memory for pictures: Single-trial learning 2500 visual stimuli. *Psychonomic Science, 19,* 73–74.

Staples, S. L. (1996). Human response to environmental noise: Psychological research and public policy. *American Psychologist*, **51**, 143–150.

Staw, B. M. (1984). Organized behavior: A review and reformation of the field's outcome variables. *Annual Review of Psychology*, **35**, 627–666.

Steadman, H. J., Mulvey, E. P., Monahan, J., & Robbins, P. C. (1998). Violence by people discharged from acute psychiatric facilities and by others in the same area. *Archives of General Psychiatry*, **55**, 393–401.

Steblay, N. M., & Bothwell, R. K. (1994). Evidence for hypnotically refreshed testimony: The view from the laboratory. *Law and Human Behavior*, **18**, 635–652.

Stechler, G., & Halton, A. (1982). Prenatal influences on human development. In B. B. Woolman (Ed.), *Handbook of developmental psychology*. Englewood Cliffs, NJ: Prentice-Hall.

Steele, C. M., & Aronson, J. (1995). Stereotype threat and the intellectual test performance of African-Americans. *Journal of Personality and Social Psychology*, **69**, 797–811.

Steele, C. M., Spencer, S. J., & Aronson, J. (2002). Contending with group image: The psychology of stereotype and social identity threat. In M. Zanna (Ed.), *Advances in experimental social psychology* (Vol. 23, pp. 379-440). New York: Academic Press.

Steele-Johnson, D., & Hyde, B. G. (1997). Advanced technologies in training: Intelligent tutoring systems and virtual reality. In M. A. Quinones & A. Ehrenstein (Eds.), *Training for a rapidly changing workplace: Applications of psychological research*. Washington, DC: American Psychological Association.

Steenbarger, B. N. (1994). Duration and outcome in psychotherapy: An integrative review. *Professional Psychology: Research and Practice*, **25**, 111–119.

Stein, B. A. (1983). *Quality of work life in action: Managing for effectiveness*. New York: American Management Association.

Stein, J. A., Newcomb, M. D., & Bentler, P. M. (1990). The relative influence of vocational behavior and family involvement on self-esteem: Longitudinal analyses of young adult women and men. *Journal of Vocational Behavior*, **36**, 320–328.

Stein, M. B., Walker, J. R., & Forde, D. R. (1996). Public-speaking fears in a community sample: Prevalence, impact on functioning, and diagnostic classification. *Archives of General Psychiatry*, **53**, 169–174.

Steinberg, L. (1999). *Adolescence (5th ed.)*. Boston: McGraw-Hill.

——. (2001). We know some things: Parent-adolescent relationships in retrospect and prospect. *Journal of Research on Adolescence*, **11**, 1-19.

Steinberg, L., & Morris, A. S. (2001). Adolescent development. *Annual Review of Psychology*, **52**, 83–110.

Steinberg, L., Darling, N., & Fletcher, A. C. (1995). Authoritative parenting and adolescent adjustment: An ecological journey. In P. Moen, G. H. Elder, & K. Luscher (Eds.), *Examining lives in context: Perspectives on the ecology of human development* (pp. 423-466). Washington, DC: American Psychological Association.

Steinberg, L., Dornbusch, S. M., & Brown, B. B. (1992). Ethnic differences in adolescent achievement: An ecological perspective. *American Psychologist*, **47**, 723-729.

Steinberg, L., Elmen, J. D., & Mounts, N. S. (1989). Authoritative parenting, prosocial maturity, and academic success among adolescents. *Child Development*, **60**, 1424-1436.

Steinberg, L., Lamborn, S. D., Darling, N., Mounts, N. S., & Dornbusch, S. M. (1994). Over-time changes in adjustment and competence among adolescents from authoritative, authoritarian, indulgent, and neglectful families. *Child Development*, **65**, 754-770.

Steinberg, L, Mounts, N., Lamborn, S., & Dornbusch, S. (1991). Authoritative parenting and adolescent adjustment across varied ecological niches. *Journal of Research on Adolescence*, **1**, 19-36.

Steiner, M., Steinberg, S., Stewart, D., Carter, D., Berger, C., Reid, R., Grover, D., & Steiner, D. (1995). Fluoxetine in the treatment of premenstrual dysphoria. *New England Journal of Medicine*, **332**, 1529–1534.

Steinhausen, H. C., Göbel, D., Breinlinger, M., & Wolleben, B. (1986). A community survey of infantile autism. *Journal of the American Academy of Child Psychiatry*, **25**, 186–189.

Stenchever, M. A., Williamson, R. A., Leonard, J., Karp, L. E., Ley, B., Shy, K., & Smith, D. (1981). Possible relationship between in utero diethylstilbestrol exposure and male infertility. *American Journal of Obstetrics and Gynecology*, **140**, 186–193.

Stephan, W. (1985). Intergroup relations. In G. Lindsey & E. Aronson (Eds.), *Handbook of social psychology (3rd ed.)*. New York: Random House.

Stephanides, S. L., Wilson, M., & Sinert, R. (2001). Hypernatremia. *Emedicine*. Available at http://www.emedicine.com/emerg/topic263.htm.

Stern, D. (1977). *The first relationship*. Cambridge, MA: Harvard University Press.

Stern, L. (1985). *The structures and strategies of human memory*. Homewood, IL: Dorsey Press.

Stern, P. C. (1992). Psychological dimensions of global environmental change. *Annual Review of Psychology*, **43**, 269–302.

Sternberg, R. J. (1981). Testing and cognitive psychology. *American Psychologist*, **36**, 1181–1189.

——. (1985). *Beyond IQ*. New York: Cambridge University Press.

——. (1988). *The triarchic mind*. New York: Viking Press.

——. (1990). *Metaphors of mind: Conceptions of the nature of intelligence*. New York: Cambridge University Press.

——. (1997). The concept of intelligence and its role in lifelong learning and success. *American Psychologist*, **52**, 1030–1037.

——. (1999). The theory of successful intelligence. *Review of General Psychology*, **3**, 292–316.

——. (2001). What is the common thread of creativity? Its dialectical relation to intelligence and wisdom. *American Psychologist*, **56**, 360–362.

——. (2004). Culture and intelligence. *American Psychologist*, **59**, 360–362.

Sternberg, R. J., & Lubart. (1996). Investing in creativity. *American Psychologist*, **51**, 677–688.

Sternberg, R. L., Grigorenko, E. L., & Kidd, K. K. (2005). Intelligence, race, and genetics. *American Psychologist*, **60**, 46–59.

Stewart. S., Stinnett, H., & Rosenfeld, L. B. (2000). Sex differences in desired characteristics of short-term and long-term relationship partners. *Journal of Social and Personal Relationships*, **17**, 843-854.

Stice, E. (2001). A prospective test of the dual pathway model of bulimic pathology: Mediating effects of dieting and negative affect. *Journal of Abnormal Psychology*, **110**, 124–135.

Stiles, W. B., Shapiro, D. A., & Elliot, R. (1986). "Are all psychotherapies equivalent?" *American Psychologist*, **41**, 165–180.

Stinnett, N., Walters, J., & Kaye, E. (1984). *Relationships in marriage and family (2nd ed.)*. New York: Macmillan.

Stokes, P. D. (2001). Variability, constraints, and creativity: Shedding light on Claude Monet. *American Psychologist*, **56**, 355–359.

Stokols, D. (1972). On the distinction between density and crowding: Some implications for future research. *Psychological Review*, **79**, 275–277.

Stokols, D. (1990). Instrumental and spiritual views of people-environment relations. *American Psychologist*, **45**, 641–646.

Stoner, J. A. F. (1961). *A comparison of individual and group decisions involving risk*. Unpublished master's thesis, Massachusetts Institute of Technology, Cambridge.

Storandt, M. (1983). Psychology's response to the graying of America. *American Psychologist*, **38**, 323–326.

——. (2008). Cognitive deficits in the early stages of Alzheimer's disease. *Current Directions in Psychological Science*, **17**, 198–202.

Strahan, E. J., Spencer, S. J., & Zanna, M. P. (2005). Subliminal priming and persuasion: How motivation affects the activation of goals and the persuasiveness of messages. In F. R. Kardes, P. Herr, & J. Nantel (Eds.). *Applying social cognition to consumer-focused strategy*, pp. 267–280). Mahwah, NJ: Erlbaum.

Strassberg, Z., Dodge, K. A., Petit, G. S., & Bates, J. E. (1994). Spanking in families and subsequent aggressive behavior toward peers by kindergarten students. *Development and Psychopathology*, **6**, 445–461.

Straus, M. A., & Stewart, J. H. (1999). Corporal punishment by American parents: National data on prevalence, chronicity, severity, and duration, in relation to child and family characteristics. *Clinical Child and Family Psychology Review*, **2**, 55–70.

Straus, M. A., Sugarman, D. B., & Giles-Sims J. (1997). Corporal punishment by parents and subsequent antisocial behavior in children. *Archives of Pediatrics and Adolescent Medicine*, **155**, 761–767.

Strauss, R. S., & Pollack, H. A. (2001). Epidemic increase in childhood overweight, 1986-1998. *Journal of the American Medical Association*, **286**, 2845–2848.

Strayer, D. L., & Drews, F. A. (2007). Cell-phone-induced driver distraction. *Current Directions in Psychological Science*, **16**, 128–131.

Strayer, D. L., Drews, F. A., & Crouch, D. J. (2006). A comparison of the cell phone driver and the drunk driver. *Human Factors*, **48**, 381–391.

Strayer, D. L., & Johnston, W. A. (2001). Driven to distraction: Dual-task studies of simulated driving and conversing on a cellular telephone. *Psychological Science*, **12**, 462–466.

Streissguth, A. P., Aase, J. M., Clarren, S. K., Randels, S. P., La Due, R. A., & Smith, D. F. (1991). Fetal alcohol syndrome in adolescents and adults. *Journal of the American Medical Association*, **265**, 1961–1967.

Streissguth, A. P., Bookstein, F. L., Barr, H., Sampson, P. D., O'Malley, K., Kieran, M. B., & Young, J. K. (2004). Risk factors for adverse life outcomes in fetal alcohol syndrome and fetal alcohol effects. *Journal of Developmental and Behavioral Pediatrics*, **25**, 228-238.

Strickland, B. R. (1992). Women and depression. *Psychological Science*, **1**, 132–135.

Striegel-Moore, R. H., Wilfley, D. E., Pike, K. M., Dohm, F., & Fairburn, C. G. (2000). Recurrent binge eating in Black American women. *Archives of Family Medicine*, **9**, 83-87.

Strober, M., Freeman, R., Lampert, C., Diamond, J., & Kaye, W. (2000). Controlled family study of anorexia nervosa and bulimia nervosa: Evidence of shared liability and transmission of partial symptoms. *American Journal of Psychiatry*, **157**, 393–401.

Strong, K., Mathers, C., Leeder, S., & Beaglehole, R. (2005). Preventing chronic diseases: How many lives can we save? *Lancet*, Published online October 5. http://lancet/DOI: 10.1016/SO140-6736(05)67341.

Strupp, H. H. (1986). Psychotherapy: Research, practice, and public policy (How to avoid dead ends). *American Psychologist*, **41**, 120–130.

——. (1996). The tripartite model and the Consumer Reports study. *American Psychologist*, **51**, 1017–1024.

Stumpf, H. (1993). The factor structure of the Personality Research Form: A cross-national evaluation. *Journal of Personality*, **61**, 27–48.

Stunkard, A. J. (1988). Some perspectives on human obesity: Its causes. *Bulletin of the New York Academy of Medicine*, **64**, 902–923.

Stunkard, A. J., Harris, J. R., Pederson, N. L., & McClearn, G. E. (1900). The body-mass index of twins who have been reared apart. *New England Journal of Medicine*, **322**, 1483–1487.

Stunkard, A. J., Storensen, T. I. A., Hanis, C., et al. (1986). An adoption study of human obesity. *New England Journal of Medicine*, **314**, 193–198.

Sturm, R. (2003). Increases in clinically severe obesity in the United States, 1986-2000. *Archives of Internal Medicine*, **163**, 2146–2148.

Sudesh, K., Swanson, M., & Trevathan, G. E. (1987). Persistence of sleep disturbances in preschool children. *Journal of Pediatrics*, **110**, 642–646.

Sue, D. W., & Sue, D. (1990). *Counseling the culturally different: Theory and practice (2nd ed.)*. New York: Wiley.

Sue, D., Sue, D. M., & Ino, S. (1990). Assertiveness and social anxiety in Chinese-American women. *Journal of Psychology*, **124**, 155–163.

Sue, S. (1998). In search of cultural competence in psychotherapy and counseling. *American Psychologist*, **53**, 440–448.

Sue, S., Zane, N., & Young, K. (1994). Research on psychotherapy on culturally diverse populations. In A. Bergin & S. Garfield (Eds.), *Handbook of psychotherapy and behavior change* (pp. 783-817). New York: Wiley.

Suinn, R. M. (1980). *Psychology in sports: Methods and applications*. Minneapolis: Burgess.

Suler, J. R. (1985). Meditation and somatic arousal: A comment on Holmes's review. *American Psychologist*, **40**, 717.

Sullivan, P. F. (1995). Mortality in anorexia nervosa. *American Journal of Psychiatry*, **152**, 1073–1074.

Sulthana, P. (1987). The effect of frustration and inequity on the displacement of aggression. *Asian Journal of Psychology and Education*, **19**, 26–33.

Surgeon General. (1988). *The health consequences of smoking, Nicotine addiction*. Rockville, MD: U.S. Department of Health and Human Services.

Surtman, R. J. (1985). Alzheimer's disease. *Scientific American*, **247**, 62–74.

Surwit, R. S., Feinglos, M. N., & Scovern, A. W. (1983). Diabetes and behavior. *American Psychologist*, **38**, 255–262.

Sussman, E. (1996). Cocaine's role in drug-exposed babies' problems questioned. *Brown University Child and Adolescent Behavior Letter*, **12**, 1–3.

Sussman, L. K., Robins, L. M., & Earls, F. (1987). Treatment-seeking for depression by Black and White Americans, *Social Science and Medicine*, **24**, 187-196.

Suter, A. H. (1991). *Noise and its effects*. Washington, DC: Administrative Conference of the United States.

Suzuki, B. H. (1980). The Asian-American family. IN R. Cardenas, & M. D. Fantini (Eds.). *Parenting in a multicultural society* (pp. 74-102). New York: Longman.

Suzuki, L. A. & Valencia, R. R. (1997). Race-ethnicity and measured intelligence: Educational implications. *American Psychologist*, **52**, 1103–1114.

Swaim, R. C., Oetting, E. R., Thurman, P. J., Beauvais, F., & Edwards, R. W. (1993). American Indian adolescent drug use and socialization characteristics: A cross-cultural comparison. *Journal of Cross-Cultural Psychology*, **24**, 53–70.

Swedo, S. E., Rapoport, J. L., Leonard, H., Lenane, M., & Cheslow, D. (1989a). Obsessive-compulsive disorder in children and adolescents. *Archives of General Psychiatry*, **46**, 335–341.

Swisher, K. G. (1990). Cooperative learning and the education of American Indian/Alaska Native students: A review of the literature and suggestions for implementation. *Journal of American Indian Education*, **29**, 36-43.

Switzer, R., & Taylor, R. B. (1983). Sociability versus privacy of residential choice: Impacts of personality and local social ties. *Basic and Applied Social Psychology*, **4**, 123–136.

Szasz, T. S. (1960). *The myth of mental illness*. New York: HarperCollins.

——. (1982). The psychiatric will: A new mechanism for protecting persons against "psychosis" and psychiatry. *American Psychologist*, **37**, 762–770.

Takagi, Y., Takashashi, J., Saiki, H., Morizone, A., Hayashi, T., Kishi, Y., et al. (2005). Dopaminergic neurons generated from monkey embryonic stem cells function in a Parkinson primate model. *Journal of Clinical Investigation*, **115**, 102-109.

Takahashi, Y. (1990). Is multiple personality disorder really rare in Japan? *Dissociation*, **3**, 57–59.

Takanishi, R. (1993). The opportunities of adolescence-research, intervention, and policy. *American Psychologist*, **48**, 85–87.

Talarico, J. M., & Rubin, D. C. (2003). Confidence, not consistency, characterizes flashbulb memories. *Psychological Science*, **14**, 455–461.

Tannenbaum, S. I., & Yukl, G. (1992). Training and development in work organizations. *Annual Review of Psychology*, 43, 399–441.

Tanner, J. M. (1973). Growing up. *Scientific American*, **179**, 34–43.

——. (1981). Growth and maturation during adolescence. *Nutrition Review*, **39**, 43–55.

Tarnow, E. (2000). Self-destructive obedience in the airplane cockpit and the concept of obedience optimization. In T. Blass (Ed.), *Obedience to authority: Current perspectives on the Milgram paradigm*. Mahwah, NJ: Lawrence Elrbaum.

Tashkin, D. P., Zhang, Z. F., Greenland, S., Cozen, W., Mack, T. M., & Morganstern, H. (2006). Marijuana use and lung cancer: Results of a case-control study. Paper presented at the American Thoracic Society International Conference, San Diego, CA, May 24.

Tasto, D. L. (1969). Systematic desensitization, muscle relaxation, and visual imagery in the counterconditioning of a four-year-old phobic child. *Behavior Research and Therapy*, **7**, 409–411.

Taub, A. (1998). Thumbs down on acupuncture. *Science*, **279**, 159.

Taylor, H. G., Klein, N., Minich, N. M., & Hack, M. (2000). Middle-school age outcomes in children with very low birthweight. *Child Development*, **71**, 1495–1511.

Taylor, R. (1994). *Brave new nose: Sniffing out human sexual chemistry* [On-line]. http://www.erox.com/SixthSense/StoryTwo.html.

Taylor, S. E., Klein, L. C., Lewis, B. P., Gruenewald, T. L., Gurung, R. A. R., & Updegraff, J. A. (2000). Biobehavioral responses to stress in females: Tend-and-befriend, not fight or flight. *Psychological Review*, **107**, 411–429.

Taylor, S. M. (2008). Electroconvulsive therapy, brain-derived neurotropic factor, and possible neurorestorative benefit of the clinical application of electroconvulsive therapy. *The Journal of ECT*, **24**, 160–165.

Taylor, W., Pearson, J., Mair, A., & Burns, W. (1965). Study of noise and hearing in jute weaving. *Journal of the Acoustical Society of America*, **4**, 144–152.

Tedeschi, R. G., Park, C. L., & Calhoun, L. G. (Eds.) (1998). *Posttraumatic growth*. Mahwah, NJ: Erlbaum.

Temple, E., Deutsch, G. K., Poldrack, R. A., Miller, S. L., Tallal, P., Merzenich, M. M., & Gabrieli, J. D. E. (2003). Neural deficits in children with dyslexia ameliorated by behavioral remediation: Evidence from functional MRI. *Proceedings of the National Academy of Sciences*, **100**, 2860-2865.

Tenopyr, M. L. (1981). The realities of employment testing. *American Psychologist*, **36**, 1120–1127.

Teplin, L. A., Abram, K. M., & McClelland, G. M. (1994). Does psychiatric disorder predict violent crime among released jail detainees? A six-year longitudinal study. *American Psychologist*, **49**, 335–342.

Terenius, L. (1982). Endorphins and modulation of pain. *Advances in Neurology*, **33**, 59–64.

Termine, N., Hrynick, T., Kestenbaum, R., Gleitman, H., & Spelke, E. S. (1987). Perceptual completion of surfaces in infancy. *Journal of Experimental Psychology: Perception and Performance,* **13**, 524–532.

Tesser, A. (1993). The importance of heritability in psychological research: The case of attitudes. *Psychological Review,* **100***,* 129–142.

Tesser, A., & Shaffer, D. R. (1990). Attitudes and attitude change. *Annual Review of Psychology,* **41**, 479–523.

Tetlock, P. E., Peterson, R. S., McGuire, C., Shi-jie Chang, & Feld, P. (1992). Assessing political group dynamic: A test of the group-think model. *Journal of Personality and Social Psychology,* **63**, 4.3–425.

Tevis, M. (2001). *Handbook of Texas online, Sanchez, George Isidore.* http://www.tsha.utexas.edu/handbook/online/articles/SS/fsa20.html (accessed August 2, 2005).

Thannickal, T., Moore, R.Y., Nienhuis, R. Ramanathan, L., Gulyani, S., Aldrich, M., Comford, M., & Siegel, J.M. (2000). Reduced number of hypocretin neurons in human narcolepsy. *Neuron,* **27**, 469–474.

Thayer, W. P. (1983). Industrial/organizational psychology: Science and application. In C. J. Scheirer & A. M. Rogers (Eds.), *The G. Stanley Hall lecture series (Vol. 3).* Washington, DC: American Psychological Association.

Thibault, J. W., & Kelley, H. H. (1959). *The social psychology of groups.* New York: Wiley.

Thoma, S. J., & Rest, J. R. (1999). The relationship between moral decision making and patterns of consolidation and transition in moral judgment development. *Developmental Psychology,* **35**, 323–334.

Thomas, A., & Chess, S. (1977). *Temperament and development.* New York: Brunner/Mazel.

Thomas, B. S. (1996). A path analysis of gender differences in adolescent onset of alcohol, tobacco and other drug use (ATOD), reported ATOD use and adverse consequences of ATOD use. *Journal of Addictive Diseases,* **15**, 33–52.

Thomas, J. J., & Daubman, K. A. (2001). The relationship between friendship quality and self-esteem in adolescent girls and boys. *Sex Roles,* **45**, 53–65.

Thomas, L. L., Curtis, A. T., & Bolton, R. (1978). Sex differences in elicited color lexicon size. *Perceptual and Motor Skills,* **47**, 77–78.

Thomas, M. B. (1992). *An introduction to marital and family therapy.* New York: Macmillian.

Thompson, B. (1994). Food, bodies, and growing up female: Childhood lessons about culture, race, and class. In P. Fallon, M. Katzman & S. Wooley, (Eds.), *Feminist perspectives on eating disorders.* New York: The Guilford Press.

Thompson, C. I. (1980). *Controls of eating.* Jamaica, NY: Spectrum.

Thompson, J. K., & Stice, E. (2001). Thin-ideal internalization: Mounting evidence for a new risk factor for body-image disturbance and eating pathology. *Current Directions in Psychological Science,* **10**, 181–183.

Thompson, J. K., Heinberg, L. J., Altabe, M. N., & Tantleff-Dunn, S. (1999). *Exacting beauty: Theory, assessment and treatment of body image disturbance.* Washington, DC: American Psychological Association.

Thompson, J. W., & Blaine, J. D. (1987). Use of ECT in the United States in 1975 and 1980. *American Journal of Psychiatry,* **144**, 557–562.

Thompson, R. F. (2005). In search of memory traces. *Annual Review of Psychology,* **56**, 1–23.

Thompson. R. F., & Krupa, D. J. (1994). Organization of memory traces in the mammalian brain. *Annual Review of Neuroscience,* **17**, 519–549.

Thorndike, E. L. (1911). *Animal intelligence.* New York: Macmillan.

Thorne, A. (1995). Developmental truths in memories of childhood and adolescence. *Journal of Personality,* **63**, 139-163.

Thornton, G. C., III, & Cleveland, J. N. (1990). Developing managerial talent through simulation. *American Psychologist,* **45**, 190–199.

Thurstone, L. L. (1938). Primary mental abilities. *Psychometric Monographs (No. 1).*

Tice, D. M., & Baumeister, R. F. (1985). Masculinity inhibits helping in emergencies: Personality does predict the bystander effect. *Journal of Personality and Social Psychology,* **49**, 420–428.

Tice, D. M., & Baumeister, R. F. (1997). Longitudinal study of procrastination, performance, stress, and health: The costs and benefits of dawdling. *Psychological Science,* **8**, 454–458.

Tice, D. M., Butler, J. L., Muraven, M. B., & Stillwell, A. M. (1995). When modesty prevails: Differential favorability of self-presentation to friends and strangers. *Journal of Personality and Social Psychology,* **69**, 1120–1138.

Tiitinen, H., May, P., Reinikainen, K., & Näätänen, R. (2002). Attentive novelty detection in humans is governed by pre-attentive sensory memory. *Nature,* **372**, 90–92.

Tilley, A. J., & Empson, J. A. C. (1978). REM sleep and memory consolidation. *Biological Psychology,* **6**, 293–300.

Toades, D. P. (1997). From the machine to the ghost within: Pavlov's transition from digestive physiology to conditioned reflexes. *American Psychologist,* **52**, 947-955.

Tobin-Richards, M., Boxer, A., & Peterson, A. C. (1984). The psychological impact of pubertal change: Sex differences in perceptions of self during early adolescence. In J. Brooks-Gunn & A. C. Peterson (Eds.), *Girls at puberty: Biological, psychological, and social perspectives.* New York: Plenum.

Todd, P. M., Penke, L., Fasolo, B., & Lenton, A. P. (2007). Different cognitive processes underlie human mate choices and mate preferences. *Proceedings of the National Academy of Sciences,* **141**, 15011–15016.

Todosijević, B., Ljubinković, S., & Arančić, A. (2003). Mate selection criteria: A trait desirability assessment study of sex differences in Serbia. *Evolutionary Psychology,* **1**, 116–126.

Tohen, M., Waternaux, C. M., & Tsuang, M. T. (1990). Outcome in mania. *Archives of General Psychiatry,* **47**, 1106–1111.

Tolman, C. W. (1969). Social feeding in domestic chicks: Effects of food deprivation of non-feeding companions. *Psychonomic Science,* **15**, 234.

Tolman, E. C. (1932). *Purposive behaviorism in animals and men.* Englewood Cliffs, NJ: Prentice-Hall.

Tolman, E. C., & Honzik, C. H. (1930). Introduction and removal of reward and maze performance in rats. *University of California Publication in Psychology, 4*, 257–275.

Tombs, S., & Silverman, I. (2004). Pupillometry: A sexual selection approach. *Evolution and Human Behavior, 25*, 221–228.

Tomes, H. (2004). The case—and the research—that forever connected psychology and policy. *Monitor on Psychology, 35*, 28.

Tomkins, S. S. (1962). *Affect, imagery, consciousness: Vol. I. The positive affects.* New York: Springer.

Toro, P. A., Trickett, E. J., Wall, D. D., & Salem, D. A. (1991). Homelessness in the United States: An ecological perspective. *American Psychologist, 46*, 1208–1218.

Torpy, J. M. (2005). JAMA Patient Page: Smoking and pregnancy. *Journal of the American Medical Association, 293*, 1286.

Torres-Gil, F., & Bikson, M. K. (2001). Multiculturalism, social policy, and the new aging. *Journal of Gerontological Social Work, 36*, 13–32.

Torrey, E. F. (1988). *Surviving schizophrenia: A family manual.* New York: HarperCollins.

——. (2001). *Surviving schizophrenia: A manual for families, consumers, and providers (4th ed.).* New York: HarperCollins.

Torrey, E. F., Taylor, E. H., Bracha, H. S., et al. (1994). Prenatal origin of schizophrenia in a subgroup of discordant monozygotic twins. *Schizophrenia Bulletin, 20*, 423–432.

Torrey, T. W., & Feduccia, A. (1979). *Morphogenesis of the vertebrates.* New York: Wiley.

Tracey, I. (2005). Nociceptive processing in the human brain. *Current Opinion in Neurobiology, 15*, 478–487.

Treffert, D. A. (1988). The idiot savant: A review of the syndrome. *American Journal of Psychiatry, 145*, 563–572.

Tremblay, L., & Frigon, J-Y. (2005). Precocious puberty in adolescent girls: A biomarker of later psychosocial adjustment problems. *Child Psychiatry and Human Development, 36,* 73–94.

Trepka, C., Rees, A., Shapiro, D. A., Hardy, G. E., & Barkham, M. (2004). Therapist competence and outcome of cognitive therapy for depression. *Cognitive Therapy and Research, 28*, 143-157.

Triandis, H. C. (1993). Collectivism and individualism as cultural syndromes. *Cross-Cultural Research, 27*, 155–180.

Triandis, H. C. & Suh, E. M. (2002). Cultural influences on personality. *Annual Review of Psychology, 53*, 133–278.

Triplett, N. (1898). The dynamogenic factors in pacemaking and competition. *American Journal of Psychology, 9*, 507–533.

Troiano, R. P., & Flegal, K. M. (1998). Overweight children and adolescents: Description, epidemiology, and demographics. *Pediatrics, 101*, 497-504.

True, W. R., Rice, J., Eisen, S. A., Heath, A. C., Goldberg, J., Lyons, M. J., & Nowak, J. (1993). A twin study of genetic and environmental contributions to liability for posttraumatic stress symptoms. *Archives of General Psychiatry, 50*, 257–264.

Trzaska, K. A., & Rameshwar, P. (2007). Current advances in the treatment of Parkinson's disease with stem cells. *Current Neurovascular Research, 4,* 99–109.

Tse, D., Langston, R. F., Kakeyama, M., Bethus, I., Spooner, P. A., Wood, E. R., Witter, M.P., & Morris, R. G. M. (2007). Schemas and memory consolidation. *Science, 316*, 76–82.

Tucker, D. M. (1981). Lateral brain function, emotion, and conceptualization. *Psychological Bulletin, 89*, 19–46.

Tuiten, A., Van Honk, J., Koppeschar, H., Bernaards, C., Thihssen, J., & Verbaten, R. (2000). Time course of effects of testosterone administration on sexual arousal in women. *Archives of General Psychiatry, 57*, 149–153.

Tulving, E. (1962). Subjective organization in free recall of "unrelated" words. *Psychological Review, 69*, 344–354.

——. (1972). Episodic and semantic memory. In E. Tulving & W. Donaldson (Eds.), *Organization of memory.* New York: Academic Press.

——. (1983). *Elements of episodic memory.* New York: Oxford University Press.

——. (1985). How many memory systems are there? *American Psychologist, 40*, 385–398.

——. (1986). What kind of a hypothesis is the distinction between episodic and semantic memory? *Journal of Experimental Psychology: Learning, Memory, and Cognition, 12*, 307–311.

——. (2003). Episodic memory: From mind to brain. *Annual Review of Psychology, 53*, 1–25.

Tulving, E., & Thompson, D. M. (1973). Encoding specificity and retrieval processes in episodic memory. *Journal of Experimental Psychology: Learning, Memory, and Cognition, 8*, 336–342.

Tune, L. E. (2001). Anticholinergic effects of medication in elderly patients. *Journal of Clinical Psychiatry, 62,* (Supplement 21), 11–14.

Tung, R. (1988). *The new expatriates: Managing human resources abroad.* New York: HarperCollins.

Turk, D. C. (1994). Perspectives on chronic pain: The role of psychological factors. *Current Directions in Psychological Science, 3*, 45–48.

Turkheimer, E. (1998). Heritability and biological explanation. *Psychological Review, 105*, 782–791.

Turnbull, C. (1961). Some observations regarding the experiences and behaviors of the Bambuti pygmies. *American Journal of Psychology, 74*, 304–308.

——. (1963). *The forest people.* London: Reprint Society.

Turner, C. F., Villarroel, M. A., Chromy, J. R., Eggleston, E., & Rogers, S. M. (2005). Same gender sex among U.S. adults: Trends across the twentieth century and during the 1990s. *Public Opinion Quarterly, 69*, 439-462.

Turner, J. A., Deyo, R. A., Loesser, J. D., Von Korff, M., & Fordyce, W. E. (1994). The importance of placebo effects in pain treatment and research. *The Journal of the American Medical Association, 271*, 1609–1615.

Turner, J. S., & Helms, D. B. (1987). *Contemporary adulthood.* New York: Holt, Rinehart & Winston.

Tuttle, T. C. (1983). Organizational productivity: A challenge for psychologists. *American Psychologist, 38*, 479–486.

Tversky, A., & Kahneman, D. (1974). Judgment under uncertainty: Heuristics and biases. *Science, 125*, 1124–1131.

Twenge, J., & Crocker, J. (2002). Race, ethnicity, and self-esteem: Meta-analyses comparing whites, blacks, Hispanics, Asians, and Native Americans, including a commentary on Gray-Little and Hafdahl. (2000). *Psychological Bulletin, 128*, 371-408.

Tyrer, P., & Shawcross, C. (1988). Monoamine oxidase inhibitors in anxiety disorders. *Journal of Psychiatric Research, 22* (Suppl. 1), 87–98.

Ulett, G. A. (2003). Acupuncture, magic, and make-believe. *The Skeptical Inquirer, 27*, 47–50.

Ulrich, R. E., Stachnick, T. J., & Stainton, N. R. (1963). Student acceptance of Generalized Personality Inventory. *Psychological Reports, 13*, 831–834.

UNAIDS/WHO (2007). *AIDS epidemic update: December 2007*. Geneva, Switzerland: UNAIDS.

Unger, R., & Crawford, M. (1992). *Women and gender: A feminist psychology*. New York: McGraw-Hill.

U. S. Bureau of the Census. (1991). *Statistical Abstract of the United States (111th ed.)*. Washington, DC: U.S. Government Printing Office.

——. (1994). *Statistical Abstract of the United States (114th ed.)*. Washington, DC: U.S. Government Printing Office.

——. (2005). *Facts for Features: 15th anniversary of Americans with Disabilities Act: July, 26, 2005*. Downloaded on November 10, 2005 from www.census.gov.

U. S. Department of Health and Human Services. (1999). *Mental health: A report of the Surgeon General*. Rockville, MD: DHHS.

——. (2000). *Healthy people 2000. Conference Edition*, pp. 57–60.

U. S. Department of Labor. (2002). *Occupational Outlook Handbook*. Retrieved February, 2003, from http://www.bls.gov/oco/ocos056.htm.

——. (2006). Women in the labor force in 2006. Retrieved on May 29, 2008 from http://www.dol.gov/wb/factsheets/Qf-laborforce-06.htm.

U. S. General Accounting Office. (1992). *Elderly Americans: Health, housing, and nutritional gaps between the poor and the nonpoor*. Washington, DC: United States General Accounting Office.

USDHHS (2006). *The health consequences of involuntary exposure to tobacco smoke: A report of the Surgeon General*. Washington, DC: U. S. Department of Health and Human Services. [Also available on the Internet at www.cdc.gov/tobacco]

Vaes, J., Paladino, M. P., Castelli, L., Leyens, J-P., & Giovanazzi, A. (2003). On the behavioral consequences of infrahumanization: The implicit role of uniquely human emotions in intergroup relations. *Journal of Personality and Social Psychology, 85*, 1016-1034.

Vaidya, C. J., Zhao, M., Desmond, J. E., & Gabrielli, J. D. E. (2002). Evidence for cortical encoding specificity in episodic memory: Memory-induced reactivation of picture processing areas. *Neuropsychologia, 40*, 2136–2143.

Valenstein, E. S. (1980). *The psychosurgery debate: Scientific, legal, and ethical perspectives*. San Francisco: Freeman.

——. (1986). *Great and desperate cures*. New York: Basic Books.

Vallerand, R. J., Colavecchio, P. G., & Pelletier, L. G. (1988). Psychological momentum and performance inferences: A preliminary test of the antecedents-consequences psychological momentum model. *Journal of Sport and Exercise Psychology, 10*, 92–108.

Valliant, G. E. (1983). *The natural history of alcoholism: Causes, patterns and paths to recovery*. Cambridge, MA: Harvard University Press.

Valliant, G. E., & Valliant, C. O. (1990). Natural history of male psychological health, XII: A 45-year study of predictors of successful aging at age 65. *American Journal of Psychiatry, 147*, 31–37.

Valtes, P. B., & Baltes, M. M. (1990). Selective optimization with compensation. In P. B. Baltes & M. M. Baltes (Eds.), *Successful aging: Perspectives from the behavioral sciences*. New York: Cambridge University Press.

Vamos, M. (2008). The cognitive side effects of modern ECT: Patient experiences or objective measurement? *The Journal of ECT, 24*, 18–24.

VandenBos, G. R. (1986). Psychotherapy research: A special issue. *American Psychologist, 41*, 111–112.

——. (1996). Outcome assessment of psychotherapy. *American Psychologist, 51*, 1005–1006.

Van den Pol, A. N. (1999). Hypothalamic hypocretin (orexin): Robust innervention of the spinal cord. *Journal of Neuroscience, 19*, 3171–3182.

VanderHam, T., Meulman, J. J., VanStrien, D. C., & vanEngland, H. (1997). Empirically based subgrouping of eating disorders in adolescents: A longitudinal perspective. *British Journal of Psychiatry, 170*, 363-368.

VanderPlate, C., Aral, S. O., & Magder, L. (1988). The relationship among genital herpes simplex virus, stress, and social support. *Health Psychology, 7*, 159–168.

van der Pompe, G., Antoni, M. H., & Heijen, C. (1998). The effects of surgical stress and psychological stress on the immune function of operative cancer patients. *Psychological Health, 13*, 1015–1026.

Vander Wall, S. B. (1982). An experimental analysis of cache recovery in the Clark's nutcracker. *Animal Behavior, 30*, 84–94.

Van Etten, M. L., & Anthony, J. C. (1999). Comparative epidemiology of initial drug opportunities and transitions to first use: marijuana, cocaine, hallucinogens and heroin. *Drug and Alcohol Dependence, 54*, 117-125.

Van Gundy, A. B. (1995). *Brain boosters for business advantage*. San Diego, CA: Pfeiffer.

Van Horn, J. D., & McManus, I. C. (1992). Ventricular enlargement in schizophrenia: A meta-analysis of studies of the ventricle/brain ratio (vbr). *British Journal of Psychiatry, 160*, 687–697.

van Ijzendoorn, M. H., & Kroonenberg, P. M. (1988). Cross-cultural patterns of attachment: A meta-analysis. *Child Development, 59*, 147–156.

Vansteelandt, K., & Van Mechelen, I. (1998). Individual differences in situation-behavior profiles: A triple typology model. *Journal of Personality and Social Psychology, 75*, 751–765.

Varca, P. E. (1980). An analysis of home and away game performance of male college basketball teams. *Journal of Sport Psychology, 2*, 245–257.

Vargha-Khadem, F., Gadian, D. G., Watkins, K. E., Connelly, A., Ban Paesschen. W., & Mishkin, M. (1997). Differential effects of early hippocampal pathology on episodic and semantic memory. *Science, 277*, 376–380.

Vasquez, J. (1990). Teaching to the distinctive traits on minority students. *The Clearinghouse, 63*, 299-304.

Vaughn, B. E., & Langlois, J. H. (1983). Physical attractiveness as a correlate of peer status and social competence in preschool children. *Developmental Psychology, 19*, 561–567.

Verghese, J., Lipton, R. B., Katz, M. J., Hall, C. B., Derby, C. A., Kuslansky, G., et al. (2003). Leisure activities and the risk of dementia in the elderly. *The New England Journal of Medicine, 348,* 2508–2516.

Verillo, R. T. (1975). Cutaneous sensation. In B. Scharf (Ed.), *Experimental sensory psychology.* Glenview, IL: Scott, Foresman.

Vernon, P. E. (1960). *The structure of human abilities (rev. ed.).* London: Methuen.

——. (1979). *Intelligence: Heredity and environment.* San Francisco: Freeman.

Vertes, R. P. (1984). Brainstem control of the events of REM sleep. *Progress in Neurobiology, 22,* 241–288.

Viguera, A. C., Baldessarini, R. J., Hegarty, J. D., van Kammen, D. P., & Tohen, M. (1997). Clinical risk following abrupt and gradual withdrawal of maintenance neuroleptic treatment. *Archives of General Psychiatry, 54,* 40–55.

Vitiello, B., & Lederhendler, I. (2000). Research on eating disorders: Current status and future prospects. *Biological Psychiatry, 47,* 777–786.

Vitz, P. C. (1990). The use of stories in moral development. *American Psychologist, 45,* 709–720.

Voevodsky, J. (1974). Evaluations of a deceleration warning light for reducing rear-end automobile collisions. *Journal of Applied Psychology, 59,* 270–273.

Vokey, J. R., & Read, J. D. (1985). Subliminal messages: Between the devil and the media. *American Psychologist, 40,* 1231–1239.

Volkmar, F. R., Klin, A., & Schultz, R. T. (2005). Pervasive developmental disorders. In B. J. Sadock & V. A. Sadock (Eds.). *Kaplan and Sadock's comprehensive textbook of psychiatry (pp. 3164–3182).* Philadelphia: Lippincott, Williams & Wilkins.

Völlm, B. A., Taylor, A. N. W., Richardson, P., Corcoran, R., Stirling, J., McKie, S., Deakin, J. F. W., & Elliott, R. (2006). Neuronal correlates of theory of mind and empathy: A functional magnetic resonance imaging study in a nonverbal task. *Neuroimage, 29,* 90–98.

Vorhees, C. F., & Mollnow, E. (1987). Behavioral tertatogenesis: Long-term influences on behavior from early exposure to environmental agents. In J. O. Osofsky (Ed.), *Handbook of infant development (2nd ed.).* New York: Wiley.

Vostag, B. (2003). Effort launched to study stem cell lines, train researchers how to use them. *Journal of the American Medical Association, 289,* 1092.

Vroom, V. (1964). *Work and motivation.* New York: Wiley.

Vurpillot, E. (1968). The development of scanning strategies and their relation to visual differentiation. *Journal of Experimental Child Psychology, 6,* 632–650.

Wade, T. J., Cairney, J., & Pevalin, D. J. (2002). Emergence of gender differences in depression during adolescence: National Panel results from three countries. *Journal of the American Academy of Child and Adolescent Psychiatry, 41,* 190-198.

Wadsworth, B. J. (1971). *Piaget's theory of cognitive development.* New York: David McKay Company, Inc.

Wagner, L. A., Kessler, R. C., Hughs, M., Anthony, J. C., & Nelson, C. B. (1995). Prevalence and correlates of drug use and dependence in the United States. *Archives of General Psychiatry, 52,* 219–229.

Wakefield, H., & Underwager, R. (1992). Recovered memories of alleged sexual abuse: Lawsuits against parents. *Behavioral Sciences and the Law, 10,* 483–507.

Wakefield, J. C. (1999). Evolutionary versus prototype analysis of the concept of disorder. *Journal of Abnormal Psychology, 108,* 374–399.

Walker, E., Kestler, L., Bollini, A., & Hochman, K. M. (2004). Schizophrenia: Etiology and course. *Annual Review of Psychology, 55,* 401-430.

Walker, E. A., Katon, W., Russo, J., Ciechanowski, P., Newman, E., & Wagner, A. W. (2003). Health care costs associated with post-traumatic stress disorder symptoms in women. *Archives of General Psychiatry, 60,* 369–374.

Walker, L. J. (1989). A longitudinal study of moral reasoning. *Child Development, 60,* 157–166.

Walker-Andrews, A. S., Bahrick, L. E., Raglioni, S. S., & Diaz, I. (1991). Infants' bimodal perception of gender. *Ecological Psychology, 3,* 55–75.

Wallace, P. (1977). Individual discrimination of humans by odor. *Physiology and Behavior, 19,* 577–579.

Wallace, R. K., & Benson, H. (1972). The physiology of meditation. *Scientific American, 226,* 85–90.

Wallach, H. (1987). Perceiving a stable environment when one moves. *Annual Review of Psychology, 38,* 1–28.

Wallas, G. (1926). *The art of thought.* New York: Harcourt Brace Jovanovich.

Walsh, B. T. (1995). Pharmacotherapy of eating disorders. In K. D. Brownell & C. G. Fairburn (Eds.), *Eating disorders and obesity: A comprehensive handbook.* New York: Guilford Press.

Walsh, B. T., Hadigan, C. M., Devlin, M. J., Gladis, M., & Roose, S. P. (1991). Long-term outcome of antidepressant treatment for bulimia nervosa. *American Journal of Psychiatry, 148,* 1206–1212.

Walsh, B. T., Kissileff, H. R., Cassidy, S. M., & Dantzic, S. (1989). Eating behavior of women with bulimia. *Archives of General Psychiatry, 46,* 54–58.

Walsh, B. T., Wilson, G. T., Devlin, K. L., Pike, K. M., Roose, S. P., Fleiss, J., & Waternaux, C. (1997). Medication and psychotherapy in the treatment of bulimia nervosa. *American Journal of Psychiatry, 154,* 523–531.

Walster, E., & Festinger, L. (1962). The effectiveness of "overheard" and persuasive communications. *Journal of Abnormal and Social Psychology, 65,* 395–402.

Walster, E., Aronson, V., Abrahams, D., & Rottman, L. (1966). Importance of physical attractiveness in dating behavior. *Journal of Personality and Social Psychology, 4,* 508–516.

Walters, G. C., & Grusec, J. E. (1977). *Punishment.* San Francisco: Freeman.

Walton, G. E., & Bower, T. G. R. (1993). Newborns form "prototypes" in less than 1 minute. *Psychological Science, 4,* 203–205.

Walton, G. E., Bower, N. J. A., & Bower, T. G. R. (1992). Recognition of familiar faces by newborns. *Infant Behavior and Development, 15,* 265–269.

Wampold, B. E., & Brown, G. (2005). Estimating therapist variability in outcomes attributable to therapists: A naturalistic study of outcomes in managed care. *Journal of Consulting and Clinical Psychology*, **73**, 914–923.

Wampold, B. E., Mondin, G. W., Moody, M., Stich, F., Benson, K., & Ahn, H. (1997). A meta-analysis of outcome studies comparing bona fide psychotherapies: Empirically, "all must have prizes." *Psychological Bulletin*, **122**, 203–215.

Wang, L., McCarthy, G., Song, A. W., & LaBar, K. S. (2005). Amygdala activation to sad pictures during high-field (4 Tesla) functional magnetic resonance imaging. *Emotion*, **5**, 12-22.

Wang, P. S., Berglund, P., & Kessler, R. C. (2000). Recent care of common mental disorders in the United States. *Journal of General Internal Medicine*, **25**, 288-292.

Wang, P. S., Lane, M., Olfson, M., Pincus, H. A., Wells, K. B., & Kessler, R. C. (2005). Twelve-month use of mental health services in the United States: Results from the National Comorbidity Survey Replication. *Archives of General Psychiatry*, **62**, 629-640.

Wang, Z., Sindreu, C. B., Aaron, V. L., Nudelman, A., Chan, G. C.-K., & Storm, D. R. Pheromone detection in male mice depends on signaling through the Type 3 Adenylyl Cyclase in the main olfactory epithelium. *The Journal of Neuroscience*, **26**, 7375–7379.

Ward, A., Ramsay, R., Turnbull, S., Benedettini, M., & Treasure, J. (2000). Attachment patterns in eating disorders: Past in the present. *International Journal of Eating Disorders*, **28**, 370-376.

Warner, L. A., Kessler, R. C., Hughes, M., Anthony, J. C., Nelson, C. B. (1995). Prevalence and correlates of drug use and dependence in the United States: Results from the National Comorbidity Survey. *Archives of General Psychiatry*, **52**, 219–229.

Warrington, E. K., & Weiskrantz, L. (1968). New method of testing long-term retention with special reference to amnesic patients. *Nature*, **217**, 972–974.

——. (1970). Amnesic syndrome: Consolidation or retrieval? *Nature*, **228**, 629–630.

Washburn, M. F. (1908). *The animal mind: A textbook of comparative psychology*. New York: McMillan.

Waterman, A. S. (1985). Identity in the context of adolescent psychology. *New Directions in Child Development*, **30**, 5–24.

Waters, E., Merrick, S., Treboux, D., Crowell, J., & Albersheim, L. (2000). Attachment security in infancy and early adulthood: A twenty-year longitudinal study. *Child Development*, **71**, 684–689.

Watkins, L. R. & Mayer, D. J. (1982). Organization of endogenous opiate and nonopiate pain control systems. *Science*, **216**, 219–229.

Watkins, M. J. (1990). Mediationism and the obfuscation of memory. *American Psychologist*, **45**, 328–335.

Watson, C. J. (1981). An evaluation of some aspects of the Steers and Rhodes model of employee attendance. *Journal of Applied Psychology*, **66**, 385–389.

Watson, J. B. (1919). *Psychology from the standpoint of a behaviorist*. Philadelphia: Lippincott.

——. (1925). *Behaviorism*. New York: Norton.

——. (1926). What is behaviorism? *Harper's Monthly Magazine*, **152**, 723–729.

——. (1913). Psychology as the behaviorist views it. Retrieved May 6, 2008 from http://psychclassics.yorku.ca/Watson/views.htm.

Watson, M. W., & Amgott-Kwan, T. (1984). Development of family-role concepts in school-age children. *Developmental Psychology*, **20**, 953–959.

Waugh, N. C., & Norman, D. A. (1965). Primary memory. *Psychological Review*, **72**, 89–104.

Weaver, C. N. (1980). Job satisfaction in the United States in the 1970s. *Journal of Applied Psychology*, **65**, 364–367.

Webb, W. B. (1975). *Sleep, the gentle tyrant*. Englewood Cliffs, NJ: Prentice-Hall.

——. (1981). The return of consciousness. In L. T. Benjamin (Ed.), *The G. Stanley Hall lecture series (Vol. I)*. Washington, DC: American Psychological Association.

Webb, W. B., & Cartwright, R. D. (1978). Sleep and dreams. *Annual Review of Psychology*, **29**, 223–252.

Weber, R., Ritterfeld, U., Mathiak, K. (2006). Does playing violent video games induce aggression? Empirical evidence of a functional magnetic resonance imaging study. *Media Psychology*, 8, 39–60.

Wechsler, D. (1958). *The measurement and appraisal of adult intelligence (4th ed.)*. Baltimore: Williams & Wilkins.

——. (1975). Intelligence defined and undefined: A relativistic reappraisal. *American Psychologist*, **30**, 135–139.

——. (1981). *Manual for the Wechsler Adult Intelligence Scale-Revised*. New York: The Psychological Corporation.

Weeden, J., & Sabini, J. (2005). Physical attractiveness and health in Western societies: A review. *Psychological Bulletin*, **131**, 635-653.

Weekes, J. R., Lynn, S. J., Green, J. P., & Brentar, J. T. (1992). Pseudomemory in hypnotized and task-motivated subjects. *Journal of Abnormal Psychology*, **101**, 356–360.

Weekley, J. A., & Gier, J. A. (1987). Reliability and validity of the situational interview for a sales position. *Journal of Applied Psychology*, **72**, 484–487.

Weidman, J. R., Dolinoy, D. C., Murphy, S. K., & Jirtle, R. L. (2007). Cancer susceptibility: Epigenetic manifestations of environmental exposures. *The Cancer Journal*, **13**, 9–16.

Weil, A. T., Zinberg, N., & Nelson, J. M. (1968). Clinical and psychological effects of marijuana in man. *Science*, **162**, 1234–1242.

Weinland, J. (1996). Cognitive behavior therapy: A primer. *Journal of Psychological Practice*, **2(1)**, 23–35.

Weinstock, H., Berman, S., & Cates, W. (2004). Sexually transmitted diseases among American youth: Incidence and prevalence estimates, 2000. *Perspectives on Sexual and Reproductive Health*, **36**, 6–10.

Weisberg, R. W. (1986). *Creativity: Genus and other myths*. San Francisco: Freeman.

——. (1993). *Creativity: Beyond the myth of genius*. New York: Freeman.

Weiskrantz, L. (1986). *Blindsight: A case study and implications*. Oxford, UK: Oxford University Press.

Weiss, A., Bates, T. C., & Luciano, M. (2008). Happiness is a personal(ity) thing: The genetics of personality and well-being in a representative sample. *Psychological Science*, **19**, 205–210.

Weissman, M. M. (1988). The epidemiology of anxiety disorders: Rates, risks and familial patterns. *Journal of Psychiatric Research*, **22** (Suppl. 1), 99–114.

——. (1993). The epidemiology of personality disorders: A 1990 update. *Journal of Personality Disorders: Supplement,* Spring, 44-62.

Weissman, M. M., Bland, R. C., Canino, G. J., Faravelli, C. et al. (1997). The cross-national epidemiology of panic disorder. *Archives of General Psychiatry,* **54**, 305–309.

Weissman, M. M., Klerman, G. L., Markowitz, J. S., & Ouellette, R. (1989). Suicidal ideation and suicide attempts in panic disorders and attacks. *The New England Journal of Medicine,* **321**, 1209–1214.

Welch, W. W., Anderson, R. E., & Harris, L. J. (1982). The effects of schooling on mathematics achievement. *American Educational Research Journal,* **19**, 145–153.

Wellman, H. M., & Gellman, S. A. (1992). Cognitive development: Fundamental theories of core domains. *Annual Review of Psychology,* **43**, 337–375.

Wells, G. L. (1993). What do we know about eyewitness identification? *American Psychologist,* **48**, 553–571.

Wells, G. L., & Olson, E. A. (2002). Eyewitness identification: Information gain from incriminating and exonerating behaviors. *Journal of Experimental Psychology: Applied,* **8**, 155–167

——. (2003). Eyewitness testimony. *Annual Review of Psychology,* **54**, 277–295.

Wells, G. W., Luus, C.A.E., & Windschitl, P. D. (1994). Maximizing the utility of eyewitness identification evidence. *Current Directions in Psychological Science,* **3**, 194–197.

Wen, C. P., Chen, T., Tsai, Y., Tsai, S. P., Chung, W. S. I., Cheng, T. Y., Levy, D. T., Hsu, C. C., Peterson, R., & Liu, W. (2005). Are marketing campaigns in Taiwan by foreign tobacco companies targeting young smokers? *Tobacco Control,* **14**, i38-i44.

Wender, P. H. (2000). *ADHD: Attention-deficit hyperactivity disorder in children and adults.* Oxford: University Press.

Werker, J. F. (1989). Becoming a native listener. *American Scientist,* **77**, 54–59.

Wertheimer, M. (1961). Psychomotor coordination of auditory and visual space at birth. *Science,* **134**, 1692.

Wessinger, C. M., & Fendrich, R. (1997) Islands of residual vision in hemianopic patients. *Journal of Cognitive Neuroscience,* **9**, 203. Retrieved from the World Wide Web on October 5, 2000. http://ehostvgw15.epnet.com/.

West, M. A. (1985). Meditation and somatic arousal reduction. *American Psychologist,* **40**, 717–719.

Westen, D. (1998). The scientific legacy of Sigmund Freud: Toward a psychodynamically informed psychological science. *Psychological Bulletin,* **124**, 333–371.

Whalen, P. J., Shin, L. M., McInerney, S. C., Fischer, H., Wright, C. I., & Rauch, S. L. (2001). A functional MRI study of human amygdala responses to facial expressions of fear versus anger. *Emotion,* **1**, 70-83.

Whaley, A. L. (2001). Cultural mistrust and mental health services for African Americans: A review and meta-analysis. *The Counseling Psychologist,* **29**, 513-531.

Wheeler, M. A., & McMillan, C. T. (2001). Focal retrograde amnesia and the episodic-semantic distinction. *Cognitive, Affective, and Behavioral Neuroscience,* **1**, 22–37.

Wheeler, M. E., Petersen, S. E., & Buckner, R. L. (2000). Memory's echo: Vivid remembering reactivates sensory-specific cortex. *Proceedings of the National Academy of Sciences,* **97**, 11125–11129.

Whetzel, D. L. & McDaniel, M. A. (1997). Employment interviews. In D. L. Whetzel & G. R. Wheaton (Eds.), *Applied Measurement Methods in Industrial Psychology* (pp. 185–206). Palo Alto, CA: Consulting Psychologists Press.

White, J. L. (1989). *The troubled adolescent.* New York: Pergamon.

White, J. L., & Cones, J. H. III. (1999). *Black man emerging: Facing the past and seizing a future in America.* New York: Routledge.

White, J. L., & Parham, T. A. (1990). *The psychology of Blacks: An African-American perspective.* Englewood Cliffs, NJ: Prentice-Hall.

White, M. A., McKee, S. A., & O'Malley, S. S. (2007). Smoke and mirrors: Magnified beliefs that cigarette smoking suppresses weight. *Addictive Behaviors,* **32**, 2200–2210.

White, V., Tan, N., Wakefield, M., & Hill, D. (2003). Do adult focused anti-smoking campaigns have an impact on adolescents? The case of the Australian National Tobacco Campaign. *Tobacco Control,* **12**, ii23.

Whitehurst, G. (1982). Language development. In B. Wolman (Ed.), *Handbook of developmental psychology.* Englewood Cliffs, NJ: Prentice-Hall.

Whiting, B., & Edwards, C. P. (1973). A cross-cultural analysis of sex differences in the behavior of children ages three through eleven. *Journal of Social Psychology,* **91**, 177–188.

Whitman, F. L., Diamond, M., & Martin, J. (1993). Homosexual orientation in twins: A report on 61 pairs and three triplet sets. *Archives of Sexual Behavior,* **22**, 187–206.

Whyte, G. (1989). Groupthink reconsidered. *Academy of Management Review,* **14**, 40–56.

Wichstrom, L. (1999). The emergence of gender differences in depressed mood during adolescence: The role of intensified gender socialization. *Developmental Psychology,* **35**, 232-245.

Wickelgren, I. (2005). Autistic brains out of sync? *Science,* **308**, 1856–1858.

Wickens, C. D. (1992). *Engineering psychology and human performance (2nd ed.).* New York: HarperCollins.

Wickens, D. D. (1973). Some characteristics of word encoding. *Memory and Cognition,* **1**, 485–490.

Widiger, T. A., & Sankis, L. M. (2000). Adult psychopathology: Issues and controversies. *Annual Review of Psychology,* **51**, 377–404.

Widner, H., Tetrud, J., Rehncrona, S., et al. (1992). Bilateral fetal mesencephalic grafting in two patients with Parkinsonism induced by 1-methyl-4-phenyl-1,2,3,6 tetrahydropridine (MPTP). *The New England Journal of Medicine,* **327**, 1556–1563.

Wiggins, J. S., & Pincus, A. L. (1992). Personality: Structure and assessment. *Annual Review of Psychology,* **43**, 473–504.

Wijkstra, J., & Nolan, W. A. (2005). Successful maintenance electroconvulsive therapy for more than seven years. *The Journal of ECT,* **21**, 171-173.

Wilcox, D., & Hager, R. (1980). Toward realistic expectations for orgasmic response in women. *Journal of Sex Research,* **16**, 162–179.

Wilhelm, K., Roy, K., Mitchell, P., Brownhill, S., & Parker, G. (2002). Gender differences in depression risk and coping factors in a clinical sample. *Acta Psychiatrica Scandinavica,* **106**, 45-53.

Wilkes, J. (1986). Conversation with Ernest R. Hilgard: A study in hypnosis. *Psychology Today*, **20(1)**, 23–27.

Williams, D. R., & Williams-Morris, R. (2000). Racism and mental health: The African American experience. *Ethnicity and Health*, **5**, 243–268.

Williams, D. R., González, H. M., Neighbors, H., Nesse, R., Abelson, J. M., Sweetman, J., & Jackson, J. S. (2007). Prevalence and distribution of major depressive disorder in African Americans, Caribbean blacks, and non-Hispanic whites. *Archives of General Psychiatry*, **64**, 305–315.

Williams, J. E., & Best, D. L. (1990). *Measuring sex stereotypes: A multination study.* Newbury Park, CA: Sage.

Williams, J. M., & Dunlap, L. C. (1999). Pubertal timing and self-reported delinquency among male adolescents. *Journal of Adolescence*, **22**, 157–171.

Williams, K., Nida, S. A., Baca, L. D., & Latané, B. (1989). Social loafing and swimming: Effects of identifiability of individual and relay performance of intercollegiate swimmers. *Basic and Applied Social Psychology*, **10**, 73–82.

Williams, W. M., & Ceci, S. J. (1997). Are Americans becoming more or less alike: Trends in race, class, and ability differences in intelligence. *American Psychologist*, **52**, 1226–1235.

Williams, R. W., & Herrup, K. (1988). The control of neuron number. *Annual Review of Neuroscience*, **11**, 423–453.

Willis, M. (1992). Learning styles of African-American children: A review of the literature and interventions. In A. K. Burlew, W. Banks, H. McAdoo, & D. Azibo (Eds.), *African-American psychology: Theory, research, and practice* (pp. 260-278). Newbury Park, CA: Sage.

Wilson, R. S., & Bennett, D. A. (2003). Cognitive activity and risk of Alzheimer's disease. *Current Directions in Psychological Science*, **12**, 87–91.

Wilson, T. D., Lindsey, S, & Schooler, T. Y. (2000). A model of dual attitudes. *Psychological Review*, **107**, 101–126.

Wilson, W. J. (1998). Personal Communication.

Wincze, J. P., & Carey, M. P. (1992). *Sexual dysfunctions: A guide for assessment and treatment.* New York: Guilford.

Winett, R. A., Southard, D. R., & Walberg-Rankin, J. (1993). Nutrition promotion and dietary change: Framework to meet year 2000 goals. *Medicine, Exercise, Nutrition, and Health*, **2**, 7–26.

Wing, L. (1989). *Diagnosis and treatment of autism.* New York: Plenum.

Wing, L., & Gould, J. (1979). Severe impairment of social interaction and associated abnormalities in children: Epidemiology and classification. *Journal of Autism and Developmental Disorders*, **9**, 11–29.

Wingrove, J., Bond, A. J., Cleare, A. J., & Sherwood, R. (1999). Plasma tryptophan and trait aggression. *Journal of Psychopharmacology*, **13**, 235–237.

Winkielman, P., & Berridge, K. C. (2004). Unconscious emotion. *Current Directions in Psychological Science, ***13***, 120–123.

Winner, E. (1996). *Gifted children: Myths and realities.* New York: Basic Books.

——. (2000). Giftedness: Current theory and research. *Current Directions in Psychological Science*, **9(5)**, 153–155.

Winter, D. G. (1987). Leader appeal, leader performance, and the motive profiles of leaders and followers: A study of American presidents and elections. *Journal of Personality and Social Psychology*, **52**, 196–202.

——. (1988). The power motive in women-and men. *Journal of Personality and Social Psychology*, **54**, 510–519.

Winter, D. G., & Stewart, A. J. (1978). The power motive. In H. London & J. E. Exner (Eds.), *Dimensions of personality.* New York: Wiley.

Winters, K. C., Weintraub, S., & Neale, J. M. (1981). Validity of MMPI code types in identifying DSM-III schizophrenics. *Journal of Consulting and Clinical Psychology*, **49**, 486–487.

Winton, W. M. (1987). Do introductory textbooks present the Yerkes-Dodson Law correctly? *American Psychologist*, **42**, 202–203.

Wise, P. M. (2003). Creating new neurons in old brains. *Science of Aging, Knowledge, and Environment*, **22**, 13.

Wisensale, S. K. (1992). Toward the 21st century: Family change and public policy. *Family Relations*, **41**, 417–422.

Witenberg, S. H., Blanchard, E. B., McCoy, G., Suls, J., & McGoldrick, M. D. (1983). Evaluation of compliance in home and center hemodialysis patients. *Health Psychology*, **2**, 227–238.

Witkin, H. A., Moore, C. A., Goodenough, D. R., & Cox, P. W. (1977). Field dependent and field independent cognitive styles and their educational implications. *Review of Educational Research*, **47**, 1-64.

Witmer, J. F., & Geller, E. S. (1976). Facilitating paper recycling: Effects of prompts, raffles, and contests. *Journal of Applied Behavior Analysis*, **9**, 315–322.

Wolf, S. (1979). Behavioral style and group cohesiveness as sources of minority influence. *European Journal of Social Psychology*, **9**, 381–395.

Wollen, K. A., Weber, A., & Lowry, D. H. (1972). Bizarreness versus interaction of mental images as determinants of learning. *Cognitive Psychology*, **3**, 518–523.

Wolpe, J. (1958). *Psychotherapy by reciprocal inhibition.* Stanford, CA: Stanford University Press.

——. (1969). Basic principles and practices of behavior therapy of neuroses. *American Journal of Psychiatry*, **125**, 1242–1247.

——. (1981). Behavior therapy versus psychoanalysis. *American Psychologist*, **36**, 159–164.

——. (1982). *The practice of behavior therapy (3rd ed.).* New York: Pergamon Press.

——. (1997). Thirty years of behavior therapy. *Behavior Therapy*, **28**, 633–635.

Wong, M. M., & Csilzenthmihalyi, M. (1991). Affiliation motivation and daily experience. *Journal of Personality and Social Psychology*, **60**, 154–164.

Wood, C. (1986). The hostile heart. *Psychology Today*, **20**, 10–12.

Woodruff, V. (1994). Studies say the kids are all right. *Working Woman*, October, p. 12.

Woods, S. C., & Ramsy, D. S. (2000). Pavlovian influences over food and drug intake. *Behavioral Brain Research*, **110**, 175-182.

Woodworth, R. S., & Schlosberg, H. (1954). *Experimental psychology (revised ed.).* New York: Henry Holt.

Worchel, S., Cooper, J., Goethals, G. R., & Olson, J. M. (2000). *Social psychology.* Belmont, CA: Wadsworth.

Worchel, S., Rothgerber, H., Day, E. A., Hart, D., & Butemeyer, J. (1998). Social identity and individual productivity within groups. *British Journal of Social Psychology,* **37**, 389-413.

World Health Organization. (2000). *Tobacco kills—Don't be duped, says WHO on World No Tobacco Day.* Press Release WHO/38, May 30, 2000.

Worringham, C. J., & Messick, D. M. (1983). Social facilitation of running: An unobtrusive study. *Journal of Social Psychology,* **121**, 23-29.

Worthen, J. B. (1997). Resiliency of bizarreness effects under varying conditions of verbal and imaginal elaboration and list composition. *Journal of Mental Imagery,* **21**, 167-194.

Worthen, J. B. & Marshall, P. H. (1996). Intralist and extralist sources of distinctiveness and the bizarreness effect: The importance of contrast. *American Journal of Psychology,* **109**, 239-263.

Wright, B. A., & Zecker, S. G. (2004). Learning problems, delayed development, and puberty. *Proceedings of the National Academy of Sciences,* **101**, 9942-9946.

Wright, D. B., Gaskell, G. D., & O'Muircheartaigh, C. A. (1998). Flashbulb memory assumptions: Using national surveys to explore cognitive phenomena. *British Journal of Psychology,* **89**, 103-121.

Wright, I. C., Rabe-Hesketh, S., Woodrugg, P. W. R., David, A. S., Murray, R. M., & Bullmore, E. T. (2000). Meta-analysis of regional brain volumes in schizophrenia. *American Journal of Psychiatry,* **157**, 16-25.

Wright, J. C., & Vlietstra, A. G. (1975). The development of selective attention: From perceptual exploration to logical search. In H. W. Reese (Ed.), *Advances in child development and behavior (Volume 10).* New York: Academic Press.

Wright, L. (1988). The Type A behavior pattern and coronary artery disease. *American Psychologist,* **43**, 2-14.

Wright, P., Takei, N., Rifkin, L., & Murray, R. M. (1995). Maternal influenza, obstetric complications, and schizophrenia. *The American Journal of Psychiatry,* **152**, 1714-1720.

Wright, S.W., Lawrence L.M., & Wrenn K.D., et al. (1998). Randomized clinical trial of melatonin after night-shift work: Efficacy and neuropsychologic effects. *Annals of Emergency Medicine,* **32**, 334-340.

Wrosch, C., & Schultz, R. (2008). Health-engagement control strategies and 2-year changes in older adult's physical health. *Psychological Science,* **19**, 537-541.

Wrosch, C., Dunne, E., Scheier, M. F., & Schultz, R. (2006). Self-regulation of common age-related challenges: Benefits for older adult's psychological and physical health. *Journal of Behavioral Medicine,* **29**, 299-306.

Wrosch, C., Schultz, R., Miller, G. E., Lupien, S., & Dunne, E. (2007). Physical health problems, depressive mood, and cortisol secretion in old age: Buffer effects of health engagement control strategies. *Health Psychology,* **26**, 341-349.

Wundt, W. (1874). *Principles of physiological psychology.* Leipzig, Germany: Engelmann.

Wyatt, R. J. (1996). Neurodevelopmental abnormalities and schizophrenia. *Archives of General Psychiatry,* **53**, 11-15.

Wyatt, R. J. & Henter, I. D. (1997). Schizophrenia: The need for early treatment. *The Harvard Mental Health Letter,* **14(1)**, 4-6.

Wyndham, C. H., & Strydam, N. B. (1969). The danger of an inadequate water intake during marathon running. *South African Medical Journal,* **43**, 893-896.

Wysowski, D. K., & Baum, C. (1989). Antipsychotic drug use in the United States, 1976-1985. *Archives of General Psychiatry,* **46**, 929-932.

Xu, J., Kobayashi, S., Yamaguchi, S., Iijima, K., Okada, K., & Yamashita, K. (2000). Gender effects on age-related changes in brain structure. *American Journal of Neuroradiology,* **21**, 112-118.

Yaggi, H. K., Concato, J., Kernan, W. N., Lichtman, J. H., Brass, L. M., & Mohensin, V. (2005). Obstructive sleep apnea as a risk factor for stroke and death. *The New England Journal of Medicine,* **353**, 2034-2041.

Yalom, I. D. (1985). *The theory and practice of group psychotherapy.* New York: Basic Books.

Yan, L. L., Liu, K., Matthews, K. A., Daviglus, M. L., Ferguson, F., & Kiefe, C. I. (2003). Psychosocial factors and risk of hypertension: The Coronary Artery Risk Development in Young Adults (CARDIA) Study. *Journal of the American Medical Association,* **290**, 2138-2148.

Yaniv, I., & Meyer, D. E. (1987). Activation and metacognition of inaccessible stored information: Potential basis for incubation effects in problem solving. *Journal of Experimental Psychology: Learning, Memory, and Cognition,* **13**, 187-205.

Yanovski, S. Z. (2000). Eating disorders, race, and mythology. *Archives of Family Medicine,* **9**, 88.

Yapko, M. (1993). The seduction of memory. *The Family Therapy Networker,* **17**, 42-43.

Yates, A. (1989). Current perspectives on the eating disorders: I History, psychological and biological aspects. *Journal of the American Academy of Child and Adolescent Psychiatry,* **28**, 813-828.

——. (1990). Current perspectives on eating disorders: II Treatment, outcome, and research directions. *Journal of the American Academy of Child and Adolescent Psychiatry,* **29**, 1-9.

Yates, F. A. (1966). *The art of memory.* Chicago: University of Chicago Press.

Yee, B. W. K., Huang, L. N., & Lew, A. (1998). Families: Life-span socialization in a cultural context. In L. C. Lee & N. W. S. Zane (Eds.), *Handbook of Asian American psychology* (pp. 83-135). Thousand Oaks, CA: Sage.

Yen, S. H., Liu, W. K., Hall, F. L., Yan, S. D., Stern, D., & Dickson, D. W. (1995). Alzheimer neurofibrillary lesion: Molecular nature and potential roles of different components. *Neurobiology of Aging,* **3**, 381-387.

Yerkes, R. M. & Dodson, J. D. (1908). The relation of strength of stimulus to rapidity of habit-formation. *Journal of Comparative Neurology and Psychology,* **18**, 459-482.

Yong, F., & Ewing, N. (1992). A comparative study of the learning-style preferences among gifted African-American, Mexican-American and American born Chinese middle-grade students. *Roeper Review*, **14**, 120-123.

Young, A. S., Klap, R., Sherbourne, C. D., & Wells, K. B. (2001). The quality of care for depressive and anxiety disorders in the United States. *Archives of General Psychiatry*, **58**, 55-61.

Youngstrom, N. (1991, May). Serious mental illness issues need leadership. *APA Monitor*, p. 27.

Yuille, J. C. (1993). We must study forensic eyewitnesses to know about them. *American Psychologist*, **48**, 572–573.

Yusuf, S., Hawken, S., Ounpuu, S., Bautista, S., Franzosi, M. G., Commerford, P., Lang, C. C., Rumboldt, Z, et al. (2005). Obesity and the risk of myocardial infarction in 27,000 participants from 52 countries: A case-control study. *The Lancet*, **366**, 1640-1649.

Zadeh, L. (1965). Fuzzy sets. *Information and Control*, **8**, 338–353.

Zajonc, R. B. (1968). Attitudinal effects of mere exposure. *Journal of Personality and Social Psychology (Monograph Suppl.)*, **9**, 1–27.

Zajonc, R. B., & Markus, H. (1982). Affective and cognitive factors in preferences. *Journal of Consumer Research*, **9**, 123–131.

Zalla, T., Koechlin, E., Pietrini, P., Basso, G., Aquino, P., Sirigu, A., & Grafman, J. (2000). Differential amygdala responses to winning and losing: A functional magnetic resonance imaging study in humans. *European Journal of Neuroscience*, **12**, 1764-1770.

Zedeck, S. (1987). *The science and practice of industrial and organizational psychology*. College Park, MD: Society for Industrial and Organizational Psychology.

Zedeck, S., & Cascio, W. F. (1984). Psychological issues in personnel decisions. *Annual Review of Psychology*, **35**, 461–518.

Zedeck, S., Tziner, A., & Middlestadt, S. E. (1983). Interviewer validity and reliability: An individual analysis approach. *Personnel Psychology*, **36**, 230–237.

Zelezny, L. C. (1999). Educational interventions that improve environmental behaviors: A meta-analysis. *Journal of Environmental Education*, **31**, 5–14.

Zelnik, M., & Kantner, J. F. (1980). Sexual activity, contraceptive use, and pregnancy among metropolitan-area teenagers; 1971-1979. *Family Planning Perspectives*, **12**, 230–237.

Zeman, A. (1998) The consciousness of sight. *British Medical Journal*, 12/19/98, 1696. Retrieved from the World Wide Web on October 5, 2000, http://ehostvgw15.epnet.com/.

Zhang, A. Y., & Snowden, L. R. (1999). Ethnic characteristics of mental disorders in five U. S. communities. *Cultural Diversity and Ethnic Minority Psychology*, **5**, 134-146.

Zhdanova, I. V., & Wurtman, R. J. (1997). Efficacy of melatonin as a sleep-promoting agent. *Journal of Biological Rhythms*, **12**, 644–651.

Zhdanova, I. V., Wurtman, R. J., Morabito, C., Piotrovska, V. R., & Lynch, H. J. (1996). Effects of low oral doses of melatonin, given 2-4 hours before habitual bedtime, on sleep in normal young humans. *Sleep*, **19**, 423–431.

Zigler, E., & Hodapp, R. M. (1991). Behavioral functioning in individuals with mental retardation. *Annual Review of Psychology*, **42**, 29–50.

Zilbergeld, B., & Evans, M. (1980). The inadequacy of Masters and Johnson. *Psychology Today*, **14**, 28–43.

Zillmer, E. A., & Spiers, M. V. (2001). *Principles of neuropsychology*. Belmont, CA: Wadsworth.

Zimbardo, P. G. (2004). A situationist perspective on the psychology of evil: Understanding how good people are transformed into perpetrators. In A. G. Miller (Ed.), *The social psychology of good and evil* (pp. 21–50). New York: Guilford Press.

Zimbardo, P. G., & Leippe, M. R. (1992). *The psychology of attitude change and social influence*. New-York: McGraw-Hill.

Zimmerman, M., Posternak, M. A., Attiullah, N., Friedman, M., Boland, R. J., Baymiller, S., et al. (2005). Why isn't Buropion the most frequently prescribed antidepressant? *Journal of Clinical Psychiatry*, **66**, 603-610.

Zinbarg, R. E., Barlow, D. H., Brown, T. A., & Hertz, R. M. (1992). Cognitive-behavioral approaches to the nature and treatment of anxiety disorders. *Annual Review of Psychology*, **43**, 235–267.

Zohar, D. (1980). Safety climate in industrial organizations: Theoretical and applied implications. *Journal of Applied Psychology*, **65**, 96–102.

Zubieta, J., Heitzeg, M. M., Smith, Y. R., Bueller, J. A., et al. (2003). COMT val158met genotype affects μ-opiod neurotransmitter responses to a pain stressor. *Science*, **299**, 1240–1243.

Zubieta, J-K., Bueller, J. A., Jackson, L. R., Scott, D. J., Xu, Y., Koeppe, R. A., Nichols, T. E., & Stohler, C. S. (2005). Placebo effects mediated by endogenous opioid activity on μ-opioid receptors. *The Journal of Neuroscience*, **25**, 7754–7762.

Zuckerman, B., & Bresnahan, K. (1991). Developmental and behavioral consequences of prenatal drug and alcohol exposure. *The Pediatric Clinics of North America*, **38**, 1387–1406.

Zuckerman, M. (1978). Sensation seeking and psychopathology. In R. D. Hare & D. Shalling (Eds.), *Psychopathic behavior*. New York: Wiley.

Zuckerman, M., Buchsbaum, M. S., & Murphy, D. L. (1980). Sensation seeking and its biological correlates. *Psychological Bulletin*, **88**, 187–214.

Zuckerman, M., Eysenck, S., & Eysenck, H. J. (1978). Sensation seeking in England and America: Cross-cultural, age, and sex comparisons. *Journal of Consulting and Clinical Psychology*, **46**, 139–149.

Zurad, E. G. (2001). New treatments of Alzheimer disease: A review. *Drug Benefit Trends*, **13**, 27–40.

CREDITS

Index